THE YEAR'S BEST

Fantasy & Horror

Also Edited by Ellen Datlow and Terri Windling

The Year's Best Fantasy: First Annual Collection

The Year's Best Fantasy: Second Annual Collection

The Year's Best Fantasy and Horror: Third Annual Collection

The Year's Best Fantasy and Horror: Fourth Annual Collection

The Year's Best Fantasy and Horror: Fifth Annual Collection

The Year's Best Fantasy and Horror: Sixth Annual Collection

The Year's Best Fantasy and Horror: Seventh Annual Collection

The Year's Best Fantasy and Horror: Eighth Annual Collection

The Year's Best Fantasy and Horror: Ninth Annual Collection

The Year's Best Fantasy and Horror: Tenth Annual Collection

The Year's Best Fantasy and Horror: Eleventh Annual Collection

The Year's Best Fantasy and Horror: Twelfth Annual Collection

The Year's Best Fantasy and Horror: Thirteenth Annual Collection

The Year's Best Fantasy and Horror: Fourteenth Annual Collection

The Year's Best Fantasy and Horror: Fifteenth Annual Collection

Snow White, Blood Red

Black Thorn, White Rose

Ruby Slippers, Golden Tears

Black Swan, White Raven

Sirens and Other Daemon Lovers

Silver Birch, Blood Moon

Black Heart, Ivory Bones

A Wolf at the Door

Sirens

The Green Man

THE YEAR'S BEST

Fantasy & Horror

SIXTEENTH ANNUAL COLLECTION

Edited by

Ellen Datlow & Terri Windling

St. Martin's Griffin New York

 For information, address St. Martin's Press, 175 Fifth Avenue, New York, N.Y. 10010.

www.stmartins.com

ISBN 0-312-31425-6 (paperback)
ISBN 0-312-31424-8 (hardcover)

First Edition: August 2003

10 9 8 7 6 5 4 3 2 1

This last one is for teammates Ellen Datlow and Tom Canty, and for coach Jim Frenkel. Also for Kelly Link and Gavin Grant. It's your turn at bat now.

—T. W.

Grateful acknowledgment is made for permission to reprint the following material:

"Lull" by Kelly Link. Copyright © 2002 by Kelly Link. First published in *Conjunctions 39: The New Wave Fabulists.* Reprinted by permission of the author.

"Egyptian Avenue" by Kim Newman. Copyright © 2002 by Kim Newman. First published in *Embrace the Mutation,* edited by William Schafer and Bill Sheehan; Subterranean Press. Reprinted by permission of the author.

"A Letter of Explanation" by Corey Marks. Copyright © 2002 by Corey Marks. First published in *Renunciation;* University of Illinois Press. Reprinted by permission of the author.

"Details" by China Miéville. Copyright © 2002 by China Miéville. First published in *The Children of Cthulhu,* edited by John Pelan and Benjamin Adams; Del Rey Books. Reprinted by permission of the author, and the author's agent, Mic Cheetham Literary Agency.

"The Assistant to Dr. Jacob" by Eric Schaller. Copyright © 2002 by Eric Schaller. First published in *Nemonymous,* Issue 2. Reprinted by permission of the author.

"The Pagodas of Ciboure" by M. Shayne Bell. Copyright © 2002 by M. Shayne Bell. First published in *The Green Man,* edited by Ellen Datlow and Terri Windling; Viking. Reprinted by permission of the author.

"The Coventry Boy" by Graham Joyce. Copyright © 2002 by Graham Joyce. First published in *The Third Alternative,* Issue 32. Reprinted by permission of the author.

"The Wild Hunt" by Helga M. Novak. Copyright © 2002 by Helga M. Novak. First published in English in *The Chicago Review,* Vol. 48, No. 2/3, Summer 2002. Reprinted by permission of the original publisher, Schöffling & Co. Verlag.

"The Green Word" by Jeffrey Ford. Copyright © 2002 by Jeffrey Ford. First published in *The Green Man,* edited by Ellen Datlow and Terri Windling; Viking. Reprinted by permission of the author.

"Stitch" by Terry Dowling. Copyright © 2002 by Terry Dowling. First published in *Eidolon: Australian SF Online,* December 2002. Reprinted by permission of the author.

"Puce Boy" by Michael Libling. Copyright © 2002 by Michael Libling. First published in *On Spec,* Winter issue. Reprinted by permission of the author and the author's agents, Virginia Kidd Literary Agency.

"The Violin-Maker" by Zoran Živković. Copyright © 2002 by Zoran Živković. First published in the English language in *Interzone,* February 2002. Reprinted by permission of the author.

"Maya's Mother" by Bentley Little. Copyright © 2002 by Bentley Little. First published in *The Collection;* Signet Books. Reprinted by permission of the author.

"Porno in August" by Carlton Mellick III. Copyright © 2002 by Carlton Mellick III. First published in *Random Acts of Weirdness,* edited by Brian Knight; Catalyst Press. Reprinted by permission of the author.

"Nesting Instincts" by Brian Hodge. Copyright © 2002 by Brian Hodge. First published in *Lies & Ugliness;* Night Shade Books. Reprinted by permission of the author.

"The Machine" by Conrad Williams. Copyright © 2002 by Conrad Williams. First published in *The Third Alternative 31.* Reprinted by permission of the author.

"Hansel, A Retrospective, or The Danger of Childhood Obesity" by Tom Disch. Copyright © 2002 by Tom Disch. First published in *The Antioch Review,* Fall 2002. Reprinted by permission of the author.

"Aquerò" by Melissa Hardy. Copyright © 2002 by Melissa Hardy. First published in *The Atlantic Monthly*, December 2002. Reprinted by permission of the author, and the author's agent, Acacia House Publishing Services Ltd.

"The Receivers" by Joel Lane. Copyright © 2002 by Joel Lane. First published *in Dark Terrors 6*, edited by Stephen Jones and David Sutton; Victor Gollancz, Ltd. Reprinted by permission of the author.

"Standard Gauge" by Nicholas Royle. Copyright © 2002 by Nicholas Royle. First published in *Thirteen*; The Do Not Press Limited. Reprinted by permission of the author.

"Creation" by Jeffrey Ford. Copyright © 2002 by Jeffrey Ford. First published in *The Magazine of Fantasy & Science Fiction*, May 2002. Reprinted by permission of the author.

"Seven Pairs of Iron Shoes" by Tracina Jackson-Adams. Copyright © 2002 by Tracina Jackson-Adams. First published in *Star*Line* 25.2, March/April 2002. Reprinted by permission of the author.

"What I Didn't See" by Karen Joy Fowler. Copyright © 2002 by Karen Joy Fowler and SCIFI.COM. First published in *SCI FICTION*, July 10, 2002. Reprinted by permission of the author.

"Reading Myth to Kindergartners" by Jackie Bartley. Copyright © 2002 by Jackie Bartley. First published in *The Louisville Review*, Spring 2002. Reprinted by permission of the author.

"Mermaid Song" by Peter Dickinson and "A Pool in the Desert" by Robin McKinley, from *Water: Tales of Elemental Spirits* by Robin McKinley and Peter Dickinson. Copyright © 2002 by Robin McKinley and Peter Dickinson. Used by permission of G. P. Putnam's Sons, a division of Penguin Young Readers Group, a member of Penguin Group (USA) Inc. All rights reserved.

"Pages from a Journal Found in a Shoebox Left in a Greyhound Bus Somewhere Between Tulsa, Oklahoma, and Louisville, Kentucky" by Neil Gaiman. Copyright © 2002 by Neil Gaiman. First published in *Tori Amos 2002 Tour Book*. Reprinted by permission of the author.

"No End of Fun" by Ramsey Campbell. Copyright © 2002 by Ramsey Campbell. First published in *Embrace the Mutation*, edited by William Schafer and Bill Sheehan; Subterranean Press. Reprinted by permission of the author.

"Swiftly" by Adam Roberts. Copyright © 2002 by Adam Roberts and SCIFI.COM. First published in *SCI FICTION*, April 3, 2002. Reprinted by permission of the author.

"The Green Man" by Christopher Fowler. Copyright © 2002 by Christopher Fowler. First published in *The Third Alternative*, Issue 31. Reprinted by permission of the author.

"Some Other Me" by Brian Hodge. Copyright © 2002 by Brian Hodge. First published *in Lies & Ugliness*; Night Shade Books. Reprinted by permission of the author.

"The Snow Queen" by Robert Phillips. Copyright © 2002 by Robert Phillips. Reprinted by permission from *The Hudson Review*, Vol. LV, No. 2, Summer 2002.

"Hides" by Jay Russell. Copyright © 2002 by Jay Russell. First published in *Stranger: Dark Tales of Eerie Encounter*, edited by Michele Slung; Perennial, an imprint of HarperCollins Publishers. Reprinted by permission of the author.

"Mr. Mendoza's Paintbrush" by Luis Alberto Urrea. Copyright © 2002 by Luis Alberto Urrea. First published in *Six Kinds of Sky*; Cinco Puntos Press. Reprinted by permission of the publisher. www.cincopuntos.com.

"Five Poems" by Margaret Lloyd. Copyright © 2002 by Margaret Lloyd. First published in *Poem*, May 2002. Reprinted by permission of the author.

"Little Dead Girl Singing" by Stephen Gallagher. Copyright © 2002 by Stephen Gallagher. First published in *Weird Tales,* Spring 2002 issue; Terminus Publishing. Reprinted by permission of the author.

"Thailand" by Haruki Murakami. Copyright © 2002 by Haruki Murakami. Copyright © 2002 by Haruki Murakami. First published in *After the Quake;* Alfred A. Knopf. Reprinted by permission of Random House, Inc.

"The Rose in Twelve Petals" by Theodora Goss. Copyright © 2002 by Theodora Goss. First published in *Realms of Fantasy,* April 2002. Reprinted by permission of the author.

"Road Trip" by Kathe Koja. Copyright © 2002 by Kathe Koja. First published in the *World Fantasy Convention Program Book.* Reprinted by permission of the author.

"Unspeakable" by Lucy Taylor. Copyright © 2002 by Lucy Taylor. First published in *The Darker Side: Generations of Horror,* edited by John Pelan; Roc. Reprinted by permission of the author.

"Inside Out: On Henry Darger." Copyright © 2002 by Elizabeth Hand. First published in *The Magazine of Fantasy & Science Fiction,* May 2002. Reprinted by permission of the author.

"The Green Children" by Kevin Brockmeier. From *The Truth About Celia* by Kevin Brockmeier. Copyright © 2003 by Kevin Brockmeier. Used by permission of Pantheon Books, a division of Random House, Inc.

"After the Chuck Jones Tribute on Teletoon" by Sharon McCartney. Copyright © 2002 by Sharon McCartney. First published in *The Malahat Review,* Fall 2002. Reprinted by permission of the author.

"Feeders and Eaters" by Neil Gaiman. Copyright © 2002 by Neil Gaiman. First published in *Keep Out the Night,* edited by Stephen Jones; PS Publishing. Reprinted by permission of the author.

"Roofwalker" by Susan Power. Copyright © 2002 by Susan Power. First published in *Roofwalker;* Milkweed Editions. Reprinted by permission of the publisher, Milkweed Editions.

"The Prospect Cards" by Don Tumasonis. Copyright © 2002 by Don Tumasonis. First published in *Dark Terrors 6,* edited by Stephen Jones and David Sutton; Victor Gollancz, Ltd. Reprinted by permission of the author.

"Hide and Seek" by Nicholas Royle. Copyright © 2002 by Nicholas Royle. First published in *Dark Terrors 6,* edited by Stephen Jones and David Sutton; Victor Gollancz, Ltd. Reprinted by permission of the author.

"The Wolf's Story" by Nan Fry. Copyright © 2002 by Nan Fry. First published in *Lady Churchill's Rosebud Wristlet,* No. 11. Reprinted by permission of the author.

"The Least Trumps" by Elizabeth Hand. Copyright © 2002 by Elizabeth Hand. First published in *Conjunctions 39: The New Wave Fabulists.* Reprinted by permission of the author.

Contents

Acknowledgments

The Year's Best Fantasy and Horror series requires the cooperation of a number of people. I'd like to thank the publishers, editors, writers, and readers who send material and make suggestions every year. And this year I'd particularly like to thank Bill Congreve, Justine Larbalestier, Kelly Link, Jim Rockhill, and Paul Witcover for their recommendations and help.

Special thanks to Jim Frenkel, our hardworking packager, and his assistants, and to Tom Canty for his unflagging visual imagination. Finally, thanks to my coeditor and friend Terri Windling, for her moral support and friendship during the past sixteen years of our literary partnership.

I'd like to acknowledge the following magazines and catalogs for invaluable information and descriptions of material I was unable to obtain: *Locus, Chronicle, Publishers Weekly, Washington Post Book World* Web site, *The New York Times Book Review, Hellnotes, Jobs in Hell, Prism* (the quarterly journal of fantasy given with membership to the British Fantasy Society). I'd also like to thank all the magazine editors who made sure I saw their magazines during the year.

—E. D.

Each year, it takes a team of people to produce a book as extensive as this one. Thanks are due to Jim Frenkel, the series packager and creator; to Ellen Datlow, my partner in crime; to Tom Canty, art partner and cover artist; to Marc Resnick, our patient editor at St. Martin's Press; and to Ed Bryant, Charles Vess, Joan Vinge, and Charles de Lint, who all contribute to the "year in review" portion of the book. Special thanks are due to Emma Hardesty, Richard Kunz, and Mardelle Kunz for their invaluable help with the fantasy half of this volume. Thanks also to Ellen Kushner, Delia Sherman, Midori Snyder, Kelly Link, Gavin Grant, Anita Roy Dobbs, Thomas Harlan, Joe Monti, Liz Hand, Jane Yolen, Debbie Notkin, Sharyn November, Patrick Nielsen Hayden, and Christopher Schelling. I'm grateful to the publishers, editors, publicists, writers, and readers who sent in material and made suggestions last year. I'm also grateful to the University of Arizona library staff, and the following review sources: *Publishers Weekly, Library Journal, Kirkus, The New York Times Book Review, The Women's Review of Books*, the DreamHaven catalog, and especially *Locus Magazine*. Readers interested in submitting fantasy material to future volumes of *Year's Best* should note that there is a new submissions address. (Please don't use the old one!) Kelly Link and Gavin Grant will be the Fantasy Editors for this series as of Volume 17. Their submission guidelines can be found on the Web at www.lcrw.net/yearsbest/.

—T. W.

As our editors have noted, this is a most collaborative effort. My profound thanks to Terri, who has been an angel from the start, and to Ellen, with whom Terri has made a wonderful tandem. I won't duplicate their thanks but I hope everyone involved knows how much I appreciate their help and cooperation. My own bailiwick wouldn't survive this annual project without the help of the University of Wisconsin's Memorial Library Reference Desk. Nor could this be the book it is without the efforts of my assistant, Stephen Smith, and our interns, Jacqueline Jo Hass, Ben Hojem, Andrea Helene Nelson, Kellen O'Brien, Derek Tiefenthaler, and most especially Jordan Zweck, who rode shotgun on this volume and was invaluable in weaving together the many strands of this tapestry.

I also owe much to my family, especially to my wife, Joan D. Vinge, who produced her anime and manga column under difficult circumstances, and our son, Joshua, who showed great understanding and also helped with production.

—J. F.

Summation 2002: Fantasy

Terri Windling

Welcome to the sixteenth edition of *The Year's Best Fantasy and Horror*, an anthology series created as an annual celebration of magical literature in all its guises—from traditional fantasy (à la Tolkien) to magical realism (à la Màrquez), from mythic fiction to surrealism, from dark fantasy to horror. While there are other Year's Best anthologies designed to honor stories published within the boundaries of the fantasy and horror genres, our purpose here is a different one. In these pages, we'll take a broader look at what contemporary writers of all stripes are doing with the material of the fantastic—in genre fiction, in mainstream fiction, in fiction for children and young adults, and in contemporary poetry.

Fantasy and horror are areas of fantastic literature with separate but linked histories, sharing some of the same literary techniques. Where they overlap, they form the shadowed subgenre of dark fantasy, which in turn has had a fascinating influence on both fantasy and horror. By placing tales drawn from the full spectrum of fantasy, dark fantasy, and horror together under one cover, we find that an interesting conversation takes place between them . . . and yet we realize that there will always be some readers with a strong preference for one kind of story over another. Those readers can identify the horror selections by looking for Ellen's initials after the story introductions; introductions to the fantasy selections carry my initials; and works of dark fantasy carry both.

The various Summations that open this volume provide an overview of fantasy and horror publishing in the year just past, with lists of recommended novels, story collections, anthologies, children's books, art books, nonfiction, and so forth. Separate Summations cover fantasy and horror in media arts, in comics, and in anime and manga, followed by an Obituaries section noting the passing of people who have contributed to these fields.

2002 is the last year I'll be coediting *The Year's Best Fantasy and Horror* annuals. After this volume, I'm retiring from the series (in order to devote more time to my own writing), and handing the reins over to two excellent new editors. Starting with next year's edition, Volume 17, the fantasy portion of the book will be edited by the team of Kelly Link and Gavin Grant, while the horror portion of the book will still be edited by the estimable Ellen Datlow.

Because of this upcoming change, I find myself looking back over the sixteen long years since Jim Frenkel (the book's packager), Ellen, and I began *The Year's Best Fantasy and Horror,* reflecting on the ways the series and the field of fantasy have changed in the intervening years. Our first edition, published in 1988, was a conservative one, sticking close to familiar genre territory (with tentative forays out to the nearby field of children's fantasy fiction)—but with the next edition we roamed much farther, mixing tales from *F&SF, Asimov's, OMNI,* and other reliable genre sources with works by nongenre writers such as Sara Maitland, Robert Kelly, and Sandra M. Gilbert. I came to this project neither as an academic theorist nor a literary critic, but as a working fantasy editor. Thus, my reason for including out-of-genre material wasn't due to a hidden critical agenda; it was simple and straightforward: these were damn good stories making damn good use of fantasy material. I enjoyed them and I thought that other fantasy readers would enjoy them, too. Like many of my generation, I was introduced to fantasy by Lin Carter's famous Sign of the Unicorn series (and his various anthologies) in which works by authors as diverse as Ariosto, William Morris, James Branch Cabell, Hope Mirrlees, Mervyn Peake, and Clarke Ashton Smith were all presented as "Fantasy Classics," blithely ignoring genre boundaries. Through Mr. Carter's editorial selections, I learned at an early, impressionable age (I first read the Sign of the Unicorn books in high school) that good fantasy could be found in many places on the library shelves, not just buried in the science fiction section.[1] When *The Year's Best Fantasy and Horror* began, I felt that it was my job to provide two services to our readers. One was the usual mission of any Best Of The Year series: to honor and preserve the top stories of the year by collecting them into one handy volume. The other was to search through the myriad out-of-the-way places where magical stories might be found (mainstream magazines and collections, small literary journals, foreign works in translation) in order to make such tales more easily available to fantasy readers. This didn't seem a particularly controversial task to me, yet in the atmosphere of fantasy publishing in the late 1980s, a mixed-genre Best Of The Year volume like ours ended up raising some eyebrows. Critical reaction was decidedly mixed. While many readers were grateful for the chance to read a broad range of fantasy material without having to search through the primarily realist offerings of journals like *The Chicago Review* and *TriQuarterly* themselves, other readers were flatly uninterested in stories that challenged the notion of what could and couldn't be read as fantasy. Fortunately there were enough of the former to keep our series going.

Fifteen years later, certain things have changed. First, there are now two new Best Of The Year series specifically devoted to genre fantasy (one edited by David G. Hartwell and Kathryn Kramer, the other edited by Robert Silverberg and Karen Haber), which is a welcome change. There's no longer any need for fans of fantasy short stories to pick up our mixed-genre book unless they genuinely want to read a mixed-genre book. Second, the use of the material of the fantastic by writers outside the genre has grown considerably over the years—

[1]Other anthology editors, of course, also ignored the genre/mainstream divide when it suited them to do so, such as the influential Judith Merril and Terry Carr.

while concurrently, the use of stylistic tropes from mainstream fiction has become more prevalent in the literary end of the fantasy genre. Third, traffic across the border between the countries of genre fiction and mainstream fiction (to borrow a metaphor from Delia Sherman's essay "An Introduction to Interstitial Arts"[2]) is now, increasingly, going both ways. Not only are mainstream authors appearing in fantasy annuals like this one, but authors with their roots in genre fiction (such as Kelly Link, Jonathan Lethem, Neil Gaiman, and Nalo Hopkinson) are now turning up in mainstream venues (*Conjunctions* and *McSweeneys*, for example). The boundary between fantasy and mainstream literature is simply not as firmly drawn as it used to be. As critic Gary K. Wolfe points out in an excellent essay in *Conjunctions:* 39, "the signal development of the last few decades has been the emergence of a generation of writers—though 'generation' is a misnomer, since these writers currently range in age from the twenties to the seventies—whose ambitions lay in what we might call recombinant genre fiction: stories which effectively decompose and reconstitute genre materials and techniques from an eclectic variety of literary traditions, even including the traditions of domestic realism."

Wolfe's essay comes from a journal that is itself an example of how fantasy has changed in the last sixteen years. *Conjunctions*, a mainstream literary journal published by Bard College and edited by Bradford Morrow, recently invited horror writer Peter Straub to guest-edit their Autumn 2002 edition. The result is a challenging volume containing seventeen cutting-edge, fantastical stories by some of the very best writers in the fantasy and horror genres today, along with a story by John Crowley that I'm not yet convinced is either fantasy or horror (although I've heard Straub make a compelling case for reading it as such) but which is simply brilliant nonetheless. The volume finishes with Wolfe's perceptive essay paired with a fascinating essay by the British critic John Clute—two pieces which are essential reading for understanding the contemporary fantasy field.

While at one time it seemed that our field's best writers dreamed of escaping the "ghetto" of genre fiction (if only to find some critical respect), now, by contrast, many of the writers on the literary cusp of the fantasy and horror fields are simply ignoring the ghetto walls, passing right through them and back again, producing work firmly rooted in the fantastic but partaking of the conventions and tropes of other genres as well (including the "genre" of realism), as they see fit. We see this in the work of new writers like Kelly Link, China Miéville, and Andy Duncan; and of established writers like Jonathan Carroll, Karen Joy Fowler, and M. John Harrison. We see it in all the subgenres that are cropping up like mushrooms after the rain: "new wave fabulism" (promoted by *Conjunctions*), "slipstream" fiction (promoted by the *Polyphony* anthology series); "decadent fantasy" (promoted by the *Leviathan* anthology series), the "new weird" fiction in Britain (by writers like China Miéville), "mythic fiction" (by writers like Charles de Lint), "Trollopean fantasy" (by writers like Ellen Kushner); and the broader, umbrella movement under which all of these categories can fall: Interstitial Arts defined as works that fall into the interstices between genres, categories, and artistic disciplines (www.artistswithoutborders.org).

[2]This essay can be read in its entirely on the Interstitial Arts Web site: www.artistswithoutborders.org.

While all this activity is going on at the edge of the fantasy field, the center of the genre is far from moribund. Here, too, we see a mix of established writers (such as Patricia A. McKillip and Robin Hobb) and new writers (such as Sean McMullen and Jaqueline Carey) keeping the traditional fantasy form alive, well, and relevant to a new generation, producing works that use familiar magical and folkloric tropes but revitalize or subvert them in innovative ways. In the subgenre of historical fantasy, writers such as Lisa Goldstein and Frances Sherwood have written memorable works, braiding fiction, fact, and folklore together; while in the area of alternate history, Kim Stanley Robinson and Christopher Priest have published novels that stretch the boundaries of the form. In children's fiction, fantasy is positively thriving, thanks to new fantasy publishing programs launched in the wake of the Harry Potter books' success. Midori Snyder, Holly Black, Sonya Hartnett, and others published extraordinary Young Adult books in 2002; and Neil Gaiman produced a novel for younger readers that may well become an all-time classic.

That's the good news. The bad news, as usual, is that it's continuing to get harder and harder for midlist authors (the ones who don't hit the bestsellers lists) to get published these days or to keep their books in print. We're seeing too many formerly established writers with several books under their belt and loyal (if not enormous) readerships suddenly finding themselves, mid-career, without a publisher. As for first novels—they're still getting published despite the high odds against them, but I wouldn't recommend new writers giving up their day jobs in any hurry. Small presses are picking up some of the slack by publishing hard-to-market books, such as novellas and short-story collections. I suspect we'll see more and more small-press editions, now that computer technology is making such editions easier to produce and distribute. The downside of this is that lately I've been seeing a profusion of small-press volumes that are poorly made, poorly designed, and in need of a good editor, featuring works by writers who would be better advised to spend more time polishing their craft before presenting it to the public. By contrast, there are a few small presses that are thoroughly professional operations, publishing some of our field's best (and most attractive) books—Golden Gryphon Press, Small Beer Press, and Subterranean Press among them.

Another noticeable change from fifteen years ago is that the quality of small-press magazines publishing fantasy fiction is considerably higher. Back then, it was rare for me to find much of interest in the smaller magazines, many of which were barely professional (with a few sterling exceptions). In the last several years, however, I've been paying close attention to small magazines such as *Century* (currently on hiatus), *Lady Churchill's Rosebud Wristlet*, and *Strange Horizons*. There one can find emerging writers (such as Alex Irvine, Theodora Goss, Christopher Barzak, Alan de Niro, Kristin Livdahl, Barth Andersen, Ray Vukcevich, and others) who are pushing the envelope of the fantasy form; and who, I suspect, will play a part in shaping the field in the years to come.

Overall, I see a field that has grown wonderfully diverse over the last sixteen years, with something to offer every kind of reader from fans of wizards-and-dragons novels to fans of postmodern surrealism. For specific examples, let's take a look at notable books published in the year just past, starting with the Top Twenty fantasy novels of 2002.

Top Twenty

The following novels are ones that, in my humble opinion, no fantasy lover should miss. As a group, they demonstrate the diversity of modern magical fiction, drawn from the "subgenres" of Imaginary World fantasy, historical fantasy, magical realism, and dark fantasy on the borderline of horror. In alphabetical order by author:

Paths of the Dead by Steven Brust (Tor) is a swashbuckling adventure fantasy and an homage to Alexander Dumas. "Swords and sorcery" is a form of fantastic literature that doesn't always command respect, so writers like Brust who are doing interesting, subversive things with the form can easily be overlooked—particularly with novels like this one, requiring an intimate familiarity with all Brust's previous Dragaera books to appreciate. Critical response to Brust's latest was mixed, but I found *Paths of the Dead* clever and surprising. This is a writer who takes risks.

White Apples by Jonathan Carroll (Tor) is another highly original, somewhat metaphysical novel from this master of contemporary fantasy—a suspenseful tale about a man who has mysteriously returned from the dead. Carroll uses this premise to reflect on the nature of death, life, the universe, and everything . . . all the while telling a cracking good, character-driven story with a satisfying conclusion. This is more sentimental than Carroll's usual fiction, which is not a bad thing in Carroll's case. In fact, this is one of his very best.

The Translator by John Crowley (Morrow) is a quiet book but a damn near perfect one—perfectly crafted, perfectly pitched, and with so many layers of subtext that it deepens with each re-reading. Set during the years of the Cuban Missile Crisis, the plot revolves around an American college coed and the exiled Russian poet who is her teacher. The interesting thing is that one could read this novel and never notice the fantasy elements, but pay close attention to the angelic mythology in the background and a further layer of the story stands revealed.

Baudolino by Umberto Eco (Harcourt), translated from the Italian by William Weaver, is historical fiction with rich mythic elements—a fat, dazzling, complex work involving stories within stories within stories. Eco's protagonist is a twelfth-century Italian peasant who becomes an adopted son of Holy Roman Emperor Frederick Barbarossa and leads an expedition to find the fabled lands of Prester John . . . to follow just one of the many plot threads. It's a picaresque story, a meditation on the nature of truth, and a fascinating read.

The Portrait of Mrs. Charbuque by Jeffrey Ford (Morrow) is another fine historical novel consisting of stories within stories and the elusive nature of truth (if not quite as flamboyantly as the Eco book above). This one is set among artists in New York City in the nineteenth century, and involves a man commissioned to paint a portrait of a woman he may not lay eyes on. Ford spins this premise into a suspenseful thriller that is darkly magical and beautifully written.

The Alchemist's Door by Lisa Goldstein (Tor) is the first of two historical fantasies set in Prague at the time of Emperor Rudolf II (a.k.a. Mad Rudolf), involving the Elizabethan alchemist John Dee and Rabbi Judah Loew, creator of the golem—a monster intended to protect the Jewish population from pogroms. Goldstein brews Czech history and Jewish folklore into a short but bewitching fantasy novel rooted in the principles of alchemical magic that is entertaining and memorable.

Evening's Empire by David Herter (Tor) is a mystery novel, a contemporary fantasy, and a "lost world" novel all rolled into one. Set on the coast of Orgeon in a small, seemingly placid town, Herter's eerie tale centers on a composer coming to terms with the death of his wife while working on an opera based on Jules Verne's *Twenty Thousand Leagues Under the Sea*. It's an unusual story, not entirely flawless but engrossing nonetheless, recommended to fans of Jonathan Carroll and James P. Blaylock.

A Fistful of Sky by Nina Kiriki Hoffman (Ace) is fabulous coming-of-age novel set in Northern California, particularly recommended to fans of contemporary fantasy of the Charles de Lint or Alice Hoffman sort. I've come to expect a lot from this writer, and still *A Fistful of Sky* simply knocked my socks off. On one level it's a fantasy story about a family of witches and a girl with a troublesome gift; on another, it's a penetrating exploration of family dynamics—a remarkable tale that deepens and darkens as it unfolds.

The Iron Grail by Robert Holdstock (Earthlight, U.K.), the sequel to *Celtika* and the second book in the Merlin Codex, is another atmospheric, complex tale from a master of mythic fiction. Here, Holdstock brings Merlin back to Alba (England), braiding Celtic history and legend with strands of Greek mythology to create a compelling portrait of the great magician at the center of Arthurian legend.

Castles Made of Sand by Gwyneth Jones (Gollancz, U.K.) is an interstitial novel that rests somewhere in the borderland between near-future science fiction and alternate history fantasy, with elements of a fairy tale, and Arthurian myth at its heart. It's the sequel to *Bold as Love* (winner of the Arthur C. Clarke Award), the second volume in a projected five-book sequence about rock-and-roll, relationships, and counterculture politics in a near-future version of a dramatically altered United Kingdom. Absolutely terrific.

The Facts of Life by Graham Joyce (Gollancz, U.K.) is one of the very finest books of the year—a dark historical fantasy by a four-time winner of the British Fantasy Award. It's the story of seven sisters in Coventry, England, during and after World War II—and about the child of one of them, a fey and magical boy with unusual abilities. Graham has always been a fine writer, but he seems to get even better with each book. *The Facts of Life* is haunting, insightful, and highly recommended.

Fresh Eggs by Rob Levandoski (The Permanent Press) is a surprising, outstanding novel that manages somehow to be ironic and warmhearted at the same time. Set in rural Ohio, it's the story a troubled chicken farmer, his wife, and his young daughter, a girl who mysteriously starts to sprout feathers. Levandoski uses this premise to explore modern farming, the corporate food business, and life in modern America—but most of all to tell a moving tale about fathers and daughters. *Fresh Eggs* is particularly recommended to fans of Jack Cady and W. P. Kinsella.

Fire Logic by Laurie J. Marks (Tor) is a novel that looks, from the packaging, like a standard "warrior woman" book, and I confess I approached it with some hesitation—if only because I've read far too many mediocre books of this sort in the years that I've been reviewing for this anthology series. Within just a few pages, however, it becomes evident that *Fire Logic* is something different and special, and that Marks deserves much more attention that she's been getting. This is smart, tough, psychologically acute, skillfully written fantasy that truly sweeps you into another world. I'd recommend it to fans of Ursula K. Le Guin, C. J. Cherryh, and Elizabeth A. Lynn.

The Scar by China Miéville (Del Rey) is the bleak and brilliant sequel to *Perdido Street Station*—less sprawling than that book, more focused, and ultimately more powerful. Set in a floating pirate city in the dark, weird, vividly rendered world of Bas-Lag, Miéville's deeply layered, highly textured urban saga seems to be, almost singlehandedly, redefining the epic fantasy form, while still acknowledging a debt to previous writers from Mervyn Peake to M. John Harrison. For fiction at the cutting edge of our field, don't miss this accomplished young writer's work.

The God Who Begat a Jackal by Nega Mezlekia (Picador) is an absolutely splendid first novel by an Ethiopian-born Canadian writer, set in a mythical version of precolonial North Africa. It's a love story about the daughter of a feudal lord and a family slave; it's also a hard-hitting political novel. Most of all, it's a fine work of African magical realism, passionate and wise.

The Fall of the Kings by Ellen Kushner and Delia Sherman (Bantam Spectra) is a delicious read—atmospheric, suspenseful, intellectual, sexy, and wickedly funny by turns. Set in the city Kushner created in her now-classic first novel, *Swordspoint*, this is a sensual, fiercely intelligent novel about academics, aristocrats, artists, wizards, the power of myth, the perils of scholarship, and the making of history. Like Miéville (above), Kushner and Sherman are redefining the fantasy form.

A *Bed of Earth* by Tanith Lee (Overlook) is an intricate dark fantasy story set in the city of Venu—a shadowy, magical version of Venice during the Renaissance. This is the third and most accomplished volume in Lee's Secret Books of Venus quartet, the books all linked by their common setting, but also easily read alone. Each novel in the sequence is thematically based on one of the four elements—first water, then fire, and now earth. This ingenious, almost Shakespearean tale centers on a gravedigger and a young noblewoman—a story of family feuds, doomed love, and death, elegantly written.

Ombria in Shadow by Patricia A. McKillip (Ace) is the latest lyrical book from a writer I consider to be the greatest American fantasist of her generation, quietly turning out one gem of a novel after another. Like all McKillip's work, *Ombria in Shadow*—an Imaginary World novel about sorcery, shadows, and the magic of art—is gorgeously written and emotionally powerful, weaving the threads of folklore and fairy tales into bright new tapestries. For fans of tradition fantasy fiction, this is as good as it gets.

The Isle of Battle by Sean Russell (Avon Eos) is the second volume in The Swan's War trilogy, following *The One Kingdom.* This is panoramic epic fantasy by an intelligent and sophisticated writer who is helping to rescue this form of the literature from a pit filled with Tolkien clones. Although *The Isle of Battle* has some of the problems common to the middle books of trilogies (a confusing number of characters to remember and catch up with; lots of exposition in the first part of the book), this is still terrific high fantasy, recommended to all those readers looking for something new to read after *The Lord of the Rings*. Stay away from the clones (you know which ones they are) and try Russell instead.

The Book of Splendor by Frances Sherwood (Norton) is the second of two historical novels about Prague at the time of Mad Rudolph, Rabbi Judah Loew, his golem, and the alchemist John Dee. Unlike the Goldstein book (above), this time John Dee is in the background while the golem's story is center stage, paired with the story of a young Jewish seamstress. Sherwood does a fine job of bringing Prague and her cast of characters vividly to life.

Also of Note

The following two novels straddle the divide between science fiction and fantasy, and should certainly be considered among the very best of the year. *The Watch* by Dennis Danvers (Avon Eos) is a time-travel novel in which the Russian "anarchist prince" Peter Kropotkin is brought forward in time (for mysterious, possibly sinister reasons) to contemporary Richmond, Virginia. This unlikely premise makes for a marvelous book in Danvers's competent hands. It's a well-written, moving, eloquent novel about anarchy and ethics. *The Impossible Bird* by Patrick O'Leary (Tor) has to be called a science fiction novel in that the plot involves the manipulation of humankind by aliens, yet it reads like contemporary fantasy of the Jonathan Carroll sort. At its core, this gorgeous, complex work full of aliens, ghosts, and hummingbirds is the tale of two brothers, the woman they both loved, and the bonds of family. It's remarkable.

First Novels

In genre fiction, the best first novel of the year was *Fires of the Faithful* by Naomi Kritzer (Bantam Spectra), an author who has been making a name for herself with memorable short stories published in *Realms of Fantasy* and other magazines. At first glimpse, Kritzer's debut novel seems to tell a familiar tale: a coming-of-age saga about a young protagonist (in this case, a music student) whose life is changed by magic, politics, and war, set in a fantasy land where new and old religious beliefs stand in conflict. What's different here is that Kritzer skillfully avoids the potential clichés of this material, giving us an Imaginary World novel that's thought-provoking and interestingly subversive. Different in tone but equally good is Alexander Irvine's *A Scattering of Jades* (Tor), an ingenious historical fantasy set in nineteenth-century America but rooted in ancient Aztec myth. The setting ranges from New York City to rural Kentucky, with mythic and historical elements stitched carefully together. I'd recommend this one to fans of Tim Powers and Jeffrey Ford. Also noteworthy is *The Eye of Night* by Paula J. Alama (Bantam Spectra), a quest-style high fantasy concerning three unlikely heroes in search of a magical object. This is standard fantasy material, of course, but Alama uses these materials so well that her tale has a genuine magic.

On the mainstream shelves, the best magical first novel of the year was *The God Who Begat a Jackal* by Nega Mezlekia (described above in the Top Twenty), while the best first novel for young adult readers was *Tithe* by Holly Black (Simon & Schuster). *Tithe* is a heartfelt, character-driven story about a streetwise girl on the Jersey shore embroiled in the world of Faery. It's an enchanting tale, and fans of Charles de Lint, Emma Bull, and Francesca Lia Block should be sure to check this one out.

Traditional Fantasy

2002 was a reasonably good year for high fantasy (à la J. R. R. Tolkien) and "swords and sorcery" (à la Fritz Leiber) set largely or entirely in imaginary lands. In addition to the Brust, Marks, McKillip, Miéville, and Russell books listed in the Top Twenty, and the Kritzer and Alama books listed under First Novels, I particularly recommend the following titles: *Kushiel's Chosen* by Jacqueline Carey (Tor) is the sequel to Carey's impressive debut novel, *Kushiel's Dart*—an unabashedly sensual, epic, exotic story about a female courtesan and spy as she threads her way through mysteries and conspiracies in her Renaissance-like world. It's stylish, original, and Carey is a superb storyteller. For fans of epic fantasy adventures, *Voyage of the Shadowmoon* by Sean McMullen (Tor) is first-rate. Set in a land devastated by magical weapons of mass destruction, it's a novel with layer—a sprawling swashbuckler on the surface covering a more serious story beneath. *Sorcery Rising* by Jude Fisher (DAW) is the first volume in a fine new series from England. Fisher is the pseudonym of British fantasy editor Jane Johnson, who also publishes collaborations with M. John Harrison under the name Gabriel King. Johnson knows her fantasy. The book contains standard ingredients (a land of exotic cultures in conflict, where magic is rising into a potent force), but the author's skillful use of these fantasy tropes makes them vivid and fresh. If you like the work of Robin Hobb or Barbara Hambly, check this one out. Speaking of which, Robin Hobb has published a clever new volume in her Tawny Man series, *Fool's Errand* (Bantam Spectra); and Barbara Hambly has followed up *Dragonstar* with *Dragonsbane* (Del Rey). Both these books subvert fantasy clichés with complex heroes who have hit middle age.

Wolf's Head, Wolf's Heart by Jane Lindskold (Tor) is the satisfying sequel to Lindskold's fine coming-of-age novel, *Through Wolf's Eyes*—the story of a young woman raised by wolves, making her way in the human world. The author makes good use of wolf lore and behavior to create a memorable heroine. *The Lady of Sorrows* by Cecilia Dart-Thornton (Warner Aspect) is the middle book of the Bitterbynde trilogy, and more tightly written than the previous volume. I'd recommend this lyrical tale to fans of Patricia C. Wrede and Tamora Pierce. Newcomer Lian Hern's *Across the Nightingale Floor* (Riverhead) is the first book in The Tales of the Otari series—a coming-of-age, martial-arts saga set in a land much like feudal Japan. It's an atmospheric, subtle, intelligent tale, and this series shows real promise. *The King* by David Feintuch (Ace) is a much grittier coming-of-age story, well written and action packed. In this sequel to *The Still*, Feintuch continues the tale of a youthful king striving to hold the throne he recently reclaimed. *Tides of Darkness* by Judith Tarr (Tor) is a welcome return to her Avaryan high-fantasy series—told with the same high color and drama she brings to her historical novels. Dave Duncan's *Paragon Lost* (Avon Eos) is loosely connected to his Tales of the King's Blades series—a swords-and-courtly-intrigue novel, fast-paced and entertaining. *A Crown Disowned* by Andre Norton and Sasha Miller (Tor) is the latest novel from one of the field's best-loved authors, collaborating—as Norton so often does these days—with an up-and-coming writer. This action-packed swords-and-sorcery tale is the third and concluding volume in The Cycle of Oak, Yew, Ash, and Rowan. If you're looking for fast-paced reads that won't insult your intelligence, try: *Shadow and Light* by Anne Bishop (Roc), *Witch's Honour* by Jan Siegel (Voyager), *The Sea Lark's Song* by Diana Marcellas (Tor), *Sisters of the Raven* by Barbara Hambly (Warner Aspect), *Restoration* by Carol Berg (Roc), *Prince of Fire and Ashes* by Katya Reimann (Tor), *Never After* by Rebecca Lickiss (Ace), *A Sorcerer's Treason* by Sarah Zettel (Tor), and *Rules of Ascension* by David B. Coe (Tor).

Two reprints of note: Evangeline Walton's absolutely gorgeous fantasy novels based on Welsh mythology (*The Children of Llyr, The Song of Rhiannon, The Prince of Annwn, The Island of the Mighty*) have been collected and reprinted in *The Mabinogion Tetralogy* (Overlook), with an introduction by Betty Ballantine. *Black Gods and Scarlet Dreams* by C. L. Moore (Gollancz Fantasy Masterworks Series) is another volume that shouldn't be missed. This omnibus edition contains Moore's complete Jirel of Joiry stories (groundbreaking swords-and-sorcery tales penned for the Golden Age pulp magazines) along with science fiction tales from her popular Northwest Smith series.

Contemporary and Urban Fantasy

This category consists of contemporary tales in real-world settings infused with magic, including works of magical realism published in the fantasy genre. A number of memorable novels of this sort were published in 2002: the Jonathan Carroll, David Herter, Nina Kiriki Hoffman, and Graham Joyce books listed in the Top Twenty; the Holly Black book listed in First Novels; and the Midori Snyder, Michael Chabon, Isabel Allende, and Alice Hoffman books listed below in Children's Fantasy. In addition, try *The Other Canyon,* a short novel (or perhaps it's a long novella) by Patricia Geary, illustrated by Penny McElroy (Gorsky Press). Set among cowboys and Indians and other colorful characters on the reservations of northern Arizona, it's a magical "road novel" of sorts, quirky and fun.

Historical, Alternate-History, and Arthurian Fantasy

In addition to the Jeffrey Ford, Lisa Goldstein, and Frances Sherwood books listed in the Top Twenty, and the Alex Irvine book listed under First Novels, several other fine historical fantasy novels are worthy of attention. To start, I'd like to mention *Fitcher's Brides* by Gregory Frost—though I'll admit to personal bias here as it comes from the Tor Books Fairy Tales series, which I edit. Based on the French fairy tale "Bluebeard" (and its odd German variant, "Fitcher's Bird"), *Fitcher's Brides* is a dark, engrossing novel set among the nineteenth-century doomsday religious cults prevalent in upstate New York. Frost uses one of the darkest stories in the Western fairy-tale cannon to illuminate a bizarre and little-known aspect of American history. *Child of the Prophecy* by Juliet Marillier (Tor) is final volume in the Sevenwaters Trilogy, which began with the lovely fairy-tale-inspired novel *Daughter of the Forest,* followed up by *Son of the*

Shadows. The new volume makes a satisfying conclusion to the saga of three generations of a mystical family in early Ireland. *Piper in the Night* by Dave Smeds (Wildside Press) is an unusual tale set in Hawaii during the Vietnam War era. It's a dark fever dream of a novel weaving the story of a Navy medical corpsman together with Pan and other characters from Greco-Roman myth. *Picture Maker* by Penina Keen Spinka (Dutton) is the first adult novel from an award-winning writer of children's fiction. Set in North America and Greenland during the fourteenth century, the story follows its protagonist (a girl who draws pictures that foretell the future) from captivity by the Algonquin people to life among the Inuit of the far North.

I'm never quite sure if the subgenre of "alternate history" novels should be considered science fiction or fantasy (they're generally listed under science fiction)—but there were several good novels of this sort that fantasy readers may enjoy. First of all, don't miss Kim Stanley Robinson's splendid *The Years of Rice and Salt* (Bantam). In this richly textured, panoramic novel, Robinson portrays an alternate history of the world dominated by the peoples, cultures, and religions of the East—a world in which Europe (decimated by the Black Death) has little importance. It's a dazzling book and an important one, worthy of award consideration. *The Separation* by Christopher Priest (Scribners) is a fascinating work of historical speculation set in a Europe whose history diverged from ours during World War II. Like the Robinson book, this is a sophisticated, thought-provoking novel that takes the alternate history form to a whole new level. *Lion's Blood* by Steven Barnes (Tor) is a clever novel set in the slave culture of the American South. In Barnes's world, however, Africa, Asia, and the lands of Islam are the dominant powers, while the slaves are white European Christians. Barnes handles this provocative theme with sensitivity and skill. *Dark Lord* by Thomas Harlan (Tor) is the fourth and final book in Harlan's sweeping Oath of Empire series, set in a seventh century where the Roman Empire still stands. Rooted in detailed historical speculation, this series is a treat for history buffs.

Fans of the sub-sub-genre of "Shakespearean fantasy" have two new books to choose from. The first is *Ruled Britannia* (NAL), an alternate-history novel from Harry Turtledove. Set in an alternate version of England where a Spanish queen sits on the throne and Elizabeth is imprisoned in the Tower of London, Turtledove's Shakespeare is a young man drawn into pro-Elizabeth conspiracies in this captivating story of players, playwrights, and political intrigue. Lighter, but also fun, is *All Night Awake* by Sara A. Hoyt (Ace), a charming concoction involving Shakespeare, Kit Marlowe, and a court full of English fairies. It's the sequel to Hoyt's previous Shakespearean fantasy, *Ill Met by Moonlight*.

Fantasy based on Arthurian myth was thin on the ground in 2002, but I can highly recommend Rosalind Miles's new novel *Isolde: Queen of the Western Isle* (Crown), the first book in a new series based on the "Tristan and Isolde" legend. In her sumptuous retelling of this famous story about a pair of star-crossed lovers, Miles draws on all her considerable skills as a feminist historian to recreate medieval life in Ireland and Cornwall. If you liked Bradley's *Mists of Avalon*, give Roselind Miles a try. Like Bradley, she brings the women of Arthurian myth to life, but she does so while grounding her work in sound historical scholarship.

Also of note: *Islandia* by Austin Tappan Wright (Tusk) is the story of a young

American diplomat's journey to a mysterious country called Islandia in the early years of the twentieth century. This classic of American fantasy, and of world utopian literature, is now available in a new edition introduced by John Silbersack.

Humorous Fantasy

For fans of humorous fantasy, the following books are recommended: *Night Watch* by Terry Pratchett (HarperCollins) is Book 28 in this author's best-selling Discworld series, set in a colorful imaginary world. Pratchett's books are funny and wise in equal measure—often silly, always entertaining, and occasionally even profound. For a different kind of humor, try *Lamb: The Gospel According to Biff, Christ's Childhood Pal* (Morrow), the latest from satirist Christopher Moore. It's a goofy, irreverent look at Christ's life from childhood to crucifixion. *Lost in a Good Book* by Jasper Fforde (Hodder & Stoughton, U.K.) is a sequel to his dazzling first novel, *The Eyre Affair.* This fantasy/comedy/mystery/thriller continues the adventures of Fforde's feisty literary detective, Thursday Next—and while it's not quite as tight as Fforde's first book, it's still a lot of fun. *The Woad to Wuin* by Peter David (Pocket) is a lighthearted sequel to *Sir Apropos of Nothing*—a pun-saturated send-up of Tolkienesque high-fantasy novels.

Fantasy in the Mainstream

Magical novels published as mainstream fiction are harder to spot than those labeled as fantasy, so each year we make a special effort to identify books that you might otherwise overlook. In addition to the excellent Umberto Eco, Rob Levandoski, and Nega Mezlekia novels listed in the Top Twenty, I particularly recommend seeking out the following books on the mainstream shelves: *The Mermaid That Came Between Them* by Carol Ann Sima (Coffee House Press) is an original, bewitching little novel, set in contemporary New York, about fathers and sons, husbands and wives, men and women, and some frisky mermaids. Sima, refreshingly, makes no apologies for the fantasy elements in her book but uses them boldly to explore the nature of love, passion, and desire. It's strange but terrific. *A Santo in the Image of Cristóbal García* by Rick Collignon (BlueHen Books) is the lovely sequel to Collignon's *The Journal of Antonio Montoya* and *Perdido.* Once again, Collignon explores daily life in a Spanish village in New Mexico, embellishing his affecting tale with gentle touches of magical realism. *Life of Pi* by Yann Martel (Harcourt), winner of the Booker Prize, is a beautifully crafted, fablelike story about the son of an Indian zookeeper who ends up in a lifeboat adrift on the Indian Ocean, along with a Bengal tiger. Published in Canada in 2001, this is the first American edition. *Insect Dreams: The Half-Life of Gregor Samsa* by Marc Estrin (BlueHen Books) is a witty, surprisingly appealing book about Samsa the cockroach from Kafka's famous story, "Metamorphosis." In Estrin's version of Samsa's life, the cockroach is mercifully saved from the dustbin, then journeys through the decades meeting remarkable figures from Rilke to Einstein to F. D. R. As implausible as it sounds, Estrin makes this premise work and tells a good story. *Balthasar's Odyssey* by Amin Maalouf (Arcade), translated from the French by Barbara Bray, is a picaresque tale of high adventure, set in the seventeenth century. The protagonist is an antique dealer roaming through Europe and the Middle East as he searches for a book containing the magical hundredth name of God.

Other notable works: *Achilles* by Elizabeth Cook (Picador) is a beautiful little book revisiting the life of this great Greek hero. It's not quite a novel, not quite a prose poem, but something in between. *Shadow Theatre* by Fiona Cheong (Soho Press) is a lush, stylistically inventive novel told through the voices of women from many different backgrounds now living in Singapore—portraying a world steeped in legends of vampires, ghosts, and other spirits. *Fatma: A Novel of Arabia* by Raja Alem with Tom McDonough (Syracuse University Press) is a lyrical if not terribly linear novel by a celebrated Arab woman writer. Alem draws upon Arabian mythology and magical symbolism to portray the life of a Saudi woman imprisoned by her marriage. If you like the work of Anaïs Nin, give this poetic story a try. *Boxwood* by Camilo José Cela (New Directions), translated from the Spanish by Patricia Haugaard, is even less linear than the Alem book and thus won't be for every reader—but it's a fascinating look at the land and culture of the Galician coast of Spain, wound through with Galician folklore. Another intriguing work of European magical realism is *The Return of the Caravels* by the Portuguese writer António Lobo Antunes, translated by Gregory Rabassa (Grove Press). Antunes explores the legacy of Portuguese colonial history in a story involving characters from both the sixteenth and twentieth centuries. *Tales of Protection* by Erik Fosnes Hansen, translated from the Norwegian by Nadia Christensen (Farrar, Straus, Giroux), is a novel composed of four interlinked stories. Although each section of the book has some slight magical realist elements, the section set in Renaissance Italy, concerning a painting with miraculous healing powers, is of particular interest to fantasy readers.

April Witch by Majgull Axelsson, translated from the Swedish by Linda Schenck (Villard), is the tale of a disabled woman who is able to leave her own body to spy on the lives of her three foster sisters—one of whom, she believes, has stolen her life. I found Axelsson's characters too relentlessly unpleasant to sustain my interest, but other readers may have better luck. This book, a best-seller in Europe, was apparently inspired by a Ray Bradbury story. *Anna in the Afterlife* by Merrill Joan Herber (Syracuse University Press), published in the Library of Modern Jewish Literature series, is another story told from the point of view of a woman who has left her body. In this case the protagonist, who has recently died, is awaiting her burial. In this limbo state, she looks down on her family and reflects on the events of her life. *The Lovely Bones* by Alice Sebold (Little Brown) is also told from the point of view of a dead protagonist—a young girl looking down on her family and neighbors after she's been raped, murdered, and buried in the neighborhood cornfield. Sebold's book (a first novel) was a bit overly sentimental for my taste despite its gruesome topic, yet it had some lovely passages, and I'd recommend giving it a try. *Abou and the Angel Cohen* by Claude Campbell (Bridge Works), inspired by the Leigh Hunt poem "Abou Ben Adhem," is the story of a Muslim man living in the Gaza strip who is visited by a Jewish angel fond of American slang. Campbell uses this offbeat premise to address the Palestinian-Israeli conflict. *Polar* by T. R. Pearson (Penguin) involves a missing girl and a porn-obsessed clairvoyant in the Blue Ridge Mountains of North Carolina. Watch out for Pearson. Underneath his folksy style, his work has a sharp satiric bite. *Bingo Under the Crucifix* by Laurie Foos (Coffee House

Press) is the latest novel from the talented author of *Portrait of a Walrus as a Young Man.* Once again, Foos makes use of fantasy to explore issues of contemporary life—in this case, the life of a doll maker whose brother has literally retreated into infancy, and the life of a girl who secretly gives birth at her senior prom. It's an insightful tale about family dynamics, recommended to fans of Carol Emshwiller and Kelly Link.

More Oddities

The "Best Peculiar Book Award" this year goes to *Lemony Snicket: The Unauthorized Autobiography* (HarperCollins), depicting the imaginary life of a pseudonymous author. Like his books for children (*A Series of Unfortunate Events,* etc.), Snicket's clever, confounding autobiography is as dire as an Edward Gorey drawing and equally filled with sardonic black humor. This book's a hoot—but requires a familiarity with Snicket's fiction to appreciate. The runner-up is *The Double* by Greg Boyd (Leaping Dog Press), a slim, small-press volume illustrated by the author. Described as an "annotated novel," it's the story of a man haunted by his doppelganger, and no longer quite certain which one of them is real. This ironic, surrealistic tale comes complete with annotations, footnotes, and *fourteen* appendixes, all of which contain interconnected stories of their own.

Briefly Noted

The following fantasy novels were among those that hit the various best-seller lists in 2002. Beloved by large numbers of readers, they deserve a mention: *The Voyage of the Jerle Shannara: Antrax* by Terry Brooks, *The Curse of Arkady* by Emily Drake (DAW), *Stormrider* by David Gemmell (Del Rey), *The Pillars of Creation* by Terry Goodkind (Tor), *The Gates of Sleep* by Mercedes Lackey (DAW), *The Fifth Sorceress* by Robert Newcomb (Del Rey), and *Transcendence* by R. A. Salvatore (Del Rey).

Children's Fantasy

Good fantasy books for younger readers have been in plentiful supply since the successes of J. K. Rowling and Philip Pullman put children's fantasy back on the map. In addition to Nina Kiriki Hoffman's *A Fistful of Sky* (listed in the Top Twenty), which I'd recommend to older teen readers, and Holly Black's *Tithe* (listed under First Novels), here's a baker's dozen of the best children's fantasy novels I read last year, listed alphabetically by author.

The Rope Trick by Lloyd Alexander (Dutton) is one of the best books yet from this master fantasist. It's both a quest novel of sorts and a character study—somewhat darker than usual for Alexander. The plot follows the journey of a young magician and conjurer as she travels around a land much like nineteenth-century Italy, seeking the man who can teach her a famous secret rope trick. It's terrific.

City of the Beasts by Isabel Allende (HarperCollins) is this celebrated author's first book for children—a mystical adventure tale about a fifteen-year-old California boy who journeys to the Amazon with his aunt in search of a fabled nine-foot-tall Beast. Allende's got ecological points to make here, but she doesn't let the message overwhelm her story. Read this one for its lush Amazonian setting and shamanic imagery.

Forbidden Forest: The Story of Robin Hood and Little John by Michael Cadnum (Orchard) tells the story of Robin Hood's famous sidekick and shows us what led Little John to seek an outlaw's life in Sherwood Forest. Cadnum's novels are gritty and realistic, even when working with legendary subjects of this kind. Like his previous Robin Hood novel, *A Dark Wood,* focused on the Sheriff of Nottingham, *Forbidden Forest* is a riveting and entertaining read.

Summerland by Michael Chabon (Talk Miramax), according to the publisher, is Chabon's attempt to create a fantasy land as resonant as Narnia but rooted in North American myth. The result is a tale about baseball, "ferishers" (American fairies), giants, goblins, Coyote the Trickster—and an eleven-year-old boy from Washington State whose job it is to save the world. The text could have used some serious pruning, and Chabon's reputation in the world of adult fiction may raise reader expectations a bit too high—writing for kids is a different kettle of fish. Nonetheless, he's created a fun, folkloric story with some charming twists and surprises. Particularly recommended for young baseball fans.

The Thief Lord by Cornelia Funke (Scholastic), translated from the German by Oliver Latsch, is an atmospheric novel set in the labyrinthine streets of Venice. The story concerns two orphaned brothers who run away from nasty relatives, traveling from Hamburg, Germany, to Venice, Italy. There, they become involved with the Thief Lord—a young Faginlike character who rules over an underground world of feral and homeless children. Funke's tale is distinctly Dickensian, steeped in the magic of an extraordinary city. Despite a somewhat unsatisfying ending (or so it seemed to me), I still recommend this one very highly.

Coraline by Neil Gaiman (HarperCollins) is aimed at adolescent readers, but adults will also find much to enjoy in this inventive and thoroughly creepy book, illustrated by the talented Dave McKean. It's the story of a young girl trapped in a "mirror world" where her home and her parents are strange and *wrong.* Her quest to get back to her real family makes for a marvelous story. Fans of Roald Dahl should seek out this one.

Thursday's Child by Sonya Hartnett (Candlewick Press) is a gorgeously written historical novel set in the rural outback of Australia during the years of the Great Depression. It follows the life of a young girl raised in painfully difficult circumstances, and her brother (the fantastic element in the book) who creates a world for himself underground. This exceptional novel is recommended to fans of David Almond and Katherine Patterson.

Stravaganza: City of Masks by Mary Hoffman (Bloomsbury) is a fantastic story in all senses of the word. Hoffman's protagonist is a London boy with cancer, undergoing chemotherapy, who finds himself able to "stravagate" (which means to travel between worlds), ending up in the magical city of Belleza, much like sixteenth-century Venice. Although Hoffman's plot works out a little too easily in the latter half of the book, it's still an inventive, enormously enjoyable novel with a truly marvelous setting.

Indigo by Alice Hoffman (Scholastic) is a lovely tale from a master of American magical realism. Though quite short (barely novella length), it's every bit as enchanting as Hoffman's better-known adult fiction. The story involves ocean myths and three adolescent misfits in a town far from the sea. It's a sequel of sorts to *Aquamarine*, but can easily be read alone.

Wolf Queen by Tanith Lee (Dutton) is an Imaginary World novel that follows a resourceful young heroine as she makes her way in a dangerous land, seeking the woman who may be her mother. This book is the final volume in The Claidi Journals trilogy (following *Wolf Tower* and *Wolf Star*)—a suspenseful saga set in a well-constructed world, rich in mythic symbolism.

Hannah's Garden by Midori Snyder (Viking) is a contemporary fantasy for older teens about a fiddle player, her difficult mother, her grandfather (a famous painter), and her grandmother's mysterious garden. On one level, Snyder's fine novel is the magical story of young woman's encounter with Faery in both its dark and bright guises; on another level, it's an insightful exploration of family dynamics, death, and creativity. This first-rate story is highly recommended to fans of Alice Hoffman, Nina Kiriki Hoffman, and Charles de Lint.

Growing Wings by Laurel Winter (Viking/Firebird) is a beautifully penned novel about an eleven-year-old girl who finds herself growing wings, as (she discovers) her mother did before her. Winter has created a deeply affecting tale that works beautifully on both magical and metaphorical levels.

The Bagpiper's Ghost by Jane Yolen (Harcourt) is the third book in the Tartan Magic series for preteen readers—charming books about American twins on vacation in Scotland who keep stumbling into magical adventures and into magical trouble. This time the story revolves around ghosts, as young Peter is possessed by the twin brother of the ghostly White Lady in a Scottish graveyard. Yolen, as usual, is in good form here, creating a tale that is both funny and spooky, as well as simply beautifully told.

Also of note: *Abarat* by Cliver Barker (HarperCollins), illustrated by the author, follows a troubled young girl from Minnesota to a magical land composed of twenty-five islands, where she becomes embroiled in the struggle between two men who seek to control the realm. Though chock-full of colorful characters, rich in "Abarat" history and myth, the writing isn't quite as assured as in Barker's best-selling fiction for adults. The book is the first in a series, however, and may be worth keeping an eye on. *A Wizard Alone* by Diane Duane (Harcourt) is Book 6 in the Young Wizards series, a lively saga about adolescent wizards-in-training (predating the Harry Potter books). The new volume explores the subject of autism, while the young wizards' lives continue to unfold. Duane does a fine job of rooting her magic in the joys and sorrows of the real world. *Paint by Magic* by Kathryn Reiss (Harcourt) is a "time-travel mystery" about a boy who journeys to the 1920s, where his mother is involved with a painter using evil magic from the Italian Renaissance. The premise is so intriguing that one could wish for a book with more substance to it, but it's nonetheless a fun and fast-paced read for young mystery fans. *Quiver* by Stephanie Spinner (Knopf) is a beautifully crafted short novel retelling the Greek legend of Atalanta—a mortal girl raised by Artemis, renowned for her skills as a runner and archer. Spinner knows her mythology and does a fine job bringing the teenaged Atalanta to life. *Hippolyta and the Curse of the Amazons* by Jane Yolen and Robert J. Harris (HarperCollins) is another good book based on Greek myth, this one for Middle Grade readers. It's a heroic tale introducing young readers to the legend of an Amazon princess. *Lionclaw: A Tale of Robin Hood* by Nancy Springer (Philomel) is the sequel to *Rowan Hood: Outlaw Girl of Sherwood Forest* (although it can be read alone). Like the previous volume, this short novel is lyrical, magical, and affecting. The protagonist is a gentle boy banished from home by his warrior father.

The Healer's Keep by Victoria Hanley (Holiday House), sequel to *The Seer and the Sword,* is a high fantasy novel with few surprises yet one that is better crafted than most. The protagonist is a young would-be healer, running from enslavement by an evil man who can harm people in their dreams. *Hunted* by N. M. Browne (Bloomsbury) is an unusual tale that unfolds in two separate worlds. In our world, the protagonist is a young girl lying in a coma after a savage beating. In an alternate world, where she's incarnated as a fox, she soon finds herself involved in a peasant rebellion against an oppressive king. *The Doll Mage* by Martine Leavitt (Red Deer College Press) is another unusual Imaginary World fantasy, dark and intricately plotted. Set in a land where the village doll maker shapes the lives of the people around her, the plot involves the children who may someday take on the doll maker's mantle. *The Water Trilogy: Ascension, Reunion,* and *Transformation* by Kara Dalkey (Avon), all three volumes published in 2002, is the saga of a sixteen-year-old girl of a "mermyd" clan in the watery realm of Atlantis. These books are light but enjoyable reads from a dependably good storyteller.

The Waterstone by Rebecca Rupp (Candlewick) makes good bedtime reading for younger fantasy fans. It's epic fantasy in miniature, brimming with folklore and myth, involving the tiny "Fisher tribes" who make their home on a dying green pond. The hero is a Fisher boy on a quest to find the Waterstone that will save his people. *The Troll King* by John Vornholt (Aladdin) is shorter and lighter—a droll little tale for Middle Grade readers about a young troll who leads his people in an uprising against oppression. *The Thorn Ogres of Hagwood* by Robin Jarvis (Harcourt) is the start of a new fantasy series about the small "Werling" folk of a woodland populated by fairies, ogres, dwarves, and other magical creatures. Though there's nothing particularly innovative here, and the plot's somewhat predictable, it's also action packed, full of colorful folklore, and will probably be a hit with kids. Also by Jarvis, *The Crystal Prison* (SeaStar) is Book 2 in The Deptford Mice Trilogy, a dark, entertaining saga about a community of mice living in an old house in London. And speaking of mice, *Triss* by Brian Jacques (Philomel) is Book 15 in Jacques' vastly popular Redwall series—a swashbuckling animal fantasy involving mice, squirrels, ferrets, and other creatures from the woodlands of Redwall Abbey. Full of swordplay, intrigue, and derring-do, Jacques's books are a lot of fun.

The Moon Robber and *The Winter King* by Dean Morrissey and Stephen Krensky (HarperCollins) are Books 1 and 2 in the Magic Door Series—magical adventures for younger readers, distinguished by Morrissey's sumptuously detailed, Norman Rockwell–like paintings. *Sea-Cat and Dragon King* by Angela Carter (St. Martin's Press) is the first U.S. edition of this brief but charming children's story, with black-and-white illustrations by Eva Tatcheva. *The World Before This One* by Rafe Martin (Arthur A. Levine/Scholastic) is a novel composed of linked Seneca legends, illustrated with fantastic paper sculptures by Calvin Nicholls.

Single-Author Story Collections

2002 was another good year for short-story collections, thanks mostly to small-press publications. The following four collections, in particular, should not be missed: *The Fantasy Writers' Assistant and Other Stories* by Jeffrey Ford (Golden Gryphon Press), collects the dazzling short stories of this World Fantasy Award–winning author. Ranging from contemporary fantasy to Imaginary World and allegorical fiction, it's a varied, outstanding collection, published in an attractive small-press edition, with cover art by John Picacio, and introduced by Michael Swanwick. *Tapping the Dream Tree* by Charles de Lint (Tor), who is also a World Fantasy Award winner, contains tales linked by a common setting: de Lint's magical city of Newford, somewhere in modern North America. These are character-driven stories beautifully rooted in myth, folklore, and folk music—with charming cover art by another World Fantasy Award winner, Charles Vess. *Report to the Men's Club and Other Stories* by Carol Emshwiller (Small Beer Press) is a well-produced small-press volume (cover art by Shelly Jackson) containing original and reprint stories ranging from contemporary fantasy to surrealism and science fiction. Emshwiller is a challenging, innovative writer and a modern master of the short-fiction form. *The Ogre's Wife: Fairy Tales for Grown-ups* by Richard Parks (Obscura Press), introduced by Parke Godwin, contains fifteen wide-ranging fantasy tales, many with mythic or folkloric themes (not all based on fairy tales, as the subtitle might imply). Parks is a versatile, talented writer and deserves to be better known.

Also of note: *Lord Stink and Other Stories* by Judith Berman and *Rossetti Song: Four Stories* by Alexander Irvine are excellent chapbook editions available from Small Beer Press. Each contains four stories, most of them fantasy, all of them first-rate. *Stories from a Lost Anthology* by Rhys Hughes (Tartarus Press) is an elegant hardcover edition containing Hughes's stylish dark fantasy stories, introduced by Michael Moorcock. These stories haunt the shadowed borderlands between fantasy and horror. *One More for the Road* by Ray Bradbury (William Morrow) is a volume of gently magical tales by this master of American fantasy. The book contains seven original tales along with reprints of recent publications. *Stories of Your Life and Others* by Ted Chiang (Tor), *Little Doors* by Paul Di Filippo (Four Walls Eight Windows), and *The Collected Stories of Greg Bear* by Greg Bear (Tor) are volumes devoted primarily to science fiction—but all contain some very good fantasy tales and are worth seeking out. *Blood and Ivory: A Tapestry* by P. C. Hodgell (Meisha Merlin) consists of four traditional fantasy stories—colorful Imaginary World tales connected to Hodgell's memorable novel, *Godstalk. Strangers and Beggars* by James Van Pelt (Fairwood Press) contains sixteen reprints and one original story, ranging from atmospheric dark fantasy to supernatural horror. Three reprint volumes present the tales of past masters of fantasy fiction: *Bright Segment* (North Atlantic) is Volume Seven in a series collecting the complete stories of Theodore Sturgeon; *Smoke and Other Apparitions* (Midnight House) is Volume Two in a series devoted to the stories to Fritz Leiber; and *The Far Side of Nowhere* (Arkham House) collects the weird tales of pulp writer Nelson Bond.

On the mainstream shelves, I recommend four collections in particular: *Six Kinds of Sky* by Luis Alberto Urrea (Cinco Puntos Press) contains a mix of terrific magical realist and realist stories from one of the very best writers working in America today. *Quake* by Haruki Murakami (Knopf) is the latest volume from one of the best-loved writers in Japan. This book contains stories that were inspired, one way or another, by the devastating Kobe earthquake, and that make deft use of magical, allegorical, and surrealist elements. *Roofwalker* by Susan Power (Milkweed Editions) is the first collection of stories by a talented young Sioux writer. Powers weaves myth and magical realism into her poignant explorations of Native American life. *Lands of Memory* by Felisberto Hernández, translated from the Spanish by Esther Allen (New Directions), contains two novellas and four short stories from a Uruguayan writer called "the father of magical realism," known to have influenced Márquez, Cortázar, and Calvino. These are dreamlike, drifting, haunting stories on the subject of memory. In addition to these first-rate collections, you might also want to try the following: *You're an Animal, Viskovitz!* by Alessandro Boffa, translated from the Italian by John Casey and Maria Sanminiatelli (Knopf), twenty short animal fables by a Russian author living in Italy; *One Way Donkey Ride* by Mark E. Cull (Asylum Arts), a slim collection of brief, ironic, surrealist tales; and *Mariah of the Spirits* by Sherry Austin (The Overmountain Press), a collection of folksy, ghostly stories set throughout the South.

In Young Adult fiction, the best original collection of the year was *Water: Tales of Elemental Spirits* by Peter Dickinson and Robin McKinley (Putnam's), a marvelous volume of fantasy stories on a watery theme, ranging from historical and mythic fantasy to contemporary and Imaginary World fiction. This book is billed as the first of four, each based on one of the elements—and if every volume is as good as this one, I'm eager to read the rest. The best reprint collection was *Waifs and Strays* by Charles de Lint (Viking), an appealing volume intended to introduce this writer's work to teenage readers. Collecting stories from 1986 to the present (including one original to the book), *Waifs and Strays* includes several "Newford" stories but also ranges beyond this now-familiar milieu to Ottowa, "Borderland" and other settings both real and imaginary. I also recommend David Almond's gorgeous collection of autobiographical stories, *Counting Stars* (Delacorte)—although only a few of the stories have magical elements; and *Aphrodite's Blessings: Love Stories from the Greek Myths* by Clemence McLaren (Atheneum), a terrific volume containing three classic stories retold with a feminist slant. For younger children, *A Gift of Dragons* by Anne McCaffrey (Ballantine) features stories from the author's Pern series (science fiction tales with a fantasy feel) illustrated by Thomas Kidd; and *Mirror, Mirror* by Silverman (Chicken House/Scholastic) contains ten "twisted tales," which are sly modern fables.

Anthologies

2002 was a good year for original anthologies, ranging from traditional fantasy tales to edgy, innovative works. In the latter category, I was intrigued by *Polyphony*, the first volume in a new series devoted to "slipstream" fiction, published and edited by Deborah Layne and Jay Lake (Wheatland Press). Layne and Lake define slipstream as cutting-edge stories that fall between the cracks of literary genres and categories, and note that they created *Polyphony* because of the dearth of markets for this kind of fiction. The volume contains unusual works by established writers such as Lucius Shepherd, Carol Emshwiller, and Andy Duncan mixed with strong entries from up-and-comers such as Elisabeth Victoria Garcia, Vandana Singh, and Carrie Vaughan. Although one could wish for better production values on the book and for a more informative, critical introduction (addressing the subject of slipstream in more depth), nonetheless this is an ambitious, interesting series that deserves the field's support. *Rabid Transit: New Fiction by the Ratbastards* (Velocity Press) is another publication of works from fantasy's cutting edge. Like *Polyphony*, this chapbook contains strong tales that fall between the genre cracks—one story apiece from Barth Anderson, Christopher Barzak, Alan DeNiro, and Kristin Livdahl. All four are members of the Ratbastards, a Midwestern writers' collective; and judging by this and other recent works, these are writers to keep an eye on. *Leviathan* 3, edited by Forrest Aguirre and Jeff VanderMeer (Ministry of Whimsy Press) is the latest volume in another unusual and ambitious undertaking: a series of anthologies dedicated to "decadent fantasy"—atmospheric, highly stylized dark fantasy tales with gothic and surrealist elements. If you love Dunsany, Peake, and Clark Ashton Smith, this is the anthology for you. Volume Three contains particularly good contributions from Stepan Chapman, L. Timmel Duchamp, Jeffrey Ford, and Brian Stableford.

If you prefer your fantasy in a more traditional vein, try *Thirtieth Anniversary DAW Fantasy*, edited by Elizabeth R. Wollheim and Sheila E. Gilbert (DAW), a celebration of DAW Books' thirty years as a major publisher of fantasy fiction. This fine volume showcases DAW writers such as Tanith Lee, Andre Norton, Tanya Huff, Melanie Rawn, Jennifer Roberson, and Michael Shea. I particularly recommend Michelle West's contribution to the book, a richly textured Imaginary World novella that I regret was simply too long to reprint in this volume of the year's best. *Shelf Life: Fantastic Stories Celebrating Bookstores*, edited by Greg Ketter (DreamHaven Books), is an attractive, well-constructed anthology containing original fantasy, horror, and science fiction stories involving bookstores, with an introduction by Neil Gaiman. For fantasy readers, entertaining tales by P. D. Cacek, Nina Kiriki Hoffman, and A. R. Morlan are particularly recommended. On the Young Adult fiction shelves, try *The Green Man* (Viking), which Ellen Datlow and I coedited. This book for older teen readers contains original tales based on forest and nature myths by Emma Bull, Charles de Lint, Nina Kiriki Hoffman, Jeffrey Ford, Tanith Lee, Midori Snyder, Patricia A. McKillip, Delia Sherman, and others, with illustrations by Charles Vess.

There were also three notable reprint anthologies published in 2002. *The Year's Best Fantasy, Volume 2*, edited by David G. Hartwell and Kathryn Cramer (Avon Eos) is an excellent collection of tales celebrating works published in the fantasy genre, reprinting stories by Ursula K. Le Guin, Patrick O'Leary, Ted Chiang, Charles de Lint, and numerous others. *Fantasy: The Best of 2001*, edited by Robert Silverberg and Karen Haber (ibooks) is the first volume in yet another Year's Best series—this one, like the Hartwell and Cramer volume, also focused on genre fantasy. Volume One reprints works by Le Guin, Poul Anderson, Jeffrey Ford, Brian Hopkins, Rosemary Edghill, and others. *The American Fantasy Tradition* edited by Brian M. Thomsen (Tor), contains stories ranging from classic works by Washington Irving, Nathanial Hawthorne, Mark Twain,

Frank Stockton, and L. Frank Baum to modern tales by Manly Wade Wellman, Stephen King, Ursula K. Le Guin, Ray Bradbury, and Gene Wolfe. Although I quibble with Thomsen's choices for the contemporary portion of this book, where women writers are all but nonexistent (despite the enormous impact of women writers on the American fantasy field in the last two decades), the historical portion of the book is sound, making it an interesting, useful, and welcome volume.

Other anthologies you may want to take a look at: *Angel Body and Other Magic for the Soul* edited by Chris Reed and David Memmott (Wordcraft/Back Brain Recluse) is an edition celebrating twenty years of publication from Wordcraft Press in Oregon, with fiction and poetry by Lorraine Schein, Bruce Boston, and others. *Agog! Fantastic Fiction: 29 New Tales of Fantasy, Imagination, and Wonder* edited by Cat Sparks and introduced by Sean Williams (Agog! Press) features the work of up-and-coming Australian writers. *Legends of the Pendragon,* edited by James Lowder (Pendragon Fiction/Green Knight), contains original stories about "Camelot's founding" by Keith Taylor, Phyllis Ann Karr, Darrell Schweitzer and others. *A Quest Lover's Treasury of the Fantastic,* edited by Margaret Weis (Warner) is a swords-and-sorcery collection with stories of varying quality, the best of them by such stalwarts as Poul Anderson, C. J. Cherryh, and Michael Moorcock. You'll also find a few fantasy tales in *In the Shadow of the Wall,* edited by Byron R. Tetrick (Cumberland House), containing fiction inspired by Vietnam and the Vietnam Veterans Memorial in Washington, D.C., and in *Passing Strange: Australian Speculative Fiction,* edited by Bill Congreve (MirrorDanse Books). The prolific anthologist Martin H. Greenberg had several new fantasy publications in 2002: *Alternate Gettysburgs,* coedited with Brian M. Thomsen (Berkley), containing original alternate-history stories; *Pharaoh Fantastic,* coedited with Brittiany A. Koren (DAW), original tales set during the time of the Pharaohs; *Knight Fantastic,* coedited with John Helfers (DAW); and *Apprentice Fantastic,* coedited with Russell Davis (DAW). Although "theme" anthologies like this might not be to every reader's taste, Greenberg is to be commended for continuing to provide commercial markets for original short fiction.

Magazines and Journals

The most noteworthy publication of the year among periodicals was the Fall 2002 issue of *Conjunctions,* the biannual journal of new writing published by Bard College, edited by Bradford Morrow. As I mentioned earlier in this Summation, Issue 39 was devoted to The New Wave Fabulists—fiction on the literary cusp of the fantasy and horror genres—guest-edited by Peter Straub and illustrated by Gahan Wilson. This unapologetically literary volume contained excellent stories by an impressive list of authors: John Crowley, Kelly Link, M. John Harrison, James Morrow, Nalo Hopkinson, Jonathan Lethem, Joe Haldeman, China Miéville, Andy Duncan, Gene Wolfe, Patrick O'Leary, Jonathan Carroll, John Kessel, Karen Joy Fowler, Paul Park, Elizabeth Hand, Neil Gaiman, and Straub himself, along with two insightful essays by Gary K. Wolfe and John Clute. Straub's selections stretch the boundaries of fantastic literature in a number of interesting and challenging ways. Even more than the anthologies mentioned above (*Polyphony, Leviathan* 3, etc.), this volume of interstitial, transgenre stories rooted in the fantastic and the weird sits at what is presently the cutting edge of the fantasy and horror fields. Nestled right up beside it is *Lady Churchill's Rosebud Wristlet* (Small Beer Press), a small 'zine edited by Gavin Grant and Kelly Link, which is a reliable source for innovative fantasy fiction, poetry, and more. I also recommend *. . . is this a cat?* and *Say . . . was that a kiss?* (Fortress of Words), two quirky little 'zines edited by Christopher Rowe; and *Floodwater* (Tropism Press), an intriguing 'zine containing tales by Heather Shaw and Tim Pratt, art by Richard Doyle.

For more traditional fantasy fare, *The Magazine of Fantasy and Science Fiction*, in the capable hands of editor Gordon Van Gelder, remains the single best source for short fantasy fiction. Month after month, Van Gelder presents stories that are dependably well-crafted, entertaining, and often surprising—by the likes of Jeffrey Ford, Lucius Shepard, Rick Bowes, Carol Emshwiller, Jack Cady, Scott Bradfield, Esther M. Friesner, and talented newcomers including Charles Coleman Finlay, and Chris Willrich. *Realms of Fantasy*, edited by Shawna McCarthy, has been getting better with each passing year. Despite the emphasis on swords-and-dragons on the cover, McCarthy has been reaching beyond swords-and-sorcery (without abandoning this core readership) to publish a wider range of fantasy fiction, much of it by promising new writers such as Theodora Goss, Naomi Kritzer, Richard Parks, Liz Williams, and Carrie Vaughan. *Asimov's Science Fiction Magazine*, edited by Gardner Dozois, seems to be publishing less fantasy these days, although what does get published is reliably good. Tales by Robert Silverberg and James Patrick Kelly were particularly memorable last year. For dark fantasy and swords-and-sorcery, the venerable *Weird Tales* is still alive and kicking under the guidance of editor Darrell Schweitzer, publishing stories in the tradition of Lovecraft, Howard, Leiber, et al. The best magazines for stories by the many fine fantasy writers working in the U.K. continue to be *Interzone*, edited by David Pringle, and *The Third Alternative*, edited by Andy Cox. A new magazine, *3SF*, began publication in 2002—devoted to "Science Fiction, Speculative Fantasy, Strange Facts," edited by Liz Holliday. In Australia, fantasy fiction can be found in *Aurealis*, the speculative fiction magazine edited by Keith Stevenson, and in *Redsine*, a handsome journal devoted to dark fantasy, edited by Trent Jamieson and Garry Nurrish. In Canada, *On Spec* mixes fantasy tales with science fiction and horror, edited by Diane L. Walton. *Aurealis*, *Redsine*, and *On Spec* are all places for emerging writers to practice their craft. Reviews of the above magazines and others, as well as links to their Web sites (and subscription addresses), can be found on the informative *Tangent Review* site: www.tangentonline.com. Book reviews and news about the fantasy publishing industry can be found in *Locus* magazine, both the print version and *Locus Online* (www.locusmag.com) and *Chronicle* (formerly *Science Fiction Chronicle*). *Locus* reached its five hundredth issue this year under the steady guidance of founder, publisher, and editor in chief Charles N. Brown. Brown has now retired from the latter of these roles, and Jennifer A. Hall has taken up the reins as executive editor. Congratulations to them both.

For readers interested in myth, folklore, and fairy tales, the best magazines continue to be *Parabola*, edited by David Appelbaum, published by the Society for the Study of Myth and Tradition, and the scholarly *Marvels and Tales: Journal of Fairy Tale Studies*, edited by Donald Haase. New in 2002, *TYR: Myth, Culture, and Tradition*, is a quirky annual review for "radical traditionalist and antimodernist thought" (including articles on myth and folk culture), edited by Joshua Buckley, Collin Cleary, and Michael Moynihan.

On the Web, *SciFiction* at *SciFi.com*, edited by Ellen Datlow (www.scifi.com/scifiction), remains the very best Webzine bar none for literary speculative fiction—including fantasy, American magical realism, and slipstream or interstitial tales. *The Infinite Matrix* edited by Eileen Gunn (www.infinitematrix.net) is also good, but focused more on science fiction than fantasy. It's worth checking out, though, in particular for the "Sleep of Reason" series of short-short stories by Michael Swanwick, written to accompany the art of Francisco Goya. *Strange Horizons*, edited by Mary Anne Mohanraj (www.Strangehorizons.com) is the best place on the Web for fiction by up-and-comers in the speculative-fiction field. Mohanraj does a good job of keeping editorial standards high when working with emerging writers. For book reviews, essays, interviews, and news about the fantasy field, try *The SF Site* edited by Rodger Turner (www.sfsite.com), *SF Revu* edited by Ernest Lilley (www.sfrevu.com), the aforementioned *Locus Online* (www.locusmag.com), *The Green Man Review* edited by Cat Eldridge (www.greenmanreview.com), and *Rambles* edited by Tom Knapp (www.rambles.net). For children's books: *The Children's Literature Web Guide* (www.acs.ucalgary.ca/~dkbrown/index.html) and *Achuka* (www.achuka.com). For myths and fairy tales: *The SurLaLune Fairy Tale Pages* edited by Heidi Anne Heiner (www.surlalunefairytales.com) and *The Endicott Studio Journal of Mythic Arts* (www.endicott-studio.com). For fantasy art, try *The SurLaLuneFairy Tale Illustrators* site (www.surlalunefairytales.com/illustrations/index.html) and *Art Magick* (www.artmagick.com). The Web Site of the Year for 2002 is *Born Magazine* (www.bornmagazine.com), a wonderful, wildly innovative journal where artists and writers work together in fascinating, often magical ways. *Born Magazine* is edited by Anmarie Trimble, with contributing editors Jennifer Grotz, Tenaya Darlington, Bruce Smith, and Monica Drake, and art director Gabe Kean. Be sure to check this one out.

The following print magazines, both big and small, provided stories and poetry for the fantasy half of this volume: *The Atlantic Monthly*, *Conjunctions*: 39, *Interzone*, *The Magazine of Fantasy and Science Fiction*, *Realms of Fantasy*, *The Antioch Review*, *The Chicago Review*, *The Hudson Review*, *The Louisville Review*, *The Malahat Review*, *Star*Line*, and *Poem*. Stories also came from the Web journals *SciFi.com* and *Arkansas Literary Forum*. We have no stories from *The New Yorker* this time, which is rare for us—but not for lack of trying. Alas, we were unable to obtain reprint rights this year to *New Yorker* stories by A. S. Byatt and John Berger (because each was scheduled to appear elsewhere), but they're listed at the end of this Summation, and again in the Honorable Mentions section. I hope you'll seek them out.

Fantasy stories and poems chosen for the 2002 Honorable Mentions list came from the same magazines and also from the following: *The Antigonish Review*, *Beloit Fiction Journal*, *Black Gate*, *Calyx*, *Connecticut Review*, *Dark Illuminati*, *Dark Terrors*. *Full Unit Hookup*, *The Georgia Review*, *Harpur Palate*, *Ideomancer*. *The Iowa Review*, *. . . is this a cat?*, *Lady Churchill's Rosebud Wristlet*, *LatinoLA*, *The Magazine of Speculative Poetry*, *Michigan Quarterly Review*, *The New Yorker*, *Not One of Us*, *On Spec*, *Pleiades*, *Poet Lore*, *Prairie Schooner*, *Quarterly West*,

Redsine, Rosebud, Say . . . was that a kiss?, The Sewanee Review, Shenandoah, The Silver Web, Supernatural Tales, Talebones, TAR, The Third Alternative, This Magazine, TriQuarterly, Weird Tales, The William and Mary Review, and *Wind*. Stories were also chosen from the Web journals *Strange Horizon, Infinite Matrix*, and *Born Magazine*.

Art

I didn't find large numbers of "must have" art books in 2002, but nonetheless there were a few I can recommend. Foremost among them is *Lady Cottington's Fairy Album* by Brian Froud (Abrams), the sequel to his best-selling "squashed fairies" saga, *Lady Cottington's Pressed Fairy Book*. Just as bawdy and irreverent as the previous book, but with a more substantive, rather moving story concerning the girlhood of the fictional Lady Cottington, it's a treat for fans of Victoriana, and of fairies squashed or whole. Another book for fans of Victoriana is *Dreaming in Pictures: The Photography of Lewis Carroll*, edited by Douglas R. Nickel (Yale University Press), published to coincide with a traveling exhibition on the subject. Carroll, author of *Alice in Wonderland*, was a passionate photographer with a particular penchant for photographing little girls in fantastical guises. Apparently there are some who share that penchant to this very day, as is evident in A *Fairy's Child* by Ann Dahlgren and Douglas Foulke (Abrams), which contains misty black-and-white photographs of children dressed up as fairies. *Fées, elfes, dragons & autres créatures des royaumes de féerie (Fairies, Elves, Dragons, and Other Creatures of the Realm of Faery)*, edited by Claudine Glot and Michel Le Bris (Editions Hoëbeke), is a very beautiful art book published in France to coincide with an exhibition of fairy tale art from the twelfth to the twenty-first centuries—ranging from medieval manuscript illustrations to the Pre-Raphaelites and Victorian fairy painters to a brief section of modern fantasy art. You needn't travel to Paris to find the book; copies are available through Amazon.com—just follow the links to their French pages.

I highly recommend *Seven Wild Sisters*, a thoroughly enchanting small-press edition containing a long story by Charles de Lint and illustrations by Charles Vess (Subterranean Press). Text and art work seamlessly together in this inspired collaboration. *The Art of Jeffrey Jones* by Cathy and Arnie Fenner (Underwood) is a retrospective of the gorgeous work of this master painter whose art graced the fantasy and comics fields primarily in the seventies and eighties. Jones is an artist who excels in both the Heroic and Romantic modes of fantasy illustration. His work has influenced many subsequent artists, and this edition will show you why. *GOAD: The Many Moods of Phil Hale* (Donald M. Grant) is a book we recommended last year, but since it seems to be ending up on 2002 Best of the Year lists, it's worth mentioning again. Hale is the polar opposite of Jeffrey Jones, without a Romantic bone in his body, but his skill with a paintbrush is equally dazzling. It's a handsome volume, filled with the exuberant work of a truly singular artist.

Spectrum 9, edited by Arnie and Cathy Fenner (Underwood), is the latest volume in an annual juried showcase of art from the science fiction, fantasy, and horror fields. This edition features work by Leo and Diane Dillon, Michael Whelan, James Gurney, Brom, and many others. *Storybook Culture: The Art of Popular*

Children's Books by Joseph and Cheryl Homme (Collector's Press) looks at American children's book illustrations from classic works by Howard Pyle and Maxfield Parrish to the covers of *Nancy Drew* and *The Hardy Boys*. *Rackham's Fairy Tale Illustrations in Full Color*, edited by Jeff Menges (Dover) reprints exquisite fairy tale paintings by this English master illustrator from the turn of the last century.

For books *about* art and artists, some interesting volumes I came across last year were: *The Correspondence of Dante Gabriel Rossetti: The Formative Years, 1855–1862*, edited by William E. Fredeman (Boydell and Brewer); *Aubrey Beardsley and British Wagnerism in the 1890s* by Emma Sutton (Oxford University Press); and *Surrealism and the Sacred: Power, Eros, and the Occult in Modern Art* by Celia Rabinovitch (Westview Press). I also recommend *The Portable Magritte* (Universe Books)—a handy little edition containing biographical material, an essay by Magritte himself, and over four hundred paintings by this master of surrealism. There were several new books about the Mexican surrealist painter Frida Kahlo in 2002, no doubt taking advantage of the popularity of the recent film *Frida*. *Beauty is Convulsive: The Passion of Frida Kahlo* by Carole Maso (Counterpoint) is a terrific, unusual volume which the author calls "a meditation" on Kahlo's life and work—not quite a biography, not quite a novel, but something in between. Less lucidly written but still interesting is *The Incantation of Frida K.* by Kate Braveman (Seven Stories Press), a fictionalized biographical work as narrated by a morphine-addicted Frida on her deathbed. *Imaging Her Selves: Frida Kahlo's Poetics of Identity and Fragmentation* by Gannit Ankori (Greenwood) is one of the few books to provide an in-depth look at the artist's paintings without getting sidetracked by her flamboyant life. I loved this informative, illuminating volume—but it's on the pricey side. Thank heavens for libraries. *Frida Kahlo, Diego Rivera and Mexican Modernism: The Jacques and Natasha Gelman Collection* is a handsome new art book from the National Gallery of Australia, with an informative text edited by Anthony White.

Picture Books for Children

Some of the best fantasy art and storytelling today can be found over on the children's book shelves. The following ten picture books are the best that came across my desk in 2002, and shouldn't be missed.

At the top of the list is a new retelling of *Sleeping Beauty*, written and illustrated by K. Y. Craft (SeaStar)—an artist whose distinctive paintings also grace the covers of adult fantasy novels. Craft's rendition of this classic fairy tale is a hauntingly beautiful one, with sumptuous, richly detailed art and a well-told story.

Next, we have two books based on the "Cinderella" fairy tale. *Cinderella* by Charles Perrault, translated from the French by Anthea Bell and illustrated by Loek Koopmans (North-South), is a charming version first published in Switzerland in 1999. Bell's translation is excellent, as always, but even better are Koopman's delicate watercolor paintings, which look something like a cross between Carl Larssen and Lizbeth Zwerger. *Adelita* by Tomie dePaola (Putnam's) is an unusual Mexican version of the fairy tale, illustrated by dePaola's appealing, deceptively simple paintings.

I also recommend two different versions of a Hans Christian Andersen story:

The Nightingale retold by Stephen Mitchell, with watercolor paintings evocative of Chinese art by the Russian artist Bagram Ibatoulline (Candlewick Press); and *The Nightingale*, skillfully retold and illustrated by the African American artist Jerry Pinkney (Putnam's). The Pinkney version moves the setting from China to Morocco.

Two lovely versions of the Russian "Firebird" legend came out in 2002: *The Tale of the Firebird*, translated from the Russian by Tatiana Popova and illustrated by the great Russian painter Gennardy Spirin; and *The Firebird*, beautifully retold by Jane Yolen, with illustrations by another fine Russian artist, Vladimir Vagin (HarperCollins).

The Red Wolf by Margaret Shannon (Houghton Mifflin) is the story of a rebellious princess who knits a magical outfit that turns her into a big red wolf. The story is hilarious and Shannon's paintings (created during this Australian artist's sojourn in the Czech Republic) are fabulous.

Frida, written by Jonah Winter, illustrated by Ana Juan (Scholastic) is simply splendid. This "picture book biography" tells the story of the life of Mexican artist Frida Kahlo through Winter's simple yet vivid prose, accompanied by the stunning artwork of the Spanish fine artist Ana Juan. In her first book for children, Juan uses many of the same Mexican folk motifs that Frida herself drew upon—creating art more accessible to children than Frida's own, yet with something of the same spirit. It's a magnificent collaboration.

A Story for Bear, written by Dennis Haseley and illustrated by Jon LaMarche (Silver Whistle/Harcourt), is a tale guaranteed to win the heart of book lovers—a poignant fantasy about a woman reading to a brown bear in the woods. The story is a gentle, magical one, and the pictures (drawn in pastel) are utterly charming. Though it's a quieter book, *A Story for Bear* ties with *Frida* as my personal favorite of the year.

Other recommendations, noted briefly: *King Midas: The Golden Touch* by Demi (Margaret K. McElderry Books); *All the Way to Lhasa: A Tale from Tibet* by Barbara Helen Berger (Philomel); *The Rumor: A Jataka Tale from India* by Jan Thornhill (Maple Tree Press); *When Animals Were People: A Huichol Indian Tale* retold by Bonnie Larson, illustrated by Modesto Rivera Lemus (Clear Light Publishing; English/Spanish bilingual edition); *The Stolen Sun: A Story of Native Alaska* by Amanda Hall (Eerdmans); *The Lands of the Dead* (Tales of the Odyssey series, Book 2) by Mary Pope Osborne, illustrated by Troy Howell (Hyperion Press); *Goodnight Fairies*, written by Kathleen Hague, illustrated by Michael Hague (SeaStar), *The Book of Dragons: Tales and Legends From Many Lands*, edited by O. Muiriel Fuller, illustrated by Alexander Key (Dover), and *If the Shoe Fits: Voices From Cinderella*, with poems by Laura Whipple and illustrations by Laura Beingessner (Margaret K. McElderry).

Reprint editions: Frederick Warne & Co. is publishing a series of oversize editions of the Cecily Barker "flower fairy" books, containing Barker's classic fairy illustrations and poems from the early twentieth century. *Flower Fairies of the Summer*, *Flower Fairies of the Wayside*, and *A Flower Fairy Alphabet* all came out in 2002. *Merry Adventures of Robin Hood* by Howard Pyle is another reprint of an early twentieth-century classic, published in the Great Illustrated Classics series from Abdo and Daughters. *Robin Hood* (Chronicle) is a handsome volume that reprints Evelyn Charles Vivian's 1906 version of the tale along with art compiled by Cooper Edens: over one hundred Robin Hood illustrations from the twelfth to the twentieth centuries.

General Nonfiction

Nonfiction titles published in 2002 that may be of interest to fantasy readers: *Mervyn Peake: My Eyes Mint Gold* by Malcolm Yorke (Overlook Press) is a biography of the British writer and artist who created the Gormenghast trilogy. *L. Frank Baum: Creator of Oz* by Katherine M. Rogers (St. Martin's) is a new exploration of the life of this American fantasist. *Bradbury: An Illustrated Life* by Jerry Weist (William Morrow), billed as a "visual biography," is a lavishly illustrated coffee-table book devoted to Ray Bradbury's lengthy, diverse career in fiction, comics, film, the theater, and visual art. *Joseph Campbell: A Fire in the Mind* by Stephen and Robin Larsen (Inner Traditions) is the authorized biography of this influential writer, teacher, and tireless advocate for the importance of myth in modern life. *Speaking of the Fantastic* by Darrell Schweitzer (Wildside Press) is a volume of interesting interviews with fantasy writers such as Ursula K. Le Guin, Ellen Kushner, Fritz Leiber, Robert Holdstock, Jonathan Carroll, and Gene Wolfe. *The Age of Chaos* by Jeff Gardiner (The British Fantasy Society) examines the "multiverse" created in the fiction of Michael Moorcock. *The Fiction of Angela Carter*, edited by Sarah Gamble (Palgrave Macmillan), is an insightful look at Carter's fiction and essays, including her adult fairy tale works.

Three interesting books focused on the works of British fantasists Lewis and Tolkien: *Imagination and the Arts in C. S. Lewis: Journeying to Narnia and Other Worlds* by Peter J. Schakel (University of Missouri Press); *Celebrating Middle-earth: The Lord of the Rings As a Defense of Western Civilization*, containing six essays by Tolkien scholars, edited by John G. West Jr. (Inkling Books); and *Splintered Light: Logos and Language in Tolkien's World* by Verlyn Flieger (Kent State University Press). *Frodo's Quest: Living the Myth in the Lord of the Rings* by Robert S. Ellwood (Quest Books) turns the trilogy into a pop-psyche manual, God help us. *Myth & Middle-earth: Exploring the Medieval Legends Behind J. R. R. Tolkien's Lord of the Rings* by Leslie Jones (Open Road Press) is a very readable guide, for nonacademics, to Tolkien's mythic source material. To learn more about the Norse legends Professor Tolkien loved, also try *Norse Mythology: A Guide to the Gods, Heroes, Rituals, and Beliefs* by John Lindow (Oxford University Press), an excellent volume.

Myth, Folklore, and Fairy Tales

There were several new works I highly recommend for fantasy readers and writers interested in the source material of myth, folklore, and fairy tales. At the top of the list is *The Annotated Classic Fairy Tales* by Maria Tatar (W. W. Norton), a beautifully designed edition containing twenty-six traditional tales along with annotations examining the history of each tale, accompanied by classic fairy tale illustrations. It's a handsome, informative volume that belongs in every fairy tale lover's library. For those interested in a deeper examination of fairy tale history, try *Breaking the Magical Spell: Radical Theories of Folk and Fairy Tales* by Jack

David Zipes (The University Press of Kentucky), a fascinating, challenging look at this subject from one the field's very best scholars. Also for fairy tale fans, Kate Bernheimer's *Mirror, Mirror on the Wall: Women Writers Explore Their Favorite Fairy Tales* (Random House/Anchor) has been re-released in an expanded edition that adds four new essays (by Ursula K. Le Guin, Midori Snyder, Carole Maso, and myself) to a collection of sterling essays by A. S. Byatt, Margaret Atwood, Joyce Carol Oates, Fay Weldon, and other writers, along with an informative new introduction. Another excellent volume of essays is *Flight of the Wild Gander: Explorations in the Mythological Dimension: Select Essays, 1944–1968* by Joseph Campbell (New World Library), a lively, engrossing, wide-ranging collection covering myth, fairy tales, and mythic themes in modern life. *Writings on Irish Folklore, Legend and Myth* by William Butler Yeats, edited by Robert Welch (Penguin Twentieth-Century Classics), collects the Irish poet's extensive writing on the subject into one edition. *The Modern Construction of Myth* by Andrew Von Hendy (Indiana University Press) and *Mythical Thinking: Philosophical Contributions to the Study of Myth*, edited by Kevin Schilbrack (Routledge) are both provocative new studies looking at the role of myth and modernity. *Myth and Ritual School: J. G. Frazer and the Cambridge Ritualists* by Robert Ackerman (Routledge) is a study of the author of *The Golden Bough* and other influential folklorists (such as Jane Harrison and Gilbert Murray) who gathered at Cambridge University at the turn of the last century.

Japanese Tales, edited by Royall Tyler (Pantheon), was the best collection of folktales that I came across in 2002—a splendid volume of over two hundred magical stories from medieval Japan. I also highly recommend *Nart Sagas from the Caucasus: Myths and Legends from the Circassians, Abazas, Abkhaz, and Ubykhs* by John Colarusso (Princeton University Press), a rare look at a rich mythic tradition that is little known in the West. The modestly titled *A Glimpse of Vietnamese Oral Literature: Mythology, Tales, Folklore* by Loc Dinh Pham (Xlibris) provides a nice introduction to this subject. *A Chinese Bestiary: Strange Creatures from the Guideways Through Mountains and Seas* by Richard E. Strassberg (University of California Press) is a good guide to mythical beasties of the East. For a more general survey of magical creatures from around the world, *The Book of Dragons and Other Mythical Beasts* by Joseph Nigg (Barron's) is a small, lively introductory book—almost more of an art book, with illustrations by eight different artists. *Hausland Tales from the Nigerian Marketplace* by Gavin McIntosh (Linnet Books) is an interesting collection of folktales from the sub-Sahara. A *Treasury of Afro-American Folklore*, edited by Harold Courlander (Marlowe and Co.), looks at "the oral literature, traditions, recollections, legends, tales, songs, religious beliefs, customs, sayings, and humor of peoples of African American descent in the Americas," following up Courlander's A *Treasury of African Folklore* (Marlowe and Co.)—which is also available from Marlowe and Co. in a new edition. *The Myth of Quetzalcoatl* by Enrique Florescano (Johns Hopkins University Press) is an in-depth exploration of this important Mesoamerican mythic figure, translated from the Spanish by Lysa Hochroth and illustrated by Raul Velazquez. The best book on Native American myth I read last year was *Being in Being: The Collected Works of a Master Haida Mythteller, Skaay of the Qquuna* by Skaay, translated by Robert Bringhurst (University of Nebraska Press). Other good volumes: *Surviving Through the Days*, Native Californian stories and songs edited by Herbert W. Luthin (University of California Press); *The Bearskin Quiver*, pan-tribal tales from the Southwestern states, edited by Gregory McNamee (Daimon Verlag); and *Elderberry Flute Song*, a quirky, slim volume of contemporary Coyote tales by Peter Blue Cloud/Aroniawenrate (White Pine Press).

The prolific, Oxford-based Arthurian scholars John and Caitlín Matthews had several new publications last year: *King Arthur and the Goddess of the Land: The Divine Feminine in The Mabinogion* by Caitlín Matthews (Inner Traditions); *Taliesin: The Last Celtic Shaman* by John Matthews (Inner Traditions); and *The Song of Arthur: Celtic Tales from the High King's Court* by John Matthews (Quest). Fans of Arthurian myth may also be interested in *Merlin and Wales: A Magician's Landscape* by Michael Danes (Thames and Hudson), an examination the Merlin legend thickly illustrated with related art, artifacts, and photographs of mythic sites in Wales.

Music

Traditional music is of interest to many fantasy lovers because it draws on some of the same cultural roots as do folk tales and other folk arts. Each year writer/folklorist/musician Charles de Lint kindly gives me a hand by recommending new releases that fantasy readers may enjoy. There is such a wealth of traditional music available these days, however, that we have room to mention only a handful of favorites from 2002 here—so for further recommendations, see reviews on the following Web sites: *The Green Man Review* (www.greenmanreview.com) and *Rambles* (www.rambles.net).

From Charles de Lint: "Being immersed in writing a book set in the American Southwest for the past year gave my recent music listening a decided Latin slant. And considering long Canadian winters, Latin music's also a good way to keep cabin fever at bay. The classic soundtrack to *Walker* by the late (and much-missed) Joe Strummer and a mix tape of the instrumentals from Calexico's back catalogue made an excellent base for both needs (and also work as a fine soundtrack by which to read your favorite magical realists), but there are plenty of new recordings as well, beginning with Calexico's brilliant *Feast of Wine*, a collection of ragged alt-rock and Americana imbued with a peppery salsa of Mariachi music and Ennio Morricone. Other high points included Salsa Celtica's *El Agua de la Vida*, where Scottish music meets Latin, and *Cybertropic Chilango Power* by Los de Abajo, where urban music meets Mariachi. Monica Ramos delivered a romantic, Latin-flavored follow-up to Alan Stivell's *Renaissance of the Celtic Harp* with her own harping on *Behind That Light*, and vocalist Lila Downs shone on the *Frida* film soundtrack. With *India Morena*, Argentinian singer Barbara Luna has produced one of my favorite recordings of the year—gorgeous, emotive vocals sung against a backdrop of indigenous South American instruments, touching everything from salsa and candombe to original material. The self-penned title track, which translates to 'Black Indian Woman,' is particularly evocative as it explores Luna's own mixed-race heritage.

"I didn't listen to as much Celtic music last year, but a real find was Clan Terra from the Canadian Prairies with their twin fiddle–based album, *Waiting for the Wickerman*; and England's Kate Rusby delivered another astonishing set of traditional ballads with *Ten*, marking her tenth anniversary in the field. And after highly successful collaborations with saxophonist Andy Sheppard and the curious musical permutations of the Ensemble Mystical, Kathryn Tickell showed that she still has her traditional chops on *Back to the Hills*, an album of solos, duets and trios, featuring, among others, the inimitable Willie Taylor on fiddle. Under unclassifiable, file British Columbia's The Bill Hilly Band and their album *All Day Every Day*, which visits pretty much every acoustic music tradition in the world and creates a joyous blend of the results. You *have* to see this band live. As I rapidly run out of space here, let me leave you with two last recommendations: *Down the Old Plank Road* has the indefatigable Chieftains visiting Appalachia to produce Celtified versions of ballads that are known on, and fit comfortably into the musical traditions of, both sides of the Atlantic, with the outstanding cut being Alison Krauss's angelic rendering of the tragic 'Molly Bawn.' And for those of you who like a little more grit in your trad music, try the final recording of one of the last concerts by Blue Mountain, the two-CD set, *Tonight It's Now or Never*. A mix of traditional ballads and original material, it's a punchy, infectious farewell performance by a great band."

I'll enthusiastically second Charles's recommendations (particularly Salsa Celtica, Lila Downs, and Barbara Luna) and add a few more of my own—such as *Anglicana* by Eliza Carthy, the talented daughter of veteran folk singers Martin Carthy and Norma Waterson. If you've been disappointed by the pop direction the younger Carthy has been wandering in, take heart—she hovers closer to her trad roots here, while losing none of her originality. Two new recordings have made me sit up and pay attention to all the good music coming out of Wales recently: Carreg Lafar's *Profiad (Experience)*, which is lovely, and the straightforwardly titled *Celtic Music from Wales* by Ffynnon. Celtic ballad lovers ought to give a listen to *Heart's Desire* by Niamh Parsons, *Three Ravens* by Malinky, and *Where the Sky Meets the Sea* by The McCalmans (along with the aforementioned *Ten* by Kate Rusby). Also check out *Sugarcane* by Shine, featuring harmonic vocals in Scots Gaelic and English by Alyth McCormack, Mary MacMaster, and Corrina Hewat. For music with a little more kick to it, there's *Hotel Kaledonia* by Keltik Electrik, Celto-punk instrumental dance music; and *East to West* by Baka Beyond, a terrific recording that combines Celtic tunes with Baka Pygmy music from Cameroon and other rhythms from around the world, stirring it all together into a wonderfully danceable concoction. The mystical traditional of Gnawa music from ancient Morocco is powerfully updated by Hassan Hakmoun on his latest, *The Gift*, which is a gift indeed. Finland's Gjallerhorn does an interesting riff on traditional Finnish and Swedish tunes on their new release, *Grimborg*, with soaring vocals by Jenny Wilhelms. Azam Ali's *Portals of Grace* mixes medieval French songs, Latin chants, Nordic music, Sephardic music, and Celtic music from Brittany and Spain. It sounds like it should be a mess, but it's really quite captivating. Two exceptional Native American music releases are *Fourth World* by the Ute/Navajo musician R. Carlos Nakai, a rich combination of symphonic music for orchestra and Native American flute, and *Peace and Power: The Best of Joanne Shenandoah*, a gorgeous introduction to this Oneida singer's work for those who don't already know it.

Awards

The World Fantasy Convention was held in Minneapolis last year. The guests of honor were Jonathan Carroll, Dennis Etchison, Stephen Jones, Kathe Koja, David McKean and William F. Nolan, and the awards were hosted by Greg Ketter.

The 2002 World Fantasy Awards (for works published in 2001) presented at the conventions were: Lifetime Achievement: George Scithers and Forrest J. Ackerman; Best Novel: *The Other Wind* by Urusla K. Le Guin; Best Novella: "The Bird Catcher" by S. P. Somtow; Best Short Fiction: "Queen for a Day" by Albert E. Cowdrey; Best Collection: *Skin Folk* by Nalo Hopkinson; Best Anthology: *The Museum of Horrors* edited by Dennis Etchison; Best Artist: Allen Koszowski; Special Award—Professional: (tie) Stephen Jones and Jo Fletcher; Special Award—Nonprofessional: Raymond Russel and Rosalie Parker. The judges for the 2002 Awards were Peter Adkins, Meg Davis, Jason Van Hollander, Michele Sagara West, and F. Paul Wilson.

The 2002 Mythopoeic Awards were presented at Mythcon in Boulder, Colorado. Scholar Guest of Honor: Alexei Kondratiev; Author Guest of Honor: Connie Willis; Best Adult Literature: *The Curse of Chalion* by Lois McMaster Bujold; Best Children's Literature: *The Ropemaker* by Peter Dickinson; Scholarship Award for Inklings Studies: *Tolkien's Legendarium: Essays on the History of Middle-earth*, edited by Verlyn Flieger and Carl F. Hostetter; Scholarship Award for General Myth and Fantasy Studies: *The Owl, the Raven and the Dove: The Religious Meaning of the Grimms' Magic Fairy Tales* by G. Ronald Murphy. The awards are judged by members of the Mythopoeic Society.

The International Conference for the Fantastic in the Arts was held again last year in Fort Lauderdale, Florida. The guests of honor were: Charles De Lint, Ramsey Campbell, S. T. Joshi, and Brian Aldiss.

The winner of the 2002 William L. Crawford Award for the best first fantasy novel was Jasper Fforde for *The Eyre Affair*. The award was presented at the I.C.F.A.

WisCon was held again last year in Madison, Wisconsin. It is a forum for writers, artists, publishers, fans, and academics to explore feminism and gender roles and relationships in speculative fiction. The guests of honor were Nalo Hopkinson and Nina Kiriki Hoffman. The James Tiptree, Jr. Memorial Award for the best gender-bending fiction for 2002 went to: (tie) M. John Harrison for *Light* and to John Kessel for *Stories for Men*.

That's an overview of the year in fantasy; now on to the stories themselves. Each year, the number of stories I would like to put in this volume is larger than we have space to print. Novellas, in particular, rarely make it into the final volume. The following stories are ones that I consider among the year's very best, and I hope you'll seek them out if you haven't run across them already.

"The Courtesy" by John Berger, from the June 17–24, 2002 issue of *The New Yorker*.

"In for a Penny, or The Man Who Believed in Himself" by James P. Blaylock, from the February 20 edition of *SciFiction* (SciFi.com).

"The Thing in the Forest" by A. S. Byatt, from the June 3, 2002 issue of *The New Yorker.*

"Seven Wild Sisters" by Charles de Lint, a novella first published by Subterranean Press, with illustrations by Charles Vess, and reprinted in *Tapping the Dream Tree.*

"Big Rock, Candy Mountain" by Andy Duncan, from *Conjunctions*: 39.

"From Across the River" by Hiromi Goto, from the November/December 2002 issue of *This Magazine*.

"Pavane for a Prince of Air" by Elizabeth Hand, from *Embrace the Mutation.*

"In the Witch's Garden" by Naomi Kritzer, from the October 2002 issue of *Realms of Fantasy.*

"The Drive-In Puerto Rico" by Lucius Shepherd, from the October/November issue of *The Magazine of Fantasy and Science Fiction.*

"A World Painted by Birds" by Katherine Vaz, from *The Green Man.*

"The Memory of Stone" by Michelle West, from *30th Anniversary DAW: Fantasy.*

"Our Friend Electricity" by Ron Wolfe, from the June 2002 issue of *The Magazine of Fantasy and Science Fiction.*

"Dark Seed, Dark Stone" by Jane Yolen, from the February issue of *Realms of Fantasy.*

I hope you'll enjoy the stories and poems chosen for this volume as much as I did. Many thanks to the authors, agents, and publishers who allowed us to reprint them there. I also want to thank all the readers who have supported this anthology series for sixteen years. It's been a privilege to work on this series, and a joy to work with Ellen and the rest of the Year's Best team.

—Terri Windling
Devon, U.K., and Arizona, U.S.A.
2002–2003

Summation 2002: Horror

Ellen Datlow

Book News

John Jarrold left Simon & Schuster's Earthlight, U.K. imprint unexpectedly in August. He created the imprint in 1997 and built an excellent list, featuring authors including Robert Holdstock, Christopher Priest, Jon Courteney Grimwood, Guy Gavriel Kay, Michael Moorcock, and Ray Bradbury. Reportedly he was asked to leave after paying too much for books and acquiring more than other sf lines. Darren Nash was appointed senior editor as Jarrold's replacement in September.

Houghton Mifflin was put on the block for sale by its owner Vivendi Universal in August, and late in the year announced a preliminary agreement to sell the company to a private equity consortium headed by Thomas H. Lee and the Blackstone Group.

New York publisher Perseus Books bought Running Press, a Philadelphia publisher that occasionally publishes genre titles such as *Stephen King Country: The Illustrated Guide to the Sites and Sights That Inspired the Modern Master of Horror* by George Beahm. Running Press continues to handle its own distribution.

Phyllis Grann left her short-lived position as vice chairman of Random House, complaining of boredom, and took a position in the private equity firm of Leeds, Weld & Company.

In early 2002 Stealth Press ran out of funds and let go the rest of its staff (most had already been laid off earlier) except for a skeleton crew. The press, founded by author Craig Spector and venture capitalist firm Wellspring FV, Inc. as an Internet-distributor bookseller of titles with small print runs, had released thirty-one titles since its November 1, 2001 launch. It brought back into print some very worthy titles, including a few of the Nebula Award Books, an early novel by Peter Straub, work by Chelsea Quinn Yarbro, and others.

Invisible Cities Press, publisher of the anthologies *Ghost Writing: Haunted Tales of Contemporary Writers* edited by Roger Weingarten and *Whispers From the Cotton Tree Root* edited by Nalo Hopkinson, and the collection *Redgunk Tales* by William R. Eakin, is no longer publishing fiction.

In late June, DarkTales Publications owned by David Nordhaus, Keith Herber, and Nick Kaufmann ceased operations. Earlier in the year the press cut back on its titles in response to the "grim business climate." Some of the books it published were *Moon on the Water* by Mort Castle, *Dead Times* by Yvonne Navarro, *Clickers* by J. F. Gonzalez and Mark Williams, and *Scary Rednecks and Other Inbred Horrors* by David Whitman and Weston Ochse.

Shane Ryan Staley, editor in chief of Delirium Books, announced that as the result of a flood in his office that destroyed his entire paperback inventory he was forced to cancel several planned books because the money kept in reserve for new titles was needed for restocking existing titles.

In December, Catalyst Press announced that new titles would be placed on hold for six months while the company reorganizes, and that publishing would resume in the summer of 2003. No books have been cancelled, only postponed. Current titles remain available.

Darkside Press has been resurrected as an imprint of classic science fiction and fantasy. Upcoming releases include: *Day Dark, Night Bright* by Fritz Leiber, *No Place Like Earth* by John Wyndham, and *My Rose and My Glove* by Harvey Jacobs.

Telos Publishing, Ltd., announced a new range of horror/fantasy titles. The launch titles were a horror thriller by Paul Finch called *Cape Wrath*, and a U.K.-only reprint of Graham Masterton's first novel *The Manitou*, featuring a new introduction and both standard and original endings to the book.

PS Publishing is expanding from the novella series it started with a few years ago into novels and collections. Planned for 2003 and beyond are novels by Lucius Shepard and Tim Lebbon, collections by Ramsey Campbell and Lucius Shepard, and essay collections by Adam Roberts and Michael Bishop.

Effective January 1, 2003, the Ministry of Whimsy Press, founded by Jeff VanderMeer, became an imprint of Night Shade Books. VanderMeer retained creative control, with Forrest Aguirre running the imprint's day-to-day operations. The Ministry will return in 2004 with *Leviathan 4*, edited by Aguirre, and Zoran Živković's novel *The Fourth Circle*. The Ministry of Whimsy will publish two books per year, in trade paperback. The Leviathan series will constitute one of those books each year.

Magazine News

Gary W. Conner announced that after four years of publication, his on-line horror magazine *Twilight Showcase* ceased publication with its mid-August Issue 32.

Mark McLaughlin, editor of *The Urbanite: Surreal and Lively and Bizarre*, stopped taking subscriptions June 1, 2002, in order to change over to an annual paperback anthology format.

In August, David B. Silva and Paul F. Olson announced that they would pass the reins of *Hellnotes* to Garrett Peck, who has written book reviews for the newsletter since early on in its publishing history. Peck took over the magazine August 30.

"We just began to burn out," Silva said. "Five years of doing a weekly newsletter takes a toll." The hard-copy edition was discontinued, and those who received that edition were offered the option to switch to the e-mail edition or receive a prorated refund for the balance of their subscription. But in December the new editor/publisher Garrett Peck announced his intention to close down the newsletter February 1, 2003. A week later Peck announced that Judi Rohrig stepped forward to take over the reins. Rohrig handled the HWA Internet newsletter, and she and her husband ran a weekly newspaper.

Late November, Paula Guran was dismissed as editor of the horror/music magazine *Horror Garage.* The periodical, an eccentric mix of indie-punk-garage music and original dark fiction, was published under Guran's editorship for three years. During that time the magazine won the International Horror Guild Award for Best Publication for the Year 2000. Guran's last issue was #6. Assistant Editor Michele Patterson resigned after Guran's dismissal. Publisher Rich Black took over all editorial duties, saying he planned to continue to run horror fiction.

Kealan-Patrick Burke was named fiction editor at *gothic.net* October 1, replacing Seth Lindberg, who was fiction editor for the previous four years. Burke resigned four months later to focus on other projects.

DNA Publications announced in July that John R. Douglas was taking over as the news editor for *Science Fiction Chronicle.* He replaced Andrew I. Porter, who founded the magazine in 1978 and had continued as news editor after selling it to DNA's Warren Lapine in 2000. Douglas has previously worked for Berkley, Pocket Books/Simon & Schuster, Avon, and HarperCollins, and as a freelance editor and publishing consultant. The magazine changed its name to *Chronicle* with the September issue.

The twenty-one-year-old sf/f/h bookstore run by Lydia Marano and Arthur Byron Cover, Dangerous Visions, closed its doors for the last time November 10, but continues to sell books on-line. The bookstore was a victim of the downturn in the economy and a decrease in walk-in trade.

The 2002 International Horror Guild awards recognizing outstanding achievements in the field of horror and dark fantasy from the year 2001 were given out Saturday, April 13, 2002, during the World Horror Convention at the Radisson O'Hare near Chicago, Illinois. The Design Image Group sponsored the 2002 awards.

The following were honored: Novel: *Threshold* by Caitlín R. Kiernan (Roc); First Novel: *Ordinary Horror* by David Searcy (Viking); Long Fiction: "Cleopatra Brimstone" by Elizabeth Hand (*Red Shift*); Short Fiction: "Onion" by Caitlín R. Kiernan (Wrong Things); Collection: *Through Shattered Glass* by David B. Silva (Gauntlet Press); Anthology: *Night Visions 10,* edited by Richard Chizmar (Subterranean Press); Illustrated Narrative: *Just a Pilgrim* (five-issue miniseries) by Garth Ennis, writer, and Carlos Ezquerra, artist, (Titan Books); Nonfiction: *Wild Hairs* by David J. Schow (Babbage Press); Publication: *The Spook* (Film City Productions; editor/publisher Anthony Sapienza); Film: *Ginger Snaps,* directed by John Fawcett, screenplay by Karen Walton; Art: John Picacio. William F. Nolan was given the Living Legend award, as previously announced.

The British Fantasy Awards for 2002 were presented September 21 at the British Fantasy Convention at Champagne Charlie's in London. Best Novel: *The*

Night of the Triffids by Simon Clark (Trafalgar Square Books), Best Short Fiction: "Goblin City Lights" by Simon Clark (*Urban Gothic*, Telos); Best Collection: *Aftershocks* by Paul Finch (Ash-Tree Press); Best Anthology: *The Mammoth Book of Best New Horror, Volume 12*, edited by Stephen Jones (Robinson); Best Artist: Jim Burns. Best Small Press: Peter Crowther, for PS Publishing. The annual awards are recommended and then voted on by members of the British Fantasy Society.

The Aurealis Awards are judged by a committee of experts in the field, chosen by Chimaera Publications. The 2002 awards were given in Melbourne, Australia, March 28. The winners are: Science Fiction Novel: *Transcension* by Damien Broderick (Tor); Science Fiction Short Story: "Walk to the Full Moon" by Sean McMullen (*The Magazine of Fantasy & Science Fiction*, December); Fantasy Novel: *The Storm Weaver and the Sand* by Sean Williams (HarperCollins); Short Story: No award; Horror Novel: *The White Body of Evening* by A. L. McCann (Flamingo/HarperCollins); Short Story: "Oracle" by Kim Westwood (*Redsine* 9); Young Adult Novel: *The Hand of Glory* by Sophie Masson (Hodder Headline); Young Adult Short Story: No Award; Children's (8–12 years) Long Fiction: *In the Garden of Empress Cassia* by Gabrielle Wang (Puffin); Children's Short Fiction: "Tashi and the Haunted House by Anna Fienberg and Kim Gamble (Allen & Unwin); The Peter McNamara Convenors' Award: Robbie Matthews, for his important contribution to local genre publishing both with the Canberra Speculative Fiction Guild and *Andromeda Spaceways Inflight Magazine*.

The 2001 Bram Stoker Awards for Superior Achievement were presented by the World Horror Association in New York City's New York Helmsley Hotel Saturday, June 8, 2002. The winners are: Novel: *American Gods* by Neil Gaiman (William Morrow); First Novel: *Deadliest of the Species* by Michael Oliveri (Vox 13); Long Fiction: "In These Final Days of Sales" by Steve Rasnic Tem (Wormhole Books); Short Fiction: "Reconstructing Amy" by Tim Lebbon (*As the Sun Goes Down*, Night Shade); Fiction Collection: *The Man with the Barbed-Wire Fists* by Norman Partridge (Night Shade); Anthology: *Extremes 2: Fantasy and Horror from the Ends of the Earth*, edited by Brian A. Hopkins (Lone Wolf Publications); Nonfiction: *Jobs in Hell* edited by Brian Keene (JIHad Publications); Illustrated Narrative: No Award; Screenplay: *Memento* by Christopher and Jonathan Nolan (Newmarket); Work for Young Readers: *The Willow Files* 2 by Yvonne Navarro (Pocket Books); Poetry Collection: *Consumed, Reduced to Beautiful Grey Ashes* by Linda Addison (Space & Time Press); Alternative Forms: *Dark Dreamers: Facing the Masters of Fear* by Beth Gwinn and Stanley Wiater (Cemetery Dance Publications); Lifetime Achievement Award: John Farris.

Novels

As a result of spending most of my time during the year reading short fiction, I have very little time to read many novels in or out of the field. So the following is just a taste of those novels I read and enjoyed during 2002:

Hunted Past Reason by Richard Matheson (Forge) is a fast-paced thriller in the traditional men's adventure/survival vein, in which two longtime friends go backpacking and discover that they have less in common than they thought. Matheson knows how to grab and hold his audience for the long haul.

The Snowman's Children by Glen Hirshberg (Carroll & Graf) is a dark, haunting first novel by an author who is already an expert teller of ghost stories. It's partly a coming-of-age story and partly about the fragility of childhood friendships. The book shifts between the 1994 homecoming of the protagonist and his boyhood in mid-1970s Detroit during a winter of fear generated by a serial child-killer dubbed the Snowman. Although marketed as mainstream, there is a shadow of impending doom over the characters that should attract and satisfy many readers of horror.

Coraline by Neil Gaiman (HarperCollins) with illustrations by Dave McKean is a deliciously creepy confection for children of all ages. Coraline's boredom prompts her to explore her family's new flat, discovering a secret doorway that leads her to excitement and danger. A quick, enjoyable read.

The Scream by Joan Aiken (Macmillan's Children's Books, U.K.) is an extraordinarily unsettling tale of a witchy, very focused little girl and her brother, who has been crippled in the car crash that killed their parents. The children live in the city with their grandmother, a strange old woman who had been the "ridder" (exterminator of pests) for her community on a remote Scottish island.

Trauma by Graham Masterton (Signet, first published in 2001 as *Bonnie Winter* in the Cemetery Dance Publications novella series) is an excellent short novel about a harried wife and mother with two jobs: selling cosmetics and running a company that cleans up crime scenes. She is faced with the horrific, grisly, and inexplicably gruesome murders of families by one of their members, while her own family life is deteriorating, her husband is jobless, and their teenage son is taking more and more after his dad.

White Bizango by Stephen Gallagher (PS Publishing, U.K.) is a dark, fast-moving novella about a New Orleans police detective's search for a creepy con man who uses his apparent voodoo powers to intimidate and bilk unsuspecting victims. Gallagher has a good feel for New Orleans and keeps up the suspense. Joe R. Lansdale provides an introduction. Available in hardcover and paperback editions, all are numbered and signed by the author.

White Apples by Jonathan Carroll (Tor) is imaginative, charming, fierce, scary, and strange. An admitted philanderer discovers that he has been brought back from the dead by his lover. As in all of Carroll's fiction the reader will be taken by surprise as events unfold in their surreal manner. (Notice: I am Carroll's editor at Tor).

The Scar by China Miéville (Del Rey) is a darkly intelligent and ambitious novel set in the same world as *Perdido Street Station.* It tells the story of a political fugitive who has found passage on a huge ship to a colony that needs her linguistic talents. But pirates take her, the other passengers, and the crew to a giant floating city created by the bits of pieces of pirated vessels. There she becomes caught up in the secret intrigues of the strange rulers of the floating city: The Lovers. The world brims with fascinating races, including vampires, cactus people, and mosquito people—a brilliant mixture of sf/f/h.

Kisscut by Karen Slaughter (William Morrow) begins when a teenage quarrel at the local skating rink in a small southern town explodes into unexplained violence, and the police chief is forced to shoot one of the teenagers. He and the pediatrician/medical examiner gradually uncover ugly secrets, with repercussions throughout the community. Some shocking bits and good twists.

The Straw Men by Michael Marshall (Jove) is Michael Marshall Smith's pseudonymous first suspense novel, and it's a doozy. Three mysterious strands of events come together into a complex and evil global conspiracy to create a new fascist society: a massacre in a small town in Pennsylvania, the return home of man whose parents have died in an auto accident, and the seemingly random snatchings of teenagers in broad daylight.

Acid Row by Minette Walters (Putnam's)—Despite a slow start during which the reader is introduced to a depressing cast of characters who live or work in the seething, crime-ridden housing project called Bassindale Estate, known by residents as Acid Row, the story very quickly becomes a riveting thriller that hits all the right buttons.

Lullaby by Chuck Palahniuk (Doubleday) is funny, biting, and dark. Who could expect less from the author of *Fight Club*? By horrible accident, a journalist discovers that a rhyme in a children's book is a culling song, killing anyone who hears it. He ends up on a road trip across the United States with some very odd companions desperately trying to destroy all copies before it gets out into the world.

Quietus by Vivian Schilling (Hannover House) is a compelling novel about a woman who survives an airplane crash against all odds and comes to believe that she and those of her companions who also survived should have died, and that something is stalking them. There are some amazing passages about adjusting to one's impending death and some very creepy bits. But the novel as it is now is overlong and contains at least one major plot hole. Word is that there will be some major revisions before the novel is released by Penguin in 2003.

Novel Listings

Malachi's Moon by Billie Sue Mosiman (DAW); *The Centaur* by Algernon Blackwood (Wildside Press); *Once. . . .* by James Herbert (Tor); *Sorcerers of the Nightwing* by Geoffrey Huntington (ReganBooks); A *Winter Haunting* by Dan Simmons (William Morrow); *Reflections of a Vampire* by Damion Kirk (RahuBooks); *Sasso* by James Sturz (Walker & Company); *Third Ring* by Phillip Tomasso III (Barclay Books); *The Dead Shall Inherit the Earth* by Vince Churchill (Booklocker); *The Book of Shadows* by James Reese (Morrow); *Silver Nails* by Jack Yeovil (Black Library); *From a Buick 8* by Stephen King (Scribner); *Vampire Vow* and *Blood Brothers* by Michael Schiefelblein (Alyson Publications); *The Blood Within* by Jax Laffer, (Yard Dog Press); *Void* by Teri A. Jacobs (Leisure); *The Restless Dead* by Hugh B. Cave (Leisure); *The Things That Are Not There* by C. J. Henderson (Marietta Publishing); *Slain in the Spirit* by Melanie Tem (Leisure); *Wounds* by Jemiah Jefferson (Leisure); *Cathedral of Vampires* by Mary Ann Mitchell (Leisure); *The Heat Seekers* by Katherine Ramsland (Pinnacle); *The Birds and the Bees* by Séphera Girón (Leisure); *Cat's-Paw* by Mark Sutton (Double Dragon Press); *Gifted Trust* by John Paul Allen (1st Books Library); *The Burden of Indigo* by Gene O'Neill (Prime); *Fear Itself* by Barrett Schumacher (Forge); *Jackdaw* by Derek M. Fox (Prime Books) with fantastic cover art by Theo Badiu; *The Ferryman* by Christopher Golden (Signet); *Midnight Predator* by Amelia Atwater-Rhodes (Delacorte); *Before the Cradle Falls* by James David (Forge); *The Blues Ain't Nothin'* by Tina L. (Design Image Group); *The Red Church* by Scott Nicholson (Pinnacle); *The Cabinet of Curiosities* by Douglas

Preston and Lincoln Child (Warner); *All That Lives* by Melissa Sanders-Self (Warner); *The White Road* by John Connolly (Hodder & Stoughton, U.K.); *Demon Crossing* by Louise Cooper (Hodder & Stoughton, U.K.); *Face to Face* by Sandra Glover (Corgi, U.K.); *Sex and Violence in Hollywood* by Ray Garton (Subterranean Press); *Living Dead in Dallas* by Charlaine Harris (Ace); *One Way Ticket to Midnight* by Gary Jonas (Yard Dog Press); *The Fixer* by Jon F. Merz (Pinnacle); *The Invoker* by Jon F. Merz (Pinnacle); *Where Darkness Lives* by Robert Ross (Pinnacle); *Fiddleback* by J. M. Morris (Macmillan, U.K.); *The Fallen* by Dale Bailey (Signet); *Charisma* by Steven Barnes (Tor); *A Scattering of Jades* by Alexander C. Irvine (Tor); *Midnight Voices* by John Saul (Ballantine); *Dark Blood* by James M. Thompson (Pinnacle); *Unidentified* by Matthew J. Costello (Berkley); *The Mount* by Carol Emshwiller (Small Beer Press); *Breed* by Owl Goingback (Signet); *A Bed of Earth* by Tanith Lee (Overlook Press); *Suffer the Flesh* by Monica J. O'Rourke (Prime); *Coffins* by Rodman Philbrick (Forge); *Snowfall* by Mitchell Smith (Forge); *Martyrs* by Edo Van Belkom (Design Image Group); *One Door Away from Heaven* by Dean Koontz (Hodder Headline, U.K.); *Darkest Heart* by Nancy A. Collins (White Wolf); *Red* by Jack Ketchum (Leisure) (the novel with a novella, "The Passenger"); *Wilding Nights* by Lee Killough (Meisha Merlin); *Atmosphere* by Michael Laimo (Delirium/Leisure); *Resurrection* by Karen E. Taylor (Pinnacle); *The Haunted Air* by F. Paul Wilson (Forge) is a new Repairman Jack novel and was also published in a limited edition by Gauntlet; *Abarat* by Clive Barker (HarperCollins, U.K./HarperCollins/Joanna Cutler, U.S.); *The Hour Before Dark* by Douglas Clegg (Leisure); *The Return* by Bentley Little (Signet); *Last Things* by David Searcy (Viking); *The Lovely Bones* by Alice Sebold (Little, Brown); *Tithe* by Holly Black (Simon & Schuster); *A Coldness in the Blood* by Fred Saberhagen (Tor); *Spider Moon* by John Shirley (Cemetery Dance Publications); *The Horned Man* by James Lasdun (Norton); *Stay* by Nicola Griffith (Nan A. Talese/Doubleday); *Demons* by John Shirley (Ballantine) includes the original novella published in 2000 by Cemetery Dance Publications and a sequel; *Nightmare House* by Douglas Clegg (Cemetery Dance Publications); *Sins of Blood and Stone* by John Urbancik (Catalyst Press); *The Villages* by Dave Hutchinson (Cosmos Books); *Hard Freeze* by Dan Simmons (St. Martin's Press); *Blood on the Tongue* by Stephen Booth (Scribner); *The Sight* by David Clement-Davies (Dutton); *The Cutting Room* by Louise Welch (Canongate, U.K.); *Chasing the Dime* by Michael Connolly (Little, Brown); *Driven* by W. G. Griffiths (Warner); *The Holy* by Daniel Quinn (Context); *Night of the Beast* by Harry Shannon (Medium Rare Books) *Angel Rock* by Darren Williams (Knopf); *Family Tradition* by Edward Lee and John Pelan (ShadowLands Press); *Sleepyhead* by Mark Billingham (Morrow); *The Heaven of Mercury* by Brad Watson (Norton); *Straydog* by Kathe Koja (Frances Foster Books/Farrar, Straus & Giroux); *Number9 Dream* by David Mitchell (Random House); *The Alchemist's Door* by Lisa Goldstein (Tor); *Beasts in Velvet* by Jack Yeovil (Black Library); *In the Forest* by Edna O'Brien (Harcourt); *The Golems of Gotham* by Thane Rosenbaum (HarperCollins); *Smoking Poppy* by Graham Joyce (Pocket); *My Loose Thread* by Dennis Cooper (Canongate, U.K.); *The Haunting of L* by Howard Norman (Farrar, Straus & Giroux); *Harlan* by David Whitman (DarkTales); *Hardcase* by Dan Simmons (St. Martin's Press); *The Portrait of Mrs. Charbuque* by Jeffrey Ford (William Morrow); *Crimson Shadows* by Trisha Baker (Pinnacle); *Hamlet II:*

Ophelia's Revenge by David Bergantino (Pocket Star); *Hybrid* by Shaun Hutson (Little, Brown, U.K.); *Blackwood Farm: The Vampire Chronicles* by Anne Rice (Knopf); *The H. P. Lovecraft Institute* by David Bischoff (Wildside); *Fitcher's Brides* by Gregory Frost (Tor); *The Killing Kind* by John Connolly (Atria); *Orangefield* by Al Sarrantonio (Cemetery Dance Publications); *Prey* by Michael Crichton (HarperCollins); *Sleep No More* by Greg Isles (Putnam); *The Blood Within* by Jax Laffer (Yard Dog Press); *Out of Sight* by T. J. MacGregor (Pinnacle); *The Eyes of the Virgin* by Thomas F. Monteleone (Forge); *The Mantra* by Dmitry Radyshevsky (Jove); *Stranger* by Simon Clark (Robert Hale, U.K.); *Hiding from the Light* by Barbara Erskine (HarperCollins, U.K.); *Dorian* by Will Self (Viking, U.K.).

Surprisingly and happily, 2002 was an exceptionally strong year for short horror fiction. There were a number of excellent original anthologies and collections with terrific stories and novellas. For the first time since beginning this series I feel that the horror section could have been twice as long as I'm allowed.

Collections

The Collection by Bentley Little (Signet) is a huge (almost 450 pages) showcase for Little's short stories, from his early appearances in *The Horror Show* in 1987 to four excellent original stories. This is one of the major collections of the year. One of the originals, "Maya's Mother," is reprinted herein.

Knuckles and Tales by Nancy A. Collins (Cemetery Dance Publications) is the author's second collection and collects her southern gothic stories. Four of the stories are published for the first time. Collins has always been at her best when writing about the South. Two of the reprints appeared in previous editions of *YBFH*. The jacket art is by J. K. Potter. *Dead Roses for a Blue Lady* (Crossroads Press) brings together all of Collins's Sonja Blue stories for the first time. Three of the seven stories are original, and two of the new ones are very good. The book includes an interview with the author conducted by Stanley Wiater. It has terrific jacket and interior art by Stephen R. Bissette.

Everything's Eventual by Stephen King (Scribner) is another excellent collection by a writer who is continually stretching his writerly muscles. It's consistently entertaining, with fourteen stories, including two that were reprinted in earlier editions of *YBFH*. The collection mixes what the author dubs his "all-out screamers" with his more literary work.

Cat in Glass and Other Tales of the Unnatural by Nancy Etchemendy (Cricket) is an excellent, suitably illustrated collection of eight weird and chilling horror stories aimed at the young adult market—the title story was reprinted in an earlier *YBFH*.

The Devil in Me by Christopher Fowler (Serpent's Tale, U.K.) is the author's seventh collection of stories. Fowler infuses his horror stories with an extra bite of satire, and when they work they're terrific. Half of the twelve stories are published for the first time, and while they're all good and some are twisted, none of the originals are all that dark. Among the reprints is "Crocodile Lady," chosen last year for both *YBFH* and *Best New Horror*.

Lies & Ugliness by Brian Hodge (Night Shade Books) is the author's third collection. His short fiction gets better and better. The book features twenty-one stories published between 1989 and 2002, two appearing for the first time anywhere and a third that previously appeared only as an audio drama. This is an important collection by a talented and versatile writer. The effective jacket illustration and design are by John Picacio. "Nesting Instincts" and "Some Other Me" are both reprinted herein.

Guises by Charlee Jacob (Delirium Books) showcases ten stories and novellas (three original to the collection) and forty poems of varying length (several also original to the collection). The jacket art is by Chris Mars.

Caliban and Other Tales by Robert Devereaux (Leisure) has four stories, one novella, and a short novel by this author whose reputation was assured by his outrageously perverse novel that disembowels the sacredness of an icon, *Santa Steps Out*. His stories may not be as outrageous as that capper, but some of them come pretty close. One ("Ridi Bobo") was reprinted in an earlier volume of *YBFH*.

Suspicions by Elizabeth Engstrom (Triple Tree Publishing) showcases a selection of twenty-five fantasy, dark fantasy, and horror stories. Five of the stories are original to the collection. Two of the stories appeared in previous volumes of *The Year's Best Fantasy and Horror*.

The Evil Entwines by John B. Ford (Hardcastle, U.K.) collects twelve of the author's collaborations with writers including Thomas Ligotti, Ramsey Campbell, Tim Lebbon, Simon Clark, and others.

Dark Shadows on the Moon by John B. Ford (Hive Press) showcases thirty-five stories by this promising British writer, all published since 1996. Several of the stories are published for the first time. Simon Clark wrote the introduction. The disturbingly macabre cover art is by Ken Whitlow.

Claremont Tales II by Richard A. Lupoff (Golden Gryphon) is an overview of the author's thirty-plus-year career during which he has been telling enjoyable Lovecraftian tales, science fiction, fantasy, and crime stories. The book includes thirteen stories from 1972 to 2002. In the foreword Lupoff asserts that this volume and two earlier collections: *Claremont Tales* and *Before . . . 12:01 . . . and After* comprise all of his short fiction that he thinks good enough to be reprinted. The playful wraparound jacket art by Nicholas Jainschigg is charming, showing Lupoff as a conjuror of magic.

The Unspeakable and Others by Dan Clore (Wildside Press) is a very odd volume of stories heavily influenced by Lovecraft and Poe. The author also includes at least one pseudo-scientific essay on flying saucers and a serious essay about Lovecraft. S. T. Joshi provides an introduction.

Immaterial by Robert Hood (MirrorDanse Books, Australia) is this Australian fantasist's second collection of stories—the fifteen ghost stories (three published for the first time) were mostly published in Australian magazines and anthologies. Hood has been publishing professionally since 1973. The attractive cover art is by Cat Sparks.

Right to Life by Jack Ketchum (Gauntlet Publications/EDGE Books) contains the first paperback edition of the author's powerful 1998 novella plus two excellent original short tales. The provocative cover art is by Neal McPheeters.

Dragonfly by Brian Knight (Catalyst Press) has thirteen stories, seven previously unpublished. There is some very good work in here—Knight is a writer to watch. The attractive cover art is by Matt Lombard and is designed by J. T. Lindroos.

Touching the Flame by Paul Kane (Rainfall Books, U.K.) has eighteen stories, two original to the collection, which includes an introduction by Simon Clark and story notes by the author.

Wrestling Rings and Other Things by John Weagly (Twilight Tales) is a chapbook of eleven lightweight short-shorts about everything from wrestling to cats, almost half of them first published in 2002.

Cranberry Gothic: Tales of Horror, Fantasy, and the Macabre by Edward Lodi (Rock Village Publishing) has twenty-two stories and vignettes, mostly original, taking place in New England.

Mariah of the Spirits and Other Southern Ghost Stories by Sherry Austin (Overmountain Press) has thirteen ghost stories.

Nameless Cults: The Cthulhu Mythos Fiction of Robert E. Howard by Robert E. Howard (Chaosium) has eighteen stories, including a round robin tale written by C. L. Moore, A. Merritt, H. P. Lovecraft, and Frank Belknap Long. Robert Price provides an introduction on Howard's Lovecraftian work.

Dark Karma by John Grover, Eric S. Brown, and Jason Brannon (Incubusvane Publishing) has ten short stories. Cover art is uncredited.

Familiar and Haunting: Collected Stories by Philippa Pearce (Greenwillow) is a YA omnibus of four of the author's previous collections, with twenty of the thirty-seven stories being supernatural.

The Emperor of Dreams by Clark Ashton Smith (Orion, U.K.) collects forty-five stories, most published between 1926 and 1938, and an article and poem by the author. Compiled, edited, and with an afterword by Stephen Jones.

Ancient Sorceries and Other Weird Stories by Algernon Blackwood (Penguin) has nine stories, with introduction and notes by S. T. Joshi.

Frights and Fancies by R. Chetwynd-Hayes (Robert Hale, U.K.) is a posthumous collection edited by Stephen Jones. It brings together nineteen previously uncollected stories of fantasy and the supernatural from the past four decades, including four previously unpublished.

Thirteen by Rick Kennett (Jacobyte Books, Australia) is a second excellent collection by the talented Australian coauthor of *472 Cheyne Walk* (see below). This one, all reprints, contains ghost stories unrelated to Carnacki the Ghost Finder. One, "Due West" appeared in an earlier volume of *YBFH*. Unfortunately, though the content is great, the presentation and production are not, with no copyright or first-publication information, minimal attention to jacket or interior design, no running heads, and not even a biography of the author. This was published in 2001 but not seen until 2002.

Ash-Tree Press: *472 Cheyne Walk* by A. F. Kidd and Rick Kennett, is a lively collection of twelve stories (most appearing for the first time) inspired by William Hope Hodgson's *Carnacki the Ghost Finder.* The stories are excellent. Four of them were originally published as a booklet in 1992 by the Ghost Story Society as *472 Cheyne Walk.* The introduction published with that chapbook is reprinted, along with a new introduction. The horrific jacket art is by Paul Lowe. *Figures in Rain* by Chet Williamson, who has been writing graceful weird and ghostly tales for over twenty years. This collection—his first—contains twenty-five of the best, plus two originals. The two new ones are less frightening than moving. Jacket art is by Paul Lowe and the introduction is by Joe R. Lansdale. *The Mirror and Other Strange Reflections* by Arthur Porges is this mystery and horror author's first collection of horror tales, although he has published hundreds of stories over the past twenty-five years in such venues as *Alfred Hitchcock's Mystery Magazine*, *If*, *Argosy*, and *The Magazine of Fantasy & Science Fiction*. The preface is by Mike Ashley and the jacket art is by Paul Lowe. *Off the Sand Road* by Russell Kirk is the first of two volumes of ghost stories by an American writer who some say assumed the mantle of the British ghost story tradition of M. R. James and Sheridan Le Fanu. His stories were collected in three volumes over the years and his most famous story, "There's a Long, Long Trail A-Winding," won the World Fantasy Award in 1977. Kirk's essay "A Cautionary Note on the Ghostly Tale" is included, along with an introduction by John Pelan. The beautiful woodcut on the jacket is by Annette Kirk. *Hauntings* by Vernon Lee is a comprehensive collection of the author's supernatural short fiction. Lee, the pseudonym of Violet Paget (1856–1935), was a cultural historian, poet, novelist, and essayist as well as the author of short stories. This new edition of *Hauntings* collects stories from four early collections and includes one story never collected previously. The volume is edited by David G. Rowland, who provides the introduction. There is also a brief essay about the author by Irene Cooper Willis. The jacket art is a painting of Lee by John Singer Sargent. *Sinister Romance* by Mary Heaton Vorse collects seven of the author's ghost stories. Vorse might be better known as a political activist for women's and workers' rights than for her fiction. Jane Yolen provides an appreciation and Jessica Amanda Salmonson, who edited the volume, provides an extensive introduction to the author and her fiction. The cover illustration is by Deborah McMillion-Nering. *The Amazing Dreams of Andrew Latter* by Harold Begbie, edited by Jack Adrian, is the fourth volume in the Occult Detective Library. The six stories were originally published in 1904 in the *London Magazine*. Adrian provides the introduction. The cover illustration is by Deborah McMillion-Nering. *Not Exactly Ghosts* by Andrew Caldecott collects two volumes of the author's work that were originally published 1947–1948: *Not Exactly Ghosts* and *Fires Burn Blue*. The introduction is by Stefan Dziemianowicz. Jacket art is by Paul Lowe. *The Invisible Eye* by Erckmann-Chatrian, edited by Hugh Lamb, is the first collection of these longtime collaborators who were natives of Alsace-Lorraine. They mostly wrote military history and fiction, but it is their macabre fiction that survives. They wrote together for about forty years before a violent quarrel destroyed their working relationship. They both slipped into obscurity soon after their deaths. The grim cover painting is by Richard Lamb. *Schalken the Painter and Others: Ghost Stories 1838–1861* by Sheridan Le Fanu is edited, and contains an introduction by Jim Rockill. It covers the period from when Le Fanu's first short story was published in the *Dublin University Magazine* to 1861. The jacket art is by Douglas Walters. *Lady Stanhope's Manuscript*, containing five supernatural stories, was the first publication of the Ash-Tree Press, published in a 150-copy edition in 1974 for members of The Ghost Story Society and now long out of print. The stories have been reset in perfect bound, gloss, laminated boards as part of the Ash-Tree Press Occasional Booklet series. Illustrations are by Pat Walsh, Dallas Goffin, Nick Maloret, and Alan Hunter.

In addition, Ash-Tree Press debuted its paperback series New Century Macabre with Matt Cardin's ambitious *Divinations of the Deep,* a collection of five original horror stories that deal with faith, dread, and chaos. The cover painting and design are by Jason Van Hollander.

A second Ash-Tree Press paperback series, Vampire Classics, debuted with *Vampires Overhead* by Alan Hyder, a novel that was first published in 1935 and whose first edition is very rare. This new edition has an introduction by Jack Adrian and suitably pulpy cover art by Jason Van Hollander.

Delirium Books: *Visions Through a Shattered Lens* by Gerard Houarner, collecting twenty stories by this up-and-coming writer—half of them published for the first time. Cover art and design is by Colleen Crary. *Dark Demons: Tales of Obsession, Possession and Unnatural Desire* by Kurt Newton, the author's second collection, has sixteen stories, more than half of them published for the first time. He's a good storyteller and shows a lot of promise. An introduction is provided by Michael Arnzen. *Luster* by Shane Ryan Staley (Corrosion Press, an imprint of Delirium) collects six original stories of sex and violence in a colorful chapbook. The stories are brutal, occasionally funny, and sometimes even hit their intended marks. Jacket art is by Sean Madden.

Mythos Books: *My Work is Not Yet Done: Three Tales of Corporate Terror* by Thomas Ligotti, featuring a new novella and two short stories about corporate life. Think of the protagonists as crazed, darker versions of Dilbert. The handsome jacket art and frontispiece is by Harry O. Morris. This is Mythos Books' first, and so far only hardcover title. *The Taint of Lovecraft* by Stanley C. Sargent consists of heavily Lovecraft-influenced stories and poems, two articles, and interspersed illustrations. Also included is a new novella and two previously unpublished poems. Richard A. Lupoff provides the introduction. Allen Koszowski, Jeffrey Thomas, Daniel Allen Ross, and Stanley C. Sargent are the illustrators, and D. L. Hutchinson did the striking cover art.

Five Star: *Charnel House and Other Stories* by Graham Masterton is a good-looking hardcover with a fine selection of four reprints that demonstrate the range of the author's talents. *The Retrieval Artist and Other Stories* by Kristine Kathryn Rusch with nine stories.

Prime: *All Too Surreal* by Tim Waggoner presents eighteen stories, three first published in 2002, by a promising young horror writer. The highly effective cover art is by Mike Bohatch and is designed by Garry Nurrish. *Nations of the Living, Nations of the Dead* by Mort Castle contains a wide range of the author's short fiction and poetry published between 1974 and 2002 (some poems are original to the collection) in mystery and horror magazines and anthologies. Cover art by Mark Evans. *Incantations* by L. H. Maynard and M. P. N. Sims collects fourteen stories and one new novella by these longtime and prolific collaborators. More than half the stories were first published in 2002, either in the collection or in magazines. The cover art by Simon Duric and cover design by Garry Nurrish are excellent. *Selling Dark Miracles* (Cosmos) combines two earlier Maynard and Sims collections, adding some uncollected and previously unpublished stories. There is an introduction by Hugh Lamb and an interview with the authors conducted by William P. Simmons. And *The Secret Geography of Nightmare* combines two other early collections by the collaborators into a collection of one hundred thousand words of supernatural and crime fiction, essays, and interviews. The introduction is by Stephen Jones and the impressive cover art is by Geoff Priest (with design by Nurrish). *Old Ghosts and Other Revenants* by J. F. Gonzales is the author's first collection and has twelve stories, two published for the first time. The others were published between 1994 and 2001 in a variety of magazines, e-zines, and anthologies. Nice cover art and design by Audre. Delirium Books also published a collection by Gonzales, *Maternal Instinct,* with four stories and one short novel. The disturbing artwork for that title is by Matt Lombard.

iUniverse: *Aaaiiieee!!!: The Best Horror Stories of Jeffrey Thomas* collects twenty stories originally published in magazines such as *Lore, Dark Regions, Not One of Us, Redsine,* and *Terminal Fright.* Tentacles, criminals, demons, and ghosts inhabit many of the stories. Although enjoyable, compared to Thomas's last two collections, this is a relatively minor effort. Also, *Christmas Trees and Monkeys: Collected Horror Stories, Volume 1* by Daniel G. Keohane contains fifteen stories, five published for the first time. The reprints are from mostly small-press magazines and Webzines, and a few are reprinted from anthologies.

Wormhole Books: *In the Spirit* by P. D. Cacek, the seventh in the Wormhole Contemporary Chapbook series is a minicollection of three ghost stories, one original. One of the reprints, "Dust Motes," won the World Fantasy Award and was reprinted in *YBFH.* Jack Ketchum provides an introduction and the author provides an afterword. The cover artwork is by David Martin. Interior art is by Joanna Erbach. *Edgar Allan Poe's Dark Dreams* has color and interior artwork throughout by Alan M. Clark and is a wonderful, collectible Wormhole Vintage chapbook. It consists of three stories and three poems by Poe. There are four full-color illustrations by Clark, one also used for the jacket art. Edward Bryant provides an introduction and Dawn Dunn provides a short history of the author. This would make a great gift for Edgar Allan Poe or Alan M. Clark fans.

Flesh & Blood Press: *A Halloween Harvest* by Paul Melniczek features three stories taking place during the horror field's favorite holiday. The cover illustration is by Keith Minnion. *Shadows, Legends and Secrets* by John Urbancik has eight vignettes, six of them original. Jacket art is by John Pierro. *Becoming October* by William Simmons is a chapbook with three stories, one a reprint. The introduction is by T. M. Wright. Cover art is by Chad Savage.

Double Dragon Press: two collections by newcomer Paul Melniczek: *Frightful October,* with eleven Halloween stories, five original to the collection, and *Restless Shades: Tales of Lurking Horror,* with ten stories, five of them original to the collection. Also, *Five Days on the Banks of the Acheron* by Jason Brannon has twelve stories, five first published in 2002.

Medium Rare Books: *Spectres and Darkness* is a selection of twelve stories by Drew Williams and Joe Nassise, two relative newcomers to the horror field. Most are original to the dual collection. The nice-looking cover art is by John Turi. Brian Keene provides an introduction to the two writers.

Tor: *Nightmare at 20,000 Feet* by Richard Matheson collects twenty of the author's horror stories, including classics like the title story, "Dance of the Dead," "Prey," and "Children of Noah." Introduction is by Stephen King. *Beneath the Moors and Darker Places* by Brian Lumley consists of nine stories, including the titular short novel, most of them based on Lovecraftian themes. There is an introduction by Lumley. *Scared Stiff: Tales of Sex and Death* by Ramsey Campbell adds three stories to the original Scream Press collection.

Yard Dog Press: *In the Shadows* by Bradley H. Sinor has six stories reprinted from various anthologies. *Tales of the Lucky Nickel* by Ken Rand has five stories that take place in the eponymous bar and are mostly humorous despite the fact that some ghosts and the Grim Reaper make appearances.

Tartarus Press: *A Damask of the Dead* by John Gale is a series of fourteen prose poems in the decadent manner, several of them original to the collection. This kind of sensuous gothic mannered writing really isn't to my taste, so it's difficult for me to comment, but for those who enjoy it this is a lovely volume. *Written With My Left Hand* by Nugent Barker is a straight reprint of the author's only book—presumed to contain his entire literary output—originally published in 1951. Douglas Anderson provides a foreword. *Nightmares of an Ether-Drinker* by Jean Lorrain and translated by Brian Stableford represents the first English publication of the French decadent author's drug-inspired, overwrought fever-dream/nightmares. In an introduction, Stableford discusses how the author's addiction permeated his writing. *Various Temptations* by William Samson is the first collection of this underrated author's work in over thirty years. It includes twenty-five of some of his best fantastical and macabre tales. The introduction is by Mark Valentine. Although I only read a smattering of the stories, those I did read were excellent. I highly recommend this title. *Prince Zaleski* by M. P. Shiel has six stories about a decadent detective who rarely leaves his divan when solving crimes. Three of the stories are by Shiel alone, and the second three are collaborations with John Gawsworth. There is an introduction by Brian Stableford about the prince and a note by R. B. Russell about the genesis of the collaborations. The beautiful frontispiece and tailpiece are by Robert Arrington in the style of Aubrey Beardsley, whose design on the boards and title page are from the first edition of Prince Zaleski published in 1895. Also, the cover illustration is by R. B. Russell. *The Other Sacrifice and Other Stories* by Sarban is the fourth collection of the author's work by this press. Two of the four novellas are original and are very good. The two other novellas were previously published in earlier Tartarus collections of Sarban's work. *Undesirable Guest and Other Stories* by William Charlton is the first collection by this still active, relatively little-known author. Of the fourteen stories, more than half are original, and they run the gamut from well-told traditional horror tales to the surreal.

Midnight House published *Feesters in the Lake and other stories*, the first collection by Bob Leman. Leman's horror stories were mostly published in *The Magazine of Fantasy & Science Fiction* between 1967 and 1988, although one story in the collection is previously unpublished. His most famous story, "Window," was nominated for a Nebula Award and was recently filmed for television. Leman is still alive but apparently no longer writing. Edited and with an introduction by Jim Rockhill, jacket and interior art is by Allen Koszowski. Also, *Smoke Ghost and Other Apparitions* by Fritz Leiber has eighteen stories by the master, including a humorous erotic story that's never been published before. The book, edited by John Pelan and Steve Savile, is the second in a series of Leiber collections and has a brief introduction by Ramsey Campbell. An uncredited illustration by Allen Koszowski graces the jacket. *The Return of the Soul and Other Stories* by Robert Hitchens collects eight stories and is the first of a two-book "comprehensive" collection of the author's supernatural stories, edited and with an introduction by S. T. Joshi and cover art by Allen Koszowski. *The Harlem Horrors: Stories of the Macabre* by Charles Birkin, selected by John Pelan. It is the second of five volumes to be published over the next few years. One of Birkin's most powerful contributions to the conté cruel is included, "A Lovely Bunch of Coconuts." This book's a must for horror readers.

The prolific Welsh writer Rhys Hughes had three collections of his weird dark fantasy published in 2002: *Stories from a Lost Anthology* (Tartarus Press) contains twenty-one (fifteen published for the first time) unclassifiable stories that are quirky, clever, surreal, and occasionally dark. *Nowhere Near Milkwood* (Prime Books), the only one of the three to be published as a paperback (with gorgeous cover art by Theo Badiu), doesn't have anything that I would consider horrific in it. *Journeys Beyond Advice* (Sarob Press) has seven stories and three novellas (original to the collection) that are highly effective. Jacket and interior art is by Justin Phillips.

Also from Sarob Press: *The Dark Tales* by Jessica Amanda Salmonson collects her weird and high-fantasy stories published over a period of fifteen years in various, mostly small-press magazines, the earliest published in 1974. Jacket art is by Lara Bandilla. *Ghosts & Other Lovers* by Lisa Tuttle includes thirteen stories written over twenty years, two of which were previously reprinted in earlier *YBFH* volumes. Cover and interior art is by Paul Lowe. *Cold Hand on My Shoulder* by Basil Copper is the eighth collection of a writer whose first stories were published in 1964 in the Pan Books of Horror series and who has been writing ever since. In it are nine tales, four previously unpublished. Richard Dalby provides the introduction. The cover art and interior illustrations are by Randy Broecker.

Subterranean Press: *For a Few Stories More* by Joe R. Lansdale, Volume Four of the Lost Lansdale series—stories that are not among the author's best but might be of interest to his readers. Some are experimental, others feel like fragments that just didn't go anywhere. Each story or vignette has an introduction by the author. Eleven are original to the collection. It's a great-looking book with jacket art by Mark A Nelson and interior design by Tim Holt. Dan Simmons's *Worlds Enough and Time* contains five speculative fiction novellas, one original. The author provides an overall introduction and introductions to each novella. *From Weird and Distant Shores* by Caitlín Kiernan collects thirteen of Kiernan's stories—several originally published in shared-world or theme anthologies—and demonstrate her ability to shape even the most seemingly limited material into something fresh. Two of the pieces are original: a story fragment and a collaboration with Poppy Z. Brite. The book itself is beautiful, with marigold-orange textured endpapers, interior illustrations by Richard Kirk, and a striking jacket illustration by Bob Eggleton. *Crimes and Punishments: The Lost Bloch, Volume Three* by Robert Bloch, edited by David J. Schow, is the final book in the series and a wonderful book it is, reprinting novellas and novelettes by the master for the first time since their original publications. Schow provides an entertaining and illuminating introduction, Gahan Wilson supplies a gracious foreword, and the appendix includes an expanded version of Douglas E. Winter's discussion with Robert Bloch for Winter's nonfiction book about horror writers, *Faces of*

Fear, plus an afterword by Robert Bloch's widow, Eleanor. The jacket art is by Bernie Wrightson and is designed by Schow.

Lone Wolf Publications brought out the following CD-ROMs: *Dark Rhythms: The Selected Short Fiction of Steve Beai* has thirteen stories, five original by a relative newcomer to horror. One, "The Scatterbrains," is particularly good. Cover art is by Alan M. Clark. Also, *The Subtle Ties That Bind* by David Niall Wilson is a good selection of the author's recent work with eighteen stories, two of them original, and one with minimal previous distribution. The cover art is by Thomas Arensberg. *Storytellers 2: Dead Teeth Chattering* edited by Richard Wright is an audio collection of stories written and read by Derek M. Fox, Brian Keene, and Mark McLaughlin. Art is by M. W. Anderson.

Mixed-Genre Collections

The Fantasy Writer's Assistant by Jeffrey Ford (Golden Gryphon) is a marvelous introduction to this talented author's short fiction. The sixteen stories, three of them original to the collection, range from science fiction, metafiction, and mythic fantasy to imaginative, darkly tinged morsels; *The Ogre's Wife: Fairy Tales for Grownups* by Richard Parks (Obscura Press) is the author's first collection, with fourteen previously published stories and one very powerful original; *Die Laughing* by John R. Platt (Medium Rare Books) has half original and half reprint stories and poems about clowns—very few are actually frightening (unless you find clowns inherently scary) with nice cover art by Barry Barnes; *Stories of Your Life and Others* by Ted Chiang (Tor) collects all of this remarkable writer's fiction, and although the stories are mostly sf, some of them have enough dark edges that aficionados of the dark might enjoy them. One story appears for the first time; *Little Doors* by Paul Di Filippo (Four Walls, Eight Windows) is the author's fifth collection and clearly demonstrates his oddball sensibilities and satirical wit. One of the stories was first published in *Night Cry: Strangers and Beggars* by the up-and-coming James Van Pelt (Fairwood Press) has seventeen stories—one published in 2002 for the first time—of sf, fantasy, dark fantasy, and horror; *One More for the Road* by Ray Bradbury (William Morrow) has twenty-five new stories by the master, mostly original, and although most are fantasy, there are a few darker ones; *If Lions Could Speak and other stories* by Paul Park (Cosmos Books) is the author's first collection. The thirteen stories are magical, eerie, funny—science fiction, fantasy, and occasionally extraordinarily dark; *The Butterfly Artist* by Forrest Aguirre (Flesh & Blood) features ten odd stories in chapbook form. Six appear for the first time; *Under Cover of Night* by Mary SanGiovanni (Flesh & Blood) has seven stories, five first published in 2002; *Selected Stories of Philip K. Dick* (Pantheon) showcases twenty-one stories from over the career of this great writer of paranoia, self-doubt, and imaginative psychosis. The introduction is by Jonathan Lethem; *Embracing the Starlight* by Dave Smeds (Dark Regions Press/Tachyon Publications) has some excellent dark fiction among its twelve stories (one original to the collection), and the author supplies informative introductions for each story; *Tapping the Dream Tree* by Charles de Lint (Tor) is a big collection by the writer whose work defines the subgenre of urban fantasy. The book includes a harrowing original dark fantasy and a short novel that was previously published as a limited edition; *Waifs and*

Strays by Charles de Lint (Viking) is a YA collection of sixteen stories, one original; *i-o* by Simon Logan (Prime) is an all-original collection of eight hard-edged science fiction stories tinged with violence and brutality that occasionally spill over into the horror realm; *Rest Area* by Clay McLeod Chapman (Theia) is an oddball first collection of twenty brief stories by a promising writer. Most are odd, some are horrific; *Tangled Webs and Other Imaginary Weaving* by Laura J. Underwood (Dark Regions Press) has fifteen fantasy and dark fantasy tales, five original; *Report to the Men's Club* by Carol Emshwiller (Small Beer Press) is a joy. It collects nineteen of this writer's weird, moving, and horrific stories, several of which are original to the collection. Emshwiller has been producing some of her best work in the past couple of years in a burst of creativity and is finally beginning to get her due with a Nebula Award and the 2002 Philip K. Dick Award; *The Woman Who Gave Birth to Rabbits* by Emma Donoghue (Harcourt Brace) has weird stories based on true bits of news reports and historical records; *Hans Christian Andersen: Stories and Tales* (Routledge, U.K.) is a new, very attractive trade paperback edition of the author's work, with an introductory essay from 1910 by Herman Hesse and the original illustrations by A. W. Bayes; *The Great Escape* by Ian Watson (Golden Gryphon) is this prolific writer's ninth collection of sf/f/h stories. *Stories for an Enchanted Afternoon* by Kristine Kathryn Rusch (Golden Gryphon) is, surprisingly, the author's first collection. Her darkest story might be "The Gallery of His Dreams," a novella about Civil War photographer Matthew Brady; North Atlantic continued its Sturgeon series with *Bright Segment: The Complete Short Stories of Theodore Sturgeon, Volume 8*. This volume covers stories written from 1953 to 1955, plus two earlier short-shorts recently discovered. The foreword is by William Tenn, and it is edited with story notes by Paul Williams; *The Collected Stories of Greg Bear* (Tor) is a an excellent overview of this versatile writer's short work. Although better known as a hard science fiction writer, Bear has also written terrific dark fantasy. His individual story introductions put the stories in context; *Swift Thoughts* by George Zebrowski (Golden Gryphon) has at least one story darkly tinged; *The Far Side of Nowhere* by Nelson Bond (Arkham House) is welcome as the first new collection in decades by an author who made a reputation for his writing in the 1930s–60s, subsequently retiring from writing fiction. Some of the twenty-nine stories show Bond to be possessed of a dark edge. The beautiful jacket concept and art is by Alan Fore and is designed by Jengraph; *City of Saints and Madmen* by Jeff VanderMeer (Prime) is an expansion of his book with the same title from 2001 and a beautiful looking collectable as well as a good read. Of the new material, the novella "The Cage" is especially fine; *Ebb Tides and Other Tales* by Mary Soon Lee (Dark Regions Press) is the second small-press collection by this promising writer whose work is occasionally dark; *Impact 20* by William F. Nolan (Gauntlet) is an expanded version of the author's first collection with three stories from the same period that were not originally included. It's a mixture of fantasy, horror, and mainstream.

Anthologies

Dark Terrors 6: The Gollancz Book of Horror, edited by Stephen Jones and David Sutton (Gollancz, U.K.) is an excellent anthology—in fact, possibly the best in the series so far. The massive hardcover has two hundred thousand words of disquieting, scary, and varied horror fiction. This is a must for any reader interested in contemporary horror fiction.

Stranger: Dark Tales of Eerie Encounters, edited by Michele Slung (Perennial), is a consistently literate and unsettling anthology of mostly reprints by the likes of Thomas Tessier, John Wyndham, Ray Bradbury, Patricia Highsmith, Richard Matheson, and others. At least two of the five originals are excellent and highly recommended. The Jay Russell story, "Hides," is reprinted herein.

Phantoms of Venice edited by David Sutton (Shadow Publishing, U.K.) was published on the cusp of 2001/2002 and was received too late to cover for *YBFH 15*. It's a very good, atmospheric anthology about the exotic city of Venice, with ten stories about ghosts, vengeful humans and spirits, and lots of history. Included are original stories by Brian Stableford, Tim Lebbon, Conrad Williams, and others, also highly recommended.

Darkness Rising Volume Three: Secrets of Shadows (Cosmos Books) is an original anthology (with one classic reprint) of seventeen stories, some very good, particularly those by Chico Kidd, Andrea J. Cooke, and Andrew Roberts. *Darkness Rising Volume Four: Caresses of Nightmare* (Prime) has twenty stories (all original but with two classic reprints) with notable ones by William P. Simmons, Andrew Roberts, and Martyn Prince. *Darkness Rising Volume Five: Black Shroud of Fear* (Prime) has twenty-three originals, several of them excellent, particularly those by Cyril Simsa and Pierre Louys. Amanda Sutton's cover art is also very good, a change from the comic book–like art of the three volumes. All three volumes were edited by L. H. Maynard and M. P. N. Sims.

Riddle Stories edited by Julian Hawthorne (Wildside Press) contains fourteen reprinted stories by Ambrose Bierce, Nathaniel Hawthorne, F. Marion Crawford, and other earlier American writers.

The Children of Cthulhu, edited by John Pelan and Benjamin Adams (Del Rey), is an entertaining anthology of stories intended to add to the mythos created by H. P. Lovecraft. The best move furthest away from the gee-whiz type of overwritten pastiches that have been so prevalent in the past. Two long pieces by Brian Hodge and Paul Finch stand out, as do excellent shorter stories by China Miéville, Caitlín Kiernan, Michael Reaves, Steve Rasnic Tem, and others. The Miéville is reprinted herein.

The Darker Side, edited by John Pelan (Roc), is a follow-up to Pelan's 1996 nontheme horror anthology *Darkside*. Most of the twenty-seven stories are good, but the standouts for me were those by Simon Clark, Lucy Taylor, Shikhar Dixit, Joel Lane, and Charlee Jacob. Taylor's is reprinted herein.

Decadence One, edited by Monica O'Rourke (Prime), is an erotic horror anthology with notable stories by newer writers such as Charlee Jacob, John Urbancik, and E. C. McMullen, Jr. *Decadence Two*, edited by Monica O'Rourke (Flesh & Blood) bills itself as erotic but is decidedly unerotic—combining sex and violence and obscenity in some pretty ugly ways. Six of the twenty tales are reprints. The best of the originals are by Gerard Houarner, Richard Gavin, and John Graham. The jacket of this hardcover has good-looking art by Mike Bohatch and a design by Feo Amante. *Dreaming of Angels*, edited by Gord Rollo and Monica J. O'Rourke (Prime), is a cross-genre anthology of twenty-three stories more or less divided between reprints and originals, The writers include Jack

Ketchum, Robert Devereaux, Ramsey Campbell, Peter Crowther, Charlee Jacob, and others. The book was published to benefit the Downs Syndrome Society. *Tourniquet Heart*, edited by Christopher Teague (Prime), is an anthology of nasty love stories. The majority of the thirty-six pieces are predictable vignettes. Only a handful of the originals (there are three reprints) contain enough characterization or plot to be memorable. Readers should check out the stories by P. Curren, Carol Anne Davis, Steve Rasnic Tem, Paul Finch, Kirstyn McDermott, and Duane Swiercynzski. The trade paperback has professional-looking cover art and design by the reliable team of Simon Duric and Garry Nurrish.

J. K. Potter's Embrace the Mutation, edited by William Schafer and Bill Sheehan (Subterranean Press), is an excellent, mostly original anthology inspired by the photographic mutant art of Potter, with original fiction by a roll call of wonderful writers such as Elizabeth Hand, Poppy Z. Brite, Peter Crowther, John Crowley, Dennis Etchison, Michael Bishop, and Norman Partridge, among others. Their stories range from the wacky to the grotesque. Stories by Ramsey Campbell and Kim Newman are reprinted herein.

Annual Macabre 2002: Ghosts at "The Cornhill" 1920–1930, edited by Jack Adrian (Ash-Tree Press), is the first of two volumes that will highlight the supernatural fiction published in *The Cornhill*, a British magazine that existed between 1860 and 1975. This volume has fourteen stories and is introduced by Adrian. Rob Suggs did the jacket illustration.

Vengeance Fantastic, edited by Denise Little (DAW), is an all-original anthology of revenge tales that are more cheeky than horrific, but there are good pieces by Kristine Kathryn Rusch, Nina Kiriki Hoffman, and Gary A. Braunbeck.

Queer Fear II, edited by Michael Rowe (Arsenal Pulp Press), contains twenty-two varied stories by writers such as Gemma Files, David Nickle, Edo van Belkom, Michael Marano, Stephen Dedman, Poppy Z. Brite, and other writers in and out of the horror genre. It is definitely worth a look.

Four Dark Nights by Bentley Little, Douglas Clegg, Christopher Golden, and Tom Piccirilli (Leisure) is a book of four original novellas, each of which takes place during one night. None of the four is meaty enough to justify its length—I suspect they would have worked better as tighter short stories.

Reckless Abandon, edited by David Sparks and Bob Strauss (Catalyst Press), is a nontheme anthology of twenty stories, mostly original to the book. There were a few notable originals by Phil Locasio, d. g. k. Goldberg, Robert Dunbar, and Peadar Ó Guilin. The varied, mostly original *Random Acts of Weirdness: An Anthology of Strange Behaviors*, edited by Brian Knight (Catalyst Press), includes—in addition to the usual disgusto blood-and-guts entries—the truly bizarre "Porno in August" by Carlton Mellick III (reprinted herein) and some other goodies. With great cover art by GAK and nice cover design by Feo Amante.

Dead But Dreaming, edited by Kevin Ross and Keith Herber (DarkTales Publications), is a Lovecraft-inspired anthology that attempts to go beyond the usual pastiches but only intermittently succeeds. All fifteen stories but the Ramsey Campbell are published for the first time. The attractive cover and book design is by co-editor Herber. *The Asylum: Volume 2: The Violent Ward*, edited by Victor Heck (DarkTales Publications), is another bunch of original stories about psychopaths. Some of the more notable tales are by Michael Laimo, Lawrence Connelly, James S. Dorr, and Gerard Houarner.

Midnight Rose: A Celebration of the Women of Horror Fiction, edited by Shannon Riley (Southern Rose Productions), has fifteen stories about women and is dedicated to Eudora Welty and Marian Zimmer Bradley. Although the foreword implies that all the stories are going to be by women, only three of the fifteen stories are.

Frontiers of Terror edited by Bruce R. Gehweiler (Marietta Publishing) is an all original (except for one reprint) nontheme horror anthology with eighteen stories of varying quality. The best were by David B. Silva, A. R. Morlan, Trey R. Barker, Richard Lee Byers, and Jeffrey Thomas. *Lin Carter's Anton Zarnak Supernatural Sleuth,* edited by Robert M. Price (Marietta Publishing), collects all of Lin Carter's Zarnak stories, and also all those written by others. Half of the sixteen stories (none Carter's) are original to the anthology.

Octoberland, edited by Jack Fisher (Flesh & Blood Press), is an entertaining original anthology about Halloween. Strong work by Robert Morrish, Len Maynard and Mick Sims, Monica O'Rourke, and Wendy Rathbone. The nice jacket art is by Mike Bohatch.

Strangewood Tales, edited by Jack Fisher (Eraserhead Press), has an evil clown face dripping with blood on the cover (no art credit), an image that doesn't really complement the publisher's expressed intention of publishing tales that can "only be described as surreal, experimental, postmodern, absurd, avant-garde or perhaps just plain bizarre." There are a few good horror stories in here and even a few strange tales by some of the usual suspects—Jeff VanderMeer, Scott Thomas, Mark McLaughlin, and Jeffrey Thomas—that might be termed absurdist. But if you want excellent cross-genre material check out the special *Conjunctions* issue of "New Wave Fabulists," *Polyphony,* or the *Leviathan* series of original anthologies.

Songs From Dead Singers . . . and Other Eulogies, edited by Michael Kelly (Catalyst Press), is a ghost story anthology with fourteen original stories and three reprints. Although the stories overall didn't have enough variation in tone or background, a few stood out. The best of the originals were by Charlee Jacob, Marie Alexander, Iain Rowan, and Joel Lane. The evocative cover art by Chad Savage is marred by a large block of quotes on the cover.

Royal Aspirations III, edited by Monica J. O'Rourke (Catalyst Press), is the third volume of stories by young writers yearning "to be Stephen King or at least write as well as he does." Unfortunately, none of the stories measure up to the master of characterization and place, although there are a few decent entries.

The Book of More Flesh, edited by James Lowder (Eden Studios, Inc.), is a worthy follow-up to the 2001 zombie anthology, *The Book of all Flesh,* itself inspired by the Eden Studios' role-playing game of the same title. I freely admit that I dreaded reading another zombie story, so I was pleasantly surprised by the variety and verve of many of the twenty-three original stories by writers such as Tom Piccirilli, Scott Edelman, Paul Finch, Darrell Schweitzer, and others.

Lighthouse Hauntings, edited by Charles G. Waugh and Martin Harry Greenberg (Down East Books), has twelve original stories. There is not enough variety or scares, but there are a few unusual, effectively written tales by Janet Berliner, Nina Kiriki Hoffman, and Gary A. Braunbeck.

Lone Wolf Publications published the following in CD-ROM format viewable in Adobe Acrobat: *Extremes 4: Darkest Africa,* edited by Brian A. Hopkins, has twenty original stories, most of them horror, and some with multimedia additions by the authors. About half the stories are very good, the rest okay, with good-looking cover art by GAK. *Stones*, edited by Judi Rohrig, has fifteen original stories and ten original photo galleries related to cemeteries. Most of the stories were pretty good, but my favorites were those by Nicholas Kaufmann, Ed Gorman, and Joel Arnold. The funerary photography was nicely varied. *Tooth and Claw Volume 1*, edited by J. F. Gonzalez and Garrett Peck, has some impressively disgusting artwork by Allen Koszowski and a lot of new pulpy stories about giant spiders, dinosaurs, crocodiles, and so forth that are unfortunately less interesting than those published in the 1930s.

Shivers, edited by Richard Chizmar (Cemetery Dance Publications), is a non-theme horror anthology with twenty-two stories, half original, half reprints. The best of the originals is a collaboration by Brian Keene and Tim Lebbon. Unfortunately, unlike most books from CD, *Shivers* has an unfinished quality to it as a result of there being no introduction, no author bios, or even cover copy providing context for the stories. Also, the copyright page is incorrect in that all stories, regardless of first publication, are copyrighted 2002.

Dark Testament, edited by Shane Ryan Staley (Delirium Books) is a nice-looking hardcover with cover and interior art by GAK. The theme is Bible stories told as horror tales. The cover copy says that the stories are told as "new, modern day stories" but that just isn't so. Most of the stories take place in biblical times and are modern only in the addition of graphic blood and guts. Still, there are some notable stories by Miriam Auden, John Rosenman, Jeffrey Thomas, Michael McCarty and Mark McLaughlin, Michael Oliveri, and Shikhar Dixit.

Darker Dawning 2: Reign in Black (Dark Dawn Industries) is a chapbook of seven stories, about half original, by some of the newer writers in the field, with art by GAK throughout.

Be Very Afraid!, selected by Edo Van Belkom (Tundra Books, Canada), is the follow-up to *Be Afraid*, an anthology from a couple of years ago aimed at teens. There are notable stories by Tanya Huff, Ed Greenwood, and Tom Piccirilli.

Other anthologies: *The 13 Best Horror Stories of all Time*, edited by Leslie Pockell (Warner Books), has a lot of the basics including stories by Edgar Allan Poe, Charlotte Perkins Gilman, Arthur Machen, H. P. Lovecraft, Shirley Jackson, and others; *The Literary Werewolf*, edited by Charlotte F. Otten (Syracuse University Press), has twenty-two werewolf tales ranging from Ovid to Stephen King; *The American Fantasy Tradition*, edited by Brian M. Thomsen (Tor), is a good introduction to a varied group of fantasists. Of the forty-four stories, over a dozen are in the horror tradition and others are borderline cases; *Witches' Brew*, edited by Yvonne Jacobs (Berkley), contains thirty-eight stories, excerpts, and poems about witches and witchcraft written by writers ranging from Ben Franklin, H. P. Lovecraft, Anton Chekhov, and Emily Dickinson to Erica Jong, Shirley Jackson, Ursula K. Le Guin, Ray Bradbury, Harlan Ellison, and Kathryn Ptacek; *The World's Finest Mystery and Crime Stories: Third Annual Collection*, edited by Ed Gorman and Martin H. Greenberg (Forge), includes stories by Lawrence Block, Joyce Carol Oates, Jeffery Deaver, Ed McBain, Anne Perry, and others; *The Book of Eibon* by Clark Ashton Smith, Lin Carter, and Divers Hands, selected and introduced by Robert M. Price (Chaosium), has stories and poetry by new writers such as Michael Cisco, Ann K. Schwader; *Great Tales of Terror*, edited by S. T.

Joshi (Dover), has twenty-three stories; *Night Shadows: Twentieth-Century Stories of the Uncanny*, edited and introduced by Joan Kessler (David R. Godine, Publisher), has fifteen reprints by writers such as Shirley Jackson, John Collier, Ray Bradbury, William Trevor, Joyce Carol Oates, and Ramsey Campbell; *The Colour Out of Space*, edited by D. Thin (New York Review of Books), has twelve stories of "cosmic horror" by authors such as Arthur Machen, H. P. Lovecraft, and Ambrose Bierce, with a cover by Charles Burns; *The Mammoth Book of Best New Horror 13*, edited by Stephen Jones (Robinson, U.K./Carroll & Graf), overlapped with *YBFH 15* on four stories. It has an extensive summary of the year and necrology; *Scary!2: More Stories to Make You Scream!*, edited by Peter Haining (Souvenir, U.K.), is a YA anthology with twelve horror stories.

Mixed-Genre Anthologies

Polyphony Volume 1, edited by Deborah Layne and Jay Lake (Wheatland Press) is a new slipstream anthology series intended to publish stories that don't quite fit within genre boundaries but are by sf/f writers. None of the stories are dark enough to be considered horrific, but readers of darker fiction might enjoy the stories by Carol Emshwiller, Maureen McHugh, and Douglas Lain; *Leviathan Three*, edited by Forrest Aguirre and Jeff VanderMeer (Ministry of Whimsy/Prime), is a fascinating stew of fantasy, a bit of sf, a bit of horror, and some utterly unclassifiable stories. The best darker pieces are by Brian Stableford and Lance Olsen; the much-anticipated *Conjunctions: 39 The New Wave Fabulists*, guest-edited by Peter Straub, has only a little horror, but it's an entertaining look at some of the best writers working in the field of fantastic fiction today. And it's got great cover art by Gahan Wilson. Kelly Link's story "Lull" is reprinted herein; *Dark Offspring*, edited by Brian Knight (Catalyst Press), is an interesting experiment that showcases fiction, poetry, and art by over thirty-five sons and daughters of writers ranging from eight to sixteen years of age. The most original and interesting darker pieces were by Kristen Stewart, Benjamin Wade Eakin, and Haitham Jendoubi; *Best of the Rest 3*, edited by Brian Youmans (Suddenly Press), picks sf/f/h from what *it* considers small-press magazines, Webzines, anthologies, and collections, although most of the venues (*Weird Tales, Talebones, On Spec, Strange Horizons*, and *Horror Garage*) are generally covered by the other editors of year's bests; *The Best American Mystery Stories 2002*, edited by James Ellroy (Houghton Mifflin), has an interesting mix of twenty short stories from various mystery/crime anthologies and magazines, including tales by Joe R. Lansdale, Joyce Carol Oates, Sean Doolittle, Michael Connolly, Thomas H. Cook, and others; *Angel Body and other Magic for the Soul*, edited by Chris Reed and David Memmott (Back Brain Recluse 24), is a welcome return for BBR, formerly a magazine but now a trade paperback. This "issue" is an interesting mix of originals and reprinted prose and poetry; *Freaks, Geeks & Sideshow Floozies*, edited by Tina L. Jens & John Weagly (Twilight Tales), has some dark fantasy and a wee bit of horror, but is mostly fantasy; *Whispers and Shadows*, edited by Jack Fisher (Prime), mixes sixteen horror and fantasy stories, originals with reprints. Some of the stories are good, but with no publication credits it's impossible to know which stories are reprints. Neither are there introductions or biographical notes on the authors; *Shelf Life: Fantastic Stories*

Celebrating Bookstores, edited by Greg Ketter (Dreamhaven Books), was published in honor of the twenty-five years of Dreamhaven Books and Comics' existence. There are some lovely magical fantasies, a touch of sf, and a smattering of horror by such authors as diverse as Jack Williamson, Ramsey Campbell, Nina Kiriki Hoffman, and Harlan Ellison (his is the only reprint). The introduction is by Neil Gaiman and luscious cover illustration and design is by John Picacio; *Passing Strange*, edited by Bill Congreve (MirrorDanse Books, Australia), showcases thirteen original stories of sf, fantasy, and horror from Australia in an attractive trade paperback with cover design by Cat Sparks; *Agog! Fantastic Fiction: 29 New Tales of Fantasy, Imagination and Wonder*, edited by Cat Sparks (agog! Press, Australia), also hails from Australia and has a wee bit of horror, the best by the always reliable Rick Kennett; *Birmingham Noir*, edited by Joel Lane and Steve Bishop (Tindal Street Press, U.K.), is a crime anthology with some stories veering into the horrific; *Dead Cat Bouncing*, edited by Gerard Houarner and GAK (Bedlam Press/Necro), is obviously a labor of love that extrapolates upon a story by Houarner published in 2000 about the adventures of a dead cat. The premise is so silly that it's impossible to judge as horror but for those into it the book is entertaining, with original stories by Jack Ketchum, Edward Lee, Yvonne Navarro, Charlee Jacob, Tom Piccirilli, Paul Di Filippo, and others, plus wonderful illustrations throughout by GAK; *Infinity Plus One*, edited by Keith Brooke and Nick Gevers (PS Publishing), is an anthology of thirteen stories, one of them original, selected by the editors of the on-line reprint fiction showcase, *Infinity Plus*. Introduction is by Peter F. Hamilton.

Artists

The artists who work in the small press toil hard and receive too little credit (forget money), and I feel it's important to recognize their good work. The following created art that I thought was noteworthy during 2002: Angus Pecover, Grant Leier, Caniglia, Mike Bohatch, Glenn Chadbourne, Tim Kirk, Allen Koszowski, Simon Duric, Bob Libby, Rob Middleton, John Myroshnychenko, Bruce Richardson, Chris Nurse, Nigel Potter, Peter Gric, Douglas Walters, Dallas Goffin, Jason C. Eckhardt, Paul Lowe, H. E. Fassl, Carter Humphrey, Mark Roberts, Geoff Priest, Rico J. C., Ian McDowell, Jeff de Boer, David Ho, Joachim Luetke, Richard Marchand, Roddy Williams, Scott Craig, Russell Dickerson, Richard Kirk, Bob Hobbs, D. Crockell, Augie Wiedemann, Headless, Adam Duncan, David Walters, André Sanchez, Bob Libby, Desmond Knight, Trevor Denyer, Cynthia Brock, Bob Crouch, Rick Hudson, Eric Yates, D. L. Hutchinson, George Ostashov, GAK, and Randy Russo.

I'd like especially to note and praise the art and design work of Simon Duric and Garry Nurrish, respectively, who created most of Prime Books' output in 2002. Their collaboration is consistently excellent, and I congratulate them for their vision and technical proficiency at designing memorable looking books.

Magazines and Newsletters

Small-press magazines come and go with amazing rapidity, so it's difficult to recommend buying a subscription to those that haven't proven their longevity. But I urge readers to at least buy single issues of those that sound interesting. The following handful are those that I thought were the best in 2002.

Some of the most important magazines/Webzines specialize in news of the field, market reports, and reviews. *Hellnotes* has changed hands twice, as noted earlier. Paula Guran's *Darkecho* is currently being sent out as an irregular e-mail newsletter. *The Gila Queen's Guide to Markets*, edited by Kathryn Ptacek, and *Jobs in Hell*, edited by Kelly Laymon, are excellent fonts of information for markets in the field. The two major venues specializing in reviewing short fiction are *Tangent Online* (www.tangentonline.com) and the print magazine, *The Fix*. *Locus* and *Chronicle* (formerly *Science Fiction Chronicle*) also cover horror but not thoroughly.

Most magazines have Web sites with subscription information, eliminating the need to include it here. For magazines that do *not* have a Web site, I provide that information:

Scarlet Street, edited by Richard Valley, for the first time seemed to concentrate more on horror movies than mystery movies in 2002. The magazine covers everything from different film adaptations of H. Rider Haggard's *She* (with cheesecake photos of Ursula Andress) and Oscar Wilde's *The Picture of Dorian Gray* to an overview of "Columbia Horrors in the 30s." It's an enjoyable magazine that keeps the past of horror films alive while not ignoring the present completely—it reviews contemporary horror DVDs and CDs.

Video Watchdog, edited by Tim Lucas, has got to be the most exuberant film magazine around—and seems especially gleeful when its reviewers discover variant versions of videos and DVDs. It's invaluable for the connoisseur of trashy, pulp, and horror movies and enjoyable for just about everyone.

Weirdly Supernatural: a journal dedicated to the weird and supernatural in literature, film and art edited by Christopher Barker, is a promising new spiral-bound magazine rich with essays on the supernatural and about specific writers, plus some fiction. The first issue has a reminiscence by T. E. D. Klein about his meeting with the late Robert Aickman in 1974, a spotlight on Marion Fox, author of several novels of the supernatural in the early twentieth century, a short biography by Peter Haining of Guy Thorne, and reviews of nonfiction books and reprinted classics of the supernatural. There are also two stories by Remy de Gourmont, translated by Brian Stableford, and a handful of original contemporary fiction with good black-and-white artwork by Doug Walters and David Fletcher.

On Spec, edited by Derryl Murphy, Holly Phillips, Jena Snyder, Diane L. Walton, and Peter Watts, is the major Canadian sf/f magazine. The excellent winter issue of this quarterly contained several very dark stories, including Michael Libling's story "Puce Boy," reprinted herein. The spring issue also had good dark fiction. The cover art was uniformly good in 2002.

Horror Garage, edited by Paula Guran, brought out an issue with several original stories about homelessness intended for *Desolation Street*, a charity anthology project proposed by John Shirley that didn't work out. In addition to some good stories, Guran interviews Clive Barker to see what he's up to. The only other issue that came out in 2002 was the last that Guran worked on, and it had five original stories and an interview with Ed Gorman.

Cemetery Dance, edited by Richard Chizmar and Robert Morrish, in its fourteenth year, continues to publish a varied selection of dark supernatural and psychological fiction, book, and movie reviews by Paula Guran, Ray Garton, Michael Marano, and others, Thomas F. Monteleone's straight-shooting "The Mothers and Fathers Italian Association," and interviews with horror notables. This continues to be one of the major magazines of the genre.

Supernatural Tales, edited by David Longhorn, is an excellent horror magazine published in the U.K. It's only been publishing a short time, trying to get out two issues a year. Although two issues were planned for 2002, it was not clear whether the magazine would continue because of the lack of subscriptions. The presentation is simple two-color but the fiction is interesting. Issue 2 had an essay about the golem by Steve Duffy and Issue 3 had an essay about the history of supernatural fiction by Joel Lane, Issue 4 had a piece about Carl Jacobi by John Howard. Anyone interested in good horror stories is urged to subscribe, or at least to try an issue.

The Spook, edited by Anthony Sapienza, was an extraordinarily promising downloadable publication when it debuted in 2001. It looked good, published some good horror fiction by better-known writers, and paid well. Unfortunately, during 2002 it lost its way, devolving from an exciting showcase for horror into a mishmash with no focus. Although there was still some fiction by prominent horror writers, the columns were about anything *but* horror, the articles were mostly trivial, and the tone became more fannish than professional.

Talebones, edited by Patrick and Honna Swenson, is an excellent mixed-genre magazine that often has fine dark fiction and is well worth checking out.

Flesh & Blood, edited by Jack Fisher, changed to full color covers with Issue 9. The magazine has fiction, poetry, and the occasional interview. Jack Ketchum was the interview subject in Issue 9.

The Third Alternative, edited by Andy Cox, is *the* major cross-genre magazine. The stories are always interesting, if only occasionally dark enough to be termed horror, although Issue 31 had enough dark fiction to satisfy this horror reader. The smart and lively articles on filmmakers such as the Coen brothers and the Brothers Quay are a welcome antidote to media magazines only concerned with the big Hollywood blockbusters. And the art is consistently excellent. Three stories from 2002 were chosen for this year's *YBFH*.

Redsine, edited by Trent Jamieson and Garry Nurrish, is an elegant-looking, quarterly perfect-bound magazine that publishes dark fantasy and horror fiction. During 2002 it also published interviews with Elizabeth Hand, Brian Stableford, and Tim Powers, and book reviews by Nick Gevers. The beautiful cover art and design are by Garry Nurrish.

Wicked Hollow, edited by Jon Hodges, is a new, nicely produced pint-sized magazine worth looking at for its fiction and poetry. It's made an excellent start in 2002.

Not One of Us, edited by John Benson and published biannually, is a reliable source for interesting dark prose and poetry. Single copies are $4.50 plus $1.00

postage and handling. Three-issue subscriptions are $13.50 postpaid. Checks payable to John Benson, 12 Curtis Road, Natick, MA 01760.

All Hallows: The Journal of the Ghost Story Society, edited by Barbara and Christopher Roden, is an attractive perfect-bound magazine published thrice yearly in February, June, and October. As it's only available to members of the Ghost Story Society, this is another good reason to join the organization dedicated to providing admirers of the classic ghost story with an outlet for their interest. *All Hallows* is an excellent source of news, articles, and ghostly fiction. For more information, visit the Ash-Tree Press Web site at www.Ash-Tree.bc.ca/gss.html.

Weird Tales, edited by George H. Scithers and Darrell Schweitzer, is a quarterly now, in its seventy-eighth year. The magazine's fiction generally provides a who's who in dark fantasy/ horror. In 2002 there was strong fiction by Tanith Lee, Ian McDowell, Ian Watson, and Stephen Gallagher. The latter's story was chosen for reprint herein. S. T. Joshi and Douglas E. Winter alternate columns.

New Genre (horror editor, Adam Golaski) is an elegant-looking, perfect-bound mixed-genre magazine that has published three issues since its debut in 2001. It began as a biannual but will be continuing as an annual. The one issue from 2002 had a very good dark novella by Steve Duffy and a strange dark fantasy by Thomas Dunford. This is a magazine to keep an eye on. For more information visit www.ngenre.com.

Gothic Studies (not seen) is a thrice yearly academic journal published by Manchester University Press in April, August, and December. A subscription includes membership in the International Gothic Association. Each issue is under the direction of a guest editor. The journal considers the field of Gothic Studies from the eighteenth century to the present day, and looks at the gothic in film, art, and literature. Abstracts from each article and subscription information are available at www.manchesteruniversitypress.co.uk/.

Crypt of Cthulhu, edited by Robert M. Price, is for readers interested in Lovecraftian fiction, poetry, essays, and reviews. Three issues were published in 2002, including one with a series of new stories about Herbert West, reanimator (two previously published), and another with three stories influenced by the fiction of August Derleth. For more information, visit www.mythosbooks.com.

nemonymous two: a journal of parthenogentic fiction and late labelling, edited by D. F. Lewis, is the second volume of an experiment to publish stories without author credit until the subsequent issue. Although the contrivance does nothing to enhance the magazine or the stories inside, happily, most of the stories *are* very good. The second issue is an elegant ninety-six-page perfect-bound magazine with a beautifully spare color cover and eighteen stories ranging from the surreal to the very dark. "The Assistant to Dr. Jacob" by Eric Schaller has been reprinted herein. Contact Nemonymous@hotmail.com for subscription information.

Dark Horizons, edited by Debbie Bennett, is a wonderful bonus for members of The British Fantasy Society. The magazine is published twice a year and the stories are always readable. It is highly recommended for those interested in traditional supernatural fiction. The British Fantasy Society is open to everyone. Members receive the informative bimonthly newsletter *Prism* in addition to *Dark Horizons*. The society organizes Fantasycon, the annual British Fantasy Convention, and its membership votes on the British Fantasy Awards. For information, write The British Fantasy Society, the BFS Secretary, 201 Reddish Road, Stockport SK5 7HR, England. Or check out their Web site at www.britishfantasysociety.org.uk.

The Web has become increasingly more important to all readers by providing a cheap venue for nonfiction and fiction. The best horror Web sites that I've seen are:

- *www.feomante.com,* edited by E. C. McMullen Jr., is a flashy and informative site covering every aspect of horror including art, comics, upcoming conventions, movie and book reviews—all with attitude.
- *www.gothic.net,* edited by Darren McKeeman, is another all-purpose horror site, but this one regularly runs short fiction and poetry that are well worth a look, although the fiction editorship has changed twice in the past year.
- *www.horrorfind.com,* edited by Brian Keene, is primarily a search engine but also has been publishing some very good fiction.
- *www.chizine.com—Chiaroscuro: Treatments of Light and Shade in Words,* or *chizine,* as it's been dubbed, is edited by Brett Alexander Savory and has high quality reviews and fiction and poetry. The Web site is easy to navigate, is nicely designed and has a terrific art gallery. It deservedly won the Bram Stoker Award for Superior Achievement in the Other Media category in 2000.

Cross-Genre Magazines and Webzines

Crimewave, edited by Andy Cox, is the best mystery/crime magazine available, and although it only occasionally has stories that are out-and-out horror, the stories are usually dark enough to satisfy those with an interest in dark crime. *The Magazine of Fantasy & Science Fiction,* edited by Gordon Van Gelder, is the oldest of the digest-sized magazines, and although it concentrates on sf and fantasy, it always publishes at least some horror—much of it notable—during the year. *Asimov's Science Fiction Magazine,* edited by Gardner Dozois, rarely publishes out-and-out horror but often has dark fiction, and once in awhile publishes an sf horror story. *Lady Churchill's Rosebud Wristlet,* edited by Gavin J. Grant and Kelly Link, is published twice a year and is a personal yet professional cross-genre 'zine full of poetry, short stories, and the occasional nonfiction article. *Aurealis: Australian Fantasy and Science Fiction,* edited by Keith Stevenson, is published twice a year in Australia and only occasionally publishes horror stories. Also hailing from Australia is a new magazine published every ten months or so called *Orb—Speculative Fiction,* edited by Sarah Endacott. I missed the first two issues but the Double Issue 3/4 had some interesting dark fiction. The quarterly *Black Gate,* edited by John O'Neill, is a fantasy magazine with an occasional darker tale. *The Silver Web,* edited by Ann Kennedy, published only one issue in 2002, but it was a wonderfully eclectic mix of mostly dark surrealism. The excellent front-and-back cover art is by Scott Eagle. *Space and Time,* edited by Gordon Linzner, is one of the oldest of the small-press magazines running sf/f/h and featured a few notable horror tales in 2002.

Poetry

Dreams and Nightmares, edited by David C. Kopaska-Merkel, is one of the longest running poetry magazines having published for over fifteen years. It's a good bet for literate, enjoyable horror and dark fantasy poetry.

Frisson: Disconcerting Verse, edited by Scott H. Urban, is another long-running poetry magazine that publishes horror or dark material.

*Star*line,* edited by David C. Kopaska-Merkel, is the Journal of the Science Fiction Poetry Association and one of the benefits of membership in the organization, which was established in 1978. In addition to publishing poetry, the journal also has market reports and small-press reviews. Check out the Web site for more information: www.dm.net/~bejay/sfpa.htm.

The 2002 Rhysling Anthology: The Best Science Fiction, Fantasy, and Horror Poetry of 2001 is also published by the Science Fiction Poetry Association. The anthology is made up of all nominated works to be considered for the Rhysling Award, chosen by members of the SFPA, and as such provides easy reference for the membership to consider all those works. In addition to being available to members of the organization, other interested parties can acquire the anthology. For information, visit www.dm.net/~bejay/sfpa.htm.

Sidecar Preservation Society: *Red Harvest* by Karl Edward Wagner, a compilation of fourteen verses about the late author's character, the immortal warrior-sorcerer Kane. Illustrated and introduced by Stephen Jones. *Recall Dark Memories* by W. Paul Ganley, which has twenty-five poems, five original. The introduction is by Brian Lumley, and the cover artwork is by Alan Servoss.

Flesh & Blood: *Dark Voices: A Collection of Poetry from the Writers of Wicked Verse,* co edited by Jack Fisher and Nancy Bennett, is an anthology of poetry by twenty-three members of the WickedVerse Internet e-mail list started by Sandra DeLuca in 1999. There is some notable horror poetry in the chapbook. Cover art is by Marge Simon. *Professor LaGungo's Exotic Artifacts & Assorted Mystic Collectibles* by Mark McLaughlin collects all new wacky poetry by the clown prince of horror. Chris Whitlow did the cover illustration.

The Gossamer Eye by Mark McLaughlin, Rain Graves, and David Niall Wilson (Meisha Merlin) showcases poetry and some prose by these three writers. Most but not all of the work included is horror.

This Cape is Red Because I've Been Bleeding by Tom Piccirilli (Catalyst Press) is a very personal yet entertaining collection by this author of ten novels. The cover art by Jeremy Caniglia and jacket design by J. T. Lindroos makes this a very attractive package.

Dark Illuminati Issue Zero (Miniature Sun Press) *appears* to be the first of a proposed series of poetry anthologies, although this isn't clear because, in addition to having no introduction, no editorial or art credit or biographical material, there is also no context provided. The booklet itself is attractive, with a black cover. Happily, the unusual editorial sloppiness doesn't detract from the enjoyment of the poetry itself, which includes reprinted and original works by Charlee Jacob, Lucius Shepard, Bruce Boston, Vance Aandahl, David Kopaska-Merkel, and others.

Quixsilver Press published *In Far Pale Clarity* by Bruce Boston with art by Margaret Ballif Simon. This is an attractive limited-edition broadside by one of sf/f/h's best poets. Also, *Night Smoke* by Bruce Boston and Marge Simon (Miniature Sun Press and Quixsilver Press) is a collection of fifteen collaborative poems with art by Simon. Four of the poems are original to the collection.

She Was There for Him the Last Time by Bruce Boston (Miniature Sun Press) is an excellent long poem. It is Volume 4 of the Aphelion limited-edition chapbook series. The wraparound cover art is created and designed by collagist Brandon Totman.

Your Handy Office Guide to Corporate Monsters by Mark McLaughlin (Richard Geyer) is a chapbook of eleven humorous poems about monsters in the workplace. An adorable little booklet with front-and-back cover art by the poet.

Psycho-Hunter's Casebook by Kurt Newton (DarkVesper Publishing) is laid out as the casebook of a detective who served on the San Francisco police force for twenty-three years. In it are poems written by some of the psycho killers he caught. Within the poems (some original to the volume) is a complex story only revealed at the end in an afterword—a cute idea with some pretty good poetry. The cover artwork is by Keith Minnion. It's the first publication from this new press.

The Darkside of Eden by Christina Sng (Allegra Press) is the first collection by a poet whose poetry has been published in various U.S. and British magazines, Webzines, and anthologies. One poem is original to the collection.

Nonfiction Books

Bad Blood: An Illustrated Guide to Psycho Cinema by Christian Fuchs (Creation) examines the crimes of over forty killers and the films that were inspired by their gory exploits. Black-and-white illustrations are of true crime photos and film stills; *Terence Fisher: Horror, Myth and Religion* by Paul Leggett (McFarland) is an illustrated critical study written from the religious perspective of this director, who worked mainly for Hammer films; *Brian De Palma: Interviews* is edited by Laurence F. Knapp (University of Mississippi Press); *Glory and Terror: Seven Deaths Under the French Revolution* by Antoine de Baecque (Routledge) examines, with graphic description, contemporary literary and visual representations of executions, funerals, processions, and ceremonies; *Grave Matters* by Mark C. Taylor and Dietrich Christian Lammerts (Reaktion Books) is a portfolio and meditation on the gravesites of 160 modern artists, writers, philosophers, and theologians such as Vincent Van Gogh, Emily Dickinson, and Thomas Jefferson; *Irish Witchcraft & Demonology* by St. John D. Seymour (Lethe Press) is a reissue, although there is no publishing or copyright history provided; *Dracula's Crypt: Bram Stoker, Irishness, and the Question of Blood* by Joseph Valente (University of Illinois Press) interprets *Dracula* as an ironic commentary on England's preoccupation with racial purity, maintaining that the real threat in the novel is not racial degeneration but the destructive force of racialized anxiety. And that *Dracula* is a critique of the anxieties concerning the decline of the British Empire, the deterioration of Anglo-Saxon culture, and the contamination of the Anglo-Saxon race; *Bloody Mary in the Mirror: Essays in Psychoanalytic Folkloristics* by Alan Dundes (University Press of Mississippi) is a fairly dry book of seven essays that attempt to illuminate such folklore genres as legend (in the vampire tale), folktale (in the ancient Egyptian tale of two brothers), custom (fraternity hazing and ritual fasting), and games (in the modern Greek game of "Long Donkey"); *Scottish Witches and Wizards* by H. M. Fleming (Dufour Editions) features true accounts from the late sixteenth century up to 1724; *Monsters, Mushroom Clouds, and the Cold War; American Science Fiction and the Roots of Postmodernism, 1946–1964* by Keith M. Booker (Greenwood Press) looks at sf literature as social criticism and covers film treatments of aliens, monsters, and postholocaust themes; *The Supernatural in Short Fiction of the Americas: The Other World in the New World* by Dana Del George (Greenwood Press); *The Frankenstein Archive: Essays on the Monster, the Myth, the Movies, and More* by Donald F. Glut (McFarland) has fifteen essays on the theme of Frankenstein; *Horror Films of the 1970s* is by John Kenneth Muir (McFarland); *The Fantastic Vampire: Studies in the Children of the Night,* edited by James Craig Holte (Greenwood Press), is a collection of papers from the 1997 International Conference on the Fantastic in the Arts: *Gothic Writers: A Critical and Bibliographical Guide,* edited by Douglass H. Thomson, Jack G. Voller and Frederick S. Frank (Greenwood Press), is a collection of fifty-four essays, most of them focusing on individual authors; *Once There Was a Magazine: A Personal View of* Unknown *and* Unknown Worlds by Fred Smith (Beccon Publishers, U.K.) is a reference guide to those two magazines, compiled, annotated, and with an introduction by Smith, and illustrated by Sue Mason. It is available through Roger Robinson, 75 Rosslyn Avenue, Harold Wood, Essex RM3 ORG, U.K.; *The Science of Vampires* by Katherine Ramsland (Berkley Boulevard) is an accessible investigation into the nature of vampirism, including possible scientific explanations for vampires; *Hauntings and Horrors: The Ultimate Guide to Spooky America* by Daniel and Susan Cohen (Dutton's Children's Books) is broken down into six regions and provides anecdotes about enough ghostly events to satisfy most anybody, child or adult; *The Brian Lumley Companion,* edited by Brian Lumley and Stanley Wiater (Tor), is a critical and popular analysis of the author's work with sixteen pages of color art and photographs; *Science and Social Science in Bram Stoker's Fiction* by Carol Senf (Greenwood Press); *The Biology of Horror: Gothic Literature and Film* by Jack Morgan (Southern Illinois University Press); *Skin: On the Cultural Border Between Self and the World* by Claudia Benthien (Columbia University Press), while academic in approach, is accessible enough for the layperson and occasionally touches on subjects of interest to the horror reader, including flaying, in history and in books and movies such as *The Silence of the Lambs.* Also, there is a chapter about the Australian artist Stelarc, who in performances between 1976 and 1988 was regularly suspended by large fishhooks embedded in his skin; *Death Makes a Holiday: A Cultural History of Halloween* by David J. Skal (Bloomsbury) is an entertaining dissection of the holiday horror aficionados love best by an expert in pop culture. I was hooked from the first chapter, which exposes the urban myth of poisoned and booby-trapped trick-or-treat candy. Skal surveys the holiday from its roots to its current commercialization and includes a chapter about the rise of the use of Halloween motifs in Hollywood monster films; *Christopher Lee: The Authorised Screen History* by Jonathan Rigby (Reynolds & Hearn Ltd., U.K.); *Tokyo Scope: The Japanese Cult Film Companion* by Patrick Macias (Cadence Books/Viz Communications); *Amicus: The Studio That Dripped Blood,* edited by Allan Bryce (The Dark Side/Stray Cat Publishing Ltd., U.K.); *Science Fiction Confidential: Interviews with 23*

Monster Stars and Filmmakers by Tom Weaver (McFarland & Co.); *So You Want to be in Pictures: From Will Hay to Hammer Horror and James Bond* by Val Guest (Reynolds & Hearn Ltd., U.K.); *Spawn of Skull Island* by George E. Turner and Orville Goldner, expanded and revised by Michael H. Price and Douglas Turner (Luminary Press), originally published in 1975 as *The Making of King Kong* and long out of print; *The Outer Limits Companion* by David J. Schow (GNP Crescendo Records Publishing Division); *H. G. Wells on Film: The Utopian Nightmare* by Don G. Smith (McFarland & Co.); *The Strange Case of Dr. Mabuse* by David Kalat (McFarland & Co.); *Lovecraft's Library: A Catalogue* is "revised and enlarged" from its original publication in 1980 by S. T. Joshi (Hippocampus Press). In his introduction, Joshi explains the importance of the library of over one thousand volumes in understanding Lovecraft's mind and imagination; *Mysteries of Time and Spirit: Letters of H. P. Lovecraft and Donald Wandrei* by H. P. Lovecraft and Donald Wandrei, edited by S. T. Joshi and David E. Schultz (Night Shade Books), is the first of a projected multivolume series of letters between Lovecraft and Arkham House cofounder-to-be Wandrei. The series will organize the letters thematically—uncut and mostly previously unpublished—each volume dedicated to a specific subject, time, or place; *Mervyn Peake: My Eyes Mint Gold, A Life* by Malcolm Yorke (Overlook) is a major biography of the man best known for his classic dark fantasy the Gormenghast Trilogy. Peake, born of missionary parents in revolutionary China, was a painter, dramatist, poet, and illustrator as well as a writer, and he lived among a circle of friends including Graham Greene, Walter de la Mare, and Dylan Thomas. The biography is richly illustrated with Peake's drawings and has a section of photographs of his family. He died at age fifty-seven after failing in mind and body for twelve years; *Science Fiction/Horror: A Sight and Sound Reader*, edited by Kim Newman (BFI Publishing, U.K.), is the fourth in a series that, according to editor Newman, draws contents almost entirely from articles and reviews published in *Sight and Sound* since 1991. The new volume provides an overview of trends that have shaped sf and horror in the last decade. There are articles by Marina Warner, Iain Sinclair, Howard Waldrop (the single original piece in the book) and reviews by Kim Newman and Jonathan Coe; *Reading the Vampire Slayer: An Unofficial Critical Companion to Buffy and Angel*, edited by Roz Kaveney (Tauris Parke), is the kind of book that provides enough information about its subject to entertain even those who've never seen the TV series; *Haunted Places in the American South* by Alan Brown (University of Mississippi Press) is an entertaining tour, organized state by state, of supposedly haunted houses, nightclubs, jails, and plantations throughout the American South. Each entry gives the history of the site, then describes the apparently supernatural events that occurred there; *Ramsey Campbell. Probably: Thirty Years of Essays and Articles* (PS Publishing, U.K.) is edited by S. T. Joshi, with an introduction by Douglas E. Winter. It collects essays from the late lamented *Necrofile*, articles from *Shock Xpress*, *Fantasy Review*, and www.thespook.com, introductions that Campbell wrote for books by Tim Powers, Dennis Etchison, Thomas Ligotti, and other writers, plus introductions and afterwards to his own books. The highly recommended cover and interior art for the slipcased hardcover edition is by J. K. Potter. *Horror*, edited by Steffen Hantke, is Issue 17 of the scholarly journal *Paradoxa*. It's filled with essays and reviews of horror literature and movies by both academics and horror writers, and it contains interviews with Kathe Koja and Graham Joyce; *Supernatural Fiction Writers: Contemporary Fantasy and Horror Volume I and II*, Richard Bleiler, editor (Thomson Gale), is part of The Scribner's Writers Series and is the update of an invaluable and very readable reference book. This is the kind of reference book that is a joy to dip into. The downside is having multiple contributors, some more proficient than others in fulfilling their briefs. In two unfortunate cases, the essayists seemed stuck on the novel rather than short-fiction form—even if that form is not representative of the author's fantasy and supernatural work. A good example is Pat Cadigan, all of whose novels are science fiction. The space spent discussing those novels could have been better used to discuss her many fantasy-and horror-stories. Yet there is not even a mention of her brilliant stories "Angel" (fantasy) and "The Power and the Passion" (horror). Another case is Dan Simmons. Almost a whole page is spent on his hard science fiction Hyperion series, while only a small paragraph is devoted to all of his short fiction—a mere half a line to his horrifying, award-winning novella "Dying in Bangkok." Notwithstanding the occasional lapses, this book is highly recommended.

Chapbooks and Small-Press Items

Earthling Publications: *El Dia De Los Muertos* by Brian A. Hopkins is a tragic, poignant, and powerfully told novella about an archaeologist who plans to call up the old gods of Mexico on the Day of the Dead in order to resurrect his dead daughter. The story is rich in historical detail and beautifully told. The book—with striking jacket art by John Picacio—is signed by the author and the artist. Peter Crowther's story "The Longest Single Note" was published as a terrific looking chapbook with a jacket cutout that creates a peek-a-boo effect over the illustration by Deena Holland. Peter Crowther provides an introduction.

Midnight House: *Echo of a Curse* is by R. R. Ryan, a virtually unknown British author of thrillers whose entire output was seven novels written during the 1930s. Her books are celebrated by Ramsey Campbell and the late Karl Edward Wagner. *Echo of a Curse*, originally published in 1939, is described by Midnight House as "one of the most deeply disturbing and perverse works ever to appear in the genre." This edition is edited and has an introduction by D. H. Olson. Allen Koszowski's artwork is on the jacket. *Fingers of Fear* by J. U. Nicholson is the first and only novel by the author, who published poetry and translations of Villon and Chaucer and was a business executive by profession. The book was last published (in paperback) thirty-five years ago and has been unavailable in hardcover for sixty years. It is edited and has an introduction by Douglas A. Anderson.

Old Earth Books did a good deed by reprinting all five of the late, great Edward Whittemore's novels: *Quin's Shanghai Circus* and the Jerusalem Quartet, comprised of *Sinai Tapestry*, *Jerusalem Poker*, *Nile Shadows*, and *Jericho Mosaic*. Whittemore's years as a CIA operative gave him plenty of material for his phantasmagoric, horrific, anarchic, hilarious, and often tragic novels. *Quin's Shanghai Circus* takes the reader from medieval Japan to Shanghai in the 1930s. The Jerusalem Quartet is no less than the secret history of the Middle East.

Cemetery Dance Publications: *Cast in Dark Waters* by Ed Gorman and Tom

Piccirilli is a wonderful, fast-moving period piece about a female privateer who takes on a commission to track down a young woman who has run off with a pirate. All through the tale Crimson, the protagonist, is plagued by dreams about her dead sailor husband, who she believes has a become a blood drinker. *Sims, Book Three: Meerm* by F. Paul Wilson is part of the author's futuristic novella series about genetically engineered chimpanzees. Jacket art is by Phil Parks. *Darkness* is Book One of the new Forever Twilight series of novellas by Peter Crowther, about the human survivors of an alien invasion. The jacket art and interior illustrations are by Alan M. Clark.

Subterranean Press: Caitlín Kiernan's novella "In the Garden of Poisonous Flowers," a prequel to her award-winning novel *Threshold* is a gorgeous little book, illustrated throughout and with sexy and gory endpapers by Dame Darcy, who also provided the jacket art.

Undaunted Press: *Plainfield Dreams* by James Futch and Weston Price has a story by each author and a poem by Price about the infamous Ed Gein. Each piece is surprisingly effective, considering how much has already been inspired by the murderer/cannibal. The cover art is by Futch. Also, *A Clicking in the Shadows and Other Tales* by Chad Hensley and W. H. Pugmire showcases one original collaboration and six other stories by one or the other. The introduction is by Robert M. Price. Interior and cover art is by Allen Koszowski.

PS Publishing: *The Uglimen* by Mark Morris, a creepy story about two English brothers who in the swinging sixties stay for a short time in a California commune run by a charismatic man around whom a strange religious cult has developed. In the present day the repercussions of that short visit become apparent when a young man's father apparently commits suicide. The introduction is by Stephen Laws, and the evocative cover art is by Edward Miller. *The Fairy Feller's Master Stroke* by Mark Chadbourn is a marvelous tale of a young genius who is nurtured through a difficult youth by his loving mother, who provides him with a mystery to solve. What is the meaning of Pre-Raphaelite patricide Richard Dadd's most famous fairy painting, the work of the title? As the narrator delves into the mystery, he sinks into drinking, drugging, and despair, simultaneously seeing things in the corner of his eye that may be "real" or his druggy imagination. *The Tain* by China Miéville is a dark fantasy about the war between humans and the tain, creatures imprisoned for thousands of years in mirrors and other reflective objects by humans' gaze. Once they escape, they transform into all sorts of strange and deadly creatures. One man believes he can stop the continued slaughter of humanity. Miéville once again demonstrates his powerful imagination. All the novellas are available in paperback and hardcover. Also, *The Darkest Part of the Wood* by Ramsey Campbell is a new novel, with an introduction by Peter Straub. It's the first supernatural novel Campbell has published since *Nazareth Hill*. The wraparound jacket art by Edward Miller is beautiful—the slipcase repeats the cover art from a slightly different perspective.

Sidecar Preservation Society: "Hain's Island" is an sf story by Ramsey Campbell with cover artwork by Rodger Gerberding. *Tales of the Backveld* by Francis H. Sibson contains two short stories by a writer born in England in 1899 who emigrated to South Africa in 1913. D. H. Olson provides an introductory essay about the author. Cover art is by Sabastian Van Esch.

American Fantasy: *A Walking Tour of the Shambles: Little Walks for Sightseers*

#16 is a charming dark fantasy guide to an imaginary Chicago neighborhood, published for the 2002 World Horror Convention. Illustrations are by Randy Broecker and Earl Geier. This thin trade paperback comes in two variant editions, one by Gaiman and Wolfe, the other by Wolfe and Gaiman, with slightly different colors. *The Broecker Sampler: The Artwork of Randy Broecker* is a chapbook of the artist's black-and-white illustrations, with an introduction by Robert T. Garcia. Tentacles, skulls, skeletons, demons—illustrations that would be right at home in the horror comics of yesteryear—Broecker takes such glee in his work that he drags you into his imagination before you know it.

Necro Publications: *Skins of Youth* by Charlee Jacob and Mehitobel Wilson, the second of the Necro Chapbook series. This one showcases a story each by two up-and-coming writers. Cover art is by Chris Trammell and interior art is by Erik Wilson. *Edward Lee's Quest for Sex, Truth & Reality* by Edward Lee is the third in the series and is a reprint of a hard-to-find chapbook by the author. It has four stories, with cover art by Chris Trammell and interiors by Erik Wilson. *Bastards of Alchemy*, fourth in the series, has one story each by Tom Piccirilli and Gerard Houarner, with cover art by David G. Barnett and interior art by Erik Wilson. *Sex, Drugs & Power Tools* by Edward Lee is a hardcover collection of three novellas, "The Pig" and "Header" reprints, and a new one, "The Horn-Cranker," which is the Perseus myth gone mad. Lee's work is often so over-the-top gross that it's impossible to believe that it's not tongue in cheek. The cover art is by David G. Barnett and the interior illustrations are by Erik Wilson.

Gauntlet Press's new imprint Edge Books brought out *Pride*, a collaboration between Richard Matheson and his son, Richard Christian Matheson. The oversized paperback is comprised of several different versions of a "notion," as Richard Matheson puts it in his introduction, one that is developed over various drafts that each writes and that becomes, finally, a chilling teleplay. Also from Gauntlet: *He Wanted to Live* by Richard Matheson, a chapbook given away as a premium for those who bought the limited edition of *A Stir of Echoes* directly through the publisher.

Hippocampus Press: Clark Ashton Smith's *The Black Diamonds* is an Arabian Nights adventure novel written when the author was fourteen years old and never before published, edited and with an introduction by S. T. Joshi. The charming jacket art and interior illustrations are by Jason C. Eckhardt. *The Last Oblivion: Best Fantastic Poems of Clark Ashton Smith*, edited by S. T. Joshi and David E. Schultz, showcases Smith's wonderfully evocative verse in the realms of the fantasy, dark fantasy, and horror. The attractive trade paperback has jacket art by Smith and an introduction by the editors, who also provide a glossary for unfamiliar words and the first line of each poem. *From the Pest Zone: The New York Stories* by H. P. Lovecraft contains five stories written in response to Lovecraft's unhappy stay in New York City, 1924–1926. Edited by S. T. Joshi and David E. Schultz. Merritt's *The Metal Monster*, the first volume in the new Lovecraft's Library Series, is intended to bring back affordable print editions of selected works that Lovecraft praised in his famous monograph and in his letters. The charming pulpy cover and interior art is by Virgil Finlay. Stefan Dziemianowicz provides a thorough introduction.

True Tales of the Scarlet Sponge by Wayne Allen Sallee (DarkTales Publications) is an unputdownable account of the real-life influences on the author's author's writing, plus a journal of a series of surgeries and hospitalizations he underwent between 1989 and 1995. The writing here is as sharp as Sallee's fiction. Brian A. Hopkins wrote the introduction. Sean Madden did the cover art.

Cape Wrath by Paul Finch (Telos) is a novella about a team of student archeologists and their professor who explore a deserted island off Britain's most northerly point and discover a Viking treasure trove. The author keeps up the suspense and writes some powerful grisly scenes of violence. Cover art is by David J. Howe with cover design by Anh Nguyen.

Where the Southern Cross the Dog by Trey R. Barker (Fairwood Press) is a very attractive chapbook of three stories taking place in the southern town of Green River. Cover and art is by Eric M. Turnmire, and the chapbook has an introduction by Steve Rasnic Tem and foreword by the author. Good fiction by an up-and-coming writer.

Veil of the Soul, also by Barker (Yard Dog Press), is a moving and tragic novella about Edgar Allan Poe and his demons. Cover art is by Mary Bullock.

Station Two by Jack Ketchum (Camelot Books and Gifts, Inc. copyright 2001) is a fast-and-furious urban nightmare of a group of people in the wrong place just as someone loses their cool and wigs out. The cover illustration is by J. K. Potter (and very unlike most of his work).

Thy Kingdom Come by Simon Morden (Lone Wolf Publications) is an apocalyptic story cycle on CD-ROM. Art is by Marge Simon.

The Hidden Language of Demons, a novella by L. H. Maynard and M. P. N. Sims (Prime), has cover art by Simon Duric and cover design by Garry Nurrish.

Catskin: a swaddled zine by Kelly Link (Jelly Ink Press) is an odd little tale about witches and cats.

Snow, Glass Apples: A Play for Voices by Neil Gaiman (Biting Dog Press), with woodcuts by George Walker and an introduction by fairy-tale scholar Jack Zipes, is a beautifully designed limited edition scripted version of the short story by Gaiman (reprinted in an earlier volume of this series).

Sherlock Holmes and the Terror Out of Time by Ralph E. Vaughn (Gryphon Publications) is a Lovecraftian novella with cover art by Alfred Klosterman.

Family Tradition by Edward Lee and John Pelan (Shadowlands Press) is a new collaborative novel about rednecks with lots of sex, gross-outs, and humor by the duo who brought you the over-the-top *Goon* and *Shifters*. The dust jacket and interior art are by Glenn Chadbourne.

Odds and Ends

Imagination Box by Steve and Melanie Tem (Lone Wolf Publications CD-ROM) is an excellent example of multimedia used to showcase the authors' fiction, poetry, plays, and art. There are even a card game, a graphic novel, and two flash cartoons written and narrated by Steve, and a virtual tour of their house. This would make a wonderful gift for those who enjoy the work of these two fine writers. Lone Wolf is ahead of the pack in creating attractive, easy to navigate, interesting CD-ROMs.

The Tree is My Hat by Gene Wolfe, adapted for voice and directed by Lawrence Santoro, was originally produced live at the 2002 World Horror Convention. I had the privilege of attending the one-hour performance and it was a brilliant rendition of a very creepy story (reprinted in an earlier *YBFH*). Now it can be heard on CD, special effects and all. To purchase contact: Larry@LarrySantoro.com.

The Last Halloween by Alan M. Clark and Friends (IFD Publishing) is a fun multimedia interactive "story sculpture" with music, painting, and animation created by this well-known horror artist.

Cautionary Tales for Children by Hilaire Belloc and illustrated by Edward Gorey (Harcourt) is a typically jaundiced view of the awful things that can happen to children who inhabit the late great Edward Gorey's world and don't listen to their elders.

Mütter Museum by Gretchen Worden (Blast Books) is a coffee-table book about this remarkable museum of the College of Physicians of Philadelphia. The museum is one of the last medical museums from the nineteenth century, and its pathological and anatomical collection was begun by Dr. Thomas Dent Mütter, who collected specimens for teaching purposes. For several years the museum produced a wall calendar, with photos of its collection taken by Joel-Peter Witkin, Arne Svenson, Rosamond Purcell, and other excellent photographic artists. No longer. However, this book has many of the photos from the calendar and others besides. The photos run the gamut from a collection of needles and pins removed from different parts of the body of "a young hysterical female in the 1940s–50s" mounted on a piece of isinglass (mica), to albumen prints of a man with a huge tumor on his face, to eight fetal skeletons.

Fakir Musafar Spirit + Flesh (Arena Editions) is a portfolio of photographs, many self-portraits, taken by the body-modification artist who has been tattooing, binding, piercing, cosseting, and otherwise manipulating his body in order to seek spiritual transcendence for over fifty years. An essay explains how Fakir, born in 1930, began his odyssey at age seventeen, secretly experimenting in his family's basement until he "came out" publicly in 1977 at the first international tattoo convention in Reno, Nevada. Some readers/viewers might find the photographs more disturbing than they'd like.

A new facsimile edition of Lewis Carroll's *Alice's Adventures in Wonderland* illustrated by Arthur Rackham (A Peter Glassman Book: Sea Star Books) is an absolute treat to those who—like me—adore Alice and Rackham. It contains thirteen full-color plates and fourteen black-and-white drawings. Peter Glassman, owner of the New York City bookstore and publisher Books of Wonder, which specializes in books for children, provides an afterword about Rackham's contribution.

The H. P. Lovecraft Tarot with a manual written by Eric C. Friedman and art by Daryl Hutchinson (Mythos Books) is a reissue of the functional tarot deck originally published in 1996 and currently out of print. The deck uses Cthulhuian characters and references and comes with an eighty-page book explaining the deck's use as a divination tool. This would make a great gift for aficionados of Lovecraft or art collectors.

The publication of a new Glen Baxter book is a joy, and in 2002 *Trundling Grunts* was published by Bloomsbury, U.K., in hardcover. Baxter is a satirist whose books and postcards are masterpieces of odd juxtapositions. One example is a drawing of a guy dressed for a safari holding a butterfly net and faced with two male lions about to attack. The caption: "All I had to do now was to coax them into the net." See why Don Tumasonis's story "The Prospect Cards" (reprinted herein) has been compared to Baxter's work.

Goad: The Many Moods of Phil Hale (Donald M. Grant, Publisher, Inc., 2001) is for anyone who enjoys the work of this artist, whose art has been on the covers and inside the Grant editions of Stephen King's Dark Tower series. The book includes sketches, paintings, photographs, and reproductions of book-jacket art. The paintings are dark and beautiful, and the text is by Tray Batey. The cover art comes in two variations. A trade and a limited edition were published, and the limited comes with a full-page original sketch by Hale.

Pictures that Tick, Short Narrative Book One by Dave McKean (Hourglass/Allen Spiegel Fine Art, 2001) is as the title suggests, a series of illustrated short narratives with interstitial material—sketches, thoughts, and just enough introductory material to intrigue the reader.

Underwood Books: *The Art of Jeffrey Jones*, edited by Cathy Fenner and Arnie Fenner, is a good introduction to an artist whose work in the sixties and seventies influenced a generation of artists. Jones illustrated a lot of dark fantasy during that period. He is best known for his lush paintings of women and warriors. There is a nice section at the beginning with the artist's memories and images of his early life that obviously stayed with him, providing fertile soil for his art. *Spectrum 9: The Best in Contemporary Fantastic Art*, edited by Cathy Fenner and Arnie Fenner, is a beautiful annual showcase of science fiction, fantasy, and horror art. In the volume covering 2001, the talented Grand Master recipient, Kinuko Y. Craft, is profiled and Arnie Fenner provides a survey of the year. The jury—all artists themselves—convene and decide on gold and silver awards in several categories. This is a book for anyone interested in art of the fantastic, whether dark or light.

The Spider and the Fly, based on the cautionary tale by Mary Howett and illustrated by Tony DiTerlizzi (Simon & Schuster Books for Young Readers), is a fresh look at the poem written in 1829 by Howett to warn her children about sweet-talking strangers. The art is inspired by old movie villains—black mustache and all—as the sinister yet elegant spider seduces a sweet and silly young thing with his charm.

Cabinets of Curiosities by Patrick Mauries (Thames & Hudson) is a coffee-table book about the seventeenth-century collections of two-headed calves, shell masks, exotic artifacts, preserved crocodile embryos, and many other bits and pieces put together by merchants, scholars, or royalty. The practice made a resurgence in the twentieth century and influenced André Breton and the surrealists, Joseph Cornell, and others.

Small Press Addresses

American Fantasy Press: Garcia Publishing Services, PO Box 1059, Woodstock, IL 60098. www.american-fantasy.com.

Arsenal Pulp Press: 103-1014 Homer Street, Vancouver, British Columbia, V6B 2W9, Canada. www.arsenalpulp.com.

Ash-Tree Press: PO Box 1360, Ashcroft, BC VOK 1A0, Canada. www.Ash-Tree.bc.ca/ashtreecurrent.html.

BBR Distributing: PO Box 625, Sheffield S1 3GY, U.K. www.bbr-online.com.

Catalyst Press: PO Box 755, New York, NY 10009. www.catalystpress.net.

Cemetery Dance Publications: PO Box 943, Abingdon, MD 21009. www.cemeterydance.com.

Chaosium, Inc: 900 Murmansk Street Suite #5, Oakland CA 94607. www.chaosium.com.

Crossroads Press: PO Box 10433, Holyoke, MA 01041.

Dark Regions Press: PO Box 1558, Brentwood, CA 94513. http://darkregions.hypermart.net.

DarkTales Publications: PO Box 19514, Shawnee Mission KS 66285-9514. http://darktales.com.

Delirium Books: PO Box 338, N. Webster, IN 46555. www.deliriumbooks.com.

The Design Image Group: PO Box 2325, Darien, IL 60561. http://www.designimagegroup.com.

Earthling Publications: 12 Pheasant Hill Drive, Shrewsbury, MA 01545. www.earthlingpub.com.

Eden Studios, Inc.: 3426 Keystone Avenue #3, Los Angeles, CA 90034-4731. www.edenstudios.net.

Fedogan & Bremer: 3721 Minnehaha Avenue South, Minneapolis, MN 55406. www.charlesmckeebooks.com/~fedogan.

Flesh & Blood Press: 121 Joseph Street, Bayville, NJ 08721. http://zombie.horrorseek.com/horror/fleshnblood.

Gauntlet Publications: 5307 Arroyo St., Colorado Springs, CO 80922. www.gauntletpress.com.

Greenwood Press: 88 Post Road West, PO Box 5007, Westport, CT 06881. www.greenwood.com.

Gryphon Publications: PO Box 209, Brooklyn, NY 11228-0209.

Haffner: 5005 Crooks Road, Suite 35, Royal Oak, MI 48073-1239. www.rust.net/~haffner.

Hippocampus Press: PO Box 641, New York, NY 10156. www.hippocampuspress.com.

IFD Publishing: PO Box 40776, Eugene OR 97404. www.ifdpublishing.com.

Kelp Queen Press: c/o Sandra Kasturi, 3-334 Westmount Avenue, Toronto, Ontario, M6E 3N2, Canada.

Lone Wolf Publications: 13500 SE 79th Street, Oklahoma City, OK 73150. www.lonewolfpubs.com.

Marietta Publishing: PO Box 3485, Marietta, GA 30061-3485. http://www.mariettapublishing.com.

McFarland & Co.: Box 611, Jefferson NC 28640. www.mcfarlandpub.com.

Meisha Merlin Publishing: PO Box 7, Decatur, GA 30031. http://www.meishamerlin.com.

Midnight House: 4128 Woodland Park Ave. N., Seattle, WA 98103. http://www.darksidepress.com/midnight.html.

Miniature Sun Press: PO Box 11002, Napa Valley, CA 94581. http://www.miniaturesunpress.com.

The Ministry of Whimsy: PO Box 4248, Talahassee, FL 32315. http://www.ministryofwhimsy.com.

MirrorDanse Books: PO Box 3542, Parramatta, NSW 2124, Australia. www.tabula-rasa.info/MirrorDanse.

Mythos Books: 218 Hickory Meadow Lane, Poplar Bluff, MO 63901-2160. www.mythosbooks.com.

Necro Publications: PO Box 540298, Orlando, FL 32854-0298. www.necropublications.com.

Night Shade Books: 3623 SW Baird St., Portland, OR 97219. www.nightshadebooks.com.

Old Earth Books: PO Box 19951, Baltimore, MD 21211. http://www.oldearthbooks.com.

Overlook Connection Press: PO Box 526, Woodstock, GA 30188. http://www.overlookconnection.com.

Prime Books, Inc.: PO Box 36503, Canton, OH 44735. www.primebooks.net.

PS Publishing: LLP, Hamilton House, 4 Park Avenue, Harrogate, HG2 9BQ, England. www.pspublishing.co.uk.

Richard Geyer, Publisher: 1338 West Maume, Idlewilde Manor #136, Adrian, MI 49221. www.geocities.com/rgeyer_2000/index.html.

Sarob Press: Ty Newydd, Four Roads, Kidwelly, Carmarthenshire, SA17 4SF, Wales UK. http://home.freeuk.net/sarobpress.

Shadow Publishing: 194 Station Road, Kings Heath, Birmingham, B14 7TE, UK. http://shadowpublishing.com.

ShadowLands Press: Bereshith Publishing, PO Box 2366, Centreville, VA 20122. www.bereshith.com.

Small Beer Press: 176 Prospect Avenue, Northampton, MA 01060. www.lcrw.net.

Space and Time: 138 W. 70th Street, New York, NY 10023-4468. www.cith.org/space&time.html.

Subterranean Press: PO Box 190106, Burton, MI 48519. http://www.subterraneanpress.com.

Tartarus Press: Coverley House, Carlton, Leyburn, North Yorkshire, DL8 4AY, UK. http://homepages.pavilion.co.uk/users/tartarus/welcome.htm.

Undaunted Press: PO Box 70, St. Charles, MO 63302. www.undauntedpress.com.

Underwood Books: PO Box 1609, Grass Valley, CA 95945. http://www.underwoodbooks.com.

Wormhole Books: 7719 Stonewall Run, Fort Wayne, IN 46825. http://www.wormholebooks.com.

Yard Dog Press: 710 W. Redbud Lane, Alma, AR 72921-7247. http://www.yarddogpress.com.

The Year in Media of the Fantastic: 2002

Edward Bryant

The Big Screen

THE ALMIGHTY MADE ME DO IT

For my money, the best 2002 movie of the dark fantastic is actor/director Bill Paxton's pet project *Frailty*. Aside from being beautifully made and suspenseful, it does what few horror films truly accomplish: it is dangerous. Popular entertainment rarely ventures very far into provocation. The idea is to sell tickets, not to accumulate refund demands from the crowd.

One could discuss for a long time why few serious Christian films are made in Hollywood, at least movies of the fantastic, utilizing Christian materials. The last good one was probably Michael Tolkin's quietly apocalyptic *The Rapture* (1991). Okay, okay, I'm not mentioning funny exceptions like Kevin Smith's *Dogma* (1999) or *Monty Python's Life of Brian* (1979). I'm thinking about serious speculative drama in which the premise is that Christian dogma is literally real. Usually only committed evangelicals tackle that sort of material and they invariably do it badly.

Frailty's script, written by Brent Hanley, takes the Old Testament seriously. Texas blue-collar widower Bill Paxton, a decent man with two young sons, one day gets a private message from God telling him that the world is full of demonic entities, creatures that will cause untold pain and destruction to virtuous human beings (read devout Christians). Paxton's mission will henceforth be to act as the Almighty's agent, ferreting out these monsters and destroying them, preferably with an old-fashioned axe labeled with the name of the original owner, Otis. Trouble is, the demons can construct perfect simulacra of human beings. To do his task properly, Paxton must have faith. He must believe implicitly in what God has asked of him.

So he does exactly that. And eventually he enlists the aid of his two young boys. The movie flips back and forth in time, travelling ahead to the present day where one now-adult son (Matthew McConaughey) has reason to bring the truth behind the unsolved killings to FBI agent Powers Booth.

Ultimately the film is a psychological litmus test for the viewer. Is Paxton's character a homicidal looney? Or is he a pious man who really is getting his marching orders from God and who truly *is* destroying agents of evil?

I watched the film with fascination and care and believe I saw the internal evidence to bolster my belief that the film is genuinely an example of the supernatural in action. I know full well there are plenty of other viewers who think Paxton's character is simply nutso.

In any case, it's a pleasure to see a movie on the multiplex screen that takes some worthwhile risks and triggers thought and debate. Director Bill Paxton and writer Brent Hanley should be extremely proud of themselves.

THE REST OF THE PACK

The Ring, directed by Gor Verbinski, is a taut and nasty piece of business with a convoluted genesis. The script by Ehren Kruger is a remake of the 1998 Japanese smash *Ringu* (scripted by Hiroshi Takahashi), based on a series of popular novels by Koji Suzuki. There since have been Japanese sequels. I'm told there's an even *scarier* Korean version, but that one I haven't been able to track down.

In any case, the American remake is quite effective on its own. Naomi Watts, whom you may recall fondly from David Lynch's *Mulholland Drive*, gets involved with a sublimely dangerous videotape. People who watch the cassette find themselves dying horribly a finite amount of time later. Consider this something of a contemporary version of the joke that kills.

Beautifully shot and tightly edited, *The Ring* offers genuine creepiness and a few solid shocks. It is far superior to the similar but vastly less adroit exploitive attack on the same materials, *fear.dot.com*.

Blade II's got a terrific director, Guillermo del Toro, the solid competent presence of actor Wesley Snipes, and a decent supporting cast in the presence of Kris Kristofferson (contortedly revived from the first *Blade*), along with Ron Perlman and a variety of other decent sorts. It's also got a reasonable story idea: the vampire establishment has to form a hunter/killer strike unit to combat a new strain of rogue vampires who prey on their "normal" fellows. What results is hash. But it's *beautiful* hash. This is another defensible no-brainer. Switch off your critical faculties when you watch it. *Blade II* is a couple hours of hyperkinetic physicality and absolutely beautiful visuals. Watch, don't think.

Signs is M. Night Shyamalan's third run at the fantastical. *Sixth Sense* was terrific; *Unbreakable* was intriguing but less successful. Now *Signs*, with its mysterious crop circles and largely offstage invasion of earth, is not terribly encouraging for the director's artistic development. Could this be entropy at work? True, disillusioned and widowed clergyman Mel Gibson has some amusing moments with his kids and alien mind control–thwarting aluminum foil hats, but those giggles and a few sinister moments out in the nighttime cornfields do not a successful full-length thriller make. One direction the film takes is laudable in that one could consider this a brave alternative to the bloated extravagance of *Independence Day*. That blockbuster showed us the macroview of alien invasion, the wide-screen spectacle of it all. *Signs* admirably adopts a microview, depicting one family trying to survive what is apparently a possible global catastrophe. Most of the alien incursion is merely suggested rather than shown. Unfortunately, when the extraterrestrial monsters eventually show up, the rubber-suit approach is a disappointment. This is a feature film that probably would have benefited from being compressed into an old-line Rod Serling *Twilight Zone* episode.

Richard Gere imparted some desperately needed professional energy to *The Mothman Prophecies*, but that wasn't nearly enough. Laura Linney added more energy as the local sheriff, but that also was insufficient. Based on the "true story" of a mysterious east-coast winged creature, the movie works as a visually entertaining no-brainer. And there's something to be said for honest giggles after the human-scaled mothman suddenly smooshes on a car windshield rather like his younger bug cousins do in the course of a night drive.

THINGS YOU MAY HAVE MISSED BUT SHOULD TRACK DOWN

Here are some interesting films that may have slipped past your attention like shadows. Indie filmmaker Larry Fessenden's *Wendigo* is a lovely small movie about an apparently ideal young family heading to an isolated area of upstate New York on a winter vacation. Their nuclear virtues are sorely tested by encounters with rednecks and evil forces—perhaps not actually evil, but rather elemental powers of Native Americans with little affection for whitey. Fessenden's film is taut and affecting, and only starts to come apart at the seams at the very end.

It's an utter mystery to me why David Twohy's *Below* made such a small impact on movie audiences. The maker of *Pitch Black* gave us an eerie *Twilight Zone* twist on World War II submarine movies. The U.S. vessel *Tigershark* picks up three survivors from a torpedoed British hospital ship. Then, as the craft tries to elude a determined German sub-chaser, things get weird. Who—or what—has taken up residence on board?

Session 9 actually hails from 2001, but I missed it then so I'm mentioning it now. This small supernatural thriller about a decontamination crew cleaning the asbestos out of a mothballed and perhaps haunted gothic insane asylum in New England sports a solid cast headed up by a highly effective David Caruso. As the men struggle against the tight deadline imposed by a ruinous low-bid arrangement, it becomes apparent that some sort of malign *genius loci* inhabits the place. Ultimately it's about apparently decent people coming apart under acute stress. Check out the DVD if you can. It's instructive to view the deleted scenes, a solid lesson in why it's a good thing sometimes to second-guess the initial shooting and tighten the editing.

Another rental delight is the low-budget British thriller, *Dog Soldiers*. Created in part by some of the people who worked on *Hellraiser*, *Dog Soldiers* gives us a small British Army detachment on maneuvers in the remote Scottish hinterlands. Unfortunately for them, they get tangled up with a passel of good old-fashioned lycanthropes. There's some effective writing and acting here, a solid mix of action, thrills, and humor.

I'll give a qualified but mostly enthusiastic thumbs-up to *Wes Craven Presents: They*. It's directed by Robert Harmon, who made a noisy debut at Telluride a few years ago with the Rutger Hauer thriller, *The Hitcher*. *They* is a remarkably restrained supernatural thriller about some adults who thought they were over childhood night fears, but turn out to be terribly wrong. Filmed in Vancouver, the film's got only one really recognizable face, Mark Blucas from *Buffy*. But that's okay; high-profile faces would distract from the growing tension. The script could have used a few editing changes, but that's about my only real complaint. What I liked quite a lot were the menaces, only shown in nasty, disquieting bits, without the kind of eventual full-frontal disclosure that killed *Signs*. What I liked even more was the monochrome visual look, drawn both from classic *Twilight Zone* and, intriguingly enough, from the even more classic first version of *Cat People*.

Look for *Dahmer* in the darker corners of your video store. Filmmaker David Jacobson used plenty of Milwaukee location shooting to set the stage for this bleakly intriguing docudrama about the grotesquely fascinating Jeffrey Dahmer (played well by Jeremy Renner). Bruce Davison portrays Dahmer's dysfunctional dad. The film attempts to delve speculatively into Dahmer's childhood, looking for reason within the psychopathic chaos. It doesn't really come up with a convincing set of keys to Dahmer's murderous adulthood, other than to submit poignantly that he was an unhappy kid. One of the film's most striking set pieces is Dahmer sitting alone in the lunchroom of the Milwaukee candy factory in which he worked as an adult, placidly munching on chocolate Santas. Could refined sugar be the villain in Dahmer's psyche?

LIMITED GUILTY PLEASURES

I'm a great fan of big arachnid flicks, so I was guardedly optimistic when *Eight Legged Freaks* opened. Actually, I went to a sneak preview where the theatre staff handed out souvenir plastic spiders and a welcoming committee of local exterminators greeted us all, then gave away prizes based on trivia questions: "True or false: Colorado is infested with brown recluses. Answer: false. People keep mistaking those darned fiddlebacks for recluses." Anyhow. *Eight Legged Freaks* has its moments as prodigal son David Arquette returns to his desert hometown and then has to join with single-mom sheriff Kari Wuhrer as a local arachnid scholar-and-freak's collection mutates horribly. It's reasonably amusing if you get a kick out of seeing obnoxious townie teens on motocross bikes get chased down by big, leaping, eight-legged predators. On the eternal spider movie scale, with *Tarantula* being up at the top and William Shatner in *Kingdom of the Spiders* being way down low, *Eight Legged Freaks* is somewhere in the dreary middle.

I'm usually suspicious of movies based on video games. But I went to see *Resident Evil* anyway. It was a free pass and I knew it starred Milla Jovavich as a memory-impaired secret agent who finds herself in a high-tech death-trap environment infested by hideous zombies. What's not to like? This'll never be an Oscar nominee in *our* parallel world track, but it does possess a high-gloss, chilly presence that kept me diverted for its duration. And a friend who has even less of a life than I do commented that this was one of the best video game representations on the screen he'd ever seen. So there.

I actually enjoyed *Queen of the Damned*, may the gods have mercy on my soul. Mix a bit of the titular Anne Rice novel with a dash of *The Vampire Lestat* and the resulting mix ranges from dumb to pretentious to pretty cute. It's probably telling that the high point is the desert concert extravaganza when the real vampires start blasting each other on stage—and the mosh-pit thugs go crazy, thinking they're tripping on the cool fx. . . .

If you love the first extravagant effects-drenched scene in *Ghost Ship*, then you might as well go out to the lobby for popcorn for, oh, the next hour and a half or so. It's a great, grisly scene as a terrible thing happens a few decades ago to a luxurious Italian cruise ship, but then the plot founders and sinks fast. In the present, an airplane pilot (Desmond Harrington) with investment money and hidden depths enlists a desperate salvage crew to go out looking for the ghost ship, newly appeared in the fog of the North Atlantic. Gabriel Byrne, Julianna Margulies, Ron Eldard, Isaiah Washington, and the rest of the unlucky salvage crew choose greed over smarts in this top-heavy morality tale. Director Steve Beck (*Thirteen Ghosts*) can't keep the whole thing from capsizing in the rough seas of cliché.

CALL IT SUSPENSE OR CALL IT THRILLERS, BUT DON'T CALL ME LATE FOR DINNER

Written and directed by the clearly talented Mark Romanek, *One Hour Photo* is terrific. Period. I'll elaborate. Robin Williams, as a middle-aged photo technician in a big-box retail store, estranged from everyone and everything and nearly terminally lonely, "adopts" the attractive young nuclear family who bring in their snapshots to him. Creepy? Yeah, but empathic as well. I think accomplished comedians are often well qualified to evoke creepiness. Williams decorates his apartment with duplicate prints of the family's holidays and fantasizes he's their loving Uncle Sy. He loves them; they love him; it's a critical dream for a man who shows people a photograph of his mom that is actually a picture he picked up at a thrift store. But then the avuncular Sy, by sheer chance, discovers the proverbial serpent in Eden. The family's dad is not being a faithful guy. Uncle Sy decides that strong measures are needed. *One Hour Photo* is a beautifully delineated psychological thriller that never forgets the heart while it tightens the noose of suspense. Ultimately it's an expertly crafted exercise in twisting audience expectations. Between this and playing the killer in the same year's *Insomnia*, Robin Williams demonstrates how effectively he can evoke the troubled mind.

Just as we didn't need in 1998 for the talented Gus Van Sant to make a shot-for-shot remake of Hitchcock's *Psycho*, so we also didn't much need in 2002 a new version of Thomas Harris's *Red Dragon* starring a digitally rejuvenated Anthony Hopkins as Hannibal Lecter. Michael Mann's 1986 adaptation, titled *Manhunter*, did just fine. But the profit motive speaks stridently, and author Thomas Harris only turns out novels according to some arcane Jovian tidal table. So, obviously, something had to be done to keep the franchise fiscally kicking. The production looks great, the cast with Hopkins and Edward Norton and Ralph Fiennes is fine, but it's all *so* unnecessary.

Okay, so you don't necessarily expect a whole lot from an adapted Tom Clancy novel with Ben Affleck picking up the CIA analyst Jack Ryan character Harrison Ford earlier appropriated for his own. The devilish fun here is in the plot details. Speaking as a resident of Denver, I was reassured that the scriptwriters moved the terrorist nuclear detonation from the Mile-High City to Baltimore. And frankly, the nuclear destruction of a Super Bowl Sunday football stadium, along with a few square miles of Baltimore, is awfully well executed. The apocalyptic disaster is ingeniously evoked through telling details rather than wide-screen mushroom clouds.

WE PAUSE, BELIEVE IT OR NOT, FOR A WORD FROM THE SPONSORS

I couldn't help but notice Tony Scott's new directorial effort, *Beat the Devil.* It's a dark fantasy with a stellar cast. It's also a commercial, being underwritten by Audi, the auto manufacturers. It also lasts for about six minutes and can be found in better movie houses all over town. I saw it instead of the usual package of trailers preceding *Standing in the Shadows of Motown*. On the story level, it's essentially another version of *Crossroads*. The editing is a paean to quick cutting, the effects are good, the makeup's fabulous, but hey, it's a Faustian bargain on all levels. You can tart it up, but it's still a goddamn commercial.

James Brown plays himself, starting as a young man in the fifties who leaves a business assignation with the Force of Darkness and finds he can immediately do the most incredible splits. But fifty years later, he wants to renegotiate his contract. Gary Oldman, looking like a profoundly weird version of the wheelchair-bound professor in *Rocky Horror,* is Old Scratch. The incomparable Danny Trejo's his assistant. Clive Owen plays Brown's driver. And Marilyn Manson is the pious Christian down the hall.

The abbreviated plot revolves around a street race between the devil and Brown, starting at sunrise on Sunset Boulevard and lasting until the sun sets. What transpires is noisy and hyperkinetic. Chuck Jones would have been proud. It's all well and good, and certainly diverting enough. But do we want to see this level of talent devoted to cranking out a higher level of diverting commercials before movies?

The space of this essay and much, much more could be devoted to the philosophical and esthetic debate. Suffice it to note that Audi is very cagily getting in on the real ground floor of this kind of insidious promotion. You also saw an animated Audi placed in the first scenes of the stellar *Spirited Away.* Those Bavarian elves do know what they're doing.

Now think about it. Q-shipping commercials into minifeatures? It's a clever novelty, but a really, *really* bad idea. As an extension of the proliferating industry of product placement, we'll probably be seeing it more and more.

HERE'S *MY* FAVORITE FANTASY—WHAT'S YOURS?

Arguably the best pure fantasy film of 2002 is also the best animated feature of the year—and maybe, as well, the best *movie* of the year. That's why the Oscar went to *Miyazaki's Spirited Away.* Fresh, colorful, spirited (no pun intended), exciting and affecting, *Spirited Away* is what we dilettantes always hope Japanese anime will be. The English script is by Cindy Davis Hewitt and Donald H. Hewitt. And if you're *really* obsessive about this sort of detail, the original title is *Sen to Chihiro No Kamikakushi*.

From the first sequence, in which two parents and their little girl take a wrong turn on the way to their new home and wind up trapped in a ghostly realm of spirit spas and weird creatures, watching the film is just like opening a picture book of freshly minted myth. The resourceful girl initially is motivated to survive and rescue her parents after they're turned to swine; later on she recognizes the necessity of strong action, bred by realizing the pigs are destined for bacon.

Hayao Miyazaki is one of today's master animators. *Spirited Away* clears the bar for what defines a classic. It reaches both kids and adults in the audience and is a visually stunning experience.

THE BIG BOYS OF SUMMER—AND FALL

Being the center chunk of a huge cinematic triptych is rarely an enviable position. After all, your fellows have the advantage of being either a) the beginning, or b) the end. Being stuck in the middle again poses some interesting challenges. But then, the first *Star Wars* trilogy solved that problem just fine with the arguably best of the series being the center episode, *The Empire Strikes Back,* cowritten by the incomparable Leigh Brackett in collaboration with Lawrence Kasdan.

Being an interstitial third turns out to be no problem at all for Peter Jackson's *The Lord of the Rings: The Two Towers.* Here's another three hours of gorgeous New Zealand countryside, various worthy parties traversing from point A to point *B,* enormous hordes of orcs and other evil creatures, plenty of clanking, smashing battle scenes, the promise of growing love, the pain of love dying, betrayal, honor, and the stage beginning to set itself for Middle-Earth's final great war against the forces of Sauron and all that's unholy.

Oh, then there's the intriguing animation approach to Gollum, with credit to human actor Andy Sirkis who modeled all the mutant hobbit's movements. The ents, the leafy green giant tree-herders, also deserve praise.

All in all, *The Two Towers* amply deserves the appellation "epic." On the other hand, there *is* that problematic moment toward the end when the hobbits babble on, wondering interminably whether they, themselves, will ever be the subject of epic storytelling. There's never an armed and murderous uruk-hai around when you need one.

While *Harry Potter and the Chamber of Secrets* is not the middle third of a three-part megawork, it *is* the successor to a highly successful box-office champ in 2001. And what do you know, it also is a greater achiever on most scores than its predecessor. For one thing, *Chamber of Secrets* struck me as far darker than *The Sorcerer's Stone,* and that always tends to give fantasy greater weight. There's plenty of spider material here, along with big snakes and other general creepiness.

Director Chris Columbus says he's bowing out after this round, and it's nip and tuck whether the child actors who do far better in their present roles than they did the year before will manage to finish the next installment before reaching puberty. The genuine sadness of *Chamber* is that re-viewings are done with the knowledge that Richard Harris, the Hogwarts School Headmaster, Albus Dumbledore, died after filming was completed.

The near-future apocalyptic dragon tale, *Reign of Fire,* is a near miss. It's a dark, dark fantasy. What if, it wonders, Britain's dragons are slumbering underground, waiting to be awakened in the present by a curious kid? Flash forward a couple of decades to when the developed world has been laid waste by the proliferating dragons. A group of *Mad Max*–level survivors led by the kid grown up (Christian Bale) encounters a bunch of American military men led with missionary zeal by Matthew McConaughey, on an obsessive mission to destroy the fire-breathers once and for all. Nothing makes a whole lot of sense, but the bleak, ruined landscape is impressive, and so is McConaughey. With a beard, less hair, and a mad gleam in his eye, he looks nothing like he has in any of his other roles. So dragon-slaying's a stretch, it seems.

The superhero hit of the year was, of course, *Spider-Man*. Perfect innocent Tobey McGuire worked out just fine as Peter Parker, the poor geek who gains superhuman arachnid powers after being bitten by a radioactive spider. Clearly director Sam Raimi loves this project and understands his materials. We who were once teenaged boys are naturally more sympathetic to fictional metaphors about guys who move from geek to cool. As an entertainment, Spidey ticks along just fine, and Willem Dafoe does well as the industrialist who unluckily morphs into the villainous Green Goblin. It's all in fun. And yes, the notorious and rain-soaked inverted kiss scene with Kirsten Dunst as Mary Jane is startlingly effective.

While Robert Rodriguez's follow-up to *Spy Kids, Spy Kids II: The Island of Lost Dreams,* didn't do nearly as well at the box office as student wizards and orc hunters, it should be overlooked by no one. Perhaps the best way to think of Rodriguez's sequel is to envision a kid-based James Bond spoof for all ages with a terrific cast and a largely amusing script. Its great strengths are imaginative reality for kids and nostalgia for adults.

This film is a shopping list of all manner of toys that kids (and probably grownups as well) would dearly love to have and use. It's true wish-fulfillment fantasy. And it also boasts Danny Trejo, one of the great villainous-looking actors, as a benign uncle.

So how do you feel about mice? If you're an adult, don't feel *too* self-conscious about checking out *Stuart Little II,* the sequel to the 1999 children's hit based on E. B. White's classic kids' book. This movie continues the tale of the mouse who's adopted by a nice New York family (Geena Davis, Hugh Laurie, and Jonathan Lipnicki) as their very own child. Michael J. Fox voices Stuart well, as does Melanie Griffith as his bird buddy. From a technical standpoint, this is an accomplished blending of digital animation with live action.

THE MOST EFFECTIVE REALITY IS USUALLY IN FANTASY

Director Julie Taymore had already proved herself as a talented creator of fantastical visions with such films as *Titus* and the imaginatively staged Broadway adaptation of *The Lion King.* She worked in partnership with Salma Hayek to bring to life the latter's dream project, the biofilm of troubled Mexican artist Frida Kahlo; the resulting movie is a visual triumph. Purists have called many of *Frida*'s details into factual question, but for those who can suspend their disbelief and accept the work as a creative blend of fact and fiction, it's a striking piece of filmmaking. At any rate, the broad strokes of Kahlo's difficult life offer a reasonably accurate account of her sadly truncated career. The supporting cast is interesting, what with Alfred Molina as husband Diego Rivera, Ashley Judd playing sensual photographer Tina Modotti, and Geoffrey Rush taking a peculiar turn with the expatriate Russian revolutionary Leon Trotsky. The wonderful fantasy elements manifest visually with a variety of puppetry and animation-charged scenes. *Frida*'s dream-and-nightmare scenes are sensational.

Give a shot, as well, to Pedro Almodovar's *Talk To Her.* No matter what he directs, while you may not always like it, the film is *always* interesting. Passion, heat, and humor are always present. Fantasy and reality interweave well in this tale of two men and their comatose, hospital-bound women. Traditionalists will either be enormously amused or else enraged by the spin Almodovar gives to a new take on *The Incredible Shrinking Man.*

On the Science Fiction Side

EVERY NEW YEAR DESERVES A DICK

Actually 2002 had two. I suspect the irony's lost on Hollywood that after a long, arduous, and productive writing life, author Philip K. Dick died at the very moment his name was about to become known widely throughout general popular culture via the expanding list of movies based on his fiction.

The year began with *Impostor,* based on Dick's grim short story from the fifties. It is a low-budget effort with Gary Sinise starring as a government scientist on the run. His bosses think he's been replaced with a humanoid replica sent by aliens in a cold war with Earth, a struggle in which the ETs are suspected of sending in suicide bombers to blow the planet to smithereens. Naturally, Sinise's character is not delighted with the idea of being vivisected to find a bomb he knows could not conceivably exist in his body because, after all, he'd *know* if he were a human simulacrum, right? Well, *wouldn't* he? The film does a creditable job with Dick's obsession with the nature of identity and paranoia. Ultimately it's surprisingly faithful to the original story.

The year's big-budget Phil Dick adaptation was Steven Spielberg's lovingly directed *Minority Report.* Tom Cruise plays future cop John Anderton, who gets into bad trouble after suspecting that someone's screwing around with the psychic trio of precognitives (one of whom's Samantha Morton) who make up the pre-crime unit, the seers who send the police out to arrest potential criminals before they actually do their dirty work. Spielberg fleshes out Dick's repressive society with a variety of clever touches.

After seeing the movie, I dug out Dick's original story for comparison. Interestingly, Dick's characters tended to be a stock cast dealing with Big Problems. Again, it's the macroview of a world in dire straits. Spielberg's movie elects to treat the same issues by irising down to a microview, trying to set things into more human perspective by putting a personal and human face on them. Spielberg being Spielberg, he can't resist the temptation to bring things down to the level of sentimentality, but fortunately that's kept to a minimum. All in all, *Minority Report* functions well as solid sf.

TOMORROWS PAST AND FUTURE

Call me crazy. Call me lonely. But I must admit to an admiration for Steven Soderbergh's remake of *Solaris.* But then, I also liked Andrei Tarkovsky's 1972 version of Stanislaw Lem's novel. I stayed awake through the entirety of Tarkovsky's deliberately paced work, eventually falling prey to the film's hypnotic rhythms. Ditto with Soderbergh. I suspect that a number of the disaffected viewers this time around were innocent victims of the studio's electing to push the movie as some sort of George Clooney romantic drama with spaceships.

Of course it's not. Clooney plays the astronaut sent out to an alien planet to find out why orbital explorers are dying or disappearing or simply going crazy and seeing unaccountable phenomena. In Clooney's case, he no sooner arrives on the space station when an apparent exact duplicate of his dead wife (Natascha McElhone) appears at his bunk.

Solaris possesses heart, indisputably, but the emphasis here is on ideas. This is science fiction in the classic mold. What is the enigmatic planet outside the space station's viewports? *Who* is the planet? A patient viewer, at least one not hell-bent on immediate titillation, will be rewarded.

So why am I now going to place *The Bourne Identity* into the science fiction list? Well, director Doug Liman's kinetic and engaging version of Robert Ludlum's 1980 thriller apparently *is* not only a crackerjack chase film, it's also a quietly cyberpunk/*Six Million Dollar Man* stealth sf melodrama. But that's more frosting than substance.

The centerpiece is amnesiac government agent Matt Damon trying to recover fragments of his past with the aid of *Run Lola Run*'s Franka Potente, even as government bad guy Chris Cooper provides sinister opposition. But for all the standard well-oiled plot machinery rocketing Damon to and from Paris, there are constant low-level hints that he's not altogether standard-issue humanity. But it's never spelled out. It's more like a game that we either get and enjoy, or totally miss and never notice. In any case, the possibility of our hero's being something more than human lends extra mystery, even charm, to the whole proceeding.

Every year needs a *1984*/*Brave New World* knockoff. It's generally good for you. In 2002, the candidate is *Equilibrium*, a post–World War III dystopia in which a repressive government foists off an emotion-suppressant to the population. One can surmise that songs such as "Feelings" are publicly banned. Christian Bale and Emily Watson are the star-crossed lovers who find reason to rebel and stop taking the drugs. There's plenty of action to carry the message that—surprise!—emotional expression is anathema to a repressive political system.

And now for something completely different. Alien invasion is rarely as genuinely amusing as it's depicted in Disney's animated feature *Lilo and Stitch*. For almost surreal reasons, the story's set in Hawaii as an alien bioweapons experiment gone wonky is dumped here on Earth thanks to a maladroit mad scientist. The experiment in question is a gremlin variant named Stitch, a little critter that can display big, big teeth when he wishes to. For reasons too strange to summarize easily, Stitch gets adopted as a pet by young Lilo, a girl who lives with her older sister after their parents die. Even as Lilo and her sis try to deal with social services in the form of the very strange man in black voiced by Ving Rhames, alien peacekeepers arrive to retrieve Stitch. In the meantime, Stitch has cottoned to Terran pop culture and has become enamored of performing Elvis impressions, along with learning to surf. It's all weird and warm and charming.

For more weird, warm, and charming, you might try renting Jackie Chan's vehicle, *The Tuxedo*. Another offshoot of the James Bond spoof subgenre, Chan plays a poor innocent who makes the mistake of donning a government-issue high-tech tux customarily employed to impart cyborgian superhuman powers to the wearer. Metaphorically speaking, the tux is a little tight around the shoulders and the seams keep wanting to split. In other words, the film betrays some strain.

OOPS, DID I FORGET . . .

Star Trek: Nemesis? It's for dedicated Trek fans.

Men in Black II? It's for *really* dedicated fans of the amusing original. Cleverness has transmuted to slog.

Treasure Planet? It's for truly dedicated animation aficionados.

Star Wars: Episode II—Attack of the Clones? Okay, so it really *is* better than *Episode I*. It's brighter, flashier, faster, and has fewer kid actors and less Jar Jar Binks face time. I'm not just being charitable. The chase scenes through the stratospheric skyscrapers of the Trantoresque planetary city of Coruscant are pretty darned cool.

The Small Screen

LOOMING LARGE

ABC scored with the miniseries *Rose Red*, directed by Craig Baxley from the original script by Stephen King. While pretty much standard haunted-house fare about a gaggle of self-interested academics and others spending increasingly dire time in an old spirit-infested mansion in the urban Northwest, King injected sufficient energy to keep us all awake. As can be done effectively with a six-hour dramatic frame, care was given to the buildup and so the audience was expecting a pretty terrific payoff at the end. While not disappointing, there was still a sense that more could have been accomplished. Much had been made of the sentient mansion's ability to shape-change its architecture. That largely got lost in the shuffle.

The Sci Fi Channel gave us all a lovely Halloween gift with *Clive Barker's Saint Sinner*, an original movie directed by Joshua Butler. The script, from a story by Barker, was written by Hans Rodionoff and popular sf novelist Doris Egan. In 1815, two demons escape from the Catholic Church's not-completely-secure repository of unholy and accursed relics at an isolated monastery. The unlucky custodial monk is obliged to follow them through time to contemporary Seattle—plenty of temptation, shaken faith, corruption, and bloody consequences. It's good to see Clive Barker keep his oar in the roiled Hollywood waters, whatever his level of participation.

Steven Spielberg's Taken, the massive ten-part miniseries about the modern history of alien abduction, extraterrestrial visitation, and government conspiracy, juiced up the Sci Fi Channel's autumn ratings considerably. Many of the best notices went to young Dakota Fanning as The Girl. While pretty much a conglomeration of *The X-Files* and *Dark Skies* and just about any other project about almond-eyed grays you can think of, *Taken* was still slickly executed and entertaining. It is true popcorn fare for the paranoid.

FRESH FACES

While a cable translation of *Firestarter* stumbled ineptly and perished with little regret on anyone's part, the USA Network's introduction of *The Dead Zone*, a weekly series based on Stephen King's novel, turned out well and became something of a surprise hit. By both producing and starring as Johnny Smith, the young man who comes out of a six-year coma with paranormal powers, Anthony Michael Hall finally banished the adult audience's lingering *Breakfast Club* memories. The scripts are often both diverting and intelligent, and the casting is superb.

One might wonder why I'm lauding Alan Ball's HBO series, *Six Feet Under*, in this venue. Well, to my mind, the series is what horror is all about. On the surface, this is a high-class soap opera with a talented ensemble cast, tracing the lives of an L.A. family-owned independent funeral home. True, ghosts appear from time to time and interact with the living characters, but that's not the prime horror element. Horror and dark fantasy are particularly interweaved with the natural human dread of and interest in our common final destination—death itself. And that's what *Six Feet Under* concerns itself with. Death and life are inextricably intertwined. It's your basic truth. And *Six Feet Under* is among the few popular entertainments to recognize that.

Here's a significator. At the most recent World Horror Convention in Kansas City, at an awards ceremony where the horror field's IHG Awards final-nominations ballot was announced, the mention that *Six Feet Under* was a finalist in the TV category drew widespread spontaneous applause from the audience.

The surviving component of Fox's onetime Friday night sf lineup (the other being the lamented *Firefly*) is *John Doe*. Or it *maybe* is sf. The premise of the pilot was that a guy woke up naked on a beach on an island just off Seattle with zero memory of who he was or from where he came. The man has an enigmatic tattoo, no color vision, and possesses an absolutely encyclopedic range of human knowledge. It's a one-trick pony the writers have attempted to remedy with mixed results, as John Doe makes his way in our modern world doing things such as consulting for the police, even as he tries to ferret out his identity. Government experiment gone wonky? Alien? Who knows? As John Doe, Dominic Purcell does a more than decent job. It probably helps that he resembles, particularly around the eyes, a young Mel Gibson.

WIN SOME, LOSE SOME: THE LIFE OF JOSS

Long out of Sunnydale High School as a student now, Buffy (Sara Michelle Gellar) manages to luck into a job at her old alma mater as a guidance counselor. Sunnydale and its environs are still as infested by blood-suckers and menaced by apocalyptic evil as ever. While *Buffy the Vampire Slayer* starts to wind down toward its final season, the series continues to maintain its remarkable level of writing and invention. Creator, producer, and occasional writer Joss Whedon knows his pop culture to a *T*, and obviously continues to love his characters. Will there be a final attempted spin-off with the characters other than Gellar, who wants to consolidate her feature-film career? At this point no one knows.

The earlier spin-off, *Angel* (co-created by Whedon and David Greenwalt), in which good-guy vamp Angelus (David Boreanaz) headed south to L.A. with onetime high school bitch Cordelia (Charisma Carpenter) and started a haphazard detective agency, has survived. Over three seasons, the series has quietly built its own life and persona. Neither burning up the ratings nor tanking, it's got an uncertain future. But one can hope for survival.

The real programming tragedy of 2002 for Whedon's productions was the debut, relatively short life, and unwarranted early demise of Fox's *Firefly*. Whedon's shot at establishing a Friday night science fiction series had a lot going for it. The terrific ensemble cast (especially Adam Baldwin as a mercenary named Jayne) of the eponymous tramp space transport, the well-worked-out and definitely lived-in future of heroic losers in an interstellar war, the trademarked Whedon high level of writing, and a combination of manic excitement with tongue still occasionally in cheek all seemed to appeal to a growing audience. The network, unfortunately, nixed starting the series with the two-hour pilot, deeming the introduction and background of the characters too talky and not sufficiently action-oriented. So the pilot ended up being the series' swansong after about a dozen episodes. *Firefly*'s life was short but sweet, along with a variety of other tangy flavors.

MILESTONES

The amusing, softly erotic, and often surreal "evil sister to *Star Trek*," *Lexx*, came to the end of its Sci Fi Channel run. There was a suitably strange final episode in which the characters pretty much got what they wanted, including the dead guy.

Also on the Sci Fi Channel, Rockne O'Bannon's series, *Farscape*, came to a more unexpected termination, a network decision that enraged the substantial (but apparently not substantial enough) audience of enthusiasts. The final season had been marked, idiosyncratically enough, by a seeming peculiar script fascination with bodily fluids. The climactic episode contained a colorful cliffhanger that confused many inveterate watchers. And *no one* in the audience seemed mollified that they'd soon be able to enjoy the Friday night pleasures of *Tremors: the Series* and the cheapjack reality TV, *Scare Tactics*, appropriately hosted by Shannon Doherty.

Roswell jumped its broadcast network traces and moved to the SciFi Channel, there to lurch, then quickly go into hiatus for retooling.

WB's *Birds of Prey* started out terrifically well as a female superheroes melodrama. Then it almost instantly lost its way, watering down the scripts, turning sharp edges into irritating fluff. And so it perished.

Fox's anthology *Night Visions*, a deadly rip of *The Twilight Zone*, managed to produce one halfway decent episode, an adaptation of Bob Leman's "The Window." The most terrifying misstep of the series was the total miscasting of the extremely talented writer and singer Henry Rollins as a tattooed and muscle-shirted Rod Serling surrogate. Didn't work. Not at all.

TNT's Yancy Butler vehicle, *Witchblade*, started winding down and then came to a screeching halt after the star got into trouble out in the mundane world.

ABC's *Dinotopia*, based on the James Gurney books and artwork, discovered that even large reptiles couldn't compete with *Survivor* and *Friends*. Those small, irritating, scurrying mammals always win.

AMONG THE SURVIVORS

UPN's latest revival of *The Twilight Zone* lurched along with the genial Forrest Whitaker hosting. Unfortunately, the scripts tended to slide to the lame side, or, at best, the level of the innocuous.

The current *Star Trek* franchise, *Enterprise*, has continued fairly smoothly on

UPN. Nothing too spectacular, though an episode in which Vulcan science officer T'Pol's great-grandmother, surviving a time-warp disaster with companions, visits Earth in the 1950s, is extremely amusing.

The WB's *Smallville*, that retro history of Superman's young adulthood out in the sticks, continues to hum along. Truth to tell, the series is frequently stolen by the equally young Lex Luthor (Michael Rosenbaum).

Stargate SG-1 with Richard Dean Anderson has done well in its new home on SciFi, and is continuing handily in its fifth season.

Finally, *Andromeda* is continuing in syndication, and the production people claim it'll continue to take on more and more of a *Star Trek* explore-the-galaxy appearance.

Your Sound System: Music for the Darkest Soul

Every year I hope for a new tune of the macabre by the Dixie Chicks, something along the lines of "Goodbye Earl." Alas, nothing from the Chicks this time. Probably they were too busy with their own real-life horror, discovering the massive First Amendment intolerance catalyzed by lead singer Natalie Maines's dissing of President Bush at a London concert.

But I did find a few things of interest, particularly Lou Reed's concept album, *The Raven* (Sire/Reprise 48372–2). How's this sound for a backing lineup? Laurie Anderson, Antony, The Blind Boys of Alabama, Ornette Coleman, Elizabeth Ashley, Steve Buscemi, Willem Dafoe, Amanda Plummer, Katie Valk, Fisher Stevens, Kate and Anna McGarrigle—and David Bowie, among many others.

The CD's got 21 tracks, a wide variety of approaches, and stunning execution. Lou Reed says in his liner notes that he recently rediscovered Edgar Allan Poe, and the ideas for the album kindled in his head. Reed feels that Poe is the spiritual godfather of the likes of Hubert Selby and William Burroughs.

Eclectic and dark, *The Raven* is a convincing reminder that the unique Mr. Reed has lost nothing with age and moderation. He reminds us all that Edgar Allan Poe *rocks*. Was that ever in doubt?

I didn't think so!

For a very different take on music and fantasy, you might check out the newest CD by Tri-Destiny, a mother and two daughters from Utah. Their exquisite harmonies on *Dragon Wine* (tridestiny@networld.com) soar from traditional folk arrangements of new music.

Tri-Destiny's usually at its best with sometimes sly, usually not-altogether-subtle infusions of humor in their work. "Chicks in Church," "Sensitive Guy," and "Chicks in Chainmail" are good examples of that approach. On their new album, I was amazed to hear a *Star Trek* tribute song that, in the abstract, would ordinarily make me want to throw the jewel case across the room. But no—"Mr. Spock" actually turns out to be witty and amusing.

The Toy Box: Bring in the B-Team

Last year I reported on Todd MacFarlane's partnership with Clive Barker that resulted in *Tortured Souls*, a series of six articulated action figures, each grotesque toy accompanied by one section of an original novella.

2002 saw MacFarlane's follow-up, *Tortured Souls II: The Fallen*, with another six action figures. Unfortunately, there's no new story to go with the toys. The figures are distorted and mutilated enough, true, but somehow the joy seems to have leached out of the project. The graphic violence just isn't as fresh as last year.

Go ahead and check out *The Fallen*, anyway. Camille Noir and Szaltax are beauteous young ladies with significant body modification. They'll look great in a tableaux, seducing your Ken doll.

Trailers

There'll be some new stuff. There always is. But 2003 will be seeing a surfeit of franchise work, ranging from the new Harry Potter chapter to the final episode of *Lord of the Rings*.

Many viewers will be painfully slipping on their vinyl jumpsuits, getting ready for sneaks of the two-part *Matrix* finale. Presumably you're all ready after seeing the slickly animated featurette, *The Last Voyage of the Osiris*, run as a bonus with first-run screenings of *The Two Towers*.

It'll be a wildly mixed year. Isn't it always?

Fantasy and Horror in Comics: 2002

Charles Vess

Over the last two decades the comic-book medium has been struggling against every boundary that has been arbitrarily placed on it: subject matter, printing technology, format, and so on. Each of these seemingly inconsequential matters has had far-reaching effects on the acceptance of this medium as a legitimate art form. Nonetheless, the medium is now alive with very personal storytelling that uses a full spectrum of themes, ranging from complex adult issues to simple tales of delight that any child may enjoy.

Much as in mainstream book-and-magazine publishing, recent advances in digital printing technologies have lowered the costs associated with color printing as well as making it much easier to control the oftentimes complex nature of color reproduction. This lowering of costs has lead to an explosion of aesthetically beautiful books produced by smaller, less commercially minded publishers, which has in turn helped elevate the prosaic design of most "mainstream" comic books. These new formats have allowed some comic books to evolve from a serially based, thirty-two-page, stapled pamphlet into a new book format with more pages, board covers, and a sturdy spine, called the graphic novel. With this single development the medium has achieved one of its most important advances.

Consider the difficulty that a typical mainstream reader has in reading those thirty-two-page pamphlets that are issued on a monthly basis. First, they would have to seek out a comic-book shop. Once there, if they were to find a book they enjoy, the comic that they now hold in their hands is only a chapter of a larger, continuing story. This reader will then have to remember to return to this same shop in subsequent months and hope that there will be copies available of each successive issue (or to try to find previous issues to catch up on the story). If that reader misses even one issue, the tale will be incomplete. Imagine if the latest Stephen King or Robert Jordan novel were to be issued in monthly installments, available only in scattered, out-of-the-way shops. Missing an installment would not be an option if you, the reader, wished to truly enjoy the tale. How much easier it is for a reader to pick up a graphic novel with its complete, all-in-one-package story.

Fortunately, the graphic-novel format has become well established in recent years, both in comic shops and in mainstream bookstores. Whether these books offer an entirely new tale or a collection of previously serialized stories, it is an ideal format for the casual reader and, I believe, in the future will be the dominant form of publication in the comic-book field.

There has been good news all year long for lovers of the graphic-novel medium, as its presence in the national bookstore outlets has been legitimized by critical media coverage. *Publishers Weekly, Entertainment Weekly,* as well as other mainstream magazines and newspapers are prime examples, and we were finally "rewarded" with a year-end, two-page review in, of all places, *The New York Times.* Partly as a consequence of this attention, sales reports have been steadily climbing, and this has helped stabilize a still weak comic-book industry.

But before we sit back complacently and contemplate a job well done, we should consider that most of this attention has been focused on graphic novels whose themes echo those of the prose-only that are most often covered by these same critical voices: autobiography, political commentary, and contemporary adult concerns. It is still very difficult to escape the ghetto of fantasy and horror (as well as that of science fiction). As a form of mere "popular entertainment," the genres that are our concern still fall well within the land of shadow where few critics shine their spotlights, and thus, as a whole, these forms continue to be disregarded by the literary establishment.

Just as in our own genre, where deserving authors such as Nina Kiriki Hoffman, Delia Sherman, Midori Snyder, and Charles de Lint receive very little mainstream critical attention due to their use of literary conventions particular to our field, so, too, this exists in the world of the graphic novel. A powerful depiction of the effects of child molestation that intertwines the fairy tale elements of the work of Beatrix Potter with the experiences of a contemporary teenage runaway—as Bryan Talbot employed in his *The Tale of One Bad Rat*—is still often considered "just a comic book" and thus relegated to those same shadowlands.

Even within the ranks of those comic-industry magazines that do keep a judgmental eye on this burgeoning medium, their critical prejudice favors the same explorations of angst-ridden contemporary lives that are constantly being extolled in the mainstream press rather than discussing so-called popular entertainment filled with genre elements.

It would do us all well to remember that popular entertainment can be directly responsible for developing a healthy, life-long habit of reading. I, for one, would not be the voracious reader that I am without my discovery early on of the books of Edgar Rice Burroughs. Also crucial were the comic-book exploits of Uncle Scrooge and Donald Duck, so beautifully brought to life by writer and artist Carl Barks. The reading that was being assigned at the same age in school (*Silas Marner, Great Expectations,* etc.) offered me literary worlds that seemed dark and dreary and aroused in me no great desire to continue reading them. If left to only those same school reading assignments I fear I never would have discovered the sheer joy of submerging myself in a world captured in the pages of a book.

Of course, any medium that extols the merits of popular entertainment risks the possibility of not being taken seriously as an art form. The graphic novel, with its roots directly in the popular comic book that has long been looked on in the United States as a mongrel combination of words and pictures fit only for children and the reading impaired, continues to be such a medium. The simple, almost primitive stories so prevalent in the early days of this medium are still considered to be the norm by those who haven't fully explored what the graphic novel has to offer.

To any serious reader of our genre this sounds all too familiar. Fantasy and horror have their own roots buried deep within the detritus of pulp fiction and still struggle to be seen as legitimate literary forms. Most high-brow critics continue to see our efforts as child's play.

There is one other matter of some concern to practitioners as well as readers of this medium of expression. For the graphic novel, much like film, there is no commonly accepted critical language to effectively deal with the seamless integration of word and picture that is the hallmark of a successful graphic narrative. Critics continue to approach the graphic novel as if it were simply a work of literature. Their concerns often revolve solely around characterization and the rise and fall of the plot, which are admittedly important elements to any successful novel. But they seem to have forgotten or even to have ignored that what they are critiquing is an entirely different literary beast. These critics mention only in afterthought the visual aspects of the graphic novel: the very element that is able to add so much depth and meaning to the sparse use of prose common to this medium. A new critical language is called for, and when this new terminology is developed and used, the graphic novel may be one more step toward being accepted as the vital, legitimate medium that it is.

Those of us who have an abiding love of the graphic novel can only hope for a slow critical attrition and public acceptance to occur. At the moment we remain a deliciously subversive medium capable of presenting a complex weave of narratives and thematic motifs that remain in that interstitial borderland between underground cult status and mainstream acceptance; between accepted genre conventions and wild experimentation of words, images, and their associated meanings. I hope that this sublime "subversiveness" will not be lost as we slowly emerge into the spotlight of mainstream attention.

As works do appear from out of the massed ranks of our genre and suddenly leap into the realm of "best seller," they come to the attention of the keepers of the mainstream critical flame. The critics then reason (much as they did with Art Spiegelman's Pulitzer Prize–winning *Maus*): "If I am paying attention to this 'work of literature' then it must not be a comic book." We must remember to keep our laughter to ourselves.

A possibly brighter future was spurred along by two major events last year. The first was the annual American Library Association convention last summer that placed particular attention onto the graphic-novel form in preparation for National Teen Read Week, scheduled to take place in the fall. A full day of the convention was devoted to prominent creative individuals within the graphic-novel field who gave presentations on their work and how this genre could be used to get young adults interested in reading. This was a major statement about the legitimacy of this field from an institution that has traditionally considered the reading of comic books as subliterate.

The second event came from a meeting of a little-heard-of but very influential book-industry advisory board, The Metadata Committee's Codes and Values Subcommittee of the Book Industry Study Group, Inc., that decided to designate graphic novels as its own subdivided genre within the bookstore market. This committee is responsible for all the categories now in place in the modern bookstore system, so these new designations are very important and will almost certainly be used as a universal guideline in the future. No longer will the overworked sales clerk, not knowing where else to put them, place *Watchman*, *Jimmy Corrigan*, *Dilbert*, *Strangers in Paradise*, *Tin Tin*, *Asterix*, and all the Dungeons & Dragons gaming material onto one sagging shelf. In the years to come, when this program begins to take effect, there will be an entire section dedicated to the graphic novel with its appropriate subgenres. This will make it much easier for the bookstores to place stock and for you to find the books that you seek.

The years ahead look bright, but there is much work to be done, especially in elevating our own genre to much-deserved critical recognition. And so, let us turn to the art at hand and recognize the best that those works within the fantasy and horror genres had to offer us last year. If you are headed off to a desert island and need to take some reading with you, I would suggest these ten graphic novels as essential to the art form from 2002.

No lover of the graphic-novel medium should miss the brilliant new adaptation of Robert Louis Stevenson's classic Victorian horror novel, *Dr. Jekyll & Mr. Hyde*, produced by Lorenzo Mattotti and Jerry Kramasky (NBM Publishing). Mattotti, a master of the medium, has brought his long years of experience to bear on this beautiful rendition of a time-honored story. Stevenson's dark streets and gloomy curtained drawing rooms are rendered in a phantasmagoria of expressionistic color, bringing to vivid new life this often retold tale of a scientific experiment gone dangerously wrong. His depiction of the bestial Mr. Hyde is quite original as well as truly horrifying. I can't recommend this one highly enough.

Carla Speed McNeil has been collecting her long-running series Finder (Lightspeed Press) into very attractive trade collections for some time now. With this new collection, *Talisman*, McNeil has reached a new level of storytelling maturity in both the complexity of her characters and the richness of her narrative. Her story, set in a detailed alternative universe, presents a poignant tale of one character's quest for a dimly remembered book that she had read in childhood. Her search for this tantalizingly memory serves as a magic portal into a world of creativity and learning that she had never realized was hers for the asking.

On the humorous side is *Max Hamm, Fairy Tale Detective* by Frank Cammusco (Nite Owl Comix). His protagonists are many of the fairy tale characters that we know and love, but given an odd slant. Our detective-for-hire is one of the Three Pigs, Little Bo Peep has been forced into a life of prostitution, Mother Goose runs a film studio, and so forth. Cammusco uses these new perceptions of old characters for all they are worth and has launched his film noir detective parody into a delightfully offbeat and wacky orbit. *Fairy Tale Detective* is a short, brisk, and hilarious story.

Bill Willingham's ongoing series *Fables* (DC/Vertigo) covers some of the same territory as Cammusco's book, but its tone is much more serious. Willingham's tale begins with an interesting concept: The Adversary has conquered all the

Lands of Fable, displacing its inhabitants onto the mean streets of modern-day Manhattan. Who or what The Adversary is has not been revealed so far, but Willingham has begun to slowly explore the complicated life of these exiles. The enforcer of their laws is Snow White, their chief of police Bigsby Wolf, their mayor, Old King Cole, and so on—fascinating material to work with. Writer Willingham and artists Lan Medina, Steve Leialoha, and Craig Hamilton are having a good time tearing down the walls of typical fairy tale conventions and erecting a fascinating new world.

The Yellow Jar, written and drawn by newcomer Patrick Atangan (NBM), is his first published work. It is a delicate and delightful adaptation of two Japanese folktales, the title story and "The Fisherman and the Sea Princess." This assured debut features subtle writing, clean, well-developed drawing, and an aesthetically pleasingly use of color and text. I look forward to future delights from this artist.

Jeff Smith's exciting, ongoing series *Bone* (Cartoon Books) is nearing its dramatic conclusion. The newest collection, *Treasure Hunters,* features extensively reworked dialogue and art. The care with which Smith develops his characters and his imaginary world is evident in each stroke of his brush, each nuance of his characters. Alternately hilarious and dramatic, *Bone* is a tale that fully repays the time readers invest in following this high-fantasy, epic story line.

The second volume of adventures following those stalwart heroes of Victorian England, *The League of Extraordinary Gentlemen,* is brought to us by writer Alan Moore and artist Kevin O'Neill (DC/Wildstorm). This time the earth is being invaded by all manner of literary Martians. The invading force teams Edgar Rice Burrough's green, four-armed denizens of the Red Planet alongside H. G. Wells's mechanized aliens. Our heroes Mina Harker, Allan Quatermain, Captain Nemo, The Invisible Man, and Dr. Jekyll/Mr. Hyde are once again employed by the British government in a dramatic effort to destroy this new enemy to all of humankind. The series continues to be great fun as it romps through great swaths of Victorian literature in a tale that is densely populated with characters taken from late-eighteenth-century novels.

Humanoids Publishing has translated into English the first lavishly produced hardcover volume in a complex and hugely entertaining fantasy/sf series, *Morgana.* In Book One, *Heaven's Gate,* creators Alberti and French open a door into their intricately developed world full of magic, immense warring armies, and swashbuckling woman warriors out for vengeance.

Another much-welcomed translation of a well-established European series is *The Towers of Bois-Maury* and the stand-alone *Rodrigo* by Hermann Huppen (Dark Horse), a master of the art of comic storytelling. His historical adventures depicting lonely knights chasing vanished dreams of glory through a richly detailed medieval world—ever so slightly touched by magic—are as engrossing as they are beautifully drawn.

Much to my delight, NBM Publishing has brought Dave McKean's magnum opus *Cages* back into print. *Cages* is a rumination on the meaning of art, music, writing, and life, all played out amongst a set of acquaintances living in contemporary London. Powerfully drawn and deeply felt, this hardcover collection of some five hundred pages was years in the making, and it is a grand testament to one artist's personal vision of the sometimes inscrutable workings of the mad universe that we all live in.

Of course, if there is more shelf space in your desert island home than you thought at first, you would do well to bring along at least some of these books as well.

Linda Medley has at last completed the Solicitine story arc in her ongoing self-published series, *Castle Waiting* (Olio Press). This time her deliciously witty storyline involves a holy order of nuns—bearded nuns. How they meet and claim a home of their own is the stuff of high drama and infectious delight. Medley's wonderfully clear drawing style and enjoyable dialogue make the reading of this tale all the more pleasurable.

Shuck, an ongoing series by creators Rick Smith and Tania Menesse (Shuck Comics), is a whimsical tale featuring a goat-headed demon who wears a human face mask, a young girl named Thursday Friday, and her talking cat. This story for adults unfolds using dialect-filled speech patterns that can only be described as poetic, and a simple yet effective approach to its art. I don't know where this very idiosyncratic series is headed, but I am charmed by its imaginative cast of characters and am willing to follow it to any destination it cares to take me.

Beginning with the poetic simplicity of a folktale, the wordless graphic novel *Bloodsong* by Eric Drooker (Harcourt) takes the reader through a complex tale told with bold iconic drawings. The limited color palette used by Drooker suddenly explodes into glorious Technicolor when the events of the story call for it. Political unrest destroys an idyllic jungle paradise, propelling a young woman across a raging sea and into a huge contemporary city. There she finds the same ruthless political reality that she had thought she left behind her, a reality that seeks the destruction of individual freedom and creative thought. Part folktale, part political statement, this drawn story will reward anyone who takes the time to carefully consider the images that Drooker offers.

Obergeist by Dan Jolley and Tony Harris (Image) is a horrific tale of personal redemption. An obsessed German doctor experiments on victims from a Nazi concentration camp, and when he dies he is given a second chance at life. He is reborn into a new era where once again fascist right-wing extremists threaten to take over the world, a world he seeks to change, this time for the better. The beautiful, moody artwork by Tony Harris is by turns wildly exaggerated and subtly realistic, enhancing this powerful, harrowing tale.

Leave It to Chance by James Robinson and Paul Smith (Image) has returned after too long an absence. Fourteen-year-old Chance Falconer is ready to take up her family's traditional business when her father informs her that magic is too dangerous for girls. With the help of her friends, including a pet dragon, she sets out to prove him wrong. Clearly rendered art with clever scripts provides the readers with a palatable sense of fun. *Shaman's Rain*, Book One, collects the first adventure.

Creator P. Craig Russell has had a busy year with the publication of his adaptation of Neil Gaiman's *Murder Mysteries* as well as the collected edition of his monumental adaptation of Wagner's *The Ring of the Nibelung* (both from Dark Horse). These publications feature high production values and serve as a showcase for Russell's elegant line and virtuoso depictions of mythic worlds and a hell right here on earth.

George Pratt's evocative painting style enhances the impressionistic storytelling that he uses to portray *Wolverine, Netsuke* (Marvel Comics). Pratt spins his yarn with compelling force and drama set in a mythic rather than a realistic Japan filled with ancient snow demons and ghostly samurai out of Asian folktales. With its abundant use of Eastern philosophy and its Zenlike conclusion, this tale features the seminal Marvel Comics superhero Wolverine, and it is a testament to Pratt's skills as a storyteller.

Mike Mignola has given us another adventure featuring his delightful continuing character, Hellboy, in *The Third Wish* (Dark Horse). This time Mignola has forsaken his obsession with crumbling middle-European castles, Nazis, and horrors from the Lovecraftian dark, and replaced them with creatures from African myth and folktale. It is a splendid and refreshing change of pace. We can all hope that Mignola will continue this exploration of various world mythologies with all the vast wealth of visual opportunity that they have to offer.

In *Promethea*, Volume 3 by writer Alan Moore and artists J. H. Williams and Mick Gray (DC/Wildstorm), the creators continue their exploration of the world of "true" magic and its meaning in our lives. The art by Williams and Grey offers the patient reader splendidly detailed drawings of worlds within worlds where myth and magic weave a sinuous dance of creation, all the while allowing for a complex sea of words from Moore.

A new *Sock Monkey* tale is always something to look forward to. This time writer/artist Tony Millionaire gives us *The Glass Doorknob* (Dark Horse) a delicately colored, whimsical story that has the outward appearance of a turn-of-the-last-century picturebook. The sly, sometimes macabre humor that is Millionaire's trademark signals to the perceptive reader that this is not just a children's tale. It is, however, most delightful.

With simple cartoonlike drawing, award-winning writer/artist Kyle Baker allows us to enter the world of ancient Israel and experience the iconic Biblical story of *King David* (DC/Vertigo). From his youthful adventure with Goliath through ascending the throne of his kingdom, Baker gives us an exciting and very humorous interpretation of this classic tale.

Colonia, Islands and Anomalies by Jeff Nicholson (AiT/PlanetLar) is a collection of this ongoing humorous adventure series. Bold seafaring pirates, gold-fevered ghosts, and a talking duck confront three visitors from contemporary America after the visitors have been mysteriously transported to a world that could only exist in a wacky alternate history just one step away from the textbooks that you read in the school.

Writer Mike Carey and artist John Bolton bring us *The Furies* (DC/Vertigo), an original graphic novel that spins off some of the characters and situations from the wildly popular *Sandman* series and stands on its own very sturdy story legs. Letia Hall becomes involved with a traveling theatre troupe in contemporary Greece that becomes redolent of true Greek tragedy. Creatures from ancient mythology come to all-too-threatening life, forcing her into a reunion with her long-lost son, the new Dream King. The art by Bolton is lush and photo-realistic, breathing new life into old visual tropes.

Gary Gianni, one of the most extraordinary artists in the comics field, has self-published an elegant edition of *Corpus Monstrum* (Hieronomous Press). Printed at a giant size to better showcase his intricately rendered tale of pulp horror, this book is black-and-white art at its finest. Bravo!

Hilarious and delightfully drawn, *Amy Unbounded* by Rachael Hartman has been a treasure for several years now, but very difficult to find in its individual issues. With this new trade collection, *Belondweg Blossoming* (Pug House Press), I hope that the talented Ms. Hartman has remedied that lack of visibility, because hers is a story that will delight any who pick it up. In a misty medieval landscape of stone castles and vast churches, ten-year-old Amy learns to read and soon sets out to make her life as exciting as those of the glittering knights and fair ladies in the stories.

In *Boneyard* by Richard Moore (NBM), it's love at first sight when boy meets girl. The problem is that the girl in question is a vampire, and the local cemetery where she and her fiendish friends live is slated to be bulldozed to make room for a new housing development. This amusing tale is filled with humorous dialogue and charming reinventions of all the monsters that lurk in your bedroom closet at night.

The brilliant C. Scott Morse brings us *Ancient Joe* (Dark Horse), a collection of tales featuring an odd protagonist in search of identity and love. In the course of his journey he falls afoul of demons and gods, stepping from the shadows of world mythology into the bright Caribbean sunlight. Morse's black-and-white line work is simple but effective, redolent with mystery and magic, setting the perfect stage for his sparse but enjoyable writing.

Writer Brian Azzarello and artist Marcelo Frusin bring us a horrific look at the dark underbelly of contemporary life in small-town America with *Hellblazer: Good Intentions* (DC/Vertigo). This complete story arc from the ongoing series offers a bleak but effective tale. John Constantine is a no-nonsense and extremely cynical protagonist. His efforts to reconnect with a woman from his past expose a very black heart of darkness amongst the inhabitants of a remote Midwestern town.

Unmanned (DC/Vertigo) is a splendid collection of the first six issues of *Y: The Last Man,* a series written by Brian K. Vaughan and illustrated by Pia Guerra. An unknown plague has wiped out the males of all the animal species on the earth except for one puzzled young man and his pet monkey. This exciting road story follows our bemused hero as he searches for answers about the plague and tries to outwit various factions of the remaining female population who wish to manipulate his choices.

Gary Spencer Millidge has been self-publishing his extended saga, *Strangehaven* (Abiogenesis Press), to much critical acclaim. His adventure features a young man who accidentally stumbles into a remote English village and is unable to leave. He slowly builds a life for himself there, all the while uncovering a deepening mystery that all the villagers are privy to. This new collection, *Arcadia,* offers a satisfying piece of Millidge's compelling puzzle of a story, while his strongly naturalistic art features instantly recognizable portraits of the many idiosyncratic characters that populate his tale.

The third volume of *Raptors* by Dufaux and Marini (NBM) was released this year. A brother and sister, renegades from a worldwide conspiracy of vampires that only allows human life to continue so that it can provide "food" for their unwholesome appetites, continue the duo's war on their former allies. With slick, stylish art all the back alleys of decadent European cities and steamy erotic couplings are rendered in rich, moody watercolors.

The Wind in the Willows (NBM), the fourth volume of French artist Michael

Plessix's adaptation of this classic fantasy by Kenneth Grahame, was published this year. The art, filled with delicate depictions of an English countryside awash in summer sunlight, is populated by a charmingly drawn cast of characters who cavort through this gentle, humorous adventure, possessing all the subtlety of the original much-loved prose.

British writer Alan Moore is one of the major architects of the mid-1980s shift within the comics genre to stories with more subtle and adult concerns. His work on the *Swamp Thing* (DC/Vertigo) series is the cornerstone of that reconstruction. There are several trade collections of this material available.

Sitting there on your private island, comfortably lazy in your hammock after a full day of reading, you might try these other books if you're not quite ready to go to sleep.

Delicate Creatures by J. Michael Straczynski and Michael Zuili (Image) is an original fairy tale with suitably delicate drawings and text.

Deicide 1: Rage Against the Gods by Carlos Portela & Das Pastoras (Humanoids Publishing) is a European adventure tale with amazing painted art.

Son of the Gun, Vol. 4: Sinner and Saint by Alejandro Jodorowsky and Georges Bess (Humanoids Publishing) is a violent but extremely well-drawn post-apocalyptic saga set in the Mexican desert.

The Invisible Frontier by artist Francois Schuiten and writer Benoit Peeters (NBM) is another in their series of dreamlike existential adventures involving faceless bureaucracy and astonishing, grandiose architectural realities.

Hammer of the Gods, Mortal Enemy, a trade collection by Michael Oeming and Mark Wheatley (Image), features their Nordic hero and his justifiable rage against the gods and demons that are responsible for his hell on earth.

Weasel by the extraordinary artist and writer Dave Cooper (Fantagraphics) offers more utterly horrifying tales drawn with a charming touch that immediately draws readers into the story and just as immediately makes their toes curl with dread.

If you have trouble locating any of these books through your local bookstore, you might try calling the official Comic Shop Locator Service at 1-888-266-4226. Those fine folks will assist you in finding a full-service comic shop near you. Then, too, many of these trade collections are carried by the friendly and well-stocked Bud Plant Comic Art (www.budplant.com).

Good luck, happy reading, and enjoy your stay on the island.

Manga and Anime 2002: The Light and Dark Fantastic

Joan D. Vinge

Ahayo, minisan! (Hi, everyone). Welcome to the second annual review, all-new, and totally fresh, of the Year's Best manga (Japanese comics and graphic novels) and anime (the Japanese term for animated films and TV series).

What's News

2002 will hopefully be remembered as the year anime and manga became fixtures of American entertainment. In April 2003 Hayao Miyazaki's *Spirited Away* won the newly created Oscar for Best Animated Film—topping off a year when the anime "Adult Swim" was the only programming that showed growth on the suddenly abashed Cartoon Network, characters from the anime series *Yu-Gi-Oh!* appeared on the cover of *TV Guide*, and not only articles about M&A but also the actual books and DVDs began to appear everywhere (at least, everywhere I go). As a result, I'm awash in new M&A.

Trends: (1) Empire building—In 2002, the head of ADV, the largest anime distributor in the United States, was named one of the 100 Most Influential People in Genre Entertainment. ADV has been expanding its horizons rapidly ever since, acquiring more of the best new anime, offering special-edition packages (boxed sets with T-shirts, and so on) for their big releases; and even entering the print market with an American edition of *Newtype*, the gorgeous, best-selling Japanese M&A news magazine. ADV has also started a new all-anime cable channel. (Call your cable company and demand it, now.)

Pioneer, another primary distributor of anime, is making a new line of soundtrack CDs available here, plus importing more anime-related merchandise, and licensing rights to do guidebooks for its series to the gaming publisher Guardians of Order.

(2) Retro nostalgia—*Thundercats, Transformers, He-Man, GI Joe, Micronauts,*

Voltron, Battle of the Planets, Robotech—they're all being resurrected in comic-book form and as cartoon shows, most of them redesigned for a more sophisticated audience (i.e., nostalgic parents watching with their kids). Not all were originally Japanese creations, but many had their animation done there or in Korea. Osama Tezuka's beloved *Astro Boy* is also back, at least in manga paperback form.

And if you want to see what our TV network censors used to do to all those imported shows you loved so well, check out the release of *Ronin Warriors* on DVD (from Bandai). Each DVD also includes the same (subtitled) Japanese episodes, complete and uncut, and originally titled *Samurai Troopers.*

(3) **Magazines**—Not only a shipload of new books and DVDs, but an armload of new M&A-related magazines also appeared in 2002. Joining Viz's venerable *Animerica* (anime news) and *Animerica Extra* (an anthology) is the American edition of Japan's *Shonen Jump*, probably the most popular manga anthology among Tokyo *otaku* ("M&A fans"), and containing some of the most popular ongoing manga both here and in Japan, including *Yu-Gi-Oh!* and *Dragon Ball Z.*

Wizard's quarterly *Amime Invasion* newszine continues, along with Dark Horse's *Super Manga Blast* and Antarctic's *MangaZine* (both anthologies); and, as mentioned above, ADV introduced the American version of *Newtype.*

Gutsoon! Entertainment also brought out *Raijin Magazine*, a weekly rather than monthly manga anthology—that's the way it's done in Japan. *Raijin G&A* is a much smaller, but glossier, newsletter/magazine reporting on games, toys, and other gotta-get-it peripherals (but unless you can find them on-line, they're only for sale in Japan). *Raijin* contains both well-established and lesser-known (here) manga series, and it seems to be aimed at an older, predominantly male audience (i.e., more gratuitous T&A and violence). It is rumored to be having financial problems; the publisher is planning to put out individual manga series in trade paperback (TPB) form—also done in Japan, as well as here—which may be a good move for them.

Newtype Shonen Jump, and *Raijin* are all published "authentically . . . oops, make that pseudo-authentically." The magazines are laid out in what we would consider "backwards" order, because Japanese is read from right to left and English from left to right. It isn't that hard to get used to reading backwards, as long as you're reading something that contains mostly pictures. However, when you start mixing columns of prose in with the pictures—which *Newtype* does a lot, and the others a little—then lay out the columns on *each page* (pay close attention here) so they have to be read from *left* to *right*, "because it's in English, not Japanese"—you have a recipe for chronic brainstrain. There has got to be a better way—lay out the columns right to left, and put little arrows on the bottoms! It's not brain surgery, folks . . . it's good *editing.*

(4)**DVD Only**—VHS tapes are as dead as dinosaurs—it's official. Content yourself with the knowledge that *you* are getting "two for the price of one"—both the dubbed and the subtitled versions of your chosen anime on one disc.

What's What

Before I launch into what's best in M&A from 2002, I'd like to talk about why I think you'll care, or ought to, about—um—"those foreign comic books and cartoons." Also, I'm going to throw a little more of the otaku dictionary at you, because every little bit helps.

Diffusion: The motto of manga and anime distributor Central Park Media is "World peace through shared popular culture." Short and sweet, it's as true as it ever was and more timely than ever, with the lamentable political developments of this past year. Our country needs to fling open our windows on the world and breathe in some fresh air. The timing could hardly be better for an influx of anime and manga.

And yet, time and again what I read in the media amounts to "East is East and West is West, and never the twain shall meet." (That line is from a Kipling poem—and usually quoted out of context.) Whether it's *The New York Times*, Amazon.com reviews, or the Ku Klux Klan newsletter, failure to do one's homework equals forever failing to get the point.

The point is that we are all human.

The variety and complexity of human culture should be honored, and I do not dismiss it lightly; furthermore, everyone on the planet has their own unique personality. Yet every day, complete strangers discover they have enough in common to become friends, or even to fall in love. How is it possible? Because the differences between different cultures, and individuals, *are* only skin-deep compared to the things we share "to the bone." Our most profoundly human behaviors are universal, across the board.

It's a new millennium—at least on our calendars. The age of the World Wide Web and the multinational corporation is here. It's time to expand, not contract, our horizons so that we truly become citizens of the world.

Resolved: Anime and manga provide an excellent source of gentle but effective "brain bran," and, consumed in large quantities, may even support renewal of atrophied brain tissue. An item of special interest to f/sf&h fans interested in supplementing a healthful diet.

As for everyone else . . . Mary Poppins had a point when she said, "a spoonful of sugar helps the medicine go down." This article must confine itself to the "best of f/sf&h." But the complete range of subject matter in M&A is as varied as life itself. There is almost certainly something for everyone. You only need to sit back and pick up a book or boot up your TV, kick back, and enjoy.

Confusion: Getting into anime and manga is a modest proposal for the typical reader of an anthology such as this one. However, there are terms and symbolism in M&A that might as well be from outer space as far as many people are concerned—including some readers of f/sf&h.

So, here's a shortlist of the more common M&A terms and imagery, just to give you a jumpstart in a time-pressured world:

• *shonen*—M&A appealing to teenage boys and young men; the more muscular art style associated with it.

• *shojo*—M&A appealing mainly to teenage girls and young women; the graceful, large-eyed art style associated with it.

Culture Note: Sexual Stereotyping—Contemporary M&A is much less stereotypic than the above, overly brief definitions would make one assume. *Shonen* and *shojo* art styles and storylines have begun to merge visibly, because there is considerable crossover in readership among young Japanese M&A fans, 30 percent of whom are female.

• *chibi*—goofy caricatures, figuratively the "inner child" of some character, who literally escape whenever they act childish; comic relief that makes a potentially dark story accessible to a broader audience.

• *bishonen, bishojo*—boy or girl characters "drawn extra sexy"—beautiful sensitive guys with long flowing hair, zaftig schoolgirls in very short skirts—referred to as "fan service," and essentially the carrot on the stick that lures teens (and adults) to read or watch something they might *learn* from.

• *biseinen*—mature (young) men "drawn extra sexy."

• *yaoi*—fiction where the main characters are young gay men engaged in a (usually meaningful) sexual relationship.

• *hentai*—hardcore porn, plain and simple—available only to adults. It is often misogynistic and sometimes gives mainstream M&A a bad name over here, because it may be the only kind of M&A some American adults have ever seen.

Culture Note: Sexuality in M&A—The popularity and easy access to hentai, for adults, is apparently associated with *fewer*, rather than more, sex crimes being committed in Japan, relative to the United States.

Japanese culture is generally more comfortable with human sexuality (and bodily functions) than ours; expect more casual nudity and mature sexual relationships, just as you should expect more "realistic" or ambiguous endings to shows.

Prime-time TV is monitored for "unsuitable material" in Japan, too; although "kids' shows" such as *Dragon Ball Z* and *Salior Moon*, when imported to the United States, are further edited for content, sometimes drastically. (A lot more naked female breasts get by in stories for teen audiences; but penises seem to be just as taboo over there as they are here; apparently it's male insecurity about "measuring up" that's the real neurosis worldwide, and not "fragile feminine sensibilities.")

• *salaryman*—businessman, office workers.

• *nosebleed* (usually male; occasionally, discreetly, female)—sexual arousal.

• *sneezing*—someone is talking about you behind your back.

• *big sweat drop*—nervousness.

• *shoes*—traditionally removed when entering a house.

• *mecha*—giant humanoid robots, functioning on their own AI, or piloted by humans; also human-sized, high-tech, superpowered suits; plus other often-transformable equipment—used for work, or more often, for fighting.

Culture Note: The Play's the Thing—Traditional forms of theater—and puppetry—influence many plotlines and often the imagery in M&A:

• *Noh*—the oldest existing style, is rooted in Shinto religious tradition and tells tales of the gods in a highly ritualized manner. (Noh appears in the anime series *Gasaraki* as a character's way of channeling spiritual power.)

• *kabuki*—began in feudal Japan, when traveling actors performed plays based on "everyday life" ("everyday life" included demons, ghosts, and witches, just as it did for Shakespeare). Striking freeze-frame moments—"Who killed whom?" or "Stand-off at sword-/gunpoint"—as well as recurring demonic villain types who show up in series from *Rurouni Kenshin* to *Trigun* originated on the kabuki stage.

• *takarazuka*—all-female acting troupes; they evolved because Shogunate Japan (like Elizabethan England) forbade coed acting. Like kabuki, it is still popular; female actors specializing in male roles often have big female fan followings. (The alien-battling "mecha" corps in the steampunk series *Sakura Wars* are a performing takarazuka troupe as cover.)

The fact that kabuki and takarazuka continue to be popular may be one reason why androgynous heroes (of both sexes) are so common, and popular, in M&A.

• *bunraku*—puppet theater. Like clowns, puppets are vaguely unnerving: bizarre looking or soulless, they still act as if they're alive and perfectly human. Evil puppet masters, spiderlike hair-demons, and ninjas armed with invisible wire to ensnare or slash up their victims show up in many M&A.

Culture Note: Religious and Mythic Symbolism—Taoism, Buddhism, and Confucianism are just some of the myriad religious traditions that have become part of Japan's rich cultural heritage. Indigenous Shintoism is still the religion of the majority of Japanese, but Hinduism, Christianity, and other Western religions—and a world-ful of myth—are also familiar enough to be used in stories told by creators of M&A.

What imagery belongs to which religion hardly matters in regard to its use in popular fiction; but recognizing certain symbols common to Asian tradition can help you get far more symbolic depth and meaning from a story:

• *Taoism*—not just the philosophical creation of Lao-Tsu, but a far more ancient tradition, "the first cousin of Shintoism," with its real roots buried deep in human prehistory. The basic Taoist ideal is a balanced life lived in harmony with the world around you; it also acknowledges that balance is hard to maintain. (*The Irresponsible Captain Tylor* comes close to being the perfect Taoist hero; he believes in "go with the flow," which is why he is so infuriating to most people around him. Even he has things to learn, however; when evil, in the form of war or corrupt superiors, is about to cause unnecessary death and destruction, sometimes the only way to maintain balance is to push back.)

• *yin/yang*—two "paisley," or teardrop, shapes enclosed in a circle. Either black and white, or blue-green and red, they are equal opposites; when conjoined, they represent perfect balance, either cosmic or spiritual. But "balance" is meant as a verb, not a noun, and so the two sides are in constant flux. Each also contains a dot of the other's color—meaning that you can't achieve balance with one alone; each contains the seed of the other.

A symbolic yin/yang formation when you least expect it—in the coiled bodies of battling dragons or a cup of coffee with cream—tells you what's at stake: The characters are struggling to maintain balance, within themselves, or by opposing an "unbalanced" enemy out to destroy the world (usually both at once).

• *Feng Shui*—means "wind and water," and is not just a trendy home-decorating fad; it is the belief that the earth contains "ley lines" of energy flow, and certain precautions must be taken to guard against negative spirit energy bringing catastrophe to you, your home, or your town.

• *Feng Shui "compass"*—a complex, compasslike instrument that contains wheels within wheels of astrological information; it can be manipulated in three dimensions to provide cosmic guidance and power. It may appear as an arcane magic device, or disguised as high-tech: a spatial navigation unit, or other futuristic object.

• *Shintoism*—the indigenous religion of Japan, one of the oldest continually practiced religions in the world.

• *kami*—"sacred spirit" or "god energy"; may occupy a tree, a stone, a body of water; from the Ainu word *kamui*.

• *oni*—demon; demons are not *always* evil, as they are in Christianity, but are powerful spirit beings.

• *torii*—a "pi"-shaped sacred arch that marks an object or place sacred to Shinto.

• *miko*—a Shinto priestess; once the religious leader/shaman of a community (see *Princess Mononoke* or *Inu-Yasha*, below). Her classic outfit was a white top and red *hakama* (long, full pants); she gained her spiritual power upon reaching womanhood: Teenage "magical girls" (and boys, these days) gain powers when they hit puberty. Watch for any girl or woman wearing red and white; she most likely has special powers whether she knows it yet or not.

• *shrine Shintoism*—influenced by Buddhism. Shinto changed into a system with actual shrines to worship in, located at sacred sites, and added male priests, reducing the mikos to "assistants."

• *numerology*—the mystic power of numbers and the geometric forms related to them; a part of every religion since ancient times, they supposedly possess special qualities, which recur worldwide. Three (as in third eye possessed by spirit beings, sometimes hinted at by a small design or mark above the eyes), four, five, six, and eight (and pentagrams, hexagrams, and octograms) are "powerful" numbers/symbols appearing the most frequently in M&A.

• *dragons*—originally associated with the sea and storms; fire dragons came later. Asian dragons are more serpent- or eel-like than reptilian; they are extremely powerful, whether good or evil. Pearls were believed to be "dragon eggs" and to possess spiritual power. Dragons spit shining balls of energy that may transform into fire or lightning—storm energy. Dragons are a part of almost all battles based on yin- vs. yang-energy; even the bolts of high-tech energy weapons may take on the form of dragons.

• *colors*—like numbers, certain colors—red, white, black, and blue-green—have particular symbolic power; each has a dual nature, befitting Taoist principles.

• *white*—yang, energy, the sun, fire, maleness, cherry blossoms (young love); also energy out of control, or bones, ghosts, death, frozen wintertime. White-haired characters are almost always supernatural; they may be anti-heroes, but they are rarely good guys.

• *black*—entropy, passivity, night fears, femaleness; but also female procreative energy, rich earth, and controlled energy. Heroes (male and female) tend to have black hair.

• *red*—similar to white, it is associated with passion, fire, killing summer heat, red flowers, and blood—as a sign of life or of war and killing. Red-haired heroes (male and female) tend to be impulsive and immature; they need to find inner balance, to "grow up," or to overcome a youthful trauma that keeps them from maturing emotionally. Red dragons tend to be fire dragons, either good or bad.

• *blue-green*—similar to black, it is associated with calm, reason, water, and sky, also with storm dragons (a combination of water and wind), monsoons, and floods—potentially destructive forces. Blue-green hair is unusual, though blue or green highlights on black hair are common. (Unusual hair color often indicates good magic powers, but sometimes it's just for variety).

• *different-colored eyes*—people whose eyes are a different color (brown and blue, blue and red, etc.) usually have magical or demonic powers; it's odd—a bad sign. Blue eyes often mean clarity—innocence not a foreigner.

• *prayer seals*—slips of paper with spells written on them, used by priests of various traditions, which can lock away an evil demon or freeze it in its tracks. *Origami* (folded paper) rings may be seen circling sacred trees or stones; prayers are tacked to the posts of Buddhist grave markers. Probably they are the inspiration for all the "magical card decks" and "Tarot card" story elements in M&A—modern artifacts that stand in for ancient ones.

• *Christianity*—often appears oddly distorted to Western eyes, viewed through the filter of M&A. Most Japanese still find Western religions to be rather "exotic" and vague—like the "mysterious powers learned in the Orient" by characters in pulp fiction written here in decades past. (Not that we are really much better informed about Eastern religions now—just a little more "PC." It's a start. . . .)

• *crosses*—originally a (universal) sun symbol. The Christian symbolism associated with the cross is direct and poignant, and recognized so widely now that it often appears alongside Asian icons like the yin/yang symbol in M&A. (In *Trigun*, for example.)

• *Christian churches*—like any sacred ground (including Japanese shrines, in M&A), they provide classic, painful irony when used as a site for bloody battles between a hero and a villain. (Stained glass also makes a great backdrop.)

Fusion: The universal shines through all varieties of human culture, for anyone willing to "see what you can see with eyes unclouded by hate," as the village *miko* tells Prince Ashitaka in Miyazaki's *Princess Mononoke*. And so, assuming your cosmic third eye is open and seeing clearly, lets take a look at M&A's Best of the Year.

This year I'm going to list things primarily by distributors and publishers, so that you get to know the main suppliers. And, since "what's best" in manga and anime varies like everyone's favorite food, I'll make it an eclectic banquet; you're bound to enjoy something here. Dig in.

Recommended Anime

MOVIES

Actual theatrical movies are, unsurprisingly, less common than TV series or manga. The first theatrical film of 2002 (which actually made it into the theaters here), and my favorite, is *Metropolis*. It's based on a work by the "father of modern manga," the late artist/writer Osamu Tezuka. He wrote his original story after seeing a news photo of the robot *femme fatale* in Fritz Lang's silent film of the same name.

The creators of the film—scriptwriter Katsuhiro Otomo (of *Akira* fame) and well-known anime director Rintaro—are both fans of Tezuka's oeuvre, with its themes of tolerance and understanding. Though Tezuka always felt that *Metropolis*, one of his earliest manga, fell short of its goal, in retrospect Otomo and Rintaro could see its great potential. Using Tezuka's original as a starting point, they made *Metropolis* into a symphony of a movie, based on his favorite leitmotifs of "what really defines a human being?" and "how can we understand each other better?"

The plot resonates with the actual sociopolitical milieu of the twenties and thirties (which had inspired Lang's movie), set in a fabulously detailed, retro-futuristic Art Deco world. The creators cast some of their heroes and villains from the "repertory company" of characters who play recurring roles in Tezuka's other works. The character designs are true to Tezuka's art (influenced by early Twentieth Century cartoon style); but their deceptively simple, open faces reveal emotions as complex as the backgrounds against which their story unfolds, while also fitting perfectly into the period *mise-en-scene*. And underlying it all—as if this weren't enough—there is still another, sublimely subtle, layer of symbolism taken from Babylonian mythology.

The soundtrack, appropriately, is pure, bluesy Jazz Age. But as the metaphoric passion play reaches its climax, suddenly Ray Charles's heartbreaking, "I Can't Stop Loving You" is all you hear, while disparate plot strands and desperate souls come together, and Irony drops its wrench into the works of Machine Age predestination. Otomo and Rintaro have said they don't think Tezuka would like their movie. I disagree.

Most of Tezuka's work, including the original manga of *Metropolis* and the anime features made from it, is now available over here for you to explore further.

And *The New York Times* wins this year's Ninja Screw Award, for its know-nothing review of *Metropolis*'s New York City premiere. Its reviewer scored a near-perfect goose egg: no understanding of animation (Japanese or American) or its evolution as an art form; no apparent knowledge of Twentieth Century socioeconomic history; and zip on ancient Near Eastern myth. Add a Dishonorable Mention for his casual dismissal of modern Japanese cinema, and for calling the movie's character designs "primitive"—a word better suited to the *Times*'s worldview. It's so hard to find good help these days. . . .

The other outstanding movie this year was, obviously, Miyazaki's *Spirited Away*, distributed here by Disney. It is also a wonderful, richly textured, beautifully animated film—a kind of Jungian waking-dream-world modern myth. Its plot follows the pattern of "classic childrens' tales" in the West, meaning it's about a child-figure who loses her parent-figures. (Why this is considered ideal story material for young children—who invariably find movies like *Bambi* and *The Wizard of Oz* nightmarish—is beyond me.) Miyazaki, the "father of Japanese animation" and an auteur who oversees every aspect of the making of his films, said that he intended this for a ten-and-older audience.

The protagonist, Chihiro, is a modern, bored, ten-year-old girl who follows her oblivious parents through a gateway into the Japanese spirit world. There she is forced to begin an archetypal journey of self-discovery, until at last she realizes that all the courage, resourcefulness, and wisdom she needs to get her parents and herself safely home again already exist inside her.

Spirited Away's magical beings are charming, whimsical, grotesque, and terrifying—or all of the above, though rarely at the same time. In Miyazaki's enchanted imagination, ancient Japanese spirits mingle freely with their world-myth counterparts and strange companions. (For example—Yubaba, the crow-spirited "old woman" who runs the bath house of the Spirit World, looks like a cross between *Alice in Wonderland*'s Queen of Hearts and Baba Yaga—a Russian "fairy tale" hag who flies in a mortar and pestle, and lives in a house on chicken legs. In Yubaba's case, a "witch's wart" symbolizes her demonic third eye.) The settings are equally awe-inspiring—beautifully, frighteningly surreal—and draw the viewer completely into both Chihiro's strange new world and her state of mind.

Both *Spirited Away* and *Metropolis* are top-notch films. But of the two, *Metropolis* is more complex, more thought-provoking, and in the end, more deeply moving. So why did *Spirited Away* win that Oscar? Timing, for one thing—arriving early, vs. late, in the year. Also, Miyazaki is better known among serious filmmakers, and one certainly can't ignore Disney's marketing clout. But the fact that *Spirited Away* was *supposed* to be mysterious and dreamlike may have been the biggest plus of all. No one voting for it need ever fear that someone, somewhere, was sniggering behind their back because they couldn't understand a "cartoon."

OTHER RECOMMENDED FILMS

Other new movies, and movies new to DVD, include the so-called "real ending" to the megahit series *Neon Genesis Evangelion* (the *2001: A Space Odyssey* of anime), which left most viewers as mystified as they had been before; and *Escaflowne: the Movie*, which retold the entire series in one film, with strikingly good animation but far too little time to explore the characters and the web of relationships among them. Also new in 2002 was *Armitage III: Dual-Matrix*, a movie sequel to the *Armitage III*: *Polymatrix* OAV (Original Animation Video—a miniseries). The first *Armitage* was recut as a movie; it told the story of a tough-as-nails female android cop (virtually indistinguishable from a human being), her once-biased partner (who fell in love with her), and the government of Mars, which wanted to destroy her.

The lovers survived, and in this sequel even have a child; but Naomi Armitage is drawn out of her new life to solve a mystery on Earth involving the fates of other androids like herself—and, suddenly, her own fate, and that of her family. Better than the original, it's a grim but ultimately very satisfying movie, with big-screen-worthy animation.

Movies that feature "further adventures" of characters from a series (ongoing or not) tend to be a mixed bag. The *Nadia: Secret of the Blue Water* movie was, disappointingly, more of the same—even though it took place some years later. The *Yu Yu Hakusho* "movie" simply seemed to be an extra-long episode of the ongoing series.

A few further-adventure movies do have good enough plots to justify their existence, whether they feature better animation or not: *Samurai X: The Movie*, based on the *Rurouni Kenshin* TV series (not to be confused with either the excellent "prequel" or the so-called "sequel"—see below) had the same animation as the TV show; but the storyline was complex and gripping, and the "guest" characters were engaging enough to give it real emotional impact.

The new (early 2003) *Cowboy Bebop* movie is also a "further adventure," but both the story and animation are terrific; if it comes to a theater near you, go see it! And bring your friends—anime made for the big screen needs, and deserves, all the friends it can get.

Gundam Nation: Several miniseries and movies from the "Mobile Suit Gundam" (earth vs. cislunar space colonies) future- and alternate history were released on DVD in 2002—including the original Gundam movies (and corresponding manga series). If you've only seen the *Gundam Wing* series and the *Endless Waltz* movie ("bishonen in space"—a lot of fun, but not much substance), you owe it to the other part of your brain to watch some of these:

- The original Gundam Mobile Suit storyline—both *First Gundam*, the TV series, and a three-part movie (war refugees flee the enemy, and a fifteen-year-old hero grows up the hard way, piloting a Gundam Mobile Suit—a mecha killing machine).
- *Gundam 08th Mobile Team* (oh, to be torn 'twixt love and duty).
- *Gundam 0080* (you'll never say "hamburger" again without cringing).
- *Gundam 0083* (worlds, loyalties, and hearts, in collision).
- *Char's Revenge*—movie sequel to the first Gundam story (the consequences of *bushido*—a warrior's code of honor—in space).

"All the best war stories are really antiwar stories," as one reviewer observed. If none of the above shows move you, or make you wonder, when you watch the evening news, about whether "the enemy" doesn't really mean "people just like us" . . . well, march yourself down to the store and get *Grave of the Fireflies.* Available on DVD for the first time, this movie, based on a semi-autobiographical novel, is the story of two small children trying to survive alone in the wasteland of post–World War II Japan. That should get your yin and yang back into balance in a hurry.

ANIME TV SERIES

The tendency of most series to come out *slowly* on DVD can save an otaku from bankruptcy, but it makes it a difficult call to decide when they should be reviewed. As a result, the list below may seem eccentric; but I calls 'em as I sees 'em.

Therefore, we start, unceremoniously, with the obituary for *Rurouni Kenshin* (put out by Anime Works). It grieves me to report that my favorite series of last year wasted away and died in its final season, with uninspired episodes and barely a whisper of character growth for Kenshin and "family." (Apparently the manga on which it was based had not finished coming out, and that fact seemed to paralyze the show's creators.)

It gets worse: Not only was the third season the end of the series, leaving the characters and audience without the resolution they deserved; but ADV, which owns the rights to the "prequel" and the "movie" (and renamed its *Rurouni Kenshin* holdings *Samurai X*), has released a "sequel"—a killing blade deceptively called *Samurai X: Reflection. Reflection* was not written by the manga's creator; the people who did the series are not to blame, either. It is not considered by them to belong to the series at all. I have no idea how it got made, but I can gue$$ why.

Reflection, after an hour wasted recapping the entire series, continues Kenshin's story past the manga's end—in a way that utterly negates the life-affirming themes that were the soul and strength of the series, and cuts the heart out of all Kenshin fought to attain. Worst of all, it cuts out *his* heart: this "bedeviled twin" is never allowed the hard-won peace and much-deserved happiness that Kenshin finally achieved at the end of the manga; instead, cursed with eternal guilt, he abandons his family constantly to do "good works"; his son hates him; he contracts an incurable, wasting disease, comes home just long enough to infect long-suffering Kaoru with it, and leaves again. Sanosuke (who hasn't changed a bit) fetches him home from a foreign shore, just so he and Kaoru can die in each others' arms. . . . Oh. Maybe I should have said "Spoiler Alert." . . . But the only thing "spoiled" here is this rotten, *doujinshi* ("fan fiction") postscript to a wonderful series.

Viz now has rights to the manga, which was originally published in *Shonen Jump*, and will begin publishing a translated version sometime soon in their American version of the magazine. If you want the true ending *now*, on-line stores sell the (untranslated) Japanese manga, and fan Web sites offer "fansubs" (free English translations) of them. Check out animenation.com for books and links.

Speaking of manga, the eerily cool noir series *Big O*, which was cancelled (with a cliffhanger ending) after one season, has spawned a manga (available in English from TokyoPop), and has gone back into production on season two of the anime—all because of its popularity as part of the Cartoon Network's "Adult Swim" manga bloc.

Rurouni Kenshin is now showing on the 'Toon Network. The DVD series was a consistent anime bestseller even before that . . . How about it, Anime Works—or Viz, owner of the manga rights: How about contracting with the original series producers for a fourth season faithful to the real ending of the manga? Do right by a wonderful story. The good karma you accrue is sure to translate into good profit.

The Rest of the Best

Kenshin fans can deal with withdrawal by checking out a number of anime and manga series, including *Tsukikage Ran*—the picaresque adventures of a butt-kicking, hard-drinking female samurai and her irksome sidekick Miao. Or try *Sakura Wars* (both the OAVs and the upcoming series), set in an alternate-history Japan with great period detail and steampunk mecha.

Or, last but not least, try my current favorite "rewatch" show, *Trigun* (now in a boxed set). It may start out like a pratfall comedy, but this samurais-in-space saga is just whistling in the dark: The deceptively innocent eyes and loopy grin of Vash, the hapless, donut-loving outlaw/hero, hide painful secrets and serious questions about what it means to be human; the underlying themes are very reminiscent of *Rurouni Kenshin*.

Prefer to wait for the manga (all twenty-eight volumes of it . . .)? Keep occupied with the continuing manga series *Blade of the Immortal* (Dark Horse), *Vagabond* (Viz), or the recently completed reprint run of *Lone Wolf and Cub* (Dark Horse). They're enough to satisfy anyone's need for beautiful art, savage swordfights, and gallows humor.

However, after reading any one of those, you'll understand why a little absurd "chibi relief" can be just that—a relief. Seek out or revisit the far less graphic, but still seriously human comedy of rabbit samurai *Usagi Yojimbo* (Viz), who wanders an alternate-world Japan getting into a lot of nongraphic sword fights, and making refreshingly nonhuman friends and enemies.

More Good Anime, by Distributor

ADV: *Sakura Wars* (see above); *Cosmo Warrior Zero* (set in the "Captain Harlock" future-history); *Bubblegum Crisis 2040* (bargain boxed set; mecha and strong female leads); *Neon Genesis Evangelion* (see above); *Gasaraki* (see above); *Generator Gawl* (bargain boxed set—excellent time travel/horror/sf); *Excel Saga* (maniacally funny fantasy/anime spoof . . . though I swear the "dog" is a cat!); *Zone of Enders* (a "dysfunctional family" saga featuring a mecha with a penis-shaped cockpit [giving the word a whole new meaning] that becomes a protective womb when "she" wakes with the AI personality of a young girl); *Dai-Guard* ("office workers saving the world"—fans of *Patlabor*, and anyone who's ever cursed a corporate board, will grin from ear to ear); *Wild Arms* (*Mad Max* meets *The Body Snatchers*, played for grins-with-grit-in-the-teeth).

Anime Works/Media Blasters (the first company to put voice actors' outtakes on DVDs): *Rurouni Kenshin* ('nuff said); *Babel II* (new version of a myth-based fantasy); *Knight Hunters* (bishonen guys do battle by night against vicious—but equally gorgeous—agents of a murderous secret cabal; DVDs include an interview with the voice actors/rock group who play the characters); *Kurogane Communication* (bargain boxed set; last human girl on Earth, and her robot "family"—but, is she really the last human?)

TokyoPop: *Samurai Girl: Real Bout High School* (modern fantasy; too short, but fun); *Reign* (Alexander the Great, done by the creator of *Aeon Flux*); *Great Teacher Onizuka* (every truly creative student's—and teacher's—fantasy of a good high school teacher . . . a bleached-blond biker bum with a heart of gold).

Pioneer: *Trigun* (see above); *Soul Taker* (horror/fantasy, with stunning stained-glass-effect animation); *Hellsing* (vampire horror/adventure/drama; wait for the final DVD's payoff, it's worth it); X, *the Series* (CLAMP's famous manga, now a TV series, giving it more time to capture all the anguish and complexity of the protagonists' mythic struggle; CGI has improved animation so rapidly that it looks as good as the movie); *Vandread* (the battle of the sexes—literally—in outer space; better thought out, fairer, more interesting and affecting, and more fun than you'd expect); *Patlabor* (only the movies; watch the series first).

Bandai: *Tsukikage Ran* (see above); *Betterman* (eerie horror/fantasy of underground war for the future, seen through the eyes of a boy who looks like Harry Potter—thank god for those innocent-looking glasses); *Big O* (see above); *Crest of the Stars* and *Banner of the Stars* (same series, different seasons; unusually intelligent and well-thought-out drama of humans under alien occupation, focused on a Human boy and an Abh girl who struggle to find common ground); *Cowboy Bebop* (the original series, still just as fresh, full of lost souls, dark humor, pain, irony, and the Real Folk Blues)—watch it while waiting for *Cowboy Bebop: Knockin' on Heaven's Door* (the new movie, see above).

Funimation: *Dragon Ball* and *Dragon Ball Z* (megapopular teen hits, edited for TV, full tilt versions available on DVD; originally based on the "Monkey King" Chinese epic, this story developed a life of its own); *Lupin III* (TV series and most of the movies, super-thief tales from the seventies—the still-cool "Pink Panther"–like antics of Lupin and his pals get a boost from updated scripts; the style of this series influenced the creators of *Cowboy Bebop*); *Yu Yu Hakusho* (exciting, funny, and sometimes touching series about two soft-hearted, hard-headed delinquents who demon-bust for the pacifier-sucking god of the underworld); *Blue Gender* (horror/adventure with mecha; imagine waking from cryogenic sleep to find you still have an incurable disease, and furthermore the world has been taken over by The Blob . . . it ends well, believe it or not); *Fruits Basket* (unlikely-named but delightful fantasy about the shapeshifting lords [and ladies] of the zodiac, and the orphaned schoolgirl busily straightening out their tangled family life; not to mention the Cat. Highly recommended: *Do not overlook this one!!*).

Viz (expect more DVDs from them in the future; they have a new distribution deal with Ventura): *Inu-Yasha* (the long-awaited series based on Rumiko Takahashi's horror/adventure/comedy manga; it's also a *long* series, so far being reissued at just three episodes per DVD—please, Viz, give us a break, and make it four, or five?); *Project Arms* (a nightmarish adventure based on a manga by the creator of *Spriggan*, and intriguingly linked to Lewis Carroll's poem "Jabberwocky").

Manga Entertainment: *Neon Genesis Evangelion* movies (see above); *Patlabor* (TV series—"cops with mecha," but far more about quirky human characters than robotic slugfests); *Ghost in the Shell* (rewatch this classic while you wait for the new sequel).

Right Stuf: *Irresponsible Captain Tylor* (series and OAVs; see above); *Boogiepop Phantom* (surreal "urban legend" horror; intertwined fates of several people when Phantom returns to old haunts).

US Manga (CPM's anime logo): *Descendants of Darkness* (bishonen/biseinan/yaoi) tale of two spirit agents working for an odd bureaucracy of the afterlife, gently leading the deceased to their new existence while hiding dark, unresolved secrets about their own former lives); *Record of Lodoss War*, and *Record of Lodoss War: Legend of the Heroic Knight* (classic high fantasy, based on a manga; more effective as full-color animation).

GOOD SERIES FROM SMALLER DISTRIBUTORS

FLCL (Synch-Point): a.k.a. *Fooly Cooly*, another series highly anticipated by fans, for good reason—it makes *Excel Saga* look calm and reasonable. By turns outrageous, delirious, teeth-grittingly real, hysterically funny, and just plain hysterical; done in an eye-boggling, experimental animation style that has an "anything goes—whoops, there it went" manner that must be glorious hell to translate. The plot involves a typical teenage sad-sack hero with a new girl at school who is either insane or an alien, a robot that suddenly grows out of his forehead, baseball, loneliness, and the family problems of all his friends . . . oh, yeah, *and* an alien invasion. This one deserves—indeed, demands—your complete attention. *It's a keeper*: you'll want the rest of your life to really take it all in!

Hyper Police (Image Entertainment): If you like *Usagi Yojimbo*, or simply like the idea of a world where humans, intelligent beasts, and demons coexist, try this charming, oddball series about a motley crew of crossbreed bounty hunters, including "underage" cat-girl Natsuke, who has some mean superpowers but not much of a clue; Batanan, the wolfman who loves her, and longs for her to figure out what "mating season" means; and Sakura, an eight-and-a-half-tailed fox-demon who wants Natsuke's powers . . . at least until she meets a handsome, time-displaced samurai. He thinks he died and went to hell; but after he falls for foxy Sakura, he decides this is "close enough" to feudal Japan. I have no idea where this ride is going, but the scenery is great.

Best Manga of the Year

So many new manga have come out this year—in comics, trade paperbacks, and anthology magazines—that it almost literally defies description. Tackling it by publisher and speaking in generalities is about all I have room for here; but being largely made up of art, manga are at least easier to browse than novels before you lay down your hard-earned cash. Aside from that, I can only hope that this rain of good fortune continues, both for the publishers and for the readers.

TokyoPop (formerly Mixx): TokyoPop has put out a jaw-dropping number of manga new and old, in every imaginable genre, during the past year. Virtually every series I've tried has been fun to read, well translated, handsome to look at . . . and addictive. (Though frankly some of the small print requires a magnifying glass.)

TokyoPop has also put out DVDs of anime series related to some of their books (*Real Bout High School*—the manga is much longer—and *GTO*, for example); but more and more they've been offering manga that are the source for other anime—a welcome event. "See the movie, read the book—how?" has been the question, until now. Now, you can read it in English, thanks to TokyoPop.

They have been bringing over some of the best Korean manga (*manhwa*) recently as well—titles like *Island* (a good horror series) and *Ragnarok* (Norse *and* Korean mythology).

TokyoPop has been at the forefront of the popular "authentic manga" trend as well: They publish many series without "flopping"—reversing—the art, which allows it to be read exactly as the creators drew it. For American readers, that means "back to front"; but since the reading matter is primarily pictures, it takes very little brain adjustment.

One of the series on their lists is the *Cowboy Bebop* manga (originally done after the anime, by popular demand in Japan), and they have published the translated six-part Official Guide to *Cowboy Bebop*. They also offer translated "Technical Manuals" for *Gundam* manga series that they publish, as well as *Sailor Moon* "Scout Guides," and even a few anime art books. (That's a trend I would love to see more of: there are countless import art books and anime series guides filled with wonderful pictures but otherwise inaccessible to a non-Japanese-speaking reader.) Next up seem to be translated novels. They have also put out CD soundtracks; whether they can continue this diversity and feverish pace, I don't know. But I wish them well!

Viz: Long the major publisher of manga in the U.S., Viz is clearly not about to be left sitting on its laurels. Viz is also "empire building," acquiring new manga titles and reprinting their already-impressive backlist—including a beautiful boxed set of Hayao Miyazaki's *Nausicaä of the Valley of the Wind.* He did the movie (hopefully we'll see it soon); he also wrote and drew this classic graphic novel. The story, with its ecological theme, is more timely now than ever.

Viz also publishes comic books and TPBs in the "authentic manga" format, and has also begun offering some translated novels. Besides their list of comics and TPBs, they have the *Gundam* series TokyoPop doesn't. Viz puts out the anime versions of several manga they publish (most notably *Inu-Yasha* and *Project Arms*). As mentioned above, expect to see a lot more DVDs from them soon.

They also have a fistful of magazines: *Animerica* is the longest running American news 'zine for anime, a good read they have made even better lately. Viz's adult anime anthology *Pulp* folded in summer 2002; but its best series found a new home in their other anthology, *Animerica Extra.* The rights to their newest publication, the American edition of *Shonen Jump,* include the rights to do TPBs of all the manga ever published in it . . . and it has run some truly excellent series.

They also scored the rights to do English versions of all the books related to Miyazaki's *Spirited Away,* perhaps because they had prior rights to other Miyazaki works, such as *Nausicaä* (it can't have been easy to retain the rights to anything when the Disney Co. was involved). Their *Spirited Away* books were wonderful; they have also done a few other translated art TPBs of their best-selling manga and anime series. I hope the success of *Spirited Away* leaves a lot of readers asking, "What's next?"

CPM (Central Park Media): Another publisher that's been putting out manga and also anime titles (U.S. Manga) for some years now; a modest-sized company compared with Viz or TokyoPop, but its motto, "World Peace through Shared Popular Culture," makes me want to write this column, and perhaps sums up the entire genre better than anything else I can imagine. CPM has several classic manga series in its list, including the *Record of Lodoss War* chronicles, Kia Asamiya's *Dark Angel* and *Nadesico* series, and the (broad) swords-and-sorcery comedy *Slayers,* along with numerous other backlist and ongoing manga series.

Dark Horse: This indie publisher has always included some excellent manga (both Japanese and Amerimanga) in its diverse line of titles. It's establishing a higher profile in both comic and TPB format; it also has a growing line of tie-in merchandise, and advertises its Web site/store more prominently.

Dark Horse has reprinted the entire *Lone Wolf and Cub* classic manga in pocket-sized TPBs, and is now running a *Lone Wolf 2100* series (with the full approval of the original creators). Another impressive new series is the sequel to Matasume Shirow's *Ghost in the Shell. Ghost in the Shell 2: Man Machine Interface* has been coming out, slowly but surely, in comic format, with full color art reproduced on quality paper; definitely worth collecting, while you wait for the new anime to get here.

ComicsOne: A new publisher that has found a niche reprinting Hong Kong manga (*manhua*) in full-color, large-format TPBs that showcase the stunning art while still managing to keep their prices reasonable. They are having a great deal of success as a result.

Chinese manhua storytelling is very different from the minimalist-dialog style of modern manga, or even the slightly more prolix modern American comics. It's reminiscent of "old-fashioned" comic books, if anything, where events are explained in the caption (and large stunning picture, in this case), and the dialog doesn't add much to it. The formal storytelling takes some getting used to, and some of the writers are more lively than others, but the art is just aces, which makes it well worth your while to make the stylistic transition.

Andy Seto is at present my favorite—a writer/illustrator whose characters are particularly appealing, and who tells a good story, too. He does *Saint Legend* (which features the ubiquitous Monkey King, along with the legendary Eight Immortals, in modern dress—and, oddly, the Greek god of the sea, Poseidon). He also does a *Crouching Tiger, Hidden Dragon* series. (Ang Lee's Oscar-winning movie was based on one of a series of novels; there are prequels, and apparently also sequels(!) to the story chosen for the movie: How strong is *your* faith . . . ?) It's said that Seto will be illustrating a *Batman* series for DC sometime soon.

Amerimanga in Bloom

Twenty years or so ago, M&A were lumped together as "Japanimation"—an exotic genre even to most readers of f/sf&h. Now it has become necessary to coin a retro term for the creative work of American serial artists who have been drawing in the manga style (some for their entire careers): It's about time they got some appreciation; so, "analog watch," meet "Amerimanga."

Dreamwave: The largest, most impressive line dedicated entirely to Amerimanga titles—all in full color. They focus primarily on miniseries, most of which have been set in one of two alternate worlds:

• *Warlands*—A fantasy scenario populated by elves, vampires, and the other unusual suspects, including human beings; *Shidima*, a samurai-style action tale, is set in a far corner of it.

• *Darkminds*—a future-scenario, part *Blade Runner*, part *Akira*, featuring a male cop and his partners—one a female android, the other a human woman; they have, like it or not, on-and-off contact with a motorcycle gang, the Neon Riders (who also had their own miniseries).

The latest *Darkminds* series, *Macropolis*, is a harrowing, *Seven*-ish thriller with drop-dead terrific art by Jo and Christian Chen. . . . I really hope the second half comes out faster than the first four issues, or frustration may kill me before the suspense does. Have a heart, guys. (Not mine—)

Dreamwave has been especially successful with their recent *Transformers* series license: Originally a Japanese creation (designed to sell robot toys . . . people *are* alike all over), the *Transformers* TV series and comics (and toys) became outrageously popular, both in Japan and here. Now it seems that future-history has repeated itself.

(Guilty secret—I have trouble recognizing individual mecha, no matter how distinctive their personalities are. I look forward to Dreamwave having time to spin more of its own dreams again, like the promising new series *Sandscape* . . . and the finale of *Macropolis*.)

Antarctic Press: Another all-Amerimanga publisher; it has gone quietly along its own path, with a variety of entertaining series, from the satiric *Ninja High School* to the brave new (action-filled) world of *Twilight X*, and the Kia Asamiya–style *Dragon Arms*. After making do on a shoestring budget for some years, Antarctic has been gaining a higher profile, too, wisely taking advantage of manga madness and Web-site shopping by selling tie-in merchandise, six-hundred-page "brick" TPBs and even its own anime series of *Gold Digger*, one of its most popular animanga titles.

Even tiny Anarchy Press has a potential hit with *Xin*, another take on the "Monkey King/Journey to the West" legend, done manga-style and in color. (There's no escape from him, at least this year: an archetypal "bad boy with a heart of gold," usually he no more looks like a monkey than Logan of the X-Men really looks like a wolverine.)

The Big Guys: What Are They Doing About It?

Almost every publisher has artists working on mainstream series whose styles are mangalike—some of these artists have been "infiltrating" for years. They've also responded more directly by adding some Amerimanga to their lines.

DC: Amerimanga is part of its creator-owned Wildstorm line; there have been a number of entertaining miniseries such as *Black Sun* in the past year, although here, too, the time lag between issues can get frustrating. It also publishes the new revivals of *Robotech* and *Thundercats*; Vertigo also published the bloody-serious *Fight for Tomorrow* miniseries; and noted Japanese artist/writer Kia Asamiya did a *Batman* story (originally printed in Japan) that DC has translated and published as a classy (yet affordable) hardcover. Various DC superheroes get to roam new terrain, including the worlds of Japanese myth and history, in its Elseworlds stories.

Marvel: The success of their *Mangaverse* miniseries in 2001 led to a variety of manga-inspired experiments, including several more "Mangaverse" tales, and the "Tsunami" line, which gives actual well-known Japanese *mangaka* ("manga creators") an opportunity to do their own takes on popular Marvel characters.

For my money, Marvel's most successful experiment was *Eden's Trail*, a little sleeper gem of a story in "Marvelvision" (drawn and printed sideways to simulate a widescreen movie). It was manga to the extreme, with some of the simplest yet most beautifully expressive faces I've seen, plus striking landscapes, all colored very subtly and accompanied by a minimum of dialog.

It left me wanting more—and, unfortunately, with a snowball's chance in hell of getting it. Steve Uy, the creator, and Marvel's editors had "creative differences," resulting in a six-issue series being cut down to five. Small wonder the dialog seemed *so* minimal, even by manga standards, and the plot seemed to be missing some jigsaw pieces. The full script is said to exist on-line somewhere. . . . Someday I may yet find the true end of *Eden's Trail*.

CrossGen: The newest big publisher in the comics field has been an experimental company in many ways—getting its books out on time, for one thing—which seems for the most part to have paid off for them. Their bargain-priced color anthologies may be fading away; but they are adding new independently owned series, including the brilliant *Red Star*, to their core line of titles, which is good news.

They've added some new manga-flavored series to their own CrossGen universe, as well—including *The Path*, a dark, moody warrior-monk series reminiscent of *Lone Wolf and Cub*; and *Way of the Rat*, the picaresque tale of Boon, a poor thief cursed with a great destiny and an inescapable, Yoda-like mentor—a sardonic monkey named Po Po. Both stories are set somewhere in the vast alternate universe created for their entire, very diverse line of comics.

Two of their first "core" titles, *Scion* and *Meridian*, have storylines containing plot twists, imagery, and art that are also very mangalike: a disfiguring scar gained in ritual combat sets off a bloody war between two clans; inhabited islands drift in the sky above a planet's surface.

Furthermore, the unifying theme that underlies all the disparate titles has a distinctly Taoist flavor—a yin/yang balance of energy in constant flux. If a god "gifts" some unsuspecting mortal, blessing or cursing him/her with the kind of power only gods possess, then someone that person interacts with will also be "gifted," to maintain cosmic balance.

There are even series about the very gods who spy on, bicker about, and watch over the universe's evolution. Occasionally, a protagonist will unexpectedly encounter one of the gods who toy with them like chess pawns; the results are very unpredictable. Everything that happens affects everything else, forever keeping "balance" running in circles: a concept you'll also find at the heart of much good manga and anime.

Image: Dreamwave was originally an Image imprint. Since they parted ways, Image, which has continued to add more diversity to its line of creator-owned books, has produced a number of manga-style series to fill the gap: miniseries like *Bastard Samurai*: ongoing series like Colleen Doran's long-running, addictive sf saga, *A Distant Soil*; the horrific goth beauty of *Defiance*, and mecha adventures *Rotogin* and *Tech Jacket*. (*Black Tide*, which recently departed Image, is also worth seeking out at its new address, Angel Gate.) As with most other publishers, the time between issues of Image books can be extremely long and unpredictable. It's something M&A fans simply have to get used to, unfortunately.

Image also has several updated revival series: *Battle of the Planets*, *Micronauts*, *Voltron*, *Masters of the Universe*, and *GI Joe*, which has been popular enough to support two new series. (It's all in the relationships, really: Scarlett and Snake-Eyes, reunited at last . . . it just doesn't get much better than that.)

Resources

If you wish I'd named more names in my M&A dream-list this year, I can help you fix that. (Quick, before Samurai Editor beheads me.) Get hold of the magazines listed above; get on the mailing lists of some of the specialty stores listed below; and get a copy of *Previews—the Comic Shop's Catalog*. You can thumb through one of those at a comic store, or buy your own huge copy, full of pictures, for only $3.95. It's essentially one big ad catalog; but it tells you what's out there, who publishes it, and enough info to give you some clue as to whether you really want to buy it.

Where to Buy (or Rent): And make new friends . . . at your local independent comic shop, whenever possible. If they don't carry what you want, they're usually glad to special-order it. Call the Comic Shop Locator Service if you need to (888-266-4226, toll free).

If you have a good independent video store in town, it probably carries much more anime than Blockbuster; again, it's a good way to find out whether you like something enough to buy it. Suncoast Video stores usually have a good selection of the latest anime; they also have a "discount points" card, which helps, because their DVDs are usually full price. Best Buy also has a lot of anime, at good prices, though not as current.

On-line ordering: Specialty import stores can be few and far between, in real time; thank god for cyberspace.

Two very well-stocked and very reliable on-line sites for M&A are The Right Stuf (www.rightstuf.com) and Anime Nation (www.animenation.com). The Right Stuf has a better-than-most supply of older anime, often at bargain prices, as well as all the newest M&A; they've had some fantastic sales in the past year, and they publish an encyclopedic hard-copy catalog. Their customer service is exceptional. You can also join their Got Anime club and get an additional 10 percent off.

Anime Nation has a better-than-average selection of import soundtracks, along with the latest anime and manga. They also have a print catalog, and their "Ask John" information column is a great resource.

Both sites offer other merchandise, too, such as imported (untranslated) manga, art books, T-shirts, and posters, plus e-mail newsletters and links to related Web sites.

Try the vast resources of Mile High Comics (milehighcomics.com), for hard-to-find back issues of translated manga, especially in comic form, and lost gems like Tim Eldred's Amerimanga versions of *Captain Harlock.* They also have a great newsletter.

Amazon.com (www.amazon.com) carries the latest anime—with preorder discounts—as well as translated manga and even some import soundtracks and books. Its "Z-Shops" are a generally reliable resource for used and/or hard-to-find anime at lower prices. Mail-order service is usually prompt and reliable; however, their customer service is controlled by an artificial intelligence.

Thanks: Once again to Westfield Comics' loyal crew; ever-excellent manager Bob, who Never Forgets, and the still diabolically charming Chadi, Nick, and Josh (*Domo arigato,* Josh Crawley, for the "heads-up" about brainwarp while trying to read a right-to-left magazine with left-to-right columns). It's more than just a store, it's a font of wisdom. . . . Thanks also to Atomic Comics in Phoenix and R-Galaxy in Tucson for providing my weekly dose of reading materials and friendly smiles when I was out in Arizona. And, once again, *domo arigato* to Loren Hekke-*sensei* and the West High School Japanese and Anime Clubs.

Sayonara (goodbye) until next time, *minasan.*

Obituaries: 2002

James Frenkel

Each year, even as formerly unknown, creatively talented individuals come to public attention, the talents of others who have already contributed to the creative community are silenced. The year 2002 was no exception, marking the death of many people whose works—whether in the written media, the performing arts, or in illustrative arts—became part of our shared cultural heritage. We mention these people in the hope that readers will note their artistry, perhaps seek out their work, or be inspired by their example to pursue their own creative work. The works of those no longer among us will live on as long as we who survive them know their work and it moves us to laughter, tears, or perhaps to create something that has never been seen before.

Chuck Jones, 89, was one of the most influential animators of the twentieth century. He worked on over three-hundred animated films, was the co-creator of such iconic Warner Brothers Cartoon characters as Road Runner, Wile E. Coyote, Pepe LePew, Michigan J. Frog, and others; he directed 1966's *How the Grinch Stole Christmas* and 1971's *Horton Hears a Who*; his short films include "What's Opera, Doc." He worked at Warner Brothers until 1962, then headed the MGM Studios Animation department from 1963 to 1971, where he worked on new Tom and Jerry cartoons. He won three Academy Awards for animated films and a Lifetime Achievement Oscar.

Ron Walotsky, 58, was a major award-winning fantasy and science fiction artist and illustrator for more than thirty years. His art has been used on over five hundred book and magazine covers, and in such widely disparate media as psychedelic posters of the 1960s, classical record albums, and advertising. He also created sculptures, most notably masks and other *objets d'art* based on horseshoe crab shells. Using a variety of realistic and surreal styles, he was a major influence in the field.

R. A. Lafferty, 87, was the author of many novels and over two hundred short stories. He received a World Fantasy Award and won a Hugo Award in 1973. His work was utterly original and defied classification, except as a new classification: the "lafferty." A modern fabulist, a magical realist, and an irrepressible iconoclast, Lafferty was never enormously popular, but his influence has been profound.

Astrid Lindgren, 94, was a Swedish children's book author who wrote the *Pippi Longstocking* books among her eighty works. She also was a children's book editor from 1946 to 1970 and the winner of numerous awards, including the Hans Christian Anderson Medal (1958) and UNESCO's International Book Award.

Virginia Hamilton, 65, was the author of *M. C. Higgins the Great*, which won the Newbery Medal and the National Book Award, *The Magical Adventures of Pretty Pearl*, and over thirty-five books of sf, fantasy, folk stories, and mystery, often celebrating African American culture.

John Buscema, 74, a comics artist for Stan Lee at Marvel, worked on Conan the Barbarian, The Mighty Thor, and The Fantastic Four, among others.

Alan Lomax, 87, was a legendary collector of folk music as well as an author, disc jockey, photographer, talent scout, producer, and musicologist. He discovered and recorded artists such as Leadbelly and Muddy Waters. He was a major figure in folk music and was integral in preserving the music for future generations.

Bill Peet, 87, was a Disney animator who worked on *Fantasia, Dumbo, Sword in the Stone,* and others. He claimed to have based Merlin in *Sword* on Disney; he also was a children's author of books such as *The Pinkish, Purplish, Bluish Egg* and *Chester, the Worldly Pig*.

Rod Steiger, 77, actor, won an Oscar for *In the Heat of the Night*. He had roles in *Marty, On the Waterfront, Al Capone,* in the Broadway version of *Rashomon,* and in the title role in *The Illustrated Man* (based on Ray Bradbury's linked collection of stories) and other films.

Virginia Kidd, 81, was the first female literary agent in the speculative fiction genre and represented many prominent authors, including Ursula K. Le Guin, Anne McCaffrey, and Gene Wolfe. She was editor of several anthologies of speculative fiction, among others, *Edges* with Ursula K. Le Guin.

Henry Slesar, 74, was an sf, mystery, and thriller author. He also wrote for TV, including for *Alfred Hitchcock Presents* and *The Twilight Zone*. In the 1950s and early 1960s, Slesar was a mainstay of those two series and a consistently entertaining author of stories of the uncanny and the dark. He continued to contribute short fiction until his death.

Roy Huggins, 87, was a producer and writer for TV. He often wrote as John Thomas James. Shows he either wrote or produced included *Maverick, The Fugitive, The Rockford Files, 77 Sunset Strip,* and *Run For Your Life*.

Cherry Wilder, 71, was the author of the Rulers of Hylor trilogy, the Torin trilogy, *Cruel Designs*, and many short stories Her work drew upon her New Zealand roots and melded other influences in unusual and powerful ways.

Monique Wittig, 67, was a French feminist whose writing tried to create a new mythology for the women's movement. Through vivid imagery she incorporated evocative subjects and nontraditional forms to challenge the conventions of the novel. Her highly praised novel *Les Guerillieres* is her best-known work.

George Alec Effinger, 55, was a brilliantly talented and versatile author of science fiction, fantasy, and crime. His first novel, *What Gravity Means to Me,* marked him as a rising talent in the mid 1970s. He wrote the cyberpunk series Marîd Audran and was the author of the Maureen Birnbaum stories (sf parody).

His novelette "Schroedinger's Kitten" won both the Nebula and Hugo awards. His work challenged convention and classification.

Richard Cowper, 73, John Middleton Murry, Jr., was the author of the Corlay trilogy, including *The Road to Corlay*, a Nebula and British Fantasy Award nominee; his story, "Piper at the Gates of Dawn," was nominated for a Hugo, a Nebula, and a British Fantasy Award. Cowper was a fine writer with an unusual sensibility.

Sharon Anne Hogan, 57, librarian, was involved in the initiative in the past twenty years to bring libraries into the new millennium with electronic advances, particularly Internet access; she also worked to protect free speech, copyright, and privacy rights.

Spike Milligan, 83, British comedian and founding member of *The Goon Show*, acted in several films including BBC-TV's miniseries *Gormenghast* and *Monty Python's Life of Brian*. He published poetry, novels, war memoirs, and children's fantasy, and his short stories appear in fantasy and horror anthologies.

George Sidney, 85, was a director of movie musicals, a child actor, and a producer for Columbia; he worked on *Anchors Aweigh* with Gene Kelly and Jerry the Mouse. He also financed and founded Hanna-Barbera Productions.

Herman Cohen, 76, was famous for producing *I Was a Teenage Werewolf* in 1957, which starred an unknown Michael Landon. He produced several other films, including *I Was a Teenage Frankenstein*, *A Study in Terror*, and *Berserk*.

Dudley Moore, 66, was a comic actor who starred in the first film production of *Bedazzled*. He and Peter Cook were a comic team in that film, and others, and before that, on television. He also starred in *10* and *Arthur*, and was a concert pianist.

Jeff Corey, 88, character actor and acting instructor, was barred from his field in the 1950s for past associations with the Communist Party and was eventually blacklisted in Hollywood. He became an acting instructor at the encouragement of friends and trained actors such as Robin Williams, Anthony Perkins, and Rita Moreno.

Mary Scott, 54, was the author of short-story collection *Nudists May Be Encountered*, a novel, *Not in Newbury*, and a reviewer of crime fiction. **Betsy Curtis**, 84; wrote short stories including "The Steiger Effect," nominated for a Hugo; she was also a costume designer who won awards at several World Science Fiction Conventions. **A. L. Barker**, 83, novelist and short story writer, was the author of ghost stories, and his novel *John Brown's Body* was shortlisted for the Booker Prize. **Pablo Antonio Cuadro**, 89, was a Nicaraguan poet influenced by peasant folklore and Indian legends. **Bartholomew Gill**, 58, whose real name was Mark McGarrity, wrote mystery novels set in Ireland; he created detective Peter McGarr, his *Death of a Joyce Scholar* was nominated for an Edgar Award. **Laurence M. Janifer,** 69, author and creator of Gerald Knave, wrote under a variety of pen names; with Randall Garrett he wrote, as Mark Phillips, the Kenneth J. Malone telepathic spy series.

William A. S. Sarjeant, 66, a geologist and paleontologist, as Antony Swithin wrote the fantasy quartet Perilous Quest for Llyonesse. **Roberto Drummond**, 68, was an author of magic realism. His first book, *A Marte de D. J. em Paris*, won a Jabuti award for Best New Writer. **Kathleen M. Massie-Ferch**, 47, wrote fantasy short stories and was the editor of *Ancient Enchantresses* and *Warrior En-*

chantress with Martin H. Greenberg. **Vincent D. Kohler**, 53: sf reviewer, wrote mysteries with sf/f influence featuring detective Eldon Larkin, including *Rainy North Woods* and *Rising Dog*. **James Mitchell**, 76, an author of espionage and suspense novels, featured Callan; sometimes wrote as James Munro. **Juan José Arreola**, 83; Mexican author, wrote short stories that used fantasy and created a genre named for his story "Varia Invención" (Diverse Inventions). **Dan Brennan**, 85; author of crime novels and the speculative fiction work *Insurrection*; sometimes used the pen name Jack Aureen.

Bruce Pelz, 65, was in the middle of the publication of many fanzines throughout the past four decades. He helped coordinate several conventions, including the World Organization of Fanpublishers (WOOF). **Jack C. (Jay) Haldeman**, 60, published nine novels and dozens of short stories and novellas in major sf magazines over the years.

Donald L[ewis] Franson, 85, was a president of the National Fantasy Fan Federation, author of sf stories, and coauthor of *A History of the Hugo, Nebula, and International Fantasy Awards*. **Dave Van Arnam**, 67; sf author and fan; principal author of *The Reader's Guide to Barsoom and Amber*; also wrote several works of fiction. **John B[arry] Spencer,** 57; rock musician and author; wrote *The Electric Lullaby Meat Market*, Charley Case mysteries, and Bloodline crime novels; founded Young Artists art agency. **Ian McAuley Hails**, 45, was the author of the conspiracy thriller *Back Door Man*.

Craig [Allan] Mills, 47, a fantasy author, wrote *The Bane of Lord Caladon*. **Ivor A. Rogers**, 72; scholar and fan, wrote *J. R. R. Tolkien: A Critical Biography* with his wife. **R(onald) V(erlin) Cassill**, 82, was a novelist, editor, and teacher. **Raymond T[homas] McNally**, 71, a Dracula scholar, theorized that Bram Stoker's Dracula was based on Vlad the Impalar. He wrote several books with Radu Florescu. **Mary Aline Siepmann (Mary Wesley)**, 90, was the author of three young-adult sf/fantasy novels, *The Sixth Seal*, *Speaking Terms*, and *Haphazard House*; she also wrote one adult novel, *Jumping the Queue*.

Clark Jones, 81, tv director; directed nearly twenty years of Tony Awards; directed broadcasts of *Carmen*, *Peter Pan*, and *Cinderella*. **Julia Phillips**, 57, was a film producer. She coproduced *Close Encounters of the Third Kind* and *The Sting*. **Barry Took**, 73, was a founder of Monty Python's Flying Circus. **Harry Gerstad**, 93, was an Oscar-winning film editor; he also worked in TV on the *Adventures of Superman*.

Norman Jolley, 86, wrote for *Space Patrol*, TV's first space exploration show; other TV shows he wrote for include *Wagon Train*, *The F. B. I.*, and *Barnaby Jones*; he also acted in westerns and on the radio.

Dave Berg, 81, was a longtime cartoonist for *Mad* magazine; he created "The Lighter Side of" strip for *Mad* and worked for Stan Lee at Timely Comics before it became Marvel. **Denis McLoughlin**, 84, illustrator and comic artist; created the *Swift Morgan* comic strip. **Tom Sutton**, 65, a science fiction and comic book artist, drew for sf and horror magazines. He worked for Marvel, DC, and also on *Frankenstein* and *Conan the Barbarian*. **Robert Kanigher**, 86; comics writer, editor, and creator; worked on many superhero comics; creator of *Sgt. Rock*. **Kurt Schaffenberger**, 81, drew Captain Marvel during the 1940s–1950s. **John W. Locke**, 87, was an artist's agent who represented Edward Gorey and Ronald Searle, among others.

Josef Svoboda, 81, a Czech stage designer, designed sets for *Carmen* and the Ring Cycle; he was cocreator of Laterna Magika; he incorporated film, lasers, mirrors, and more into his sets. **Martin Aronstein**, 65, was a lighting designer for Broadway shows including *Peter Pan. Medea,* and *Ain't Supposed to Die a Natural Death.* **Richard Sylbert**, 73, Oscar-winning designer of film sets including *Dick Tracy;* worked on *Chinatown, The Manchurian Candidate,* and *Catch-22.* **Richard Lippold**, 87, sculptor; "lyric poet of space and light" (*New York Times*); designed *World Tree* at Harvard and *Ad Astra* at the National Air and Space Museum. **Joshua Ryan Evans**, 20, a young actor, had a recurring role in *Ally McBeal,* appeared as Tom Thumb in *P. T. Barnum,* an A&E miniseries, appeared in *Poltergeist: The Legacy,* and was the young grinch in the film of Dr. Seuss's *How the Grinch Stole Christmas.*

Nigel Hawthorne, 72, was an actor in *Demolition Man;* he provided voices for characters in *Watership Down, The Black Cauldron,* and *Tarzan* (1999), among much film and stage work. **Sihung Lung**, 72, was an actor in such Ang Lee movies as *Eat Drink Man Woman;* he played Sir Te in *Crouching Tiger, Hidden Dragon,* **Bill McCutcheon**, 77, an actor, won a Tony for *Anything Goes,* played Uncle Wally on *Sesame Street,* and was in the film *Mr. Destiny,* among others. **Ron Taylor** created the voice of Audrey II in the off-Broadway production of the musical *Little Shop of Horrors.* **Kevin Smith**, 38, actor; played Ares, the God of War on *Xena: Warrior Princess.* **Sheldon Allman**, 77, singer, provided Mr. Ed's singing voice; made an album, *Sing Along with Drac,* which included "Fangs for the Memory." **Lucille Lund**, 89, an actress played in 1934's *The Black Cat* with Boris Karloff. **Signe Hasso**, 91, was an actress whose career spanned nine decades. She is most famous for her role in *A Double Life,* the 1947 drama with Ronald Colman. **Ted Ross**, 68, an actor, won a Tony for *The Wiz* and was in the film version as well. He had many other and TV roles. **Michael Elphick**, 55, played the Empire officer Darth Vader choked with the Force in *Star Wars.*

Thor Heyerdahl, 87; anthropologist and adventurer, was the author of *Kon-Tiki.* **Stephen Jay Gould**, 60, was a biologist and evolutionary theorist who challenged Darwinian evolution and wrote popular books on natural science. **Joseph L. Steiner**, 95, was the cofounder of Kenner, which made Spirograph and other creative toys.

Charles Ede, 80, was the founder of the Folio society, which produces fine books at affordable prices. **Cele Goldsmith Lalli**, 68, was an editor of *Amazing* and *Fantastic* magazines. **Cathleen Jordan**, 60, was editor of *Alfred Hitchcock's Mystery Magazine* and primary editor at Doubleday for Isaac Asimov, Loren D. Estleman, and Charlotte MacLeod. She won the 2002 Ellery Queen Award. **Zena Sutherland**, 86, a reviewer of children's books, served on committees for the Newbery and Caldecott Awards. **Betty Shapian**, 73, a West Coast book publicist, worked with Ray Bradbury and many other authors. **Franco Lucentini**, 81, an Italian author, translator, and editor translated authors such as Lovecraft and Jorge Luis Borges, wrote mysteries, and edited sf anthologies.

Thomas E[dward] Fuller, 54, head writer for the Atlanta Radio Theater Company, received a Georgia Science Fiction Fandom award, three silver awards in the Mark Time competition for radio drama, an Ogle award for best horror-fantasy audio, among other kudos. **Stan Rice**, 60, the husband of Anne Rice and poet and painter, was the physical inspiration for the handsome vampire Lestat in *Interview with the Vampire.* **Wendy Hilton**, 71, was a specialist in recreating Baroque dance. **Noel Young**, 79, founded Capra Press and published several fantasy-related titles, including *Zen and the Art of Writing* by Ray Bradbury and *Wild Angels* by Ursula K. Le Guin.

They will be missed.

THE YEAR'S BEST Fantasy & Horror

KELLY LINK

Lull

Kelly Link's stories have recently appeared in Conjunctions *and McSweeney's* Mammoth Treasury of Thrilling Tales. *Her first collection,* Stranger Things Happen, *was published to critical acclaim in 2001. She has won a World Fantasy Award, a Nebula Award, and the James Tiptree, Jr. Award. She works with her husband, Gavin J. Grant, on the 'zine* Lady Churchill's Rosebud Wristlet, *and is the editor of* Trampoline, *an anthology forthcoming from Small Beer Press. She lives in Massachusetts.*

About "Lull" Link says: "Time-travel, palindromes, and poker. I'm not really very good at any of these." Perhaps not, but she has masterfully created a delightfully chilling and original nesting doll of light and dark elements. The story was originally published in Conjunctions 39: The New Wave Fabulists.

—E. D., T. W.

There was a lull in the conversation. We were down in the basement, sitting around the green felt table. We were holding bottles of warm beer in one hand, and our cards in the other. Our cards weren't great. Looking at each others' faces, we could see that clearly.

We were tired. It made us more tired to look at each other when we saw we weren't getting away with anything at all. We didn't have any secrets.

We hadn't seen each other for a while and it was clear that we hadn't changed for the better. We were between jobs, or stuck in jobs that we hated. We were having affairs and our wives knew and didn't care. Some of us were sleeping with each others' wives. There were things that had gone wrong, and we weren't sure who to blame.

We had been talking about things that went backwards instead of forwards. Things that managed to do both at the same time. Time travelers. People who weren't stuck like us. There was that new movie that went backwards, and then Jeff put this music on the stereo where all the lyrics were palindromes. It was something his kid had picked up. His kid, Stan, was a lot cooler than we had ever been. He was always bringing things home, Jeff said, saying, *you have got to listen to this. Here, try this. These guys are good.*

Stan was the kid who got drugs for the other kids when there was going to be a party. We had tried not to be bothered by this. We trusted our kids and we hoped that they trusted us, that they weren't too embarrassed by us. We weren't cool. We were willing to be liked. That would have been enough.

Stan was so very cool that he hadn't even minded taking care of some of us, the parents of his friends (the friends of his parents), although sometimes we just went through our kids' drawers, looked under the mattresses. It wasn't that different from taking Halloween candy out of their Halloween bags, which was something we had also done, when they were younger and went to bed before we did.

Stan wasn't into that stuff now, though. None of the kids were. They were into music instead.

You couldn't get this music on CD. That was part of the conceit. It only came on cassette. You played one side, and then on the other side the songs all played backwards and the lyrics went forwards and backwards all over again in one long endless loop. *La allah ha llal. Do, oh, oh, do you, oh do, oh, wanna?*

Bones was really digging it. "Do you, do you wanna dance, you do, you do," he said and laughed and tipped his chair back. "Snakey canes. Hula boolah."

Someone mentioned the restaurant downtown where you were supposed to order your dessert and then you got your dinner.

"I fold," Ed said. He threw his cards down on the table.

Ed liked to make up games. People paid him to make up games. Back when we had a regular poker night, he was always teaching us a new game and this game would be based on a TV show or some dream he'd had.

"Let's try something new. I'm going to deal out everything, the whole deck, and then we'll have to put it all back. We'll see each other's hands as we put them down. We're going for low. And we'll swap. Yeah, that might work. Something else, like a wild card, but we won't know what the wild card was, until the very end. We'll need to play fast—no stopping to think about it—just do what I tell you to do."

"What'll we call it?" he said, not a question, but as if we'd asked him, although we hadn't. He was shuffling the deck, holding the cards close like we might try to take them away. "DNA Hand. Got it?"

"That's a shitty idea," Jeff said. It was his basement, his poker table, his beer. So he got to say things like that. You could tell that he thought Ed looked happier than he ought to. He was thinking Ed ought to remember his place in the world, or maybe Ed needed to be reminded what his place was. His new place. Most of us were relieved to see that Ed looked okay. If he didn't look okay, that was okay too. We understood. Bad things had happened to all of us.

We were contemplating these things and then the tape flips over and starts again.

It's catchy stuff. We could listen to it all night.

"Now we chant along and summon the Devil," Bones says. "Always wanted to do that."

Bones has been drunk for a while now. His hair is standing up and his face is shiny and red. He has a fat stupid smile on his face. We ignore him which is what he wants. Bones' wife is just the same, loud and useless. The thing that makes the rest of us sick is that their kids are the nicest, smartest, funniest, best kids. We can't figure it out. They don't deserve kids like that.

Brenner asks Ed if he's found a new place to live. He has.

"Off the highway, down by that Texaco, in the orchards. This guy built a road and built the house right on top of the road. Just, plop, right in the middle of the road. Kind of like he came walking up the road with the house on his back, got tired, and just dropped it."

"Not very good feng shui," Pete says.

Pete has read a book. He's got a theory about picking up women which he's always sharing with us. He goes to the Barnes and Noble on his lunch hour and hangs around in front of displays of books about houses and decorating, skimming through architecture books. He says it makes you look smart and just domesticated enough. A man looking at pictures of houses is sexy to women.

We've never asked if it works for him.

Meanwhile, we know, Pete's wife is always after him to go up on the roof and gut the drains, reshingle and patch, paint. Pete isn't really into this. Imaginary houses are sexy. Real ones are work.

He did go buy a mirror at Pottery Barn and hang it up, just inside the front door, because otherwise, he said, evil spirits go rushing up the staircase and into the bedrooms. Getting them out again is tricky.

The way the mirror works is that they start to come in, look in the mirror, and think a devil is already living in the house. So they take off. Devils can look like anyone—salespeople, Latter Day Saints, the people who mow your lawns—even members of your own family. So you have to have a mirror.

Ed says, "Where the house is, is the first weird thing. The second thing is the house. It's like this team of architects went crazy and sawed two different houses in half and then stitched them back together. Casa Del Guggenstein. The front half is really old—a hundred years old—the other half is aluminum siding."

"Must have brought down the asking price," Jeff says.

"Yeah," Ed says. "And the other thing is there are all these doors. One at the front and one at the back and two more on either side, right smack where the aluminum siding starts, these weird, tall, skinny doors, like they're built for basketball players. Or aliens."

"Or palm trees," Bones says.

"Yeah," Ed says. "And then one last door, this vestigial door, up in the master bedroom. Not like a door that you walk through, for a closet, or a bathroom. It opens and there's nothing there. No staircase, no balcony, no point to it. It's a Tarzan door. Up in the trees. You open it and an owl might fly in. Or a bat. The previous tenant left that door locked—apparently he was afraid of sleepwalking."

"Fantastic," Brenner says. "Wake up in the middle of the night and go to the bathroom, you could just pee out the side of your house."

He opens up the last beer and shakes some pepper in it. Brenner has a thing about pepper. He even puts it on ice cream. Pete swears that one time at a party he wandered into Brenner's bedroom and looked in a drawer in a table beside the bed. He says he found a box of condoms and a peppermill. When we asked what he was doing in Brenner's bedroom, he winked and then put his finger to his mouth and zipped his lip.

Brenner has a little pointed goatee. It might look silly on some people, but not on Brenner. The pepper thing sounds silly, maybe, but not even Jeff teases Brenner about it.

"I remember that house," Alibi says.

We call him Alibi because his wife is always calling to check up on him. She'll say, so was Alec out shooting pool with you the other night, and we'll say, sure he was, Gloria. The problem is that sometimes Alibi has told her some completely different story and she's just testing us. But that's not our problem and that's not our fault. She never holds it against us and neither does he.

"We used to go up in the orchards at night and have wars. Knock each other down with rotten apples. There were these peacocks. You bought the orchard house?"

"Yeah," Ed says. "I need to do something about the orchard. All the apples are falling off the trees and then they just rot on the ground. The peacocks eat them and get drunk. There are drunk wasps, too. If you go down there you can see the wasps hurtling around in these loopy lines and the peacocks grab them right out of the air. Little pickled wasp hors d'oeuvres. Everything smells like rotting apples. All night long, I'm dreaming about eating wormy apples."

For a second, we're afraid Ed might tell us his dreams. Nothing is worse than someone telling you their dreams.

"So what's the deal with the peacocks?" Bones says.

"Long story," Ed says.

So you know how the road to the house is a private road, you turn off the highway onto it, and it meanders up some until you run into the house. Someday I'll drive home and park the car in the living room.

There's a big sign that says Private. But people still drive up the turnoff, lost, or maybe looking for a picnic spot, or a place to pull off the road and fuck. Before you hear the car coming, you hear the peacocks. Which was the plan because this guy who built it was a real hermit, a recluse.

People in town said all kinds of stuff about him. Nobody knew. He didn't want anybody to know.

The peacocks were so he would know when anyone was coming up to the house. They start screaming before you ever see a car. So remember, out the back door, the road goes on down through the orchards, there's a gate and then you're back on the main highway again. And this guy, the hermit, he kept two cars. Back then, nobody had two cars. But he kept one car parked in front of the house and one parked at the back so that whichever way someone was coming, he could go out the other way real fast and drive off before his visitor got up to the house.

He had an arrangement with a grocer. The grocer sent a boy up to the house once every two weeks, and the boy brought the mail, too, but there wasn't ever any mail.

The hermit had painted in the windows of his cars, black, except for these little circles that he could see out of. You couldn't see in. But apparently he used to drive around at night. People said they saw him. Or they didn't see him. That was the point.

The real estate agent said she heard that once this guy had to go to the doctor.

He had a growth or something. He showed up in the doctor's office wearing a woman's hat with a long black veil that hung down from the crown, so you couldn't see his face. He took off his clothes in the doctor's office and kept the hat on.

One night half of the house fell down. People all over the town saw lights, like fireworks or lightning, up over the orchard. Some people swore they saw something big, all lit up, go up into the sky, like an explosion, but quiet. Just lights. The next day, people went up to the orchard. The hermit was waiting for them—he had his veil on. From the front, the house looked fine. But you could tell something had caught fire. You could smell it, like ozone.

The hermit said it had been lightning. He rebuilt the house himself. Had lumber and everything delivered. Apparently kids used to go sneak up in the trees in the orchard and watch him while he was working, but he did all the work wearing the hat and the veil.

He died a long time ago. The grocer's boy figured out something was wrong because the peacocks were coming in and out of the windows of the house and screaming.

So now they're still down in the orchards and under the porch, and they still came in the windows and made a mess if Ed forgot and left the windows open too wide. Last week a fox came in after a peacock. You wouldn't think a fox would go after something so big and mean. Peacocks are mean.

Ed had been downstairs watching TV.

"I heard the bird come in," he says, "and then I heard a thump and a slap like a chair going over and when I went to look, there was a streak of blood going up the floor to the window. A fox was going out the window and the peacock was in its mouth, all the feathers dragging across the sill. Like one of Susan's paintings."

Ed's wife Susan took an art class for a while. Her teacher said she had a lot of talent. Brenner modeled for her, and so did some of our kids, but most of Susan's paintings were portraits of her brother, Andrew. He'd been living with Susan and Ed for about two years. This was hard on Ed, although he'd never complained about it. He knew Susan loved her brother. He knew her brother had problems.

Andrew couldn't hold down a job. He went in and out of rehab, and when he was out, he hung out with our kids. Our kids thought Andrew was cool. The less we liked him, the more time our kids spent with Andrew. Maybe we were just a little jealous of him.

Jeff's kid, Stan, he and Andrew hung out all the time. Stan was the one who found Andrew and called the hospital. Susan never said anything, but maybe she blamed Stan. Everybody knew Stan had been getting stuff for Andrew.

Another thing that nobody said: what happened to Andrew, it was probably good for the kids in the long run.

Those paintings—Susan's paintings—were weird. None of the people in her paintings ever looked very comfortable, and she couldn't do hands. And there were always these animals in the paintings, looking as if they'd been shot, or gutted, or if they didn't look dead, they were definitely supposed to be rabid. You worried about the people.

She hung them up in their house for a while, but they weren't comfortable paintings. You couldn't watch TV in the same room with them. And Andrew had this habit, he'd sit on the sofa just under one portrait, and there was another one, too, above the TV. Three Andrews was too many.

Once Ed brought Andrew to poker night. Andrew sat a while and didn't say anything, and then he said he was going upstairs to get more beer and he never came back. Three days later, the highway patrol found Ed's car parked under a bridge. Stan and Andrew came home two days after that, and Andrew went back into rehab. Susan used to go visit him and take Stan with her—she'd take her sketchbook. Stan said Andrew would sit there and Susan would draw him and nobody ever said a word.

After the class was over, while Andrew was still in rehab, Susan invited all of us to go to this party at her teacher's studio. What we remember is that Pete got drunk and made a pass at the instructor, this sharp-looking woman with big dangly earrings. We were kind of surprised, not just because he did it in front of his wife, but because we'd all just been looking at her paintings. All these deer and birds and cows draped over dinner tables, and sofas, guts hanging out, eyeballs all shiny and fixed—so that explained Susan's portraits, at least.

We wonder what Susan did with the paintings of Andrew.

"I've been thinking about getting a dog," Ed says.

"Fuck," we say. "A dog's a big responsibility." Which is what we've spent years telling our kids.

The music on the tape loops and looped. It was going round for a second time. We sat and listened to it. We'll be sitting and listening to it for a while longer.

"This guy," Ed says. "The guy who was renting this place before me, he was into some crazy thing. There's all these mandalas and pentagrams painted on the floors and walls. Which is also why I got it so cheap. They didn't want to bother stripping the walls and repainting; this guy just took off one day, took a lot of the furniture, too. Loaded up his truck with as much as he could take."

"So no furniture?" Pete says. "Susan get the dining room table and chairs? The bed? You sleeping in a sleeping bag? Eating beanie weenies out of a can?"

"I got a futon," Ed says. "And I've got my work table set up, the TV and stuff. I've been going down to the orchard, grilling on the Hibachi. You guys should come over. I'm working on a new video game—it'll be a haunted house—those are really big right now. That's why this place is so great for me. I can use everything. Next weekend? I'll fix hamburgers and you guys can sit up in the house, keep cool, drink beer, test the game for me. Find the bugs."

"There are always bugs," Jeff says. He's smiling in a mean way. He isn't so nice when he's been drinking. "That's life. So should we bring the kids? The wives? Is this a family thing? Ellie's been asking about you. You know that retreat she's on, she called from the woods the other day. She went on and on about this past life. Apparently she was a used car salesman. She says that this life is karmic payback, being married to me, right? She gets home day after tomorrow. We get together, maybe Ellie can set you up with someone. Now that you're a free man, you need to take some advantage."

"Sure," Ed says and shrugs. We can see him wishing that Jeff would shut up, but Jeff doesn't shut up.

Jeff says, "I saw Susan in the grocery store the other day. She looked fantastic. It wasn't that she wasn't sad anymore, she wasn't just getting by, she was radiant, you know? That special glow. Like Joan of Arc. Like she knew something. Like she'd won the lottery."

"Well, yeah," Ed says. "That's Susan. She doesn't live in the past. She's got this new job, this research project. They're trying to contact aliens. They're using household appliances: satellite dishes, cell phones, car radios, even refrigerators. I'm not sure how. I'm not sure what they're planning to say. But they've got a lot of grant money. Even hired a speech writer."

"Wonder what you say to aliens," Brenner says. "Hi, honey, I'm home. What's for dinner?"

"Your place or mine?" Pete says. "What's a nice alien like you doing in a galaxy like this?"

"Where you been? I've been worried sick," Alibi says.

Jeff picks up a card, props it sideways against the green felt. Picks up another one, leans it against the first. He says, "You and Susan always looked so good together. Perfect marriage, perfect life. Now look at you: she's talking to aliens, and you're living in a haunted house. You're an example to all of us, Ed. Nice guy like you, bad things happen to you, Susan leaves a swell guy like you, what's the lesson here? I've been thinking about this all year. You and Ellie must have worked at the same car dealership, in that past life."

Nobody says anything. Ed doesn't say anything, but the way we see him look at Jeff, we know that this haunted house game is going to have a character in it who walks and talks a lot like Jeff. This Jeff character is going to panic and run around on the screen of people's TVs and get lost.

It will stumble into booby traps and fall onto knives. Its innards will sloop out. Zombies are going to crack open the bones of its legs and suck on the marrow. Little devils with monkey faces are going to stitch its eyes open with tiny stitches and then they are going to piss beautiful ribbons of acid into its eyes.

Beautiful women are going to fuck this cartoon Jeff in the ass with garden shears. And when this character screams, it's going to sound a lot like Jeff screaming. It will scream for a while, which might attract other things. Ed's good at the little details. The kids who buy Ed's games love the details. They buy his games for things like this.

Jeff will probably be flattered.

Jeff starts complaining about Stan's phone bill, this four hundred dollar cell phone charge that Stan ran up. When he asked about it, Stan handed him a stack of twenties just like that. That kid always has money to spare.

Stan also gave Jeff this phone number. He told Jeff that it's like this phone sex line, but with a twist. You call up and ask for this girl named Starlight, and she tells you sexy stories, only, if you want, they don't have to be sexy. They can be any kind of story you want. You tell her what kind of story you want, and she makes it up. Stan says it's Stephen King and sci-fi and the Arabian nights and Penthouse Letters all at once.

Ed interrupts Jeff. "You got the number?"

"What?" Jeff says.

"I just got paid for the last game," Ed says. "The one with the baby-heads and the octopus girlies, the Martian combat hockey. Let's call that number. I'll pay. You put her on speaker and we'll all listen, and it's my treat, okay, because I'm such a swell guy."

Bones says that it sounds like a shit idea to him, which is probably why Jeff went and got the phone bill and another six-pack of beer. We all take another beer.

Jeff turns the stereo down—

Madam I'm Adam Madam I'm Adam

—and puts the phone in the middle of the table. It sits there, in the middle of all that green, like an island or something. Marooned. Jeff switches it on speaker. "Four bucks a minute," he says, and shrugs, and dials the number.

"Here," Ed says. "Pass it over."

The phone rings and we listen to it ring and then a woman's voice, very pleasant, says hello and asks if Ed is over eighteen. He says he is. He gives her his credit card number. She asks if he was calling for anyone in particular.

"Starlight," Ed says.

"One moment," the woman says. We hear a click and then Starlight is on the line. We know this because she says so. She says, "Hi, my name is Starlight. I'm going to tell you a sexy story. Do you want to know what I'm wearing?"

Ed grunts. He shrugs. He grimaces at us. He needs a haircut. Susan used to cut his hair, which we used to think was cute. He and Andrew had these identical lopsided haircuts. It was pretty goofy.

"Can I call you Susan?" Ed says.

Which we think is strange.

Starlight says, "If you really want to, but my name's really Starlight. Don't you think that's sexy?"

She sounds like a kid. A little girl—not even like a girl. Like a kid. She doesn't sound like Susan at all. Since the divorce, we haven't seen much of Susan, although she calls our houses sometimes, to talk to our wives. We're a little worried about what she's been saying to them.

Ed says, "I guess so." We can tell he's only saying that to be polite, but Starlight laughs as if he's told her a joke. It's weird hearing that little-kid laugh down here.

Ed says, "So are you going to tell me a story?"

Starlight says, "That's what I'm here for. But usually the guy wants to know what I'm wearing."

Ed says, "I want to hear a story about a cheerleader and the Devil."

Bones says, "So what's she wearing?"

Pete says, "Make it a story that goes backwards."

Jeff says, "Put something scary in it."

Alibi says, "Sexy."

Brenner says, "I want it to be about good and evil and true love, and it should also be funny. No talking animals. Not too much fooling around with the narrative structure. The ending should be happy but still realistic, believable, you know, and there shouldn't be a moral although we should be able to think back later and have some sort of revelation. No *and suddenly they woke up and discovered that it was all a dream.* Got that?"

Starlight says, "Okay. The Devil and a cheerleader. Got it. Okay."

THE DEVIL AND THE CHEERLEADER

So the Devil is at a party at the cheerleader's house. They've been playing spin the bottle. The cheerleader's boyfriend just came out of the closet with her best friend. Earlier the cheerleader felt like slapping him, and now she knows why. The bottle pointed at her best friend who had just shrugged and smiled at her. Then the bottle was spinning and when the bottle stopped spinning, it was in her boyfriend's hand.

Then all of a sudden an egg timer was going off. Everyone was giggling and they were all standing up to go over by the closet, like they were all going to try to squeeze inside. But the Devil stood up and took the cheerleader's hand and pulled her backwards-forwards.

So she knew what exactly had happened, and was going to happen, and some other things besides.

This is the thing she likes about backwards. You start out with all the answers, and after a while, someone comes along and gives you the questions, but you don't have to answer them. You're already past that part. That was what was so nice about being married. Things got better and better until you hardly even knew each other any more. And then you said goodnight and went out on a date, and after that you were just friends. It was easier that way—that's the dear, sweet, backwards way of the world.

Just a second, let's go back for a second.

Something happened. Something has happened. But nobody ever talked about it, at least not at these parties. Not anymore.

Everyone's been drinking all night long, except the Devil, who's a teetotaler. He's been pretending to drink vodka out of a hip flask. Everybody at the party is drunk right now and they think he's okay. Later they'll sober up. They'll think he's *pretentious*, an *asshole*, drinking air out of a flask like that.

There are a lot of empty bottles of beer, some empty bottles of whiskey. There's a lot of work still to be done, by the look of it. They're using one of the beer bottles, that's what they're spinning. Later on it will be full and they won't have to play this stupid game.

The cheerleader guesses that she didn't invite the Devil to the party. He isn't the kind of guy that you have to invite. He'll probably show up by himself. But now they're in the closet together for five minutes. The cheerleader's boyfriend isn't too happy about this, but what can he do? It's that kind of party. She's that kind of cheerleader.

They're a lot younger than they used to be. At parties like this, they used to be older, especially the Devil. He remembers all the way back to the end of the world. The cheerleader wasn't a cheerleader then. She was married and had kids and a husband.

Something's going to happen, or maybe it's already happened. Nobody ever talks about it. If they could, what would they say?

But those end of the world parties were crazy. People would drink too much and they wouldn't have any clothes on. There'd be these sad little piles of clothes in the living room, as if something had happened, and the people had disappeared, disappeared right out of their clothes. Meanwhile, the people who belonged to the clothes would be out in the backyard, waiting until it was time to go home. They'd get up on the trampoline and bounce around and cry.

There would be a bottle of extra-virgin olive oil and sooner or later someone was going to have to refill it and go put it back on the pantry shelf. You'd have had these slippery naked middle-aged people sliding around on the trampoline and the oily grass, and then in the end all you'd have would be a bottle of olive oil, some olives on a tree, a tree, an orchard, an empty field.

The Devil would stand around feeling awkward, hoping that it would turn out he'd come late.

The kids would be up in their bedrooms, out of the beds, looking out the windows, remembering when *they* used to be older. Not that they ever got that much older.

But the world is younger now. Things are simpler. Now the cheerleader has parents of her own, and all she has to do is wait for them to get home, and then this party can be over.

Two days ago was the funeral. It was just how everyone said it would be.

Then there were errands, people to talk to. She was busy.

She hugged her aunt and uncle goodbye and moved into the house where she would live for the rest of her life. She unpacked all her boxes, and the Salvation Army brought her parents' clothes and furniture and pots and pans, and other people, her parents' friends, helped her hang her mother's clothes in her mother's closet. (Not this closet.) She bunched her mother's clothes up in her hand and *sniffed*, curious and hungry and afraid.

She suspects, remembering the smell of her mother's monogrammed sweaters, that they'll have fights about things. Boys, music, clothes. The cheerleader will learn to let all of these things go.

If her kids were still around, they would say *I told you so*. What they did say was, *Just wait until you have parents of your own. You'll see.*

The cheerleader rubs her stomach. *Are you in there?*

She moved the unfamiliar, worn-down furniture around so that it matched up old grooves in the floor. Here was the shape of someone's buttocks, printed onto a seat cushion. Maybe it would be her father's favorite chair.

She looked through her father's records. There was a record playing on the phonograph, it wasn't anything she had ever heard before, and she took it off, laid it back in its empty white sleeve. She studied the death certificates. She tried to think what to tell her parents about their grandchildren, what they'd want to know.

Her favorite song had just been on the radio for the very last time. Years and years ago, she'd danced to that song at her wedding. Now it was gone, except for the feeling she'd had when she listened to it. Sometimes she still felt that way, but there wasn't a word for it anymore.

Tonight, in a few hours, there will be a car wreck and then her parents will be coming home. By then, all her friends will have left, taking away six-packs and boyfriends and newly applied coats of hair spray and lipstick.

She thinks she looks a bit like her mother.

Before everyone showed up, while everything was still a *wreck* downstairs, before the police had arrived to say what they had to say, she was standing in her parents' bathroom. She was looking in the mirror.

She picked a lipstick out of the trash can, an orangey-red that will be a favorite because there's just a little half-moon left. But when she looked at herself in the mirror, it didn't fit. It didn't belong to her. She put her hand on her breastbone, pressed hard, felt her heart beating faster and faster. She couldn't wear her mother's lipstick while her mother lay on a gurney somewhere in a morgue: waiting to be sewn up; to have her clothes sewn back on; to breathe; to wake up; to see the car on the other side of the median, sliding away; to see her husband, the man that she's going to marry someday; to come home to meet her daughter.

The recently dead are always exhausted. There's so much to absorb, so many things that need to be undone. They have their whole lives ahead of them.

The cheerleader's best friend winks at her. The Devil's got a flashlight with two dead batteries. Somebody closes the door after them.

Soon, very soon, already now, the batteries in the Devil's flashlight are old and tired and there's just a thin line of light under the closet door. It's cramped in the closet and it smells like shoes, paint, wool, cigarettes, tennis rackets, ghosts of perfume and sweat. Outside the closet, the world is getting younger, but in here is where they keep all the old things. The cheerleader put them all in here last week.

She's felt queasy for most of her life. She's a bad time traveler. She gets timesick. It's as if she's always just a little bit pregnant, *are you in there?* and it's worse in here, with all these old things that don't belong to her, even worse because the Devil is always fooling around with time.

The Devil feels right at home. He and the cheerleader make a nest of coats and sit down on them, facing each other. The Devil turns the bright, constant beam of the flashlight on the cheerleader. She's wearing a little flippy skirt. Her knees are up, making a tent out of her skirt. The tent is full of shadows—so is the closet. The Devil conjures up another Devil, another cheerleader, mouse-sized, both of them, sitting under the cheerleader's skirt. The closet is full of Devils and cheerleaders.

"I just need to hold something," the cheerleader says. If she holds something, maybe she won't throw up.

"Please," the Devil says. "It tickles. I'm ticklish."

The cheerleader is leaning forward. She's got the Devil by the tail. Then she's touching the Devil's tail with her pompoms. He quivers.

"Please don't," he says. He giggles.

The Devil's tail is tucked up under his legs. It isn't hot, but the Devil is sweating. He feels sad. He's not good at being sad. He flicks the flashlight on and off. Here's a knee. Here's a mouth. Here's a sleeve hanging down, all empty. Someone knocks on the closet door.

"Go away," the cheerleader says. "It hasn't been five minutes yet. Not even."

The Devil can feel her smile at him, like they're old friends. "Your tail. Can I touch it?" the cheerleader says.

"Touch what?" the Devil says. He feels a little excited, a little nervous. Old enough to know better, brand new enough, here in the closet, to be jumpy. He's taking a chance here. Girls—*women*—aren't really domestic animals at the moment, although they're getting tamer, more used to living in houses. Less likely to bite.

"Can I touch your tail now?" the cheerleader says.

"No!" the Devil says. "I'm shy," he says. "Maybe you could stroke my tail with your pompom, in a little bit."

"We could make out," the cheerleader says. "That's what we're supposed to do, right? I need to be distracted because I think I'm about to have this thought. It's going to make me really sad. I'm getting younger, you know? I'm going to keep on getting younger. It isn't fair."

She puts her feet against the closet door. She kicks once, like a mule.

She says, "I mean, you're the Devil. You don't have to worry about this stuff. In a few thousand years, you'll be back at the beginning again and you'll be in good with God again, right?"

The Devil shrugs. Everybody knows the end of that story.

The cheerleader says, "Everyone knows that old story. You're famous. You're like John Wilkes Booth. You're historical—you're going to be really important. You'll be Mr. Bringer-of-Light and you'll get good tables at all the trendy restaurants, choruses of angels and maitre d's, et cetera, la, la, la, they'll all be singing hallelujahs forever, please pass the vichyssoise, and then God unmakes the world and he'll put all the bits away in a closet like this."

The Devil smirks. He shrugs. It isn't a bad life, hanging around in closets with cheerleaders. And it gets better.

The cheerleader says, "It isn't fair. I'd tell him so, if he were here. He'll unhang the stars and pull Leviathan right back out of the deep end of the vasty bathwater, and you'll be having Leviathan tartar for dinner. Where will I be, then? You'll be around. You're always around. But me, I'll get younger and younger and in a handful of years I won't be me at all, and my parents will get younger and so on and so on, whoosh. We'll be gone like a flash of light, and you won't even remember me. Nobody will remember me. Everything that I was, that I did, all the funny things that I said, and the things that my friends said back to me, that will all be gone. But you go all the way backwards. You go backwards and forwards. It isn't fair. You could always remember me. What could I do so that you would remember me?"

"As long as we're in this closet," the Devil says, he's magnanimous, "I'll remember you."

"But in a few minutes," the cheerleader says, "we'll go back out of the closet and the bottle will spin, and then the party will be over, and my parents will come home, and nobody will ever remember me."

"Then tell me a story," the Devil says. He puts his sharp, furry paw on her leg. "Tell me a story so that I'll remember you."

"What kind of story?" says the cheerleader.

"Tell me a scary story," the Devil says. "A funny, scary, sad, happy story. I want everything." He can feel his tail wagging as he says this.

"You can't have everything," the cheerleader says, and she picks up his paw and puts it back on the floor of the closet. "Not even in a story. You can't have all the stories you want."

"I know," the Devil says. He whines, "But I still want it. I want things. That's my job. I even want the things that I already have. I want everything you have. I want the things that don't exist. That's why I'm the Devil." He leers, and it's a shame because she can't see him in the dark. He feels silly.

"Well, what's the scariest thing?" says the cheerleader. "You're the expert, right? Give me a little help here."

"The scariest thing," the Devil says. "Okay, I'll give you two things. Three things. No, just two. The third one is a secret."

The Devil's voice changes. Later on, one day the cheerleader will be listening to a preschool teacher say back the alphabet, with the sun moving across the window, nothing ever stays still, and she'll be reminded of the Devil and the closet and the line of light under the door, the peaceful little circle of light the flashlight makes against the closet door.

The Devil says, "I'm not complaining," (but he is) "but here's the way things used to work. They don't work this way anymore. I don't know if you remember. Your parents are dead and they're coming home in just a few hours. Used to be, that was scary. Not anymore. But try to imagine: finding something that shouldn't be there."

"Like what?" the cheerleader says.

The Devil shrugs. "A child's toy. A ball, or a night-light. Some cheap bit of trash, but it's heavier than it looks, or else light. It shines with a greasy sort of light or else it eats light. When you touch it, it yields unpleasantly. You feel as if you might fall into it. You feel light-headed. It might be inscribed in a language which no one can decipher."

"Okay," the cheerleader says. She seems somewhat cheered up. "So what's the next thing?"

The Devil shines the flashlight in her eyes, flicks it on and off. "Someone disappears. Gone, just like that. They're standing behind you in a line at an amusement park—or they wander away during the intermission of a play—perhaps they go downstairs to get the mail—or to make tea—"

"That's scary?" the cheerleader says.

"Used to be," the Devil says. "It used to be that the worst thing that could happen was, if you had kids, and one of them died or disappeared. Disappeared was the worst. Anything might have happened to them."

"Things are better now," the cheerleader says.

"Yes, well." The Devil says, "Things just get better and better nowadays. But—try to remember how it was. The person who disappeared, only they didn't. You'd see them from time to time, peeking in at you through windows, or down low through the mail slot in your front door. Keyholes. You might see them in the grocery store. Sitting in the backseat of your car, down low, slouching in your rearview mirror. They might pinch your leg or pull your hair when you're asleep. When you talk on the phone, they listen in, you hear them listening."

The cheerleader says, "Like, with my parents—"

"Exactly," says the Devil. "You've had nightmares about them, right?"

"Not really," the cheerleader says. "Everyone says they were probably nice people. I mean, look at this house! But, sometimes, I have this dream that I'm at the mall, and I see my husband. And he's just the same, he's a grownup, and he doesn't recognize me. It turns out that I'm the only one who's going backwards. And then he does recognize me and he wants to know what I've done with the kids."

The last time she'd seen her husband, he was trying to grow a beard. He couldn't even do that right. He hadn't had much to say, but they'd looked at each other for a long time.

"What about your children?" the Devil says. "Do you wonder where they went when the doctor pushed them back up inside you? Do you have dreams about them?"

"Yes," the cheerleader says. "Everything gets smaller. I'm afraid of that."

"Think how men feel!" the Devil says. "It's no wonder men are afraid of women. No wonder sex is so hard on them."

The cheerleader misses sex, that feeling afterwards, that blissful, unsatisfied itch.

"The first time around, things were better," the Devil says. "I don't know if you remember. People died, and no one was sure what happened next. There were all sorts of possibilities. Now everyone knows everything. What's the fun in that?"

Someone is trying to push open the closet door, but the cheerleader puts her feet against it, leaning against the back of the closet. "Oh, I remember!" she says. "I remember when I was dead! There was so much I was looking forward to. I had no idea!"

The Devil shivers. He's never liked dead people much.

"So, okay, what about monsters?" the cheerleader says. "Vampires? Serial killers? People from outer space? Those old movies?"

The Devil shrugs. "Yeah, sure. Boogeymen. Formaldehyde babies in Mason jars. Someday someone is going to have to take them out of the jar, unpickle them. Women with teeth down there. Zombies. Killer robots, killer bees, serial killers, cold spots, werewolves. The dream where you know that you're asleep but you can't wake up. You can hear someone walking around the bedroom picking up your things and putting them down again and you still can't wake up. The end of the world. Spiders. *No one was with her when she died.* Carnivorous plants."

"Oh goody," the cheerleader says. Her eyes shine at him out of the dark. Her pompoms slide across the floor of the closet. He moves his flashlight so he can see her hands.

"So here's your story," the cheerleader says. She's a girl who can think on her feet. "It's not really a scary story. I don't really get scary."

"Weren't you listening?" the Devil says. He taps the flashlight against his big front teeth. "Never mind, it's okay, never mind. Go on."

"This probably isn't a true story," the cheerleader says. "And it doesn't go backwards like we do. I probably won't get all the way to the end, and I'm not going to start at the beginning, either. There isn't enough time."

"That's fine," the Devil says. "I'm all ears." (He is.)

The cheerleader says, "So who's going to tell this story, anyway? Be quiet and listen. We're running out of time."

She says, "A man comes home from a sales conference. He and his wife have been separated for a while, but they've decided to try living together again. They've sold the house that they used to live in. Now they live just outside of town, in an old house in an orchard.

"The man comes home from this business conference, and his wife is sitting in the kitchen and she's talking to another woman, an older woman. They're sitting on the chairs that used to go around the kitchen table, but the table is gone. So is the microwave, and the rack where Susan's copper-bottomed pots hang. The pots are gone, too.

"The husband doesn't notice any of this. He's busy looking at the other woman. Her skin has a greenish tinge. He has this feeling that he knows her. She and the wife both look at the husband, and he suddenly knows what it is. It's his wife. It's his wife, two of her, only one is maybe twenty years older. Otherwise, except that this one's green, they're identical: same eyes, same mouth, same little mole at the corner of her mouth.

"How am I doing so far?"

"So-so," the Devil says. The truth (the truth makes the Devil itchy) is, he only likes stories about himself. Like the story about the Devil's wedding cake. Now that's a story.

The cheerleader says, "It gets better."

IT GETS BETTER

The man's name is Ed. It isn't his real name. I made it up. Ed and Susan have been married for ten years, separated for five months, back together again for three months. They've been sleeping in the same bed for three months, but they don't have sex. Susan cries whenever Ed kisses her. They don't have any kids. Susan used to have a younger brother. Ed is thinking about getting a dog.

While Ed's been at his conference, Susan has been doing some housework. She's done some work up in the attic which we won't talk about. Not yet. Down in the spare bathroom in the basement, she's set up this machine, which we get around to later, and this machine makes Susans. What Susan was hoping for was a machine that would bring back Andrew. (Her brother. But you knew that.) Only it turns out that getting Andrew back requires a different machine, a bigger machine. Susan needs help making that machine, and so the new Susans are going to come in handy after all. Over the course of the next few days, the Susans explain all this to Ed.

Susan doesn't expect Ed will be very helpful.

"Hi, Ed," the older, greenish Susan says. She gets up from her chair and gives him a big hug. Her skin is warm, tacky. She smells yeasty. The original Susan—the Susan Ed thinks is original, and I have no idea if he's right about this, and, later on, he isn't so sure, either—sits in her chair and watches them.

Big green Susan: am I making her sound like Godzilla? She doesn't look like Godzilla, and yet there's something about her that reminds Ed of Godzilla, the way she stomps across the kitchen floor—leads Ed over to a chair and makes him sit down. Now he realizes that the kitchen table is gone. He still hasn't managed to say a word. Susan, both of them, is used to this.

"First of all," Susan says, "the attic is off limits. There are some people working up there. (I don't mean Susans. I'll explain Susans in a minute.) Some visitors. They're helping me with a project. About the other Susans, there are five of me presently—you'll meet the other three later. They're down in the basement. You're allowed in the basement. You can help down there, if you want."

Godzilla Susan says, "You don't have to worry about who is who, although none of us are exactly alike. You can call us all Susan. We're discovering that some of us may be more temporary than others, or fatter, or younger, or greener. It seems to depend on the batch."

"Are you Susan?" Ed says. He corrects himself. "I mean, are you my wife? The real Susan?"

"We're all your wife," the younger Susan says. She puts her hand on his leg, and pats him like a dog.

"Where did the kitchen table go?" Ed says.

"I put it in the attic," Susan says. "You really don't have to worry about that now. How was your conference?"

Another Susan comes into the kitchen. She's young and the color of green apples or new grass. Even the whites of her eyes are grassy. She's maybe nineteen, and the color of her skin makes Ed think of a snake. "Ed!" she says. "How was the conference?"

"They're keen on the new game," Ed says. "It tests real well."

"Want a beer?" Susan says. (It doesn't matter which Susan says this.) She picks up a pitcher of green foamy stuff, and pours it into a glass.

"This is beer?" Ed says.

"It's Susan beer," Susan says, and all the Susans laugh.

The beautiful snake-colored nineteen-year-old Susan takes Ed on a tour of the house. Mostly Ed just looks at Susan, but he sees that the television is gone, and so are all of his games. All his notebooks. The living room sofa is still there, but all the seat cushions are missing. Later on, Susan will disassemble the sofa with an axe.

Susan has covered up all the downstairs windows with what looks like sheets of aluminum foil. She shows him the bathtub downstairs where one of the Susans is brewing the Susan beer. Other Susans are hanging long, mossy clots of the Susan beer on laundry racks. Dry, these clots can be shaped into bedding, nests for the new Susans. They are also edible.

Ed is still holding the glass of Susan beer. "Go on," Susan says. "You like beer."

"I don't like green beer," Ed says.

"You like Susan, though," Susan says. She's wearing one of his T-shirts, and a pair of Susan's underwear. No bra. She puts Ed's hand on her breast.

Susan stops stirring the beer. She's taller than Ed, and only a little bit green. "You know Susan loves you," she says.

"Who's up in the attic?" Ed says. "Is it Andrew?"

His hand is still on Susan's breast. He can feel her heart beating. Susan says, "You can't tell Susan I told you. She doesn't think you're ready. It's the aliens."

They both stare at him. "She finally got them on the phone. This is going to be huge, Ed. This is going to change the world."

Ed could leave the house. He could leave Susan. He could refuse to drink the beer.

The Susan beer doesn't make him drunk. It isn't really beer. You knew that, right?

There are Susans everywhere. Some of them want to talk to Ed about their marriage, or about the aliens, or sometimes they want to talk about Andrew. Some of them are busy working. The Susans are always dragging Ed off to empty rooms, to talk or kiss or make love or gossip about the other Susans. Or they're ignoring him. There's one very young Susan. She looks like she might be six or seven years old. She goes up and down the upstairs hallway, drawing on the walls with a marker. Ed isn't sure whether this is childish vandalism or important Susan work. He feels awkward asking.

Every once in a while, he thinks he sees the real Susan. He wishes he could sit down and talk with her, but she always looks so busy.

By the end of the week, there aren't any mirrors left in the house, and the windows are all covered up. The Susans have hung sheets of the Susan beer over all the light fixtures, so everything is green. Ed isn't sure, but he thinks he might be turning green.

Susan tastes green. She always does.

Once Ed hears someone knocking on the front door. "Ignore that," Susan says, as she walks past him. She's carrying the stacked blades of an old ceiling fan, and a string of Christmas lights. "It isn't important."

Ed pulls the plug of aluminum foil out of the eyehole, and peeks out. Stan is standing there, looking patient. They stand there, Ed on one side of the door, and Stan on the other. Ed doesn't open the door, and eventually Stan goes away. All the peacocks are kicking up a fuss.

Ed tries teaching some of the Susans to play poker. It doesn't work so well, because it turns out that the Susans all know what cards the other Susans are holding. So Ed makes up a game where that doesn't matter so much, but in the end, it makes him feel too lonely. There aren't any other Eds.

They decide to play spin-the-bottle instead. Instead of a bottle, they use a hammer, and the head never ends up pointing at Ed. After a while, it gets too strange watching Susan kiss Susans, and he wanders off to look for a Susan who will kiss him.

Up in the second-story bedroom, there are always lots of Susans. This is where they go to wait when they start to get ripe. The Susans loll, curled in their nests, getting riper, arguing about the end of some old story. None of them remember it the same way. Some of them don't seem to know anything about it, but they all have opinions.

Ed climbs into a nest and leans back. Susan swings her legs over to make room for him. This Susan is small and round. She tickles the soft part of his arm, and then tucks her face into his side.

Susan passes him a glass of Susan beer.

"That's not it," Susan says. "It turns out that he overdosed. Maybe even did it on purpose. We couldn't talk about it. There weren't enough of us. We were trying to carry all that sadness all by ourself. You can't do something like that! And then the wife tries to kill him. I tried to kill him. She kicks the fuck out of him. He can't leave the house for a week, won't even come to the door when his friends come over."

"If you can call them friends," Susan says.

"No, there was a gun," Susan says. "And she has an affair. Because she can't get over it. Neither of them can."

"She humiliates him at a dinner party," Susan says. "They both drink too much. Everybody goes home, and she breaks all the dishes instead of washing them. There are plate shards all over the kitchen floor. Someone's going to get hurt; they don't have a time machine. We knew that they still love each other, but that doesn't matter anymore. Then the police showed up."

"Well, that's not the way I remember it," Susan says. "But I guess it could have happened that way."

Ed and Susan used to buy books all the time. They had so many books they used to joke about wanting to be quarantined, or snowed in. Maybe then they'd manage to read all the books. But the books have all gone up to the attic, along with the lamps and the coffee tables, and their bicycles, and all Susan's paintings. Ed has watched the Susans carry up paperback books, silverware, old board games, and musical instruments. Even a kazoo. *The Encyclopedia Britannica*. The goldfish and the goldfish bowl and the little canister of goldfish food.

The Susans have gone through the house, taken everything they could. After all the books were gone, they dismantled the bookshelves. Now they're tearing off the wallpaper in long strips. The aliens seem to like books. They like everything, especially Susan. Eventually when the Susans are ripe, they go up in the attic, too.

The aliens swap things, the books and the Susans and the coffee mugs for other things: machines that the Susans are assembling. Ed would like to get his hand on one of those devices, but Susan says no. He isn't even allowed to help, except with the Susan beer.

The thing the Susans are building takes up most of the living room, Ed's office, the kitchen, the laundry room—

The Susans don't bother with laundry. The washer and the drier are both gone and the Susans have given up wearing clothes altogether. Ed has managed to keep a pair of shorts and a pair of jeans. He's wearing the shorts right now, and he folds the jeans up into a pillow, and rests his head on top of them so that Susan can't steal them. All his other clothes have been carried up to the attic.

—and it's creeping up the stairs, spilling over into the second story. The house is shiny with alien machines.

Teams of naked Susans are hard at work, all day long, testing instruments, hammering and stitching their machine together, polishing and dusting and stacking alien things on top of each other. If you're wondering what the machine looks like, picture a science fair project involving a lot of aluminum foil, improvised, homely, makeshift, and just a little dangerous-looking. None of the Susans is quite sure what the machine will eventually do. Right now it grows Susan beer.

When the beer is stirred, left alone, stirred some more, it clots and makes more Susans. Ed likes watching this part. The house is more and more full of shy, loud, quiet, talkative, angry, happy, greenish Susans of all sizes, all ages, who work at disassembling the house, piece by piece, and, piece by piece, assembling the machine.

It might be a time machine, or a machine to raise the dead, or maybe the house is becoming a spaceship, slowly, one room at a time. Susan says the aliens don't make these kinds of distinctions. It may be an invasion factory, Ed says, or a doomsday machine. Susan says that they aren't that kind of aliens.

Ed's job: stirring the Susan beer with a long, flat plank—a floor board Susan pried up—and skimming the foam, which has a stringy, unpleasantly cheese-like consistency, into buckets. He carries the buckets downstairs and makes Susan beer soufflé and Susan beer casserole. Susan beer surprise. Upside-down Susan cake. It all tastes the same, and he grows to like the taste.

The beer doesn't make him drunk. That isn't what it's for. I can't tell you what it's for. But when he's drinking it, he isn't sad. He has the beer, and the work in the kitchen, and the ripe, green fuckery. Everything tastes like Susan.

The only thing he misses is poker nights.

Up in the spare bedroom, Ed falls asleep listening to the Susans talk, and when he wakes up, his jeans are gone, and he's naked. The room is empty. All the ripe Susans have gone up to the attic.

When he steps out into the hall, the little Susan is out there, drawing on the walls. She puts her marker down and hands him a pitcher of Susan beer. She pinches his leg and says, "You're getting nice and ripe."

Then she winks at Ed and runs down the hall.

He looks at what she's been drawing: Andrew. Scribbly crayon portraits of Andrew, all up and down the walls. He follows the pictures of Andrew down the hall, all the way to the master bedroom where he and the original Susan used to sleep. Now he sleeps anywhere, with any Susan. He hasn't been in their room in a while, although he's noticed the Susans going in and out with boxes full of things. The Susans are always shooing at him when he gets in their way.

The bedroom is full of Andrew. There are Susan's portraits of Andrew on the walls, the ones from her art class. Ed had forgotten how unpleasant and peculiar these paintings are. In one, the largest one, Andrew, life-size, has his hands around a small animal, maybe a ferret. He seems to be strangling it. The ferret's mouth is cocked open, showing all its teeth. A picture like that, Ed thinks, you ought to turn it towards the wall at night.

Susan's put Andrew's bed in here, and Andrew's books, and Andrew's desk. Andrew's clothes have been hung up in the closet. There isn't an alien machine in the room, or for that matter, anything that ever belonged to Ed.

Ed puts a pair of Andrew's pants on, and lies down on Andrew's bed, just for a minute, and he closes his eyes.

When he wakes up, Susan is sitting on the bed. He can smell her, that ripe green scent. He can smell that smell on himself. Susan says, "If you're ready, I thought we could go up to the attic together."

"What's going on here?" Ed says. "I thought you needed everything. Shouldn't all this stuff go up to the attic?"

"This is Andrew's room, for when he comes back," Susan says. "We thought it would make him feel comfortable, having his own bed to sleep in. He might need his stuff."

"What if the aliens need his stuff?" Ed says. "What if they can't make you a new Andrew yet because they don't know enough about him?"

"That's not how it works," Susan says. "We're getting close now. Can't you feel it?"

"I feel weird," Ed says. "Something's happening to me."

"You're ripe, Ed," Susan says. "Isn't that fantastic? We weren't sure you'd ever get ripe enough."

She takes his hand and pulls him up. Sometimes he forgets how strong she is.

"So what happens now?" Ed says. "Am I going to die? I don't feel sick. I feel good. What happens when we get ripe?"

The dim light makes Susan look older, or maybe she just *is* older. He likes this part: seeing what Susan looked like as a kid, what she'll look like as an old lady. It's as if they got to spend their whole lives together. "I never know," she says. "Let's go find out. Take off Andrew's pants, and I'll hang them back up in the closet."

They leave the bedroom and walk down the hall. The Andrew drawings, the knobs and dials and stacked, shiny machinery, watch them go. There aren't any other Susans around at the moment. They're all busy downstairs. He can hear them hammering away. For a minute, it's the way it used to be, only better. Just Ed and Susan in their own house.

Ed holds on tight to Susan's hand.

When Susan opens the attic door, the attic is full of stars. Stars and stars and stars. Ed has never seen so many stars. Susan has taken the roof off. Off in the distance, they can smell the apple trees, way down in the orchard.

Susan sits down cross-legged on the floor and Ed sits down beside her. She says, "I wish you'd tell me a story."

Ed says, "What kind of story?"

Susan says, "A bedtime story? When Andrew was a kid, we used to read this book. I remember this one story about people who go under a hill. They spend one night down there, eating and drinking and dancing, but when they come out, a hundred years have gone by. Do you know how long it's been since Andrew died? I've lost track of time."

"I don't know stories like that," Ed says. He picks at his flaky green skin and wonders what he tastes like. "What do you think the aliens look like? Do you think they look like giraffes? Like marbles? Like Andrew? Do you think they have mouths?"

"Don't be silly," Susan says. "They look like us."

"How do you know?" Ed says. "Have you been up here before?"

"No," Susan says. "But Susan has."

"We could play a card game," Ed says. "Or I Spy."

"You could tell me about the first time I met you," Susan says.

"I don't want to talk about that," Ed says. "That's all gone."

"Okay, fine." Susan sits up straight, arches her back, licks her green lips with her green tongue. She winks at Ed and says, "Tell me how beautiful I am."

"You're beautiful," Ed says. "I've always thought you were beautiful. All of you. How about me? Am I beautiful?"

"Don't be sarcastic," Susan says. She slouches back against him. Her skin is warm and greasy. "The aliens are going to get here soon. I don't know what happens after that, but I hate this part. I always hate this part. I don't like waiting. Do you think this is what it was like for Andrew, when he was in rehab?"

"When you get him back, ask him. Why ask me?"

Susan doesn't say anything for a bit. Then she says, "We think we'll be able to make you, too. We're starting to figure out how it works. Eventually it will be you and me and him, just the way it was before. Only we'll fix him the way we've fixed me. He won't be so sad. Have you noticed how I'm not sad any more? Don't you want that, not to be sad? And maybe after that we'll try making some more people. We'll start all over again. We'll do everything right this time."

Ed says, "So why are they helping you?"

"I don't know," Susan says. "Either they think we're funny, or else they think we're pathetic, the way we get stuck. We can ask them when they get here."

She stands up, stretches, yawns, sits back down on Ed's lap, reaches down, stuffs his penis, half-erect, inside of her. Just like that. Ed groans.

He says, "Susan."

Susan says, "Tell me a story." She squirms. "Any story. I don't care what."

"I can't tell you a story," Ed says. "I don't know any stories when you're doing this."

"I'll stop," Susan says. She stops.

Ed says, "Don't stop. Okay." He puts his hands around her waist and moves her, as if he's stirring the Susan beer.

He says, "Once upon a time." He's speaking very fast. They're running out of time.

Once, while they were making love, Andrew came into the bedroom. He didn't even knock. He didn't seem to be embarrassed at all. Ed doesn't want to be fucking Susan when the aliens show up. On the other hand, Ed wants to be fucking Susan forever. He doesn't want to stop, not for Andrew, or the aliens, or even for the end of the world.

Ed says, "There was a man and a woman and they fell in love. They were both nice people. They made a good couple. Everyone liked them. This story is about the woman."

This story is about a woman who is in love with somebody who invents a time machine. He's planning to go so far into the future that he'll end up right back at the very beginning. He asks her to come along, but she doesn't want to go.

What's back at the beginning of the world? Little blobs of life swimming around in a big blob? Adam and Eve in the Garden of Eden? She doesn't want to play Adam and Eve; she has other things to do. She works for a research company. She calls people on the telephone and asks them all sorts of questions. Back at the beginning, there aren't going to be phones. She doesn't like the sound of it. So her husband says, fine, then here's what we'll do. I'll build you another machine, and if you ever decide that you miss me, or you're tired and you can't go on, climb inside this machine—this box right here—and push this button and go to sleep. And you'll sleep all the way forwards and backwards to me, where I'm waiting for you. I'll keep on waiting for you. I love you. And so they make love and they make love a few more times and then he climbs into his time machine and whoosh, he's gone like that. So fast, it's hard to believe that he was ever there at all. Meanwhile she lives her life forward, slow, the way he didn't want to. She gets married again and makes love some more and has kids and they have kids and when she's an old woman, she's finally ready: she climbs into the dusty box down in the secret room under the orchard and she pushes the button and falls asleep. And she sleeps all the way back, just like Sleeping Beauty, down in the orchard for years and years, which fly by like seconds, she goes flying back, past the men sitting around the green felt table, now you can see them, now they're gone again, and all the peacocks are screaming, and the Satanist drives up to the house and unloads the truckload of furniture, he unpaints the pentagrams, soon the old shy man will unbuild his house, carry his secret away on his back, and the apples are back on the orchard trees again, and then the trees are all blooming, and now the woman is getting younger, just a little, the lines around her mouth are smoothing out. She dreams that someone has come down into that underground room and is looking down at her in her time machine. He stands there for a long time. She can't open her eyes, her eyelids are so heavy, she doesn't want to wake up just yet. She dreams she's on a train going down the tracks backwards and behind the train, someone is picking up the beams and the nails and the girders to put in a box and then they'll put the box away. The trees are whizzing past, getting smaller and smaller and then they're all gone too. Now she's a kid again, now she's a baby, now she's much smaller and then she's even smaller than that. She gets her gills back. She doesn't want to wake up just yet, she wants to get right back to the very beginning where it's all new and clean and everything is still and green and flat and sleepy and everybody has crawled back into the sea and they're waiting for her to get back there too and then the party can start. She goes backwards and backwards and backwards and backwards and backwards and backwards and backwards and backwards and backwards and backwards and backwards and backwards—

The cheerleader says to the Devil, "We're out of time. We're holding things up. Don't you hear them banging on the door?"

The Devil says, "You didn't finish the story."

The cheerleader says, "And you never let me touch your tail. Besides, there isn't any ending. I could make up something, but it wouldn't ever satisfy you. You said that yourself! You're never satisfied. And I have to get on with my life. My parents are going to be home soon."

She stands up and slips out of the closet and slams the door shut again, so fast the Devil can hardly believe it. A key turns in a lock.

The Devil tries the doorknob, and someone standing outside the closet giggles.

"Shush," says the cheerleader. "Be quiet."

"What's going on?" the Devil says. "Open the door and let me out—this isn't funny."

"Oh, I'll let you out," the cheerleader says, "eventually. Not just yet. You have to give me something first."

"You want me to give you something?" the Devil says. "Okay, what?" He rattles the knob, testing.

"I want a happy beginning," the cheerleader says. "I want my friends to be happy too. I want to get along with my parents. I want a happy childhood. I want things to get better. I want them to keep getting better. I want you to be nice to me. I want to be famous, I don't know, maybe I could be a child actor, or win state-level spelling bees, or even just cheer for winning teams. I want world peace. Second chances. When I'm winning at poker, I don't want to have to put all that money back in the pot, I don't want to have to put my good cards back on top of the deck, one by one by—

Starlight says, "Sorry about that. My voice is getting scratchy. It's late. You should call back tomorrow night."

Ed says, "When can I call you?"

Stan and Andrew were friends. Good friends. It was like they were the same species. Ed hadn't seen Stan for a while, not for a long while, but Stan stopped him, on the way down to the basement. This was earlier. Stan grabbed his arm and said, "I miss him. I keep thinking, if I'd gotten there sooner. If I'd said something. He liked you a lot, you know, he was sorry about what happened to your car—"

Stan stops talking and just stands there looking at Ed. He looks like he's about to cry.

"It's not your fault," Ed said, but then he wondered why he'd said it. Whose fault was it?

Susan says, "You've got to stop calling me, Ed. Okay? It's three in the morning. I was asleep, Ed, I was having the best dream. You're always waking me up in the middle of things. Please just stop, okay?"

Ed doesn't say anything. He could stay there all night and just listen to Susan talk.

What she's saying now, is, "But that's never going to happen, and you know it. Something bad happened, and it wasn't anyone's fault, but we're just never going to get past it. It killed us. We can't even talk about it."

Ed says, "I love you."

Susan says, "I love you, but it's not about love, Ed, it's about timing. It's too late, and it's always going to be too late. Maybe if we could go back and do everything differently—and I think about that all the time—but we can't. We don't know anybody with a time machine. How about this, Ed—maybe you and your poker buddies can build one down in Pete's basement. All those stupid games, Ed! Why can't you build a time-machine instead? Call me back when you've figured out how we can work this out, because I'm really stuck. Or don't call me back. Goodbye, Ed. Go get some sleep. I'm hanging up the phone now."

Susan hangs up the phone.

Ed imagines her, going down to the kitchen to microwave a glass of milk. She'll sit in the kitchen and drink her milk and wait for him to call her back. He lies in bed, up in the orchard house. He's got both bedroom doors open, and a night breeze comes in through that door that doesn't go anywhere. He wishes he could get Susan to come see that door. The breeze smells like apples, which is what time must smell like, Ed thinks.

There's an alarm clock on the floor beside his bed. The hands and numbers glow green in the dark, and he'll wait five minutes and then he'll call Susan. Five minutes. Then he'll call her back. The hands aren't moving, but he can wait.

KIM NEWMAN

Egyptian Avenue

Kim Newman has worked extensively in the theater, radio, and television as a novelist, critic, and broadcaster. His most recent novels include Anno Dracula, Judgment of Tears: Anno Dracula 1959 *(aka* Dracula Cha Cha Cha*), and* Life's Lottery. *Under the name Jack Yeovil, he has written a series of gaming novels including* Genevieve Undead *and* Orgy of the Blood Parasites. *His short stories are collected in* The Original Dr. Shade and Other Stories, Famous Monsters, Seven Stars, *and* Where the Bodies Are Buried.

His nonfiction books include Millennium Movies: End of the World Cinema *and* BFI Classics: Cat People. *He has won the Bram Stoker Award, the British Science Fiction Award for Best Short Fiction, the Children of the Night Award, the Fiction Award of the Lord Ruthven Assembly, and the International Horror Critics' Guild Award for Best Novel (twice). He's been working on* An English Ghost Story, *simultaneously as a novel and a movie script, and seems to have been sidetracked into writing more odd film projects.*

Kim Newman says: " 'Egyptian Avenue' is an entry in a series of 1970s–set occult/sf/mystery stories I've been working at on and off since 'End of the Pier Show.' Richard Jeperson has also appeared in 'You Don't Have to Be Mad,' 'Seven Stars: The Biafran Bank Manager,' and 'Tomorrow Town'; for my entry in the revived Night Visions series, I've written 'Swellhead,' a novella that brings Jeperson's story up to the present day, though I've still not solved all the ongoing mysteries. 'Egyptian Avenue' was written for Embrace the Mutation, *a collection in which writers were given their pick of pre-existing J. K. Potter illustrations and asked to write something inspired by one of them. I assume from the picture I chose that J. K. once took the same tour of Highgate Cemetery that I did—the old one, not the one where Karl Marx is buried."*

And how could anyone resist a story that contains the phrase: "glam rock ghouls gutting groupies at the Glastonbury Festival"? Now, I ask you!

—E. D.

This tomb's leaking sand," said Fred Regent. "And beetles."

Fine white stuff, hourglass quality not bucket and spade material, seeped from a vertical crack, fanning out around and between clumps of lush, long green grass. Black bugs glittered in morning sunlight, hornlike protrusions rooting through the overgrowth, sand-specks stuck to their carapaces. Fred looked up at the face of the tomb, which was framed by faux-Egyptian columns. The name BUNNING was cut deep into the stone, hemmed around by weather-beaten hieroglyphs.

It was the summer of 197-. Fred Regent, late of the Metropolitan Constabulary, was again adventuring with the supernatural. As before, his guide off life's beaten track was Richard Jeperson, the most resourceful agent of the Diogenes Club, which remained the least-known branch of Britain's intelligence and police services. All the anomalies came down to Jeperson. Last month, it had been glam rock ghouls gutting groupies at the Glastonbury Festival and an obeah curse on Prime Minister Edward Heath hatched somewhere inside his own cabinet; this morning, it was ghosts in Kingstead Cemetery.

Jeperson, something of an anomaly himself, scooped up a handful of sand and looked down his hawk nose at a couple of fat bugs.

"Were we on the banks of the great river Nile rather than on a pleasant hill overlooking the greater city of London," said Jeperson, "I shouldn't be surprised to come across these little fellows. As it is, I'm flummoxed. These, Fred, are *scarabus* beetles."

"I saw *Curse of the Mummy's Tomb* at the Rialto, Richard. I know what a scarab is."

Jeperson laughed, deepening creases in his tanned forehead and cheeks. His smile lifted black moustaches and showed sharp teeth-points. The Man from the Diogenes Club sounded as English as James Mason, but when suntanned he looked more like an Arab, or a Romany disguised as Charles II. His mass of black ringlets was not a wig, though. And no gypsy would dress as gaudily as Richard Jeperson.

"Of course you do, Fred. I elucidate for the benefit of exposition. Thinking out loud. That is Sahara sand and these are North African beasties."

"Absolutely, Guv'nor. And that bloody big dead one there is a scorpion."

Jeperson looked down with amused distaste. The scorpion twitched, scuttled and was squashed under Jeperson's foot.

"Not so dead, Fred."

"Is now."

"Let us hope so."

Jeperson considered his sole, then scraped the evil crushed thing off on a chunk of old headstone.

For this expedition to darkest N6, he wore a generously bloused, leopard-pattern safari jacket and tight white, high-waisted britches tucked into sturdy fell-walker's boots. His ensemble included a turquoise Sam Browne belt (with pouches full of useful implements and substances), a tiger's-fang amulet that was supposed to protect against evil, and an Australian bush hat with three corks dangling from the rim. Champagne corks, each marked with a date in felt-tip pen.

"The term for a thing so out of place is, as we all know, an 'apport,' " said Jeperson. "Unless some peculiar person has for reasons unknown placed sand, scarabs and scorps in our path for the purpose of puzzlement, we must conclude that they have materialized for some supernatural reason. Mr. Lillywhite, this is your belief, is it not? This is yet another manifestation of the spookery you have reported?"

Lillywhite nodded. He was a milk-skinned, fair-haired middle-aged man with burning red cheeks and a peacocktail-pattern smock. His complaint had been passed from the police to the Diogenes Club, and then fielded to Jeperson.

"What is all this doing here?" asked Vanessa, Jeperson's other assistant—the one everyone noticed before realizing Fred was in the room. The tall, model-beautiful redhead wore huge sunglasses with swirly mint-and-yellow patterns on the lenses and frames, a sari-like arrangement of silk scarves that exposed a ruby winking in her navel, and stack-heeled cream leather go-go boots. Beside the other two, Fred felt a bit underdressed in his Fred Perry and Doc Martens.

"Appearing supernaturally, I should say, Vanessa," said Jeperson. "That's generally what apports do."

"Not just the apports," she went on. "All the obelisks and sphinxes. Oughtn't this to be in the Valley of the Kings, not buried under greenery in London North Six?"

Jeperson dropped the sand and let the scarabs scuttle where they might. He brushed his palms together.

Vanessa was right. Everything in this section of Kingstead Cemetery was tricked out with Ancient Egyptian statuary and design features. The Bunning tomb was guarded by two human-headed stone lions in pharaonic headdresses. Their faces had weathered as badly in a century as the original sphinx in millennia. All around were miniature sandstone pyramids and temples, animal-headed deities, faded blue and gold hieroglyphs and ankh-shaped gravestones.

"I can explain that, Miss . . . ah?" said Lillywhite.

"Vanessa. Just Vanessa."

"Vanessa, fine," said the scholarly caretaker, segueing into a tour guide speech. "The motif dates back to the establishment of the cemetery in 1839. Stephen Geary, the original architect, had a passion for Egyptiana which was shared by the general public of his day. From the first, the Cemetery was planned not just as a place for burying the dead but a species of a morbid tourist attraction. Victorians were rather more given to visiting dead relatives than we are. It was expected that whole families would come to picnic by grandmama's grave."

"If my gran were dead, we'd certainly have a picnic," said Fred. Lillywhite looked a little shocked. "Well, you don't know my gran," Fred explained.

"They held black-crepe birthday parties for the many children who died in infancy," the caretaker continued, "with solemn games and floral presents. Siblings annually gathered around marble babies well into their own old age. It's not easy to start a graveyard from scratch, especially at what you might call the top end of the market. Cemeteries are supposed to be old. For a Victorian to be laid to rest in a new one would be like you or me being bundled into a plastic bag and ploughed under a motorway extension."

"That's more or less what Fred has planned," said Jeperson.

"I can't say I'm surprised. To circumvent the prejudice, Geary decided to trade on associations with ancient civilizations. If his cemetery couldn't be instantly old, then at least it would look old. This area is Egyptian Avenue. Geary himself is buried here. Originally, there were three such sections, with a Roman Avenue and a Grecian Avenue completing the set. But the fashionable had a craze for

Egypt. The Roman and Grecian Avenues were abandoned and overtaken. It was no real scholarly interest in Egyptology, by the way, just an enthusiasm for the styles. Some of the gods you see represented aren't even real, just made up to fit in with the pantheon. A historian might draw a parallel between Ancient Egyptian obsession with funerary rites and the Victorian fascination with the aesthetics of death."

Fred thought anyone who chose to spend his life looking after a disused cemetery must have nurtured some of that obsession himself. Lillywhite was an unsalaried amateur, a local resident who was a booster for this forgotten corner of the capital.

"It's certainly ancient now," said Fred. "Falling to pieces."

"Regrettably so. Victorian craftsmen were good on surface, but skimped everything else. Artisans knew the customers would all be too dead to complain and cut a lot of corners. Impressive stone fronts, but crumbling at the back. Statues that dissolve to lumps after fifty years in the rain. Tombs with strong corners but weak roofs. By the 1920s, when the original site was full and children and grandchildren of the first tenants were in their own grave-plots, everything had fallen into disrepair. When the United Cemetery Company went bust in the early '60s, Kingstead was more or less abandoned. Our historical society has been trying to raise money for restoration and repair work. With not much luck, as yet."

"Put me down for fifty quid," said Jeperson.

Fred wasn't sure if restoration and repair would improve the place. The tombs had been laid out to a classical plan like miniature pyramids or cathedrals, and serpentine pathways wound between them. Uncontrolled shrubbery and ivy swarmed everywhere, clogging the paths, practically burying the stonework. A broken-winged angel soared from a nearby rhododendron, face scraped eyeless. It was the dead city of a lost civilization, like something from Rider Haggard. Nature had crept back, green tendrils undermining thrones and palaces, and was slowly taking the impertinent erections of a passing humanity back into her leafy bosom.

"This is the source of your haunting?" asked Jeperson, nodding at the Bunning tomb.

Fred had forgotten for a moment why they were here.

"It seems to be."

There had been a great deal of ghostly activity. Yesterday, Fred had gone to the newspaper library in Colindale and looked over a hundred and twenty years of wails in the night and alarmed courting couples. As burial grounds went, Kingstead Cemetery was rather sporadically haunted. Until the last three months, when spooks had been running riot with bells and whistles on. A newsagent's across the road had been pelted with a rain of lightning-charged pebbles. A physical culture enthusiast had been knocked off his bicycle by ectoplasmic tentacles. And there had been a lot of sightings.

Jeperson considered the Bunning tomb. Fred saw he was letting down his guard, trying to sense what was disturbed in the vicinity. Jeperson was a sensitive.

"According to your report, Lillywhite, our spectral visitors have run the whole gamut. Disembodied sounds . . ."

"Like jackals," said Lillywhite. "I was in Suez in '56. I know what a jackal sounds like."

". . . phantom figures . . ."

"Mummies, with bandages. Hawk-headed humans. Ghostly barges. Crawling severed hands."

". . . and now, physical presences. To whit: the scarabs and other nasties. Even the sand. It's still warm, by the way. Does anyone else detect a theme here?"

"Spirits of Ancient Egypt," suggested Vanessa.

Jeperson shot her a finger-gun. "You have it."

Fred would have shivered, only . . .

"Richard, isn't there something funny here?" he said. "A themed haunting? It's a bit Hammer Horror, isn't it? I mean, this place may be done up with Egyptian tat but it's still North London. You can see the Post Office Tower from here. Whoever is buried in this tomb . . ."

"Members of the Bunning Family," put in Lillywhite. "The publishing house. Bunning and Company, Pyramid Press. You can see their offices from here. That black building, the one that looks like the monolith in *2001: A Space Odyssey*. It's called the Horus Tower."

Fred knew the skyscraper, but had never realized who owned it.

"Yes, them. The Bunnings. They were just Victorians who liked the idea of a few hierogylphs and cat-headed birds in the way they might have liked striped wallpaper or a particular cut of waistcoat. You said it was a fashion, a craze. So why have we got authentic Egyptian ghosts, just as if there were some evil high priest or mad pharaoh in there."

"George Oldrid Bunning was supposedly buried in a proper Egyptian sarcophagus," said Lillywhite. "It was even said that he went through the mummification process."

"Brains through the nose, liver and lights in canoptic jars?"

"Yes, Mr. Jeperson. Indeed."

"That would have been irregular?"

"In 1897? Yes."

"I withdraw my objection," said Fred. "Old Bunning was clearly a loon. You might expect loon ghosts."

Jeperson was on his knees, looking at the sand. The scarabs were gone now, scuttling across London in advance of a nasty surprise come the first frost.

"I've been trying to get in touch with the descendants for a while," said Lillywhite. "Even before all this fuss. I was hoping they might sponsor restoration of the Bunning tomb. The current head of the family is George Rameses Bunning. He must maintain the family interest in Egypt, or at least his parents did. It appears George Rameses has his own troubles."

"So I'd heard," said Jeperson. "All dynasties must fail, I suppose."

Fred had vaguely heard of the Bunnings but couldn't remember where.

"Pyramid Press are magazine publishers," said Jeperson, answering the unspoken query. "You've heard of *Stunna*."

Vanessa made a face.

Stunna was supposedly a blokes' answer to *Cosmopolitan*, with features about fast cars and sport and (especially) sex. It ran glossy pictures of girls not naked enough to get into *Playboy* but nevertheless unclad enough for you not to want your mum knowing you looked at them. The magazine had launched last year with a lot of publicity, then been attacked with a couple of libel suits from a rival publisher they had made nasty jokes about, Derek Leech of the *Daily Comet. Stunna* had just ceased publication, probably taking the company down with it. Fred realized he had heard of George Rameses Bunning after all. He was doomed to be dragged into bankruptcy and ruin, throwing a lot of people out of work. The scraps of his company would probably be gobbled up by the litigious Leech, which may well have been the point.

"Bunning and Company once put out *British Pluck* and *The Halfpenny Marvel*," said Jeperson. "Boy's papers. At their height of popularity between the wars. And dozens of other titles over the years. Mostly sensation stuff. Generations of lads were raised on the adventures of Jack Dauntless, RN, and the scientific vigilante, Dr. Shade. I think the masthead of *Stunna* bears the sad legend 'incorporating *British Pluck*.' "

"You think there's a tie-in," said Fred. "With all the pluck business. It's a penny dreadful curse."

Jeperson's brow furrowed. He was having one of his "feelings," which usually meant bad news for anyone within hailing distance.

"More than that, Fred. I sense something very nasty here. An old cruelty that lingers. Also, this is one of those "hey, look at me" hauntings. It's as if our phantoms were trying to tell us something, to issue a warning."

"Then why start making a fuss in the last month? Any ghosts around here must have been planted . . ."

"Discorporated, Fred."

"Yes, that . . . they must have been dead for eighty years. Why sit quietly all that time but kick up a row this summer?"

"Maybe they object to something topical," suggested Vanessa. "Like what's Top of the Pops?"

"It's not dreadful enough to be after the Bay City Rollers, luv," said Fred.

"Good point."

Jeperson considered the Bunning tomb, and stroked his 'tache.

Fred looked around. The cemetery afforded a pleasant green dappling of shadow, and swathes of sunstruck grass. But Jeperson was right. Something very nasty was here.

"Vanessa," said Jeperson. "Pass the crowbar. I think we should unseal this tomb."

"But . . ." put in the startled Lillywhite.

Jeperson tapped his tiger fang, "Have no fear of curses, man. This will shield us all."

"It's not that . . . this is private property."

"I won't tell if you don't. Besides, you've already established that George Rameses Bunning has less than no interest in the last resting place of his ancestors. Who else could possibly object?"

"I'm supposed to be a guardian of this place."

"Come on. Haven't you ever wanted to open one of these tombs up and poke around inside?"

"The original Mr. Bunning is supposed to have had an authentic Egyptian funeral. He might be surrounded by his treasures."

"A bicycle to pedal into the afterlife? Golden cigar cuspidors? Ornamental funerary gaslamps?"

"Very likely."

"Then we shall be Howard Carter and Lord Carnaervon."

Fred thought that wasn't a happy parallel. Hadn't there been an effective curse on the tomb of King Tutankamun?

Vanessa produced a crowbar from her BOAC hold-all. She was always prepared for any eventualities.

Fred thought he should volunteer, but Jeperson took the tool and slipped it into a crack. He strained and the stone didn't shift.

"Superior workmanship, Lillywhite. No skimping here."

Jeperson heaved again. The stone advanced an inch, and more sand cascaded. Something chittered inside.

Vanessa had a trowel. She cleared some of the sand and picked out dried-up mortar.

"Good girl," said Jeperson.

He heaved again. The bottom half of the stone cracked through completely, then fell out of the doorway. The top-half slid down in grooves and broke in two pieces. A lot more sand avalanched.

Fred tugged Lillywhite out of the way. Jeperson and Vanessa had already stepped aside.

A scarecrow-thin human figure stood in the shifting sands, hands raised as if to thump, teeth bared in a gruesome grin. It pitched forward on its face and broke apart like a poorly-made dummy. If it were a guy, it would not earn a penny from the most intimidated or kindly passerby.

"That's not George Oldrid Bunning," gasped Lillywhite.

"No," said Jeperson. "I rather fear that it's his butler."

There were five of them, strewn around the stone sarcophagus, bundles of bones in browned wrappings.

"A butler, a footman, a cook, a housekeeper and a maid," said Jeperson. Under his tan, he was pale. He held himself rigidly, so that he wouldn't shake with rage and despair. He understood this sort of horror all too well—having lost the memory of a boyhood torn away in a Nazi camp—but never got used to it.

The servant bodies wore the remains of uniforms.

Lillywhite was upset. He was sitting on the grass, with his head between his knees.

Vanessa, less sensitive than Jeperson, was looking about the tomb with a torch.

"It's a good size," she called out. "Extensive foundations."

"They were alive," bleated Lillywhite.

"For a while," said Jeperson.

"What a bastard," said Fred. "Old George Oldrid Bunning. He got his pharaoh's funeral all right, with all his servants buried alive to shine his boots and tug their forelocks through all eternity. How did he do it?"

"Careful planning," said Jeperson. "And a total lack of scruples."

Lillywhite looked up. He concentrated, falling back on expertise to damp down the shock.

"It was a special design. When he was dying, George Oldrid contracted a master-mason to create his tomb. It's the only one here that's survived substantially intact. The mason died before Bunning. Suspiciously."

"Pharaohs had their architects killed, to preserve the secrets of their tombs from grave robbers. There were all kinds of traps in the pyramids, to discourage looters."

A loud noise came from inside the tomb. Something snapping shut with a clang.

Jeperson's cool vanished.

"Vanessa?" he shouted.

Vanessa came out of the tomb, hair awry and pinned back by her raised sunglasses. She had a nasty graze on her knee.

"I'm fine," she said. "Nothing a tot won't cure."

She found a silver flask in her hold-all and took a swallow, then passed it round. Fred took a jolting shot of brandy.

"Who'd leave a man-trap in a tomb? Coiled steel, with enough tensile strength after a century to bisect a poor girl, or at least take her leg off, if she didn't have a dancer's reflexes."

"George Oldrid Bunning," said Jeperson.

"Bastard General," clarified Fred.

"Just so. He must have been the *bastardo di tutti bastardi*. It would have been in the will that he be laid personally to rest by his servants, with no other witnesses, at dead of night. They were probably expecting healthy bequests. The sad, greedy lot. When closed, the sarcophagus lid triggered a mechanism and the stone door slammed down. Forever, or at least until Vanessa and her crowbar. The tomb is soundproof. Weatherproof. Escapeproof."

"There's treasure," said Vanessa. "Gold and silver. Some Egyptian things. Genuine, I think. Ushabti figures, a death-mask. A lot of it is broken. The downstairs mob must have tried to improvise tools. Not that it did them any good."

The now-shattered stone door showed signs of ancient scratching. But the breaks were new, and clean.

"How long did they . . . ?"

"Best not to think of it, Lillywhite," said Jeperson.

"In death, they got strong," said Vanessa. "They finally cracked the door, or we'd never have been able to shift it."

The little maid, tiny skull in a mobcap, was especially disturbing. She couldn't have been more than fourteen.

"No wonder the ghosts have been making a racket," said Fred. "If someone did that to me, I'd give nobody any rest until it was made right."

Jeperson tapped his front tooth, thinking.

"But why wait until now? As you said, they've had a hundred years in which to manifest their understandable ire. And why the Egyptian thing? Shouldn't they be Victorian servant ghosts? I should think an experience like being buried alive by a crackpot with a King Tut complex would sour one on ancient cultures in general and Egypt in particular."

"They're trying to tell us something," said Vanessa.

"Sharp girl. Indeed they are."

Fred looked away from the tomb. Across the city.

The Horus Tower caught the light. It was a black glass block, surmounted by a gold pyramid.

"George Rameses Bunning is dying," said Lillywhite. "A recurrence of some tropical disease. News got out just after Derek Leech Incorporated started suing Pyramid Press. It's had a disastrous effect on the company stock. He's liable to die broke."

"If he's anything like his great-great, then he deserves it," said Vanessa.

Jeperson snapped his fingers.

"I think he's a lot like his great-great. And I know what the ghosts have been trying to tell us. Quick, Fred, get the Rolls. Vanessa, ring Inspector Price at New Scotland Yard, and have him meet us at the Horus Tower immediately. He might want to bring a lot of hearty fellows with him. Some with guns. This is going to make a big noise."

Fred didn't care to set foot inside the Horus Tower. Just thinking about what had been done in the building made him sick to his stomach. He was on the forecourt as the coughing, shrunken, handcuffed George Rameses Bunning was led out by Inspector Euan Price. Jeperson had accompanied the police up to the pyramid on top of the tower, to be there at the arrest.

Employees gathered at their windows, looking down as the boss was hauled off to the pokey. Rumors of what he had intended for them—for two hundred and thirty-eight men and women, from senior editors to junior copy-boys—would be circulating already, though Fred guessed many wouldn't believe them. Derek Leech's paper would carry the story, but few people put any credence in those loony crime stories in the *Comet*.

"He'll be dead before he comes to trial," said Jeperson. "Unless they find a cure."

"I hope they do, Richard," said Fred. "And he spends a good few years buried alive himself, in a concrete cell."

"His Board of Directors was wondering why, with the company on the verge of liquidation, Bunning had authorized such extensive remodeling of his corporate HQ. It was done, you know. He could have thrown the switch tomorrow, or next week. Whenever all was lost."

Now Fred shivered. Cemeteries didn't bother him, but places like this—concrete, glass and steel traps for the enslavement and destruction of living human beings—did.

"What did he tell what's-his-name, the architect? Drache?"

"It was supposed to be about security, locking down the Tower against armed insurrection. Rioting investors wanting their dividends, perhaps. The spray nozzles that were to flood the building with nerve-gas were a new kind of fire-prevention system."

"And Drache believed him?"

"He believed the money."

"Another bastard, then."

"Culpable, but not indictable."

The Horus Tower was equipped with shutters that would seal every window, door and ventilation duct. When the master-switch was thrown, they would all come down and lock tight. Then deadly gas would fill every office space, instantly preserving in death the entire workforce. Had George Rameses Bunning intended to keep publishing magazines in the afterlife? Did he really think his personal tomb would be left inviolate in perpetuity with all the corpses at their desks, a monument to himself for all eternity? Of course, George Oldrid Bunning had got away with it for a century.

"George Rameses knew?"

"About George Oldrid's funerary arrangements? Yes."

"Bastard bastard."

"Quite."

People began to file out of the skyscraper. The workday was over early.

There was a commotion.

A policeman was on the concrete, writhing around his kneed groin. Still handcuffed, George Rameses sprinted back towards his tower, shouldering through his employees.

Jeperson shouted to Price. "Get everyone out, now!"

Fred's old boss understood at once. He got a bullhorn and ordered everyone away from the building.

"He'll take the stairs," said Jeperson. "He won't chance us stopping the lifts. That'll give everyone time to make it out."

Alarm-bells sounded. The flood of people leaving the Horus Tower grew to exodus proportions.

"Should I send someone in to catch him?" asked Price. "It should be easy to snag him on the stairs. He'll be out of puff by the fifth floor, let alone the thirtieth."

Jeperson shook his head.

"Too much of a risk, Inspector. Just make sure everyone else is out. This should be interesting."

"Interesting?" spat Fred.

"Come on. Don't you want to see if it works? The big clockwork trap. The plans I saw were ingenious. A real economy of construction. No electricals. Just levers, sand and water. Drache kept to Egyptian technology. Modern materials, though."

"And nerve gas?" said Fred.

"Yes, there is that."

"You'd better hope Drache's shutters are damn good, or half London is going to drop dead."

"It won't come to that."

Vanessa crossed the forecourt. She was with the still-bewildered Lillywhite.

"What's happening?" she asked.

"George Rameses is back inside, racing towards his master-switch."

"Good grief."

"Never fear, Vanessa. Inspector, it might be an idea to find some managerial bods in the crowd. Read the class register, as it were. Just make sure everyone's out of the tower."

"Good idea, Jeperson."

The policeman hurried off.

Jeperson looked up at the building. The afternoon sun was reflected in black.

Then the reflection was gone.

Matt shutters closed like eyelids over every window. Black grilles came down behind the glass walls of the lobby, jaws meshing around floor-holes. The pyramid atop the tower twisted on a stem and lowered, locking into place. It was all done before the noise registered, a great mechanical wheezing and clanking. Torrents of water gushed from drains around the building, squirting up fifty feet in the air from the ornamental fountain.

"He's escaped," said Fred. "A quick, easy death from the gas and it'll take twenty years to break through all that engineering."

"Oh, I don't think so," said Jeperson. "Fifteen at the most. Modern methods, you know."

"The ghosts won't rest," said Lillywhite. "Not without revenge or restitution."

"I think they might," said Jeperson. "You see, George Rameses is still alive in his tomb. Alone, ill and, after his struggle up all those stairs, severely out of breath. Though I left the bulk of his self-burial mechanism alone, I took the precaution of disabling the nerve gas."

"Is that a scream I hear?" said Vanessa.

"I doubt it," said Jeperson. "If nothing else, George Rameses has just soundproofed his tomb."

COREY MARKS

A Letter of Explanation

Corey Marks's first book, Renunciation, *was a National Poetry Series Open Competition winner published by University of Illinois Press. His work has appeared in a number of journals, including* Antioch Review, Black Warrior Review, New England Review, the Paris Review, *and* TriQuarterly. *A 2003 NEA Creative Writing Fellowship recipient, Marks teaches at the University of North Texas. Marks's delightful poem "A Letter of Explanation" comes from* Renunciation.

—*T. W.*

By now, sir, you expect a second installment.
What novel is worth its ink if the hero's ship
never finishes sinking, if the cold tide
never tumbles him ashore into the provincial care
of two strolling shepherds?
But I'm not writing to beg leniency;

rather, to offer warning.
For so long I thought myself irreversibly
singular, but I've met another who shares
features almost indistinguishable
from my own and with them seeks to steal
everything I call my own.

When I first saw him, he was innocuous,
staring from a strategic corner in a café.
He learned to read lips so he could order
what *I* ordered. One by one, he acquired my habits
the way a lexicographer compiles a dictionary,
noting first the most rudimentary usages,

gradually adding nuance, context,
until his approximation was exhaustive.
What a performance! What unnerving self-reference.
His shadow play followed me everywhere.
Once, my novel in its first flush upon the page,
I—we—took a train all night through the mountains,

to think, to be driven further inside my story.
I spoke to him then, my double, my shadow,
and he listened, attentive, all nods
and approving hums. The perfect audience.
Then he spoke. Imagine, never having seen one,
you find yourself before a mirror.

Shock, at first. An inability to fit your mind
around the clear fact of your outward self,
the stranger agape before you.
Soon, though, you tame a stray wisp of hair.
Check your teeth, the fit of your overcoat.
Imagine how others see you, what they miss.

The mirror becomes indispensable,
a page of reference to an aspect of yourself.
It pales before what I found in him.
He was the book, perfect and whole.
You see the cruelty in his disappearance.
I've returned to the mountains, scoured trains, villages.

So often I want to call his name,
but what name would I call? My own?
I've asked after him on the streets, in cafés, hotels.
I've described him, pointing to my own face.
I've seen the glances, shoulders turning away. I'm not blind
no matter how blind the world becomes to me.

You must understand my negligence,
why my ambitions are all postponed,
peering into the yawning waves.
The amputee who still feels the ache of a missing limb
knows nothing of my state. I do not feel an arm
still attached, but rather that it is elsewhere,

perched on a desk behind a door I've yet to find,
clutching a pen that descends a page
filled with waves of script—*my* script—
conducting the body's business on its own.
I implore your patience, sir, and your caution,
for we are not always who we are.

CHINA MIÉVILLE

Details

China Miéville is the author of several short stories and three novels: King Rat, Perdido Street Station *(which won the Arthur C. Clarke and British Fantasy Awards), and* The Scar. *Born in 1972, he lives and works in London.*

Miéville says: " 'Details' was an attempt to write an homage to Lovecraft that was un-Lovecraftian in style. It was serendipity that John Pelan and Benjamin Adams were putting together an anthology with the same idea—tribute, not imitation or parody."

The story succeeds brilliantly in evoking Lovecraftian horror without invoking any specifically Lovecraftian tropes. No small feat!

"Details" was originally published in The Children of Cthulhu.

—E. D.

When the boy upstairs got hold of a pellet gun and fired snips of potato at passing cars, I took a turn. I was part of everything. I wasn't an outsider. But I wouldn't join in when my friends went to the yellow house to scribble on the bricks and listen at the windows.

One girl teased me about it, but everyone else told her to shut up. They defended me, even though they didn't understand why I wouldn't come.

I don't remember a time before I visited the yellow house for my mother.

On Wednesday mornings at about nine o'clock I would open the front door of the decrepit building with a key from the bunch my mother had given me. Inside was a hall and two doors, one broken and leading to the splintering stairs. I would unlock the other and enter the dark flat. The corridor was unlit and smelled of old wet air. I never walked even two steps down that hallway. Rot and shadows merged, and it looked as if the passage disappeared a few yards from me. The door to Mrs. Miller's room was right in front of me. I would lean forward and knock.

Quite often there were signs that someone else had been there recently. Scuffed dust and bits of litter. Sometimes I was not alone. There were two other children I sometimes saw slipping in or out of the house. There were a handful of adults who visited Mrs. Miller.

I might find one or another of them in the hallway outside the door to her flat, or even in the flat itself, slouching in the crumbling dark hallway. They would be slumped over or reading some cheap-looking book or swearing loudly as they waited.

There was a young Asian woman who wore a lot of makeup and smoked obsessively. She ignored me totally. There were two drunks who came sometimes. One would greet me boisterously and incomprehensibly, raising his arms as if he wanted to hug me into his stinking, stinking jumper. I would grin and wave nervously, walk past him. The other seemed alternately melancholic and angry. Occasionally I'd meet him by the door to Mrs. Miller's room, swearing in a strong cockney accent. I remember the first time I saw him, he was standing there, his red face contorted, slurring and moaning loudly.

"Come on, you old slag," he wailed, "you sodding old *slag*. Come on, please, you cow."

His words scared me but his tone was wheedling, and I realized I could hear her voice, Mrs. Miller's voice, from inside the room, answering him back. She did not sound frightened or angry.

I hung back, not sure what to do, and she kept speaking, and eventually the drunken man shambled miserably away. And then I could continue as usual.

I asked my mother once if I could have some of Mrs. Miller's food. She laughed very hard and shook her head. In all the Wednesdays of bringing the food over, I never even dipped my finger in to suck it.

My mum spent an hour every Tuesday night making the stuff up. She dissolved a bit of gelatin or cornflour with some milk, threw in a load of sugar or flavorings, and crushed a clutch of vitamin pills into the mess. She stirred it until it thickened and let it set in a plain white plastic bowl. In the morning it would be a kind of strong-smelling custard that my mother put a dishcloth over and gave me, along with a list of any questions or requests for Mrs. Miller and sometimes a plastic bucket full of white paint.

So I would stand in front of Mrs. Miller's door, knocking, with a bowl at my feet. I'd hear a shifting and then her voice from close by the door.

"Hello," she would call, and then say my name a couple of times. "Have you my breakfast? Are you ready?"

I would creep up close to the door and hold the food ready. I would tell her I was.

Mrs. Miller would slowly count to three. On three, the door suddenly swung open a snatch, just a foot or two, and I thrust the bowl into the gap. She grabbed it and slammed the door quickly in my face.

I couldn't see very much inside the room. The door was open for less than a second. My strongest impression was of the whiteness of the walls. Mrs. Miller's sleeves were white, too, and made of plastic. I never got much of a glimpse at her face, but what I saw was unmemorable. A middle-aged woman's eager face.

If I had a bucket full of paint, we would run through the routine again. Then I would sit cross-legged in front of her door and listen to her eat.

"How's your mother?" she would shout. At that I'd unfold my mother's careful queries. She's okay, I'd say, she's fine. She says she has some questions for you.

I'd read my mother's strange questions in my careful childish monotone, and

Mrs. Miller would pause and make interested sounds, and clear her throat and think out loud. Sometimes she took ages to come to an answer, and sometimes it would be almost immediate.

"Tell your mother she can't tell if a man's good or bad from that," she'd say. "Tell her to remember the problems she had with your father." Or: "Yes, she can take the heart of it out. Only she has to paint it with the special oil I told her about." "Tell your mother seven. But only four of them concern her and three of them used to be dead.

"I can't help her with that," she told me once, quietly. "Tell her to go to a doctor, quickly." And my mother did, and she got well again.

"What do you not want to do when you grow up?" Mrs. Miller asked me one day.

That morning when I had come to the house the sad cockney vagrant had been banging on the door of her room again, the keys to the flat flailing in his hand.

"He's begging you, you old tart, please, you owe him, he's so bloody angry," he was shouting, "only it ain't you gets the sharp end, is it? *Please*, you cow, you sodding cow, I'm on me knees. . . ."

"My door knows you, man," Mrs. Miller declared from within. "It knows you and so do I, you know it won't open to you. I didn't take out my eyes and I'm not giving in now. Go home."

I waited nervously as the man gathered himself and staggered away, and then, looking behind me, I knocked on her door and announced myself. It was after I'd given her the food that she asked her question.

"What do you not want to do when you grow up?"

If I had been a few years older her inversion of the cliché would have annoyed me: It would have seemed mannered and contrived. But I was only a young child, and I was quite delighted.

I don't want to be a lawyer, I told her carefully. I spoke out of loyalty to my mother, who periodically received crisp letters that made her cry or smoke fiercely, and swear at lawyers, bloody smartarse lawyers.

Mrs. Miller was delighted.

"Good boy!" she snorted. "We know all about lawyers. Bastards, right? With the small print! Never be tricked by the small print! It's right there in front of you, *right there in front of you*, and you can't even *see* it and then suddenly it *makes you notice it!* And I tell you, once you've seen it it's got you!" She laughed excitedly. "Don't let the small print get you. I'll tell you a secret." I waited quietly, and my head slipped nearer the door.

"The devil's in the details!" She laughed again. "You ask your mother if that's not true. The devil is in the details!"

I'd wait the twenty minutes or so until Mrs. Miller had finished eating, and then we'd reverse our previous procedure and she'd quickly hand me out an empty bowl. I would return home with the empty container and tell my mother the various answers to her various questions. Usually she would nod and make notes. Occasionally she would cry.

After I told Mrs. Miller that I did not want to be a lawyer she started asking me to read to her. She made me tell my mother, and told me to bring a newspaper or one of a number of books. My mother nodded at the message and packed me a sandwich the next Wednesday, along with the *Mirror*. She told me to be polite and do what Mrs. Miller asked, and that she'd see me in the afternoon.

I wasn't afraid. Mrs. Miller had never treated me badly from behind her door. I was resigned and only a little bit nervous.

Mrs. Miller made me read stories to her from specific pages that she shouted out. She made me recite them again and again, very carefully. Afterward she would talk to me. Usually she started with a joke about lawyers, and about small print.

"There's three ways not to see what you don't want to," she told me. "One is the coward's way and too damned painful. The other is to close your eyes forever which is the same as the first, when it comes to it. The third is the hardest and the best: You have to make sure *only the things you can afford to see* come before you."

One morning when I arrived the stylish Asian woman was whispering fiercely through the wood of the door, and I could hear Mrs. Miller responding with shouts of amused disapproval. Eventually the young woman swept past me, leaving me cowed by her perfume.

Mrs. Miller was laughing, and she was talkative when she had eaten.

"She's heading for trouble, messing with the wrong family! You have to be careful with all of them," she told me. "Every single *one* of them on that other side of things is a tricksy bastard who'll kill you soon as *look* at you, given half a chance.

"There's the gnarly throat-tipped one . . . and there's old hasty, who I think had best remain nameless," she said wryly. "All old bastards, all of them. You *can't trust them* at all, that's what I say. I should know, eh? Shouldn't I?" She laughed. "Trust me, trust me on this: It's too easy to get on the wrong side of them.

"What's it like out today?" she asked me. I told her that it was cloudy.

"You want to be careful with that," she said. "All sorts of faces in the clouds, aren't there? Can't help noticing, can you?" She was whispering now. "Do me a favor when you go home to your mum: Don't look up, there's a boy. Don't look up at all."

When I left her, however, the day had changed. The sky was hot, and quite blue.

The two drunk men were squabbling in the front hall and I edged past them to her door. They continued bickering in a depressing, garbled murmur throughout my visit.

"D'you know, I can't even really remember what it was all *about*, now!" Mrs. Miller said when I had finished reading to her. "I can't remember! That's a terrible thing. But you don't forget the basics. The exact question escapes me, and to be honest I think maybe I was just being *nosy* or *showing off*. . . . I can't say I'm proud of it but it could have been that. It could. But whatever the question, it was all about a way of seeing an answer.

"There's a way of looking that lets you read things. If you look at a pattern of tar on a wall, or a crumbling mound of brick or somesuch . . . there's a way of unpicking it. And if you know how, you can trace it and read it out and see the things hidden *right there in front of you*, the things you've been seeing but not noticing, all along. But you have to learn how." She laughed. It was a high-pitched, unpleasant sound. "Someone has to teach you. So you have to make certain friends.

"But you can't make friends without making enemies.

"You have to open it all up for you to see inside. You make what you see into a window, and you see what you want through it. You make what you see a sort of *door*."

She was silent for a long time. Then: "Is it cloudy again?" she asked suddenly. She went on before I answered.

"If you look up, you look into the clouds for long enough and you'll see a face. Or in a tree. Look in a tree, look in the branches and soon you'll see them just so, and there's a face or a running man, or a bat or whatever. You'll see it all suddenly, a picture in the pattern of the branches, and you won't have *chosen* to see it. And you can't *unsee* it.

"That's what you have to learn to do, to read the details like that and see what's what and learn things. But you've to be damn careful. You've to be careful not to disturb anything." Her voice was absolutely cold, and I was suddenly very frightened.

"Open up that window, you'd better be damn careful that what's in the details doesn't look back and see you."

The next time I went, the maudlin drunk was there again wailing obscenities at her through her door. She shouted at me to come back later, that she didn't need her food right now. She sounded resigned and irritated, and she went back to scolding her visitor before I had backed out of earshot.

He was screaming at her that she'd gone too far, that she'd pissed about too long, that things were coming to a head, that there was going to be hell to pay, that she couldn't avoid it forever, that it was her own fault.

When I came back he was asleep, snoring loudly, curled up a few feet into the mildewing passage. Mrs. Miller took her food and ate it quickly, returned it without speaking.

When I returned the following week, she began to whisper to me as soon as I knocked on the door, hissing urgently as she opened it briefly and grabbed the bowl.

"It was an accident, you know," she said, as if responding to something I'd said. "I mean of *course* you know in *theory* that anything might happen, you get *warned*, don't you? But oh my . . . oh my *God* it took the breath out of me and made me cold to realize what had happened."

I waited. I could not leave, because she had not returned the bowl. She had not said I could go. She spoke again, very slowly.

"It was a new day." Her voice was distant and breathy. "Can you even imagine?

Can you see what I was ready to do? I was poised . . . to change . . . to see everything that's hidden. The best place to hide a book is in a library. The best place to hide secret things is there, in the visible angles, in our view, in plain sight.

"I had studied and sought, and learnt, finally, to see. It was time to learn truths.

"I opened my eyes fully, for the first time.

"I had chosen an old wall. I was looking for the answer to some question that I told you I can't even *remember* now, but the question wasn't the main thing. That was the opening of my eyes.

"I stared at the whole mass of the bricks. I took another glance, relaxed my sight. At first I couldn't stop seeing the bricks as bricks, the divisions as layers of cement, but after a time they became pure vision. And as the whole broke down into lines and shapes and shades, I held my breath as I began to see.

"Alternatives appeared to me. Messages written in the pockmarks. Insinuations in the forms. Secrets unraveling. It was bliss.

"And then without warning my heart went tight, as I saw something. I made sense of the pattern.

"It was a mess of cracks and lines and crumbling cement, and as I looked at it, I saw a pattern in the wall.

"I saw a clutch of lines that looked just like something . . . terrible . . . something old and predatory and utterly terrible . . . staring right back at me.

"And then I saw it move."

"You have to understand me," she said. "*Nothing changed*. See? All the time I was looking I saw the wall. But that first moment, it was like when you see a face in the cloud. I just *noticed* in the pattern in the brick, I just *noticed* something, looking at me. Something angry.

"And then in the very next moment, I just . . . I just *noticed* another load of lines—cracks that had always been there, you understand? Patterns in broken brick that I'd seen only a second before—that looked exactly like that same thing, a little closer to me. And in the next moment a third picture in the brick, a picture of the thing closer still.

"Reaching for me."

"I broke free then," she whispered. "I ran away from there in terror, with my hands in front of my eyes and I was *screaming*. I ran and ran.

"And when I stopped and opened my eyes again, I had run to the edges of a park, and I took my hands slowly down and dared to look behind me, and saw that there was nothing coming from the alley where I'd been. So I turned to the little snatch of scrub and grass and trees.

"And I saw the thing again."

Mrs. Miller's voice was stretched out as if she was dreaming. My mouth was open and I huddled closer to the door.

"I saw it in the leaves," she said forlornly. "As I turned I saw the leaves in such a way . . . just a *chance conjuncture*, you understand? I noticed a pattern. I *couldn't not*. You don't choose whether to see faces in the clouds. I saw the monstrous thing again and it still reached for me, and I shrieked and all the mothers and fathers and children in that park turned and gazed at me, and I turned my eyes from that tree and whirled on my feet to face a little family in my way.

"And the thing was there in the same pose," she whispered in misery. "I saw it in the outlines of the father's coat and the spokes of the baby's pushchair, and the tangles of the mother's hair. It was just another mess of lines, you see? But you *don't choose what you notice*. And I couldn't help but notice *just the right lines* out of the whole, just the lines out of all the lines there, just the ones to see the thing again, a little closer, looking at me.

"And I turned and saw it closer still in the clouds, and I turned again and it was clutching for me in the rippling weeds in the pond, and as I closed my eyes I swear I felt something touch my dress.

"You understand me? You understand?"

I didn't know if I understood or not. Of course now I know that I did not.

"It lives in the details," she said bleakly. "It travels in that . . . in that perception. It moves through those chance meetings of lines. Maybe you glimpse it sometimes when you stare at clouds, and then maybe it might catch a glimpse of you, too.

"But it saw me *full* on. It's jealous of . . . of its place, and there I was peering through without permission, like a nosy neighbor through a hole in the fence. I know what it is. I know what happened.

"It lurks before us, in the everyday. It's the boss of *all the things* hidden in plain sight. Terrible things, they are. Appalling things. Just almost in reach. Brazen and invisible.

"It caught my glances. It can move through whatever I see.

"For most people it's just chance, isn't it? What shapes they see in a tangle of wire. There's a thousand pictures there, and when you look, some of them just appear. But now . . . the thing in the lines chooses the pictures for me. It can thrust itself forward. It makes me see it. It's found its way through. To me. Through what I see. *I opened a door into my perception*."

She sounded frozen with terror. I was not equipped for that kind of adult fear, and my mouth worked silently for something to say.

"That was a long, long journey home. Every time I peeked through the cracks in my fingers, I saw that thing crawling for me.

"It waited ready to pounce, and when I opened my eyes even a crack I opened the door again. I saw the back of a woman's jumper and in the detail of the fabric the thing leapt for me. I glimpsed a yard of broken paving and I noticed just the lines that showed me the thing . . . *baying*.

"I had to shut my eyes quick.

"I *groped* my way home.

"And then I taped my eyes shut and I tried to think about things."

There was silence for a time.

"See, there was always the easy way, that scared me rotten, because I was never one for blood and pain," she said suddenly, and her voice was harder. "I held the scissors in front of my eyes a couple of times, but even bandaged blind as I was I couldn't bear it. I suppose I could've gone to a doctor. I can pull strings, I could pull in a few favors, have them do the job without pain.

"But you know I never . . . really . . . reckoned . . . that's what I'd do," she said thoughtfully. "What if you found a way to close the door? Eh? And you'd already put out your eyes? You'd feel such a *fool*, wouldn't you?

"And you know it wouldn't be good enough to wear pads and eyepatches and all. I tried. You catch glimpses. You see the glimmers of light and maybe a few of your own hairs, and that's *the doorway right there*, when the hairs cross in the corner of your eye so that if you notice just a few of them in just the right way . . . they look like something coming for you. That's a doorway.

"It's . . . unbearable . . . having sight, but trapping it like that.

"I'm not giving up. See . . ." Her voice lowered, and she spoke conspiratorially. "*I still think I can close the door*. I learnt to see. I can unlearn. I'm looking for ways. I want to see a wall as . . . as bricks again. Nothing more. That's why you read for me," she said. "*Research*. Can't look at it myself of course, too many edges and lines and so on on a printed page, so you do it for me. And you're a good boy to do it."

I've thought about what she said many times, and still it makes no sense to me. The books I read to Mrs. Miller were school textbooks, old and dull village histories, the occasional romantic novel. I think that she must have been talking of some of her other visitors, who perhaps read her more esoteric stuff than I did. Either that, or the information she sought was buried very cleverly in the banal prose I faltered through.

"In the meantime, there's another way of surviving," she said slyly. "Leave the eyes where they are, but *don't give them any details*.

"That . . . thing can force me to notice its shape, but only in what's there. That's how it travels. You imagine if I saw a field of wheat. Doesn't even bear *thinking* about! A million million little bloody *edges*, a million lines. You could make pictures of damn *anything* out of them, couldn't you? It wouldn't take any effort at *all* for the thing to make me notice it. The damn *lurker*. Or in a gravel drive or, or a building site, or a lawn . . .

"But I can outsmart it." The note of cunning in her voice made her sound deranged. "Keep it away till I work out how to close it off.

"I had to prepare this blind, with the wrappings round my head. Took me a while, but here I am now. Safe. I'm safe in my little cold room. I keep the walls *flat white*. I covered the windows and painted them, too. I made my cloak out of plastic, so's I can't catch a glimpse of cotton weave or anything when I wake up.

"I keep my place nice and . . . simple. When it was all done, I unwrapped the bandages from my head, and I blinked slowly . . . and I was alright. Clean walls, no cracks, no features. I don't look at my hands often or for long. Too many creases. Your mother makes me a good healthy soup looks like cream, so if I accidentally look in the bowl, there's no broccoli or rice or tangled up spaghetti to make *lines and edges*.

"I open and shut the door so damned quick because I can only afford a moment. *That thing is ready to pounce*. It wouldn't take a second for it to leap up at me out of the sight of your hair or your books or whatever."

Her voice ebbed out. I waited a minute for her to resume, but she did not do so. Eventually I knocked nervously on the door and called her name. There was no answer. I put my ear to the door. I could hear her crying, quietly.

I went home without the bowl. My mother pursed her lips a little but said nothing. I didn't tell her any of what Mrs. Miller had said. I was troubled and totally confused.

The next time I delivered Mrs. Miller's food, in a new container, she whispered harshly to me: "It preys on my eyes, all the *white*. Nothing to see. Can't look out the window, can't read, can't gaze at my nails. Preys on my mind.

"Not even my memories are left," she said in misery. "It's colonizing them. I remember things . . . happy times . . . and the thing's waiting in the texture of my dress, or in the crumbs of my birthday cake. I didn't notice it then. But I can see it now. My memories aren't mine anymore. Not even my imaginings. Last night I thought about going to the seaside, and then the thing was there in the foam on the waves."

She spoke very little the next few times I visited her. I read the chapters she demanded and she grunted curtly in response. She ate quickly.

Her other visitors were there more often now, as the spring came in. I saw them in new combinations and situations: the glamorous young woman arguing with the friendly drunk; the old man sobbing at the far end of the hall. The aggressive man was often there, cajoling and moaning, and occasionally talking conversationally through the door, being answered like an equal. Other times he screamed at her as usual.

I arrived on a chilly day to find the drunken cockney man sleeping a few feet from the door, snoring gutturally. I gave Mrs. Miller her food and then sat on my coat and read to her from a women's magazine as she ate.

When she had finished her food I waited with my arms outstretched, ready to snatch the bowl from her. I remember that I was very uneasy, that I sensed something wrong. I was looking around me anxiously, but everything seemed normal. I looked down at my coat and the crumpled magazine, at the man who still sprawled comatose in the hall.

As I heard Mrs. Miller's hands on the door, I realized what had changed. The drunken man was not snoring. He was holding his breath.

For a tiny moment I thought he had died, but I could see his body trembling, and my eyes began to open wide and I stretched my mouth to scream a warning, but the door had already begun to swing in its tight, quick arc, and before I could even exhale the stinking man pushed himself up faster than I would have thought him capable and bore down on me with bloodshot eyes.

I managed to keen as he reached me, and the door faltered for an instant, as Mrs. Miller heard my voice. But the man grabbed hold of me in a terrifying, heavy fug of alcohol. He reached down and snatched my coat from the floor, tugged at the jumper I had tied around my waist with his other hand, and hurled me hard at the door.

It flew open, smacking Mrs. Miller aside. I was screaming and crying. My eyes hurt at the sudden burst of cold white light from all the walls. I saw Mrs. Miller rubbing her head in the corner, struggling to her senses. The staggering, drunken man hurled my checked coat and my patterned jumper in front of her, reached down and snatched my feet, tugged me out of the room in an agony of splinters. I wailed snottily with fear.

Behind me, Mrs. Miller began to scream and curse, but I could not hear her well because the man had clutched me to him and pulled my head to his chest. I fought and cried and felt myself lurch as he leaned forward and slammed the door closed.

He held it shut.

When I fought myself free of him I heard him shouting.

"I told you, you slapper," he wailed unhappily. "I bloody told you, you silly old whore. I warned you it was time. . . ." Behind his voice I could hear shrieks of misery and terror from the room. Both of them kept shouting and crying and screaming, and the floorboards pounded, and the door shook, and I heard something else as well.

As if the notes of all the different noises in the house fell into a chance meeting, and sounded like more than dissonance. The shouts and bangs and cries of fear combined in a sudden audible illusion like another presence.

Like a snarling voice. A lingering, hungry exhalation.

I ran then, screaming and terrified, my skin freezing in my T-shirt. I was sobbing and retching with fear, little bleats bursting from me. I stumbled home and was sick in my mother's room, and kept crying and crying as she grabbed hold of me and I tried to tell her what had happened, until I was drowsy and confused and I fell into silence.

My mother said nothing about Mrs. Miller. The next Wednesday we got up early and went to the zoo, the two of us, and at the time I would usually be knocking on Mrs. Miller's door I was laughing at camels. The Wednesday after that I was taken to see a film, and the one after that my mother stayed in bed and sent me to fetch cigarettes and bread from the local shop, and I made our breakfast and ate it in her room.

My friends could tell that something had changed in the yellow house, but they did not speak to me about it, and it quickly became uninteresting to them.

I saw the Asian woman once more, smoking with her friends in the park several weeks later, and to my amazement she nodded to me and came over, interrupting her companions' conversation.

"Are you alright?" she asked me peremptorily. "How are you doing?"

I nodded shyly back and told her that I was fine, thank you, and how was she?

She nodded and walked away.

I never saw the drunken, violent man again.

There were people I could probably have gone to to understand more about what had happened to Mrs. Miller. There was a story that I could chase, if I wanted to. People I had never seen before came to my house and spoke quietly to my mother, and looked at me with what I suppose was pity or concern. I could have asked them. But I was thinking more and more about my own life. I didn't want to know Mrs. Miller's details.

I went back to the yellow house once, nearly a year after that awful morning. It was winter. I remembered the last time I spoke to Mrs. Miller and I felt so much older it was almost giddying. It seemed such a vastly long time ago.

I crept up to the house one evening, trying the keys I still had, which to my surprise worked. The hallway was freezing, dark, and stinking more strongly than ever. I hesitated, then pushed open Mrs. Miller's door.

It opened easily, without a sound. The occasional muffled noise from the street seemed so distant it was like a memory. I entered.

She had covered the windows very carefully, and still no light made its way through from outside. It was extremely dark. I waited until I could see better in the ambient glow from the outside hallway.

I was alone.

My old coat and jumper lay spreadeagled in the corner of the room. I shivered to see them, went over, and fingered them softly. They were damp and mildewing, covered in wet dust.

The white paint was crumbling off the wall in scabs. It looked as if it had been left untended for several years. I could not believe the extent of the decay.

I turned slowly around and gazed at each wall in turn. I took in the chaotic, intricate patterns of crumbling paint and damp plaster. They looked like maps, like a rocky landscape.

I looked for a long time at the wall farthest from my jacket. I was very cold. After a long time I saw a shape in the ruined paint. I moved closer with a dumb curiosity far stronger than any fear.

In the crumbling texture of the wall was a spreading anatomy of cracks that—seen from a certain angle, caught just right in the scraps of light—looked in outline something like a woman. As I stared at it it took shape, and I stopped noticing the extraneous lines, and focused without effort or decision on the relevant ones. I saw a woman looking out at me.

I could make out the suggestion of her face. The patch of rot that constituted it made it look as if she was screaming.

One of her arms was flung back away from her body, which seemed to strain against it, as if she was being pulled away by her hand, and was fighting to escape, and was failing. At the end of her crack-arm, in the space where her captor would be, the paint had fallen away in a great slab, uncovering a huge patch of wet, stained, textured cement.

And in that dark infinity of markings, I could make out any shape I wanted.

ERIC SCHALLER

The Assistant to Dr. Jacob

Eric Schaller is a plant biologist, artist, and writer currently teaching at the University of New Hampshire and will be moving to Dartmouth College in the fall of 2003. He lives in New Hampshire with his wife, Paulette Werger, a jeweler who makes use of botanical images in her own work. Schaller's recent work includes illustrations for Jeff VanderMeer's The Exchange *and Vander-Meer's marvelous hardcover collection* The City of Saints and Madmen, *an art/text piece in* The Silver Web, *and a contribution to that essential medical companion* The Thackery T. Lambshead Pocket Guide to Eccentric and Discredited Diseases, *recently published by Nightshade Books.*

Eric Schaller says: "'The Assistant to Dr. Jacob' is about a loss of innocence. It is also about the tools by which we attempt to define a world that resists definition."

"The Assistant to Dr. Jacob" was first published in Nemonymous, *edited by Des Lewis.*

—E. D.

Past a certain age, one lives in memories instead of dreams.

I stand before the kitchen window, Whiskers cradled in my arms, and I feel the soft vibration as she purrs, voicing the unconcern of all her species. She does not care about tomorrow. Or yesterday. Just that her food dish is filled, that she has a warm place to sleep, and that the songs of birds entertain her at suitable intervals. I do not believe she has ever been disappointed.

I am not so lucky as she is. I know that with each new year, the window through which I gaze will add another layer of grime and the wind that rattles the glass will only blow more chill.

Winter and the new year are two curses on my bones.

As if hearing my thoughts, the policeman passing below turns his collar up and pulls his coat tighter across his shoulders.

Still, I remember a more expansive time when the first winter snowfall was a magical act of creation and cold seemed incapable of penetrating even the thinnest fabric. Once again, I am eight years old and running along the sidewalk, puffs of snow evading my footsteps, my breath visible and streaming. I slip rounding the turn to my house, but recover and take the three steps that lead up to the front door in a single bound. I sit at the lunch table, my coat still on, and spoon down tomato soup and chomp half-moons out of my salami sandwich. My cheeks prickle with warmth and returned circulation. Behind me and beside me, my mother is a hovering angel with red hair and freckles; she kisses my forehead, thanks me for coming home at lunchtime without being called, and busies herself with a floral arrangement on the table. "There," she says and steps back to admire her handiwork. "How do you like that?"

This is the scene preserved in the crisp winter light of that long ago afternoon, but there is something wrong here—I no longer trust the memory.

Any memory.

But of this I said nothing to the policeman when we spoke earlier.

The policeman, a plain-clothes man, sat across from me on the edge of a stuffed chair over which I had draped a patterned blanket. In the corner, by the bookcase, Whiskers eyed the man who had usurped her seat.

He held a small notepad and tapped it with a gnawed ballpoint pen.

"Do you remember a Dr. Samuel Jacob?" he asked me. He had a scar or birth defect that twisted the left side of his mouth; it gave him the appearance of constantly smirking.

My face must have revealed my lack of comprehension, for he leaned forward and said again more loudly, "Dr. Samuel Jacob. He lived at 224 Maple Street in Danbury. In the house next to yours." He smelled of mustard and corned beef.

Still I looked at him, not knowing whom he was asking about.

Then I knew.

"Dr. Jacob! But that was fifty years ago. At the very least. I was just a boy."

Once again, in memory, I was that boy.

I did know Dr. Jacob, although I doubt if I ever knew his first name and, if I did at one point, I would never have addressed him by it—he was a well-respected man and those were respectable times. He owned the largest house on the block, a rambling white colonial built over a century before, and although he was a wealthy man he had no family with which to share his good fortune. Perhaps it was for this reason that he noticed me, the neighbor's child. Young and noisy, how could he not notice me. I was only too happy to spend a portion of my afterschool hours and weekends with him. His house was a treasure trove of books and memorabilia. But it was not these, not even the extensive collection of wooden and ivory sailing vessels that lined mantle and bookshelves, or the large black camera on tripod, to which I was most attracted. It was simply this—Dr. Jacob was a gardener. He was not the sort you find grubbing in the backyard dirt. He had his own hothouse, a small crystal palace abutting his home, a secret kingdom sheltered from prying eyes by shrubs and hedgerows. I would spend uncounted hours with him among his orchids, lilies, and roses, as he watered, trimmed, and otherwise coddled those sometimes fragile blooms.

He was a consummate artist in his chosen hobby, and he must have belonged to a variety of garden clubs for an endless parade of vegetation passed through his glass house. I remember a profusion of color—although Dr. Jacob dressed in somber gray suits, he did not expect his wards to share his wardrobe—colors both garish and sexual, so much so in the orchids that sometimes I would blush and feel my stomach churn, and not know why I could not look at the blooms for long. I remember also how, as Dr. Jacob moved about the pots, as he handled his pruning shears with the deft sobriety of his profession, he named each plant and flower, giving both the common and the Latin phrasing. He would lift a scarlet bloom between his fore and middle fingers, other digits curled into his palm, and say softly, caressing the foreign tongue, "Haemanthus coccineus." He would then glance down to where I hovered at his elbow and say, "To you, the blood lily."

Do I remember the many and varied tongue twisters he pressed upon me?

No.

But I do remember how his eyes sparkled and how sometimes, with a sly look, as if ashamed of pleasure, he would snip off a fragrant bloom and insert it into the buttonhole of his jacket. Then he would seem to bloom himself, turning slowly toward me, chest thrown out to show off that single brilliant splash of color in the midst of the most neutral of grays.

That was a simple pleasure and one might think that there could be none greater for the amateur horticulturist.

But there were other days when Dr. Jacob brought in new plants, rarities, and on those days from the look on his face you might have thought that he heard the angels singing, for his broad shiny face beamed with an uncontainable joy made manifest.

Of particular beauty were the massive rose bushes that he occasionally set up in the hot house. These came wrapped in burlap around the roots, the body of the plant nothing to speak of at first, with perhaps only a few tender buds revealing the thinnest lips of pink and red. Under his ministrations, the clipping of stray branches, a nip here and there with his shears and Japanese knife, small chocks of wood to spread certain branches, and wires twisted around others, the plants would take on more perfect form. I would watch in awed fascination as he circled one of his massive rose bushes, then darted in with sharpened tools. He seemed to be always circling, responding to each change in the plant with further changes of his own device. Later, I held my breath as the bushes came into full bloom for, depending on Dr. Jacob's earlier handling, the flowers might open gradually, radiating outward from one initial location such that a wave of color passed across the bush, while in other cases the flowers might hold themselves back day after day, until it seemed that the buds must burst, and then they would burst, an explosion of color that transformed the bush from green to burning red in the space of a single night.

I say I watched Dr. Jacob, and I did, through a long humid summer and a chill winter during which the kerosene heaters roared and that hothouse seemed transplanted from a foreign jungle into our snow-carpeted suburbs. I watched for a year, and then Dr. Jacob handed me a pair of pruning sheers. He said, "You have watched enough," and pointed me toward a small rosebush in one corner. "She is yours."

I lived next door to Dr. Jacob for only two years, but those two years remain etched in my mind with all the intensity of youth.

To the policeman I said, still unsure as to the exact nature of his business, "Yes. I knew him. But not too well. I was very young."

"He died recently," said the policeman. "He was ninety-one."

He paused and looked at me to gauge my reaction, working his tongue at a piece of meat stuck in his teeth.

I said nothing and waited for him to continue.

"He still lived at the Danbury residence, from which you would know him. Lived there all his life. He lived alone, but had a nurse on call. She was the one who found his body. No known relatives."

I wondered if perhaps I had been named in Dr. Jacob's will.

"Some interesting items turned up in his house when preparing it for auction. Photographs. That's why we were called in." He set his notebook down upon his knee—the upturned page was covered with small crosshatched doodles. He then burrowed into his jacket pocket, pulled out an envelope, and extracted a stack of photographs from the envelope. "These are not the originals, of course."

He laid the photographs on the coffee table and pushed them across toward me. "Have a look. It's not pleasant."

The photographs were of dead people.

They were the close-up photographs of a surgeon's handiwork: sections of the body from which the skin had been cut, then peeled back to reveal the fat and muscle beneath; and deeper explorations, where muscle had been stripped from bone and the interior of the body laid open, the rib cage sawed and bent back to expose the organs.

I saw a hand, naked of skin and lacking its thumb, on which the fingers were spread so wide apart that they described a full half-circle.

I saw the head of a woman, her eyes exhumed from their sockets and braced upon her cheekbones, her lips removed so that she grinned hideously into the camera.

Dr. Jacob was a doctor after all.

But the images were more disturbing than their graphic nature might indicate for they did not seem consistent with the normal process of surgery. They were more like what one would find in an anatomy text, rendered personal by the intimacy of a photograph. However, even granting this, there seemed an excess of blood. The skin was stained in dark patches, and elsewhere blood coagulated in gelatinous knots and obscured the wounds.

I would have expected the results of an anatomy lesson to be more thoroughly cleaned.

I did not think that corpses bled.

The policeman watched as I thumbed through the photographs and, as I continued, it became apparent that he had established a certain order within the photographs.

The initial photographs had shown details of the surgery, but now I came upon ones that showed the bodies in their entirety. Rather than laid out on a hospital or mortuary table, the bodies were vertical, trussed to and supported by poles, and held in strange animation—legs caught as if in midstep, arms gesticulating, heads turned as if to speak—these effects maintained by wires or string twisted about and in some cases penetrating the bodies. I could also see the blood. Every wound or laceration, and there were many, had released a dark stream of blood, black in the grainy photographs, that slid down the body and outlined the tortured forms beneath. The patterns of blood were not simply those dictated by gravity, but in places had been smeared by hand, the indecipherable calligraphy of a madman.

My eyes filled with tears.

I shook my head and handed the photographs back to the policeman.

"I didn't know," I said, I meant to say. My mouth moved but no words came out.

"Did you see where the photos were taken?" he asked. "It was in the greenhouse he had behind his house. That's why you have the better lighting. More windows. See." He pushed a photograph toward me of a bloody woman meshed in chickenwire. The shot was overexposed and the woman's skin, where not darkened by blood, seemed to glow white. Behind her were shelves with pots and foliage. "It would have been too dark indoors in the big house."

I nodded my head numbly.

He pulled the photo out of my hand and added it back to his stack, making sure to place it in the same position from which he had removed it.

"After finding these, we did a search of the grounds. We thought there might be bodies buried on the property. Didn't find a thing. Only the bones of a dog beside the porch."

That would have been Blackie, I thought. But perhaps there had been other dogs later of which I knew nothing.

"He was a doctor, and they have different avenues of disposal. The victims were probably buried in a cemetery or cremated. Just like anyone else. Very hard to trace."

"But of one thing I want you to be sure. One thing we do know." He leaned across the table and glared into my eyes with such intensity that I was afraid to look away. "That man was a murderer. Those people when he started on them were alive."

I thought of the blood, the black blood on the bodies in photographs.

"I don't know how long he kept them alive. But there were gags on some of their mouths in the pictures. Others had their tongues cut out; their throats mutilated. So they couldn't scream."

I swallowed.

"You may be wondering why I'm telling you this. Or even showing you these things."

I nodded my head. My reflection bobbed up and down in his dark eyes.

"There was a photo in there which you may not have looked at closely. One photo that interested us in particular." He settled back a little bit and looked at me expectantly. "Did you see it?"

He riffled through the photos like a card deck. "This one." He handed the photograph across to me.

Yes, I had seen the photograph. I had seen it the first time I went through the stack, but I had said nothing. I wasn't surprised that he had singled it out, that he was now asking me about it.

That was what I expected.

There were two children in the photograph. The first was a girl, her blond hair flipped out like wings, maybe five or six years old. Her face was butchered past recognition, and one of her arms was bent back, apparently broken, so as to twist behind her head, fingers pointed upward. The second child was a boy. He kneeled beside the girl. He did not look at the camera but, with knife in his right hand, carved within her exposed stomach cavity, engrossed in the removal of her internal organs.

The policeman reached over and tapped the picture with his pen. "It's the boy we're wondering about."

The boy beneath his pen was turned away from the camera.

"Do you know who he is? One of the kids from around your neighborhood? Look closely. I know it's not an easy thing to do."

In addition, although the brutalized body of the girl was clearly in focus, the boy's image was slightly blurred, a result of his movements while the photography was in progress.

I shook my head and mumbled "No."

"What?"

"No," I said.

I press my forehead against the cold window and watch the policeman get into his car. The policeman with his photographs.

That photograph: the boy, the girl, and the blood.

Warm tears gather in my eyes again and spill over, and I hear the distant sound as they impact the floor.

Whiskers tenses in my arms and I pet her clumsily.

I recognize the girl from memory. I knew her as soon as I saw the photograph, the way she twisted toward the sun, her outstretched limbs seeming to both yearn and shrink from the sky, the way the roses bloomed in patches at face and belly. I knew every blossoming turn of her.

I remember how I trimmed and cajoled her, emulating Dr. Jacob, the patience of his approach, the knowledge that sometimes certain blooms, beautiful in their own right, had to be sacrificed to the overall appearance of the shrub, that by cutting back parts of the plant, one could obtain larger and healthier blooms later. I strove to demonstrate that although I could not match his accomplishment, I could pursue the same vision.

So it is this image that I hold in my memory, that of a rose bush growing toward the sun of a winter's day, and of a young boy emulating his mentor.

There must be something false about the photographs the policeman held. Perhaps the light entering a camera's lens can shift and take on new forms, alien to the original subject. Or perhaps time itself alters the nature of things, adapting them to the dark dreams of the viewer, such that a rose bush can metamorph into a bloody child.

I cannot accept the alternative.

For I remember holding the shears, the knife, and cutting back the flowers. I remember the thick fragrance and the warmth within the hothouse.

I had come over in the morning, a Saturday with many precious hours to spend, and when next I looked up, I realized that the sun had moved considerably, and I had promised my mother that I would be home for lunch at noon.

Dr. Jacob sat on a wooden stool, bent over his pots of orchids, a small trowel in his hand, chips of wood and spongy moss in tidy piles on the bench beside him. I apologized for disturbing his work and asked the time. He smiled. He wiped his hands on a towel, then pulled a gold watch from his pocket and pressed the fob so that the cover swung back. "Twelve-o-five," he said. "Time for you to go home, I suppose. Your mother will be waiting for you."

He looked over to where I had been working on the rose bush and I, following his gaze, saw the loose twigs, leaves, and snipped blooms beneath it, which I did not have time to clean up.

"Beautiful," Dr. Jacob said. "You have done well. Very well. Tell your mother that she should be proud of you." He waved a hand in the direction of my handiwork.

I blushed with pride.

"Hurry now. I will clean up here."

Then I was running through the house. I deftly avoided the camera on its tripod, grabbed my coat from the rack by the front door, and ran along the sidewalk, my coat unzipped and billowing behind me. The snow that had fallen the previous night swirled about my footsteps and glinted in perfect crystalline beauty.

I turned up the walkway to my house, still running, and there, inside the house, was warmth, lunch and my mother.

She looked down at me as I came bursting in the door. She smiled and her crooked teeth shone.

"Here you are, my little general."

Seeing my arm hidden behind my back, she said, "Oh, and what have you brought me?"

She craned her head so that she could peer over my shoulder and I, in response, backed up against the wall to obstruct her view. "Nothing. Nothing at all," I said.

But I could not keep up the charade, nor did I want to. I held out the roses to her, presenting them as a knight might to his queen, the ones from the hothouse, the ones that I had trimmed from my rose bush. There were five of them, each perfect with concentric rings of petals, a deep burgundy red with the velvety texture of skin. A few droplets of water glistened on them from where flakes of snow kicked up in my mad rush home had melted.

All this is as I remember it. My memory.

But what I want to know is what did my mother see there in my outstretched hands? What was it that she took from me, and arranged upon the dining room table as I sat eating?

What did *she* see?

M. SHAYNE BELL

The Pagodas of Ciboure

M. Shayne Bell is the author of one novel, Nicoji, *and numerous short stories published in* F&SF, Asimov's, Interzone, Amazing Stories, Realms of Fantasy, Science Fiction Age, Tomorrow, gothic.net, *and various anthologies. He lives in Salt Lake City.*

"The Pagodas of Ciboure" is a charming work of historical fantasy about the childhood of composer Maurice Ravel and the pagodas of French folklore. Pagodas are mysterious creatures found in a number of old French fairy tales, haunting remote woodlands with the eerie sound of their tinkling music. The story appeared in The Green Man: Tales of the Mythic Forest *(Viking) and was subsequently nominated for the 2002 Nebula Award.*

—T. W.

On a day of the summer Maurice nearly died, his mother carried him to the banks of the Nieve River and his life changed forever. He was ten years old then. It was a warm day around noon in June of 1885. A gentle breeze blew off the bay, and from where they sat Maurice and his mother could smell the salt of the sea. His mother believed such breezes could heal.

"When will Papa be here?" he asked his mother.

"Any day," she said. "His letter said he would come soon."

"Will he bring a doctor to bleed me?"

"Hush," she said. She brushed the hair across his forehead. "No one will bleed you in Ciboure, Maurice. I won't let them."

Maurice leaned against his mother and slept for a time in the sunlight. When he woke, he wanted to walk along the river. Yes he had a fever, and yes he did not feel well, but he wanted to walk upstream. He felt drawn to something in that direction, curious about what might lie just out of sight. His mother watched him totter along. "Don't go too far," she said, glad that he felt well enough to do this on his own but anxious that he not hurt himself.

Maurice worked his way slowly up the riverbank. He picked a reed and swished it at the grasses ahead. The grasses gave way to flowered bushes, and the land rose gently to a forest. The water of the little river gurgled over rocks as it rushed clear and cold down from the Pyrenees.

Not far into the trees, in a wide glen, Maurice came upon the walls of an abandoned pottery. Five hundred years earlier this workshop had sold sparkling dinner plates and soup bowls to Moorish and Christian princes. After the region had passed to France, its wares had been treasured in the palaces and mansions of Paris, Lyon, and Marseilles. But most of the wealthy family who owned the pottery had been guillotined in the Revolution. The few survivors had not returned to open it again.

The roof was now caved in. Windows in the stone walls were sunny holes. Maurice stood on his tiptoes and looked through one of the windows. He saw grass growing where workers had once hurried about polished floors.

Maurice walked around the ruined building and stopped in surprise. Three high mounds down by the river glittered in the sunlight as if covered in jewels. He had never seen anything like it. Among the daisies and the wild roses and the lacy ferns sunlight gleamed and sparkled on what looked from a distance like gems. It was as if he had wandered into a fairy treasury.

"Mother!" he called because he wanted her to see this. "Mother!"

But she was too far away to hear. Then he decided to be quiet: if there were jewels on those mounds he did not want to attract anyone else walking in the forest. He would fill his pockets first, then he would lead his mother here. If he had found jewels, they could buy a seaside mansion and he would get well and his father would come to live with them. They would all be happy again.

He walked slowly down to the mounds. His feet crunched on the ground, and he realized he was walking on broken china and glass. When he got to the mounds, he could see that that was what sparkled in the sunlight—broken dishes. The mounds were the old trash heaps of the pottery. There would be no fortune here.

Maurice scooped up a big handful of the shards, careful not to cut himself, and he carried them to the river. He held them down into the water and let the water wash away the dirt that had blown over the shards all these years. After a moment he shook out the water and spread his handful of broken china, wet and glittery, on the riverbank. Some shards were edged with a gold rim. One had a black fleur-de-lys entirely complete. Three pieces were from a set of blue china so delicate and clear he could see shadow through them when he held them up to the light.

Maurice was tired and hot. He sat breathing heavily for a time. When the breeze moved the branches overhead, sunlight sparkled on the broken china that had washed into the shallow riverbed. Maurice liked this place. Even if there were no jewels, it was nice to dream about being rich. It was nice to dream about being well again. This was a place that invited dreams.

He sat quietly—just long enough for the things that had gone still at his approach to start moving and singing again. First the birds, then the butterflies, then Maurice saw clusters of pieces of china moving slowly over the ground: one cluster, then another, then more than he could count. They moved slowly between the flowers and around the stands of grass.

Maurice sat very, very still. He did not know what was making the pieces of china cluster together and move. He shivered, but he did not dare run. He watched very carefully, hardly daring to breathe. Sometimes only three shards moved together. Sometimes a handful. The pieces that moved were bright and clean, and the sharp edges had all been polished away. One small clump of six snowy-white shards came upon the pieces Maurice had washed. It stopped by one of the blue ones, and drew back as if amazed.

It was then that Maurice heard the singing. It was an odd music, soft and indistinct, and he had to struggle to hear it at all. The simplest birdsong would drown it out. But the white china shards tinkled as they moved, and amidst the tinkling a high, clear voice sang. He thought the music sounded Chinese.

Other clusters of shards hurried up—pink clumps and white clumps and some with each shard a different color or design. With so many gathered around him Maurice could hear their music clearly. Somehow, surrounded by music, Maurice forgot to be afraid. Creatures that made music would not hurt him, he thought. They seemed to debate in their songs the merits of each piece he had washed. Maurice slowly reached out and picked up the white shard with the black fleur-de-lys. He set it down by a small cluster of terra-cotta shards and thought it made a fine addition.

All movement and song stopped. The clusters sank slowly to the ground. No one walking by would have noticed them or thought them special at all. Maurice put his hand back in his lap and sat still. He wanted them to move once more. He wanted them to sing.

It took some time for it to happen again. After the birds had been singing by themselves for a long time and when the butterflies were fluttering about Maurice's head, the terra-cotta pieces slowly drew themselves up into a terraced pattern, the larger pieces on the bottom, the smaller on top. It held the fleur-de-lys shard in the middle, as if it were a shield.

You look like a pine tree, Maurice thought.

But the more he looked at it, the more he realized it looked like a Chinese temple. He knew then what these creatures were. "Pagodas," he whispered. "Pagodas!"

His mother had told him stories about the pagodas. She'd said they looked like little Chinese temples. They were creatures made of jewels, crystal, and porcelain who lived in the forests of France. If you were good to them, they could heal you. He had thought the stories mere fairy tales.

He looked at the glittery river and the sparkling mounds and then at the shining shards around him. "Please heal me," he whispered. "I want to get better. Please help me."

He did not know how it would happen. He thought that maybe he should touch one of them. Some power might flow into him and make him well if he did. He reached out and gently touched the terra-cotta shards.

They sank down at once. He picked up each piece, then put it back in its place. He saw nothing among them. He found no hint of what a pagoda inside its shell of shards might look like. "Please help me," he whispered. "Mother's doctors can't, and I don't want Papa's to bleed me again."

Nothing around him moved now. When he heard his mother calling, he stood up very carefully. He did not want to step on the pagodas. He took off his shoes and planned each footstep before he took it. He tried to walk on grass and flowers, not the broken china. He hoped he had not hurt a single pagoda.

His mother met him at the steps of the pottery where he sat lacing his shoes. "You have been gone a long time," she said. She looked around as she waited for him. "Oh, this is pretty here. The trash heaps glitter so. You shouldn't walk barefoot to the river, Maurice—you could cut your feet on the glass!"

"I was careful, Mother," Maurice said.

She smiled and took his hand. They walked home slowly.

She did not have to carry him.

That night, while the fever made him wobbly, Maurice pulled the box that held his favorite things out from beneath his bed. Inside were all the letters from his father carefully tied with a red ribbon. He set them aside. There were the thirteen francs he'd been able to save, wrapped in a note to his parents asking them to divide the money. He set that aside as well. There was the bright red, white, and blue pouch that held the set of seven tin soldiers his grandmother had sent him from Switzerland.

And there was his kaleidoscope. It was his most treasured possession. It was a shiny brass tube filled with mirrors. A person looked through one end to see the glorious patterns; the other was a chamber that could be screwed off and opened. Into that chamber Maurice would put pieces of broken glass and the beads and the strips of colored paper and string that made the intricate images in the kaleidoscope. The most common objects could become beautiful there. He could change the images whenever he wanted, and he and his mother had spent pleasant hours walking along the roadsides looking for broken, colored glass small enough to fit inside. He unscrewed the chamber and picked out three bright blue glass shards and one crystal bead. He took the tin soldiers out of their pouch and laid them in a row along the bottom of the box. Then he put the pieces of glass and the bead in the pouch.

He would take them to the pagodas, he thought. Maybe if he gave them something they would help him.

In the morning, his nose would not stop bleeding. He kept old pieces of rag stuffed up his nose and his mother made him lie down, but every time he removed the rags, his nose would bleed again.

"Will Papa come today?" he asked.

"He may, or he may arrive tomorrow morning. It won't be long."

Maurice thought about that. He wanted to see his papa. He felt better when his papa held him. But he did not like the doctor his papa took him to, and neither did his mother. The good doctors, as his mother called them, had said to keep him comfortable and to give him medicines to take away the pain. The doctor Papa had found believed he could cure Maurice if he bled him. Papa had had to hold him down while the doctor had cut his arm and let his blood drip into a bowl. It had made him dizzy and sick, and he had embarrassed everyone by crying. It was why his mother had taken him away from Paris to his grandmother's house in Ciboure.

"Can we walk to the river again?" he asked.

His mother laughed, but then she looked out the window and put down her sewing. How many mornings would he want do to something like this, she wondered? A nosebleed was manageable.

She packed them a lunch and extra rags for his nose. They walked slowly to the river. Maurice could not wait to be gone. After eating a few bites, he stuffed some of the rags into his pockets and started for the trees. His mother was glad to see him take exercise, but she could not help herself. "Be careful, Maurice," she called.

The day was chill, and Maurice wore a heavy sweater. He took off his shoes when he came to the old rubbish heaps. He stepped very carefully down to the river, careful not to crush clumps of china shards and careful not to cut his feet. He started to be able to distinguish the shards that made up a pagoda's shell: they were the shiny and polished ones, the ones with bits of color, not the ones caked with mud or dust.

He inspected the ground before he sat down, and he sat where he had sat the day before. He listened, but he heard no Chinese music. "Pagodas?" he whispered. "Pagodas?"

Nothing stirred. He looked around and saw a few clumps that he recognized: the terra-cotta shards, still with the black fleur-de-lys; the light pink shards; clumps that were all white.

"Don't be afraid," he whispered. "I've brought you presents."

He took the pouch out of his pocket and opened it in his lap. He took out one of the pieces of blue glass and set it by the nearest snowy white clump. He wasn't sure, but he thought it might have shivered ever so slightly at his touch. He waited for a time, then he set the crystal bead by the terra-cotta shards.

Slowly, shard by shard, the terra-cotta pieces rose up. He watched the bead roll along the different shards, passed from one to another until it stood balanced on the very top.

Other pagodas began to move then. They rose up and gathered warily around Maurice, keeping their distance. He could hear their tinkly music again, and all at once he understood part of what they were asking him.

"I'm Maurice," he said. "My name is Maurice Ravel."

They sang at him, and he imagined that they were telling him their names. He had never heard one of those names before. He thought the terra-cotta shards were saying "Ti Ti Ting."

"You *are* all Chinese!" he laughed.

Then he started coughing, and he could not stop coughing for a time. Most of the pagodas sank down to the ground while he coughed. But not Ti Ti Ting. It edged a little closer.

"Can you help me?" Maurice asked it. "Can you make me well? Tell me what to do, and I will do it."

All the shards grew quiet. The music stopped completely.

"I know my presents are not very valuable, but it was all I could think to bring you today."

Nothing happened. The pagodas did not tell him anything more then. After a time, Maurice could see pagodas moving all around him. The mounds were covered with them. He could see places where they were digging into the mounds—mining, he imagined, for shards to weave into their shells. In other places, they were forming what looked like protective walls four or five inches high with sharp-edged pieces of china poking out from them. He wondered what small enemies they could fear? Whatever it was, they were going about their business unconcerned with his presence.

When he heard his mother calling, he made his way barefoot back to the steps of the pottery. His mother met him there.

"Is your nose still bleeding?" she asked.

Maurice took out the rags, but no blood followed. He threw the rags aside, and he and his mother walked home.

His nose did not bleed again that day.

Before bed, his grandmother brewed him a tea from herbs she had sent for from Spain. A priest in San Sebastian had blessed the tea, and his grandmother had even paid to have the priest touch the cross of Saint Teresa of Avila to the little packet. His grandmother was sure the tea would cure Maurice. He drank the whole cup to please her. It did not taste bad.

His mother brought out her silver-handled brush from her bedroom and started brushing his grandmother's hair. She did this every night before they went to bed. He liked to lay his head in his grandmother's lap and watch her face while his mother brushed her hair. She would close her eyes and hold herself very still and lean her head back into the brushing. Sometimes Maurice fell asleep while he watched his grandmother, and his mother would have to wake him to take him to bed. He did not fall asleep that night. He lay awake on his grandmother's lap till his mother finished brushing, then she led him to bed.

"Tell me about pagodas," he asked as his mother tucked the blankets around his chin.

"Oh, they are magic creatures!" she said. "They live in crystal and porcelain cities hidden in the forests. Few people see them or their cities these days. But when I was a little girl, your grandmother told me about an evil man who had found one of their cities not far from here. He tried to steal their jewels, but the pagodas attacked him with their crystal swords. He ran away, but bore the scars on his hands and feet the rest of his life. Because of those scars, everyone in Ciboure knew he was a thief so they could watch out for him."

She stood up to go.

"Can pagodas heal people?" Maurice asked. "You told me before that they could."

She looked at Maurice, then she sat down on the edge of his bed and held his hands. "Sometimes in your sleep you can hear them singing," she said. "They weave healing spells in their music. I hope you hear their music tonight, Maurice. I wish we had pagodas in the back garden. I'd set them on your windowsill and let them sing to you all night."

When his mother had gone, Maurice touched his nose. It still was not bleeding, though it had bled most days since winter. He thought of the walks he could take now on his own, despite the fevers.

The pagodas were helping him. He was sure of it. If he could stay here long enough, they would cure him.

Maurice slept soundly but heard no music. He woke to the sound of his parents arguing softly in the kitchen. His father had come. Part of him wanted to jump out of bed and run to his father's arms, but he did not do that. Instead he lay listening to what his parents were saying. He could not hear the words clearly.

He got out of bed and crept to the door. He heard his father say "doctor" and "bleeding." Then, "I want him to get well too! He's my son."

"I won't let anyone bleed him again!" his mother said.

"Does he still bruise easily? Does he still have fevers?"

"Yes, but—"

"Then Dr. Perrault knows how to help him! He uses ancient treatments for fevers and swelling, nosebleeds and abnormal bruising in children. I trust his techniques more than herbs and priests' blessings."

"Maurice is improving here. What Mother and I are doing is helping, though whether priests' blessings have anything to do with it I don't know. He is strong enough now to take walks every day. He sleeps through the nights. How could he ever sleep in Paris with all the street traffic?"

"You are wearing yourself out," his father said. "You can't do everything for him. None of us knows enough, Marie."

"I know enough not to hurt him."

"The other doctors we took him to had given up—they said to just keep him comfortable. At least Dr. Perrault had reason to think he could save him. Don't you think we should try, Marie? Don't you think we'd wonder the rest of our lives if we didn't try?"

Maurice had heard enough. He stood and opened the door. He looked out at his parents sitting at the big wooden table in front of the fireplace. His grandmother was still locked in her bedroom.

"Maurice," his father said. He stood and hurried to his son. Maurice did not want his father to touch him, but his father knelt and hugged him close. "Look at you!" he said. "So brown from the sun. Our neighbors in Paris will think I've adopted a peasant boy when I bring you back home."

"I don't want to go back to Paris," Maurice said. "Don't take me there again."

"Never go back to Paris? Who could say such a thing? Our home is in the greatest city in the world."

"I love the forest here, Papa. It's magic."

"All forests are magic," his father said.

His mother was setting out dishes for breakfast, and when Grandmother came out they all sat at the table. There was cheese and fresh bread, strawberries and milk.

"Don't ever take me back to Paris," Maurice said before any of them could take a bite.

His mother and father looked at each other. They all ate in silence for a time.

His father cleared his throat. "When do you set out on your walks, Maurice?" he asked. "May I go with you today? I want to see this magic forest of yours."

Maurice felt he had no choice but to take him. At noon that day, they set out. Maurice was nervous. He did not want his father accidentally stepping on the pagodas and crushing them. He decided not to take his father to the mounds of broken china. They would stop at the old pottery or even before they reached the trees. He'd claim to be sick, and his father would have to take him home.

His father carried a basket with a lunch in one hand, and he held Maurice's hand in the other. They passed his grandmother in her garden. She straightened up at their approach and bent her back.

"What a lovely summer this is," she said. "I find practically no slugs in the vegetables. The lettuce is free of slugs, and I found only one in the strawberries last week. Now if I could just keep the birds away."

"I'll make you a scarecrow when we return," Maurice's father said. "That should help."

She smiled and turned back to her hoeing. Maurice and his father walked to the river. Maurice was not very hungry. "You should eat to build up your strength," his father said. "Here, take more of this rabbit breast. Meat will make you strong."

"Yes, Papa," he said, and he did eat the meat. It was salty and good.

"Are those trees the forest you walk to?" his father asked, pointing.

They were soon among the trees and at the ruined pottery. They walked slowly. Maurice's legs hurt, and he was not making that up. "Can we just sit here for a time?" Maurice asked, and they sat on the steps.

His father rubbed Maurice's legs, then he put an arm around Maurice's shoulders and hugged him close. "I—" he started to say something, but he stopped. He looked away. He just held Maurice.

Maurice looked down at the mounds. They glittered, but his papa said nothing about that. Maurice looked all over the ground for the pagodas, but he saw none. That didn't surprise him. They would have taken cover at their approach.

But there were things moving on the nearest mound. Dark things. Maurice sat up straight. His father kicked at something at their feet, and Maurice saw that it was a shelled slug. It lay for a moment in the dirt where his father had kicked it, then it started crawling toward the mounds.

"Are those slugs on that mound, Papa?" Maurice asked.

His father looked where Maurice was pointing. "I think so," he said. "How odd. I've never seen them gather like that." He stood to walk over to the mound.

Maurice grabbed his hand. "Don't, Papa!"

"It's just slugs, Maurice."

"We have to be careful where we walk. We could crush things and not mean to."

"The slugs? Your grandmother would be grateful if we stepped on them."

"No, you don't understand. If we walk over there, let me show you where to step."

His father sat down beside him again. "So the magic begins here, does it? What is it we're trying not to crush?"

His papa had a merry smile. Maurice knew that Papa thought this was a game he had made up, but Maurice didn't care. He had to get over to the mound to see what was happening.

"Take off your shoes and step where I step," Maurice said.

They unlaced their shoes, and his father followed along behind him. Maurice worried about his father's bigger feet, but he saw no pagodas along the way that his father might step on. None of the shards they passed were washed and polished.

The nearest mound was a frightening sight. It was covered in shelled slugs. They heaved themselves about it in a dark mass sometimes three or four deep.

"Testacella," his father said, "carnivorous slugs. They eat earthworms and other slugs. No wonder your grandmother's garden is free of slugs. If these testacella migrated through this region on their way here they would have cleaned out all the other varieties in their path."

Maurice was looking for the pagodas. Where would they have gone to escape this blight of slug-eating slugs?

"I've never seen so many in one place," his father said. "I wonder if it's their mating season?"

Maurice felt a growing panic inside him. He knew it was selfish to think only of himself, but if the slugs had done something to the pagodas or if they had driven them away and he could not find them again he would never get well.

"They seem to be trying to reach those other two mounds, but something is holding them back," his father said.

It was the pagoda walls. Maurice understood now what the pagodas feared and why they had had to build walls. But what did the slugs want here? Where were the pagodas?

Then he saw the terra-cotta shards with the black fleur-de-lys scattered on the ground on the wrong side of the wall. Three slugs were nosing among the pieces.

"No!" Maurice screamed.

He started for Ti Ti Ting.

"Come back, Maurice!" his father said. "You'll cut your feet!"

But Maurice did not cut his feet. He stepped on the grass and the flowers and the slugs. He was glad to crush the slugs underfoot. He threw the three slugs on Ti Ti Ting into the river and knelt to pick up the pieces of the pagoda.

"What is it?" his father asked softly. He was standing next to him.

"A pagoda," Maurice said. He could barely talk. He would not cry, he told himself. He would not let himself cry in front of his father.

His father knelt down next to him. "What was the pagoda?"

Maurice held out the terra-cotta shards in his hands for his father to see. He picked up the piece with the black fleur-de-lys. "I gave it this piece," he said. "And I gave it a crystal bead. I can't find the bead."

"There it is, by your right foot." His father picked up the bead and handed it to Maurice.

"I watched them building these walls," Maurice said, nodding at the low walls in front of them. "I didn't know why they were doing it."

"Your pagoda was a brave one then. He was fighting outside the walls."

Maurice saw some of the pagodas he recognized lying on the ground on the safe side of the walls: the pink one, the white one with the piece of blue glass he had given it, clumps of multicolored shards.

"We have to go, Papa. They won't stand to fight if you are watching."

His father stood. He picked up a handful of slugs and threw them into the river.

Maurice stepped forward and set the pieces of Ti Ti Ting down by the other pagodas. Maybe they could do something for him. He wiped his eyes and watched for a moment, but none of the pagodas stood up. He wished he could make them trust his papa and get up to help Ti Ti Ting or at least get up to fight the slugs.

"They've breached your wall over here," his father said. "Let's get the slugs that have crawled onto that mound."

"It's not my wall," Maurice said.

"The pagodas' wall, I meant," he said.

Maurice went after the slugs that had crossed the wall. They were nosing down among the pagoda shards on the ground in the area. They *were* eating them! Maurice knew as he stepped along that he was probably stepping on pagodas, not just slugs. He didn't know what was worse: his crushing weight or the carnivorous slugs. He threw handful after handful of slugs into the river. His legs hurt and his arms hurt, and his nose started bleeding again.

"Maurice," his father called. "Let's go home. You've done all you can do to help here."

They sat on the steps of the ruined pottery and pulled off their slimy socks. "Just throw them away," his father said. "No one would want to wash them."

They rubbed their feet on the grass, then pulled on their shoes. Maurice had to turn his head so blood wouldn't drip onto his shoes while he tied them. He found the bloody rags he had thrown away days before and stuffed them back up his nose. He could see more slugs in the grass making their way slowly toward the mounds.

"The pagodas were helping me, Papa. They were healing me."

His papa considered that for a moment. "I'm sure they were," he said. "We all want to help you. Your grandmother tries with her priests. Your mother gives you good food, rest, and quiet. I would do anything for you too, Maurice. I've tried. I'm sure the pagodas did what they could."

He took his son's hand and led him away. When they came to the road, he had to carry Maurice.

But Maurice decided he had not done everything he could to help the pagodas. He lay feverish in his bed and listened to his parents talk quietly at the table. His father was trying to convince his mother to go back to Paris in a week or so. He knew what would happen there. Never mind Dr. Perrault and the bleeding. He knew what would happen to him without the pagodas.

And the pagodas themselves needed help. He could not let the slugs eat them whether they helped him or not. No one would believe him about the pagodas, of course. They thought he had made it all up.

After his parents and his grandmother had gone to bed, and after he had listened to his father snore for some time, Maurice crept out from under the covers. He had kept on his clothes and covered up before his mother had come to tuck him in, so no one had guessed that he was still dressed. He pulled on a sweater. He picked up his shoes, opened the bedroom door, and looked around the main room. No one was up. He walked barefoot to the kitchen and set a chair carefully by the cupboard. He stood on the chair and opened the top cupboard. He took out his grandmother's sack of salt. He would give her some of his money later to pay for it. Slugs hated salt. He'd use it to drive them away from the pagodas.

He closed the front door quietly behind him and set out down the road. There was a bright moon, and the road shined clearly ahead. He had to rest by the river, but soon he was at the ruined pottery.

It was darker there among the trees. The wind sighed in the branches. It felt different being among the trees at night. Maybe the slugs had changed the feeling of the forest, Maurice thought. He hurried up to the mounds. The slugs had breached the wall again and had covered half of the second mound. He looked frantically about for the pagodas, but saw none. He looked for the pieces of Ti Ti Ting, but they had been moved from where he had set them. The pagodas he had lain Ti Ti Ting next to had all moved somewhere else, too.

He looked around for the pagodas. "Don't be afraid," he called. "It's Maurice. I've come to help you fight!"

He started scattering salt onto the slugs at his feet. They curled up quickly into little balls at the slightest touch of salt. He took a handful of salt and threw it onto a mass of heaped slugs higher up the mound by the opening of what Maurice had thought was a pagoda mine. The slugs writhed and rolled around when the salt touched them. They would pull back into their segmented shells, then stick all the way out, then pull back inside. How the salt must hurt them, Maurice thought, but he had to try to help the pagodas. There was no stopping now.

"Where are you?" Maurice called to the pagodas. "I have only one bag of salt. Show me how best to help you before it's all gone."

Then he saw a pagoda, one of the white ones—the white one with the piece of blue glass. It was standing just around the edge of the second mound. It held up the piece of glass as if in salute. But then Maurice saw that it was pointing. He looked and saw a huge mass of slugs slowly crawling over the wall and swarming over the depression between the second and third mounds.

Maurice had an idea what they were swarming over—what they were eating there!

"I'm coming!" Maurice called.

He surprised the slugs from behind. He scattered salt over the slugs massed at the wall and left them writhing there. He started scattering salt on the huge heap of slugs in the depression, but there were so many. He picked up handful after handful and threw them into the river, then he scattered more salt.

He saw more pagodas, the pink ones and the white ones and all the multicolored ones. They were standing in a defensive line at the base of the third mound—and they did carry crystal swords! Maurice saw them glitter in the moonlight. The swords were as thin as needles. He watched them stab the slugs in the mouth with them. They would wait till a slug loomed over them, its mouth gaping open, then they would strike with their swords and pull back quickly. The slugs would snap about and try to bite them, but some fell over and did not move again.

The pagodas were stabbing through the mouth into the brain, Maurice realized.

He did not see Ti Ti Ting.

"Ti Ti Ting!" Maurice called. "Ti Ti Ting!"

But he could not see him.

"Did the slugs kill him?" he asked the other pagodas, but they did not have time to sing answers to his questions.

Maurice kept scattering salt and throwing slugs into the river. He started to conserve the salt. He threw only slugs he hadn't salted into the river. The pagodas advanced on the slugs he had salted, and they could easily dispatch them with their swords as they writhed about in salty agony. Maurice threw unsalted slugs until he had to rest. He sat down on a part of the third mound free of slugs and free of pagodas and changed the rags in his nose. His nose was bleeding steadily. He tried to stopper it up tight, though he knew the blood would soak through the rags and start dripping onto his clothes again.

He wanted to sleep. He was tired. He was feverish. But there were more and more slugs.

Then he saw Ti Ti Ting. He was drooping in a depression of the third mound. Maurice stood up to look down into that area. There were other drooped pagodas there, and some just lying on the ground. Three intact pagodas were singing to the hurt ones—he could hear the music softly. They were trying to heal their friends.

"Get well Ti Ti Ting!" Maurice said. "I know what it feels like to be sick. Get well!"

Ti Ti Ting stood a little straighter and looked at Maurice. He seemed to be trying to tell him something, but Maurice could not hear what it was. Maurice reached out and touched Ti Ti Ting softly, then he hurried off to scatter more salt.

When he ran out of salt, he filled the bag with slugs and emptied it into the river then went back for more. He dropped unsalted slugs onto the salted ones, trying to get twice the use for the salt. He worked for hours it seemed. The night grew darker, as it does before dawn. All the wind hushed. Maurice and the pagodas had cleared the slugs from the depression between the second and third mounds. Pagodas were manning their wall again. Others were securing the second mound and the wall there, and some were advancing even on the first mound.

Maurice could do no more. His arms ached, and his legs ached so badly that he had to sit down. He lay back for a moment to slow the blood dripping from his nose.

He watched the pagodas. They were still fighting hard to save themselves, but Maurice thought they had the advantage now. He and his grandmother's salt had changed the outcome of the battle.

He knew he should be getting back before someone missed him. "Good-bye pagodas!" he said. "Good-bye Ti Ti Ting. I'll try to come back before we leave for Paris."

None of them noticed him now. They were all too busy. Maurice was tired and cold, but he decided to lie there just a little longer till maybe his legs felt a little better. He was not sure he could walk all the way home just then.

He woke with a start. Pagodas stood all around him, singing. There were more pagodas around him than he had ever seen. Ti Ti Ting stood right by his head.

The battle was over.

Maurice felt so at peace surrounded by the music he did not move. His head felt different somehow, clearer, not feverish. His nose had stopped bleeding.

A soft morning light burnished the glen and the mounds. A gentle breeze blew east off the bay. Yet it was so quiet he could hear the pagodas' music clearly.

They were singing for him.

Maurice closed his eyes. His legs did not ache. His nose throbbed, but it was not bleeding. He felt certain his body was healed. "Thank you," he whispered.

It seemed that Ti Ti Ting was singing thank you in return.

He woke again when he heard his mother and father calling his name. It was full light now. The pagodas had moved away. He could see them on all the mounds, even the first. He saw only dead slugs. He stepped carefully away from the mounds and walked steadily up to the pottery steps. He lay there waiting for his parents.

"Maurice!" he heard his mother call. "Maurice?"

"I'm here, Mother," he called.

He saw her running up the path. Soon he was in her arms, and Papa and Grandmother were there, too.

"I'm better now," Maurice said. "The pagodas sang to me last night. I went to sleep hearing them sing after we defeated the slugs, and I feel better now. They helped me."

"Oh, Maurice," his mother said.

But Maurice was right. He was still weak, and he had to work to regain his strength, but his nose did not bleed again. His legs did not bruise abnormally again. The fevers did not return. His grandmother thought her priests and their blessings had done it. His mother thought it had been all their tender care, and maybe a miracle. His father did not care how it had happened, just that his son was well again.

On their last day in Ciboure before returning to Paris, they all picnicked by the river. They let Maurice walk alone up to the old pottery.

He went straight to the mounds. The pagodas were there. None of them sank down at his approach. He looked around for Ti Ti Ting and found him standing guard on the repaired wall. Maurice knelt in front of him. He opened his tin soldier pouch and scattered the broken pieces of a dish his grandmother had dropped the day before. "I brought you presents," he said.

The pagodas all gathered around. He set down a big bag of salt in front of them. "You know how to use this," he said. "I'll bring you more next summer when we visit Grandmother."

The pagodas started singing. Maurice listened. He tried to catch a melody he could remember and hum, but it was all too different. The music seemed so foreign to him then. But Ti Ti Ting seemed insistent about something. Maurice leaned down to listen to what he might be saying. Maurice listened and listened—and suddenly he understood. Ti Ti Ting was telling Maurice that he would understand their music in time, that Maurice would write down some of it and present it to the world. They knew this about him: that Maurice would become a composer who would give beautiful music to a world that needed beauty.

Maurice sat up and laughed. "Oh, I hope so!" he said. "That would be such fun."

They said their good-byes, and Maurice made his way up the path. He met his father standing in shadows under the trees at the edge of the glen. He had an odd look on his face. Maurice just smiled and took his father's hand as they walked back to the others.

In the coming years, Maurice always took salt and bits of broken china to the pagodas when they visited his grandmother. His illness never returned, and he grew into a strong young man. In time, all the world knew the name "Maurice Ravel" because of the beautiful music he wrote. He remembered what Ti Ti Ting had told him, and when he could finally make sense of it, he used some of the pagoda music in his *Mother Goose Suite* and a ballet before that and a set of piano pieces before that. The music delights audiences to this day. Maurice hoped it might heal some of them.

One day, a letter arrived from his grandmother. She told him that a corporation had bought the ruined pottery with plans of establishing a shoe factory on the site. Maurice rushed to Ciboure. The men loading his trunks onto the train wondered why he took so many empty trunks, but when he returned they were not so empty. Maurice bought a house in the forest of Rambouillet outside Paris, and over time he purchased all the land around it. The neighbors wondered at the many happy parties the Ravel family held among the trees there, at all the tinkling lights and the Chinese-sounding music.

Maurice always donated to charities helping children with leukemia. From time to time he let his friends bring their children to his estate, if they were sick. They'd take them home well again weeks later.

The Ravels keep that forest estate to this day. It is a wild, brambly place with secret, flowered glens. No one will ever build on that land.

Other things have built there.

GRAHAM JOYCE

The Coventry Boy

Graham Joyce is a British writer whose work falls into the interesting interstitial realm at the intersection of horror, contemporary fantasy, and mainstream fiction. His novels include Requiem, Dark Sister, Indigo, The Tooth Fairy, Smoking Poppy, *and* The Facts Of Life, *all of which are highly recommended. His short fiction has been collected in* Partial Eclipse and Other Stories *(Subterranean Press). Joyce lives in Leicester, England, and has won four British Fantasy Awards.*

Although "The Coventry Boy" works as a stand-alone story, it is part of The Facts of Life. *Joyce says: " 'The Coventry Boy' deals with the night of November 14, 1940, when Coventry, a deeply historical English city, had all its visible and architectural history erased in a single night by a ferocious and sustained Nazi bombing raid. Coventry is my home town, by the way."*

"The Coventry Boy" was originally published in the British magazine The Third Alternative, *Issue 32.*

—E. D.

Everyone suspected that the big storm was coming, but Cassie seemed to know exactly when. There had already been numerous raids between June and October of 1940, when bombs had rained down on Coventry. Factories, shops and cinemas left twisted and smoking. There were even incidents of German planes machine-gun strafing civilians in the street. The civilian injury list was high, and almost two hundred people were killed outright in these early raids.

After all, Coventry was located exactly at the heart of the country and Adolf Hitler wanted to show what a surgeon he was; show how the heart could be cut out. A beautiful mediaeval and Georgian rosette town boasting resplendent cathedrals and antiquarian buildings, Coventry was a heritage showpiece of the English Midlands. And after all again, Coventry manufactured the Armstrong-Whitworth Whitley bomber, the first plane to penetrate German airspace, and the main instrument of the torment of Munich. No, not surgery: the Fuhrer wanted to show he could bring his fist down and turn it to dust. The storm *would* come, but if only the city might know *when* then the fatalities might be minimised.

But Cassie knew. Sixteen years old, going on seventeen, exactly how she knew is unspeakable, but she knew it in her water, in her bowels. Her blood coursed differently. Perhaps the moon fattening in the night sky spoke to her; whatever it was she knew better than to tell. She'd already learned that if she did try to tell, no one would believe her; and that after they'd failed to listen they would call her a jitterbug. So she knew with certainty, but did not speak.

Like the dead.

"The dead can hear you," her mother Martha had said. Martha, who smoked a pipe and who never moved from her place by the fireside. "But they can't speak. They can't get their words out."

It started for Cassie when she woke early one morning with music playing in her head. Her sleep patterns, already disrupted by the nights spent in the Anderson shelter at the bottom of the back garden and by the sirens, had broken like an egg yolk, spilling something of her. She felt a mild flow inside her and put her hands between her legs. The wetness she found there made her think of the residue of sleep, a slippery vernix left behind by her dreams. While elder sister Beatie and Martha still slept she pulled on her dressing gown and went downstairs.

The haunting music was still playing in her head. It was a piece she'd heard several times, familiar, comforting. Cassie switched on the radio. It was tuned to the BBC Home Service, and the same piece was playing, perfectly segued with the version sounding in her head. She switched the radio off and although it became fainter, she continued to hear the music, without it missing a beat or dropping a note. After switching the radio back on again she sat on a chair and stared hard at the radio until the piece had finished playing. When the music stopped on the radio, it stopped inside her head, too.

Cassie went upstairs to her room, dressed hurriedly and reached under her bed for a tin tea-caddy, Japanese lacquer-style. In it were her savings. After emptying the caddy into her purse she went downstairs again, put on her coat and allowed the door to click quietly behind her as she let herself out. The morning was cold and sharp and there was a rime of frost on the ground. She walked into the city.

Up Trinity Street to the top of the town and directly to Paynes music shop. Too early: it was closed. She stood in the doorway and waited. It was an hour and a half before the manager of the store arrived to open up. "You're keen," he said, producing his glittering bunch of keys. He had to wave his hand at Cassie to get her to stand aside for him.

"I want a record player," Cassie said as soon as they'd got inside the shop. "A new one."

The store manager switched on the lights. "Let me get my coat off," he said. "Where's the fire?"

Coming, said the voice in Cassie's head.

He took her over to the latest box-players. Cassie was mesmerized by the little explosions of hair in his nostrils and earholes. "This is a HMV gramophone. It has a Bakelite playing arm and it comes in this beech cabinet—"

"Yes."

"Yes?"

"Yes. I'll have it."

"You haven't asked me how much it is." The manager eyed this slip of a girl suspiciously. "How much can you afford?"

Cassie emptied her savings out of her purse. The manager sighed. "I've got some second-hand cabinets over here. Let's see what we can do."

Cassie could just afford one of the machines on offer. It took her last penny. Then she said, "I want a record. I don't know what it's called. But you'll know it. It goes like this." She hummed the music that had been playing both on the radio and in her head that morning.

" 'Moonlight Serenade.' I've got it in stock but how are you going to pay for it? I've just let you off a few shillings on that cabinet and that's cleaned you out, hasn't it?"

Cassie merely fixed her eyes on the man and crossed her legs at the ankles. She swayed, very slightly.

The manager seemed cross, but he stepped behind his counter and sorted through the discs until he found the Glenn Miller recording. "I'll let you have it but you're going to have to bring the money in when you've got it. Understand? I don't know why I'm doing this."

It's because I've got power over you.

Cassie lugged the record-playing cabinet home by its carrying-handle. It was heavy and she had to keep stopping to switch hands, but she was unwavering. On the way home an ARP officer in a tin hat, hands on hips, interposed himself on the pavement before her. "Oi girlie, where's your gas mask?" he shouted in a bullying tone.

She stepped round the ARP man, leaving him to gaze after her.

Martha and Beatie were up and about when she got home. Cassie bustled into the sitting room and squeezed by them without a word. "Where've you been?" Martha called. "Do you want some breakfast?"

"Whatever have you got there?" Beatie said, eyeing the record player. But Cassie only bumped upstairs without a word. "She's getting to be a proper moody girl." Beatie complained.

"Not like someone I could name," Martha said.

Beatie was about to fire back an answer, but there came to stop her lips the strains of Glenn Miller's 'Moonlight Serenade,' drifting from Cassie's room. The sound filled the house like a dew-backed mist.

In the next few days, Cassie played the piece over and over and over. She would lie on her bed, sometimes naked, listening. At first, Beatie and Martha were merely irritated. Martha quizzed her daughter about why she'd blown her savings on the record player without getting an answer. Beatie actually went out and bought Cassie two more Glenn Miller hits, and an armload of stuff a friend at the bomber factory—where Beatie punched rivets for the war effort—had found too sad to keep because it had all belonged to a brother in the navy killed at sea. But Cassie didn't play any of it. She sat upstairs in her room, spinning 'Moonlight Serenade.' And if Martha or Beatie complained too aggressively, then she merely went out, and stayed out, for long periods of time.

At night, wide awake with whatever it was that had broken her sleep and when her mother and sister absolutely would not tolerate any sound coming from her room, she huddled in a blanket on the edge of her bed, watching the moon fattening slowly, maturing, feeding her with more energy as if on a silver umbilical cord. If the sirens came she was ready, and would help the others pull a few things together for the shuffle to the Anderson shelter; have the kettle boiled for a flask of tea while they were still blinking and complaining; especially helpful to Beatie who was doing ten-hour shifts riveting bombers and who needed the sleep, unlike Cassie. Most of the sirens at that time were false alarms, and Cassie knew it; knew they might as well sleep on, that it would be Birmingham or maybe Liverpool catching a tanning that night. But even in the shelter she couldn't nap. One night some time before dawn Beatie got up to relieve herself in the tin pail. Martha, blinking, dozy, said, "Hark! Is that the all-clear?"

"No, Mum, it's Beatie pissing in the bucket. Go back to sleep."

Beatie was having a hard time for sleep. Like many of the women of Coventry she was under pressure to work ten and sometimes twelve-hour shifts for the war effort.

Buck up girls! Let's bomb the hun! This she did readily, and since the pay was good she'd never had so much money in her pocket; but the sirens going off on so many nights like this left her exhausted and irritable.

One evening Cassie heard her sister calling up the stairs, "Cassie if you play that bloody thing one more time—just one more time—I'm coming up these stairs to sort you out! You hear me, Cassie?"

Cassie didn't answer. She lay on her bed in bra and pants. 'Moonlight Serenade' played on. When it stopped, Cassie languidly reached over to put it on again. After a moment, the thundering of shoes on the stairs. Beatie threw open the door, made straight for the record player, lifted the stylus arm, plucked up the record from the turntable and broke it over her knee. Then she turned to look Cassie in the eye.

Cassie didn't flinch. Beatie screamed and went thundering back down the stairs. Cassie didn't mind. She'd got the music lodged in her head, and perfectly, note for note, beat for beat. She could switch it on or off any time she wanted to.

What's more she could repeat that trick with the radio over and over. Many times she heard music playing in her head, would go to switch on the Home Service and find the same tune broadcasting loud and clear. Without saying anything she tested this ability scientifically. It was clear to her that she could somehow 'hear' radio broadcasts in the thin air. She didn't need radio receiving equipment. She somehow *was* the equipment.

Though she was not so stupid as to try to tell anyone about this.

Other things were going on in her body. Her breasts had plumped slightly, and her nipples were tender and sensitive. The lips of her vagina, too, were swollen, and she felt an itch or a trickle deep inside her. She needed to masturbate often, and before Beatie snapped the slate disc she would lie under a sheet on her bed stroking her clitoris and squeezing her nipples while 'Moonlight Serenade' teased her on. And in the street, too, it was obvious all this wasn't just one-way. Even as a virgin she knew the effect she was having on men. Off-duty soldiers and sailors and airmen were burning for her, it was plain from the way they sized her up. Plus she could make men's heads turn—not in the usual figure of speech but literally: all she had to do was focus her gaze on the back of the neck of a man somewhere in her vicinity, perhaps on the bus or while waiting in a queue with her ration-card, and after a moment the subject would have to turn and look at her. It worked without fail. She was accreting powers to herself, she knew that. What powers they were she had no idea, but they were extraordinary. She'd used them on that man in the record shop, but he didn't know it. They never did know. They were easy. Men were easy.

And that was just part of it. It was knowing that the storm was coming that most excited her. Terrified and excited her.

On the night of 12 November she went to a dance with Beatie. Martha had stopped worrying about what the girls got up to a long time ago. Though Cassie was only sixteen she could easily pass for a twenty-year-old, and Martha had given up trying to keep her in. Though she'd been stricter with her other daughters, something about the incidence of death all around had relaxed her with Cassie; and she'd learned early that Cassie would go her own way whatever obstacles were placed before her. But she did extract a promise from both her daughters that they would seek proper shelter, and *not* to try to find their way home should they get caught in a raid.

Cassie was in a highly excitable state as the two stepped into town together. The moon was moving into its fullness, like an autumn gourd, and though it was a clear and rather frosty night, the searchlights sweeping the starry sky passed across the three spires of the city, prickling the night. Beatie was trying to get her to calm down.

She might not have bothered. As soon as they barrelled into the dance hall, Cassie heard the band and broke away from Beatie's side. When Beatie caught up with her she was already jiving with an airman, his hair slicked back and his eyes dripping with ardor. "Don't give it all away too quick," was all Beatie could whisper, but Cassie was spinning and waving her hands in the air.

That jitterbug.

Within the hour Cassie was in the shadows of the great gothic cathedral in Bayley Lane, her back against the cold, damp mediaeval wall and her skirt around her waist. There were no streetlights because of the blackout. "Wow, you're in a hurry," said her airman as she fumbled with his belt.

"We might never see each other again," Cassie said, clinging to the fleecy collar of his leather flying jacket. "Imagine that. And then we'd have missed the chance to fuck." *And I'd never lose my cherry,* she thought.

"Hey, and you think like a bloke," he said.

"Does it put you off?"

"No, no . . . it's just . . . and, oh you smell good."

"Stop talking. Let's do it."

A siren began moaning, very close. "Fuckanddamn."

"Ignore it," Cassie said. "It's not tonight."

"What?"

"Maybe tomorrow night. Or the next night. But it's not coming tonight."

"Hey, they should have you down at Bletchley, if you know all that. You know, Telligence service. I'm sorry I can't do much with that siren going off in my ears. How old are you anyway?"

Cassie dug her hand into the airman's trousers, stroking the bell of his cock with her thumbnail. He flinched, and settled back into her arms again. "Can't do what?" Cassie shouted. She was having to bellow to make herself heard above the siren. Someone ran past them on their way to a shelter. Then she put her tongue in his ear.

"Christ! God you're lovely!"

Cassie glanced up at the cathedral spire and at the searchlights raking the sky overhead. She knew the airman wanted to get himself off to the nearest air-raid shelter, but with his cock fattening in her hand he couldn't tear himself away. "Do it," she said.

He tugged his trousers down and he hooked the back of Cassie's leg over his arm. He had to push her knickers out of the way and come at her from the side, almost lifting her from the ground as he made to enter her, their eyes locked together in that ancient place, under the sky-pricking spire, under the crossbeams of the searchlights, inside the demonic and melancholy howl of the siren. He fell back. "It's no good. I can't—not with that thing going off right in my ear."

"What's the matter?"

The airman fumbled. He looked up at the sky, at the searchlights raking the clouds. Then he looked down again. "It's just not happening for me. Can we please go to the shelter? My arse is getting cold."

Cassie pulled up his trousers for him. Hand-in-hand they strolled towards the shelter on Much Park Street. An ARP man standing outside the shelter said, "Don't 'urry yourselves, will you?"

"It's all right," said the airman glumly. "It's not coming tonight."

"Another bleedin' know-it-all," the ARP man said sourly.

The airman whispered as they went down into the basement of Draper's Hall, "Don't mind him. He just needs to get laid."

Not the only one, Cassie's voice said.

They spent an hour in the shelter together before the all-clear came. His name was Peter and he was a navigator. He was twenty, and seemed worldly and mature to Cassie. She was cold so he pulled his leather flying helmet out of his pocket and put it on her head. He walked her all the way home and they kissed again in the alley running between the houses. He put his hand on her forehead. "You've got a fever."

"I'm all right," Cassie said. "Really I am."

But the moment had passed. Cassie sighed when she knew it wasn't going to happen. She made to give him back his flying helmet. "You keep it," he said.

"Won't you get in trouble for losing it?"

"Yeah. Goodnight Cassie. You're too lovely, you are. Too lovely."

And he went back to his war.

The next day Cassie lay in bed late, touching herself, thinking of her airman and other handsome men, sleeping fitfully. Now as well as the music her head was full of other sounds: high frequency whistles and intermittent morse-signals and snatches of foreign language. When she rose the house was empty. Beatie had gone to work and Martha had left a note on the kitchen table to say that she had popped out to do some shopping.

Cassie parked a stray curl behind her ear with a delicate finger and switched on the radio, fiddling with the tuning dial. The frequency whistle rose and fell, throbbed and hummed. There was morse code. There was guttural language.

She didn't need an interpreter. It was going to be the following night for sure. Last night the moon had been almost full. Tomorrow night it would be complete. Cassie shook with excitement. It was plain. Adolf Hitler would send his men, his bombers, his demons to Coventry tomorrow night. That is what he would do.

"There you are," Martha said, letting herself in, pulling off her hat. "Sleeping the sleep of the dead. It'll do you no good, all this lying in."

"Tomorrow night. They're going to bomb us tomorrow night."

"Eh? What's that?"

"More than before. More than last month. The big raid. It's tomorrow night. I know."

"Know? How can you know?"

"It's a full moon tomorrow night. It's coming. It's going to rain fire here in Coventry, Mum."

Martha walked over and put her hand on Cassie's forehead. "You're shivering. You're burning up. Do you want to go back to bed?"

Cassie hadn't even known what the airman had meant in his reference to the intelligence mansion at Bletchley, the government code and cypher school. Its very existence was supposed to be top secret. But the day before Cassie met her airman at a dance the Bletchley school had decoded a recent German transmission. The transmission laid down the signal procedures for an operation codenamed not Moonlight Serenade but Moonlight Sonata, implying that a three-pronged attack would be launched against a British city on the night of the full moon. On the same day a captured German pilot was overheard telling his cellmate that a three-phase raid would be made on either Coventry or Birmingham on or around 15 November.

The Germans had invented a radio navigational system known as the X-Gerat, guiding a plane to its target and automatically triggering the bomb-release on arrival. The X-Gerat used four radio transmitters sending radio beams from different locations. It comprised one main beam aligned on the target and three intersecting beams. The German pathfinder pilots flew parallel to the main beam until they hit the first intersecting beam. That was their instruction to change course and fly directly along the main beam. Twenty miles from the target they passed through the second intersecting beam: a signal to press a button starting a clock. Five miles from target they crossed the third beam: an instruction to press another button that stopped the first hand of the clock and started a second hand ticking. The bombing run had begun. When the two hands came together, the bomb load was automatically released on the people below. It was an efficient system for obliteration bombing.

Bletchley had uncovered signals to special bombing units, all starting with the code-word Korn. They also decrypted information revealing that special Luftwaffe calibration signals would commence at one P.M. on 14 November.

At 13.00 hours on the afternoon of 14 November the German calibration signal was detected. Two hours later British Fighter Command were satisfied that the X-Gerat beams were aligned on Coventry. The Air Ministry warned the RAF home commands that Coventry had become a special target.

They might also have warned Coventry. The city's anti-aircraft batteries and barrage-balloon units might have appreciated the tip-off; not to mention the Coventry Fire Brigade, the Chief of Police, and the local ARP. They might have tipped the wink to the mayor of the city, or rumored it at the Coventry and Warwickshire hospital.

They chose not to. Cassie was the only person in Coventry who had been informed.

At one o'clock that afternoon, Martha and Cassie were about to sit down to lunch. Martha switched on the radio for the news. Just as it came on Cassie felt something click in her head, like a switch being thrown. "It's started," she said.

"Yes yes," Martha said, bringing the teapot to the table, thinking Cassie referred to the news broadcast.

"I don't mean the news. Do you think you should all go out to the farm? That would be best. You should go out to Wolvey where Tom and Una are. Safer, Mum."

"I can't be bothered with that game," Martha said. "If Adolf wants me he'll have to come and get me." When the early raids had started in June they had, like many other Coventry citizens, all gone out together to stay in the country. But what with the small aerodrome at Bramcote so close to the farm, they had found the concentration of bombs denser and somehow more immediate than when they stayed shivering under the stairs in the days before the Anderson shelter was erected.

"Well I'm glad. I don't want to go to the farm. I want to stay. Stay and be here. Stay and help. That's it. I want to help." Cassie spoke rapidly. Martha had seen it before in her. A repetitive but cheerful chatter. "But you and Beatie, Mum, I want you and Beatie to stay in the shelter. While I'm out. Helping."

"Is it your time of the month?" Martha said.

Some time after six o'clock that evening Cassie changed from her dress into a pair of slacks, pulled on a pair of Beatie's work boots, donned her coat and scarf and went out without telling her mother. She stopped by the park to light a cigarette and to look up at the night sky. A Harvest Moon, they had called it before the war. The moon was indeed loaded, and one great thing about the blackout, Cassie thought, was the restoration of the stars in the sky. The evening was crisp and cold and the cigarette smoke reared up like white horses' heads briefly painted on the air. And if she swung her head the black night ran with tiny beads of color, and she knew that these were radio signals that she could not just hear but could see tracking across the sky, and it was pointless trying to fix your gaze on these tiny iridescent parabolas because they would be gone in a twinkling anyway and the only way to apprehend them with the human eye was to acknowledge the brevity of the leap they made into and out of the visible spectrum, and it was an extraordinary thing how few people understood that.

Cassie was chipped out of her reverie by a burn on her hand. The cigarette wedged between first and second fingers had burned down to a stick of ash, unsmoked. The stub sparked as it fell to the flagstones, and she stamped it out under her shoe. She took her compact out of her bag and reapplied her lipstick by the light of the moon. She checked her hair in her pocket mirror, clipped it shut and returned her compact to her bag. "And the night," she said; though she didn't know why, because her mind was racing. Turning her collar against the chill of the evening, she proceeded to walk slowly towards Coventry city center.

At around seven P.M. she developed a strange feeling in her stomach, or perhaps in her bowels. A vibration. Then it spread across her body to her ears, until she understood that the vibration was not inside her, but was the familiar air-raid warning sirens. She'd somehow anticipated it by several seconds. That sour, almost forlorn howl dragged up from the lowest place on earth, fattening and rising into a despairing moan, climbing at last until it wails, fighting to live at its uppermost note until it falls back, uselessly, defeated, and then climbs again, wanting to infect with its own panic. Cassie heard the whistles of nearby ARP men as they went through their drill. Soon, she, knew, there would be more urgency. Within ten minutes she was right. The throbbing of incoming aircraft could be heard like a great rumor in the distance, behind the moan of the air-raid siren. The ARP men began to whistle more spiritedly and shout along the streets, some of them jocular, "Run rabbits, run my little rabbits!" The search-lights were thrown on, crisscrossing the night sky from points in the center of town.

Cassie pressed on. Then something beautiful illuminated the sky. It was a parachute flare, strontium-white and blazing brilliantly, hanging in the air. Then more, several, parachute flares hanging in formation, dropped on the east side of the city and floating west in the light breeze. Ack-ack guns replied from ground placements in nearby villages, uselessly thumping rounds of shells into the sky; then Bofors guns from nearby, louder.

In Swan Lane a voice from the dark said, "Come on girlie, let's have you off the streets."

"Hello Derek," Cassie said. "Where've you been these past weeks?"

Derek was an old friend of Beatie's. He'd been turned down for active service because his right leg was three inches longer than his left. "Cassie! What are you doing? Why don't you get home? This one's for real."

"I can see that. I'm out to help. Official, like."

Derek squinted at her. "Official?"

"Go and do your rounds. Get some rest. It's going to be a long night."

Derek snorted at this sixteen-year-old advising him. But she was already gone. Derek put his whistle to his lips but merely stared after her.

Cassie took Thackall Street alongside the football stadium. There was a cut-through alley behind the football ground, and she hoped that route into town would help her dodge most of the ARP men. As she slipped through the alley towards Hill fields, Cassie could see families getting into their Andersons, and she thought she heard a snigger. Then another, and another, and she realized the sniggers were coming from the air. The sky was sniggering. They were incendiary bombs, producing an eerie sound as they twisted in the air. They thumped the ground without exploding, but spread fire where they fell, and they began to rain down in great number. Someone saw her from a garden by the light of one such flame and shouted, beckoning. But even when a different type of incendiary dropped with a flaring, phosphorescent flash, Cassie wasn't going to be deflected.

Why am I unafraid? she said to herself. This isn't natural. It's because, she told herself, it's because I am *meant* to be here.

Isolated minor fires broke out around her as she moved towards the heart of the town, and away from the sniggering rain of incendiaries. There was another sound in the air, like a beating of leathery wings as something fluttered around her head. It raised the gooseflesh on her arms, but she hadn't time to think what had caused it because the incendiaries were followed by the crump-blasts of high-explosive bombs falling all over the city.

A fire engine with its bell ringing sped past her on Primrose Hill. Most of the incendiaries around her were burning without effect in the middle of the road; others spread their fire. One licked at a gatepost in Cox Street and she tried to kick the flames away with her toe before a man rushed out of the house, smothering the small fire with a blanket. The man grabbed her arm and tried to drag her inside but she pulled free of him.

The drone of planes overhead got louder, and it occurred to Cassie that there must be many, many bombers in the air above her head, otherwise the throbbing noise would have passed. She looked up and she could see them. Hundreds of them, in beautiful geometric formation. Some of them near enough to reflect the light of their own flares, others tiny specks caught in the crossbeams of the searchlights. She could see tracers, and the brief orange puffball explosions of anti-aircraft fire, and still around her she heard both the sniggering and the unexplained, loathsome batwing flutter. In the sky she could also detect—briefly visible, now gone—the iridescence of radio waves, sparkling but following an undeviating route across the sky and she knew that the bombers were somehow following this rainbow route. Another parachute was falling behind her. It had something dangling on the end. She thought it was a paratrooper, that the Germans were actually going to land. The parachute swung hither and thither in perfect time to the beat of "Moonlight Serenade." But then she saw that the parachute carried a cylindrical box, and after it disappeared behind the houses it rocked the earth with a fantastic blast that left Cassie's ears ringing. She reached in her pocket and found the leather aviation helmet her airman had given her two nights ago, and she put it on, tying the strap under her chin.

It was plain to her by now that each new cascade of incendiaries and explosives was coming down at approximately thirty-second intervals. That must have been the distance between each bank of planes, half-a-minute. She began to punctuate her movements accordingly.

By the time she got to the cathedral there were small fires burning everywhere and crews of firemen putting them out. No sooner would they extinguish one small fire than another packet of incendiaries fell within yards. Cassie saw four men on the roof of the cathedral trying to put out the flames. She stood behind a policeman who stared up at the roof.

The policeman glanced at her and, seeing her in her aviation helmet, took her to be a messenger. "Son, get down to the Command Center and tell 'em we need firemen here if we're going to save it."

She was gone. She knew that Command Center for Civil Defense was in the basement of the Council House. A Home Guard soldier stopped her at the door and said he'd pass the message along. "Don't hold out much hope. The phone lines are gone already. Try to get a crew along yourself."

Cassie ran up Jordon Well. Another fire engine was active in Little Park Street, where a small factory was alight. A fireman was screwing his hose to a hydrant. Then another wave of bombs landed and three buildings went up like matchwood. An empty double-decker bus was turned on its nose to come crashing down, belly-up, in a great groaning and splintering of metal. The fireman stopped what he was doing and stared at the destruction. Cassie had to tug his arm. "Cathedral," she said. "They need you."

The fireman's face was streaked with soot. "I can't leave this," he shouted above the thudding of anti-aircraft fire. "The entire block'll go. Tell 'em I'll come if I can."

Cassie ran back up Jordan Well. A crater had appeared in the road and an ambulance had driven into it. The driver was climbing out of his cab. Back at the cathedral the policeman was gone. There were still men on the roof, but acrid, yellow smoke writhed off it like fat worms making an escape from the conflagration. The men tore up the lead to get to the incendiaries that had fallen through to the timbers beneath. Cassie knew they were wasting their time. She looked up in the air again and saw the sky was still filled with planes.

They are riding on a secret beam, she thought. *They can't go anywhere else.*

More incendiaries came sniggering, metal clanging or thumping depending where they hit, all landing on the roof above the north door. From nearby came a massive, vibrating explosion. The men on the roof turned from their work to see where the newest parachuted land mine had hit. Then they went back to the scrabbling job of tearing up the lead. But the new basket of incendiaries had gone through and took hold. "Where's the fucking firemen?" someone screamed.

"Putting out the other fucking fires," Cassie screamed back.

The men on the roof looked down at her. Then one said, "We're coming down. Help us save what's inside."

The interior was choked with twisting yellow fumes. They all went in and saved what they could. Everything on the altar, some paintings, a couple of tapestries. But the cathedral was a museum of priceless medieval artworks. No one knew where to begin. Cassie rescued a gilt-framed painting of Lady Godiva. Within half an hour the smoke was overwhelming. One of the men put an arm out to stop Cassie going back in again. "It's all over," he said. "We don't want to lose you as well." One of the others, a young man, broke down in tears. They all stood together at the south porch and they watched the flames grow higher. Outside more explosions rocked the city. Inside, history burned and the jewel of the city melted.

At about nine-thirty a group of firemen from Solihull battered their way through the rubble-strewn streets and set up hoses. When they trained water on the interior of the burning roof, violent billowing geysers of steam howled back at them in a reverse draught. There was a moment of hope before, without warning, the hoses stopped running, dribbled. The water mains had been hit. An exploding incendiary injured a policeman still involved in salvage. "It's gone," a voice said quietly.

Another policeman put a hand on her shoulder. "Look sharp," he said firmly, "the phones are down and they need more messengers over at central." Then he squinted at her. The giant red flames from the cathedral roof illuminated Cassie's face. "Are you a lass?"

"I'm a messenger," Cassie said.

"You're a bloody angel."

She skipped away.

The entire city was aflame. The fire crew on Little Park Street had given up and moved on, leaving the street burning, a row of three-story scooped out front walls. Cassie could see that Broadgate, the heart of the city, was spectacularly aflame. At the Council House Command Center the soldier on duty recognized her this time and waved her through. She went down the stone steps to the basement. Three men and half a dozen women were chalking on blackboards or conferring. The telephone lines were still dead. They worked away under insipid yellow emergency lighting

"Who the hell are you?" said one bespectacled, sweating man, shirtsleeves rolled. He had a cigarette squashed between his fingers but it had gone out.

"Messenger Vine," Cassie said.

"Right then, Messenger Vine, get down the fire station—speed of light—and take this list of water hydrants. On you go."

"First I've got a message for you."

"Let's have it then."

"The message is: we will win through this."

Everyone looked up from his or her task. The man took off his spectacles. He grimaced. His lips twitched and his mouth shaped to speak but no words came out. Then he said, "Who is the message from?"

"From me. Messenger Vine."

The man put his cigarette to his lips, took a drag on it, then remembered that it had gone out. Then he started laughing, and within a moment everyone in the basement was laughing. The man stepped forward and crushed her in a bear hug, and he kissed her cheek. "You beauty!" he shouted at her. "You little beauty!" Then everyone in the basement was applauding her. "Somebody please give her a tin 'at!" the man shouted. One of the women found her an oversized ARP helmet and squashed it over Cassie's flying cap. Cassie ran back up the stairs, clutching her note, flushed and embarrassed by the applause. *People are strange,* she thought.

But when she got into Broadgate she was shocked into paralysis by what she saw. The height of the town was in flames. Fire crews were fighting uselessly. The fires and the bombs had stripped department stores. Steam rose from the water directed by the hoses; bible-black smoke belching where it wasn't. It was too hot to pass through Broadgate. She stood back and watched the flames and the vile beat of leathery wings at her ears returned. She swatted wildly at the small tormenting demons in the air about her. Then she saw her first corpse.

It was propped against a shop doorway. The glass from the shopfront had blown out and crystalled the street before her, and every winking shard of glass reflected the red flames. The sparkling rubies crunched under her boots as she approached the figure, its face and clothes white with plaster dust; eyes wide open, trickles of blood glistening at ears, nostrils and mouth. It was a man, middle-aged, in uniform, though she couldn't tell which uniform because it was caked in dust. He looked like one who, exhausted, had squatted down in the doorway for a moment's rest. Cassie thought she should try to close the staring eyes, not out of respect or religious practice but because she thought that was what you should do. But the eyelids wouldn't stay closed. She tried again and said, "You can go now." The eyelids sprung open again. Cassie shivered and walked backwards from the staring corpse, and turned to run, prepared to take her chances amidst the flames of Broadgate.

The flames were climbing. Not one building in Broadgate seemed untouched, and still the bombs and incendiaries were raining down, and for a moment Cassie lost the center of herself and the unassailable confidence that had so far been guiding her. She retreated to the white stone steps under the portico of the National Provincial Bank and looked down at Broadgate aflame. The drone of the bombers, the snigger and the howl of bombs, the leather wings, the roar and crackle of the flames was not going to go away. The planes in the night sky became demons, exulting, stretching their wings in effortless displays of aerial prowess, gloating, exulting, making merry. They fanned winds with their wings to make the flames dance higher. Was this hell, then? Cassie thought. Is this what they meant? If it was, she knew she must walk through it. Wasn't that the only way to move about in hell, to be defiant?

Snigger. Another stick of incendiaries falling.

Cassie turned to see the beautiful globe of a parachute, its silk reflecting pearl and pink, moon and fire, waltzing low in the air currents, tugged down by its land-mine basket. It dropped in Broadgate and the blast punched Cassie's ears and the black wind that followed flung her on her back. Then came a shuffling sound, almost like water, like the sound of someone taking a loose shit in a backyard outhouse, and Cassie lifted her head to see a four-story building shredding itself into the street.

She got to her feet and moved away from the swirling, hot dust. She clapped her ears. She hadn't been deafened, but all sound had become muted. The roar of fire had become a low surf. The blast of further bombs had become the crackle of sticks on a fire. The air was warm and bitter. It scorched her lungs. She retreated to the white stone steps, the pillared portico of the National Provincial Bank.

Hunkered in the corner of the portico was another corpse. It was a young boy of her own age, about sixteen. He was also a messenger: she saw the insignia on his epaulette. This time the eyes were closed in death and his face was pancaked with white masonry dust. Red worms of blood soaked into the dust from his ears and his nostrils. Cassie reached out, very, very slowly, her forefinger and second finger extended in a probing V, and touched the boy's closed eyes. His eyelids shot open, and his blank, bloodshot eyes stared back at her.

Snigger in the air. Another stick falling. Flutter of leather wings.

She leaned forward and put her lips very close to his. "You can't go," she said. She exhaled a kiss into him. *Still a virgin, like me.* She took dust and ash on to the moistness of her own lips. The boy shivered.

His eyes were now wide with terror and he cowered from her touch. She peered hard at him. His teeth chattered. Cassie moved very slowly, squatting next to him, and put her hand on his head.

He moved his mouth, saying something, but with the recent blast muffling her ears, Cassie couldn't make out what he said. She remembered the fire hydrant list, still clutched in her hand. "Come with me," she said. "We'll help each other."

He twitched slightly, grimacing, making an effort to stir. He spoke again but Cassie couldn't hear it. She guessed from his lip motion that he said, "I can't move."

"Are you injured?"

Perhaps he said something like, "No. I just can't move."

There was a sound in her head when he tried to speak. But it was out of sync with his lip movement.

"If you stay there you will die of shame. You must get over your fear and come with me now. What's your name?"

Something. Again he moved his lips, but no clear sound came.

"I can't hear. My ears are damaged."

"Michael." Maybe, he said his name was Michael.

Cassie placed her hands either side of his face, and she leaned into him, kissing him full on the mouth once more, sucking more dust and ash from his lips. He trembled and his teeth continued to chatter, so she kissed him harder. "Coventry boy," she said at last. "Coventry boy. Are you coming with me?"

The boy wept and tried to hide his eyes from her. She stood up, as if to go, and he scrambled to his feet.

"Which way to the fire station?" Cassie asked.

He pointed that they would have to go along Broadgate.

"Cut through Pepper Lane?" Cassie said, putting the tin hat back on the boy's head. "No, we won't get. Hold my hand and we'll find a way through."

Together they moved into the inferno of Broadgate. Though St Michael's Cathedral was lost, Holy Trinity church was untouched. They ran down Broadgate between the blazing shops and into Trinity Street. When they got to the fire station it had been abandoned. The roof had completely collapsed.

They passed the twisted skeletons of double-decker buses and clambered over the brick and broken plaster and melted girders. The bodies of two women ARP workers spilled from an ambulance. They stepped over the corpses. The tires of the ambulances had liquefied in black puddles. The women had blast-blood leaking from eyes, nose and ears.

They managed to find the relocated Fire Service headquarters and deliver the message. An air of numb resolution gripped the emergency services now. They worked fiercely but blindly. The need for messages was giving way. No one stopped working but there was a sense that planning, strategy, co-ordination in the face of these odds was useless. There was just the need to fight the fires and ferry the wounded. So they went back to the Command Center to see if they could be useful.

On the way Cassie heard the fluttering of leather wings again, and one of her aerial tormentors clanged on her tin helmet. "They give me the creeps," she said.

"What does?" At first she thought her hearing was coming back, but it just seemed that she was better able to intuit Michael. He spoke and she heard his words in her brain, and the words came before his lips moved.

"These bat-things. These creatures fluttering around. Listen." Michael strained his ears. The thirty-foot flames lighted the perspiration on his face. "There! Did you hear it?"

Michael pointed at a piece of smoking metal on the ground. "Shrapnel. Spinning to the ground. From our own ack-ack guns. What do you think happens to the shells after they burst?"

Cassie felt stupid.

A man ran past them, very fast, with his hair on fire and the soles of his boots smoking. They watched him run into a side street.

Together they spent the night running messages for the Command Center. They were given tea and cigarettes, and told to rest for ten minutes. One of the workers there pulled Cassie aside. "Are you all right?" he said. Cassie could hear him more clearly than she could hear Michael.

"Yes. We're all right."

"We?"

"We're okay."

"I think you're in shock."

"Well, we're all in shock."

"Blown if that's not true. But get someone to look at you if you get a chance."

The news of the city's losses couldn't be kept from them. Hundreds dead. Wounded incalculable. The library destroyed, churches burned out, shops obliterated, monuments smashed. History had been pulled from the town like a set of back molars. Seven hours after the raid had started it was still going on. The German planes, it was calculated, had had time to go back to their bases, reload and return.

When they went outside again, it was obvious that there was nothing to be done. Roads were blocked and ambulances couldn't get through. Fire engines had no water. Buses and cars lay tossed around in the streets like toys. There were the bodies of policemen in Cross Cheaping and a dead messenger boy in Pepper Lane. They had to leave them. Fires on either side of the streets were joining up in the middle, like theater curtains closing on some hideous show. The heat sucked oxygen from the air and made the mouth taste of ashes and plaster dust and charcoal. And there was the smell of sewage and corruption. Rats ran squeaking amongst the rubble. Still the buildings burned. Coventry was going to be punched into powder. Even the ack-ack guns were giving up.

"Why aren't the guns firing?" Cassie asked Michael.

"Out of ammunition," she thought he said.

"Shall we bring one down, Michael? A Nazi plane, I mean? You and me? We could do it."

"You're mad, Cassie."

"Do you trust me?"

"Somehow."

"Then hold my hand and follow me." She led him down Cuckoo Lane and into Priory Row, perilously close to the burning cathedral. All attempts to put it out had ended and the roof had collapsed entirely. Only the smoking gothic shell remained, a pulsating ruby of vile heat. Every prayer to hope in half a millennium spitting and roasting and smoking. But the tower and the spire were untouched. The door to the tower had burned off. She beckoned him in.

Michael laughed bitterly. "Not up there."

"It's the safest place in the city," she said. "That's why it's still standing. Trust me, Michael. More than anything I need you to trust me." She took his hand and pulled him towards the base of the spire. Though it stood apart from the dense smoldering and smoking at the other end of the cathedral it was like walking into an oven. The spire acted like a chimney, sucking up heat, but after the first few twists of spiral steps the updraft blew out of the open mullioned lightwells and it became cooler. Together they climbed the one hundred and eighty spiralling, echoing stone steps.

When they stepped out on to the parapet of the tower the wind whipped at Cassie's hair, and she realized what a cold evening it was and how the fires raging below had made an oven of the city. The sky overhead glowed cherry-red. She poked her head between the crenellations of the gothic spire and looked down.

From below she could hear nothing, and up here only the wind, and that muted, like a sad murmuring at her ears, like the whispering of an inconsolable, defeated angel. The city was a broken bowl, spilling fire. It was like looking into the heart of Satan. Rivers of flame, grinding sparks, belching black puffs of smoke. Miles of red glowing earth at all compass points. She ran to the other side. A filthy strand of smoke, twisting up like a giant worm. Silvery tongues of flame. Crimson jaws working away. Sudden flares. Puddles of combustion. A writhing, as if the flames were a maggoty infestation on the underbelly of the city. For a moment it seemed to Cassie that the tower too dropped away beneath her; she felt her stomach flip, but she was borne up by hot currents of air and she went flying over the inferno, over a city of three hundred thousand burning souls. Then she was back again, her feet planted firmly on the stone parapet of the medieval tower, with the wind in her ears. She heard a new drone.

More German aircraft coming in from the south-east, ten, no twenty, no twenty-five or so, flying in perfect formation. She put her hand out behind her and found Michael's hand, drawing her to him. He was shivering uncontrollably.

"My God, you're freezing," Cassie said.

Michael's teeth chattered wildly. Cassie unbuttoned her coat and wrapped him inside. "Come here," Cassie said. "Take some of my warmth."

Michael tried to say something, shaped his lips, but he was unable to speak. He was unbearably cold, his fingers like frost. She took his hand and put it inside her blouse, on to her breast. He stared at her in anguish.

"Look at them, Michael," Cassie said, indicating the incoming bombers. "They think they are beautiful. They think their engines are keeping them in the sky. We know different, don't we? Don't we? Smell that? It's aviation fuel. Close enough to smell, aren't they? Look! It's almost possible to see the pilots in the cockpits, isn't it? If you imagined him a little closer you could talk with him, Michael. Which one? Pick one for yourself. Which one will you choose? Which one must pay? Which one shall we say will not be going home?"

Michael didn't answer. Cassie drew his other hand under her skirt and placed it between her thighs, rubbing his icy fingers against herself. "No one should die a virgin, should they Michael?"

Michael shivered as she unbuttoned his trousers and massaged his erection, stroking her thumb over the head of his cock, whispering to him, encouraging him, as if she were expert. "We'll have to fly to him, Michael. Scare him. Fly at him like a demon from out of the night." She hoisted her leg over the crook of his elbow, just as the airman had taught her. Michael was wide-eyed, shocked, but yielding. As she guided him inside her they both gasped, grabbing each other to steady themselves against the surpassing pleasure of the penetration. All words had gone. They were paralyzed and the sky was ripping open in a fire-breathing ejaculation. Cassie tipped back her head and tried to look up into the moon-flooded fuel-drenched sky. And they fell, upwards, soaring, locked together, the wind streaming in their hair, Cassie's jet-black curls lashing behind her, making a banshee of her, swooping on the incoming aircraft.

Oh Michael. Let's choose one. Let's choose one for you. For you and for the city. Don't be afraid and you mustn't feel guilty. After all, they have chosen us. This one? This one coming in a little lower than the others? Shall we punish his beautiful daring? Shall we? He won't know how it's done. He'll have no idea.

And they swooped on one of the German airplanes, arcing through the night, burning silver moonglow in their wake, coming upon the cockpit canopy, and they fastened upon the glass of the canopy with their sucking fingers and mouths, seeing the pilot look up from his controls, seeing his hideous smile of bowel-loosening, uncomprehending fear.

That's it. That's it, Michael. Fly to him. See his face. Look at his eye. Fix your eye on his. It will be like glue. Our eyes. Will be glued. Iris to his iris. We'll be angels. In his cockpit. Or demons. Look at his terror. Look at the terror in his eye. That's it. That's it. That's it. It's done, Michael, oh it's done. He won't get home. That one. No way home for him. It's done. You can let go.

Back on the parapet of the spire Cassie watched the targeted plane, saw it bank and turn and climb, and head north-east of the city. A single puff of ack-ack fire burst in the air nearby, but not close enough to damage the plane. The defensive Bofors and ack-ack guns were depleted and exhausted now, offering only token fire. The plane disappeared safely into the darkness.

But she knew it made no difference. The plane was doomed. She knew in the same way she knew what song was playing on the radio even before she switched it on. The plane was locked into its course. It would come down seven miles from the city. Only Cassie knew that it wouldn't return home safely. Only Cassie and Michael.

"Michael," Cassie whispered. "Michael? Where are you?" She walked around the parapet, twice, calling softly to him.

He was gone. Cassie felt the wind at her ears. She buttoned her coat around her and descended the tower, feeling the heat return to her as she spiralled down the steps of the tower. Back on the ground the hot air was like a reeking and bitter pepper.

She knew where to find Michael. She retraced her steps, through the dripping fire and the acrid fog of smoke, dodging the fluttering airborne cinders and the maggoty cascading sparks, to the white stone steps under the portico of the National Provincial Bank. She found him hunkered in the corner of the portico, his face white with dust, dried blood in his nose and ears and eye sockets. She put a hand to his neck. His body was cold. This time she didn't touch his eyelids, and they stayed shut. "You can go now," she whispered.

More fire-crews and emergency teams were finding their way into the city, but it was all over. Desperate salvage jobs were failing. Men were weeping or consoling the weeping. Cassie passed a pile of archaic manuscripts someone had pulled from the smoking ruins of the library but had then abandoned on the pavement. Gothic script and illuminated letters, handwritten by an ancient monk, left to char and blow along the street.

Cassie drifted through the streets with the surety of a sleepwalker, passing fire crews hosing mechanically and without hope. One fireman nodded to her, with a blackened face and with an insane grin twisting his mouth, as if he wanted her to share in some joke. It was all over. It was burning, and everything was gone. A fine, cold drizzle started to descend, mixed in with the swirling ash and soot and dust, mixing a warm smog that brushed the face like hot cobwebs. The reek was one of cooked filth, of cracked drains and broken sewers, the spices of hell's kitchen.

No more raids came in, but it was not until six-fifteen that the all-clear sounded, mournful and hollow in the gray light. The drizzle made for steam, and where black smoke wasn't belching from the rubble, white smoke added to the dense, evil pall draped over the city. Cassie wandered without purpose, feeling herself like smoke, thinning, vague, unable to remember her purpose. Almost a ghost.

The city itself was a specter. The steam and the mist and the smoke rendered the remaining walls and angles of broken buildings like vague pencil sketches, or photographic negatives, or perhaps they were only after-images of toppled buildings. Unrecognizable shells stood on weird stilts. Landmarks had vanished into rubble. Millions of bricks, splinters of wood, twisted girders, clumps of plaster and shards of glass spread in huge barrow-mounds across the streets. Cassie wandered down Cross Cheaping, alongside the remains of a department store and saw a tailor's dummy hanging from a window. Amid a pile of rubble an ironwork lamp stand boasted an untouched sign reading BUSES FOR KERESLEY STOP HERE. Beneath it was the twisted, melted skeletal frame of a double-decker.

And the people began to emerge. They picked their way over the bricks and the rubble, and they didn't speak. Cassie watched them, saw them making internal inventory, trying to orient themselves. They moved about in huddles. They touched their faces a great deal as they moved, silently, through the desolation.

Some business proprietors and shopkeepers arrived, bent on getting into the remains of their stores. Brief arguments broke out with police and ARP men. One tobacconist, finding only a single wall remaining, had salvaged a few bales of tobacco. He found a piece of card and wrote on it: TOBACCO SALE, SLIGHTLY SMOKED. HALF PRICE. Then he sat down on a timber joist and waited for trade.

"I'd like a smoke," Cassie told him.

The tobacconist looked up at her. "Been at it all night, have you?" he said brightly. "You look all in. Here, help yourself. On the bleedin' house."

"Would you roll one for me? My fingers are numb."

"I'll tell you what I'll do. I'll roll one for you, and one for me. And we'll sit down here together and we'll smoke 'em, and we'll say we're glad to be alive. How about that?"

"Sounds good."

"Right then." The tobacconist made a big show of finding Cassie a spot on the timber beside him, dusting it off for her before she sat down. "Shouldn't have a problem finding a light," he said. Cassie smiled. He rolled two neat cigarettes, lighting them both before handing one to her. They sat and smoked, each in honor of the other, and not taking their eyes from the other until the cigarettes were done. And during that time Cassie hummed a tune, very softly.

" 'Moonlight Serenade,' " said the tobacconist. "Funny. I had that tune going round in my head afore you sat down."

Cassie grinned, as if she knew something. People stopped to look at them, and everyone cracked a thin smile at his sign. "You need to go home, darlin'," said the tobacconist. "If you've a home to go to."

"Hadn't thought of that," Cassie said.

She trudged through streets now thronged with people. Incredibly, most of them seemed to be up and dressed and on their way to their places of employment, as if they thought the morning ritual in preparation for work might change the events of the raid. They wheeled their bicycles through the rubble, they carried their knapsacks or their briefcases. A large number of houses outside the city center had been demolished or damaged, and as she approached home Cassie's footsteps quickened.

The house was untouched. The front door was slightly ajar. Martha stood inside with Beatie. When they saw her come in, Cassie with blackened face and filthy clothes and with her tin helmet they peered hard at her. Then Martha screamed and ran to her and hugged her and howled and beat her child's back and head with her fists, hard, so hard that Beatie had to pull her away, before letting their mother hug Cassie to her.

"Cassie," Martha wailed. "What are you, Cassie? What must we do with you? Wherever have you been?"

"I've been helping the dead," said Cassie. "Beatie, you can have my record player."

And she sat down and slept.

HELGA M. NOVAK

The Wild Hunt

Helga M. Novak was born in 1935 and grew up in the German Democratic Republic, from which she was expelled in 1966. After spending time in Yugoslavia, Czechoslovakia, and Portugal, Novak currently lives and writes in Poland. She has been awarded the Bremen Literature Prize, the Kranichstein Literature Prize, and the Brandenburg Literature Prize, amongst others. Among her varied work in poetry and prose are the acclaimed autobiographies Die Eisheligen *and* Vogel Federlos.

"The Wild Hunt" is based on a piece of folklore known throughout the countries of northern Europe in which supernatural figures, accompanied by spectral hounds with blood-red eyes, hunt stray travelers and unbaptized souls on stormy nights. The poem appeared in the Chicago Review's *"New Writing in German" issue, Summer 2002.*

Translator Andrew Duncan is a critic, editor, and poet himself.

—T. W.

the Wild Hunt off the leash twelve nights
before Epiphany secret uncanny brotherhoods
ruined errant knights let themselves go
to the roughest habits of the forest
field exercises of a ranting army
swinging torn-out trees dropouts
and primitives caught often with their pelt of hair
with oakleaves clinging to it they are at once
forced to perform chain dances on the market places
where with firebrands pitched at them they go up in flames
no breach of the game laws

Wild Hunt army of spirits by night
twelve nights are between Christmas
and Epiphany Woden shining huntsmen gabriel hounds
roars through the sky and through us through
Theoderic the Goth and him of Rodenstein
jolareidi oskureidi odinsjakt is coming
oh all you dead huntsmen
and silvatica are living yet as wild women
and Artemis is living yet

JEFFREY FORD

The Green Word

Jeffrey Ford has quickly made a name for himself as one of the leading writers in the fantasy field today. His first novel, The Physiognomy, *won the 1998 World Fantasy Award and was a* New York Times *Notable Book; his second novel,* Memoranda, *was also a* New York Times *Notable Book; and his third novel,* The Beyond, *was selected as one of the Best Fiction Books of 2001 by* The Washington Post Book World. *His short stories have appeared in* F&SF, The Northwest Review, MSS, Lady Churchill's Rosebud Wristlet, SCI FICTION, *and other journals. His most recent publications are* The Portrait of Mrs. Charbuque, *a novel, and* The Fantasy Writer's Assistant and Other Stories. *Ford lives in New Jersey with his wife and two sons, and teaches at Brookdale Community College in Monmouth County.*

"The Green Word" is a richly mythic tale inspired by ancient "Green Man" legends. It first appeared in the anthology The Green Man: Tales of the Mythic Forest.

—T. W.

On the day that Moren Kairn was to be executed, a crow appeared at the barred window of his tower cell. He lay huddled in the corner on a bed of foul straw, his body covered with bruises and wounds inflicted by order of the king. They had demanded that he pray to their God, but each time they pressed him, he spat. They applied the hot iron, the knife, the club, and he gave vent to his agony by cursing. The only thing that had prevented them from killing him was that he was to be kept alive for his execution.

When he saw the crow, his split lips painfully formed a smile, for he knew the creature was an emissary from the witch of the forest. The black bird thrust its head between the bars of the window and dropped something small and round from its beak onto the stone floor of the cell. "Eat this," it said. Then the visitor cawed, flapped its wings, and was gone. Moren held out his hand as if to beg the bird to take him away with it, and for a brief moment, he dreamed he was flying out of the tower, racing away from the palace toward the cool green cover of the trees.

Then he heard them coming for him, the warder's keyring jangling, the soldiers' heavy footsteps against the flagstones of the circular stairway. He ignored the pain of his broken limbs, struggled to all fours, and crept slowly across the cell to where the crow's gift lay. He heard the soldiers laughing and the key slide into the lock as he lifted the thing up to discover what it was. In his palm, he held a round, green seed that he had never before seen the likes of. When the door opened, so did his mouth, and as the soldiers entered, he swallowed the seed. No sooner was it in his stomach than he envisioned a breezy summer day in the stand of willows where he had first kissed his wife. She moved behind the dangling green tendrils of the trees and when a soldier spoke his name it was in her voice, calling him to her.

With a gloved hand beneath each arm, they dragged him to his feet, and he found that his pain was miraculously gone. The noise of the warder's keys had somehow become the sound of his daughter's laughter, and he laughed, himself, as they pulled him roughly down the steps. Outside, the midsummer sunlight enveloped him like water, and he remembered swimming beneath the falls at the sacred center of the forest. He seemed to be enjoying himself far too much for a man going to his death, and one of the soldiers struck him across the back with the flat side of a sword. In his mind, though, that blow became the friendly slap of his fellow warrior, the archer Lokush. Moren had somehow forgotten that his best bowman had died not but a week earlier, along with most of his other men, on the very field he was now so roughly escorted to.

The entirety of the royal court, the knights and soldiers and servants, had gathered for the event. To Kairn, each of them was a green tree and their voices were the wind rippling through the leaves of that human thicket. He was going back to the forest now, and the oaks, the alders, the yews parted to welcome him.

The prisoner was brought before the royal throne and made to kneel.

"Why is this man smiling?" asked King Pious, casting an accusatory glance at the soldiers who had accompanied the prisoner. He scowled and shook his head. "Read the list of grievances and let's get on with it," he said.

A page stepped forward and unfurled a large scroll. Whereas all in attendance heard Kairn's crimes intoned—sedition, murder, treachery—the warrior himself heard the voice of the witch, chanting the beautiful poetry of one of her spells. In the midst of the long list of charges, the queen leaned toward Pious and whispered, "Good lord, he's going green." Sure enough, the prisoner's flesh had darkened to a deep hue the color of jade.

"Finish him before he keels over," said the king, interrupting the page.

The soldiers spun Moren Kairn around and laid his head on the chopping block. From behind the king stepped a tall knight encased in gleaming red armor. He lifted his broadsword as he approached the kneeling warrior. When the deadly weapon was at its apex above his neck, Kairn laughed, discovering that the witch's spell had transformed him into a seed pod on the verge of bursting.

"Now," said the king.

The sharp steel flashed as it fell with all the force the huge knight could give it. With a sickening slash and crunch of bone, Kairn's head came away from his body and rolled onto the ground. It landed, facing King Pious, still wearing that inscrutable smile. In his last spark of a thought, the warrior saw himself, a thousandfold, flying on the wind, returning to the green world.

All but one who witnessed the execution of Moren Kairn that day believed he was gone for good and that the revolt of the people of the forest had been brought to an end. She, who knew otherwise, sat perched in a tree on the boundary of the wood two hundred yards away. Hidden by leaves and watching with hawklike vision, the witch marked the spot where the blood of the warrior had soaked into the earth.

Arrayed in a robe of fine purple silk King Pious sat by the window of his bedchamber and stared out into the night toward the tree line of the forest. He had but an hour earlier awakened from a deep sleep, having had a dream of that day's execution—Kairn's green flesh and smile—and called to the servant to come and light a candle. Leaning his chin on his hand and his elbow on the arm of the great chair, he raked his fingers through his white beard and wondered why, now that the threat of the forest revolt was eradicated, he still could not rest easily.

For years he had lived with their annoyance, their claims to the land, their refusal to accept the true faith. To him they were godless heathens, ignorantly worshiping trees and bushes, the insubstantial deities of sunlight and rain. Their gods were the earthbound, corporeal gods of simpletons. They had the audacity to complain about his burning of the forest to create new farmland, complained that his hunting parties were profligate and wasted the wild animal life for mere sport, that his people wantonly fished the lakes and streams with no thought of the future.

Had he not been given a holy edict by the pontiff to bring this wild territory into the domain of the church, convert its heathen tribes, and establish order amidst this demonic chaos? All he need do was search the holy scripture of the Good Book resting in his lap and in a hundred different places he would find justification for his actions. Righteous was his mission against Kairn, whom he suspected of having been in league with the devil.

Pious closed the book and placed it on the stand next to his chair. "Be at ease, now," he murmured to himself, and turned his mind toward the glorious. He had already decided that in midwinter when what remained of the troublesome rabble would be hardest pressed by disease and hunger, he would send his soldiers into the maze of trees to ferret out those few who remained and return them to the earth they claimed to love so dearly.

As the candle burned, he watched its dancing flame and decided he needed some merriment, some entertainment to wash the bad taste of this insurrection from his palate. He wanted something that would amuse him, but also increase his renown. It was a certainty that he had done remarkable things in the territory, but so few of the rulers of the other kingdoms to the far south would have heard about them. He knew he must bring them to see the extraordinary palace he had constructed, the perfect order of his lands, the obedience of his subjects.

While he pondered, a strong wind blew across the fields from out of the forest, entered the window by which he sat, and snuffed the flame of the candle. At the very moment in which the dark ignited in his room and swiftly spread to cover everything in shadow, the idea came to him. A tournament—he would hold a tournament and invite the knights from the southern kingdoms to his palace in the spring. He was sure that his own Red Knight had no equal. The challenge would go out the following morning, and he would begin preparations immediately. The invitation would be so worded to imply that his man could not be beaten, for he, Pious, had behind him the endorsement of the Almighty. "That should rouse them enough to make the long journey to my kingdom," he whispered. Then he saw the glorious day in his imagination and sat for some time, laughing in the dark. When he finally drifted off to sleep, he fell into another nightmare in which a flock of dark birds had rushed into his bedchamber through the open window.

The witch of the forest, doubly wrapped in black, first by her long cloak and then by night, crouched at the edge of the tree line, avoiding the gaze of the full autumn moon, and surveyed with a keen eye the field that lay between herself and the palace. She made a clicking noise with her tongue, and the crow that had perched upon her shoulder lit into the sky and circled the area in search of soldiers. In minutes it returned with a report, a low gurgling sound that told her the guards were quite a distance away, just outside the protective walls. She whistled the song of a nightingale, and a large black dog with thick shoulders padded quietly to her side over fallen leaves.

She pulled the hood of the cloak over her head, tucking in her long white hair. Although she had more years than the tallest of trees looming behind her had rings, she moved with perfect grace, as if she was a mere shadow floating over the ground. The dog followed close behind and the crow remained on her shoulder, ready to fly off into a soldier's face if need be. The same memory that gave her the ability to recall, at a moment's notice, spells containing hundreds of words, all of the letters in the tree alphabet, the languages of the forest creatures, and the recipes for magical concoctions, worked now to help her pinpoint the spot where Moren Kairn's blood had soaked the earth three months earlier.

When she knew she was close, she stopped and bent over to search through the dark for new growth. Eventually she saw it, a squat, stemless plant, bearing the last of its glowing berries and yellow flowers into the early weeks of autumn. She dropped down to her knees, assuming the same position that Kairn had the day of his execution, and with her hands, began loosening the dirt in a circle around the plant's thick base. The ground was hard, and an implement would have made the job easier, but it was necessary that she use her hands in order to employ the herb in her magic.

Once the ground had been prepared, she started on a circular course around the plant, treading slowly and chanting in whispers a prayer to the great green mind that flows through all of nature. As she intoned her quiet plea in a singsong melodic voice, she thought of poor Kairn and her tears fell, knowing she would soon join him.

From within her cloak, she retrieved a long length of rope woven from thin vines. Taking one end, she tied it securely around the base of the plant. With the other end in hand, she backed up twenty paces and called the dog to her with the same whistled note she had used earlier. He walked over and sat, letting her tie that end of the rope around his neck. Once the knot was tight, she petted the beast and kissed him atop the head. "Stay now, Mahood," she whispered and the dog did not move as she backed farther away from it. Then she took four small balls of wild sheep wool from a pouch around her waist. Carefully, she stuffed one into each of the dog's ears and one in each of her own.

The moon momentarily passed behind a cloud, and as she waited for it to reappear, the crow left her shoulder. Eventually, when the moon had a clear view of her again, she motioned with both hands for the dog to join her. Mahood started on his way and then was slowed by the tug of the plant. She dropped to her knees, opened her arms wide and the dog lurched forward with all his strength. At that moment, the root of the plant came free from the ground, and its birth scream ripped through the night, a piercing wail like a pin made of sound for bursting the heart. Both witch and dog were protected from its cry by the tiny balls of wool, but she could see the effects the terrible screech still had on Mahood, whose hearing was more acute. The dog stopped in his tracks as if stunned. His eyes went glassy, he exhaled one long burst of steam, and then sat down.

The witch did not hesitate for a heartbeat but began running. As she moved, she reached for the knife in her belt. With a smooth motion she lifted the exposed root of the plant and tugged once on the vine rope to warn Mahood to flee. Then she brought the knife across swiftly to sever the lead, and they were off across the field, like flying shadows. She made for the tree line with the crow flapping in the air just above her left shoulder. The bird cawed loudly, a message that the soldiers had heard and were coming on horseback. The hood fell from her head, and her long white hair flew out behind her, signaling to her pursuers.

When she was a hundred yards from the boundary of the forest, she could hear the hoofbeats closing fast. The mounted soldier in the lead yelled back to those who followed, "It's the crone," and then nocked an arrow in place on his bow. He pulled back on the string and aimed directly for her back. Just as he was about to release, something flew into his face. A piece of night with wings and sharp talons gouged at his right eye. The arrow went off and missed its mark, impaling the ground in the spot where the witch's foot had been but a second before.

Mahood had bounded ahead and already found refuge in among the trees of the forest. The crow escaped and the witch ran on, but there was still fifty yards of open ground to cover and now the other horsemen were right on her heels. The lead soldier drew his sword and spurred his horse to greater speed. Once, twice, that blade cut the air behind her head and on both passes severed strands of her long hair. Just when the soldier thought he finally had her, they had reached the boundary of the trees. He reared back with the sword to strike across her back, but she leaped before he could land the blow. The height of her jump was miraculous. With her free hand, she grabbed the bottom branch of the closest tree and swung herself up with all the ease of a child a hundred years younger. The other soldiers rode up to join their companion at the tree line just in time to hear her scampering away, like a squirrel, through the dark canopy of the forest.

The black dog was waiting for her at her underground cave, whose entrance was a hole in the ground amidst the vast stand of willows. Once safely hidden in her den, she reached beneath her cloak and pulled out the root of the Mandrake. Holding it up to the light from a burning torch, she perused the unusual design of the plant's foundation. Shaped like a small man, it had two arms extending from the thick middle part of the body and at the bottom a V shape of two legs. At the top, where she now cut away the green part of the herb, there was a bulbous lump, like a rudimentary head. This root doll, this little wooden mannikin, was perfect.

She sat on a pile of deerskins covering a low rock shelf beneath the light of the torch. Taking out her knife, she held it not by the bone handle but at the middle of the blade, so as to have finer control over it. The technique she employed in carving features into the Mandrake root was an ancient art called *simpling*. First, she carefully gouged out two eyes, shallow holes precisely equidistant from the center of the head bump. An upward cut beneath the eyes raised a partial slice of the root. This she delicately trimmed the corners off of to make the nose. Next, she made rudimentary cuts where the joints of the elbows, knees, wrists and ankles should be on the limbs. With the tip of the blade, she worked five small fingers into the end of each arm to produce rough facsimiles of hands. The last, but most important job was the mouth. For this opening, she changed her grip on the knife and again took it by the handle. Applying the sharp tip to a spot just below the nose, she spun the handle so as to bore a deep, perfect circle.

She laid the knife down by her side and took the Mandrake into the crook of her arm, the way in which one might hold a baby. Rocking forward and back slightly, she began to sing a quiet song in a language as old as the forest itself. With the thumb of her free hand she persistently massaged the chest of the plant doll. Her strange lullaby lasted nearly an hour, until she began to feel a faint quivering of the root in response to her touch. As always with this process, the life pulse existed only in her imagination at first, but as she continued to experience it, the movement gradually transformed from notion to actuality until the thing was verily squirming in her grasp.

Laying the writhing root in her lap, she lifted the knife again and carefully sliced the thumb with which she had kneaded life into it. When she heard the first peep of a cry come from the root child, she maneuvered the self-inflicted wound over the round mouth of the thing and carefully let three drops of blood fill the orifice. When the Mandrake had tasted her life, it began to wriggle and coo. She lifted it in both hands, rose to her feet and carried it over to a diminutive cradle she had created for it. Then looking up at the crow, who perched on a deer skull resting atop a stone table on the other side of the vault, she nodded. The bird spoke a single word and flew up out of the den. By morning, the remaining band of forest people would line up before the cradle and each offer three drops of blood for the life of the strange child.

King Pious hated winter, for the fierce winds that howled outside the palace walls in the long hours of the night seemed the voice of a hungry beast come to devour him. The cold crept into his joints and set them on fire, and any time he looked out his window in the dim daylight all he saw was his kingdom buried deeply beneath a thick layer of snow the color of a bloodless corpse. During these seemingly endless frigid months, he was often beset by the thought that he had no heir to perpetuate his name. He slyly let it be known that the problem lay with the queen, who he hinted was obviously barren, but whom, out of a keen sense of honor, he would never betray by taking another wife. The chambermaids, though, knew for certain it was not the queen who was barren, and when the winds howled so loudly in the night that the king could not overhear them, they whispered this fact to the pages, who whispered it to the soldiers, who had no one else to tell but each other and their horses.

To escape the beast of winter, King Pious spent much of the day in his enclosed pleasure garden. Here was summer confined within four walls. Neat, perfectly symmetrical rows of tulips, hyacinths, roses, tricked into growth while the rest of nature slept, grew beneath a crystal roof that gathered what little sunlight there was and magnified its heat and light to emulate the fair season. Great furnaces beneath the floor heated the huge chamber and butterflies, cultivated for the purpose of adding a touch of authenticity to the false surroundings, were released daily. Servants skilled in the art of recreating bird sounds with their voices were stationed in rooms adjoining the pleasure garden, and their mimicked warblings were piped into the chamber through long tubes.

In the afternoon of the day on which the king was given the news that the first stirrings of spring had begun to show themselves in the world outside the palace walls, he was sitting on his throne in the very center of the enclosed garden, giving audience to his philosopher.

On a portable stand before him lay a device that the venerable academician had just recently perfected, a miniature model with working parts that emulated the movement of the heavens. The bearded wise man in tall pointed hat and starry robe lectured Pious on the Almighty's design of the universe. The curious creation had a long arm holding a gear train attached to a large box with a handle on the side. At the end of the arm were positioned glass balls, connected with wire, representative of the Sun and Earth and other planets. Pious watched as the handle was turned and the solar system came to life, the heavenly bodies whirling on their axes while at the same time defining elliptical orbits.

"You see, your highness," said the philosopher, pointing to the blue ball, largest of the orbs, "the Earth sits directly at the center of the universe, the Almighty's most important creation which is home to his most perfect creation, mankind. All else, the Sun, the Moon, the planets and stars, revolve around us, paying homage to our existence as we pay homage to God."

"Fascinating," said the king as he stared intently at the device that merely corroborated for him his place of eminence in the far flung scheme of things.

"Would you like to operate the device?" asked the philosopher.

"I shall," said the king. He stood up and smoothed out his robes. Then he advanced and placed his hand on the handle of the box. He gently made the world and the heavens spin and a sense of power filled him, easing the winter ache of his joints and banishing, for a moment, the thought that he had no heir. This feeling of new energy spread out from his head to his arm, and he began spinning the handle faster and faster, his smile widening as he put the universe through its paces.

"Please, your highness," said the philosopher, but at that instant something came loose and the entire contraption flew apart, the glass balls careening off through the air to smash against the stone floor of the garden.

The king stood, looking perplexed, holding the handle, which had broken away from the box, up before his own eyes. "What is this?" he shouted. "You assassinate my senses with this ill-conceived toy of chaos." He turned in anger and beat the philosopher on the head with the handle of the device, knocking his pointed hat onto the floor.

The philosopher would have lost more than his hat that afternoon had the king's anger not been interrupted. Just as Pious was about to order a beheading, the captain of the guard strode into the garden, carrying something wrapped in a piece of cloth.

"Excuse me, your highness," he said, "but I come with urgent news."

"For your sake, it had better be good," said the king, still working to catch his breath. He slumped back into his chair.

"The company that I led into the forest last week has just now returned. The remaining forest people have been captured and are in the stockade under guard. There are sixty of them, mostly women and children and elders."

Pious straightened up in his seat. "You have done very well," he told the soldier. "What of the witch?"

"We came upon her in the forest, standing in a clearing amidst a grove of willows with her arms crossed as if waiting for us to find her. I quietly called for my best archer and instructed him in whispers to use an arrow with a poison tip. He drew his bow and just before he released the shaft, I saw her look directly at where we were hiding beneath the long tendrils of a willow thirty feet from her. She smiled just before the arrow pierced her heart. Without uttering a sound, she fell forward, dead on the spot."

"Do you have her body? I want it burned," said Pious.

"There is no body, your highness."

"Explain," said the king, beginning to lose his patience.

"Once the bowman hit his mark, we advanced from the trees to seize her, but before we could lay hands on her, her very flesh, every part of her, became a swirling storm of dandelion seed. I swear to you, before my very eyes, she spiraled like a dust devil three times and then the delicate fuzz that she had become was carried up and dispersed by the wind."

Pious nodded, thought for a second and then said, "Very well. What is that you carry?"

The soldier unwrapped the bundle and held up a book for the king to see. "We found this in her cave," he said.

The king cleared his eyes with the backs of his hands. "How can this be?" he asked. "That is the copy of the Good Book I keep in my bedchamber. What kind of trickery is this?"

"Perhaps she stole it, your highness."

Pious tried to think back to the last time he had picked the book up and studied it. Finally he remembered it was the night of Kairn's execution. "I keep it near the open window. My God, those horrid birds of my dream." The king looked quickly over each shoulder at the thought of it. "A bag of gold to the bowman who felled her," he added.

The captain nodded. "What of the prisoners, your highness?" he asked.

"Execute the ones who refuse to convert to the faith, and the others I want taught a hymn that they will perform on the day of the tournament this spring. We'll show our visitors how to turn heathens into believers."

"Very good, your highness," said the captain and then handed the book to the king. He turned and left the garden.

By this time, the philosopher had crept away to hide and Pious was left alone in the pleasure garden. "Silence!" he yelled in order to quell the birdsong, which now sounded to him like the whispers of conspirators. He rested back in his throne, exhausted from the day's activities. Paging through the Good Book, he came to his favorite passage—one that spoke elegantly of vengeance. He tried to read, but the idea of the witch's death so relaxed him that he became drowsy. He closed his eyes and slept with the book open on his lap while that day's butterflies perished and the universe lay in shards scattered across the floor.

The tournament was held on the huge field that separated the palace from the edge of the forest. Spring had come, as it always did, and that expanse was green with new-grown grass. The days were warm and the sky was clear. Had it not been for the tumult of the event, these would have been perfect days to lie down beneath the sun and daydream up into the bottomless blue. As it was, the air was filled with the cheers of the crowd and the groans of agony from those who fell before the sword of the Red Knight.

Pious sat in his throne on a dais beneath a canvas awning, flanked on the right and left by the visiting dignitaries of the southern kingdoms. He could not recall a time when he had been more pleased or excited, for everything was proceeding exactly as he had imagined it. His visitors were obviously impressed with the beauty of his palace and the authority he exhibited over his subjects. He gave orders a dozen an hour in an imperious tone that might have made a rock hop to with a "Very good, your highness."

Not the least of his pleasures was the spectacle of seeing the Red Knight thrash the foreign contenders on the field of battle. That vicious broadsword dislocated shoulders, cracked shins, and hacked appendages even through the protective metal of opponents' armor. When one poor fellow, the pride of Belthaena, clad in pure white metal, had his heart skewered and crashed to the ground dead, the king leaned forward and, with a sympathetic smile, promised the ambassador of that kingdom that he would send a flock of goats to the deceased's family. So far it had been the only fatality of the four day long event, and it did little to quell the festivities.

On the final day, when the last opponent was finished off and lay writhing on the ground with a broken leg, Pious sat up straight in his chair and applauded roundly. As the loser was carried from the field, the king called out, "Are there any other knights present who would like to test our champion?" Since he knew very well that every represented kingdom had been defeated, he made a motion to one of his councilors to have the converted begin singing. The choir of forest people, chained at the ankles and to each other shuffled forward and loosed the first notes of the hymn that had been beaten into their memories over the preceding weeks.

No sooner did the music start, though, than the voice of the crowd overpowered its sound, for now there was a new contender on the tournament field. He stood, tall and gangly, not in armor, but wrapped in a black, hooded cloak. Instead of a broadsword or mace or lance, he held only a long stick fashioned from the branch of a tree. When the Red Knight saw the surprised face of the king, he turned to view this new opponent. At this moment, the crowd, the choir and the dignitaries went perfectly quiet.

"What kind of mockery is this?" yelled Pious to the figure on the field.

"No mockery, your highness. I challenge the Red Knight," said the stranger in a voice that sounded like a limb splintering free from an oak.

The king was agitated at this circumstance that had been no part of his thoughts when he had imagined the tournament. "Very well," he called, and to his knight, said, "Cut him in half."

As the Red Knight advanced, the stranger undid the clasp at the neck of his cloak and dropped it to the ground. The crowd's response was a uniform cry torn between a gasp and a shriek of terror, for standing before them now was a man made entirely of wood. Like a tree come to life, his branch-like limbs, though fleshed in bark, somehow bent pliantly. His legs had the spring of saplings, and the fingers with which he gripped his paltry weapon were five-part pointed roots, trailing thin root hairs from the tips of the digits. The gray bark of his body held bumps and knots like a log, and in certain places small twigs grew from him, covered at their ends with green leaves. There was more foliage simulating hair upon his pointed head and a fine stubble of grass across his chin. Directly in the center of his chest, beneath where one's heart might hide, there grew from a protruding twig a large blue fruit.

The impassive expression that seemed crudely chiseled into the face of the wooden man did not change until the Red Knight stepped forward and with a brutal swing lopped off the tree root hand clutching the stick. Then that dark hole of a mouth stretched into a toothless smile, forming wrinkles of joy beneath the eyes. The Red Knight stepped back to savor the pain of his opponent, but the stranger exhibited no signs of distress. He held the arm stump up for all to see and, in a blur, a new hand grew to replace the one on the ground.

The Red Knight was obviously stunned, for he made no move as the tree man came close to him and placed that new hand up in front of his enemy's head. When the king's champion finally meant to react, it was too late. For as all the crowd witnessed, the five sharp tips of the root appendage grew outward as swiftly as snakes striking and found their way into the eye slits of the knight's helmet. Ghastly screams echoed from within the armor as blood seeped out of the metal joints and onto the grass. The knight's form twitched and the metal arms clanked rapidly against the metal sides of the suit. The broadsword fell point first and stuck into the soft spring earth. When the stranger retracted his hand, the fingers growing back into themselves, now wet with blood, the Red Knight tipped over backward and landed with a loud crash on the ground.

Pious immediately called for his archers. Three of them stepped forward and fired at the new champion. Each of the arrows hit its mark, thunking into the wooden body. The tree man, nonchalantly swept them off him with his arm. Then he advanced toward the dais, and the crowd, the soldiers, the visiting dignitaries fled. The king was left alone. He sat, paralyzed, staring at the advancing creature. So wrapped in a rictus of fear was Pious that all he could manage was to close his eyes. He waited for the feel of a sharp root to pierce his chest and puncture his heart. Those moments seemed an eternity to him, but eventually he realized nothing had happened. When he could no longer stand it, he opened his eyes to an amazing scene. The tree man was kneeling before him.

"My liege," said the stranger in that breaking voice. Then he stood to his full height, and said, "I believe as winner of the tournament, I am due a feast."

"Quite right," said Pious, trembling with relief that he would not die. "You are an exceptional warrior. What is your name?"

"Vertuminus," said the tree man.

A table had been hastily brought into the pleasure garden and laid with the finest place settings in the palace. The feast was prepared for only Pious and the wooden knight. The visiting ambassadors and dignitaries were asked if they would like to attend, but they all suddenly had pressing business back in their home kingdoms and had to leave immediately after the tournament.

The king dined on roasted goose, whereas Vertuminus had requested only fresh water and a large bucket of soil to temporarily root his tired feet in. Soldiers were in attendance, lining the four walls of the garden, and were under orders to have their swords sharp and to keep them drawn in case the stranger's amicable mood changed. Pious feared the tree man, but was also curious as to the source of his animation and bizarre powers.

"And so my friend, you were born in the forest, I take it?" asked the king. He tried to stare into the eyes of the guest, which blinked and dilated in size though they were merely gouges in the bark that was his face.

"I was drawn up from the earth by the witch," he said.

"The witch," said Pious, pausing with a leg of the goose in his hand.

"Yes, she made me with one of her spells, but she has abandoned me. I do not know where she has gone. I have been lonely and needed other people to be with. I have been watching the palace from a distance, and I wanted to join you here."

"We are very glad you did," said the king.

"The witch told me that you lived by the book. She showed me the book and taught me to read it so that I would know better how to wage war on you."

"And do you wish me harm?" asked Pious.

"No, for when I read the book it started to take hold of me and drew me to its thinking away from the forest. I joined the tournament so that I could win a place at the palace."

"And you have," said Pious. "I will make you my first knight."

Here Vertuminus recited the king's favorite passage from the good book. "Does it not make sense?" he asked.

Pious slowly chewed and shook his head. "Amazing," he said, and for the first time spoke genuinely.

"You are close to the Almighty?" asked Vertuminus.

"Very close," said the king.

There was a long silence, in which Pious simply sat and stared as his guest drank deeply from a huge cup.

"And if you don't mind my asking," said the king, pointing "what is that large blue growth on your chest?"

"That is my heart," said Vertuminus. "It contains the word."

"What word?" asked Pious.

"Do you know in the book, when the Almighty creates the world?"

"Yes."

"Well, how does he accomplish this?" asked the tree man.

"How?" asked the king.

"He speaks these things into creation. He says, 'Let there be light,' and there is. For everything he creates, he uses a different word. This fruit contains the green word. It is what gives me life."

"Is there a word in everything?" asked Pious.

"Yes," said Vertuminus, whose index finger grew out and speared a pea off the king's platter. As the digit retracted, and he brought the morsel to his mouth, he said, "There is a word in each animal, a word in each person, a word in each rock, and these words of the Almighty make them what they are."

Suddenly losing his appetite, the king pushed his meal away. He asked, "But if that fruit of yours contains the green word, why is it blue?"

"Only its skin is blue, the way the sky is blue and wraps around the earth."

"May I touch it?" asked Pious.

"Certainly," said Vertuminus, "but please be careful."

"You have my word," said Pious, as he stood and slowly reached a trembling hand across the table. His fingers encompassed the blue fruit and gently squeezed it.

The wooden face formed an expression of pain. "That is enough," said the tree man.

"Not quite," said the king, and with a simple yank, pulled the fruit free from its stem.

Instantly, the face of Vertuminus went blank, his branch arms dropped to his sides, lifeless, and his head nodded.

Pious sat back in his throne, unable to believe that defeating the weird creature could have been so easy. He held the fruit up before his eyes, turning it with his fingers, and pondered the idea of the word of God trapped beneath a thin blue skin.

The ruler sat in silent contemplation, and in his mind formulated a metaphor in which the acquisition of all he desired could be as easy as his plucking this blue prize. It was a complex thought for Pious, one in which the blue globe of the world from the philosopher's contraption became confused with the fruit.

He nearly dropped the precious object when suddenly his lifeless guest gave a protracted groan. The king looked up in time to see another blue orb rapidly growing on the chest of the tree man. It quickly achieved fullness, like a balloon being inflated. He gave a gasp of surprise when his recently dead guest smiled and brought his branch arms up.

"Now it is my turn," said Vertuminus, and his root fingers began to grow toward the king.

"Guards," called Pious, but they were already there. Swords came down on either side, and hacked off the wooden limbs. As they fell to the floor, Pious wasted no time. He dove across the table and plucked the new blue growth. Again, Vertuminus fell back into his seat, lifeless.

"Quickly, men, hack him to pieces and burn every twig!" In each of his hands he held half of his harvest. He rose from his throne and left the pleasure garden, the sound of chopping following him out into the corridor. Here was a consolation for having lost his Red Knight, he thought—something that could perhaps prove far more powerful then a man encased in metal.

When Pious ordered that one of the forest people be brought to him, he had no idea that the young woman chosen was the daughter of Moren Kairn. She was a tall, willowy specimen of fifteen with long blonde hair that caught the light at certain angles and appeared to harbor the slightest hues of green. Life in the stockade, where the remaining rebels were still kept was very difficult. For those who did not willingly choose the executioner over conversion to the faith, food was used as an incentive to keep them on the path to righteousness. If they prayed they ate, but never enough to completely satisfy their hunger. And so this girl, like the others, was exceedingly thin.

She stood before the king in his study, a low table separating her from where he sat. On that table was a plate holding the two blue orbs that had been plucked from Vertuminus.

"Are you hungry, my dear?" asked the king.

The girl, frightened for her life, knowing what had become of her father and having witnessed executions in the stockade, nodded nervously.

"That is a shame," said Pious. "In order to make it up to you, I have a special treat. Here is a piece of fruit." He waved his hand at the plate before him. "Take one."

She looked to either side where soldiers stood guarding her every move.

"It's quite all right," said Pious in as sweet a tone as he was capable.

The girl reached out her hand and carefully lifted a piece of fruit. She brushed her hair away from her face with her free hand as she brought the blue food to her mouth.

The king leaned forward with a look of expectation on his face as she took the first bite. He did not know what to expect and feared for the worst. But the girl, after tasting a mouthful, smiled, and began greedily devouring the rest of it. She ate it so quickly he barely had time to see that its insides, though green, were succulent like the pulp of an orange.

When it was finished and she held nothing but the pit in her hand, Pious asked her, "And how was that?"

"The most wonderful thing I have ever tasted," she whispered.

"Do you feel well?" he asked.

"I feel strong again," she said and smiled.

"Good," said Pious. He motioned to one of the soldiers to escort her back to the stockade. "You may go now," he said.

"Thank you," said the girl.

"Once she and the soldier had left the room, the king said to the remaining guard, "If she is still alive by nightfall, bring me word of it."

It tasted, to him, something like a cool, wet ball of sugar, and yet hidden deeply within its dripping sweetness there lay the slightest trace of bitterness. With each bite, he tried to fix more clearly his understanding of its taste, but just as he felt on the verge of a revelation, he found he had devoured the entire thing. All that was left in his hand was the black pit, shaped like a tiny egg. Since the blue-skinned treat had no immediate effect on him, he thought perhaps the secret word lay within its dark center and he swallowed that also. Then he waited. Sitting at the window in his bedchamber, he stared out into the cool spring night, listening, above the din of his wife's snoring, to the sound of an unseen bird, calling plaintively off in the forest. He wondered what, if anything, the fruit would do for him. At worst he might become sick unto death, but the fact that the girl from the forest was still alive but an hour earlier was good insurance that he would also live. At best, the risk was worth the knowledge and power he might attain. To know the secret language of the Almighty, even one green word, could bring him limitless power and safety from age and death.

Every twinge of indigestion, every itch or creak of a joint, made him think the change was upon him. He ardently searched his mind, trying to coax into consciousness the syllables of that sacred word. As it is said of a drowning man, his life passed before the inner eye of his memory, not in haste but as a slow stately procession. He saw himself as a child, his parents, his young wife, the friends he had had when he was no older than the girl he had used to test the fruit. Each of them beckoned to him for attention, but he ignored their pleas, so intent was he upon owning a supreme secret.

The hours passed and instead of revelation, he found nothing but weariness born of disappointment. Eventually, he crawled into bed beside his wife and fell fast asleep. In his dreams, he renewed his quest, and in that strange country made better progress. He found himself walking through the forest, passing beneath the boughs of gigantic pines. In those places where the sunlight slipped through and lit the forest floor, he discovered that the concept of the green word became clearer to him.

He went to one of these pools of light and as he stood in it, the thought swirled in his head like a ghost as round as the fruit itself. It came to him that the word was a single syllable comprised of two entities, one meaning life and one death, that intermingled and intertwined and bled into each other. This knowledge took weight and dropped to his tongue. He tried to speak the green word, but when he opened his mouth, all that came out was the sound of his own name. Then he was awake and aware that someone was calling him.

"King Pious," said the captain of the guard.

The man was standing next to his bed. He roused himself and sat up.

"What is it?" he asked.

"The forest people have escaped from the stockade."

"What?" he yelled. "I'll have your head for this!"

"Your highness, we found the soldiers who guard them enmeshed in vines that rooted them to the ground and, impossible as it sounds, a tree has grown up in the stockade overnight and the branches bend down over the high wall to touch the ground. The prisoners must have climbed out in the night. One of the horseman tried to pursue them but was attacked by a monstrous black dog and thrown from his mount."

Pious threw back the covers and got out of bed. He meant to give orders to have the soldiers hunt them down and slay them all, but suddenly a great confusion clouded his mind. That ghost of the green word floated and turned again in his mind, and when he finally opened his mouth to voice his command, no sound came forth. Instead, a leafed vine snaked up out of his throat, growing with the speed of an arrow's flight. He clutched his chest, and the plant from within him wound itself around the soldier's neck and arms, trapping him. Another vine appeared and another, until the king's mouth was stretched wide with virulent strands of green life, growing rapidly out and around everything in the room. At just this moment, the queen awoke, took one look at her husband and fled, screaming.

By twilight, the palace had become a forest. Those who did not flee the onslaught of vegetation but stayed and tried to battle it were trapped alive in its green web. All of the rooms and chambers, the kitchen, the tower cell, the huge dining hall, the pleasure garden, and even the philosopher's hiding place were choked with a riot of leafy vine. The queen and those others who had escaped the king's virulent command, traveled toward the south, back to their homes and roots.

Pious, still planted where he had stood that morning, a belching fountain of leaf and tendril, was now the color of lime. Patches of moss grew upon his face and arms, and his already arthritic hands had spindled and twisted into branches. In his beard of grass, dandelions sprouted. On the pools that were his staring eyes, minuscule water lilies floated. When the sun slipped out of sight behind the trees of the forest, the last of that part of the green word he knew to be *life*, left him and all that remained was *death*. A stillness descended on the palace that was now interrupted only by the warblings of nightingales and the motion of butterflies escaped from the pleasure garden into the wider world.

It was obvious to all of the forest people that Moren Kairn's daughter, Alyessa, who had effected their escape with a startling display of earth magic, was meant to take the place of the witch. When they saw her moving amidst the trees with the crow perched upon her shoulder, followed by Mahood, they were certain. Along with her mother, she took up residence in the cave beneath the stand of willows and set to learning all that she could from what was left behind by her predecessor.

One day near the end of spring, she planted in the earth the seed from the blue fruit, the origin of her magic, that Pious had given her. What grew from it was a tree that in every way emulated the form of Vertuminus. It did not move or talk, but just its presence was a comfort to her, reminding her of the quiet strength of her father. With her new powers came new responsibilities as the forest people looked to her to help them in their bid to rebuild their village and their lives. At the end of each day, she would come to the wooden knight and tell him of her hopes and fears, and in his silence she found excellent council and encouragement.

She was saddened in the autumn when the tree man's leaves seared and fell and the bark began to lift away from the trunk, revealing cracks in the wood beneath. On a cold evening, she trudged through orange leaves to his side, intending to offer thanks before winter devoured him. As she stood before the wooden form, snow began to lightly fall. She reached out her hand to touch the rough bark of his face, and just as her fingers made contact, she realized something she had been wondering about all summer.

It had never been clear to her why the fruit had been her salvation and gift and at the same time had destroyed King Pious. Now she knew that although the king had the green word, he had no way to understand it. "Love," she thought, "so easy for some and for others so impossible." In the coming years, through the cycle of the seasons, she planted the simple seed of this word in the hearts of all who knew her, and although, after a long life, she eventually passed on, she never died.

TERRY DOWLING

Stitch

Terry Dowling was born in 1947 in Sydney, Australia, and always expected that his creative efforts would be directed into music and songwriting. After time as a soldier and primary school teacher, he completed two degrees and spent eight years performing his songs on Mr. Squiggle & Friends, *one of the world's longest-running children's television shows. He made his first professional sale in 1982 and continues to be one of Australia's most respected and internationally acclaimed writers of science fiction, dark fantasy, and horror. In addition to editing* Mortal Fire: Best Australian SF *and* The Essential Ellison, *Dowling is the author of the linked collections* Rynosseros, Blue Tyson, Twilight Beach, *and* Wormwood, *and his short fiction is collected in* The Man Who Lost Red, An Intimate Knowledge of the Night, Antique Futures: The Best of Terry Dowling, *and* Blackwater Days. *His work has appeared in numerous "Best of" anthologies and he has won many awards for his storytelling, the most recent being the Grand Prix at Utopiales in France for his computer game adventure,* Schizm: Mysterious Journey.

The following story was inspired by an actual cross-stitch hanging in a real bathroom, seen during an overnight stay in Canberra.

—E. D.

Soon Bella would find the nerve to go upstairs. Soon she would be able to excuse herself from her uncle and aunt and climb the familiar old stairs, counting every one, enter the toilet in the alcove of the upstairs bathroom, and confront Mr Stitch.

She couldn't leave without seeing him. Not this time. It was Auntie Inga's birthday, occasion enough, yes, but this time Mr Stitch *was* the reason for being here. Bella had always tried to see him once or twice a year, just to make sure he was still there, shut tight behind the glass, locked in his frame. This time it had to be more.

"Your boyfriend couldn't make it, Bel?" Auntie Inga asked, but gently, in case there was a point of delicacy involved.

"Roger? No. He had to work, like I said." Bella knew she had said. It had been the third or fourth line out of her mouth when she arrived. "Sends his best wishes though. 'Manniest happiest returns'—quote, unquote. His exact words." What he would have said anyway. "He has to work every second Saturday."

Bluff and hearty as ever, but it's what you often had to do where Roger was concerned. Maybe it would have been better if he *were* here. Having someone to be with her through it. Through this. Bella couldn't remember feeling such dread.

But this time she had to be alone. This time she wanted more.

"This photo of your mom was always my favorite," Auntie Inga said, returning to the page in the old album, going through them as she always did when Bella visited. Possibly when anyone visited.

Bella ignored the mention of her mother, concentrated instead on what Uncle Sal was doing. He smiled kindly at them both and poured more coffee. Bella couldn't remember him any other way. It was as if at some point in his life he had discovered the word "avuncular" and had resolved to be precisely that for the rest of his days. With Mr. Stitch upstairs, it made him seem positively sinister, a gleefully distracting conspirator. An avuncular usher, Bella thought, then was reminded of the old witch in the story of Hansel and Gretel. And witch rhymed with stitch, so back she went, into the panic loop again, with both hands steadying her coffee cup, her heart hammering and her feet flexing inside her shoes, itching to run. If only Roger *could* have been here, could have at least made an effort to understand what this meant. Stayed close. That would have made all the difference.

Though alone, alone. Some things had to be done alone. And today had to be different. Today she had to change it all.

"Auntie Inga, do you still have that old sampler on the wall in the upstairs toilet? The one with the two Dutch children in the street?" Bright voice. Light voice. Smiling all the while. No big deal. As if she hadn't been up there in years, hadn't *made* herself go up and see it on each and every one of those terrifying visits.

"What's that dear?" Auntie Inga said. "Dutch children?"

Summoned by name, the rosy-cheeked sixty-seven-year-old came tracking across the years from where the photographs had taken her. Smile for smile, here she was: Auntie Inga, always Hansel and Gretel witch (stitch!) friendly. She'd never been any different. But forgetful today. Mentioning her mother.

What *was* the female form of avuncular? Bella wondered. Because here it was, tidied up, presented and displayed: more in terms of velour and Hush Puppies than gingham and gingerbread, but just as real.

"The sampler?" her aunt added, as if only a few words ever got through at a time, drip-feed fashion. "That old thing! Of course. Been there forever."

This was the moment. "Of all your cross-stitch pieces, that's my favorite." Bold and direct. Tell a big enough lie and people will believe. Could she pull it off?

"Really, Bel? I would have done that when I was thirty-one. Just before you were born. Landscapes. Street scenes. I suppose they are Dutch children when I think of it. I did so many. Gave them as gifts too." She considered the framed pieces on the walls of the cosy living-room. "I did a lot of these pieces then."

Bella dutifully let herself be seen to be admiring the embroideries. Yes, and both you and Uncle Sal are so like the smarmy, neighborly, *avuncular* people in them. Made up of so many tiny squares, a neat and orderly mosaic. Four stitches in the aida backing to give a really good square. Four to make each black square of Mr. Stitch. But, yes, neat and tidy like that, Inga and Sal. Chock full of smarm. Terminal avuncular.

Though one of the cliched pieces did charm Bella, she had to admit: the road leading off from the open door towards a sunset, with words set in the doorway, picked out vividly against the light.

Westering home,
And a song in the air,
Light in the eye,
And it's good-bye to care;
Laughter o'Love,
And a welcoming there;
Isle of my heart,
My own one!

The door, the setting sun, the sentiments, the sheer belonging: such precious things. It brought her parents' faces, always did, but she was skilled at pushing those aside. She'd dealt with that, and so could almost let herself go there, through that door. But no bidding care good-bye today. And that door, pulled right back, inviting in, inviting out, showing the road and the setting sun, was the absolute opposite of her own dark green front door, always locked these past ten, fifteen years. Double locked. Triple locked. Because of Stitch. Mr. Stitch. Because of all that her life had ended up being.

Even as Bella pulled back, accepting how the world was, there was Auntie Inga. A new thought, *that* thought, had occurred to her.

"Funny that you like it now. You were frightened of it as a girl."

Frightened. An understatement in the ratio of Hitler being misguided, or the atomic bomb at Hiroshima causing collateral damage.

"Oh?" Said calmly enough. Interested. This was the part Bella had to get through.

Auntie Inga was looking off up the stairs, as if a part of herself had been sent off to check the piece or, better yet, was running replays of a tinier, younger Bella Dillon sobbing, yelling, refusing to use *that* bathroom, *that* toilet. "You hated going into that bathroom. Lise—your mother—we always noticed it. That cross-stitch upset you. Two little kids in a street and you'd run away screaming."

Her mother again. Aunt Inga *was* forgetting.

Can't stop. Can't stop. Can't stop now. Bella pretended to be easy. Pretended to remember. "They were facing away, looking off up the street," Bella said, feet wanting to run. *Don't mention Mr. Stitch.*

"It wasn't that I couldn't do faces," Auntie Inga insisted, some old point of pique and a welcome show of larger humanity, a blemish on the sugar rose. "It's how the picture came in the kit. I liked doing faces. Look at *The Man in the Golden Helmet* there."

Bella glanced briefly, dutifully, but stayed on track. "Well, I'm very fond of it now. Just being sentimental, I guess. That one in the bathroom." Bella added the last remark to keep Auntie Inga on the piece upstairs. Even Uncle Sal stayed with her. He was nodding: Uncle Sal on Avuncular Setting #3.

"You're welcome to go up and see," he said. "It's still there."

At one level, Bella would never need to see it again. She knew it intimately. Two children holding hands seen from behind, looking off up a street. The boy in long-sleeved blue top and white pants, long brown hair, a brown Dutch or Flemish hat—soft, shaped like a bucket, definitely a hat worn by boys from another time and place; the little girl in a dark red dress with a white lace collar, long blonde hair. Two houses foreshortened, leading off up the street, then a wall and a tree beyond; an old-style lamp-post in the middle distance on the footpath just at the edge of the road.

And the face of a woman, probably their mother, looking down at them from a partly opened leadlight window as if reminding them what to get at the village shop, possibly warning them to beware of strangers.

And that had been the crux of it.

For along that foreshortened street, off in its tidy, converging cross-stitch distances near where the wall met the tree, was just such a stranger. A pedestrian on the sidewalk, stylised, minimalist, no doubt meant to be a token figure to fill out the scene, sketched in, stitched in with exactly seventy and a half black cross-stitch squares. Small, yet large enough, exactly seventy and a half squares big in fact, each set of four making a bold black larger square, squares set oddly so he was jagged and jigsawed down one side. A jigsaw man.

Bella could never forget that figure beyond the lamp-post, beyond the houses, small and sketchy, jagged with distance. Give her a pen and she could draw him, could tell his bits like marking squares in a hopscotch rhyme. It had been the mantra of her years.

Four in a true square
Then eight more in two lines
Four in another square
And four for shoulders fine
Six in a body line
Then six to get it right
Five more make it odd one out
Like someone took a bite.
Six more in a body line
Then six to keep it strong
Five again is odd one out
Like someone got it wrong
Three begins to give him legs
Then three and a half—it's true!
Four in a line is almost there
But not like me and you.
One and a half—space—a half and one
One and a half—space—a half and one
Now Mr. Stitch can run run run!

It was all in *how* they were set together. A man in a thick-brimmed black hat (or with a hideously deformed head), with two bites out of his left side, ruining his body, a third snipped out of his legs. A lopsided, jigsaw man.

And here was Bella about to confront him again. The figure who stood behind her days, who determined things like the extra locks on her big green front door, on the inner doors as well, the green Keep Away doors, because she'd read somewhere that dark green kept demons and devils at bay.

"I will go up and take a look, if you don't mind," Bella said. "Guess I'm sentimental like you, Aunty Inga."

"Sentimental is good, dear," her aunt said. "Too much nastiness in the world. Too many bad people. Old values are best."

"Why don't I keep you company, Bel?" Uncle Sal said, totally unexpected. "I have to get something upstairs. Inga, we could sure use some of that new Darjeeling you bought. I'm sure Bella would."

Bella was surprised, pleased, shocked all in an instant. When had Uncle Sal ever initiated anything? When had he shown such strategic thinking too, any kind of thinking that put him at odds with the Inga and Sal show?

There had to be a reason.

And before Inga could veto it, ask him to help with the tea—it was her birthday, after all—Sal was out of his chair and leading the way.

Another first.

Bella was after him in a flash, ready for that climb to that landing and that bathroom. But there had to be a reason.

"Uncle Sal," she said at the foot of the stairs. "You really don't have to."

"Nonsense, Bel. When do I ever get to do anything for myself?"

Again he'd surprised her. So why now? Why this? Bella decided to be direct.

"So why this time?" Sharp and hard, considering, and he blinked at her as she took the first few steps ahead of him.

"Just wanted to see you were okay," he said, following her up the staircase. "That cross-stitch bothers me too."

Bella could have stumbled and fallen in amazement. What had he said?

"What's that, Uncle Sal?" She heard the tremble in her voice.

"Bothers me. Bothers you," he said from behind. "Always hated it. Figure in the distance. Small and wrong."

Exactly! Exactly that! Small and wrong. Jagged and incomplete.

They were halfway to the landing when Bella slowed, hearing his breathing, labored, agitated somehow.

For it had dawned on her.

He's serving me up. Making sure I get there. They're in collusion.

Bella stopped on the stairs.

It made terrible sense. The *new* Uncle Sal, the odd behavior.

Bring her to me!

Bella turned, pressed her back hard against the wall.

"Don't think I will," she said.

"What, Bel? What is it?"

"This." *You.* "I can't do this today." *You're different.*

"Bel, I'm being brave. I'm doing it right. Should have done it years ago."

"What?" She gasped the word and so said it again. "What?"

"Should have told you. Said something about Benny."

"Benny? What's Benny got to do with anything?"

But it was all there in the instant. Benny in his stupid blue plaid shirt. Benny eight years older, surprising her in the bathroom. In the toilet. Benny and Stitch.

Time was frozen on the stairs: Bella against the wall, Uncle Sal two steps lower, back to the rail, Aunt Inga lost in the impossibly far reaches of the kitchen.

"We know what he did, Bel. Your aunt won't have it. A mother can't. But we know. I know."

Part of Bella stayed on the old safe track.

What's he going on about? They haven't seen Benny in years. Benny went from their lives. Upped and went, just like that. Just like anyone can.

Part of Bella was in the other fork of that eternal moment. Benny against her. The smell of his blue plaid shirt. The hand over her mouth. And Stitch. Mr. Stitch urging him on. Stitch behind it all, looming on the wall, waiting off along the street, there but not all there. Jagged. Dark man-thing in a funny thick hat or with a big cross-shaped hammer head. Benny breathing hard. "My word against yours! No-one believes a kid!" Hard against her. Then inspired, worried, improvising. "That's Stitch! Mr. Stitch! He'll get you. It was his idea. He's coming for you, see! He'll get you if you tell!"

Both tracks running, playing out on the stairs, Uncle Sal's eyes catching hers at last, pulling her back, but the walls pounding, drumming, thundering with the mighty secret heartbeat of the house.

"You're safe now, Bel. We're all safe. You can go see."

Bella was back with him, five steps from the top. Blue-plaid Benny was gone and Uncle Sal was here and Bella was back and doing what she still had to do, always had to do.

"Thanks for knowing," she said.

"You can't go home again. Had to be said."

"I can do it alone."

"Never doubted it. I'll be outside."

"Th-Thanks."

And into the bathroom she went. The door to the toilet was ajar. She couldn't see the back wall, of course, just the strip of dim blue through the crack.

You can't go home again.

The truth in those words.

But I keep trying. Keep coming here.

She couldn't see the back wall, or the frame, or the children.

A warning to the Dutch children. *You can't go home again! You'll never see your mother!*

That word.

Bella had closed the bathroom door behind her. Old habit. But she hadn't locked it. Hadn't locked it then, hadn't now.

Put on your blue-plaid shirt, Sal, and bring her to me!

But she could lock the toilet door. Lock it this time. Just in case. Though that would be locking her in. And Benny, something of Benny, might be off in the cross-stitch distance. Two of them now, along that terrible, too tidy street.

She had to know. Had to act. Now or never.

She grabbed the door-knob and pushed back the door.

There was the old patterned lino, so well known, the old toilet and cistern, the air freshener in its container, the two frosted window panes on the right, the pale blue walls. There—letting her gaze move up—was the frame, brown wood, the neatly braided world forming, the children and the street, the lamp-post in the middle distance, the wall and the tree.

The black ragged form.

Hello, Bella.

"Bastard!" She said it quietly.

Sal's putting on his blue-plaid shirt.

"Bastard! Bastard!"

Like father, like son. He's bigger. Older but bigger.

"Bastard! Bastard! Bastard!"

Put your hands on the cistern like before. There's a good girl.

"Bastard! Bastard! Bastard!"

You could ask for me. Take me home. Get me through your Green Door.

Reading her mind. "Bastard!"

Language, Bel. Get a needle and thread then. Make me complete.

Tears were hot and brimming, running down her cheeks.

"Bastard! Bastard!"

Mr. Stitch was moving in her tears. Her tears were making him run.

You like me jagged. Ragged. Here I come!

Bella wiped her eyes with the back of her hand, freed herself from him. Steadied herself. Her hands were on the cistern.

"Bastard! Bastard!"

She snatched them away.

You want it! You were ready!

"No! No! Bastard!"

Scaredy cat! Ready cat!

"Bastard!"

And Sal was pushing at the toilet door. "Bella! What's wrong? What is it?"

She hadn't locked it! Meant to. Thought to. Hadn't.

Says it all, Bel!

Stitch was running in her tears. Jigging. Jagging. Running.

"Bel, what's wrong?"

Sal pushing at the door. Stitch running.

One hand was on the cistern, but to steady her, so she could turn. Nothing like before.

"You bastard!"

"What, Bel? What is it?" Sal's voice.

And the door was finally open far enough and Sal was there and no blue-plaid shirt.

Bella stole a final glance. Stitch was back along the street, back by the wall and the tree. The children were safe. *All* the children were safe.

"Oh, Uncle Sal! I thought—for a moment, I just thought—it's all right. It's fine now!"

"What happened?"

"You know. Old memories. Dealing with old memories. Would Aunt Inga let me have this?"

Yes! Take me home!

Sal, bless him, understood.

"Bel, just take it. Sneak it out. I'll distract her."

It was beyond all expectation, Uncle Sal saying this.

"But—"

"You mightn't have noticed, but your aunt—she's getting forgetful. Repeating herself, things like that. We can say she gave it to you. I'll put another one in here. She won't remember, won't—be certain."

"Uncle Sal, it's not—you know?"

"Can't be sure yet. But Alzheimer's is a possibility, the doctor says. The thing is, she doesn't come in here much. She uses the en suite. So take it. She's got so many. It's never been a favorite."

Yes! Bella thought, so relieved, so grateful, then hesitated.

Too easy. Too easy. What if Sal were an accomplice after all?

Get me through the Green Door, Stitch had said.

And was quiet now, down by the tree all jagged and waiting. With not a word.

It was what she wanted too—crazily, what they both wanted. Unless this impulse came from Stitch via her mind, via Sal's. Stitch using them all.

He never said a word. Just stood off in the real, never-real, cross-stitch world, just seventy and a half stitches himself, but trying to be more, embroidering back.

How could she know? How could she be sure of anything now?

"Probably shouldn't," she said.

"Your choice, hon," Sal said.

They stood in the bathroom, Bella staring in at the piece in its frame, waiting for some reply. Stitch would be thwarted if she went without him. Furious. Bella laughed at the word-play. *Cross* Stitch. But he would still *be here,* in this blue-plaid, hands-on-the-cistern place. And she'd be back again and again because of it.

Her need was as great as his, that's what it came down to. And this was her chance to be free of it. To move it along. Stop it being something here and now. Now and then.

"Sal, why don't you bring it over tomorrow? Tell Aunty Inga she promised it. See if she goes along with it.

"Bel, one more thing."

"Yes?"

"Your mom and dad—"

"Uncle Sal, let it go, please!"

"Has to be said, darlin'. Now that we're talking, just let me—"

"No!"

"Bel, you've managed this much. Go the rest of the way. They weren't to blame. They couldn't protect you—"

"Listen, Uncle Sal—"

"It wasn't their fault. None of it. What happened on *Sea Spray*. The explosion. Of course you feel responsible—"

No! No! No! No! No!

Bella actually had her hands over her ears. "Uncle Sal!"

"It was an accident! If we'd found their bodies, maybe that would've made a difference. They didn't leave you with this! Didn't desert you!"

Stitch hadn't said a word.

"You promised, Uncle Sal! You promised!"

Stitch was out there, up there, back there, listening.

"Okay. Okay. Enough. But it had to be said. I'm sorry!"

Bastard, bastard, Uncle Sal.

Or Stitch was putting his words in Sal's mouth. Had a thin, jagged, cross-stitch arm up Sal's back, working Sal's jaws.

But Bella saw the resignation in the eyes, the strain on the old face.

This wasn't Stitch. This was Sal, torn loose from avuncular, reinventing himself second by second for this desperate task, with only a few known aces up his sleeve. Known cards every one.

"I'm sorry, Uncle Sal," she said into the silence, the terrible end-time silence of these haunted upstairs.

Stitch was nowhere to be found. Back on the wall. Back in his frame. Seventy and a half meagre twists of black. Barely made.

"It's just—hon, you couldn't do anything. They didn't fail you."

Again. Bella added the word. *Get it right, Uncle Sal. You meant to say didn't fail me again.*

"We'll play it your way," Sal said then, saving what he could. "We'll come over tomorrow. I'll tell your aunt we promised. We'll bring the cross-stitch."

Better. Much better.

"Can't guarantee that your aunt—you know—won't mention certain things. Won't."

"Listen, Uncle Sal, let's take it over now! You said Auntie Inga forgets things. Let's just do it! Tell her we arranged it. A special outing for her birthday. It's a surprise! I'll take you over in my car, bring you back. You said Auntie Inga's always wanted to see—mom's place again. What I've done with it. This is her birthday treat!"

"I don't know, hon. It's so sudden. Your aunt—"

"I'll have you back inside the hour, two at the most. Say it's important to me. Important that she sees where I'm going to hang it! We can do it, Sal!"

Panic was driving her, determination to do it before her courage failed, before Stitch came back.

"I'll go see, okay?" Sal turned towards the stairs.

"We can do it, Uncle Sal. It'll really help."

He looked back, smiled his old safe smile. "Anything for closure, they say."

Stitch was too quiet. It had been too long.

"Anything. Look, I'll come down with you now. Tell her I've got a birthday cake or something. We can get one on the way."

Pride, vanity and panic of another kind helped. Auntie Inga wasn't about to admit that she had forgotten their outing, or that she couldn't remember promising the cross-stitch. Bella felt a stab of guilt and shame at the duplicity, using such a desperate condition against the person suffering from it, but her own need was greater. Having the person who had created Stitch carry him across the threshold, through the green door; now that was perfect. Suddenly important. Closure, Sal had said. This would do it.

They left the pot of new Darjeeling cooling on the kitchen bench. While Bella jollied Aunt Inga along, helped her into the front passenger seat of the Lexus, got the seatbelt done up, Sal fetched Stitch, brought him down swathed in an old towel and put him in the back.

Bella could never have done it. She felt a giddiness, an intense, irrational joy, a sudden certainty. This was right in every sense. Inga doing the honors. Inga bringing Stitch. All so perfect.

Bella couldn't remember what she said as she drove, just that she was babbling happily all the while, going on about a special birthday treat and how important it all was. Aunt Inga blossomed under the attention. This was her day, her outing. Bella was being, well, avuncular.

Stitch never said a word.

He was there in the back next to Sal, hidden under his towel. This was what he wanted too, no doubt, staying close like this, but at least he was out of the upstairs bathroom, *that* place.

They stopped for a birthday cake as Sal and she had agreed: a store-bought mudcake with *Happy Birthday* in white looping letters. Then, in another two minutes, they were at Eltham Street, tree-lined and shady, and there was the big white house with the green door.

"It looks wonderful, dear," Aunt Inga said. "Your mother liked the white with the green trimming. It's nice that you've kept it. She'd be very proud, Bel."

Bella endured it, forced herself to say thanks, again half-expecting a refrain from Stitch: *She'd be very proud.* But nothing came. Again nothing. Perhaps he thought he could still win. Perhaps he was saving his best till last. Perhaps—it suddenly occurred to her—being out in a *real* day on a *real* street was simply too much. Either way, she'd prepared. She was ready for him.

Bella swung into the sheltered driveway, opened the garage with the remote and drove in. A wink and a smile at Sal in the rear-view mirror, then more fussing over Auntie Inga, helping her out, drawing her attention to the marigolds and geraniums in the big planters while Sal hauled Stitch out after him. Who would have thought that it could go so smoothly?

Then they were through the first green door and in the hall, then through the second and in the sitting room at last.

Inga and Sal never expected it. Even as their noses twitched at the odd smell, even as their eyes widened, making sense of what they saw, Bella had the stiletto off the sideboard and into Inga's throat. Had it in before her aunt knew it had happened, before her little shard of a scream died in a gurgle. Then Bella had the blade out and into Sal's neck at the exact moment he dropped the shrouded frame and managed: "Bella, what on earth—?"

But he saw what it was and had to know. His eyes were wide as they glazed, as the light in them died. He'd know. He had seen the figures—Bella's mother and father, and Benny and Roger—sitting upright in their chairs, had seen them totally stitched over with black, head to toe, every surface covered with precious dark thread, protected forever from the jagged man.

Bella closed and locked the door, old instinct, old habit, then reached down and removed the towel from the frame with its broken glass and tiny helpless figure. She wiped the stiletto clean, then sat cross-legged on the floor and began the unpicking. Seventy and a half stitches, then they would be safe. All the children.

MICHAEL LIBLING

Puce Boy

Michael Libling lives in Montreal with his wife, Pat, a writer of children's books. He has three bright and beautiful daughters and a neurotic mutt named Woody who continues to be terrified of aluminum foil, snowflakes and buttered toast.

When he's not writing fiction he makes his living writing other things. He's been a newspaper columnist, radio talk-show host, speechwriter, and creative director of an ad agency. Most recently, he's put the finishing touches on a new novel.

Libling says about his story: "The story was inspired by a young girl who heckled my daughters and me while we were playing mini-golf in a tourist town in upstate NY. As it turned out, the girl's father owned the mini-golf course and she spent her days both playing and harassing customers."

"Puce Boy," thus propelled, tells a tale that may do for miniature golf what George R. R. Martin's "The Pear Shaped Man" did for cheese curls. A story with a large emotional vocabulary, it is as disquieting as it is chilling. It was first published in the Winter issue of the Canadian magazine On Spec.

—E. D.

Dumb.

Dumb as a gull humping a 747 dumb.

Fool stupid loser ass-backward idiot cretin moron sucker brain-dead dumb.

Ten thousand routes to NYC and he takes 87. Twenty-four years of every excuse in the book and overnight the interstate is okay by him. "Okay by me, Holly." Exactly what he said. Barely gave her AAA maps a second look. As if time had healed the wounds, made everything all better. Which it sure as hell hadn't. As if, at last, he was ready to fight the demons. Which he sure as hell wasn't. Seemed to think he could just drive by. Hardly pay it any notice. Trouble was, he never figured on the billboards. Never figured the place would still be standing. Not after all this time.

19 HOLES OF ROOTIN', TOOTIN', SHOOTIN' FUN!
FORT BUMPPO'S MINI-PUTT

EXIT 21-SOUTH ON 9
LAKE ARNOLD

Boys squealing in the back. "We wanna go, Daddy."

Holly pleading their case. "We have the time, Orry. We really do."

He shudders, guzzles air as if entering the final stage of natural childbirth, grits teeth, and whispers, "No. I don't like mini-golf." And on the eddies of his breath, already sour from the fear: "I don't like death sports."

Holly winces. "What?" Begins to giggle, catches herself, not really sure of what the heck she actually heard him say. "You don't like . . . what?"

He flicks off the cruise control and kicks down on the accelerator. Only interest he has in Exit 21 is in putting it behind him.

"Please, Orry, slow down," she begs, voice calm, mindful not to alarm the children. But with that spooked rabbit look. Worry descending in an ashen veil. Steeling herself, as his secrets roil to the surface yet again. "You're going too fast. . . ."

He had never told her the story. Never once told anyone, in fact. Holly could live with most of his quirks—the fast-food burger phobia, for one. The moods. But adding miniature golf to the mix would have been a risky stretch. Too damn loopy, for sure. He could explain it, of course, but not without exposing himself to be a downswing less than sane.

Dumb as a dick on a scarecrow dumb.

It had been just him and his mother then. In the Datsun 510.

"Orry, wake up, we're here." Left hand on the wheel, she reached behind and gently shook him by the shoulder. "C'mon, honey."

"Gee, Mom." Sprawled across the back seat, sneakers propped on vinyl sill, he yawned, stretched arms, opened eyes, and caught his first glimpse of Bumppo's in passing.

Anyone who ever summered at Lake Arnold knew Fort Bumppo's Mini-Putt. A half mile south of the interstate, nestled on the terraced hillside where old highway 9 doubles back on itself before doddering down into the village proper, you could hardly miss it.

"Looks like fun, doesn't it?" his mother said. She eased up on the gas and downshifted through the rusty hairpin.

Flags panted damp and lifeless along the stockade that fronted the course, rough-hewn uprights alternating red, white, and blue. A sprawling coonskin cap roofed a trio of ramshackle huts: a ticket booth, an ice cream stand, a souvenir shop; *Welcome Settlers*, scripted in red, ran boldly to the tip of the curlicued tail. Behind, a plaster Indian towered, keeping grim watch, arms folded across bare chest, a tomahawk in hand, legs straddling the path, paint worn to gray on calves, thighs and crotch.

Orry blinked. Took a second look. Cocked his head, confused, defensive. Blinked again. A girl appeared to be waving to him from the steps leading up from the parking lot. At least, he thought it was a girl. More like some crazed gnome, really. Squat. Spongy. Flowing into the concrete rather than standing upon it. Gag shop glasses, with googly eyes sprung from frosted panes. Teeth, ivory monoliths that may well have glowed green in the dark. Someone you might expect to find with pointy ears and sharper shoes, assisting a dime store Santa or, more likely, bludgeoning the old guy to death beneath the tree. Beside her, taller, a blond girl brandished two putters, twirling them above her head as if she were a helicopter beating for takeoff. Hair tumbling in waves to shoulders. Hot-pink hot-pants and long, long legs.

"In Lake Arnold for less than a minute and it looks as if you've already made friends," observed his mother.

He reddened, turned away quickly. "Don't even know them," he grumbled. *Why would they be waving at him, anyway?* "Stupid girls." But he stole a second glance before Bumppo's vanished round the bend. The place looked kind of neat. Girls or no girls, he would check it out up close. He would have plenty of time to kill.

Orry had put up quite a stink at first. Shot back with every argument he could muster; some even made good sense. But not enough to sway his mother. She accepted the job at Goodkind's Resort without his approval. "With everything that's happened, honey, we need to get away. It will do the both of us a lot of good. You'll see." When in doubt, she always chose empathy, and the two had come to savor the closeness that inevitably followed.

"But what am I going to do all day while you're off working?"

She laughed. "Believe me, keeping yourself busy will be the least of your worries. You're going to have a great time, Orry. I promise."

"But I still think it's weird, Mom. I never heard of any hotel that had a nurse."

"Well, some do. And Goodkind's is one of them."

"So how come they never needed one before?" He couldn't help himself; he had to bait her, force her to admit how the job had come to be. How Ray Goodkind had invented it for her.

But she refused to bite. Merely rambled on with the now familiar refrain. As if she had memorized the lines for school. "The nearest hospital is way over in Saratoga. Ray says a nurse will let him take better care of his guests. A lot of them are older, and prone to more than just black fly bites and sunburn. Ray says I'll make them feel safer, and that's good for business."

Ray says. Ray says. Ray says. "Ray sure says a lot."

"Don't be a smart aleck," she said, her disappointment in him more heartfelt than he had expected. "You've no reason to talk to me like that. We're friends, remember? Ray is a very nice man."

He lowered his eyes, guilt like graffiti on his cheeks. "I still never heard of any hotel nurse," he pouted.

"At fourteen, you'll find there's a lot you've never heard."

"Wanna bet?" he said, immediately regretting he had spoken the challenge aloud.

"Yes," she snapped, imposing closure. "And if you're as smart as you think you are, you'll quit before you say something you'll really be sorry for."

Who did Ray Goodkind think he was anyhow? Jerk. Why couldn't she see that?

Where so many of its competitors had crumbled by the wayside, foundations overrun by scrub or lakefront development, Goodkind's Resort had managed to survive. An earnestly rustic welter of sprightly painted gables, gutters and hammered down shutters. The collective upchuck of a dozen failed schools of architecture. All keen on porches and exotic cornices.

In the main lodge, on the wall opposite the reception desk, a sepia chronology told all. From the founding in '21 to the ascendancy of Ray, "following the tragic death of Mr. Leonard Goodkind." Photos of the three big fires: August '33, July '44 and October '68. Photos of proud men smiling beside dead fish.

Rebuilt. Refinanced. Restored. So much so, the latest incarnation of Goodkind's won Ray and his "state-of-the-art smoke detection and sprinkler system" the cover of *Resort Management Monthly*. **GOODKIND, THE HOSTELRY WÜNDERKIND** was how that August issue heralded him. Orry's mother kept a copy on her night table. It was Orry's first clue.

"Since when do you read this?" he asked.

"Since the man on the cover gave it to me in the hospital."

"You know this wunderkind guy? Really?"

"Uh-huh. He was a patient of mine."

"What was the matter with him?"

"He had an allergic reaction."

"To what?"

"Peanuts."

"Peanuts?"

"Uh-huh. Almost killed him. He was in very bad shape when they brought him."

"And now?"

"He's fine. As a matter of fact, you're going to get the chance to meet him. He'll be visiting soon."

"Visiting? Who?"

"Me," she said, followed by an unconvincing "Us."

After that, Orry made sure *Resort Management Monthly* lay on the night table with the cover face-down.

The more Ray tried to win him over, the less Orry wanted to be won.

"Consider yourself a guest, Orson," he said, hips tilted in a stationary swagger, the salmon from lunch fresh upon his breath. "The resort is yours to use as you please—as long as you obey the rules, of course."

"Orry. I've told you, I'm Orry. Nobody calls me Orson." He edged closer to the bike stand, feigning interest in a battered blue Schwinn.

"I know. But mark my words, when you grow up, you'll prefer something more formal." That was one of the problems with Ray, he knew everything. Even things he didn't know.

"Then how come you don't call yourself Raymond?"

Goodkind chuckled, the humor curdling in the space between them. "Well, you got me there, except for the fact my name is Raybourne, son."

"I'm not your son."

"I didn't mean it that way. You know that." He extended a bony and conciliatory palm. "C'mon, Ors? Truce?"

Ors? Cripes! That was a new one. Orry hoisted the Schwinn out of the rack. "I got to go."

Ray pocketed his hand. "For a haircut, I hope? It's getting mighty shaggy."
Orry pretended not to hear.
"I don't care what you say, son, we're going to be friends. You'll see."
Orry coasted up the beaten path and swung into the saddle, muttered: "Eat some peanuts, why don't you?" Pedaled the road to Fort Bumppo's Mini-Putt without looking back.

The third hole was a par 5 doozy. **TICONDEROGA'S TEEPEE TERROR.** A drive dead center promised to send smoke signals up through the teepee roof and almost guaranteed a hole-in-one. Slice a tad to the right or left, however, and the ball would die in a gravel rough.
Orry shot. The ball struck the wall of the teepee and dribbled back to his feet.
Someone cackled behind him, but he didn't look. Playing solo was embarrassing enough.
He shot again. The ball struggled up the ramp, gasped in failure, and retreated meekly.
The cackles grew louder. But he refused to acknowledge them.
Again. The ball hooked left, rattled into the hole, skittered through the teepee and into the rough.
"I can see why you play alone. How else could you bear the shame?"
He turned to face his tormentors, knowing it would be them—the girls he had seen on that first day. The shapeless gnome, with the goofy glasses and big teeth. *Even creepier up close.* And the tall, pretty one. *Even prettier up close.*
"You're a horrible player," said the gnome with immense disgust, as if her pronouncement would be a revelation to him. Voice high and nasal. A castrato with hay fever. He couldn't place her age. Maybe 12, maybe 20, maybe God-knows-what.
He fired back, venting the anger reserved from his earlier encounter with Ray. "Jesus! Gimme a break. It's just my first time. What makes you so darn special, anyhow?"
She smirked a snotty "This!" and set the ball upon the tee.
"Show him, Keitha," said the blond.
Keitha showed him.
Smoke signals puffed through the top of the teepee. "Usually that's a hole-in-one," she said, tipping the ball into the cup. "But I guess this isn't my day."
"Okay, I'm impressed," he said, trying hard not to be impressed. He stepped toward the fourth hole. **THE DEERSLAYER.** Hoped the gnome would get the hint and find another mark to pester.
"Don't let it bother you," the blond smiled.
Orry shrugged, wary, assessing whether her concern was genuine. He kneeled, absorbed with the intricacies of the green.
"Keitha's father owns Fort Bumppo's. She plays a lot. This is her eleventh round since last night."
"Twelfth, Tess," Keitha corrected. Grin huge and hollow, nostrils concealed by upper lip. And then she hit him smack between the eyes: "How long has your father been dead?"
He froze. "Huh? What?" Ice down his spine, razors in his belly.

Keitha huffed impatiently, raised her voice. "It is a simple question. How long has your father been dead?"

He cleared his throat, breathed in ragged syllables: "How do you know about my father?"

"Because you look like your father's dead," she said flatly.

Now he was the castrato. "What's that supposed to mean?" No one had ever phrased it quite so bluntly. *Passed away. Deceased. Departed. In Heaven. Gone to his reward. No longer with us. Even kicked the bucket. But never dead. Not ever.*

"It's not supposed to mean anything. It means what I said."

He rose slowly, pondering his choices. "Did Ray tell you about my father? Is that how you know?"

"Ray? Who's Ray."

"Then who told you?"

Hands at her mouth, sucking fingers, watching him. Coyness oozing like rancid musk.

"Tell me!" Orry looked to Tess for support, but she appeared more concerned with the yellow golf ball in her hand.

Keitha hissed exasperation. "Puce," she said to him. "Puce."

"I don't know anybody named Puce."

"Oh, God!" she groaned. "Let me guess: you were raised by wolves, you're Helen Keller, or you're a tourist? Puce is a color, idiot."

"A color?"

"Yes. Sort of purplish brown," Tess said quietly, avoiding his eyes. She lingered on her friend a moment, then, not quite sure of herself, confided: "Keitha sees people in colors."

"And you are puce," Keitha barked, jabbing him sharply in the ribs. "And puce boys have dead fathers."

His throat was tight, as if he had swallowed a jawbreaker whole. "What are you talking about?"

"If you need simultaneous translation, I suggest you visit the United Nations, Puce Boy."

"My name is Orry."

Keitha snorted. "Nice name. But you still don't have a father."

"You shut up about my father already. Just shut up." He threw down the putter, booted his ball out of the rough, and stomped down the hill toward the entrance. "You're crazy."

"What do you think you're doing?" Keitha shouted, face like a fist wrapped round a red balloon. "It's against the rules not to return your ball and club. Look, it's there in writing on your scorecard."

"You're nuts," he shouted back, crumpling the card and pitching it at her. *His father was dead, gone for almost two years—and out of nowhere, after all this time, the tears were finally coming. Of all the times, of all the places!*

"There are no refunds, you know?" She yapped at his heels as he drove for the gate. "No refunds ever. Just rain checks when it rains."

He wiped wet cheeks with the back of his wrist. Dodged a woman towing two boys in Speedos and rubber thongs. Cried hoarsely over their heads: "You're crazy. Really crazy."

He rapped his shoulder off the Indian's left knee and tripped hip-first into the revolving gate. But it would not budge.

They were biding their time now, sizing him up. Keitha, putter pressed against her mouth, tongue teasing metal. Tess alongside, lips tight, bloodless.

"What are you staring at?" Again, he thumped the gate without success.

Tess cupped a hand over Keitha's ear, whispered, then withdrew. "Please. For me?"

Keitha sighed. "All right, if that's what you want, Tess. But you better do it quickly. Tell the puce boy now."

"Damn, stupid gate. Stuck or. . . ."

"That's because you're pushing the wrong way, Orry," said Tess.

Just what he needed. The bike was gone.

He made his way back to Goodkind's on foot. Dreamed up excuse upon excuse along the way. Spotted Ray just outside the dining hall, a few minutes before dinner. And blurted out the truth.

Orry was ready for anything, except Ray's reaction.

"I'm glad you had the courage to come and tell me. The bike was old. Not even any need to tell your mother. We'll just keep this between us men. Deal?"

Ray offered his hand and Orry accepted. "Deal."

"But I do have one favor to ask."

Orry swallowed, suspicious. "Yeah?"

"The next time you take a bike off the property, make sure you bring a lock, too. Okay, Orson?"

"I—uh—okay, Raybourne."

"And get a haircut. You trying to be a hippie or something?"

Orry might well have made it through the summer, never once returning to Bumppo's. Fully expected to. But one night, after dinner, his mother had a craving for a scoop of pistachio, and Ray, gushing over her as always, was eager to oblige: "I've a mind for chocolate ripple, myself." He winked inexplicably, saliva running high.

The three drove into Lake Arnold village.

When Ray took her hand to cross the street, Orry knew it was time to cut out. They were hardly bothering to hide it anymore, even caught them kissing once. "I don't feel like ice cream," he said.

They agreed on when and where to meet and went their separate ways.

Orry was sitting on the bench outside the Wonderland Arcade, contemplating a thick slab of fudge, when she came up behind him. "Rocky Road is my favorite, too."

July. Mid-week in Lake Arnold. Humidity neck-deep. Neon swirling through orphaned puddles. Moths sparring under street lights. Kids slavering for fried dough and snow cones. Moms and dads hemming and hawing over local arts and crafts no locals ever touched. Honeymooners billing and cooing, each silently suspecting the Poconos would have been a more memorable destination. Bikers dragging up Champlain Avenue, cops roaring in pursuit. Punks with packs of Camels up their sleeves, hassling nervous mothers and curious daughters for lights. School kids without shirts or shoes bitching at the doors of restaurants with signs that read NO SHIRT, NO SHOES, NO SERVICE. And Orry fumbling for something to say to Tess.

"Going to eat that all yourself?" she asked, eyes wide, bluer than he had remembered.

He offered up the fudge and caught her on the nose. *Idiot.*

She laughed, wiped the smudge away, licked it off her finger. "Mmmm . . . nice and creamy."

"Have some more," he said. Then, as if someone else were speaking: "I really like your hair that way." And wondered immediately if it was a too-corny thing to say.

She tossed her ponytail from left to right. "Thanks," she said, as if every boy she'd ever known had said the same. "I like your hair, too."

And not once did he stop to mull the fact and panic, that a conversation with this terrific girl was actually taking place, and he was holding his own.

Telling her where he was from.

Her telling him where she was from.

How Lake Arnold was more fun than he had expected.

How she hated living there. Too small.

How he liked scary movies.

How she liked peanut brittle.

How he liked club sandwiches.

How she hoped the rumors about the Beatles breaking up weren't true.

How he was 15. Almost.

How she was 16. Barely.

His sign of the zodiac.

Her sign of the zodiac.

How he wanted to be a newspaper reporter or a writer for MAD Magazine.

How she wanted to be an actress, but how everyone said secretary made more sense.

How his mother was a nurse. And about Ray, of course.

How a lot of people in the area worked at Goodkind's, and how she and Keitha had seen Old Man Goodkind play at Bumppo's not long before he drowned.

How *his* father had died. The fall, the broken neck, and all. The suddenness. No chance to say goodbye.

How terrible that must have been for him and his mother.

More about his Mom and Ray. How Ray wasn't so bad. But. But. But.

How Keets—Keitha—wasn't too bad either, once you got to know her. How, if it wasn't for Tess, Keitha wouldn't have a friend in the world—and how it was important to remind her every once in a while. How, after Keitha was born, her parents began to sleep in bunk beds. "Which is pretty odd, if you ask me." And how she had *heard* Keitha before she actually met her face-to-face. "She was singing happy birthday to herself. Imagine. Someone singing happy birthday to themself. I think that must be the loneliest sound in the world."

"Yeah," Orry quavered, coughed, "that's lonely, all right." Tears welled up in his eyes as he choked on his laughter.

Tess glared at him quizzically, anger rising, then she suddenly saw the joke. She shrieked hysterically, "Singing happy birthday to herself. . . ."

"And bunk beds too," he howled.

"Mom on top."

"Dad on the bottom."

They sat, their bellies aching. Touching each other. Tears streaming down their cheeks. Hiccuping. Gulping air. Until they and the night were spent or, more accurately, Ray honked the horn.

"C'mon, get in here, you hippie."

"Oh, Ray," his mother chided.

Orry saw Tess a lot after that night, despite Ray's doubts. *"She's a little old for you, isn't she?"* Took her rowing on Lake Meserve. Went berry-picking up on Mount Beechwood. Swam lengths in the pool. Hugged her below the surface in the deep end, and came up sputtering when she kissed him on the mouth—his first kiss ever. Went horseback riding without a guide and without permission, and barely minded the lecture from Ray that followed. *"I knew she'd be trouble, putting ideas like that in your head. I've heard stories about that girl. . . ."* Even let her coax him back to Bumppo's for a complete round, compliments of a surprisingly subdued Keitha.

The girls trounced him, their margins of victory too many strokes to count. But he did get a rise out of them when he drove the ball up the rattler's spine and down the gullet of the cougar for a hole-in-one on the bonus 19th, **THE LAST OF OUR MOHICANS.**

This outing, Keitha reserved her heckling for others on the course.

"Nothing wrong with your putting a frontal lobotomy wouldn't cure."

"Is your seeing-eye dog in the car?"

"This can't be the first time your girlfriend has seen you fail to put it in the hole."

"Any more strokes on your scorecard and we'll have to call in a heart specialist."

Most took it well, laughing her off as the oddity she was. But some couldn't handle it.

A bean-shaven troglodyte in a Penn State t-shirt and denim cutoffs, his wisp of a girlfriend simpering restraint, blustered, "I'd kick your face in if it wasn't already kicked in, you little bitch."

Keitha didn't blink. "Remind me to wave a colorful bye-bye to him," she said to Tess. "He won't be leaving blue, I promise you."

An older man with a Canada flag pinned to his shirt, caddying two grandchildren as his wife watched from a wheelchair at the stockade, took Keitha aside at **LEATHER-STOCKING LUNGE**, and wagged a lethal finger in her face: "You're a very nasty young lady and I've a mind to report you to both the proprietor and the New York State Tourist Authority."

Keitha yawned aloud. "Ho hum," she said. "You can report anything you want, but my father has owned Fort Bumppo's for over twenty years and absolutely nothing will come of it." And then quietly to Tess: "Already a perfect white. Should be any day now."

After each incident, Orry asked, "What are you talking about?"

Each time, Tess replied, "Nothing you need to worry about, Orry."

"And that's the whole puce and nothing but the puce," Keitha quipped.

"Do you like Ray?" his mother asked him one morning.

He had seen it coming for weeks.

She eased herself beside him on the bed. Tentative. "You know I like Ray a lot, don't you?"

He reached for his socks.

"And you know that Ray likes me?"

He shrugged, intent on an ant as it sprinted down the blind and onto the window sill.

"I know what you're thinking, Orry, but Daddy's not coming back. You know that. We have to get on with our lives, Orry. Living in the past isn't good for either of us."

He moved to the window, stared blankly out.

"Ray asked me to marry him, Orry."

Rigid. Eyes on the ant.

"I told him 'yes.' "

Incapable of facing her.

"I'll always be your mother, Orry, no matter what. Loving Ray doesn't mean I love you any less. Orry, please. . . ."

The ant zigged, and Orry crushed it with his thumb before it had a chance to zag.

There was BINGO in the dining hall that night, but Orry passed. "I just can't stand looking at the two of them," he told Tess.

She tried to make him see otherwise. "It doesn't sound like a raw deal to me, Orry. The Goodkinds are really nice people. Everybody in town says so."

"I don't like him, Tess. Honest, I've tried. I just don't like him. He's not my Dad. He could never be my Dad."

"And there's another thing, too, Orry." She ran her finger down his nose and to his lips. "We wouldn't have to say goodbye when summer's over. You'd be living here."

"Ray wouldn't make it easy for us. Some of the things he says, Tess. . . ."

"He doesn't like me, does he?"

The moon cast a streamer of yellow crepe across the surface of the lake. He rowed until the night enveloped them and any noise from shore was distant and indistinct, then pulled the oars aboard. They drifted, lying together, the lake and starry sky as one, and they a solitary mote upon it.

A long while passed before, at last, she said, "If you really hate him that much, Orry, there is a way." The boat rocked as she stepped gingerly to the stern. "Something could happen to Ray."

He pulled himself up onto the bench at the bow. Hands clasped between knees, a baseball catcher, readying to snag her every word.

She measured him carefully, the furrows of his brow, the telltale heaving of his chest. But not until the stillness of the night had tightened its grip upon them did she begin to tell the story, not unlike a mother comforting her child at bedtime. "Bumppo's is a place where peoples' futures are decided—good or bad. And the colors Keitha sees tell her what those futures will be."

"Like a crossroads or something . . . ?"

"Uh-huh." A throaty, nervous giggle. "But Keitha calls them . . . *fate stations*."

She dipped a hand into the water and surveyed the lake as if someone might be listening from afar. "But there are only a few of them over here. That's why most of us go through life and nothing bad ever happens. But in other places—like India and China, Keitha says fate stations are everywhere. At watering holes, pagodas—wherever people gather. That's why they have all those disasters and a million people get wiped out in a single shot."

"How does she know all this?" he asked, his skepticism like a dart.

"I don't know," she snapped, her anger instantly eclipsed by understanding. "She just does. You don't have to believe me, Orry. But she says we're going to have fate stations all over America, too, one day. But not like in India or China. Here, they'll be mini-putts and hamburger places, mostly."

He was sure he would spill his guts right then and there, maybe capsize the boat. "Mini-putts and burger places!" He trembled from scalp to sole as he wrestled with his laughter. "You're kidding me, right? Her parents tell her that stuff?" *How gullible could Tess be? How gullible did she expect him to be?*

"No. They don't know anything. They never come onto the course anymore—except when it's real busy and Keitha needs them. Whatever Keitha knows, she just knows."

"So if she looked at Ray, she'd know if something was going to happen to him?"

Tess nodded gravely. "But she only sees the colors at Bumppo's."

"And what if she sees nothing is going to happen?"

"That's not how it works, Orry." Again, she searched the lake, as if rethinking her strategy. "Peoples' colors change all the time—sometimes from hole to hole. The only color that matters is the color you are when you leave Fort Bumppo's."

"But she said I was puce. My color didn't change?"

"The puce is only your aura; the rest of you did change. Keitha just made sure you left with a safe color. I asked her to do that."

"Safe colors? This is way too much, Tess, c'mon. . . ."

"Whites are the worst. They mean something bad will happen real soon. Blues are best. Especially lavender blue. That's what Keitha likes me to be. Nothing bad ever happens to blues. And then there are all the colors in between. Tangerine. Amaranth. Keitha knows more colors than even the Crayola people."

"So if I bring Ray to Bumppo's . . . ?"

"It would be just a matter of getting him to leave . . . at the right moment."

"And then?"

"I don't know. Keitha never knows exactly. Only thing certain is that something *will* happen."

"This is crazy."

"But it's all true, Orry. *Keitha knew about your dad.* And a couple of years ago, when Ray's father, Old Man Goodkind, played at Bumppo's with a bunch of men from the Rotary Club, he left white. Keitha said he didn't have long, and a few days later he drowned. Just like that. She didn't know he'd drown, but she knew he'd be dead."

Orry gulped, took a deep breath. "I hate Ray, but not that much, Jesus." He swallowed, inhaled again. "I don't want him to die; I don't want that."

"Then maybe you just want him to leave with one of those in-between colors?"

"Yeah. Something to just scare him away from my Mom and me. For good."

Keitha wasn't happy. "You told him everything, Tess? Everything?"

"He needed my help. He won't tell anybody. He promises."

Orry nodded, sincerity his mantra.

"But you promised, too, Tess, and now look what you've done? I knew you were seeing too much of him. I knew this would happen."

"He won't tell anyone, Keitha. He won't."

"I won't, I swear."

"That was supposed to be between me and you, Tess. No one else. *Our* secret. That's what made it special."

Tess examined the buckles of her sandals, toes crossed. "I'm sorry," she said, pouting, tongue moistening her lips, gauging her friend's reaction from the corner of her eye, sharing a secret smile with Orry. "But you'll do this for me, won't you, Keets? Us best friends and all . . . ?"

Keitha snatched the glasses from her nose, spit harshly on each lens and buffed them on the hem of her dress. "Tell me, Puce Boy," she said, "when were you planning to bring *your friend*?"

"As soon as I can, I guess."

"Then bring him."

"But remember, I don't want him to die or anything."

"He wants an in-between color, Keets."

Ray Goodkind drove a hard bargain. "I'll play on one condition, Ors. You get your hair cut first."

Orry didn't hesitate. The sacrifice would be worth it. Besides, his hair would come back while Ray presumably would not.

"That's nice," his mother said. "You boys have fun." To say anything more, she feared, would surely jeopardize the moment.

As agreed, Orry and Ray arrived late on a Wednesday night, just after the curtain had rung down on the Goodkind weekly talent show. The finale had dragged on—**"Yesterday"** rendered consecutively by trumpet, mandolin, accordion, and mezzo-soprano from New Rochelle. Ray hummed the tune as Tess greeted them beneath the tail of the coonskin roof. "Hello, Mr. Goodkind," she said, followed by a disbelieving, "My god! What happened to your hair, Orry?"

"It was Ray's idea," he said glumly.

"You must admit, young lady, he looks significantly more human."

Tess smiled, as if an earwig were creeping across her tongue, and handed them their balls, putters and scorecard.

Keitha locked up the ticket booth and switched off the neon sign that beckoned on route 9. Orry and Ray would be the final twosome of the night.

Keitha and Tess kept watch from the stockade. When Ray's color was right, Keitha would step forward, announce she was forced to close early because her father had taken ill, and then rush the two through the exit with rain checks. Simple. Effective. Foolproof. Except nothing happened. They played hole after hole after hole and Keitha did not budge.

Discouraged, Orry pressed on, enduring Ray's persistent volleys, noxious amalgams of guidance and gloating.

"Bend your knees more, Ors. Straighten that back. Chin up. Chin up! I said, 'chin up!' "

"Coordination of hand and eye. That's all there is to it, Ors."

"Don't be a namby-pamby, son. Address the ball."

"Luck, Ors, is merely good planning, brilliantly executed."

By the 18th, **NATTY'S NIGHTMARE**, Orry was certain Keitha's *talent* was a sham; Ray would be a part of his life forever. Worse yet, Ray was whupping him by thirty strokes. *The jerk was under friggin' par!*

Eight punching bags swung suspended around and over the putting tee, leaving little room for a player to maneuver. Painted on each bag was a ferocious Iroquois warrior, tomahawks and knives poised for the kill. It was called the gauntlet, and, somehow, players were expected to putt through to the hole. There lay the second part of the challenge: three dwarf grizzlies guarded the cup, prowling about it in circles, rearing onto their hindquarters at random intervals. The best way to play the hole changed constantly.

Orry crammed himself among the swaying Iroquois and putted. The ball trickled timidly out from under the warriors and stopped well short of the grizzlies.

Ray elbowed his way to the tee. "Let me show you how it's done, son." He twisted his left arm awkwardly behind him and heaved two warriors aside, keeping them at bay, his arm straight, but trembling against the pendulous weight. Face flushed, he teetered, struggling to *address the ball* with his free hand. He swung and simultaneously the two Iroquois broke loose. Fury unleashed, they slammed against him, hurling him headlong into the plastic turf. His ball shot from the tee and struck Orry's dead-on, propelling it under a grizzly; it rimmed the hole, skittered left under the butt of a second bear, before the third unceremoniously pawed it into the cup. Ball sunk, the grizzlies froze.

Orry beheld his ball agape. "Um . . . does that count as a hole-in-one for me?"

Ray wriggled out from under his attackers and wobbled to his feet. His lip was bleeding. "Damn," he said, "I think I chipped a tooth. Jesus. Can you believe that?"

"Does that count as a hole-in-one?" Orry asked again.

Ray massaged his cheek, feeling for damage. "For chrissake, no," he sputtered.

"But I only took one shot. . . ."

"It's not a hole-in-one, Ors, that's all there is to it. The ball comes out."

"But—"

Keitha interrupted, Tess a step behind. "Excuse me," she said politely, quite unlike herself.

Orry's heart began to gallop. He stared at Ray, straining to materialize a color. Any color.

Keitha tendered the story, about her father taking ill.

"Now wait a minute," Ray protested. "I almost kill myself and now. . . ."

She stuck with the script. Handed him a pair of rain checks.

Ray frowned, inspecting the chits. "Well, I guess that's fair, seeing as how we're almost done."

"Please, I really must close up." Keitha collected their clubs and herded them toward the exit.

Ray folded the coupons into his wallet. "Must have turned my ankle, too," he grimaced, limping forward. "That 18th is dangerous."

Orry lagged behind. "What color?" he whispered to Tess.

She shook her head.

"You asked for an in-between . . . ," Keitha assured, her mouth a flat line. "Quickly now, before it changes. Before yours changes, too."

"Pardon me?" said Ray.

"Nothing," said Orry, clipping Ray's heels as he prodded him through the gate.

Orry's mother tended to Ray's scrapes and bruises while Orry went off to bed. "I never imagined miniature golf could be such a rough sport," she said, clearly amused.

Orry had expected to lie awake the entire night. Didn't think he would sleep at all until the *in-between color* did whatever it was supposed to do. But nary a disturbing thought intruded, and he fell fast and deep asleep.

Sunrise leaked round the edges of the window shade, but it was the commotion outside that awoke him. He peeked through to morning, but saw only the row of cedars and a dirty sky overhead. Smelled smoke.

"Ma," he called. "Mom?" But her bed was empty. Untouched from the night before. Panic knocked the wind from him. He gulped for the door, stopped. Scrambled back for his jeans. Pulled them up over his jockey shorts and ran outside.

The main lodge was in flames. Although the fire had yet to reach the gables or Ray's quarters, it was swiftly spreading in that direction. "Mom!" he shouted. But all eyes and ears remained focused on the fire, the bucket brigade in full swing and a Lake Arnold pumper wheezing up the road.

In-between colors didn't kill. He had been told they didn't kill. *Unless Keitha had lied? Sent Ray out with something other than in-between?*

He had to save his mother. Had to. But how?

The porch was ablaze. There was no way in, no way out. Except through the windows. *Why weren't they at the windows? Was he already too late?* Once, years before, there had been a fire in a house on his street. When the firemen entered, they discovered the couple who lived there on the floor beside their bed, unscarred, but dead from the fumes. *Had Ray and his mother met the same fate?*

Mind set, steps deliberate, he trudged up the path to the lodge. Felt the heat flush his face, scorch his chest. Then heard the shriek behind him. "Orry. My god, Orry! What are you doing?" Turned. Saw his mother at the front of the crowd. In her housecoat. Ray beside her. Arm about her waist. Hand on her shoulder. Holding her back.

Relief rushed through him in torrents. Relief for the *both* of them. "Mom," he tried to say, throat seared raw. "Mom," he tried to shout, but only rasped.

Timbers cracked, braying in agony, as the ceiling bellowed painfully to the floor, and twisters of spark and flame ripped into the second storey, lapping at the rafters, blackening, then shattering the windows.

Shards flew. Cinders peppered his back. He saw the horror in his mother's face, the dread in Ray, and hauled himself towards them, miraculously unscathed.

The bucket brigade had now given way to the Lake Arnold volunteers. Pumps were being primed. Hoses snaked up from lakeside.

But something wasn't right. The onlookers, who had been gathered about his mom and Ray, were retreating, scattering to the sides, isolating the pair whose attention remained solely on him. Orry saw why.

A big, baby blue Chrysler was barreling toward them, gaining momentum as it rolled silently down the roadway that sloped from cabins 1 to 12. Orry raised his hands to warn them, voice nowhere to be found.

His mother turned. Too late. The Chrysler smacked her harshly aside, discarding her into the shrubbery as if she were too small a catch. But Ray. Ray was another story altogether.

The vehicle scooped him off the ground and splayed him to the hood like a virgin bound for sacrifice. Pajama crotch wrapped round the ornament of the hood. Housecoat crumpled up about his neck, belt loop hooked on wiper blade.

Orry glanced down at the license plate. *Ontario*. And as the car rumbled by, he saw an old man slumped behind the wheel, same old man he had seen at Fort Bumppo's, the old guy who had been caddying his grandkids and then threatened Keitha. From the back seat, his wife looked on. Helpless. Her wheelchair folded away.

"Ray," Orry whimpered, reaching out. But Ray heard nothing, eyes fixed in disbelief on the inferno dead ahead. *Where in the hell was his state-of-the-art sprinkler system?*

Orry did not watch as the Chrysler tore through what remained of the porch. Did not watch as the flames eagerly wolfed it down. Did not hear Ray's screams. Did not wait for the explosion.

He ran to his mother, but others were already attending to her. He could not tell if she were alive or dead; he was too frightened to ask. He backed off. Willed himself invisible. Began to walk. Trot. Jog.

He did not stop until he arrived at the feet of the big Indian. For the first time, he noticed the brass plaque screwed to a moccasin: **In memory of CHINGACHGOOK**. And then, above him, he saw Keitha. An avenging angel clipped of its wings.

"You said he was an in-between color. That's what *you* said."

She looked down from the ladder, squeegee in hand, not the least bit ruffled by the intrusion. "What brings you out so bright and early, Puce Boy? Did your wish come true?"

"I didn't wish for *that*."

"Oh? Really?" She dipped the squeegee into the pail and scraped it across Chingachgook's chest.

"Orry!" Tess called from the 16th. She propped a rake against a buck with broken antlers and shuffled down the gravel slope, pebbles spraying in her wake. "My god, what happened?"

His foot was cut. His chest and shoulders were streaked with soot. He struggled to explain, tears flowing freely. "Ray. And my mother, too," he said. "Fire. The whole lodge."

"Oh, Orry, I'm so sorry." She threw her arms around him, buried her face in his neck and sobbed along with him.

Tenderly, he pulled Tess aside. Again, he challenged Keitha. "You said he was going to leave with an in-between color."

"No. That's what *you* said. That's what *Tess* said." She flung the squeegee into the bucket and hoisted it down from the ladder. "I never promised anything." The bucket dropped with a damp thud; water sloshed over the sides and pooled beneath the Indian.

"And my mother . . . what about my mother?" His fists were clenched. "Nobody said anything about hurting her."

Keitha leaned close, her breath a shroud across his face. "That's life now, isn't it, Puce Boy?"

Tess stroked the back of his hand. "Sometimes, Orry, people with bad fates take others down with them. Happens all the time. Plane crashes, for instance. All it takes is a single *white* and everybody pays the price—no matter what color they may be."

"Even lavender blues," Keitha added, glancing softly at Tess.

"She can't get away with this, Tess. I'm going to tell."

"But who would you tell, Orry?"

"Yes, Puce Boy. Who?"

"Think about it, Orry: there is nothing for Keitha to get away with. She didn't really do anything. She simply saw the colors and no one can prove or disprove that."

Keitha smirked, the corners of her smile reaching ever closer to her ears. "On the other hand, maybe you *should* tell someone, Puce Boy."

"Stop bullying him, Keitha," Tess said sharply.

Keitha stamped her foot and spun about. She toppled the ladder onto its side and slammed it shut.

Tess gently wiped a tear from Orry's cheek. "If you tell, they'll only think you're crazy."

"And even if they do believe you, Puce Boy, you'll be guiltiest of all." Wrath cleaved Keitha's face into a ruptured hock of blood and bone, sinews aquiver. "You were the one who brought Ray Goodkind here. Before last night, he'd never been to Bumppo's."

Tess held him close. "There's nothing you can do, Orry. Nothing we can do."

He backed away, hesitated. "Come with me, Tess. I got to go . . . to see about my mother."

"Yes. Go, Tess." The ladder clattered noisily as Keitha dragged it towards the shed.

Tess swallowed. "I can't," she said, ashamed. "She won't tell me what color I am until you're gone, Orry. Gone from Lake Arnold for good. And you can't go either, Orry, not without knowing. Please tell him, Keitha. Please."

The ladder crashed to the ground, skidded up against a cast-iron toadstool. Keitha crept closer, paused beside a plaster beaver, and raked her fingernails down its spine. "And I hope you leave very, very soon, Puce Boy."

"Mind your own business."

"What a brilliant comeback! Puce Boy is quite the wit."

"You haven't seen the last of me."

"Oh, haven't I?" Keitha bristled, eyebrows squirming like newborn tentworms. "That all depends on the color you are when you pass through the gate."

"I don't care what color I am."

"Good. Because I certainly won't tell you."

He grabbed Tess by the wrist. "Come."

She kissed him on the cheek. "No," she sobbed. "And you can't go either, not without knowing. Tell him, Keitha. Please." But her friend remained unmoved.

He squeezed her hand, released it with reluctance. "I'll come back for you," he whispered gallantly, shut his eyes, and committed himself to the exit.

The barred gate shut with a loud clank behind him. The finality thundered through his skull.

Keitha dangled the key for him to see. She smiled, teeth like ivory daggers. "You're lucky, Puce Boy. You shifted colors at the last moment and, I'm afraid, escaped with a rather tame in-betweener." She sighed. "I'm afraid we'll all just have to be patient."

Orry steadied himself on the turnstile bars, tried to speak, but nothing came to mind or mouth. He reeled into the parking lot as if on the cusp of a fifth of vodka.

Keitha shouted to him from atop the stockade. "There's one more thing."

Head up. Swaying.

"Puce boys with a hint of vermilion also have dead mothers."

He was well up the road, unaware that Tess had chosen to chase after him. Didn't find out or put two and two together until the day Aunt Con and Uncle Neil came to get him. Just happened to notice the paper lying on the sheriff's desk, her picture, and the story—about a local girl being the victim of a hit and run, just outside the gates of Fort Bumppo's Mini-Putt.

Dumb.

Dumb as a cliff diver working at low tide dumb.

"I knew this would happen," Holly says, more smug than angry.

The state trooper hands him the ticket. "Three kids and a fine-looking wife. . . . Ain't worth risking the lives of loved ones, pal."

Eyes fixed on Exit 21.

"You take it easy, now." The trooper slaps the roof of the mini-van and saunters back to his car, the lights still flashing red and blue.

"Nice man," Holly says cheerfully.

Breath on hold. He turns the key. Shifts to drive. But the van does not agree to go. A fat, metal cow lowing in tar sand.

"What now?" Holly seems to think he might have the answer.

Eyes fixed on Exit 21.

The cop taps on the window. "You musta run over something on the shoulder. You got a couple of flats, pal. Ripped pretty bad."

They climb out. Examine the damage.

"There's a real fine mini-putt just down the road, run by a real nice lady," the trooper says. "Why don't I take you and your boys over while hubby waits for the tow? It could be a spell."

"No," he says. "They stay with me."

Holly stares at him queerly. Quickly concludes a little time apart, right now, will do them all a bit of good. "Don't be silly, Orry. Meet us there. It's not fair to the kids."

The boys cheer.

She is right, of course. Besides, what more can he do without sounding like an idiot? With the cop hovering nearby?

Holly and the kids pile into the police car. "You won't believe it," Holly says, "but the boys have been begging us to stop at this mini-putt for miles."

"Must be fate," says the trooper.

Eyes fixed on Exit 21.

Crickets serenade at roadside. An orchestra of tambourines, but without the whack and thump. Strange to hear them so active by daylight.

He watches in the rear-view mirror. Stomach queasy. Mind unsettled.

Reviews the road map. The AAA Tour Guides. The comic books. Steps out to stretch his legs.

Notes the Greyhound on the horizon. A white Honda Civic scurrying behind.

An ideal time to start smoking again. If only he had a pack of anything.

No sign of tow truck.

Sees the Greyhound, closer. Much closer.

Sees the white Honda Civic cutting in front, a car length too soon. Much too soon.

Stands rigid. Tries to throw himself clear. Tries his damnedest. Really. Though he has long deserved it. Sees the plaster Chingachgook guarding Fort Bumppo's, elbow bent and fist extended, middle finger pointing insolently upwards. Sees the kids, Holly shepherding them to the ticket booth beneath the coonskin cap, *Welcome Settlers* scripted in red along the tail. Sees the woman at the cash. Short. Pear-shaped. Body flowing in folds over stool. Sees the grin grease her face. Hears her ask: "How long has your father been dead, boys?"

ZORAN ŽIVKOVIĆ

The Violin-Maker

Zoran Živković is a leading writer and critic of speculative fiction in Yugoslavia. Born in Belgrade in 1948, he received his undergraduate, masters, and doctoral degrees from the University of Belgrade. He currently lives in Belgrade with his wife and their twin sons. Živković is the author of numerous books including The Fourth Circle, Time-Gifts, Impossible Encounters, The Library, *and* Steps Through the Mist. *His enigmatic story "The Violin-Maker" (translated from the Serbian by Alice Copple-Tošić) comes from his story suite* Seven Touches of Music, *serialized by the British magazine* Interzone *between late 2001 and early 2002. A book edition of* Seven Touches of Music *has been published in Belgrade under the Polaris imprint.*

—T. W.

To the police inspector, it was an open-and-shut case. Mr. Tomasi, master violin-maker, had committed suicide by jumping from the window of the garret of the three-storey building where he lived and ran his celebrated workshop. The tragic incident was reported by two eye-witnesses, a baker's roundsmen, delivering bread and rolls, who had been crossing the square early that morning. After hesitating a moment they had fearfully approached the place where the unfortunate man lay. He showed no signs of life, even though they could not see any external injuries.

Inspector Muratori quickly arrived at the scene of the incident and found out from the agitated young men, who had never seen death at first-hand before, that nothing had heralded the falling body. They had heard no sounds before the dull thud on the sidewalk, which had frightened the pigeons at the little fountain in the middle of the square like a sudden detonation. Most suicides who take their lives by jumping from a height make their intentions known by shouting once they have stepped into the abyss and it is too late to change anything. Only those who are firmly convinced that they are doing the right thing remain silent to the end.

One glance at the three-storey building told Inspector Muratori where Mr. Tomasi had jumped from. The only open window was in the garret. Actually, he could have jumped off the roof, but there was no reason to choose such a inaccessible place since the window was much more suitable and served purpose equally well. Although one might not expect that of a suicide, the policeman knew that they did not, as a rule, make their last moments more difficult than necessary.

His examination of the inside of the house revealed nothing to conflict with the suicide hypothesis—on the contrary. When he climbed up to the garret that looked out on the square, the inspector found the door locked from the inside. This was a precautionary measure typical of someone who did not want to be deterred from carrying out his intention. The door had to be forced, because there was no way to push the key out of the lock so as to open it with a skeleton key. The small room was sparsely furnished: a table and four chairs, a single bed, a washstand with a basin and pitcher in the corner, a large mirror. There was no rug on the floor, no curtains at the window, no pictures on the walls.

Mr. Umbertini, the tall, thin man in his late twenties who was the late master violin-maker's assistant and lived alone with him in the house, explained that the garret was used exclusively for the final test of a new instrument. Mr. Tomasi would go inside and play there alone for some time. Then he would come out, either with a smile on his face, which meant that he was satisfied with his work, or with a handful of firewood and broken strings; then it was best to stay away from him.

The inspector's efforts, with the help of the visibly distressed Mr. Umbertini, to find a farewell letter that his master might have left somewhere produced no results. This was not unusual. Those who did not actually want to kill themselves, even though they actually did in the end, were the most frequent writers of such messages. Determined suicides did not find it necessary to interpret or justify their actions to the world, or to make their farewells.

By all appearances, Mr. Tomasi belonged to that category. Obviously the man had been firmly resolved to take that step, and had set about it without hesitation. This case was one for the textbooks, clear and unambiguous. There was nothing more to investigate. The causes that had led the esteemed master violin-maker to commit suicide had not been established, but were of no interest to earthly justice. Let divine justice handle them, for it alone could know what had been on the suicide's mind.

Inspector Muratori ordered Mr. Umbertini to pack his things and leave the house so that it could be sealed pending probate. For a moment it seemed that the assistant wanted to make a comment or add something, about this or some other matter, but he held back. That was just as well. Everything had already been said, and the policeman could by no means help the poor man who was suddenly out on the street. But Inspector Muratori had seen far worse fates. This fellow would manage. A man who had learned the violin-maker's trade under maestro Tomasi need never be without an income. Such a recommendation would easily find him a job with another violin-maker, or he might even open his own shop.

The experienced policeman was rarely mistaken in his conclusions about people and their fates, but he was wrong this time. Mr. Umbertini neither looked for new employment nor tried to set up making violins on his own. With the savings he been putting aside for years, he rented a small room in one of the narrow little streets off the square where he used to live. The rent was not high because the room was partially below street level and quite humid. This did not bother him very much. In any event he only went there to sleep.

Mr. Umbertini spent most of his time in a tavern not far from the maestro's house. He had not frequented the place before, primarily because he hadn't been the least inclined to drink, but also because it had a bad reputation as a hangout for the demi-monde. Now neither reason mattered. He started to drink, first moderately, just enough to feel slightly intoxicated; then more and more. He hardly felt when he crossed the line and became addicted. The tavern only served cheap, low quality wines and spirits that made Mr. Umbertini's head ache for a long time after waking in his dirty basement bed, but that did not deter him from going there every day.

At first the other tavern regulars were suspicious of the new patron, avoiding his company. With his genteel manners and appearance, he was not part of their world. But as time passed and he became more and more like them in his person and behavior, they slowly started to warm to him. He no longer drank alone; they began to join him until finally all the places at his table were occupied almost all the time. They were a motley collection, and just a few months ago he certainly could not have imagined himself among them: frowning mercenaries from a regiment camped near the town, rotten-toothed and withered prostitutes, pickpockets on their way back from forays to the outdoor markets, tattered beggars, blemished and maimed.

Although Mr. Umbertini had no desire to talk about the suicide, with these people or anyone else, the topic could not be avoided once their relations with the former assistant to the celebrated violin-maker, by now a thoroughly unkempt drunk, became familiar enough to remove their inhibitions. Unlike the police, who found it unnecessary to delve into what had forced the maestro to suicide, this mystery had never stopped intriguing prying minds, even in such a hole as this. Mr. Umbertini was subjected to a variety of approaches, from flattery through cajolery to threats, to get him to explain what had happened, but he withstood all such pressures without uttering a word. However, he could not avoid listening to the conjectures expounded by his fellow-drinkers at the table in the tavern, through the dense, stale cigarette smoke and sharp smell of sour wine.

One of the mercenaries, a man with a black patch over his left eye and a face full of scars, claimed that he had heard from a reliable source that a legacy of madness in the family lay behind it all. Mr. Tomasi's paternal grandfather, a carpenter from a nearby village, had also taken his life, but in a far better way. When his mind had gone black he had shut himself in his workshop and started to stick every sharp tool he could find into his body. Not a single wound was fatal, but he died in prolonged agony, from blood loss, without uttering a single cry during that multiple, self-inflicted impalement. When his household forced their way into the workshop they beheld a horrible sight. The carpenter's body on the floor, arms outstretched like some horizontal crucifixion, resembled a hedgehog with thirty-three quills sticking out of it. His wife, who was five months pregnant, had a miscarriage and his only son, who was four at the time, was haunted his whole life by nightmares that made him wake up screaming.

Mr. Umbertini could easily have refuted this awful story, but he didn't. In the early days of his apprenticeship he had met the maestro's paternal grandfather. He had been a watch-mender here in town and had died in his sleep, at an advanced age, from heart failure. He had outlived his wife by several years, leaving seven children. The third of them, the first son after two daughters, was Mr. Tomasi's father, a cheerful and rather unruly man, certainly unburdened by dark stains from childhood, who died of suffocation on a fishbone, having been so incautious as to refill his mouth before he had finished laughing. Although not yet full grown, the younger of his two sons, Alberto, who had inherited his mother's fine ear for music, took over his father's workshop where musical instruments were made and repaired. Not long afterwards he narrowed his activities exclusively to making violins, and over time earned a reputation for his exceptional workmanship.

One of the prostitutes, whose original beauty could still be discerned despite her dilapidated state, though she was barely over thirty, had a completely different story. She had learned from someone completely trustworthy that the cause of Mr. Tomasi's suicide was unrequited love. A travelling circus had camped near the town the previous summer and given performances on the square. Three musicians accompanied most of the acts, among them a young Gypsy woman who played the violin. At first the master violin-maker had complained about the noisy disturbance every evening in front of his house, but when he saw and heard the girl he became more cordial.

He went to the window evening after evening and pretended to watch the events on the square, but never actually took his eyes off the young Gypsy. Finally, he went up to her at the end of a show, bringing the best instrument he had ever made. He invited her to his house and proposed that she play this violin for him alone during the coming night, promising to pay her generously in return. The girl whispered briefly to one of the other two musicians, and then accepted. When she left Mr. Tomasi's house the next morning she was carrying the precious instrument wrapped in brown felt.

The next evening the master violin-maker waited impatiently on the terrace for the customary circus performance, but no one appeared. In the meantime the travelling show had decamped and continued on its way. Mr. Tomasi hired a horse at daybreak and set out in frantic search for them. He went to many of the nearby towns without finding a trace of the entertainers. The earth seemed to have swallowed them up. Completely crushed, he had been forced to give up in the end. He returned home, hoping that time would heal his wounds and he would somehow forget the beautiful violinist, but he couldn't get over her. He fell into deeper and deeper depression, slowly losing the will and ability to make any more instruments. Finally, sunk into total despair, he decided to end his suffering.

The late master violin-maker's assistant knew from the outset that this story hadn't a grain of truth, but he didn't say so, among other things so as not to ruin the woman's pleasurable excitement as she recounted her tale. There was, in truth, a sad tale of love in the violin-maker's life, but it dated from his much younger days, while he was still learning the skills of his trade. Love blossomed between him and a close cousin on his mother's side. Although forbidden and clandestine, it was tempestuous, as often happens at that age. Who knows how things might have ended had illness not intervened. The girl came down with galloping tuberculosis and died only a few weeks later. He never became attached to a single woman after that, although he did not renounce them. He tried to be as inconspicuous as possible when he slaked his urges, usually going to other towns for that purpose.

One of the pickpockets, a man with long, clever fingers, but a face that was the very incarnation of innocence, swore on his honor that he had first-hand knowledge about the real reason why Mr. Tomasi had killed himself. It was because of a huge gambling loss he had suffered. The violin-maker had been in the clutches of this obsession for some time, although no one knew anything about it, not even his assistant who lived under the same roof. A group of gamblers used to meet secretly at his house every Friday, going up to the garret from which he had finally jumped to his death. They would cover the window with the blanket from the bed so no one from outside suspected anything, and then the game that would start by candlelight often lasted until dawn.

As an honorable man, the violin-maker had been convinced that his companions were his equals in integrity. He had had not the slightest inkling that he had fallen into a network of shrewd and unscrupulous cheats. At first they bet small amounts, and he mostly won. Then Lady Luck suddenly turned her back on him. He started losing, not only his money but his common sense. He agreed to increase the bets in the futile hope that he would win back what he had lost, but he only sank deeper and deeper into debt. When his cash and valuables disappeared, he started to write IOUs. First he lost his large estate in the country, then his house in town. He still managed to hold up somehow, but when the cards took away the last of his expensive instruments, he realized he had hit rock bottom. In the end he caught on, realizing he had been the victim of a hoax, but there was no turning back. Unable to live with the thought that his violins were in the hands of cunning thieves, he sentenced himself to the ultimate punishment.

That was pure invention, of course, but Mr. Umbertini still made no comment. Gambling organized every Friday, however discreetly, would never have escaped his attention. Moreover, Mr. Tomasi had never had a country estate to lose. Far more important than these details, however, was the fact that gambling was the last vice to which the maestro would have succumbed; without ever being touched by it personally, he had experienced the grievous consequences of this addiction.

The violin-maker's older brother, Roberto Tomasi, had been a regular attender at large casinos since he was a young man. He had left his share of their father's inheritance in them long ago, but for some time afterwards continued to gratify this irresistible vice thanks to his brother's generous support. Alberto had shown a strange compassion for Roberto's weakness, agreeing to pay his gambling debts, until one day he refused to give him the large amount he had come for.

Thereupon Roberto had, in a fit of rage, seized a newly finished violin and smashed it against the wall. The two brothers never saw each other again after that, even though the older brother had sent many letters of apology and even gone to plead at his younger brother's door.

A crippled beggar, who claimed to be the illegitimate son of a duke, patiently listened to all three stories and announced self-confidently that none of them was true. The master violin-maker had not committed suicide at all, whatever thought. He did not jump from the window, he was thrown out of it. There was a third eyewitness to this tragedy, as well as the two baker's men. He was a beggar who had left town in a hurry immediately after the fateful event, fearing what he had seen, and pausing only long enough to confide in his lame friend.

The beggar had spent the night on the square and was sleeping under some stairs, when he was awakened at daybreak by banging from somewhere above. He looked around drowsily, then realized that the noise was coming from the open window in the garret of the violin-maker's house. It seemed as if someone was trying to break something in there, but he could see nothing from below. Then everything quieted down and a brief silence reigned. Just as the two baker's boys arrived in the square from a side street, each carrying baskets full of freshly baked bread and rolls, the terrified maestro appeared at the window. He held tightly onto the frame, trying to resist whoever was pushing him from behind. It was a silent struggle, which was why the young men were completely unaware of it. They crossed the square, unsuspecting among the pigeons, chatting in low voices.

The unrelenting pressure on the maestro's back grew stronger and stronger until his resistance yielded. As if hurled by a huge hand, he flew out of the window and plunged helplessly towards the pavement, still without uttering a sound. Behind him, however, the window was not empty as it would have been had he jumped of his own free will. A terrifying figure appeared for just an instant, curdling the blood in the observer's veins as he lay hidden under the stairs. It disappeared at once, but that fleeting look was enough for the beggar to recognize it beyond all doubt. He remained hidden for quite some time, not daring to move. It was only after the police inspector had completed his investigation and the dead man's body was removed that the beggar mustered the courage to come out.

It should surprise no one, the lame beggar concluded didactically, that Mr. Tomasi finally fell victim to the Tempter. Anyone who pledges his soul to the Devil for the sake of some vain and evanescent acclaim must be assured that the Devil will get his due—sooner or later. The master violin-maker had no reason to complain; he had gloried for many years in his reputation as the unsurpassed creator of magnificent violins, although it was clear to everyone that such talent could not be natural.

That was when Mr. Umbertini was first tempted to contribute a comment of his own. Unlike the other stories, this one was at least partially credible. The storyteller himself had probably been the eye-witness on the square that morning, rather than this nameless friend who had so conveniently disappeared. Most likely he was reluctant to admit it so as to avoid being questioned by the police, but he had given too many convincing details for one who was merely recounting another's experience. The supplementary parts which he had invented were understandable in the circumstances; without them his story would not have been exciting enough for the listeners in the tavern. On the other hand, although he could not have known, they were not completely unfounded. Nonetheless, the ex-assistant decided once again not to say anything, principally because of his unwillingness to enter into the inevitable discussion about this aspect of the maestro's accident, for the secret at its heart greatly surpassed his own understanding.

He might never have spoken about it at all, had his hand not been forced by an extraordinary chain of events. The vagabonds and good-for-nothings who kept him company in the tavern started to lose interest in the violin-maker's suicide as it became clear they would get nothing out of his former assistant. They also found the man himself less and less interesting, since he passed most of his time withdrawn into gloomy silence, concentrating on the bottle. They gradually started to drop away, finally leaving him alone at the table. At last only the large, bearded innkeeper sometimes exchanged a word or two with him.

One rainy day in late autumn, Mr. Umbertini arrived at the tavern early, while there were still no other guests. He sat at a small table with two chairs in the corner, close to the hearth, and the innkeeper, without asking and giving just a brief nod, brought him three bottles of red wine and a glass. He peered briefly at his customer's thin, unshaven face, inflamed eyes and red nose, but said nothing. The innkeeper couldn't care less about the appearance of those who frequented his establishment as long as they had money to pay for what they ordered. It was not his job to warn immoderate drunks that every new glass only shortened what little life they had remaining. He picked up the coins that Mr. Umbertini put on the table without a word and slipped them in the deep pocket under his stained apron, then went behind the bar.

Mr. Umbertini was already halfway through the second bottle when new guests started to appear in the tavern. They were certainly not those he was accustomed to seeing there. First a little boy came in. He could not have been more than six or seven years old, but he went up to the largest table, sat at the head, took out a piece of paper and pen from somewhere, bowed his head and started to write something in a tiny script. From time to time he took out a handkerchief and held it briefly to his nose. After him came a middle-aged woman holding a bunch of rolled-up scrolls under her arm. She sat next to the boy, unrolled a scroll and became engrossed in reading. The refined-looking, older man who soon joined them brought a snow-white cat with him. He stroked it gently in his lap, whispering in its ear. The older woman who next arrived stood at the entrance, looking in bewilderment first at the innkeeper and then at the master violin-maker's assistant as though she had seen ghosts. She sat down stiffly on one of the three unoccupied chairs and put her muff on the table in front of her without taking her hands out of it. The man who came in after her was a painter. As soon as he joined the others he opened a large sketching block, took a stick of charcoal and started sketching in brisk, rough strokes. Finally, the last to arrive was a rather casually dressed man with dishevelled gray hair. He rummaged through his pockets for a few moments, finally found a piece of chalk and without the least hesitation began to write on the uncovered wooden table, erasing something here and there with the leather-patched elbow of his jacket.

The sight of six such strangers at the big table was extremely unusual in this establishment. During all the months that Mr. Umbertini had spent in the tavern he had never seen anyone even slightly resembling them. But what seemed to him almost as unbelievable was the fact that the innkeeper paid them absolutely no attention. He, who took great pains that no guest was ever left even momentarily without a glass or a plate on the table in front of him, who kept an eye on empty glasses in order to fill them at once, and never recoiled from showing the door to anyone who contemplated sitting inside for free, had not even approached these dignified guests, although they clearly promised a good tab. Instead, he went up to the assistant's table, waved at the other chair with the dirty rag he constantly wore over his arm, and sat down.

He came straight to the point. He maintained that he knew why Mr. Tomasi had killed himself—a most unexpected statement as he had never taken part in the conversations on the subject. He had seemed totally uninterested, just idly listening to the stories told by others. The master violin-maker, the innkeeper now asserted, had wanted to make a perfect violin. He had invested years of effort and everything indicated that he was on the right track. Unfortunately, no human hands, not even the most gifted, are able to reach perfection. Although appearing perfect in every way, the violin was nonetheless not divine, as he had hoped. When he realized this after testing it that morning, the violin-maker understood that there was only one way out of this defeat, and he took it.

This time Mr. Umbertini could hold back no longer. Had the innkeeper's story simply been wrong, he certainly would not have reacted, gliding over it as he had the others. But he had found one essential aspect of this story deeply offensive, and only he could now stand up to defend the maestro's besmirched honor. That was a debt he owed his teacher, and it rose above the pledge the assistant had made to himself never to reveal what had happened in the garret.

The innkeeper had been right, although Mr. Umbertini could not even imagine how that simple and greedy seller of bad wine could have found out something which the maestro had kept secret even from his faithful pupil. For eighteen years, with endless devotion and patience, he had indeed been working on a perfect violin. It was only towards the end that the assistant finally understood what lay hidden behind the violin-maker's periodic retreats to the highest room in the house. He would stay locked inside for hours, although he had taken no instrument with him to test, and no one dared to disturb him.

The innkeeper, however, was wrong when he said, with an edge of malice in his voice, that the master violin-maker had been unsuccessful in his efforts. Sneaking up to the garret on that fateful morning when the unique violin was given its final test, Mr. Umbertini heard the sound of divine harmony for the first and only time in his life. Even though the closed door dampened the music, the magic of that experience had been so powerful that he had felt compelled to stay close to the maestro's house instead of going somewhere else, where he might hope to enjoy a more useful and fulfilling life—even though he was conscious that he would never again be given an opportunity to hear it.

Mr. Umbertini knew the question the innkeeper would ask next, just as he knew that he had no answer. If the maestro had truly created a perfect violin, what had happened to it? Or to its remains, if the crashing that the beggar on the square had heard meant that the maestro had broken it? (Although why would he do such a thing to his masterpiece?) When the inspector had forced the door, nothing was found inside: neither a whole instrument nor its wreckage. So, there must have been a secret entrance into the garret, concluded the cunning innkeeper, which the assistant had used before the inspector's arrival in order to remove all traces.

This was a logical assumption that offered an explanation for both possibilities: that the violin had been perfect and that it hadn't been. Its only defect was that it was incorrect. There was no secret entrance to the highest room in the building. When he finally entered the garret with the inspector, the assistant encountered his second wonder of that morning. Although the instrument had to be there, and in one piece, it was not. And the fact that it should have been in one piece constituted the first wonder.

As Mr. Umbertini stood in front of the door, still dazzled by the music that had just ended, he suddenly heard something inside that terrified him. He was quite familiar with that sound. The crashing could mean only one thing: the master violin-maker was destroying his life's work! But why? Not knowing what else to do, the assistant quickly dropped to his knees and tried to peer inside through the keyhole. Had there been no key in the lock, he could have seen more, but even this way he was able to catch at least partial sight of the maestro's crazed figure as he swung the violin, holding it by the neck. He hit it against whatever he found: the table, chair back, bed-frame, walls.

Even though the full force of his unbridled rage went into it, the instrument was not the least scratched. The violin steadfastly resisted all his attempts to shatter it, remaining untouched, as though he was merely swinging it through the air. When he threw it to the floor and started to jump on it, again without damaging it, he finally collapsed, sat on the edge of the bed, thrust his head in his hands and stayed there without moving for a while. And then he got up slowly, went to the large window, grabbed the frame, stayed in that position a few moments, then let go of his hands and simply leaned forward. The dumbfounded assistant took his eye off the keyhole and slid to the floor next to the door. It was not until the inspector banged the knocker on the front door of the house that he was startled out of his paralysis.

The innkeeper shook his head. Of all the stories he had heard, he said, this one seemed the most far-fetched. Thank heavens Mr. Umbertini had not told it to the police, because that would surely have focused suspicion on himself. He personally still thought that the only true explanation lay in the secret entrance. As far as the noise was concerned, it didn't have to come from breaking the violin, rather its maker might have banged the furniture around him in frustration over his failure, as people do when they are infuriated.

In any case, the innkeeper concluded, after the master violin-maker jumped through the window, Mr. Umbertini had gone into the garret and stowed the instrument somewhere. He had waited for the situation to calm down, then sold it under the counter. The violin might not have been perfect according to Mr. Tomasi's criteria, but the seller certainly would have received a pretty sum for it that would enable him to lead a comfortable life. For example, he could amuse himself at the tavern day after day without having to work. But Mr. Umbertini had no need to worry. The innkeeper certainly would not turn him in. What benefit would that bring him? He would only be losing a regular customer who had never asked for credit.

Seeing there was nothing more to say, he returned to the bar. He started to wipe glasses idly, continuing to neglect the six visitors at the other table. They sat there briefly, involved in their preoccupations, and then, as though at an invisible signal, stood up and left the tavern together, probably offended at being so rudely ignored. Mr. Umbertini watched them leave, and then, as though remembering something, quickly got up and headed after them, leaving almost a bottle and a half of wine, paid for but not drunk. He was never seen in there again.

For a while stories were concocted in the tavern regarding his disappearance. It was heard with great reliability that thieves had slaughtered him and thrown him into the river, that he had left for the New World to seek his fortune, that he had opened his own workshop in another town, and that he had come down with leprosy and was now living the miserable remainder of his days in an asylum on some island. Only the sober innkeeper, who was not to be cheated, knew that they were all fabrications and that, as usual, the simplest explanation was the soundest: the late master violin-maker's assistant had fled, fearing that someone might denounce him to the police after he had spent all of his dishonestly acquired money.

BENTLEY LITTLE

Maya's Mother

Bentley Little was born in Arizona and currently divides his time between that state and Southern California. He is the author of twelve novels including The Association, The Walking, The Town, *and* The House. *His first published novel,* The Revelation, *won the Bram Stoker Award.*

"Maya's Mother" is the third of Little's stories set in contemporary Phoenix, Arizona, and featuring a noirish detective as its protagonist. It was first published in his story collection, The Collection.

—E. D.

It was hot as I drove through the desert to the Big Man's. The place was out past Pinnacle Peak and at one time had probably been the only house out here, but now the city was creeping in, and there were only a few miles of open space between the last subdivision and the dirt road that led to the Big Man's compound.

I turned onto the unmarked drive, slowing down, peering through my dusty windshield. The Big Man had made no effort to landscape his property, but there was a lot more out here than just cactus and rocks. Doll parts were hanging on the barbed wire fence: arm and leg, torso and head. Mesquite crosses stood sentry by the cattle guard. A blood-drenched scarecrow with a coyote skull on its shoulders faced the road, arms raised.

I hadn't expected him to be so spooked—or at least not so superstitious—and I was starting to get a little creeped out myself as I ventured farther into the desert and away from civilization. He wouldn't say over the phone why he wanted to hire me, had said only that he had a case he wanted handled, but the few details he'd given me were enough to pique my interest.

His house sat on a small rise, surrounded by saguaros, and was one of those Frank Lloyd Wrightish structures that had bloomed out here in the late fifties/early sixties when the Master himself had set up his architectural school north of Scottsdale. It was, I had to admit, damned impressive. Low, geometric, all rock and windows, it blended perfectly with the environment and bespoke an optimism for the future that had died long before they'd built the square shoebox that was my dingy Phoenix apartment complex.

One of the Big Man's men was out front to greet me, and he ushered me inside after allowing me to park my dirty shitmobile next to a veritable fleet of gleaming Mercedes Benzes. The interior of the house was just as impressive as the outside. Lots of light. Potted palms. Hardwood floors and matching furniture. I was led to an extra wide doorway and ushered into a sunken living room approximately five times the size of my entire apartment. "He's here," the flunky said by way of introduction.

And I finally got to meet the Big Man.

I'd heard of him of course. Who in Phoenix hadn't? But I'd never met him, seen him or even spoken to him. I looked at the man before me, underwhelmed. I'd been expecting someone more impressive. Sydney Greenstreet, maybe. Orson Welles. Instead, this Richard Dreyfuss look-alike stood up from the couch, shook my hand and introduced himself as Vincent Pressman.

Time was when I wouldn't have even returned the man's phone call. I worked strictly for the good guys, followed all of the guidelines necessary to maintain my investigator's license, dealt only with the law-abiding who had been screwed or were in some type of jam. I still try to keep it that way whenever possible, but there are grey areas now, and while I try to rationalize my behavior, I sometimes sit alone at night and think about what I do and realize that perhaps I'm not as pure and honest as I like to think I am.

Which is a long way of saying that I now take cases that interest me. There are only so many lost dogs and missing teenagers and two-timing spouses that a man can handle.

And the Big Man's case interested me.

As I said, he didn't tell me much, but the hints had been tantalizing. Water turned to blood. A shadow that followed him from room to room, building to building. Obscene calls received on a disconnected phone. He claimed he didn't know who was behind all this, but I had the feeling he did, and I figured I could act as an intermediary between the two, bring them together and settle things out of court, as it were, without any bloodshed.

At least that was my plan.

I sat down as directed on a white loveseat, facing the Big Man across a glass coffee table. He cleared his throat. "I've heard you're into this stuff, this supernatural shit."

I shrugged.

"I've had this place bugged and debugged, scanned by every electronic device known to man, and no one's been able to come up with an explanation for what's happening here."

"But you don't think your house is haunted."

He glared at me with cold steely eyes and, Richard Dreyfuss look-alike or not, I saw for the first time a hint of what made Vincent Pressman the most feared underworld figure in the Southwest. "I told you, someone's after me."

I nodded, acting calmer than I felt. "And I asked you who it was."

He sighed, then motioned for everyone else to leave the room. He stared at me, his eyes never leaving my own, and I held the gaze though it was beginning to make me feel uncomfortable. He did not speak until we heard the door click shut. Then he leaned back on the couch, glanced once toward the door, and started talking.

"I had this maid working for me. Guatemalan bitch. She looked like a goddamn man, but her daughter was one fine piece of poon. Maya, her name was. Skinny little thing. Big tits. Always coming on to me. I don't usually like 'em young—I'm not a pedophile, you understand—but this babe got to me. She was sixteen or so, and she was always lounging around in her bikini, going to the fridge for midnight snacks in panties and a t-shirt. You know the drill.

"Anyway, bitch mama gives me this warning, dares to tell me that I'd better stay away from her little girl. I see the daughter later, and she's got this bruise on her cheek, like she's been hit, beaten. I call mama in, give *her* a warning, tell her if she ever touches one hair on that girl's head I'll have her cut up and fed to the coyotes." He smiled. "Just trying to put a scare into her, you understand."

I nodded.

"So the girl comes back later, thanks me. One thing leads to another, I take her into my room and . . . I fucked her." The Big Man's voice dropped. "The thing is, after I came, after I finished, I opened my eyes, and she was . . . she wasn't there. She was a rag doll. A full-sized rag doll." He shook his head. "I don't know how it happened, how they did it, but it happened instantly." He snapped his fingers. "Like that! One second I was holding her ass, rubbing my face in her hair, the next I felt her ass turn to cloth, was rubbing my face in yarn. Scared the fuck out of me. I jumped out of bed, and that doll was smiling at me, a big old dumbass grin stitched onto her head."

He licked his lips nervously. "It didn't even look like Maya. Not really. I called on the intercom, ordered my men to make sure the girl and her mom didn't leave the house, told them to hunt them down and find them, especially the mom. When I turned back around, the bed was empty. Even the doll was gone."

He was silent for a moment.

"They were gone, too," I prodded. "Weren't they?"

He nodded. "Both of them, and it was after that that the weird shit started happening. I put the word out, told my men to find the maid, have her picked up, but, as you know, she seems to have disappeared off the face of the fucking earth."

"So you want me to find the woman."

He leaned forward. "I want you to stop this shit. I don't care how you do it, just do it. Find her if you have to, leave her out of it, I don't care. I just want this curse gone." He sat back. "Afterward, after it's over, then I'll decide how to deal with her."

I nodded. We both knew how he was going to deal with her, but that was one of those things he didn't want to spell out and I didn't want confirmed.

I thought of Bumblebee, and while the memory of that situation remained sharp, the emotions had faded, and it seemed somehow more fun in retrospect.

Well, maybe not fun.

Interesting.

Kind of like this seemed interesting.

"How did you find me?" I asked. "Phone book?"

"I told you: I heard you handle this stuff."

"From who?"

He smiled. "I have my sources."

I didn't like that. I hadn't told anyone about Bumblebee, and the only people who knew were either dead or fled.

"Word is that you're in tight with the wetbacks, too. I figured that can't hurt."

"You hear a lot of words."

"I wouldn't be where I am if I didn't."

I looked at him for what seemed an appropriate length of time. "All right," I said. "I'll do it. But it'll be twenty-five hundred plus expenses." That was far more than I usually charged, but I knew the Big Man could afford it.

He agreed to my terms without question, and I knew that I could have and should have asked for more. But I'd always been bad at this part of the game, and once again my stupidity had screwed me out of a big payday.

"You have a picture of this maid?" I asked. "And a name?"

He shook his head.

"Not even her name?"

"I never used her name. Didn't matter to me." He motioned toward the foyer. "Maybe Johnny or Tony knows."

The arrogance of the powerful. I'd forgotten to take that into consideration.

One of the flunkies came hurrying up. Pressman asked the maid's name but the flunky didn't know, and he hurried out, returning a few moments later, shaking his head.

The Big Man smiled. "I guess that means we forgot to pay her Social Security tax."

"But the girl's name is Maya?" I said.

He nodded.

"Maya's mother, then. I'll start there."

"Do what you have to," he told me. "But I want results. I expect people to complete the jobs I hire them to do, and I don't like to be disappointed. Are we understood?"

It was one of those movie moments. He'd probably seen the same movies I had and was playing his role to the hilt, but I felt as though I'd just sold my soul to the Mob, as though I'd jumped in over my head, painted myself into a corner and was being forced to sink or swim. It was a scary feeling.

But it was also kind of cool.

I nodded, and Pressman and I shook hands. I had to remind myself not to get too caught up in the glamour of it all. These were the bad guys, I told myself. I was only working for them on a temporary basis. I was not one of them and never wanted to be.

I drove back through the desert. There was only one person I knew who might be able to decipher this: Hector Marquez. Hector was a former fighter, a local light heavyweight who'd gotten railroaded by Armstrong and his goons a few years back for a payroll heist he'd had nothing to do with. I'd gotten him a good lawyer—Yard Stevens, an old buddy who still owed me a slew of favors—but even that had not been enough to counter the manufactured evidence and coerced witnesses Armstrong had lined up, and Yard had told me, off the record, that probably the best thing for Hector would be if he disappeared. I'd relayed the message, and ever since there'd been a warrant out for Hector's arrest.

I hadn't seen him after his disappearance, but I knew someone who knew someone who could get in touch with him, and I put the word out. I expected a long-distance phone call, expected Hector to be hiding either in Texas or

California, but he was still right here in the Valley, and the woman who called on his behalf said that he wanted to meet with me personally.

We set up the meeting for midnight.

South Mountain Park.

A lot of bodies had been dumped here over the years, and though the city had been trying for decades to clean up its image, the park remained a haven for gangbangers, drunken redneck teens and the occasional naive couple looking for a lover's lane.

In other words, not exactly a family fun spot.

The view was spectacular, though, and as I got out of my car and looked over the edge of the parking lot, I could see the lights of the Valley stretching from Peoria to Apache Junction. Phoenix looked cleaner at night. The lights cut clearly through the smog, and everything had a sweeping cinematic quality that reminded me of how it had been in the old days.

I was suddenly spotlighted by headlights, and I turned around to see three silhouetted men standing in front of a parked Chevy. One of them started toward me.

It had been three years since I'd seen Hector, and he definitely looked the worse for wear. He was probably in his late twenties but he looked like a man in his early fifties, and his old smooth-faced optimism had been buried under lines and creases of disillusionment and disappointment. His fighter's body had long since softened into pudge.

"Hector," I said.

He walked up to me, hugged me. The hug lasted a beat longer than was polite, and I understood for the first time that he had really and truly missed me. I didn't know why he'd stayed away if he was still living in the Valley, but I could only assume that it was because he hadn't wanted to get me into trouble, and I felt guilty for not making an effort to keep in touch.

He pulled back, looked me over. "How goes it, man?"

"My life doesn't change."

"Solid."

"As a rock."

He laughed, and I saw that he had a new silver tooth in the front.

"I don't know if Liz told you what I'm looking for, but I'm working on a case and I need to find a Guatemalan witch used to work as a maid. Her daughter's named Maya. I thought you might be able to introduce me to someone, set me up."

Hector thought for a moment. "I don't know much about Guatemalans. But you talk to Maria Torres. She run a small bodega on Central between Southern and Baseline. In an old house by the Veteran's Thrift. Her son is married to a Guatemalan girl. She can get you in."

"You couldn't've told me that over the phone?" I ribbed him. "I had to come all the way out here in the middle of the night?"

"I wanted to see you again, bro."

I smiled at him. I'm not a touchy-feely guy, but I grasped his shoulder. "I wanted to see you, too, Hector. It's good to see you again."

We caught up a bit on our respective lives, but it was clear that Hector's friends were getting antsy, and when the lights flashed and the horn honked, he said he'd better get going.

"I'll call," I promised. "We'll get together somewhere. In the daytime. Away from Phoenix."

He waved.

The next morning I learned that Hector had been followed.

Armstrong was the one who called me. Gleefully, I thought. He told me they'd found Hector in a Dumpster, burned beyond recognition. His teeth had been knocked out first and his fingertips sliced off so there'd be no possibility of positive identification. The cops had been able to ID the men with him, however, and one of the women who'd come down to claim the body of her husband said that Hector had been hanging with these guys and had ridden with them last night and was in all probability the other man.

The lieutenant paused, savoring his story. "That Dumpster smelled like a fuckin' burnt tamale."

I hung up on him, feeling sick. Immediately, I picked up the phone again and dialed the Big Man's number. I was so furious that my hand hurt from gripping the receiver so tightly, and when he answered the phone himself and gave me that silky smooth "Hello," it was all I could do not to yell at him.

"You killed Hector Marquez," I said without preamble.

"Is this—?"

"You know damn well who this is, and you killed Hector Marquez."

"Sorry. I don't know anyone by that name."

"I'm off this case. You can find some other sucker to do your dirty work."

"I wouldn't do that." The Big Man's voice was low, filled with menace.

"Fuck you."

He sighed. "Look, I'm sorry. If something happened to someone you know—and I'm not saying it did or that I'm in any way involved—then it was probably a mistake. If you'd like, I could look into it for you."

"I want you to make sure it never happens again. If I'm going to continue, I need to have your word that no one is going to be murdered, no one I talk to is going to be attacked. You want to follow me, fine. But just because I'm getting information from someone doesn't mean they're involved with this. You let me handle this my own way, or I'm off. You can threaten me all you want, but those are my terms, those are my rules, that's the deal. Take it or leave it."

"I understand," he said smoothly. "A slight misunderstanding. As I said, I am in no way connected to the death of your friend, but I think I have enough clout that I can assure you nothing like it will ever happen again. You have my word, and I'm sorry for your loss." He paused. "Do you have any leads?"

"Hector was a friend."

"I said I'm sorry."

I was still furious, but I knew enough not to push it. I might be brave when I'm angry, but I'm not stupid. I took a deep breath. "Hector gave me the name of a woman who might offer me an in to the Guatemalan community. I'll ask around. See what I can find out about this Maya and her mother."

There was silence on the line, but I knew he was nodding. "Keep me informed," he said.

"Of course."

I was still furious, but I pretended I wasn't, and we ended on a false note of rapprochement. I wondered after I hung up what kind of man could treat human life so casually, could order deaths as other people ordered dinner, and I told myself that the kind of man who could do that was the kind of man who would statutorily rape the daughter of his housekeeper.

The kind of man I would take on as a client.

I didn't want to think about that, and I walked into the kitchen to make my morning wakeup coffee.

Maria Torres's bodega was closed when I arrived, so I went to a nearby McDonald's to get some coffee. There were gang members signing near the blocked bathrooms and a host of hostile faces among the silently staring people at the tables, so I paid for my order, took the covered cup, and went out to wait in my car.

I didn't have to wait long. Before the coffee was even cool enough to drink, a dark, overweight woman in a white ruffly skirt walked down the street and stopped in front of the barred door of the bodega. She sorted through a massive keyring, used one of the keys to open the door and flipped the CLOSED sign in the window to OPEN.

I went over to talk to her.

The woman was indeed Maria Torres, and when I told her that Hector had said she could put me in touch with a Guatemalan woman who might know Maya's mother, she nodded and started telling me in broken English a long involved story about her son and how he'd met and married this Guatemalan girl over the wishes of her and her family. It was clear that she hadn't heard what had happened to Hector, and I didn't want to be the one to tell her, so I simply waited, listened, nodded, and when she finally got around to telling me her daughter-in-law's name and address, I wrote it down.

"Does she speak English?" I asked.

"Therese?" Maria smiled wide. "More better than me."

I thanked her, and to show my appreciation, I bought a trinket from her store, a little rainbow-colored "friendship bracelet" that I could either give to my niece or toss away, depending on how the mood struck me.

The Guatemalans lived in a ghetto of a ghetto in the slums of south Phoenix. It was a bad area on a good day, and there hadn't been a lot of good days since the beginning of this long hot summer.

I found the house with no problem, a crummy plywood shack on a barren lot with no vegetation, and I got out of my car and walked up to the section of plywood that I assumed to be the door.

I should've brought a tape recorder, I thought as I knocked. But it didn't really matter, because no one was home. I walked over to the neighbors on both sides, but one of the houses was empty and the tired skinny old man in the other spoke no English. My attempts at pidgin Spanish elicited from him only a blank look.

I decided to head home, get my tape recorder, then come back and see if Therese had returned, but when I reached the front door of my apartment, the phone was ringing, and it continued to ring as I unlocked and opened the door. Someone was sure anxious to talk to me, and I hurried over, picked up the receiver.

It was the Big Man.

I recognized the voice but not the tone. Gone was the arrogant attitude the sureness and confidence born of long-held power.

The Big Man sounded scared.

"She's hit me!" he said.

"Maya's mother?"

He was frantic. "Get over here now!"

"What happened?"

"Now!"

I drove like a bat out of hell. I did not slow down even through Paradise Valley with its hidden radar cameras, and I sped up Scottsdale Road at nearly twice the speed limit, figuring I'd have the Big Man pay off any tickets that were sent to me through the mail.

One of Pressman's flunkies was waiting for me at the door of the house, and I was quickly ushered in and taken to the bedroom, where the Big Man was seated on a chair next to the gigantic waterbed, stripped to the waist. He looked at me with frightened eyes as I entered.

I felt a sudden coldness in my gut.

His right arm had withered to half its normal size and was blackening with rot. No less than three doctors, all of them obviously very highly paid specialists, were standing around him, one of them injecting something into the arm, the other two talking low amongst themselves.

"That bitch cursed me!" he shouted, and there was both anger and fear in his voice. "I want her found! Do you understand me?"

The flunkies and I all nodded. None of us were sure who he was talking to, and it was safer at this point not to ask.

The Big Man grimaced as the needle was pulled out of his arm. He looked at me, motioned me over, and one of the doctors stepped aside so I could get close.

"Is there any way to reverse this?" he asked through gritted teeth. "Can I get this curse taken off me somehow?"

"I don't know," I admitted.

"Well, find out!"

He screamed, and the arm shrunk another six inches before our eyes. The doctors looked at each other, obviously at a loss. They seemed nervous, and it occurred to me for the first time that though they might be tops in their field, the best and the brightest the Mayo Clinic had to offer, they were just as afraid of the Big Man's wrath as anyone else. It was a sobering thought.

I started out of the bedroom, intending to find a phone, make a few calls and see if anyone of my acquaintance knew anything about the lifting of Guatemalan arm-shrinking spells. I turned around in the doorway, wanting to ask the Big Man something else, but he screamed again and with a low, sickeningly wet *pop*, his arm disappeared, its tail-end nub sucked into his shoulder, the skin closing behind it as if it had never existed.

I hurried out of the room.

No one I knew had any info or any ideas, so I figured the best idea was to once again stake out Therese's shack. I told one of the Big Man's flunkies to let him know that I'd gone to find out about the spell and Maya's mother. The flunky looked about as thrilled as I felt to be telling the Big Man anything right now, and I quickly left before he could decline and insist that I do it myself.

Luckily for me, Therese was home. Alone. I put on my most official-looking expression in order to intimidate her into talking. I told her I was working for Vincent Pressman, hoping that the name carried weight even down here, and said that he wanted to know the current whereabouts of his former maid and her daughter Maya.

Word about the situation must have already spread through the Guatemalan community because Therese blanched at Pressman's name, and quickly crossed herself when I mentioned Maya.

"You know something about this," I said.

She nodded, obviously frightened. I got the feeling she wasn't supposed to be talking to outsiders.

"What's going on?" I asked. "What's happening to Mr. Pressman?"

The woman looked furtively about. "He mess with the wrong woman. She a . . . how you call it? . . . Very powerful, uh . . ."

"Witch?" I offered helpfully.

"Yes? Witch! She curse him. She will kill him but she want him to suffer first." Therese crossed herself again.

"What about her daughter, Maya?"

"Daughter dead."

"What?"

"Mother kill her. She have to. Cannot live with shame. Now she blame him for daughter's death, too. His fault she have to kill girl." She shook her head. "It bad. Very bad."

I asked about removing the curse, asked if there was anyone else who could do it, another witch perhaps, but Therese said that only the one who applied the curse could lift it. She told me the other limited options for dealing with the situation, but they were all horrible, and I asked if I could talk to someone who knew more about the black arts than she did, but she would not give me any names, not even for a pair of Andrew Jacksons.

I wanted to stop by my place, pick up a few phone numbers, some people I knew who weren't Guatemalan but might be able to tell me something about lifting curses, but Armstrong was waiting for me outside my apartment, and with typically piggish glee he told me that since I was one of the last people to see Hector alive, I was automatically a suspect in his murder. I denied everything as I desperately tried to think of who could have seen me with him, who could have ratted me out, but Armstrong motioned for me to get in the cruiser so we could go down to the station and talk.

All the way over, my stomach was tied up in knots. Not because of Hector—I was innocent, and I knew there was no way that even Armstrong could make that stick—but because I needed to talk to the Big Man. He was waiting with his one arm to hear what I'd found, but I sure as hell couldn't call from a police station, and I sat in the interrogation room as I waited for someone to talk to me, and pretended I was in no hurry to do anything.

An hour or so later, a smirking Armstrong joined me. He asked me a shitload of stupid questions, then leaned smugly back in his chair. "In my estimation, you're a flight risk," he said. "I can keep you in custody for twenty-four without cause, and I think I'm going to do that while we sort through what you said and check out your alibis."

He grinned at me. He knew I was innocent, but this was his idea of fun, and I made no comment and pretended as though I didn't care one way or the other as I was led to a holding cell.

I was awakened in the middle of the night by a cowed young sergeant who was accompanied by an intimidating man in a smartly fitted business suit, and I knew that the Big Man had tracked me down and had me sprung.

I was happy to be out, but I didn't like being this close to someone that powerful, and I vowed to be careful in the future who I took on as clients—no matter how interesting their cases might be.

A limo was waiting outside, and we drove in silence out to the desert.

It was late at night, but the Big Man was awake. He was also limping. It looked like he was wearing a diaper, but I saw the grimace of pain on his face as he sat down, and I knew something else had happened, something far worse than mere incontinence.

I was afraid to ask, but I had to know. "What happened?"

"My cock," he said, his voice barely above a mumble. "It attacked me."

"What?"

"I woke up, and it'd turned into a snake. It was biting my leg and whipping around and biting my stomach, and I could feel its poison going into me. So I ran into the kitchen and got a knife and I cut it off."

It took a moment for that to sink in. Pressman had cut off his own penis? I imagined Maya's mother cackling to herself as she wove that spell.

"The doctors sewed me up, but they couldn't sew it back on. It was still alive. We had to kill it." He grimaced, using his arm to grab the side of the sofa and support himself. "So what'd you find out?"

I told him the truth. "Maya's dead. Her mother killed her. Now she blames you for that, too." I motioned toward his crotch. "So this is going to go on. You're going to be tortured until you die. And then she'll own you after death. She'll be able to do whatever she wants with your soul."

"I'll kill her," he said. "I'll find that bitch and kill her."

"Won't do any good. The whammy's on, and as I understand it, killing her won't stop it. All of the Guatemalans are terrified. She's one powerful woman."

"So what are my options?"

I shrugged. "Only three that I see. One: get her to stop, convince her to lift the curse, which, considering the situation, I don't think is going to happen. Two: put up with this shit until you die and then go gently into her vindictive little hands . . ." I trailed off.

"And three?"

I looked at him. "You can take your own life. That will put an end to it. Her curse is meant to kill you . . . eventually. But if you take matters into your own hands, if you interrupt it and thwart her plans, all rights revert back to you."

I was playing it cool, playing it tough, but the truth was, I was scared shitless. Not of the Big Man, not anymore, but of what I'd gotten into here, of the powers we were dealing with. I was out of my depth, but Pressman was still putting it all on my shoulders. I was supposed to be the expert, and it was a role I neither deserved nor wanted.

He was actually considering the benefits of suicide.

"So if I eat my gun—"

"No," I said. "It has to be stabbing or hanging."

He slammed his hand down on the back of the couch. "Why?" He glared at me. "What fucking difference does that make?"

"I don't know why," I said. "But it does make a difference. I don't make the rules, I just explain them. And for some reason, those are the only two ways that are guaranteed to get you out from under the curse. A shooting *might* work, but then again, it might not. And you'll only get one chance at this, so you'd better make sure it counts."

He shook his head, lurched away from the sofa. "Fuck that. There's no way in hell I'm going to off myself because some little wetback bitch put her voodoo on me. I'll take my chances. I'm going to find her and get rid of her and we'll see if *that* works."

That's what he said on Thursday.

On Friday, his teeth fell out.

On Saturday, he began shitting rocks.

His men did find the maid, and the cops found her later, her teeth knocked out, her arm amputated, her private parts cut open, her anus stuffed with gravel. Like Hector, she was in a Dumpster, having been left there to die, and over the next few days several other Guatemalans, who I suppose had some relationship to Maya's mother, were also found murdered.

But it didn't stop for the Big Man. His travails grew worse, and by mid-week, he was able to walk only with the help of serious painkillers.

I asked around, checked my other sources, even went out to see Bookbinder, but the first facts proved true, and no one knew of a way to get around the witch's handiwork.

I stayed away, stayed home, tried to stay out of it, tried not to think about it, but finally he called me in, and I went. There was almost no trace left of that hard, confident crimelord I'd met the first day. He was broken and blubbering, drunk and wasted, and he told me that he wanted to hang himself.

Only he was too weak to do it on his own.

I told him he could have some of his men help him, but he said he didn't want them to do it and they probably wouldn't anyway. He also wanted to make sure he did everything right, that nothing went wrong.

"You're the only one who knows that shit," he said, his voice slurred.

I nodded reluctantly.

He grabbed my shoulder. I think he wanted to make sure he had my full attention, but it seemed more as though he used me to steady himself. "I don't want to suffer after death," he whispered. His eyes were feverish, intense. "And I don't want that wetback bitch to win." His voice rose. "Your daughter was the best fuck I ever had!" he shouted to the air. "I took that whore the way she liked it! I gave her what she wanted! I gave her what she wanted!"

I left him in the bedroom, went out to the garage and found a rope, and set it up, throwing it over the beam, tying the knots.

He changed his mind at the last minute. A lot of people do. It's a hard way to go, a painful ugly way, and the second he jumped off the chair, he started to claw at the rope and flail away in the air.

I thought about helping him. Part of me wanted to help him.

But I didn't.

I let him thrash about until he was still, watching him die. I'll probably go to hell for that, but I can't seem to muster up much remorse for it. I wish I could say that I let him die for his own sake, so Maya's mother wouldn't own his soul, but the truth was that I did it because I *wanted* him dead. I thought we'd all be better off without him.

"That's for Hector," I said softly.

I stood there for a moment watching him swing, and I actually did feel bad. No one deserved what had happened, and I was glad he'd escaped, glad he wouldn't have to suffer it anymore.

But I was also glad he was gone.

I walked out of the bedroom, down the hallway to the front of the house, where I found one of his men eating crackers in the kitchen.

"Call the cops," I said. "He's dead."

The flunky looked at me dumbly. He knew what had gone down, but it still seemed to catch him off guard. "What'll I tell them?"

I patted his cheek on my way out. "Don't worry. You'll think of something."

I walked outside and got in my car, driving as quickly as I could away from the house. The air in the vehicle was stifling, but I didn't mind, and I felt as though I'd just been released from a prison as I followed the dirt road through the desert, past the crosses and the doll parts and the skull-headed scarecrows, toward the distant white smog of Phoenix, shimmering in the heat.

CARLTON MELLICK III

Porno in August

Carlton Mellick III specializes in the surreal and bizarre. His books include Razor Wire Pubic Hair, Satan Burger, Electric Jesus Corpse, Sunset with a Bear, *and the forthcoming* Teeth and Tongue Landscape. *He lives in Portland, Oregon and his Web site is: http://www.avantpunk.com.*

"Porno in August" is his first appearance in this series. Aside from its prosaic title, it is a marvelously bizarre amalgam of the grotesque, the horrific, and the mystically baffling. Think of one of Gene Wolfe's more layered stories, but with sex and a very odd cast to it. It was first published in the anthology Random Acts of Weirdness.

—E. D.

Chapter One

They dropped us off by helicopter in the middle of the Atlantic Ocean, wearing speedos and sexy bathing suits, and now we are waiting for the director and crew to arrive. Staring at each other, wading in the ocean water miles and miles from any type of land.

"So what's this movie about?" asks the puffy blonde actress beside me, inside a child's floating tube with zebra patterns, trying to hold her hair away from the water.

Unlike any of the others, I am in a wetsuit with diving gear, even an oxygen tank. I have to take the mask and breathing tube from my face to respond. "Didn't you read the script?"

"I tried," says the woman, her breasts floating in the water under the tiny bikini top, "but it was too confusing to me."

"Well," I begin, "it's about . . ." My mind draws a blank. "We're in the middle of the ocean and . . ."

I don't remember.

I swear I read it just the other night, every line of it. I remember saying: "At last, a porn flick I'd be proud to act in. So new, so groundbreaking." But I don't remember a single word from it anymore. All I know is that it takes place in the middle of the ocean. I must be losing more brain cells than I thought.

I just stare at the blonde woman—Jenna, I think her name is—with a dumb/

blank look. Then I just turn and swim to another cast member, Randy, the only thing close to a friend in this business, probably because we both have a fascination with AMC automobiles, especially Matadors.

Randy is closing and opening his eyes, a zombie in the water, water wings on his arms to keep him afloat.

"Hey Randy, do you have a copy of the script?"

Salt water makes his eyes itchy and the sunblock on his nose doesn't seem to be helping. Turns to me, "No, I never got one. They said I'd get it last week. When I told them I never got one, they said one of the crew would give me a copy on the helicopter but the crew wasn't on the helicopter."

"They are coming by boat."

"Yeah, so I've never even seen the script. Did you forget yours?"

"I left it at home, we rarely follow the script anyway." I gaze down into the water to watch my flippers waving forth and back; inches below my flippers the deep blue water becomes darkness. "It's bugging me. I read the script, but I can't remember a thing about it. I remember really liking it, really-really liking it, but that's all."

Randy shrugs his beefy shoulders at me. "All I know is it's the biggest budget porn film this company has ever been willing to try." Chewing on a pruned finger, "And that it's shot entirely on location in the middle of the ocean."

Randy turns to the bald woman with a full suit of tattoos, who didn't bother to wear a bathing suit because she already has one tattooed on her privates. "Shady, do you have a copy of the script?"

The bald girl smiles at him, always smiling and twitching. "No, they wouldn't let anyone take it on the helicopter." She holds up her arm to scratch, tattooed up and down with sun-faces and dragon scales. "They didn't want them ruined in the water."

Randy calls to the entire cast of porn performers, "DOES ANYONE KNOW WHAT THIS FILM IS ABOUT? I WAS NEVER GIVEN A SCRIPT . . ."

Everyone looks at each other, frozen in question-faces, struggling with thoughts. I don't think anyone of them can give us an answer.

"I know what it's about," one of them says, deep voice.

Yes, it is King Soul, the big name of the film, the older well-endowed black actor whose been doing these films for nearly twenty years. A real professional. Of course, he probably knows the script by heart, memorized it word for word, even the scenes he doesn't perform in. He's been known to treat porno scripts like he's acting in a real movie, or maybe even a play.

We all swim to him, circle around the King. He likes the attention. Big smile in his salty water goatbeard, scraggly like pubic hair.

"So what's it about?" I ask.

"Well, it's about a bunch of people stranded in the middle of the ocean. There's some sex. Parts of it are filmed on an island. Lots of other weird stuff too."

"Kinky stuff?" Shady asks, curling her fingers excitedly.

"Freaky stuff?" Jenna seems concerned.

"I mean . . . Well . . ." King Soul begins. "Well, just weird stuff. Unusual stuff. Like that stuff in art theaters."

"Like what?" I ask.

The King thinks about that for a minute, a hand in his crusty facial hair.

"Not sure," he says, and we groan in response. "I read it so long ago it might all be false memory. I had a couple dreams about the movie. Not sure what was the script and what was dream now."

"I can't believe how unorganized this is!" Randy squawks. "They said how important it was for us to actually read the script for once, but not a single one of us can remember a single detail!"

"Speaking of unorganized . . ." I say, softly. "Does anyone know when the crew is going to get here?"

We wander our eyes for the director's ship, looking to the horizons. Nothing. The ocean stretches for miles in all directions with no foreseeable end.

"How are they going to find us?" Jenna, like a little child though the oldest woman here. "They promised they wouldn't lose me. I'm scared of oceans."

"They can't lose us," King Soul says.

He holds up a small mechanism like a walky-talky with a blinking red light on it. "I was given this tracking device. They know exactly where to find us. They's just late, that's all."

You got to look up to Soul, everyone in the business does. He's so calm, has everything under control. They say he even graduated from college but doesn't ever brag about it. Half of us didn't even make it through high school. Hell, I only got a GED. But he's not the only one, we look up to Shady as well sometimes. She's been taking art classes at the community college for as long as I can remember.

We are able to relax for now, but my legs are getting tired from treading water. I have to let myself float sometimes to allow the muscles a rest. Good thing we all have strong lower bodies from doing so many of these films. We are all in great shape, even old Soul, for this kind of legwork.

The eleven of us hold tightly together, keeping each other warm as the wind begins to pick up.

We stop talking to each other when the sun goes down.

Water smacking against our bodies in the quiet, skin shriveled and numb, thirsty.

The water begins to get warm around us, hugging us, like a bed.

Chapter Two

I open my eyes. I see half the sky is murder-black, but there's a deep blue line on the other horizon, the sun about to come up.

I move my legs and my mind jerks clear. I remember where I am. My lower half numb in the warm water, waving my bare feet back and forth in the dark salty ocean. I am no longer wearing the wetsuit or diving gear, but now am in a speedo that is not at all mine. Perhaps I traded costumes with someone.

I'm lying on my back, my upper half floating on something soft and comfortable. I turn to my left. No one is in that direction. I look to the right. No one. I look behind me, in front of me. I'm all alone.

I feel something rub against me under the water. *Screech* and leap, splashes in the ocean, looking for what had touched me. It was a hand, a human hand. Jenna. She is floating face down in the water, still in her floating tube. I had been on her corpse, sleeping on her this whole time. Perhaps I am the cause of her drowning. I don't remember at all. Shivers creep down my back as I watch her body rocking in the dim lighting.

"Where is everyone?" I ask the water, but the water is busy whispering to itself.

I lift Jenna's face up. In a delayed burst, liquid burst-pours out of her mouth and nose and ears and eyes. I tremble at the sight, looking closer. Her eyes are wide open but the eyeballs are missing. And there is nothing inside of her beyond the eyeballs either, hollow. She is empty inside, just a shell filled with water. Her skin, on the inside and out, has been bleached white, her mouth hanging open greasy tongue dripping out. Like a fish's mouth.

"What happened to you?" I ask her.

She looks blank. Not horrifying or morbidly disfigured, just blank. Empty and sad. I let her slip through the floating tube and slowly sink into the shadowy depths, her empty corpse refilling itself with water.

I take her place in the tube, a tight fit but I'll be able to last for a long time without having to tread water.

The strip of light in the horizon is not growing any bigger. The sun doesn't want to come up anymore.

Did everybody drown? Perhaps they killed themselves. . . . It wouldn't have been difficult, just take a deep breath of water and then all black. Maybe they are with Jenna now.

But Jenna . . .

What happened to her? Her insides . . . just disappeared. Perhaps she never had any insides. Perhaps—

A voice.

Somewhere in the distance. I can hear it slightly. From the darkness. I can't see that far. There's a fog in that direction.

I hear the voice again. A little more distant. It is real though. I'm sure. Definitely someone trying to find me. Perhaps the director and crew have finally arrived by boat. Or they might have sent a search party for us.

"Over here," I holler to the distance.

Those assholes. Fucking assholes. They came too late. I'm the only one left now. Yeah, I guess I should be happy I'm actually being rescued, but everyone else is dead.

"Over here, over here," I scream.

I get closer to the voice, it gets closer to me. But . . . there aren't any boat sounds. Just a voice.

I recognize who it is. Randy. He's still alive.

"Randy!" I call to him.

His distant voice grows a little louder and louder until we are able to understand each other. Though we are still unable to see each other in the fog.

"What happened?" Randy cries. "I don't remember anything. Did the helicopter crash?"

"What do you mean?" I ask.

"The last thing I remember is getting on a helicopter to film the new movie on some island. Then I woke up alone in the middle of the ocean. It scared the shit out of me. Where are you?"

"I'm over here."

His voice is so close to me, but the fog gets thicker. I can't see anything.

"Keep talking," he says.

"Don't you remember yesterday at all?" I ask him, paddling furiously.

"Yeah, we went to the bar and bought an eight-ball."

"No, that was the day before yesterday."

"No, it was last night, remember?"

"You must be delirious," I tell him. "Yesterday we were dropped off in the ocean. How could you forget? That was the whole catch to the film. It was going to be filmed in the middle of the ocean. We were waiting for the director's boat to get here, but they never showed up."

"What are you talking about?" Randy yells, I think I can make him out in the distance. "The film was going to be some stupid runofthemill porno on a deserted island. It was going to be a Gilligan's Island parody."

"No it wasn't, Soul said it was an avant-garde porn flick set in the middle of the ocean."

"What are you talking about? That's impossible. For one, Americans do not do avant-garde flicks. And two, how the heck are we supposed to fuck in the middle of the ocean?"

My mind becomes dizzy. Is he confused or am I the confused one? I don't think I can think straight. My head's in pain from dehydration.

"It doesn't matter what happened," I tell him. "We're both probably delirious. In either case, we're in a shit of trouble."

Still swimming to each other, but we have yet to meet.

"Have you seen anyone else?" he asks.

"I woke up next to Jenna," I tell him. "She's dead."

"Do you think anyone else survived?"

"I doubt it. I only remember you and Jenna having stuff to float on. The rest of them would have been treading water all this time. I don't think they made it."

"So you think they'll find us?"

"Not if this fog doesn't clear up, I can't even find you."

And then Randy came into view, lying on his back to keep afloat. His water wings stretched to his sides.

"There you are," I tell him, paddling my feet in his direction.

His eyes closed. I grab his leg and pull him to me, just watching him in his relaxed position.

But he doesn't end this relaxed posture.

"Randy . . ." I reach my hand to his shoulder. "Come on, stop fucking around."

And I jerk him to wake.

A popping noise. Randy opens his eyes and water boils out of the sockets, flowing out of his mouth and nostrils. I splash backwards, almost out of the floating tube, fumbling my limbs. Face dunks into the hot ocean. Try to reclaim myself, huffing/choking breaths.

A few minutes of calm-breathing and I slip the water wings from Randy, let him sink out of view.

"You too, Randy," I say to his silhouette beneath me. "You were empty inside just like Jenna."

They must not have had souls. Just hollow sad creatures without anything on the inside. I guess most people in the adult film business are without soul. Eventually, as I believe Jenna once told me, the business squeezes it out of you like juice, and then you don't really care about anything anymore.

Chapter Three

A gush of water goes into my lungs and I cough myself into consciousness.

"Hey, look who's awake," Shady says, splashing water at me. And my eyes go in and out to see her face, her bald head shining in the dim light.

"Told you he'd wake up eventually," I hear King Soul from beside me.

I clear my head and look around. There are five of them with me.

"What happened?" I ask them. "The last thing I remember is finding Randy dead."

"That's all you remember?" Shady asks. "You didn't go unconscious until two days after we found you. And you told us you found Randy empty that morning."

"I don't remember seeing any of you since the first day. How long have we been out here?"

"How long, Grim?" Shady asks the skinny bearded biker guy to my left.

"Eleven days," he says in a feminine voice.

Wait a minute.

"ELEVEN DAYS?"

Shouldn't we be dead by now?

"The jellyfish have been keeping us alive," Shady says.

My questioning face wrinkles into more questions.

"You're the one who found them," Grim tells me, his face very bisexual in its features.

"Look," Shady says, jerking her dragon hand into the water and pulling out a transparent jellyfish as big as a head, squirreling at her wrist. "The first night we were out here you reached into the water and pulled one out."

"There's enough juices and nutrients to sustain us," Soul tells me, "But now we're starting to think they're poisonous, making us lose our memory."

"Here, we haven't fed you in awhile," Shady gives the curling jellyfish to me. "Eat this."

Biting into the live creature, twisting limbs around my face. Water. Cold fresh water gushes down my throat, and the creature stops moving.

"It's fresh water," I say.

"Yeah," Shady tells me. "Like a living water balloon."

A rubbery exterior with only water inside.

"There's hundreds of them all around us," some girl says. "But you can't see them 'cause they're clear."

After I chew its stretchy meat down, I gaze into the water looking for them. But there is nothing. Just crystal water.

"What happened to the others?" I ask.

King Soul: "Well, you said Jenna and Randy drowned. Toby and Camesis disappeared the first night like you. And Norma . . . Well, there's been . . . a shark that's been after us for the past few days. It picked off the weakest of us yesterday. You probably would've been next."

"What about the tracking device?" I ask.

"What tracking device?" Shady blinks her tattooed eyes.
"Soul has a tracking device," I tell them.
They have confused looks.
King Soul digs into his bag around his shoulder.
"Everything they gave me is in here," Soul says. "But I don't remember a . . ."
He's so shocked to see the device in his hand that he nearly drops it.
"That's it," I say. "But it was blinking before."
Soul clicks a button and the red light starts blinking again. "It was turned off . . ."
"We're saved," one of the girls says. "They'll find us now!"
Shady: "Thank God you remembered."
A wave of relief blows through them, but I am amazed they had forgotten about it. It's something I would never let leave my mind.
"By the way, wasn't there twelve of us supposed to be in the movie?" a girl asks us. She's the girl who was supposed to work with Shady in the lesbian underwater scenes.
"What do you mean?" Shady asks.
"They always have twelve cast members in every film they make."
"I don't know what you're talking about."
"No, that's right," Soul says. "They were always strict about that. But wasn't there twelve of us dropped off in the ocean?"
"No, there were eleven of us," the girl says.
"Vixen," Shady puts her hand on the girl. "I think you're right. Hold on . . . There are the six of us, Norma, Randy and Jenna, Toby and Camesis. That's eleven."
"Who was the twelfth?" Vixen asks.
Shady: "You and I were going to fuck, Randy and Mark were going to fuck Jenna, Soul was going to fuck Norma and Camesis, Grim was going to fuck Toby. Who's left?"
The shy girl behind me, a newbie in the business, "I don't know who I am screwing?"
We all turn to her. Cyl I think her name is. Yeah, pretty sure it's Cyl.
A moment of clarity and my hand reaches up in the air.
"The little guy!" I scream.
"Who?" they ask.
"You know, the little man."
Soul: "Oh yeah, the midget."
"I'm screwing a midget!" Cyl screams.
"Not a midget," I say. "A little person. Remember, he always gets mad when you call him a midget."
"What's it matter?" says Soul. "Midget is just another word for little."
Vixen: "But what happened to him?"
"He was never on the helicopter," Grim says.
"Yeah, he was," Soul says. "The entire helicopter ride seems like a dream now, but I swear he was on it."
"Did he ever get off?" I ask.
"Yeah," Soul says. "He was swimming with us, making us laugh with his tricks."

Me: "Where is he then?"
Soul: "He must have disappeared like the others."
"Are you sure you didn't dream him?" Vixen asks.
"No," he says. "Of course not, I always confuse my dreams with memories."
"I'm glad he's dead," Cyl says. "I don't want to fuck a midget."
"Who was I supposed to sleep with?" I ask them.
"I already told you," Shady says. "You and Randy were going to do Jenna."
"No," I tell her. "You said *Mark* and Randy were."
They gaze at me annoyingly.
"You *are* Mark," they say.
"No it's not . . ."
Wait a minute. What is my name?
"It's not Mark, it's . . ." I shake my head.
"Mark," Shady puts a dragon arm around me, "this is hard for us all."
"My name isn't Mark!" I shove her away.
"Then what should we call you?" Shady asks.
"Don't call me anything," I say, swimming away from her.

Chapter Four

I wake one morning in the wetsuit again, praying I am not lying on another dead/empty body.

My eyes searching. I see King Soul sleeping, Grim holding him up. Cyl sleeping, with Vixen holding her.

And I turn my head, noticing Shady is behind me, making sure I don't drown in my sleep.

"You didn't sleep long," she tells me.

"I feel like I've been asleep for days," I tell her, rubbing my red eyes with salty numb fingers.

"You've been awake for days," she tells me, "and only slept for an hour."

"How long have we been out here?"

"You've forgotten again?"

I nod.

"We stopped counting a long time ago. A month or two, maybe."

My eyes burn spicy at her words, wanting to cry.

Shady says, "Our memories keep going in and out, especially after we sleep. We don't know how truthful our memories are anymore."

"I don't remember very much at all."

"Nothing's been worth remembering. We just take turns sleeping and eating jellyfish all day. And sometimes one of us loses most of our memory and we have to explain a lot of things."

"What about the tracking device?" I ask.

"There is no tracking device," Shady says in a bent voice.

"What happened to it? Did it break? Sink?"

"No," Shady says. "Soul opened it. There was nothing inside. Just a box with a blinking red light."

"Are you sure?" I ask.

"It was just a prop for the film," she says. "Not a real tracking device."

"Well, what about the shark?" I ask.

Shady pauses.

"What shark?"

"There was a shark, they said it killed Norma."

"No," Shady says. "Norma drowned. There's been nothing but jellyfish out here."

"No, they said it was a big shark that killed her in one bite."

"Your memory is playing tricks."

A high-pitched scream and everybody jerks upright. A fin is in the water, violently splashing next to Cyl. Vixen pulling the young girl away from the splashing fin.

"A shark," Grim screams and everyone swims together in a tight ball.

The shark fin lowers into the water. Cyl shrieking at the top of her lungs. We hold her from thrashing, arms whipping at us.

"My feet," she screams. "Watch my feet."

We pull her into the floating tube, exposing the shark bite to us.

We jump away from her when we see it. Her feet are missing. But there is no blood. Her legs are hollow, nothing inside at all. Water gushes out of the holes and into the ocean.

When she sees her legs, Cyl stops screaming. Like she was never really in pain. Her eyes drop wide. Just staring at the stream of water draining out of her hollow limbs.

"What the hell are you?" Vixen screams.

The shark is circling in the background, but all of our attentions are on Cyl now.

Cyl is confused, shocked maybe, not saying a word, not breathing. She lifts her wrist to her eyes and examines it closely. Then she pokes a hole with a fingernail. A thin line of water sprays out like a cut vein. Everyone watching her, the shark behind us, as she begins to drink from her arm. Then she looks up and smiles.

"I'm like the jellyfish," she tells us.

And then she falls back, exhausted.

"I'm hot," she says. "I'm so hot. The water . . ."

Shady swims to her, staring into her hollow legs.

"She's right," Shady says. "She's like a jellyfish."

They all sigh, like the whole mystery has been solved.

Then Shady bites into her arm, ripping the rubbery skin from her. Cyl doesn't scream, watching Shady chew her like a jellyfish. The rest of them join her, gnawing on Cyl's skin, water squirting out into their mouths.

I swim behind her as Shady chews the back of her head away. She's totally hollow inside. And I can see the back of her face.

"Stop doing that," Cyl says, and seeing her mouth move from the inside sends nails into my cricky neck. No vocal chords, no brain, no blood. How can she function?

"She's a jellyfish, Mark," Shady says, stuffing one of Cyl's empty breasts into my mouth. "Eat her."

Chapter Five

"Wake up!" somebody screams through a megaphone.

I open my eyes to a small speedboat in front of me. A camera is pointed in my direction.

My vision clears and I see three men standing in the boat. A camera man, a sound man, and the director with his megaphone.

"We have a porno to make," he says. "No more sleeping on the job."

I don't recognize the man. He is not the director I remember. Actually, I don't remember any of these men. We've had the same director for years, we go drinking together, baseball games together, but these people are utter strangers, yelling at me like a drill sergeant. I'm not sure what the original crew looks like or what their names were, but these people are not them I'm sure of it.

"Start fucking," the director yells at me.

I see King Soul and Grim are double-teaming Vixen over there, lying on floating tubes, struggling to get a decent position.

I turn around to Shady who was cradling me in my sleep.

"When did they get here?" I ask her.

"A couple days ago," she whispers. "They've been working us day and night. I don't think we can do it anymore. They won't let us in the boat until they have enough decent footage for the movie."

"Go under water," the director screams, pointing his finger like God.

Shady and I are sucked under the water, jellyfish pulling us down, curling around our limbs and sucking us under the water. Invisible creatures forcing us together, my wetsuit rubbing against her tattooed flesh. We use my oxygen tank to take turns breathing as they pull us into the darkness. They open up a pocket in the crotch of my wetsuit, they slide up the insides of her legs, and then they shift us together like puzzle pieces.

I watch Shady through the mask, her eyes closed tight with fear and maybe pleasure, the jellyfish caressing our back thighs and shoulders. But my mind jerks awake as I realize I feel nothing inside her. She is hollow/empty in there. I'm just moving in open space. I go soft. I cannot continue.

Over Shady's shoulders, the shark is returning, plunging at us for an attack. I grab her, force our way through the slippery jellyfish, her hollow body light enough to carry. We explode through the surface and Shady takes a gasping breath.

"Get back down there," the director screams at us.

"Shark! Shark!" Shady yells at him.

And the shark leaps out of the water, flying over our heads like its fins are wings. We all tweak our eyes when we see the shark has pink-peach skin and large human-like breasts underneath it. And it lands on the unsuspecting Grim, who had been hard at work between Vixen's legs until it came crashing on top of him. The shark begins squirming on top of him. It is screwing him. He screams at us for help, but we cannot move. He tries to scream again but the shark bites into his face, tears off his mouth.

Water gushes out of Grim's face, his head is hollow inside. His lower face missing, Grim's eyes look around, watching the shark/woman as she rapes him.

"Keep going! This is great!" the director screams, cheering for the shark. "This is what we've been waiting for!"

Vixen is pinned under Grim. King Soul slowly swims away without considering to help. Vixen pushing on Grim but they are hooked together by the floating tube and the weight of the shark.

Jerking arms, punches, but the shark will not stop fucking Grim and begins to eat more of his meat, ripping his arms from the sockets and slurping them down, devouring the rest of his head, chewing on his chest as she rubs her shark-breasts all over him.

"Oh, what a picture!" screams the director.

Vixen kicks the shark, trying to get away, and the shark snaps at her, taking her entire face off, and the shark continues its rampage on Grim's lower half. Faceless Vixen swimming blindly away.

"Mark," the director screams, "go fuck the shark in the ass!"

"My name isn't Mark," I respond, swimming away from the rapist fish.

At a safe distance, I turn to see Shady and King Soul sneaking onto the speedboat. The director shouts at me to return to have sex with the shark.

Soul, in his leopard speedo, has a sharp object in his hand. A knife maybe, or a broken beer bottle, something that he found close to him on the boat. And as the sound man turns to him, Soul slashes him in half, his whole body cut into two, folding backwards, empty inside. Water splashes at Soul, blinding him as the director and camera man turn to attack.

Vixen's faceless body is swimming to my direction, following my splashes. I try ignoring her, the horrifying look of a woman alive and swimming without the front half of her head.

I watch Shady out of the water. Her tattoos are like fish scales covering her skin, fighting the director with the boom stand, in her nudity, but with her illustrations she never really looks naked. She's a beautiful woman, even though a porn actress. But she's empty inside now, all of her beauty is only on the outside.

She punches the rod right through the director's chest, but the director continues swinging the megaphone at her. King Soul cuts the camera man's leg off, water emptying into the boat.

Vixen, the faceless creature, is behind me now. She grabs me and holds me, caressing my flesh.

The shark leaps into the boat, tearing into the camera man, and Soul is ripped in half longways.

His water empties out of him, but one half of him is still standing. One leg one arm balancing.

The sounds of the shark eating rubbery meat. Soul's left half stays upright just long enough to cut the director's head off, leaning to one side and popping his head right off of its neck, both of them crashing into the water.

Shady standing alone in the boat: Her face has a confused look as if waking into the situation without any memory of it ever happening. She jerks when she notices the shark in the boat, fucking and eating a man. And then she shrieks when she sees Soul's right half lying in the boat, wiggling at her. One by one, she tosses the men into the water, and the shark chases after them.

I try screaming at Shady, but she doesn't seem to hear me. She must be horribly confused. And Vixen holds me tight in place, won't let me swim to her, wrapping her legs around me.

Shady turns on the boat and speeds into the distance, the shark following close behind.

And I am alone in the ocean again. Alone with Vixen, the faceless abomination.

She is still caressing my body. I look into the back of her head because she has no eyes to look into. She moves me forward, hand around my skull to pull me closer to kiss her. But without a mouth, my face slides into her empty head and kisses the insides. The back wall of her head is slick and salty. I close my eyes, holding her tightly in the water.

Chapter Six

I wake on a beach, staring up at a bright sun. Salt-foamy water simmering around me.

I sit up.

My clothes are a white tuxedo. My mind feels just as white, like a blank piece of paper.

The island is lush with vegetation and hills, a stream of water leaking from my nose. Walking up the beach, the sun following me like a camera. Like I am a television show to the sun. After a ways, I find a table with two seats. A white cloth covering it, with a centerpiece of wildflowers.

I sit down in one of the chairs, brushing the sand off of my tuxedo and hands. My face goes into the tablecloth, eyes drifting.

"Can I get you something, monsieur?" a scratchy voice asks me.

I lift my head and see a little man of three and a half feet standing on a log and wearing a white tuxedo almost identical to mine. He also wears a matching eye patch.

"Excuse me?" my mind spinning.

"Can I take your order, monsieur?"

I look at my hands as if a menu and then look back at the little man, my mouth agape, squinting my eyes.

"Yeah," I tell him. "Give me the roast beef."

"Very good, monsieur," says the little man, writing it down in a notebook. "What would you like as beverage?"

"Just water," I tell him.

"Very good, monsieur," he says, scribbling words in his notebook. "Are you meeting someone, monsieur? Or dining alone?"

"I don't know," I tell him.

There is a woman in my view striding along the beach. She sees me and waves, smiling wide. I do not recognize her but she seems to recognize me. The woman is nude but has a white dress tattooed to her body. Her head is bald of hair but has a white dinner hat tattoo, tilted to one side.

The smile grows even bigger once she sits at the little table across from me, saying, "Hello, Charles, isn't it a wonderful day today?"

"Yes," I say, half-smiling back to her. "One of the best I've seen."

Her vision lowers to my hand and her smile turns angry, shocked. "Oh my God! Your ring is crooked!"

She rips my hand from its resting place and adjusts a wedding ring that has been on my finger. Then she holds our hands together and I see she has a similar ring tattooed on her finger.

Once she decides my ring is lined up perfectly with hers, she pops her face up into my sight and brings back her very large smile.

"Your water, monsieur," the little man says as he taps a sandy glass on the table.

And the little man closes his one good eye and places his thumb into his mouth, biting it off at the tip. Then he fills my glass with the water from inside him.

I sigh as I take a drink, my hand still prisoner to the woman's grasp, trying to pull it away.

The small man scurries to her, "And for madame?" as I gaze into the distance to find another happy couple on the beach. A woman missing the front of her head, burying half of a black man in the beach soil, and the tide flows in without the consent of the moon.

BRIAN HODGE

Nesting Instincts

Brian Hodge is the author of eight novels ranging from horror to crime-noir, most recently Wild Horses *and its forthcoming successor* Mad Dogs. *He's also written around eighty short stories and novellas, many of which have been forced at gunpoint into three highly acclaimed collections,* The Convulsion Factory, Falling Idols, *and* Lies & Ugliness. *He lives in the shadow of the Colorado Front Range, where he also periodically shuts himself away with an ever-growing studio of keyboards, samplers, didgeridoos, and other assorted noise-inducing gear, for an alter-ego recording project dubbed Axis Mundi.*

"Nesting Instincts" is one of the most unusual tales in this anthology. While it is definitely a tale of horror, it is also something quite different, which is why it qualifies as one of the most notably intriguing stories of the year. It was first published in Hodge's collection Lies & Ugliness.

—E. D.

Call it another day he won't remember by the time the next one gets here, nothing much to commend it even if there's nothing much to condemn it, either. The whole idea of average is really starting to weigh on him, a kind of giant beige trash bin that the majority of everything gets swept into sooner or later. Average is the standard that special is judged against, which means that most of what anyone does in a day ends up being pretty pointless. It's like the acres of wallpaper surrounding the framed photo or painting that's actually all you're really interested in looking at.

Micah points this out to Charisse four blocks from his house—maybe not the best time to get into heavy conversation, especially not at the speeds she likes to drive, but it sort of slips out anyway.

"You're probably right," she says, sounding neither pleased nor displeased about it. "But that's just the way it is and it's not like anybody gets any say in the matter, do they?"

Really, he's not trying to put a damper on the afternoon, only figure a few things out. It's not like he has actual parents who can be relied upon to pitch in on that endeavor, even though if he did he would be probably be expected to pretend he wouldn't really welcome their input. There's Lydia, of course, but even if she were to agree that this was part of her domestic job description, and most likely she would, by all indications she's still working on figuring things out for herself. And right now he would prefer to think that's just a fluke instead of the norm.

"You know what we need?" Micah says. "We need a good terminal illness. Or a near-death experience. That always seems to straighten people out. They come out of it and everything's so clear from then on."

"Except when they don't come out of it at all." She's laughing now, and when Charisse laughs, he can't help but join in. Yeah, as if riding with her isn't enough of a near-death experience in itself at least once a day. "You're sick," she tells him then.

"I guess. But not in a good way."

Another intersection and half a block later, she cuts over to the curb in front of his house. Ranch-style, with two-and-a-half trees in front. Could they have possibly made it any more average? Some days he'll rotate through a series of imaginary dwellings as long as he's somewhere else and not being confronted with the real thing. One day it's a palace to look forward to coming home to, the next day a grass shack on a Tahitian beach, the day after that a New York subway station where he'll go deep underground to rejoin the rest of the mole people. And then, on other days, as much as he hates to admit it, average isn't really all that bad, because at least it's predictable, it's *there*, it'll *always* be there.

"I could come in. Want me to come in?" Charisse says. "I've got a little time before I have to go to work."

It hurts to shake his head no. Physically hurts. "Evan's home." Not that he can see past the closed garage doors but the main door is standing open on the other side of the screen door, and it's sure not Lydia, not this early.

"I'll have to meet him someday, won't I, if he and Lydia stay together?"

What she really means to say, even if she doesn't realize it, is *if you and I stay together*. That's the scary thing she actually means.

"Just not today, though, okay? It really should be when Lydia's around too. It'd be too weird with Evan on his own."

"Want to hear my theory? The only reason you keep stalling is because there's no way he can live up to what you keep saying he's like."

She's fearless in her way, Charisse is. As if somebody or something stepped down from the sky and with a voice so deep it left no room for doubt told her that nothing could ever go wrong for her. That everyone she would ever meet would like her, that her hair would forever twine effortlessly down around her face in perky loose curls, that she would always score ninety or above on every test, that traffic lights would stay yellow a little longer just for her. Imagine being able to go through life with that kind of assurance.

Although it's not that Evan is *like* anything, exactly. More that Micah would rather have him figured out first before Charisse gets to take a crack at him, probably diagnose his every neurosis from a psych class she's taken that same afternoon.

They kiss, then he grabs his bookbag by the straps and hoists it into his lap and levers the door handle.

"You're beautiful," she tells him. It's what she usually says instead of *I love you*. At first it used to bother him, figuring that it was her easy way out, her escape clause, her subtle declaration of noncommitment—that in her view, he could still go on being beautiful whether she was around to love him or not. *I'm off to go live with another guy in a grass shack on the beach in Tahiti . . . and don't forget, you're beautiful.* Lately, though, it seems like there's more wrapped up in it than he first gave it credit for, since he's never once heard her say this to anyone else. Maybe what she's telling him is that she could never love anything she found ugly, or leave anything she found ugly's opposite.

Then he's out of the car and she's off, roaring down the street as he stares after her a moment, her arm out the window as she waves while veering around the corner. Charisse. For some of the guys at school, it's already obvious what they are, the first thing they wrap their drooling senses around. Leg-men, some of them. Ass-men, others. Breast-men. *Charisse*—Micah tastes the word for the millionth time and has to wonder if he isn't some sort of freak, a name-man. Sight unseen, he would've walked a thousand miles to meet someone named Charisse.

Up by the house, he notices a few spiny dark shapes buzzing lazily under the eaves. He stops a moment at the door to watch them, a few more crawling over an alien gray wad stuck into the angle between the wall and the roof: wasps, and their nest. Why did they always have to build someplace like this, just a few feet from the door, where you couldn't ignore them? Never in a spot where nobody went, like the side of the house facing the neighbors, so everyone could go about their lives peacefully, whether they walked or buzzed. No, it had to be someplace that was sure to doom them.

Now he'll have to go buy one of those spray cans that fires a solid chemical stream at them, soaking them with poison. The whole tiny civilization of them, nuked because they've got no sense of compromise. It's the kind of task you'd think that Evan could handle, might even feel was his *duty* to handle, but no. Evan doesn't do bugs. Just like Evan doesn't do rugs. As long as the sun's up, Evan doesn't appear to do a whole lot of anything that's useful.

Micah is conscientious about banging the screen door good and loud when he walks in, make sure that Evan hears him. The worst thing he can think of is coming home some day and finding Evan playing with himself. He'd rather be a wasp in the nest on the day of its annihilation than endure such a trauma. Really, you'd have to leave home after an ordeal like that, and if there's one thing Micah's sure about, it's that he's fresh out of other homes.

He's not sure if guys Evan's age still do that, but it's safer to assume that the possibility exists. The guy's forty or forty-one, around there, so on the one hand, ha ha, why should they as long as they have their own women, like Evan has Lydia. But then, on the other, it's not like Micah can imagine just waking up one day and tossing out the magazines after realizing that, what do you know, he's had enough of it, guess he won't be going back to pump *that* particular well ever again.

After ditching his bookbag in the kitchen and grabbing a bottle of guava juice from the fridge, he wanders back into the family room, although it's always seemed that it should have a reserve name for houses where "family room" doesn't quite fit. All he's had to do is follow the music back here, Evan listening to the stereo like he does during so much of his down-time. Jazz, always jazz. If the man wanted to kill him, all he'd have to do would be kick back with some rap or metal when Micah comes home, and that would do it. Boom—instant coronary.

No chance, though, because it's like Evan has to steep himself in jazz, the way a teabag steeps in hot water, before he can head to the uptown club where he plays most nights. Where the paper-tearing fits into this routine, Micah can't begin to guess, Evan just sitting on the edge of the easy chair and tearing paper—junk mail, catalogs, older newspapers, pretty much whatever he gets his hands on.

"How was school?" he asks.

"Ample," Micah says, just to say something different for a change. Every day he says okay, he has *got* to start being less predictable.

Except Evan doesn't appear to have even noticed this break in routine, intent only on tearing paper. He's not making confetti, either. There's a deliberate method to it, and quality control—nothing but straight strips, torn slowly to maximize each ripping noise. Only then are they released, to flutter to the floor and join the pile. It's a new twist in the entity that is Evan, something he took up two or three weeks ago, like he woke up one afternoon and decided from then on he was going to be a human paper shredder.

Micah doesn't know how he can stand it, listening to that steady tearing sound, it's enough to drive you bugshit—but then, wouldn't you have to be a little whacked in the head to make such a habit of this to begin with? As far as Micah knows, Lydia has no idea her boyfriend does it.

Maybe it's some kind of mystical exercise for finger dexterity known only to jazz musicians. Until Evan, Micah had never met anyone whose entire bodily focal point seemed to be his hands. The rest of Evan, from his lanky legs to his narrow shoulders to his severely clipped hair and small round glasses, is only there to provide a context for his hands. Even if you don't shake, have your attention called to them that way, you're still going to end up staring at his hands—larger than you would think judging by the rest of him, but not in a thick, clumsy way. What swans are to ducks, Evan's hands are to everyone else's.

If there are leg-men and ass-men, surely there must be hand-women, and maybe Lydia's one of them.

"There's something I've wondered about, but never got around to asking," Evan looks up and says. "Do you mind?" He seems to pause, waiting for Micah to say no, leave the room, puncture his own eardrums, something. "Before I moved in, did Lydia give you a chance to vote on it?"

"Not that I remember, exactly." How much time were they talking about here? Five or six months, it would be. It's hot and sticky out now, and when Evan had moved in the day was cold and damp. "More like all she did was tell me it was gonna happen, and that's all there was to say about it." After a few moments, he feels compelled to add, "Not that she was mean about it or anything."

That brings a sort-of grin out of Evan, even though he directs it at the latest careful strip he's tearing. "No . . . mean is the one thing that's impossible to picture her being. You have to have a good heart if you take in strays the way she has."

Can't argue with that, then he knows the question is on its way even before it hits the air, Evan wanting to know, okay, if Lydia *had* given him the chance to say no, just leave that guy at the jazz club where she found him, what would've been the verdict? As if there can be an honest answer to a question like this—*Sure,* I told *Lydia, in fact bring home two or three why don't you, maybe they can all tear paper together in a disassembly line*—when Micah knows he's under this roof by her good graces every bit as much as Evan is.

In truth, the relationship they've had here has been one of benign tolerance. Having Evan move in was like the arrival of a charmless dog. You don't want to pet him, and he doesn't show any tendency to bite, so the two of you wind up leaving each other alone most of the time.

He's blissing on the music now, and with most normal people that's a good thing, but there's something about the way Evan does it that gives you reason to worry—three parts appreciation to one part smoldering resentment that comes to the surface at all the wrong times. A flurry of trumpet notes terminates in a single tone held for an inhumanly long time, and the way Evan seems to ride it, it's so obvious he wishes he'd been around to play in some earlier, smokier, more intoxicated and dangerous era instead of now, when all he's doing is going to the club every night and furnishing wallpaper that you can barely hear above the clink of martini glasses. Micah's overheard him complain about it to Lydia.

Evan nods toward the stereo. "Sometimes you hear Miles play and you know he realizes that even though he and the audience may have been in the same room, they weren't anywhere near being in the same place. You can really understand why sometimes he used to turn his back on the audience and play like that." Evan scowls and tears another strip. "You don't have that luxury with a piano."

"Maybe you should take up the accordian instead."

To look at him, you'd think Evan didn't realize it was a joke; worse, that he actually thought about it for a moment, then decided no only because it sounded like too much effort.

"And what you should do is quit school," Evan tells him. "Quit school and have some real adventure in your life before it's too late."

"And pay for it how?"

"That's where the adventure part comes in, I suppose."

Sure. Easy for Evan to say, as easy as it is for Micah to dream about roaming free, just him and Charisse, except dreaming is *all* he can manage to do about it. And if he's too dumb to know the difference, well then, how convenient for Evan, who gets Lydia and her place all to himself.

He's smooth when he wants to be, you have to give him that.

"Anyway," Micah says, more to spite him than anything, make Evan look at the prospect of sharing the same shower soap for years to come, "who says it's not too late already?"

He leaves the room to Evan and Miles and the abuse of processed wood pulp, taking his bookbag into his room to let it acclimate awhile before he can even begin to consider learning anything else for one day. Once there he realizes he's left his guava juice behind, where he set it down on a tabletop for a few moments.

Micah backtracks, but decides to leave the bottle of sweet nectar right where it is as soon as he sets foot in the doorway to the family room, without Evan noticing him, Evan thinking he's by himself as he feeds a strip of paper into his mouth and chews. Then another. And another.

It's always strange to him to consider how he's lived with Lydia for more years than he ever got to spend with his own mother, and not once during that time has he called her anything other than her name. Probably she's earned something more by now, but it's just like that deal with "family room," nobody's come up with a better alternative.

"Do you miss her?" she used to ask him long ago, about his mother, and it wasn't that Lydia didn't already know the answer, it was just her way of getting the conversation going when she sensed it was something that had to be gone through. Stroking the hair back from his forehead and listening for as long as it took, or waiting with him through the silence when he had no voice for it.

Do you miss her?

A fierce nod against Lydia's newly damp shoulder.

Do you miss her?

Uh huh . . . but it doesn't hurt as bad as it used to.

Until the day:

Do you miss her?

Sure . . . I just don't remember her much anymore.

What a surprise hearing that come from his own lips. Like he'd gone into a room looking for a big bag of agony that he was certain he'd left in its usual place, only it wasn't there anymore. Hunt around, but it wasn't in the corner, either, or under the bed, or in the closet; it was like the most he could turn up were a few photos, already starting to look faded and washed-out. Put together the captions from the photos and maybe you could whip up a little biography: She married Dad and they had a son who for some unfathomable reason they named Micah and she made great spaghetti and meatballs and used to yell a lot around once a month and one day she tripped over a bucket of soapy water and fell down a flight of stairs and she lived in the hospital for a couple of days after but never regained consciousness, just gave in to the skull fracture. A terrible story, really, but it was hers.

Do you miss her?

I suppose . . . but why'd she have to be so clumsy in the first place?

After Lydia had drawn it all out of him, over time, it was as though she knew precisely when to quit asking. She'd never once asked him to call her Mom, even seemed to discourage it when after a year or two, when he was just eight or nine, he was showing signs that maybe he could transfer the title over and no harm would be done. But not a good idea, apparently.

The best explanation he could ever come up with was that being needed was title enough for her.

"I need you to do me a favor," she asks that weekend. "If you're out today I want you to pick up something to spray at those wasps by the front door and take care of them."

"Oh—okay," he tells her, like it's the first he's ever heard of them instead of having expected this for days. Dreading it: becoming a mass murderer. Anthills demolished when he was a kid don't count. Now he's old enough to be tried as an adult. "Do you want them to suffer?"

Lydia pretends to consider it, then shakes her head. "As quickly and humanely as possible, please."

Hey, let's go drown whole families in neurotoxins. It'll be very humane.

"And *please* don't think you'll take a shortcut and get after them with charcoal starter instead." She starts to laugh. "I remember, your dad had a client once, a new listing, and that's how the man thought he'd get rid of a nest before we started showing the place. He burned out the whole side of it two days before the open house. And then . . . ! Then he had the nerve to suggest we could just knock forty thousand off the asking price and everything would be fine."

He laughs with her. Lydia tells a story well, very animated. But it's the only way she ever brings up his dad anymore: as a stepping stone to something else.

It's never hard for him to recognize what his father must have seen in her a decade ago. Since she's not really his mother, it's not like the territory is that creepy. She's blond like a fading sun, her face softly square, and even though she's put on a few extra pounds over the last few years, it doesn't detract. She worked in the same real estate agency as Dad, and right after his wife died, sure, everywhere he turned there was a gush of sympathy, but like a watering hole in a drought, that's got to dry up eventually. Except for Lydia. The way Micah has always imagined it, Lydia's was the last shoulder left for him to lean on. It took him more than four years to decide he didn't want to lean there after all, although he could leave his kid behind as a consolation prize.

"Evan tells me you two had a pretty good conversation the other day," she says then.

He tries to remember one remarkable or even above-average detail about it and can't come up with a single thing. Maybe that's what passes for good conversation with guys who sit around tearing paper and eating it like potato chips, but Micah supposes he's got higher standards. Lying back on a blanket spread on thick grass, sharing a contraband bottle of wine with Charisse as they stare up at the stars and talk about what their lives are going to be like, and life on other planets—now *that's* a conversation.

"I guess we did," he lies. Because it at least makes Lydia happy.

"I'm so glad. I hope you're starting to warm up to him." She says it with such earnest hope that it breaks his heart. "It's important that my two guys get along."

"Do you love him?" Jesus. Did he really say that out loud? "Or, I'm sorry, is that too personal a question?"

It isn't, by the look of her, but she sidesteps it anyway, like she's gotten good at dodging questions from years of showing people empty houses and hearing them ask if the basement leaks.

"He needs somebody in his life," she says. "Evan's had a hard life."

Lydia *has* to know what he's thinking, hearing her say that.

"And *you've* had a hard life, I *know* that. Same as I've had a hard life. One way or another, we've all had hard lives, okay?"

He nods. As long as they're at it, the lives of those stupid wasps out there are about to get a whole lot harder, too.

"Hard, horrible lives and it's a miracle we all haven't hanged ourselves by now." She starts to grin, to let him know she's only kidding, even though he caught on to her years ago, the way she gets a kick out of exaggerating in weird moments. Then she turns serious. "It's what life is. Life's hard, Micah. I hate to be so blunt about it, but that's the plain truth of it. And the only way we can keep it from turning us hard along with it is to give of ourselves."

He's already given back both parents—that wasn't enough? Maybe not, since he never even got a receipt.

"Give 'til it hurts. *Especially* 'til it hurts," she says, sounding like she has plenty of experience at this. "That's when it does the most good."

He has no doubt that she knows what she's talking about. But is this system of hers even relevant when life hasn't made you hard, hasn't even come close—you only wish it had?

And even though she hasn't answered his question in so many words, she's answered it in other ways: No, she doesn't love Evan. Just the empty spaces inside him, and all his needs that take up residence to fill the empty spaces of her own.

The next afternoon Micah decides he's put it off long enough, and borrows Lydia's car and a few dollars from the grocery money to buy the lethal aerosol can from the nearest hardware store. The label looks like the stuff really means business—extra-strength formulated for hornets, wasps, and yellowjackets. But the art doesn't take it far enough to show them dead, flat on their backs with X's for eyes. Instead, they're drawn to appear as foul-tempered and vicious as alien invaders, like all it's supposed to take is one look to make you lunge for the can, realizing that these things *deserve* to die.

As he stands beside the foundation of the house, shaking the can and looking up at the target zone, he wonders what they would say if they could talk. If all their deranged waspy fury would prove to be an act and they would plead, or if they were too proud for that, just say bring it on. Or do the unexpected and send their finest diplomats, ones who could be counted on not to sting first and ask questions later, to see if they couldn't work something out.

Instead, they just buzz around in the heat. Oblivious, you'd have to imagine. From inside the nest comes a lower hum, and he wonders if this might be their way of singing lullabies to the next generation.

"I know," he says. "What'd you ever do to me, right?"

He uncaps the can and raises it and, after a couple of false starts, lets them have it. Nothing personal, just following orders. It comes out in a thin liquid jet, splashing and spattering wasps, nest, and wall alike. Some of the airborne troops he catches in mid-flight and they go into death spirals, trying to keep it together but now they've got no control, banging into the house on their way to the ground. Others come scrambling out of the nest and tumble straight down, joining the earliest casualties in a litter of twitching legs and spastic wings and throbbing abdomens, while the overall buzzing builds with a heightened new intensity. He doesn't speak their language but is that even necessary to translate? Probably just choking and coughing, maybe even crying out to him, too—what's wrong with you, you monster, don't you realize there are larvae here?

Which ones are the fathers, he wonders, and would they have left early if they'd known?

"Do you miss him?" Lydia used to ask long ago, and it wasn't that she didn't already know the answer, it was just her way of getting the conversation going when she sensed it was something that had to be gone through. She would try stroking the hair back from his forehead the way she had when he was younger and she'd listened to him talk about his mother, but he was older this time, twelve, and didn't want her messing with what he'd worked so hard to achieve with the comb.

Do you miss him?

Shaking his head no as he glared at the floor.

Do you miss him?

Probably more than he misses me.

Until the day:

Do you hate him?

Hell yes, and if he was here, I'd tell him so to his face.

What a surprise hearing that come from his own lips. Nearly as big a surprise as Lydia's expression, since he'd assumed the question was some kind of contrived lead-in for her to sermonize about forgiveness, but instead she looked as though she not only understood but approved. For the first time he wondered if this sort of thing might've happened to her before, if inside her heart she carried around a gallery of photos, kept bright and vibrant by frequent polishing.

As for their captions and the story they told, he could only be sure about the ones from the last few years: She worked alongside his father and felt sorry for his loss, then for some unfathomable reason maybe even decided she loved him, and opened up her home to not just him but his son Micah and took care of them, did it for years, until the day there came more yelling than Micah had ever heard at once and the same woman's name was repeated several times, and within a few days Dad was out the door without a word to anyone, although he'd left a cashier's check on the kitchen counter for child care, or as Lydia called it, "conscience money," and eventually she started to date again, always guys who seemed sad-looking no matter how hard they tried to smile. A pathetic story, really, but it was hers.

Do you wish he was dead?

He couldn't recall ever answering that one.

Micah stoops down to the miniature killing field he's created, where the struggles are growing more feeble—a leg here, a wing there, one especially tough victim dragging itself in a slow circle. He's still got plenty left in the spray can and, feeling hugely guilty of genocide already, wonders if using more would be merciful or merely adding insult to fatal injury. Funny, how they never sell an antidote spray in case you should change your mind. Although it's hard to imagine the wasps coming out of it just laughing it off: Good one, Micah, you really had us going for a few minutes.

"There's probably a lesson there to be learned," he hears from behind him; hasn't even known that Evan is outside, much less standing a few feet away. He's always thought of musicians as noisy people, that you should be able to hear them coming from a mile away.

"Oh yeah?" It's the weekend. He shouldn't have to be learning anything. He stands up. Maybe from a higher perspective the wasps will look like they're only sleeping. "What kind of lesson?"

For a moment, Evan stands with his oversized hands in his pockets as he regards the toxified nest. "They thought they knew their place in the scheme of things. They had it all figured out, didn't they . . . knew right where they belonged. Now look where they are."

Micah doesn't say anything, just wishes he had the courage to tell Evan to go eat a magazine or something. That talk of place and belonging and being wrong . . . it sounds like a threat, a very subtle threat.

"I don't know if you ever thought about anything like this before," Evan says next, kind of bumbling about it, a completely new and unexpected direction, "but if you were ever interested in piano lessons, maybe I could get you started. I had to sell my baby grand last year, during the divorce, but I'm thinking about buying a good digital piano. Kawai makes them pretty close to the real thing. You'd be welcome to practice on it whenever you wanted."

"I don't suppose you'd know anything about guitar, instead, would you?"

"Afraid not."

"That's okay," Micah tells him, and doesn't know why he says things like what's about to pop out, things he doesn't mean, it just happens: "Anyway, nobody makes *real* music anymore. They just sample what somebody else has already done. Kinda makes you a chump if you take up something you have to practice, instead of just pushing some buttons."

Evan blinks at him from the other side of his little round glasses. This is the cleanest man he's ever seen, Micah realizes. Never a smudge or a fiber out of place. Maybe it's the hair, not even long enough to blow.

"A chump," Evan says, almost whispering.

And now, the guilt. "I just . . . meant for me, you know? I didn't mean you. They didn't have the kind of technology they do now when you were my age."

But Evan tells him it's okay, he hasn't said anything wrong, that this would hardly be the first time he's thought the word applied to himself. He starts to look as though he wishes he were someplace else, or maybe it's a hungry look, like he could really go for a nice candy wrapper about now.

Piano lessons. Of all the lame-brain ideas.

"You never had kids, did you?"

"That lived?" Evan says. "No."

Abruptly, Micah is overcome with a powerful awareness of the can he's holding, and it's a good thing that his normal-sized hands seem to be under greater control than his vocal cords, because he can't help wondering what would happen if he turned the spray on Evan, and again, if it would be an act of cruelty, or just another name for mercy.

A few days later he takes the snow shovel from the garage and uses the front of the blade to scrape the barren nest from the side of the house. It hits the ground with a rattly, papery sound, pieces of it flaking away, but most remains intact, still looking like something from another world, or at least something that doesn't belong in this one. Micah steps on it, feels its dry crunch through his sneaker, and when he takes his foot away can see the shiny broken husks of the unborn glittering in the wreckage.

He's a moron, of course. Feeling sorry for a bunch of bugs that, if the spray can's label was accurate, existed only to sting you full of welts. And so much for Lydia's system of personal development, too. If giving is supposed to prevent you from getting hardened by life, it makes sense that taking would promote it. Well, he took, all right, took on an epic scale as far as those wasps were concerned, and the act hasn't accomplished a thing. He's got plenty of pity left inside, more than ever it seems, although maybe it *is* misdirected, because probably he should be slopping some of it Evan's way.

But the guy sure doesn't make it easy.

And could be Evan doesn't really need it, either. Overall, things must be going pretty much the way Evan wants in the Lydia department. They must think he isn't hearing them in their bedroom lately, and maybe he wouldn't if not for his new habit of sneaking out his own window late nights to link up with Charisse for an hour or two, whatever they can steal away. After sneaking back in and lying in bed awake, like sleep is something for other people, most nights Micah can't help but have his nose rubbed in the fact that Evan's getting a whole lot more action than he is. Although Micah figures that potential is working in his favor, at least.

The weird part is, this whole time, he's never figured Evan for a dynamo of passion. And ever since catching him gnoshing strips of paper, Micah's wondered if Evan might not actually prefer paper women, if maybe to him the act of eating a centerfold would be better than the idea of having sex with the actual model.

Turns out Evan must know his business behind a closed bedroom door after all. Either that, or Lydia's just uncommonly good at faking it, but does it make sense that she'd fake it so enthusiastically every night? Not to Micah it doesn't. Because if she's not into it to the degree that she sounds like, surely not even Lydia would want to give a man *that* much encouragement. The kind of encouragement that, if they were in an apartment building instead, with thin walls, concerned neighbors would be calling the police.

Most nights it sounds like she's dying in there for a minute or two before dissolving into her strange, satisfied little whimpers.

More now than ever before, he's glad he has at least a few recollections of his real mother, enough to realize that her memory and Lydia are nothing alike. He's got that little bit of distance left intact, and maybe this, finally, is the reason Lydia has always insisted upon things staying that way, that even though she's been just like a mom for the last decade, she still wanted to hang onto the privilege of turning into a wildwoman without him totally freaking over it.

Which is only validated by Charisse when he tells her about it one night, to get her perspective on the situation.

"Good for Lydia," is all she says, like she doesn't see anything one bit weird about it.

"So you don't think it's perverted?" he has to know.

"That they're not afraid of having a good time? What's perverted about that?"

"Well," Micah says, only tossing this out for consideration, not that he's made any determinations on it yet, "their age, for one thing."

"Let me tell you a secret," she says, under the stars and with the taste of berry wine on her lips. "I wish my mother still remembered how to cut loose and enjoy herself that much. She'd be a lot more fun to live with, I think. Mostly she just seems to look at my sisters and me like we stole it away from her."

And it's comments like this that make him realize one thing above all: He will never come close to understanding the way women think. Even at the best of times, they seem to him as alien as anything that came out of that nest he nuked.

"Where does she think you stashed it?" he asks.

Charisse stares at the sky with her arms around her knees, like she really has to think about this one. "I guess we're supposed to have kept it for ourselves. Just sucked it out of her and held onto it. Like it was our birthright or something."

More bug imagery—he can't help it. Maybe it's the sticky almost-summer air and the expectation of what it'll soon be bringing. He pictures Charisse and her four sisters, most known only through photographs, as mosquitos surrounding their mother and bleeding her of any ability to get it on with abandon. No matter which way she turns, she can't escape the sharp hollow probes they jam into her for another extraction of *joi de vivre*. Her exhausted cry of heartbreak and defeat: How am I supposed to live like this, love like this, you ungrateful little whores? A word he can't even imagine the woman saying . . . which may be part of the problem.

"So, all that pent-up energy, it's, like, inside *you* now," Micah says, clarifying, with so much hope it could power a city.

"Don't let it give you ideas. That's not what I was driving at."

Again. Shot down in flames so many times he could qualify for frequent flier miles. His craving, his absolute need, to be inside her churns away like a turbine.

"You're beautiful," she tells him then, cheerfully, as if that's supposed to be enough to quench every urgent yearning.

Maybe it's even good for Lydia, he decides eventually—that much attention, that much desire, that much satisfaction.

These noisy nocturnal bouts between her and Evan have been going on for three or so weeks by the time Micah concludes that it's not just his imagination: She really is losing weight. And not just those extra pounds she put on starting the year after his dad left them. At first that's all it was, as if she were flipping through the pages of the last few calendars in reverse, restoring herself into the person that he remembers first taking him in. But soon it goes beyond this, and he's never known her to be so thin, Lydia throwing an ever-narrower shadow, until she's as gangly as any of Charisse's friends that he's hardly ever seen eat more than two bites. Except Lydia still has that soft little pad of jowl beneath her chin.

"Are you feeling okay?" he asks her one day. Has to. It's what sons do, even if he's no one's son anymore. What, he's supposed to ignore it when she seems to have a bit of trouble walking?

"Never better!" she says, very chirpy about it.

She tries to reassure him with that same confident smile she must use whenever house-hunters say we'll take it, where do we sign. Except he finds it impossible to believe her. Secrets between them, at last. Secrets and lies. It's what mothers do, even if they didn't give birth: lie so the kids won't worry. Where did they ever get the idea this worked, anyway?

Until now, he and Lydia have always been so open, because they can afford it, not one single chromosome in common. What could finally be so awful that she won't tell him? It's Evan-related, obviously. He's brought home some appalling disease, the way musicians are prone to doing. Or maybe she's gone into the club one night to listen to him play and seen some other woman drape herself over him, a stick figure with nipples, and has decided she's got to compete.

No fair, Micah thinks. Lydia's turning him into a detective right here in his own home, and her timing sucks. What kind of thing is that to force on him now, with the school year winding to a close and final exams to worry about?

In this role as detective, it's not like he can get anyone to answer questions; he's forced to rely on observation. Which only creates more questions, and he sort of wishes that he never noticed the way Lydia wears nothing but long sleeves now, no matter how hot the days are getting. It's been weeks since he's seen her elbows.

Likewise her knees. She wears only slacks now. She was never that prone to wearing shorts, being sensitive about a couple patches of spidery blue veins on her thighs, but used to be, it wasn't like she'd *never* wear them. Some days, comfort got the better of pride. Except it's not only shorts he knows she won't be wearing again anytime soon. Even her skirts and dresses seem to have become obsolete.

One evening his watchful vigilance pays off when Lydia gets careless. He sees her reach for the day's mail, or what's left of it after Evan gets through with the junk, except her sleeve isn't buttoned. It rides up past her wrist and he sees the lower inches of a gauze bandage wrapped around her forearm, and the edge of a yellowish stain that's seeped up from below. Sees it for two seconds maybe, hardly enough time to know for sure that his eyes aren't playing tricks, then her arm is close to her dwindling body again. He pretends not to have noticed anything as Lydia's other hand scurries to secure her sleeve and she pretends she's not eyeing him to see if she got away with it.

They've become junkies, he imagines. Suburban junkies. Evan's found a connection and is trying in his own demented way to bring back the great dangerous age of jazz that he was cheated out of by being born too late. Except they don't know how to do it right yet, and already they've made an infected mess out of her limbs by wrecking vein after vein.

So maybe that's the cause of the Lydia-sounds he hears at night. She hates the needles but loves what they bring.

No fair, Micah thinks. Lydia's turning him into a pervert right here in his own home, because now he actively listens for her—the moans, the cries, the whimpers, the sighs. He's becoming something that his friends used to razz him about, back when all these guys started showing a freedom to admire Lydia that they wouldn't have if she'd really been his mother. Telling him how they wished they were in his position, because since she'd only raised him for the last few years, she would probably be the one to fuck him the first time, too.

So Micah listens for her sounds and excuses it by reimagining them as the soundtrack to his own life. Same sounds, different source, and he's the one who inspires them. It's a unique form of ventriloquism, throwing these anguished and delicious cries across town so they're emerging from Charisse instead.

Except . . .

If all that about them being junkies is really true, how come Evan hasn't started to diminish?

Micah's been turning that one over and over in his mind awhile, watching the creeping dawn brighten his window after a night without sleep. It's Saturday, though, so maybe he can do some catching up. Saturday morning—garbage day for their part of town, he remembers after hearing the grind of the truck and the clang and thud of emptying cans coming from the end of the block.

A whole week's worth of their trash is sitting out beside the alley behind the house, waiting to be hauled away and made anonymous. If he's going to get to the bottom of any mysteries, there may not be a better time.

Micah grabs a pair of jeans, wrestles them up to his self-tenderized groin and fastens them on the run while, behind their closed and inviolable door, Lydia and Evan soundlessly guard their secrets. He doesn't waste time with shoes and barely makes a sound himself as he rushes through the house and out the back door. He crosses the dew-slick back lawn with wet whisking footslaps.

The truck and crew are four houses away, which doesn't leave much time if he has to do any real digging to find anything. In the sticky-cool dawn, with a scab of pebbles and dirt forming on the soles of his feet, he stands over the pair of big round green plastic cans and waves away the flies that find them so appealing. Not both cans so much as just one.

At first it seems reasonable that it's only kitchen scraps they're after, but two seconds' thought and this theory doesn't hold up. They eat a lot of carry-in in this household. How are you going to have kitchen scraps when hardly anyone ever cooks?

He clutches the handle of the lid and yanks it from the can.

More flies—they flurry upward into a dense cloud. Their buzzing is so thick it has legs of its own, so loud it nearly drowns out the rumble and hydraulic crush of the approaching truck. He swats at them with the lid like it's a shield, feels the hailstone pop of their hard little bodies against the plastic and his stomach does slow rolls at the thought of something so many, so mindless, so greedy.

When he's cleared away the worst of them, Micah thrusts his free hand down into the can, not knowing the first thing about what he's looking for. If it's used-up needles, then he figures he's doing a really stupid thing because he'll be sure to get one through the palm.

The stink hits him only after he remembers he should be breathing. He's smelled worse—it's not quite like something spoiled, or fast-food dumpsters on a hot day. It's a stink with some mystery to it, a pliable odor that hasn't yet tipped into full rot, but still has a richness of suppuration and decay. It's like no smell he's ever encountered rising out of a garbage can.

He finds the source in a big white plastic bag forced into the can and subjected to a halfass job of trying to conceal it, with a few other bits of trash scattered on top. It's filled as tight as a sausage with soiled bandages, just like the one he saw bound around Lydia's arm, except here there are wads and wads of them—so many that he might as well have ripped open a trash bag behind a hospital.

He scatters the more benign rubbish back over them, like more than anything it's still important to maintain household secrets, and slams the lid back into place.

He needn't have bothered. By now the truck has pulled up to carry it all away.

The ground trembles underfoot and until this moment he never thought he could be so glad to smell diesel exhaust.

"That ready to go?" asks one of the garbage men. Barely six in the morning and already he looks like he's made of grime. He points at the can and its halo of flies. "Or are you looking for something you lost?"

Micah doesn't know how to even begin to answer that.

In hindsight, it seems inevitable that she would stop going to work. That one morning he would get up and the bedroom door at the end of the hall would still be closed. That there would be no coffee smell wafting from the kitchen, no Lydia rushing around with her day planner and trying to remember where she last laid her cell phone. That Charisse would drop him off after school and Lydia's car would appear not to have moved an inch.

Maybe she took a sick day, is all. If anybody's entitled, Lydia is, judging by what he found in the garbage. And then a second sick day after that?—well, okay fine, but he can't keep from wondering if she shouldn't actually be in the hospital, instead of just replicating the trash from one.

And shouldn't he *see* her?

"Maybe she's depressed," Charisse tries. "It happened to my mom once, a few years ago. She shut herself up in her room and drew the blinds and we hardly saw her for three weeks."

They're on lunch break, except it turns out that the last thing he's interested in is that greasy burger in his hand. Just like there are two days of school left and the last thing he wants is more time to spend at home.

"But you did see her *some*, right?" he asks.

"Sure. But we had to force our way into the room."

That's the difference between them. He could never do that. Another side-effect of not being related to the woman. Since he's not bone of her bone and flesh of her flesh, he doesn't have the full Bill of Rights. He can stand out in the hallway and look at the door like any pet thwarted by the knob.

"The only thing is," he says, "she doesn't *sound* depressed."

"Then she's probably pretending it's not even happening. My mom, if you mention that time to her now, she just looks at you like 'What are you talking about?' " Charisse makes a big flourish with her hands, introducing something that isn't there. "Ladies and gentlemen . . . our role models!" She laughs, and it's the first time Micah can remember her laughter sounding like he's not supposed to join in. Like maybe this time she's worried she might not be able to overcome every bad example set for her. "What does Evan say?"

"Evan doesn't say anything." Micah stares at the liquefying shake in his hand. He's been downing them since before time began but this one suddenly seems unnatural and nauseating. They can't call these things milkshakes because no milk ever gets anywhere near them. He's heard they're made of aerated chemical foam. "When he's not in there with her, Evan just smiles and plays his new piano."

Like now he's got everything he wanted, Micah thinks but doesn't say out loud, because it too would be an admission of failure, since to get it Evan at least had to know what that was.

It's the third day and he's decided enough's enough. He's going to get some answers. Which is only fitting, since he can't shake the nagging suspicion that he's given a lot of wrong ones during this past week of test questions.

Today's the right day for it, too, since this is one of those rare afternoons when Evan's car is gone. He's run down to the jazz club, maybe, to pick up his paycheck while it's still banking hours.

Weird, how long a hallway can feel when you're not that eager to get to the other end. If Charisse had known he was going to do this, she could've wished him good luck, told him he could handle it, that he was beautiful.

He knocks on the closed bedroom door. Lightly, in case she's sleeping.

"Lydia?" he calls. "Can I come in for a minute and talk to you?"

"Micah?" she calls back. Like who else would it be? "No . . . no, I'd really rather you didn't. Not right now."

He listens carefully, trying to hear if there's a rustle of sheets, or any other movement of a depressed, sluggish body, and decides there isn't. Just this strange distant quality to her voice, as if it were coming through an extra door or two.

"Well . . . when, then?"

"I don't know, Micah. Whenever I'm feeling better, I guess."

She's starting to sound irritated and defensive, then softens when he tells her all he wants to do is talk the way they used to when it was just the two of them, when they used to need each other to make it through some of those earliest days. *That* gets her; he's speaking Lydia's native language now. She knows exactly the days he means: both of them hating the same man and for a long time too chicken to come right out and admit it.

"We can talk this way," she says. "Nothing has to change."

"But I can't even *see* you."

She makes a noise that sounds a little like her most carefree laugh. "You don't know what I look like by now?"

Taking great care to do it silently, Micah grips the knob and gives it a slow twist. It turns only millimeters before it stops. Locked. He leans against the door frame, stalling for time while he schemes. Telling her that today was the last day of school for the year—did she know that?

"You're kidding." She sounds legitimately surprised. "It seems like only a week or two ago it was spring break."

Yeah, he thinks, losing all track of time is always what happens when you start to lose yourself in the wrong guy. He has to wonder if for Lydia there even exists such a thing as the right one.

"So you're on summer vacation now?" she says. "What are you going to do?"

"I figured I'd just get a crappy job somewhere."

"No . . . no, that's a bad idea. Maybe you should take off and travel . . . did you ever think of that?" she says from faraway, from what sounds like a small cave. "You should have some adventure in your life. . . ."

There's something about hearing her echo Evan now, in very nearly his exact words, that makes Micah want to be sick. She tells him how wonderful traveling would be for him, how it would broaden his horizons, except all he can hear is what she's *really* saying: that he no longer belongs here and maybe never has.

A thing like that and she can't even say it to his face?

He looks at the doorknob. How good a lock can it be, anyway? Locks inside the house are only meant for the people you live with, so you can't accidentally walk in on them while they're in the process of deciding to hate you. It's not like they're meant to keep out thieves. Once the thieves are inside the house—and some even come in by invitation—it's too late.

He slides the wallet from his pocket and slips out his student I.D. It's as stout as a credit card, and with another year survived, useless. Except maybe as a break-in tool. He wiggles it between the door and the frame, working it into the latch until it gives with a soft pop, and so much for home security. He can't think of one thing he learned in school this year that was half this useful.

Even though it's not nearly as strong here, the same smell is in the bedroom that he remembers all too well from the garbage can. Except there's something about it now that's cleaner, purer, less diseased and more a fact of biology.

The last thing he was expecting to find was no Lydia. Not only is she not on the bed, the bed doesn't even look slept in, doesn't look like anyone's so much as reclined on it. It's made up as neat as a barracks bunk.

The curtains and blinds are pulled halfway shut, making a pleasant light actually, enough for him to walk in and see how worthless his and Charisse's theories have been. There's no junkie paraphernalia. None of the stuff that would accumulate where someone depressed was holing up, whatever that would be—food and magazines and sleeping pills and liquor bottles, he imagines. And for sure there's no swirling vortex into which someone could just disappear.

He checks beneath the bed—nothing but luggage and boxes of old pictures.

The only other alternative is the closet, although that seems way peculiar, since it's not big enough, deep enough, to be a walk-in. It's just two sliding doors on rollers in a track, like in a motel, only not as cheap-looking. He pushes one door aside, right to left, and lets in the light.

When he looks downward, Micah backs away with a start and probably a loud cry, then has to stare for a few moments simply to process the presence of what he's seeing. How about those eyes—they can really play tricks on you sometimes, can't they? At first he can't believe it has the remotest connection with Lydia. It's a science project. It's an industrial accident. It's something one of them has brought home from an anatomy lab, then form-fitted into the corner of the closet.

He remembers from school that the skin is the body's largest organ, and yeah, he supposes it would take something like that to have created what he's seeing—this fleshy hollow, its opening nearly as big around as a barrel. Its inner walls are surprisingly thick, pink as muscles. The edges of the structure cling to the floor and the closet wall like they've been fastened with some sort of natural adhesive.

The worst part about this? Those two wide, familiar eyes staring out at him from the shadows at the very back of the inside of . . . it? her? They seem to reflect their own unique brand of shame and guilt, like the time a few years ago when she loaned money to a boyfriend who then split town in his new car, no forwarding address.

He can't fathom how such a thing can begin to be possible, no more than he can figure out what sustains her. It looks so painful and raw, what she's been made into; if her cries at night were any indication, it *had* been. But Lydia had to have wanted this, because it couldn't have happened all at once. Micah imagines that Evan must've used his teeth. And lots of patience, along with architectural skills learned from . . . where? Strange gray things clinging to the outside of the house?

Every impulse is telling him to run, that what he's seeing is overload and if he stares at it any longer something terrible will happen, over and above his insides feeling as chewed up and reprocessed as Lydia's body.

Because what else is this but the ultimate proof of how much it must actually take to keep someone loving you?

But when he does run, he doesn't get far, running smack into Evan out in the hallway. Immediately Evan knows what's up—can't put anything past Evan—and for a guy who's always seemed so passive, he can look awfully enraged. Before Micah has even recovered from the collision, Evan's grabbed him by the shoulders with those oversized hands and hurled him into the wall. He's bounced all the way to the floor before he hears Lydia's oddly reverberant voice crying out, "Don't hurt him, don't hurt him," except Micah doesn't know which of them she's calling to.

He lies face-down while feeling Evan's legs swing over him, hearing the footsteps proceed into the bedroom. There's a murmur of voices, maybe the sound of someone crying, and the sound of someone getting undressed.

Micah debates it for a few moments, but it's no debate of intellect, more like warring instincts, and finally one side wins and he squirms forward along the floor and gets as far as his shoulders through the bedroom doorway. Just enough to see what's going on over at the closet, where Evan is pulling the last of himself into the cell that they've made of her.

And could it really only have been minutes ago that he was thinking about Lydia after so many wrong men, doubting if for her there could be such a thing as the right one?

Listening to them, to the sounds they make together, he knows he shouldn't have been so quick to judge.

Now, at least, this time, the fit is perfect.

CONRAD WILLIAMS

The Machine

Born in 1969, Conrad Williams is the author of Head Injuries *and* Nearly People *(nominated for an International Horror Guild Award and a British Fantasy Award) as well as around eighty short stories. His most recent work has appeared in* The Museum of Horrors, Dark Terrors 6, Cemetery Dance, Phantoms of Venice, Best New Horror 13, Best New Erotica 2, Crimewave 6, *and* The Third Alternative. *Next up is a story in Maxim Jakubowski's anthology,* The Mammoth Book of Future Cops, *and a new novella,* The Scalding Rooms.

"The Machine" was written as part of a deal between the author and his wife, the writer Rhonda Carrier. One of the first dates they went on was a trip to Dungeness, which is arguably one of the weirdest coastlines in the world. While walking among the fish-heads and rusting hulks of hardware, they challenged each other to write something based in the area. While Rhonda finished her story, "Twice," in double-quick time, Conrad found himself blocked at barely two and a half pages into the story. "It took another six months for me to get going on it again," he says. "But I don't panic when these things happen. Sometimes you need that distance for the ideas to come together properly in your head, so even when you're not thinking about it, not writing, in fact you are, all the time, at some unknowable level."

"The Machine" was first published in the British magazine The Third Alternative, *Issue 31.*

—E. D.

When he asked her, she said: "A car, wasn't it? Or was it a bus?" There was a little smear of mayonnaise on her mouth and her hair was scrunched like dead spiders' legs at the back, where she had not been able to see it to comb in the mirror. Graham had parked the car by a pub. The Britannia, that overlooked the flat, greasy edge of sea. Inside he had bought them halves of bitter. The barmaid seemed preoccupied, unable to look them in the eye when he ordered. The only other couple were sitting at a table inspecting a camera.

"Don't you remember resting your hand on mine? On the gear lever?"

Julia looked at him as if he had asked her to perform an indecent act. Maybe, in asking her to remember, he had. He watched her as she moved her glass on the table, spreading rings of moisture across the cracked varnish. He could smell beef and onion crisps, smoke from the little train that traveled between Hythe and Dungeness, and an underlying tang; the faint whiff of seawater.

"Can you—" he began, but stopped himself. Her answers didn't matter anymore. He didn't know how long they should stay here. He didn't know how long it would take.

Three months ago, he didn't need to mash her food for her or accompany her up and down the stairs. She wouldn't slur his name or regard him with a lazy eye. "Where are we?" she said, one Sunday morning as he re-entered the bedroom with a tray of tea and toast. "I don't know where we are."

He sipped his beer. It tasted sour, as if what had filled it previously had not been properly purged from the glass. The symptoms of brain cancer—or *glioblastoma multiforme* as the specialist revealed to them (with an unwelcome flourish, as if he were introducing an unusual item on a menu)—are headaches and lethargy, seizures, weakness and motor dysfunction, behavior changes and unorthodox thought processes. This form of cancer, the specialist said, was particularly aggressive. If it were a dog, it would be a *toza inu*.

"I don't want the rost of is," she said, pushing her drink to one side. "In bastes faddy."

He rubbed her knuckles, white and papery, and tried to smile. "It's okay," he said. "Come on."

Outside they headed towards the sea, compelled by an unspoken mutual need. She was not to know that he had been here before, many years ago. She just wanted to see the ocean one more time before her sight deteriorated. He allowed her to lean on him and they went slowly over the uneven shingle; it didn't matter. Time had lost its meaning. Time was nothing anymore other than now and the next thing. "Next week" was as alien to his vocabulary as a phrase of Russian.

The tide was a long way out, visible only as a seam of pale grey that stitched the lead of the sky to the dun of the beach. Fishing boats trapped on the shingle faced the sea, their bows raised as if impatient to return. Explosions of static from their communication radios made her start. She moved into the collapsed light as though immersing herself. The air was thick here. It seemed to coat the beach. Her footsteps in the shingle beat at the friable crust of his mind and in the shape of her progress, the delicacy of her step, he saw how near the end was.

The sea was affecting the light in some subtle way that he had not recognized before. It erased an area above the horizon, a band of vague ochre that she would stare at during the moments when she stopped to rest, as if it might contain words, or the barest outline of them, some code to unpick. An explanation. Around them, the beach slowly buried its secrets. Great knots of steel cable, an anchor that had lost its shape through the accretion of oxidant, cogs so large they might well drive the Earth's movement. All of it was slowly sinking into the endless shingle.

Us too, he thought, blithely. *If we don't keep moving.*

"He isn't here," she said, panic creeping into her voice.

"He'll come," he insisted. "He'll come. He always does."

"You saib he would be fere."

She wasn't going to be pacified. He was tiring, and sat back against one of the drifts of shingle, watched her move away from him, a gently wailing wraith in black clothes that were now too big for her. He lost her for a moment, against the distant flutter of black flags on the boats, and when she reemerged, it was to drop, exhausted, to the stones. He hoped she would be able to sleep, at least for a little while.

A wind was rising, drawing white flecks to the crest of the waves. It was getting rough out there. Small fishing boats tipped and waggled on the surf, bright and tiny against the huge expanses of cobalt pressing in all around them. Behind him, urgent bursts of white noise from the radios wrapped voices that nobody received. The deserted boats looked too blasted by salt and wind to be up to the task of setting sail for dab, pout and whiting.

An elderly couple picked their way through the shingle, hunting for sponges perhaps, or other similarly useless booty. All he remembered seeing on these beaches were rotting fish-heads and surgical gloves, thin, mateless affairs flapping in the stones like milky, viscous sea creatures that had been marooned by the quick tides. The couple reached Julia, then passed her by, giving her a wide berth.

He hauled himself out of the shingle, noticing how the flinty chips had crept over the toes of his shoes; always the beach was in the process of sucking under, of burying. He tried to understand the motivation for building on something so unsubstantial: the sheds and houses dotting the beach were grim little affairs, colorless, uninviting, utilitarian in the extreme.

He caught up with Julia; she looked withdrawn to the point of translucence. Her skin was a taut, grey thing that shone where her bones emerged. Salt formed white brackets around her mouth. The shingle had shifted across her boots, completely concealing her feet. He gently drew her upright and picked the strands of hair away from her eyes. Her scalp gleamed palely through a scant matting that had once been thick, black and silky. When she opened her eyes though, everything else became superfluous. He felt scorched by her gaze, as he had for the past twenty years. Even with her flesh failing so quickly, she could not be anything other than beautiful if she had strength enough to open her eyes and look around her.

"Are you hungry?"

She shook her head. "Where is he?"

He smiled. "You've always been impatient, haven't you? I told you he doesn't come till dark. We've got an hour yet. At least."

"I want to walk," she said, looking around her as if assessing the landscape for the first time.

"You sure you aren't too tired?" he said. "Okay. Come on."

They trudged up the beach, the strange, stunted vegetation like hunks of dried sponge or stained blotting paper trapped between the stones: sea campion, kale, Babington's orache. Angling towards the row of weatherboard cottages that lined the Dungeness Road he looked back to the great hulk of the gas-cooled reactors of the power station. Maybe they were causing the sizzle in the air, or perhaps it was the taut lines of the fishermen, buzzing with tension as lugworm and razor clam were cast far beyond the creaming tides. He told Julia that special grilles had been constructed over the cold water intake pipes for the reactors because seals kept being drawn into them. She nodded and shook her head. One eye was squeezed shut, her lank hair swung about her lowered face. A vein in her temples reminded him of mold in strong blue cheese. The color of decay. Nature consuming itself. He reached for her hand but she snatched it away as if burned.

They toured the strange, attractive garden at Prospect Cottage where he took a picture of her standing by a circular pattern of stones that were adorned with pieces of colored glass and a single, brilliant white crab's claw. A rusting, battered trumpet had been nailed to the back door but it was so deteriorated, he couldn't tell if it was the right way up. Though the day was overcast, it had a dry, scorched smell and the air was unpleasantly metallic in his mouth, as if he had pressed a spoon against his fillings.

The previous time he had been here—the only other time—had been with his school on a field trip as part of his geography course. The teacher who accompanied them, Mr. Wilson, spoke with what Fudgey, his best mate, had said was an "X-rated lisp." His sibilants weren't so much softened as slurred. He always sounded drunk and though the boys had suspected he might be, they never smelled any booze on him; only the musty depth of the tweed that he wore or stale pipe smoke. Mint imperials.

"It's because he's missing a few teeth on his top set," one of the more liberal teachers explained, when Fudgey had been overhead mimicking him. "You should see him trying to eat a banana. I have to leave the staff room."

Mr. Wilson was more interested in birdspotting than the shape and behavior of the land. At lunch one day, he had taken some of the more interested boys with him—squeezed into his beige Rover—to the reservation and passed around binoculars that smelled of the clothes he wore. He pointed out gargancy and greenshank and Balearic shearwater. On the way back, he allowed the boys half an hour on the beach while he went to post some letters and make a phone call. "You can take off your ties but leave your blazers on. This isn't a holiday. You are still representing your school."

"*You are shhhhtill represhhhhenting your shhhhhchool,*" Fudgey intoned, spot on. "Represhhenting my arshhe, more like."

They kicked about in the shingle and threw stones at the half-submerged gears and cogs and bolts. They agreed that this is what the world would be like after America and the Soviets swapped H-bombs. Merce found a fish-head and forced it on to the end of a stick then chased Bebbo around—"Snog it! Snog it Bebbo! Snog the fish, you fishy-faced pisspant!"—until he was crying. Fudgey and Graham broke away from the other three boys and headed towards the water. A naturally formed ledge gave way to a steep slope of shingle. At the edge, they could see what had been concealed from them until two or three feet away from where the land sank towards the water.

The woman was on her knees, her jacket and blouse discarded. Her bra was lost for a moment against the shocking white of her flesh. She was weeping, trying to cut into the skin of her forearms with a piece of shingle. To her right, his back to her desperation, a man in a panama hat was sitting cross-legged in a deck chair, smoking a cigarette as he watched the horizon. All the boys could see of him was a fat, neatly barbered nape bulging over a collar; the merest edge of brow.

"Lovely view," Fudgey said, a little queasily. "Let's get back to the car."

"Wait," Graham said, but he couldn't explain what it was he wanted them to wait for. After a while, Fudgey's insistent tugging at his elbow broke through his fascination and he allowed himself to be led away.

The following day, the final day of their week in Dungeness, Mr. Wilson gave them another period of free time. Fudgey wanted to play football, but Graham declined, explaining that he had a headache and just wanted to go for a walk on his own, to clear his mind. He made his way back to the spot on the beach where they had seen the woman. The deck chair was still there. Where she had been kneeling, he found a smooth, glistening curve of steel buried in the shingle. He dug at it a little, moving away the stones from each side until he had unearthed a disc as large as a train's wheel. What looked like caterpillar tracks, clean and freshly oiled, snaked around the wheel and deep into the ground. As hard as he pulled, Graham couldn't budge it. He saw too, once he rocked back on to his heels, breathing hard with the exertion, how some of the stones were spattered with black spots of blood.

He stopped at a hot dog stall on his way back to the Bed and Breakfast and ordered a Coke and a packet of ready salted crisps. It was only as he was handing over the money to the woman that he recognized her.

"Hello," he said, and his voice cracked on the second syllable like a recording on perished tape. The woman regarded him as if he were a retard; rightly so, he realized. Hellos were gambits, usually, not something you said when you were about to be on your way.

"Sorry," he explained. "I saw you on the beach yesterday. You were—"

"I *know* what I was doing," she hissed, her eyes flicking away from his to scan their immediate surroundings. She came down the few steps at the rear of the van and grabbed him by the collar. Her cuff slid away from her wrist a little as she dragged him inside and he saw a pinkish bandage pinned tightly around her forearm. She closed the door and bolted it, unclasped the latch that kept the serving hatch opened. It was very hot inside, and heavy with the smells of enthusiastically recycled cooking oil and raw onions. Graham fed crisps into his mouth, trying hard not to appear frightened.

"Would you like some Coke?" he asked, offering her the unopened tin. She slapped it from his hands. He stopped eating and neatly closed the bag with a few twists.

"I'm sorry," she said, her voice gusting from her collapsed mouth like heat from an oven. She tousled his hair and sat on her stool, pinching the bridge of her nose between her fingers. "He said that I would have an answer before nightfall tonight. The wheels had been greased, he said. He said that the technology, though old, was of a perfection you would not find anywhere else. Ancient technology. He told me that it wasn't certain if it had been made by man or not."

She snorted, a sudden, bitter sound that was devoid of any laughter she might have meant for it. "Anyway, I don't care about that. As long as it brings him back to me." She stared intently at Graham. "My husband," she said, spicily, as if it were obvious. "A sweet, sweet man. He would help anybody. Stupid, lovely man."

Her left hand had moved to her forearm and worried at the bandage. The pinkness at its core deepened. Graham stared at the bolt on the door. He retrieved his can of Coke and pulled the ring opener. Beige froth fizzed out over his hand. The woman didn't pay him any attention. It was as if the memory of what had happened to her husband numbed her to extraneous sensation.

"There was a car on a dual carriageway. The A12 going north, towards Ipswich. A nasty bitch of a night. Wind. Rain. So hard it was coming at you side on. The car hit the central reservation and went out of control. End over end job. Came to a stop in the middle of the road. Eddie, my husband, and me, we were about a hundred yards behind. He pulled over and put his hazard lights on, ran over to help. I sat there because we were on our way to a party and I didn't want to get my hair wet. I'd just had it done, especially.

"Seconds later he was hit by a Ford Mondeo doing ninety miles an hour. Do you know . . . the force of the impact knocked him out of his shoes. Lace-ups. And they pinched him a little, those shoes. He was always going on about them, how he ought to get another pair."

Graham rubbed the back of his hand across his mouth. The saltiness of the crisps had made his lips sore. "What happened on the beach?" he asked.

The woman closed her eyes and then clenched them even tighter, as if the darkness behind them was not deep enough. "You don't need to know anything. I'm sorry you saw it. I didn't mean to upset you."

"Who was that man?"

By degrees she relaxed. Her eyes reopening, she reached behind her to unbolt the door. "You can go," she said, and her voice was soft and likeable now.

"Was he your boyfriend?" Graham asked.

The trace of a smile. She shook her head and then she frowned. "Yes," she said. "I suppose he was, after a fashion."

"I don't remember how I got back to the Bed and Breakfast."

"Sorry?"

They were sitting on a bench watching the colors in the sky warp as the sun ground itself out against the black mass of the power station. Julia's skin was stippled from the cold; what color it had enjoyed now thinned to that of cooked chicken, but she refused Graham's jacket when he offered it to her.

"I was just remembering," he said, turning his face away from hers, "the first time I came here. With the school."

"Where was I?"

"I didn't know you then. We didn't meet for another fifteen years."

"Were you seeing someone else?"

Graham watched the edge of the sun slip behind the reactors. Parts of the sky were green. The sunsets here were always spectacular.

"No, Jules. I was only fourteen."

She giggled. "You were neber fourteej."

The last three of the day-trippers that had come to Dungeness for a dose of stinging surreality got into their Ford Focus and backed out of the pub car park. They all turned to look out of their windows as they trundled past the bench, their faces partially eclipsed by the oily flash of weak streetlamps on the glass.

"How are you feeling?" he asked.

"It could be workse," she said. "I mean, God, I could have a brain tuzor."

He drew Julia gently upright and kissed the top of her head. Sometimes, when she slept, he would nuzzle her hair, enjoying the clean, warm smell of her scalp. He endured a second or two of real panic when he thought of her gone, her and her unique smell, and it seemed more unspeakable, for a moment, that he might not be able to recall her scent rather than the way she spoke or talked or touched him.

"We should go now," he said. "He might be here."

The strange buzzing noise persisted, though it was not so much in his ears anymore as deep within him, like the thrum one feels in the chest at a rock concert. It was as if the vibrations were rising from the stones themselves and, if he trained his view on the trembling shoreline, they appeared to writhe in the gloaming, pretending to be the leading edge of a tide long retreated.

He makes things perfect she had said, all those years ago. He had come across her one more time, on the morning of their departure. She was sitting in a bus shelter and the gin was coming off her in sharp waves, like the poisonous veils of a deep sea fish repelling unwanted attention.

Well, not so much him as the beach he tends, and what lies beneath it. Even before him, before there was that stretch of Kent, before the stones and the sea, even, there was something that moved and rotated and ticked off the seconds, and all the while it was rusting and seizing up. Like an old person. Exactly like an old person.

Her eyes, when she looked up at him, were clownishly large, filmed with tears.

But it won't die. My husband came back to me last night. The tears in his body, they were all gone, like he had zipped them up, as easy as that. He's . . . he's perfect. But I'm scared of what perfection means.

He had gone back to the bus, his mind burning with her words. How, as a child, she had watched two girls playing in the surf. And one had been sucked out by a surge of water. And the other girl had been crying and somehow, minutes later, managed to grasp hold of her limp, outstretched arm and pull her from the water. They had lain together on the stones, one of them heaving and wailing, the other as still as the beached fishing boats that gathered shadows beneath their cracked, peeling bows.

She had stared at them for an age, while everything surrounding the girls, everything beyond her focus, seethed and blurred and warped. And she had blinked and the girls had risen and walked away up the beach, their hands linked, laughing, laughing, with wet hair and the white impressions of the stones on their legs and arms. She found a highly polished lever, brassy with oil, sticking out of the stones where they had lain. When she tried to move it, she felt a deep ratcheting under her toes and the lever sank out of sight.

There was a deckchair on the beach now, the alternating white stripes of its ballooned fabric like ghostly ribs floating above the ground. Graham smelled cigarette smoke and thought he could see a pulsing coal hovering a little way to the right of the chair.

"I'm tired, Gray," Julia said. He removed his jacket and pressed her back into the pebbles, cushioning her head, which looked tiny and white and punched in with too many dark holes and shadows. There was a moon low in the sky, like an albino's eyelash. What light there was came from the stars, or the ineffectual blocks of orange in the pub windows. A great arm of rusted steel reached out of the stones further up the beach, the hinges where its elbow might had long been gritted up with salt and time. Perhaps it was a crane, or a digger, a model of which he had enthusiastically played with as a boy. He had seen other heavy plant around the beach at Dungeness, silent, slowly being subsumed by the stones, like mammoths caught in tar. Nothing moved here, but change was constant.

Graham approached the figure. "Do you look after the beach?" he asked. The man looked no different, despite the intervening years. When he turned around, Graham could not meet his eyes. The mouth wore a sweet smile and he inclined his head towards the chair. Graham went to sit down, but saw that the man intended for him to take what was lying there. He picked the stone up and moved away. Behind him, the creak of the deck chair and the rasp of a match.

"Here?" he called. "Is here okay?" There was no reply. The sound of the sea was almost lost to distance now. There was the barest whisper, but that might well have been his own breath, hurrying on his lips as he bared his arm to a beach that suddenly seemed to whiten, as if the moisture on the pebbles had evaporated in an instant.

The stone in his fingers felt warm and familiar. It had been honed, and he pressed the edge against his skin. Beneath him ran a tremor, from the north end of the beach to the south. The pebbles chuckled as they realigned themselves. When the blood came, Graham looked up at the night sky and waited. Despite the wheeling areas of nothing at his shoulders, he had never felt so smothered. After a little while he was able to return his attention to the wound. Blood tigered his arm. It had drizzled the patch of stones by his foot. From somewhere, what looked like spark plugs and the teeth of a partially concealed cog had emerged. They gleamed in the subtle light, shop fresh, it seemed, oiled, primed for use. Infinitesimally, the cog turned. He heard Julia shift in the stones, a couple of meters away but he could not see any detail in the black shape she made.

He thought of the woman, and her failed attempts to perfect her husband. Unlike the girl she had witnessed on the beach, he was too far removed from what it was to be human. All that had happened was that his injuries had been bettered, had reached a sublime point that could not be bested by the crude materials that had served him previously.

Perfection, he could see now, never had to mean something good.

The man in the deckchair had gone. The pebbles shifted again. Graham's feet were buried in them. He felt something mesh with the leather of his shoes. A metallic taste filled his mouth. A chain had wound itself around his hand and was binding the muscles of his arm. Blood coursed along the links, oil-black in the night. Where was the difference here? He was soft and it was hard, but they were both machines, in the end. Machines needed other people in order to work properly. An hour, two hours later, his body hardened by fatigue and the attentions of the machine, Graham, by degrees, felt himself being released.

He remembered how he had thought the machinery was slowly being buried. How he had attributed its sounds to other things. He had been wrong in so many other aspects of his life that to be mistaken now was hardly unexpected. He trudged over to the shockingly small shape of his wife. He held her close to him, feeling her bones through the twill of his jacket. When he heard Julia's breath leave her body, the tired echo of the surf collapsing on the stones, that too came as no surprise. He watched the sky at the horizon slowly flood with color. The sun would rise before long but he didn't need it to be able to see the shining grid of machinery pumping and gyrating across the beach. For a little while it seemed rejuvenated, super-real like an image manipulated by computers. He watched until spent, it grew still. The stones shifted and soon there were just the occasional glimpses of gears and pistons, as it was when he had arrived many years ago.

Like Julia, the beach was striving for perfection. Unlike her, it had yet to attain it. She was real to him and yes, even beautiful in the dawn. The smell of her was deep in him, *of* him. He would not forget. A part of her, at least, was perfect now.

TOM DISCH

Hansel, A Retrospective, or, The Danger of Childhood Obesity

Tom Disch is best known to speculative fiction readers as the author of groundbreaking SF novels such as Camp Concentration, 334, *and* On Wings of Song*—yet he has also published numerous works of children's fiction, criticism, and poetry. His most recent publications are* A Child's Garden of Grammar *and* Burn This and Other Essays on Criticism. *The following poem, making clever use of the Hansel and Gretel fairy tale, comes from the Fall 2002 edition of* The Antioch Review, *published in Ohio.*

—*T. W.*

When this tale is chronicled,
  Some centuries from now,
I doubt the teller will think to tell
  Just exactly how
Long it took for a boy my age
  To pork up to the point
A hungry witch might consider him
  A reasonable joint.

The gingerbread that trimmed her house,
  The shingles of her roof,
Were all consumed, by me, to yield
  A *daube* of decent *boeuf*.
Hunger is precipitous,
  But art is long, and she
Wished for more than a boney loin
  From a promising lad like me.

She fed me grits and polished her spits
  And studied Julia Child.
One must respect such circumspect
  Behavior in the wild.
And I, in my cage, fared well as I could
  For someone so overfed,
And never once did I think I would
  Soon be better off dead.

My sister visited from time to time
  To discuss our situation.
Gretel believed it was a crime
  To be fed to satiation,
While I, as selfishly, repined
  Only at my captivity,
For still I comfortably dined
  On marzipan and Brie.

The day would come, as come it did,
  When reality intruded:
The witch behaved as Gretel bid,
  And kindly Fate colluded.
Now I, though not exactly thin,
  Enjoy the witch's wealth,
While still possessing sister, skin,
  And the boon of perfect health.

MELISSA HARDY

Aquerò

Melissa Hardy is quietly becoming one of the best writers of short fiction working today, equally at ease with modern realist fiction, historical fiction, magical realism, and pure fantasy (such as her Cornish fairy story "The Bockles," reprinted in last year's edition of The Year's Best Fantasy and Horror*). Her short stories have been published in a wide variety of magazines; her books include* A Cry of Bees, Constant Fire, *and (most recently)* The Uncharted Heart. *Hardy lives in London, Ontario.*

"Aquerò" is a beautifully penned, engrossing tale that falls somewhere between historical fantasy and magical realism. It comes from the December issue of The Atlantic Monthly.

—T. W.

Testimony of Mother Marie-Thérèse Vauzou
February 2, 1899

Mother Marie-Thérèse Vauzou, once the mistress of novices at the Convent of Saint-Gildard but now her order's superior general, judiciously lowered her bulk into the very armchair in which her former charge, Bernadette Soubirous, had died so many years before. The elderly nun was not padded so much as plated with fat, like a stately rhinoceros. The angle of the chair was intended to promote reclining. Nevertheless, the Benedictine brother charged with taking the superior general's testimony understood that Mother Vauzou was determined to sit erect, which feat, after some adjustment and repositioning, she managed to accomplish. Now, perched on the edge of the chair, one liver-spotted hand folded over the other in her lap, she might have appeared quite composed were it not for a tic that made her right cheek jump every few seconds.

"So, if I'm to understand you correctly, Brother, they are talking of canonizing the little Soubirous?" Mother Vauzou spat out the question like a bad taste.

"They are," the Benedictine conceded.

She turned to look at him; her large face, wreathed in a wimple of starched white linen, hovered like a full moon over the blackness of her habit. She had wide-open eyes the color of smoked glass and an enormous beaked nose; her expression was disdainful. "A mistake, if you ask me!" the old nun hissed.

First Identification of the Body
September 22, 1909

Thirty years after the interment of the body of Bernadette Soubirous, to whom the Mother of God had appeared eighteen times in the Grotto of Massabielle, just outside the Pyrenean town of Lourdes, the Bishop of Nevers, Monsignor Gauthey, dispatched a messenger with a request that a Dr. David and a Dr. Jourdan attend at an exhumation to take place at the Convent of Saint-Gildard the following week.

"At long last, the work of the episcopal commission charged with investigating the merits of Bernadette Soubirous's case has been completed and the saintly virtues of the Little Shepherdess thoroughly confirmed," Monsignor Gauthey wrote. "Our next step must be to identify the body and to determine the extent to which it has remained intact. It is incumbent upon my office to do this in accordance with both civil and canon law, in order to do which successfully, I require your assistance."

Accordingly, the two physicians and Monsignor Gauthey met at eight-thirty on the morning of the appointed day at the Chapel of Saint-Joseph in the Convent of Saint-Gildard, where the body of Bernadette Soubirous had been laid to rest. They were joined by five others: Abbé Perreau; Mother Superior Marie-Josephine Forestier and her deputy, Sister Alexandrine; and the mayor and deputy mayor of Nevers. Also in attendance were two stonemasons and two carpenters, who were to see to the practical matters at hand.

Acting on the bishop's instructions, the two stonemasons lifted the massive stone from the vault and, with some difficulty, managed to half pry and half wrestle the wooden coffin out of it.

"Not exactly light as a feather, was she?" one mason muttered to his colleague in mid-negotiation.

"A lead coffin is inside the wooden one," the second mason snapped back. "Standard procedure in these cases. Why do you think I brought the 'can opener'?" Then, to the carpenters, "You there! How about some help carrying this thing!"

The four men staggered under the coffin's weight into the room adjacent to the chapel, where the examination was to take place. They set it down carefully on two trestles and proceeded first to unscrew the lid and then to shear open the lead coffin within. As the masons bent over this task and the metal cutters bit into the lead, everyone stiffened in expectation of a terrible stench: the nuns discreetly applied handkerchiefs to their nostrils and turned slightly away, while the gentlemen concentrated their expressions in such a way that their lips were pursed shut and their nostrils reduced to mere slits.

Then Dr. David spoke. "I say, Jourdan!" he exclaimed. "There's not a trace of an odor!"

The nuns removed the handkerchiefs from their noses and sniffed the air hesitantly. "It's true!" the mother superior said. "How very extraordinary!"

By now the masons had managed to peel back the metal lid. Everyone took two tentative steps nearer to the coffin and peered in.

"Only look, Monsignor!" the deputy mayor said to the bishop. "The body is perfectly preserved! Apart from seeming . . . rather wan."

"Only to be expected under the circumstances," the mayor commented to the mother superior.

Sister Alexandrine inhaled deeply. "I smell something!" she announced. "I smell . . . lilies!"

"You smell no such thing, Alexandrine!" Mother Forestier chastised her. "You're overexcited."

As for the carpenters and stonemasons, they only stared at the body of the beautiful Bernadette, gulping, their eyes wide with astonishment. Then one of the masons crossed himself and his three colleagues quickly followed suit.

Testimony of Mother Marie-Thérèse Vauzou
February 2, 1899

"I am here on the instructions of the episcopal commission, Mother Vauzou," the Benedictine informed the superior general, as dry as toast. "Naturally they are interested in your opinion, although, as you will surely have heard, we have learned of cures. Miraculous ones, and well documented. The commission cannot afford to ignore such apparent manifestations of Our Lady's grace. Surely you understand."

Mother Vauzou snorted. " 'Manifestations of Our Lady's grace,' " she muttered. "For the record, I should just like to state my great sadness that of all the good works I have done in my long life, of all my triumphs and achievements, the only thing anyone wishes to discuss with me is that wretched peasant girl. Proceed, sir."

He consulted his list of questions. "When did you first meet Bernadette Soubirous?" he asked.

"Sister *Marie-Bernard*, as I knew her, came to me some eight years after the last apparition," Mother Vauzou replied. "She was twenty-two years old. The reason for whisking her away to Nevers, so far from her native Bigorre, was not bruited about, for fear of scandal. The nuns in whose charge she had been placed feared for her virtue."

"Why was that?" the Benedictine asked.

"She was demonstrating signs of female weakness," the superior general replied stiffly. "Imagine, if you can, the distress of the poor sister who discovered Marie-Bernard trying to widen her skirt to create the effect of a crinoline underneath. And that is not all! Later she was surprised in the act of introducing pieces of wood into her corset in an attempt to stiffen it further! Such acts were considered by the sisters in whose charge she was placed to be nothing less than diabolical."

"I see!" the Benedictine said.

"Marie-Bernard was terribly vain," Mother Vauzou continued. "She once told a fellow novice that she had joined the Sisters of Charity and Christian Instruction because she preferred our headpiece to that of the Sisters of the Cross, which she compared to a funnel, and our habit to that of the Sisters of Saint Vincent de Paul, which she described as dowdy! Of course, I must concede both her points. But there was more."

"Yes?" the Benedictine said encouragingly.

"An infatuated medical student from Nantes had written the Bishop of Tarbes asking for her hand in marriage," Mother Vauzou exclaimed. " 'If I am not permitted to marry her,' the distraught youth wrote, 'I think I will quit this world.' And perhaps he was compelled to do so, for it was inconceivable that anyone—however humble and, for want of a more precise word, simple—to whom the Holy Virgin was believed to have appeared should be permitted to breed."

"Naturally!" the Benedictine agreed.

Second Identification of the Body
April 3, 1919

On August 13, 1913, thirty-four years after the death of the Little Shepherdess, Pope Pius X, by virtue of signing the Decree of Venerability, authorized the process by which Bernadette Soubirous might attain beatification and, ultimately, should her virtues be proved authentic, recognition as a saint of the Holy Roman Catholic Church. Unfortunately, the Great War interfered with the progress of Bernadette's case; but on April 3, 1919, the Seer of Lourdes's body was exhumed for the second time. This time the examination was conducted by Drs. Talon and Comte before witnesses who included Monsignor Gauthey's successor, Monsignor Chatelus; Mother Forestier; and her deputy, Sister Alexandrine. Also in attendance were the commissioner of police, representatives of the municipalities, and members of the Church tribunal.

Following the examination, the two men of science retired to write up their reports. They were dispatched to separate rooms to ensure that they could not consult each other as to this detail or that, and thus that one man's observations would not taint or in any way color the other's.

Later, after Bernadette's body had been placed in a new coffin and reburied in the Chapel of Saint-Joseph, the bishop met with the two doctors in Mother Forestier's parlor and reviewed their reports over tea.

"Remarkably, I find that your reports coincide perfectly, not only with each other but also with those of Dr. Jourdan and Dr. David, made at the first exhumation, on September 22, 1909," Monsignor Chatelus told the two physicians. "Except in those several small particulars you mention, of course. Sister Alexandrine, if I could trouble you for another one of those delightful *langues-de-chat?*"

"But of course, Monsignor!"

"Indeed!" Dr. Comte replied. "The only changes I could observe in the lady's condition were those patches of mildew on the body and quite a notable layer of salt . . ."

"*Calcium* salts, I think," Dr. Talon clarified.

"Probably the result of the body's having been washed the first time it was exhumed," his colleague speculated. "Precisely why I suggested dispensing with a second such bath, Mother Forestier."

"But of course, dear Dr. Comte," the mother superior murmured, a trifle embarrassed. "We were perhaps a little overzealous on the last occasion."

"So exciting!" Sister Alexandrine agreed. "To find our wondrous sister so uncorrupted, I mean. May I freshen your tea, Doctor?"

"Please," Dr. Talon replied.

"As for the skeleton, it is remarkably complete," Dr. Comte declared. "If it had not been, we could not possibly have conveyed the body to the examining table. Without its falling apart, I mean."

"And, not to be indelicate on this, but we detected no smell of putrefaction," Dr. Talon said. He glanced around the room. "No one present experienced any discomfort, I presume?" All shook their heads vigorously.

"Indeed," Sister Alexandrine trilled, "I would have to say that the exercise has been an entirely pleasant one. Who would like a petit four? Sister Casimir makes them, and they are so very good!"

Testimony of Mother Marie-Thérèse Vauzou
February 2, 1899

"Her family was perfectly dreadful," Mother Vauzou told the Benedictine. "They lived like pigs in a sty, all six of them crowded together into one tiny room."

"The father, I understand, was a bit of a ne'er-do-well," the Benedictine said. "Arrested twice. Once for stealing two bags of flour, and the second time for removing a plank of wood from the street. They were very poor. Did you know that Bernadette's little brother Jean-Marie was once caught eating the wax that had dripped from the candles in their parish church?"

"Their own fault, if you ask me!" Mother Vauzou said gruffly. "No fortitude. No self-control. No discipline. Oh, I suppose they were well-meaning enough, but inept! Do you know what Marie-Bernard was *doing* when she first saw Our Lady? She was looking for bones to sell to the local ragpicker!"

" 'Blessed are the poor . . . ,' " the Benedictine began, but the nun cut him short.

"Don't start in on that!" she said.

Third Identification of the Body
April 18, 1925

On November 18, 1923, His Holiness declared Bernadette's virtues to be authentic. Her beatification was imminent.

"We may not yet refer to our famous sister as the *Blessed* Marie-Bernard," the mother superior informed her charges, "but we soon shall."

She immediately set about making arrangements for the third identification of the body, as required by canon law. "We shall need to avail ourselves of your services once again," she wrote Dr. Talon. To Dr. Comte, who was a surgeon, she added, "We hope you will be so kind as to remove a few tiny relics . . . for Rome, Lourdes, and, of course, for ourselves here at Saint-Gildard and other houses of our order."

"I should be honored," Dr. Comte replied by letter.

Accordingly, on April 18, 1925, the bishop, the vicars general, the Church tribunal, and nuns from the community assembled in the little chapel of Saint-Joseph to witness the exhumation. Also in attendance, representing the municipal authorities, were the commissioner of police and a Monsieur Bruneton.

While the masons and carpenters were swearing an oath, "We hereby promise that we shall accomplish the task entrusted to our care to the utmost of our abilities!," Bruneton leaned over and murmured out of the corner of his mouth to the police commissioner, "Given the number of times they've exhumed her, they might have been better off to install her in a jack-in-the-box."

"*Shhh!*" the commissioner enjoined roughly. He was more devout than Bruneton, a freethinker. Besides, being newly appointed to his position, he had not been present at the previous identification, and was therefore intensely curious to see what a corpse looked like after so many years in the grave.

Testimony of Mother Marie-Thérèse Vauzou
February 2, 1899

"You have written to the commission that you object—'vigorously' is, I believe, the word you used—to this investigation," the Benedictine said. "Would you be so kind as to explain why?"

Mother Vauzou sniffed and sat up even straighter than before, throwing back her shoulders and tossing her head. "The ecclesiastical authorities prevailed upon Marie-Bernard to take the veil because they could not allow her to remain in the world," she replied. "They were afraid that she might embarrass the Church. Their fears, I must say, were well founded, given her nature and her family background. Unfortunately, because of the fame attached to her by the apparitions, once she had completed her novitiate, we had nowhere to send her where she would not have been a curiosity, a carnival sideshow, a freak. All the Sisters of Charity and Christian Instruction who served their novitiate at Saint-Gildard received assignments elsewhere; none stayed on to live at the Mother House. Only Marie-Bernard."

"But surely you cannot blame her for that, madame!" the Benedictine protested. "She was, as it were, a prisoner of her own fame."

"An undeserved fame!" Mother Vauzou cried. "Marie-Bernard Soubirous was an ordinary scullery nun, monsieur, fit for scraping carrots and scrubbing floors and little else. She was vain and stupid and stubborn and sly and common."

"Nevertheless, the Mother of God chose her—" the Benedictine began.

The nun cut him off. "Nonsense! Oh, Marie-Bernard saw something. I will admit to that. She saw *something*. Just what it was I am not prepared to say."

"But bishops believed her," the Benedictine pointed out. "The pontifical curia . . ."

"I am not denying that *others* believed her," Mother Vauzou clarified. "She took so many people in right from the start, and they could not be dissuaded. Nor can they be dissuaded now, apparently. What I am saying is that *I* didn't believe her."

Third Identification of the Body
April 18, 1925

"Now, what is it that you would like?" Dr. Comte said, turning to the Bishop of Nevers with the air of a guest at the table who has been asked to carve.

"Whatever you can manage without making too much of a mess," the bishop replied. "In these matters one can rarely afford to be too picky. A few ribs should do nicely, eh, Mother Forestier?"

"We would prefer that the Venerable's heart remain in her body," the mother superior told the surgeon. "Apart from that, anything that can be covered up by her habit would be fine." She turned to the bishop. "Did I tell you? Given the remarkable condition of the Venerable's body, we have decided to display her."

"In a glass coffin?" the bishop asked.

"A crystal-and-gilt reliquary, actually," the mother superior replied. "The Armand Caillat Cateland workshop, in Lyons, does beautiful work. We have already placed the order."

"A splendid idea!" the bishop exclaimed.

"I say, Talon, the trunk is slightly supported on the left arm," Dr. Comte pointed out. "Might be a bit tricky to go in there without doing noticeable damage."

"Right you are," his colleague replied. "We'll start with the other side, then. Scalpel, Sister Clémence, please!"

Testimony of Mother Marie-Thérèse Vauzou
February 2, 1899

"It seems to me, Mother Vauzou . . . if you don't mind my saying so . . . that you are displaying a prideful nature in insisting that you are right about Sister Marie-Bernard whereas so many eminent ecclesiastics—men better equipped than you to judge these matters, I might add—are wrong." This old harridan with the twitching cheek was beginning to try the Benedictine's patience. "Not to mention the thousands of devout Catholics who champion her cause!"

"Eminent ecclesiastics! Devout Catholics!" Mother Vauzou snorted. "I suppose you're referring to those countless bishops and cardinals, not to mention wealthy ladies, who would convene in the parlor to hear Marie-Bernard's account of the apparitions and, in the course of conversation, casually drop a handkerchief in the hopes that she might pick it up and so transform it into a holy object!" She laughed. "Not that she enjoyed talking about the apparitions, mind you! 'Do I have to tell the story again?' she would complain petulantly. 'How tiresome!' Or, sulking and turning away, 'I'm sorry, Mother, but I forget.' As if anyone could forget one moment of an encounter with Our Lady! That was when I began to suspect her."

"So she did not vaunt herself on account of the apparitions?" the Benedictine said, writing this down. "Some people would relish the attention."

"Not Marie-Bernard!" Mother Vauzou shook her head. "She was a secretive little thing. You recall that the Holy Mother was supposed to have given her messages?"

"I do."

"She wouldn't tell me what they were!" Mother Vauzou was indignant. " 'You must tell me what the Queen of Heaven said,' I'd tell her.

" 'No,' she'd reply, shaking her head. 'They were secrets.'

" 'But I am the mistress of novices,' I would remind her. 'You cannot have any secrets from me!'

" '*Aquerò* said, "Tell no one!" ' She always referred to the Virgin Mother as *Aquerò*—a pronoun in her native langue d'oc, best translated as 'That one there.' I thought it very disrespectful!

" 'But what about the Pope?' I would counter. 'Would you not tell His Holiness if he asked you?'

" 'Certainly not!' she would reply. 'My secrets have nothing to do with him either.' You see how bold she was? How insolent? Why it was necessary to . . . do as I did?"

Third Identification of the Body
April 18, 1925

Carefully the surgeon made an incision in the right side of Bernadette Soubirous's thorax and detached and then removed the rear section of the fifth and sixth right ribs. He handed these to Sister Clémence, the convent's infirmarian, who promptly dropped them on the slate floor.

"Mother of God!" Sister Clémence cried out in a strangled voice.

"What?" Dr. Comte asked.

"They're warm!" she declared.

"That is impossible!" the doctor countered.

"Sister Clémence!" The mother superior took charge of the situation. "Get ahold of yourself!" Stooping, she picked up the two pieces of rib and popped them into the basin of holy water designated for that purpose. "You are overwrought," she told the infirmarian. "The holy relics are not in the least warm. Indeed, they are cold." She handed Sister Clémence a towel of white linen. "Now dry them off and place them on the silver tray."

But Sister Clémence burst into noisy tears. "I felt the dear saint's life tremble in her bones!" she sputtered. "I assure you, Mother Forestier, they were quite warm! Oh, thanks be to our Holy Mother in Heaven! Blessed Bernadette!" In the end she had to be led, gulping and hysterical, from the chapel. Poor Sister Philomène, her assistant, reluctantly took her place.

Testimony of Mother Marie-Thérèse Vauzou
February 2, 1899

"To do as you did . . . ?" the Benedictine repeated, feigning ignorance.

"Oh, don't tell me you haven't heard the rumors!" Mother Vauzou scoffed. "Read the reports! It was all over the newspapers at the time. The convent's physician told a journalist that the years of scrubbing stone floors on her hands and knees had given rise to that grotesque tumor on her right knee, which contributed to her eventual demise. He implied that I was somehow to blame . . . that I had worked Marie-Bernard too hard, given the ever fragile state of her health. Of course, the mother superior promptly dismissed him, but the harm was done."

"Let me assure you . . . ," the Benedictine began.

Mother Vauzou cut him short. "You will no doubt be surprised to hear that I concede his point. I was too hard on Marie-Bernard. I was *obviously* too hard on the wretched girl. She died, didn't she?"

"I'm sure you didn't mean . . ." The Benedictine faltered.

"*However,*" the elderly nun said, "*nonetheless*, I must remind the episcopal commission that it was my job to humble Marie-Bernard. The Mother of Our Lord was supposed to have elected to appear to her. That she would be proud of this fact would be inevitable, and pride, as you have so recently pointed out, is the devil's own snare. Then, too, I had the other nuns in my charge to think of. We could not have them venerating Marie-Bernard and so putting their own mortal souls in peril."

"Still . . ." The Benedictine consulted his notes. "She was quite ill. Asthma that became, over time, chronic, not to mention chest pains and shortness of breath. Then there was that aneurysm she had and, of course, the bone decay."

"Yes! Yes!" Mother Vauzou admitted. "No need to go on and on about it! She was a veritable bundle of infirmities! She was forever hawking up blood. Basin after basin of it. One would never have thought she had so much in her. However, I still maintain that receiving extreme unction four times in one lifetime is excessive."

Third Identification of the Body
April 18, 1925

"What have we here?" Dr. Comte said, poking around in the opening in Bernadette's thorax with his thumb.

"Let's have a look!" Dr. Talon suggested, moving alongside his colleague and bending over the body. "Offhand I would say that that would be the liver, covered by the diaphragm."

"Excellent!" Dr. Comte replied. "Let's take a sliver!" Carefully he removed a piece of the diaphragm and cut into the liver below. "*Mon Dieu!*" he exclaimed softly.

"What?" the bishop asked.

"The liver is still . . . viable!" Dr. Comte replied. "Observe!" Straightening up, he dangled a slice of the organ from his forceps. "The liver," he explained to the assembled witnesses, "is a soft organ and inclined to crumble. Normally it decomposes very rapidly, or else hardens to a chalky consistency. That it should be so well preserved in this case is . . . well, wouldn't you agree with me, Talon, that it might be called preternatural?"

"Indeed!" Dr. Talon said, nodding gravely. "Preternatural!"

"A viable liver! Our Bernadette is blessed indeed!" the bishop cried, while the nuns fluttered and made sounds like those of birds when a gentle spring rain commences.

Testimony of Mother Marie-Thérèse Vauzou
February 2, 1899

"So, in brief, you feel that Marie-Bernard did not exhibit the attributes of a saint as you understand them, and you question the authenticity of the apparitions. Is that correct?"

"That is correct," Mother Vauzou replied.

The Benedictine closed his notebook and started to rise. "Well, Mother Vauzou, this has been most enlightening . . ."

"That is not to say that she didn't have a way about her," Mother Vauzou said hastily, as if seeking to detain him.

"What do you mean?" the Benedictine asked.

"She drew people to her," Mother Vauzou explained. "She had, for lack of a better word, a sort of charisma."

"Charisma?" the Benedictine repeated.

"And, of course, she was . . . I suppose you might say fetching."

"I don't grasp your meaning," the Benedictine said.

"Attractive," the nun said. "She was very attractive."

"I have seen photographs," the Benedictine said.

"Well, they do not do her justice." The old nun's expression softened momentarily, becoming almost wistful. "Marie-Bernard had a certain otherworldly quality that became even more pronounced over time," she continued, but in a gentler tone. "Even when she came to us, a fresh-faced girl and, if the truth be told, too much like a dumpling for my taste, something about her eyes was compelling." Mother Vauzou paused, remembering. Then she glanced away and said hurriedly, "Prolonged illness greatly refined her beauty even as it rendered her poor body grotesque. By the end she was . . . quite inexplicably lovely. Transfigured, you might say."

"You did not hate her so much as you pretend," the Benedictine said, guessing.

"On the contrary!" the former mistress of novices confessed in a constricted voice. "I loved her as I have loved no other human being. I loved her, to my great shame, more than I loved the Bridegroom! She had seen God, you see—just not yours and mine!"

A single tear inched its way through the labyrinth of wrinkles that was the old nun's ruined face, while her right cheek vibrated like the plucked string of a standing bass.

The Beatification of Bernadette Soubirous
Spring 1925

Once the relics had been removed from Bernadette's thorax, everyone left the chapel with the exception of the handful of Sisters of Charity and Christian Instruction upon whom the mother superior had bestowed the signal honor of assisting in the preparation of the body of the soon to be Blessed Bernadette Soubirous. On Mother Forestier's instructions they swathed Marie-Bernard with bandages, leaving only her hands and face uncovered, and replaced her in her coffin. Then the mother superior sent Sister Clémence to fetch a Monsieur

Bourgeot to the chapel. He was from the firm of Pierre Imans, a mannequin manufacturer in Paris, and had been waiting in her parlor.

"Although you will see that Sister Marie-Bernard's body is perfectly mummified," she told him, "you can't help noting a somewhat blackish tinge to her face and hands and a rather sunken quality to her nose and eyes. As we have decided to display her to the public, we are naturally concerned that these slight imperfections might distress our visitors. That is the reason we have approached your firm."

"You have done the right thing," Monsieur Bourgeot said. "We French are not like the Italians, who insist on displaying their saints regardless of how hideous they appear. Have you ever seen Santa Chiara, madame, in Assisi? Black as an Ethiope! Very unbecoming!"

He then proceeded to make a precise imprint of the Seer's face and hands, from which to fashion a light wax mask and a set of paraffin gloves.

"I have some photographs for you as well," the mother superior said, handing the artisan a packet. "They should assist you in perfecting the likeness."

"Trust Pierre Imans, madame!" Monsieur Bourgeot said. "The Blessed Bernadette will look as beautiful in death as in life, and no one shall suspect a thing!"

The coffin was transferred to the Chapel of Saint-Helen (which was more easily sealed off not only from the curious public but also from the other nuns, whose devotion to Marie-Bernard might distract them from other obligations) and was left open until such time as the firm of Armand Caillat Cateland had finished the crystal-and-gilt reliquary. "I want these doors locked and sealed until the Pope has proclaimed our Marie-Bernard blessed," Mother Forestier instructed the sacristan.

For the next three months the body of Bernadette, tightly bound in bandages, lay alone in the shadowy chapel, listening to the prayers of nuns who knelt, whispering, beyond the padlocked doors.

Bernadette Soubirous
Spring 1925

"Are they all gone, *Aquerò*? Such a noise they make, and so much fuss! The little Forestier . . . she was just beginning her novitiate when the doctor said, 'It's the White Chapel for you, my girl!' and off to the infirmary I went for the last time. Do you remember my White Chapel, *Aquerò*? That's what I used to call my little bed in the infirmary, with its white curtains. So pretty! I must say Forestier looks rather the worse for wear. Was her chin always that long? But she was never good-looking. Not like me, *Aquerò*. Not like you.

"I can't say I was very happy when that fellow with the goatee cut me open. 'Like slicing beef jerky!' he muttered under his breath to that other monsieur, the stout one with the pince-nez. He should try being dead for forty-six years! And his breath smelled of whiskey and garlic.

"Hmm . . .

"So this is what you meant when you said I would be immortal. Put in a glass case for all to see, like the Star of India, or Snow White. And apparently I will look my best. I have to say I'm pleased about that. How angry horrid old Mother Vauzou was when I wouldn't tell her my secret. But really, now, when you think of it, how could I? You told me not to, and you are much, much more powerful than Mother Vauzou. Besides, if I had told the old terror, she would only have beaten me some more for being too proud. She was strange. Sometimes I'd catch her looking at me, just staring—with the most peculiar expression on her face, as though I were something in a store window that she wanted to buy but couldn't afford.

"I wonder if poor Raoul, who wanted so to marry me, is still alive. If he is, he must be a very old man . . . eighty-five at least. Perhaps he will come to see me from Nantes. How I would enjoy that!

"*Aquerò? Aquerò?* You are still here, aren't you? Oh, good! I am so glad. Locked away in that vault all by myself. It was dark and cold and so tedious. To tell the truth, I thought you were never coming. Not that I doubted your promise. No, not for an instant!

"Do you think you could come a little closer? I cannot move my head, you see. So many years have passed since Massabielle, and I have missed you very much.

"Ah, there you are! You are as beautiful as I remember. So much more beautiful than they imagined. I know you were disappointed with the statue at Lourdes, but the sculptor insisted on making you look like Mary, though you are so much more beautiful. But they had it in their heads, you know. 'It's the Mother of God you saw!' they'd insist. 'Why, it must be!' And they believed it. Yet I never said so, *Aquerò*. I never used her name, only that which belonged to you. I was faithful all those years, in spite of everything.

"And now they will call me blessed and venerate me, and I will have a shrine like those that my friends and I used to build for you out of stones back in Lourdes every May—only much grander, apparently. Miraculous cures will be attributed to me and people will implore me to intercede on their behalf with God. Little do they know I am your handmaiden and yours alone, *Aquerò*. Beautiful, terrible Goddess."

The Enshrinement of the Blessed Bernadette Soubirous
July 18, 1925

On June 14, 1925, Pope Pius XI signed the official edict: the Venerable Bernadette, now the Blessed Bernadette, was launched on the road to sainthood, which she would attain, finally, in 1933.

However, delays occurred at the firm of Armand Caillat Cateland; not until the first week of July did the gilt-encrusted crystal reliquary in which Marie-Bernard's body was to be displayed arrive on the train. It was then carted to the novices' hall in the Convent of Saint-Gildard, where it was lovingly unpacked and polished.

On July 18 the body of Bernadette Soubirous, clothed in a new habit and outfitted with the wax mask and gloves made for her in Paris by the firm of Pierre Imans, was borne to the Hall of Novices on a white stretcher. Following the chant for the Office of the Virgins, the body was, with great gentleness born of reverence, placed in the reliquary. On August 3 it was transferred to its permanent position in the beautiful principal chapel of the Convent of Saint-Gildard, where it is on view to this day.

JOEL LANE

The Receivers

Joel Lane is the author of a book of short stories, Earth Wire, *a book of poems,* The Edge of the Screen, *and two novels,* From Blue to Black *and* The Blue Mask. *He has edited an anthology of subterranean horror stories,* Beneath the Ground, *and he and Steve Bishop have edited an anthology of crime and suspense fiction,* Birmingham Noir. *His short stories have appeared in various anthologies and magazines.*

"The Receivers" is one of an intermittent series of supernatural crime stories he is working on, all rooted in the geography and culture of England's West Midlands. It possesses a quality of horror laced with pathos that infuses what might have been merely frightening with an ambiguity that makes this story even more effective than a simpler tale might have been.

"The Receivers" appeared in Dark Terrors 6, *edited by Stephen Jones and David Sutton.*

—E. D.

People don't talk about it now. They've forgotten, or pretended to forget, just how bad it was. New people have moved in, and new businesses have started up. "Regeneration" would be putting it a bit strongly, but most of the damage has been repaired. Or at least covered up. As for the madness—well, nothing healed it, so maybe it's still hidden. When you've seen what people are capable of, it's hard to believe that they can change.

To begin with, it was nothing out of the ordinary. The local branch of Safeway reported a sharp increase in the level of shoplifting. No one had been caught. In the same week, a Warwick-based building firm reported the theft of a truck-load of bricks. Ordinary items are the hardest to track down. Once they go missing, it's already too late.

At the time, a much more serious theft was concerning us. A former local councillor whom we'd been investigating for corruption had died of blood poisoning at Solihull Hospital—the result of a ruptured bowel, apparently. I don't think we'd ever have got enough on him for a conviction. We'd just closed the case when his body went missing, three days before the funeral. The security guard at the mortuary swore he'd not seen or heard anything. But there was clear evidence of a break-in, in the form of a missing windowpane. Not broken: missing.

I won't tell you the ex-councillor's name. It's all over Birmingham in any case, on plaques set in hotels and shopping arcades and flyovers. He'd have attended the opening of an eyelid. I don't even remember what party he belonged to. It doesn't matter these days. He'd been cozy with the building firm that had some materials nicked. That was the first hint I got of how this might all be connected up.

That October was hazy and overcast, the clouds dropping a veil of warm rain. I remember things were difficult at home. Julia had just turned eighteen, and Eileen was torn between wanting her to stay and wanting her to move in with her boyfriend. It was a kind of territorial thing. Julia was too old to stay in her room when she was at home: she needed the whole house. As usual, I tried to stay out of it, using my awkward working hours as an excuse to keep my distance. I believe in peace and harmony; I've just never been able to accept how much work they need.

It was a while before the police in Tyseley, Acocks Green and Yardley got round to comparing notes on recent theft statistics. What we were dealing with was an epidemic of shoplifting. No one much was getting caught, and the stolen goods weren't turning up anywhere. Most of it was basic household stuff anyway, hardly worth selling on. Shoes, DIY equipment, frozen food, soft-porn magazines, cheap kitchenware, bottles of beer. If there was an organization behind all this, what the fuck was it trying to prove? Of course, we had our doubts. Rumors of invisible thieves were a gift to dishonest shop staff—or even owners working a scam. It was happy hour on the black economy.

To start with, we encouraged shop owners to tighten up their security. A lot of younger security staff got sacked and replaced by trained professionals, or by hard cases from the shadows of the hotel and club scene. Suspects were more likely to end up in casualty than the police station. We put more constables on the beat to cut down on burglaries. But stuff still went missing—at night or in broad daylight, it didn't seem to matter. Cash disappeared from pub tills. A couple of empty freezers vanished from an Iceland stockroom. A junk shop lost a shelf of glassware. It made no sense.

Walking out of the Acocks Green station at night became an unsettling experience. There was hardly anyone around. The barking of guard dogs shattered any sense of peace there might have been. Dead leaves were stuck like a torn carpet to the rain-darkened pavement. The moon was never visible. Every shop window was heavily barred or shuttered. Slogans began to appear on metal screens and blank walls: HANG THE THEIVES, THIEVING GYPPOS, SEND THE THIEFS HOME. I must admit, I laughed out loud when I saw someone had painted with a brush on the wall of the station car park: WHO STOLE MY SPRAY CAN?

People were being shopped to us all the time, but we never got anywhere. Without the stolen goods, there was no evidence. Some of our informants seemed to feel that evidence was an optional extra when it came to prosecution. Being Asian, black, European, unusually poor or new to the area was enough. As the problem escalated, letters started to appear in the local evening paper accusing the police of protecting criminals, or insisting that the homes of "suspicious characters" be searched regularly. *If they have nothing to hide, they have nothing to fear.* In truth, we were questioning a lot of people. And getting a lot of search warrants. We were even catching the odd thief. But not as odd as the ones we weren't catching.

Julia really summed it up one evening, during one of our increasingly rare family meals. "It's like some children's gang," she said. "Nicking all the things they see at home. Then hiding somewhere, dressing up, smoking cigarettes. Pretending to be their own parents." She looked sad. Playfulness was slipping away from her. I wondered if she could be right. Maybe it was some whimsical game, a joke played by kids or the members of some lunatic cult. But the consequences weren't funny. People were getting hurt. Homes were getting broken up.

I remember the day, in late October, when I realized just how serious things had become. I was interviewing some people who'd been involved in a violent incident at the Aldi supermarket on the Warwick Road. A Turkish woman shopping with two young children had been attacked by several other shoppers. She'd suffered a broken hand, and her four-year-old daughter was badly bruised. No stolen goods had been found in her bag or her bloodstained clothes. She told me a young woman had started screaming "Stop thief!" at her in the toiletries section, near the back of the store. People had crowded round, staring. A man had grabbed her arm and held her while the young woman started throwing jars of hair gel at her. Someone else had knocked her down from behind. She'd woken up in hospital, and it had been a while before she'd found out that her two children were safe.

Then I talked to the young woman who'd thrown the jars. She was only nineteen, a hard-faced AG girl with china-white skin and hair tied back. She chain-smoked throughout the interview, flicking ash over the table between us. Her answers were mostly monosyllables, but a few times she interrupted me with sudden outbursts. "She wouldn't let go of her little girl. That means she was using her as a human shield." And later, "Are you a copper or a fucking social worker? Wake up and join the real world." I don't think she really heard a word I was saying.

A couple of days later, a tiny padded envelope was sent to the Acocks Green station. It was full of crushed stink bombs. The smell lingered in the building for days. Groups of neo-fascists took to patrolling the streets in combat jackets, led by dogs on steel chains. Meanwhile, the thefts continued. In desperation, all the local police stations joined forces in a massive raid on the homes of suspects. We found next to nothing. But local racists used the operation as a cover for their own little *Kristallnacht*. Asian shops were broken into and smashed up, and a few homes were set on fire. We were caught off balance, too busy hunting for stolen goods to stop the violence. I still wonder if our superiors knew what was going to happen and turned a blind eye.

November was unexpectedly cold. It never seemed to become full daylight. The frost made everything slippery or tacky, difficult to handle. Car fumes made a smoky haze above the streets. I spent the days and nights rushing from one crime scene to another, from thefts to fights to arson attacks, my hands and face numb with cold and depression. It felt like the meaning was being sucked out of everything.

Julia's boyfriend moved to Coventry to start a new job. She started moving her own stuff over there in batches, a suitcase at a time. It was strange to find things missing—pictures, books, ornaments—that I'd come to take for granted as part of the house. Maybe Elaine was letting Julia take some things that weren't strictly hers, just to avoid arguments. I felt too tired to mediate between them; all I wanted to do at home was sleep. Without Julia there, filling the house with her scent and music, I was reminded of how things had been before she was born. When Elaine and I had first set up home together. Maybe we could get some of that back.

It was maudlin retreat into the past that sent me to the allotments in Tyseley, near the street where I'd lived as a child. The allotments occupied a strip of land between an industrial estate and a local railway line that carried only freight trains. There was a patch of waste ground at one end, with some derelict railway shacks and a heap of rusting car bodies. It was overgrown with fireweed and pale, straggly grass. I'd spent a lot of time there at the age of ten or eleven, getting into fights and spying on couples. Somehow I remembered the place as having a kind of mystery about it, a promise that was never fulfilled.

It was my day off—either Monday or Tuesday, I'm not sure. Another chilly, overcast day. I'd been walking around Tyseley all afternoon, trying to make sense of things. How quickly it had all changed, once the fear had taken hold. I wasn't immune either. How easy it was to blame. How hard it was to know. In some way I couldn't understand, the police were being used. Not to find the truth, but to cover it up. There was a time, I thought, before I was caught up in this. There must be a part of me that can stand outside it. The light was draining away through the cracks in the world. By the time I reached the alley at the back of the allotments, a red-tinged moon was staring through the ragged trees.

I was so far up my own arse by then that the first time I saw the child, I thought he was one of my own memories. The light was fading anyway; his face was indistinct. He was reaching through the chain-link fence from the railway side. I remember his fingers were unusually thin and pale; they looked too long for his hands. He glanced at me without making eye contact. His eyes were large and very dark, but his skin was so white it seemed translucent. His brand-new ski jacket made him look bulkier than he probably was. Something about his posture suggested need. I wondered what he was looking for.

A flicker in the half-light distracted me. Another child, ducking behind the derelict shacks. Then a third, somewhere beyond the fence. I realized I was surrounded. But I felt more tired than scared. There was a smell in the air like ash and burned plastic; probably there'd been a bonfire nearby on the fifth. The evening light felt dry and brittle, like old cellophane. There was no color anywhere in this world. I could see a double exposure of my own hands as I moved from side to side, trying to catch one of the paper-faced children. The way they jittered and grabbed and hid reminded me of silent films. I wondered how far they'd go to become what they appeared to be.

It was getting too dark to see anything much. I stumbled to the end of the line of shacks, where three old brick garages backed onto an alley. I'd once stood here and watched an Asian kid getting beaten up by skinheads. There was a smell of mold and cat piss. No one was around. I glimpsed two of the film children in a garage doorway, pretending to be a courting couple. I lunged at them, but caught only a rusty metal screen. One of them touched my wrist with soft fingers. It took me a few seconds to realize that he'd taken my watch. My mind kept asking me what was wrong with the garages. I looked around the alley in the unreal glow of city lights reflected off the clouds. Three garages. When I'd been here as a child, there'd only been two.

I hardly said a word at home that evening. Near midnight, I came back with a torch and a spade. The children were gone. The third garage had been clumsily knocked together with bricks of different sizes, mortar slapped on to cover the gaps. It was a *faux* building, made from stolen materials. I pried the metal door loose and stepped inside. The ground was soft under my feet.

Between the uneven walls, every kind of stuff was heaped up: clothes, food, cushions, magazines, all of it beginning to molder. There was a pane of glass attached to the inside of the brick wall. Beetles stirred in the waning light of my torch. I saw bags of pet food that had been torn open by rats, flesh gleaming from the damp cases of porn videos, soft pizzas rotting in an open freezer that couldn't be plugged in here. My foot slipped on dead leaves, and I put my weight on the spade.

Have you ever dug into a cat litter tray and realised what was buried under the wafer of soil? The blade sank inches into the ground, then lifted a sticky wedge that smelled like a museum of disease. I pushed my left hand against my mouth and bit down. My torch fell and stuck, its light reflecting from pale spots in the exposed slime. Metal glittered. A face swam into view on a scrap of paper, then vanished.

I dug for a while. The ground was full of cash: crumpled fivers and tenners, verdigris-covered coins, all slippery from the layer of nearly liquid excrement they'd been buried in. I gagged and retched any number of times, but I hadn't eaten since lunchtime. Daylight seemed a long time ago. Eventually I got down far enough to reach a number of yellowish, brittle sticks wrapped in dark cloth. There was nothing left of his flesh. I did as much damage as I could with the spade, then covered up the fragments with the strange earth I'd removed from them. The contents of the garage had drained my torch; I doubted it would ever work again. I left it there with the other rubbish.

The moon's small, bloodshot face peered at me as I stood in the allotments, wiping my shoes with dead leaves. I thought about the power of damaged lives. How a corrupt politician might try to come back, feeding on money like a vampire on blood. How he could attract followers desperate for an illusion of normality. No wonder the police couldn't make a difference.

Money talks. But you wouldn't want to hear its accent.

As I walked home, the streets around me were deserted. The sodium light gave the pavement a faint tinge of gold. There were no thieves, no vigilantes, no children, no beggars. If anyone had got in my way, I'd have killed them. I needed someone to blame. We all do. But there was nothing except a smell of shit, and an icy chill in the air.

NICHOLAS ROYLE

Standard Gauge

Nicholas Royle was born in Manchester, England, in 1963. He is the author of four novels: Counterparts, Saxophone Dreams, The Matter of the Heart, *and* The Director's Cut, *and has published more than one hundred short stories. He has also edited eleven anthologies. Since becoming a full-time writer in 2001 he has been writing a sequel to* The Director's Cut, *entitled* Straight to Video, *and researching a nonfiction project about breaking into abandoned buildings.*

He says: " 'Standard Gauge' appeared in a book of photographs of female nudes by Marc Atkins. The idea behind the book, Thirteen, *was that thirteen writers would each be sent a randomly selected nude from Atkins's collection and asked to write a piece to 'illustrate' the photograph. For this story's reappearance here, you'll just have to imagine the nude. For years now, people have been talking of Shepherd's Bush, the rather scruffy neighborhood where the story is set, as the new Notting Hill, a trendy district a mile and a half up the road. Efforts are being made to tart up the Bush, but as long as the winos and madmen continue to rub shoulders with the BBC executives, and perhaps each be mistaken for the other, it'll never shed the vital contradictions that make it such an interesting place to live."*

—E. D.

There are two things you can be sure of with west London estate agents. One is that the prices will always be higher than the last time you looked. The other is that among the properties for sale or rent, there will always be at least one in Sinclair Road.

Sinclair Road runs from behind Olympia to the top of Addison Gardens in Shepherd's Bush. It's a long straight road lined with big Victorian terraced houses divided up into flats. Nothing unusual in that, you might think, but Sinclair Road is actually very unusual indeed.

Late one blowy afternoon towards the end of last year, I was looking in the window of an estate agents close to Shepherd's Bush Green when I noticed a couple of places in Sinclair Road. I went into the office intending to score a flat list and get back out on the street as quickly as possible—I've nothing against estate agents, I just wish they didn't always demand your soul in return for a flat list—but both the agents, a man and a woman, were busy and there was no other visible source of information. The man, a well-built dark-skinned guy in his early thirties, was on the phone, twirling a set of keys around his index finger as he exaggerated the charms of a studio flat in Hammersmith Grove to someone on the other end of the line.

The woman, pipe-cleaner thin, cigarette-lined, looking ten years older than her thirty-odd years, was fielding some bizarre questions from the only other person in the place, apart from me. Having dismissed the woman's invitation to sit down, the questioner used his hands to press against the edge of the woman's desk. Essentially he wanted to know if the properties they sold were divided up vertically or horizontally. It didn't matter how many different ways he phrased it, the woman seemed unable to give him an answer.

"We sell flats and houses," she kept saying. "Some of the houses are divided up into flats."

"Horizontally or vertically?" he wanted to know, chopping his hands through the air. "This way or that?"

Deep gridlines of stress had appeared on the woman's forehead as if etched there by the man's hand movements. "I'm sorry," she said finally. "I don't think I can help you."

Her colleague continued to spiel and twirl, appearing to drag out the conversation. I had no doubt, however, that the caller had hung up.

What interested me in particular was that as I had entered the office the first words I had heard the crazy guy say were "Sinclair Road."

Abruptly, the madman scowled and spun away from the woman's desk. I saw his face for the first time; his eyes blazed with an unsettling intensity. He pulled open the door and left. I noted the direction he took, then turned to raise my eyebrows at the woman, but she was still wound up, so I quickly requested a flat list. She pulled one out of a drawer and handed it to me without a word. I left the shop and headed down Goldhawk Road. The sky above the Hammersmith & City line bridge was turning a deep pink. Within half an hour it would be that uniform orangey purple that passes for night in London. The crazy guy turned and went into Vesbar. I stopped outside and watched through the window as the young, the fashionable and the beautiful parted to allow the interloper to approach the bar, where I saw him growl at the staff until they relented, presenting him with what I assumed was a glass of tap water.

I went in and asked for two beers, pointing to a row of bottles in the chiller.

"Want a beer?" I asked him.

He glared at me.

"I was in the estate agents," I explained. "I'm interested in this vertical/horizontal thing. Have a beer and tell me about it."

He turned away.

"I think I know what you're talking about," I lied.

He turned back.

"What's it to you?" he asked, taking the beer.

"I'm interested."

And so he told me. The normal way in which a street is divided up—one house, consisting of a ground floor, first floor and perhaps second floor, next to another—did not reflect the actual reality of these spaces. There was more homogeneity between one first floor space and the next than between any first floor space and the ground floor beneath it or the second floor above.

"I see," I said, wishing I'd saved my beer money.

"Anyway," he muttered, turning away again. "She wasn't tall enough."

"What?"

"The estate agent woman. She wasn't tall enough."

"How could you tell? She was sitting down."

"I can tell."

He kept looking away, watching people around him, as if an attack could come from any quarter.

"What's your name?" I asked him.

"Marco."

"Tall enough for what, Marco?" I asked.

"It ran just south of here, you know."

"What did?"

"Two minutes' walk."

I thought about buying him another beer, out of pity, and making myself scarce. But I didn't like to leave him there. He was in the wrong place. Very soon after it had opened, Vesbar had started to fill up from early evening onwards with the sort of people you didn't normally see in Shepherd's Bush. Young, trendy, furiously smoking; tote bags, tight jackets, Hoxton fins. Where did they come from? They didn't live in the Bush; you never saw them carrying shopping or entering houses. From which branch of Central Casting did they get bussed in? They weren't of the same stripe as the good-time girls and boys who shivered in shirtsleeves outside the Walkabout, on the west side of the Green, or even drawn from the same subset as the exhibition drinkers who had packed out the Slug & Lettuce on the north side the moment it opened. Nor would they be likely to wander down to the Bush Bar & Grill for expensive eats after a couple of swift ones. They were there for the duration. (Earlier in the day it was a different story. The place was almost empty at lunchtime. It was good for meetings with BBC producers who wanted to get out of the office. I'd take my iBook down there and show them my stuff over a mineral water, and they'd say "Mmm, yes. Very nice," and then never call.)

"D'you wanna see it?" Marco asked, looking up at me through dirty wisps of hair.

"See what?" I asked, running a hand over my shaved skull.

"The old line, the disused line. What I've been talking about all this time, for fuck's sake."

I had to admit I had almost no idea what he'd been talking about, even less now, but I left with him because I rather liked the unnecessary cursing and I didn't have him pegged as dangerous. We turned off Goldhawk Road into Richford Street.

Richford Street is mixed. Dentists, psychologists, foreign editors and private finance types rub shoulders with hookers, crackheads, murderers and various victims of violent crime. I knew a bunch of people down there, primarily drawn from the former group. I wondered where Marco was taking me. I wasn't carrying my camera, my standard piece of armor in awkward situations.

At the bottom of Richford Street we kept going. At Trussley Road, Marco stopped.

"Over there," he said. To our left was a viaduct carrying the Hammersmith & City line south to Hammersmith. The railway arches had been colonized by car workshops, separate businesses specialising in different makes of vehicle. Marco was pointing across the street to the remains of another railway viaduct. "There."

"So what?" I said.

"That's it, the disused line I was talking about."

I looked at him.

Footsteps approached from Hammersmith Grove. We each turned and watched a young woman of medium height coming towards us. She crossed the road to avoid us and carried on down towards the railway arches.

"Too short, I suppose?" I said, when she had turned the corner.

"By a good six inches."

If I had known then why he was interested in tall women, I would never have made the comment.

For the next few days I concentrated on my own project, my film about Sinclair Road, which I was hoping to flog to one of the new BBC digital channels that were soon to come on line. Nobody would see it, but that wasn't the point. I'd get paid, there'd be a bit of press and the next one might actually get commissioned. It was a plan, not an especially clever one, but a plan nevertheless, which I'd come up with after several years of trying to set stuff up with the BBC and countless small production companies. I'd been to enough meetings to last a lifetime, all of them fruitless.

The conceit of the film was that everybody in London has lived in Sinclair Road or will do so at some point in the future. It seemed a neat way in to make a little film about a road that actually is a bit special. It does have an unusually high turnover of residents. I am forever meeting people who live there, or who tell me they've lived there in the past. An academic I met at a party a year ago, and an architect she knew who lived there too; a musician I met via some writer friends; a lad I gave a lift home to after playing football under the Westway. It got to the point where I was expecting people to say "Sinclair Road" when I asked them where they lived.

At home I edited various bits of footage on the iBook while working my way through a bottle of vodka. I replayed a panning shot of top-floor flats along Sinclair Road and it struck me how similar it was to a clip I'd shot the day before of a train on the Hammersmith & City line near Latimer Road. Playing both clips forward and back and varying the speeds, I remembered what Marco had said about streets full of houses being divided up horizontally rather than vertically. His theory ended up influencing the way I edited the film, as I intercut shots of Sincair Road with shots of the train.

Tired and half-pissed, I decided to log on to the net for half an hour before crashing out. I looked into Marco's story about a disused line and discovered that it was true. There had been a line, going from Addison Road station (now Kensington Olympia) to Hammersmith and then on to Richmond. It had run north alongside the West London line, parallel with Sinclair Road, as far as Addison Gardens, then had peeled off to the left.

Normally, in the mornings, I waited for the post before going out anywhere, and especially around that time, as I had placed an ad for an actress or model in the *Stage*. "Possible nudity," I had specified, and "no fee upfront," so the CVs were not exactly flooding in. First thing the next day, however, before the post came, I wandered over to Sinclair Road with the camera.

The line's former route was easy to identify. Because it had run in a cutting just below street level, there were noticeable humps where various roads had bridged the line. On the west side of Shepherd's Bush Road there was even a parapet where you could look down on to a row of lock-up garages where once there had been a station serving Shepherd's Bush. On the east side of the road, an imposing block of flats, the Grampians, had been built in the Art Deco style of the day only fifteen years or so after the line's closure in 1916. It occurred to me that I had walked over that former bridge hundreds of times and wondered why it was there. When you looked west you somehow expected a slightly grander view than a line of lock-ups and a few old cars. It had always seemed an unsatisfactorily resolved landscape.

The old line had passed underneath the Hammersmith & City line just south of Goldhawk Road station and then straightened to mount its own viaduct, a fragment of which Marco had shown me at Trussley Road.

I headed back towards Sinclair Road via the Green, then cut behind the petrol station, but as I did so I noticed a figure disappearing up the ramp into the residents' car park at the foot of one of the tower blocks. It's funny how with some people you think you recognize them in the street, but you're not quite sure, even though you can see them right there in front of you, and so you don't know whether or not to acknowledge them, and if you do and it's not them, you look stupid, and you look no less stupid if you fail to acknowledge someone you do know; and yet with other people, you recognize them in a split second, a hundred percent, even from the back as they're disappearing into a car park.

Instead of hailing Marco, I followed him. I had never had reason to enter this or any other nearby car park. I lived in a two-bedroom flat that cost more than I could afford above a twenty-four-hour supermarket on the north side of the Green and parked my Mazda in the street.

At the top of the ramp there was a covered section. I waited until Marco had reached the other end and turned left into daylight again. I passed a couple of 4×4s and a newish Jaguar. Smart cars for a block of council flats. Beyond the covered area was an open-air extension to the car park. At the far side, a low wall and a wire-mesh fence separated the parked cars, among them two new Minis, from a twenty-foot drop to the rear of the Deco apartment block, the Grampians. I realized this represented part of the track-bed of the disused line. Marco was standing close to the fence further along. From what I could make out, he was trying to see into the flats. Every few seconds he lowered his gaze to the cutting where, a hundred years before, trains would have run. It was at that point that I started to suspect that his interest in the old line went beyond that of a local historian. Before I knew what I was doing I had the camera to my eye and was filming him. Local nutter or neighborhood visionary, he'd look good in the film, whether his taking part was agreed to or not. If he fancied it, we could shoot some more stuff in Sinclair Road; if not, he'd just be a long-haired bystander in a dirty coat, a tatty figure in a scruffy landscape. There'd be a stark contrast with the female nude, if ever I found one.

Marco registered my presence. I lowered the camera, but he didn't seem that bothered. I walked over to him.

"I'm making a film," I said, "about Sinclair Road. Since you told me about the old line, I realize that's got to be in it. It ran just down here, didn't it?"

"Can you hear them, too?"

I raised my eyebrows at him.

"The trains."

"Did one just go by? Did I miss it?"

He laughed to himself, somewhat hollowly.

"There's a good view from my place," he said.

"Where's that?"

"Where do you think?"

We walked together to Sinclair Road. His place was on the east side close to Addison Gardens and the bridge over the railway. We climbed to the top floor, where he had a studio flat that smelled of incense and damp.

"Nice place," I said.

"It's a shithole," he muttered.

My brain went into overdrive. My visits to estate agents had served two purposes. I wanted to gather evidence that Sinclair Road had an unusually high turnover, as I've said, but I was also on the lookout for a cheap flat to rent, to use in the film. Maybe I'd found it, rent free. The studio room was relatively uncluttered: a vinyl settee, a portable TV and a free-standing bookcase full of books on magic and biographies of Aleister Crowley. I looked out of the front window. It was only really when you saw the road from this angle that you appreciated how big these houses were and how many people must live in the street at any one time. What looked like three-story houses to the casual passer-by in fact comprised five stories if you counted the lower-ground floor and the attics that most of them seemed to have.

Hearing the sound of tearing paper, I turned to look at Marco. He was opening his post by ripping the tops and bottoms of envelopes right across.

"Do you always open your mail like that?" I asked him.

"Of course," he said.

"Why 'of course'?"

Again he laughed to himself and held up a brown A5-size envelope.

"Open one of these in a darkened room," he said, "and you'll see why."

When I continued to look baffled, he went and pulled the curtains, front and back, plunging the room into semi-darkness. He tossed the envelope to me.

"You open it," he said. "Pull it apart where the glue's stuck together."

I realized what he was going on about, but opened the envelope, all the same, according to his instructions. As I expected, where the glue parted, in long stringy filaments, a faint phosphorescent glow appeared. I'd seen this before, but had no idea what caused it.

"You don't like that then?" I asked him. "The phosphorescent thing."

"What's there to like? That they're trying ever more bizarre ways to get at me? I'm not stupid, you know."

"No. I can see that," I said, opening the curtains at the rear and looking down at the railway line. "So that's the West London line?" I said.

"Yes."

"And the disused line ran alongside?"

"On this side, yes. And can I sleep at night? No. The noise of it is constant. Constant. The trains never stop. They never stop."

Marco was pressing the heel of his hand to his forehead like a method actor with a headache.

"Right," I said. "And what's this, if you don't mind my asking?" I pointed to a small pile of soil on the carpet near the window, and an indecipherable series of chalk marks on the wall.

"That's my business," he said darkly.

"Whatever."

Walking home, I thought about the soil. I vaguely recalled reading up on magic and divination for an unsuccessful pitch to Channel Four. Geomancy had something to do with seeing the future in patterns of scattered soil. The contents of Marco's bookshelves attested to more than a passing interest in the dark arts. I wondered how far he took it.

I pictured the flat and imagined ripping up the ratty carpet to expose the bare boards that must lie beneath. All I needed was the right face, and more, to situa.te in that space and have it looking out at Sinclair Road from the inside.

And when I got home I found that face.

There was a small pile of mail on the doormat. I took the mail into the front room. Then I did something I'd never done before. I don't know why I did it—whether in homage to Marco, or as a way of rather pointlessly taking the piss out of the poor fucker—but I selected the biggest item and opened it in the way I'd seen him do it, by ripping off the top and the bottom. Too late I realized the envelope had contained a response to my ad in the *Stage*: a letter, a CV and a black and white ten-by-eight.

I gingerly withdrew what remained of the photo. The respondent had taken heed of my warning about nudity and gamely got herself snapped in the buff. Her arms and legs looked dark, making me think she might be Asian or Arab. Her torso and abdomen were awash with light from the adjacent open window. It could have been the window in Marco's flat. Between her breasts and her navel was a series of broken-up horizontal lines that I assumed to be some sort of henna pattern. Her left hand was placed across her breastbone, just below her throat, which seemed a strangely vulnerable gesture for a woman willingly posing nude.

I picked the remaining contents of the envelope up off the floor. The woman's head, which I had so cavalierly ripped from her body, was turned towards the window, a distant, melancholy look on her face. On the other strip that I'd unwittingly torn from the photograph were the model's feet. Around her ankles were more henna designs like dotted lines. Only when I reassembled the three pieces did I appreciate fully her tall, statuesque figure.

I looked at the letter and CV. Her name was Vita Ray, which I took to be a stage name. She wanted the work, she said, because she wanted to get into films. Modeling for the picture had demonstrated that she was at ease in front of a camera. She gave a mobile number and what looked like a temporary address in Paddington.

I knew I should really give it a few more days for some more CVs to come in, but I felt bad about mistreating Vita Ray's portrait, and she looked right for Sinclair Road, so I picked up the phone.

Our first meeting took place in Sinclair Road itself. Vita Ray arrived by cab. As she stepped out and paid the driver, I saw for the first time how tall she was. At least two inches taller than my five foot seven. We walked the length of Sinclair Road while I explained to her what the film was about. As we approached the far end I glanced up at the attic window of number 148. Did I see the curtain move? It was impossible to be sure, especially with the sun reflecting off the glass.

I found her a little nervous, but keen to get started. I got her to walk towards me while looking into the windows she was passing.

"I want you to appear curious about who lives here and what they do," I explained.

She was a natural. Unaware of the camera and a graceful mover. I began, prematurely, to congratulate myself on having chosen her. I asked her to unbutton her coat. As soon as she did so I saw that she had another intricate henna pattern, one that postdated the photograph, around her throat like a necklace. I then wondered if it could have been there, after all, and I had torn along the line of it when opening the envelope.

As we reached the bottom of the street, we ran into Marco, who was walking up from the Olympia end, so either I'd been mistaken about the curtain in his flat, or he'd seen us and come straight out, going the long way round and doubling back. I introduced them to each other. The way Marco stole glances at Vita, while she was looking elsewhere, appeared sly and calculating. It was only later that I realized precisely how calculating.

"So you're working on his film?" he asked her, somehow managing to offend both of us at the same time. "Me too."

Vita looked less than thrilled at the prospect.

"We've got to go," I said, taking her arm. "I'll be in touch."

I walked Vita down to Olympia and put her in a black cab. She turned round to watch me through the rear window as the cab pulled away. I gave a self-conscious wave. It was the last time I would see her alive.

I fixed a meeting for a couple of days later at Marco's place. If I could actually get Marco out of the flat for half an hour, get him to run some invented errand, then Vita and I would be able to shoot some stuff. I didn't need long and my instinct told me she'd be a fast worker, too.

My plan was to get there first, so she didn't have to hang around on her own with Marco. Typically, however, a BBC producer rang me on the morning of the day we were to do the filming. Some woman I'd had a couple of inconclusive meetings with in the past. Something had just come up, she said, an opportunity that was too good to miss. A BBC2 thing. Could I come in and knock a few ideas around? She suggested a time. I asked if we could make it any earlier or even the following day.

"It's *just* come up," she repeated, from which I inferred that it could just as quickly go away again.

"OK, I'll be there," I said. "But I've got to be away by three."

I should have said no, but I didn't know that then. Obviously I know it now, but I didn't know it then, although you could argue, and I often do, that I should have done.

I was still pacing up and down in the White City lobby at ten to three when Amanda finally showed up, trotting down to the security barriers. I considered telling her I had to go, but these meetings have a way of sucking you in, draining you of the power to resist. I went through and we went upstairs and we knocked a few ideas around and she said she'd get back to me and I knew she wouldn't. Or she would, but it would be six weeks down the line and she'd remind me I knew what it was like.

It was four when I got to Sinclair Road. There was no response to my repeated leaning on Marco's bell, nor to my hammering on the door.

"You gave her to me," Marco would later whisper, when I visited him.

Vita's body was found by the lock-up garages on the west side of Shepherd's Bush Road. She lay across the track-bed of the disused line, albeit on asphalt laid down over its long-dead remains. Her feet were found closest to the garages, severed just above the ankle. Her head had rolled a few inches in the direction of the block of flats served by the garages. It was quickly established, from the amount of blood spilled at the site, not only that the beheading and double amputation had taken place right there in broad daylight and in full view of residents and passersby, but that Vita had still been alive at the time.

Marco was picked up soaked in blood outside Vesbar. He never denied taking Vita to the lock-up garages and being present at the moment of her death, which he attributed not to his own efforts and the hacksaw bearing his bloody fingerprints found on the roof of one of the garages, but to a train that had emerged from the tunnel under Shepherd's Bush Road and failed to stop. It should have stopped at the station, he maintained.

In the opinion of the court, Marco was not insane, merely trying his hardest to give that impression. I asserted otherwise, having cooperated fully with the authorities. Not only did I believe there was a danger I might face charges myself, I would have welcomed them. As it was, I was cleared of any impropriety and left free to judge myself. It wasn't long before the offers started coming in. Meetings would be an informality this time, it seemed. I could choose my own projects. Set my own budgets. Publicity guaranteed.

I turned down the offers, despite the fact I had even less work now than before. My landlord gave me notice to quit the flat.

Whenever I began to feel I had sacrificed enough and might try to return to a normal life, I arranged to visit Marco.

"You gave her to me," he whispered.

"She was tall," I said. "Why did she have to be tall?"

"Standard gauge is four foot eight-and-a-half inches."

I looked at him. His gaze had lost its intensity.

"I've got nowhere to live," I told him.

"Move into my place," he said. "You've always wanted to live in Sinclair Road."

It wasn't so much that I'd always wanted to, more that I'd always believed I would at some point. It wasn't long after I'd moved in that I, too, started hearing the trains. They came in the middle of the night when there was no traffic on the West London line.

I measured my head in the mirror in Marco's bespattered bathroom. Roughly nine inches from crown to Adam's apple. From the sole of my foot to above my ankle bone was four inches. Nine and four made thirteen. Subtract thirteen inches from five foot nine and a half—Vita's height, as stated in court—and you're left with four foot eight and half. Standard gauge.

I'm just that little bit shorter, so I'd have to stretch a bit.

JEFFREY FORD

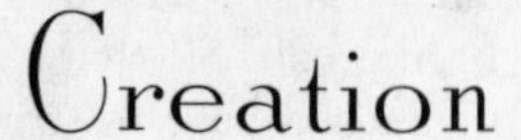

Jeffrey Ford published an astonishing number of first-rate short stories in 2002. "Creation" is the second of two stories we've chosen to reprint in this year's edition of The Year's Best Fantasy and Horror. *(Other Ford stories can be found in our Honorable Mentions list.)*

"Creation" is a wise, wistful, understated work of contemporary fantasy, which first appeared in the May issue of The Magazine of Fantasy & Science Fiction. *The tale was subsequently reprinted in the author's collection,* The Fantasy Writer's Assistant and Other Stories *(Golden Gryphon Press).*

—T. W.

I learned about creation from Mrs. Grimm, in the basement of her house around the corner from ours. The room was dimly lit by a stained-glass lamp positioned above the pool table. There was also a bar in the corner, behind which hung an electric sign that read *Rheingold* and held a can that endlessly poured golden beer into a pilsner glass that never seemed to overflow. That brew was liquid light, bright bubbles never ceasing to rise.

"Who made you?" she would ask, consulting that little book with the pastel-colored depictions of agony in hell and the angel-strewn clouds of heaven. She had the nose of a witch, one continuous eyebrow, and tea-cup-shiny skin—even the wrinkles seemed capable of cracking. Her smile was merely the absence of a frown, but she made candy apples for us at Halloween and marshmallow bricks in the shapes of wise men at Christmas. I often wondered how she had come to know so much about God and pictured saints with halos and cassocks playing pool and drinking beer in her basement at night.

We kids would page through our own copies of the catechism book to find the appropriate response, but before anyone else could answer, Amy Lash would already be saying, "God made me."

Then Richard Antonelli would get up and jump around, making fart noises through his mouth, and Mrs. Grimm would shake her head and tell him God was watching. I never jumped around, never spoke out of turn, for two reasons, neither of which had to do with God. One was what my father called his size ten, referring to his shoe, and the other was that I was too busy watching that sign over the bar, waiting to see the beer finally spill.

The only time I was ever distracted from my vigilance was when she told us about the creation of Adam and Eve. After God had made the world, he made them too, because he had so much love and not enough places to put it. He made Adam out of clay and blew life into him, and once he came to life, God made him sleep and then stole a rib and made the woman. After the illustration of a naked couple consumed in flame, being bitten by black snakes and poked by the fork of a pink demon with horns and bat wings, the picture for the story of the creation of Adam was my favorite. A bearded God in flowing robes leaned over a clay man, breathing blue-gray life into him.

That breath of life was like a great autumn wind blowing through my imagination, carrying with it all sorts of questions like pastel leaves that momentarily obscured my view of the beautiful flow of beer: Was dirt the first thing Adam tasted? Was God's beard brushing against his chin the first thing he felt? When he slept, did he dream of God stealing his rib and did it crack when it came away from him? What did he make of Eve and the fact that she was the only woman for him to marry? Was he thankful it wasn't Amy Lash?

Later on, I asked my father what he thought about the creation of Adam, and he gave me his usual response to any questions concerning religion. "Look," he said, "it's a nice story, but when you die you're food for the worms." One time my mother made him take me to church when she was sick, and he sat in the front row, directly in front of the priest. While everyone else was genuflecting and standing and singing, he just sat there staring, his arms folded and one leg crossed over the other. When they rang the little bell and everyone beat their chest, he laughed out loud.

No matter what I had learned in catechism about God and hell and the ten commandments, my father was hard to ignore. He worked two jobs, his muscles were huge, and once, when the neighbors' Doberman, big as a pony, went crazy and attacked a girl walking her poodle down our street, I saw him run outside with a baseball bat, grab the girl in one arm and then beat the dog to death as it tried to go for his throat. Throughout all of this he never lost the cigarette in the corner of his mouth and only put it out in order to hug the girl and quiet her crying.

"Food for the worms," I thought and took that thought along with a brown paper bag of equipment through the hole in the chain link fence into the woods that lay behind the school yard. Those woods were deep, and you could travel through them for miles and miles, never coming out from under the trees or seeing a backyard. Richard Antonelli hunted squirrels with a BB gun in them, and Bobby Lenon and his gang went there at night, lit a little fire and drank beer. Once, while exploring, I discovered a rain-sogged *Playboy*; once, a dead fox. Kids said there was gold in the creek that wound among the trees and that there was a far-flung acre that sank down into a deep valley where the deer went to die. For many years it was rumored that a monkey, escaped from a traveling carnival over in Brightwaters, lived in the treetops.

It was mid-summer and the dragonflies buzzed, the squirrels leaped from branch to branch, frightened sparrows darted away. The sun beamed in through gaps in the green above, leaving, here and there, shifting puddles of light on the pine-needle floor. Within one of those patches of light, I practiced creation. There was no clay, so I used an old log for the body. The arms were long, five-fingered branches that I positioned jutting out from the torso. The legs were two large birch saplings with plenty of spring for running and jumping. These I laid angled to the base of the log.

A large hunk of bark that had peeled off an oak was the head. On this I laid red mushroom eyes, curved barnacles of fungus for ears, a dried seed pod for a nose. The mouth was merely a hole I punched through the bark with my pen knife. Before affixing the fern hair to the top of the head, I slid beneath the curve of the sheet of bark those things I thought might help to confer life—a dandelion gone to ghostly seed, a cardinal's wing feather, a see-through quartz pebble, a twenty-five-cent compass. The ferns made a striking hairdo, the weeds, with their burr-like ends, formed a venerable beard. I gave him a weapon to hunt with: a long pointed stick that was my exact height.

When I was finished putting my man together, I stood and looked down upon him. He looked good. He looked ready to come to life. I went to the brown paper bag and took out my catechism book. Then kneeling near his right ear, I whispered to him all of the questions Mrs. Grimm would ever ask. When I got to the one, "What is Hell?" his left eye rolled off his face, and I had to put it back. I followed up the last answer with a quick promise never to steal a rib.

Putting the book back into the bag, I then retrieved a capped, cleaned-out baby-food jar. It had once held vanilla pudding, my little sister's favorite, but now it was filled with breath. I had asked my father to blow into it. Without asking any questions, he never looked away from the racing form, but took a drag from his cigarette and blew a long, blue-gray stream of air into it. I capped it quickly and thanked him. "Don't say I never gave you anything," he mumbled as I ran to my room to look at it beneath a bare light bulb. The spirit swirled within and then slowly became invisible.

I held the jar down to the mouth of my man, and when I couldn't get it any closer, I unscrewed the lid and carefully poured out every atom of breath. There was nothing to see, so I held it there a long time and let him drink it in. As I pulled the jar away, I heard a breeze blowing through the leaves; felt it on the back of my neck. I stood up quickly and turned around with a keen sense that someone was watching me. I got scared. When the breeze came again, it chilled me, for wrapped in it was the quietest whisper ever. I dropped the jar and ran all the way home.

That night as I lay in bed, the lights out, my mother sitting next to me, stroking my crewcut and softly singing, "Until the Real Thing Comes Along," I remembered that I had left my catechism book in the brown bag next to the body of the man. I immediately made believe I was asleep so that my mother would leave. Had she stayed, she would have eventually felt my guilt through the top of my head. When the door was closed over, I began to toss and turn, thinking of my man lying out there in the dark woods by himself. I promised God that I would go out there in the morning, get my book, and take my creation apart. With the first bird song in the dark of the new day, I fell asleep and dreamed I was in Mrs. Grimm's basement with the saints. A beautiful woman saint with a big rose bush thorn sticking right in the middle of her forehead told me, "Your man's name is Cavanaugh."

"Hey, that's the name of the guy who owns the deli in town," I told her.

"Great head cheese at that place," said a saint with a baby lamb under his arm.

Another big bearded saint used the end of a pool cue to cock back his halo. He leaned over me and asked, "Why did God make you?"

I reached for my book but realized I had left it in the woods.

"Come on," he said, "that's one of the easiest ones."

I looked away at the bar, stalling for time while I tried to remember the answer, and just then the glass on the sign overflowed and spilled onto the floor.

The next day, my man, Cavanaugh, was gone. Not a scrap of him left behind. No sign of the red feather or the clear pebble. This wasn't a case of someone having come along and maliciously scattered him. I searched the entire area. It was a certainty that he had risen up, taken his spear and the brown paper bag containing my religious instruction book, and walked off into the heart of the woods.

Standing in the spot where I had given him life, my mind spiraled with visions of him loping along on his birch legs, branch fingers pushing aside sticker bushes and low hanging leaves, his fern hair slicked back by the wind. Through those red mushroom eyes, he was seeing his first day. I wondered if he was as frightened to be alive as I was to have made him, or had the breath of my father imbued him with a grim food-for-the-worms courage? Either way, there was no dismantling him now—Thou shalt not kill. I felt a grave responsibility and went in search of him.

I followed the creek, thinking he would do the same, and traveled deeper and deeper into the woods. What was I going to say to him, I wondered, when I finally found him and his simple hole of a mouth formed a question? It wasn't clear to me why I had made him, but it had something to do with my father's idea of death—a slow rotting underground; a cold dreamless sleep longer than the universe. I passed the place where I had discovered the dead fox and there picked up Cavanaugh's trail—holes poked in the damp ground by the stride of his birch legs. Stopping, I looked all around through the jumbled stickers and bushes, past the trees, and detected no movement but for a single leaf silently falling.

I journeyed beyond the Antonelli brothers' lean-to temple where they hung their squirrel skins to dry and brewed sassafras tea. I even circled the pond, passed the tree whose bark had been stripped in a spiral by lightning, and entered territory I had never seen before. Cavanaugh seemed to stay always just ahead of me, out of sight. His snake-hole footprints, bent and broken branches, and that barely audible and constant whisper on the breeze that trailed in his wake drew me on into the late afternoon until the woods began to slowly fill with night. Then I had a thought of home: my mother cooking dinner and my sister playing on a blanket on the kitchen floor; the Victrola turning out The Ink Spots. I ran back along my path, and somewhere in my flight I heard a loud cry, not bird nor animal nor human, but like a thick limb splintering free from an ancient oak.

I ignored the woods as best I could for the rest of the summer. There was basketball, and games of guns with all of the children in the neighborhood ranging across everyone's backyard, trips to the candy store for comic books, late night horror movies on Chiller Theatre. I caught a demon jab of hell for having lost my religious instruction book, and all of my allowance for four weeks went toward another. Mrs. Grimm told me God knew I had lost it and that it would be a few weeks before she could get me a replacement. I imagined her addressing an envelope to heaven. In the meantime, I had to look on with Amy Lash. She'd lean close to me, pointing out every word that was read aloud, and when Mrs. Grimm asked me a question, catching me concentrating on the infinite beer, Amy would whisper the answers without moving her lips and save me. Still, no matter what happened, I could not completely forget about Cavanaugh. I thought my feeling of responsibility would wither as the days swept by; instead it grew like a weed.

On a hot afternoon at the end of July, I was sitting in my secret hideout, a bower formed by forsythia bushes in the corner of my backyard, reading the latest installment of *Nick Fury*. I only closed my eyes to rest them for a moment, but there was Cavanaugh's rough-barked face. Now that he was alive, leaves had sprouted all over his trunk and limbs. He wore a strand of wild blueberries around where his neck should have been, and his hair ferns had grown and deepened their shade of green. It wasn't just a daydream, I tell you. I knew that I was seeing him, what he was doing, where he was, at that very minute. He held his spear as a walking stick, and it came to me then that he was, of course, a vegetarian. His long thin legs bowed slightly, his log of a body shifted, as he cocked back his curled, wooden parchment of a head and stared with mushroom eyes into a beam of sunlight slipping through the branches above. Motes of pollen swirled in the light, chipmunks, squirrels, deer silently gathered, sparrows landed for a brief moment to nibble at his hair and then were gone. All around him, the woods looked on in awe as one of its own reckoned the beauty of the sun. What lungs, what vocal chords, gave birth to it, I'm not sure, but he groaned; a sound I had witnessed one other time while watching my father asleep, wrapped in a nightmare.

I visited that spot within the yellow blossomed forsythias once a day to check up on my man's progress. All that was necessary was that I sit quietly for a time until in a state of near-nap and then close my eyes and fly my brain around the corner, past the school, over the treetops, then down into the cool green shadow of the woods. Many times I saw him just standing, as if stunned by life, and many times traipsing through some unknown quadrant of his Eden. With each viewing came a confused emotion of wonder and dread, like on the beautiful windy day at the beginning of August when I saw him sitting beside the pond, holding the catechism book upside down, a twig finger of one hand pointing to each word on the page, while the other hand covered all but one red eye of his face.

I was there when he came across the blackened patch of earth and scattered beers from one of the Lenon gang's nights in the woods. He lifted a partially crushed can with backwash still sloshing in the bottom and drank it down. The bark around his usually indistinct hole of a mouth magically widened into a smile. It was when he uncovered a half a pack of Camels and a book of matches that I realized he must have been spying on the revels of Lenon, Cho-cho, Mike Stone, and Jake Harwood from the safety of the night trees. He lit up and the smoke swirled out the back of his head. In a voice like the creaking of a rotted branch, he pronounced, "Fuck."

And most remarkable of all was the time he came to the edge of the woods, to the hole in the chain link fence. There, in the playground across the field, he saw Amy Lash, gliding up and back on the swing, her red gingham dress billowing, her bright hair full of motion. He trembled as if planted in earthquake earth, and squeaked the way the sparrows did. For a long time, he crouched in that portal to the outside world and watched. Then, gathering his courage, he stepped onto the field. The instant he was out of the woods, Amy must have felt his presence, and she looked up and saw him approaching. She screamed, jumped off the swing, and ran out of the playground. Cavanaugh, frightened by her scream, retreated to the woods, and did not stop running until he reached the tree struck by lightning.

My religious instruction book finally arrived from above, summer ended and school began, but still I went every day to my hideout and watched him for a little while as he fished gold coins from the creek or tracked, from the ground, something moving through the treetops. I know it was close to Halloween, because I sat in my hideout loosening my teeth on one of Mrs. Grimm's candy apples when I realized that my secret seeing place was no longer a secret. The forsythias had long since dropped their flowers. As I sat there in the skeletal blind, I could feel the cold creeping into me. "Winter is coming," I said in a puff of steam and had one fleeting vision of Cavanaugh, his leaves gone flame red, his fern hair drooping brown, discovering the temple of dead squirrels. I saw him gently touch the fur of a stretched-out corpse hung on the wall. His birch legs bent to nearly breaking as he fell to his knees and let out a wail that drilled into me and lived there.

It was late night, a few weeks later, but that cry still echoed through me and I could not sleep. I heard, above the sound of the dreaming house, my father come in from his second job. I don't know what made me think I could tell him, but I had to tell someone. If I kept to myself what I had done any longer, I thought I would have to run away. Crawling out of bed, I crept down the darkened hallway past my sister's room and heard her breathing. I found my father sitting in the dining room, eating a cold dinner and reading the paper by only the light coming through from the kitchen. All he had to do was look up at me and I started crying. Next thing I knew, he had his arm around me and I was enveloped in the familiar aroma of machine oil. I thought he might laugh, I thought he might yell, but I told him everything all at once. What he did was pull out the chair next to his. I sat down, drying my eyes.

"What can we do?" he asked.

"I just need to tell him something," I said.

"Okay," he said. "This Saturday, we'll go to the woods and see if we can find him." Then he had me describe Cavanaugh, and when I was done he said, "Sounds like a sturdy fellow."

We moved into the living room and sat on the couch in the dark. He lit a cigarette and told me about the woods when he was a boy; how vast they were, how he trapped mink, saw eagles, how he and his brother lived for a week by their wits alone out in nature. I eventually dozed off and only half woke when he carried me to my bed.

The week passed and I went to sleep Friday night, hoping he wouldn't forget his promise and go to the track instead. But the next morning, he woke me early from a dream of Amy Lash by tapping my shoulder and saying, "Move your laggardly ass." He made bacon and eggs, the only two things he knew how to make, and let me drink coffee. Then we put on our coats and were off. It was the second week in November and the day was cold and overcast. "Brisk," he said as we rounded the corner toward the school, and that was all he said until we were well in beneath the trees.

I showed him around the woods like a tour guide, pointing out the creek, the spot where I had created my man, the temple of dead squirrels. "Interesting," he said to each of these, and once in a while mentioned the name of some bush or tree. Waves of leaves blew amidst the trunks in the cold wind, and with stronger gusts, showers of them fell around us. He could really walk and we walked for what seemed ten miles, out of the morning and into the afternoon, way past any place I had ever dreamed of going. We discovered a spot where an enormous tree had fallen, exposing the gnarled brainwork of its roots, and another two acres where there were no trees but only smooth sand hills. All the time, I was alert to even the slightest sound, a cracking twig, the caw of a crow, hoping I might hear the whisper.

As it grew later, the sky darkened and what was cold before became colder still. "Listen," my father said, "I have a feeling like the one when we used to track deer. He's nearby, somewhere. We'll have to outsmart him."

I nodded.

"I'm going to stay here and wait," he said. "You keep going along the path here for a while, but, for Christ's sake, be quiet. Maybe if he sees you, he'll double back to get away, and I'll be here to catch him."

I wasn't sure this plan made sense, but I knew we needed to do something. It was getting late. "Be careful," I said, "he's big and he has a stick."

My father smiled. "Don't worry," he said and lifted his foot to indicate the size ten.

This made me laugh, and I turned and started down the path, taking careful steps. "Go on for about ten minutes or so and see if you see anything," he called to me before I rounded a bend.

Once I was by myself, I wasn't so sure I wanted to find my man. Because of the overcast sky the woods were dark and lonely. As I walked I pictured my father and Cavanaugh wrestling each other and wondered who would win. When I had gone far enough to want to stop and run back, I forced myself around one more turn. Just this little more, I thought. He's probably already fallen apart anyway, dismantled by winter. But then I saw it up ahead, treetops at eye level, and I knew I had found the valley where the deer went to die.

Cautiously, I inched up to the rim, and peered down the steep dirt wall overgrown with roots and stickers, into the trees and the shadowed undergrowth beneath them. The valley was a large hole as if a meteor had struck there long ago. I thought of the treasure trove of antlers and bones that lay hidden in the leaves at its base. Standing there, staring, I felt I almost understood the secret life and age of the woods. I had to show this to my father, but before I could move away, I saw something, heard something moving below. Squinting to see more clearly through the darkness down there, I could just about make out a shadowed figure standing, half hidden by the trunk of a tall pine.

"Cavanaugh?" I called. "Is that you?"

In the silence, I heard acorns dropping.

"Are you there?" I asked.

There was a reply, an eerie sound that was part voice, part wind. It was very quiet but I distinctly heard it ask, "Why?"

"Are you okay?" I asked.

"Why?" came the same question.

I didn't know why, and wished I had read him the book's answers instead of the questions the day of his birth. I stood for a long time and watched as snow began to fall around me.

His question came again, weaker this time, and I was on the verge of tears, ashamed of what I had done. Suddenly, I had a strange memory flash of the endless beer in Mrs. Grimm's basement. At least it was something. I leaned out over the edge and, almost certain I was lying, yelled, "I had too much love."

Then, so I could barely make it out, I heard him whisper, "Thank you."

After that, there came from below the thud of branches hitting together, hitting the ground, and I knew he had come undone. When I squinted again, the figure was gone.

I found my father sitting on a fallen tree trunk back along the trail, smoking a cigarette. "Hey," he said when he saw me coming, "did you find anything?"

"No," I said, "let's go home."

He must have seen something in my eyes, because he asked, "Are you sure?"

"I'm sure," I said.

The snow fell during our journey home and seemed to continue falling all winter long.

Now, twenty-one years married with two crewcut boys of my own, I went back to the old neighborhood last week. The woods and even the school have been obliterated, replaced by new developments with streets named for the things they banished—Crow Lane, Deer Street, Gold Creek Road. My father still lives in the same house by himself. My mother passed away some years back. My baby sister is married with two boys of her own and lives upstate. The old man has something growing on his kidney, and he has lost far too much weight, his once huge arms having shrunk to the width of branches. He sat at the kitchen table, the racing form in front of him. I tried to convince him to quit working, but he shook his head and said, "Boring."

"How long do you think you can keep going to the shop?" I asked him.

"How about until the last second," he said.

"How's the health?" I asked.

"Soon I'll be food for the worms," he said, laughing.

"How do you really feel about that?" I asked.

He shrugged. "All part of the game," he said. "I thought when things got bad enough I would build a coffin and sleep in it. That way, when I die, you can just nail the lid on and bury me in the backyard."

Later, when we were watching the Giants on TV and I had had a few beers, I asked him if he remembered that time in the woods.

He closed his eyes and lit a cigarette as though it would help his memory. "Oh, yeah, I think I remember that," he said.

I had never asked him before. "Was that you down there in those trees?"

He took a drag and slowly turned his head and stared hard, without a smile, directly into my eyes. "I don't know what the hell you're talking about," he said and exhaled a long, blue-gray stream of life.

TRACINA JACKSON-ADAMS

Seven Pairs of Iron Shoes

Tracina Jackson-Adams lives, she says, in the Snow Belt and rides big horses. Her fiction and poetry have appeared in Strange Horizons, Weird Tales, Speculon, Icarus Ascending, The Magazine of Speculative Poetry, The Modern Art Cave, *and other journals. "Seven Paris of Iron Shoes" is based on the fairy tale "East of the Sun, West of the Moon," in which the heroine must travel in search of her lover (the victim of a malign spell) while wearing out seven pairs of iron shoes in the process. Jackson-Adams's insightful exploration of this story comes from the March/April edition of* Star*Line.

—*T. W.*

The first pair of shoes I wore out
was for your forgiveness. Racked with guilt,
I pursued you with single intent,
barely ate or slept, accepted the heat,
the cold, the wet misery and stumbling weariness
as my due. I had failed you. It was only just.

Throughout the second pair, I hated you.
I followed you only because I forgot I could stop.

Many places looked familiar by the third pair,
and I found I knew the coming weather by the taste
of the wind. I was no longer afraid of snakes,
and I placed my feet with care
so as not to trample small things. By the fourth,
I moved silently and did not realize it.

From then on, I roamed for wonder alone,
and slipped through the years like a wolf
through tall grass. I had long since stopped counting
when I heard stories of a land east
of the sun and west of the moon,
and I thought, *There's one place I haven't walked to yet.*

So here we stand, face to face at last,
both of us older, and both of us changed.
I look at you across the distance
of seven pairs of iron shoes,
and I am glad I found you not one moment sooner,

for iron, they say, will break enchantments,
and I have no illusions about us now.
Now my sight is true, and now
is the moment when I can choose,
as I could not have chosen before,
whether to offer you my hand, or kiss you once,
for memory's sake, and walk on.

KAREN JOY FOWLER

What I Didn't See

Karen Joy Fowler is the author of the acclaimed novels Sarah Canary, The Sweetheart Season, *and* Sister Noon. *Her short stories have been published in numerous magazines and anthologies (including previous volumes of* The Year's Best Fantasy and Horror), *and she has published two story collections:* Artificial Things *and* Black Glass. *Fowler also teaches writing and is one of the founders of the James Tiptree, Jr. Awards for works of speculative fiction exploring issues of gender. She lives in Davis, California.*

"What I Didn't See" is a provocative work of interstitial fiction, resting between the borders of several genres: fantasy, horror, mystery, historical fiction, adventure fiction, and feminist mainstream fiction—with a nod to science fiction (in that the story forms a literary dialogue with the famous Tiptree SF story "The Women Men Don't See"). "What I Didn't See" first appeared in the July 10 edition of SCI FICTION, an on-line journal. It's a powerful, controversial tale, and easily one of the very best of the year.

—T. W.

I saw Archibald Murray's obituary in the *Tribune* a couple of days ago. It was a long notice, because of all those furbelows he had after his name, and dredged up that old business of ours, which can't have pleased his children. I, myself, have never spoken up before, as I've always felt that nothing I saw sheds any light, but now I'm the last of us. Even Wilmet is gone, though I always picture him such a boy. And there is something to be said for having the last word, which I am surely having.

I still go to the jungle sometimes when I sleep. The sound of the clock turns to a million insects all chewing at once, water dripping onto leaves, the hum inside your head when you run a fever. Sooner or later Eddie comes, in his silly hat and boots up to his knees. He puts his arms around me in the way he did when he meant business and I wake up too hot, too old, and all alone.

You're never alone in the jungle. You can't see through the twist of roots and leaves and vines, the streakish, tricky light, but you've always got a sense of being seen. You make too much noise when you walk.

At the same time, you understand that you don't matter. You're small and stuck on the ground. The ghosts of paths weren't made for you. If you get bitten by a snake, it's your own damn fault, not the snake's, and if someone doesn't drag you out you'll turn to mulch just like anything else would and show up next as mold or moss, ferns, leeches, ants, millipedes, butterflies, beetles. The jungle is a jammed-alive place, which means that something is always dying there.

Eddie had this idea once that defects of character could be treated with doses of landscape: the ocean for the histrionic, mountains for the domineering, and so forth. I forget the desert, but the jungle was the place to send the self-centered. We seven went into the jungle with guns in our hands and love in our hearts. I say so now when there is no one left to contradict me.

Archer organized us. He was working at the time for the Louisville Museum of Natural History and he had a stipend from Collections for skins and bones. The rest of us were amateur enthusiasts and paid our own way just for the adventure. Archer asked Eddie (arachnids) to go along and Russell MacNamara (chimps), and Trenton Cox (butterflies), who couldn't or wouldn't, and Wilmet Siebert (big game), and Merion Cowper (tropical medicine), and also Merion's wife, only he turned out to be between wives by the time we left, so he was the one who brought Beverly Kriss.

I came with Eddie to help with his nets, pooters, and kill jars. I was never the sort to scream over bugs, but if I had been, twenty-eight years of marriage to Eddie would have cured me. The more legs a creature had, the better Eddie thought of it. Up to a point. Up to eight.

In fact Archer was anxious there be some women and had specially invited me, though Eddie didn't tell me so. This was smart; I would have suspected I was along to do the dishes (though of course there were the natives for this) and for nursing the sick, which we did end up at a bit, Beverly and I, when the matter was too small or too nasty for Merion. I might not have come at all if I'd known I was wanted. As it was, I learned to bake a passable bread on campfire coals with a native beer for yeast, but it was my own choice to do so and I ate as much of the bread myself as I wished.

I pass over the various boats on which we sailed, though these trips were not without incident. Wilmet turned out to have a nervous stomach; it started to trouble him on the ocean and then stuck around when we hit dry land again. Russell was a drinker, and not the good sort, unlucky and suspicious, a man who thought he loved a game of cards, but should have never been allowed to play. Beverly was a modern girl in 1928 and could chew gum, smoke, and wipe the lipstick off her mouth and onto yours all at the same time. She and Merion were frisky for Archer's taste and he tried to shift this off onto me, saying I was being made uncomfortable, when I didn't care one way or the other. I worried that it would be a pattern and every time one of the men was tired on the trail they'd say we had to stop on my account. I told Eddie right away I wouldn't like it if this was to happen. So by the time we were geared up and walking in, we already thought we knew each other pretty well and we didn't entirely like what we knew. Still, I guessed we'd get along fine when there was more to occupy us. Even during those long days it took to reach the mountains—the endless trains, motor cars, donkeys, mules, and finally our very own feet—things went smoothly enough.

By the time we reached the Lulenga Mission, we'd seen a fair bit of Africa—low and high, hot and cold, black and white. I've learned some things in the years since, so there's a strong temptation now to pretend that I felt the things I should have felt, knew the things I might have known. The truth is otherwise. My attitudes toward the natives, in particular, were not what they might have been. The men who helped us interested me little and impressed me not at all. Many of them had their teeth filed and were only ten years or so from cannibalism, or so we were informed. No one, ourselves included, was clean, but Beverly and I would have tried, only we couldn't bathe without the nuisance of being spied on. Whether this was to see if we looked good or only good to eat, I did not wish to know.

The fathers at the mission told us that slaves used to be led through the villages in ropes so that people could draw on their bodies the cuts of meat they were buying before the slaves were butchered, and with that my mind was set. I never did acknowledge any beauty or kindness in the people we met, though Eddie saw much of both.

We spent three nights in Lulenga, which gave us each a bed, good food, and a chance to wash our hair and clothes in some privacy. Beverly and I shared a room, there not being sufficient number for her to have her own. She was quarreling with Merion at the time though I forget about what. They were a tempest, those two, always shouting, sulking, and then turning on the heat again. A tiresome sport for spectators, but surely invigorating for the players. So Eddie was bunked up with Russell, which put me out, because I liked to wake up with him.

We were joined at dinner the first night by a Belgian administrator who treated us to real wine and whose name I no longer remember though I can picture him yet—a bald, hefty man in his sixties with a white beard. I recall how he joked that his hair had migrated from his head to his chin and then settled in where the food was plentiful.

Eddie was in high spirits and talking more than usual. The spiders in Africa are exhilaratingly aggressive. Many of them have fangs and nocturnal habits. We'd already shipped home dozens of button spiders with red hourglasses on their backs, and some beautiful golden violin spiders with long delicate legs and dark chevrons underneath. But that evening Eddie was most excited about a small jumping spider, which seemed not to spin her own web, but to lurk instead in the web of another. She had no beautiful markings; when he'd first seen one, he'd thought she was a bit of dirt blown into the silken strands. Then she grew legs and, as we watched, stalked and killed the web's owner and all with a startling cunning.

"Working together, a thousand spiders can tie up a lion," the Belgian told us. Apparently it was a local saying. "But then they don't work together, do they? The blacks haven't noticed. Science is observation and Africa produces no scientists."

In those days all gorilla hunts began at Lulenga, so it took no great discernment to guess that the rest of our party was not after spiders. The Belgian told us that only six weeks past, a troupe of gorilla males had attacked a tribal village. The food stores had been broken into and a woman carried off. Her bracelets were found the next day, but she'd not yet returned and the Belgian feared she never would. It was such a sustained siege that the whole village had to be abandoned.

"The seizure of the woman I dismiss as superstition and exaggeration," Archer said. He had a formal way of speaking; you'd never guess he was from Kentucky. Not so grand to look at—inch-thick glasses that made his eyes pop, unkempt hair, filthy shirt cuffs. He poured more of the Belgian's wine around, and I recall his being especially generous to his own glass. Isn't it funny, the things you remember? "But the rest of your story interests me. If any gorilla was taken I'd pay for the skin, assuming it wasn't spoiled in the peeling."

The Belgian said he would inquire. And then he persisted with his main point, very serious and deliberate. "As to the woman, I've heard these tales too often to discard them so quickly as you. I've heard of native women subjected to degradations far worse than death. May I ask you as a favor then, in deference to my greater experience and longer time here, to leave your women at the mission when you go gorilla hunting?"

It was courteously done and obviously cost Archer to refuse. Yet he did, saying to my astonishment that it would defeat his whole purpose to leave me and Beverly behind. He then gave the Belgian his own thinking, which we seven had already heard over several repetitions—that gorillas were harmless and gentle, if oversized and overmuscled. Sweet-natured vegetarians. He based this entirely on the wear on their teeth; he'd read a paper on it from some university in London.

Archer then characterized the famous Du Chaillu description—glaring eyes, yellow incisors, hellish dream creatures—as a slick and dangerous form of self aggrandizement. It was an account tailored to bring big game hunters on the run and so had to be quickly countered for the gorillas' own protection. Archer was out to prove Du Chaillu wrong and he needed me and Beverly to help. "If one of the girls should bring down a large male," he said, "it will seem as exciting as shooting a cow. No man will cross a continent merely to do something a pair of girls has already done."

He never did ask us, because that wasn't his way. He just raised it as our Christian duty and then left us to worry it over in our minds.

Of course we were all carrying rifles. Eddie and I had practiced on bottles and such in preparation for the trip. On the way over I'd gotten pretty good at clay pigeons off the deck of our ship. But I wasn't eager to kill a gentle vegetarian—a nightmare from hell would have suited me a good deal better (it scared me a great deal more). Beverly too, I'm guessing.

Not that she said anything about it that night. Wilmet, our youngest at twenty-five years and also shortest by a whole head—blond hair, pink cheeks, and little rat's eyes—had been lugging a tin of British biscuits about the whole trip and finishing every dinner by eating one while we watched. He was always explaining why they couldn't be shared when no one was asking. They kept his stomach settled; he couldn't afford to run out and so on; his very life might depend on them if he were sick and nothing else would stay down and so forth. We wouldn't have noticed if he hadn't persisted in bringing it up.

But suddenly he and Beverly had their heads close together, whispering, and he was giving her one of his precious biscuits. She took it without so much as a glance at Merion, even when he leaned in to say he'd like one, too. Wilmet answered that there were too few to share with everyone so Merion upset a water glass into the tin and spoiled all the biscuits that remained. Wilmet left the table and didn't return and the subject of the all-girl gorilla hunt passed by in the unpleasantness.

That night I woke under the gauze of the mosquito net in such a heat I thought I had malaria. Merion had given us all quinine and I meant to take it regularly, but I didn't always remember. There are worse fevers in the jungle, especially if you've been collecting spiders, so it was cheerful of me to fix on malaria. My skin was burning from the inside out, especially my hands and feet, and I was sweating like butter on a hot day. I thought to wake Beverly, but by the time I stood up the fit had already passed and anyway her bed was empty.

In the morning she was back. I planned to talk to her then, get her thoughts on gorilla hunting, but I woke early and she slept late.

I breakfasted alone and went for a stroll around the Mission grounds. It was cool with little noise beyond the wind and birds. To the west, a dark trio of mountains, two of which smoked. Furrowed fields below me, banana plantations, and trellises of roses, curving into archways that led to the church. How often we grow a garden around our houses of worship. We march ourselves through Eden to get to God.

Merion joined me in the graveyard where I'd just counted three deaths by lion, British names all. I was thinking how outlandish it was, how sadly unlikely that all the prams and nannies and public schools should come to this, and even the bodies pinned under stones so hyenas wouldn't come for them. I was hoping for a more modern sort of death myself, a death at home, a death from American causes, when Merion cleared his throat behind me.

He didn't look like my idea of a doctor, but I believe he was a good one. Well-paid, that's for sure and certain. As to appearances, he reminded me of the villain in some Lillian Gish film, meaty and needing a shave, but handsome enough when cleaned up. He swung his arms when he walked so he took up more space than he needed. There was something to this confidence I admired, though it irritated me on principle. I often liked him least of all and I'm betting he was sharp enough to know it. "I trust you slept well," he said. He looked at me slant-wise, looked away again. I trust you slept well. I trust you were in no way disturbed by Beverly sneaking out to meet me in the middle of the night.

Or maybe—I trust Beverly didn't sneak out last night.

Or maybe just I trust you slept well. It wasn't a question, which saved me the nuisance of figuring the answer.

"So," he said next, "what do you think of this gorilla scheme of Archer's?" and then gave me no time to respond. "The fathers tell me a party from Manchester went up just last month and brought back seventeen. Four of them youngsters—lovely little family group for the British museum. I only hope they left us a few." And then, lowering his voice, "I'm glad for the chance to discuss things with you privately."

There turned out to be a detail to the Belgian's story judged too delicate for the dinnertable, but Merion, being a doctor and maybe more of a man's man than Archer, a man who could be appealed to on behalf of women, had heard it. The woman carried away from the village had been menstruating. This at least the Belgian hoped, that we'd not to go up the mountain with our female affliction in full flower.

And because he was a doctor I told Merion straight out that I'd been light and occasional; I credited this to the upset of travel. I thought to set his mind at ease, but I should have guessed I wasn't his first concern.

"Beverly's too headstrong to listen to me," he said. "Too young and reckless. She'll take her cue from you. A solid, sensible, mature woman like you could rein her in a bit. For her own good."

A woman unlikely to inflame the passions of jungle apes was what I heard. Even in my prime I'd never been the sort of woman poems are written about, but this seemed to place me low indeed. An hour later I saw the humor in it, and Eddie surely laughed at me quickly enough when I confessed it, but at the time I was sincerely insulted. How sensible, how mature was that?

I was further provoked by the way he expected me to give in. Archer was certain I'd agree to save the gorillas and Merion was certain I'd agree to save Beverly. I had a moment's outrage over these men who planned to run me by appealing to what they imagined was my weakness.

Merion more than Archer. How smug he was, and how I detested his calm acceptance of every advantage that came to him, as if it were no more than his due. No white woman in all the world had seen the wild gorillas yet—we were to be the first—but I was to step aside from it just because he asked me.

"I haven't walked all this way to miss out on the gorillas," I told him, as politely as I could. "The only question is whether I'm looking or shooting at them." And then I left him, because my own feelings were no credit to me and I didn't mean to have them anymore. I went to look for Eddie and spend the rest of the day emptying kill jars, pinning and labeling the occupants.

The next morning Beverly announced, in deference to Merion's wishes, that she'd be staying behind at the mission when we went on. Quick as could be, Wilmet said his stomach was in such an uproar that he would stay behind as well. This took us all by surprise as he was the only real hunter among us. And it put Merion in an awful bind—we'd more likely need a doctor on the mountain than at the mission, but I guessed he'd sooner see Beverly taken by gorillas than by Wilmet. He fussed and sweated over a bunch of details that didn't matter to anyone and all the while the day passed in secret conferences—Merion with Archer, Archer with Beverly, Russell with Wilmet, Eddie with Beverly. By dinnertime Beverly said she'd changed her mind and Wilmet had undergone a wonderful recovery. When we left next morning we were at full complement, but pretty tightly strung.

It took almost two hundred porters to get our little band of seven up Mount Mikeno. It was a hard track with no path, hoisting ourselves over roots, cutting and crawling our way through tightly woven bamboo. There were long slides of mud on which it was impossible to get a grip. And always sharp uphill. My heart and my lungs worked as hard or harder than my legs and though it wasn't hot I had to wipe my face and neck continually. As the altitude rose I gasped for breath like a fish in a net.

We women were placed in the middle of the pack with gun-bearers both ahead and behind. I slid back many times and had to be caught and set upright again. Eddie was in a torment over the webs we walked through with no pause as to architect and Russell over the bearers who, he guaranteed, would bolt with our guns at the first sign of danger. But we wouldn't make camp if we stopped for spiders and couldn't stay the course without our hands free. Soon Beverly sang out for a gorilla to come and carry her the rest of the way.

Then we were all too winded and climbed for hours without speaking, breaking whenever we came suddenly into the sun, sustaining ourselves with chocolate and crackers.

Still our mood was excellent. We saw elephant tracks, large, sunken bowls in the mud, half-filled with water. We saw glades of wild carrots and an extravagance of pink and purple orchids. Grasses in greens so delicate they seemed to be melting. I revised my notions of Eden, leaving the roses behind and choosing instead these remote forests where the gorillas lived—foggy rains, the crooked hagenia trees strung with vines, golden mosses, silver lichen; the rattle and buzz of flies and beetles; the smell of catnip as we stepped into it.

At last we stopped. Our porters set up which gave us a chance to rest. My feet were swollen and my knees stiffening, but I had a great appetite for dinner and a great weariness for bed; I was asleep before sundown. And then I was awake again. The temperature, which had been pleasant all day, plunged. Eddie and I wrapped ourselves in coats and sweaters and each other. He worried about our porters, who didn't have the blankets we had, although they were free to keep a fire up as high as they liked. At daybreak, they came complaining to Archer. He raised their pay a dime apiece since they had surely suffered during the night, but almost fifty of them left us anyway.

We spent that morning sitting around the camp, nursing our blisters and scrapes, some of us looking for spiders, some of us practicing our marksmanship. There was a stream about five minutes walk away with a pool where Beverly and I dropped our feet. No mosquitoes, no sweat bees, no flies, and that alone made it paradise. But no sooner did I have this thought and a wave of malarial heat came on me, drenching the back of my shirt.

When I came to myself again, Beverly was in the middle of something and I hadn't heard the beginning. She might have told me Merion's former wife had been unfaithful to him. Later this seemed like something I'd once been told, but maybe only because it made sense. "Now he seems to think the apes will leave me alone if only I don't go tempting them," she said. "Lord!"

"He says they're drawn to menstrual blood."

"Then I've got no problem. Anyway Russell says that Burunga says we'll never see them, dressed as we're dressed. Our clothes make too much noise when we walk. He told Russell we must hunt them naked. I haven't passed that on to Merion yet. I'm saving it for a special occasion."

I had no idea who Burunga was. Not the cook and not our chief guide, which were the only names I'd bothered with. I was, at least (and I do see now, how very least it is) embarrassed to learn that Beverly had done otherwise. "Are you planning to shoot an ape?" I asked. It came over me all of sudden that I wanted a particular answer, but I couldn't unearth what answer that was.

"I'm not really a killer," she said. "More a sweet-natured vegetarian. Of the meat-eating variety. But Archer says he'll put my picture up in the museum. You know the sort of thing—rifle on shoulder, foot on body, eyes to the horizon. Wouldn't that be something to take the kiddies to?"

Eddie and I had no kiddies; Beverly might have realized it was a sore spot. And Archer had made no such representations to me. She sat in a spill of sunlight. Her hair was short and heavy and fell in a neat cap over her ears. Brown until the sun made it golden. She wasn't a pretty woman so much as she just drew your eye and kept it. "Merion keeps on about how he paid my way here. Like he hasn't gotten his money's worth." She kicked her feet and water beaded up on her bare legs. "You're so lucky. Eddie's the best."

Which he was, and any woman could see it. I never met a better man than my Eddie and in our whole forty-three years together there were only three times I wished I hadn't married him. I say this now, because we're coming up on one of those times. I wouldn't want someone thinking less of Eddie because of anything I said.

"You're still in love with him, aren't you?" Beverly asked. "After so many years of marriage."

I admitted as much.

Beverly shook her golden head. "Then you'd best keep with him," she told me.

Or did she? What did she say to me? I've been over the conversation so many times I no longer remember it at all.

In contrast, this next bit is perfectly clear. Beverly said she was tired and went to her tent to lie down. I found the men playing bridge, taking turns at watching. I was bullied into playing, because Russell didn't like his cards and thought to change his luck by putting some empty space between hands. So it was me and Wilmet opposite Eddie and Russell, with Merion and Archer in the vicinity, smoking and looking on. On the other side of the tents the laughter of our porters.

I would have liked to team with Eddie, but Russell said bridge was too dangerous a game when husbands and wives partnered up and there was a ready access to guns. He was joking, of course, but you couldn't have told by his face.

While we played Russell talked about chimpanzees and how they ran their lives. Back in those days no one had looked at chimps yet so it was all only guesswork. Topped by guessing that gorillas would be pretty much the same. There was a natural order to things, Russell said, and you could reason it out; it was simple Darwinism.

I didn't think you could reason out spiders; I didn't buy that you could reason out chimps. So I didn't listen. I played my cards and every so often a word would fall in. Male this, male that. Blah, blah, dominance. Survival of the fittest, blah, blah. Natural selection, nature red in tooth and claw. Blah and blah. There was an argument then as to whether by simple Darwinism we could expect a social arrangement of monogamous married couples or whether the males would all have harems. There were points to be made either way and I didn't care for any of those points.

Wilmet opened with one heart and soon we were up to three. I mentioned how Beverly had said she'd get her picture in the Louisville Museum if she killed an ape. "It's not entirely my decision," Archer said. "But, yes, part of my plan is that there will be pictures. And interviews. Possibly in magazines, certainly in the museum. The whole object is that people be told." And this began a discussion over whether, for the purposes of saving gorilla lives, it would work best if Beverly was to kill one or if it should be me. There was some general concern that the sight of Beverly in a pith helmet might be, somehow, stirring, whereas if I were the one, it wouldn't be cute in the least. If Archer really wished to put people off gorilla-hunting, then, the men agreed, I was his girl. Of course it was not as bald as that, but that was the gist.

Wilmet lost a trick he'd hoped to finesse. We were going down and I suddenly saw that he'd opened with only four hearts, which, though they were pretty enough, an ace and a king included, was a witless thing to do. I still think so.

"I expected more support," he said to me, "when you took us to two," as if it were my fault.

"Length is strength," I said right back and then I burst into tears, because he was so short it was an awful thing to say. It took me more by surprise than anyone and most surprising of all, I didn't seem to care about the crying. I got up from the table and walked off. I could hear Eddie apologizing behind me as if I was the one who'd opened with four hearts. "Change of life," I heard him saying. It was so like Eddie to know what was happening to me even before I did.

It was so unlike him to apologize for me. At that moment I hated him with all the rest. I went to our tent and fetched some water and my rifle. We weren't any of us to go into the jungle alone so no one imagined this was what I was doing.

The sky had begun to cloud up and soon the weather was colder. There was no clear track to follow, only antelope trails. Of course I got lost. I had thought to take every possible turn to the right and then reverse this coming back, but the plan didn't suit the landscape nor achieve the end desired. I had a whistle, but was angry enough not to use it. I counted on Eddie to find me eventually as he always did.

I believe I walked for more than four hours. Twice it rained, intensifying all the green smells of the jungle. Occasionally the sun was out and the mosses and leaves overlaid with silvered water. I saw a cat print that made me move my rifle off of safe to ready and then often had to set it aside as the track took me over roots and under hollow trees. The path was unstable and sometimes slid out from under me.

Once I put my hand on a spider's web. It was a domed web over an orb, intricate and a beautiful pale yellow in color. I never touched a silk so strong. The spider was big and black with yellow spots at the undersides of her legs and, judging by the corpses, she carried all her victims to the web's center before wrapping them. I would have brought her back, but I had nothing to keep her in. It seemed a betrayal of Eddie to let her be, but that sort of evened our score.

Next thing I put my hand on was a soft looking leaf. I pulled it away full of nettles.

Although the way back to camp was clearly downhill, I began to go up. I thought to find a vista, see the mountains, orient myself. I was less angry by now and suffered more from the climbing as a result. The rain began again and I picked out a sheltered spot to sit and tend my stinging hand. I should have been cold and frightened, but I wasn't either. The pain in my hand was subsiding. The jungle was beautiful and the sound of rain a lullaby. I remember wishing that this was where I belonged, that I lived here. Then the heat came on me so hard I couldn't wish at all.

A noise brought me out of it—a crashing in the bamboo. Turning, I saw the movement of leaves and the backside of something rather like a large black bear. A gorilla has a strange way of walking—on the hind feet and the knuckles, but with arms so long their backs are hardly bent. I had one clear look and then the creature was gone. But I could still hear it and I was determined to see it again.

I knew I'd never have another chance; even if we did see one later the men would take it over. I was still too hot. My shirt was drenched from sweat and rain; my pants, too, and making a noise whenever I bent my knees. So I removed everything and put back only my socks and boots. I left the rest of my clothes folded on the spot where I'd been sitting, picked up my rifle, and went into the bamboo.

Around a rock, under a log, over a root, behind a tree was the prettiest open meadow you'd ever hope to see. Three gorillas were in it, one male, two female. It might have been a harem. It might have been a family—a father, mother and daughter. The sun came out. One female combed the other with her hands, the two of them blinking in the sun. The male was seated in a patch of wild carrots, pulling and eating them with no particular ardor. I could see his profile and the gray in his fur. He twitched his fingers a bit, like a man listening to music. There were flowers—pink and white—in concentric circles where some pond had been and now wasn't. One lone tree. I stood and looked for a good long time.

Then I raised the barrel of my gun. The movement brought the eyes of the male to me. He stood. He was bigger than I could ever have imagined. In the leather of his face I saw surprise, curiosity, caution. Something else, too. Something so human it made me feel like an old woman with no clothes on. I might have shot him just for that, but I knew it wasn't right—to kill him merely because he was more human than I anticipated. He thumped his chest, a rhythmic beat that made the women look to him. He showed me his teeth. Then he turned and took the women away.

I watched it all through the sight of my gun. I might have hit him several times—spared the women, freed the women. But I couldn't see that they wanted freeing and Eddie had told me never to shoot a gun angry. The gorillas faded from the meadow. I was cold then and I went for my clothes.

Russell had beaten me to them. He stood with two of our guides, staring down at my neatly folded pants. Nothing for it but to walk up beside him and pick them up, shake them for ants, put them on. He turned his back as I dressed and he couldn't manage a word. I was even more embarrassed. "Eddie must be frantic," I said to break the awkwardness.

"All of us, completely beside ourselves. Did you find any sign of her?"

Which was how I learned that Beverly had disappeared.

We were closer to camp than I'd feared if farther than I'd hoped. While we walked I did my best to recount my final conversation with Beverly to Russell.

I was, apparently, the last to have seen her. The card game had broken up soon after I left and the men gone their separate ways. A couple of hours later, Merion began looking for Beverly who was no longer in her tent. No one was alarmed, at first, but by now they were.

I was made to repeat everything she'd said again and again and questioned over it, too, though there was nothing useful in it and soon I began to feel I'd made up every word. Archer asked our guides to look over the ground about the pool and around her tent. He had some cowboy scene in his mind, I suppose, the primitive who can read a broken branch, a footprint, a bit of fur and piece it all together. Our guides looked with great seriousness, but found nothing. We searched and called and sent up signaling shots until night came over us.

"She was taken by the gorillas," Merion told us. "Just as I said she'd be." I tried to read his face in the red of the firelight, but couldn't. Nor catch his tone of voice.

"No prints," our chief guide repeated. "No sign."

That night our cook refused to make us dinner. The natives were talking a great deal amongst themselves, very quiet. To us they said as little as possible. Archer demanded an explanation, but got nothing but dodge and evasion.

"They're scared," Eddie said, but I didn't see this.

A night even more bitter than the last and Beverly not dressed for it. In the morning the porters came to Archer to say they were going back. No measure of arguing or threatening or bribing changed their minds. We could come or stay as we chose; it was clearly of no moment to them. I, of course, was given no choice, but was sent back to the mission with the rest of the gear excepting what the men kept behind.

At Lulenga one of the porters tried to speak with me. He had no English and I followed none of it except Beverly's name. I told him to wait while I fetched one of the fathers to translate, but he misunderstood or else he refused. When we returned he was gone and I never did see him again.

The men stayed eight more days on Mount Mikeno and never found so much as a bracelet.

Because I'm a woman I wasn't there for the parts you want most to hear. The waiting and the not-knowing were, in my view of things, as hard or harder than the searching, but you don't make stories out of that. Something happened to Beverly, but I can't tell you what. Something happened on the mountain after I left, something that brought Eddie back to me so altered in spirit I felt I hardly knew him, but I wasn't there to see what it was. Eddie and I departed Africa immediately and not in the company of the other men in our party. We didn't even pack up all our spiders.

For months after, I wished to talk about Beverly, to put together this possibility and that possibility and settle on something I could live with. I felt the need most strongly at night. But Eddie couldn't hear her name. He'd sunk so deep into himself, he rarely looked out. He stopped sleeping and wept from time to time and these were things he did his best to hide from me. I tried to talk to him about it, I tried to be patient and loving, I tried to be kind. I failed in all these things.

A year, two more passed, and he began to resemble himself again, but never in full. My full, true Eddie never did come back from the jungle.

Then one day, at breakfast, with nothing particular to prompt it, he told me there'd been a massacre. That after I left for Lulenga the men had spent the days hunting and killing gorillas. He didn't describe it to me at all, yet it sprang bright and terrible into my mind, my own little family group lying in their blood in the meadow.

Forty or more, Eddie said. Probably more. Over several days. Babies, too. They couldn't even bring the bodies back; it looked so bad to be collecting when Beverly was gone. They'd slaughtered the gorillas as if they were cows.

Eddie was dressed in his old plaid robe, his gray hair in uncombed bunches, crying into his fried eggs. I wasn't talking, but he put his hands over his ears in case I did. He was shaking all over from weeping, his head trembling on his neck. "It felt like murder," he said. "Just exactly like murder."

I took his hands down from his head and held on hard. "I expect it was mostly Merion."

"No," he said. "It was mostly me."

At first, Eddie told me, Merion was certain the gorillas had taken Beverly. But later, he began to comment on the strange behavior of the porters. How they wouldn't talk to us, but whispered to each other. How they left so quickly. "I was afraid," Eddie told me. "So upset about Beverly and then terribly afraid. Russell and Merion, they were so angry I could smell it. I thought at any moment one of them would say something that couldn't be unsaid, something that would get to the Belgians. And then I wouldn't be able to stop it anymore. So I kept us stuck on the gorillas. I kept us going after them. I kept us angry until we had killed so very many and were all so ashamed, there would be no way to turn and accuse someone new."

I still didn't quite understand. "Do you think one of the porters killed Beverly?" It was a possibility that had occurred to me, too; I admit it.

"No," said Eddie. "That's my point. But you saw how the blacks were treated back at Lulenga. You saw the chains and the beatings. I couldn't let them be suspected." His voice was so clogged I could hardly make out the words. "I need you to tell me I did the right thing."

So I told him. I told him he was the best man I ever knew. "Thank you," he said. And with that he shook off my hands, dried his eyes, and left the table.

That night I tried to talk to him again. I tried to say that there was nothing he could do that I wouldn't forgive. "You've always been too easy on me," he answered. And the next time I brought it up, "If you love me, we'll never talk about this again."

Eddie died three years later without another word on the subject passing between us. In the end, to be honest, I suppose I found that silence rather unforgivable. His death even more so. I have never liked being alone.

As every day I more surely am; it's the blessing of a long life. Just me left now, the first white woman to see the wild gorillas and the one who saw nothing else—not the chains, not the beatings, not the massacre. I can't help worrying over it all again, now I know Archer's dead and only me to tell it, though no way of telling puts it to rest.

Since my eyes went, a girl comes to read to me twice a week. For the longest time I wanted nothing to do with gorillas, but now I have her scouting out articles as we're finally starting to really see how they live. The thinking still seems to be harems, but with the females slipping off from time to time to be with whomever they wish.

And what I notice most in the articles is not the apes. My attention is caught instead by these young women who'd sooner live in the jungle with the chimpanzees or the orangutans or the great mountain gorillas. These women who freely choose it—the Goodalls and the Galdikas and the Fosseys. And I think to myself how there is nothing new under the sun, and maybe all those women carried off by gorillas in those old stories, maybe they all freely chose it.

When I am tired and have thought too much about it all, Beverly's last words come back to me. Mostly I put them straight out of my head, think about anything else. Who remembers what she said? Who knows what she meant?

But there are other times when I let them in. Turn them over. Then they become, not a threat as I originally heard them, but an invitation. On those days I can pretend that she's still there in the jungle, dipping her feet, eating wild carrots, and waiting for me. I can pretend that I'll be joining her whenever I wish and just as soon as I please.

JACKIE BARTLEY

Reading Myth to Kindergartners

Jackie Bartley is currently an adjunct assistant professor at Hope College in Holland, Michigan. Her poems have appeared in a number of journals, including Spoon River Poetry Review, Iron Horse Literary Review, Phoebe, *and* Crab Orchard Review. *Her first full-length collection,* Bloodroot, *was recently published by Mellen Poetry Press. The following poem is reprinted from the Spring 2002 edition of* The Louisville Review.

—*T. W.*

Today I read them the story of Persephone and Hades,
the telling of it brief, a child's version of the tale.
I am beginning to think of each story the way
a doctor thinks of vaccination; part of my task
to see they've had their shots,
these small doses of stunning loss,
seeds of grief planted early so that later,
when their own lives bear down on them,
they will remember these tales,
recall how, on first hearing this one,
they held their breath and sat,
unmoving and absolutely silent in their chairs,
stricken by what the flowers and birds
say to Demeter in her sorrow:
Gone, gone. Persephone
is gone.

PETER DICKINSON

Mermaid Song

Peter Dickinson was born in Zambia, raised in Africa and England, and now lives in the south of England. He is, quite simply, one of the very finest writers in the fantasy field. He has published close to fifty books in a long and distinguished career, winning the Carnegie Medal, the Whitbread Children's Award, the Guardian Fiction Award, the Printz Honor Prize, and many other honors. In addition to his fantasy novels and stories (most of them published for young readers), he is also well known as the author of several superb detective novels. His books include King and Joker, The Changes Trilogy, The Gift, The Blue Hawk, Healer, Giant Cold, Tulku, The Seventh Raven, Eva, *and* A Bone from a Dry Sea. *His most recent novel,* The Ropemaker, *is highly recommended.*

"Mermaid Song" is a deceptively quiet tale, with powerful magic at its core. It comes from Water: Tales of Elemental Spirits, *a first-rate collection of stories for young readers by Dickinson and his wife, writer Robin McKinley.*

—T.W.

Her name was Pitiable Nasmith.

Her grandfather had chosen Pitiable so that she and others should know what she was, he said. All the People had names of that kind. He was Probity Hooke, and his wife was Mercy Hooke. Their daughter had been Obedience Hooke until she had married Simon Nasmith against their will and changed her second name to his. Because of that, the People had cut her off from themselves, and Probity and Mercy had heard no more of her until Simon had come to their door, bringing the newborn baby for them to care for, and told Probity of his daughter's death. He said he was going away and not coming back. Probity had taken the baby from him and closed the door in his face without a word.

He had chosen a first name for the baby because she had neither father nor mother. She was pitiable.

The Hookes lived in a white wooden house on the edge of the town. Their fields lay a little distance off, in two separate odd-shaped patches along the floor of the steep valley, where soil deep enough to cultivate had lodged on the underlying granite. The summers were short, but desperately hot, ending usually in a week of storms, followed by a mellow autumn and then a long, bitter winter, with blizzards and gales. For night after night, lying two miles inland in her cot at the top of the ladder, Pitiable would fall asleep to the sound of waves raging along the outer shore, and wake to the same sound. Between the gales there would be still, clear days with the sun no more than a handsbreadth above the horizon, and its light glittering off mile after mile of thigh-deep snow. Then spring, and thaw and mud and slush and the reek of all the winter's rubbish, rotting at last. Then searing summer again.

It was a hard land to scrape a living off, though there was a good harbor that attracted trade, so some of the People prospered as merchants. Fishermen, and others not of the People, came there too, though many of these later went south and west to kinder, sunnier, richer places. But the People stayed "in the land the Lord has given us," as they used to say. There they had been born, and their ancestors before them, all the way back to the two shiploads who had founded the town. The same names could be read over and over again in their graveyard, Bennetts and Hookes and Warrens and Lyalls and Goodriches, but no Nasmiths, not one.

For eight years Pitiable lived much like any other girl-child of the People. She was clothed and fed, and nursed if she was ill. She went to the People's school, where she was taught to read her Bible, and tales of the persecution of her forebears. The People had few other books, but those they read endlessly, to themselves and to each other. They took pride in their education, narrow though it was, and their speech was grave and formal, as if taken from their books. Twice every Sunday Pitiable would go with her grandparents to their church, to sit still for two hours while the Word was given forth.

As soon as she could walk, she was taught little tasks to do about the house. The People took no pride in possessions or comforts. What mattered to them in this world was cleanliness and decency, every pot scoured, every chair in its place, every garment neatly stitched and saved, and on Sundays the men's belts and boots gleaming with polish, and the women's lace caps and collars starched as white as first-fall snow and as crisp as the frost that binds it. They would dutifully help a neighbor who was in trouble, but they themselves would have to be in desperate need before they asked for aid.

Probity was a steady-working, stern old man whose face never changed, but Mercy was short and plump and kindly. If Probity was out of the house, she used to hum as she worked, usually the plodding, four-square hymn tunes that the People had brought with them across the ocean, but sometimes a strange, slow, wavering air that was hardly a tune at all, difficult to follow or learn, but once learned, difficult to let go of. While Pitiable was still very small, she came to know it as if it had been part of her blood, but she was eight before she discovered what it meant.

The summer before that, Mercy had fallen ill. At first she would not admit it, though her face lost its roundness and became grey and sagging, and sometimes she would gasp and stand still while a shudder of pain ran through her and spent itself. Probity for a while did not notice, and for another while chose not to, but Pitiable found herself doing more and more of her grandmother's tasks while Mercy sat on one of the thin upright chairs and told her what she did not already know. By winter Mercy could not even sit and was forced to lie, and the neighbors had come to see why she no longer came to church, but Probity had sent them away, saying that he and the child could manage between them. Which they did, but Pitiable's days were very long for a child, from well before dawn until hours after dark, keeping the house clean and decent, and seeing to her grandfather's meals and clothes, and nursing her grandmother.

On a Sunday near Christmas (though the People did not keep Christmas, saying it was idolatrous) there was a storm out of the west, driving snow like a million tiny whips, fiery with cold. Still, Probity put on his leather coat and fetched out his staff and snowshoes, and told Pitiable to get ready so that he could drag her to church on the log sled.

"Let her stay," said Mercy. "I am dying, Probity. I may perhaps die while you are gone. May the Lord deal with me as He will, but I am afraid to die alone."

Probity stared at her with his face unchanging, then nodded and tied on his snowshoes and went out into the storm without a word. Mercy watched the door close.

"He had love in him once," she said. "But he buried it the day your mother left us and set the tombstone on it the day she died. Bear with him, Pitiable. Deal with him as best you may. It will not be easy."

"Are you really going to die?" said Pitiable.

"As we all are, when the Lord calls to us."

"To-day? Now?"

"Not to-day, I think. I am better to-day. The pain is almost gone, which is a bad sign. My body has no more messages to send me."

Pitiable knelt by Mercy's cot and put her head on the quilt and wept, while Mercy stroked her shoulders and told her she was glad to be going, because she trusted in God to forgive her the small harms she had done in her life. She told Pitiable to fetch a stool and sit by her and hold her hand.

"I have a story to tell you," she said. "My mother told it to me, and her mother to her, through seven generations since *The Trust in God* was lost. You remember the story of Charity Goodrich, our ancestress, yours and mine?"

Pitiable nodded. Every child among the People, even those who were not directly descended from her, knew about Charity Goodrich. It was almost the only story they knew, outside the ones in the Bible. They were told that the stories other children knew were superstitious nonsense, inventions of the devil, to distract believers from the narrow path to salvation. Two hundred years ago, three small ships had set out to cross the great ocean. They had been given new names before they left, *The Lord is Our Refuge, The Deliver Us from Bondage* and *The Trust in God*. Apart from their crews they carried the People, 287 men, women and children who had determined to leave the country where they were oppressed and imprisoned and burned for their beliefs, and settle in new land where they could worship as they chose. After a dangerous voyage they were in sight of land when a storm separated them. Two ships came safe into the providential bay which was now the harbor of the town, but the third, *The Trust in God*, was driven against the cliffs to the north of it and lost with all hands. All hands but one, that is, for five days later a child was found wandering on the shore, unable to say how she had come there. Her name was Charity Goodrich.

"I am going to tell you how Charity was saved," said Mercy. "But first you must promise me two things. You must remember it so that you can tell it to your daughters when they are old enough to understand. And you must tell it to nobody else, ever. It is a secret. You will see why. Charity Goodrich was my great-grandmother's great-grandmother. There are other descendants of hers among the People, but I have never asked, never even hinted, and nor must you. Do you understand?"

"Yes, and I promise," said Pitiable.

"Good. Now this is the story Charity told. She remembered the storm, and the breaking of the mast, and the shouts of the sailors, and the People gathering on the deck, standing all together and singing to the Lord Who made the sea, while they clutched at ropes and spars and the ship heaved and wallowed and waves swept foaming around their legs. Some of them were washed away, still singing, and then the ship was laid on its side and the deck stood upright and they all went tumbling down into the roaring sea. Charity remembered her hand being torn from her father's grasp, and then a loose sail tangled round her and she remembered nothing more.

"Nothing more, that is, until she woke. A shuddering cold roused her and told her too that she was not dead, but alive. Her clothes were soaked, but she was lying on dry sand. She sat up and looked around. She saw a dim, pale light to one side of her. It was just enough for her to make out the black water that stirred at her feet, and the black rock all around her and over her. Somehow she had been washed up in a small cave whose entrance was beneath the water.

"Beside her was a small sea chest of the sort that the People had used to store their possessions for the voyage. With numbed fingers she opened it and found that it had been well packed, with all its contents wrapped tight in oilskins. There were dry clothes, far too large for her, but she stripped off, spreading out her own clothes to dry on the rocks, and wrapped herself in these others, layer on layer, and nursed her body back to warmth.

"Now she began to wonder what had happened to her and how she had come to this cave. She remembered the sinking of the ship, and herself being tumbled into the sea and tangled in the sail, and remembering that she saw that the sail was lying half out of the water, over against one wall of the cave. So she supposed that some current had washed her in here, and the sea chest too, and the tide had then gone out and left her in air. But why was it not dark? The light came from the other side of the cave, low down, and when she went to look she found that the water washed in along that wall, making as it were an inlet in the waterline, and partway up this was a pool where lay a coiling fish like a great eel, which shone with points of light all along its flanks. It stirred when it saw her and the light grew stronger, and now she saw that it was trapped in that place by a wall of small boulders, piled neatly against one another across the inlet.

"Then she grew afraid, for she could see that the wall had not come there by chance. She searched the cave, looking for a place to hide, but there was none. Only she found that the inlet was formed by a little stream of water, sweet to drink, that ran down the back of the cave. After that she prayed and sang, and then fell asleep, weeping for the mother and father she would never see again.

"When she woke she knew before she opened her eyes that she was not alone. She had heard the whisper of a voice.

"She sat up and looked at the water. Two heads had risen from it. Four eyes were gazing at her. She could not see them well in the faint light, but her heart leaped and her throat hardened. Then one of the heads spoke, in a weak human voice, in a language she did not know, though she understood it to be a question.

" 'Who are you?' she whispered, and they laughed and came further out of the water, so that she could see that they were human-shaped, pale-skinned and dark-haired, wearing no clothes but for what seemed to be collars or ruffs around their necks. She stood and put her palms together and said the Lord's Prayer in her mind while she crept down to the water's edge. As she came, the creatures used their arms to heave themselves up through the shallows. Closer seen, she thought they were children of about her age, until she saw that instead of legs each had a long and shining tail, like that of a fish. This is what Charity Goodrich said she saw, Pitiable. Do you believe her?"

"If you believe her, I do too."

"Then you believe her. Now it came to her that these two were children of the sea-people, and the cave was a place they had found and made their own, as children like to do. They had caught the fish and prisoned it here to give light to the cave, for their own amusement, and in the same way they had found Charity and brought her here, and the chest, floating them in when the tide was high and dragging them onto dry land.

"They fetched the sail and by signs showed her that somehow a pocket of air had been caught in it with her, allowing her to breathe for a little beneath the water. All this and other things Charity learned as the days passed. She could count those days by the coming and going of the tide.

"They had brought food for the shining fish, so she made signs that she wanted to eat and they swam off. She was afraid that they would bring her raw fish, but instead they came with human stores from the wrecked ship. Some were spoiled with salt, but some were in canisters that had kept the water out, wormy bread and dried apples and oatmeal which she mixed with fresh water from the stream at the back of the cave.

"She tried to talk with the sea-children. Their voices were weak, and they could not breathe for long out of the water. What she had thought to be ruffs around their necks were plumy growths with which they seemed to breathe the sea-water, as a fish does with its gills. Their language was strange. She told them her name, but they could not say it, nor she theirs. Instead they sang, not opening their mouths but humming with closed lips. You have often heard me humming the song of the sea-people."

"This one?" said Pitiable, and hummed the slow, wavering tune that she had heard so often. Mercy joined her, and they hummed it together, their voices twining like ripples in water. When they finished, Mercy smiled.

"That is how I used to sing it with my own mother," she said. "And then with yours. It needs two voices, or three. So Charity sang it with the sea-children in their cave, and they hummed the tunes she taught them, *The Old Hundredth* and *Mount Ephraim* and such, so that they should be able to praise their Creator beneath the waves. So as the days went by a kind of friendship grew, and then she saw that they began to be troubled by what they had done. At first, she supposed, she had seemed no more than a kind of toy, or amusement, for them, a thing with which they could do as they chose, like the shining fish. Now they were learning that this was not so.

"They made signs to her, which she did not understand, but supposed them to be trying to comfort her, so she signed to them that she wished to return to her own people, but they in their turn frowned and shook their heads, until she went to the place where the shining fish was trapped and started to take down the wall they had built. They stopped her, angrily, but she pointed to the fish as it sought to escape through the gap she had made, and then at herself, and at the walls that held her, and made swimming motions with her arms, though she could not swim. They looked at each other, more troubled than before, and argued for a while in their own language, the one trying to persuade the other, though she could see that both were afraid. In the end they left her.

"She sat a long while, waiting, until there was a stirring in the water that told her that some large creature was moving below the surface. She backed away as it broke into the air. It was a man, a huge, pale man of the sea-people. If he had had legs to walk upon, he would have stood as tall as two grown men. She could feel the man's anger as he gazed at her, but she said the Lord's Prayer in her mind and with her palms together walked down to the water's edge and stood before him, waiting to see what he would do.

"Still he stared, furious and cold. She thought to herself and closed her lips and started to hum the music the sea-children had taught her, until he put up his hand and stopped her. He spoke a few words of command and left.

"She waited. Twice he came back, bringing stuff from the wreck, spars and canvas and rope, which he then worked on, in and out of the water, making what seemed to be a kind of tent which he held clear of the water and then dragged back in, with air caught inside it, so that it floated high. He then buoyed it down with boulders to drag it under. He took it away and came back and worked on it some more, and then returned, having, she supposed, tried it out and been satisfied. Meanwhile she had gathered up her own clothes and wrapped them tightly in oilskin, and stripped off the ones she was wearing, down to the slip, and tied her bundle to her waist.

"When he was ready, the man, being unwilling himself to come ashore, signalled to her to break down the wall that held the shining fish, which she did, and it swam gladly away. So in utter darkness she walked down into the water, where the man lifted his tent over her and placed her hands upon a spar that he had lashed across it for her to hold and towed her away, with her head still in the air that he had caught within the canvas and her body trailing in the water. She felt the structure jar and scrape as he towed it through the opening and out into the sea. By the time they broke the surface, the air had leaked almost away, but he lifted the tent from her and she looked around and saw that it was night.

"The storm was over, and the sea was smooth, with stars above, and a glimmer of dawn out over the ocean. Charity lay along the sea-man's back with her arms around his shoulders as he swam south and set her down at last in the shallows of a beach. Oyster Beach we call it now.

"She waded ashore, but turned knee-deep in the water to thank him. He cut her short, putting the flat of his hand against his lips and making a fierce sideways gesture with his other hand—so—then pointed at her, still as angry-seeming as when she had first seen him. She put her palms crosswise over her mouth, sealing it shut, trying to say to him: Yes, I will keep silent. She had already known she must. She did not know if any of the People were left alive after the storm, but they were the only folk she knew, and who of them would believe her, and not think she was either mad or else talking profane wickedness? Then she bowed low before him, and when she looked up, he was gone.

"She took off the slip she had worn in the sea and left it at the water's edge, as though the tide had washed it there. Then she dressed herself in her own clothes, dank and mildewy though they were, and walked up the shore. Inland was all dense woods, so she walked along beside them, past Watch Point to Huxholme Bay, where three men met her, coming to look for clams at the low tide.

"So. That is the story of Charity Goodrich. Tomorrow you shall tell it to me, leaving nothing out, so that I can be sure you know it to tell it truly to your own daughters when they are old enough to understand."

Probity sat by Mercy's bed throughout the night she died, holding both her hands in his. They prayed together, and from time to time they spoke of other things, but in voices too soft for Pitiable, in her cot at the top of the ladder, to hear. In the end she slept, and when she came down before dawn to remake the fire, she found Probity still in his clothes, sitting by the fire with his head between his hands, and Mercy stretched out cold on her cot with her Bible on her chest. For two days Probity would not eat or dress or undress or go to bed. He let the Church Elders make the arrangements for the funeral, simply grunting assent to anything that was said to him, but for the ceremony itself he pulled himself together and shaved carefully and polished his belt and boots and dressed in his Sunday suit and stood erect and stern by the graveside with his hand upon Pitiable's shoulder, and then waited with her at the churchyard gate to receive the condolences of the People.

Mercy in her last hours must have spoken to him about their granddaughter, and told him to take comfort in her and give her comfort in return, and this he tried to do. He read the Bible with her in the evenings, and sometimes noticed if she seemed tired and told her to rest. And around Christmas, when all the children of the townspeople were given toys, he whittled a tiny horse and cart for her to set upon the mantelshelf. By day he worked as he always had to see that the two of them were warm and fed, fetching in the stacked logs for the stove, and bringing in more from the frozen woods to make next season's stack, and digging turnips and other roots from the mounds where they were stored, and fetching out grain from the bins and salted meat from the barrels, and mending the tools he would need for next summer's toil, while Pitiable cooked and stitched and cleaned as best she could, the way Mercy had shown her. She was young for such work, and he did not often scold her for her mistakes. So the neighbors, who at first had felt that in Christian duty they must keep an eye upon the pair, decided that all was well and left them alone.

Spring came with the usual mud and mess, followed by the urgent seed-time when the ground dried to a fine soft tilth and had not yet begun to parch. It was then that Probity, after brooding for a while, went to the Elders of the People and asked for their permission to bring his daughter's body up from the town cemetery and bury it beside Mercy's in the graveyard of the People. The Elders did not debate the question long. They were all of one grim mind. Obedience Hooke had cut herself off from the People by marrying the outwarder, Simon Nasmith. When the Lord came again in Glory, he would raise the bodies of His faithful People from their graveyard to eternal life, but Obedience Hooke had by her own act cast herself into damnation and would not be among them.

Probity sowed his crops as usual, but then, as June hardened into its steady, dreary heat, he seemed to lose heart. The leafy summer crops came quick and easy, and there was always a glut of them, but the slow-grown roots and pulses that would be harvested later, and then dried or salted or earthed into clamps, were another matter. He did not hoe them enough, and watered irregularly, so that the plants had no root-depth and half of them wilted or wasted. He neglected, too, to do the rounds of his fences, so that the sheep broke out and he had to search the hills for them, and lost three good ewes.

Pitiable was aware that the stores were barely half-filled, but said nothing. Probity was her grandfather, her only protector, and absolute master in his own house. He did what he chose, and the choice was right because it was his.

September brought a great crop of apples from the two old trees. Mercy had always bottled them into sealed jars, but that was a skill that had to be done just right, and Pitiable did not know how. Probity could well have asked a neighbor to teach her, but he was too proud, so he told her to let them fall and he would make cider of them. Most of the People made a little cider, keeping it for special days, but this year Probity made a lot, using casks he would not now need for storage as he had less to store. He shook himself out of his dull mood and took trouble so that the cider brewed strong and clear. He took to drinking a tankard of it with his supper, and became more cheerful in the evenings.

Winter came, with its iron frosts, and Probity started to drink cider with his dinner, to keep the cold out, he said. And then with his breakfast, to get the blood moving on the icy mornings. By the time the sunrise turned back along the horizon, he was seldom without a tankard near by, from the hour he rose until the hour at which he fell snorting, and still in his day clothes, onto his bed.

He began to beat Pitiable, using his belt, finding some fault and punishing her for it, though both of them knew that that was not the cause. He was hurt to the heart, and sick with his own hurt, and all he could think of was to hurt someone or something else, and doing so himself to hurt himself worse, dulling the pain with new pain. One night Pitiable watched as he took the horse and cart he had made her and broke them into splinters with his strong hands and dropped them into the fire.

Pitiable did not complain or ask anyone for help. She knew that anything that happened to her was a just punishment for her having been born. Her mother and father should never have wed. By doing so they had broken God's law. And then Obedience, Probity's lovely lost daughter, had died giving birth to Pitiable. So Pitiable was both the fruit of her parents' sin and the cause of her mother's death, and of Probity's dreadful hurt. Nothing that was done to her could be undeserved.

On Sunday mornings Probity did not drink. He shaved and dressed with care and took Pitiable to church. They made an impressive pair, the big, gaunt man and the pale and silent child. Neighbors remarked how much they meant to each other, now Mercy was gone. Once a woman asked Pitiable why she wept in church, and Pitiable replied that it was because of her grandmother dying. The woman clucked and said that she was a good little girl—how could she have known that Pitiable had been weeping with the pain of having to sit still on the hard bench after last night's beating?

They came through the winter, barely, scraping out the old and moldy stores from the year before. Probity butchered and salted one of his ewes, saying she was too old for bearing, which was not true. So they did not quite starve.

The mush of spring dried to the blaze of summer, and Probity pulled himself together and drank less and worked in his fields and brought home food and kept his belt around his waist, but he did almost nothing to provide for the coming winter. One noon in the late summer heat wave, Pitiable went out to tell him that his dinner was on the table and found him at the door of his store shed, staring into its emptiness, as if lost in a dream. He started when she spoke and swung on her, and snarled, "The Lord will provide." That evening he undid his belt and beat her for no reason at all.

From then on he was as harsh as he had been last winter, but at the same time strangely possessive. He seemed unable to bear to let her out of his sight. Having no harvest to gather, he took to wandering along the shore, in the manner of the truly poor and shiftless townspeople, looking for scraps of the sea's leavings, driftwood and such, which he might use or sell. Almost at once he was lucky, finding a cask of good sweet raisins, unspoilt, which he sold well in the town. After that he would go almost every day, taking Pitiable with him to help search and carry, but the quiet days of the heat wave brought little to land.

That dense stillness broke, as usual, with a week of storm. There was a proverb in the town, "The hotter burns the sun, the wilder blows the wind," and so it proved that year, with gales that brought down trees and chimneys and stripped roofs and scattered haystacks, while day and night huge rollers thundered against the shore. On the ninth night the storm blew itself out and was followed by a dawn of pearly calm.

Probity was up before sunrise and gulped his breakfast and pulled on his boots and told Pitiable to leave the dishes unwashed and the hearth unlaid.

"The Lord spoke to me in the night," he said. "We must be first down on the shore, for this is the day on which He will provide."

The town was barely stirring as they hurried towards the harbor, and left up Northgate to the beaches. On Home Beach there were men about, seeing to their boats, many of which, though drawn well up above the tide-lines, had been tossed about by the storm, overturned, piled together or washed inland. Probity hurried past, and on over Shag Point to Huxholme Bay, which was steep small shingle. Here they stopped to search. The waves had brought in a mass of new stuff, piles of wrack and driftwood, tangles of half-rotted cording, torn nets, broken casks and crates, as well as sea-things, shells and jellyfish and small squid and so on. Probity had a piece of chalk with which to mark anything he wanted to collect on his way back, but he was not looking for timber or firewood to-day and marked nothing.

Next came Watch Point, both sandy and rocky. Here Pitiable picked out of the sand an ancient leather boot with a spur, which Probity tested with his jackknife to see if it might be silver. It was not, but he put it in his sack and poked around with his staff in the sand, in case it might be part of some buried hoard exposed by the storm, but again it was not.

Beyond Oyster Bay lay the Scaurs, two miles of tilted rocky promontories with inlets between, like the teeth of a broken comb, and beyond them black unscalable cliffs. The Scaurs were the best hunting ground, but slow work, full of crannies and fissures where trove might lodge. If Pitiable had been less sore from last night's beating—lengthy and savage after Probity had been nine days cooped up by the storm—she might have enjoyed the search, the jumping and scrambling, and the bright sea-things that lurked in the countless pools. As it was, she searched numbly, dutifully, her mind filled with the dread of their homecoming, having found nothing. That failure would be made her fault, reason enough for another beating.

She searched the upper half of the beach and Probity the lower. They were about half way to the cliffs, and could already hear the screaming of the tens of thousands of gulls that nested there, when her way was blocked by the next jut of rock, a vertical wall too high for her to climb. She was hesitating to go shoreward or seaward to get past the barrier when she heard a new noise, a quick rush of water followed by a slithering, a mewling cry and a splash. After a short while the sounds were repeated in the same order. And again. And again.

They seemed to come from beyond the barrier to her right, so she turned left, looking for a place where she could climb and peer over without whatever was making them becoming aware of her. She came to a pile of rocks she could scramble up. The top of the barrier was rough but level. Crouching, she crept towards the sea and discovered a large, deep pool, formed by the main rock splitting apart and then becoming blocked at the seaward end by an immense slab, trapping into the cleft any wave that might be thrown that far up the shore. The seal at the top end wasn't perfect, and enough water had drained away for the surface to be several feet down from the rim, leaving a pool about as wide as one of the fishing boats and twice as long, or more.

As Pitiable watched, the surface at the seaward end of the pool convulsed and something shot up in a burst of foam. She saw a dark head, a smooth, pale body, and a threshing silvery tail that drove the creature up the steep slope of the slab that held the pool in. A slim arm—not a leg or flipper but an arm like Pitiable's own—reached and clutched, uselessly, well short of the rim, and then the thing slithered back with its thin despairing wail and splashed into the water. From what Mercy had told her of Charity Goodrich's adventure, Pitiable understood at once what she had seen.

Amazed out of her numbness, she watched the creature try once more, and again, before she silently backed away and looked down the shore for her grandfather. He was standing near the water's edge but gazing landward, looking for her, she guessed. She waved to him to come and he hurried towards her. She held her finger to her lips and made urgent gestures for silence with her other hand. By now he must have heard the sounds and understood that something living was concerned, which must not be alarmed, so he made his way round and climbed cautiously up the same way that she had. She pointed and he crept forward to peer into the pool.

She lost count of the cries and splashes while he stared, but when at length he backed away and turned she saw that his eyes were glistening with a new, excited light. He climbed down, helped her to follow, chalked his mark onto the rock and led her up the beach.

"The Lord has indeed provided," he whispered. "Blessed be His name. Now you must stand guard while I fetch nets and men to bring this thing home. If anyone comes, you must tell them that the find is mine. See how excellent are His ways! This very week He brings the fair to town! Stay here. Do not go back up the rock. It must not see you."

He strode off, walking like a younger man, picking his way easily across the broken rocks. Pitiable sat on a sea-worn slab and waited. She felt none of Probity's excitement. She was now appalled at what she had done. Probity and his helpers would catch the sea-child and sell her—from what she had seen, Pitiable was almost sure it was a girl—sell her to the showmen at the fair. That in itself was dreadful. The People had no dealings with the fair that came each autumn. It was an occasion of frivolity and wickedness, they said. But now Probity was going to take the sea-child to them and haggle for a price. More than anything else, more than the ruined farm, more even than her own beatings, this made Pitiable see how much he had changed.

Obediently she sat and watched him go. When he came to Oyster Bay, he turned back, shading his eyes, so she stood and waved and he waved back and vanished into the dip, leaving her alone with the sea and the shore and the strange, sad cries from the pool. By now Pitiable was again too wrapped in her own misery to hear them as anything more than cries, as meaningless to her as the calling of the gulls. It struck her perhaps that Probity would perhaps not sell the sea-girl, but would join the fair, taking Pitiable with him, and show her himself. She would be dead by then, of course—in Charity Goodrich's story the sea-people could not live long out of water—but people would pay money to see even a dead sea-child.

The cries and splashes stopped for a while. Probably the sea-child was resting for a fresh attempt, and yes, when it came the swirl of the water was stronger and the slap of the body against the rock was louder, and the wail as the child fell back yet more despairing than before—so lost, so hopeless, that this time Pitiable heard it for what it was, and when it came again she felt it was calling to her, to her alone, in a language she alone knew, the language of a child trapped in a pit of despair by things too powerful for her to overcome.

Weeping, she realized that she could not bear it.

She dried her eyes and rose and climbed back up to the pool. This time as she watched the sea-child's desperate leapings she saw that there must be something wrong with the other arm, which dangled uselessly by the slim body as it shot from the water. Still, one arm should be enough, if Pitiable could lean far enough to reach it, so she made her way round to the sloping rock, knelt and craned over.

The sea-girl was on the point of leaping again. For a moment Pitiable gazed down at the wan, drawn face with its too-small mouth and its too-large dark eyes, but then the sea-girl twisted from her leap and plunged back below the surface, leaving nothing but the swirl of her going. Pitiable reached down, calling gently and kindly, telling the girl she wanted to help her, though they must hurry because her grandfather would soon be back. But the girl hid in the depths, invisible behind the sky-reflecting surface and did not stir.

Pitiable stood up and looked along the Scaurs, but there was still no sign of Probity. He must have reached Home Beach by now, but perhaps the men there were too busy with their boats to listen to him. Well, she thought, though I cannot swim, if the girl will not come to me, I must go to her. At its shoreward end the pool narrowed almost to a slit, into which a few boulders had fallen and wedged, so she made her way round, sat down and took off all her clothes. Then she lowered herself into the slimy crack and, using the boulders for footholds, climbed down to the water.

Despite the hot summer it was chill from the storm, which had churned up the underdeeps and thrown them here ashore. The salt stung the weals where Probity's belt had cut, but she forced herself down and down, clutching a jag of rock beside her. With her chin level with the water she spoke.

"Please come. Please trust me. I want to help you. I will take you back to the sea."

Nothing happened. She was about to plead again, but then changed her mind and lowered herself a little further, drew a deep breath and ducked beneath the surface. Through closed lips she started to hum the music Mercy had taught her, and now she discovered why it needed to be hummed, not sung. It wasn't just that she couldn't open her mouth under water—the sea-people spoke with words, so they must be able to. It was because now her whole body acted as a sort of sounding-board from which the slow notes vibrated. She could feel them moving away from her through the water, and when she rose to draw breath and sank again, they were still there, the same wavering air that she had heard Mercy hum so often, but this time coming out of the depths where the sea-child lay hidden.

Pitiable joined the music, weaving her own notes through it as she had learned to do with Mercy those last days, until she needed to draw breath again, but before she sank back, the surface stirred and the sea-girl's head appeared, staring at her from only a few feet away, lips parted, desperate with fear.

Pitiable smiled at her and hummed again, in the air this time. The sea-girl answered and moved closer, slowly, but then came darting in and gave Pitiable a quick, brushing kiss and swirled away. Pitiable smiled and beckoned. Now the girl came more gently, and stayed, letting Pitiable take her good arm by the wrist and wind it around her own neck and then turn so that the girl's body lay along Pitiable's back and Pitiable could try to climb out the way she had come.

She gestured first, trying to explain that though they had to start inland, she would turn seaward as soon as they reached the top of the rock. The girl seemed to understand, and hummed the tune again, with a querying rise at the end.

"Yes," said Pitiable. "I will take you to the sea."

The great fish tail became desperately heavy as she dragged it from the water, but the girl understood the need and spoke and knocked with her closed knuckles against Pitiable's shoulder to stop her climbing while she deftly swung her tail sideways and up so that it lodged among the fallen boulders and Pitiable was now lifting only half her weight as she climbed on. Pitiable's small body was wiry from its household tasks, and since Mercy had fallen ill, she had had to learn how to lift and shift burdens beyond her apparent strength, so she strove and grunted up the cleft, with the girl helping as best as she could, until she could roll her out onto the surface and climb gasping beside her.

From then on she could crawl, with the sea-girl's arm round her neck and the chilly body pressed against her back and the tail slithering behind. The rock promontory that held the pool tilted steadily down towards the incoming tide. It had weathered into sharp ridges, painful to crawl on, but Pitiable barely noticed, because a tremendous thought had come to her and given her fresh strength. She herself belonged body and soul to Probity, to beat and use in whatever way he chose until he finally killed her. Until then she was utterly trapped in that pit, with no escape. But here, now, there was this one thing she could prevent him from doing. He would not have the sea-girl, to join her in the pit. Not now, not ever.

So she crawled on. Soon the sea-girl was gulping and panting from being too long in the air, but she lay still and trusting as the sea came slowly nearer. At last one flank of the promontory sloped down with the small waves washing in beside it, and Pitiable could crawl down until the sea-girl, judging her moment, was able to convulse herself sideways into the backwash and slither on through the foam to deeper water. In the haze of her huge effort Pitiable barely saw her go, but when her vision cleared and she looked out to sea, she saw the girl beckoning to her from beside the tip of the promontory.

Wearily she rose and staggered down. The sea-girl gripped the rock with her good hand and dragged herself half out of the water. Pitiable sat beside her with her feet dangling into the wave-wash. Her knees and shins, she noticed, were streaming with blood. The sea-girl saw them and made a grieving sound.

"It's all right," said Pitiable. "It is only scratches."

Face to face they looked at each other.

"You must go now," said Pitiable. "Before he comes back."

The sea-girl answered. She craned up. Pitiable bent so that they could kiss.

"I must dress myself before the men come," she said. "Good-bye."

She gestured to herself, and up the shore, and then to the sea-girl and the open sea. The sea-girl nodded and said something that must have been an answering good-bye. They kissed again, and the sea-girl twisted like a leaping salmon and shot off down the inlet, turned in the water, rose, waved and was gone.

As Pitiable dressed, she decided that now Probity would very likely kill her for what she had done, take her home and beat her to death, half meaning to, and half not. And then, perhaps, he would kill himself. That would be best all round, she thought.

And then she thought that despite that, she had done what Mercy would have wanted her to. It was why she had told her the story of Charity Goodrich, though neither of them could have known.

When she was dressed she shook her hair out and sat combing her fingers through it to help it dry in the sun, but still he did not come, so she tied it up under her shawl and waited where he had left her. Her mood of gladness and resignation ebbed, and she was wrapped in terror once again.

The men came at last, four of them, carrying nets and ropes, a stretcher, and a glass-bottomed box of the sort that crab-catchers used to see below the surface of the water. From their dress Pitiable saw that the three helpers were townspeople, as they would have to be—Probity would not even have tried to persuade any of the People to come on such an enterprise. From the way they walked, it was obvious that even these men were doubtful. A tall, thin lad in particular kept half-laughing, as if he was convinced that he was about to be made a fool of. But Probity came with a buoyant, excited pace and reached her ahead of the others.

"Has anyone been near?" he whispered.

"No one, grandfather."

"And have you heard anything?"

"Only the gulls and the sea."

He stood and listened and frowned, but by now the helpers had come up, so he told them to wait with Pitiable and make no noise, and himself climbed up onto the ridge and crept out of sight. After a while he climbed down and fetched the glass-bottomed box, and this time he allowed the others to come up with him, but Pitiable stayed where she was. She heard his voice, gruff and stubborn, and the others answering him at first mockingly and then angrily, until he came down again and strode over to where she sat, with the others following.

Pitiable rose and waited. She could see how the others glanced at one another behind Probity's back, and before he spoke, she knew how she must answer.

"I tell you, the child saw it also," he shouted. And then to Pitiable, "Where has it gone? How did it get free?"

"What do you speak of, grandfather?"

"The sea-child! Tell them you saw the sea-child!"

"Sea-child, grandfather?"

He took a pace forward and clouted her with all his strength on the side of her head. She sprawled onto the shingle, screaming with the pain of it, but before she could rise, he rushed at her and struck her again. She did not know what happened next, but then somebody was helping her to her feet and Probity and the others were shouting furiously while she shook her head and retched in a roaring red haze. Then her vision cleared though her head still sang with pain, and she saw two of the men wrestling with Probity, holding his arms behind him.

"The wicked slut let her go!" he bellowed. "She was mine! Mine! You have no right! This is my grandchild! Mine!"

His face was terrible, dark red and purple, with the veins on his temples standing out like exposed tree roots. Then he seemed to realize what he had done and fell quiet. In silence and in shame he let them walk him back to the town, with the young man carrying Pitiable on his back.

Though there were magistrates in the town, there was so seldom any wrongdoing among the People that it was the custom to let them deal with their own. After some debate the men took Probity to the Minister and told him what they had seen, and he sent for three of the elders to decide what to do. They heard the men's story, gave them the money Probity had promised them, thanked them and sent them away. They then questioned Probity.

Probity did not know how to lie. He said what he had seen, and insisted that Pitiable had seen the sea-child too. Pitiable, still dazed, unable to think of anything except how he would beat her when he had her home, stuck despairingly to her story. She said that she had been looking at the pool when Probity had climbed up beside her and looked too and become very excited and told her to wait down on the shore and let no one else near while he went for help.

At this Probity started to shout and his face went purple again and he tried to rush at Pitiable, but the elders restrained him, and then a spasm shook him and he had to clutch at a chair and sit down. Even so, but for his story about the sea-child, the elders might have sent Pitiable home with him. She was, after all, his granddaughter. But a man who says he has seen a creature with a human body and a shining fish tail cannot be of sound mind, so they decided that in case there should be worse scandal among the People than there already was, Pitiable had best be kept out of his way, at least until a doctor had examined him.

Pitiable spent the night at the Minister's house, not with his own children but sleeping in the attic with the two servants. First, though, the Minister's wife, for whom cleanliness was very close indeed to godliness, insisted that the child must be bathed. That was how the servants came to see the welts on Pitiable's back and sides. Her torn knees they put down to her fall on the beach when Probity had struck her. The elder servant, a kind, sensible woman, told the Minister. She told him too that if the child received much more such handling, she would die, and her blood would be not only on her grandfather's hands.

The elders did not like it, but were forced to agree. A home would have to be found for the child. As a servant, naturally—she was young, but Mercy Hooke had trained her well. So on the second day after the business on the Scaurs, a Miss Lyall, a very respectable spinster with money of her own, came to inspect Pitiable Nasmith. She asked for a private room and the Minister lent her his study.

Pitiable was brought in and Miss Lyall looked her up and down. Not until the door closed and they were alone did she smile. She was short and fat with bulgy eyes and two large hairy moles on the side of her chin, but her smile was pleasant. She put her head to one side and pursed her lips and, almost too quietly to hear, started to hum. Pitiable's mouth fell open. With an effort she closed it and joined the music. At once Miss Lyall nodded and cut her short.

"I thought it must be so," she said softly. "As soon as I heard that story about the sea-child."

"But you know the song too!" whispered Pitiable, still amazed.

"You are not the only descendant of Charity Goodrich, my dear. My mother taught me her story, and the song, and said I must pass them on to my own daughters, but I was too plain for any sensible man to marry for myself, and too sensible to let any man marry me for my money, so I have no daughters to teach them to. Not even you, since you already know them. All the same, you shall be my daughter from now on and we shall sing the song together and tell each other the story. It will be amusing, after all these years, to see how well the accounts tally."

She smiled, and Pitiable, for the first time for many, many days, smiled too.

NEIL GAIMAN

Pages from a Journal Found in a Shoebox Left in a Greyhound Bus Somewhere Between Tulsa, Oklahoma, and Louisville, Kentucky

Neil Gaiman's many books include the novels American Gods, Neverwhere, Stardust *(with Charles Vess), and* Good Omens *(with Terry Pratchett); the story collection* Smoke and Mirrors; *the* Sandman *series of graphic novels; and two children's books,* The Day I Swapped My Dad for Two Goldfish *and* Coraline. *He has won the World Fantasy Award, the Bram Stoker Award, and the Hugo Award. Originally from England, Gaiman now lives in Minnesota.*

"Pages from a Journal . . ." is a wonderfully mysterious fantasia—a modern rendition of an epic quest, condensed into just a few pages. It first appeared in the 2002 Tour Book of the singer/songwriter Tori Amos.

—T. W.

Monday the 28th

I guess I've been following Scarlet for a long time now. Yesterday I was in Las Vegas. Walking across the parking lot of a casino, I found a postcard. There was a word written on it in crimson lipstick. One word: *Remember*. On the other side of the postcard was a highway in Montana.

I don't remember what it is I'm meant to remember. I'm on the road now, driving north.

Tuesday the 29th

I'm in Montana, or maybe Nebraska. I'm writing this in a motel. There's a wind gusting outside my room, and I drink black motel coffee, just like I'll drink it tomorrow and the night after that. In a small town diner today I heard someone say her name. "Scarlet's on the road," said the man. He was a traffic cop, and he changed the subject when I got close and listened.

He was talking about a head-on collision. The broken glass glittered on the road like diamonds. He called me "Ma'am," politely.

Wednesday the 30th

"It's not the work that gets to you so bad," said the woman. "It's the way that people stare." She was shivering. It was a cold night and she wasn't dressed for it.

"I'm looking for Scarlet," I told her.

She squeezed my hand with hers, then she touched my cheek, so gently. "Keep looking, hon," she said. "You'll find her when you're ready." Then she sashayed on down the street.

I wasn't in a small town any longer. Maybe I was in Saint Louis. How can you tell if you're in Saint Louis? I looked for some kind of arch, something linking East and West, but if it was there I missed it.

Later, I crossed a river.

Thursday the 31st

There were blueberries growing wild by the side of the road. A red thread was caught in the bushes. I'm scared that I'm looking for something that does not exist any more. Maybe it never did.

I spoke to a woman I used to love today, in a café in the desert. She's a waitress there, a long time ago.

"I thought I was your destination," she told me. "Looks like I was just another stop on the line."

I couldn't say anything to make it better. She couldn't hear me. I should have asked if she knew where Scarlet was.

Friday the 32nd

I dreamed of Scarlet last night. She was huge and wild, and she was hunting for me. In my dream, I knew what she looked like. When I woke I was in a pick-up truck, parked by the side of the road. There was a man shining a flashlight in the window at me. He called me "Sir" and asked me for ID.

I told him who I thought I was and who I was looking for. He just laughed, and walked away, shaking his head. He was humming a song I didn't know. I drove the pick-up south, into the morning. Sometimes I fear this is becoming an obsession. She's walking. I'm driving. Why is she always so far ahead of me?

Saturday the 1st

I found a shoebox that I keep things in. In a Jacksonville McDonald's I ate a quarter pounder with cheese and a chocolate milkshake, and I spread everything I keep in the shoebox out on the table in front of me: the red thread from the blueberry bush; the postcard; a Polaroid photograph I found in on some fennel-blown wasteland beside Sunset Boulevard—it shows two girls whispering secrets, their faces blurred; an audio cassette; some golden glitter in a tiny bottle I was given in Washington DC; pages I've torn from books and magazines. A casino chip. This journal.

"When you die," says a dark-haired woman at the next table, "they can make you into diamonds now. It's scientific. That's how I want to be remembered. I want to shine."

Sunday the 2nd

The paths that ghosts follow are written on the land in old words. Ghosts don't take the interstate. They walk. Is that what I'm following, here? Sometimes it seems like I'm looking out through her eyes. Sometimes it feels like she's looking out through mine.

I'm in Wilmington, North Carolina. I write this on an empty beach, while the sunlight glitters on the sea, and I feel so alone.

We make it up as we go along. Don't we?

Monday the 3rd

I was in Baltimore, standing on a sidewalk in the light fall rain, wondering where I was going. I think I saw Scarlet in a car, coming toward me. She was a passenger. I could not see her face, but her hair was red. The woman who drove the car, an elderly pick-up truck, was fat and happy, and her hair was long and black. Her skin was dark.

I slept that night in the house of a man I did not know. When I woke, he said, "She's in Boston."

"Who?"

"The one you're looking for."

I asked how he knew, but he wouldn't talk to me. After a while he asked me to leave, and, soon enough, I did. I want to go home. If I knew where it was, I would. Instead I hit the road.

Tuesday the 4th

Passing Newark at midday, I could see the tip of New York, already smudged dark by dust in the air, now scumbled into night by a thunderstorm. It could have been the end of the world.

I think the world will end in black and white, like an old movie. (Hair as black as coal, sugar, skin as white as snow.) Maybe as long as we have colors we can keep going. (Lips as red as blood, I keep reminding myself.)

I made Boston in the early evening. I find myself looking for her in mirrors and reflections. Some days I remember when the white people came to this land, and when the black people stumbled ashore in chains. I remember when the red people walked to this land, when the land was younger.

I remember when the land was alone.

"How can you sell your mother?" That was what the first people said, when asked to sell the land they walked upon.

Wednesday the 5th

She spoke to me last night. I'm certain it was her. I passed a payphone on the street in Metairie, LA. It rang, I picked up the handset.

"Are you okay?" said a voice.

"Who is this?" I asked. "Maybe you have a wrong number."

"Maybe I do," she said. "But are you okay?"

"I don't know," I said.

"Know that you are loved," she said. And I knew that it had to be her. I wanted to tell her that I loved her too, but by then she'd already put down the phone. If it was her. She was only there for a moment. Maybe it was a wrong number, but I don't think so.

I'm so close now. I buy a postcard from a homeless guy on the sidewalk with a blanket of stuff, and I write *Remember* on it, in lipstick, so now I won't ever forget, but the wind comes up and carries it away, and just for now I guess I'm going to keep on walking.

RAMSEY CAMPBELL

No End of Fun

Ramsey Campbell was born in Liverpool and still lives on Merseyside with his wife, Jenny. He has been described by the London Times *as "the nearest thing to an heir to M. R. James." He was presented with the World Horror Convention's Grand Master Award and the World Horror Association's Bram Stoker Award for Life Achievement in 1999. His most recent novels are* The Darkest Part of the Woods *and* The Overnight, *and his nonfiction is collected in* Ramsey Campbell, Probably. *An expanded edition of his erotic horror stories,* Scared Stiff, *was published in 2002, and he has a new short story collection,* Told by the Dead, *due this summer. He is working on two novels:* Secret Stories *and* Spanked by Nuns.

"No End of Fun" is typically creepy Campbell at its best.

—E. D.

You don't mind, do you, Uncle Lionel? I've given you mother's old room."

"Why should I mind anything to do with Dorothy?"

"I expect you've got happy memories like us. Is it all right if Helen sees you up? Only we've got paying guests arriving any minute."

"You really ought to let me pay something towards my keep."

"You mustn't think I meant that. Mother never let you and I'm not about to start. Just keep Helen amused like always and that'll be more than enough. Helen, don't let my uncle lug that case."

"Are you helping with the luggage now, Helen? Will that be a bit much for you?"

"I've done bigger ones."

"That sounds a bit cheeky, doesn't it, Carol? The sort of thing the comics used to say at the Imperial. Is that old place still alive? That can be one of your treats then, Helen."

"Say thank you, Helen, and will you please take up that case. Here are the boarders now."

When the thirteen-year-old thrust her fingers through the handle, Lionel let it go. "You're a treasure," he murmured, but she was apparently too intent on stumping upstairs to give him his usual smile. Remarking "She's a credit to you" brought him no more than a straight-lipped nod from her mother. He had to admit to himself that Helen's new image—all her curls cropped into auburn turf, denim overalls so oversized he would have assumed they'd been handed down if she'd had an older sibling—had rather startled him. "So how have you been progressing at school?" he said as he caught up with her, and in an attempt to sound less dusty, "You can call me Lionel if you like."

"Mum wouldn't let me."

"Better make it uncle, then, even if it's not quite right. Great-uncle is a mouthful, isn't it, though you liked it one year, didn't you? You said I was the greatest one you had, not that there was any competition."

All this, uttered slowly and with pauses inviting but obtaining no responses, brought them to the third floor, where he held onto the banister and regained his breath while Helen preceded him into the room. Dorothy's sheets had been replaced by a duvet as innocently white, but otherwise the place seemed hardly to have changed since her girlhood, when children weren't expected to personalize their rooms: the same hulking oaken wardrobe and chest of drawers she'd inherited at Helen's age along with Dorothy's grandmother's room, the view of boarding-houses boasting of their fullness, the only mirror her grandmother's on the windowsill. As he stepped into the July sunlight that had gathered like an insubstantial faintly lavender-scented weight in the room, he thought he saw Dorothy in the mirror.

It was Helen, of course. She resembled Dorothy more than Carol ever had—elfin ears, full lower lip, nose as emphatic as an exclamation mark, eyes deep with secrets. As she dumped Lionel's suitcase by the bed, the mirror wobbled with the impact. The oval glass was supported by two pairs of marble hands, each brace joined at the wrists; the lower of the left hands was missing its little finger. He lurched forward to steady the mirror, and his arm brushed the front of Helen's overalls. He expected the material to yield, and the presence of two plump mounds of flesh came as more than a shock.

She twisted away from him, and her face reappeared in the mirror, grimacing. For a moment it exactly fitted the oval. The sight set his heart racing as though a knot of memories had squeezed it. "Sorry," he mumbled, and "I'll see you at dinner" as she slouched out of the room.

Laying his socks and underwear in Dorothy's chest of drawers and dressing her padded hangers in his shirts and suits made him wonder if that was more intimate than she would have liked. By the time he'd finished he was oppressively hot. He donned the bathrobe that was waiting for him every year and hurried to the attic bathroom, to be confronted by a crowd of Carol's and Helen's tights pegged to a clothesline over the bath as though to demonstrate two stages of growth. Not caring to touch them, he retreated to his room and transferred the mirror to the chest of drawers so as to raise the sash as high as it would wobble. Hours of sunlight had left the marble hands not much less warm than flesh.

He might have imagined he heard the screams of people drowning if he hadn't recognized the waves as the swoops of a roller coaster. Soon he was able to hear the drowsing of the sea. Its long, slow breaths were soothing him when he saw a passerby remove her topmost head. She'd lifted her small daughter from her shoulders, but the realization came too late to prevent Lionel from remembering a figure that had parted into prancing segments. He lay down hastily and made himself breathe in time with the sea until the summons of the dinner gong resounded through the house.

Even in their early teens he and his cousin had squabbled over who sounded the gong, until Dorothy's mother had kept the task for herself. While it was meant to call only the guests, it reminded him that he didn't know when he was expected for dinner. He was changing, having resprayed his armpits, when a rap at the door arrested him with trousers halfway up his greying thighs. "Would you mind taking dinner with the others?" Carol called. "We're not as organized as mother yet."

"I'd be happy to wait till you have yours."

"We eat on the trot at the moment. You'd be helping."

In the dining room a table in the corner farthest from the window was set for one. All his fellow diners were married couples at least his age. A few bade him a wary good evening, but otherwise none of the muted conversations came anywhere near him. He felt like a teacher attempting to ignore a murmurous classroom, not that he ever would have. As soon as he'd finished dinner—thin soup, cold ham and salad, brown bread and butter, a rotund teapot harboring a single bag, a pair of cakes on a stand, everything Dorothy used to serve—he followed Helen into the kitchen. "Would you be terribly upset if we didn't go anywhere tonight?" he said.

"Don't suppose."

"Only driving up from London isn't the picnic it was."

"She wouldn't have been joining you anyway. It's dirty sheet night," Carol said, wrinkling her nose.

He did all the washing-up he could grab, and would have helped Helen trudge to the machine in the basement with armfuls of bedclothes if Carol hadn't urged him to tell her his news. Now that he'd retired from teaching there wasn't much besides the occasional encounter with an ex-pupil, and so he encouraged Carol to talk. When her patient responses betrayed that she regarded his advice about the multitude of petty problems she'd inherited with the boarding-house as at best uninformed, he pleaded tiredness and withdrew to his room.

At first exhaustion wouldn't let him sleep. Though he left the window open, the heat insisted on sharing his bed, Dorothy's ever since she was Helen's age. He found himself wishing he hadn't arrived for the funeral last December too late to see her. "We never said goodbye," he whispered into the pillow and wrapped his arms around himself, covering his flaccid hairy dugs.

He wakened in the middle of the night and also of the heat with the notion that Dorothy had grown an unreasonable number of legs. He raised himself on his elbows to peer sleepily about, and realized she was staring at him. Of course it was her oval photograph, except that there was no picture of her in the room. As he jerked upright he saw her face balanced on the marble hands, crammed into the mirror. She looked outraged, unable to believe her fate.

Lionel snatched at the overhead cord to drag light into the room. The mirror was deserted apart from a patch of wallpaper whose barely discernible pattern gave him the impression of gazing straight through the frame at the wall. When the illusion refused to be dispelled he turned the light off, trying not to feel he'd used it to drive Dorothy into the dark. She was gone wherever everyone would end up, that was all; how could dreaming summon her back? Nevertheless he felt as guilty as the only other time he'd seen her in the mirror.

It had been the year when she'd kept being late for dinner. One evening her mother had sent him to fetch her. He'd swaggered into Dorothy's room without knocking; they'd never knocked at each other's doors. Although it wasn't dark the curtains had been drawn, and at first he'd been unsure what he saw—Dorothy stooping to watch her face in the oval mirror as she'd squeezed her budding breasts. While she hadn't been naked, her white slip had let the muted light glow between her legs. The smile of pride and quiet astonishment she had been sharing with herself had transformed itself into an accusing glare as she'd caught sight of him in the mirror. "Go away," she'd cried, "this is my room," as Lionel fled, his entire body pounding like an exposed heart. He hadn't dared venture downstairs until he'd heard her precede him.

The breakfast gong quieted his memories at last. In the bathroom he was relieved to find the tights had flown. He showered away most of his coating of mugginess, and thought he was ready for the day until he opened the kitchen door to hear Carol tell Helen "You're not to go anywhere near him, is that understood?"

Surely she couldn't mean Lionel, but he would have been tempted to sidle out of reach of the idea if she hadn't given him a wink behind Helen's eloquently sulky back. "A boyfriend she's too young to have," she said. "Do you mind sitting where you did again?"

Lionel had hoped they could have breakfast together, but tried to seem happy to head for the dining room. "Morning all," he declared, and when that stirred no more than muted echoes "I'm her uncle, should anyone be wondering."

Did explaining his presence only render it more questionable or suggest he thought it was? He restrained himself from explaining that Carol had divorced her husband once she'd resolved to move in with her aging mother. He made rather shorter work of his breakfast than his innards found ideal so that he could escape to the kitchen. "Are we going for a roam?" he asked Helen as he set about washing up.

"Too many rooms to change," Carol said at once. "Maybe we can let her out this evening if you can think how to occupy her."

He strolled up to the elongated Victorian garden that was the promenade and clambered down a set of thick hot stone steps to the beach. The sand was beginning to sprout turrets around families who'd staked out their territories with buckets and spades the colors of lollipops. He paced alongside the subdued withdrawn waves until screams rose from the amusement park ahead, and then he labored up another block of steps to the Imperial.

The theater was displaying posters for the kind of summer show it always had: comedians, singers, dancers, a magician. It took the mostly blonde girl in the ticket booth some moments to pause her chewing gum and see off a section of her handful of paperback, which was proportionately almost as stout as its reader. When she said "Can I help you?" she sounded close to refusing in advance.

"Could you tell me whether there are any, you won't take offense if I call them dwarfs?"

She met that with a grimace she supplemented by bulging her cheek with her tongue. "Any . . ."

"Small performers. You know, a troupe of dinky fellows. They used to perform here when I was a child. I don't know if you'd have anything like them these days." When she only tongued her cheek more fiercely he grew desperate. "Tiny Tumblers, one lot were called," he insisted. "Squat little chaps."

"The only little people we've got are Miss Merritt's Moppets."

"That's fine, then," Lionel said with an alacrity she appeared to find suspicious. "Any chance of a pair of your best seats for tomorrow night?"

"Best for what?"

For persuading Carol to give Helen an evening off, he hoped: she was working the child harder than Dorothy had ever worked her. "For watching, I should think," he said.

From the theater he wandered inland. Behind the large hotels facing the sea a parallel row of bed and breakfast houses kept to themselves. Victorian shopping arcades led between them to the main street, which was clinging to its elegance. Among the tea shops and extravagant department stores, not a pub nor an amusement arcade was to be seen. Crowds of the superannuated were taking all the time they could to progress from one end of the street to the other, while those that were wheeling or being wheeled traversed the wide pavements more slowly still. When Lionel discovered that matching the speed of the walkers made him feel prematurely old, or perhaps not so prematurely, he turned aside into the park that stretched opposite half the shops.

Folding chairs could be hired from a spindly lugubrious youth decorated with a moustache like two transplanted eyebrows. Lionel plumped himself and the swelling that was breakfast onto a chair close to the bandstand. The afternoon concert was preceded by an open-air theater of toddlers on the lawns and secretaries with lunch-boxes, a spectacle he found soporific. By the time the elderly musicians in their dinner jackets assembled on the bandstand, he was dozing off.

A medley of Viennese waltzes failed to rouse him, as did portions of Mozart and Mendelssohn. He was past being able to raise his head when the orchestra struck up a piece he would have thought too brash to win the applause, much of it gloved, of the pensioned audience. Though he couldn't name the opera responsible, he recognized the music. It was the Dance of the Tumblers. Far from wakening him, it let a memory at him.

A few days after he'd seen Dorothy at the mirror, her mother had taken her and Lionel to the Imperial. She'd made them sit together as if that might crush whatever had come between them, but Dorothy had sat aside from him, knees protruding into the aisle. She had seemed to take half the evening to eat a tub of ice cream, until the scraping of the wooden spoon had started to grate on his nerves. As she'd lifted yet another delicate mouthful to her lips, the master of ceremonies had announced the Tiny Tumblers, and then her spoon had halted in mid-air. Two giant women had waddled onstage from the wings.

He'd never known if Dorothy had cowered against her seat because of their size or from guessing what was imminent. The long-haired square-faced figures had swayed to the footlights before the flowered ankle-length dresses had split open, each of them disgorging a totem-pole composed of three dwarfs in babies' frilly outfits. The dwarfs had sprung from one another's shoulders, leaving the dresses to collapse under the weight of the wigs, and piled down the stairs that flanked the stage. "Who's coming for a tumble?" they'd croaked.

Lionel had felt Dorothy flinch away from the aisle, pressing against him. If she'd asked he would have changed places with her, but he'd thought he sensed how loath she was to touch him after his glimpse in her room. As two dwarfs had scurried towards her, swivelling their blocky heads and widening their eyes, he'd dealt her a covert shove. Her lurch and her squeak had attracted the attention of the foremost dwarf, who'd shambled fast at her. She'd jumped up, spilling ice cream over the lap of her skirt, and fled to the sanctuary of the Ladies'. Her mother had needed to ask Lionel more than once to let her past to follow, he remembered with dismay. Part of him had wanted to find out what would happen if the dwarfs caught his cousin.

He came back to himself before the thought could reach deeper. He'd grown unaware of the music in the park, and now there was only clapping. He was awakened less by the discreet peal than by a sense that his body was about to expel some element it was no longer able to contain. His midriff strained itself up from the chair as the secret escaped him—a protracted vibrant belch that the applause faded just in time to isolate.

He excused himself as quickly and as blindly as he could—he had a childish half-awake notion that if he didn't see he wouldn't be seen either—but not before he glimpsed couples staring as if he'd strayed from the Imperial, which they barely tolerated for its appeal to tourists. Several pensioners on the main street frowned at his excessively boisterous progress, but he was anxious to take refuge in his room. Since Carol and Helen were busy in the kitchen, only shortness of breath delayed him on the stairs. He manhandled the door open and slumped against it, but took just one step towards the bed.

Whoever had tidied up had returned the mirror to the windowsill. It must be himself he could see in the oval glass, even if the face appeared to recede faster than he stumbled forward. Presumably his having rushed back to the hotel made him see the face dwindle beyond sight, carried helplessly into a blackness that had no basis in the room. He rubbed his eyes hard, and once the fog cleared he saw nothing in the mirror except his own confused face.

The marble hands had stored up warmth. They brought back the touch of flesh, which he'd avoided since losing his parents, not that he'd encountered much of it while they were alive. He planted the hands on the chest of drawers and turned the glass to the wall, then lay on top of the duvet, trying harder and more unsuccessfully to relax than he ever had after a day's teaching, until the gong sent its vibrations through his nerves.

He didn't eat much. Besides being wary of conjuring another belch, he felt though someone who knew more about him than he realized was observing him. When he took the last of his plates into the kitchen, Carol gave him a harassed disappointed blink. "Dinner was excellent," he assured her, though it had been something of a repeat performance of last night's, with cold beef understudying ham. "I'm just not very peckish. I expect I'm too excited at the prospect of a date with my favorite young lady."

"Do you still want to go out with my uncle tonight?"

Helen had kept her back to his comment, but turned with a quick bright smile. "Yes please, Uncle Lionel."

That was more like the girl he remembered. It lasted as far as the street, where he said "Shall we just go for an amble?"

"To the rides."

"Best save those till I've been to the bank."

"I've got some money. If we aren't going to the rides I don't want to go."

He felt as if she knew he'd manufactured his excuse. "It's your treat," he said. All the way along the promenade he had to remind himself that the screams from the tracks etched high on the glassy sunset expressed pleasure. The sight beyond the entrance to the amusement park of painted horses bobbing like flotsam on an ebb tide provided some relief. He halted by the old roundabout to regain his breath. "Shall we," he said, and "go on here?"

Helen squashed her lower lip flat with its twin. "That's for babies."

He might have retorted that she hadn't seemed to think so last year, but said "What shall it be, then?"

"The Cannonball."

"I thought you didn't care for roller coasters any more than I do."

"That was when I was little. I like it now, and the Plunge of Peril, and Annihilation."

"Will you be awfully offended if I watch?"

"No." The starkness of the word appeared to rouse her pity for him, since she added "You can win me something, Uncle Lionel."

He felt obliged to see her safely onto the roller coaster. Once she was installed in the middle carriage, next to a boy with an increasingly red face and the barest vestige of hair, Lionel headed for the sideshows. Too many of the prizes were composed of puffed-up rubber for his taste—he remembered a pink horse whose midriff had burst between his adolescent legs, dumping him in the sea—but they were out of reach of his skill. He had yet to ring a single bell or cast a quoit onto a hook when Helen indicated she was bound for the Plunge of Peril.

He was determined to win her a present. Eventually rolling several pounds' worth of balls down a chute towards holes intermittently exposed by a perforated strip of wood gained him an owl of shaggy orange cloth. He would have felt more triumphant if he hadn't realized he'd betrayed that he wouldn't have needed to go to the bank. He was just in time to see Helen leave the Plunge of Peril.

She glanced about but didn't notice him behind a bunch of teddy bears pegged by their cauliflower ears. As he watched through the tangle of legs she shared a swift kiss with her companion, the red-faced boy crowned with grey skin, and tugged him in the direction of a virtually vertical roller coaster. Lionel didn't intervene, not even when they staggered off the ride, though he was unsure whether he was being discreet or spying on them or at a loss how to approach them. He was pursuing them through the crowds when their way was blocked by two figures with the night gaping where their faces ought to be.

They were life-size cartoons of a man and a woman sufficiently ill-dressed to be homeless, painted on a flat with their faces cut out for the public to insert their own. Lionel saw Helen scamper to poke hers out above the woman's body. Her grimace was meant to be funny—she was protruding at the boy the tongue she'd recently shared with him—but Lionel realized that too late to keep quiet. "Don't," he cried.

For a moment Helen's face looked trapped by the oval. Perhaps her eyes were lolling leftward to send the boy that way, since that was the direction in which he absented himself. She emerged so innocently it angered Lionel. "I think it's time we went back to your mother," he said, and thrust the owl at Helen as she mooched after him. "This was for you."

"Thanks." On the promenade she lowered a mournful gaze to the dwarfish button-eyed rag-beaked soft-clawed orange lump, and then she risked saying, "Are you going to tell Mum?"

"Can you offer me any reason why I shouldn't?"

"Because she'd never let me see Brandon again."

"I thought that was already supposed to be the arrangement."

"But I love him," Helen protested, and began to weep.

"Good heavens now, no need for that. You can't be in love at your age." The trouble was that he had no idea when it was meant to start; it never had for him. "Do stop it, there's a good girl," he pleaded as couples bound for the amusement park began to frown more at him than Helen, and applied himself to taking some control. "I really don't like being used when I haven't even been consulted."

"I won't ever again, I promise."

"I'll hold you to it. Now can we make that the end of the tears? I shouldn't think you'd like your mother wondering what the tragedy is."

"I'll stop if you promise not to tell."

"We'll see."

He was ashamed to recognize that he might have undertaken more if she hadn't dabbed her eyes dry with the owl, leaving a wet patch suggesting that the bird had disgraced itself; should Carol learn of Helen's subterfuge she would also know he'd neglected to supervise her. Carol proved to be so intent on her business accounts that she simply transferred her glance of surprise from the clock to him. "I've a job for you as long as you're here," she told Helen, and Lionel took his sudden weariness to his room.

As he fumbled for the light switch he heard a scream. It sounded muffled, presumably by glass—by the window. He couldn't tell whether it signified delight or dismay or a confusion of both, but he would have preferred not to be greeted by it. A memory was waiting to claim him once he huddled under the quilt in the dark.

Yet had he done anything so dreadful? Days after the incident at the Imperial, her mother had taken him and Dorothy to the amusement park. On the Ghost Train his cousin had sat as far from him as the bench would allow, though when the skull-faced car had blundered into the daylight they'd pretended to be chums for her mother's camera. For her benefit they'd lent their faces to the painted couple, ancestors of the pair behind which Helen had posed. Lionel had been growing impatient with the pretense and with Dorothy's covert hostility when he'd seen all six dwarfs, dapper in suits and disproportionately generous ties, strutting towards them.

He must have been too young to imagine how she might feel, otherwise he would surely have restrained himself. He'd grabbed her shoulders, wedging her head in the oval. "Look, Dorothy," he'd whispered hotly in her ear, "they're coming for you." In what had seemed to him mere seconds he'd released her, though not before her struggles had caused her dress to ride up, exposing more of her thighs than he'd glimpsed in her room. As she'd dashed into the darkness behind the cartoon he'd heard her mother calling "Where's Lionel? Where are you going, Dorothy? What's up now?"

In time nothing much was, Lionel reassured himself: otherwise Dorothy wouldn't have invited him to spend summers at the boarding-house after she'd inherited it. Or was it quite so straight-forward? He'd always thought that, having forgotten their contentious summer, she had both taken pity on his solitariness and looked to him for company once Carol had married and Dorothy's husband had succumbed to an early heart attack, but now it occurred to him that she had kept him away from her daughter. He withdrew beneath the covers as if they could hide him from his undefined guilt, and eventually sleep joined him.

He thought walking by the sea might clear his head of whatever was troubling him. There was just one family on the beach. He assumed they were quite distant until he noticed the parents were dwarfs and the children pocket versions of them. They must work in a circus, for all of their faces were painted with grins wider than their mouths, even the face of the baby that was knocking down sandcastles as it crawled about. Lionel had to toil closer, dragging his inflated toy, before he understood that the family was laughing at him. When he followed their gazes he found he was clutching by one breast the life-size naked rubber woman he'd brought to the beach.

He writhed himself awake, feeling that his mind had only started to reveal its depths. As he tried to rediscover sleep he heard a scratching at the window. It must be a bird, though it sounded like fingernails on glass, not even in that part of the room. When it wasn't repeated he managed to find his way back to sleep.

He felt he hadn't by breakfast time. Being glanced at by more people than bade him good morning left him with the impression that he looked guilty of his dream. There wasn't much more of a welcome in the kitchen, where a disagreement had evidently occurred. When Carol met his eyes while Helen didn't, he said "She'll be all right for this evening, won't she?"

"Quite a few things aren't all right, I'm afraid. Torn serviettes, for a start, and tablecloths not clean that should be." She was aiming her voice upwards as if to have it fall more heavily on Helen. "We've standards to keep up," she said.

"I think they're as high as your mother's ever were, so don't drive yourself so hard. You deserve a night or two off. Is the show at the Imperial your kind of diversion?"

"More like my idea of hell."

"Then you won't be jealous if I take Helen tonight? I've got tickets."

"You might have said sooner."

"You were busy."

"Exactly."

"I think you could both benefit from taking it easier. You and your mother managed, didn't you?"

Carol unloaded a tray into the sink with a furious clatter and twisted to face him. "You've no idea what she was like when you weren't here. Used me harder than this one ever is, and my dad as well, poor little man. No wonder he had a heart attack."

Lionel had forgotten how diminutive Dorothy's husband had been, and hadn't time to brood about it now. "Let me hold the fort while you two have an evening out," he said.

"Thanks for the offer, but this place is our responsibility. Make that mine." Carol sighed at this or as a preamble to muttering "Take her as long as you've bought tickets. As you say, I'll just have to manage."

He thought it best to respond to that with no more than a sympathetic grimace and to keep clear of her and Helen for a while. He stayed in his room no longer than was necessary to determine he had nothing to wear that would establish a holiday mood. He bought a defiantly luxuriant shirt from a shop in a narrow back street to which the town seemed reluctant to own up, and wandered with the package to the park, where he found a bench well away from the bandstand in case any of the musicians identified him as yesterday's eructating spectator. The eventual concert repeated its predecessor, which might have allowed him to catch up on his sleep if he hadn't been nervous of dreaming—of learning what his mind required unconsciousness to acknowledge it contained.

It was close to dinnertime when he ventured back to his room. Rather than examine his appearance, he left the mirror with its back to him. His new shirt raised eyebrows and lowered voices in the dining room. At least Carol said "You're looking bright," which would have heartened him more if she hadn't rebuked Helen: "I hope you'll be dressing for the occasion as well."

Perhaps Helen had changed her black T-shirt and denim overalls and chubby shoes when he found her waiting on the pavement outside; he couldn't judge. He told her she looked a picture, and thought she was responding when she mumbled "Uncle Lionel?"

"At your service."

She peered sideways at him. "Will you be sad if I don't come with you?"

"I would indeed."

"I told Brandon last night I'd meet him. I wouldn't have if you'd said you'd got tickets."

"But you've known all day."

"I couldn't call him. Mum might have heard."

"You mustn't expect me to keep covering up for you." Lionel supposed he sounded unreasonable, having previously complained of not being let into the secret. "Very well, just this once," he said to forestall the moisture that had gathered in her eyes. "You two go and I'll meet you at the end of the performance."

"No, you. You like it."

It was clear she no longer did. "Where will you be?" he said, and immediately "Never mind. I don't want to know. Just make certain you're waiting at the end."

"I will."

She might have kissed him, but instead ran across the promenade to her boyfriend. Lionel watched them clasp hands and hurry down a ramp to the beach. He stayed on the far side of the road so as not to glimpse them as he made for the Imperial.

The stout girl in the booth seemed even more suspicious of his returning a ticket than she had been of the purchase. At last she allowed him to leave it in case it could be resold. In the auditorium he had to sidle past a family with three daughters, loud in inverse proportion to their size. He was flattening a hand beside his cheek to ward off some of the clamor of his neighbor, the youngest, when someone tapped him on the shoulder. Seated behind him were two of Carol's guests: a woman with a small face drawn tight and pale by her sharp nose, her husband whose droopy empurpled features had yet more skin to spare underneath. "Will you be stopping this show too?" the woman said.

Could she have seen Dorothy chased by the dwarfs? "I don't," Lionel said warily, "ah . . ."

"We saw you at the concert yesterday."

"Heard me, you mean." When that fell short of earning him even a hint of a grin, Lionel said "I expect I'll be able to contain myself."

The man jabbed a stubby finger at the empty seat. "On your own?"

"Like yourselves."

"Our granddaughter's one of Miss Merritt's Moppets."

His tone was more accusing than Lionel cared to understand. "Good luck to her," he said, indifferent to whether he sounded sarcastic, and turned his back.

As the curtains parted, the child beside him turned her volume up. He put the empty seat between them, only to hear the sharp-nosed woman cough with displeasure and change seats with her husband. Before long Lionel's head began to ache with trying not to wonder how Helen and her boyfriend were behaving, and he couldn't enjoy the show. He squirmed in his seat as the moppets in their white tutus pranced onstage. At least they weren't dwarfs, he thought and squirmed again, growing red-faced as another cough was aimed at him.

He had no wish to face the couple at the end of the show. He remained seated until he realized they might see Helen outside and mention it to Carol. He struggled up the packed aisle and succeeded in leaving the theater before they did. Helen was waiting on the chipped marble steps. She half turned, and he saw she was in tears. "Oh dear," he murmured, "what now?"

"We had a fight."

"An argument, I trust you mean." When she nodded or her head slumped, he said "I'm sure it'll turn out to be just a hiccup." She only turned away, leaving him to whisper "Shall we hurry home? We don't want anybody knowing you were meant to be with me."

They were opposite the ramp down which she'd vanished with her boyfriend when she began to sob. Lionel urged her over to the far corner of her street while Carol's guests passed by. Once they'd had ample time to reach their room and Helen's sobs had faltered into silence he said "Will you be up to going in now, do you think?"

"I'll have to be, won't I?"

Her maturity both impressed and disconcerted him. Each of them pulled out a key, and he would have made a joke of it if he'd been sure she would respond. He let her open the front door and followed her in, only to flinch from bumping into her. Carol and the couple from the theater were talking in the hall.

They fell silent and gazed at the newcomers. As Lionel struggled to decide whether he should hurry upstairs or think of a comment it would be crucial for him to make, the sharp-nosed woman said "I see you found yourself a young companion after all."

Her husband cleared his throat. Presumably he thought it helpful to tell Carol "My wife means he was on his own at the show."

Carol stared at Helen and then shifted her disapproval to Lionel. Her face grew blank before she told them "I think you should both go to bed. I'll have plenty to say in the morning."

"Mummy . . ."

"Don't," Carol said, even more harshly when Lionel tried to intervene.

"I think we'd better do as we're told," he advised Helen, and trudged upstairs ahead of her. Just now his room offered more asylum than anywhere else in the house, and he attempted to hide in his bed and the dark. His guilt was lying in wait for him—his realization that rather than make up for anything he might have done to Dorothy, he'd let down both Carol and Helen. He heard Helen shut her door with a dull suppressed thud and listened apprehensively for her mother's footfall on the stairs. He'd heard nothing further when exhaustion allowed sleep to overtake him.

A muffled cry roused him. Heat and darkness made him feel afloat in a stagnant bath. As he strained his ears for a repetition of the cry he was afraid that it might have been Helen's—that he'd caused her mother to mistreat her in some way he winced from imagining. When he heard another sound he had to raise his shaky head before he could identify it. Some object was bumping rhythmically against glass.

He kicked off the quilt and stumbled to drag the curtains apart. There was nothing at the window, nothing to be seen through it except guest-houses slumbering beyond a streetlamp. He hauled the sash all the way up and leaned across the sill, but the street was deserted. He was peering along it when the muffled thumping recommenced behind him.

As he stalked towards it he refused to believe where it was coming from. He took hold of the mirror by its bunch of wrists, which not only felt unhealthily warm but also seemed to be vibrating slightly in time with the sound. He gripped them with both hands and turned the glass towards him. It was full of Dorothy's outraged face, glaring straight at him.

She was so intensely present that he could have thought there was no mirror, just her young woman's face balanced on the doubly paralyzed hands. More and worse than shock made his arms tremble, but he was unable to drop the mirror. In a moment Dorothy's forehead ceased thudding against the glass and shrank into it as though she was being hauled backwards. The ankle-length white dress she wore—the kind of garment in which he imagined she'd been buried—was bulging vigorously in several places. He knew why before a dwarf's head poked up through the collar, ripping the fabric, to fasten on Dorothy's mouth. His outline made it clear that he'd shinnied up by holding onto her breasts. Her left sleeve tore, revealing the squarish foot of a dwarf who was inverted somewhere under the dress. Then she was borne away into darkness so complete she oughtn't to be visible, even for Lionel's benefit. He saw a confusion of feet scurrying beneath the hem. One pair vanished up the dress, and her body set about jerking in the rhythm of the dwarf who had clambered her back.

The worst thing was that Lionel recognized it all. It had lived in his mind for however many years, too deep for thought and so yet more powerful, and now Dorothy had become the puppet of his fantasy. He supposed that to be at his mercy the dwarfs were dead too. He didn't know if he was desperate to repudiate the spectacle or release the participants as he flung the mirror away from him.

It was toppling over the windowsill when he tried to snatch it back. He saw Dorothy's face plummeting out of reach as though he'd doubled her helplessness. As he craned over the sill, the button at the waist of his pyjamas snapped its thread. The mirror struck the roof of his Mini, which responded like a bass drum. One marble finger split off and skittered across the dent the impact had produced. The mirror tottered on the metal roof, and Lionel dashed out of the room.

He was scrabbling at the front-door latch while he clutched his trousers shut when he heard the mirror slide off the car and shatter. The chill of the concrete seized his bare feet like a premonition of how cold they would end up. The marble hands had been smashed into elegant slivers surrounded by fragments of glass, but the oval that had contained the mirror was intact. He hardly knew why he stooped to collect the glass in it. When his trousers sagged around his ankles he had no means of holding them up. Not until lights blazed between curtains above him did he realize that several of Carol's guests were gazing down at him.

In the morning Carol said very little to him beyond "I'm sorry you're leaving, but I won't have anyone in my house going behind my back."

This reminded him of his last glimpse of Dorothy, and he had to repress a hysterical laugh. He bumped his suitcase all the way downstairs in the hope that would bring Helen out of her room, but to no avail. "Shall I just go up and say goodbye?" he almost pleaded.

"Madam isn't receiving visitors at the moment."

He couldn't tell if that was Helen's decision or her mother's. He lugged the suitcase to the Mini and dumped it in the boot. "You're sure you don't mind if I take the mirror," he said.

"If you want to try and mend it, be my guest. I've never had any use for it," Carol said, doling him a token wave to speed him on his way before she shut herself in the house.

As the Mini backed onto the street he muttered "Here you go, old bones," crouching his lanky frame lower so that the dent in the roof didn't touch his scalp. On the seat beside him shards of glass stirred in the marble frame, but he could see nothing other than the underside of the roof in even the largest piece of mirror. He scarcely knew why he was taking the mirror with him; could it somehow help him gain control of the depths of his mind and let Dorothy go? The boarding-house swung away behind him, and he wondered what the people in it might be thinking about him—worse, what they might be storing up about him unexamined in their minds. For the first time in all his years he dreaded living after death.

ADAM ROBERTS

Swiftly

Adam Roberts has published short stories, novellas, and three novels: Salt, On, *and* Stone. *He teaches literature and culture at Royal Holloway, University of London, and lives just west of London with his wife and daughter.*

"Swiftly" is a beautifully crafted story rooted in the works of the eighteenth-century satirist Jonathan Swift. Like the older fiction on which it is based, Roberts's story is a droll adventure tale that also explores more serious questions in the realms of politics, culture, and ethics. "Swiftly" first appeared in the March 3rd edition of SCI FICTION, an on-line journal.

—T. W.

[1]
7 November 1848

Swiftly, expertly, the tiny hand worked, ticked up and down, moved over the face of the miniature pallet. The worker was wearing yellow silk trousers, a close-woven cotton blue waistcoat; it (Bates could not see whether it was a *he* or a *she*) had on spectacles that shone like dewdrops in the light. Its hair was black, its skin a golden-cream. Bates could even make out the creases of concentration on its brow, the tip of its tiny tongue just visible through its teeth.

Bates stood upright. "It hurts my back," he said, "to lean over so."

"I quite understand," said Pannell. "Might I fetch you a chair?"

"Ah, no need for that, thank you," said Bates. "I think I have seen all I need. It is, indeed, fascinating."

Pannell seemed agitated, shifting weight from one foot to another. "I never tire of watching them work," he agreed. "Pixies. Fairies! Creatures from childhood story." He beamed. *You smile sir,* thought Bates. *You smile, but there is sweat on your lip. Perhaps you are not altogether lost to shame. Nerves, sir, nerves.*

"What is it, eh, making exactly?"

"A mechanism for controlling the angle, pitch and yaw, in flight you know. I could give you its technical name, although it is Mr. Nicholson who is the greater expert on this matter."

"Is it a sir or a madam?"

"It?"

"The creature. The workman."

"A female." Pannell touched Bates's elbow, herding him gently towards the staircase at the far end of the workshop. "We find they have better hands for weaving the finest wire-strands."

Bates paused at the foot of the wooden stairs, taking one last look around the workshop. "And these are Lilliputians?"

"These," replied Pannell, "are from the neighboring island, Blefuscu. We believe Blefuscans, sir, to be better workers. They are less prone to disaffection, sir. They work harder and are more loyal."

"All of which is," said Bates, "very interesting."

Up the stairs and through the glass door, Bates was led into Pannell's office. Pannell guided him to a chair, and offered him brandy. "When my superior heard of the terms you were offering," he gushed, wiping the palms of his hands alternately against the sleeves of his coat as Bates sat down, "he was nothing less than overwhelmed. Mr. Burton is not an excitable man, sir, but he was impressed, very impressed, more," Pannell went on, hopping to the drinks cabinet in the corner of the room, "more than impressed. Very generous terms, sir! Very favorable on both sides!"

"I am pleased you think so," said Bates.

From where he was sitting the view was clear through the quartered window of Pannell's office. Grime marked the bottom right hand corners of each pane like grey lichen. Each patch of dirt was delineated from clean glass by a hyperbolic line running from bottom left to top right. *X equals y squared*, thought Bates. The pattern on the glass was distracting, the eye hardly noticed the view that was actually through the window, the dingy street, the grey-brick buildings.

He shifted his weight in the chair. It complained, squeaking like a querulous baby. I, too, am nervous, he thought to himself.

"Brandy?" Pannell asked for the second time.

"Thank you."

"Mr. Burton expressed his desire to meet you himself."

"I would be honored."

"Indeed . . ."

A bell tinkled, as tiny a sound as ice-glass breaking. A Lilliputian sound. Bates looked to the patch of wall above the door. The bell was mounted on a brass plate. It shivered again, and silver sound dribbled out.

Pannell stood, staring at the bell like a fool, a glass of brandy in his hands. "That means that Mr. Burton is coming here directly. It rings when Mr. Burton is on his way here directly. But I was to bring you to Mr. Burton's office, not he to come here . . ."

And almost at once the door shuddered, as with cold, and snapped open. Burton was a tall man who carried a spherical belly before him like an O of exclamation. His jowls were turfed with black beard, but his forehead was bald, as pink and curved as a rose petal. He moved with the fierce energy of the financially successful. As Bates got up from his chair he tipped his glance down with a respectful nod of the head: Burton's shoes were very well-made, tapering to a point, the uppers made of some variety of stippled leather. Standing to his full height brought Bates's glance up along the fine cloth of Burton's trousers, past the taut expanse of dark waistcoat and frock, to the single bright item of clothing on the man: a turquoise and scarlet bow tie, in which actual jewels had been fitted.

He faced the proprietor with a smile, extending his hand. But the first thing Burton said was: "No, sir."

"Mr. Burton," gabbled Pannell, "may I introduce to you Mr. Bates, who has come in person to negotiate the contract. I was just telling him how generous we considered the terms he offered . . ."

"No sir," repeated Burton. "I'll not stand it."

"Not stand it, sir?" said Bates.

"I know who you are, sir," fumed Burton. He stomped to the far side of the office, and turned to face them again. Bates noticed the bone-colored walking stick, capped at each tip with red gold. "I know who you are!"

"I am Abraham Bates, sir," replied Bates.

"No sir!" Burton raised the cane, and brought it down on the flat of Pannell's desk. It reported like a rifle discharge. Pannell jerked at the sound, and even Bates found sweat pricking out of his forehead again.

"No sir," bellowed Burton. "You'll not weasel your way here! I know your type, and you'll not come here with your *false* names and *false* heart. No."

"Mr. Burton," said Bates, trying to keep his voice level. "I assure you that Bates is my name."

"You are a liar, sir! I give you the *lie*, sir." The cane flourished in the air, inadvertently knocking a picture on the wall and tipping a perspective of the South Seas through forty degrees.

"I am not, sir," retorted Bates.

"Gentlemen," whimpered Pannell. "I beg of you both . . ."

"Pannell, you'll hold your tongue," declared Burton, emphasising the last word with another flourish of the cane. "If you value your continued employment at this place. Do you *deny*, sir," he added, pointing the cane directly at Bates, "do you deny that you came here to infiltrate? To weasel your way in?"

"I came to discuss certain matters," insisted Bates. "That is all. Sir, do you refuse even to talk with me?"

"And if I do?" said Burton, his voice dropping a little. "Then? You'll have your members of parliament, your newspaper editors, your many friends, and with them you'll turn on me? A pack of dogs, sir! A pack of dogs!"

"I admire your cane," said Bates, lowering himself back into his chair in what he hoped was a cool-headed manner. "Is it bone, sir?"

This took the wind from Burton's sails. "We'll not discuss my cane, sir."

"Is it Brobdingnagian bone? From which part of the body? A bone from the inner-ear, perhaps?"

"There is nothing illegal," Burton began, but then seemed to change his mind. The sentence hung in the air for a while. "Very well," he said, finally, somewhat deflated. "You have come to talk, sir. We will talk, sir. Pannell, you will stay in this room. Pour me a brandy, in fact, whilst I and this . . . *gentleman* discuss the affairs of the day. Then, Mr. Bates, I'd be obliged if you left this manufactory and did not return."

"One conversation will satisfy me, sir," said Bates, rounding the sentence off with a small sigh, like a full-stop given breath.

Burton settled into a chair by the window, and Pannell poured another glass of brandy with visibly trembling fingers. "This *gentleman*," Burton told his employee, "is an agitator, sir. A radical, I daresay. Are you a radical?"

"I am one of Mr. Martineau's party."

"Oh!" said Burton, with egregious sarcasm. "A party man!"

"I am honored to be so styled."

"And no patriot, I'll lay any money."

"I love my country, sir," replied Bates, "love her enough to wish her better managed."

"Faction and party," Burton muttered grimly, raising the brandy glass to his face like a glass muzzle over his bulbous nose. "Party and faction." He drank. "They'll sunder the country, I declare it." He put the empty glass down on the table with an audible *ploc*.

Pannell was hovering, unhappy-looking, by the door.

"We can agree to differ on the topic, sir," said Bates, a little stiffly.

"Well, sir," said Burton. "What conversation is it you wish to have with me? I own this manufactory, sir. Yes, we employ a cohort of Blefuscans."

"Employ, sir?"

"They cost me," said Burton, bridling. "A fortune. Regular food does not sit in their stomachs, so they must be fed only the daintiest and most expensive. Regular cloth is too coarse for their clothing, so they must be given the finest silks. The expense is very much greater than a regular salary would be. True, I own them outright, and this makes them slaves. But they are well treated, and they cost me more as slaves than employees ever could. I suppose Mr. Bates here," Burton added, addressing Pannell in a raised voice that aimed for sarcasm, but achieved only petulance, "would see them *free*. Mr. Bates considers slavery an *evil*. Is it not so, Mr. Bates?"

Bates shifted in his chair. It squeaked again underneath him. "Since you ask, I do consider such slavery as you practice here an evil. How many of your employees die?"

"I lose money with each fatality, sir," said Burton. "I've no desire to see a single one die."

"And your cane, sir? How many Brobdingnagians are left alive in the world?"

"I have nothing to do with those monsters. Indeed not. One of their kind could hardly fit inside my building."

"Yet you carry a cane made from their bodies, sir. Do you not consider that a small wickedness? A celebration of their pitiable state?"

"*Some* people, Pannell," said Burton, addressing his employee again. "Some people have leisure and predisposition to be sympathetic towards animals. Others are too busy with the work they have at hand."

"Your Lilliputians . . ."

"Blefuscans, sir."

"Your little people, sir—and the giant people also—are hardly animals."

"No? Have you worked with them, Mr. Bates?"

"I have devoted many years now to their cause."

"But actually *worked with them*? No, of course not. The midgets are mischievous, and their wickedness is in the bone. And the giants—they are a clear and present danger to the public good."

"The Brobdingnagians have endured homicide on an appalling scale."

"Homicide? But that implies man, don't it? Implies killing *men*, don't it?"

"Are not the Brobdingnagians made in God's image, sir? As are you and I? As are the Lilliputians?"

"So," said Burton, smiling broadly. "It's God, at the heart of your disaffection, is it?"

"Our nation would be stronger," said Bates, struggling to keep the primness out of his voice, "if we followed God's precepts more, sir. Or are you an atheist?"

"No, no."

"Let me ask you a question, Mr. Burton: are your Blefuscan workers—are they white-skinned, or black?"

"What manner of question is this, sir? You've just examined my workers out there. You know the answer to your own question."

"Their skins are as white as mine," said Bates. "Now, the Bible is clear on this. God has allotted slavery to one portion of his creation, and marked that portion by blackening their skins—Ham's sons, sir. There are enough blacks in the world to fill the places of slaves. But it mocks God to take some of his most marvellous creations and enslave them, or kill them."

"I do not kill my workers, sir," insisted Burton.

"But they *are* killed, sir. Worldwide, only a few thousand are left. And the Brobdingnagians—how many of them remain alive? After the affair with the *Endeavour* and the *Triumph*?"

"I have met the Captain of the *Triumph*, sir," said Burton, bridling up again. "At a dinner party of a friend of mine. An honorable man, sir. Honorable. He followed the orders he was given. What naval gentleman could do otherwise? And," he continued, warming to his theme, "was it so great a crime? These giants are twelve times our size. Had they organized, had they known cannon, and ordnance, and gunpowder, they could have trampled us to pieces. Not only England neither, but the whole of Europe—they *would* have come over here and trampled us to pieces. Who'd have been the slaves then? You may answer me that question, if you please. With an army of monstrous giants trampling England's green fields, who'd have been the slaves then?"

"The Brobdingnagians are a peace-loving people," said Bates, feeling his own color rise. "If you read the account of the mariner who discovered their land . . ."

Burton laughed aloud. "That fellow? Who'd believe a word he wrote? Riding the nipple of a gentlewoman like a hobby-horse, begging your pardon—it was nonsense. And the reality? A race of beings big enough to squash us like horseflies, and destroy our nation. Our nation, sir! Yours and mine! We had but one advantage over them, and that was that we possessed gunpowder and they did not. The King did well to destroy the majority of that population and seize their land. Our people are the best fed in the world, now, sir. Perhaps you do not remember how things were before the gigantic cattle were brought here, but I do: many starved in the streets. Now there's not a pauper but eats roast beef every day. Our army is the strongest and manliest on the continent. Would we have had our successes invading France and Holland without them?"

"You speak only of temporal advantages," insisted Bates. "But to do so is short purely material terms—but the spiritual, sir? The spiritual?"

"God," said Burton.

"Indeed, my friend. God created all these creatures as marvels. We have spat upon his gift. Lilliputians may seem small to us, but they are part of God's universe."

"There are giants in Genesis, I believe," said Burton. "Did not the flood destroy them?"

"The flood may not have reached the northwestern coast of America," said Bates. "At least, this is one theory as to the survival of these peoples."

"It hardly seems to me that God's Providence was greatly disposed towards these monsters. He tried to destroy them in the flood, and again in the form of two British frigates." His face twitched with smiling.

"After much prayer," Bates insisted, not wanting to be distracted. "After much prayer, it has become obvious to me . . ."

At this Burton laughed out loud, a doggy, abrasive noise; each laugh parcelled into sections, like the "ha! ha! ha!" of conventional orthography, although the noise he made was not so aspirated as this representation implies. More like: nugh! nugh! nugh! It broke through Bates's speech. "Pannell," said Burton. "Mr. Bates has come to vex us, not to divert us, and yet how diverting he is!"

"Mockery is," began Bates, his anger rising. He swallowed his words. Better to turn the other cheek. "I come, sir, to *invite* you. To invite you to join a communality of *enlightened* employers and financiers—a small core, sir, but a vital one. From us will grow a more proper, a more holy society."

"A society? So that's it. And if I joined your communality, I would not be allowed to possess any slaves, I suppose?"

"You might own slaves, sir, provided only they *were* slaves—blacks I mean. The Lilliputians are not slaves, sir, in God's eye, and it is God you mock by treating them so. God will not be mocked."

"I daresay not," agreed Burton, hauling his cumbersome body from its chair. "It's been a pleasure, sir, talking with you. Mr. Pannell here will show you out."

Bates rose, flustered, unsure exactly where he had lost the initiative in the interview. "Am I to take it, sir, that you . . ."

"You are to take it any way you choose, sir. I had thought you a spy for Parliament, sir: there are MPs who would gladly outlaw slavery in all its forms, and they have the power to do actual harm. But you, sir, do not—I doubt nothing but that you are harmless, as are your God-bothering friends. Good day, sir!"

Bates's color rose fiercely. *Godbothering*! The insolence! "You are rude sir! Believe me, God is more powerful than any parliament of men."

"In the next world sir, the next world."

"You veer towards blasphemy."

"It is not *I*," Burton growled, "who attempted to infiltrate an honest workman's shop with lies and deceit, not I who broke the commandment about bearing false witness to worm my way inside a decent business and try to tear it down. But you knew that you would not gain admittance if you spoke your true purpose. Good day, sir."

[2]

Bates paced the evening streets of London, the long unlovely streets. He passed gin-shops and private houses. He walked past a junior school with ranks of windows arrayed along its brick walls like the ranks of children within. He passed churches, chapels and a synagogue. Up the dog-leg of Upper St. Martin's Lane and past the rag-traders of Cambridge Circus, now mostly putting away their barrows and boarding up their shops. Bates, lost in his own thoughts, walked on, and up the main thoroughfare of Charing Cross Road.

Around him, now, crowds passed. Like leaves at autumn, drained of their richness, dry and grey and rattling along the stone roads before the wind. He thought of the French word: foule. A true word, for what was of greater folly than a crowd? The stupidity of humankind, that cattle-breed. Hiding, unspeaking, in some crevice of his mind was a sense of the little Lilliputians as daintier. More graceful. More *faery*. But he didn't think specifically of the little folk as he walked the road. There was an oppressive weariness inside him, as grey and heavy as a moon in his belly. Melancholia was, he knew it of course, a sin. It sneered at God's great gift of life. It was the sin against hope. It was to be fought, but the battle was hard. It was hard because melancholia corroded precisely the will to fight; it was a disease of the will.

Over his head, one of the new clockwork flying devices buzzed, dipping and soaring like a metal dragonfly, long as his arm. It croaked away through the air up Charing Cross Road, flying north and carrying who knew what message to who knew what destination. Only the wealthy could afford such toys, of course; the wealthy and the government. Perhaps it was the noise, the self-importance humming of it, that always gave the impression of a creature hurrying off on an errand of the mightiest importance. The war! The empire! The future of humankind!

Probably a financial facilitator, a manufactor, somebody with nouveau riches in the city, one of that type, had sent it flying north to let his servants know he would be late home from work.

The thought was sour in Bates's belly, a tart, undigested pain. He should not have drunk the brandy.

He stopped to buy the *Times* from a barrow-boy, and ducked into a mahogany ceilinged coffee shop to read it, sitting with hot chocolate breathing fragrant steam at his elbow. Gaslight from four lamps wiped light over the polished tabletops, reflecting blurry circles of light in the waxed wood of the walls. He brought his face close to the newsprint, as much to bury himself away from the stare of the other coffee-drinkers as to make out the tiny printface. Miniature letters, like insects swarming over the page.

News.

British forces had seen action again at Versailles; the famous palace had been pocked with cannonshells. There was little doubt that Christmas would see the flag of St. George flying over Paris. Anxiety of the French people; reassurance from the King that there would be no anti-Catholick repression after an English victory. The mechanics of the Flying Island had been thoroughly analyzed by the Royal Society, and a paper had been read before the King. It seemed that a particular ore was required, against which a magnetic device of unusual design operated. This ore was found only rarely in His Majesty's dominions, and in Europe not at all. But deposits were known to lie in portions of the North American and Greater Virginian continent. The way was clear, the paper announced, for a new island to be constructed as a platform for use in the war against the Spanish in that continent.

Still Bates's spirits sank. He could not prevent it: some malign gravity of the heart dragged him down.

He turned to the back of the paper, and studied the advertisements. For sale, one Lilliputian, good needleworker. For sale, two Lilliputians, a breeding couple; four hundred guineas the pair. For sale, stuffed Lilliputian bodies, arranged in poses from the classics: Shakespeare, Milton, Scott. For sale, prime specimen of the famed Intelligent Equines, late of His Majesty's Second Cognisant Cavalry; this Beast (the lengthy advertisement spooled on) speaks a tolerable English, but knows mathematics and music to a high level of achievement. Of advanced years, but suitable for stud. And there, at the bottom, swamped and overwhelmed by the mass of Mammonite hawking and crying, was a small box: Public Lecture, on the Wickedness of Enslaving the Miniature Peoples from the East India Seas. Wednesday, no entrance after eight. Wellborough Hall. Admission one shilling.

Hopeless, all hopeless.

For Bates, the sinking into the long dark night of the soul had begun. It had happened before, but every time it happened there was never anything to compare it to, never any way to fight it off. He stumbled down Oxford Street in a fuggy daze of misery. Where did it come from? Chapels littered both sides of the road, some polished and elegant, some boxy and unpretentious, and yet none of them held the answer to his indigestion of the spirit. If only some angel would swoop down to him, calling and weeping through the air like a swift, varicolored wings stretching like a cat after a sleep, the feather-ends brushing the street itself in the lowest portion of Its flying arc, its face bland and pale and still and beautiful. If only some angel could bring God's blessing down to him. Or perhaps the angel would actually be a faery, a tiny creature with wings of glass and a child's intensity of innocence. Grace was Grace, even in the smallest parcels.

[3]
11 November 1848

By the time Bates next rose from his bed he had been on the mattress for two days and two nights. His man put his insolent white head through the doorway to his cubby and chirruped. "Feeling better today?"

"Go away, Baley," Bates groaned. "Leave me in peace."

"Off to your club today? It's Thursday—you told me most particularly to remind you of Thursday."

"Yes," he muttered, more to himself than to his servant. "Yes, Thursday. I will be getting up today. My . . . stomach feels a little better."

"There you go sir." The head withdrew, with only the faintest of smirks upon it that seemed to say *we all know there's nothing the matter with your stomach, you old stay-a-bed.*

Bates turned over in the bed. The sheet underneath him was foul with two days' accumulated stink, creased and wrinkled like the palm of a white hand. His bedside cabinet was littered with glasses, bottles, a newssheet, an ivory pipe. The curtain was of cotton-velvet, and muffled off most of the daylight. The joints between knuckles and fingers'-ends ached in both hands; the small of his back murmured complaint. His feet hurt from inaction. A series of bangs, miniature sounds, *goh, goh, goh*. Bates could not tell whether the thrumming sound was the spirit of Headache rapping inside his scull, or the sound of something thudding far away. The volatile acid of his melancholia had even eroded away the boundaries of self and world, such that Bates's misery spread out and colonized reality itself, it became a universal pressure of unhappiness. It seemed to Bates at that moment that the Biblical flood had been, symbolically speaking, a *type* or *trope* for Melancholia itself, washing away strength, joy, will, hope, diluting the very energy of life itself and spreading it impossibly weakly about the globe. Grey waves washing at a rickety waterfront.

He pulled the pot from under the bed and pissed into it without even getting up, lying on his side and directing the stream over the edge of the mattress. Flecks of fluid messed the edge of the bed, but he didn't care. Why should he care? What was there to care about? When he had finished he did not even bother pushing the pot back under the bed. He turned on his other side and lay still. There was a faint noise, a repeated thud-thud-thud.

It stopped. Bates turned over again.

Turned over again. Ridiculous, ridiculous.

He pulled himself upright, and snatched at the paper. Baley had brought it to him the night before, but Bates's fretful, miserable state of mind had not allowed him to concentrate long enough to read the articles. He started on the first leader, an imperial puff about the prospects for a British European Empire once France had been defeated. He read the third sentence three times—*our glorious history reasserts itself, our generals revitalize the dreams of Henry the Fifth*—without taking it in at all. The words were all there, and he knew the meaning of each, but as a whole the sentence refused to coalesce in his mind. Senseless. It was hopeless. In a fit of petty rage, he crushed the whole paper up into a ragged ball and threw it to the floor. It started, creakily, to unwind, like a living thing.

He lay down again.

"Gentleman at the door, sir." It was Baley, his head poking into crib.

"I'm not at home," Bates said into the mattress.

"Won't take that for an answer, sir," said Baley. "A foreign gentleman. Says he's High Belgium, but I'd say France, sir."

Bates hauled himself upright. "His hair black, in a long knout at the back of his head?"

"A what, sir?"

"Long hair, idiot, long hair?"

"Continental fashion, yes sir."

Bates was struggling into his gown. "Show him through, you fool." He pressed the crumbs of sleep from his eyes and wiped a palm over his sleep-ruffled hair. Here? D'Ivoi had never before come to his rooms, they had always met in the club. Perhaps Baley had made a mistake—but, no, coming through to the drawing room there was D'Ivoi, standing facing the fire, with a turquoise hat under his arm, the sheen of his silk suit gleaming, and his ridiculous tassel of hair dangling from the back of his head. Baley was loitering, and Bates shooed him away.

"My friend," said D'Ivoi, turning at the sound of Bates's voice.

"I was coming to the club today," said Bates at once. "Perhaps I seem unprepared, but I was about to get dressed."

D'Ivoi shook his head very slightly, no more than a tremble, and the smile was not dislodged from his face. "There is no need for us to meet at the club." His *th*s were brittle, *tare* is no need for us to meet at *tea* club, but otherwise his accent was tolerably good. "I regret to say my friend, that I leave this city this afternoon." *Tat* I leave *tiss* city.

"Leave?" Bates reached without thinking for the bell-rope, to call for tea; at the last minute he remembered that this was a conference to which the servant must not be privy.

"I regret to say it. And before I depart, I bring a warning of sorts. Events in the war are about to take a turn . . . shall we say, dramatic?"

"Dramatic? I don't understand. The paper says that we . . . that, ah, the English are on the edge of capturing Paris. When that happens, surely the . . ."

"No my friend," said D'Ivoi. "You will find tomorrow's newspapers tell a different story. France and the Pope have declared a common right with the Pacificans."

It was all a great deal for Bates to take in at once. "They have?" he said. "Why that's excellent news. Excellent news for our cause. Common right with Lilliputians and Brobdingnagians, both?"

"Certainly, with both. The petite folk, and the giant folk, both are made in God's image. The talking horses, not; the Pope has decreed them devilish impostures. But of course he does so more because the English has its cavalry regiment of sapient horses. And the French army now has its own regiments. Regiments of the little folk would be useless enough, I suppose, but the giants make fearsome soldiers, I think."

"The French army has recruited regiments of Brobdingnagians?" repeated Bates, stupidly.

"I have not long, my friend," said D'Ivoi, nodding his head minutely. "I come partly to warn you. There are other things. The President of the Republic has relocated to Avignon, as you know. Well, there have been great things happening in Avignon, all in the south you know. And these great things are about to emerge to the day's light, for all the world to see. It will be terrible to be an English soldier before them."

"Monsieur," said Bates. "Are you . . . ?"

"Forgive me, my friend," interrupted D'Ivoi. "When these things happen, it will be uncomfortable to be a French national in London, I think. And so I depart. But I warn you too: your cause, your pardon our cause, for the liberation of the Pacificans, has aligned you with the nation of France. Your government may take action against you for this reason."

"I am no traitor," Bates asserted, though his tongue felt heavy in his mouth uttering the sentiment.

"No no," assured the foreigner. "I only warn you. You know best, of course, how to attend to your own safety. But before I depart (and time is close, my friend), let me say this: contemplate a French victory in this war. I advise it. Believe that, with the Pope and the President now allied formally to the petites and the giants, believe that a victory for France will spell freedom for these people. Perhaps one smaller evil counterbalances a larger good? Perhaps?"

Bates did not know what to say to this. "I know that my actions here," he started saying, speaking the words slowly, "have benefited the French government. And I am not ashamed of this."

"Good! Excellently good! Because it will be less time than you think before French soldiers arrive here in London town, and you would be well to consider how your duty lies. Your duty, my friend, to God above all. No?"

"Monsieur," said Bates again anxiously.

But D'Ivoi was putting his top hat on and bowing, stiffly. "I regret I must depart."

"French soldiers here?"

"Ah, yes. I will say only this, at last. There has been a very great series of inventions. We have a machine, a thinking and calculating machine . . . have you heard of this?"

"A machine?"

"Mister Babbage, and his French mistress, have been working in Uzes, in France's south, for many years now. You have heard, perhaps, of mister Babbage?"

"The name is familiar . . ." said Bates. His head was starting to buzz unpleasantly. This conference was a shock, there was no mistaking it.

"He has built a machine. It can undertake a week's calculations in a moment. It is nothing more than a box, the size of a piano I think, but it gives great power of calculation and ratiocination, of the power of thought in this box. Forgive me, I am forgetting my English already. But our engineers now use this box, and with it they design fantastic new machines. Our generals use it, and with it they plan all possible military strategies. This box will win the war, for us."

And he bowed again and was gone.

[4]
11–12 November 1848

Where does it go, the melancholia, when some startling event evaporates it, sublimes it into vapor that dissolves into the wind? Bates's downheartedness vanished. He washed, shaved, dressed, ate and bustled from his rooms in an hour. Everything had been turned topsy-turvy, and the evil spirit squatting spider-like in his head had somehow fallen free.

He hurried. D'Ivoi had been his only contact with the French, and perhaps by limiting his contact to a single individual he had, at some level, believed that he limited his treason too. And for a day or two the very notion of a French victory—of French troops marching up the Mall—was too shocki
think about it at all. But the idea percolated through his mind any
he was almost welcoming it. It would bring his cause to fruition. T
would be freed, the Brobdingnagians reprieved from race-death.

He was up, up, up.

He went to his club, and wrote three letters. Then he caught a cab (a rare expense for him) and visited a sympathetically minded gentleman in Holborn. He spent the evening with a gaggle of churchmen, duck-like individuals who paced about the room with their heads forward and their hands tucked into the smalls of their backs, talking ponderously of God. He told the sympathetically minded gentleman little, but he told the churchmen all. Their worry, it transpired, was not of French political rule, so much as the danger of an oppressive Catholicism being imposed as the official religion. Bates was too excited, too elevated in spirit, to worry about this.

"Are you certain that these events are going to come to pass?" one of the clerics asked him. "Are you sure?"

"I am sure," gabbled Bates. He tended to talk too rapidly when the mood was on him, when his blood was hurtling through his body, but it couldn't be helped. "Now that they have declared themselves for the humanity of the Lilliputians and Brobdingnagians, all of the civilized world will support them, surely. And their alliance has meant that they could recruit a regiment of giants to fight us. To fight the English. Moreover," he went on, wide-eyed, "they have perfected a device, a machine, a thinking machine. Have you heard of Mister Babbing?"

Babbing? Babbing?

"Do you mean *Babbage*," said one elderly churchman, a whittled, dry-faced old man who had been a main agent in the campaign since its first days. "The computational device?"

"The French have perfected it," said Bates. "And with it they have constructed new engineering devices, and plotted new techniques of war-making."

"Incredible!"

"It is credible indeed."

"The computing device has been perfected!"

On the Saturday he attended a tea-party at which he was the only male present. He sat on a chair too small for him, and listened politely to half-a-dozen wealthy matrons and maidens expatiate upon how beautiful the little people were, how marvelous, and how wicked it was to chain them with tiny chains and make them work in factories. Nobody mentioned the Brobdingnagians, of course, who lacked the daintiness to appeal to this class of person. But Bates smiled and nodded, and thought of the money these women might gift to the cause.

One woman confided in him. "Since my husband passed through the veil," she said in a breathy tone of voice, "my life has become divided between these darling little creatures, and my cats."

The Sunday, naturally he went to chapel. But he could not bring his mind to focus on the sermon. Something fretted at its margins, some piece of thought-grit. *These darling little creatures*. But, Bates thought, there was so much more to the Lilliputians than this! They were messengers, in some way or other. He had not managed to clear the thought thoroughly enough through his brain to fully understand it, but he felt it, he felt it genuinely and thoroughly. Messengers. There was something about them, something special, that deserved preservation in the way few ordinary-sized people did.

She had sat next to him, with purple crinoline and a lacecap covering her hair, but with these intense, beautiful air-blue eyes, and had said: *these darling little creatures, and my cats.*

Cats preyed on them, of course. One of Bates's acquaintances declared that he had first become interested in their cause after watching two cats fighting over a stray Lilliputian, in the kitchen of his uncle's house.

And so it slid again, dropping like leaves from a tree until the tree has lost all its leaves. Bates went to bed Sunday night with a heart so heavy it registered not only in his chest, but in his throat and belly too. And waking the following morning was a forlorn, interfered-with sensation. The urge not to rise was very strong: merely to stay in bed, to turn the heavy-body and heavy-head and lie there. After a few days of energetic living, Bates's life had been usurped again by melancholia.

His rooms, on Cavendish Square, looked over an oval of parched winter grass and four nude trees. Some days he would sit and stare, emptying one cigarette after another of its smoke, and doing nothing but watching the motionlessness of the trees.

When he had been a young man, some six or seven years earlier, Bates had had an intrigue with a tobacconist's daughter called Mary. The romance had strayed into physical impropriety. To begin with, Bates had felt a glow in his heart, something fueled by equal parts pride and shame. The necessary secrecy had built him up inside his suit. He felt the sin, but he also felt elevated, enlarged. He could walk the streets of London, looking at the others, and knowing something they did not know. The aftermath, the potent stew of good and bad emotions, was more pleasurable than the physical enjoyment of the act itself, pleasurable though that act is.

Then Mary told him that she was carrying a child. This changed the balance of feelings inside him to a form of fear. He could not bring himself to confront his own father (still alive at that time) to declare himself the destined parent of an infant. It was impossible. Inner shame is, perhaps, a sensation so powerfully mixed of delight and disgust it approximates glory; but public shame is a very different matter. Bates senior was not a wealthy man, but he was proud. Marriage to a tobacconist's daughter was out of the question. And Mary was a sweet girl. But what could he do? What could be done.

Of course nothing could be done.

There was a very uncomfortable interview between the former lovers. There were tears and recriminations from her. They made it easier for him to adopt a stony exterior manner. Afterwards he spent the evening in his club, and drank most of a bottle of claret. A walk home and a half-hour in a chapel along the way. Prayer blended his awkwardness, his shame, his self-loathing, his weakness, into a cement of strength. He would be strong from this moment, which was all that Christ required. He would sin no more.

His resolution included a blanking out of Mary, which he managed by pretending that she did not exist. For weeks this strategy worked well. For hours at a time he forgot that there was such a person in the world. Only when he indulged in occasional, night-time bouts of impure thought and manual stimulation did her image pop into his mind, and this only encouraged him to quit that degrading business anyway.

Then, a month or more later, he saw her at the booth, paying to cross London Bridge. He hurried after her, uncertain whether the face glimpsed under the bonnet was indeed hers. "Excuse me, madam," he called. And she turned.

She looked blankly into his face, neither pleased nor displeased to see him.

"Mary," he said, catching up with her.

Her stomach was flat.

"You're looking," she chided, following his gaze. "Tis not decent."

Light made painterly effects on the river, speckles of brightness spread in a swathe.

He didn't know how to ask the question.

"Don't worry yourself, sir," she said, blushing plum-red, her voice as angry as Bates had ever heard it. "No child will come and threaten your family honor." She pronounced this last word *on 'er*.

"I don't understand."

She was quiet for a time. "Well, a friend of mine knows a doctor. Not that I'd call him a real doctor, if you see what I say."

"Oh," said Bates, soft, realizing what had happened. They were a third of the way over the bridge now. The sunlight swelled, and the Thames was glittering and sparkling like a solid. Bates's mouth was dry.

"What did you do with it?" he asked, a pain growing in his chest as if his ribs were contracting and squeezing his lungs.

"It?" she replied.

"The," he said, his voice sounding somehow different to himself, "child."

She stared at him, stared for half a minute, her face immobile but her eyes wide. "I buried him," she said. "I dug under the hedgerow in Somer's Town, beside the churchyard, and buried him there."

For days Bates had been unable to get this image out of his mind. His child, his son, buried and mixed into the earth. Like ore. He dreamt of the little creature, its eyes closed and its mouth pursed against the chill. He imagined it with hair, long blonde strands of hair. He imagined it miniature, Lilliputian in size. In the dream he scuffed at the dirt with his feet, knowing his child was interred beneath the spot. A strand of gold grazed his wrist. Boys in brown, crossing-sweepers, leaned together to talk, somewhere in the distance. Through a window, perhaps. One of them yawned. But he was in a room, with velvet curtains. The strands of gold were woven into a cobweb. A strand of gold grazed his wrist. The baby's tiny hand was reaching for him, and when it touched him its skin was so cold he yelped out loud.

At that point he awoke.

[5]

On 19 November, French forces crossed the Channel. The fighting in the north-east was the hardest, British troops having pulled back with a military alacrity to trenches dug earlier in the campaign and then sticking to their positions in and around Saint Quentin. But the French army was renewed. Three battalions of regular troops attacked the British positions; but then the *premier corps de géants* stormed the eastern flank. They carried enormous weaponry, great hoops of iron ringing massive planks of treated wood, cannonaders that the Brobdingnagians could fire from their shoulders, sending fissile barrel-shaped charges hurtling onto troops below. The packages were filled with Greek Fire. The giants proved remarkably resistant to rifle fire; although cannon-shells would tend to bring them down.

The battle fought at Saint Quentin was the major engagement of the whole war, with conventional troops charging the English line-of-defense from two sides at once, and a platoon of Brobdingnagians wading amongst the fighting with studied, slow-footed seriousness, smashing and killing about them with long, weighted pikes—sixty foot long, and carrying nearly a ton of metal shaped at the killing end. And the cannonaders wrought havoc. One colonel lost his color completely as he read the paper containing the casualty figures after the battle. "If this number were pounds rather than corpses," he told his aide de camp, "we would be wealthy indeed." His bon mot went around the camp. The English army, the soldier joked grimly, was wealthy indeed in corpses, but poor in terms of the sovereign. The Commander in Chief was still hanging men for High Treason, because this joke had passed their lips, when the rest of the army had retreated to the coast. He himself left on a sapient horse as French forward-troops broke through the camp and past the dangling bodies.

From Quentin the English fell back across the Pas de Calais. Orders to establish a series of redoubts were ignored, or heroically followed to the death of everyone concerned. Commanders attempted to co-ordinate an evacuation on the beaches around Calais-town, but the French pressed their advantage and embarkation turned to rout. Eventually the Brobdingnagians swam through again, pulling boats down to perdition from underneath. Commanders fled the scene in small skiffs. There was screaming, weapon's-fire, commotion and confusion. The English losses were even worse than they had been at the battle of Saint Quentin.

Corpses sank to the bottom of the Manche as stones, or bobbed on the surface, tangled with the waves, or rolled and trundled dead in the surf, sand in their mouths and in their hair, in their sightless eyes.

Bates followed the news, reading the hastily printed news-sheets with a fearful avidity. He wanted the French repulsed, like any Englishman. But he wanted the French victorious, and with it the noble God-endorsed cause to which he had devoted so much of his adult life. He didn't know what he wanted. He wanted to sleep, but he could only toss and roll on his dirty sheets.

His servant vanished. This abandonment didn't surprise him. Everywhere, people were leaving the capital.

The *premier* and *troisième corps de géants* walked and swam the channel, pulling troop-barges behind them. The army beached at Broadstairs. The English army, with all reserves called up and all available men under orders, assembled themselves on the hills south of Canterbury. Travelers and passengers began carrying word-of-mouth reports of the fighting. *Terrible, like the end of the world,* they said. *It be the world's end, a preacher was saying on Gad's Hill. These gigantic men are God's wrath.*

The flood of people from London increased.

Bates found his mood undergoing one of those peculiar bubblings-up that correlated only poorly to his surroundings. He took to rising relatively early, and walking the streets of London with a dispassionate, observer's eye. He watched servants load belongings onto carts outside lankily opulent town houses in Mayfair; watched shopkeepers fitting boards over their windows, whilst their wives wrapped whimpering Lilliputians in handkerchiefs for the journey. On the Great North Road a great worm of humanity pulsed away to the horizon, people walking, trudging, hurrying or staggering, hand-carts and horse carts, men hauling packs stacked yards high with clinking pots and rolled cloth, women carrying children, animals on tight tethers. Bates stood for an hour or more watching the stream of people trudge on, as seemingly sourceless and endless as the Thames itself. Militiamen trotted by on horseback, hawkers cried wares to the refugees, clockwork aerial craft buzzed up and down the rank, left and right across it.

Eventually, Bates wandered back into the city, and went to his club to take luncheon. Only Harmon was there, and one cook in the back-room. "Dear me," Bates muttered. "What's happened here." Harmon was all apologies, a good man in trying times. "Luncheon should not present problems, sir, if you'd care to eat."

Bates ate. His thoughts kept returning to the war. Could the generals, perhaps, be persuaded that England was losing the war *because* it had flouted God's ordinance? A general proclamation from Parliament freeing the Lilliputians, and God's radiance would smile on His people again—surely? Surely?

He wandered, pensive, taking twice his normal time back to Cavendish Square. A stranger, dressed in an anonymous brown, was waiting outside his front door.

"Sir?" he said, starting forward. "You are Mr. Bates?" The words were enough to reveal that his accent was French.

Bates felt suddenly panicky, he wasn't sure why. "What do you want?"

"Calm yourself, sir, calm yourself," said the stranger. "You are a friend of Mr. D'Ivoi, I believe?"

"D'Ivoi," said Bates. "Yes."

"I bring a message from him. Could we go inside your apartment?"

"Your army is in Kent, sir," said Bates, his fight-or-flight balance teetering towards the aggressive again. "It loots Kent as we speak, sir."

The stranger only said: "I bring a message from him."

The stranger did not introduce himself, or give a name. He carried a leather attaché case, and his boots were well worn at toe and heel. Inside, as Bates unclasped his own shutters (having no servant to do the job for him), the man placed his case carefully on a table, took off his three-cornered-hat, and bowed.

"Swiftness is to be desired, sir," he said. "I apologize for my English, for the speaking. You will pardon my expression?" Without waiting for an answer, he went on. "Mr. D'Ivoi has asked for you particularly." He enunciated every syllable of this latter word with care. "He, and I, ask for your help. You have faith in our cause, I believe."

"Cause."

"For the Pacificans. For the little and the great, of the people. The Holy Father has declared the war a holy war, to free these creatures from their bondage. Yes?"

"Yes."

"Our army will soon be in London. We wish for you to do something for us, which it will make more swift the ending of the war. If you do this thing for us, the war will end sooner, and the holy cause achieved."

"Yes," said Bates. His mouth was dry.

"In this satchel there is a person."

"Satchel?"

The stranger bowed. "Is the word incorrect? I apologize. This sack, this bag."

"No, sir, I understand the word."

"Please, will you take this satchel to the Tower of London. It is this tower which is the command position for the defense of London, as we believe. The generals, the munitions, the forces, they gather there. The person inside the satchel will be able to work such things as to . . . to make more swift the ending of the war."

"There is a Lilliputian in the bag?"

The stranger bowed, and opened the flap of the satchel. A Lilliputian unhooked himself from a small padded harness inside and climbed out to stand, at attention, on the tabletop. Bates, as amazed and as unsettled as he always was in the presence of these tiny beings, smiled, made his smile broader, opened his mouth to show his teeth as if he were going to eat the thing. The Lilliputian stood, motionless.

"He has a training, a special training," said the stranger. "He is a warrior of great courage, great value. If I were to approach the Tower I would be shot, of course. And the naked streets are dangerous places for the little men, with traps and cats and all things like this. But if you were to bear the satchel, you would be able to release him inside the fort. Yes?"

"I know nobody in the Tower of London," said Bates. "I have no contacts in the army."

"You go to the Tower, and tell them that you bear a message from Colonel Truelove."

"I do not know the gentleman."

"He is captured, but we believe that the . . . English, excuse me, that you . . . do not know that he is captured. You will present to the guards and tell them that you bear a message from him, for attention of General Wilkinson only, for the General only. Once inside, find a quiet place to release the warrior from the satchel."

Sunlight laid squares on the floor. Light is a weight upon the earth, a mighty pressure from above, and yet it is constituted of the tiniest of particles.

Bates felt as if the moment of choice had already passed behind him. He did not have the language to phrase a rejection. All he could say was: "I will do this thing."

[6]
27 November 1848

You are a strange figure, somebody told Bates. Sometimes your spirit is enormous; sometimes it shrinks to nothing. To nothing, Bates thought, and I lie abed for days. But not now, he thought. Now I have a task, to test myself, to prove myself to God.

The Frenchman had insisted on the urgency of his mission, and had pressed Bates until he offered up a promise to undertake it the following dawn. "Dawn, mind, sir," said the Frenchman, before leaving. "If we co-obstinate . . ."

"Co-ordinate," corrected Bates.

"Just so. If we co-obstinate, such that the little warrior is inside the Tower at the right moment, then we can complete the war much sooner. Much sooner."

He departed, with a gait that looked to Bates like an insolent jauntiness. But it was much too late for regrets. He shut his door, pulled up a chair and sat opposite the miniature human on the tabletop.

"Good evening, my friend," he said.

The Lilliputian was silent.

There was some uncanny aspect to them, Bates thought to himself. He could not feel comfortable in their company. They unsettled him. He tried to visualize them as toys, or marionettes, but then they would shiver in some inescapably human way, or their little eyes would swivel and stare, as if penetrating beneath the decorous levels of manner and behavior. They carried within them a strange elision. They were sylphs, but they were also and at the same time devils.

But it was too late for regrets.

"You are reticent, my friend," he said. "I cannot blame you if you harbor resentment against the English peoples. My people have committed . . . terrible crimes against . . . your people."

The Lilliputian said nothing. Was his silence the outward sign of some savage indignation?

"Believe me," Bates went on, "I am your friend. I have devoted my life to your cause."

Nothing.

It occurred to Bates that the Lilliputian might not speak English. "Mon ami," he began, but his French was not good. "Mon ami, j'espère que . . ."

The Lilliputian turned on his heel, clambered back inside the satchel, and was gone.

In the small hours of the morning Bates discovered that the Lilliputian did indeed speak English. He had somehow mounted the arm of the *chaise longue* on which Bates was sleeping, and called in his wren-like voice: "Awake! Awake! For the sun will soon scatter darkness like a white stone scattering crows in flock."

Sleepy-headed, Bates found this hard to follow.

"We must be on our way," cried the Lilliputian. "We must be on our way."

"It is still dark," Bates grumbled, rubbing the sleep from his eyes with the calf of his arm.

"But it will be light soon."

"You speak English."

The Lilliputian did not say anything to this.

Bates rose and lit a lamp, dressing rapidly. He used yesternight's bowl of water to rinse his face, laced his feet into his boots and looked about him. The Lilliputian was standing beside the satchel.

"You are eager to go to war, my little friend," Bates said.

The morning had a spectral, unreal feel about it: the citrus light of the lamp, the angular purple shadows it threw, the perfect scaled-down human being standing on the table.

"I am a warrior," it piped.

"But we must remember that Jesus is the Prince of Peace."

The little figure slanted his head minutely, but did not reply.

"Well well," said Bates. "Well well, we shall go."

The little figure slipped inside the case.

Locking the door to his rooms felt, to Bates, like sealing off his life entire. Perhaps I shall die, he said, but his mind was so muzzy with tiredness that the thought carried no sting. Perhaps I shall never return here. But he didn't believe that, not really. He did not truly believe that.

His fingers slipped and fumbled at his coat buttons, and then hoisting the case with its precious cargo and striding out.

The light was growing, as his heels sounded on the pavement in Cavendish Square. The air was chill. The western horizon was still a gloomy and impressive purple, but the sky to the east was bright, the color of malaria, with the morning star a dot of sharp light like a tiny window, immeasurably far off, open in the wall of an immense yellow citadel.

At the top of Charing Cross Road Bates saw a solitary person in the otherwise deserted streets, a hunched-over infantryman stumbling, or hurrying, north. He was nervous enough to draw back into the shadow of a doorway, and then rebuked himself and strode on. He imagined sentry-questions. *Who goes there?* An Englishman! A loyal Englishman! God save the King! *What's in the bag?* Nothing—sir—nothing at all, save some personal belongings . . . but that would be easily disproven, a quick search would reveal his true carriage. Papers! Papers for the general . . . to be perused by him alone. To be seen by his eyes only! Would that satisfy a sentryman?

He walked on, and the dawn swelled in brightness all around him.

By the time he reached Holborn the sounds of fighting were unignorable.

From a distance the cannon-fire sounded like the booming of bitterns over estuary flats, or the stomach-rumble of distant thunder. But once down the dip and up the other side of Holborn the battle seemed to swoop out of the imaginary into the real with appalling swiftness. Knocks and bangs three streets away, two, and then rifle fire tattering the air, men in beetroot uniforms with bayoneted rifles trotting en masse, or hurrying singly from firing-position to firing-position.

Bates was fully awake now.

He ducked down one side street, and then another, trying to stay clear of the scurrying military action. He was vividly aware of the stupidity of his position; a civilian, an unarmed and inexperienced man wandering the streets in the midst of a war. A bomb swooned through the air, exploding somewhere away to his left with a powerful crunch.

Panic took him for ten minutes, during which time he dropped the satchel and tried to claw his way through a barred oak door. When his right fingernails were bloody the panic seemed to ebb from him, leaving him panting and foolish. He retrieved the satchel, hurried to the end of the street, turned a dog-leg and found himself on the riverside.

The sun at its low angle, with sunlight trembling off the water, turned the river to metal. Bates hurried on. Fifty yards downriver and he was at the deserted toll-booth of London Bridge's Middlesex side.

"You there!" called somebody. "Hold yourself! Friend or foe!"

Bates stopped. "An Englishman!" he called.

From where he was standing he could look down upon the bridge, and across the pale brown rush of the river. The Thames's flow seemed enormous, the water standing up at the leading face of the bridge's pillars in burly, muscular lips, the trailing edge leaving deep scores in the surface that broke into wakes and ripples hundreds of yards further downstream. Riflemen hurried along the half-completed embankment, ducking behind the unplaced stone-blocks, or jumping into the holes where such blocks were yet to be placed. The sound of horses' whinnying, like metal skittering over ice, was in the air from somewhere on the other side of the river. An artillery unit labored with a recalcitrant field gun, poking its snub over the bridge's parapet. On the river's surface, a boat jockeyed against the fierce pull of the water, three sets of oars flicking up and down like insect legs to keep the boat alongside a small quay onto which soldiers were alighting.

And then, with the sounds of multiple detonation, smoke flowered into the air. French dart-shells hurtled over the horizon, threads against the sky, and careered into the masonry alongside the river with astonishing vehemence. The ground shook; ripples shuddered across the face of the water; stone cracked and puffed into the air as smoke. Bricks, pillars and blocks tumbled and clattered. More explosions. The tick-tock of bullets, British rifle fire, although Bates couldn't see what they were firing at. Then the giants came; heads rearing up like the sun over the horizon, but these suns followed by bodies, and the bodies supported on enormous legs. They strode up the river, the water blanching into foam about their shins. They were dressed in crazily-patched leather clothes, padded with numerous metal plates that were too poorly burnished to gleam in the light. With the sun behind them, four marched.

He was so stunned by the sight as to not understand how much in shock he was. He blinked, and turned. People were rushing on all sides, faces distorted as they shouted. He blinked again, turned again. The French, soldiers of ordinary size, were visible on the south bank, some firing over the water, some attempting to cross the bridge. English troops were defending the position. Bates stood in the midst of it, a single gentleman in modest but expensive clothing, his coat buttoned all the way to his chin, carrying a leather satchel briefcase. One of the English soldiers, hurrying to the bridge, caught his eye. "You!" he yelled. "You!"

Still numb to his surroundings, Bates turned to face him. Smoke misted up and swirled away, to an orchestral accompaniment of clattering explosions.

Everybody was looking north. Bates followed their glances. Another thunder-stroke.

One of the Brobdingnagians was standing over the dome of Saint Paul's. He had driven his metal-tipped staff through the shell of it, as if breaking the blunt end of an egg. He lifted it out, and struck again, and the dome collapsed leaving a fuzzy halo of dust.

Bates turned to look for the soldier who had accosted him. He was not standing where he had been standing. Bates looked around, and then looked down, and saw him lying spreadeagled on the floor. Blood, dark and taut like poured molasses, was pooled all around him.

Bates stumbled, half-awake, from the tollbooth and down a side-street. A crazy trajectory. He ran clumsily past a row of scowling arches, and then turned into a doorway, pressing himself up into the shadow and against the side wall.

The sounds of battle became chuckles and creaks. It took him a moment to realize that the fighting was moving away, sweeping round beyond the wrecked cathedral and into the fields to the north. He fiddled with the catch on the briefcase and whispered inside, although as he did so he was struck by how peculiar it was to be whispering.

The street was deserted.

The Lilliputian's high-pitched voice warbled from its hidden place. "You must go on."

"I will be killed," said Bates, a trill of nerves shaking the last word. He felt close to tears.

"Death is the soil of the world," said the Lilliputian, the oddness of the sentiment made stranger still by the ethereal, piping voice that uttered it.

"I will wait here until the fighting has stopped," said Bates. Saying so brought him a trembly sense of satisfaction: to be safe, not to die, to stay hidden until the danger had passed.

"No," said the Lilliputian. The timbre of his voice had changed. Somehow, Bates could not see how, he had slipped out of the case and climbed up the coat. He stood on Bates's shoulder, and with a shimmer was on his face. Tiny pressure on his ear, a tickling sensation of an insect on his cheek. Bates could not repress a shudder, a raising of his eyes to swat the spider that had the *gall* to touch his face—to touch his face! Only an effort of will, consciousness, prevented him from slapping at the little creature. I must not! He thought. God's creature! So easy to crush it out of life . . . but no, no, I must not, never, never.

Blurrily close to his eyeball, the pink-yellow shape of a head, a lash-like hand, dissolved by nearness. "This thorn," warbled the Lilliputian, "is a weapon. I can thrust it into your eye, and it will explode, a bomb." Bates blinked furiously. "If you attack me I will have your eye." Bates blinked again. His eye was watering; his breaths were coming much more swiftly. "If you do not move *now*, to go to the Tower, I will have your eye."

"My dear little friend," said Bates, high-pitched. "Mon share amy."

"The Brobdingnagians live to be a hundred and fifty years of age," came the sing-song rapid little voice. "They are wary of death, for death is a rarity to them. But we of Lilliput live a quarter as long, and hold death in a quarter as much worth. We are a nation of warriors."

"My dear little friend," said Bates, again.

"Go now." And the tickling sensation vanished from his face, the ornament-like pressure removed from his ear. When Bates had regained his breath the Lilliputian was back in the satchel.

The battle seemed to have passed entirely away. Cautious as a mouse, Bates ducked from doorway to doorway, but the only people he saw were British soldiers. He hurried down Eastcheap, and came out from the tall houses directly before the Tower.

He had no idea of the time. Certainly the morning was advanced now, the sky was crowded with ivory-colored thunderheads. Spots of rain touched his face, and Bates thought of contemptuous Lilliputians spitting upon his skin.

There was a great deal of military activity around the Tower; mounted troops jittered by, their horses glittery with sweat, or rain, or both; cannons were positioned at all places, sentries doing their clockwork sentry-business, chimney-smoke and noise and business and camp-followers, all the melee. It seemed odder to Bates than the battle he had just witnessed. He shouldered the satchel, its occupant like some wasp, striped with its own uniform; and yet, who could say, why not angelic as well? And there was the tower itself, London's tower as white as ice, blocky like teeth, standing taller over him, his parent, his nationhood's parent. It did not look inviting.

Nobody challenged him as he marched up the causeway until he had come within ten yards of the closed main gate, with its lesser gate inset and open. "Who goes there?" yelled the sentryman, although he was only a foot or so from Bates. "General Wilkinson!" shouted Bates, startled into life. "I bring a message for General Wilkinson!" His heart stuttered. "I have a message for the General's ears only! From Colonel Truelove!"

[7]

He spent much of the rest of the day hiding inside a well-appointed house whose door had been blown, or beaten, from its hinges. The kitchen was messed and food looted, but the other rooms had been left untouched: beautiful furniture, with legs curled and slender as string, ornaments with the intricacy of clockwork but without function or movement, globes of glass holding preserved flowers, a new design of tallboy-clock, whose metronomic timekeeper rocked back and forth on its hinged base like a tree swaying in the breeze. The walls were hung with oils of society beauties.

Entering the Tower had been simple in the end. The guard had looked inside the satchel, but only cursorily and without penetrating deep enough to unearth the miniature warrior concealed inside. He had slipped through the inset door, the flap a twelfth the size of the great gates which were not opened, and hurried past the buzz of people within, over the inner quad, through another door and to a coign in an empty corridor. And there he had released the Lilliputian warrior, who had emerged from the bag with threads of rope coiled over his shoulder, and his own miniature satchel on a belt around his waist. He had not bade Bates farewell, but had scurried off.

Bates had loitered, nervously, around the Tower, and then had slipped amongst a crowd of engineers and kitchen-servants as they exited the Tower, and after that had slipped into deserted streets in Whitechapel.

Perhaps he expected to hear some titanic explosion, the arsenal beneath the Tower exploded by the fierce little Lilliputian; perhaps he expected the cheers of French troops. But although his ear was repeatedly distracted by bangs, knocks, creases of sound in the air, yells, tatters of song, aural flotsam, he heard nothing that matched the imagined cataclysm of his heart.

Much later in the afternoon, ashamed at his own instincts for cowardice, he had ventured out from this house, and wandered the city. He came across one body, in a British uniform, and then a clutch more of them. A print shop's windows had been broken in to make a placement for a field gun, but the gun's barrel was sheared and broken as a daisy, and its crew lay in a tangle of blackened arms and legs around it. Southward brought Bates out on the river again. Here there were more bodies. Bates went to the water's edge and sat down. On the far side of the river broken buildings bannered smoke into the evening air.

There was nobody around. It was as if London were a dead city.

The river hushed below him, like breathing.

I have killed my city, thought Bates, his mood flowing away from him now like the river itself, his spirits draining into the hidden sinks of despair. I am a traitor, and I have killed my city.

An irregular splashing to the west intruded on his attention. Upriver he could see one of the giants, sitting on the bank with its legs in the water for all the world like a small boy beside a tiny stream. The giant kicked his legs, languidly, intermittently, sending up house-sized bulges of water up to trouble the surface. Behind him, the tip of the sun dipped against the river, color bleeding from it into the water like watercolor paint from a paintbrush being washed after a day's work.

With desperate, self-detesting resolution Bates started towards the figure; this giant surveying the ruins he had made of the world's greatest city. "Monsieur!" he called. "Monsieur!"

He ran for ten minutes before he was close enough for his gnat's-voice to reach the great flappy ears. "Monsieur! Monsieur!"

The Brobdingnagian turned his head with the slowness of a planet revolving.

"I am here Monsieur!" squeaked Bates. "Down here Monsieur!"

The eyelids rolled up, great blinds, and the carpet-roll lips parted. "Good day," said the giant.

And now that he was standing beside the creature, Bates realized he had no idea what he had intended in coming over. "Forgive me, sir," he said. "Forgive me for approaching you. Is the battle over?"

"I can barely hear you," grumbled the giant, its sub-bass voice rolling and coiling in the evening air. "Allow me to lift you." And with sluggish but minute patience the enormous hand presented itself, so that Bates could step into the palm. The quality of the skin was not in the least leathery, as he expected it to be; it was douce, though strong, with some of the quality of turf. And then he was lifted into the air, and brought before the enormous benign face. Bates could see the pores, a thousand rabbit-holes in the cliff-face; could see the poplar-stubs of unshaved beard, the tangle of hair in the nostril like winter trees.

"Thank you monsieur," he said. "Is the battle over?"

"It is," said the giant.

"Are the French victorious?"

Every flicker of emotion was magnified, as if the great face were acting, over-acting, each expression. "You are French?"

"No sir, no sir," Bates gabbled. "But a sympathizer, sir. I am an ally of France, an ally, that is to say, of its great cause, of freedom for Pacificans, of freedom against slavery and the upholding of God's law."

"Your voice is too small, and too rapid," rumbled the voice. "I cannot follow your speech."

"I am a friend to the Brobdingnagian people," said Bates more slowly and more loud. "And the Lilliputians."

A smile, wide as a boulevard. "The tiniest of folk. Our fleas are bigger than they. Some of my people," he grumbled on, benignly, "do not believe they exist, never having seen them. But I am assured they do exist, and I am prepared to believe it."

There was silence for a moment. The light reddened deeper into sunset.

"The day is yours?" Bates asked again.

"The army of France is victorious."

"You do not seem happy."

"Melancholia," said the giant, drawing the word out so that it seemed to rumble on and on, a sound like heavy furniture being dragged over the floor. "To observe a city broken like this. We Brobdingnagians are a peaceful people, and such destruction . . ." He trailed off.

"But your great cause," chirruped Bates. "This victory is a great thing! It will mean freedom for your people."

"The France-army," said the giant, "possesses a machine of the greatest ingenuity. I have seen it; no bigger than a snuff-box, yet it *computes* and *calculates* and solves all manner of problems at a ferocious rate. So swiftly it works! It is this machine that has won the war, I think. This machine. Its strategy, and its solution to problems. This machine." He hummed and hoomed for a while. "My people," he continued, "my people are ingenious with machines, but never so ingenious as your people. You are small, but cunning. Perhaps the others, the Lil, the Lilli . . ."

"The Lilliputians."

"Just so, perhaps *they* are more ingenious even than you? The smaller the more cunning? This may be God's way of ordering his universe. The smaller the more cunning."

"I have long been an ally of France," Bates declared. His spirits, sunken only minutes before, were rising again, following their own unfathomable logic. Perhaps, he thought, perhaps my betrayal truly followed a higher good. Perhaps it is for the best. After defeat, England will abandon its persecution of the Pacificans, and soon after that its greatness will reassert itself. In ten years . . . maybe less. And it will be a more worthwhile greatness, because it will not flout God's ordinance. "I have long been an ally of France, and a friend of the Count D'Ivoi."

"D'Ivoi," said the giant. "I know him."

"You know him?"

"Indeed. Shall I take you to him?"

"Yes!" Bates declared, his heart flaring into fervor. "Yes! I will congratulate him on his victory, and on the new age of justice for Lilliputians and Brobdingnagians both!"

The enormous hand cupped him against the giant's shoulder, and he rose to his full height. The sun seemed to pull back from the horizon with the change in perspective, and then in lengthily slushing strides the giant marched down the river. He paused at the wrecked arches of London Bridge, stepping up onto the concourse and over it into the water again. In moments he was alongside the Tower. The troops outside the citadel were in French uniform; they scurried below, insect-like, apparently as alarmed by their gigantic ally as the British had been by the giants as foes. Cannons were hauled round to bear on the figure.

"A visitor for Monsieur le Comte," boomed the Brobdingnagian. "A visitor for Monsieur D'Ivoi."

He placed Bates on the charred lawn before the main gate, and withdrew his hand.

[8]

Bates was kept waiting for an hour or more, sitting on a bench inside the main gate. The evening light thickened to full darkness, and a November chill wrapped itself around the skin. Soldiers passed back and forth, their spirits elevated by victory. Every face was grinning. Bates allowed the sense of achievement to percolate through into his own heart. Something great had happened here, after all. He thought of the little warrior he had carried past this gate only that morning. Such valor in so small an individual! Was he still alive? When he met D'Ivoi again, he would ask. Such valor. He deserved a medal. Would miniature medals be forged, to reward the part brave Lilliputians had played in their own liberation?

"Monsieur?" An aide de camp was standing in front of him. "The Comte D'Ivoi will see you now."

Bubbling with excitement, Bates followed the fellow across the court and down a series of steps. Gaslit corridors, the stone wet with evening dew. Finally into a broad-groined room, lit by two-dozen lamps, brighter than day. And there was D'Ivoi, his absurd pigtail bobbing at the back of his head. A group of gorgeously uniformed men was sitting around a table.

"Bates, my friend," called D'Ivoi. "France has much to thank you for."

Bates approached, smiling. The generals at table were examining maps of the Southern Counties. Around them strutted and passed a stream of military humanity. In the corner, the size of a piano only taller, was an ebonywood box.

Of the generals, only D'Ivoi stood up. The rest of the generals were still eating, and pausing only to drink from smoky coffee-cups as wide as skulls.

"Bates, my friend," said D'Ivoi again.

They were eating pastries glazed with sugar that glistened as if wet.

"D'Ivoi," said Bates. He felt cheered to see his old friend, but something was wrong somewhere. He couldn't put his finger on it. He could not determine exactly what was wrong. It might have been that he did not want to determine what was wrong, for that would mean dismantling his buoyant feeling of happiness and achievement. And yet, like a pain somewhere behind the eyes, Bates knew *something was wrong*.

One of the generals looked up from the table. His ugliness was breathtaking, the left eyebrow and cheek were scored with an old scar, the eye itself glass and obnoxious. "Sit," said D'Ivoi.

The air in the room was not sweet: close and stale-smelling.

"I am glad my small action," said Bates, "was able to hasten the conclusion to this wasteful war."

One of the generals at table snorted.

"Did the Lilliputian warrior I ported here . . . did he survive?"

"He did his job very well," said D'Ivoi. "Although, alas, the war is not over yet. The English are resisting at Runnymede, with some skill and some force. But it will not be long! It will not be long, in part because of your labor. We, France, salute you."

"Ours is a nobler cause," said Bates, the words for a moment swimming his head with the thrill and honor of it all.

"Cause?" asked the general with the glass eye. It was impossible to look at his bunched, seamed face without one's glance being drawn to his hideous eye. Bates snapped his gaze away, and it fell on the box in the corner of the room.

"The Pope's latest decree," said D'Ivoi, and stopped. He noticed where Bates was looking. "Ah, my friend, your eye falls on our most valuable ally. The computation device!"

"So this is it," said Bates, distantly. The fact that there was something wrong was, somehow, intruding itself again. "The famous computation device."

"Truly," said D'Ivoi. "It has brought us further, and faster. It will change the whole world, this beautiful machine. Beautiful machine!"

"The Pope's latest decree?" queried the general. "C'est quoi ce que t'as dit?"

D'Ivoi gabbled something in French, too rapidly for Bates to follow. His own smile felt fixed, now. The light was too bright in this underground cavern. It slicked the walls. Centuries of the Tower, a prison. The giants Gog and Magog, or was it Bran? Bran the giant? Buried under Tower Hill, that was the story. Buried under the hill and the Tower built above it, pressing down on the enormous bones. A giant prison squashing the bones of a buried giant. How many people had seen the inside of this chamber, and never seen the light again? Centuries of people locked away, barred and closed and buried in the ground like blind stones in the mud.

Bates was stepping towards the device now. "It is marvellous," he muttered. "How does it work?"

D'Ivoi was at his arm, a touch on his elbow. "Ah, my friend," he said. "I cannot permit you to examine it too closely. You are a friend to France, I know, but even you must respect military secrets."

The box was coffin-black. It did not display any of its secrets on its exterior. "Of course," murmured Bates.

"As to how it works," D'Ivoi continued, steering Bates back towards the door of the room. "For that you will have to ask Mr. Babbage. It is something like an abacus, I think; something like a series of switches, or rolls, or gears, or something like this. I do not know. I only know," he beamed, and took Bates's hand in his own. "I only know that it will win us the war. Goodbye, my friend, and thank you again."

Bates was half dazed as he walked from the room. A guard eyed him. He walked half-aware up the stairway. There were certain things he should not think about. That was it. That was the best way. Bury thought, like the giant buried under the hill. Certain things he should not think about. He should not think of the French troops ranging out across the fields of England, of other towns burning, of the smoke rising as a column from the heart of the kingdom. Should not think of the blood draining out of bodies, pooling like molasses, dark in the sunlight. Should not think of giant men working to the extinction of their race at brute tasks, menial tasks, hauling logs or working great engines until their sturdy bodies gave out in exhaustion. Should not think of the Computational Device in the corner of the oppressive underground room. Not imagine opening the front of the device and looking inside. Or if he did think of this last, if he must think of it, then he should think of some giant clockwork device, some great rack of toothed-wheels and pins and rods, something wholly mechanical. But not think of a tight, close, miniature prison-cage, in which sweating rows of laboring tiny people worked at wheels and abacus racks, tied into position, working joylessly in the dark and hopelessness to process some machine for computation. Not that. He was on the top step now, and about to step back into the light, and the best thing would be to leave all that behind him, buried away below.

CHRISTOPHER FOWLER

The Green Man

Christopher Fowler lives and works in central London, where he runs the Soho film and design company Creative Partnership, creating film campaigns. In his spare time he writes novels and short stories.

Although he began his career writing humor books, he shifted into what he calls "dark urban." His first short story collection, City Jitters, *featured interlinked tales of urban malevolence. Since then he's had seven further volumes of short stories published:* More City Jitters, The Bureau of Lost Souls, Sharper Knives, Flesh Wounds, Personal Demons, *and* Uncut. *His most recent collection,* The Devil in Me, *was published in early 2002. He won the British Fantasy Society Award in 1998 for his story "Wageslaves."*

His first novel, Roofworld, *is being developed as a film. Other novels by Fowler are* Rune, Red Bride, Darkest Day, Spanky *(being scripted as a feature by director Guillermo Del Toro),* Psychoville *(recently cast as a film with Jude Law and Sadie Frost in the lead roles),* Disturbia, Soho Black, *and* Calabash. *His novel* Full Dark House *was just published in the UK, and his next is called* Plastic. *His ninth story collection,* Fast Awake, *will be out in spring 2004.*

About "The Green Man" he says: "Last year I went jungle trekking, a bookish Englishman poorly prepared to experience the rougher edge of nature. I certainly didn't expect to emerge with my back covered in welts from poisonous trees, and my blood-stained socks full of leeches. Consequently, I wrote 'The Green Man,' turning to the once-popular sub-genre of the English tropical story, a tradition that peaked with Kipling and Wells and hasn't been seen much since Carl Stephenson's 'Leiningen Versus the Ants.' It's odd how many English writers are hyper-sensitive to the surreal and the mysterious. As inhabitants of a grey, damp world, I think one is drawn to seek out the exotic. . . ." "The Green Man" was first published in the British magazine The Third Alternative, *Issue 31.*

—E. D.

Josh Machen told himself that jealousy was as much part of being in love as all the other demonstrable gestures, like twiddling your partner's hair across a dinner table and giving her knowing glances on crowded tube trains, that it simply proved how much you cared. Kate teased him about it. "By your reckoning, Othello was a regular guy acting pretty much within his rights," she suggested. Being jealous meant that someone was always on your mind, which was desirable, so the subject remained a joke between them.

It stopped being a joke after Josh followed her to a hen night and accused a male stripper of touching her thighs. As they argued about the exact height of the young man's teasing hands, Kate's amused smile faded. After that, he questioned her movements, checked her mobile phone for unrecognizable addresses and her e-mail box for mysterious correspondents. Usually he apologized afterwards, but that didn't make it better.

"It's living in London," Josh told her over a conciliatory dinner in his favorite Camden restaurant, the Cypriot joint he always used for making announcements. "Ten million people all on the make, lots of men looking at you with an eye on the main chance, it's no wonder relationships don't last in this city."

"Are you telling me this is why we never eat anywhere fashionable?" she asked, only half teasing. The one-eyed owner slipped beadily between his patrons, making them uneasy.

"How different could our lives be if we were living somewhere else? Somewhere warm and dry, where the streets aren't covered in trash and every other shop isn't a fried chicken outlet? London's dying, it doesn't have residents now, it has inmates. There's more crime here than in New York, it's got a third world transport system, there are just too many people. I look at old photographs of half-deserted streets and think *that's the city I want back.*"

"You can't stop the world, Josh."

"No, but you can find a place in it that suits you better."

"You really think it would make a difference to us living somewhere else?"

"Yes, I do."

"Do you have a place in mind?"

"If I came up with an idea, would you at least consider it?"

"I suppose so," she agreed vaguely. "This isn't anything to do with getting me all to yourself on some island, is it?"

"Of course not. I think it would be good for both of us to see a little more of the planet. I never took a gap year like you."

She wondered whether it was the city he longed to run away from, or the fact that he could not trust himself to trust her here.

For a long time, Kate refused to get married. She had seen how marriage had crushed the life from her parents, and had no desire to follow in their carpet-slippered footsteps. Why else was it called wedlock? She finally relented because she thought it would answer the question of trust that hung between them once and for all. Josh centered his world too much around hers. He got under her feet. With the trust marriage brought, he might become free to find himself.

After a grimly nondescript civil ceremony which her parents boycotted, she moved in with him, shoving an extra bed into his tiny flat near Victoria Park. The marriage contract held an implicit promise, that Josh would learn to behave less like a jealous schoolboy. She wondered what had happened in his past to make him so scared of losing her.

She worried at first that life together in Victoria Park would become claustrophobic, but as they worked flexi-time in different parts of the city (she was a research scientist at the King's Cross College of Tropical Medicine, he worked as an in-house designer for an ailing record company in Kensington) they didn't see as much of each other as she had imagined. They were both Londoners, both had too many old friends, too many birthdays to celebrate, too many arrangements to squeeze into their free hours. And like centuries of Londoners before them, they respected privacy.

Then Josh lost his job.

After three months spent sitting around the flat waiting for companies to call back, he was becoming morose and frustrated. Cutbacks, retrenchment, the music business faring poorly, the same excuses were trotted out time and again. They were looking for cheap labor, and that meant buying young staff. Josh would be thirty-one this year, and as a designer working to attract teenage sales, they feared he was past his sell-by date. He maintained his old contacts and managed to keep some occasional freelance work, but it wasn't enough to pay the bills. Kate often went out in the evenings with colleagues from her department. Josh had nothing in common with these intense biologists, and stayed at home, but always waited up so that he could discreetly question her when she returned.

It didn't take either of them long to see how the strain of their new circumstances was damaging their relationship. Something, they knew, would have to be done. They loved each other very much, but too many things were getting in the way.

It was Kate who heard about the offer from a Malaysian lady who had recently joined the department.

"You're talking about a pretty severe change of lifestyle," said Josh, after she explained what the move would entail.

"You said you wanted to get out of London," she reminded him, anxiously unfolding the map across the pub table.

"London, yes, but giving up the whole Western hemisphere seems a bit extreme."

"It would be perfect for my thesis. Look, Malaysia's divided into two separate chunks, the West peninsula, and the North-West section of Borneo. Taman's supposed to be somewhere off the West coast of the peninsular." Her finger traced the line of the sea. "Here it is. You have to look carefully."

"I thought she said it was tiny."

"You're looking at Langkowi. Taman island a little further to the North. See?"

"It's a speck. What's the scale of this thing?"

"Flights go to Kuala Lumpur, then it's an internal hop to Langkowi and finally there's a short ferry ride."

"Dear God, that's a long way off the map." They examined the emerald droplet together. The island was so small that there were no towns marked on it. Kate checked the map again, looking for something positive to remark upon.

"It looks nearer to the coast of Malaysia than Langkowi Island. It's just not been opened to tourism as much. The ferry only goes twice a week at the moment, but they'll expand the service if more visitors come." She pressed her hand across his. "Think about it. One of the most futuristic cities on the planet will be just a few hundred miles away. From that point of view, it's no more remote than, say, the Isle of Man."

He ran his hand down through his hair, pressing a frown into place. "Exactly," he said gloomily.

After two meetings with the proprietors of the new hotel on Taman, Josh remained unconvinced that they should take the posting. They would be required to act as caretakers for a minimum period of four months, while the builders were finishing the rooms in the hotel's main building. The owners were a pair of Swiss bankers, and wanted someone to keep an eye on the place until they were ready to open for business in the first summer season. The money they were willing to pay for a European couple to take the job was substantial. A suite had already been furnished in the hotel's residential section, and the bankers were prepared to provide them with anything they wanted. Kate would be able to realize a cherished dream of writing up her toxicology research, something she could never find time to do in London. Josh would be able to reconsider his options, and maybe get around to the photographic career he had always wanted to pursue. But as their deadline for making a decision approached, he still he refused to commit.

Then Kate ran into an old boyfriend who announced that he was single again and wished he had never broken up with her. He offered to take her to the Gordon Ramsey restaurant at Claridges for dinner on Saturday night, and try to make amends for what had once passed between them. While she was deciding whether to go or not, Josh announced that they were leaving for Malaysia.

They signed the papers, locked up the flat and transferred through Kuala Lumpur with a single large suitcase between them. Backpackers, package tourists and businessmen crowded the shuttle to Langkowi, but only a handful of locals continued on with them to the port. It was late October, a month before the start of the island's rainy season, and the first guests on Taman were to be expected at the end of March. The sleek white ferry was more modern than anything Josh had traveled on in Britain. They cut through a smooth green sea that filled with a delicate aquamarine light where the sun hit it, and felt at once that they had made the right decision to leave behind the grey dome of London sky. All around them, improbably steep plugs of jungle rose from the glittering jade water.

At Taman's jetty they were met by the works foreman, a smiling freckled Australian named Aarun Tunn, who pumped their hands hard and insisted on carrying their suitcase, hefting it onto his shoulder as though it weighed nothing. The hotel proved to be a drive away in a juddery jeep that threatened to tip over as it climbed the slippery red tire ditches in the unlaid roads.

"This area around you is ancient rainforest," Aarun explained, pointing to the white-legged eagles that dipped into rocky outcrops behind the greenery. A streak of orange as wide as the world was settling over the jungle, pointing to the close of day.

"How old do you think it is?" asked Kate, enchanted.

"About three hundred million years, although much of it has been cut down recently. The government hasn't got a very good environmental record, but this time they're trying to get the balance right. We're dry-walling with reclaimed stone, and barely touching the foresty canopy except to bury pipes. The cut paths will have completely grown over by the end of the rainy season. You can expect a downpour every day soon, but plenty of hot sun, too."

Josh clung to the side of the jeep and focussed his eyes on the green shadows of the forest. Dusty lianas looped between the trees like the arcs of a suspension bridge. Parasitic plants grew with the same thickness and strength as the trees they clung to. Something was jumping between slender bushy branches, shaking whole trunks and violently rustling treetops.

"What about poisonous insects?" he shouted to Aarun. "Is there anything we have to look out for?"

"There are one or two bugs they don't tell the tourists about," Aarun called over his shoulder, "and a very mean breed of jellyfish that turns up in lagoons when it rains hard, but generally speaking, the fauna's safer here than it is back home in Perth. We've got about sixty men working on the site, a mix of locals and experts from Far East territories. They won't talk to you much, they just get on with their work and go home when the bell rings. Me and three of the lads are on site overnight, but we go to the mainland at weekends. That's the only time you'll be alone here." Aarun laughed. "You'll probably be glad of the peace and quiet by then."

For a brief moment Josh wondered if he was entering a hell of his own making. Sixty sweat-stained men slyly watching the fragrant white woman who walked past them to her bedroom, smirking at the skinny London lad who couldn't keep her satisfied. *You've been watching too many old movies,* he told himself.

The track led down toward the sun, and Josh realized they had reached the far northern tip of the island. The hotel was so well concealed in the undergrowth that he could not see it at first. As they drew nearer, angled stone walls could be glimpsed between the trees. It looked like an Incan city in miniature, a central block built low to the ground in natural materials that blended harmoniously with the dense olive landscape surrounding it. Set away from the main body of the building, a series of wooden-roofed villas could be discerned beneath the feathered leaves of the jungle's primary growth.

"It's a beaut, isn't it?" said Aarun, with the pride of a man who knew he had achieved something special. He stopped the jeep and jumped out, pulling back the seats. "We had you marked down for a suite in the main building, but it got flooded, so we built you a villa. We only finished it this morning, so you may find some of the wood seals a bit sticky, but apart from that it's ready to live in. They'll be a dozen of them when we open."

It was clear that the work whistle had just blown, because men were returning from the hotel's staff room in white short-sleeved shirts and jeans, carrying holdalls. They nodded politely at Aarun as they passed, but barely seemed to notice the new arrivals.

"They won't bother you," Aarun explained. "They're industrious and religious, only interested in getting paid and getting home. They don't speak much English, only Malay, but they're good men and won't get in your way. You'll enjoy it here. All you have to do is keep the site safe."

"Safe from what?" asked Josh, his eyes searching the undergrowth for leaping shapes. "Are there any dangerous locals hanging about?"

"Oh, nothing like that," Aarun replied airily, "it's just a condition of the building's insurance contract. But there are small problems. There's been some stealing. Tools, clothes, stuff left lying around."

"You think it's your workmen?"

"No, they value their jobs too highly to touch anything."

"Then who do you suspect?"

"We all know who the thieves are." Aarun set the case down on the step of their villa. "We'll talk more when you've unpacked and had a chance to freshen up."

"This will be so good for us," said Kate, folding her legs beneath the silk kimono that had been left, folded, on the bed. "Look at this place, it's incredible." The villa's teak legs had been punched into the angled, loamy floor of the forest. The suite was basically one large polished hardwood room, divided by alcoves that extended into a pair of private bathrooms. White linen drapes hung in swathes across the shuttered windows. There was no glass in the villa; the seasonal winds were likely to draw them out.

"I thought it would be quiet, but listen to all that noise outside." Josh looked uneasily at the swaying vegetation beyond the veranda. A long yellow stick suddenly sprouted legs and moved, running along the railing to jump into the bushes. The wildness of the forest would take some getting used to. Strange birds squealed like electric saws in the tops of the trees, while crickets and toads provided a low rolling trill that had begun the moment shadows fell on the leaves. Something hooted angrily near the shore, its upturned call answered by a mate or an enemy. The canopy of the forest was so close around them that it touched the roof of the villa.

"I thought it would be quieter," repeated Josh, as he tipped the blinds shut.

Aarun's helpers had set up a meal in the partially finished dining room. They sat on fat silk cushions sorting through dishes of chicken, banana-leaf wrapped rice and a splayed fried fish with hundred of small bones.

"Two monsoons a year, nine major airstreams, a rainfall of a hundred inches, eighty five percent humidity, it's a fantastic ecosystem for breeding unique plant species," said Aarun, crunching the fish bones in strong white teeth. "Birds, too. We've got hornbills, parrots, swifts, eagles. I can watch 'em for hours. The island used to deal palm-oil with the mainland, but the government protected the trees. The locals weren't too happy until organic tourism came along."

"What about animals?" asked Kate, nipping a chunk of tender chicken from its green bamboo splinter.

"Mainland's got the lot, elephants, tigers, the Eastern half even has a few rhinos left. We've got pelandok, that's kind of a small deer, dusky leaf monkeys, some small crocs, monitor lizards, and you have to keep an eye out for snakes, mostly cobras. Good news is that the mozzies are malaria-free, but you'll still get bitten to buggery around the swamps. You get the best of both worlds here. Taman has its own natural selection patterns and its own microclimate. The animals and plants grow up differently, behave differently. You won't see stuff like this anywhere else. Zoological teams from all over the world come here. Kate tells me you're into photography, Josh. You want to take pictures, this is the place to do it."

"I used to be good at it." Josh eyed the carcass of the bony fried fish with suspicion. "I don't know whether I've brought the right equipment."

"No problem, mate. The ferry will bring in anything you order from the internet."

It crossed Josh's mind that Kate might find this plain-speaking blonde Southerner attractive. "Doesn't your wife miss you out here?" he asked casually as Kate shot him a look.

"I'm not a married man, Josh, not in that sense." He popped open beers and slid them across the table. "I'm afraid I had to put the wine stock on hold because we haven't been able to drain the cellar yet. No, to answer your question, Josh, I've got a partner back on the mainland, but she runs a gardening center and can't get away often." Kate's follow-up look to Josh warned him. *Satisfied?*

"You were going to tell us about your thief," reminded Josh, anxious to move away from his clumsy display of insecurity.

"Thieves, actually. We've got a troupe of Macaques on the island, big green-haired bastards with muzzles like baboons, you can't miss 'em. That howling noise? They head for the beach around sunset. They dig up crabs and eat 'em. The Malays train them to pick coconuts. They'll take the washing from the lines, and won't give it back until you feed 'em. They're smart, but they're mean-spirited fuckers. They'll try to get you to join in with their games, but it's best not to interfere. You really don't want to get involved, believe me. So we let 'em steal a little, just not too much."

The next morning, Josh saw the Macaques, ten or twelve of them looping through the trees on long, muscular arms. As casually as waltzing around a maypole, their leader swung on his liana and dropped to the ground near the villa. Leaning on his forepaws, he raised a doglike whiskery head and sniffed the air through broad flat nostrils. After a few minutes, he scooted toward the verandah. The others held back, as if waiting for their leader to pass judgment. Josh realized that he was much larger than the rest, almost as big as a man. He had to weigh well over twenty kilos. His shaggy coat was, as Aarun had pointed out, a curious shade of brownish-green, his head framed by a center-parted lion's mane of straight, swept-back hair. Implacable silk-brown eyes stared at Josh. No, not at him—past him. He turned and followed the Macaque's gaze. Kate was standing in the doorway of the bedroom, pulling a white T-shirt above her breasts, over her head.

"Don't move," Josh warned her.

"What is it?" She snapped off the shirt.

"One of the Macaques."

"Where? Oh. My God, he's enormous. Much bigger than I imagined."

"Stay where you are."

"It's all right, he's more scared of you than you are of him." Kate smiled and turned. "Would you put some sun-block on my back?"

"Don't let him see you like that."

"Like what?"

"Without your top on."

"He's an animal, Josh."

"That's not the point."

"He doesn't look at me in the same way."

"How do you know?" Josh took a step forward. The Macaque released a startling wide-mouthed howl and bounded off, followed by the rest of the troupe.

"All right, you showed him who the man was," said Kate. "Come on, Alpha Male, put some cream on me, then let's check out the beach."

It was the perfect place to build a hotel; a crescent of cadmium yellow beach surrounded by heavy underbrush, the sand striped with stream outlets from the hills behind. Low rolling waves indicated the shallow slope of the bay, ideal for safe swimming. White birds fell from the sky, streamlining as they hit the water, to emerge with wagging fish in their beaks. Josh held Kate's hand as they walked. In the distance he could hear Aarun's men knocking hammers on posts. They had started at six that morning, and would continue until darkness.

Aarun took them on a tour of the property boundaries. Most of the hotel was finished. Only the rest of the outlying villas remained to be built. Gangs of Malays were digging out the foundations, but water filled the ditches as quickly as the earth was shoveled out. "It'll be worse when the rains come," warned Aarun cheerfully. "Look, there's Sinno." He pointed to the burly leader Macaque they had seen near the verandah earlier. He was seated in a clearing near the water's edge, cracking a large crab out of its shell by carefully prying apart its exoskeleton. The creature's disembodied legs were still waving as he levered them into his pouting mouth. The other members of the troupe foraged for smaller picking on the banks of a stream.

"How did he get his name?" asked Kate as they passed.

"From his genus, Celebes 'Cynomacaca.' He's a moor Macaque, a crab-eater, although they'll eat anything in a push. He's the most intelligent one I've ever seen, but fuckin' bad tempered. I've a book on them if you're interested."

"Yes, I'd like to see that," said Kate. "Josh, you could take pictures of them."

"Just don't get too close," Aarun warned. "He's capable of pulling your arms out of their sockets, although his shout is mostly for show."

"Listen to this." Kate flattened out the page and marked a passage. "They're arboreal, diurnal, and love the company of others. They're fast swimmers, climbers and runners. Some were used in studies that led to the development of the polio vaccine. Macaques provide the models for the Buddhist saying, 'See No Evil, Hear No Evil, Speak No Evil.' Some people believe that they are human insofar as they embody the worst traits of man."

"He's sitting outside right now," said Josh, who was shaving in the bathroom.

"Who is?"

"Sinno. The leader. Sitting in the branch of a tree. I can see him from the window."

"He's probably getting used to having new neighbors."

"He's sniffing the air like he did this morning."

"I bet he can smell my perfume. After all, no-one else here wears any."

Josh shaved bristles and foam from beneath his nose, but he could see the Macaque in his mirror. The damned thing was sitting on its haunches calmly watching his wife. He studied the monkey's face too intently; the razor slipped and the blade nicked him just below the nose.

After supper that evening Josh kept watch from the verandah, but the vast, slim trees were still and silent. The forest's nocturnal residents crept silently through the undergrowth while, somewhere far above them, Taman's troupe of monkeys dreamed away the star-filled night.

The next three weeks passed easily. As their lives decelerated into an elegance of relaxed motion, boredom became inconceivable. To hurry was to sweat and grow tired. During the mornings, Josh busied himself more than was strictly necessary with administrative chores around the hotel, where the floor tiles were being polished and relays of electric wiring were being discreetly added. Kate helped out in the main building, but spent most of the day working at her computer, mapping out a thesis on primate toxicology that remained incomprehensible and private to everyone but her. Late afternoons were passed in make-shift hammocks as the site lost its human sounds and all activity ceased. Shadows deepened, eye-searing yellows faded to cool greens, and small animals could be heard snuffling on the forest floor. Kate took languid baths while Josh lay face down on his bed reading.

When the tide turned, the Macaques would return from the beach where they had been digging out crabs, led by Sinno, who would lope past the villa, pausing to check the verandah. Josh knew that he took small items of Kate's from the deck, hairbrushes, hand-mirrors, combs, but never saw him do it. One day, the monkey left a neat pile of bulbous green fruit on Kate's sunchair. The fleshy split pericarps were crimson and yellow, and oozed sweet-smelling juice onto the teak deck until Josh cleared it away.

"He hangs around here like a lovesick suitor," Josh complained as they walked through the compound to the dining room. "And you're doing nothing to discourage him. You hardly ever wear clothes in the villa. The way he looks at you, it's not the way an animal looks at a person."

"Then how is it?"

"The way a man looks at a woman."

Kate laughed off the idea. "It's too hot in the afternoon. What do you want me to do, dress as if I was in London? I'm just someone new to him, and I smell different. Besides, it helps me that he comes so close. So much of my writing is purely theoretical, he reminds me that the subjects are flesh and blood. But they don't think like humans. For years scientists tried to teach primates the American Sign Language system, but they discovered their so-called 'trained' monkeys used exactly the same signs in the wild. People have this idea of the noble savage. Everyone from Swift to Huxley has suggested that we can learn sensitivity from the apes, but the species simply don't correspond at a sociological level." She touched his arm. "I thought you were going to concentrate on your photography. You haven't taken any shots in days."

"I haven't been in the mood. Besides, Aarun's kept me busy with the inventory."

"You know he's going to the mainland at the end of the week. You'd better make a list if you want him to pick up any supplies for you."

Aarun knew that with the coming of the rains their drainage problems would increase, and was hoping to return with the spare parts he needed to keep his pumps working.

The next morning, Josh rose earlier than usual, and sat on the verandah leafing through a catalogue of photographic materials as Sinno's troupe hooted and hollered through the branches on their way back from the beach. He tried to concentrate on the pages of sleek software options, but found his attention sliding to the shapes in the trees. Behind the hulking form of their leader he could see the troupe's females. They had never come this close before. Josh slowly reached for the small digital camera he had left on the table. He quietly switched it on and studied the LCD monitor. Several of the females nursed small babies against their breasts, but one turned away whenever Josh focused his camera on her. The other females seemed to shun her. Once or twice he caught her in the display panel, but by the time the light had adjusted to a level his equipment could read, she had sensed his attention and turned aside.

When the troupe passed in the evening, he called Kate out to the verandah. She tiptoed beside him and studied the females.

"Her baby's dead," she pointed out. Looking more closely, Josh could see now that the mother was nursing a dry furry corpse. "She won't let it go because she wants to be like the other mothers, but she knows you know that it's dead, and she's ashamed to let you see."

"You really think they can play those sorts of games?" asked Josh, surprised.

"They're nót games," said Kate, "it's human nature."

"I bet he's the father." Josh glared at Sinno, who had wedged himself into his usual position overlooking the villa's bedroom. "He's waiting for you to undress again."

Kate gave an angry sigh and went indoors.

By the end of the first month, both Kate and Josh looked physically different; leaner, blonder, shiny as leather, and Kate, at least, was more relaxed. Aarun offered to take them to the mainland, but they decided to wait until a desire for the noise and chaos of cities had returned to some degree.

The rains arrived in a deafening display of ferocity. Aarun's men splashed through the building hauling portable pumps, hunting down floods and leaks in the first real test of the building's durability. Sluices of rainwater appeared in dry alleys. Kate and Josh were increasingly confined to the villa, as getting to the main building involved crossing treacherous torrential slides. Between storms the sun blazed hard, filling the forest with steam. The air was laden with the smell of rotting vegetation. Kate worked, Josh read, and they got on each other's nerves.

"I've been watching the Macaques," said Kate one morning in December. "The females are getting thinner. They don't look well. Their fur—it's changing, losing its gloss. I don't know much about their social behavior patterns, but it looks as if they don't forage, and the males provide for them. But lately the males have stopped."

Josh knew why. Sinno was taking their supplies and daily dumpling piles of fruit at the villa as some kind of votive offering. The monkey clambered into place on his branch and waited for her to appear, but raced off when Josh appeared. Every morning he cleared the verandah, throwing it all back into the jungle before Kate came out.

The next day Josh opened the door to find an enormous injured crab lying on its back, grasping at the air. Sinno sat motionless in the tree in the falling rain, his fur dripping over his implacable eyes. "I'm not going to play your game," Josh muttered, gingerly raising the crab by a waving leg and hurling it into the bushes. "You're going to play mine."

The next morning, he waited until the troupe had passed, then climbed out into the forest with the linen bag he had filled with scraps from the kitchen.

The Macaques were omnivores, and the females were clearly being starved. They kept to a secondary route behind the males, so this was where Josh laid the trail of food. He was still shaking the last scraps of fish from the bag when he heard the troupe returning. His heart thumped in his chest as Sinno and the other males passed within feet of him. The females followed, guiltily stopping at the trail of food and shoveling the delicacies into their cheek pouches. Sinno screamed at them and slapped at their heads as they passed, then caught sight of Josh. His inexpressive face, striped in leaf-stencilled sunlight, betrayed no emotion. He continued to stare for a full ten minutes, then swung sharply up into the trees as if scampering up a set of ladders.

Josh was frightened, but excited. He had shown the monkey who was really the boss. He had undermined Sinno's command. Over the next few days, the piles of fruit left on the balcony dwindled, but Sinno soon returned to his usual place, watching Kate.

When the refridgeration units arrived on Friday morning, Aarun needed help with the stock-orders and Josh rose early to help him, leaving Kate asleep in bed. He was more concerned about missing the troupe's morning patrol.

"We need the inventory pad," said Aarun, searching under the workbenches in the new wine cellar. "You didn't take it with you last night?"

"It's my fault, you're right," Josh admitted, "I took it back to the room. I shouldn't have had that last bottle." They had been celebrating the arrival of the French wines by working their way through a crate of breakages. "I'll get it." He picked his way back across the muddy paths, passing through scorched strips of sunlight. Ahead of him a battalion of centipedes, pillarbox red and each longer than a man's hand, undulated over the dead wet leaves. He could hear water running as he approached the villa. Kate was using the outside shower, a slatted hardwood box on the verandah with a broad copper spray head. She had her back to him, and was soaping her thighs, her tanned stomach. White foam drifted down the channel of her back to her buttocks. She was humming as she washed, a song they had used to sing together as they drove across London to the apartments of friends, now a distant world away. High in the dark tree to the rear, Sinno sat in position watching her, his blank brown eyes motionless, his arms hanging below the branch, the exposed tip of his penis like a furled scarlet orchid.

Bellowing, Josh ran at the tree with a rock in his hand and threw it as hard as he could. The rock hit Sinno squarely in the face. The Macaque released a howl of pain and defiance, and vanished. Kate screamed. Josh's eyes were wild. "You knew he was there!" he yelled. "You saw him! What the hell did you think you were doing, leading him on?"

"Are you insane?" Kate shouted back, frightened by his sudden outburst. "I had no idea he was there. I never even thought to look. What kind of person do you think I am? What on earth is wrong with you?"

"Remember what Aarun said, you play games with them, they'll play games with you," said Josh, fighting to regain his breath in the heat-saturated air. "He's the leader, your alpha male, the others will follow him anywhere, do whatever he tells them to."

"Whatever he *tells* them?" Kate shut off the shower and grabbed a towel. "*My* alpha male? Listen to yourself. You did this in London, and you're doing it again, when there aren't even any humans around. These are animals you're talking about, Josh, *animals!* You don't even know you're doing it any more, do you?"

Josh suddenly felt lost. He tried to take Kate in his arms, but she moved beyond reach. "Forgive me, Kate," he whispered, "it's the way he looks at you, I know he wants you. I know it's grotesque but you must see that you're in danger. He studies you. He leaves gifts for you. He waits for me to leave so that he can spy on you alone. You once said some men have the souls of animals. Couldn't an animal have the soul of a man?"

"Not on a biological level, no."

"Perhaps this isn't about biology but something deeper than blood and tissue. So much here comes from a time before there were demarcations between man and beast. How can we hope to understand? I love you, darling, I just don't want you to get hurt."

"When we get back I think you need to get some professional help." Kate swept back inside the villa and slammed the door in his face.

Josh knew it was beyond anything either of them could understand. They were far from their own social circle, away from the rules that controlled them. When he was a child, visiting the Regent's Park Zoo, animals were something to be seen pacing behind bars, half-demented by their incarceration. Back then there had been little understanding and less respect for animal psychology; chimpanzees were dressed as humans and given tea parties each afternoon, as if their clumsy etiquette was intended to remind children of man's superiority as a species. The very word "ape" evoked mimickry of human action. But here, he and the primates were on equal footing, simply moving in different spheres.

He returned to work, but all day long his fear and anger grew.

On Saturday morning, Aarun caught the ferry to the mainland, promising to return that night, but in the afternoon rising monsoon winds put paid to any chance of his return. A storm-sky as grey and unbroken as the concrete walls Aarun's men had built raced overhead. In the distance they heard the tumble of thunder. The air so oppressively hot that it caught in Kate's mouth and blocked her sinuses. Numb with headache, she lay on the bed in her underwear, listening to the colliding treetops, waiting for the storm to break and lower the temperature.

Josh prowled the main building with his camera, taking close-up test shots of butterflies drying their wings, as large as the pages of paperbacks. A sense of unease had settled on him in a suffocating caul. The thought of being away from his wife disturbed him, but he knew that she would be angry if she suspected that he was guarding her.

That was when he realized. He had not heard from the Macaques all afternoon. He found himself at the far side of the compound. From here it was a twenty-minute walk back to the villa. He went to Aarun's locker and took the keys to the jeep, the only motorized vehicle on the island.

The fat green vehicle was parked out front on the half-graveled drive. He climbed in and tried the ignition, but the engine would not turn over. Leaning from his seat, he lowered his head over the side and followed the trail of petrol back to the external tank. He could see from here that the petrol cannister had been punctured. Kneeling beside it, he touched the indentations left by rows of wide-set teeth. The acrid contents had drained away into the earth. Could a Macaque do that, even one as large as Sinno? Could he somehow have evolved more quickly than his relatives? Josh studied the teethmarks again and felt a lurch of fear.

Aarun kept a loaded 12-gauge slide action shotgun in his locker. He had told Josh about it the first week he was here, had even shown him how to pump and fire the damned thing in case of an unspecified emergency. Josh ran toward the locker now, dragging it out by the stock and throwing it across his arm as he ran back into the forest.

The rain began just as he was within sight of the villa. He stopped for a moment to catch his breath, and heard lightning split a branch somewhere above him. The deluge fell in large hard pellets of water, hammering the leathery leaves around him, instantly churning the ground to mud. The noise was incredible. Suddenly he could no longer see the villa.

But he could see the Macaques. They were pushing their way toward the verandah in a broad semi-circle, and at the center rose the great green back of a single primate, twice as big as any of the others. He slipped on the muddy slope, his leg collapsing under him, and rolled into the undergrowth. Thick thorns jammed themselves into his arms and legs, tearing gouts of flesh as he hauled himself upright. In a fold of the rain he could see the Macaques moving in.

"Come on, you fuckers," he shouted, pumping the gun and firing it into the air, igniting a cacophony of bird screams surrounded him. The kickback wrenched his shoulder, but he stumbled on toward the scattering monkeys, bearing down as the beast headed away toward the beach. This time he stopped and steadied the gun against a tree before he fired. There was an explosion of terrified parrots, flashes of red and blue in the downpour, a mad tumble of feathers and leaves, as he smashed his way through the thinning undergrowth toward the sea.

He wondered if he had managed to wound it, because the great monkey was moving more slowly now, so that the rest of the troupe quickly overtook their leader. The Macaque was dragging his left leg. The forest cleared to rain-pocked sand and rock as Josh entered the farthest end of the beach, where the streams formed treacherous deep-sided pools. The rain was blinding him, making it hard to keep his eyes open, but he closed the distance.

"Who's got the balls now?" he shouted through the downpour, closing in on the limping Macaque. He needed to steady himself in order to take aim, and searched for a suitable rock. Sinno was trapped. All that stood ahead of him was a broad water pit filled by the rain-flattened sea. Still the creature had its back to him, as if unwilling to admit defeat. It hobbled to the far side of the pool and squatted heavily on the wet sand. Josh turned, searching for something stable on which to rest the shotgun.

It was then that he saw the others. Alarmingly close, they had drawn into a ring about him, and were moving quickly forward. He felt the sand softening beneath his feet and realized that he was sliding forward into the sand pool as the rain-soaked bank shifted with his weight. He tried to steady himself, but the weight of the gun overbalanced him.

On the other side, the great Macaque slowly turned—or rather, he split in two, not one great primate at all but a pair of the troupe's younger males, one spread across the other's shoulders, their coarse green hair ratted together. They jumped apart and found their places in the circle, turning their calm brown eyes to him.

Josh sank swiftly into the pool. There was something odd about the water, a viscous texture he had seen before when it rained hard. As the first sting penetrated his shirt like an electric shock, he remembered Aarun's warning about swimming in heavy rain; it was when the most dangerous jellyfish surfaced. The pool was alive with them, hundreds washed in by the tide and now rising like clear plastic bags as the rain drummed the surface of the water. Their stings trailed and wrapped about his limbs, sticking to his waist, his back, his neck, jolts flashing through his disrupted nervous system, ten, fifty, a hundred. He tore at the strips but they stuck to his flesh, needles burrowing like thorns. Paralyzed by the strobing pain, the endless jabbing injections of venom, he threshed and stilled, sinking into the deep green darkness, watched by the motionless members of the loyal troupe. The rain pattered and the monkeys watched, their souls ranged beyond human emotional response, their hearts only obeying the patterns of their communal life.

On the roof of the villa, Sinno scratched himself and waited until silence returned once more to the forest. Then he slid down onto the verandah and peered in through the window slats, to the bedroom where Kate lay uneasily sleeping. As quietly as Josh had ever moved, the great Macaque opened the bedroom door and slipped inside, closing it ever so gently behind him.

BRIAN HODGE

Some Other Me

"Some Other Me," a marvelously subtle piece that combines the pain of growing up in difficult circumstances with baroque urban tenement portraiture, was first published in Brian Hodge's collection Lies & Ugliness.
—E. D.

After the day we first moved in, it was months before I saw his face.

I must've been nine years old when we moved into that second floor apartment, the five of us, my parents and me and my little brother and even littler sister who was still just a baby. Neither my mom nor my dad ever called it anything other than home, but as I look back from the more critical perspective of adulthood, I now realize that our building was something less than an apartment building, if only in semantics. It was a tenement.

We lived in a tenement and all that it implied, and at the time my brother and sister didn't know enough to feel ashamed, but I felt it, that something had changed and while maybe this new place wasn't wrong, exactly, it wasn't right, either, not as right as where we'd come from.

I remembered the house we'd lived in before my dad lost his earlier job, and all the grass and the trees where I used to play with friends I never saw again. There wouldn't be any more treehouses, ever again, because there was no place to build them. We lived in a tenement now, and no matter which window I looked out of there were no trees to be seen, and very little grass for that matter, just scrubby, weedy patches that grew up around cans and bottles thrown onto plots of ground that someone had forgotten to pave. People dumped trash there as though to cover the plots entirely, as though they couldn't bear the taunting sight of something they had so little of.

We all lived in tenements, and it was months before I saw his face.

Out back, near the dumpsters, and on the stoop, and coming or going along the stairway, and at the mailslots in the vestibule, it wasn't long before we recognized most of our neighbors. We might not know anything more about them than what we could see in passing, but we knew their faces and the sounds of their voices, whether they were friendly or gruff or if it depended on the weather; if they, like us, seemed struck down by a run of bad luck and spent part of each day trying to figure out why.

His name was Mr. Cavanaugh, and it was months before I saw his face.

When we moved to the tenement it was late fall, winds already icy, and so whenever old Mr. Cavanaugh left his apartment on the first floor, all anyone could see of him was a straight, narrow figure in a tattered coat that hit him around the knees. He would turn up its collar, wearing a hat with the brim pulled low; he would pull his head into this shadowy niche like a turtle in its shell, and off he'd go.

He was old, but he wasn't slow. Even when he favored one leg, even when he stumped along with a pair of crutches under his arms, he didn't slouch, didn't shuffle. I'd watch from our window, or hidden across the street; watch until he'd stumped out of sight. He moved like a man with a mission, and his mission was to do his errand and get back inside his apartment as quickly as possible.

I had no idea what lay behind most of the doors in those four floors of apartments, but only Mr. Cavanaugh's held any mystery, because he never opened his curtains. Even on those rare, cloudless days of late autumn and winter when the sun shone bright as jewels, his curtains remained drawn. I'd walk home from school and see that every window would have its curtains flung wide to the warming light except for his, like eyes blinded by cataracts.

But some days the curtains would waver in the middle, and I'd catch a glimpse of fingers retreating through the folds.

My parents didn't seem to give him much thought, but that was only because they'd already started going blind themselves, not in their eyes but in their imaginations; they'd lost the power to realize whatever he was doing in there, it had to be awful.

I could hear him coughing, you see.

We lived in a tenement but it was old and solid, and it took a lot of sound, or a very special kind of sound, to carry through the walls and floors. He lived below us, and there would be times I wasn't doing anything special, just lying on the floor or couch, when the sound of his coughing would burrow through the barrier and fill any room I was in. There was no getting away from it, a thick, wet, strangulating cough that sounded as though he were wrestling it, forcing it up through a windpipe that could hardly contain it. He hacked and moaned and cursed, this creature with a face like a cruel, hidden smudge, down there in the dark where I was sure he spent the rest of his time clanking around with chains and the gnawed bones of kids nobody would miss.

Sometimes you could hear it while on the stairway, the sound coming from behind his door. As the months went by I guess I grew used to it, because I'd pause to stare at that door, curiosity getting the better of my fear, wondering what could do that to a person yet still leave him alive for so long.

Finally, one cold day in January, the law of probability won another absurd victory of awe and apocalypse. We were coming down the stairway, my mom and I, Saturday afternoon ruined by her need to find shoes that I might not outgrow for a while, when the knob of Mr. Cavanaugh's door scraped loudly enough to fill the stairway with its shriek. His door opened, and he stood there as though caught in some unnatural act, hidden in his usual garb, but that wasn't what mattered.

I'd been granted a rare look beyond. I saw past him, into a slice of what must've been his living room. There were no chains, only a cramped den of furniture dulled with the need to be dusted, and wallpaper and air the color of dried tobacco leaves.

But then my attention was caught by that other thing, half-blocked by the edge of his doorway, so I couldn't see how much of the far wall it covered, but it was enough to fill me with dread and curiosity that prickled from groin to throat, because here was something I hadn't anticipated.

My blind mother had me moving again as she gave Mr. Cavanaugh a cheerful hello, and out on the stoop, before he could follow into earshot, she chided me.

"Don't stare at him," she said. "He's just a poor, sick old man who doesn't have anybody in the world."

My brother turned six years old a couple of months later, as spring threatened to return any day now, but hadn't quite made it, as though its cloak had caught on a nail and it could only tug futilely. We still called him Paulie but he was starting to chafe at that, a kid's name after all, and while I called him Paulie twice as often now, I secretly welcomed this new maturity. In our old neighborhood he'd been a pesky dwarf, but here he was showing signs of being a real person and so far I hadn't made any friends.

He was determined to solve the mystery of Mr. Cavanaugh with me, and that April I could tell him to sit by the front window and watch until he saw the old man moving down the street, and he'd do it, just the most diligent little sentry you've ever seen.

Paulie would come get me then, and for the benefit of either parent who may have been watching, hold his nose high with his neck as limp as a dandelion stem, wobbling his head so anyone could tell he was bored silly, with nothing to do, half-dawdling, half-zooming to inform me that our chance had come. Again. We'd bundle ourselves against the stubborn chill and creep outside.

"Maybe he left his curtains all the way open," Paulie would say, every time. "Bet you he did."

Alongside the building's foundation, I'd lace my fingers into a stirrup and give Paulie a boost up to window level. He'd cup his hands around his eyes and try to peer through any gap between or beneath the curtains, and a few times there was cause for hope.

"I can see them!" he would report in a squealing whisper, but he couldn't furnish any details I didn't already know, so I'd let him down and brace him against the wall, climbing onto his bony back and chinning up to the window to look for myself.

I wouldn't manage any better than Paulie on details, but this stolen sight was more captivating somehow, more ripe with terrible promise, than the view I'd had through Mr. Cavanaugh's open door. With the street sounds so near, this was like peering into another world, another time, silent and mysterious.

On a rack of shelves that reached across one wall stood many dozens, if not hundreds, of jars. Some were tall and narrow, others widemouthed and squat, and while my view of them was gauzy through the window and screen and dim brown light, none seemed empty, but I couldn't make out what they held.

In some, things floated in cloudy liquids, or had sunk to the bottom. Others wouldn't have seen moisture in decades, that's how old they looked, whatever they held as dry as a desert. There were labels on most, curling at the edges, the paper and brittle tape gone the same yellow as I imagined the old man's toenails to be.

I would stare as long as I could, clinging to the windowsill until Paulie began to tremble under my weight, or, less often, a loud insane woman in the adjacent building threatened to call the police on us, and then we'd either walk or run away, depending.

Then we'd hide ourselves, and laugh and shudder and speculate on the contents of those jars, proposing new theories or repeating old favorites. We never ran out of ideas. The jars came from all over the world, inspired countless grotesque scenarios. They would invade our sleep. In the room we shared, one of us would awaken with a start and make sure the other was still breathing, whenever we weren't trying to *cause* a heart attack by plopping wet socks on each other's sleeping faces, like something escaped from its glass prison.

And now, many years later, I'm glad we had this shared dread to bring us together, because Paulie was my brother and it's only in our fears and dreams that anyone truly comes to know the real anyone else. I knew him better because of it, even though he was just six years old, and never saw seven, not even six-and-a-half.

Even today I find myself wishing that Paulie had gotten sick instead, that he'd lain in a bed and the rest of us, even my tiny sister Lindsey, who was learning to walk, had clustered around him and fallen wailing into each other's arms after his last breath.

That way, we might've steeled ourselves for it, and yes the anticipation would've been torture, but there's no less cruelty to the survivors in the terrible abruptness of accidents, and maybe even more. We could've told Paulie we loved him, one last time. We could've stood together in our rage. We could've blamed God.

Instead, they had me.

The next day my mom told me she was sorry, she hadn't meant it, and by then my dad had already told me the same thing, in case she never did I guess, but I couldn't believe them now, not a word they said. You can't look into your mother's face and see it that tear-stained, that frightened, that maniacal with grief, and believe anything other than what she's saying are the truest, most unfiltered words she's ever screamed.

What did you think you were doing up there, answer me, you had no business up there, answer me, you might as well have taken him and thrown him off yourself!

It hadn't seemed that way at the time, but once she got me thinking about it, I knew she was right.

Because it was spring, finally, genuinely, and we'd no longer needed our heavy jackets. We still missed the trees, but realized maybe we could make do. We didn't have trees. But we had roofs.

We climbed the fire escape on the back of the building, which had long been a particular temptation, but the frozen winds had made it less inviting, while now the warm breezes seemed to push us right to it. We carried a ball up with us.

First we took in the sights, all the points of the compass, a panorama of new horizons from our black tar mesa. We saw buildings we never knew existed, people we could've spit on. I was a king and Paulie a prince, and the world below there to serve us.

Inside, outside, on grass, on asphalt—we'd done it a hundred times, your basic dodgeball game for two. One point scored for a hit, none for a miss, one point lost if the other guy caught your throw. I usually tried to make it sting. As big brother, it was my right.

Soon, after a fling when I banged my knee against a steam vent, I looked back up and didn't see Paulie anywhere, gone from the spot he'd been in just seconds earlier, and the first thing I thought of was school. We'd been studying big birds and it was as though some giant condor had swooped down and carried him off and I'd missed the whole thing, and for the first few minutes I think that was what I decided to believe, it happened exactly that way except the condor had dropped him.

Our neighbors were very kind, and brought lots of food, and some of the women made offers to babysit, and the day before the funeral there came a knock at the door and when my dad opened it there stood Mr. Cavanaugh, without his coat and hat, a crutch under one arm and a plate in the other hand.

It was the first time I'd really seen his face, a creased old thing you knew had been lived in for a long time, but even so, it didn't droop, just settled there snugly across his skull under a bristly thatch of iron gray hair.

"I'm very sorry for your loss," he said, left the plate in my dad's hands, and thumped softly down the stairs.

My breath froze as we uncovered the plate, but it only held cookies—not store-bought, either. I ate one and it was warm from the oven, the chocolate chips half-gooey, and ate another because if they were poison I wanted to be the first to go. I deserved it.

But I didn't even get sick. So he did know how to make pretty good cookies, and that night when I heard him coughing down there, for the first time I felt sorry for him.

It was toward the end of the school year when a longstanding feud boiled over and sent me home bloody. The kid with the fists had taken a quick dislike not long after we'd moved and I started in this different school with the textbooks that looked as old as Mr. Cavanaugh's wallpaper. He hated me mainly for smarts but had never really acted on it until now. It wasn't fair, because if he knew how my papers were being graded now, instead of months ago, he'd see we weren't really that far apart anymore, that he was beating on an undeserving innocent, because those higher grades had been earned by some other me that we'd both lost track of.

If on my way home I'd been paying attention maybe I would've noticed a hand pulling back from Mr. Cavanaugh's curtains, but I wasn't, and didn't. I trudged through the vestibule and was two stairs up before seeing him standing in his doorway.

"Let's do your poor mother a favor, why don't we?" he said. "Let's not let her see you looking this way."

By now I was satisfied he wasn't a cannibal, plus I'd been losing weight so there was less of me anyway. I'd already braved the worst a few weeks ago, committing the once-unthinkable act of knocking on his door after my mom had sent me down to return his plate with a thank-you note.

So I went in, into that uncharted territory of his home, and it wasn't as alien as I'd thought, just a few musty old smells was all. After I washed away the blood and grime in his bathroom, Mr. Cavanaugh inspected my face and elbows and a knee that had gotten it bad through a fresh hole ground out of the denim. He doctored me with cotton balls sprayed with Bactine. It stung, but the fresh clean medicine smell reminded me of bug bites and summers past.

"Well, that's about the best we can do," he said, and I could tell he'd been hoping for better. "We're not going to be able to hide those scrapes unless we paint you."

I didn't say anything, just looked at the bathroom floor.

"The other fella," he said, graver now. "Did you get a few licks in on him too?"

I shrugged, because everything I'd done had seemed to bounce off. Then it all came back at me, the fists and how much they'd hurt and the helpless rage. I started to fight the tears and lost that one too. Mr. Cavanaugh pretended not to notice.

"I was going to pour you some lemonade," he said. "Probably take me a few minutes to make it."

He left me alone until I'd gotten it all out of my system and dried my eyes. When I came out of the bathroom he was standing at the kitchen sink, his spoon clinking inside the pitcher as his arm moved in slow circles.

"There's good timing," he said, "it's just now ready," and poured. I drank it gratefully, the coldest, sweetest drink I'd ever tasted, and carried the glass into the main room where I was drawn to what I'd deliberately been ignoring until now.

The jars.

I was finally seeing them up close, racks and racks of them in no order I could make out, clear glass with their pale murk and dusty lids and jaundiced labels, nothing here the sort of thing you'd ever dream of eating, although some jars held bits of things that once might not have been shy about eating you, instead.

In one of the largest lay the inert green coils of a snake with two heads branching from the same body. The faded ink on the label read *Corbin, KY* with a date over twenty years before. Even older was the tiny pig's head in another. Older still, a pale gray mass of spongy, fibrous tissue crowned with a cup as big around as a half-dollar; when I picked it up a cloud of particles stirred, like I'd shaken a snow globe but snow globes never made me queasy.

"That's a sucker off an octopus tentacle, washed up on the beach in Fort Lauderdale. That's in Florida."

"The whole octopus?" I said.

"Nah. Just the tentacle. Probably got bit off by a whale, way out to sea. Twenty feet of it if there was an inch."

Thrilled and horrified by the idea of actual monsters, rising from the watery dark undertow of my imagination, I continued the search, more eager with each new discovery sunk in preservative or rattling loose and dry.

Eyeballs and sharks' teeth, backbones and claws, arrow heads and sea shells.

A centipede as long as a weiner; a huge slug the same bright yellow as a banana; a scorpion, and the brain from a monkey's skull. And most pitiful of all, a tiny, hairless kitten with a fifth stunted leg jutting from its shoulder, and a ragged bite chewed from the back of its neck.

"Its mother did that," he explained. "A mother cat'll do that when something's wrong."

"Why?" I whispered. "Doesn't she love it?"

"I guess she loves it too much to let it grow up the way it is. It's a mercy to them, in the long run."

This bothered me greatly, because I felt sorry for the tiny newborn, never having a chance, never even seeing anything of its world because it had been killed before its eyes opened, and then I couldn't help but think of Paulie, and my part in that. I might as well have bitten away the back of his neck myself.

Mr. Cavanaugh said, "Maybe you shouldn't see these today."

Oh, but I had to. They'd tantalized me for so long that I couldn't turn loose of them now. I owed it to Paulie to see them all, no matter if they repelled me as much as they drew me closer.

While most had labels, not all of them did, and for some jars labels weren't necessary to know what they held, like the grinning monkey's skull that had donated the brain, but for others I had no clue. Several held glazed, dried-out curls of what looked like jerky, and others, what might've been the same thing only fresher, in thick, irregular shapes. Others held bugs, with lots of legs, but I couldn't have said what kind, and neither could he.

"This whole collection," he said, "I've been accumulating it for more than forty years. I guess that's even longer than your folks have been around."

I nodded, but didn't ask *why* he'd been doing it because this never occurred to me. Why is a question for five-year-olds. When you're ten you're focused on why not. It seemed perfectly natural to me that somebody, somewhere, would collect things like this and I just happened to live upstairs from one of them. I was lucky.

When I was ten I didn't know anything of statistics. My world wasn't big enough to need them. But now I know that more than half the couples who lose a young child split up eventually. I think I can even understand how it happens.

Paulie was gone and nothing was the same. Before, everything had been so balanced, each of us like one of the five points of a star that connects with every other point so that the whole structure is enclosed and protected. Now Paulie was gone and everything felt weak and exposed and out of balance.

Sometimes when nobody suspected—and they never did because in my own way I'd become invisible—I would watch my mom and dad and the way each of them acted around Lindsey. My little sister had learned to walk and was up to talking now, but they behaved as though she'd regressed and needed help again.

My mom would follow her around constantly, scarcely letting Lindsey out of her sight, and when she'd lose track of her for a minute, rush to scoop her up and clutch her tight and tell her to never ever run off like that again. My dad would follow her with his eyes, instead, and whenever Lindsey's short legs took her near the edge of a table, for instance, his breath would lock in his throat and his hand might slowly crumple the outer columns of the want-ads he was reading and he wouldn't even realize it.

I came home one day to find the floor covered with sawdust, because he'd taken a file and rounded off the corners of all the tables, and now was smoothing them with sandpaper. After he tried to restain the raw wood and couldn't get it to match, he and my mom got into a fight that lasted a week, because she said he was ruining the last nice things we had, and he said he'd choose that over a daughter with a split skull any day, and my mom accused him of accusing her of not being able to protect her own daughter.

They'd say just about anything in front of me now.

Because I was invisible and they didn't notice whether I was around or not, I figured I might as well not be. I roamed some, but more often stuck close to the building, hanging out on the fire escape, or with Mr. Cavanaugh.

He didn't seem to mind. I'd come in and gravitate toward the jars and ask "Anything new?" and he'd chuckle to himself and tell me he was too old to track down anything very interesting. Then he'd hold up a jar in his hand, examining what was inside, and I'd pretend to, but examine him instead, his gray hair and creases, and think *People look like this someday. Dad will look like this.*

I liked being there, because Mr. Cavanaugh really did see me instead of through me, but didn't expect anything. We didn't have to talk but if I wanted to, then he would.

"Did you ever kill anything to put it in a jar?" I asked one summer afternoon.

First he told me he didn't remember, then mused it over and said, "The starfish. I think that was probably alive when I put it in. But it would've died anyway."

"Did you ever have to throw any away? Like, you had something for a long time but then it fell all apart, so you had to throw it away because you couldn't even tell what it was anymore?"

He nodded immediately. "Two years ago I dropped my jellyfish. It wasn't any good after. Just made a big sonofabitching mess."

Then one day I got around to asking him if he'd ever killed anything that he *didn't* put in a jar.

"Hunting or fishing, you mean?" he said, and I nodded, then said, "Or anything bigger, like . . . people," and he stared at me.

"Why do you want to know a thing like that?" he asked.

So I tried to tell him without really telling him, wondering how it'd affected him, if he still had the same friends after, or if they didn't want to have anything to do with him anymore. He watched the floor for a long time, then told me he had and how long ago it had been, and I said, "Oh, okay, World War Two, I've heard of that," and I knew it wasn't the same thing at all.

What I really wanted to ask was if he ever *thought* of killing somebody, but I could tell he didn't want to talk about this, and even at ten I couldn't blame him. I felt awful about it myself.

It wasn't that I wanted to hurt Lindsey, as much as I'd been wishing she'd never been born at all. I'd look at cleaners and bug sprays in the cabinet and wonder what they'd do to her. I knew how wrong it was to think it, so I'd shut myself in my room and punch myself on the shoulder until it got red and sore, and pretty soon it would be bruised, and for the next few days if I still needed to punish myself, all I'd have to do was press it hard.

The more I visited Mr. Cavanaugh, the more I got used to his coughing on the days he had his attacks, and it wouldn't scare me so much as make me wince at the power of it. That *had* to hurt.

On the worst days he wouldn't even let me stay. He'd hobble into the kitchen and grab a dish towel and clamp it over his mouth. His face would turn deep red and he'd choke out what were almost words, furiously waving at me and then at the door, once grabbing me by my sore shoulder and pulling me there himself when I wasn't moving fast enough. The door would slam behind me and I'd hear the click of the lock, then his gruesome hacking would fade away as he went lurching back toward the bathroom.

As the months passed from summer to autumn to winter again, and my parents got worse and Mr. Cavanaugh got no better, I began to wonder if it was my imagination that his collection of jars was growing even though he always denied it. Every week or two I was sure there were more, although I couldn't find anything I didn't already recognize even if I didn't know what everything was.

I decided to test this theory by finding out how many there actually were, and one day after school I counted them. I'd made sure he was distracted first, telling him we should listen to his stereo. He had these records of organ music he liked, and I did too. They weren't anything like hymns; they didn't make me think of church at all. Low notes swirled like dark clouds, higher notes stabbing in and out like cries for help. Mr. Cavanaugh would lose himself in their desperate melancholy pace, the rhythm like a train he was riding far away from our tenement.

That first time I counted one hundred and sixty-two jars. A week later it was the same, and the week after that the count went up by one but I allowed I might've been wrong before. But by the time I counted one hundred and sixty-six, I knew I couldn't be off by that many.

So I had him fix hot cocoa for us, and while he was busy at the stove I'd methodically lift up each jar. Anything with a clean circle beneath it had to have been there a long time, while any jar sitting on top of dust was probably new.

Slowly, then, while his spoon clinked in the pan, the pattern began to emerge.

None of the newer jars held anything I recognized. None were labeled with contents or location, but some of the old dusty ones that had similarly puzzling contents had been dated. The oldest of these—the ones that had reminded me of beef jerky—dated back nearly thirty years.

The newer jars held fresher specimens, sometimes floating in preservative, sometimes not. The textures may have looked the same but their colors varied, pinks and grays, and before I knew it I'd slipped one of the new jars into the pocket of my winter coat. I knew he'd never miss it because there were a *lot* of them up there.

"Do you like marshmallows?" he called out, and I said that I did, feeling guilty for tricking him like this.

But there were so many secrets in our family now, it was a relief to concern myself with somebody else's for a change.

The main things I remember my parents telling me during those months were prohibitions. I was never to discuss family matters with anyone, whether friend or relative or stranger. Never to take Lindsey up on the roof. Never to change Paulie's side of the room we'd shared.

After all this time it remained the way it was the day he'd fallen, like a museum exhibit that I was supposed to live in but not touch. The worst of it was the stuffed clown that sat against the pillow of his smelly, half-made bed and leered at me all night long, holding its fat hands wide as though scheming to wrap them around my throat. I didn't dare drape a shirt over it at bedtime because I'd done this once and my mom had me write five hundred times that my clothes didn't belong on Paulie's furniture. She had a snapshot of the room in her mind. Any deviation caught her eye.

Sometimes I thought I could feel Paulie there, still, maybe because by holding onto the room we were holding onto him as well. Maybe this was why I'd stolen the jar. I'd brought it into the room and hidden it beneath my bed and that first night set it on the table between the two. A present, or a trophy. That I wasn't sure what it held made it that much more valuable. We didn't have to be afraid of it anymore, or the old man I'd taken it from.

Late that night, after the light was out and I'd quit trying to fall asleep, I heard a tiny tapping, totally without rhythm. First I thought a mouse was in the room with me, or at the window, but the more I listened, the closer it seemed. I turned to the jar, and in the cold moonlight coming through the window saw that the meaty little thing inside was clinging near the top, making a noise against the metal lid. It would flex like a slug, thickening in the middle and pushing itself forward as it slid around the rim of the jar, periodically testing for weak spots.

I watched it awhile, but when I turned on the lamp it froze, then let go and fell to the bottom with a plop. It lay there, playing possum. I stared at it, daring it to move, but before it would a voice from the hall yelled for me to turn out my light unless something was wrong. I left my fingers on the switch for a minute, because I couldn't make up my mind whether anything was wrong or not, then did as I was told because that was easiest.

I've said it before, but it bears repeating: It's only in our fears and dreams that anyone truly comes to know the real anyone else. In that spirit I can say I knew Mr. Cavanaugh better than anyone, because he feared death. Often, the things we've been and things we've done leave a burden inside us, and when death becomes as real as an old friend planning a visit, we dream of more days to pay for the past a little at a time instead of all at once.

The winter was cruel that year, and Mr. Cavanaugh spent too much of it coughing. He grew weak enough that it would've been dangerous for him to run his errands. I did them for him, a figure growing taller and straighter, leaning into the wind as I moved down the street, hidden in an old coat inherited from my dad, as I picked up groceries or deposited an occasional check in his bank.

From the couch where he lay, Mr. Cavanaugh would give me a dollar bill every time, and I knew he didn't have it to spare, but he insisted.

"Go on, take the damn thing, where'm I going to spend it?" he would wheeze.

"And don't you say one word to your folks. You hide it and do whatever you want with it."

Sometimes I suspected he was sending me on extra errands just to give away more dollars, without it seeming like he was raising my rate. But when he started giving them to me for listening to his records with him, then I really felt awful and wanted so badly to admit I'd stolen that jar and whatever it held, even though it seemed to have died, but I couldn't bring myself to confess.

"Are you going to die?" I asked one day, point blank, because I didn't know any better.

He was all watery eyes and gray whiskers on wilted cheeks. He didn't blink. "Don't worry, it's not catching."

"But *are* you?"

"I suppose I am," he said, then struggled to sit upright on his couch. When he was up, he gazed across the room at the jars for a long time before shaking his head. "Forty years to put that together. Sure doesn't look like much now, does it?"

I told him that *I* really liked it, and had seen things there I'd never seen anywhere else. He tried to smile at this, then said he'd once thought his collection would help him to understand and appreciate life and its diversity, but it hadn't, really. He said he didn't understand anything, and asked if I'd put on a record.

Mr. Cavanaugh started coughing halfway through, and it was a bad bout, so bad it got him moving when not much else had. I tried to help, but with a rag over his face and his eyes squinched shut, he furiously shook his head, and forced me out the door.

I stood out in the chilly hall, listening for the click of the lock, as usual. But it never came. I waited for a minute, then crept back in, because what if he needed an ambulance this time?

From the bathroom came the sounds of his sickness. I followed them back, taking careful steps while the organ music covered any trace of them, and when I was able to peer around the edge of the doorway, I saw him bent double with his mouth over a jar clutched in both hands, his back heaving in violent spasms until he coughed out a glistening clot of tissue. It sat on the bottom of the jar, stringing threads of sputum. Mr. Cavanaugh drew a ragged breath of relief and cursed before screwing the lid on the jar.

He saw me then, in the doorway, and when he realized I'd been watching, his face turned red again and full of shame. He gritted his teeth and shoved me away with the padded end of his crutch.

"Don't you ever come back down here again," he said, then used the crutch to slam the bathroom door in my face.

He didn't live long after that.

More than a week went by, then I realized I hadn't heard him coughing for at least a couple of days. When I went down to check, my knock went unanswered, but the door wasn't locked. I'd left it that way.

I found Mr. Cavanaugh on the couch, and spoke to him because I couldn't tell if he was dead or only sleeping, and then I tried to shake him awake. With one hand I grabbed his shoulder and the other I braced against his chest, but with the second good hard shake his whole chest collapsed beneath my hand, skin and bone and shirt buckling in as though I'd broken through a pie crust, and there was hardly any filling left at all.

At least that's the way I remember it.

Over the next few days everyone learned that his name wasn't really Cavanaugh and that more than thirty years ago he had killed his wife in a distant state and town, then disappeared. I couldn't say he didn't, but all I could remember was how nice he'd been to me, until the end, so I came to the conclusion that whatever he'd done had been done by some other Mr. Cavanaugh, and he'd carried it with him, paying for it a little bit at a time.

Guilt, I have learned, eats like a fiend.

Several years ago, when my daughter was born, I watched her through the nursery window and made more pledges than I could ever keep in one lifetime. How I was going to do everything so right.

It soon seemed that I had turned this into an all-or-nothing proposition. She wouldn't have any recollection of me now, I don't think. I look at the picture of the toddler she was the last time I saw her, and wonder if she'll learn to forgive this inexcusable absence I've imposed on her past, present, and future.

We are phantoms to each other, haunted by memories that don't exist.

In most ways Paulie is more real to me than she is, and not a year goes by that I don't think of something he would've just done had he still been alive. A graduation. A job. A marriage. A kid who'd be a cousin to my own. This year he probably would've lost his first few hairs in the shower drain.

Not a month goes by that I don't wonder how different things would've been for everyone if Paulie had never died. Sometimes I believe there used to be some other me who was supposed to have lived, and goddamn, I killed him too.

But the rest of the time, I know better.

I feel him deep inside, tearing his way through until there's a tickle at the back of my throat, as day by day he loosens the ties that bind.

ROBERT PHILLIPS

The Snow Queen

Robert Phillips is the author of three collections of short stories and six books of poetry. His most recent books are News About People You Know *(Johns Hopkins University Press) and* Spinach Days *(Texas Review Press). He lives in Texas, where he teaches creative writing at the University of Houston. "The Snow Queen," based on a nineteenth-century Danish fairy tale by Hans Christian Andersen, comes from the Summer 2002 edition of* The Hudson Review.

—T. W.

for A.S. Byatt

Her bedchamber is white
as a refrigerator, cold
all year as a meat locker.

No meat there. The canopy
over her four-poster bed
is hung with white lace

intricate as snowflakes.
Her windows are frosted,
to keep out the dazzle

of the Northern Lights,
the fun of polar bears
dancing on hind legs.

When she pads barefoot
she never feels the carpet's
tickle. Her nightgown

is white as a winding-sheet.
Underneath her pillow
she keeps an icicle,

just in case. Her sheets
are ice floes—white on white—
no cherries in the snow.

She is married to Winter.
It isn't as though she were
locked away by a cold groom.

He'd melt like a snowman
all over that shag carpet
if she would just let him in.

JAY RUSSELL

Hides

Jay Russell is the author of the novels Celestial Dogs, Burning Bright, *and* Greed and Stuff, *all featuring quasi-detective Marty Burns, as well as* Blood, *and World Fantasy Award nominee* Brown Harvest. *Some of his short fiction has been collected in the volume* Waltzes and Whispers. *He lives in London with his wife and daughter.*

About "Hides," he says: "Michele Slung asked me for a story for her new anthology—with the simple premise of 'strangers'—and mentioned that she wouldn't mind seeing a period piece for the book. Since Michele's books are always wonderful and I didn't want to miss the chance of inclusion, I aimed to oblige. I'd also long wanted to write a story set in the old west and reckoned this was the right opportunity. I honestly can't remember how I came to the decision to write about who I write about here, as I have no special fondness for the main character despite his importance to the genre. At the same time, the broad chronology of events is historically accurate in the context of his life. So technically I suppose this is an alternate-history story. But with teeth."

—E. D.

You ain't from here."

Stevenson did his best to smile. The smell wafting off the man was atrocious, like something that should have been buried weeks before. Stevenson hadn't noticed it so much while the man slept through the first several hours of the journey, but now that he was up and moving, waving his arms about, the smell was impossible to avoid. The others in the stage didn't seem to mind, but Stevenson couldn't stop coughing; had to will himself not to retch with every fresh wrack of his aching lungs. He spat a wad of phlegm out into his dirty handkerchief. The blonde man who smelled like a dead thing hawked up a brown lugie of his own and spat it out the window, largely missing.

"Lunger?" the man asked.

Stevenson nodded, started coughing again and lost all control. He turned, leaned over the sleeping, red-haired woman to his right and vomited out the window. Bloody wads of mucus came up along with the too-big breakfast of hotcakes, bacon and coffee he'd forced down in the dining car of the train. The train that was supposed to take him all the way to Sacramento, but which had been forced to discharge its passengers at Carson City where the track had flooded out. Stevenson had been reluctant to board the uncomfortable stagecoach, but hadn't seen any choice. Not if he wanted to get to Fanny.

And seeing her again was the only thing in the world that truly mattered. His desire had driven him across an ocean and this massive, mad continent.

Stevenson held his head outside as the stage rattled along the choppy dirt trail. The dry air did his lungs some good—just not enough. And nothing could change the smell of the man sitting across from him. Stevenson would never have gotten on board if he'd known, but the blonde man had jumped on just as the stage pulled out of Carson City. So there was nothing to do but ride it out. Reluctantly, gulping a last tubercular lungful of fresh air, Stevenson withdrew back into the coach. He started to apologize to the young woman he'd leaned across, but saw that she hadn't so much as stirred. The acid taste of bile coated his tongue and palate, but Stevenson found that it cut into his sense of smell, and he accepted the small mercy. The blonde man watched him with an unpleasant smile plastered across his unshaved face. The other passengers—a stiff-backed, elderly man in a black suit and stovepipe hat, and his horse-faced, pursed-lipped wife, also in black—simply looked bored.

"Nasty," the blonde man said.

"Aye," Stevenson agreed.

"You what?"

"Sorry?" Stevenson was confused.

"You said 'I,' but you didn't say what. Then you said 'Sorry,' but you didn't say what you's apologizing for."

"Aye," Stevenson repeated, catching on. "I meant to say yes. Aye means yes, ye see. Ken?"

"Not in these parts it don't. And my name ain't Ken. It's Jackworth." He looked at the elderly man. "You Ken?"

The old man offered the slightest, unfriendliest-possible shake of his head. His wife screwed her face up into an even uglier expression.

"No Kens here," the blonde man said.

"My mistake," Stevenson said. He sighed.

"You talk funny, mister." Jackworth hawked another wad of phlegm toward the window. Given his own condition, it didn't bother Stevenson—not like the smell—though Stevenson had now seen enough of the American West to realize that there was nothing likely wrong with the man's lungs; it was the egg-sized wad of tobacco stuffed in his cheek that was to blame.

"So where's you from then?"

The smell was starting to get to Stevenson again. He put his hand up to his mouth and nose to stem the effects. It didn't help much.

"Edinburgh," he said, and coughed.

"Enburr?" the man puzzled.

Stevenson lowered his hand, tried not to roll his *r*'s so much. "Ed-in-burgh."

Jackworth scratched his head, pulling out a louse which he briefly inspected before squashing it between thumb and forefinger. "Ed-and-burg," he repeated. "That up Nebraska way?"

Stevenson coughed again, but this time to disguise a laugh. The blonde man might be stupid—might be?—but he looked like the type who wouldn't take kindly to being mocked. And he was watching Stevenson very closely.

"Edinburgh's a city in Scotland."

Jackworth just frowned.

"Scotland. It's a country."

Nothing. A blank stare.

"It's a part of Great Britain. England?"

The man shook his head.

"Across the Atlantic Ocean."

Jackworth's eyes lit up. "I heard of that," he yelled, slapping his hat against his thigh. "Never seed it, though. Seed Wichita once. Big old town." He leaned forward—bringing his smell with him—and held a hand up to his cheek to confer on Stevenson a conspiratorial whisper. "Got me some fine cunny there, tight as a baby sheep. Ain't never forgot it."

Appalled, Stevenson nonetheless smiled and nodded, then turned toward the window for a taste of clean air and the hope of an end to the conversation.

"Where's abouts—"

The question was interrupted by a monstrous lurch of the stagecoach. The sleeping woman rolled on top of Stevenson and both fell to the far side of the compartment. Jackworth was quick—very quick—and grabbed hold of the door handle, but the old man and his wife tumbled to the floor, like a pair of coupling crows in flight. The man's stovepipe hat zipped right out the window. The wheels on the right side of the coach lifted off the ground, and for a very long second Stevenson felt certain that the vehicle was going to flip over. But with a gut and lung-shuddering thud, followed by a loud crunch from the undercarriage, the coach righted itself. The driver shouted a stream of curses as he tried to bring the horses to rein. Stevenson couldn't see much with the no-longer-sleeping woman sprawled on top of him, but he could hear the horses shriek and whinny as they went down and the rear axle of the coach was ripped out from underneath. The carriage hit the dirt trail hard, and Stevenson smacked his jaw against the wooden bench, biting into his upper lip as he did so. His mouth filled with the too-familiar taste of blood.

There was another jerk, and then everything came to a blessed stop.

Jackworth was out of the coach before Stevenson could even right himself. The woman had rolled back off of him with the coach's final lurch and spilled into the old man and woman. Stevenson pressed the back of his hand to his mouth and, examining the volume of blood, decided that the cut wasn't too bad. He got to his feet as best he could—at better than six feet tall, he couldn't stand up straight—and offered a hand to help untangle his fellow passengers. The young woman appeared dazed, but had no visible injuries. Stevenson lifted her up and sat her down on the bench, where she rubbed her stomach. The old man had gotten to his knees and now fussed over his wife, who sat whimpering on the floor. The man had a long gash across his forehead, and had torn his undertaker's suit, but the woman was hurt much worse. Her black skirt had ridden up and Stevenson saw that her leg was badly broken. An ivory cane of bone poked out through a bloody tear in her left thigh. The woman touched the bone with her finger, unable, it seemed, to recognize it for what it was. She'd gone very pale indeed, and started to cry out with the pain, but her husband, studying Stevenson's gaze, seemed more concerned with drawing the hem of her skirt back over the exposed expanse of her ghost-white thigh. The man's lips drew back in a snarl, but before Stevenson could say anything, two shots sounded from outside. Another pair swiftly followed.

Stevenson leaped out the open door, misjudged the distance and took a face-first fall into the dirt. More embarrassed than hurt, he scrambled to his feet. He came around to the front of the coach just in time to see the driver put a final bullet into the head of a dying horse. A second dead animal lay beside it.

"There's my job," the driver said, and spat onto the corpse. The pair of horses that had survived the accident whinnied nervously a dozen yards up the road.

"The old woman is hurt quite badly," Stevenson announced. "She's broken her leg clear through the skin."

The driver turned to Jackworth, who was dancing excitedly between the dead animals. "What in hell'd he say?"

"He ain't from here," Jackworth reported. "Come from 'cross the ocean. Atlantic, you know it?"

"The old woman inside the carriage is badly injured," Stevenson repeated, slowly. "Her leg is broken."

"Shee-it," the driver said, and spat again. "Ain't that just the fly on the turd."

"You a doc there, Ed-and-burg?" Jackworth asked. He practically leaped from leg to leg, like a man desperate to urinate. What was he so bloody excited about, Stevenson wondered.

"Nae . . . no. But ye can see bone through the flesh. There's not a lot of doubt as to what's wrong."

"Hot damn! Got to get me a lookee-loo at that." And Jackworth jumped back into the coach.

A moment later the younger woman leaned out, still rubbing at her belly, but looking less dazed. Stevenson went to help her out, and together they studied the wreck of the stagecoach. The rear axle had snapped in two and lay a dozen yards up the road, near the two-foot-deep gully in the trail that had caused the crash. The front axle was still attached, but it too was as broken as the old woman's leg. It was clear that they wouldn't be going any farther in this coach, though, looking at the damage, Stevenson felt lucky to be alive and essentially uninjured.

"What do we do now?" Stevenson asked the driver.

The man picked his nose and spat. He looked aggrieved to have to answer the question. Or perhaps just scared about the consequences of the crash, Stevenson considered.

"We's caught what you'd call 'twixt and 'tween and halfway to neither. Too far to the company post, especially with the womenfolk and such. There is a old way station not too far from here. Five, maybe seven miles, best I reckon. Don't generally like to stop there, though."

"Why not?"

"Company don't like it. Had some trouble there a while back. S'all I know."

"Will there be a doctor there?" Stevenson asked.

The driver chuckled. "Barely a *there* there, friend. But I reckon she'll have to do us. Feller runs things there knows some doctoring. Claims to, anyway, what I hear. Queer feller, I thought; makes your blood run like the wrong way."

Stevenson didn't much care for the sound of that. "Is there nae a better destination for us?"

"Not to make before nightfall. We put the old lady on the one horse, and the ma'am here on t'other, should make it right enough. Not too bad a hike, these things go. Bit uphill. Not that I sees much choice in the matter."

And thus did Robert Louis Stevenson, late of Edinburgh, Scotland (across the Atlantic Ocean, of which many people have heard), set out on the road to Hides.

The old woman screamed something fierce as they dragged her out of the remains of the coach, but mercifully she passed out as they settled her onto the horse, making the task that much easier. Jackworth continued to marvel at the length of bone protruding through her thigh, though to his credit he did the lion's share of carrying her without complaint. Her husband, who'd reluctantly introduced himself as Mr. Anderson Balfour—he stressed the *Mister*—looked on disapprovingly, constantly tugging her dress down over her exposed leg, and proving himself to be of little help. The driver—Grey, he called himself, though if that was his first name or last, or merely an encapsulation of his life, Stevenson never learned—was only slightly more helpful, utterly preoccupied, it seemed, with the wreckage of his stagecoach and his livelihood. Little Jackworth was a ball of energy, though, and while Stevenson felt that there was something odd about the fellow (not just his smell), he decided Jackworth's primary offense was that of being somewhat juvenile. Indeed, as he studied the blonde man, Stevenson guessed that Jackworth couldn't be much more than nineteen or twenty years old. Though he did wear a pair of guns on his belt.

The other woman, who eventually introduced herself as Mrs. Timothy Reilly, continued to clutch at her belly, while denying any specific discomfort or injury. She showed some initial reluctance at mounting the remaining horse, and in the end would only ride sidesaddle. Stevenson might have assumed she was fearful of the steed, but she seemed confident enough once in place.

Grey led the way, taking the reins of the horse bearing the unconscious old woman, along with the lockbox from the stagecoach; the other bags would have to be left behind with the wreckage, though the driver secreted the passengers' belongings in the woods off the trail to be safe, then covered his tracks. Balfour followed directly behind Grey, eyes glued to his wife's leg, then came Mrs. Reilly on her horse. Stevenson, already feeling the effects of the strain on his lungs, brought up the rear. Much to his chagrin, Jackworth fell into place beside him, swinging his arms back and forth as he walked, like a kid in a holiday parade. A light breeze from the north brought with it just a hint of storm; Stevenson took advantage of it to position himself upwind of the man.

"So, Ed, what's yer business?" Jackworth asked.

Stevenson didn't much want to talk—he was finding it difficult enough just walking and breathing—but neither did he like to be rude.

"I've trained and toiled as both a lawyer and an engineer, though neither vocation proved much to my liking. I do a wee bit of writing now, and am told I've a flair for it. And most people call me Louis." *Except for one who calls me Robbie*, he thought.

"No fooling. Sorry 'bout that, Lou. Well, gee. I always did want to learn to read, you know. Got a cousin who knows his ABCs right through, mostly. Smart as a whip and hung like a bear. Beat that if you can! What ya write?"

"Stories about my travels, mostly. People and things I've seen, and places I've visited. France and Germany most recently. And about my home in Scotland, of course."

"Hooo-weee! You been all them places? I heard of France, you know. That 'cross the Atlantic, too?"

Stevenson merely nodded. "My health compels me to travel. The climate back home is particularly unsuitable to my condition. More's the pity, because I do love it so."

"So what brings yer hell and gone out here? You fixing to write another story?"

Stevenson hesitated. He didn't much care to discuss his life and plans with this stranger. And he couldn't talk about Fanny to anyone. She was . . . hard to explain.

"In fact, I'm just now thinking about something entirely different: a work of pure fiction. A pirate story, I ken. I find that my imagination grows keener than my powers of observation with each passing year." Stevenson offered himself a slight chuckle.

"Don't know no pirates, so I can't help you there, Lou. Plenty good tales 'round these parts, though."

"Is that right?"

"You must know 'bout the Donners," Jackworth whispered.

"Not to my recollection."

Jackworth took off his hat and slapped it against his thigh. He grinned so wide, Stevenson could see all his missing back teeth. "You ain't heard of the Donner party?" he practically yelled.

The others all turned around and the driver, Grey, offered a particularly disgusted look. Jackworth slapped his hand over his mouth.

"What was the Donner party?" Stevenson asked.

When it was clear that the others were again facing front, Jackworth continued, determinedly sotto voce: "Cannibals."

Stevenson assumed he misunderstood. "I beg your pardon?"

Jackworth feverishly nodded his head. "They was cannibals. I mean, not to start, but that's how it come out in the end."

"I don't think I follow ye."

"Thirty years or so back. Donners and Reeds was travelling west. Two big families. Got trapped up in the Sierra, just a piece aways from here, by the winter snows. Damn fools, but ain't no shortage of them. Supplies run out, animals run out, luck run out, mostly. Nothing left for it but to chomp each other. Told folks after that they only et the ones what was already dead, but there's them what say elsewise. Some claim they drew lots and slaughtered the losers like sows. Others that the families set up camps and went at each other like in a war and et their enemies what they captured. Eighty-odd went into that pass in winter, forty-odd come out the other end in spring. Others all got et."

"Good Lord!"

"Yessir. There's folks 'round who still remember, can tell you the gruesome details if you can stand to hear 'em. It's a wonder, ain't it? Imagine how'd it be like to end your days getting et."

"And you're certain that this is true?"

A darkness crossed Jackworth's face. "You calling me a liar?"

"Nae, certainly not." Stevenson had learned that, in this part of the world, short of stealing a man's horse there was no offense worse than questioning his word. "I just wondered if this is not, perhaps, some wee tall tale which is told in the region. I have heard a few others. Some nonsense about a giant lumberjack for one. And it reminds me of the stories told of old Sawney Bean in and around Ballantrae."

Jackworth nodded, seemingly appeased. "Well, this ain't no tall tale, that's for sure. It's a damn historical fact. They even started to call the old canyon trail where it happened Donner Pass."

"Remarkable," Stevenson mused. "How could anyone do that?"

"How's you mean?"

Stevenson found himself intrigued and repelled by the story in equal measure. "Imagine eating human flesh. Not just eating it, but slaughtering it yourself. A friend, a cousin, a brother. Even if they were already dead, the things ye'd have to do. Draining the blood. Cutting the muscle from the bone. Carving the organs from their cavities. Cooking the meat, putting the morsels in your mouth. Chewing. Swallowing." He shuddered. "Doesn't seem possible."

"I could do it."

Stevenson studied the young man. Jackworth stared ahead with an intense, very serious expression, nodding to himself. "Ye couldn't."

Jackworth looked up at the writer. "Oh, yeah. I been hungry. I done things. I seen things."

"Not like that, surely."

"Naw, not exactly. But then I ain't never been stuck in no mountain pass in no blizzard with nothing to eat but a third cousin twice removed. I seen men kilt, though, and it were for less than not starving to death. People is funny animals, Lou. My daddy used to say never turn your back on a animal 'cause you never can tell what it's likely to do. Well, I turned my back on lots of critters and I ain't never suffered no harm. Okay, mebbe a bite on the ankle. But turn your back on a man, and you're likely as not to take a bullet in the ass. Or worser. People is just animals when day turns to night, you gotta know that. And you can't never be surprised by the things they's prone to do. Aw, hell, I got to take a piss something fierce. Burns like hell when I do it, too. Don't know what that's about."

As Jackworth dashed off into the trees, unbuttoning his fly, Stevenson increased his stride. He thought he could do with some different company for a while.

They stopped after an hour of mostly uphill walking. It was Mrs. Reilly who asked if they could rest, and though Grey glanced up at the darkening skies with a frown, he nodded his assent. Stevenson went over to help the woman down from the horse, but a fresh coughing fit overcame him, and ultimately she had to help him to sit on an outcropping of rock above a gurgling stream. He waved her away, nodding his thanks, and hawked up a bloody wad of phlegm against the white stone. He lay flat on the rocks and reached down to scoop up handfuls of clear water. It was so cold that it sent a spike of pain up through his head, but after a few swallows, the coughing once again subsided. He rolled over, breathing slowly, enjoying the dim rays of late afternoon sun that penetrated the mounting overcast.

Balfour stood guard beside his wife, still out cold. With Grey's help, they'd lowered her off the horse, to give the animal a chance to rest and drink from the stream. Jackworth kept an excited eye on the enterprise, eager, it seemed, to catch another glance at the woman's protruding leg bone. Mrs. Reilly had wandered off behind the trees, to answer nature's call no doubt. She returned a few minutes later, still rubbing her stomach, a dyspeptic expression distorting her otherwise pleasant features. She went over to see if she could be of help with Mrs. Balfour. The four of them stood in a circle around the old woman, none of them quite knowing what to do. Jackworth saw Stevenson studying the tableau and grinned at the writer. Stevenson groaned to himself as the blonde man came over to his spot on the rock. Jackworth leaned over and whispered into Stevenson's ear: "You're trying to figure which of us you'd eat, ain't ya?"

Stevenson had been thinking no such thing. Before he could say so, Jackworth added: "Well, I got dibs on the Irish cunny, hear?" and he licked his lips lasciviously. To Stevenson's relief, Jackworth stood up and wandered back toward the trail.

Mrs. Reilly was gesticulating forcefully at the old woman. Mr. Balfour crossed his arms over his chest and firmly shook his head from side to side. She then pointed at the driver, but he raised his hands in a "no sir, not me" gesture and walked away, back to the horses. Mrs. Reilly again made a pleading gesture at the old man, but he just turned his back on her. Exasperated, she walked away and sat down beside Stevenson.

"She's going to lose that leg," Mrs. Reilly informed him. "He's tied a sash around the top to stem the bleeding, but it's fastened too tight and the leg's gone all blue. The blasted man won't listen to a word I say."

"He looks a stubborn old mule."

"Impossible. I told him she'll lose the leg and he just insists that 'the Lord will provide.' And beggars will ride, I say."

Stevenson raised an eyebrow. "Not one for Providence then?"

"I didn't mean to shock you. I understood you to be a writer of tales. I always heard writers were open-minded, liberal types."

Jackworth liked to talk, Stevenson realized. "Aye, but I'm also a lay preacher's son."

"No offense meant, I'm sure."

"None taken, missus. I'm just surprised to hear a good Irish lass like yourself express such a sentiment."

"Who said I was Irish?"

Stevenson felt slightly flustered. "Well, it's just . . . your look and your hair and . . . Mrs. *Reilly* and all that."

Mrs. Reilly dragged her rear end across the rock, closer to Stevenson. "May I confess something to you?" Stevenson nodded. "My name isn't really Mrs. Reilly."

"Nae?"

She shook her head. "There is no Mr. Reilly."

"Is there not?"

She shook her head. Suddenly, a picture took shape in Stevenson's head. He didn't know how he knew, but he knew. He said it out loud. "Then who's the father of the bairn?"

The woman's eyes went wide, and the hand that had been rubbing her stomach froze.

"I didn't mean to shock ye," Stevenson said, touching a hand lightly to the woman's arm.

"How did you know?" she whispered.

"I didn't for certain. Until this second. But the way ye touch your belly, and the way ye ride the horse and, well, ye've probably heard it said before, but as I look at ye there's a kind of a glow about ye. I just put a series of observations together and invented the story that tied them up in a neat package. That's what I do, after all. It's true then?"

She nodded. "You won't say—"

"It's none of their concern," he said, patting her hand. "Nor mine. As an open-minded writer."

The woman looked relieved. "I'm travelling to find the father. Let him know the situation. I hope to *become* Mrs. Reilly. Well, a missus at least, whatever the name." She studied Stevenson carefully. "I bet you're a good writer."

Before he could reply, or recover from his blush, their attention was distracted by a piercing scream from the old woman. She'd come to, and didn't much like the feeling. As she continued to shriek, Grey had to rush over and try to settle the horses. Jackworth came running back from wherever he'd been, and made straight toward the Balfours. He stood directly over the old woman, breathing hard from his exertions, but seemingly excited by her agony. Mr. Balfour was struggling with his wife, holding her from behind, trying to calm her down. Stevenson and Mrs. Reilly both stood up, but before they could make a move to help, Jackworth hauled off and punched the old woman in the jaw with all his might. Her head rocked back and she tipped over, smacking the ground hard.

She was out cold again.

Mr. Balfour studied his wife, then glanced up at the still-grinning Jackworth. The old man nodded his thanks and Jackworth winked at him.

They loaded the women back on the horses and set off up the road.

The trail leveled out, but the early evening air took on a chill. Stevenson had left his coat in his traveling bag and had to make do with cinching tight his waistcoat. Jackworth was up in front with Grey—every so often the two men broke out in fits of ugly laughter—and Mrs. Reilly seemed to be half dozing in the saddle as they made slow progress. Stevenson had been lagging behind and increased his pace, as much to keep warm as anything else, and without really meaning to, found himself beside Mr. Balfour. He thought about walking on past, but another burst of vile hilarity from Grey and Jackworth restrained him. He matched strides with Balfour, offering a glance back at the old man's wife, still enjoying Jackworth's ministrations on the back of the horse. They walked like that for some ways.

"Has she stirred?" Stevenson asked, unable to endure any more of the uncomfortable silence.

"No."

"With fortune this gentleman at the way station will be able to help."

"Can't say."

"Do you know anything about this place? The driver doesn't seem to care for it."

"Nnnn."

Stevenson tried a different tack: "So where are ye and your wife headed?"

"West."

Stevenson coughed. "Getting a tad cold now," he said.

"You say so."

Balfour walked a little quicker. Stevenson slowed his pace again, allowing Balfour and the horse bearing his wife to advance past him once more.

Coughing, shaking his head, crossing his arms over his chilled body, Stevenson walked on alone.

There was just enough light to make out the sign. It had been crudely burned into a strip of old wood that might once have been part of a door. It dangled on frayed hemp rope from the dead branches of a lightning-struck willow tree. Just the one word:

HIDES

"There she is," Grey announced.

The building was roughly oblong, but none of the angles were quite straight. Several crude windows had been carved out of the mismatched wooden walls, but there was no glass in the frames, only flimsy shutters to keep out the wet and the cold. One whole side of the structure was black and charred, though some makeshift effort to patch up the worst of the fire damage was in evidence. Bright light glinted out through holes in the door and gaps in the frame, suggesting that someone waited inside. Though who could regard such a wreck as *home*, Stevenson couldn't imagine. His heart sank at the prospect of finding proper attention for the injured old woman from anyone residing here.

"Hides," Stevenson whispered. He shuddered.

"They say it used to be a big trading post," Grey explained. "Been here since Hector was a pup. The Yana and the Atsugewi'd come swap their pelts and beads and such for heap big firewater. Heh-heh. Don't think I even seen a Atsugewi for going on ten years now. Kilt 'em all, I reckon. Or drank 'emselves to death, filthy red buggers."

And he spat. "Don't know what keeps the place going these days. Not much from the look of her."

Mrs. Balfour began to stir again on the back of the horse. She wasn't quite awake, but she was moaning slightly and her teeth chattered like cicadas at sunrise. Stevenson saw Jackworth ball his fingers into a preparatory fist, but Mrs. Reilly slid down from her mount and stood between the blonde man and the old woman.

"We'd best get her inside," she said to Mr. Balfour. The old man glanced at

Jackworth, as if considering the fist option, then nodded at Mrs. Reilly. Jackworth looked briefly disappointed, but he was all smiles as he helped Grey carry the woman into the old trading post.

Mrs. Reilly opened the door for them as Grey and Jackworth hauled Mrs. Balfour across the threshold. Mr. Balfour scurried right behind. Mrs. Reilly held the door for Stevenson, who entered last.

The trading post consisted of a single large room, broken up only by a counter that ran the length of the far wall. The room was lit every which way by gas lamps and fat tallow candles that stank to high hell but provided an unexpectedly warm glow. All manner of furry hides had been draped across the walls and over the rough wooden floor. Stevenson didn't know his American fauna too well, but he recognized bits of beaver, raccoon, deer and an immense bearskin that covered the whole center of the room. A grizzly, possibly. The hides smelt musky and mildewed, but their softness and heat sucked the worst of the chill right out of his lungs.

Sitting in a rocking chair by a roaring fire in the corner was a rotund ball of a man with a misshapen, bald head. He wore wire-rim spectacles and was reading from a tattered yellowed copy of Beadle's Dime Novels. His dark brown eyes opened wide at the sight of the group that had intruded on his quiet evening.

"Howdy," Grey said. He hawked into a spittoon by the door. "Paul, ain't it?"

"Poole," the round man said. He had a soft, almost girlish voice. He pulled a pocket watch from his vest, frowned. "You should have passed hours ago. Why are you here?"

"Accident. Busted both axles, believe that? Been hoofing it for miles. Coach is a wreck and I had to put down two the horses. I'm through, that's for your certain."

"My," Poole replied.

Everyone stood and stared at each other then, Jackworth and Grey still supporting Mrs. Balfour between them. Her groaning had gotten louder.

"This woman needs some attention," Stevenson finally said. "She's broken her leg in the accident."

"He's from Ed-and-burg," Jackworth helpfully pointed out.

Poole continued to sit there.

"Can ye help her?" Stevenson urged. "Or is there someone else?"

"No one else. Just me now." The fat man blinked. He put down his book, pointed at the opposite corner of the room. "Bring her this way."

Jackworth and Grey carried Mrs. Balfour over to a bench and put her down—a bit roughly, Stevenson thought—then stepped away. Mr. Balfour walked around behind the bench, hovering protectively over his wife. The old woman's eyes fluttered open and she immediately began to shriek in pain. Poole waddled over and lifted the hem of her black dress without so much as a by-your-leave. Mr. Balfour gasped, but offered no more substantive objection. Poole knelt down and ran his fingers up the woman's leg, gently prodding at the exposed shank of bone. Mrs. Balfour screamed.

"Well," Poole said.

"Won't you do something?" Mrs. Reilly asked.

"This tourniquet has been fastened much too tightly," Poole announced. Mrs. Reilly issued a harrumph. Poole loosened the sash and kneaded the flesh of the woman's upper thigh. Mr. Balfour took a white-knuckle grip on the back of the bench, but held his tongue. His wife wailed in such agony that, had there been any glass in the windows, Stevenson felt sure that the sound would have shattered it. Blood oozed out of the open wound, but in lesser volume than before.

"First things first," Poole said. He got up and slowly walked behind the counter, not at all bothered by the old woman's cries. A series of ill-balanced shelves and cubbyholes along the back wall held a plethora of mismatched jars and beakers, filled to varying levels with multicolored liquids. As the old woman continued to shriek—Stevenson wanted to cover his ears—Poole calmly went about pouring drops and drains out of different bottles into a chipped whiskey glass. He glanced up and down the counter for something, shrugged to himself, then stuck his finger in the glass to stir the potion. He sniffed his finger as he withdrew it and nodded in approval. He handed the glass to Mr. Balfour.

"Make her drink that," he said.

The old man tried to put the glass in his wife's hand, but she was beyond reasoning. She flailed at him, nearly emptying the glass of its contents. Balfour didn't seem to know what to do. Poole shook his head and sighed.

"A bit of help, if you would."

Grey and Jackworth had retreated near the fire with a bottle of rye. The two men exchanged a glance and got up. Grey took the old woman's arms, Jackworth, grinning, her feet. When she opened her mouth to let out a wail, Poole snatched the glass back from her husband and poured the contents down her gullet.

Mrs. Balfour choked on the stuff at first and spat some of it out, but enough of it must have gone down, because in less than a minute she was asleep again.

"What was in that?" Stevenson asked.

"Oh, just a little elixir I know," Poole said. "She'll be out till morning if we're lucky. We could saw that leg right off, and she wouldn't feel a thing." He looked up then at Mr. Balfour. "I'm not planning on sawing it off. At least not yet. But you shouldn't have tied that knot so tight. I'll try and fix her up, but I don't know that it will take. Time, as is its wont, will be the final arbiter. And circumstance."

Mr. Balfour nodded.

Stevenson was impressed as he and Mrs. Reilly assisted Poole with setting the leg. Poole decided that Grey and Jackworth were too indelicate for the task, and though the process had its difficult moments—Stevenson had to look away as Poole forced the exposed length of bone back inside Mrs. Balfour's torn flesh, then twisted and pulled at the leg until he felt the broken ends grind together and mesh—Poole worked quickly and with a minimum of spilled blood. They used two lengths of worm-eaten board for a splint, and secured it with strips of muskrat hide. Poole couldn't decide what to do about the open wound, then opted for stitching it closed with some catgut and a needle made from bone that must have been meant for sewing hides. Stevenson again found it difficult to watch as Poole darned together the torn flaps of skin but suspected that, all in all, Mrs. Balfour could have had worse luck than to have alighted at Hides. Poole finished up by dousing the wound with rotgut whiskey. As the amber liquid washed over the stitched opening, Mrs. Balfour shuddered in her induced slumber. Poole lay a blanket on top of her, and gave another to her husband, who settled in for the night on the floor beside her.

By the time they were done with the old woman and had cleaned themselves up, Jackworth and Grey had finished off their bottle of hootch and had both passed out on the floor in front of the dying fire. "Leave them be," Poole said, and hauled out a couple of louse-ridden horse blankets which he gently laid over the sleeping men. He searched around in a trunk until he found a length of calico. He hung it up across a corner of the room, making a private sleeping space for Mrs. Reilly. He found a somewhat softer and cleaner blanket for her and piled some furs on the floor into a little mattress.

"I'm not really equipped for ladies," he said, "but you should be able to make do with that. I receive so few guests."

Mrs. Reilly gratefully retreated behind the curtain, still rubbing her belly and saying her good-nights. Poole gathered another set of furs together and flung them on the floor beside his own bed. "That should do you," he said.

"That'll be dandy," Stevenson replied.

Poole went about damping out the candles and lamps until the only light came from the embers of the fire in the corner. Stevenson removed his boots and waistcoat, unfastened the top buttons of his trousers and chemise and lay down.

The sound of snoring soon filled Hides.

The rain woke Stevenson up. The rain and the coughing.

The storm that had threatened to break all during their long hike finally arrived, and with a fury. Water sloshed into the corners of the room, from the spots where the walls and roof were poorly joined, and through gaps in the wall and windows and door. The sudden concentration of humidity and moisture in the air sat heavily in Stevenson's lungs and provoked a diabolical coughing fit.

At first, Stevenson could barely stop hacking long enough to take a breath. He crawled off his pallet of furs toward the door, made it to the spittoon to hawk up a wad of dark mucus. He was able to take several deep breaths after that, until a fresh spell of coughing possessed him. Not wanting to wake the others, he dragged himself out the door and into the wet night. His stockinged feet plunged ankle-deep into the mud, but a slight overhang in the roof kept the worst of the rain off of his head.

The coughing, however, simply wouldn't stop.

Stevenson sank back to his knees as the pain exploded through his chest. This was as bad as it had ever felt. His lungs were on fire and something wet and thick got caught in his throat; he couldn't draw sufficient breath to expel it. He opened his mouth as wide as it would go, began clawing at the air with his muddy hands as if he could physically wrench some of it into his lungs.

He was choking to death.

As veins of darkness seeped in at the edges of his vision, Stevenson saw, in his mind's eye, Fanny's sweet face. As he made one, last effort to draw a saving breath, his only regret was that he'd never kiss that face again, feel her lips on his.

Something struck him hard across the back, knocking him face-first into the mud. A hand grabbed at the hair on the back of his neck, yanked him up sharply, then another blow to the back. And another.

With the fourth hammer strike, a fist-sized chunk of phlegm exploded from his throat, passed his lips and disappeared into the black swamp around him. With a gasp like rattling bones, he drew in a wet lungful of air, and nothing had ever tasted so sweet. He exhaled, coughed, took another slap on the back—but didn't need it. Just like that he was breathing normally, though tears continued to stream from his eyes.

"Better?"

Stevenson turned around in the slick mud and saw Poole, mud-spattered as well, staring down at him. Poole put out a hand, helped Stevenson back to his feet.

"I thank ye, sir."

"I heard the ruckus. You was looking a little peaked there, friend."

"I believe, Mr. Poole," Stevenson said, through another small cough, "that ye just saved my life."

Poole shrugged, but smiled. He looked embarrassed. "Just a little pat on the back's all it was. Could have gone either way. How long you suffered the consumption?"

"Always. It's afflicted me in one way or the other since I was a boy."

The rain had slowed, but Stevenson stepped out into it, allowing the cool drops to wash the sweat and blood from his face. He breathed deep, found he wasn't coughing at all.

"That's rough," Poole said. "But you beat the odds still being alive this long. I'm impressed by that. We live with long odds and brief lives. Tried anything for the consumption?"

"Medicines are largely useless. I travel. I find some climes more amenable than others, at least for a time. I hadn't expected this one to be so . . . ungracious."

"This can be rough country."

Stevenson stepped back under the protection of the overhang, stared out into the night with Poole, who'd lit up a cheroot. "So I've been told. Though I thought only in winter."

"Heard about that, huh? Well, I guess everyone knows about the Donners by now."

"I hadn't until Mr. Jackworth in there told me the tale during our sojourn here. Quite gruesome."

"You have no idea, friend."

Stevenson raised an eyebrow. "Ye weren't . . ."

"Seen and done a lot," Poole said, not meeting Stevenson's gaze. "It's rough country and it's a rougher life. You can't really understand if you ain't a part of it. Some see things out here and call them cruelties, but everything is relative. Ever seen how a cat plays with a rat? What a fox'll do to a chicken or a bear to a sheep? Eaten alive is nature's rule and it's just our civilized—so-called—selves who've got nancy-prance ideas about such things. Ideas that we deserve better than being eaten alive. Better than nature."

"And don't we?"

Poole shrugged. "Maybe some. Not most."

"But surely the whole purpose of civilization, its primary virtue, is to escape those very cruelties of nature. To celebrate our unique ability to rise above such cruelty, to transcend nature. Even if it's our own nature."

"Think so? Think anyone rises above their nature? That that's possible to do?" Poole turned his gaze back on Stevenson, who wanted to respond in the affirmative, but who didn't fancy arguing with a man who'd just saved his life, who suddenly looked very intense. Poole answered his own questions anyway: "Just ask the Donners," he said.

As the storm swelled again Stevenson felt a fresh cough coming on, so Poole led him back inside and out of the rain. Mr. Balfour raised his head, scowled, and went back to sleep beside his still-slumbering wife. Jackworth and Grey continued to snore on the floor, Mrs. Reilly hadn't so much as stirred from behind her curtain.

"I got something here that might help you out a bit," Poole whispered, and led Stevenson back to his collection of jars and beakers. He had to stand on a chair to get a bottle of clear liquid down from a high shelf. "Try this."

"What is it?"

"Laudanum. Mostly. Ever try it?"

Stevenson nodded. "The effects are salubrious, but short-lived. The afterward is like drinking a barrel of cheap gin."

"Get you through the night," Poole suggested.

Stevenson considered, then nodded. Poole poured him a measured glassful, which Stevenson raised to his host in a toast. "You don't regard this as too intrusive of civilization on nature?" Stevenson asked. He meant it as a joke.

"Some interventions are necessary. And it'll get you through the night," Poole repeated, mirthlessly.

Stevenson downed the drink, which was extremely potent. Poole had to help him back to his makeshift bed.

Breathing comfortably, Stevenson was asleep within seconds.

And awoke to the familiar smell of blood.

Stevenson was so used to spitting up blood in the night that he didn't think much of it. He had trouble, thanks to the laudanum, thinking straight at all. The storm had passed and the morning sunlight pierced his eyes like knitting needles. Stevenson tried to lift his head, but couldn't do it. He lay there for a while, breathing deeply but without difficulty. Bits of dried mud spotted the furs and floor beneath him, flaked off his hands and arms as he raised them to rub at his bleary eyes.

The smell of blood was very strong.

Stevenson forced himself to a half-sitting position and glanced down at the front of his shirt. He saw more mud there, but no sign of having bled from his mouth in the night. He touched his fingers to his lips, came away with no trace of red there, either. The scent, however, was overpowering.

Stevenson looked behind him, saw the arc of Poole's sleeping back, the slight rise and fall of his round shoulders. Glancing across the room, he could make out Grey's and Jackworth's legs poking out from the far end of the counter. They didn't appear to have moved at all in the night. The Balfours were silent, as well. As he groggily got to his feet he stole a guilty glance at Mrs. Reilly's curtained corner.

The calico lay on the floor, revealing the exposed flesh of the young woman sprawled across the bed of furs. Embarrassed, Stevenson looked away, but even as he did so, he knew that something was very wrong.

That bloody smell had to be coming from somewhere.

Stevenson turned back toward Mrs. Reilly. He took a tentative step, saw that the pile of hides on which she slept were dark and wet. She was entirely naked, and though his gaze fell at first on the swell of her exposed breast, he saw that something dark sat upon her abdomen. As he drew nearer, his head began to swim with the sanguine odor that wafted off of and out of her. There was nothing atop her stomach, he saw as he neared her bed, but rather her abdomen had been cut open; peeled apart and turned inside out. She'd been slit from between the legs up to her navel. Most of what had been contained within was untidily piled without.

"Jackworth," Stevenson whispered.

He spun around, but there was no movement from the pairs of legs on the floor. Stevenson grabbed at an empty whiskey bottle, holding it by the neck like a club. He advanced along the counter, raising the bottle high above his head as he turned the corner.

The legs were unattached to any bodies. The bloody stumps had been neatly arranged on the floor, but the bulk of neither Grey nor Jackworth was anywhere to be seen. Stevenson dropped the bottle, opened and closed his eyes several times, convinced that he must be trapped in some laudanum-inspired nightmare.

The sight—and smell—of the Balfours' bodies, husband's head on wife's shoulders and vice versa, eventually convinced him otherwise. The old woman's carefully splinted leg was untouched.

Stevenson stared at the carnage around him, his head still fuzzy from the drug and the shock.

What had happened? Who could have done this? What kind of animal . . .

Poole.

Stevenson grabbed the bottle again and smashed it against the counter. Holding the jagged edge in front of him, he advanced on his host—his savior of only hours previous who still lay in his bed.

Stevenson could hear the fat man's heavy breathing, saw now that his blanket and straw mattress were drenched in drying blood.

Poole slowly rolled over as Stevenson approached. His eyes were glazed, his features dotted with splotches of red.

Stevenson moved closer, saw that the man's hands were cupped over his chest, something wet and dark clutched within.

Stevenson raised up the broken bottle.

Poole stared dully at him; made no move to attack or get up. He just lay there in his blood-soaked bedclothes.

"Why?" Stevenson asked.

Poole didn't respond, didn't so much as blink.

"Why?" Stevenson demanded, voice breaking. "Why did you do this?"

"Eaten alive," Poole whispered. "Eaten alive."

Stevenson waited for more. He had to blink away the fuzziness that continued to dance at the edge of his consciousness.

". . . alive," Poole croaked.

Stevenson lowered his weapon. He looked into Poole's eyes and saw only a reflection of the morning sunlight.

"Why not me?" Stevenson begged.

Poole swallowed hard, and his eyes flicked down to his chest. Stevenson followed his gaze.

Poole opened his hands to show Stevenson what he held. So tiny but so unmistakable in form.

He shovelled it into his fat mouth.

Stevenson screamed.

He lifted the sharp-edged glass high above his head.

Fanny's skin glowed in the lamplight with the sweat of their exertions. A snail's trail of semen dried on her thigh, matted the softness between her legs. Her head rested on his shoulder and he stroked her long hair. She held his spent organ delicately in her hand; his arm beneath her, his hand cupping the outer curve of her breast.

"He must have been alone out there for a very long time," she said.

"The stagecoaches passed by, stopped in when they had to. The driver, Grey, knew the place, knew the man's name. He wasn't a hermit."

"I'm trying to think how he could have . . ."

"Do ye think I'm not? Don't ye know I can't think of anything else now?"

She didn't reply.

"Other than ye," he added. And kissed her hair.

"He could have taken you, too," she said, and shuddered. "So easily. Why didn't he, Robbie? Why did he spare you?"

"I haven't a clue. Perhaps because he saved my life in the night."

"He saved the old woman, too. It didn't help her."

"Aye. I don't know. That's why I say. There was nothing but madness in his act, so where do ye look for the logic, for the reason in such a thing?"

"And there was no clue? No sense of, I don't know, danger or menace from him?"

"Not a bit. Like I say, the conversation we had in the night, about human nature and the quality of civilization, was a bit peculiar, but it was just words in the night. Or so I thought. And if ye'd seen him treating that old woman the night before—he seemed so clear-headed, so knowledgeable. But it's like there was some other man hiding inside the one I could see, ken? Imprisoned within the first, waiting to come out. But damned if I know what the key was that opened the door and set the monster free. Was it something I said to him? Is that why he spared me? Damned if I know anything at all about people."

"Eaten alive," Fanny whispered.

"What's that?"

"Isn't that what he kept repeating to you? Eaten alive?"

"Aye. That's all I could understand. Not that I do understand."

"Perhaps he was describing himself. Perhaps he was talking about something that happened to him?"

"I don't know, love, I feel like I don't know anything anymore. I just feel lost. Like a stranger even within myself."

"Eaten alive," Fanny repeated.

Stevenson turned his head, but, in spite of the topic of conversation, had grown hard again in her hand. She slipped out of his grasp and climbed astride him, slipping him back inside herself. She rocked slowly back and forth on top of him.

"Robbie?"

"Aye," he groaned.

"You didn't tell me what you did."

"Eh?" he said, understandably distracted.

"You didn't finish the story. You said you had the broken bottle, and that you raised it up. But you didn't tell me what you did. What happened to Poole."

"Oh, Fanny. Oh my, Fanny."

She grasped his head and looked hard into his eyes.

"Tell me what you did, Robbie. You know that you can tell me anything. You can tell your Fanny."

"Eaten alive," Stevenson gasped, and exploded inside her.

"Robbie?"

LUIS ALBERTO URREA

Mr. Mendoza's Paintbrush

Luis Alberto Urrea is one of the best writers working in America today, bar none. Since his first appearance in the anthology Edges, *edited by Ursula K. Le Guin in 1980, he has published a number of truly remarkable books including nonfiction (*Across the Wire, By the Lake of Sleeping Children, Wandering Time, Nobody's Son*), poetry (*The Fever of Being, Ghost Sickness, Vatos*), and one terrific novel (*In Search of Snow*). His most recent publication is* Six Kinds of Sky, *from which the following luminous story is drawn.*

Urrea was born in Tijuana of an American mother and a Mexican father. He now lives in Chicago with his wife and children, where he teaches at the University of Illinois–Chicago. He has won the American Book Award and the Western States Book Award, among other honors.

—T. W.

When I remember my village, I remember the color green. A green that is rich, perhaps too rich, and almost bubbling with humidity and the smell of mangos. I remember heat, the sweet sweat of young girls that collected on my upper lip as we kissed behind the dance stand in the town square. I remember days of nothing and rainstorms, dreaming of making love while walking around the *plazuela*, admiring Mr. Mendoza's portraits of the mayor and the police chief, and saying dashing things to the girls. They, of course, walked in the opposite direction, followed closely by their unsympathetic aunts, which was only decent. Looking back, I wonder if perhaps saying those dashing things was better than making love.

Mr. Mendoza wielded his paintbrush there for thirty years. I can still remember the old women muttering bad things about him on their way to market. This was nothing extraordinary. The old women muttered bad things about most of us at one time or another, especially when they were on their way to market at dawn, double file, dark shawls pulled tight around their faces, to buy pots of warm milk with the cows' hairs still floating in them. Later in the day, after their cups of coffee with a bit of this hairy milk (strained through an old cloth) and many spoonfuls of sugar, only then did they begin to concede the better points of the populace. Except for Mr. Mendoza.

Mr. Mendoza had taken the controversial position that he was the Graffiti King of All Mexico. But we didn't want a graffiti king.

My village is named El Rosario. Perhaps being named after a rosary was what gave us our sense of importance, a sense that we from Rosario were blessed among people, allowed certain dispensations. The name itself came from a Spanish monk—or was it a Spanish soldier—named Bonifacio Rojas who broke his rosary, and the beads cascaded over the ground. Kneeling to pick them up, he said a brief prayer asking the Good Lord to direct him to the beads. Like all good Catholics, he offered the Lord a deal: if you give me my beads back, I will give you a cathedral on the spot. The Good Lord sent down St. Elmo's fire, and directly beneath that, the beads. Bonifacio got a taste of the Lord's wit, however, when he found an endless river of silver directly beneath the beads. It happened in 1655, the third of August. A Saturday.

The church was built, obliterating the ruins of an Indian settlement, and Rosario became the center of the Chametla province. For some reason, the monks who followed Bonifacio took to burying each other in the cathedral's thick adobe walls. Some mysterious element in our soil mummifies monks, and they stood in the walls for five hundred years. Now that the walls are crumbling, though, monks pop out with dry grins about once a year.

When I was young, there was a two-year lull in the gradual revelation of monks. We were certain that the hidden fathers had all been expelled from the walls. A thunderclap proved us wrong.

Our rainy season begins on the sixth of June, without fail. This year, however, the rain was a day late, and the resulting thunderclap that announced the storm was so explosive that windows cracked on our street. Burros on the outskirts burst open their stalls and charged through town throwing kicks right and left. People near the river swore their chickens laid square eggs. The immense frightfulness of this celestial apocalypse was blamed years afterward for gout, diarrhea, birthmarks, drunkenness and those mysterious female aches nobody could define but everyone named "*dolencias.*" There was one other victim of the thunderclap—the remaining church tower split apart and dropped a fat slab of clay into the road. In the morning, my cousin Jaime and I were thrilled to find a mummified hand rising from the rubble, one saffron finger aimed at the sky.

"An evangelist," I said.

"Even in death," he said.

We moved around the pile to see the rest of him. We were startled to find a message painted on the monk's chest:

HOW DO YOU LIKE ME NOW?
DEFLATED! DEFLATE
YOUR POMP OR FLOAT AWAY!

"Mr. Mendoza," I said.

"He's everywhere," Jaime said.

On the road that runs north from Escuinapa to my village, there is a sign that says:

ROSARIO POP. 8000

Below that, in Mr. Mendoza's meticulous scrawl:

NO INTELLIGENT LIFE FOR 100 KILOMETERS.

There is a very tall bridge at the edge of town that spans the Baluarte river. Once, my cousin Jaime said, a young man sat on the railing trading friendly insults with his friends. His sweetheart was a gentle girl from a nice family. She was wearing a white blouse that day. She ran up to him to give him a hug, but instead she knocked him from his perch, and he fell, arms and legs thrown open to the wind. They had to hold her back, or she would have joined him. He called her name all the way down, like a lost love letter spinning in the wind. No one ever found the body. They say she left town and married. She had seven sons, and each one was named after her dead lover. Her husband left her. Near this fatal spot on the bridge, Mr. Mendoza suggested that we:

UPEND HYPOCRITES TODAY.

Across town from the bridge, there is a gray whorehouse next to the cemetery. This allows the good citizens of the village to avoid the subjects of death and sex at the same time. On the wall facing the street, the message:

TURN YOUR PRIDE ON ITS BACK
AND COUNT ITS WIGGLY FEET.

On the stone wall that grows out of the cobble street in front of the cemetery, a new announcement appeared:

MENDOZA NEVER SLEPT HERE.

What the hell did he mean by that? There was much debate in our bars over that one. Did Mr. Mendoza mean this literally, that he had never napped between the crumbling stones? Well, so what? Who would?

No, others argued. He meant it philosophically—that Mr. Mendoza was claiming he'd never die. This was most infuriating. Police Chief Reyes wanted to know, "Who does Mr. Mendoza think he is?"

Mr. Mendoza, skulking outside the door, called in, "I'll tell you! I think I'm Mendoza, that's who! But who—or what—are you!"

His feet could be heard trotting away in the dark.

Mr. Mendoza never wrote obscenities. He was far too moral for that. In fact, he had been known to graffito malefactors as though they were road signs. Once, Mr. Mendoza's epochal paintbrush fell on me.

It was in summer, in the month of August, Bonifacio's month. August is hot in Rosario, so hot that snapping turtles have been cooked by sitting in shallow water. Their green flesh turns gray and peels away to float down the eternal Baluarte. I always intended to follow the Baluarte downstream, for it carried hundreds of interesting items during flood-times, and I was certain that somewhere farther down there was a resting place for it all. The river seemed, at times, to be on a mad shopping spree, taking from the land anything it fancied. Mundane things such as trees, chickens, cows, shot past regularly. But marvelous things floated there, too: a green De Soto with its lights on, a washing machine with a religious statue in it as though the saint were piloting a circular boat, a blond wig that looked like a giant squid, a mysterious star-shaped object barely visible under the surface.

The Baluarte held me in its sway. I swam in it, fished and caught turtles in it. I dreamed of the distant bend in the river where I could find all these floating things collected in neat stacks, and perhaps a galleon full of rubies, and perhaps a damp yet lovely fifteen-year-old girl in a red dress to rescue, and all of it speckled with little gray specks of turtle skin.

Sadly for me, I found out that the river only led to swamps that oozed out to the sea. All those treasures were lost forever, and I had to seek a new kind of magic from my river. Which is precisely where Mr. Mendoza found me, on the banks of the post-magical Baluarte, lying in the mud with Jaime, gazing through a stand of reeds at some new magic.

Girls. We had discovered girls. And a group of these recently discovered creatures was going from the preparatory school's sweltering rooms to the river for a bath. They had their spot, a shielded kink in the river bank that had a natural screen of trees and reeds and a sloping sandy bank. Jaime and I knew that we were about to make one of the greatest discoveries in recent history, and we'd be able to report to the men what we'd found out.

"Wait until they hear about this," I whispered.

"It's a new world," he replied.

We inserted ourselves in the reeds, ignoring the mud soaking our knees. We could barely contain our longing and emotion. When the girls began to strip off their uniforms, revealing slips, then bright white bras and big cotton underpants, I thought I would sob.

"I can't," I said, "believe it."

"History in the making," he said.

The bras came off. They dove in.

"Before us is everything we've always wanted," I said.

"Life itself," he said.

"Oh, you beautiful girls!" I whispered.

"Oh, you girls of my dreams!" said he, and Mr. Mendoza's claws sank into our shoulders.

We were dragged a hundred meters upriver, all the while being berated without mercy: "Tartars!" he shouted. "Peeping Toms! Flesh chasers! Disrespectors of privacy!"

I would have laughed if I had not seen Mr. Mendoza's awful paintbrush standing in a freshly opened can of black paint.

"Oh oh," I said.

"We're finished," said Jaime.

Mr. Mendoza threw me down and sat on me. The man was skinny. He was bony, yet I could not buck him off. I bounced like one of those thunderstruck burros, and he rode me with aplomb.

He attacked Jaime's face, painting:

I AM FILTHY.

He then peeled off Jaime's shirt and adorned his chest with:

I LIVE FOR SEX AND THRILLS.

He then yanked off Jaime's pants and decorated his rump with:

KICK ME HARD.

I was next.
On my face:

PERVERT.

On my chest:

MOTHER IS BLUE WITH SHAME.

On my rump:

THIS IS WHAT I AM.

I suddenly realized that the girls from the river had quickly dressed themselves and were giggling at me as I jumped around naked. It was unfair! Then, to make matters worse, Mr. Mendoza proceeded to chase us through town while people laughed at us and called out embarrassing weights and measures.

We plotted our revenge for two weeks, then forgot about it. In fact, Jaime's "I LIVE FOR SEX" made him somewhat of a celebrity, that phrase being very macho. He was often known after that day as "El Sexi." In fact, years later, he would marry one of the very girls we had been spying on.

There was only one satisfaction for me in the whole sad affair: the utter disappearance of the street of my naked humiliation.

Years after Bonifacio built his church in Rosario, and after he had died and was safely tucked away in the church walls (until 1958, when he fell out on my uncle Jorge), the mines got established as a going concern. Each vein of silver seemed to lead to another. The whole area was a network of ore-bearing arteries.

Tunnels were dug and forgotten as each vein played out and forked off. Often, miners would break through a wall of rock only to find themselves in an abandoned mineshaft going in the other direction. Sometimes they'd find skeletons. Once they swore they'd encountered a giant spider that caught bats in its vast web. Many of these mine shafts filled with seepage from the river, forming underground lagoons that had fat white frogs in them and an albino alligator that floated in the dark water waiting for hapless miners to stumble and fall in.

Some of these tunnels snaked under the village. At times, with a whump, sections of Rosario vanished. Happily, I watched the street Mr. Mendoza had chased me down drop from sight after a quick shudder. A store and six houses dropped as one. I was particularly glad to see Antonia Borrego vanish with a startled look while sitting on her porch yelling insults at me. Her voice rose to a horrified screech that echoed loudly underground as she went down. When she was finally pulled out (by block and tackle, the sow), she was all wrinkled from the smelly water, and her hair was alive with squirming white pollywogs.

After the street vanished, my view of El Yauco was clear and unobstructed. El Yauco is the mountain that stands across the Baluarte from Rosario. The top of it looks like the profile of John F. Kennedy in repose. The only flaw in this geographic wonder is that the nose is upside-down.

Once, when Jaime and I had painfully struggled to the summit to investigate the nose, we found this message:

MOTHER NATURE HAS NO RESPECT FOR YANQUI PRESIDENTS EITHER!

Nothing, though, could prepare us for the furor over his next series of messages. It began with a piglet running through town one Sunday. On its flanks, in perfect cursive script:

Mendoza goes to heaven on Tuesday.

On a fence:

MENDOZA ESCAPES THIS HELLHOLE.

On my father's car:

I'VE HAD ENOUGH!
I'M LEAVING!

Rumors flew. For some reason, the arguments were fierce, impassioned, and there were any number of fistfights over Mr. Mendoza's latest. Was he going to kill himself? Was he dying? Was he to be abducted by flying saucers or carried aloft by angels? The people who were convinced the old "MENDOZA NEVER SLEPT HERE" was a strictly philosophical text were convinced he was indeed going to commit suicide. There was a secret that showed in their faces—they were actually hoping he'd kill himself, just to maintain the status quo, just to ensure that everyone died.

Rumors about his health washed through town: cancer, madness (well, we all knew that), demonic possession, the evil eye, a black magic curse that included love potions and slow-acting poisons, and the dreaded syphilis. Some of the local smart alecks called the whorehouse "Heaven," but Mr. Mendoza was far too moral to even go in there, much less advertise it all over town.

I worked in Crispin's bar, taking orders and carrying trays of beer bottles. I heard every theory. The syphilis one really appealed to me because young fellows always love the gruesome and lurid, and it sounded so nasty, having to do, as it did, with the nether regions.

"Syphilis makes it fall off," Jaime explained.

I didn't want him to know I wasn't sure which "it" fell off, if it was it, or some other "it." To be macho, you must already know everything, know it so well that you're already bored by the knowledge.

"Yes, I said, wearily, "it certainly does."

"Right off," he marveled.

"To the street," I concluded.

Well, that very night, that night of the Heavenly Theories, Mr. Mendoza came into the bar. The men stopped all their arguing and immediately taunted him: "Oh look! Saint Mendoza is here!" "Hey, Mendoza! Seen any angels lately?" He only smirked. Then, squaring his slender shoulders, he walked, erect, to the bar.

"Boy,", he said to me. "A beer."

As I handed him the bottle, I wanted to confess: *I will change my ways! I will never peep at girls again!*

He turned and faced the crowd and gulped down his beer, emptying the entire bottle without coming up for air. When the last of the foam ran from its mouth, he slammed the bottle on the counter and said, "Ah!" Then he belched. Loudly. This greatly offended the gathered men, and they admonished him. But he ignored them, crying out, "What do you think of that! Eh? The belch is the cry of the water-buffalo, the hog. I give it to you because it is the only philosophy you can understand!"

More offended still, the crowd began to mumble.

Mr. Mendoza turned to me and said, "I see there are many wiggly feet present."

"The man's insane," said Crispin.

Mr. Mendoza continued: "Social change and the nipping at complacent buttocks was my calling on earth. Who among you can deny that I and my brush are a perfect marriage? Who among you can hope to do more with a brush than I?"

He pulled the brush from under his coat. Several men shied away.

"I tell you now," he said. "Here is the key to Heaven."

He nodded to me once, and strode toward the door. Just before he passed into the night, he said, "My work is finished."

Tuesday morning we were up at dawn. Jaime had discovered a chink in fat Antonia's new roof. Through it, we could look down into her bedroom. We watched her dress. She moved in billows, like a meaty raincloud. "In a way," I whispered, "it has its charm."

"A bountiful harvest," Jaime said condescendingly.

After this ritual, we climbed down to the street. We heard the voices, saw people heading for the town square. Suddenly, we remembered. "Today!" we cried in unison.

The ever-growing throng was following Mr. Mendoza. His startling shock of white hair was bright against his dark skin. He wore a dusty black suit, his funeral suit. He walked into a corner of the square, knelt down and pried the lid off a fresh can of paint. He produced the paintbrush with a flourish and held it up for all to see. There was an appreciative mumble from the crowd, a smattering of applause. He turned to the can, dipped the brush in the paint. There was a hush. Mr. Mendoza painted a black swirl on the flagstones. He went around and around with the legendary brush, filling in the swirl until it was a solid black O. Then, with a grin, with a virtuoso's mastery, he jerked his brush straight up, leaving a solid, glistening pole of wet paint standing in the air. We gasped. We clapped. Mr. Mendoza painted a horizontal line, connected to the first at a ninety degree angle. We cheered. We whistled. He painted up, across, up, across, until he was reaching over his head. It was obvious soon enough. We applauded again, this time with feeling. Mr. Mendoza turned to look at us and waved once—whether in farewell or terse dismissal we'll never know—then raised one foot and placed it on the first horizontal. No, we said. He stepped up. Fat Antonia fainted. The boys all tried to look up her dress when she fell, but Jaime and I were very macho because we'd seen it already. Still, Mr. Mendoza rose. He painted his way up, the angle of the stairway carrying him out of the *plazuela* and across town, over Bonifacio's crumbling church, over the cemetery where he had never slept and would apparently never sleep. Crispin did good business selling beers to the crowd. Mr. Mendoza, now small as a high-flying crow, climbed higher, over the Batuarte and its deadly bridge, over El Yauco and Kennedy's inverted nose, almost out of sight. The stairway wavered like smoke in the breeze. People were getting bored, and they began to wander off, back to work, back to the rumors. That evening, Jaime and I went back to fat Antonia's roof.

It happened on June fifth of that year. That night, at midnight, the rains came. By morning, the paint had washed away.

MARGARET LLOYD

Five Poems

A native of Wales, Margaret Lloyd chairs the Humanities Department at Springfield College in Massachusetts, where she teaches poetry, women in literature, and Celtic literature. Her work has appeared in Poetry East, The New England Review, The Minnesota Review, The Gettysburg Review, The Literary Review, *and* Passages North. *She is the author of one book of poems,* This Particular Earthly Scene, *winner of the Alice James Books Award. Lloyd is presently working on a book-length narrative sequence inspired by Arthurian myth. The following five poems are a part of that sequence. They come from the May 2002 edition of* Poem, *published in Huntsville, Alabama.*

—T. W.

First Night with Lancelot

That first night, everything
that could be seen
was seen by the light of the moon.

But when he came to my chamber
it was like the sudden dark
when the moon travels up in a cloud.

You wonder how I suffered his loving me
only when he thought I was the queen?

Like all artists in the world,
I used my imagination,
which is not at all the same thing
as fancy or deceit.

We change one thing into another
under the dark wingspan of the night.

Second Night

The first night it was God who moved my hand
to lead him into me. Prophesy

did not require a second night. It was
what I required.

And I knew I risked his wrath or madness
to hold him close again,
for in the light of day he could not bear
to look upon my face. Awakened,
he went mad, running naked in the woods,
pelted with stones by children and beggars,
thrown into a cart with a dead pig.

But I tell you, with his body still in mine,
he slept the small hours of that second night
like a boy, sighing in his sleep.

Then I foolishly thought to myself,
surely now he will love the mother of his child.

From the Walls

When I finally found him,
he was my own court's fool,
sleeping in the garden near the well.

How close we are to love and madness every day.
How close we are to what we most desire.
Now I am the fool and bored.

Bored by women fighting over men.
Bored by prophesy which uses me.
Bored by seduction and my own beauty.

From the walls, I watched him leave,
while in the west the cattle lumbered home,
trailing in their ancient line. I might as well be

one of those plodding cows. At least then
I'd sleep through the long winter nights
in the bedstraw without shame.

Guinevere: On Hearing of Galahad's Birth

I climbed the mountain today
above the wild whinberries and kept
walking until my body was so tired
I could no longer remember
the sound of his voice.
Is this what he meant when he said
his tryst with Elaine was beyond his control?
When he said he thought he was in my arms?
Tales claim I am appeased by these excuses.

I am not. He is responsible for everything.
I have no interest in a story
which insists on preserving him
flawless, but for his love of me.

Elaine Watches Galahad

Night after night I stood over the crib
with my hand on your body, breathing
slowly to calm you, to help you sleep.

Now I watch you on the pebbled beach,
no bigger in this distance than a small bone
from a sparrow's leg used to etch the pottery.

Today I breathe slowly to keep your hawk
flying to the lure, while the fingers
of the sea's foam point always toward you.

Churning from your father's loss like a tangled knot
of seaweed on the sands, what can I give you
but this simple watching and my steady breath?

STEPHEN GALLAGHER

Little Dead Girl Singing

Stephen Gallagher was born in Salford, Lancashire, England, in 1954. After working for a TV company for four years, his frustrations with the limitations of the job spurred him to write, learning the basic craft in radio and then moving into novels and screenplays.

With the sale of his first book, Chimera, *he quit his job and headed to the United States with the intention of staying there until the money ran out. He toured extensively and settled for the longest period in Phoenix, Arizona, the setting for his later police procedural/supernatural horror novel,* Valley of Lights. *He moved back to England in 1981 but later returned to the U.S. to write* Red, Red Robin, *set in Philadelphia.*

Gallagher has written over a dozen novels, sold lots of film options, and written numerous screenplays and teleplays, including an adaptation of Chimera. *In 1998 he wrote and directed a miniseries based on his novel* Oktober. *His most recent book is* White Bizango, *a short novel.*

His short stories have been published in The Magazine of Fantasy & Science Fiction, Asimov's SF Magazine, Weird Tales, *and in various anthologies including* Shadows *and* The Dark.

"Little Dead Girl Singing" was first published in Weird Tales.

—E. D.

Here's one you won't have heard before.

If you're a parent with a musical child, then you'll know the festival circuit. I don't mean anything that is big business or in any way high-profile. I'm talking about those little local festivals run on dedication and postage stamps, where the venue's a school theatre or a draughty church hall and the top prize is nothing more than pennies in an envelope. I'm talking about cold Saturday mornings, small audiences made up of singing teachers and edgy parents, judges whose quality varies depending on how their judgments accord with your own, and shaky little juvenile voices cracking with nerves.

As you might have guessed, I have been there.

Never as an entrant, of course. Even the dog leaves the house when I sing. But every young singer needs an adult support team rather like a racing driver needs a pit crew, to provide transport and encouragement and to steer them through the day's schedule. That's where the parents come in. Some children turn out with their entire extended families in tow, decamping with them from class to class like a mobile claque.

But not us. By the time Victoria was twelve we'd reached the point where she wanted as little fuss or pressure as possible. The thought of one of those three-generation cheer squads would have filled her with horror.

"One of you can come," she'd say. "And you're not to sit right at the front. I don't want to be able to see you."

This was last year. She liked to sing and she sang well, but she didn't like to make a big deal of it. So on the Saturday of the festival just she and I made the hour's drive to this tiny little town you've never heard of, way out in the middle of the flat country between home and the coast, with her entry slips and her piano copies and a bottle of mineral water.

They'd been running an annual festival here since nineteen forty-eight, and we'd done it twice before. This year Vicky's singing teacher had entered her for four different competition classes, spread throughout the day. The room where the earliest would take place was the one we liked least, the village hall with its high ceiling and tiny stage and no acoustic to speak of. Well, you could speak of it, but you'd have to shout to be heard at the back. And it was always so cold in there that at this time of year you could see your breath.

We sat outside in the car for a few minutes.

"All right?" I said. "Anything else you need?"

She shook her head. She didn't seem keen. I knew she'd had a bad throat for a few days and wasn't feeling entirely at her best, but in we went.

They'd already started and so we waited for an interval between competitors to find a seat. When the opportunity came, we dodged around empty chairs and a photographer's tripod and made our way down the hall.

The judge had her table out in the middle, while the spot for the singers was by an upright piano before the stage. The stage had a homemade backcloth for *The Wizard of Oz*. The judge was a woman in her late fifties, straight-backed, powdered, a little severe. None of which meant anything. I'd found you could never really get the measure of them until you heard what they had to say.

Vicky's name came halfway down the program, so we settled in. The class was *Songs from the Shows* and the age group was the youngest. There was low winter sun coming in through the windows at the back of the hall and it was making the singers squint.

Early morning voices, little kids singing. Some in tune, most not, every one of them the apple of someone's eye.

Andrew Lloyd Webber was getting a real hammering. In the space of half an hour we had three "Whistle Down the Wind"s relieved only by a couple of "I'm Just a Girl Who Can't Say No"s. I recognized a few of the entrants from previous years. Only two young boys got up to sing and, bless 'em, you could tell that this was not their chosen element.

Vicky got up and did her piece. As she sat down beside me again she said, "That was rubbish."

It wasn't, but I knew that it wasn't a patch on what she could do at her best. But I also had that sneaking feeling that I'm sure I shared with every parent in the room, that out of this bunch I had the only real singer and the rest of them might just as well give up and go home.

We had a song from *Annie* and a song from *Les Miserables* and then another "Whistle Down the Wind," and then the judge did some scribbling and called the next name.

She mispronounced it the first time and I looked at my program to check . . . Cantle? But the name was Chantal, exotic enough amongst the Emmas and the Jennies. There was movement over on the other side of the room and I craned to see what a Lancashire Chantal might look like.

Up stood this little girl in a cardigan, with a bow in her top-knot and a dress that looked like funeral parlor curtains. She was tiny, and I reckoned she couldn't have been more than eight or nine years old..

She stood by the piano and waited for the judge's nod and then the accompanist started up, and then little Chantal sang a perfect piping rendition of "Don't Cry for Me, Argentina."

Let me qualify that. It was perfect, but it was also horrible in a way that I still can't quite put my finger on. Her diction was clear and her intonation was bright. She hit all the notes dead-on, and she even acted the whole thing out.

But to see this eight-year-old doing such a precise imitation of mature emotion was like watching a wind-up doll simulating sex. She'd been drilled to a frightening degree. On one line her hand moved to her heart, on the next she gestured to the crowd. When the lines were repeated later in the song, she did exactly the same movements again in exactly the same way. There was a slightly American intonation there, as if she'd learned the words by listening to the movie soundtrack so many times that it rang in her head like tintinnitus.

I looked for her mother. Sure enough, there she was. She had a little boy of about five or six beside her. The little boy was ordinary, fidgeting, eyes wandering, all his little-boy energies struggling against the imposed stillness like cats in a heavy sack.

The mother, though . . . she was as much of a study, in her way, as the little girl.

She wasn't old, or even middle-aged. But her youth was only there in traces, as if it had been harried out of her too soon. Her hair was a dirty-blonde froth of curls, cut short and pushed up high on her head above her ears. She was staring at her daughter as she sang, her lips twitching along. She wasn't mouthing the words as some of the mothers do, vicariously living the performance or, even worse, trying to conduct it from the sidelines. To me it seemed that she was just rapt, quite literally lost in the song, as the tenderest of souls might be overwhelmed by the greatest of artists.

I reckon you could have wheeled out Madonna herself and the London Symphony Orchestra, but you couldn't have given her a performance that could affect her half so much. And my cynical heart softened then, because whatever form it comes in, however it's expressed, it's hard to be critical of such uncompromising love.

The song ended. There was the standard scattering of applause, and the little girl's smile switched on like a bulb. Two seconds later it switched off again and she walked back to her seat as the next singer went up to take her place. Her mother bent over to whisper something but I was distracted then by a metallic bang from the back of the room, and I looked around to see a nondescript man noisily folding up his camera tripod.

The father, I assumed. My heart promptly hardened up again. I don't like it when people make it so obvious that they've no interest in the efforts of any other child than their own. It may be a universal truth, but I think we've all got a responsibility at least to pretend otherwise. Yet still you see them at school shows and concerts, not looking at the stage, flicking through the program book, sometimes not even bothering to join in the applause. They're here to see the Third Wise Man triumph, and to them all the rest is just noise.

We've got a camera of our own, but I'd stopped taking it along. I'd started to find that if you make a big thing out of recording the moment, what you lose is the moment itself.

They stuck it out for one more song, which was about as long as it took for him to pack the video gear away, and then in the gap between entrants the four of them got up and left. The girl went out in front and her brother got dragged along behind, bobbing around in his family's wake like a rag doll caught up on a motorboat.

We slipped out ourselves about ten minutes after that. Done quietly, it was no breach of etiquette. The class was running late and we had another one to get to, so for this one we'd check the results and pick up the judgment slip later in the day.

That was how it worked; young singers and their minders in constant motion from one hired room to another, getting nervous, doing their best, hoping for praise, fearing the worst.

We planned to get some lunch after the English Folk Song. They always set up a tearoom in the church but, being no lover of grated cheese and pickle sandwiches, I had other ideas. On our way to the car, we stopped to pick up the slip from that earlier class and to check on the list of prizewinners.

Strange little Chantal had taken the first prize. Second and third places went to performances that I couldn't remember.

Well, what can you do? You note it and move on.

We got into the car and drove out toward the coast, which was only another three or four miles. I thought a change of scene would be a good idea. I could sense that Vicky was unhappy; not peevishly so, just unhappy with her own performance, unhappy with the way she felt, unhappy with the day ahead and the sense of a course to be run that had no great promise of satisfaction in it.

After being quiet for a few minutes she said, "I don't think I want to go back."

"No?"

"I just want to go home. There's no point."

I said, "If that's what you want, then fine. I'm not going to force you to stay. But be sure in your own mind that you're not throwing it in for the wrong reasons. All right?"

"Mmm." She was looking out of the window.

We found a cafeteria over an Edwardian parade and, wouldn't you know it, they'd run out of ham for the sandwiches but had no shortage of grated cheese and pickle to offer.

Over lunch, we talked about the morning. Specifically, about Chantal's win.

"I can't say she didn't deserve it," I said. "Technically she's very impressive and in two or three years' time there's a chance she'll be really good. Right now I'd say she's been drilled too much. She's very mechanical and over-controlled. But I'd also have to say she's got an obvious natural gift. From here it'll depend upon how naturally it's allowed to develop, as opposed to being forced."

Vicky sat there sucking her Coke through a straw, not over-happy but not disagreeing, either. She needed a straw to keep the ice from bobbing against the metal of her brace.

I said, "And of course, we know for a fact that the room's got a curse on it and the judges are always peculiar."

I said it as a joke, but felt there was a grain of truth in it. This was the third time we'd had the same experience. It was a catch-all class that started the day, with the age range heavily weighted towards the very young. The prizes had always gone to shrill little girls who maybe didn't get the notes but did a lot of eye-rolling and arm-waving. The judges marked high on smiling and gestures, and some of the teachers played to that. A real singer probably flew right above the radar.

Well, it got her laughing when I said it was no insult to miss out on a prize in a freak show. And as we were walking to the car she said, "I think I *will* go back."

So instead of going home, we went back.

I was glad, because later in the day was when the big girls came in and the musicianship got more serious. Vicky was caught somewhere in between the moppets and the teenagers but when she sang amongst the best, she sounded as if she belonged there. Even if she didn't get a prize, it would be good for her to see it through. Prizes are nice. But what really matters is who your peers are. The quality of the people amongst whom you clearly belong.

We were laughing about something else in the car when it came to me. The little girl had stuck in my mind and had been troubling me for some reason, and I suddenly realized why.

I found myself recalling an image from a TV documentary that I'd once seen. It was about the second world war, the London Blitz. I don't know how old I'd been when I saw it, but it was an early and shocking memory. Outside a bombed-out house, this family had been laid on the pavement. One was a baby, clearly dead, but not in repose. Its mouth was open, as if caught in mid-chortle.

The image was in my mind now because it shared something with the face of the girl I'd seen that morning. I'd hate to say what. But if I close my eyes I can still see her now, eyes hooded with dark rings under them, her downturned mouth hanging slightly open, her tiny teeth like points.

I saw her again, about half an hour later.

We'd moved over into the church, which was a big improvement. Inside the church there were several large informal rooms as well as the wood-panelled nave, and they were decently heated. In the nave was the best acoustic of them all, and the best piano to go with it.

I slipped out while we were waiting for Vicky's turn in the British Composer set piece. She was complaining that her throat was dry and the water bottle was empty. She stayed behind in the hall.

The tea room was in the middle of the building and had no windows. Metal-legged tables and plastic chairs had been set up amongst the pillars, and service was through a hatchway from a kitchen staffed by volunteers. There were some uncleared plates and crumbs on the tables but otherwise the seating area was empty apart from me and Chantal.

I recognized her easily, even from the back. That top-knot, that cardigan. Just like a dressed-up doll. She was drawing something aimless in spilled sugar on one of the tables, and she was making a singsong whispering sound as she did.

"Hello, there," I said.

She jumped. Not literally, but you could see her start. She turned around.

I said, "I heard you this morning. Congratulations. You sang really well."

I was sorry I'd started this. She seemed panicked. I'd spoken to her and she didn't know what to do or how to respond. Her eyes were looking at me but her eyes were empty.

I didn't know what I could say now.

"Chantal," I heard from behind me.

It was her mother. I glanced back and saw her. She didn't meet my eyes but her gaze kind of slid around me to her daughter, as if she knew I was there and she ought to acknowledge me . . . and she *was* acknowledging me in her own way, but her own way was not direct.

She muttered something about being late and the two of them went off together, with me stepping aside to let them by. I don't know if she'd been speaking to me or to her daughter. I felt like an idiot, to be honest, and I wished I'd kept my mouth shut.

More than feeling stupid, I felt a little bit spooked. That was one creepy family. Chantal's eyes had been empty until her mother spoke. But I can't say for sure what I'd seen in them then.

The rest of the afternoon passed by. Other classes came and went and the voices got better and better. We heard some thrilling sopranos and one beanpole of a teenaged boy who ran in late and sang Handel like a spotty angel.

Our final session was in the nave of the church. Vicky was more or less resigned to the fact that this wasn't her best day, and she was taking something of a gonzo attitude to it all now . . . by which I mean that she wasn't worrying about placing or prizes, but was just getting in there and doing it. Which I've always liked better. Do a thing for its own sake, and let anything else that comes along be a surprising bonus. That's how to be an original. That way you can't lose.

So there we were. The first thing that I noticed on entering the church, up on the empty balcony above our heads, was the nondescript man with his tripod and camera. Once we were in our seats, I looked around for the other three.

And there *they* were. The boy was in the middle. Slumped, glowering. He was the one I felt sorry for. He looked like the normal one in the family and I could imagine his patience being tested to near-destruction by a day like this. It must have been Boy Hell, having to get scrubbed-up and endure hours of boredom and sitting still in the company of grown-ups, and all for your sister in the spotlight.

Vicky was up third. She sang her piece, and sang it well. The throat problem hadn't gone and she was up against her limit by the ends of some of the lines, but in contrast to the morning she was warmed-up and relaxed, and it was a great room to sing in. The atmosphere was completely different. The piping-little-kid factor was almost completely absent, but then I had to remind myself that all these mature and impressive young singers had probably been piping little kids once.

While Vicky was singing, there was a sharp noise from one of the rows. It didn't throw her—in fact she told me afterwards that she hadn't even noticed it—but it made me look back.

Chantal's brother had dropped something, I guessed. Probably a hymn book from the rail in front of him. His mother was giving him a kind of gritted-teeth, staring-eyes silent scolding. I looked past him to Chantal. She was completely slack, as if she'd been switched off.

That was when I started thinking of her as a little dead girl, in her funeral home curtain dress. In fact I fantasized about the whole family of them living above the funeral parlor, and climbing into the boxes to sleep at night.

But not for long. My kid was still singing.

Even the applause sounded better in here. She sat down flushed, and I could see that she was pleased with herself.

Chantal was the youngest entrant in this class. She went up about twenty minutes later.

If anything, her performance was more extreme than the one I'd seen that morning. Her diction was so sharp that it was unpleasant to the ear. Every *r* was rolled, every *t* was a gun-shot. Whatever had served her well before, she was doing more of it now. The light-bulb smile was a bizarre face-pull.

I nudged Vicky and she followed my glance over at the mother. The mother was doing it again, her mouth unconsciously making the shapes of the words, living the song with her daughter. I couldn't see the balcony from my seat but I knew for sure that Cecil B. would be up there, capturing it all on tape for endless home replay.

It was only the youngest member of the family who seemed to have used up all his reserves of team spirit. He wasn't paying his sister any attention at all. To be fair to him, he'd probably sat through this a hundred times at home. He squirmed in his seat and stuck an arm up in the air, stretching. His mother quickly pulled it down so he stuck it up again, instantly computing that he'd found a way to annoy her. She pulled it down almost violently now and he tried it a third time, but by then the damage was done. The movement must have caught the little girl's eye and distracted her for a second. She'd stumbled on her words. I'd only been half-listening but when she went wrong, I knew it at once.

So did her mother. God, now *there* was a look. Medusa would have asked for lessons.

When it came time for the judge to give his results, Chantal got a kind mention along with everybody else but Vicky got a very respectable second prize. It was all the more welcome for being unexpected, and she was only one point behind the sixteen-year-old who took the first. I'd have been happy at the fact that she'd held her own so well amongst such a high class of singers. But what the hell, it was nice to get an envelope as well.

"I bet you're not sorry you stayed," I said to her as everybody was gathering up their papers and their coats, and she made a face that could have meant anything.

Outside the church, the sky was mostly dark and streaked with red but there was just enough light to see by. Some of the sessions would go on into the evening, but quite a few of us were dispersing to our cars.

This was never my favorite kind of countryside. Far too flat and featureless. I imagine it had all been under the sea at one time, and the best thing you could say about it was that the views were uninterrupted. Looking out now, across the road and the fields beyond, I realized that I could see all the way to the far horizon. On the horizon sat the disappearing rim of the sun, on a strip of ocean that was like a ribbon of fire.

In a minute or less, the sun would have dropped and the effect would be gone. I wasn't the only one to have my attention caught by it.

I could see Chantal about halfway across the parking area. She was out where there were few cars and she was alone. She was little more than a shadow-silhouette in the fading light but, as before, she was immediately recognizable.

I saw this little ghost take a faltering step, and then another. And then I saw her break into a run.

I don't know why. But it was as if she'd seen a doorway open up between the sun and the sea, and she'd set her mind to reach it before it closed.

Whatever was in her mind, she was running straight for the road.

I wasn't near enough to reach her. I looked around for her parents and saw them, loading their stuff into a brown Allegro. I'll swear to what happened then, because I saw it. I don't think anyone else did.

Her mother looked back over her shoulder. That's all she did. She didn't call out and she didn't even change her expression. Just looked at the running child, and the running child stopped about a dozen yards short of the road.

A couple of cars zipped by. Then the child turned and started back.

She climbed into the brown car without a word and they all drove off together.

As I said, that was last year.

This year, we went again.

Vicky had picked up a first prize in one of the classes in the city festival a few months later, and it had raised her enthusiasm enough for her to want another crack at this one. When the time came around, we sent in the forms. We skipped that perverse morning session, finally giving in to the lesson of experience, and went straight for the afternoon.

I remembered little Chantal, and when we got there I looked for her name in the program. I felt a slight disappointment when I didn't see it. I was curious to see how she might have developed—at that age, a year can make a lot of difference in one way or another—but it seemed that I wasn't to find out.

Well, it was only curiosity.

But here's the odd thing. Chantal wasn't there, but her family was.

I knew it as soon as I saw Cecil B. up in the gallery with his camera. Of course I immediately looked around the pews, and saw the mother with the boy. But no little dead girl.

The boy was in short pants and a clean shirt with a little bow tie. He was behaving himself. Or was he? By the look of him, you'd think he'd been drugged.

He certainly wasn't the squirming live wire I remembered from the year before. In fact he had the same kind of slack, dead-eyed expression that I'd seen on his sister.

So if they were here, where was she? Could she have changed so much that I'd passed her outside and hadn't recognized her? I looked towards the doorway, expecting her to walk in and join them, but the stewards were closing up the room ready to begin.

The competition started, and the boy just sat there.

Until a name was called, and with a nudge from his mother he got to his feet.

Surprised, I watched him move to the piano. He took short steps. If body language could show a stammer, I reckon that walk is what you'd see. When he reached the piano, he turned to face the audience. And when the accompanist hit the first note, he switched on his smile.

The woman leaned forward in the crowd, her gaze intent, her lips already beginning to shape the first of the words. Upstairs, the man rolled the tape.

I looked at Vicky, and Vicky looked at me.

And down by the piano, when the moment came, the boy placed his hand over his heart, opened his mouth, and sang like a clockwork nightingale.

ROBIN MCKINLEY

A Pool in the Desert

Robin McKinley was born in Ohio and grew up all over the world because her father was in the army. She now lives in the south of England with her husband, writer Peter Dickinson. She is the author of several fantasy novels published for young adults but loved by readers of all ages, including Beauty, Rose Daughter, The Blue Sword *(a Newbery Honor Book), and* The Hero and the Crown *(winner of the Newbery Medal). Her most recent novel is* Spindle's End, *based on the Sleeping Beauty fairy tale. McKinley's short fiction has been published in* The Door in the Hedge, A Knot in the Grain, *and* Water: Tales of Elemental Spirits. *The latter volume is the first book in a projected series based on the four elements, written in collaboration with her husband.*

"A Pool in the Desert" first appeared in Water. *The story is loosely connected to McKinley's "Damar" novels (*The Blue Sword *and* The Hero and the Crown*), though readers needn't be familiar with Damar to enjoy this fine work of traditional fantasy.*

—T. W.

There were no deserts in the Homeland. Perhaps that was why she dreamed of deserts.

She had had her first desert dreams when she was quite young, and still had time to read storybooks and imagine herself in them; but deserts were only one of the things she dreamed about in those days. She dreamed about knights in armour and glorious quests, and sometimes in these dreams she was a knight and sometimes she was a lovely lady who watched a particular knight and hoped that, when he won the tournament, it would be she to whom he came, and stooped on bended knee, and . . . and sometimes she dreamed that she was a lady who tied her hair up and pulled a helmet down over it and over her face, and won the tournament herself, and everyone watching said, Who is that strange knight? For I have never seen his like. After her mother fell ill and she no longer had time to read, she still dreamed, but the knights and quests and tournaments dropped out of her dreams, and only the deserts remained.

For years in these desert dreams she rode a slender, graceful horse with an arched neck, and it flew over the sand as if it had wings; but when she drew up on the crest of a dune and looked behind her, there would be the shallow half-circles of hoofprints following them, hummocking the wind-ridges and bending the coarse blades of the sand-grass. Her horse would dance under her, splashing sand, and blow through red nostrils, asking to gallop on, but she would wait for the rest of her party, less wonderfully mounted, toiling behind her. Then she would turn again in the direction they were all going, and shade her eyes with one hand, talking soothingly to her restless horse through the reins held lightly in the other; and there would be the dark shadow of mountains before her, mountains she knew to call the Hills.

As the years passed, however, the dreams changed again. She left school at sixteen because her parents said they could spare her no longer, with her mother ill and Ruth and Jeff still so little and her father and Dane (who had left school two years before) working extra hours in the shop because the specialists her mother needed were expensive. When Mrs. Halford and Mr. Jonah came to visit them at home (repeated efforts to persuade her parents to come into the school for a meeting having failed), and begged them to reconsider, and said that she was sure of a scholarship, that her education would be no burden to them, her mother only wept and said in her trembling invalid voice that she was a good girl and they needed her at home, and her father only stared, until at last they went away, the tea and biscuits she had made in honour of so rare an event as visitors in the parlour untouched. Her father finally told her: "See them out to their car, Hetta, and then come direct back. Supper's to be on time, mind."

The three of them were quiet as they went down the stairs and through the hall that ran alongside the shop. The partition was made of cheap ply, for customers never saw it, which made the hall ugly and unfriendly, in spite of the old family photos Hetta had hung on the walls. The shop-door opened nearly on the curb, for the shop had eaten up all of what had been the front garden. At the last minute Mrs. Halford took Hetta's hand and said, "If there's anything I can do—this year, next year, any time. Ring me."

Hetta nodded, said good-bye politely, and then turned round to go back to the house and get supper and see what Ruth and Jeff were doing. Her father had already rejoined Dane in the shop; her mother had gone to bed, taking the plate of biscuits with her.

Ruth had been told by their father to stay out of the way, it was none of her concern, but she was waiting for Hetta in the kitchen. "What happened?" she said.

"Nothing," said Hetta. "Have you done your homework?"

"Yes," said Ruth. "All but the reading. D'you want to listen while you cook?"

"Yes," said Hetta. "That would be nice."

That night Hetta dreamed of a sandstorm. She was alone in darkness, the wind roaring all round her, the sand up to her ankles, her knees, her waist, filling her eyes, her nose, her mouth. Friendly sand. She snuggled down into it as if it were a blanket; as it filled her ears she could no longer hear the wind, nor anything else. When the alarm went off at dawn, she felt as stiff as if she had been buried in sand all night, and her eyes were so sticky, she had to wash her face before she could open them properly.

It had been a relief to quit school, because she was tired all the time. There was more than she could get done even after there was no schoolwork to distract her; but without the schoolwork she found that her mind went to sleep while her body went on with her chores, and for a while that seemed easier. Sometimes months passed without her ever thinking about what she was doing, or not doing, or about Mrs. Halford, or about how she might have used that scholarship if she had got it, if her parents had let her accept it, which they wouldn't have. Months passed while her days were bound round with cooking and housekeeping and keeping the shop accounts, looking through cookery books for recipes when her mother thought that this or that might tempt her appetite, sweeping the passage from the shop twice a day because of the sawdust, teaching Ruth and Jeff to play checkers and fold paper airplanes. When she had first started keeping the accounts, she had done it in the evening, after supper was cleared away and there were no other demands till morning, and the kitchen was peaceful while everyone watched TV in the parlour. But she found she was often too bone weary to pay the necessary attention, so she had taught herself to do it in the edgy time between breakfast and lunch, when the phone was liable to ring, and her mother to be contemplating having one of her bad days, and her father to call her down to the shop to wait on a customer. One afternoon a week she took the car to the mall and shopped for everything they had to have. After the narrow confines of the house, the car park seemed liberating, the neon-edged sky vast.

The months mounted up, and turned into years.

One year the autumn gales were so severe that ruining the harvest and breaking fences for the stock to get through out in the countryside wasn't enough, and they swept into the towns to trouble folk there. Trees and TV aerials came down, and some chimney-pots; there was so much rain that everyone's cellars flooded. The wood stored in their cellar had to come up into the parlour, whereupon there was nowhere to sit except the kitchen. Everyone's tempers grew short with crowding, and when the TV was brought in too, there was nowhere to put it except on counter space Hetta couldn't spare. The only time there was armistice was during programmes interviewing farmers about how bad everything was. Her father watched these with relish and barked "Ha!" often.

That season in spite of the weather she spent more time than ever in the garden. The garden had still been tended by her great-grandfather when she was very small, but after he died, only her grandmother paid any attention to it. As her mother's illness took hold and her father's business took off, it grew derelict, for her grandmother had done the work Hetta did now, with a bad hip and hands nearly frozen with arthritis. Hetta began to clear and plant it about a year after she stopped school; gardening, she found, was interesting, and it got her out of the house. Her father grumbled about having to contain his heaps of wood chips and discarded bits too broken to be mended, but permitted it because she grew vegetables and fruit, which lowered the grocery bills, and she canned and froze what they didn't eat in season. No one else even seemed to notice that the view from the rear of the house looked any different than the front—although Ruth liked bugs, and would sometimes come out to look at the undersides of leaves and scrape things into jars—and so long as Hetta wasn't missing when someone wanted her, nothing was said about the hours she spent in the garden. Their house was the oldest on the street and had the largest garden. It had been a pretty house once, before the shop destroyed its front, but the shop at least made it look more in keeping with the rest of the row. There were proper walls around their garden, eight foot tall on three sides, and the house the fourth. It was her own little realm.

That autumn there was a heaviness to the air, and it smelled of rain and earth and wildness even on days when the sun shone. Hetta usually left as much as she could standing over the winter, to give shelter to Ruth's bugs and the birds and hedgehogs that ate them, but this year she brought the last tomatoes and squashes indoors early (where, denied the wet cellar, she balanced them on piles of timber in the parlour), and she cut back and tied in and staked everything that was left. Even with the walls protecting it, the wind curled in here, flinging other people's tiles at her runner-bean teepees and stripping and shredding the fleece that protected the brassicas. Sometimes she stopped and listened, as if the whistle of the wind was about to tell her something. Sometimes at sunset, when there was another storm coming, the sky reminded her of her desert. But she didn't dare stop long or often, even in the garden; her mother's bedroom window overlooked it, and the sight of Hetta standing still invariably made her hungry. She would open her window and call down to Hetta that she just felt she might eat a little something if Hetta would make it up nice the way she always did and bring it to her.

When the meteorologists began predicting the big storm on its way, the family gathered round the TV set as if the weather report had become a daily installment of a favourite soap opera. Her father snorted; he hated experts in clean business suits telling him things he didn't know. But he didn't protest when the TV was turned on early and he didn't declare the forecast rubbish, and he told Hetta to do her weekly shop early, "just in case."

Two days later the sky went green-yellow, grey-purple; *soon*, sighed the prickle of wind against her skin, and for a moment, leaning on her hoe, the sky was some other sky, and the smooth wooden handle in her hands felt gritty, as if sticky with sand. Her fingers, puzzled, rolled it against her palm, and she blinked, and the world seemed to blink with her, and she was again standing in the back garden of the house where three generations of her father's kin had lived, and there was a storm coming.

When the storm came in the deep night, Hetta was asleep. She knew she was asleep, and yet she knew when the storm wind picked her up . . . no, it did not pick her up, it plunged her down, forced her down, down into darkness and roaring and a great weight against her chest, like a huge hand pressing her into. . . .

She was drowning in sand. It wasn't at all as she'd imagined it, a peaceful ending, a giving up: she did not want to die, and what was happening *hurt*. She gasped and choked, nearly fainting, and the sand bit into her skin, sharp as teeth. She could feel the tiny innumerable grains hissing over her, offering no apparent resistance as she beat at them, pouring through her fingers, down her body, into her eyes and mouth, the unimaginable multitudes of them covering her till they weighed as heavy as boulders, a river, an avalanche. . . .

Where were the others? Had they set out knowing a storm was on the way? Even in this area a storm this severe gave some warning. . . .

In this area? Where was she? There was nothing to tell her—nothing but sand

and wind roar and darkness. And . . . who were *they?* She could not remember—she would not have set out alone—even a guided party had to take care—in the last few years the storms had grown more violent and less predictable—parties rarely went mounted any more—she—remembered—

Perhaps she slept; perhaps she fainted. But there were hands upon her—hands? Had her party found her again? She tried to struggle, or to cooperate. The hands helped her up, held her up, from her wind-battered, sand-imprisoned crouch. The wind still shouted, and she could see nothing; but the hands arranged the veil over her face and she could breathe a little more easily, and this gave her strength. When the hands lifted her so that one of her arms could be pulled around a set of invisible shoulders, and one of the hands gripped her round her waist, she could walk, staggering, led by her rescuer.

For some time she concentrated on breathing, on breathing and keeping her feet under her, tasks requiring her full attention. But her arm, held round the shoulders, began to ache; and the ache began to penetrate her brain, and her brain began to remember that it didn't usually have to occupy itself with negotiating breathing and walking. . . .

It was still dark, and the wind still howled, and there was still sand in the heaving air, but it pattered against her now, it no longer dragged at and cut her. She thought, The storm is still going on all round us, but it is not reaching us somehow. She had an absurd image that they—her unknown rescuer and herself—were walking in a tiny rolling cup of sand that was always shallow to their feet just a footstep's distance before and behind them, with a close-fitting lid of almost quiet, almost sandless air tucked over them.

When the hand clutching her wrist let go, she grabbed the shoulder and missed, for her hand had gone numb; but the hand round her waist held her. She steadied herself, and the second hand let go, but only long enough to find her hand, and hold it firmly—As if I might run off into the sandstorm again, she thought, distantly amused. She looked toward the hand, the shoulders—and now she could see a human outline, but the face was turned away from her, the free hand groping for something in front of it.

She blinked, trying to understand where the light to see came from. She slowly worked out that the hand was more visible than the rest of the body it was attached to; and she had just realised that they seemed to be standing in front of a huge, rough, slightly glowing—wall? Cliff? For it seemed to loom over them; she guessed at something like a ledge or half-roof high above them—when the fingers stiffened and the hand shook itself up in what seemed like a gesture of command—and the wall before them became a door, and folded back into itself. Light fell out, and pooled in the sand at their feet, outlining tiny pits and hummocks in shadows.

"Quickly," said a voice. "I am almost as tired as you, and Geljdreth does not like to be cheated of his victims."

She just managed to comprehend that the words were for her, and she stepped through the door unaided. The hand that was holding hers loosed her, the figure followed her, and this time she heard another word, half-shouted, and she turned in time to see the same stiff-fingered jerk of the hand that had appeared to open the door: it slammed shut on a gust of sand like a sword-stroke. The furious sand slashed into her legs and she stumbled and cried out: the hands saved her again, catching her above the elbows. She put her hands out unthinkingly, and felt collarbones under her hands, and warm breath on her wrists.

"Forgive me," she said, and the absurdity of it caught at her, but she was afraid to laugh, as if once she started, she might not be able to stop.

"Forgive?" said the figure. "It is I who must ask you to forgive me. I should have seen you before; I am a Watcher, and this is my place, and Kalarsham is evil-tempered lately and lets Geljdreth do as he likes. But it was as if you were suddenly there, from nowhere. Rather like this storm. A storm like this usually gives warning, even here."

She remembered her first thought when she woke up—if indeed any of this was waking—*Even in this area a storm this severe gave some warning*. "Where—where am I?" she said.

The figure had pulled the veiling down from its face, and pushed the hood back from its head. He was clean-shaven, dark-skinned, almost mahogany in the yellow light of the stony room where they stood, black-haired; she could not see if his eyes were brown or black. "Where did you come from?" he said, not as if he were ignoring her question but as if it had been rhetorical and required no answer. "You must have set out from Chinilar, what, three or four weeks ago? And then come on from Thaar? What I don't understand is what you were doing alone. You had lost whatever kit and company you came with before I found you—I am sorry—but there wasn't even a pack animal with you. I may have been careless"—his voice sounded strained, as if he were not used to finding himself careless—"but I would have noticed, even if it had been too late."

She shook her head. "Chinilar?" she said.

He looked at her as if playing over in his mind what she had last said. He spoke gently. "This is the station of the fourth Watcher, the Citadel of the Meeting of the Sands, and I am he."

"The fourth—Watcher?" she said.

"There are eleven of us," he said, still gently. "We watch over the eleven Sandpales where the blood of the head of Maur sank into the earth after Aerin and Tor threw the evil thing out of the City and it burnt the forests and rivers of the Old Damar to the Great Desert in the rage of its thwarting. Much of the desert is quiet—as much as any desert is quiet—but Tor, the Just and Powerful, set up our eleven stations where the desert is not quiet. The first is named the Citadel of the Raising of the Sands, and the second is the Citadel of the Parting of the Sands, and the third is the Citadel of the Breathing of the Sands. . . . The third, fourth, fifth, and sixth Watchers are often called upon, for our Pales lie near the fastest way through the Great Desert, from Rawalthifan in the West to the plain that lies before the Queen's City itself. But I—I have never Watched so badly before. Where did you come from?" he said again, and now she heard the frustration and distress in his voice. "Where do you come from, as if the storm itself had brought you?"

Faintly she replied: "I come from Roanshire, one of the south counties of the Homeland; I live in a town called Farbellow about fifteen miles southwest of Mauncester. We live above my father's furniture shop. And I still do not know where I am."

He answered: "I have never heard of Roanshire, or the Homeland, or Mauncester. The storm brought you far indeed. This is the land called Damar, and you stand at the fourth Sandpale at the edge of the Great Desert we call Kalarsham."

And then there was a terrible light in her eyes like the sun bursting, and when she put her hands up to protect her face there was a hand on her shoulder, shaking her, and a voice, a familiar voice, saying, "Hetta, Hetta, wake up, are you ill?" But the voice sounded strange, despite its familiarity, as if speaking a language she used to know but had nearly forgotten. But she heard anxiety in the voice, and fear, and she swam towards that fear, from whatever far place she was in, for she knew the fear, it was hers, and her burden to protect those who shared it. Before she fully remembered the fear or the life that went with it, she heard another voice, an angry voice, and it growled: "Get the lazy lie-abed on her feet or it won't be a hand on her shoulder she next feels"—it was her father's voice.

She gasped as if surfacing from drowning (the howl of the wind, the beating against her body, her face, she had been drowning in sand), and opened her eyes. She tried to sit up, to stand up, but she had come back too far in too short a span of time, and she was dizzy, and her feet wouldn't hold her. She would have fallen, except Ruth caught her—it had been Ruth's hand on her shoulder, Ruth's the first voice she heard.

"Are you ill? Are you ill? I have tried to wake you before—it is long past sunup and the storm has blown out, but there is a tree down that has broken our paling, and the front window of the shop. There are glass splinters and wood shavings everywhere—you could drown in them. Dad says Jeff and I won't go to school today, there is too much to do here, although I think two more people with dust-pans will only get in each other's way, but Jeff will somehow manage to disappear and be found hours later at his computer, so it hardly matters."

Hetta's hands were fumbling for her clothes before Ruth finished speaking. She still felt dizzy and sick, and disoriented; but the fear was well known and it knew what to do, and she was dressed and in the kitchen in a few minutes, although her hair was uncombed and her eyes felt swollen and her mouth tasted of . . . sand. She went on with the preparations for breakfast as she had done many mornings, only half-registering the unusual noises below in the shop, habit held her, habit and fear, as Ruth's hands had held her—

—As the strange cinnamon-skinned man's hands had held her.

After she loaded the breakfast dishes into the dishwasher, she dared run upstairs and wash her face and brush her hair. . . . Her hair felt stiff, dusty. She looked down at the top of her chest of drawers and the bare, swept wooden floor she stood on and saw . . . sand. It might have been wood dust carried by yesterday's storm wind; but no tree produced those flat, glinting fragments. She stared a moment, her hairbrush in her hand, and then laid the brush down, turned, and threw the sheets of her bed back.

Sand. More pale, glittery sand. Not enough to sweep together in a hand, but enough to feel on a fingertip, to hold up in the light and look again and again at the flash as if of infinitesimal mirrors.

She fell asleep that night like diving into deep water, but if she dreamed, she remembered nothing of it, and when she woke the next morning, there were no shining, mirror-fragment grains in her bedding. I imagined it, she thought. I imagined it all—and it was the worst thought she had ever had in her life. She was dressed and ready to go downstairs and make breakfast, but for a moment she could not do it. Not even the knowledge of her father's certain wrath could make her leave her bedroom and face this day, any day, any day here, any other person, the people she knew best. She sat down on the edge of her bed and stared bleakly at nothing: into her life. But habit was stronger: it pulled her to her feet and took her downstairs, and, as it had done yesterday, led her hands and feet and body through their accustomed tasks. But yesterday had been—yesterday. Today there was nothing in her mind but darkness.

She struggled against sleep that night, against the further betrayal of the dream. It had been something to do with the storm, she thought, twisting where she lay, the sheets pulling at her like ropes. Something to do with the air a storm brought: it had more oxygen in it than usual, or less, it did funny things to your mind. . . . Some wind-roused ancient street debris that looked like sand had got somehow into her bed; some day, some day soon, but not too soon, she would ask Ruth if there had been grit in her bed too, the day after the big storm.

She took a deep breath: that smell, spicy, although no spice she knew; spice and rock and earth. She was lying on her back, and had apparently kicked free of the tangling sheets at last—no, there was still something wrapped around one ankle—but her limbs were strangely heavy, and she felt too weak even to open her eyes. But she *would* not sleep, she would not. A tiny breeze wandered over her face, bringing the strange smells to her; and yet her bedroom faced the street, and the street smelled of tarmac and car exhaust and dead leaves and Benny's Fish and Chips on the opposite corner.

She groaned, and with a great effort, managed to move one arm. Both arms lay across her stomach; she dragged at one till it flopped off to lie at her side, palm down. What was she lying on? Her fingertips told her it was not cotton sheet, thin and soft from many launderings. Her fingers scratched faintly; whatever this was, it was thick and yielding, and lay over a surface much firmer (her body was telling her) than her old mattress at home.

An arm slid under her shoulders and she was lifted a few inches, and a pillow slid down to support her head. Another smell, like brandy or whisky, although unlike either—her gardener's mind registered steeped herbs and acknowledged with frustration it did not know what herbs. She opened her eyes but saw only shadows.

"Can you drink?"

She opened her mouth obediently, and a rim pressed against her lips and tilted. She took a tiny sip; whatever it was burned and soothed simultaneously. She swallowed, and heat and serenity spread through her. Her body no longer felt leaden, and her eyes began to focus.

She was in a—a cave, with rocky sides and a sandy floor. There were niches in the walls where oil lamps sat. She knew that smoky, golden light from power cuts at home. When she had been younger and her great-grandfather's little town had not yet been swallowed up by Mauncester's suburbs, there had been power cuts often. That was when her mother still got out of bed most days, and her grandmother used to read to Hetta during the evenings with no electricity, saying that stories were the best things to keep the night outside where it belonged. Cleaning the old oil lamps and laying out candles and matches as she had done the night before last still made her hear her grandmother saying *Once upon a time. . . .* The only complaint Hetta had ever had about her grandmother's stories was that they rarely had deserts in them. Hetta had to blink her eyes against sudden tears.

A cave, she thought, a cave with a sand floor. She looked down at glinting mirror-fragments, like those she had found in the folds of her sheets two nights ago.

I have never heard of Roanshire or the Homeland, or Mauncester. The storm brought you far indeed. This is the land called Damar, and you stand at the fourth Sandpale at the edge of the Great Desert we call Kalarsham.

Her scalp contracted as if someone had seized her hair and twisted it. She gasped, and the cup was taken away and the arm grasped her more firmly. "You have drunk too much, it is very strong," said the voice at her ear; but it was not the liquor that shook her. She sat up and swung her feet round to put them on the floor—there was a bandage tied around one ankle—the supporting arm allowed this reluctantly. She turned her head to look at its owner and saw the man who had rescued her from the sandstorm two nights ago, in her dream. "Where am I?" she said. "I cannot be here. I do not want to go home. I have dreamed this. Oh, I do not want this to be a dream!"

The man said gently, "You are safe here. This is no dream-place, although you may dream the journey. It is as real as you are. It has stood hundreds of years and through many sandstorms—although I admit this one is unusual even in the history of this sanctuary."

"You don't understand," she began, and then she laughed a little, miserably: she was arguing with her own dream-creature.

He smiled at her. "Tell me what I do not understand. What I understand is that you nearly died, outside, a little while ago, because your Watcher almost failed to see you. This is enough to confuse anyone's mind. Try not to distress yourself. Have another sip of the *tiarhk*. It is good for such confusions, and such distress."

She took the cup from him and tasted its contents again. Again warmth and tranquility slid through her, but she could feel her own nature fighting against them, as it had when the doctor had prescribed sleeping pills for her a few years ago. She had had to stop taking the pills. She laced her fingers round the cup and tried to let the *tiarhk* do its work. She took a deep breath. The air was spicy sweet, and again she felt the little stir of breeze; where was the vent that let the air in and kept the dangerous sand-tides out?

"Tell me a little about this place," she said.

He sat back, willing to allow her time to compose herself. "This is the fourth of the Eleven Sandpales that King Tor the Just and Powerful set round the Great Desert Kalarsham some years after the battle of the Hero's Crown and the second and final death of Maur, when it became evident that no easy cure for the desert would be found and that Damar's ancient forest was gone forever, and Geljdreth, the sand-god, would rule us if we let him. This Fourth Pale is called *Horontolopar* in the Old Tongue, and I am its Watcher, Zasharan, fifteenth of that line, for it was my father's mother's mother's father's"—his voice fell into a singsong and she did not count, but she guessed he named fourteen forebears exactly—"mother, who was first called Zasharanth, and installed by Tor himself, and kissed by Queen Aerin, who wished her luck forever. And we have had luck"—he took a deep sigh—"even tonight, for I did find you, though it was a narrow thing. Much too narrow. I would like you to tell me more about *Roanshire*, and *Mauncester*, where you are from, and how you came to be in such state, for no guide would have led or sent you so, and my eye tells me you were alone."

"Your eye?" she said.

"My Eye," he replied, and this time she heard. "I will show you, if you wish. The Eye may see more to this puzzle that you are: how it is that a sandstorm should have come from nowhere to bring you, and yet pursue you across my doorstep so viciously that the wound it laid open on your leg took eight stitches to close. My Eye lies in the place where I Watch, and it is much of how I do what I am here to do. It is only Aerin's Luck that I looked tonight, for this is an unsettled season, and no one has set out from Thaar in weeks. Perhaps you did not come from Thaar."

She laughed, although it hurt her. "No, I did not come from Thaar. And—and I have gone away—and come back. The storm—you brought me here two nights ago."

He looked at her calmly. "You have not been here above an hour. You fainted, and I took the opportunity to dress your leg. Then you woke."

She was silent a moment. Her head swam, and she did not think another sip of *tiarhk* was advisable. "Are you alone here?"

He looked astonished. "Alone? Certainly not. Rarely does anyone else come to this end of the citadel, for I am the Watcher, and no other has reason to know of the desert door I brought you through. But there are some few of us, and the caves run far up into the Hills, and where they come out there is the filanon town Sunbarghon, although you would not find it unless they decided to allow you to, and Ynorkgindal, where they ring the Border, that the music of their bells may help keep us safe from the North, and the dlor Gzanforyar, which is mastered by my good friend Rohk. Perhaps you will meet him one day—" He blinked and gave a tiny shiver, and said, "Forgive me, lady, that was presumptuous."

She shook her head. "I should like to meet him," she said, but she heard in her voice that she believed there would be no such meeting. Zasharan heard it too, and turned his face a little away from her, and she saw how stiffly he sat. Her first thought was that she had offended him, but she remembered, *Forgive me, lady, that was presumptuous*, and before she could think, had reached to touch his arm. "But I *would* like to meet your friend, and see the caves, and your Eye, and—" She stopped. How long would the dream last this time?

He turned back to her. "There is something strange about you, I know that, and I see—I think I see—I—" He looked down at her hand on his arm, which she hastily removed. "You trouble me, lady. May I have your name?"

"Hetta," she said.

"Hetthar," he said. "Do you think you can stand, and walk? Do you wish food first? For I would like you to come to the place of my Eye, where I think you and I may both be able to see more plainly."

"I am not hungry," she said, and tried to stand; but as she did, her head swam, and Zasharan and the room began to fade, and she began to smell wood shavings and wet tarmac. "The sand!" she cried. "The sand!" And just before she lost consciousness, she flung herself on the floor of Zasharan's cave, and scrabbled at the sand with her hands.

She woke lying on her back again, her hands upon her stomach, but her hands were shut into fists, and the backs of them hurt up into her forearms, as if she had been squeezing them closed for a long time. With some difficulty she unbent the fingers, and two tiny palmfuls of sand poured out upon her nightdress. Slowly, slowly she sat up, pulling up folds of her nightdress to enclose the sand. She stood, clutching the front of her nightdress together, and went to her chest of drawers. She had been allowed to move into this room, which had been her grandmother's, when her grandmother died, but she had always been too busy—or too aware of herself as interloper—to disarrange any of her grandmother's things that weren't actively in her way. But they were friendly things, and once the first shock of grief was over, she liked having them there, reminding her of her gran, and no longer wondered if it might be disrespectful to keep them as they were. On the top of the chest there was an assortment of little lidded boxes and jars that had once held such things as bobby pins and cotton balls and powder, and were now empty. She chose one and carefully transferred the sand into it. She stood looking at its lid for a moment. She had chosen this one because it had a pretty curl of dianthus flower and leaf painted on its surface; her gran's dianthus still bloomed in the garden. She lifted the lid to reassure herself that the sand was still there—that it hadn't disappeared as soon as she closed the box—and for a moment, faint but unmistakable, she smelled the spicy smell of Zasharan's cave, and *tiarhk*.

When she dreamt of nothing again that night, she almost didn't care. When she woke up, she looked in the tiny box on her chest of drawers and the sand was still there on this second morning, and then she went downstairs to get breakfast. Today was her day to drive to the mall. Usually, if her list was not too long, she could spare an hour for herself. And today she wanted to go to the library.

It took more time to get to the mall than usual; she had had to go the long way round their block because of the fallen tree that still lay in the broken remains of their front paling, and there were other trees down elsewhere that the exhausted and overburdened county council had not yet cut up and hauled away. In one place the road had caved in where a flash flood had undermined it. There were detours and orange warning cones and temporary stoplights, and when she finally got there, some of the car park at the mall was blocked off. She'd have barely half an hour at the library, and only if she pelted through the rest first.

She didn't go to the library very often any more, since she had had to stop school. She didn't have much time for reading, and she couldn't think of any book she wanted to read: both fiction and nonfiction only reminded her of what she wasn't doing and might never do. She did read seed catalogues, intensely, from cover to cover, every winter, and the off-beat gardening books and even more bizarre popular science books Ruth bought her every birthday and Christmas, which, because Ruth had bought them, were friendly instead of accusing. The library felt like a familiar place from some other life. There were calluses on her hands that scraped against the pages that hadn't been there when she had been coming here several times a week.

None of the encyclopedias had any listings for Damar, nor the atlases, and she didn't have time to queue for a computer. They had added more computes since she had been here last, but it hadn't changed the length of the queue. She went reluctantly to the help desk. Geography had never been a strong suit, and by the time she was standing in front of the counter, she felt no more than ten and a good six inches shorter. "Er—have you ever heard of a place called Damar?" The librarian's eyes went first to the row of computers, all occupied, and she sighed. She looked up at Hetta. "Yes," said Hetta. "I've tried the encyclopedias and atlases."

The librarian smiled faintly, then frowned. "Damar. I don't recall—what do you know about it?"

It has eleven Sandpales and a Watcher named Zasharan at the fourth. "Um. It—it has a big desert in it, which used to be ancient forest." The librarian raised her eyebrows. "It's—it's a crossword puzzle clue," said Hetta, improvising hastily. "It's—it's a sort of bet."

The librarian looked amused. She tapped *Damar* into the computer in front of her. "Hmm. Try under *Daria.* Oh yes—Damar," she said, looking interested. "I remember . . . oh dear. If you want anything recent, you will have to consult the newspaper archive." She looked suddenly hunted. "There's a bit of a, hmm, gap . . . up till five years ago, everything is on microfiche, and in theory everything since is available on the computer system but, well, it isn't, you know. . . . Let me know if I can find . . . if I can try to find anything for you." She looked at Hetta with an expression that said full body armour and possibly an oxygen tank and face-mask were necessary to anyone venturing into the newspaper archive.

"Thank you," said Hetta demurely, and nearly ran back to the reference room; her half hour was already up.

> Daria. The Darian subcontinent in southwestern Asia comprises a large landmass including both inland plains, mostly desert with irregular pockets of fertile ground, between its tall and extensive mountain ranges, and a long curved peninsula of gentler and more arable country in the south. . . . Its government is a unique conception, being both the Republic of Damar under its own people and a Protectorate of the Homeland Empire and legislated by her appointed officers. See text articles. . . .

Damar. It existed.

She had been nearly an hour at the library. She ran out to the car park and banged the old car into gear in a way it was not at all used to. It gave a howl of protest but she barely heard it. Damar. *It existed!*

The ice cream had started to melt but her father never ate ice cream, and there were scones for tea with the eggs and sausages because scones were the fastest thing she could think of and her father wouldn't eat store bread. She ignored more easily than usual her mother's gently murmured litany of complaint when she took her her tray, and in blessed peace and quiet—Dane and his girlfriend, Lara, were having dinner with her parents, Jeff was doing homework in his room, their father was downstairs in the shop, and Hetta had firmly turned the still-resident TV *off*—began washing up the pots and pans that wouldn't fit in the dishwasher. She was trying to remember anything she could about Daria—they had been studying the Near East in history and current events the year her grandmother had died and her mother had first taken seriously ill, and the only thing she remembered clearly was *Great Expectations* in literature class, because she had been wishing that some convict out of a graveyard would rescue her. This had never struck her as funny before, but she was smiling over the sink when Ruth—whom she hadn't heard come into the kitchen—put her hand on her arm, and said, or rather whispered, "Hetta, what is *with* you? Are you okay?"

"What do you mean?"

"You haven't been yourself since the storm. I mean, good for you, I think you haven't been yourself in about eight years, except I was so young then I didn't know what was going on, and maybe you're becoming yourself again now. But you're different, and look, you know Mum and Dad, they don't like different. It'll turn out bad somehow if they notice. At the moment Dad's still totally preoccupied with the storm damage but he won't be forever. And even Mum—" Ruth shrugged. Their mother had her own ways of making things happen.

Hetta had stopped washing dishes in surprise but began again; Ruth picked up a dish-towel and began to dry. They both cast a wary look at the door; the hum of the dishwasher would disguise their voices as long as they spoke quietly, but their father didn't like conversations he couldn't hear, and the only topics he wished discussed all had to do with business and building furniture. "I—I'm embarrassed to tell you," said Hetta, concentrating on the bottom of a saucepan.

"Try me," said Ruth. "Hey, I study the sex lives of bugs. Nothing embarrasses me."

Hetta sucked in her breath on a suppressed laugh. "I—I've been having this dream—" She stopped and glanced at Ruth. Ruth was looking at her, waiting for her to go on. "It's . . . it's like something real."

"I've had dreams like that," said Ruth, "but they don't make me go around looking like I've got a huge important secret, at least I don't think they do."

Hetta grinned. Hetta had always been the dreamy daughter, as their father had often pointed out, and Ruth the practical one. Their grandmother had teased that she was grateful for the eight-year difference in their ages because telling stories to both of them at the same time would have been impossible. Hetta wanted fairy-tales. Ruth wanted natural history. (The two sons of the house had been expected to renounce the soft feminine pleasures of being tucked in and told stories.) The problem with Ruth's practicality was that it was turning out to have to do with science, not furniture; Ruth eventually wanted to go into medical research, and her biology teacher adored her. Ruth was fifteen, and in a year she would have to go up against their father about what she would do next, a confrontation Hetta had lost, and Dane had sidestepped by being—apparently genuinely—eager to stop wasting time in school and get down to building furniture ten hours a day. Hetta was betting on Ruth, but she wasn't looking forward to being around during the uproar.

"Do you know anything about Daria?"

Ruth frowned briefly. "It got its independence finally, a year or two ago, didn't it? And has gone back to calling itself Damar, which the Damarians had been calling it all along. There was something odd about the hand-over though." She paused. International politics was not something their father was interested in, and whatever the news coverage had been, they wouldn't have seen it at home. After a minute Ruth went on: "One of my friends—well, she's kind of a space case—Melanie, she says that it's full of witches and wizards or something and they do, well, real magic there, and all us Homelander bureaucrats either can't stand it and have really short terms and are sent home, or really get into it and go native and stay forever. She had a great-uncle who got into it and wanted to stay, but his wife hated it, so they came home, and you still only have to say 'Daria' to her and she bursts into tears, but he told Melanie a lot about it before he died, and according to her . . . well, I said she's a space case. It's not the sort of thing I would remember except that there *was* something weird about the hand-over when it finally happened and Melanie kept saying 'well of course' like she knew the real reason. Why?"

"I've been dreaming about it."

"About *Daria?*—Damar, I mean. How do you dream about a *country?*"

"Not about the whole country. About a—a person, who lives on the edge of the—the Great Desert. He says he is one of the Watchers—there are eleven of them. Um. They sort of keep an eye on the desert. For sandstorms and things."

"Is he cute?"

Hetta felt a blush launch itself across her face. "I—I hadn't thought about it." This was true.

Ruth laughed, and forgot to swallow it, and a moment later there was a heavy foot on the stair up from the shop and their father appeared at the kitchen door. "Hetta can finish the dishes without your help," he said. "Ruth, as you have nothing to do, you can have a look at these," and he thrust a handful of papers at her. "I've had an insulting estimate from the insurance agent today and I want something to answer him with. If Hetta kept the files in better order, I wouldn't have to waste time now."

She did not dream of Zasharan that night, but she dreamed of walking in a forest full of trees she did not know the names of, and hearing bird-voices, and knowing, somehow, that some of them were human beings calling to other human beings the news that there was a stranger in their forest. She seemed to walk through the trees for many hours, and once or twice it occurred to her that perhaps she was lost and should be frightened, but she looked round at the trees and smiled, for they were friendly, and she could not feel lost even if she did not know where she was, nor frightened, when she was surrounded by friends. At last she paused, and put her hand on the deeply rutted bark of a particular tree that seemed to call to her to touch it, and looked up into its branches; and there, as if her eyes were learning to see, the leaves and branches rearranged themselves into a new pattern that included a human face peering down at her. It held very still, but it saw at once when she saw it; and then it smiled, and a branch near it turned into an arm, and it waved. When she raised her own hand—the one not touching the tree—to wave back, she woke, with one hand still lifted in the air.

She did not dream of Zasharan the next night either, but she dreamed that she was walking past a series of stables and paddocks, where the horses watched her, ears pricked, as she went by, till she came to a sand-floored ring where several riders were performing a complicated pattern, weaving in and out of each other's track. The horses wore no bridles, and their saddles, whose shape was strange to her eyes, had no stirrups. She watched for a moment, for the pattern the horses were making (while their riders appeared to sit motionless astride them) was very lovely and graceful. When the horses had all halted, heads in a circle, and all dropped their noses as if in salute, one of the riders broke away and came towards her, and nodded to her, and said, "I am Rohk, master of this dlor, and I should know everyone who goes here, but I do not know you. Will you give me your name, and how came you past the guard at the gate?"

He spoke in a pleasant voice, and she answered with no fear, "My name is Hetta, and I do not remember coming in your gate. Zasharan has mentioned you to me, and perhaps that is how I came here."

Rohk touched his breast with his closed hand, and then opened it towards her, flicking the fingers in a gesture she did not know. "If you are a friend of Zasharan, then you are welcome here, however you came."

On the third night she was again walking in a forest, and she looked up hopefully, searching for a human face looking down at her, but for what seemed to be a long time she saw no one. But as she walked and looked, she began to realise that she was hearing something besides birdsong and the rustle of leaves; it sounded like bells, something like the huge bronze bells of the church tower in her town, but there were too many bells, too many interlaced notes—perhaps more like the bells of the cathedral in Mauncester. She paused and listened more intently. The bells seemed to grow louder: their voices were wild, buoyant, superb; and suddenly she was among them, held in the air by the bright weave of their music. The biggest bell was turning just at her right elbow, she could look into it as it swung up towards her, she could see the clapper fall, BONG! The noise this close was unbearable—it should have been unbearable—it struck through her like daggers—no: like sunbeams through a prism, and she stood in air full of rainbows. But now she could hear voices, human voices, through the booming of the bells, and they said: *Come down, you must come down, for when the bells stand up and silent, you will fall.*

She looked down and saw the faces of the ringers, hands busy and easy on the ropes, but the faces looking up at her fearful and worried. *I do not know how,* she said, but she knew she made no sound, any more than a rainbow can speak. And then she heard the silence beyond the bells, and felt herself falling past the music and into the silence; but she woke before she had time to be afraid, and she was in her bed in her father's house, and it was time to get up and make breakfast. That afternoon when Ruth came home from school, she bent over Hetta's chair and dropped a kiss on the top of her head, as she often did, but before she straightened up again, she murmured, "I have something for you." But Lara, on the other side of the table, was peeling potatoes with a great show of being helpful, and Ruth said no more. It was a busy evening, for both the hired cabinetmakers from the shop, Ron and Tim, had been invited to stay late and come for supper, which was one of Hetta's father's ways of avoiding paying them overtime, and it was not until they had gone to bed that Ruth came creeping into Hetta's room with a big envelope. She grinned at Hetta, said, "Sweet dreams," and left again, closing the door silently behind her. Hetta listened till she was sure Ruth had missed the three squeaky stairs on her way back to her own room before she dumped the contents of the envelope out on her bed.

Come to Damar, land of orange groves, said the flier on top. She stared at the trees in the photo, but they were nothing like the trees she had seen in her dream two nights before. She shuffled through the small pile of brochures. As travel agents' propaganda went, this was all very low-key. There were no girls in bikinis and no smiling natives in traditional dress; just landscape, desert and mountains and forests—and orange plantations, and some odd-looking buildings. What people there were all seemed to be staring somewhat dubiously at the camera. Some of them were cinnamon-skinned and black-haired like Zasharan.

There were also a few sheets of plain stark print listing available flights and prices—these made her hiss between her teeth. Her father gave her something above the housekeeping money that he called her wages, which nearly covered replacing clothes that had worn out and disintegrated off their seams; she had nonetheless managed to save a little, by obstinacy; she could probably save more if she had to. Most of her grandmother's clothes still hung in the cupboard, for example; she had already altered one or two blouses to fit herself, and a skirt for Ruth. The difficulty with this however was that while her father would never notice the recycling of his mother's old clothes, Hetta's mother would, and would mention it in her vague-seeming way to her husband, who would then decide that Hetta needed less money till this windfall had been thoroughly used up. But over the years Hetta had discovered various ways and means to squeeze a penny till it screamed, her garden produced more now than it had when she began as she learnt more about gardening, and the butcher liked her. . . .

Perhaps. Just perhaps.

She did not dream of Zasharan that night either, but she smelled the desert wind, and for a moment she stood somewhere that was not Farbellow or her father's shop, and she held a cup in her hands, but when she raised it to taste its contents, it was only water.

She thought about the taste of desert water that afternoon as she raked the pond at the back of the vegetable garden. She wore tall green wellies on her feet and long rubber gloves, but it was still very hard not to get smudgy and bottom-of-pond-rot-smelling while hauling blanket-weed and storm detritus out of a neglected pond. She didn't get back here as often as she wanted to because the pond didn't produce anything but newts and blanket-weed and she didn't have time for it, although even at its worst it was a magical spot for her, and the only place in the garden where her mother couldn't see her from her window.

She had wondered all her life how her great-grandmother had managed to convince her great-grandfather to dig her a useless ornamental pond. Her great-grandfather had died when she was four, but she remembered him clearly: in his extreme old age he was still a terrifying figure, and even at four she remembered how her grandmother, his daughter, had seemed suddenly to shed a burden after his death—and how Hetta's own father had seemed to expand to fill that empty space. Hetta's father, her grandmother had told her, sadly, quietly, not often, but now and again, was just like his grandfather. Hetta would have guessed this anyway; there were photographs of him, and while he had been taller than her father, she recognised the glare. She couldn't imagine what it must have been like to be his only child, as her grandmother had been.

But his wife had had her pond.

It was round, and there was crazy paving around the edge of it. There was a little thicket of coppiced dogwood at one end, which guarded it from her mother, which Hetta cut back religiously every year; but the young red stems were very pretty and worthwhile on their own account as well as for the screen they provided. She planted sunflowers at the backs of the vegetable beds, and then staked them, so they would stand through the winter: these sheltered it from view of the shop as if, were her father reminded of it, it would be filled in at once and used for potatoes. It was an odd location to choose for a pond; it was too well shaded by the apple tree and the wall to grow water lilies in, for example, but the paving made it look as though you might want to set chairs beside it and admire the newts and the blanket-weed on nice summer evenings; nearer the house you would have less far to carry your patio furniture and tea-tray. Maybe her great-grandmother had wanted to hide from view too. Hetta's grandmother had found it no solace; she called it "eerie" and stayed away. "She was probably just one of these smooth, dry humans with no amphibian blood," Ruth had said once, having joined Hetta poolside one evening and discovered, upon getting up, that she had been sitting in mud. Ruth had also told Hetta that her pond grew rather good newts: Turner's Greater Red-Backed Newt, to be precise, which was big (as newts go) and rare.

Hetta paused a moment, leaning on her rake. She would leave the blanket-weed heaped up on the edge of the pond overnight, so that anything that lived in it had time to slither, creep, or scurry back into the pond; and then she would barrow it to the compost heap behind the garage. She looked down at her feet. The blanket-weed was squirming. A newt crept out and paused as if considering; it had a jagged vermilion crest down its back like a miniature dragon, and eyes that seemed to flash gold in the late-afternoon sunlight—she fancied that it glanced up at her before it made its careful way down the blanket-weed slope and slid into the pond with the tiniest chuckle of broken water.

That night she woke again in Zasharan's rocky chamber. She lay again on the bed or pallet where she had woken before; and she turned her head on her pillow and saw Zasharan dozing in a chair drawn up beside her. As she looked into his face, he opened his eyes and looked back at her. "Good," he said. "I dreamed that you would wake again soon. Come—can you stand? I am sorry to press you when you are weary and confused, but there are many things I do not understand, and I want to take you to my Eye quickly, before you escape me again. If you cannot stand, and if you will permit it, I will carry you."

"Dream?" she said. "You *dreamed* I would return?" She was sitting up and putting her feet on the floor as she spoke—bare feet, sandy floor, her toes and heels wriggled themselves into their own little hollows without her conscious volition. For the first time she thought to look at what she was wearing: it was a long loose robe, dun-coloured in the lamplight, very like her nightdress at home—it could almost be her nightdress—but the material was heavier and fell more fluidly, and there seemed to be a pattern woven into it that she could not see in the dimness.

"Watchers often dream," he said. "It is one of the ways we Watch. No Watcher would be chosen who had not found his—or her—way through dreams many times." He offered her his hand. "But you—I am not accustomed to my visitors telling me they are dream-things when I am not dreaming."

She stood up and staggered a little, and he caught her under the elbows. "I will walk," she said. "I walked here before, did I not? The—the night I came here—nearly a fortnight ago now." He smiled faintly. "I would like to walk. Walking makes me feel—less of a dream-thing."

His smile jerked, as if he understood some meaning of her remark she had not meant, and they left the room, and walked for some time through rocky corridors hazily lit by some variable and unseen source. At first these were narrow and low, and the floor was often uneven although the slope was steadily upward; both walls and floor were yellowy-goldeny-grey, although the walls seemed darker for the shadows they held in their rough hollows. The narrow ways widened, and she could see other corridors opening off them on either side. She felt better for the walk—realler, as she had said, less like a dream-thing. She could feel her feet against the sand, a faint ache from the wound on her ankle, listen to her own breath, feel the air of this place against her skin. She knew she was walking slowly, tentatively, when at home she was quick and strong, and needed to be. Perhaps—perhaps they were very high here—had he not said something about hills?—perhaps it was the elevation that made her feel so faint and frail.

They had turned off the main way into one of the lesser corridors, and came at last to a spiral stair. The treads twinkled with trodden sand in the dim directionless light as far up as she could see till they rounded the first bend. "You first, lady," he said, and she took a deep breath and grasped the rope railing, and began to pull herself wearily up, step by step; but to her surprise the way became easier the higher they climbed, her legs grew less tired and her breath less laboured. They came out eventually on a little landing before a door, and Zasharan laid his hand softly on it and murmured a word Hetta could not hear, and it opened.

There were windows on the far side of the room, curtainless, with what she guessed was dawn sunlight streaming in; she flinched as the daylight touched her as if in this place she would prove a ghost or a vampire, but nothing happened but that its touch was gentle and warm. The view was of a steep slope rising above them; the room they were in seemed to grow out of the hillside.

There was a round pool in the middle of the floor and Zasharan knelt down beside it on the stone paving that surrounded it. "This is my Eye," he said softly. "Come and look with me."

She knelt near him, propping herself with her hands, for she was feeling weary again. Her gaze seemed to sink below the water's surface in a way she did not understand; perhaps the contents of the pool was not water. And as her sight plunged deeper, she had the odd sensation that something in the depths was rising towards her, and she wondered suddenly if she wanted to meet it, whatever it was.

A great, golden Eye, with a vertical pupil expanding as she saw it, as if it had only just noticed her. . . .

She gave a small gasp, and she heard Zasharan murmuring beside her, but she could not hear what he said; and then the pupil of the Eye expanded till it filled the whole of her vision with darkness, and then the darkness cleared, and she saw—

She woke in her bed, her heart thundering, gasping for breath, having pulled the bed to bits, the blankets on the floor, the sheets knotted under her and her feet on bare ticking. It was just before dawn; there was grey light leaking through the gap at the bottom of the blind. She felt exhausted, as if she had had no sleep at all, and at the same time grimly, remorselessly awake. She knew she would not sleep again. Her right ankle ached, and she put her fingers down to rub it; there was a ridge there, like an old scar.

She got through the day somehow, but she left a pot of soup on the back of the cooker turned up too high, so it had boiled over while she was scraping the seeds out of squashes over the compost heap, and her mother had called out, a high, thin shriek, that the house was burning down, although it was only burnt soup on the hob. Her mother had palpitations for the rest of the evening, was narrowly talked out of ringing the doctor to have something new prescribed for her nerves, and insisted that she might have burned in her bed. Her father complained about the thick burnt smell spoiling his tea, and that Hetta was far too old to make stupid mistakes like that. She went to bed with a headache, remembering that the blanket-weed was still waiting for her to haul it away, and found two aspirin on her pillow, and a glass of water on the floor beside it: Ruth. Their father believed that pharmacology was for cowards. The only drugs in the house were on her mother's bedside table, and Hetta would much rather have a headache than face her mother again that evening; she had forgotten Ruth's secret stash. She swallowed the pills gratefully and lay down.

When she opened her eyes she was again by the pool in Zasharan's tower, but she had moved, or been moved, a little distance from it, so she could no longer look into it (or perhaps it could no longer look out at her), and Zasharan sat beside her, head bowed, holding her hand. When she stirred, he looked up at once, and said, "I have looked, and asked my people to look, in our records, and I cannot find any tale to help us. I am frightened, for you sleep too long—it is longer each time you leave. You have been asleep nearly a day, and there are hollows under your eyes. This is not the way it should be. You live elsewhere—you have been born and have lived to adulthood in this elsewhere—where you should not be; you should be here; my Eye would not have troubled itself to look at any stranger, and my heart welcomes you whether I would or nay. There have been others who have come here by strange ways, but they come and they stay. If you wish to come here and we wish to have you, why do you not stay?"

She sat up and put her other hand on his and said, "No, wait, it is all right. I have found Damar in the atlas at home, and my sister has found out about air flights, and I will come here in the—in the—" She stumbled over how to express it. "In the usual way. And I will come here, and find you." She heard herself saying this as if she were listening to a television programme, as if she had nothing to do with it; and yet she knew she had something to do with it, because she was appalled. Who was this man she only met in dream to tell her where she belonged, and who was she to tell him that she was going to come to him—even to herself she did not know how to put it—that she was going to come to him in the real world?

"Air flights," he said thoughtfully.

"Yes," she said. "Where is the nearest airport? I could not find Thaar, or Chin—Chin—" As she said this, her voice wavered, because she remembered how hard it was to remember anything from a dream; and she was dreaming. *Remember the sand,* her dream-thought told her. *Remember the sand that lies in the little box on your chest of drawers.* "Oh—you will have to tell me how to find you. I assume there is a better way than . . ." Her voice trailed away again as she remembered being lost in the sandstorm, of being led blindly through the sand-wind, her arm pulled round Zasharan's shoulders till her own shoulder ached, remembered her curious sense that they were somehow kept safe in a little rolling bubble of air that let them make their way to the door in the cliff. *That is why he is a Watcher,* said the dream-thought. *There is little use in Watching if you cannot act upon what you see.*

"I do not know where the nearest airport is. What is an airport?" said Zasharan.

She knew, sometimes, that she spoke some language other than Homelander in her dreams; but then it was the sort of thing you felt you knew while you were dreaming and yet also knew that it was only a trick of the mind. The words she spoke to Zasharan—the words she had heard and spoken to the other Damarians she had met in other dreams—*felt* different. It was just a part of the dream, as was the different, more rolling, growlier, peaked-and-valleyed sound of the words Zasharan and the other Damarians said to her than what she spoke in Farbellow, when she was awake. (*I am awake now,* said the dream-thought.) It was only a part of the same mind-trick that when Zasharan said "airport," it sounded like a word that came from some other language than the one he was speaking.

She looked around, and saw a table in the corner, and books upon it (were these the records he had been searching for stories like hers?), and several loose sheets of paper, and a pen. She stood up—carefully, prepared to be dizzy—and gestured towards the table. Zasharan stood up with her. "May I?" she said. He nodded as anyone might nod, but he also made a gesture with his hand that was both obviously that of hospitality and equally not at all—she thought; her dream-thought thought—like the gesture she would have made if someone had asked her to borrow a sheet of paper.

She took a deep breath, and picked up the pen (which was enough like an old-fashioned fountain pen that she did not have to ask how to use it) and drew an airplane on the top sheet of paper. She was not an artist, but anyone in the world she knew would have recognised what she drew at once as an airplane.

Zasharan only looked at it, puzzled, worried, both slightly frowning and slightly smiling, and shook his head, and made another gesture, a gesture of unknowing, although not the shoulders raised and hands spread that she would have made (that she thought she would have made) in a similar situation.

Frustrated, she folded the sheet of paper, lengthwise in half, then folding the nose, the wings—she threw it across the room and it flew over the round pool where the Eye waited, bumped into the wall on the far side and fell to the ground. "Paper airplane," she said.

"Paper glider," he agreed. He walked round the pool, and picked her airplane up, and brought it back to the table. He unfolded it, carefully, pressing the folds straight with his fingers, smoothing and smoothing the wrinkles the bumped nose had made—as if paper were rare and precious, she thought, refusing to follow that thought any farther—and then, quickly, he folded it again, to a new pattern, a much more complex pattern, and when he tossed his glider in the air it spun up and then spiralled down in a lovely curve, and lit upon the floor as lightly as a butterfly.

She looked at him, and there was a sick, frightened feeling in her throat. "When you travel—long distances," she said, "how—how do you go?" She could not bring herself to ask about cars and trucks and trains.

"We have horses and asses and ankaba," he said. "You may walk or ride or lead a beast loaded with your gear. We have guides to lead you. We have waggoners who will carry you and your possessions. There are coaches if you can afford them; they are faster—and, they say, more comfortable, but I would not count on this." He spoke mildly, as if this were an ordinary question, but his eyes were fixed on her face in such a way that made it plain he knew it was not.

Slowly she said, "What year is it, Zasharan?"

He said, "It is the year 3086, counting from the year Gasthamor came from the east and struck the Hills with the hilt of his sword, and the Well of the City of the Kings and Queens opened under the blow."

"Gasthamor," said Hetta, tasting the name.

"Gasthamor, who was the teacher of Oragh, who was the teacher of Semthara, who was the teacher of Frayadok, who was the teacher of Goriolo, who was the teacher of Luthe," said Zasharan.

Gasthamor, she repeated to herself. *Goriolo*. She doubted that the encyclopedia would tell the tale of the warrior-mage who struck the rock with the hilt of his sword and produced a flow of water that would last over three thousand years, but an encyclopedia of legends might. "You—you said the Queen's City, once before," she said. "What is the name of your queen?"

"Fortunatar," he said. "Fortunatar of the Clear Seeing."

She woke to the sound of her own voice, murmuring, *Gasthamor, Fortunatar of the Clear Seeing, the year 3086*. Her heart was heavy as she went about her chores that day, and she told herself that this was only because it was two more days before she could go to the library again, and look up the kings and queens of Damar.

She made time to finish cleaning the pool at the back of the garden, hauling the blanket-weed—now a disgusting sticky brown mat—two heaped barrowloads of the stuff—to the compost heap. When she was done, she knelt on the crazy paving that edged the pool, and dipped her dirty hands in the water. The sting of its coolness was friendly, energising; her head felt clearer and her heart lighter than it had in several days. She patted her face with one wet hand, letting the other continue to trail in the water, and she felt a tiny flicker against her palm. She looked down, and there was a newt, swimming back and forth in a tiny figure eight, the curl of one arc inside her slightly cupped fingers. She turned her hand so that it was palm up, and spread her fingers. It swam to the centre of her palm and stopped. She thought she could just feel the tickle of tiny feet against her skin.

She raised her hand very, very slowly; as the newt's crested back broke the surface of the water, it gave a frantic, miniature heave and scrabble, and she thought it would dive over the little rise made by the web between her forefinger and thumb, but it stilled instead, seeming to crouch and brace itself, as against some great peril. Now she definitely felt its feet: the forefeet at the pulse-point of her wrist, the rear on the pads at the roots of her fingers, the tail sliding off her middle finger between it and the ring finger. She found she was holding her breath.

She continued to raise her hand till it was eye level to herself; and the newt lifted its head and stared at her. Its eyes were so small, it was difficult to make out their colour: gold, she thought, with a vertical black pupil. The newt gave a tiny shudder and the startling red crest on its back lifted and stiffened.

They gazed at each other for a full minute. Then she lowered her hand again till it touched the pond surface, and this time the newt was gone so quickly that she stared at her empty palm, wondering if she had imagined the whole thing.

She heard bells ringing in her dreams that night, but they seemed sombre and sad. On the next night she thought she heard Zasharan's voice, but she was lost in the dark, and whichever way she turned, his voice came from behind her, and very far away.

She stormed around the supermarket the next day, and when she found herself at the check-out behind someone who had to think about which carefully designated bag each item went into, she nearly started throwing his own apples at him. She arrived at the library with less than half an hour left, but her luck had found her at last, for there was a computer free. *Queens of Damar*, she typed. There was a whirr, and a list of web sites which mentioned (among other things) internationally assorted queens apparently not including Damarian, paint varnishes, long underwear, and hair dressing salons, presented itself to her hopefully. She stared at the screen, avoiding asking something that would tell her what she feared. At last she typed: *Who is the ruler of Damar today?*

Instantly the screen replied: *King Doroman rules with the Council of Five and the Parliament of Montaratur.*

There was no help for it. *Queen Fortunatar of the Clear Seeing*, she typed.

There was a pause while the computer thought about it. She must have looked as frustrated and impatient as she felt, because a librarian paused beside her and asked in that well-practised ready-to-go-away-without-taking-offense voice if she could be of service.

"I am trying to find out some information about the queen of Damar," she said.

"Damar? Oh—Daria—oh—Damar. Someone else was just asking about Damar a few weeks ago. It's curious how much we *don't* hear about a country as big as it is. They have a king now, don't they? I seem to remember from the independence ceremonies. I can't remember if he had a wife or not."

The computer was still thinking. Hetta said, finding herself glad of the distraction, "The queen I want is Fortunatar of the Clear Seeing."

The librarian repeated this thoughtfully. "She sounds rather, hmm, poetical, though, doesn't she? Have you tried myths and legends?"

The computer had now hung itself on the impossible question of a poetical queen of Damar, and Hetta was happy to let the librarian lean over her and put her hands on the keyboard and wrestle it free. The librarian knew, too, how to ask the library's search engine questions it could handle, and this time when an answering screen came up, there was a block of text highlighted:

> Shortly after this period of upheaval, Queen Fortunatar, later named of the Clear Seeing for the justice of her rulings in matters both legal and numinous, took her throne upon the death of her half-brother Linmath. Linmath had done much in his short life, and he left her a small but sound queendom which flourished under her hand. The remaining feuds were settled not by force of arms (nor by the trickery that had caught Linmath fatally unaware) but by weaponless confrontation before the queen and her counsellors; and fresh feuds took no hold and thus shed no blood. The one serious and insoluble menace of Fortunatar's time were the sandstorms in the Great Desert which were frequent and severe.

"Hmm," said the librarian, and scrolled quickly to the top of the document. *An Introduction to the Legendary History of Damar*:

> All countries have their folk tales and traditions, but Damar is unusual in the wealth of these, and in the inextricable linkage between them and what western scholars call factual history. Even today. . . .

Hetta closed her eyes. Then she opened them again without looking at the computer screen, made a dramatic gesture of looking at her watch, and did not have to feign the start of horror when she saw what it was telling her. "Oh dear—I really must go—thank you so much—I will come back when I have more time." She was out the door before she heard what the librarian was asking her. Probably whether she wanted to print out any of what they had found.

No.

For three nights she did not dream at all, and waking was cruel. The one moment when her spirits lifted enough for her to feel a breeze on her face and pause to breathe the air with pleasure was one sunny afternoon when she went back to her pool and scrubbed the encircling paving. She scrubbed with water only, not knowing what any sort of soap run-off might do to the pond life, and she saw newts wrinkle the water with their passing several times. When she stopped to breathe deep, she thought she saw a newt with a red back hovering at the edge of the pond as if it were looking at her, and it amused her for another moment to imagine that all the newts she saw were just the one newt, swimming back and forth, keeping her company.

That night she dreamed again, but it was a brief and disturbing dream, when she sat at the edge of Zasharan's pool where the Watcher's Eye lay, and she strained to look into the water and see it looking out at her, but the water was dark and opaque, though she felt sure the Eye was there, and aware of her. She woke exhausted, and aching as if with physical effort.

She dreamed the same the next night, and the oppression and uselessness of it were almost too much to bear. Her head throbbed with the effort to peer through the surface of the water, and she fidgeted where she sat as if adjusting her body might help her to *see*, knowing this was not true, and yet unable to sit still nonetheless. There was a scratchy noise as she moved and resettled, and grit under her palms as she leaned on them. Sand. The ubiquitous Damarian desert sand; Zasharan had told her that usually there was no sand in the Watcher's chamber but that this year it had blown and drifted even there. She dragged her blind gaze from the water and refocussed on the sand at the edge of the pool: the same glittery, twinkly sand that had first given her her cruelly unfounded hope when she had woken at home with grains of it in her hands and nightdress.

She shifted her weight and freed one hand. *Help me,* she wrote in the sand at the edge of the pool, and as she raised her finger from the final *e,* the dream dissolved, and she heard the milk float in the street below, and knew she would be late with breakfast.

A fortnight passed, and she dreamed of Damar no more. She began to grow reaccustomed to her life above the furniture shop, housekeeper, cook, mender, minder, bookkeeper, dogsbody—nothing. Nobody. She would grow old like this. She might marry Ron or Tim; that would please her father, and tie one of them even more strongly to the shop. She supposed her father did not consider the possibility that she might not be tied to the shop herself; she supposed she did not consider the possibility either. She had raised no protest when her parents had sent Mrs. Halford and Mr. Jonah and the possibility of university and a career away; she could hardly protest now that she had a dream-world she liked better than this one and wished to go there. The paperback shelves at the grocery store testified to the popularity of dream-worlds readers could only escape to for a few hours in their imaginations. She wondered how many people dreamed of the worlds they read about in books. She tried to remember if there had been some book, some fairy-tale of her childhood, that had begun her secret love of deserts, of the sandstorm-torn time of Queen Fortunatar of the Clear Seeing, of a landscape she had never seen with her waking eyes; she could remember no book and no tale her grandmother told that was anything like what she had dreamed.

It took three weeks, but Ruth finally managed to corner her one Saturday afternoon, hoeing the vegetable garden. "No you don't," she said as Hetta picked her hoe up hastily and began to move back towards the garden shed. "I want to talk to you, and I mean to do it. Those dreams you were having about Damar lit you up, and the light's gone off again. It's not just the price of the ticket, is it? We'd get the money somehow."

Hetta dropped the hoe blade back behind the cabbages, but left it motionless. "No," she muttered. "It's not just the money." Her fingers tightened on the handle, and the blade made a few erratic scrapes at the soil.

"Then what is it?"

Hetta steadied the blade and began to hoe properly. Ruth showed no sign of going away, so at last she said: "It doesn't matter. It was a silly idea anyway. Doing something because you *dreamed* about it."

Ruth made a noise like someone trying not to yell when they've just cracked their head on a low door. She stepped round the edge of the bed and seized Hetta's wrist in both hands. Ruth was smaller than Hetta, and spent her spare time in a lab counting beetles, but Hetta was surprised at the strength of her grasp. *"Talk to me,"* said Ruth. "I have been worrying about you for *years*. Since Grandma died. You're not supposed to have to worry about your older sister when you're six. Don't you think I know you've saved *my* life? Father would have broken me like he breaks everyone he gets his hands on if I'd been the elder—like he broke Mum, like he's broken Dane, like he's broken Tim and Ron and they were even grown-ups—and Lara's going, for all that she thinks she just wants to marry Dane. You are the only one of us who has been clever enough, or stubborn enough, to save a little bit of your soul from him—maybe Grandma did, when she was still alive I wasn't paying so much attention, maybe you learned it from her—and I learned from you that it can be done. I know it, and Jeff does too—you know, with that programming stuff he can do, he's already got half his university paid for. When the time comes, nobody'll be able to say no to him. We're going to be all right—and that's thanks to *you*. It's time to save *yourself* now. That little bit of your soul seems to live in that desert of yours—if I were a shrink instead of a biologist, I'm sure I could have a really good time with *that* metaphor—I've wondered where you kept it. But you're going to lose it, now, after all, if you're not careful. What are you *waiting* for? Lara can learn to do the books—I'll tell Dane to suggest it, they'll both think it's a great idea—I'll teach her. We'll eat like hell, maybe, but there's only a year left for me and two for Jeff, and the rest of 'em are on their own. Who knows? Maybe Mum will get out of bed. Hetta. My lovely sister. Go. I'll visit you, wherever you end up."

Hetta stood trembling. In her mind's eye she saw Zasharan, sand, trees, bells, horses, tree-framed faces, the Eye, the pool. For a moment they were more real to her than the garden she stood in or the bruising grip on her wrist. She realised this—realised it and lost it again as she recognised the landscape of her *real* life—with a pain so great, she could not bear it.

She burst into tears.

She was only vaguely aware of Ruth putting an arm round her shoulders and leading her back behind the storm-broken sunflower screen and sitting her down at the pool's edge, vaguely aware of Ruth rocking her as she had many times rocked Ruth, years ago, when their mother had first taken to her bed and their father shouted all the time. She came slowly to herself again with her head on Ruth's breast, and Ruth's free hand trailing drops of cold water from the pond against her face.

She sat up slowly. Ruth waited. She began to tell Ruth everything, from the first dream. She stumbled first over saying Fortunatar's name: *Queen Fortunatar of the Clear Seeing*. And she paused before she explained what had happened in the library the day before. "It's all *imaginary*. It's not only not real, it's not even history—it's just legends. I might as well be dreaming of King Arthur and Robin Hood and Puck of Pook's Hill and Middle Earth. If—if you're right that a little of my soul lives there, then—then it's an imaginary soul too." *Nothing,* whispered her mind. *Nothing but here, now, this.* She looked at the walls around the garden; even from this, the garden's farthest point, she could hear the electric buzz of woodworking tools, and the wind, from the wrong direction today, brought them the smell of hot oil from Benny's Fish and Chips.

Ruth was silent a long time, but she held on to one of her sister's hands, and Hetta, exhausted from the effort of weeping and explaining, made no attempt to draw away. She would have to go indoors soon, and start supper. First she had to pull the fleece back over her exposed cabbages; there was going to be a frost tonight. Soon she had to do it. Not just yet.

Ruth said at last: "Well, they thought for hundreds of years that bumblebees couldn't fly, and the bumblebees went on flying while they argued about it, and then they finally figured it out. It never made any difference to the bumblebees. And I met Melanie's great-uncle once and he was no fool, and Melanie and I are friends because she's not really a space case, it's just that if she pretends to be one, she can tell her uncle's stories. Haven't you ever thought that legends have a lot of *truth* in them? History is just organised around facts. Facts aren't the whole story or the bumblebees would have had to stop flying till the scientists figured out how they could."

Hetta said wearily, "That's a little too poetical for me. Legends and poetry don't change the fact that I have to go get supper now."

Ruth said, "Wait. Wait. I'm still thinking. I'll help you with supper." Her head was bowed, and the hand that wasn't holding Hetta's was still trailing in the pool, and she flicked up water drops as if her thoughts were stinging her. "You know, I think there's a newt trying to get your attention. One of these big red fellows."

"Yes, I've met him before," said Hetta, trying to sound lighthearted, trying to go with Ruth's sudden change of subject, trying to accept that there was nothing to be done about Damarian dream-legends, and that this was her life.

"Not very newt-like behaviour," Ruth said. "Look." There was a newt swimming, back and forth, as it—he or she—had swum before. "Watch," said Ruth. She dabbled her fingers near the newt and it ducked round them and continued its tiny laps, back and forth, in front of the place where Hetta sat. Ruth dabbled again, and it ducked again, and came straight back to Hetta. "Put *your* hand in the water," said Ruth.

Hetta was still in that half-trance mood of having told her secret, and so she put her hand into the water without protest. The newt swam to her and crept up on the back of her hand. She raised her hand out of the pond, slowly, as she had done once before; the newt clung on. She stared into the small golden eyes, and watched the vertical pupil dilate as it looked back at her.

"Maybe Queen Fortunatar of the Clear Seeing is trying to send you a message," said Ruth.

Hetta dreamed again that night. She came through the door she had first entered by, when Zasharan had saved her from the storm. She came in alone, the sand swirling around her, and closed the door against the wind with her own strength. She felt well and alert and clear-headed. She dropped the scarf she had wrapped around her face, and set off, as if she knew the way, striding briskly down the corridors, the sand sliding away under her soft-booted feet, and then up a series of low stairs, where the sand grated between her soles and the stairstone. The same dim light shone as it had shone the night that Zasharan had guided her, but she often put her hand against the wall for reassurance, for the shadows seemed to fall more thickly than they had done when she was with him. She was not aware of why she chose one way rather than another, but she made every choice at every turning without hesitation.

She came to the spiral stair, and climbed it. When she put her hand to the door of the Eye's chamber, it opened.

Zasharan was standing on the far side of the pool. Hetta raised her hands and pushed her hair back from her face, suddenly needing to do something homely and familiar, suddenly feeling that nothing but her own body *was* familiar. She let her palms rest against her cheekbones briefly. The sleeves of the strange, pale, loose garment she was wearing fell back from her forearms; there was a shift beneath it, and loose trousers beneath that, and the soft boots with their long laces wrapped the trousers around her calves. Her right ankle throbbed.

Zasharan made no move to approach her. From the far side of the pool of the Eye, he said, "I thought you would not return. It has been a sennight since you disappeared. If there had not been the hollow in the sand beside the pool where you had lain, I might have believed I had dreamed you. I went back to the little room by the lowest door where I first brought you, and the dressings cabinet still lay open, and the needle lay beside it with the end of the thread I had used on your ankle, and one bandage was missing; and I could see where your blood had fallen in the sand, for no one goes there but me, and I had not swept nor put things to rights. I—when you first came, I—I thought I knew why you were here. I thought—I thought I had read the signs—not only in the sand, but in your face. I was glad. But you do not wish to come here, do you? That is what I missed, when I searched the records. That is why your story is different. Sandstorms are treacherous; I knew that; I just did not see what it meant here. It is only the blood you shed here that brings you back, the blood you shed by the treachery of the sand. That is all. I must let you go. I am glad you have come back once more, to let me say good-bye, and to apologise for trying to hold you against your will."

There were tears under Hetta's palms. She smeared them away and dropped her hands. "I—I *dream* you." She meant to say *I only dream you, you are just a dream.*

Zasharan smiled; it was a painful smile. "Of course. How else could we meet? You have told me of *Roanshire,* in a land I do not know. I should have realised . . . when you never invited me to come to you in your dreams . . ."

"*I only dream you! You are just a dream!*" Hetta put her hands to her face again, and clawed at her hair. "I looked up Queen Fortunatar in the library! She is a *legend!* She is not real! Even if she were real, she would have been real hundreds of years ago! We have airports now, and cars, and electric lights and television and computers!"

Zasharan stepped forward abruptly, to the very edge of the pool. "Queen Fortunatar is in your library?" he said. "You have read about her—you sought to read about her in your waking Roanshire?"

"Yes, yes," said Hetta impatiently. "But—"

"Why?"

"Why? Why did I?—because I *wanted* her to be real, of course! Because I want you to be real! You do not want to waste your dreaming on my life—you do not want to visit me there!—although I wish Ruth could meet you—oh, this is *absurd!* I am *dreaming*, and Queen Fortunatar is a *myth*, a fairy-tale—she is not real."

"Everything that is, is real," murmured Zasharan, as if his mind were on something else. Then he walked round the pool and held his hand out towards her. "Am I real? Take my hand."

Hetta stared at him and his outstretched hand. This was only a dream; she had touched him, dreaming, many times on her visits here; he had half-carried her out of the sandstorm, he had dressed her ankle, he had held a cup for her to drink from, he had led her to this room.

She raised her hand, but curled it up against her own body. What if, when she reached out to him, her hand went through his, as if he were a ghost? As if he were only imaginary, like a legend in a book?

Like a dream upon waking?

She held out her hand, but at the last moment she closed her eyes. Her fingers, groping, felt nothing, where his hand should be. She felt dizzy, and sick, and there was a lumpy mattress against her back, and sheets twisted uncomfortably round her body, and a fish-and-chips-and-wood-shavings smell in her nostrils.

And then it was as if his hand *bloomed* inside of hers; as if she had held a tiny, imperceptible kernel which the heat of her hand had brought suddenly to blossoming; and her feet in their boots were standing on sand-scattered stone, and she opened her eyes with a gasp, and Zasharan drew her to him and he let go her hand only to put both arms round her.

He said gently, "You must find your own way to come. The way is there. I do not know where; I do not know your world, your time, with the cars and the electricithar. If you wish to come, you must find the way. I will wait for you here."

She turned her head as it lay against his shoulder, and stared at the water of the pool at their feet. Somewhere deep within it, she thought a golden eye glittered up at her.

She woke feeling strangely calm. It was just before dawn. The first birds were trying out the occasional chirp, and the chimneys across the street were black against the greying sky. She climbed out of bed and put her dressing gown on and crept down the first flight of stairs, careful of the creaking boards, to Ruth's room. Ruth woke easily; a hand on her shoulder was enough. She put her lips to Ruth's ear. "Will you come with me?"

They made their way noiselessly downstairs, past the shop, into the back room and the garden door. There they paused briefly, baffled, for that door could not be opened silently. Hetta stood with her hand on the bolt, and for a moment she thought she saw Zasharan standing beside her, his hand over her hand. He was looking at her, but then looked up, over her shoulder, at Ruth; then he looked back at Hetta, and smiled. *I thank you*, he said: she did not hear him, but she saw his lips move. *My honour is yours*, she said, formally. Then she pulled the bolt and opened the door, and it made no sound. "Whew!" Ruth sighed.

When they reached the pool at the end of the garden, Hetta pulled Ruth into a fierce hug and said softly, "I wanted to say good-bye. I wanted someone here when I—left. I wanted to thank you. I—I don't think I will see you again."

"You are going to go live in a legend," said Ruth. "I—I'll remember the bumblebees. I—make up a legend about me, will you?"

Hetta nodded. She knelt by the pool. Its surface was still opaque in the grey dawn light, but when she put her hand to the surface of the water, the newt crept up immediately into her cupped palm. As she knelt, an edge of her dressing gown slipped forward—"You're bleeding!" said Ruth.

Hetta looked down. The scar on her ankle had opened, and a little fresh blood ran down her leg. The first drop was poised to fall. . . .

She jerked upright to her knees and thrust her foot out over the pool. The blood fell into the water: one drop, two, three. The newt was still clinging to her hand. "Ruth—"

"Go," said Ruth harshly. "Go *now*."

Hetta slipped forward, into the water, and it closed over her head.

It was a long journey, through water, through sand, through storms and darkness. She often lost track of where she was, who she was, where she was going and why; and then she felt a small skipping sensation against the palm of one hand, or the weight of a small clawed thing hanging to the hair behind her ear, or saw a goldy-black glint of eye with her own eye, and she remembered. She swam through oceans, and through deserts. She was swallowed and vomited up by a green dragon in a great stinking belch of wet black smoke. She eluded sea serpents by drifting, for, like sharks, they respond to movement; and water goblins by hiding in mud, because water goblins, being ugly themselves, are determined to notice only beautiful things, even if this means missing dinner. She was guided on her way by mer-folk, who have a strong liking for romance and adventure, and in whose company she sang her first songs, although they laughed at her for only being able to breathe air, and said that her little gold-eyed friend would teach her better. She spoke to sand-sprites, who have small hissing voices like draughts under doors, and she listened to the desert feys, who rarely speak to humans but often talk to the desert. She was almost trampled by the sand-god's great armoured horses till her little friend showed her how to hide in the hollow behind their ears and cling to their manes; but Geljdreth stood between her and what she sought and longed for, and at last she had to face him with nothing but her own determination and wit and the strength of her two hands, and a little friend hanging over one ear like an ear-ring. And, perhaps because she was from Roanshire in the Homeland where there were no deserts, and she had not lived her life in fear of him, she won out against him, and loosed his horses, and crippled his power.

At last her head broke the surface in a small calm pool; and there was Zaaran, waiting to pull her out, and wrap her in a cloak, and give her *tiarhk* to drink, as he had done once before, though he had wiped her face free of grit then, not of water. She turned to look back into the pool, and she saw a gold eye looking back at her, and she could not tell if it were a very large eye or a very small one. "Thank you," she said. "I thank you."

Somewhere—not in her ear; in her heart or her belly or the bottoms of her feet—she heard *My honour is yours*.

"Welcome home," said Zasharan.

Ruth had grown up, married, had two children, and written three best-selling books of popular science concerning the apparent impossibilities the natural world presents that scientists struggle for generations to find explanations for, before she found herself one day tapping *the legends of Damar* on her computer. Her search engine produced few relevant hits; after a brief flurry of interest for a few years following independence, Damar had again drifted into the backwaters of international attention.

It only took her a few minutes to find a reference to Queen Fortunatar of the Clear Seeing. It described her half-brother, her success as an adjudicator, and the sandstorms that particularly plagued her reign. After a few compact paragraphs the article ended:

> One of the most famous Damarian bards also began telling stories during Fortunatar's reign. Hetthar is an interesting figure, for part of her personal legend is that she came out of time and place to marry Fortunatar's Fourth Sandpale Watcher, Zasharan, and it was said that after she came, no one was ever again lost to the storms of the Kalarsham, and that the sand-god hated her for this. But her main fame rests on the cycle of stories she called The Journeying, and whose central character has the strangely un-Damarian name of Ruth.

HARUKI MURAKAMI

Thailand

Haruki Murakami was born in Kyoto, grew up in Kobe, and now lives near Tokyo. He is the author of numerous works of fiction ranging from contemporary realism to magical realism, surrealism, and satire. Widely considered to be one of Japan's greatest contemporary writers, he has won numerous literary awards including, most recently, the Yomiuri Prize, and his work has been translated into twenty-seven languages. His books include The Elephant Vanishes; Hard-Boiled Wonderland and the End of the World; South of the Border, West of the Sun; Sputnik Sweetheart; *and* A Wild Sheep Chase.

"Thailand" is a quieter piece than the Murakami tales we've published in previous volumes of The Year's Best Fantasy and Horror. *It's a subtle story, with magic at its edges, exploring the mysteries of the human heart. It comes from Murakami's most recent collection of stories,* After the Quake, *containing tales written in the aftermath of the 1995 Kobe earthquake, and is translated from the Japanese by Jay Rubin.*

—T. W.

There was an announcement: *Lettuce angel men. We aren't countering some tah bulence. Please retahn to yah seat at thees time and fasten yah seat belt.* Satsuki had been letting her mind wander, and so it took her a while to decipher the Thai steward's shaky Japanese.

She was hot and sweating. It was like a steam bath, her whole body aflame, her nylons and bra so uncomfortable she wanted to fling everything off and set herself free. She craned her neck to see the other business-class passengers. No, she was obviously the only one suffering from the heat. They were all curled up, asleep, blankets around their shoulders to counter the air-conditioning. It must be another hot flash. Satsuki bit her lip and decided to concentrate on something else to forget about the heat. She opened her book and tried to read from where she had left off, but forgetting was out of the question. This was no ordinary heat. And they wouldn't be touching down in Bangkok for hours yet. She asked a passing stewardess for some water and, finding the pill case in her pocketbook, she washed down a dose of the hormones she had forgotten to take.

Menopause: it had to be the gods' ironic warning to (or just plain nasty trick on) humanity for having artificially extended the life span, she told herself for the *n*th time. A mere hundred years ago, the average life span was less than fifty, and any woman who went on living twenty or thirty years past the end of her menstruation was an oddity. The difficulty of continuing to live with tissues for which the ovaries or the thyroid had ceased to secrete the normal supply of hormones; the possible relationship between the postmenopausal decrease in estrogen levels and the incidence of Alzheimer's: these were not questions worth troubling one's mind over. Of far more importance to the majority of mankind was the challenge of simply obtaining enough food to eat each day. Had the advancement of medicine, then, done nothing more than to expose, subdivide, and further complicate the problems faced by the human species?

Soon another announcement came over the PA system. In English this time. *If there is a doctor on board, please identify yourself to one of the cabin attendants.*

A passenger must have taken sick. For a moment Satsuki thought of volunteering, but quickly changed her mind. On the two earlier occasions when she had done so, she had merely had run-ins with practicing physicians who happened to be on the plane. These men had seemed to possess both the poise of a seasoned general commanding troops on the front line and the vision to recognize at a glance that Satsuki was a professional pathologist without combat experience. "That's all right, Doctor," she had been told with a cool smile, "I can handle this by myself. You just take it easy." She had mumbled a stupid excuse and gone back to her seat to watch the rest of some ridiculous movie.

Still, she thought, I might just be the only doctor on this plane. And the patient might be someone with a major problem involving the thyroidal immune system. If that is the case—and the likelihood of such a situation did not seem high—then even I might be of some use. She took a breath and pressed the button for a cabin attendant.

The World Thyroid Conference was a four-day event at the Bangkok Marriott. Actually, it was more like a worldwide family reunion than a conference. All the participants were thyroid specialists, and they all knew each other or were quickly introduced. It was a small world. There would be lectures and panel discussions during the day and private parties at night. Friends would get together to renew old ties, drink Australian wine, share thyroid stories, whisper gossip, update each other on their careers, tell dirty doctor jokes, and sing "Surfer Girl" at karaoke bars.

In Bangkok, Satsuki stayed mainly with her Detroit friends. Those were the ones she felt most comfortable with. She had worked at the university hospital in Detroit for almost ten years, researching the immune function of the thyroid gland. Eventually she had had a falling-out with her securities analyst husband, whose dependency on alcohol had grown worse year by year, in addition to which he had become involved with another woman—someone Satsuki knew well. They separated, and a bitter feud involving lawyers had dragged on for a full year. "The thing that finally did it for me," her husband claimed, "was that you didn't want to have children."

They had finally concluded their divorce settlement three years ago. A few months later, someone smashed the headlights of her Honda Accord in the hospital parking lot and wrote "JAP CAR" on the hood in white letters. She called the police. A big black policeman filled out the damage report and then said to her, "Lady, this is Detroit. Next time buy a Ford Taurus."

What with one thing and another, Satsuki became fed up with living in America and decided to return to Japan. She found a position at a university hospital in Tokyo. "You can't do that," said a member of her research team from India. "All our years of research are about to bear fruit. We could be nominated for a Nobel Prize—it's not that crazy," he pleaded with her to stay, but Satsuki's mind was made up. Something inside her had snapped.

She stayed on alone at the hotel in Bangkok after the conference ended. "I've worked out a vacation for myself after this," she told her friends. "I'm going to a resort near here for a complete rest—a whole week of nothing but reading, swimming, and drinking nice cold cocktails by the pool."

"That's great," they said. "Everybody needs a breather once in a while—it's good for your thyroid, too!" With handshakes and hugs and promises to get together again, Satsuki said goodbye to all her friends.

Early the next morning, a limousine pulled up to the hotel entrance as planned. It was an old navy blue Mercedes, as perfect and polished as a jewel and far more beautiful than a new car. It looked like an object from another world, as if it had dropped fully formed from someone's fantasies. A slim Thai man probably in his early sixties was to be her driver and guide. He wore a heavily starched white short-sleeved shirt, a black silk necktie, and dark sunglasses. His face was tanned, his neck long and slender. Presenting himself to Satsuki, he did not shake her hand but instead brought his hands together and gave a slight, almost Japanese, bow.

"Please call me Nimit. I will have the honor to be your companion for the coming week."

It was not clear whether "Nimit" was his first or last name. He was, in any case, "Nimit," and he told her this in a courteous, easy-to-understand English devoid of American casualness or British affectation. He had, in fact, no perceptible accent. Satsuki had heard English spoken this way before, but she couldn't remember where.

"The honor is mine," she said.

Together, they passed through Bangkok's vulgar, noisy, polluted streets. The traffic crawled along, people cursed each other, and the sound of car horns tore through the atmosphere like an air-raid siren. Plus, there were elephants lumbering down the street—and not just one or two of them. What were elephants doing in a city like this? she asked Nimit.

"Their owners bring them from the country," he explained. "They used to use them for logging, but there was not enough work for them to survive that way. They brought their animals to the city to make money doing tricks for tourists. Now there are far too many elephants here, and that makes things very difficult for the city people. Sometimes an elephant will panic and run amok. Just the other day, a great many automobiles were damaged that way. The police try to put a stop to it, of course, but they cannot confiscate the elephants from their keepers. There would be no place to put them if they did, and the cost of feeding them would be enormous. All they can do is leave them alone."

The car eventually emerged from the city, drove onto an expressway, and headed north. Nimit took a cassette tape from the glove compartment and slipped it into the car stereo, setting the volume low. It was jazz—a tune that Satsuki recognized with some emotion.

"Do you mind turning the volume up?" she asked.

"Yes, Doctor, of course," Nimit said, making it louder. The tune was "I Can't Get Started," in exactly the same performance she had heard so often in the old days.

"Howard McGhee on trumpet, Lester Young on tenor," she murmured, as if to herself. "JATP."

Nimit glanced at her in the rearview mirror. "Very impressive, Doctor," he said. "Do you like jazz?"

"My father was crazy about it," she said. "He played records for me when I was a little girl, the same ones over and over, and he had me memorize the performers. If I got them right, he'd give me candy. I still remember most of them. But just the old stuff. I don't know anything about the newer jazz musicians. Lionel Hampton, Bud Powell, Earl Hines, Harry Edison, Buck Clayton . . ."

"The old jazz is all I ever listen to as well," Nimit said. "What was your father's profession?"

"He was a doctor, too," she said. "A pediatrician. He died just after I entered high school."

"I am sorry to hear that," Nimit said. "Do you still listen to jazz?"

Satsuki shook her head. "Not really. Not for years. My husband hated jazz. All he liked was opera. We had a great stereo in the house, but he'd give me a sour look if I ever tried putting on anything besides opera. Opera lovers may be the narrowest people in the world. I left my husband, though. I don't think I'd mind if I never heard another opera again for as long as I live."

Nimit gave a little nod but said nothing. Hands on the Mercedes steering wheel, he stared silently at the road ahead. His technique with the steering wheel was almost beautiful, the way he would move his hands to exactly the same points on the wheel at exactly the same angle. Now Erroll Garner was playing "I'll Remember April," which brought back more memories for Satsuki. Garner's *Concert by the Sea* had been one of her father's favorite records. She closed her eyes and let herself sink into the old memories. Everything had gone well for her until her father died of cancer. Everything—without exception. But then the stage suddenly turned dark, and by the time she noticed that her father had vanished forever from her life, everything was headed in the wrong direction. It was as if a whole new story had started with a whole new plot. Barely a month had passed after her father's death when her mother sold the big stereo along with his jazz collection.

"Where are you from in Japan, Doctor, if you don't mind my asking?"

"I'm from Kyoto," answered Satsuki. "I only lived there until I was eighteen, though, and I've hardly ever been back."

"Isn't Kyoto right next to Kobe?"

"It's not too far, but not 'right next to' Kobe. At least the earthquake seems not to have caused too much damage there."

Nimit switched to the passing lane, slipping past a number of trucks loaded with livestock, then eased back into the cruising lane.

"I'm glad to hear it," Nimit said. "A lot of people died in the earthquake last month. I saw it on the news. It was very sad. Tell me, Doctor, did you know anyone living in Kobe?"

"No, no one. I don't think anyone I know lives in Kobe," she said. But this was not true. *He* lived in Kobe.

Nimit remained silent for a while. Then, bending his neck slightly in her direction, he said, "Strange and mysterious things, though, aren't they—earthquakes? We take it for granted that the earth beneath our feet is solid and stationary. We even talk about people being 'down to earth' or having their feet firmly planted on the ground. But suddenly one day we see that it isn't true. The earth, the boulders, that are supposed to be so solid, all of a sudden turn as mushy as liquid. I heard it on the TV news: 'liquefaction,' they call it, I think. Fortunately we rarely have major earthquakes here in Thailand."

Cradled in the rear seat, Satsuki closed her eyes and concentrated on Erroll Garner's playing. Yes, she thought, *he* lived in Kobe. I hope he was crushed to death by something big and heavy. Or swallowed up by the liquefied earth. *It's everything I've wanted for him all these years.*

The limousine reached its destination at three o'clock in the afternoon. They had taken a break at a service area along the highway at precisely twelve o'clock. Satsuki had drunk some gritty coffee and eaten half a donut at the cafeteria. Her weeklong rest was to be spent at an expensive resort in the mountains. The buildings overlooked a stream that surged through the valley, the slopes of which were covered in gorgeous primary-colored flowers. Birds flew from tree to tree emitting sharp cries. A private cottage had been prepared for Satsuki's stay. It had a big bright bathroom, an elegant canopy bed, and twenty-four-hour room service. Books and CDs and videos were available at the library off the lobby. The place was immaculate. Great care—and a great deal of money—had been lavished on every detail.

"You must be very tired, Doctor, after the long trip," Nimit said. "You can relax now. I will come to pick you up at ten o'clock tomorrow morning and take you to the pool. All you need to bring is a towel and bathing suit."

"Pool?" she asked. "They must have a perfectly big pool here at the hotel, don't they? At least that's what I was told."

"Yes, of course, but the hotel pool is very crowded. Mr. Rapaport told me that you are a serious swimmer. I found a pool nearby where you can do laps. There will be a charge, of course, but a small one. I'm sure you will like it."

John Rapaport was the American friend who had made the arrangements for Satsuki's Thai vacation. He had worked all over Southeast Asia as a news correspondent ever since the Khmer Rouge had run rampant in Cambodia, and he had many connections in Thailand as well. It was he who had recommended Nimit as Satsuki's guide and driver. With a mischievous wink, he had said to her, "You won't have to think about a thing. Just shut up and let Nimit make all the decisions and everything will go perfectly. He's a very impressive guy."

"That's fine," she said to Nimit. "I'll leave it up to you."

"Well then, I will come for you at ten o'clock tomorrow . . ."

Satsuki opened her bags, smoothed the wrinkles in a dress and skirt, and hung them in the closet. Then, changing into a swimsuit, she went to the hotel pool. Just as Nimit had said, it was not a pool for serious swimming. Gourd-shaped, it had a lovely waterfall in the middle, and children were throwing a ball in the shallow area. Abandoning any thought of trying to swim, she stretched out under a parasol, ordered a Tío Pepe and Perrier, and picked up reading where she had left off in her new John le Carré novel. When she grew tired of reading, she pulled her hat down over her face and napped. She had a dream about a rabbit—a short dream. The rabbit was in a hutch surrounded by a wire-mesh fence, trembling. It seemed to be sensing the arrival of some kind of thing in the middle of the night. At first, Satsuki was observing the rabbit from outside its enclosure, but soon she herself had become the rabbit. She could just barely make out the thing in the darkness. Even after she awoke, she had a bad taste in her mouth.

He lived in Kobe. She knew his home address and telephone number. She had never once lost track of him. She had tried calling his house just after the earthquake, but the connection never went through. I hope the damn place was flattened, she thought. I hope the whole family is out wandering through the streets, penniless. When I think of what you did to my life, when I think of the children I should have had, it's the least you deserve.

The pool that Nimit had found was half an hour's drive from the hotel and involved crossing a mountain. The woods near the top of the mountain were full of gray monkeys. They sat lined up along the road, eyes fixed on the passing cars as if to read the fates of the speeding vehicles.

The pool was inside a large, somewhat mysterious compound surrounded by a high wall and entered through an imposing iron gate. Nimit lowered his window and identified himself to the guard, who opened the gate without a word. Down the gravel driveway stood an old stone two-story building, and behind that was the long, narrow pool. Its signs of age were unmistakable, but this was an authentic three-lane, twenty-five-meter lap pool. The rectangular stretch of water was beautiful, surrounded by lawn and trees, and undisturbed by swimmers. Several old wooden deck chairs were lined up beside the pool. Silence ruled the area, and there was no hint of a human presence.

"What do you think, Doctor?" Nimit asked.

"Wonderful," Satsuki said. "Is this an athletic club?"

"Something like that," he said. "But hardly anyone uses it now. I have arranged for you to swim here alone as much as you like."

"Why, thank you so much, Nimit. You *are* an impressive man."

"You do me too great an honor," Nimit said, bowing blank-faced, with old-school courtesy. "The cottage over there is the changing room. It has toilets and showers. Feel free to use all the facilities. I will station myself by the automobile. Please let me know if there is anything you need."

Satsuki had always loved swimming, and she went to the gym pool whenever she had a chance. She had learned proper form from a coach. While she swam, she was able to thrust all unpleasant memories from her mind. If she swam long enough, she could reach a point where she felt utterly free, like a bird flying through the sky. Thanks to her years of regular exercise, she had never been confined to bed with an illness or sensed any physical disorder. Nor had she gained extra weight. Of course, she was not young anymore; a trim body was no longer an option. In particular, there was almost no way to avoid putting on a little extra flesh at the hips. You could ask for only so much. She wasn't trying to become a fashion model. She probably looked five years younger than her actual age, which was pretty damn good.

At noon, Nimit served her ice tea and sandwiches on a silver tray by the pool—tiny vegetable and cheese sandwiches cut into perfect little triangles.

Satsuki was amazed. "Did you make these?"

The question brought a momentary change to Nimit's expressionless face. "Not I, Doctor. I do not prepare food. I had someone make this."

Satsuki was about to ask who that someone might be when she stopped herself. John Rapaport had told her, "Just shut up and let Nimit make all the decisions, and everything will go perfectly." The sandwiches were quite good. Satsuki rested after lunch. On her Walkman she listened to a tape of the Benny Goodman Sextet that Nimit had lent her, after which she continued with her book. She swam some more in the afternoon, returning to the hotel at three.

Satsuki repeated exactly the same routine for five days in a row. She swam to her heart's content, ate vegetable and cheese sandwiches, listened to music, and read. She never stepped out of the hotel except to go to the pool. What she wanted was perfect rest, a chance not to *think* about anything.

She was the only one using the pool. The water was always freezing cold, as if it had been drawn from an underground stream in the hills, and the first dunk always took her breath away, but a few laps would warm her up, and then the water temperature was just right. When she tired of doing the crawl, she would remove her goggles and swim backstroke. White clouds floated in the sky, and birds and dragonflies cut across them. Satsuki wished she could stay like this forever.

"Where did you learn English?" Satsuki asked Nimit on the way back from the pool.

"I worked for thirty-three years as a chauffeur for a Norwegian gem dealer in Bangkok, and I always spoke English with him."

So that explained the familiar style. One of Satsuki's colleagues at a hospital where she had worked in Baltimore, a Dane, had spoken exactly this kind of English—precise grammar, light accent, no slang. Very clean, very easy to understand, and somewhat lacking in color. How strange to be spoken to in Norwegian English in Thailand!

"My employer loved jazz. He always had a tape playing when he was in the car. Which is why, as his driver, I naturally became familiar with it as well. When he died three years ago, he left me the car and all his tapes. The one we are listening to now is one of his."

"So when he died, you became an independent driver-guide for foreigners, is that it?"

"Yes, exactly," Nimit said. "There are many driver-guides in Thailand, but I am probably the only one with his own Mercedes."

"He must have placed a great deal of trust in you."

Nimit was silent for a long time. He seemed to be searching for the right words to respond to Satsuki's remark. "You know, Doctor, I am a bachelor. I have never once married. I spent thirty-three years as another man's shadow. I went everywhere he went, I helped him with everything he did. I was in a sense a part of him. When you live like that for a long time, you gradually lose track of what it is that you yourself really want out of life."

He turned up the volume on the car stereo a little: a deep-throated tenor sax solo.

"Take this music for example. I remember exactly what he told me about it. 'Listen to this, Nimit. Follow Coleman Hawkins' improvised lines very carefully. He is using them to tell us something. Pay very close attention. He is telling us the story of the free spirit that is doing everything it can to escape from within him. That same kind of spirit is inside me, and inside you. There—you can hear it, I'm sure: the hot breath, the shiver of the heart.' Hearing the same music over and over, I learned to listen closely, to hear the sound of the spirit. But still I cannot be sure if I really did hear it with my own ears. When you are with a person for a long time and following his orders, in a sense you become one with him, like husband and wife. Do you see what I am saying, Doctor?"

"I think so," answered Satsuki.

It suddenly struck her that Nimit and his Norwegian employer might have been lovers. She had no evidence on which to base such an assumption, merely a flash of intuition. But it might explain what Nimit was trying to say.

"Still, Doctor, I do not have the slightest regret. If I could live my life over again, I would probably do exactly the same thing. What about you?"

"I don't know, Nimit. I really don't know."

Nimit said nothing after that. They crossed the mountain with the gray monkeys and returned to the hotel.

On her last day before leaving for Japan, Nimit took Satsuki to a nearby village instead of driving straight back to the hotel.

"I have a favor to ask of you," he said, meeting her eyes in the rearview mirror. "A personal favor."

"What is it?"

"Could you perhaps spare me an hour of your time? I have a place that I would like to show you."

Satsuki had no objection, nor did she ask him where he was taking her. She had decided to place herself entirely in his hands.

The woman lived in a small house at the far edge of the village—a poor house in a poor village, with one tiny rice paddy after another crammed in layers up a hillside. Filthy, emaciated livestock. Muddy, pockmarked road. Air filled with the smell of water buffalo dung. A bull wandered by, its genitals swinging. A 50cc motorcycle buzzed past, splashing mud to either side. Near-naked children stood lined up along the road, staring at the Mercedes. Satsuki was shocked to think that such a miserable village could be situated so close to the high-class resort hotel in which she was staying.

The woman was old, perhaps almost eighty. Her skin had the blackened look of worn leather, its deep wrinkles becoming ravines that seemed to travel to all parts of her body. Her back was bent, and a flower-patterned, oversize dress hung limp from her bony frame. When he saw her, Nimit brought his hands together in greeting. She did the same.

Satsuki and the old woman sat down on opposite sides of a table, and Nimit took his place at one end. At first, only the woman and Nimit spoke. Satsuki had no idea what they were saying to each other, but she noticed how lively and powerful the woman's voice was for someone her age. The old woman seemed to have a full set of teeth, too. After a while, she turned from Nimit to face Satsuki, looking directly into her eyes. She had a penetrating gaze, and she never blinked. Satsuki began to feel like a small animal that has been trapped in a room with no way to escape. She realized she was sweating all over. Her face burned, and she had trouble breathing. She wanted to take a pill, but she had left her bottle of mineral water in the car.

"Please put your hands on the table," Nimit said. Satsuki did as she was told. The old woman reached out and took her right hand. The woman's hands were small but powerful. For a full ten minutes (though it might just as well have been two or three), the old woman stared into Satsuki's eyes and held her hand, saying nothing. Satsuki returned the woman's strong stare with her timid one, using the handkerchief in her left hand to mop her brow from time to time. Eventually, with a great sigh, the old woman released Satsuki's hand. She turned to Nimit and said something in Thai. Nimit translated into English.

"She says that there is a stone inside your body. A hard, white stone. About the size of a child's fist. She does not know where it came from."

"A stone?" Satsuki asked.

"There is something written on the stone, but she cannot read it because it is in Japanese: small black characters of some kind. The stone and its inscription are old, old things. You have been living with them inside you for a very long time. You must get rid of the stone. Otherwise, after you die and are cremated, only the stone will remain."

Now the old woman turned back to face Satsuki and spoke slowly in Thai for a long time. Her tone of voice made it clear that she was saying something important. Again Nimit translated.

"You are going to have a dream soon about a large snake. In your dream, it will be easing its way out of a hole in a wall—a green, scaly snake. Once it has pushed out three feet from the wall, you must grab its neck and never let go. The snake will look very frightening, but in fact it can do you no harm, so you must not be frightened. Hold on to it with both hands. Think of it as your life, and hold on to it with all your strength. Keep holding it until you wake from your dream. The snake will swallow your stone for you. Do you understand?"

"What in the world—?"

"Just say you understand," Nimit said with the utmost gravity.

"I understand," Satsuki said.

The old woman gave a gentle nod and spoke again to Satsuki.

"The man is not dead," translated Nimit. "He did not receive a scratch. It may not be what you wanted, but it was actually very lucky for you that he was not hurt. You should be grateful for your good fortune."

The woman uttered a few short syllables.

"That is all," Nimit said. "We can go back to the hotel now."

"Was that some kind of fortune-telling?" Satsuki asked when they were back in the car.

"No, Doctor. It was not fortune-telling. Just as you treat people's bodies, she treats people's spirits. She predicts their dreams, mostly."

"I should have left her something then, as a token of thanks. The whole thing was such a surprise to me, it slipped my mind."

Nimit negotiated a sharp curve on the mountain road, turning the wheel in that precise way of his. "I paid her," he said. "A small amount. Not enough for you to trouble yourself over. Just think of it as a mark of my personal regard for you, Doctor."

"Do you take all of your clients there?"

"No, Doctor, only you."

"And why is that?"

"You are a beautiful person, Doctor. Clearheaded. Strong. But you seem always to be dragging your heart along the ground. From now on, little by little, you must prepare yourself to face death. If you devote all of your future energy to living, you will not be able to die well. You must begin to shift gears, a little at a time. Living and dying are, in a sense, of equal value."

"Tell me something, Nimit," Satsuki said, taking off her sunglasses and leaning over the back of the passenger seat.

"What is that, Doctor?"

"Are *you* prepared to die?"

"I am half dead already," Nimit said as if stating the obvious.

That night, lying in her broad, pristine bed, Satsuki wept. She recognized that she was headed toward death. She recognized that she had a hard, white stone inside herself. She recognized that a scaly, green snake was lurking somewhere in the dark. She thought about the child to which she never gave birth. She had destroyed that child, flung it down a bottomless well. And then she had spent thirty years hating one man. She had hoped that he would die in agony. In order to bring that about, she had gone so far as to wish in the depths of her heart for an earthquake. In a sense, she told herself, I am the one who caused that earthquake. *He* turned my heart into a stone; *he* turned my body to stone. In the distant mountains, the gray monkeys were silently staring at her. *Living and dying are, in a sense, of equal value.*

After checking her bags at the airline counter, Satsuki handed Nimit an envelope containing a one hundred-dollar bill. "Thank you for everything, Nimit. You made it possible for me to have a wonderful rest. This is a personal gift from me to you."

"That is very thoughtful of you, Doctor," said Nimit, accepting the envelope. "Thank you very much."

"Do you have time for a cup of coffee?"

"Yes, I would enjoy that."

They went to a café together. Satsuki took hers black. Nimit gave his a heavy dose of cream. For a long time, Satsuki went on turning her cup in her saucer.

"You know," she said at last, "I have a secret that I've never told anyone. I could never bring myself to talk about it. I've kept it locked up inside of me all this time. But I'd like to tell it to you now. Because we'll probably never meet again. When my father died all of a sudden, my mother, without a word to me—"

Nimit held his hands up, palms facing Satsuki, and shook his head. "Please, Doctor. Don't tell me anymore. You should have your dream, as the old woman told you to. I understand how you feel, but if you put those feelings into words they will turn into lies."

Satsuki swallowed her words, and then, in silence, closed her eyes. She drew in a full, deep breath, and let it out again.

"Have your dream, Doctor," Nimit said as if sharing kindly advice. "What you need now more than anything is discipline. Cast off mere words. Words turn into stone."

He reached out and took Satsuki's hand between his. His hands were strangely smooth and youthful, as if they had always been protected by expensive leather gloves. Satsuki opened her eyes and looked at him. Nimit took away his hands and rested them on the table, fingers intertwined.

"My Norwegian employer was actually from Lapland," he said. "You must know, of course, that Lapland is at the northernmost tip of Norway, near the North Pole. Many reindeer live there. In summer there is no night, and in winter no day. He probably came to Thailand because the cold got to be too much for him. I guess you could call the two places complete opposites. He loved Thailand, and he made up his mind to have his bones buried here. But still, to the day he died, he missed the town in Lapland where he was born. He used to tell me about it all the time. And yet, in spite of that, he never once went back to Norway in thirty-three years. Something must have happened there that kept him away. He was another person with a stone inside."

Nimit lifted his coffee cup and took a sip, then carefully set it in its saucer again without a sound.

"He once told me about polar bears—what solitary animals they are. They mate just once a year. One time in a whole year. There is no such thing as a lasting male-female bond in their world. One male polar bear and one female polar bear meet by sheer chance somewhere in the frozen vastness, and they mate. It doesn't take long. And once they are finished, the male runs away from the female as if he is frightened to death: he runs from the place where they have mated. He never looks back—literally. The rest of the year he lives in deep solitude. Mutual communication—the touching of two hearts—does not exist for them. So, that is the story of polar bears—or at least it is what my employer told me about them."

"How very strange," Satsuki said.

"Yes," Nimit said, "it *is* strange." His face was grave. "I remember asking my employer, 'Then what do polar bears exist for?' 'Yes, exactly,' he said with a big smile. 'Then what do *we* exist for, Nimit?' "

The plane reached cruising altitude and the FASTEN SEAT BELT sign went out. So, thought Satsuki, I'm going back to Japan. She tried to think about what lay ahead, but soon gave up. "Words turn into stone," Nimit had told her. She settled deep into her seat and closed her eyes. All at once the image came to her of the sky she had seen while swimming on her back. And Erroll Garner's "I'll Remember April." Let me sleep, she thought. Just let me sleep. And wait for the dream to come.

THEODORA GOSS

The Rose in Twelve Petals

Theodora Goss lives in Boston, Massachusetts, where she is working on her Ph.D. in English Literature. Her poetry has appeared in The Lyric, Dreams of Decadence, *and* Lady Churchill's Rosebud Wristlet, *among other journals, and has thrice received Honorable Mention designations in* The Year's Best Fantasy and Horror. *"The Rose in Twelve Petals," which first appeared in the April 2002 issue of* Realms of Fantasy, *is her first published story. This gorgeous retelling of Sleeping Beauty makes for a powerful fiction debut.*

—T. W.

I. The Witch

This rose has 12 petals. Let the first one fall: Madeleine taps the glass bottle, and out tumbles a bit of pink silk that clinks on the table—a chip of tinted glass—no, look closer, a crystallized rose petal. She lifts it into a saucer and crushes it with the back of a spoon until it is reduced to lumpy powder and a puff of fragrance.

She looks at the book again. "Petal of one rose crushed, dung of small bat soaked in vinegar." Not enough light comes through the cottage's small-paned windows, and besides she is growing nearsighted, although she is only 32. She leans closer to the page. He should have given her spectacles rather than pearls. She wrinkles her forehead to focus her eyes, which makes her look prematurely old, as in a few years she no doubt will be.

Bat dung has a dank, uncomfortable smell, like earth in caves that has never seen sunlight.

Can she trust it, this book? Two pounds 10 shillings it cost her, including postage. She remembers the notice in *The Gentle-woman's Companion*: "Every lady her own magician. Confound your enemies, astonish your friends! As simple as a cookery manual." It looks magical enough, with *Compendium Magicarum* stamped on its spine and gilt pentagrams on its red leather cover. But the back pages advertise "a most miraculous lotion that will make any lady's skin as smooth as an infant's bottom" and the collected works of Scott.

Not easy to spare 10 shillings, not to mention two pounds, now that the King has cut off her income. Rather lucky, this cottage coming so cheap, although it has no proper plumbing, just a privy out back among the honeysuckle.

Madeleine crumbles a pair of dragonfly wings into the bowl, which is already half full: orris root; cat's bones found on the village dust heap; oak gall from a branch fallen into a fairy ring; madder, presumably for its color; crushed rose petal; bat dung.

And the magical words, are they quite correct? She knows a little Latin, learned from her brother. After her mother's death, when her father began spending days in his bedroom with a bottle of beer, she tended the shop, selling flour and printed cloth to the village women, scythes and tobacco to the men, sweets to children on their way to school. When her brother came home, he would sit at the counter beside her, saying his *amo, amas*. The silver cross he earned by taking a Hibernian bayonet in the throat is the only necklace she now wears.

She binds the mixture with water from a hollow stone and her own saliva. Not pleasant this, she was brought up not to spit, but she imagines she is spitting into the King's face that first time when he came into the shop, and leaned on the counter, and smiled through his golden beard. "If I had known there was such a pretty shopkeeper in this village, I would have done my own shopping long ago."

She remembers: buttocks covered with golden hair among folds of white linen, like twin halves of a peach on a napkin. "Come here, Madeleine." The sounds of the palace, horses clopping, page-boys shouting to one another in the early morning air. "You'll never want for anything, haven't I told you that?" A string of pearls, each as large as her smallest fingernail, with a clasp of gold filigree. "Like it? That's Hibernian work, taken in the siege of London." Only later does she notice that between two pearls, the knotted silk is stained with blood.

She leaves the mixture under cheesecloth, to dry overnight.

Madeleine walks into the other room, the only other room of the cottage, and sits at the table that serves as her writing desk. She picks up a tin of throat lozenges. How it rattles. She knows, without opening it, that there are five pearls left, and that after next month's rent there will only be four.

Confound your enemies, she thinks, peering through the inadequate light, and the wrinkles on her forehead make her look prematurely old, as in a few years she certainly will be.

II. The Queen

Petals fall from the roses that hang over the stream, Empress Josephine and Gloire de Dijon, which dislike growing so close to the water. This corner of the garden has been planted to resemble a country landscape in miniature: artificial stream with ornamental fish, a pear tree that has never yet bloomed, bluebells that the gardener plants out every spring. This is the Queen's favorite part of the garden, although the roses dislike her as well, with her romantically diaphanous gowns, her lisping voice, her poetry.

Here she comes, reciting Tennyson.

She holds her arms out, allowing her sleeves to drift on the slight breeze, imagining she is Elaine the lovable, floating on a river down to Camelot. Hard, being a lily maid now her belly is swelling.

She remembers her belly reluctantly, not wanting to touch it, unwilling to acknowledge that it exists. Elaine the lily maid had no belly, surely, she thinks, forgetting that Galahad must have been born somehow. (Perhaps he rose out of the lake?) She imagines her belly as a cavern where something is growing in the darkness, something that is not hers, alien and unwelcome.

Only 12 months ago (14, actually, but she is bad at numbers), she was Princess Elizabeth of Hibernia, dressed in pink satin, gossiping about the riding master with her friends, dancing with her brothers through the ruined arches of Westminster Cathedral, and eating too much cake at her 17th birthday party. Now, and she does not want to think about this so it remains at the edges of her mind, where unpleasant things, frogs and slugs, reside, she is a cavern with something growing inside her, something repugnant, something that is not hers, not the lily maid of Astolat's.

She reaches for a rose, an overblown Gloire de Dijon that, in a fit of temper, pierces her finger with its thorns. She cries out, sucks the blood from her finger, and flops down on the bank like a miserable child. The hem of her diaphanous dress begins to absorb the mud at the edge of the water.

III. The Magician

Wolfgang Magus places the rose he picked that morning in his buttonhole and looks at his reflection in the glass. He frowns, as his master Herr Doktor Ambrosius would have frowned, at the scarecrow in faded wool with a drooping gray mustache. A sad figure for a court magician.

Gott in Himmel, he says to himself, a childhood habit he has kept from nostalgia, for Wolfgang Magus is a reluctant atheist. He knows it is not God's fault but the King's, who pays him so little. If the King were to pay him, say, another shilling per week—but no, that too he would send to his sister, dying of consumption at a spa in Berne. His mind turns, painfully, from the memory of her face, white and drained, which already haunts him like a ghost.

He picks up a volume of Goethe's poems that he has carefully tied with a bit of pink ribbon and sighs. What sort of present is this for the Princess's christening?

He enters the chapel with shy, stooping movements. It is full, and noisy with court gossip. As he proceeds up the aisle, he is swept by a Duchess's train of peau de soie, poked by a Viscountess's aigrette. The sword of a Marquis smelling of Napoleon-water tangles in his legs, and he almost falls on a Baroness, who stares at him through her lorgnette. He sidles through the crush until he comes to a corner of the chapel wall, where he takes refuge.

The christening has begun, he supposes, for he can hear the Archbishop droning in bad Latin, although he can see nothing from his corner but taxidermed birds and heads slick with macassar oil. Ah, if the Archbishop could have learned from Herr Doktor Ambrosius! His mind wanders, as it often does, to a house in Berlin and a laboratory smelling of strong soap, filled with braziers and alembics, books whose covers have been half-eaten by moths, a stuffed basilisk. He remembers his bed in the attic, and his sister, who worked as the Herr Doktor's housemaid so he could learn to be a magician. He sees her face on her pillow at the spa in Berne and thinks of her expensive medications.

What has he missed? The crowd is moving forward, and presents are being given: a rocking horse with a red leather saddle, a silver tumbler, a cap embroidered by the nuns of Iona. He hides the volume of Goethe behind his back.

Suddenly, he sees a face he recognizes. One day she came and sat beside him in the garden and asked about his sister. Her brother had died, he remembers, not long before, and as he described his loneliness, her eyes glazed over with tears. Even he, who understands little about court politics, knew she was the King's mistress.

She disappears behind the scented Marquis, then appears again, close to the altar where the Queen, awkwardly holding a linen bundle, is receiving the Princess's presents. The King has seen her, and frowns through his golden beard. Wolfgang Magus, who knows nothing about the feelings of a king toward his former mistress, wonders why he is angry.

She lifts her hand in a gesture that reminds him of the Archbishop. What fragrance is this, so sweet, so dark, that makes the brain clear, that makes the nostrils water? He instinctively tabulates: orris root, oak gall, rose petal, dung of bat with a hint of vinegar.

Conversations hush, until even the Baronets, clustered in a rustic dump at the back of the chapel, are silent.

She speaks: "This is the gift I give the Princess. On her 17th birthday she will prick her finger on the spindle of a spinning wheel and die."

Needless to describe the confusion that follows. Wolfgang Magus watches from its edge, chewing his mustache, worried, unhappy. How her eyes glazed, that day in the garden. Someone treads on his toes.

Then, unexpectedly, he is summoned. "Where is that blasted magician!" Gloved hands push him forward. He stands before the King, whose face has turned unattractively red. The Queen has fainted and a bottle of salts is waved under her nose. The Archbishop is holding the Princess like a sack of barley he has accidentally caught.

"Is this magic, Magus, or just some bloody trick?"

Wolfgang Magus rubs his hands together. He has not stuttered since he was a child, but he answers, "Y-yes, your Majesty. Magic." Sweet, dark, utterly magic. He can smell its power.

"Then get rid of it. Un-magic it. Do whatever you bloody well have to. Make it not be!"

Wolfgang Magus already knows that he will not be able to do so, but he says, without realizing that he is chewing his mustache in front of the King, "O-of course, your Majesty."

IV. The King

What would you do, if you were James IV of Britannia, pacing across your council chamber floor before your councilors: the Count of Edinburgh, whose estates are larger than yours and include hillsides of uncut wood for which the French Emperor, who needs to refurbish his navy after the disastrous Indian campaign, would pay handsomely; the Earl of York, who can trace descent, albeit in the female line, from the Tudors; and the Archbishop, who has preached against marital infidelity in his cathedral at Aberdeen? The banner over your head, embroidered with the 12-petaled rose of Britannia, reminds you that your claim to the throne rests tenuously on a former James's dalliance. Edinburgh's thinning hair, York's hanging jowl, the seams, edged with gold thread, where the Archbishop's robe has been let out, warn you, young as you are, with a beard that shines like a tangle of golden wires in the afternoon light, of your gouty future.

Britannia's economy depends on the wool trade, and spun wool sells for twice as much as unspun. Your income depends on the wool tax. The Queen, whom you seldom think of as Elizabeth, is young. You calculate: three months before she recovers from the birth, nine months before she can deliver another child. You might have an heir by next autumn.

"Well?" Edinburgh leans back in his chair, and you wish you could strangle his wrinkled neck.

You say, "I see no reason to destroy a thousand spinning wheels for one madwoman." Madeleine, her face puffed with sleep, her neck covered with a line of red spots where she lay on the pearl necklace you gave her the night before, one black hair tickling your ear. Clever of her, to choose a spinning wheel. "I rely entirely on Wolfgang Magus," whom you believe is a fraud. "Gentlemen, your fairy tales will have taught you that magic must be met with magic. One cannot fight a spell by altering material conditions."

Guffaws from the Archbishop, who is amused to think that he once read fairy tales.

You are a selfish man, James IV, and this is essentially your fault, but you have spoken the truth. Which, I suppose, is why you are the King.

V. The Queen Dowager

What is the girl doing? Playing at tug-of-war, evidently, and far too close to the stream. She'll tear her dress on the rosebushes. Careless, these young people, thinks the Queen Dowager. And who is she playing with? Young Lord Harry, who will one day be Count of Edinburgh. The Queen Dowager is proud of her keen eyesight and will not wear spectacles, although she is almost 63.

What a pity the girl is so plain. The Queen Dowager jabs her needle into a black velvet slipper. Eyes like boiled gooseberries that always seem to be staring at you, and no discipline. Now in her day, thinks the Queen Dowager, remembering backboards and nuns who rapped your fingers with canes, in her day girls had discipline. Just look at the Queen: no discipline. Two miscarriages in 10 years, and dead before her 30th birthday. Of course linen is so much cheaper now that the kingdoms are united. But if only her Jims (which is how she thinks of the King) could have married that nice German princess.

She jabs the needle again, pulls it out, jabs, knots. She holds up the slipper and then its pair, comparing the roses embroidered on each toe in stitches so even they seem to have been made by a machine. Quite perfect for her Jims, to keep his feet warm on the drafty palace floors.

A tearing sound, and a splash. The girl, of course, as the Queen Dowager could have warned you. Just look at her, with her skirt ripped up one side and her petticoat muddy to the knees.

"I do apologize, Madam. I assure you it's entirely my fault," says Lord Harry, bowing with the superfluous grace of a dancing master.

"It *is* all your fault," says the girl, trying to kick him.

"Alice!" says the Queen Dowager. Imagine the Queen wanting to name the girl Elaine. What a name, for a Princess of Britannia.

"But he took my book of poems and said he was going to throw it into the stream!"

"I'm perfectly sure he did no such thing. Go to your room at once. This is the sort of behavior I would expect from a chimney sweep."

"Then tell him to give my book back!"

Lord Harry bows again and holds out the battered volume. "It was always yours for the asking, your Highness."

Alice turns away, and you see what the Queen Dowager cannot, despite her keen vision: Alice's eyes, slightly prominent, with irises that are indeed the color of gooseberries, have turned red at the corners, and her nose has begun to drip.

VI. The Spinning Wheel

It has never wanted to be an assassin. It remembers the cottage on the Isles where it was first made: the warmth of the hearth and the feel of its maker's hands, worn smooth from rubbing and lanolin.

It remembers the first words it heard: "And why are you carving roses on it, then?"

"This one's for a lady. Look how slender it is. It won't take your upland ram's wool. Yearling it'll have to be, for this one."

At night it heard the waves crashing on the rocks, and it listened as their sound mingled with the snoring of its maker and his wife. By day it heard the crying of the sea birds. But it remembered, as in a dream, the songs of inland birds and sunlight on a stone wall. Then the fishermen would come, and one would say, "What's that you're making there, Enoch? Is it for a midget, then?"

Its maker would stroke it with the tips of his fingers and answer, "Silent, lads. This one's for a lady. It'll spin yarn so fine that a shawl of it will slip through a wedding ring."

It has never wanted to be an assassin, and as it sits in a cottage to the south, listening as Madeleine mutters to herself, it remembers the sounds of sea birds and tries to forget that it was made, not to spin yarn so fine that a shawl of it will slip through a wedding ring, but to kill the King's daughter.

VII. The Princess

Alice climbs the tower stairs. She could avoid this perhaps, disguise herself as a peasant woman and beg her way to the Highlands, like a heroine in Scott's novels. But she does not want to avoid this, so she is climbing up the tower stairs on the morning of her 17th birthday, still in her nightgown and clutching a battered copy of Goethe's poems whose binding is so torn that the book is tied with pink ribbon to keep the pages together. Her feet are bare, because opening the shoe closet might have woken the Baroness, who has slept in her room since she was a child. Barefoot, she has walked silently past the sleeping guards, who are supposed to guard her today with particular care. She has walked past the Queen Dowager's drawing room thinking: *If anyone hears me, I will be in disgrace.* She has spent a larger portion of her life in disgrace than out of it, and she remembers that she once thought of it as an imaginary country, Disgrace, with its own rivers and towns and trade routes. Would it be different if her mother were alive? She remembers a face creased from the folds of the pillow, and pale lips whispering to her about the lily maid of Astolat. It would, she supposes, have made no difference. She trips on a step and almost drops the book.

She has no reason to suppose, of course, that the Witch will be there, so early in the morning. But somehow, Alice hopes she will be.

She is, sitting on a low stool with a spinning wheel in front of her.

"Were you waiting for me?" asks Alice. It sounds silly—who else would the Witch be waiting for? But she can think of nothing else to say.

"I was." The Witch's voice is low and cadenced, and although she has wrinkles at the corners of her mouth and her hair has turned gray, she is still rather beautiful. She is not, exactly, what Alice expected.

"How did you know I was coming so early?"

The Witch smiles. "I've gotten rather good at magic. I sell fortunes for my living, you see. It's not much, just enough to buy bread and butter and to rent a small cottage. But it amuses me, knowing things about people—their lives and their future."

"Do you know anything—about me?" Alice looks down at the book. What idiotic questions to be asking. Surely a heroine from Scott's novels would think of better.

The Witch nods, and sunlight catches the silver cross suspended from a chain around her neck. She says, "I'm sorry."

Alice understands, and her face flushes. "You mean that you've been watching all along. That you've known what it's been like, being the cursed princess." She turns and walks to the tower window, so the Witch will not see how her hands are shaking. "You know the other girls wouldn't play with me or touch my toys, that the boys would spit over their shoulder, to break the curse they said. Even the chambermaids would make the sign of the cross when I wasn't looking." She can feel tears where they always begin, at the corners of her eyes, and she leans out the window to cool her face. Far below, a gardener is crossing the courtyard, carrying a pair of pruning shears. She says, "Why didn't you remove the curse, then?"

"Magic doesn't work that way." The Witch's voice is sad. Alice turns around and sees that her cheeks are wet with tears. Alice steps toward her, trips again, and drops the book, which falls under the spinning wheel.

The Witch picks it up and smiles as she examines the cover. "Of course, your Goethe. I always wondered what happened to Wolfgang Magus."

Alice thinks with relief: *I'm not going to cry after all.* "He went away, after his sister died. She had consumption, you know, for years and years. He was always sending her money for medicine. He wrote to me once after he left, from Berlin, to say that he had bought his old master's house. But I never heard from him again."

The Witch wipes her cheeks with the back of one hand. "I didn't know about his sister's death. I spoke to him once. He was a kind man."

Alice takes the book from her, then says, carefully, as though each word has to be placed in the correct order, "Do you think his spell will work? I mean, do you think I'll really sleep for a hundred years, rather than—you know?"

The Witch looks up, her cheeks still damp, but her face composed. "I can't answer that for you. You may simply be—preserved. In a pocket of time, as it were."

Alice tugs at the ribbon that binds the book together. "It doesn't matter, really. I don't think I care either way." She strokes the spinning wheel, which turns as she touches it. "How beautiful, as though it had been made just for me."

The Witch raises a hand, to stop her perhaps, or to arrest time itself, but Alice places her finger on the spindle and presses until a drop of blood blossoms, as dark as the petal of a Cardinal de Richelieu, and runs into her palm.

Before she falls, she sees the Witch with her head bowed and her shoulders shaking. She thinks, for no reason she can remember, *Elaine the fair, Elaine the lovable . . .*

VIII. The Gardener

Long after, when the gardener has grown into an old man, he will tell his grandchildren about that day: skittish horses being harnessed by panicked grooms, nobles struggling with boxes while their valets carry armchairs and even bedsteads through the palace halls, the King in a pair of black velvet slippers shouting directions. The cooks leave the kettles whistling in the kitchen, the Queen Dowager leaves her jewels lying where she has dropped them while tripping over the hem of her nightgown. Everyone runs to escape the spreading lethargy that has already caught a canary in his cage, who makes soft noises as he settles into his feathers. The flowers are closing in the garden, and even the lobsters that the chef was planning to serve with melted butter for lunch have lain down in a corner of their tank.

In a few hours, the palace is left to the canary, and the lobsters, and the Princess lying on the floor of the tower.

He will say, "I was pruning a rosebush at the bottom of the tower that day. Look what I took away with me!" Then he will display a rose of the variety called Britannia, with its 12 petals half-open, still fresh and moist with dew. His granddaughter will say, "Oh, grandpa, you picked that in the garden just this morning!" His grandson, who is practical and wants to be an engineer, will say, "Grandpa, people can't sleep for a hundred years."

IX. The Tower

Let us get a historical perspective. When the tower was quite young, only a hovel really, a child knocked a stone out of its wall, and it gained an eye. With that eye it watched as the child's father, a chieftain, led his tribe against soldiers with metal breastplates and plumed helmets. Two lines met on the plain below: one regular, gleaming in the morning sun like the edge of a sword, the other ragged and blue like the crest of a wave. The wave washed over the sword, which splintered into a hundred pieces.

Time passed, and the tower gained a second story with a vertical eye as narrow as a staff. It watched a wooden structure grow beside it, in which men and cattle mingled indiscriminately. One morning it felt a prick, the point of an arrow. A bright flame blossomed from the beams of the wooden structure, men scattered, cattle screamed. One of its walls was singed, and it felt the wound as a distant heat. A castle rose, commanded by a man with eyebrows so blond that they were almost white, who caused the name Aelfric to be carved on the lintel of the tower. The castle's stone walls, pummeled with catapults, battered by rams, fell into fragments. From the hilltop a man watched, whose nose had been broken in childhood and remained perpetually crooked. When a palace rose from the broken rock, he caused the name D'Arblay to be carved on the lintel of the tower, beside a boar rampant.

Time passed, and a woman on a white horse rode through the village that had grown around the palace walls, followed by a retinue that stretched behind her like a scarf. At the palace gates, a Darbley grown rich on tobacco plantations in the New World presented her with the palace, in honor of her marriage to the Earl of Essex. The lintel of the tower was carved with the name Elizabeth I, and it gained a third story with a lead-paned window, through which it saw in facets like a fly. One morning it watched the Queen's son, who had been playing ball in the courtyard, fall to the ground with blood dripping from his nostrils. The windows of the palace were draped in black velvet, the Queen and her consort rode away with their retinue, and the village was deserted.

Time passed. Leaves turned red or gold, snow fell and melted into rivulets, young hawks took their first flight from the battlements. A rosebush grew at the foot of the tower: a hybrid, half wild rose, half Cuisse de Nymphe, with 12 petals and briary canes. One morning men rode up to the tower on horses whose hides were mottled with sweat. In its first story, where the chieftain's son had played, they talked of James III. Troops were coming from France, and the password was "Britannia." As they left the tower, one of them plucked a flower from the rosebush. "Let this be our symbol," he said in the self-conscious voice of a man who thinks that his words will be recorded in history books. The tower thought it would be alone again, but by the time the leaves had turned, a procession rode up to the palace gates, waving banners embroidered with a 12-petaled rose. Furniture arrived from France, fruit trees were planted, and the village streets were paved so that the hoofs of cattle clopped on the stones.

It has stood a long time, that tower, watching the life around it shift and alter, like eddies in a stream. It looks down once again on a deserted village—but no, not entirely deserted. A woman still lives in a cottage at its edge. Her hair has turned white, but she works every day in her garden, gathering tomatoes and cutting back the mint. When the day is particularly warm, she brings out a spinning wheel and sits in the garden, spinning yarn so fine that a shawl of it will slip through a wedding ring. If the breezes come from the west, the tower can hear her humming, just above the humming that the wheel makes as it spins. Time passes, and she sits out in the garden less often, until one day it realizes that it has not seen her for many days, or perhaps years.

Sometimes at night it thinks it can hear the Princess breathing in her sleep.

X. The Hound

In a hundred years, only one creature comes to the palace: a hound whose coat is matted with dust. Along his back the hair has come out in tufts, exposing a mass of sores. He lopes unevenly: on one of his forepaws, the inner toes have been crushed.

He has run from a city reduced to stone skeletons and drifting piles of ash, dodging tanks, mortar fire, the rifles of farmers desperate for food. For weeks now, he has been loping along the dusty roads. When rain comes, he has curled himself under a tree. Afterward, he has drunk from puddles, then loped along again with mud drying in the hollows of his paws. Sometimes he has left the road and tried to catch rabbits in the fields, but his damaged paw prevents him from running quickly enough. He has smelled them in their burrows beneath the summer grasses, beneath the poppies and cornflowers, tantalizing, inaccessible.

This morning he has smelled something different, pungent, like spoiled meat: the smell of enchantment. He has left the road and entered the forest, finding his way through a tangle of briars. He has come to the village, loped up its cobbled streets and through the gates of the palace. His claws click on its stone floor.

What does he smell? A fragrance, drifting, indistinct, remembered from when he was a pup: bacon. There, through that doorway. He lopes into the Great Hall, where breakfast waits in chafing dishes. The eggs are still firm, their yolks plump and yellow, their whites delicately fried. Sausages sit in their own grease. The toast is crisp.

He leaves a streak of egg yolk and sausage grease on the tablecloth, which has remained pristine for half a century, and falls asleep in the Queen Dowager's drawing room, in a square of sunlight that has not faded the baroque carpet.

He lives happily ever after. Someone has to. As summer passes, he wanders through the palace gardens, digging in the flower beds and trying to catch the sleeping fish that float in the ornamental pools. One day he urinates on the side of the tower, from which the dark smell emanates, to show his disapproval. When he is hungry he eats from the side of beef hanging in the larder, the sausage and eggs remaining on the breakfast table, or the mice sleeping beneath the harpsichord. In autumn, he chases the leaves falling red and yellow over the lawns and manages to pull a lobster from the kitchen tank, although his teeth can barely crack its hard shell. He never figures out how to extract the canary from its cage. When winter comes, the stone floor sends an ache through his damaged paw, and he sleeps in the King's bed, under velvet covers.

When summer comes again, he is too old to run about the garden. He lies in the Queen Dowager's drawing room and dreams of being a pup, of warm hands and a voice that whispered "What a beautiful dog," and that magical thing called a ball. He dies, his stomach still full with the last of the poached eggs. A proper fairy tale should, perhaps, end here.

XI. The Prince

Here comes the Prince on a bulldozer. What did you expect? Things change in a hundred years.

Harry pulls back the brake and wipes his forehead, which is glistening with sweat. He runs his fingers through blond hair that stands up like a shock of corn. It is just past noon, and the skin on his nose is already red and peeling.

Two acres, and he'll knock off for some beer and that liver and onion sandwich Madge made him this morning, whose grease, together with the juice of a large gherkin, is soaking its way through a brown paper wrapper and will soon stain the leather of his satchel. He leans back, looks at the tangle of briars that form the undergrowth in this part of the forest, and chews on the knuckle of his thumb.

Two acres in the middle of the forest, enough for some barley and a still. Hell of a good idea, he thinks, already imagining the bottles on their way to Amsterdam, already imagining his pals Mike and Steve watching football on a color telly. Linoleum on the kitchen floor, like Madge always wanted, and cigarettes from America. "Not that damn rationed stuff," he says out loud, then looks around startled. What kind of fool idiot talks to himself? He chews on the knuckle of his thumb again. Twenty pounds to make the Police Commissioner look the other way. Damn lucky Madge could lend them the money. The bulldozer starts up again with a roar and the smell of diesel.

You don't like where this is going. What sort of Prince is this, with his liver and onion sandwich, his gherkin and beer? Forgive me. I give you the only Prince I can find, a direct descendant of the Count of Edinburgh, himself descended from the Tudors, albeit in the female line. Of course, all such titles have been abolished. This is, after all, the Socialist Union of Britannia. If Harry knows he is a Prince, he certainly isn't telling Mike or Steve, who might sell him out for a pack of American cigarettes. Even Madge can't be trusted, though they've been sharing a flat in the commune's apartment building for three years. Hell, she made a big enough fuss about the distillery business.

The bulldozer's roar grows louder, then turns into a whine. The front wheel is stuck in a ditch. Harry climbs down and looks at the wheel. Damn, he'll have to get Mike and Steve. He kicks the wheel, kicks a tree trunk and almost gets his foot caught in a briar, kicks the wheel again.

Something flashes in the forest. Now what the hell is that? (You and I know it is sunlight flashing from the faceted upper window of the tower.) Harry opens his beer and swallows a mouthful of its warm bitterness. Some damn poacher walking around on his land. (You and I remember that it belongs to the Socialist Union of Britannia.) He takes a bite of his liver and onion sandwich. Madge shouldn't frown so much, he thinks, remembering her in her housecoat, standing by the kitchen sink. She's getting wrinkles on her forehead. Should he fetch Mike and Steve? But the beer in his stomach, warm, bitter, tells him that he doesn't need Mike and Steve, because he can damn well handle any damn poacher himself. He bites into the gherkin.

Stay away, Prince Harry. Stay away from the forest full of briars. The Princess is not for you. You will never stumble up the tower stairs, smelling of beer; never leave a smear of mingled grease and sweat on her mouth; never take her away (thinking, *Madge's rump is getting too damn broad*) to fry your liver and onions and empty your ashtray of cigarette butts and iron your briefs.

At least, I hope not.

XII. The Rose

Let us go back to the beginning: petals fall. Unpruned for a hundred years, the rosebush has climbed to the top of the tower. A cane of it has found a chink in the tower window, and it has grown into the room where the Princess lies. It has formed a canopy over her, a network of canes now covered with blossoms, and their petals fall slowly in the still air. Her nightgown is covered with petals: this summer's, pink and fragrant, and those of summers past, like bits of torn parchment curling at the edges.

While everything in the palace has been suspended in a pool of time without ripples or eddies, it has responded to the seasons. Its roots go down to dark caverns which are the homes of moles and worms, and curl around a bronze helmet that is now little more than rust. More than two hundred years ago, it was rather carelessly chosen as the emblem of a nation. Almost a hundred years ago, Madeleine plucked a petal of it for her magic spell. Wolfgang Magus picked a blossom of it for his buttonhole, which fell in the chapel and was trampled under a succession of court heels and cavalry boots. A spindle was carved from its dead and hardened wood. Half a century ago, a dusty hound urinated on its roots. From its seeds, dispersed by birds who have eaten its orange hips, has grown the tangle of briars that surround the palace, which have already torn the Prince's work pants and left a gash on his right shoulder. If you listen, you can hear him cursing.

It can tell us how the story ends. Does the Prince emerge from the forest, his shirtsleeve stained with blood? The briars of the forest know. Does the Witch lie dead, or does she still sit by the small-paned window of her cottage, contemplating a solitary pearl that glows in the wrinkled palm of her hand like a miniature moon? The spinning wheel knows, and surely its wood will speak to the wood from which it was made. Is the Princess breathing? Perhaps she has been sleeping for a hundred years, and the petals that have settled just under her nostrils flutter each time she exhales. Perhaps she has not yet been sleeping, perhaps she is an exquisitely preserved corpse, and the petals under her nostrils never quiver. The rose can tell us, but it will not. The wind sets its leaves stirring, and petals fall, and it whispers to us: you must find your own ending.

This is mine. The Prince trips over an oak log, falls into a fairy ring, and disappears. (He is forced to wash miniature clothes, and pinched when he complains.) Alice stretches and brushes the rose petals from her nightgown. She makes her way to the Great Hall and eats what is left in the breakfast dishes: porridge with brown sugar. She walks through the streets of the village, wondering at the silence, then hears a humming. Following it, she comes to a cottage at the village edge where Madeleine, her hair now completely white, sits and spins in her garden. Witches, you know, are extraordinarily long-lived. Alice says, "Good morning," and Madeleine asks, "Would you like some breakfast?" Alice says, "I've had some, thank you." Then the Witch spins while the Princess reads Goethe, and the spinning wheel produces yarn so fine that a shawl of it will slip through a wedding ring.

Will it come to pass? I do not know. I am waiting, like you, for the canary to lift its head from under its wing, for the Empress Josephine to open in the garden, for a sound that will tell us someone, somewhere, is awake.

KATHE KOJA

Road Trip

Kathe Koja is a Detroit-area native and lives there with her husband, artist Rick Lieder, and her son, Aaron. She has been a full-time freelancer since 1984, after attending the Clarion Workshop at Michigan State University (thanks to the Susan C. Petrey scholarship), but has been a writer since she was four years old. Among her novels are The Cipher, Skin, Kink, *and* Straydog; *some of her short fiction is collected in* Extremities. *Her most recent novel is* Buddha Boy. The Blue Mirror *will follow in 2004, and* Talk *in 2005. She is currently at work on another novel.*

"Road Trip" is an excellent example of Koja's ability to create a powerful tale by using a disturbed viewpoint character to provide a disjointed, yet extremely effective, interpretation of events. The story was originally published in the World Fantasy Convention Program Book in honor of her being an Honored Guest of the convention.

—E. D.

Look for a storefront, the woman in the gas station tells you. Older woman, older than you anyway, yellow GO GATORS! t-shirt, skinny elbows planted on the counter and *Oaktree and Madison, it's in a little strip mall, next to a Cigarette King. Says BCI on the window, but the louver-blinds are always shut*. Lights then puffs on her own cigarette, cigarette queen smiling at you through the smoke, she's not going to say anything else so there's nothing to do but go back into daylight, strong sunlight and the heat of the car's front seat, it's cooking like an oven and it isn't even noon. How can people live in a climate like this? Why did you even come?

OK. In a strip mall, OK. Pass a drug store, discount store, various restaurants (The Oasis, Redd Robbin's), the Home Improvement Barn; trolling and craning through the traffic and the heat, through the secret crawl of sweat on your back, sour elixir of salt and light. The thickets of skepticism, the forests of desire, *oh sure* as you trawl down Madison, looking for Oaktree, looking for a strip mall and BCI on the window, *the louver-blinds are always shut*, what for? So no one can see what they do in there? So no one can see you, doing what no rational person would or should do, committing the cardinal sin of stupidity and need? *Gonna wade in the Jordan, wade in the Jordan, let the waters break over my head—*

—and there it is, Cigarette King, way over on the opposite side of the road so you have to pass it to turn around, *pass it and keep going*, your mind advises, the part that still can reason, the part ungripped by pain: the pain that never passes, that never wavers or abates, that wakes you dry-eyed in the night until you have to get out of bed and walk, walk, walk it down—because you can't drink it down, not any more, right? Even when you get out of rehab? Even when they give you back your car?

Where are we going?

Nowhere, baby. Just for a ride.

and the dog in the back seat, don't forget the dog, tail wagging and

there's a parking space right by the door, left just for you. The letters on the window are plain and nondescript, BCI, Before Christ Incorporated, Bullshit Created Inside, it can mean whatever you want it to mean, it can be whatever you need it to be, isn't that what that woman had said? The herbalist, spiritualist, whatever the hell she was she was Elizabeth's idea but you were the one she spoke to: *They'll be able to help you*, her hand warm on your arm, was she coming on to you or what? with Elizabeth right there, Elizabeth who could hardly bear to look at you, Elizabeth who was turning to stone right before your very eyes so *All right*, you said, because there was nothing else you could say, nothing else to do but buy the goddamned plane ticket, take the time off from work and *What will you tell them?* in the bed, in the morning, her face turned like a bas-relief towards the window, grey skies and weeping rain. *At work, I mean? How will you get the time off to—*

I already told them, you said, a lie meant to soothe her, the whole thing was meant to soothe her, wasn't it? make her look at you, come back to you again? because without her there was nothing left and no one, nothing living but the pain and so you lied and left, just another in a chain of lies laundered by noble intent, like sticking drug money in the poorbox, does that make it better? does it even matter? And why are you sitting out here like this, in the car, in the sun, in the fist of the heat? Are you stalling? Are you frightened? Of what?

They'll be able to help you, they who? but the spiritualist-herbalist had been less than precise about that: a healing group, she had called them, without specifying exactly what was done to whom and how this healing might be accomplished. Maybe just getting on the plane had done it, maybe you could turn around and go home right now, tell Elizabeth another lie, she must be used to them by now, right? *It was wonderful, honey, I went right into the light*—no, that's what you do when you're dead, right?

Where are we going?

Nowhere, baby. Just for a ride.

Two women come out of the cigarette store, glance at you, keep walking: will they go into BCI, too? but instead they step into the dry cleaner's, come out carrying suits, men's suits dark in swathing plastic, suitable for funerals; Elizabeth wore white. Mass of the Angels. Who even believes this shit? her? You? Anybody? Are you going to sit here all day?

Go in. Go on.

Air conditioning, a dry refrigerator smell; for a moment you just breathe in, cool air like a circulating gas, like anethestic. Not a big space, but adequate: folding chairs stacked on a dolly, a card table with a phone and a CD player, posters on the walls, anonymous sunsets and waterfalls, nothing overtly religious, thank God and

"Hello," a woman's voice, it makes you jump: she sees, she smiles and "Hello," again; she's young, twenties maybe, slim and blonde, that pure white-blonde like Elizabeth, like—"Are you here for the service?"

Yes.

"You're a little early," kindly, "but that's fine. Would you like to read some of our literature while you wait?"

No; but you do, hand out automatically like on the street, flyers for this or that, save 20 percent, save the whales, save yourself and the "literature" she gives you is as bland as the posters, just a lot of low-key new-ageish crap about the soul, restoring the soul, it could be an advertisement for a facelift or a spa . . . so maybe this won't be so bad, you think, sitting back in the folding chair, maybe this won't be much of anything and you can get right back in the rental car and head for the airport, maybe even get home tonight, home to lie beside Elizabeth and

"Sir? Could you—" from the blonde, smiling, struggling with the dolly's release and Here, you say, hands atop hers on the catch, her hands are so small. Here, let me.

As you help her free the chairs a small tone sounds, *ping!*, a digital doorbell and here come two more supplicants: a man your age and a very old woman, oxygen tether and terrible bright eyes, she gives you the once-over as you stand there with the blonde and "Well hello," the blonde says, "how are you?" as you keep setting out chairs, joined now by the old woman's caretaker? son? until thirty chairs are lined in three neat rows.

And all the while the door keeps pinging, people keep coming in, why so many people in the middle of a workday? Mostly woman, mostly middle-aged but there are a few young ones, and even, most dreadfully, a couple of kids, a boy and a girl but fortunately they're both dark and fat and sullen, they sit kicking the backs of the chairs and each other as their mother? no, grandmother, keeps hissing at them to hush.

"She started it, she—"

"You hush!"

And then the music begins, tinkling windchime piano and "We welcome you all here," says the blonde, in a louder, more professional voice, "we're so glad you can be with us today. We're going to start with a song, 'Love is the Light We Follow', " and off they go, most of them seem to know the words; is this a radio-type song or church or what? You don't sing, of course, you listen, listen because you can't help it, because it keeps your mind off what you came here to do—

—which is what? Ask forgiveness? weep healing tears? dump all your guilt like a steaming load of shit and float away redeemed? *I wish I was dead* you said a hundred times to Elizabeth, said it as she held you and cried, said it until *I wish you were too* with her hand over her eyes, mouth drawn down like a stroke victim's, after that you never said it again but *How do you think it is for me?* you wanted to say, walking the floor with the pain, monster baby no one else could see, *how'd you like to be in my shoes* with nothing but memory for companion, nothing but the sun and the non-smell of vodka, the dog in the back seat wagging his tail, she wriggling in the booster seat because its straps were bugging her, making her fuss and whine so *You can be a big girl*, you said, remember? *Be a big girl up front with the seatbelt* which of course she loved, up front with Daddy, with the non-smell of vodka, with the dog in the back

barking and barking

crying

and the scatter of bottle glass gleaming in the sun, bottle glass and safety glass and your own teeth—remember?—your own teeth mixed up with the glass and you were sorting through it, somehow thinking if you could find your teeth everything would be all right

as "Love is the light we follow/Love is the dream we need/Love is the new tomorrow/Love is the flowering seed," jesus who writes this crap? and look at them all singing along like it was Mozart, what are they here for anyway? And the laugh rises in your chest, black metastasizing laugh because what would they do if you started shouting, calling it out like some mad MC, anybody here with cancer? How about MS? emphysema? leukemia? AIDS? What's the matter with you, little girl, little dark girl with the big fat stomach, is it you or your brother or your grandma who needs help?

"Let's pray," and it's a new voice, a woman's voice: sweet as honey and soft as smoke, a voice so compelling you crane your head to see her face: but she's nondescript, 40-ish in oversized glasses, brown pageboy and brown blouse, with her mouth shut you'd never notice her at all.

But "Let's pray," with such seductive power, such insistence that you let the woman on your right, one of the younger ones, take your hand as you reach for the person on your left, the man with the oxygen-mother, it feels strange to hold a man's hand. The minister held your hand, remember? until you told him to stop, took your hand away, hugged it against your body as Elizabeth moaned.

don't touch me don't touch me

"We ask for healing. We ask for solace. We ask for what is broken to be made whole," says the woman with the voice, an incredibly sexy voice if you don't look at the dumpy face, what would it be like to make love to a voice like that? and "We ask for healing," the woman says again, so close now you start, is she talking to you? No, to the oxygen-woman, those bright bird-eyes closing as the woman takes her hands, birdclaw liver-spotted hands, strokes and kisses them, ugh—but the old woman is crying, and the son is crying, and "Be healed, Virginia," the woman with the voice says, the words one long caress; how does she know her name? Are they repeat visitors, regulars? and does that mean whatever this is doesn't work, you have to keep coming back? *You're* not coming back. "You want to be healed, don't you?"

Simple as that, huh? as the old woman weeps, and coughs, the oxygen line trembling like a scuba diver's, going deeper and deeper but for you the disappointment is like a gust of clean air, is that all this is going to be? Just like watching a TV evangelist, just a lot of blow-dried histrionics but what else did you expect? She'll come to you next, take your hand, murmur some crap in that sexy voice and then you can—

—but she passes you entirely, heads for the grandma and the kids, ah Christ it would have to be the kids and "Praise Jesus," says the grandma; if you turn your head a little—and you do—you can see her tears, too, long clear lines on that round dark face. "Make him whole."

"What's the matter with you, Shawn?" the woman asks the boy; and now that voice is a mother's, a sweet teacher's, the teacher you most want to please and "I got asthma," says the boy, his gaze all trust, his hand in hers. "I can't breathe good when I play."

"What do you like to play?" as the song on the CD changes, something about going home, *when I go home* and "Soccer," says the boy. "Soccer and—"

"Basketball," the girl breaks in, not to be left out; she takes the woman's other hand. "He don't play very good, though. *I* always—"

"Be healed, Shawn. You want to be healed, don't you?"

"Yes," says the boy—and then screams, just like that, screams and bucks like he's just been shot and the grandmother cries out as if she felt the bullet too—and you jerk away from all of it, stumbling into the son next to you who stares at you like *What's your problem?* as the boy shrieks again, a teakettle cry that sinks to a wheeze then becomes a whimper; but now he's smiling, the grandmother is smiling, the girl stares avidly at them both and "Better," says the woman with the voice; it's not at all a question; she knows. "Better now."

And then it's onto the next one, and the next and the next: younger woman touching her breast, older woman with crippled hands, an old man with "cancer liver," he says, with a deaf man's flat high volume, "I got cancer liver," and "You want to be healed?" she asks them all, as if she's checking it out with them first, making sure, sharp salesperson bringing the mark in on the sale which is what you want to think, what you do think—except for that smell in the air, a definite smell like thunderstorms, ozone, except for the little boy, Shawn, whose eyes are glowing, he keeps taking deep breaths and letting them out, in and out and two steps from you the old lady with the oxygen tether has slipped it from her nose, a woman in a faded blue tube top is saying "I can feel it! I can feel it!" to the fat friend beside her who's clutching her arm, everything stinks of ozone and there's sweat on the back of your neck, sweat though the room is chilly, sweat though you don't believe because this is not real, this is not *real*, who does she think she is anyway? Billy Graham? Jesus Christ? because some things just can't be healed, no matter what she says in that seductress voice, no matter what you or Elizabeth or anyone else may want or long or pray for: because time runs only forward, life runs into death and stops, stops like a brick wall crumbling from the impact, stops like a body flung into the air

like a circus trick like black magic you watched her go fly hurled free by velocity right through the windshield why didn't the airbag work? yours worked you lived she flew: bright hair black blood there in the street like the worst thing you'd ever seen it was the worst thing and the dog too jesus christ that your dog sir? and you scrabbling through glass for your teeth head spinning mouth a dark wet flap of blood and Oh no you said just like that, the simple round vowels of a clown, a liar, a killer, oh no in simple dismay because time had not stopped when your car had and now she was dead dead forever and you were drunk and alive

alive, oh

oh no

Where are we going?

Nowhere, baby

because being alive means you have to live, hospital, police station, lawyer's office, home—and home becomes worse than a prison, prison would be a relief, no Elizabeth there with her swollen eyes and ice-cold hands and *Why?* she asked you once, just once, everything there in that one word and of course you had no answer, what answer was there?

Because I was drunk. Because she was whining. Because I didn't think anything bad would happen.

Because I wanted to.

"You want to be healed, don't you?" and she's back in your row now, working her way down, hands on a massive woman in a hideous off-white blouse, she looks like a weather balloon and she's mumbling and spitting as the music changes again, going not home but up this time, *going up we're going up,* we're flying, baby, whee! "Sandra, tell me, do you want to be healed?"

"Yes," like a groaning organ, player piano running down, eyes squeezed shut and in a few minutes it'll be over, all over and you can go, *go into the light* and the heat and the rental car, back home to nothing, nothing—

and now she's in front of you, voice and bad glasses and all: and her eyes through those glasses are not what you expected, not professionally kind, not measuring or shrewd but something else, something you don't like but can't name, well she can't name you either can she? but "You're in a lot of pain, aren't you?" and she not only knows your name but your nickname, the name everyone calls you, she calls you that now as she keeps gazing at you with those eyes, that look you can't bear, you're sweating like a pig and all you want to do is run away but

"You want to be healed, don't you?"

in that voice like a lover's, staring at you in the ozone chill, staring at you like Elizabeth and the cop and the judge . . . and Caitlin, Caitlin Caitlin Caitlin flying through the air, fairy princess, baby gumdrop squashed flat as a bug and

you want to be healed don't you?

Don't you?

with her hands out and reaching: waiting in the white room of your terror, the palace of your guilt; waiting for you to make a move, to say Yes, I do. I do.

Don't you?

The smell of ozone in your mouth: the flung glass glittering like ice.

LUCY TAYLOR

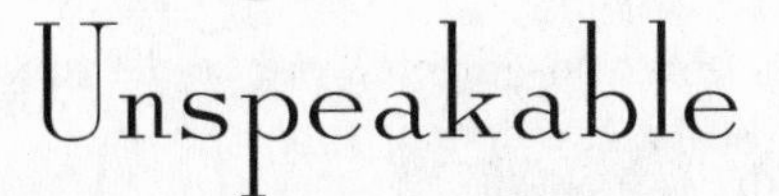

Lucy Taylor lives in Mead, Colorado, "with six wonderful cats." Her most recent book, Saving Souls, *a mystery–suspense novel, was published by Penguin in 2002. Her next book,* Left to Die, *is due out this year, also from Penguin, and is the first in what she hopes will be a detective series. It will be published under the name Taylor Kincaid.*

Overlook Press is publishing a new collection titled The Silence Between the Screams *in late 2003 and a second collection,* Girl Under Glass, *is forthcoming from Silver Salamander Press.*

About her story, Taylor says, "I have always had an interest in 'the fetishistic potential of words.' "

"Unspeakable," while not a graphically horrific story, is not for the faint of heart. It was originally published in The Darker Side.

—E. D.

Never underestimate the power of words, Christine, my stepfather, Dr. Peyton Eads, used to say. *We think they're only symbols, only sounds, but the right word is like a rare perfume—it has the power to evoke the feelings and sensations from the past and make them real again.*

I was just a kid then. I didn't know what he meant, only that Dr. Eads was a renowned psychiatrist and unquestionably the best of the various "uncles" and boyfriends who had preceded him through the revolving door to Mother's bedroom. But that was because he hadn't yet started to "train" me. Later on, I learned only too well what he meant about the power of words.

Ricky Calloway, as I was to find out years later, understood the power of words as well or better than Dr. Eads and demonstrated that knowledge more dramatically. Unlike in the case of my stepfather, though, I knew Ricky was dangerous and crazy from the start.

It had been over a year since I'd last seen Ricky Calloway when I came home one night to find the lock on my apartment door jimmied and Ricky sitting in my living room, naked, in the dark.

I knew it was Ricky by the bulk of his outline, backlit against the aquarium-green glow from the computer screen that threw the only light in the room—his sheer heft was unmistakable; his nudity—when viewed in silhouette—was shockingly apparent. His only concession to clothing was the biker bandanna holding back the mass of black hair that slid over his shoulders like an Apache warrior's.

The first question that popped into my mind—*did you do it?*—was the one I was afraid to ask. So instead I said, "Jesus, what are you doing here? Why'd you break into my place?"

"I didn't know what time you got off work, and I didn't want to wait out in the hall. Don't worry, I'll fix the door before I go."

"Damn right you will. And you'll get dressed."

"When I leave. But maybe you won't want me to leave. Maybe you'll want me to stay the night. I've got something to show you that might change things for us."

Us. What us? I thought.

"What could you show me that could change anything?" I said. "I can't be with you. I can't be with anybody. We tried that once, remember?"

"Well, let's try again," said Ricky. He held a big hand out to me. "Come over here and touch my cock."

"Do *what?*"

I knew Ricky Calloway was a little nuts and I knew I should be afraid of him, but I wasn't. If he'd come back to kill me or extort money, I figured so fucking be it. Considering what I'd set in motion, maybe I deserved it. On the other hand, I knew Ricky was once in love with me, so maybe he still was. Or maybe he just wanted to get laid and figured that I owed him. Big time.

"Christine," he said, "did you hear me?"

"Yeah, I heard you." I sidled into the room and sat across from him on the couch, looking him up and down, trying to assess the extent of his dangerousness. "Give me a minute. I need to think about this."

I first laid eyes on Ricky Calloway at my brother Andrew's funeral. Andrew committed suicide two years ago by hurling himself off the roof of the ten-story apartment building where he owned a condo. He didn't jump feet first, which I was told by the police—who tend to know about such things—is the norm, but dived headfirst, like a Mexican cliff diver—an aberration even for an act that is itself an aberration.

The funeral was modestly attended, the priest drafted for the occasion a tufted-haired old Benedictine from St. Paul's, the church that Mother used to attend before her gait grew too tipsily unsteady to make it up the broad, pink-marble steps. My sister, Anne, and her husband, Robert, were there and Andrew's colleagues from the legal firm where he'd worked as a criminal defense attorney. Our younger brother, Barnett, the baby of the family and a little slow in the head, came to eulogize his elder sibling and did so with such fervor and at such length that the priest's head drooped upon his chest and snores emanated from his ribby torso.

"Whatever the magnitude of his sin, *God* loves Andrew," Barnett yelled, fist raised as though challenging anyone to argue the point. "*God* has saved Andrew, and he is sitting at the feet of our most merciful *God* and His son, our Lord and Savior *Jesus Christ.*"

I'd never heard Barnett rant like this, churning himself into such a spiritual lather that his listeners were either appalled or simply agog at the display. Barnett shook sweat from his hair like a wet spaniel and rolled his eyes and trembled each time he invoked the name of the Lord. At a certain point, his ferocity began to make me uneasy and I searched for distraction by looking at the reactions to my surviving brother's diatribe in the faces of the predominantly well-groomed and tastefully attired mourners who had made up Andrew's social set.

A couple of people, who didn't fit in any better than Barnett did, caught my eye.

"Who's that?" I said to Anne, indicating the hulking biker type whose glaring black eyes would have been scary if not for his copious weeping.

"That's Ricky Calloway," she said. "When he was sixteen years old he caught his father molesting his sister and stabbed him to death."

I absorbed this, then said, "How'd he know Andrew?"

"Andrew defended him on an assault charge a few years back and they got to be buds. Stop staring at him, Christine. He's a career criminal. Not your type. Even if you haven't been with a man in ten years," she added, squeezing my hand to show she wasn't trying to be nasty, just acknowledging what she viewed as my bizarre and stubborn celibacy.

"Make that fifteen," I said.

Chastised, though, I stopped sneaking peeks at Ricky Calloway and turned my attention to the other person who looked out of place here—the one I figured this Calloway guy would probably end up going home with—a short, zaftig woman whose brassy blond curls stood out like yellow neon and whose dangly minichandelier earrings twisted in the breeze like tiny hanged men. She must have felt my eyes on her, because she turned suddenly, looking directly at me. Her hand came up in a tiny wave, fingers only, as one waves to a child.

After the service, as everyone drifted back to their cars, the blonde came stumblingly up the hill behind me. She wore a long black skirt, slit to the thigh, and a grey sweater unbuttoned to allow a glimpse of her pink lace bra. She was easily twice the age I'd guessed—blond hair framing a coarse, fatigue-lined face, her limbs stocky and muscular—factory worker limbs, well larded but at the same time powerful.

Then, closer still, I reassessed that thought—not a factory worker at all, but in a manner of speaking, still assembly line. She reeked of brandy and her steel-gray eyes looked slightly out of focus from a lifetime of seeing selectively.

"I'm Katrina," she gushed, forcing a sloppy hug on me. "Andrew and I were close friends, *very* close." She dabbed at her dry eyes to show sincerity. "You're his sister, right?"

"I'm Christine. He mentioned me?"

"Yes, well, not exactly. Not really, no. He wasn't a big talker, Andrew. He more liked me to talk."

She gave me a crafty sideways glance. "He left a few things at my apartment, some clothes and a few books, and you know, some other items, items of a sex'shul nature."

"Whatever things you have of Andrew's, I don't want them," I said. "The only thing I'd appreciate, if you have it, is information. Why would he do something like this?"

Her eyeballs rattled around in their sockets as though she'd taken a blow to the chin. "He had a lot of secrets," she managed finally, "but, like I said, he wasn't much of a talker."

I turned and strode away from the stench of her hundred-proof breath. I have nothing against hookers, but I'm intolerant of drunks, my mother having been one.

"Hey, wait!" she called.

Incredibly, she was grinning as she staggered after me. "Look, Christine, I liked Andrew a bunch and I got only respect for the dead, whatever way they go, but I have to ask. I gotta know . . ." She ran a pointed pink tongue along vermillion lips and whispered slyly, "I mean, I thought maybe you could tell me, what does—what did—there were some words he made me say over and over every time we were, you know, intimate—it was the only way he could get it up—but they weren't sex words. They weren't dirty. I wondered, maybe you could, you know, like satisfy my curiosity, what did they—"

"Stop it. I don't want to know."

But she was drunk and one thing I learned from my mother was that drunks neither see nor listen nor care, so she told me anyway. Three words—my brother Andrew's dirty little secrets. They weren't the same Words given me, but I damn well knew where they'd come from and how they'd gotten hard-wired into his brain. Just realizing this brought up such rage in me that for an instant I stood looking around for Ricky Calloway, patricidal son, no longer feeling shy or grief stricken, but ballsy and sexy and hot on the make.

I wanted something from Ricky Calloway.

Thank God, when I spotted him, he was roaring away on a Harley, and I watched him go, imagining what kind of knife he might have used to stab his father with, how it must have felt when he shoved in the blade.

At night, I dream Words. Not Andrew's words. Mine. The consonants whisper against my clit like the stroke of a feather, the vowels ooze wetly like a seeking tongue. I chant them in my mind, these Words that I never say aloud, that no one else has ever heard me utter except the one who first inflicted them on me.

"Say them, Christine, pronounce them slowly, lovingly," says Dr. Eads as his fingers rove and wander. He has long, beautiful pale hands capable of elegant, almost balletic movements. In my dream his hands flow over me like cool wine. They weave a lurid tapestry across a befouled loom, uniting sounds and synapses, hot-wiring lust and potent shame to sounds that, in standard English, are almost pathetically innocuous. A child could say these words and not be scolded. To the world at large, they are just words.

But to me they are Words that suck and stroke, Words that evoke my darkest memories, that set me on fire and immolate me with shame. Magic Words. The Words that accompanied my introduction to sex and to shame and to secrecy.

A few weeks after Andrew's funeral, I went over to my sister Anne's to keep her company while her husband, Robert, was out of town. We were hanging out, eating popcorn, and watching TV. I knew she was worried about something, working up to telling me. Finally, she said, "Barnett is giving me the creeps. When he gave that eulogy at Andrew's funeral, it seemed to have an effect on him."

"What do you mean?"

"I heard he's been going to the cathedral, preaching sermons, ranting and raving, God-this and Jesus-that. The priests are being good-natured about it—they like Barnett—but it's got to stop. He's interfering with the masses."

"You want me to talk to him?"

"Would you?"

"No."

We both laughed. "That's what I thought you'd say."

We talked some more, Anne trying to persuade me to pay a visit to Barnett, me coming up with reasons not to. Barnett and I are ten years apart in age and miles apart in temperament and lifestyle. "He's eccentric," I said to my sister. "It's why he can't hold down a job. This preaching thing—it's just a phase."

The sitcom we were watching ended and a trailer for a new movie came on, something about the flood of the decade in a small northwestern town. "*Hundreds in danger of drowning,*" a grim-faced actor was saying to a panicky crowd.

Anne started to giggle, stifled it, and stuffed some popcorn into her mouth, almost choking in the process, and then spitting it back out into her hand.

The giggles pealed out of her like a wildly rung bell.

"Anne, you okay?"

Anne clamped her thighs together and doubled over as the TV voice went on, "*Water rising! A town inundated . . .*" The giggling wasn't giggling anymore. It had transformed into something else, a jagged, helpless laughter with as much gaiety as a death rattle. She wrapped both arms around her belly, fighting for breath as the compulsive laughter racked her, and hissed, "Where's the goddamn remote?"

I tossed it to her

She must have been trying to hit *mute* or change the channel, but in her flustered state, she increased the volume by mistake. "*Floodwaters drown an entire valley . . .*"

She lurched to her feet and staggered into the bathroom. When she came out, her hands were trembling, and she couldn't look at me.

"Anne, what's wrong? What just happened?"

"Jesus, it's so embarrassing . . . why do they let them *talk* like that on TV? How the fuck can they allow it?"

"Allow what?"

"The obscenities! The dirty talk just then. Didn't you—" She covered her face. "Jesus, you have no fucking idea what I'm talking about."

Something cold passed under my heart. "What obscenities?"

"Oh, *you* know." She leaned toward me conspiratorially, body language and tone of voice that of a woman confessing to something torrid: banging her brother-in-law, embezzling funds from the school soccer team. "You know, the nasty words that everyone pretends aren't. Hearing them like that, when I don't expect it—fuck, I had to go jerk off. My goddamn cunt was throbbing. Why does everyone pretend those words aren't nasty when they *are*?"

"Anne," I said, "when Mom was married to Dr Eads, she was drinking more than ever, and he'd spend a lot of time with us, each individually. Making up for her absence, he'd say. Did he do something to you? Those words that made you laugh—did he link them in your mind to—other things?"

For a second, she looked at me as though I'd just landed from the moon. Then her face drooped like a crone's. "You, too?" she said, her voice barely a whisper. "Oh fuck—he did that weird shit to you, too?"

"And Andrew," I said. "I'm pretty sure."

"I always thought it was just me he played those sick games with, and I was too ashamed to tell anyone. But why the words? If he was into molesting kids, that's one thing, but why did he hook the sex up to words that aren't even sex words, that he probably picked out at random?"

"Maybe that was the point. He wanted to see if he could take ordinary words and make them erotically charged—forever—for his victims. He was always talking about the way the brain processes language. I think we were his own private experiment."

Anne folded her thin arms around herself. "The son of a bitch. I always felt so ashamed, so crazy. I mean, just hearing those stupid words sometimes will make me come."

"Did you ever ask Robert to—you know—say them when you're making love?"

"You kidding? I know those really aren't dirty words to anyone but me. I'd feel like an idiot. What about you? Have you ever asked a lover to repeat whatever it was Eads said to you?"

I tried to smile, but the corners of my mouth turned down. "It's been fifteen years, Anne. Does that answer your question?"

Her small, freckled hands curled into fists. "It isn't fair. He molested both of us, maybe Andrew, too. We should track him down to wherever he's living now and make him pay."

"I've thought about it," I said, "but I'm afraid to try that. I'm afraid it would come back to haunt me."

But God has a sick sense of humor and He proved it by letting me run into Ricky Calloway, in the least likeliest of places for either of us to be—a church. Ricky grew up in the same Irish-Catholic neighborhood that I did and, even though far from devout, he still managed to get to confession and mass a few times a year. I'd gotten a strange call from the priest who gave the eulogy at Andrew's funeral—apparently Barnett was at the cathedral delivering a sermon. He'd commandeered the church steps and was giving some sort of extemporaneous rant. *Could I please come get him*? the old priest wanted to know.

By the time I got there, Barnett was gone, and I was nearly knocked down the pink-marble stairs by a huge man with angry black eyes who came barreling through the door. Later, Ricky would tell me that he'd forgotten to put the safety lock on his Harley and had bolted out in the middle of mass, afraid hoodlums would be taking off with his prized bike. He knew how easily and profitably such a theft could be accomplished because it was one of the ways he supplemented his own income.

"Watch where you're going," I snapped.

"I was watching," he said, stopping to look me up and down the way he might appraise a communion goblet he was getting ready to filch. "I saw you at Andrew's funeral. You're his sister."

"Christine," I said. "I remember you, too. You're Ricky Calloway." Astonished at my own boldness, I added, "You headed anywhere in particular?"

He grinned. "Straight to Hell, according to the priest."

"Me, too."

He looked me over again. "That's kinda hard to believe."

"You'd be surprised."

"Surprise me."

I did—but not, undoubtedly, in the way that he'd been hoping.

Considering that we were both, in our own way, desperate, we observed an unlikely regimen of self-control, postponing sex while we became friends. I hadn't had a lover, male or female, in years, and Ricky had just broken up with a girlfriend and hadn't been with a woman in nearly a week—which somehow, for the two of us, approximated the same amount of deprivation. And we had Pasts. His, he liked to boast about. Mine, I preferred to hide. We'd meet for dinner or drinks, catch a movie. I learned his story, not little by little in dribs and drabs, but in large, nearly indigestible chunks of such mayhem, intrigue, and substance abuse that it resembled an action/adventure series. After the stint in juvie for murdering his dad, he'd worked construction and sold drugs on the side, got busted and gone to prison for drug dealing and assault, weathered two divorces, countless breakups, and the death of his mother, survived a gunshot wound to his thigh that almost severed his femoral artery.

We didn't have sex for four months, partly because I was in denial about what I really wanted from Ricky Calloway, partly because I cherished the fantasy that this time, because he was so different, so outside the conventional norms, I would be different, too, and the act of sex itself would be different. Not shameful and sordid and embarrassing, but full of raw lust and vigor and sheer animal exuberance.

When I judged that Ricky could be put off no longer and I had to take the risk, we finally lay together in his bed, kissing and caressing. His body was a tapestry of scars from various mishaps and altercations, fistfights and motorcycle accidents and bullet wounds, in addition to a number of lurid tattoos and painful-looking piercings. While in prison, as part of a gang initiation, he'd notched his right shin with a knife—three equally spaced vertical lines—and carved some sort of Celtic-looking symbol into his forearm, and he seemed proud of this self-mutilation, as though it marked some sort of rite of passage.

My fingers kept returning to the scars, especially the self-inflicted ones, tracing them over and over.

"What was it like when you killed your father?"

"A rush," he said. "Better than sex. Then later on, I just went numb, spaced it all out. But I was never sorry for what I did. He deserved it."

I knew for sure then that I wanted Ricky Calloway. From the neck up, anyway. Now if I could just convince the rest of me to want the rest of him.

But the moment he started to penetrate me, I froze and my mind seemed to exit my body like a parachutist abandoning a doomed plane. I invoked my Words, saying them in my mind, but in another human being's presence that only caused a paralyzing shame that numbed my limbs and pelvis. It was as if I was afraid that he could hear me thinking, that he would *know*.

He propped himself on his elbows. "What is it, Christine? I do something wrong?"

"No, you're fine. It's just that . . . I'm so sorry. I can't—"

"Tell me what's wrong."

"It's not your fault."

His face contorted. "It's me, isn't it? Because you're scared of me. I shouldn't have told you all the shit I've done. That stuff turns women off."

"Not necessarily."

"What is it then? I can force my way inside you, but it'll hurt you and probably me, too, and I don't want to do that."

My mouth was as dry as my pussy; the only part of me that was lubricated was my eyes.

"Ricky, I'm sorry. I haven't had a lot of practice at this. I think I'd like sex if I could just be good at it."

"Something happened to you to make you afraid of sex. Tell me."

So I did—most of it anyway.

Ricky listened with a mournful expression on his face, then asked, "What happened to the bastard?"

"The marriage to my mother fell apart because of her drinking, and Eads divorced her. The last I heard, he'd gotten a job at a psychiatric hospital back east and moved away. We never heard from him except at Mother's funeral. He sent me a condolence card. On the back he'd written a sonnet that contained the Words. His little joke. I had to leave the viewing to go masturbate."

"Christ, what a bastard," Ricky said. "Where the hell does the son of a bitch live?"

I almost told him that he'd have to track Eads down, that I wasn't really sure where he lived, but something stopped me. Maybe the fact that I really liked Ricky Calloway and didn't want him to risk another prison term in some possibly misguided quest for vengeance on my behalf. Maybe because I'd planned to at least make love with him first.

Or maybe I just wasn't angry enough.

It took a call from Anne the following week to accomplish that. She told me that Barnett had quit his job as a custodian at a local middle school to "preach" full time—on the steps of the library, outside a day-care center, in the rose garden behind city hall. His spiritual intoxication seemed to be reaching apocalyptic and dangerous new heights.

"I'm afraid for him," said Anne. "When I tried to talk to him myself—well, put it this way: When the priest talks about having a passion for God, I don't think this is what he means."

When I went to Barnett's apartment, I found him sitting in the middle of his living room with three TV sets turned on—each one to the same religious channel. On each screen, a florid-faced, pompadoured huckster-for-Jesus exhorted his audience to let God provide for food and rent and send cash *now*. The TV screens were blurry with handprints, which puzzled me till I remembered that TV preachers often exhort viewers to "pray" with them by touching the screen.

"Cut that nonsense off," I said, perhaps too harshly, for Barnett looked like a mother who's just been told her blessed newborn resembles a toy troll.

"That's God's message, Christine," he said. "Have some respect."

"Bullshit," I said. "What's going on, Barnett? I know you've always been religious, the only one of us who went to mass, but I never knew you wanted to be a preacher."

"Till Andrew's funeral, I never realized what it feels like to get up in front of a crowd of people and talk about *Jesus* and *God* and the *Holy Spirit*." He put an emphasis upon the words, drew them out across his tongue, and licked the final consonants. "I always said those words alone in prayer, never out loud. I never dreamed the thrill that comes from calling out the name of God and God's son Jesus Christ and Lord and Saviour."

As he went on, a cold finger of dread wended its way up my spine. "You like to say God's name, don't you, Barnett?"

His mouth stretched wide in a parody of ecstasy.

"The Lord God is my savior. I sure as hell do. It lifts up my spirit."

Not to mention your cock, I thought, to judge from the hard-on that had tented up his pants the first time he said the word *God*.

"Tell me something, Barnett. When we were little and Mother was married to Dr. Eads, did he touch you and do things to you? And did he maybe talk about God while he was doing it?"

Barnett scrunched his forehead as though deeply perturbed. "Why do you always call him Dr. Eads? I call him Dad."

"I know you do, Barnett. So tell me, did he?"

"Did he what?"

"Touch you."

"He calls me sometimes, you know."

"He does?"

"At night, real late. He likes to call me up and talk."

"Where does he call from?"

"A pay phone."

"A pay phone where?"

"Near Noah."

"Noah? Like Noah's ark?"

"Yeah, but new."

"New? Newark? Is that where that scumbag lives now, Barnett? Newark, New Jersey?"

"Why do you hate him, Christine? He's a good man. When he calls, we talk about God. He says God must love me a whole lot, because I haven't forgotten anything."

Oh, Barnett, I thought, *you were just a baby. Oh, fuck.*

I went home and called up Ricky Calloway and told him Newark was where he could start looking for Dr. Eads.

"Christine," says Ricky, sitting in my darkened living room almost a year later, "come here and touch my cock."

I see his hand move toward the darker shadow of his lap and look away. I want to want him, but the cold is coming over me, climbing my spine like some inner ice age, numbing my heart.

He holds out a hand. "Come here."

I shake my head. "It won't be any different than before. Nothing's changed."

"Give it a try. Please, Christine, just once."

So I do. In the bedroom, I cut off all the lights and peel out of my clothes with my eyes shut, as though this means he won't be able to see me. Then I crawl under the covers, where Ricky, having nothing to do in the way of undressing, is already waiting for me.

"I found your Dr. Eads," he says, "and I made sure where I put the body, nobody's gonna find it for another twenty years. But before I used the knife on him, we had a talk." In the dark I feel him smiling. "And then I used the knife on me."

"You what?"

"I had to stay away until I was sure the scars were going to heal up good and raised. I think you'll like the way they feel. I think you'll want to touch me now. I think you'll want me inside you."

"I don't see—"

"I know your Words, Christine," he said. "I made him tell me."

I move to clamp a hand across his mouth, but he pushes me away.

"Don't worry. I don't need to say them," he says. "They're as much a part of me now as they are of you. Run your hands over me. Feel the scars." He takes my hand and guides it down. "You can start with my dick."

ELIZABETH HAND

Inside Out: On Henry Darger

Elizabeth Hand is the author of six novels, including Waking the Moon, Winterlong, *and* Glimmering, *the short story collection* Last Summer at Mars Hill, *and the forthcoming* Bibliomancy: Four Novellas *and* Mortal Love, *a novel.*

Hand's work has received numerous honors, including the Nebula Award, the World Fantasy Award, and the James Tiptree, Jr. Award. In 2001 she was the recipient of an Individual Artist's Fellowship in Literature from the Maine Arts Commission and the National Endowment for the Arts. Her critical essays and reviews appear regularly in The Washington Post Book World, Village Voice, *and* Fantasy & Science Fiction.

Hand has had a lifelong interest in outsider and visionary art. A shorter version of this essay was originally published in Fantasy & Science Fiction. *Henry Darger's life and art, as illuminated through the lens of Hand's incisive, compassionate, and clear-eyed essay, offer a look at a strangely compelling phenomenon that defies easy characterization or dismissal.*

—E. D., T. W.

Earlier this year, people in New York lined up to gaze upon vivid, large-scale images of a world not unlike our own, populated by a childlike race engaged in an epic battle with the monstrous forces of Evil which sought to enslave them. Dragons, demonic creatures, richly detailed landscapes, carefully wrought battle-sequences and eruptions of cataclysmic weather; all sprung from the imagination of a devout Catholic, born in 1892, whose world reflected a lifelong preoccupation with Christian mythos as well as the dark matter of Twentieth Century war and technology.

Peter Jackson's first installment of *The Lord of the Rings*? No: the paintings of Henry Darger, the so-called Outsider artist whose massive body of work, painted and written, has posthumously established him as one of the major—and certainly one of the most provocative—creative figures of the last century. Since its discovery in Darger's apartment a few months before his death in 1972, the immense trove of Darger's scroll-like paintings and collages, fictional text, and autobiographical material has incited the kind of interest one might expect from the successful translation, after nearly a century of failed effort, of the

Linear A tablets from ancient Crete. Yet even as Darger's lifework is embraced by a critical establishment, that of another singular artist, J.R.R. Tolkien, continues to suffer critical condescension and often outright disdain, despite (and no doubt because of) its huge commercial success.

Tolkien and Darger were almost exact contemporaries, born a few months apart in 1892 and dying less than a year apart, Darger in late 1972 and Tolkien in September 1973. Though they lived and died in radically different worlds (Tolkien spent most of his life in England, Darger in Chicago), and had adult lives that could not be more diametrically opposed, their early years have an eerie, almost uncanny symmetry. Both were profoundly affected by early childhood losses. Darger's mother died a few weeks before his fourth birthday; Tolkien's father a few months after his. Both became orphans at an early age. After his mother's death (from diabetes) the twelve-year-old Tolkien and his younger brother came under the charge of a benevolent priest, before being taken in by a relative-by-marriage. In 1900, Darger's ailing father entered a Catholic mission; his son was consigned to a Catholic boys' home, and upon his father's death five years later, the thirteen-year-old Darger was institutionalized (in 1908 he escaped). Both began work on their epics around the same time, 1913 for Tolkien, Darger a year or so earlier. Both used visual as well as written forms for their art. And both chose as fictional oeuvres the lifelong creation of a single, epic history of an imagined world: Tolkien's Middle Earth and Darger's Realms of the Unreal.

In *Henry Darger: In the realms of the Unreal*, art historian John M. MacGregor has created a magisterial work that at times seems as immense and all-encompassing as the one which it explores. MacGregor is the author of the 1988 *The Discovery of the Art of the Insane*, a seminal study of one manifestation of the form that has been variously called Art Brut, Folk Art, Self-Taught Art, Visionary Art, but which is now commonly classed under the catch-all term Outsider Art. The phrase is frustratingly elastic. It has been applied to artists as disparate as the Victorian fairy painter Richard Dadd, a member of the Royal Academy, neither an outsider nor self-taught but unquestionably mad; Chris Mars, onetime musician for the Replacements and now a highly-regarded painter whose work deals with the familial fallout of schizophrenia; the folk artist Howard Finster, and the anatomical transcendentalist painter Alex Grey. "Visionary" is probably a more appropriate description, especially if modified with "obsessive" or "obsessional" (which could also be applied to much of Tolkien's written work).

Perhaps the most poignant reaction to such personal, intense forms of creative expression comes from the artist Nathan Lerner, Darger's landlord and the man who, with a student assistant, discovered Darger's monumental accomplishment after his death—

"What made him do all these things that didn't have to be done?"

What indeed? Henry Darger may not have been insane, but he was as close to a poster boy for the Outsider Artist as we are likely to get. A few weeks before Darger's fourth birthday, his mother died of puerperal fever after giving birth to a girl. The infant, Henry's sister, was given up for adoption; her history is unknown, but it is clear that her disappearance, following his mother's death and his father's subsequent grief, became the central event upon which the adult Darger constructed his brilliant, severely disturbed and disturbing history of The Realms of the Unreal. After his stint at a Catholic boys' home, in 1904 the twelve-year-old Darger was placed in the Lincoln Asylum for Feeble-Minded Children. His father helped fill out the committal forms before his death in 1905. Henry remained at the asylum until 1908. The reasons for his presence there were his propensity for dangerous behavior (attacking smaller children, perhaps displaced aggression towards the infant sister who had robbed him of his mother; he also attacked a teacher); setting fires; "acquired" self-abuse. This last appears to have been what motivated the assessing physician to pronounce the child "insane." Yet whatever severe psychological orders assailed him, the young Henry was not feeble-minded. He was intelligent and loved to read, particularly newspapers and military history (the Civil War was an especial passion); during his time at the boys' home he was probably impressed by the publishing business that was run by the Mission as a vocational tool for its inmates. MacGregor suggests that Darger may have suffered from Asperger's Syndrome, a comparatively mild form of autism whose traits include difficulty in establishing and maintaining human relationship, obsessional behavior and interests, and often normal or above-normal intelligence and verbal fluency.

Despite Darger's later casual dismissal—"Finally I got to like the place and the meals were good and plenty"—the asylum seems to have been a nightmarish institution, marked by violent outbursts and lacking in any compassionate interaction between its 500 employees and 1200 inmates. Summers provided a surcease, when Henry was sent to work on the State Farm outside the city. After several aborted efforts at running away, the seventeen-year-old Henry finally did so for good, returning to Chicago where he found work as a janitor at St. Joseph's Hospital.

> Now it is a strange thing, but things that are good to have and days that are good to spend are soon told about, and not much to listen to; while things that are uncomfortable palpitating, and even gruesome, may make a good tale, and take a good deal of telling anyway.

So Tolkien muses in *The Hobbit*. And while the remainder of Henry Darger's life can only with great difficulty be construed as "good," it was certainly without great event, at least to any outside observer. In 1917 he was drafted and a few months later discharged for medical reasons. After that he worked as a janitor and dishwasher at various hospitals. In later years when he grew too frail for these jobs he was given other menial tasks. He seems to have ever had only one real friend. In 1932 he moved into the rooming house where he was to spend the rest of his life, most of it in a single large room. In 1956 the building was bought by the artist Nathan Lerner, an amiably bohemian landlord who created a small floating world of artists and musicians and art students who tolerated Darger's presence and made small gestures of friendship to the lonely old man.

Lerner was an exceptionally compassionate landlord: he neither raised Darger's rent nor complained about his tenant's housekeeping. He and the other residents of 851 Webster took turns helping Darger, providing the occasional meal, assistance with medical care; most important, they provided contact with a world outside the one in Darger's head. For by the 1960s Henry Darger had become one of those lost souls who populate the edges of any urban landscape, usually glimpsed from the corner of one's eye: a furtive, slight man—he was just over five feet tall—he wore the filthy ruins of his Army overcoat and spent hours every day wandering back alleys, poking through trash cans for refuse which he then brought back to his room. MacGregor quotes a visitor to Darger's room.

> There was a tremendous amount of stuff. Newspapers and magazines piled in bundles up the ceiling. If there was one pair of glasses, there must have been a hundred. Rubber bands, boxes of rubber bands. Shoes, lots of shoes. But you went into the room and it was organized. The table was cluttered to a depth of two to three feet, except for a working area. He had all these drawings and pictures across the top. I was interested in art, and a little bit curious, but it was obvious that this was very private, a very private kind of thing.

Darger's neighbors often heard him talking to himself, carrying on lengthy conversations in which he took on different voices. He was in fact engaged in the final stages of a lifelong battle with God, a struggle which he had recorded in his vast multivolume epic, and which eventually found its way into his autobiography.

> Had trouble again with twine. Mad enough to wish I was a bad tornado. Swore at God, yet go to three morning masses. Only cooled down by late afternoon. Am I a real enemy of the cross, or a very very sorry saint?

Ah yes: the eternal problem of the struggle with twine. And yet what do our lives really consist of, most of the time, but precisely this: life-or-death battles with the shopping, the commute, the boss, the kids, the spouse, the neighbors, the neighbor's dog. God? Each age gets the art it deserves, and no doubt we get the saints we deserve as well; in which case Henry Darger is infinitely worthy of the critical canonization he has received in the decades since his death. The end came a few months after he finally left Webster Street for a Catholic nursing home. He was eighty years old. Not long before he died Nathan Lerner entered Darger's room to clean it. As he said in a personal recollection,

> It is a humbling experience to have to admit that not until I looked under all the debris in his room did I become aware of the incredible world that Henry had created from within himself. It was only in the last days of Henry Darger's life that I came close to knowing who this shuffling old man really was.

What Lerner found under the compulsively organized piles of twine and spectacles and newsprint was the eight-volume biography Darger had been working on since 1963—and, in a number of old trunks where they had been stored, the trove of original artwork that has now made Darger world famous. In MacGregor's words:

> . . . fifteen volumes, 15,145 typewritten pages, unquestionably the longest work of fiction ever written. In time the room also yielded the three huge bound volumes of illustrations for that work, several hundred pictures, many over twelve feet long and painted on both sides. By accident, the landlord had stumbled upon a concealed and secret life work which no one had ever seen: Darger's alternate world.

That world is a vast nameless planet orbited by our own Earth. The frontispiece of Volume One of its history reads

OF THE STORY OF THE VIVIAN GIRLS,
IN WHAT IS KNOWN AS THE REALMS OF THE UNREAL,
OF THE GLANDECO-ANGELINIAN WAR STORM,
CAUSED BY THE CHILD SLAVE REBELLION

The Vivian Girls! Seven plucky child princesses who, with their brother Penrod, battle the adult, male Glandelinians, enemies who exist solely to capture, imprison, and especially, torture the child-slaves of the Christian country of Abbiennia. Modelled largely upon the books he loved as a child—L. Frank Baum's Oz books, Johanna Spyri's Heidi stories, *Uncle Tom's Cabin*, Booth Tarkington's *Penrod* series—Darger's epic follows the Vivian Girls through an endless relay of scrapes, plots, imprisonments, battles, escapes and cataclysmic storms.

Still, as Darger himself admits in a tone at once wistful and minatory, "This is not the land where Dorothy and her Oz friends reside." Darger seems to have had little innate skill as a draftsman: he created his scroll-like paintings and drawing by means of collage, tracery, photocopying and enlarging pictures, then hand-coloring them, creating an imagistic impasto that is breathtaking, surreal, deliriously funny and very often horrific. The figures of the Vivian Girls and the child slaves are taken mostly from children's coloring books and newspaper cartoons, Disney figures, advertisements, illustrations from The Saturday Evening Post; the malevolent Glandelinian generals from newspaper photos and images of soldiers from the Civil War. There are also the beautiful dragon-like Blengiglomeneans and Blenglins, children with ram's-horns and gorgeous butterfly wings. The landscapes are vast, with Toon Town trees and blue-washed skies; though the usual weather consists of cyclones, tornadoes, hail, fire; the "insane fury of crazy thunderstorm." A sample of Darger's captions read "thrilling time while with bombshells bursting all around," "Children tied to trees in path of forest fires. In spite of exceeding extreme peril, Vivian Girls rescued them," and "Everything is allright though storm continues."

Within Henry Darger's mind, it continued for decades; a firestorm of conflicting impulses. Art critics make much of Darger's luminous use of color and his genius for collage, and certainly many of the paintings in the Henry Darger Collection at the American Folk Art Museum are gorgeous and genuinely breathtaking: a watercolor of the dragonlike Blengins that resembles an Edenic vision filtered through Klimt; portraits of the Glendelinian Generals that anticipate the dizzy swirl of Terry Gilliam's Monty Python animations; a nine-foot panel that shows the Vivian Girls and their followers in an idyllic, flower-strewn setting that evokes the pastoral beauty of "A Midsummer Night's Dream."

But this is not Oz. The girl slaves are usually naked (a good deal of the written text involves getting their clothes off); they often have male, but never female, genitals. There is no real economic purpose for their enslavement: the children exist solely to be tortured, in graphic and appalling detail, by the predatory Glendelinians, who crucify, disembowel, burn and flagellate them. In his exhaustive study, MacGregor compellingly suggests that in Darger's work we have the singular opportunity to gaze into the mind of someone who, under different circumstances, might well have been a pedophile and perhaps a serial killer of children.

Given America's continuing obsession with pedophilia and serial murder, it's not surprising that there would be a ready-made audience for work that has the seal of approval of a critical establishment. Yet the power of Darger's art doesn't lie in prurience, or even in the voyeuristic sense of looking upon the work of someone who, almost certainly, would have been frightened and angered by our attention. It's too strange for the former—like the Victorian art critic John Ruskin, Darger seems to have been innocent of the facts of human anatomy, and probably of human reproduction and sexual function as well—and too repellent, in many instances, to incite the sustained voyeuristic interest of most "normal" people.

Separated from his visual work, his written text has the monotonous banality of the simplest pornography (only without the sex); but taken in toto, THE REALMS is as excruciating and detailed a portrait of the human psyche that we have seen: brutal, banal, transcendental, and with flashes of the divine. As MacGregor says,

> Darger's acute awareness of violence and evil in the world, and particularly in the lives of children, was unmistakably derived from the presence of monstrous drives and desires in himself. By withdrawing from the world, the mystic, far from escaping from temptation, opens himself to the encounter with evil in its purest form as it arises from within. Darger, like the Desert Fathers, was repeatedly overwhelmed by such temptations, but by encountering them in the Realms of the Unreal he defended himself against the danger of acting on them in the world . . . Evil, carried to impossible extremes, surely must attract the attention of God.

I first heard of the Vivian Girls in 1979, in a song called "The Vivian Girls" by the late Snakefinger (Philip Lithman)—

> The Vivian Girls are the frozen ones
> The chosen ones.
> Standing on pedestals out in the sun
> The melting continues, it's barely begun
> Still, nobody knows what will happen the day
> The ice around The Vivian Girls melts away.

Now the ice around the Vivian Girls has melted away at last. Darger's paintings sell for close to a hundred thousand dollars, and the images of his exuberant dragons, plucky princesses, and murderous generals can be seen in museums and collections around the world. Their sad, frail creator has achieved, in death, the kind of fame that would surely have bewildered him if it had come during his lifetime.

In John Crowley's *Engine Summer*, a race of angelic creatures treasures a crystal globe which has recorded within it the entire memory and experiences of a single human being, a man named Rush That Speaks. In the novel's final paragraphs, the process of reading the crystal is described by an angel conversing with Rush's encoded consciousness—

Interpenetration, yes. With another . . . you'll marvel at the dome, the clouds; and tell your story again. What it is to be you when you aren't here but on your pedestal, we don't know; we only know that sometimes you come . . .

We know nothing else, Rush, but what you tell us. It's all you here now, Rush.

I think that the awe and terror and humility we feel when we contemplate Henry Darger's work is not dissimilar to this sense of interpenetration with another being: it is all you, here; it is all us. The timeless urge to create is what made the profoundly damaged, isolated and lonely man named Henry Darger human. It is also, ultimately, what may make him immortal.

KEVIN BROCKMEIER

The Green Children

Kevin Brockmeier has published innovative short fiction in numerous literary journals, winning the Italo Calvino Short Fiction Award, the Nelson Algren Award, an O. Henry Award, and a James Michener–Paul Engle Fellowship. He is the author of an excellent story collection, Things That Fall From the Sky, *and a memorable novel for children,* City of Names. *His new novel,* The Truth About Celia, *is scheduled for Summer 2003 publication. He lives in Little Rock, Arkansas.*

Although much of Brockmeier's fiction stands in the borderland between several modes of writing (realism, magical realism, surrealism, and fable), the tale that follows is a more traditional work of historical fantasy. The piece is based on an English fairy story that was recorded (as historical fact) in the medieval chronicles of William of Newburgh and Ralph of Coggeshall. Brockmeier's rendition of "The Green Children" is reprinted from Arkansas Literary Review, *an online journal featuring the works of Arkansas writers and artists, and is part of* The Truth About Celia.

—T. W.

Based on an account in the Historia Rerum Anglicarum, written in 1196 by William of Newburgh.

They say I was the first to touch them. When the reapers found the children in the wolf-pits—a boy and a girl, their skin the pale flat green of wilting grass—they shuddered and would not lay hands on them, prodding them across the fields with the handles of their scythes. I watched them approach from my stone on the bank of the river. The long, curving blades of the scythes sent up flashes of light that dazzled my eyes and made me doubt what I was seeing—a boy and a girl holding fast to each other's garments, twisting them nervously between their green fingers, their green faces turned to the sun. The reapers nudged and jabbed at them until they came to a stop at my side, where the river's green water lapped at their shoes. I allowed myself to stare.

Alden took me by the shoulder and said, "We think that it must be the rotting disease. They were calling out when we found them, but none of us could make out the tongue. We're taking them to the house of Richard de Calne."

I understand little of medicine, and in those days I understood even less, but I could see that, despite the coloring of their skin, the children were healthy. The veins beneath their arms were dark and prominent, the sharp green of clover or spinach leaves. Their breathing was regular and clear.

"Will you carry them across the river?" Alden asked me, and I took my time before answering, cleaning the gristle from my teeth with the tapering edge of a twig. I know the rules of bargaining.

"Two coins," I said. "Two coins for each. And one for the rest of you."

The reapers fished the silver from their satchels.

If I was not the first to touch the children, I was certainly the first to carry them.

I lifted the boy onto my shoulders (one of the men had to rap the girl's wrist with the butt of his scythe to make her let go of him) and was halfway across the river when Alden summoned me back. "Take some of us across first. If you leave the boy there alone, he'll run away." So I carried two of the men to the opposite shore, and then the boy, and then I returned for the girl, balancing her in the crook of my arm so that she straddled the hummock of muscle like a rider on a pony. This was years ago, when I could haul a full trough of water all the way from the river to the stables, or raise a calf over my head, or shore up the wall of a house while the sun dried the foundation. The water was as high as my waist when my foot fell on a patch of thick, jellylike moss and shot into the current. The girl wrapped her arms around my neck and began to speak in a panic, a thread of shrill, gabbling syllables that I could not understand. "Wooramywoorismifath!"

I regained my balance, throwing my arms out, and heard one of the reapers laughing at me from the river-bank. The girl was crying now, convulsive sobs that shook her entire body, and I took her chin in my fingers and turned her face toward mine. Her eyes were as brown as singed barley, as brown as my own. "I know these people," I said to her. "Look at me. I know them. No one will hurt you." A yellow slug of mucous was trailing from her nose, and I wiped it off with my finger and slung it into the water, where the fish began to nip at it. "Don't cry," I said, and with three loping strides I set her on the other shore.

As the reapers led the children into Woolpit, I kneaded the coins in my pocket, feeling their satisfying weight and the imprint of their notches. Seven birds came together in the sky. The coming week would bring a change of fortune. It was the plainest of signs.

The river spills straight through the center of town, with the fields, the church, and the stables on one side and the smithy, the tavern, and the market on the other. It is an angry foaming dragon, the current swift and violent, and only the strongest can cross it without falling. The nearest stepway is half an hour's walk downstream, a wedge of stone so slippery it seems to sway beneath you like a lily-pad, yet before I took my place on the shore, the people of Woolpit made that journey every day. I was just a boy then and liked to stand on the bank casting almond shells into the water, following beside them as they tumbled and sailed away, memorizing the trails they took. By the time my growth came upon me I knew the river well, every twist and eddy and surge of it. I soon discovered I could cross it with ease. I had found my work.

The days after the green children appeared were busy ones. I would rest on my stone no longer than a moment before a new party of townspeople would arrive, their coins gleaming in their hands, eager to see the wonders at the house of Richard de Calne. One by one I would hoist them onto my back and wade into the water, leaning against the current and rooting my feet to the ground, and one by one I would haul them back to the other shore when they returned some few hours later. At night, as I lay on my pallet, the muscles of my back gave involuntary jerking pulses, like fish pulled from the river and clapped onto a hard surface. The sensation was entirely new to me then, though I have experienced it many times since.

The people who had seen the green children spoke of little else, and I listened to their accounts as they gathered in clutches on the strand:

"The girl is covered in bugbites, and the boy just lies there and shivers."

"I hear that de Calne has hired someone to train them in English."

"Green to their gums! Green to the roots of their hair!"

"Have you seen the midget who lives at Coggeshall Abbey?"

"I made a farting noise with my tongue, and the girl smiled at me."

"The chirurgeon says that it's chlorosis—the greensickness."

"They're the ugliest specimens I've ever seen—uglier than a boil, uglier than that hag Ruberta."

"I can see them glowing like marshfire when I close my eyes."

"Did I tell you my milk-cow dropped a two-headed calf last year?"

"Mark my words—they'll be dead before the first frost."

The river was swollen with rain from a storm that had broken in the hills, but the sky over Woolpit was so windless and fine that the current ran almost noiselessly between its banks. As I carried the townsfolk through water as high as my gut, I gave my ear to them and learned that the green children had eaten nothing for several days, though bread and meat and greens had all been set before them. I learned that though they did not eat, they did drink from the dippers of water they were given, and that sometimes the girl even used the excess to clean her face and hands. One of the men who had examined the children for hidden weapons said that their hair was handsomely clipped, their teeth straight and white, and their clothing was stitched from a strange-looking material with many narrow furrows: it fell on their bodies with the stiffness of leather, yet was soft and smooth to the touch. "They huddled together as soon as I drew away," I heard him say. "They clutched their stomachs and cried."

On the third day of the children's keeping, one of the growers brought them some beans newly cut from the field. The children were plainly excited and slit the stalks open with their fingernails, examining the hollows for food, but finding nothing there, they began to weep. Then one of the kitchen-maids swept the stalks aside and showed them how to crack open the pods. She prised out a row of naked beans, and the children gasped and thrust their hands out for them. The kitchen-maid insisted on softening the beans in water first, and then, with great relish, the children devoured them. For several days after they would eat nothing else.

It was Martin, the tanner's son, who told me that the girl had spoken her name. He arrived at the river one evening carrying a palm-shaped basket of green reeds raddled so carelessly together that the fringe twisted in every direction. "Our fire went out," he said. "My dad told me to go get some more."

"Climb on," I said, and he shinnied up to my shoulders. As we crossed the water, he asked me whether I had seen the boy and the girl yet. "I have," I told him.

"Did you know the girl's started talking now? Real words, I mean."

"What has she said?"

"She can say 'water,' and she can say 'hungry,' and she can say 'more.' The boy hasn't said a damned thing, though." We had reached the shore by then, and I lifted him from my shoulders, straight into the air, so that he spat the word "Jesus" and then laughed as I planted him upright on the bank. "That's what my dad told me, anyway," and he ran up the trail into the village.

When he returned some short time later, there was a small heap of orange coals smoldering inside his basket. Each time the breeze touched them, they glimmered brightly for a moment, then gently dimmed. "You're not going to spill those on me, are you?" I asked. "Because if you do you'll be walking home wet."

"I promise," he said, and so I carried him to the other shore.

As I stood him on dry ground I asked, "Has the girl told her name yet?"

"Seel-ya," he said. "That's how she pronounced it, too. Funny." He set his basket of coals on the grass and pulled a coin from the inside of his shoe: it was clinging to the skin of his foot, and he had to peel it loose before handing it to me. I took the coin and dropped it in my satchel, heavy as a fist from the day's business. "Goodbye then," he said.

"Goodbye," I answered.

He marched off toward home, carrying his pocket of light into the graying air.

It was no later than the hunter's moon when the first travelers began to arrive. They came from the east and the south (those from the west and north having no need to cross the river) and asked how to find their way to the green children they had heard tell of. They referred to the children as oddities, or marvels, or curiosities. Some of them had been given to believe they were bedded down like goats or cattle in a grain-crib or a stable somewhere, though in truth de Calne was housing them in one of his servant's rooms. "You'll find them over there," I told them, gesturing obscurely beyond a spinney of thin, girlish elm trees. "A large house past a row of small ones. You can't miss it." I offered to ferry them to the opposite shore of the river on my back. "Only two coins," I would say—my new fee for pilgrims. "Or you can try to push your way across without me." At this I would toss a stick into the water, dropping it midstream so that the current gripped it immediately, wrenching it away. "There's an outcropping of rocks downstream where we usually retrieve the bodies."

The travelers all carried parcels and walking sticks, and after scouting along the bank for a time they always accepted my offer.

The green children had quickly become commonplace to the people of Woolpit, just another feature of the landscape, like the bluff above the maple thicket, shaped like the body of a sleeping horse, or the trio of stone wells outside the marketplace, but as the story of their discovery spread, the people who came to see them journeyed from farther and farther away. I was becoming a wealthy man.

One of these pilgrims, a boy of no more than fifteen who was traveling alone, asked me why there was no bridge by which to make the crossing. "We've built them before," I said, "but the river is too powerful. They never last the month before the rains come and the high water washes them away."

"There's a man in my town who's developed a new method of working with stone. He can shape it into a half-circle, and it will be broad enough and strong enough for even a man on horseback to pass over. I've seen him do it. For the right price, I'm sure he would build a bridge for you."

I gave the boy a flinty stare and said, "We have no need of such a service." His hair was as white as an old man's, with the flat shine of chalk. Even after he was gone, its image stayed in my eyes.

As soon as the green children began to eat the same food as the rest of us, the same bread and flesh and vegetables, the girl developed a healthy cushion of skin around her bones. The boy, however, became frailer and more feverish with each new morning, trembling with the slightest movement of the air and passing a pungent, oily shit from his bowels. A doctor bled and purged him to balance his humours, then applied a poultice to his sores, but to no effect. He merely rolled over onto his side, coughing and blinking until he fell asleep. For a single coin Richard de Calne would have him strip from his clothing so that onlookers could see the way his skin pinched tight around the corners of his body—a mottled shade of green, like a leaf fed upon by aphids.

The boy had yet to say anything more than his name, a dusty line of syllables I have long since forgotten, but the girl, Seel-ya, was now speaking in complete sentences, and she astonished her visitors by conversing with them in a tongue they understood, telling the tale of how she came to this country.

She was, she said, from a wholly different land, though she could not say where it lay in relation to our own. The people there were of her color, and when she first saw the reapers leaning over her in the wolf-pits, their skin was of so pale a shade she was not sure they were human, and she screamed for her mother and father. The sun, she claimed, was not so bright in her country, and the stars were not so many. She had been playing outside her house when she heard a great sound, like the chiming of bells, and when she turned to follow it, she found herself in this place. The boy had appeared in the wolf-pits alongside her, and though she did not know him, she could tell that he came from her land. She missed her family, she said, and she wanted to go home.

One morning, while I was waiting for my first foot passengers of the day, Joana the Cyprian came walking toward the river. It has been a long time now since she was young enough to sell her services, but in the years of which I speak she was the most beautiful woman in Woolpit, and her eyes in their black rings were as shining and open as windows. She lived in a small hut hidden in the trees at the edge of town. The sun was climbing into the sky behind her, and through the thin fabric of her dress I could see the outline of her thighs and a tangled gusset of pubic hair. "Good morning, Curran," she said to me.

"Joana," I nodded.

"Aren't you going to ask me what I'm doing out so early?" Instead I pitched a stone into the water to measure the pace of the current, watching as it drifted from the surface to the bed. "I'm headed to Richard de Calne's house," she said.

"Going to gawp at the green children, I suspect."

"Going to work with the green children." Her voice was thistleish with irritation, and I had to smother a grin. It was one of my joys to provoke her. "I'm teaching the girl her duties as a woman," she said. "De Calne plans to raise her to his wife." She swung the copper-colored horsetail of her hair over her shoulder. "So are you going to take me across or not?"

I slapped my palms against my back and said, "I'm at your service, dear," but she winked at me and declared, "No, Curran, I want to ride up front"—which is exactly what she did. She wrapped her legs around my hips and her arms around my neck. I swung forward with her into the river.

As I carried her deeper into the water, she allowed herself to sink slowly down over my crotch, exaggerating her fall with each jerk of my stride. The muscles of the current pulled at my ankles. I could feel her releasing her breath in a long, thin rope against my chest, and my nose began to prickle with her scent. "Why so quiet, Curran?" she asked. "Hmm?" When I set her on the other shore, she placed a slow-rolling kiss on my lips and ran her finger up my penis, from the root to the ember, which was visibly propping up my waistcloth. "So what do I owe you?" she whispered into my ear.

I brought her hand to my mouth and kissed the knuckles. "No charge," I said.

Sometimes I wish it was still that way.

I was leaning forward on my stone, eating a boiled egg one of the farmers had given me for his passage, on the morning the monk arrived. I watched him hobble around the end of the stables and follow the path toward the river. His robe was coated so thickly with dust I could not tell whether the cloth underneath was brown or white. "Tell me," he asked, planting his staff at my feet, "have I reached Woolpit?"

"You have." I cast the eggshell halves into the water, where they went bobbing off like two glowing boats. I have watched the river for many years, and there is nothing it won't carry away. I'm told that if you follow it far enough into the distance, past the hills and the long forest of pines, it empties into the sea, offering its cargo of sticks, bones, and eggshells to the whales, but I have never been that far.

"I've come for the monsters," said the monk. The sun shifted from behind a cloud, and he squinted into the glare.

"The children, you mean." I pointed across the river. "They're at the house of Richard de Calne."

"The soldier," he said. "Yes, so I've heard. How much for passage?"

"Three coins," I said. He drew open the pouch that was sagging from his belt, handed me the silver, and then rapped my leg with the end of his staff. "Up," he ordered.

I looked at him grayly. He was not a large man and I could have broken him over my knee, but instead I pocketed the coins, counting repeatedly to three in my head.

While we were crossing the river, I allowed him to slip a few notches lower on my spine so that the hem of his robe trailed in the water and took on weight. Snake-shapes of dirt twisted away from him downstream, but he did not notice. He told me that he had heard of the green children from a beggar in the town of Lenna, who had informed him fully of their strange condition. "They speak a language known to no Christian ear," the monk recited, "and are green as clover. The girl is loose and wanton in her conduct, and the boy shudders at the touch of any human hand. They are a corruption to all those who look upon them."

"Most of what you say is false," I said. A little whirlpool spun like a plate on the surface of the water before it wobbled and came apart. "The children have learned our own tongue now, or at least the girl has, and while I can't speak for anyone else, they've certainly done me no harm."

"You've seen them?" he asked.

"I have, and they're no danger to anyone."

He made a scoffing noise. "Yes, but you are clearly an ignorant man. I'm told they will eat nothing but beans. Beans! Beans are the food of the dead, and the dead-on-earth are the implements of Satan."

"They eat flesh and bread, just like the rest of us. It was only those first few days that they ate beans."

"The devil quickly learns to hide himself," he said dismissively, as though he had tired of arguing with me. "I aim to baptize them, and if they won't take the water, then I aim to kill them."

I stopped short, anchoring my foot against the side of a rock. I could feel the anger mounting inside me. "You won't harm them," I said.

"I will do as my conscience demands." He cuffed my ear. "Now move, you!"

At that, I whipped my body around and let him drop into the water. He sideslipped downstream, tumbling and sputtering in a fog of brown soot, before he managed to find root on the riverbottom. Then, bracing himself with his staff, which swayed and buckled in his hands, he hitched his way slowly to the other shore. By the time he staggered onto the rocks, I was already sitting against the high ledge of the bank. His robe hung on his body like a moulting skin, and his hair curtained his eyes. "You—!" he said. He flapped his arms and water spattered onto the shingle. "I want my silver returned to me."

I did not feel the need to answer him. Instead, I reached into my pocket and retrieved the coins, slinging them at him one by one. They thumped against the front of his robe and fell to the rocks with a ting. He picked them up, then straightened himself and set his eyes on me. "I have a mission," he said. "God has given it to me. I will not be discouraged from it by the muscles of any Goliath," and he went stamping up the road into Woolpit, wringing the water from his clothing. Three blackbirds landed in the path behind him, striking at the dirt.

It was late that afternoon when I heard that the boy had died.

I abandoned my post by the river that night to attend the burning of his body. The pyre had been laid with branches of white spruce and maple, and the silver wood of the one and the gold wood of the other carried a gentle, lambent glow that seemed to float free of the pyre in the air. The moon was full, and I could see the faces of the townspeople by its light. Alden was there, and Joana, and the boy Martin, along with the blacksmith and the reapers and all the other men and women of Woolpit. I had never seen so many of them gathered together in one place. The monk, though, was nowhere among them. He had indeed baptized the children, I learned—immersing them in a basin of water, each for the count of one hundred—but while the girl had survived the dunking, the boy had not. He was already weak with illness, and when his body met the water, it stiffened in a violent grip and went still as the monk pushed him under. One of the servants who was watching said that he breathed not a single bubble of air. When de Calne learned that the boy had died, he set his men on the monk with clubs, and the monk was made to flee by the western road.

There was some discussion between de Calne and Father Gervase, the town priest, as to whether or not the boy ought to be buried in church ground—had his spirit passed from him before, during, or after baptism?—but finally it was decided to follow the path of caution. They would allow the fire to consume him.

The boy was laid out on the pyre inside a white sheet painted with wax, and as we stood about the fallow field watching, de Calne signaled to his servants and a ring of torches was driven into the wood. The flames were tall and bright, the smoke so thickly woven that it blotted out the stars. Our faces were sharp in the yellow light, which was clear and steady, so that our shadows scarcely wavered. I saw the green girl holding onto Joana, her arms wrapped tightly around her waist. A moment later de Calne stooped at her side, taking her chin in his hands. He stared into her eyes with a strange, questioning zeal until she quailed away from him, hiding her face in Joana's dress.

The fire burned long into the night, and I fell into conversation with the merchant brothers Radulphi and Emmet. They were deliberating over what had killed the boy, and they had flatly differing notions on the matter, as they had on so many others. "He was not of this world," said Emmet. "That much was clear to see—and so of course he rejected the baptism. The sacraments are for members of the body of Jesus Christ. The boy was a member of no body but his own."

"But the girl accepted the water without sign of affliction." Radulphi smacked his palms together as he made his point. "And it's not at all clear that the children are from another world. They might have gotten lost in the flint mines of Fordham, nothing else, and simply wandered around the mine shafts until they came out inside the wolf-pits. It's happened before."

"Then how do you explain the color of their skin?" I asked.

"It was the greensickness, like the chirurgeon said."

"Not likely," said Emmet. "And if it wasn't the baptism that killed the boy, then what was it?"

"Starvation," said Radulphi. "His body wasn't accepting the food he ate, and so it devoured itself."

"At the very moment he touched the water?" Emmet smacked his own palms together. "Hah!"

Radulphi had been working an acorn between his fingers, and he tossed it to me. "You haven't told us what you think, Curran?"

"What do I think?" I was, as I have said, a young man then, and my answer was a young man's answer: "I think it's foolish to argue over matters that cannot be decided. Who knows why our spirits depart, and who can say where they go when they do? These things are a mystery. Nothing more can be said."

I have grown older since then, if only occasionally wiser, but I have tried to pay attention to what happens around me, and there is one sure thing my age has taught me—death is no mystery, in its cause if not in its consequences. If Radulphi were to ask me his question today, my answer would not be the same. I would tell him instead what I have seen with my own eyes: you can die of too much, and you can die of too little, and everybody dies of one or the other. That night, however, I simply fell silent. The shadow of the boy's body flickered in and out of sight inside the flames, and as the wood settled, de Calne's men prodded at it with long, forked sticks to keep it from tumbling free.

"I still believe it was the baptism," said Emmet.

"And I still believe you're an idiot," said Radulphi.

I cast the acorn into the fire, listening for the nut to explode in the heat.

It was ten years or more before I saw the girl again. The last of the trees were turning color with the end of autumn, and the air had the fine, dry smell of burning leaves that signals an early snow. I was resting against the edge of my stone, worn smooth from all my years of sitting, when a young woman emerged from the spinney of elm trees by the tavern. She walked swiftly but deliberately, turning occasionally to look behind her as though sweeping the ground for footprints. I crossed the river to be ready to meet her on the other bank.

"I need passage over the water," she said when she arrived. Her breath was coming rapidly, in thick white plumes. "Quickly. How much?" she asked.

"Four coins," I said.

She counted out the money from a leather satchel hanging at her side. A shirt that had been tucked neatly inside poked out from the broaching after she tied the straps down. "Is there anybody following me?" she asked.

The sky was hidden behind a single flat sheet of clouds, and the path into town was long and shadowless. Even the birds were resting. "No one," I said.

"Good." She handed me the silver, then shifted her satchel so that it fell over her buttock, and climbed onto my back. "Let's go."

The water was frigid that morning. It rose around my stomach in a sealed, constricting ring, and I began to shiver. I couldn't help myself. Even the year before, the chill of the water had seemed only the barest prickle to me, a tiny gnat to swat away with my fingers, but with each passing month, ever since the summer had fallen, I had noticed it more and more. The young woman tightened her arms around my chest and said, "I hate this—crossing the water. I feel sick inside."

"Don't worry," I said. "I won't let anything happen to you."

It was then that she made a clicking noise in her throat, and I could feel her seizing upon a memory or perception. You learn to recognize such things when you carry people as I do: it's in their posture and their breathing and the power of their grip. In this case, it was as if all the heaviness drained from her body into mine, then gradually returned to her. "I remember you," she said. "You were here by the river on the day I came."

Whereupon I realized who she was.

Her body had spread open into its grown-up shape and become paler over time. Her skin was now a yellow-gold, like that of the spice merchants who travel through Woolpit from Far Asia. "Seel-ya," I said.

"That's right."

"You look—different."

She almost smiled. "I know. I lost most of my color a long time ago. The chirurgeon says it was the change in my diet, but people take on new colors all the time as they grow older, don't they? They're like caterpillars turning into butterflies." She tensed suddenly. "Tell me, is there anybody following me yet?"

I looked behind me. "Still no one."

"Good," she said, and her muscles relaxed. "Then so far he hasn't realized."

I bent my thoughts to what she had said about people taking on new colors. It was not without its truth. The tillers and planters, for instance, were gray with a soil that would never wash out of their skin—you could recognize them by the stain of it on their hands and faces—and my own body had turned a rich chestnut-brown across the chest and shoulders from the hours I spent in the sun. Children were born with murky blue eyes, and only later did they become green or brown or hazel, or the lighter, more natural blue of the living. Old people faced with their last sickness turned white as tallow as they took to their beds. I caught my likeness in the water and saw the two long cords of silver in my hair. I deposited Seel-ya on the shore.

"Where are you fleeing to, child?" I asked.

"How do you know that I'm fleeing?"

I gave a snort of laughter, and her face sprang up in a slanting grin. "Very well," she said. "I suppose I have to tell somebody. I'm going to King's Lynne. There's a man that I intend to wed." She glanced over my shoulder, across the river. "In fact"—she dug into her satchel for another four coins—"if Richard de Calne or any of his servants come asking after me, will you tell them you haven't seen me? Or better yet, will you send them the wrong way?"

"I will," I told her, and I pocketed the coins. "Good luck to you."

She nodded. She lifted herself carefully onto the shelf of the bank, then turned back to me. "You were kind to me that day. I haven't forgotten. Thank you."

"You were in need of someone's kindness," I said.

She set out along the southern road, moving at a steady trot, and soon she vanished from my sight behind the stables. That was the last I saw of her.

What else is there to tell? De Calne and his men did indeed come looking for the girl, their pikestaffs held at the ready, and I directed them into the hills to the west of town, where a few meager paths had been trampled into the brush by the few travelers foolish enough to attempt passage. Packs of wolves and wild boar could be heard baying and grunting there at night, and great owls lifted from the branches of trees with a sound like someone beating the dirt from a mat.

I told de Calne that the girl said she was going to gather her strength there and make her way north when the weather cleared. He and his men came stumping back two days later, their garments split and tattered and their pikestaffs left behind them in the forest.

The winter that followed was the coldest I have ever seen. (It has been a long life, and I cannot imagine I will see one colder.) The river froze over for the first time in memory, assuming the blue-white color of solid ice, and the people of Woolpit scattered dirt across it in a continuous sheet, walking from one shore to the other as though it were simply a road. I spent the season hauling coal to the village from the mines. When spring came and the water melted, the chalk-haired boy who had visited Woolpit ten years before—I had never forgotten him—returned with the stonemason he had told me of. Together they built a bridge that spanned the water in a perfect arch. It stands there still, as sturdy and elegant as the bones of a foot.

I found new work as a lifter and plougher, and when my strength went, as a tavern-keeper. It was some few years ago that a man of Newburgh, a historian by the name of William, came to the tavern seeking reports of the green children, and I told him this story as I have told it to you. Afterwards, he asked me if I knew what had become of the girl. Had she married the man at King's Lynne? Had de Calne ever managed to find her? Though I am certain she did not return to Woolpit, and de Calne soon gave her up as lost, I know nothing else for a certainty. Some say she did indeed marry, mothering children of her own. Some say she took work as a kitchen steward in a small town to the south of Norfolk. Some say she vanished from this world as suddenly as she appeared here, following a sound like the chiming of bells. I myself could make no guesses. It was very long ago, and I was not there.

SHARON McCARTNEY

After the Chuck Jones Tribute on Teletoon

Sharon McCartney has an M.F.A. in poetry from the University of Iowa Writers' Workshop and a law degree from the University of Victoria. Her work has been published in The Fiddlehead, Prism International, Event, Frain, sub-TERRAIN, Prairie Fire, Iowa City, *and other journals; and she is the author of one book of poems,* Under the Abdominal Wall. *Her wry fantasia "After the Chuck Jones Tribute on Teletoon" appeared in the Fall 2002 edition of* The Malahat Review, *published by the University of Victoria in British Columbia.*

—*T. W.*

Swan-diving off the crewcut mesas of Monument Valley
in an Icarus contraption of fluff and paste, roadrunner
bull's-eyed far below, coyote can't help it—it's an addiction,
a disease, beyond his control. He's resigned to pain,
the blacksmith's anvil stuka-ing his skull, the Sisyphean boulder
snowballing down each time he shoulders it upward,
his crabbed frame of bones and hide steamrollered, accordion-
folded or simply incinerated. *Hope is the thing with feathers,*
he grumbles but he can't get Prometheus out of his craw;
his scrawny belly cringes under the eagle's talons, cold avian
claws on his abdomen. He paws the packed earth of the river
gorge, fear and sorrow a garment he can't shed, a raiment,
his scratchy winter coat. What else is there to do in the desert?
Experience tells him he can't win and yet he persists.
Who can predict the actions of the Gods? The chances
are slim but statistics mean nothing to the one who succeeds.
He splashes a false horizon on sandstone, sets the sun
precariously low, dots the vanishing point, steps three paces
back with his Picasso beret and palette, thumb up to correct
the perspective, and plummets off the predictable cliff.

NEIL GAIMAN

Feeders and Eaters

About the following story Gaiman says: "This story started as a dream I had in 1984, when I was living in Edgeware. I was in the dream, both me and the man in the story. Normally dreams don't make stories, but this one continued to haunt me, and in 1990-ish I wrote it as a comic for Mark Buckingham to draw. Not many people read it, and it was printed so dark that much of what was happening became almost impossible to make out.

"When asked for a story for Keep Out the Night, *I remembered that one, and I got intrigued by the idea of taking an old horror story I wrote as a comic and rewriting it as prose. It's an odd piece, like a collaboration between me age thirty and me age forty-one."*

—E. D.

This is a true story, pretty much. As far as that goes, and whatever good it does anybody.

It was late one night, and I was cold, in a city where I had no right to be. Not at that time of night, anyway. I won't tell you which city. I'd missed my last train, and I wasn't sleepy, so I prowled the streets around the station until I found an all-night café. Somewhere warm to sit.

You know the kind of place; you've been there: café's name on a Pepsi sign above a dirty plate-glass window, dried egg residue between the tines of all their forks. I wasn't hungry, but I bought a slice of toast and a mug of greasy tea, so they'd leave me alone.

There were a couple of other people in there, sitting alone at their tables, derelicts and insomniacs huddled over their empty plates. Dirty coats and donkey jackets, each buttoned up to the neck.

I was walking back from the counter, with my tray, when somebody said, "Hey." It was a man's voice. "You," the voice said, and I knew he was talking to me, not to the room. "I know you. Come here. Sit over here."

I ignored it. You don't want to get involved, not with anyone you'd run into in a place like that.

Then he said my name, and I turned and looked at him. When someone knows your name, you don't have any option.

"Don't you know me?" he asked. I shook my head. I didn't know anyone who looked like that. You don't forget something like that. "It's me," he said, his voice a pleading whisper. "Eddie Barrow. Come on mate. You know me."

And when he said his name I did know him, more or less. I mean, I knew Eddie Barrow. We had worked on a building site together, ten years back, during my only real flirtation with manual work.

Eddie Barrow was tall, and heavily muscled, with a movie star smile and lazy good looks. He was ex-police. Sometimes he'd tell me stories, true tales of fitting-up and doing over, of punishment and crime. He had left the force after some trouble between him and one of the top brass. He said it was the Chief Superintendent's wife forced him to leave. Eddie was always getting into trouble with women. They really liked him, women.

When we were working together on the building site they'd hunt him down, give him sandwiches, little presents, whatever. He never seemed to do anything to make them like him; they just liked him. I used to watch him to see how he did it, but it didn't seem to be anything he did. Eventually, I decided it was just the way he was: big, strong, not very bright, and terribly, terribly good-looking.

But that was ten years ago.

The man sitting at the Formica table wasn't good-looking. His eyes were dull, and rimmed with red, and they stared down at the table-top, without hope. His skin was grey. He was too thin, obscenely thin. I could see his scalp through his filthy hair. I said, "What happened to you?"

"How d'you mean?"

"You look a bit rough," I said, although he looked worse than rough; he looked dead. Eddie Barrow had been a big guy. Now he'd collapsed in on himself. All bones and flaking skin.

"Yeah," he said. Or maybe "Yeah?" I couldn't tell. Then, resigned, flatly, "Happens to us all in the end."

He gestured with his left hand, pointed at the seat opposite him. His right arm hung stiffly at his side, his right hand safe and hidden in the pocket of his coat.

Eddie's table was by the window, where anyone walking past could see you. Not somewhere I'd sit by choice, not if it was up to me. But it was too late now. I sat down facing him and I sipped my tea. I didn't say anything, which could have been a mistake. Small talk might have kept his demons at a distance. But I cradled my mug and said nothing. So I suppose he must have thought that I wanted to know more, that I cared. I didn't care. I had enough problems of my own. I didn't want to know about his struggle with whatever it was that had brought him to this state—drink, or drugs, or disease—but he started to talk, in a grey voice, and I listened.

"I came here a few years back, when they were building the bypass. Stuck around after, the way you do. Got a room in an old place around the back of Prince Regent's Street. Room in the attic. It was a family house, really. They only rented out the top floor, so there were just the two boarders, me and Miss Corvier. We were both up in the attic, but in separate rooms, next door to each other. I'd hear her moving about. And there was a cat. It was the family cat, but it came upstairs to say hello, every now and again, which was more than the family ever did.

"I always had my meals with the family, but Miss Corvier she didn't ever come down for meals, so it was a week before I met her. She was coming out of the upstairs lavvy. She looked so old. Wrinkled face, like an old, old monkey. But long hair, down to her waist, like a young girl.

"It's funny, with old people, you don't think they feel things like we do. I mean, here's her, old enough to be my granny and . . ." He stopped. Licked his lips with a grey tongue. "Anyway . . . I came up to the room one night and there's a brown paper bag of mushrooms outside my door on the ground. It was a present, I knew that straight off. A present for me. Not normal mushrooms, though. So I knocked on her door.

"I says, 'Are these for me?'

" 'Picked them meself, Mister Barrow,' she says.

" 'They aren't like toadstools or anything?' I asked. 'Y'know, poisonous? Or funny mushrooms?'

"She just laughs. Cackles even. 'They're for eating,' she says. 'They're fine. Shaggy inkcaps, they are. Eat them soon now. They go off quick. They're best fried up with a little butter and garlic.'

" 'I say, are you having some too?'

"She says, 'No.' She says, 'I used to be a proper one for mushrooms, but not any more, not with my stomach. But they're lovely. Nothing better than a young shaggy inkcap mushroom. It's astonishing the things that people don't eat. All the things around them that people could eat, if only they knew it.'

"I said 'Thanks,' and went back into my half of the attic. They'd done the conversion a few years before, nice job really. I put the mushrooms down by the sink. After a few days they dissolved into black stuff, like ink, and I had to put the whole mess into a plastic bag and throw it away.

"I'm on my way downstairs with the plastic bag, and I run into her on the stairs, she says 'Hullo Mister B.'

"I say, 'Hello Miss Corvier.'

" 'Call me Effie,' she says. 'How were the mushrooms?'

" 'Very nice, thank you,' I said. 'They were lovely.'

"She'd leave me other things after that, little presents, flowers in old milk-bottles, things like that, then nothing. I was a bit relieved when the presents suddenly stopped.

"So I'm down at dinner with the family, the lad at the poly, he was home for the holidays. It was August. Really hot. And someone says they hadn't seen her for about a week, and could I look in on her. I said I didn't mind.

"So I did. The door wasn't locked. She was in bed. She had a thin sheet over her, but you could see she was naked under the sheet. Not that I was trying to see anything, it'd be like looking at your gran in the altogether. This old lady. But she looked so pleased to see me.

" 'Do you need a doctor?' I says.

"She shakes her head. 'I'm not ill,' she says. 'I'm hungry. That's all.'

" 'Are you sure,' I say, 'because I can call someone. It's not a bother. They'll come out for old people.'

"She says, 'Edward? I don't want to be a burden on anyone, but I'm so hungry.'

" 'Right. I'll get you something to eat,' I said. 'Something easy on your tummy,' I says. That's when she surprises me. She looks embarrassed. Then she says, very quietly, '*Meat*. It's got to be fresh meat, and raw. I won't let anyone else cook for me. Meat. Please, Edward.'

" 'Not a problem,' I says, and I go downstairs. I thought for a moment about nicking it from the cat's bowl, but of course I didn't. It was like, I knew she wanted it, so I had to do it. I had no choice. I went down to Safeway, and I bought her a readipak of best ground sirloin.

"The cat smelled it. Followed me up the stairs. I said, 'You get down, puss. It's not for you. It's for Miss Corvier and she's not feeling well, and she's going to need it for her supper,' and the thing mewed at me as if it hadn't been fed in a week, which I knew wasn't true because its bowl was still half-full. Stupid, that cat was.

"I knock on her door, she says 'Come in.' She's still in the bed, and I give her the pack of meat, and she says 'Thank you Edward, you've got a good heart.' And she starts to tear off the plastic wrap, there in the bed. There's a puddle of brown blood under the plastic tray, and it drips onto her sheet, but she doesn't notice. Makes me shiver.

"I'm going out the door, and I can already hear her starting to eat with her fingers, cramming the raw mince into her mouth. And she hadn't got out of bed.

"But the next day she's up and about, and from there on she's in and out at all hours, in spite of her age, and I think there you are. They say red meat's bad for you, but it did her the world of good. And raw, well, it's just steak tartare, isn't it? You ever eaten raw meat?"

The question came as a surprise. I said, "Me?"

Eddie looked at me with his dead eyes, and he said, "Nobody else at this table."

"Yes. A little. When I was a small boy—four, five years old—my grandmother would take me to the butcher's with her, and he'd give me slices of raw liver, and I'd just eat them, there in the shop, like that. And everyone would laugh."

I hadn't thought of that in twenty years. But it was true.

I still like my liver rare, and sometimes, if I'm cooking and if nobody else is around, I'll cut a thin slice of raw liver before I season it, and I'll eat it, relishing the texture and the naked, iron taste.

"Not me," he said. "I liked my meat properly cooked. So the next thing that happened was Thompson went missing."

"Thompson?"

"The cat. Somebody said there used to be two of them, and they called them Thompson and Thompson. I don't know why. Stupid, giving them both the same name. The first one was squashed by a lorry." He pushed at a small mound of sugar on the Formica top with a fingertip. His left hand, still. I was beginning to wonder whether he had a right arm. Maybe the sleeve was empty. Not that it was any of my business. Nobody gets through life without losing a few things on the way.

I was trying to think of some way of telling him I didn't have any money, just in case he was going to ask me for something when he got to the end of his story. I didn't have any money: just a train ticket and enough pennies for the bus ticket home.

"I was never much of a one for cats," he said suddenly. "Not really. I liked dogs. Big, faithful things. You knew where you were with a dog. Not cats. Go off for days on end, you don't see them. When I was a lad, we had a cat, it was called Ginger. There was a family down the street, they had a cat they called Marmalade. Turned out it was the same cat, getting fed by all of us. Well, I mean. Sneaky little buggers. You can't trust them.

"That was why I didn't think anything when Thompson went away. The family was worried. Not me. I knew it'd come back. They always do.

"Anyway, a few nights later, I heard it. I was trying to sleep, and I couldn't. It was the middle of the night, and I heard this mewing. Going on, and on, and on. It wasn't loud, but when you can't sleep these things just get on your nerves. I thought maybe it was stuck up in the rafters, or out on the roof outside. Wherever it was, there wasn't any point in trying to sleep through it. I knew that. So I got up, and I got dressed—even put my boots on in case I was going to be climbing out onto the roof—and I went looking for the cat.

"I went out in the corridor. It was coming from Miss Corvier's room on the other side of the attic. I knocked on her door, but no one answered. Tried the door. It wasn't locked. So I went in. I thought maybe that the cat was stuck somewhere. Or hurt. I don't know. I just wanted to help, really.

"Miss Corvier wasn't there. I mean, you know sometimes if there's anyone in a room, and that room was empty. Except there's something on the floor in the corner going *mrie, mrie* . . . And I turned on the light to see what it was."

He stopped then for almost a minute, the fingers of his left hand picking at the black goo that had crusted around the neck of the ketchup bottle. It was shaped like a large tomato. Then he said, "What I didn't understand was how it could still be alive. I mean, it was. And from the chest up, it was alive, and breathing, and fur and everything. But its back legs, its rib cage. Like a chicken carcass. Just bones. And what are they called, sinews? And, it lifted its head, and it looked at me.

"It may have been a cat, but I knew what it wanted. It was in its eyes. I mean." He stopped. "Well, I just knew. I'd never seen eyes like that. You would have known what it wanted, all it wanted, if you'd seen those eyes. I did what it wanted. You'd have to be a monster, not to."

"What did you do?"

"I used my boots." Pause. "There wasn't much blood. Not really. I just stamped, and stamped on its head, until there wasn't really anything much left that looked like anything. If you'd seen it looking at you like that, you would have done what I did."

I didn't say anything.

"And then I heard someone coming up the stairs to the attic, and I thought I ought to do something, I mean, it didn't look good. I don't know what it must have looked like really, but I just stood there, feeling stupid, with a stinking mess on my boots, and when the door opens, it's Miss Corvier.

"And she sees it all. She looks at me. And she says, 'You killed him.' I can hear something funny in her voice, and for a moment I don't know what it is, and then she comes closer, and I realize that she's crying.

"That's something about old people, when they cry like children, you don't know where to look, do you? And she says, 'He was all I had to keep me going, and you killed him. After all I've done,' she says, 'making it so the meat stays fresh, so the life stays on. After all I've done.

" 'I'm an old woman,' she says. 'I need my meat.'

"I didn't know what to say.

"She's wiping her eyes with her hand. 'I don't want to be a burden on anybody,' she says. She's crying now. And she's looking at me. She says, 'I never wanted to be a burden.' She says, 'That was my meat. Now,' she says, 'who's going to feed me now?' "

He stopped, rested his grey face in his left hand, as if he was tired. Tired of talking to me, tired of the story, tired of life. Then he shook his head, and looked at me, and said, "If you'd seen that cat, you would have done what I did. Anyone would have done."

He raised his head then, for the first time in his story, looked me in the eyes. I thought I saw an appeal for help in his eyes, something he was too proud to say aloud.

Here it comes, I thought. This is where he asks me for money.

Somebody outside tapped on the window of the café. It wasn't a loud tapping, but Eddie jumped. He said, "I have to go now. That means I have to go."

I just nodded. He got up from the table. He was still a tall man, which almost surprised me: he'd collapsed in on himself in so many other ways. He pushed the table away as he got up, and as he got up he took his right hand out of his coat-pocket. For balance, I suppose. I don't know.

Maybe he wanted me to see it. But if he wanted me to see it, why did he keep it in his pocket the whole time? No, I don't think he wanted me to see it. I think it was an accident.

He wasn't wearing a shirt or a jumper under his coat, so I could see his arm, and his wrist. Nothing wrong with either of them. He had a normal wrist. It was only when you looked below the wrist that you saw most of the flesh had been picked from the bones, chewed like chicken wings, leaving only dried morsels of meat, scraps and crumbs, and little else. He only had three fingers left, and most of a thumb. I suppose the other finger-bones must have just fallen right off, with no skin or flesh to hold them on.

That was what I saw. Only for a moment, then he put his hand back in his pocket, and pushed out of the door, into the chilly night.

I watched him then, through the dirty plate-glass of the café window. It was funny. From everything he'd said, I'd imagined Miss Corvier to be an old woman. But the woman waiting for him, outside, on the pavement, couldn't have been much over thirty. She had long, long hair, though. The kind of hair you can sit on, as they say, although that always sounds faintly like a line from a dirty joke. She looked a bit like a hippy, I suppose. Sort of pretty, in a hungry kind of way.

She took his arm, and looked up into his eyes, and they walked away out of the café's light for all the world like a couple of teenagers who were just beginning to realize that they were in love.

I went back up to the counter and bought another cup of tea, and a couple of packets of crisps to see me through until the morning, and I sat and thought about the expression on his face when he'd looked at me that last time.

On the milk-train back to the big city I sat opposite a woman carrying a baby. It was floating in formaldehyde, in a heavy glass container. She needed to sell it, rather urgently, and although I was extremely tired we talked about her reasons for selling it, and about other things, for the rest of the journey.

SUSAN POWER

Roofwalker

Susan Power was born in Chicago and now lives in St. Paul, Minnesota, where she teaches at Hamline University. She is the author of one novel, The Grass Dancer, *which I cannot recommend too highly. Her short fiction has appeared in* The Atlantic Monthly, Paris Review, The Village Voice, The Best American Short Stories, *and* The Vintage Book of Contemporary Fiction.

Power is a member of the Standing Rock Sioux tribe (Yanktonnai Dakota), and much of her fiction is inspired by her Native American roots. In "Roofwalker," she makes skillful use of an old Sioux legend to illuminate the story of a Native American girl and her extended family. It is the title story in Power's gorgeous new collection, Roofwalker *(Milkweed Editions).*

—T. W.

It was family legend that Grandma Mabel Rattles Chasing came down from the Standing Rock Reservation in North Dakota to help deliver me. She took the Greyhound bus all the way to Chicago, stepping out of the exhaust fumes like a ghost emerging from fog, her deep paper shopping bags banging against the sides of her legs. For most of the trip she had been finishing a child-sized star quilt, touching the fabric as gently as she would her new grandchild, smoothing it in her lap. This was the quilt they would wrap me in after my first bath, the same quilt Mom pulled out in later years every time I was sick.

Grandma Mabel came to help with the delivery because my mother was terrified of going to the huge maternity ward at Chicago's Cook County Hospital. She was convinced that the white doctors would sterilize her after she gave birth, a practice once routine at many reservation hospitals. So I was born in our third-floor apartment, which was little more than a chain of narrow rooms resembling the cars of a train.

Family legend continued that I began life with a fall. My birth went smoothly until Grandma Mabel wiped my face and head with her hands. What she saw made her scream, and I slipped out of her fingers like buttered dough. My father caught me. He went down on one knee, and his slim hands with long fingers stretched beneath me like a net.

"What is it?! What's wrong?!" I can imagine Mom's voice getting frantic as she tried to sit up, afraid I was born with too many fingers, or too few toes.

"Nothing, just her hair. It's different," Dad told her.

"The color of the devil," Grandma whispered, and they made her sit down because she was trembling.

As far back as anyone in my family could remember, both sides were Indian—full-blood Sioux on my mother's side and full-blood Sioux on my dad's. Yet I was born with red hair the color of autumn maple leaves. Grandma Mabel looked at me sideways and began to recite stories of the Viking invaders.

"Hundreds of years ago, long before Columbus and his three boats got lost and stumbled upon our land, those Vikings came down from the North country, where it's always cold. They had red hair and blue eyes, and heavy hatchets made of bronze. They married into our tribes. They must have. Just look." Grandma Mabel brushed my head with the tips of her fingers.

Although I was the mysterious family skeleton pushed out of the closet with my mother's fluid still damp on my skin, Grandma Mabel didn't hold it against me for long. Soon she was cradling me in her broad lap, her round thighs ample as pillows. She traced my features with a thick finger, smoothing my forehead when it wrinkled in frustrated hunger. I know this because I have seen the photographs. I spent years playing with them, spreading them out on the coffee table. Grandma Mabel's skin was brown and wrinkled as a walnut, but her hair was mostly black, tied in one long braid. She wore shapeless cotton dresses and bowling sneakers, and I noticed that her legs looked strong but lumpy, a little like caked oatmeal. I knew her eyes were black because Mom told me, but in the photographs it was impossible to tell. Grandma Mabel's eyes were so bright they were beams of light shooting from her face, making me blink if I stared at them for too long.

Grandma Mabel was a presence in my life even though she returned to the reservation shortly after I was born. I came to know her through the photographs and the occasional phone calls she made from her tiny government-funded house. The stories she told me over the phone were better than the ones Mom told me at night before I fell asleep. Grandma asked me strange questions sometimes.

"Do you have spiders in Chicago?" she asked me once.

"Sure we do."

"I hope you don't kill them. You have to be careful because one of them might be Iktome."

"Who's that?" I asked her, smiling to myself because I knew the answer would involve a story.

"He is a spirit and sometimes he takes the form of a spider. He is clever-foolish, like your little brothers."

I knew what she meant. By this time *I* had *two* younger brothers, Billy and Grover, both of them as dark as our parents and Grandma Mabel, unburdened by my mysterious red hair, and both of them were energetically mischievous.

"Iktome is greedy," Grandma Mabel continued. "That's the bad side of him. If he has a plump duck or a haunch of venison set for dinner and he sees a chance to get something more, he will go after it. But you know what happens when he does that? Coyote sneaks behind him and steals the fat duck or the juicy venison and runs off with it. Then Iktome goes hungry."

"Grandma, I wish you were here," I told her one time. I wanted the stories to last longer. I wanted her shining eyes to light my room at bedtime like two candles burning in the dark.

"I know it," she said. "It's hard."

"Why do we live in Chicago?" I finally asked my mother after one particularly entertaining visit with Grandma Mabel, when she told me she could hear her husband's ghost singing to her from the bottom of their old well.

"Your father's job is here," Mom told me.

"Can't he work somewhere else?"

"It's not that easy." Mom sighed. "He's a political person, and political people don't always have a lot of choices."

My mother chose her words cautiously, I could tell. She spoke slowly, and the words seemed heavy as she spoke them, like dense marbles rolling off her tongue. There were other times when she flung words at my father and wasn't careful at all. She'd point to him and tell us: "Your father is a gung ho Indian. It's his job and his life!"

We were living in the uptown area of Chicago, just blocks away from the Indian Center on Wilson Avenue, which is where Dad went to work each day. I knew that he wrote proposals for the Indian community, but when I was little I didn't understand what that meant. I imagined my father writing marriage proposals for shy Indian men who couldn't find the words for themselves, who would have spent their lives alone were it not for my father's intervention. Likewise, I didn't know what a gung ho Indian was, but in retrospect, I suppose my father fits that description. He always wore jeans, cowboy boots, a western shirt with silver clips on the collar, and a heavy turquoise bolo tie. He never carried a briefcase but instead used an old backpack completely covered by pins and bumper stickers with slogans like CUSTER DIED FOR YOUR SINS, I'M SIOUX AND PROUD, INDIAN POWER, and POWWOW COUNTRY.

Dad burned tobacco on Columbus Day to mourn the arrival of the man who pressed Indians into slavery, fasted on Thanksgiving Day to show his solidarity with all those eastern tribes the Pilgrims killed off with their European strain of germs, and set off fireworks on June 26 to celebrate the anniversary of the Little Big Horn battle, when our ancestors crushed Custer like a wood tick.

I asked Grandma Mabel what it all meant.

"What is a gung ho Indian?"

"Well . . ." She paused then, and I could hear her sipping liquid, probably wild peppermint tea, which she said kept her blood healthy. "That's a good question. It used to be that your people knew who they were and what was expected of them. From the time they were born, each day was a lesson. They were close to the father over all of us, *Wakan Tanka*, the one who hears our prayers. But we have gone through many things, and now it's difficult to find the right road. Some of our people try too hard; they think they've found the old-time trail leading them to the heart of our traditions, but if they looked down, I think they would see only their footprints. It is their own lonely trail, and they are truly lost."

Was my father lost? I wanted to call him back and take him by the hand. I would walk with him, eyes cast upon the ground, looking for signs that other Sioux people had passed this way before us. I didn't want him to wander all alone, carrying nothing but his worn backpack and an angry heart.

When I was nine years old, Dad left us. My brothers and I were like those three blind mice: we didn't see it coming. I think my mother did. I am certain now that Mom could read this future in my father's face, because when the time came, she simply lived through it. She had probably noticed the way women watched my handsome father, who was tall and straight with brown skin smooth as glass and wavy long hair streaming down his back.

Of course, Dad didn't tell us there was another woman but blamed politics for our separation. He said he was going back to his own reservation in South Dakota, Pine Ridge, where so much trouble was brewing.

"I can make a difference," he said.

My mother wasn't fooled for a second. "Then take us with you," she told him.

"It's not that easy," my father answered. "These days Pine Ridge is dangerous, Indians fighting Indians and the FBI just complicating everything. I can't take you back there."

Dad bought a used Volkswagen van and painted bronze fists on each of its sides. At first I admired it, imagined it reflected his conscience and principles; it was a rugged little vehicle, hell-bent for danger and activism. But then my mother pointed out the truth with her chin as we watched it from our apartment window. My father had a young girl with hair as long as his own already living in that van.

I decided to investigate, and when Mom was busy preparing lunch for me and my brothers, I ran down the front stairs. The girl was standing outside the van, leaning against it with her arms crossed. She was watching our apartment windows three stories above her with muddy green eyes the color of the Chicago River. She's only a part-blood Indian, like me, I thought. She had on hip-hugger jeans with wide bell-bottoms that dragged on the ground, covering her feet. On top she wore a skimpy halter hanging loosely from her narrow, caved-in chest. I knew she was observing me, too, although she never glanced away from the window. I was in the doorway of our building, right in front of her, staring rudely, which I had been taught never to do.

Finally she asked, "Which one are you?"

"Jessie," I told her. I pulled myself a little straighter and wiped the limp red bangs from my forehead.

"Oh," she said. She shrugged her right shoulder and lifted suddenly on tiptoes to get a better view of our apartment. Just as I was about to leave, pushing back against the outside glass door, she looked at me again. Her green eyes fell on mine like heavy hammers. I couldn't blink, my eyes were dry, her hard look was squeezing the breath from my lungs. My fingernails cut into my palms.

"I love him," she said. We stood there silently for a while.

Finally I whispered, "I love him too." My voice was gentle, but it wasn't out of kindness or sympathy. Anger sizzled in the pit of my stomach; I felt the sparks fly inside of me, scorching my heart and lungs. She turned her back on me, retreating into the safety of the van.

I walked to the back of the building and sat on the porch steps. I wished I could become a bird of vengeance. I curled my toes inside my sneakers, feeling their terrible grip, and imagined the fierce sweep they would make at that part-blood girl's hair. My talons would tangle in her hair like barbed wire and I would carry her off, banging her useless, scrawny body against the buildings as I flew toward the lake. Halfway to Canada maybe I would let her go, hovering in the air so I could watch her fall into the deep cold center of Lake Michigan. Her heavy, angry eyes would weight her down like stones. She would never float or be recovered.

As the bird of vengeance, I would shriek and cackle loud enough that my mother would hear it and know she was avenged, powerful enough that my father would hear me and know that I had won.

The day finally came for my father to leave. My mother sat on one of the kitchen chairs. For the first time I noticed that the chair she always used was the one repaired with black electrical tape, just as she always set herself the chipped plate and bent fork. Dad was standing with one pointy-toed boot resting on a chair, his body hitched over the bent knee. My parents faced slightly apart, and I remember worrying that they wouldn't be able to hear each other, that their words would slide in different directions.

"Let's not put the kids through a big scene," Dad told her.

Mom's dry eyes hurt me more than if they had been pouring tears like the Hoover Dam burst open. She didn't flinch or rustle but was suddenly still and massive, the center of gravity become flesh in our kitchen.

"It doesn't matter what I say or what I do," she finally said, and I was convinced that her voice slipped out of her navel and not from her thin, pressed lips.

Was that all she was going to say? I was trembling, as nervous as she was motionless; my blood was sliding too quickly through my veins. I wanted to scream, *Stop him! Don't let him go!* But I had been raised too well for that. Instead I bit my tongue until I tasted blood.

Dad moved then, walked toward my mother. He scooped her hand into his but almost lost it, it was so heavy.

"You're a good woman," he said, "and I promise I'll call you. Take care of yourself." He kissed her on the cheek and replaced her hand. He was on his way out. He looked so relieved when he said his last words: "I just have to do some things that are bigger than my life."

"Don't kid yourself," Mom answered.

I know Dad must have hugged and kissed the three of us before he made it out the front door. After all, we stood there in the hallway between the kitchen and living room, his last hurdle to freedom. But I don't remember it. I must have blanked the moment out. Or maybe I was frightened because his last touch was too much like a ghost walking right through me.

I remember looking out of the front window, my mother suddenly beside me. She took my hand and I realized she was facing the wrong way, her back to the street.

"Has he gone?" she asked me. I looked out and saw the painted upraised fists slide away from our building. The rear fender gleamed when Dad stopped for a red light at the corner, and as he turned there was a flash, like the winking of an eye.

"Yes," I told her, "I can't see him anymore."

"Then that's the last time," she said, moving heavily toward the kitchen.

Dad left on July 1. The very next day a heat wave hit Chicago, which seemed associated with the hole in the world Dad left behind. There was an imbalance to things; we had lost our equilibrium and were living at extremes. With a large ice cube in my mouth, I practiced freezing my heart. Mom didn't bother to sit near a fan or wipe the sweat from her forehead with the towel I draped around her neck.

"Are you hungry?" I asked her because I was, and my brothers were chewing on dry cereal while they watched *The Three Stooges*. She didn't answer or even act as if she heard me. A tear of sweat rolled from her temple to the curve of her jawline and on down her neck to soak into her red tank top.

"Do you think he'll come back?" I asked her. The fingers of her right hand twitched, but that was her only response.

"C'mon." I herded my brothers into the kitchen and cut them slices of Colby cheese. We ate cheese and buttery Ritz crackers for lunch and later for dinner.

That week my mother became her own ghost, and I became more real. I learned to heat SpaghettiOs in a pan on the dark metal burners and to light the oven to heat up chicken potpies. At night I wiped my brothers' foreheads with ice wrapped in a washcloth and made sure the fan was blowing straight onto their small forms. It was a week of heat, quiet, and solitude.

Mom came back to us a little at a time. One night she laughed at something on TV, and we all came running to laugh with her. "What is it, Mom? What's so funny?" I sat on the edge of her easy chair and put my arm around her damp shoulder.

"Hmmm?" She peered at the three of us, taking stock, and we moved instinctively closer like wealth to be counted. Billy planted his hands on her knees and rocked toward her face.

"We heard you," he whispered, and then he laughed out loud because she bumped her nose against his. "Eskimo kiss!" Billy shouted.

One week had passed. My brothers found solace in Tonka trucks and a G.I. Joe with a furry crew cut and kung fu grip. I trailed after my mother, determined to ward off her unhappiness with my vigilance. One evening we sat together. It was later than it looked. We had all the windows pushed open as wide as they would go.

"An inch of breeze is an inch of breeze," Mom had said as we helped her tug on window sashes warped by the heat.

I sat across from Mom at the kitchen table. She was doing the *TV Guide* crossword puzzle, and I was pretending to color pictures in a coloring book while I was really keeping an eye on her.

"What's the name of that guy from *Little House on the Prairie*?" she asked me, the tip of her pen waving over the paper.

"Michael Landon," I said. "He plays the pa."

That made her look up before she finished writing his name, and she glanced at my artwork. She moved her arms, about to get up from the table, but her skin was warm and stuck to the Formica. My arms were stuck, too, and when I finally pulled them free, they were greasy, coated with toast crumbs.

Mom laughed. "Now you know what a bug stuck to flypaper feels like." Then she cocked her head at the silence. "Say, what are your brothers up to? They've been too quiet." Mom left to find Billy and Grover after wiping her arms with a dish towel. The kitchen was darker all of a sudden. I could hear cicadas thrumming from the vacant lot next door, and I had this sad, loose-ends feeling of wasted time.

Mom came back into the kitchen, brandishing her red patent-leather purse. She waved it in the air, saying, "Let's make us some black cows!" So the four of us went to the corner liquor store, where we bought vanilla ice cream, root beer, and striped plastic straws for our floats. But Grover said he wanted his ice cream in Coke, so then Billy wanted Coke too. Mom made a face but she let them switch their A&Ws for Cokes.

On the way back Mom spotted a thick patch of milkweed as high as her waist in the vacant lot. "Look at this," she said. She reached out her free hand to gauge the weight of green pods heavy with latex. "Just what you kids need, some green in your diet." Mom handed me the black cow fixings, starting to break out of the moist bottom of the paper bag, and put the keys in my pocket.

"Why don't you run this up before it melts and then come back? I'm going to collect some of these greens." By the time I returned it was almost dark and her arms were full of thick-stemmed milkweeds looking like an exotic bridal bouquet.

Grover and Billy were picking around by the Dumpster so I went to collect them. "Look, Jessie," Grover hissed. He pulled Billy out of the way so I could see. Some winos were passed out in the space between the Dumpster and the brick wall of our building. The smell rising from their niche was worse than that coming from the open garbage. I couldn't count how many there were—maybe three or four—because they were piled in a confusion of dirty clothes, their legs stacked together like wood.

"Get away from there!" Mom called us back and hefted the plants higher in her arms. "Leave those poor drunks alone. Let them sleep it off in peace."

"Are they dead?" Billy asked me as we followed Mom and the cluster of milk flowers nodding over her shoulder.

"No," I said, "they're just sleeping." I could tell Billy didn't believe me. I heard him whisper to Grover when we were walking up the stairs: "Dad wouldn't of left those dead Indians to get eaten by flies."

We both hushed him.

Dad had been gone exactly two weeks and Mom was making sounds about the future. She said, "With me going back to work, you'll have more responsibilities."

Her fingers were smoothing out a white athletic sock, one of Dad's. She caught me watching her and quickly balled the sock into a tight wad, chucking it basketball style into the tall kitchen trash can. She pressed her empty hands against the table and smiled. "Everything's going to be okay, though. It'll be all right."

"I know," I told her.

My mother held her arms out to me in a way she hadn't done since I was as young as my brothers. I moved hesitantly, but she pulled me onto her lap, and our bare legs, poking out of polyester shorts, slid together like held hands.

"I guess you're not too young for me to talk to real serious."

I couldn't see her; we were both facing the refrigerator door, taped all over with poems cut out of Indian newspapers like *News from Indian Country* and *Akwesasne Notes*. The printing was so small that from across the room it looked like trails of sugar ants crawling up and down. Mom talked over my shoulder, her warm breath sliding past my neck.

"Listen up now," she began, but interrupted herself. She leaned against me to bury her face in my hair. "Boy, it sure smells sweet," Mom said, "and it's real pretty. Always was pretty." I knew she meant my unusual red hair.

"See." She was holding pale strands near the window, where they glistened in the sunlight. "It's just like Black Hills gold. Three different colors woven together." Mom paused, my hair held close to her eyes. She was suddenly very quiet, and I could feel tears gathering in the air.

"I want to tell you something, okay? Just because your father took off on some crazy adventure doesn't mean he stopped caring about us. He's just mixed up. He thinks he's doing the right thing, but he's forgetting that a Sioux man's first duty is to his family." Mom was crying now, her tears falling on my thighs like the first warning drops of rain. "Do you hear me?"

I nodded and swallowed my own throat again and again. *Don't defend him,* I wanted to tell her, but I remained silent. I stroked Mom's hand with my fingers. I was tired of seeing my mother rub away, becoming so thin the few wrinkles on her forehead pulled taut across the bone, her face as smooth as the worry stones I saw between the fingers of old women in Greektown.

Grandma Mabel came for a visit that summer, smelling faintly of sweet grass. She entered our apartment gracefully. Her ancient carpetbag (which she said dated back to the Truman administration), heavy support hose, and worn bowling sneakers did not detract from her air of dignity.

I meant to give Grandma a tour of our apartment when I took her hand, leading her from room to room. But along the way she took over and began labeling familiar objects. She pointed to my parents' bedside table, its one short leg propped higher with a *Reader's Digest*.

She said, "*Waglutapi,*" and dropped her hand. Grandma paused, looking at me.

"*Waglutapi?*" I repeated. Grandma nodded. She pointed to the door: "*Tiyopa*"; the window, "*Ozanzanglepi.*" In the kitchen she poked her finger at the dingy stove. "*Oceti,*" she said. Billy had left a soda can on the kitchen table and Grandma snatched it, waving it before my face. "*Kapopapi,*" she told me, wiggling her eyebrows. It had a funny sound. I couldn't say it correctly because each time I tried, I sputtered laughter. Pretty soon the two of us were holding each other for support, Grandma shaking and shaking with light, almost soundless gasps that wafted like smoke rings to the ceiling.

"Oh, I've got to pee," she finally managed, and rushed past me to the bathroom. I'd never seen an old lady move so quickly.

At night the two of us shared my bed, across the room from where my little brothers slept in a tangle of bony elbows. Grandma wore white cotton anklets to bed.

"When you get old the blood doesn't reach your feet anymore," she explained. And she never wore a real nightgown. Instead she pulled on one of her old housedresses, worn away almost to gauze, the print on the fabric washed off long ago. She had a set of rosary beads that glowed in the dark. She wore them around her neck and they glared at me like little eyes unless I slept with my back to her.

After saying her prayers in Sioux, she would pull me against her, a heavy arm draped across my waist. The smell of sweet grass was so thick in the bed I imagined we were sleeping on the plains.

It was Grandma Mabel who told me about the roofwalker. "My *tunkasila*, that's my grandfather, first saw the roofwalker standing in the sky, his wings stretched so wide he covered the light of the moon and most of the stars. My *tunkasila* said the roofwalker was born out of misery, right after the Wounded Knee massacre, where so many of our people were killed for holding a Ghost Dance. They were buried in the snow and the roofwalker drifted over their mass grave, his eyes big and hungry, so empty my *tunkasila* hunched in the snow, afraid he would be eaten.

"And now that roofwalker has followed me to Chicago. Isn't he crazy? He'll get lost and never find the Dakotas again. He'll choke over those steel mills or fly straight into that John Hancock Building, won't he?"

Grandma tickled me with her stubby fingers and we almost rolled out of the bed with our giggling. To finish her story, however, Grandma became serious. She whispered as if the roofwalker were listening. I kept glancing at the window, expecting to see the smoky steam of his breath, but the window was clear black.

She told me that the roofwalker was a Sioux spirit, a kind of angel. "He isn't good or bad, though," she said. "He just is."

The roofwalker was the hungriest of all spirits, hugely, endlessly hungry, his stomach an empty cavern of echoes.

"You see," Grandma explained, "even though he's starving, he is fussy. Always holding out for a delicacy."

The roofwalker lived to eat dreams, and when he feasted on the dream of his choice, it always came true. "Did he ever get one of yours?" I asked Grandma Mabel, trying to imagine what a dream tasted like, and how you could fit it in your mouth without choking.

"Yes, he did," she said. She smoothed the hair off my forehead. "I dreamed you."

I let my head fall back against Grandma's chest. I could feel her rosary beads tangle in my hair and rub against my scalp. I dreamt that we were sleeping on the prairie, Grandma's fingers pointing out the stars, her arms so long she could reach up and dust them.

That fall, after Grandma Mabel returned to North Dakota, her voice remained in my head, repeating stories and Sioux vocabulary words. I think that is why the creature came to me. He stepped full grown from my dreams, a night visitor prowling through my thoughts, and later, quite fleshed out, hovering outside my bedroom window as if treading air. My brothers slept on in the next bed that night. I could see their gray outline and the hang of loose arms, thin as sticks.

I wanted to wake them, to ask them, "Do you see him out there? Has he gone?" But I didn't. Instead I admired the creature's brown, hairless body, glistening and smooth. He seemed eager, his mouth open and barbed tongue curled over his teeth. His eyes were penetrating, the black pupils drilled; I was convinced he could see right through my brain and spot my dreams. I knew what that tongue was for. I knew what he did. The tiny curved thorns lining the edge of his tongue like needles were for catching dreams. His tongue was flexible enough for excavation, like delicate surgery, and after he swallowed an extracted dream, it would come true.

I wasn't surprised that he looked just like my father, although his thick waist-length hair was trimmed with feathers. The handsome face and the strong arms and torso were my father's. Only the legs were different: feathered haunches, and curved talons for feet.

"You are part bird," I whispered to him through the pane of glass separating us. "You are part spirit." His eyes stared without expression, but his hand lifted a necklace worn against his chest, which was strung with bear claws, elk teeth, and rare dentalium shells. I tried to reach my hand through the glass to stroke the necklace he proffered with a graceful hand, but as I grazed the barrier, he flew upward, and I heard a backwash of wind forced by the beating of powerful wings.

In the morning I looked for scattered red and black feathers, the color of his plumage. I couldn't find any, but that didn't shake my faith. I knew the roof-walker had visited me. He was as real as I needed him to be.

When I was little I had blind faith in family legends, my grandmother's stories, and even in my handsome father, who was temporarily lost, searching for the road Grandma Mabel told me was beneath my own feet. After all, he had been the one to catch me before I slipped to the floor, the one who kept me in the world once my mother released me.

Grandma Mabel told me that life is a circle, and sometimes we coil around on ourselves like a drowsy snake. Weeks after Grandma Mabel returned to North Dakota, I decided to circle back to my own beginning. Perhaps that was where I should go to make things right, to bring my father home to his lonesome family. It seemed very clear to me what I had to do.

It was my tenth birthday. I woke before anyone else and dressed quietly so I wouldn't wake my brothers. I looked out of the front window and watched the leaves fall, tugged loose by a morning wind. I slipped out of the front door but left it unlocked for my return.

I chose the place carefully, somewhere high enough to test faith, but not so high as to be dangerous. I stood at the top of the final flight of stairs leading to our tiled vestibule. I was ten carpeted steps away from the front door of our building. I curled the edges of my feet over the top step, feeling the space slope forward and downward. I lunged chin first into the fall with eyes closed, my body as relaxed as the startled release of tension before sleep. I waited for Dad to catch me, for the roofwalker to throw back his head and open his mouth, letting my dream float up from his throat into the breeze rolling away from Lake Michigan.

DON TUMASONIS

The Prospect Cards

Don Tumasonis lives in the outskirts of a Scandinavian capital with his Norwegian wife, rambunctious cats, and space-consuming books. He has published stories in Ghosts & Scholars, All Hallows, Supernatural Tales, *and the Ash-Tree Press anthology* Shadows and Silence.

He says: " 'The Prospect Cards' draws its inspiration from many sources: stuff in booksellers' catalogues, volumes of eighteenth and nineteenth century Levantine travel writings, a walk along the Seine, Kipling, H. Rider Haggard in his usual more perverse mode, and anthropological literature. Its mood was influenced by the books of George MacDonald Fraser, Glen Baxter, and the character of John Cleese. It was meant to be humorous, but seems to have gotten out of hand."

The story, which also has a touch of the flavor of the legendary A. Merritt, was originally published in Dark Terrors 6, *edited by Stephen Jones and David Sutton.*

—E. D.

Dear Mr. Cathcart,

We are happy to provide, enclosed with this letter, our complete description of item no. 839 from our recent catalogue *Twixt Hammam and Minaret: 19th and Some Early 20th Century Travel in the Middle East, Anatolia, Nubia, etc.*, as requested by yourself.

You are lucky in that our former cataloguer, Mr. Mokley, had, in what he thought were his spare moments, worked to achieve an extremely full description of this interesting group of what are probably unique items. Certainly no others to whom we have shown these have seen any similar, nor have been able to provide any clue as to their ultimate provenance.

They were purchased by one of our buyers on a trip to Paris, where, unusually—since everyone thinks the *bouquinistes* were mined out long ago—they were found in a stall on the Left Bank. Once having examined his buy later that evening, he determined to return the following day to the vendor in search of any related items. Alas, there were no others, and the grizzled old veteran running the boxes had no memory of when or where he purchased these, saying only that he had them for years, perhaps since the days of Marmier, actually having forgotten their existence until they were unearthed through the diligence of our employee. Given the circumstance of their discovery (covered with dust, stuffed in a sealed envelope tucked away in a far corner of a green tin box clamped onto a quay of the Seine, with volumes of grimy tomes in front concealing their being), we are lucky to have even these.

Bear in mind, that as an old and valued customer, you may have this lot at 10% off the catalogue price, postfree, with insurance additional, if desired.

Remaining, with very best wishes indeed,

Yours most faithfully,

Basil Barnet

BARNET AND KORT,
ANTIQUARIAN TRAVEL BOOKS AND EPHEMERA

NO. 839

Postal view cards, commercially produced, various manufacturers, together with a few photographs mounted on card, comprising a group of 74. Mostly sepia and black-and-white, with a few contemporary tinted, showing scenes from either Balkans, or Near or Middle East, ca. 1920–30. The untranslated captions, when they occur, are bilingual, with one script resembling Kyrillic, but not in Russian or Bulgarian; the other using the Arabic alphabet, in some language perhaps related to Turco-Uighuric.

Unusual views of as yet unidentified places and situations, with public and private buildings, baths, squares, harbors, minarets, markets, etc. Many of the prospects show crowds and individuals in the performance of divers actions and work, sometimes exotic. Several of the cards contain scenes of an erotic or disturbing nature. A number are typical touristic souvenir cards, generic products picturing exhibits from some obscure museum or collection. In spite of much expended effort, we have been unable to identify the locales shown.

Entirely unfranked, and without address, about a third of these have on their verso a holographic ink text, in a fine hand by an unidentified individual, evidently a travel diary or journal (non-contiguous, with many evident lacunæ). Expert analysis would seem to indicate 1930 or slightly later as the date of writing.

Those cards with handwriting have been arranged in rough order by us, based on internal evidence, although the chronology is often unclear and the order therefore arbitrary. Only these cards—with a single exception—are described, each with a following transcription of the verso holograph text; the others, about 50 cards blank on verso, show similar scenes and objects. Our hypothetical reconstruction of the original sequence is indicated through lightly pencilled numbers at the upper right verso corner of each card.

Condition: Waterstain across top edges, obscuring all of the few details of date and place of composition. Wear along edges and particularly at corners. A couple of cards rubbed; the others, aside from the faults already noted, mostly quite fresh and untouched.

Very Rare. In our considered opinion, the cards in themselves are likely to be

unique, no others having been recorded to now; together with the unusual document they contain, they are certainly so.
Price: £1,650

CARD NO. 1

Description: A dock, in some Levantine port. A number of men and animals, mostly mules, are congregated around a moored boat with sails, from which large *tonnes*, evidently containing wine, labelled as such in Greek, are being either loaded or unshipped.
Text: not sculling, but rather rowing, the Regatta of '12, for which his brother coxswained. Those credentials were good enough for Harrison and myself, our credulity seen in retrospect as being somewhat naïve, and ourselves as rather gullible; such, however, is all hindsight. For the time being, we were very happy at having met fellow countrymen—of the right sort, mind you—in this godforsaken backwater at a time when our fortunes, bluntly put, had taken a turn for much the worse. When Forsythe, looking to his partner Calquon, asked "George, we need the extra hands—what say I tell Jack and Charles about our plans?" To that Calquon only raised an eyebrow, as if to say it's your show, go and do as you think fit. Forsythe, taking that as approval, ordered another round, and launched into a little speech, which, when I think back on the events of the past weeks, had perhaps less of an unstudied quality than his seemingly impromptu delivery would have implied. Leaning forward, he drew from his breast pocket a postal view card, and placed it on the table, saying in a lowered voice, as if we were fellow conspirators being drawn in, "What would you think if I told you, that from here, in less than one day's sail and a following week's march, there is to be found something of such value, which if the knowledge of it became common, would

CARD NO. 2

Description: A view of a mountain massif, clearly quite high and rugged, seen from below at an angle, with consequent foreshortening. A fair amount of snow is sprinkled over the upper heights. A thick broken line in white, retouch work, coming from behind and around one of several summits, continues downward along and below the ridge-line before disappearing. This evidently indicates a route.
Text:—ania and Zog. Perfidious folk! Perfidious people. Luckily, our packet steamer had arrived and was ready to take us off. A night's sailing, and the better part of the next day took us to our destination, or rather, to the start of our journey. After some difficulty in finding animals and muleteers, we loaded our supplies, hired guides, and after two difficult days, arrived at the foothills of the mountains depicted on the obverse of this card. Our lengthy and laborious route took us ultimately up these, where we followed the voie normale, the same as shown by the white hatched line. Although extremely steep and exposed, the slope was not quite sheer and we lost only one mule and no men during the 1500-yard descent. Customs—if such a name can be properly applied to such outright thieves—were rapacious, and confiscated much of what we had, including my diary and notes. Thus the continuation on these cards, which represent the only form of paper allowed for sale to the

CARD NO. 3

Description: A panorama view of a Levantine or perhaps Balkan town of moderate to large size, ringed about by snow-covered mountains in the distance. Minarets and domes are visible, as is a very large public building with columns, possibly Greco-Roman, modified to accommodate some function other than its original religious one, so that the earlier elements appear draped about with other stylistic intrusions.
Text: vista. With the sun setting, and accommodation for the men and food for the animals arranged, we were able to finally relax momentarily and give justice, if only for a short while, to the magnificence of the setting in which the old city was imbedded, like a pearl in a filigreed ring. I've seen a lot of landscapes, 'round the world, and believe me, this was second to none. The intoxicating beauty of it all made it almost easy to believe the preposterous tales that inspired Calquon, and particularly Forsythe, to persuade us to join them on this tossed-together expedition. I frankly doubt that anything will come of it except our forcing another chink in the isolation which has kept this fascinating place inviolate to such a degree that few Westerners have penetrated its secrets over the many centuries since the rumored group of Crusaders forced their

CARD NO. 4

Description: A costume photograph, half-length, of a young woman in ethnic or tribal costume, veiled. The décolletage is such that her breasts are completely exposed. Some of the embroidery and jewelry would indicate Cypriote or Anatolian influence; it is clear that she is wearing her dowry in the form of coins, filigreed earrings, necklaces, medallions, and rings. Although she is handsome, her expression is very stiff. [Not reproduced in the catalogue]
Text: Evans, who should have stuck to Bosnia and Illyria. I never thought his snake goddesses to be anything other than some Bronze Age fantast's wild dream, if indeed the reconstructions are at all accurate. Harrison, however, has told me that this shocking—i.e. for a white woman (the locals are distinctively Caucasian: red hair, blue eyes and fair skin appearing frequently, together with traces of slight Mediterranean admixture)—déshabillé was common throughout the Eastern Ægean and Middle East until a very short while ago, when European mores got the better of the local folk, except, it seems, those here. I first encountered such dress (or undress) a week ago, the day after our late evening arrival, when out early to see the market and get my bearings, and totally engaged in examining some trays of spices in front of me, I felt suddenly bare flesh against my exposed arm, stretched out to test the quality of some turmeric. It was a woman at my side who, having come up unnoticed, had bent in front of me to obtain some root or herb. When she straightened, I realized at once that the contact had been with her bare bosom, which, I might add, was quite shapely, with nipples rouged. She was unconcerned; I must have blushed at least as much

CARD NO. 5

Description: A naos or church, on a large stepped platform, in an almost impossible mélange of styles, with elements of a Greek temple of the Corinthian order mixed in with Byzantine features and other heterogeneous effects to combine in an unusual, if not harmonious, whole. The picture, a frontal view, has been taken most probably at early morning light, since the temple steps and surrounding square are devoid of people.

Text: light and darkness, darkness and light Forsythe said. "With this form of dualism, and its rejection of the body, paradoxically, until the sacrament is administered, the believers are in fact encouraged to excess of the flesh, which is viewed as essentially evil, and ultimately, an illusion. The thought is that by indulging mightily, disdain is expressed for the ephemeral, thus granting the candidate power over the material, which is seen as standing in his or her way to salvation." "What does that have to do with your little trip of this morning?" I remonstrated. We had agreed to meet at ten o'clock to see if we could buy manuscripts in the street of the scribes, for the collection. Paul reddened and replied "D'you know the large structure on the square between us and the market? I was on my way to meet you, when I happened to pass through there. It seems"—and here he went florid again—"that in an effort to gain sanctity more quickly, parents, as required by the priests, are by law for two years to give over those of their daughters on the verge of womanhood to the temple each day between 10 and noon, in a ploy to quicken the transition to holiness. Any passer-by, during that time, who sees on the steps under the large parasols (set up like tents, there to protect exposed flesh) any maiden suiting his fancy, is urged to drop a coin in the bowls nearest and

CARD NO. 6

Description: A quite imperfect and puzzling picture, with mist and fog, or perhaps steam, obscuring almost all detail. What is visible are the dim outlines of two rows of faces, some veiled, others bearded.

Text: poured more water on the coals. By now it was quite hot, and I could no longer see Forsythe, but only hear his voice. The lack of visibility made it easier to concentrate on his words, with my eyes no longer focused on details I had found so distracting. "The incongruity of it all makes my head reel—how could they have maintained all this in the face of the changes around them? After all, a major invasion route of the past three millennia lies two valleys to the west . . ." Nodding in unseen agreement, my attention was momentarily diverted by the sound of a new arrival entering the room, and seconds later, a smooth leg brushed for a second against mine; I assumed it was a woman, and durst not stir. "Not that they've rejected the modern at all costs—they've got electric generators and some lighting, a fair amount of modern goods and weaponry find their way in, there's the museum, that Turkish photography shop, the printing press, and—oh, all the rest. But they pick and choose. And that religion of theirs! All the Jews and Muslims and Christians here are cowed completely! Why hasn't a holy war been declared by their neighbors?" With Paul ranting on in the obscuring darkness, I grunted in agreement, and then, shockingly, felt a small foot rub against

CARD NO. 7

Description: Costumed official, perhaps a religious leader or judge, sitting on the floor facing the camera. He is bearded, greying, with a grim set to his mouth. One hand points gracefully towards a smallish, thick codex held by the other hand. From the man's breast depends a tall rectangular enamelled pendant of simple design, divided vertically into equal fields of black and white.

Text: Sorbonne, three years of which, I suppose, could explain a lot, as for example, his overpowering use of garlic. "Pseudo-Manicheeism" he continued, "is solely a weak term used by the uncomprehending for what can only be described as perfection, the last word itself being a watered-out expression merely, for that which cannot be comprehended through the feeble tool of rational and skeptical thinking, which closes all doors it does not understand. Oh, I know that some of you"—and here he eyed me suspiciously, as if I was running muckin' Cambridge!—"have tried to classify our belief, using the Monophysites as opposed to the Miaphysites of your religion in an analogy that neither comprehends nor grasps the subtlety of our divinely inspired thought! As if It could be explained in Eutychian terms! Our truth is self-evident and is so clear that we allow, with certain inconsequential restrictions and provisos, those of your tribe who wish, to expound their falsehoods in the marketplace, assuming they have survived the rigors of the journey here. You were better to perceive indirectly, thinking of flashing light; the colors green, and gold; the hundred instead of the one; segmentation, instead of smoothness, as metaphors that enable one

CARD NO. 8

Description: Another museum card, with several large tokens or coins depicted, which in style and shape resemble some of the dekadrachm issues of 5th century Syracuse. The motifs of the largest one shown, are, however, previously unrecorded, with a temple (see card 5) on the obverse. The reverse, with a young girl and three men, is quite frankly obscene. [Not reproduced in the catalogue]
Text: tea. I was quite struck with the wholesome appearance and modest demeanour of Mrs. Fortesque, who was plainly, if neatly dressed in the style of ten years ago—evidently, they had been out of contact with the Society for Conversion of the Unfortunate Heathen and the rest of Blighty London since their arrival! The Rev. Fortesque was holding forth on how they were, as a family, compelled by local circumstance, and frankly, the threat of force, to adhere strictly to the native code of behavior and mores when out in public, the children not being exempt from the rituals of their fellows of like age. Calquon frowned at this, and asked, "In every way, Reverend?" to which the missionary sighed, "Unfortunately, yes—otherwise, we would not be allowed to preach at all." There was a small silence while we pondered the metaphysical implications of this when a young and angelically beautiful girl of about twelve entered the room. "Gentlemen, this is my daughter, Alicia . . ." smiled Mrs. Fortesque proudly, only to be interrupted in the most embarrassing fashion by the sudden sputtering and spraying of Forsythe, whom we thought had choked on his crumpet. Thwacking him on the back, until his redness of face receded and normal breathing resumed, I thought I saw an untoward smirk lightly pass over the face of the young girl. "What is it, old man?" I solicitously enquired. Paul, after having swallowed several times, with the attention of the others diverted, whispered sotto voce, breathlessly, so that only I could hear "Yesterday—the temple

CARD NO. 9

Description: An odd view, taken at mid-distance, of a low-angled pyramidal or cone-shaped pile of stones, most fist-sized or slightly smaller, standing about one to two feet high. A number of grimacing urchins and women, the last in their distinctive public costume, stand gesticulating and grinning to either side, many of them holding stones in their hands. Given the reflection of light on the pool of dark liquid that has seeped from the pile's front, it must be—midday.

Text: brave intervention, with dire consequence. "For God's sake, Fortesque, don't . . ." shouted Forsythe, as I well remember, before his arms were pinned behind him, and with a callused paw like a bear's clamped over his mouth, in much the same situation as myself, was forced helplessly to watch the inexorable and horrific grind of events. Eager hands, unaided by any tool—such is the depth of fanaticism that prevails in these parts—quickly scooped out a deep enough hole from the loose soil of the market square. The man of the cloth, who had persevered in the face of so much pagan indifference and outright hostility for over a decade, was for his troubles and valiant intervention unceremoniously divested of his clothing and dumped in the hole, which was quickly filled—there was no lack of volunteers—immobilizing him in the same manner as Harrison, who was buried with his arms and upper breast free. They were just far enough apart so that their fingers could not touch, depriving them in fiendish fashion of that small consolation. I remember the odd detail that Fortesque was half-shaven—he had dropped everything when informed of Harrison's situation. Knowing full well what was in store, he began singing "Onward, Christian Soldiers" in a manly, booming voice that brought tears to my eyes, while Harrison, I am ashamed to say, did

CARD NO. 10

Description: Group portrait, of nine men. Six stand, wearing bandoliers, pistols with chased and engraved handles protruding from the sashes round their waists, decorative daggers, etc. The edges of their vests are heavily embroidered with metallic thread in arabesque patterns. All are heavily moustachioed. A seventh companion stands, almost ceremoniously, to their right, holding like a circus tent peg driver a wooden mallet with a large head a foot or so off the ground; a position somewhat like that of a croquet player. The eighth man, wearing a long shift or kaftan, is on all fours in the center foreground, head to the left, but facing the camera like the others. A wooden saddle of primitive type is on his back. A ninth man, dressed like the first seven, is in the saddle, as if riding the victim, who, we see, has protruding from his fundament, although discreetly draped in part by the long shift, a pole the thickness of a muscular man's forearm.

Text: no idea, being sure that all this was misunderstanding, and could easily be cleared up with a liberal application of baksheesh. This was our mistake, as Calquon was led from the judge's compartments, arms bound, to a small square outside, where there was a carved fountain missed by the iconoclasts of long ago (of whom there had been several waves), with crudely sculptured and rather battered lions from whose mouths water streamed into the large circular limestone basin. We followed, of course, vehemently protesting his innocence all the while, and were studiously ignored. Poor Calquon was untied, and forced onto his knees and hands in a most undignified and ludicrous position. A crowd of people had already gathered under the hot midday sun, including many women and children. Hawkers walked through the throng that gathered, offering cold water from tin tanks on their backs, each with a single glass fitted into a decorated silver holder with a handle, tied onto the vessel by a cord. I saw, lying off to the side, on the steps of the fountain, a wooden stake, bark removed from its narrow end, smoothed and sharpened to a nasty point. A fat greasy balding man wearing the red cummerbund of officialdom came out of the crowd, with a bright knife in

CARD NO. 11

Description: A market with various stalls and their owners. A wandering musician is off to the left, and a perambulating vendor of kebabs, with long brass skewers, is on the right.
Text: painful for everyone concerned, particularly George. A guard in crimson livery, decorated with gold thread, was sitting smoking his hubble-bubble a short distance away from our gloomy group, every now and then looking up from his reverie to make sure things were as they should be. Perhaps it was the smoke from the pipe, or sheer bravado—I have never known, to this day—but Calquon, poor George, asked for a cigarette, which Forsythe immediately rolled and put on his lips, lighting it, since this was impossible for our fellow, whose arms were bound. He took a puff, as cool as if he were walking down Regent Street to Piccadilly, and then, for the first time noticing the women and children seated at his feet, asked us in a parched voice what they might possibly be doing there. I shuffled my feet and looked away, while Paul told him in so many words that they were waiting for his imminent departure, for the same purpose that women in the Middle Ages would gather around criminals about to be executed, in hope of obtaining a good luck charm that was powerful magic, after the fact of summary punishment was accomplished. This, as we were afraid, enraged our unfortunate en brochette companion, who became livid as we tried to calm him. Writhing in his stationary upright position, would after all do him no good, given that out of his shoulder (whence I noticed a tiny tendril of smoke ascending), there was already protruding

CARD NO. 12

Description: A public square, photo taken from above at a slant angle, from a considerable distance. Some sort of framework or door, detached from any structure, has been set up in one corner. A couple of dark objects, one larger than the other, appear in the middle of that door or frame which faces the viewer, obscuring what is going on behind. A large agitated crowd of men of all ages—from quite young boys to bent, aged patriarchs, all wearing the truncated local version of the *fez*, are milling around the rear of the upright construction. A number of local police, uniformed, are in the thick of it, evidently to maintain order.
Text: wondering what the commotion was about. I was therefore shocked to see in one tight opening the immobilized head of a young woman of about twenty-five, and in the other her right hand. Instead of the ubiquitous veil, she had some sort of black silk bandage that performed the same function, closely wrapped around her mouth and nose. She was plainly emitting a sullen glare—easily understood, given the circumstance. There was no join or seam; for the life of me, I still do not understand the construction. Every now and then the

frame and the woman contained by it would violently shake and judder. The expression under her shock of unruly red hair remained stoic and unperturbed. Walking to the other side (make sure that Mildred doesn't read this!!) I saw the crowd of men—there were about 80 to 100, including about twenty or so of the few negro slaves found in these parts—with more pouring into the square—jostling in the attempt to be next: those nearest had partially disrobed, and had taken "matters" in hand, fondling themselves to arousal, for taking her in the fashion preferred here, which is of that between men and boys, from behind. Despondent as I was, I had no intention other than to continue, when I was suddenly shoved forward into the midst

CARD NO. 13

Description: A view down a narrow street, with the high tenements and their overhanging wooden balconies blocking out much of the light. The photographer has done well to obtain as much detail as is shown here. A cupola or dome, and what is perhaps a minaret behind it, are just visible at the end of the lane. Three young (from the look of their figures as revealed by the traditional dress, cf card 2) women in black, each with a necklace from which hangs a single bright large pendant, stand in the middle of the way, at mid-distance. They appear to be approaching the camera. Surprisingly, for all that they are bare-headed, etc., they are wearing veils that conceal their features utterly. There are no others in the street.

Text: said to Forsythe that there was no point to it, that we would have to, at some moment, accept our losses and the futility of going any further. With the others gone, I argued, it was extremely unlikely that we could continue on our own; we should swallow our pride, and admit that we had come greatly unprepared for what we had in mind. It was best, in other words, that we make our run as soon as backs were turned. Forsythe disagreed vehemently, and meant that on the contrary, we were obliged by the sacred memory of our companions to carry on, an odd turn of phrase, considering what we had hoped to accomplish and obtain, by any means. And then he said cryptically, "It doesn't matter in any case—the deed is done." I immediately took this as admission that the object of our expedition had been somehow achieved without my knowledge; that was the likely cause of the troubles we had experienced, and the growing agitation of the populace I had uneasily witnessed the past few days. As we discussed our dilemma outside the carpet shop, one of many lining the street, I became aware of a silence, a hush that had descended. People turned to face the wall, in fear, I thought, as I saw three females approaching. These

CARD NO. 14

Description: A poor reproduction of the second state of plate VII of Piranesi's *Carceri*. In fact, the ascription is given on the verso of the card, the artist's name (G. B. PIRANESI) appearing in Latin capitals inserted amongst the Arabic and Kyrillic letters.

Text: less than the Carceri! What everyone had once thought the malarial fever dreams of a stunted, perverse genius, I saw now only to be honest reporting. I was absolutely astounded, once the dragoman, smelling of garlic and anisette, had removed the blindfold from my eyes. A lump came to my throat, and tears threatened to engulf me, when I thought of the others done away with through treachery, foul ignorance and intolerance. I suppose rumors regarding the disappearance of the sacred entity of the valley had much to do with the situation, too. Controlling my emotions—here, for a man to weep is a sign of weakness, with all the consequences such a perception entails—I saw around me. A number of individuals, male and female, nude or partly so, were being ushered along the spiral staircase wrapped around an enormous stone column down which I myself must have descended only a few minutes before. Natural light played through a number of cleverly placed oculi in the invisible ceiling, concealed by the complex bends and angles of the place. Turning,

CARD NO. 15

Description: Another crude reproduction of a Piranesi "Prisons" plate, this number VIII, ascribed as above.
Text: I saw yet another vista of the Italian artist before me, and began to understand, for the first time, that the plan of all his mad, insane engravings was a coherent whole, either taken from the actuality before me, or perhaps plotted out from his prints, and converted to reality, by some unsung architectonic genius. The Venetians had been here, I knew, during the mid-1700s, when things had settled down. Perhaps one of their workmen was given the book, and told to produce, or . . . With my glance following the staircase from its beginning, flanked by gigantic military trophies, with plumed helmets much larger than any human head, I traced the turn upwards to the left, and saw, between two enormous wooden doors opening on an arch, a large rack. A series of ropes hung down from the supporting wall, and I could see the faint glow of a brazier and hear the distant screams of the poor women and men, white bodies glistening with the sweat of fear, who hung

CARD NO. 16

Description: tinted, clearly a display of gemstones, perhaps from a museum of natural history or local geology. One of the larger groups, arranged separately from the others, with green coloring obviously meant to indicate emeralds, appears to be the fragments, longitudinally shattered, of what must have been a single enormous stone.
Text: subincision being the technical expression. As you can imagine, I was wildly straining against my bonds, in fact, you could say I was struggling to the point of extreme violence, to, as it turned out, no avail. In spite of all my agitated effort, I was clamped to some sort of heavy metal framework or stand that immobilized me more or less completely. Naked, helpless, dreading whatever was in store, I saw the same three young women approach into the torchlight from the encircling darkness. Without a word, my jailers and the others left and I was alone with the unholy trio. As if at a signal, they simultaneously removed their veils and I was momentarily stunned, almost drugged, by the sight of their incredible beauty. Remember, this was the first time I had ever seen one of the local women unmasqued—if these were representative of the rest, it would easily explain any number of puzzling local rituals and customs. In spite of my extreme situation, I could not help myself—the ravishing faces, the fulsome breasts with their shapely crimsoned nipples, the long black glistening hair

CARD NO. 17

Description: A market place, with many and various stands and displays. An ironmonger, a merchant of brass teapots, a seller of cured leather are all easily discerned. In the center, arms like a Saint Andrew's cross before his chest, holding a large knife in the one hand, a two-pronged fork in the other, is a seller of grilled and roasted meats. On the small portable gridiron in front of him, a number of sizable sausages are warming, split neatly lengthwise.

Text: darted out with the tip of her tongue, and then slowly extended it again. To my horror, I saw it was no tongue: it was a long razor-sharp dagger or splinter of green glass or stone; a smaragd dirk that was somehow attached or glued to the root of what remained of her tongue. The other two, kneeling close on either side of her, each reverentially held, both with two hands, the one heavy breast nearest them of their chief colleague, as if ritually weighing and supporting these at the same time. This observation was made on the abstract, detachedly, as if I were outside my own body. More mundanely, I was screaming and thrashing—or attempting uselessly to thrash. Praise to the gods that be, I passed out completely, and awoke with the foul deed done, blood running down me and pooling on the cold flagging, and the three dark sisters gone. Looking down, as my original captors reentered the chamber, I saw that the operation had been carried out, just as had been described to me by the temple priest, and I fainted once more. When

CARD NO. 18

Description: Not a postal card, but rather a half-length portrait photograph mounted on thick pasteboard, of a family group from about the 1920s. The two parents are quite young, and formally dressed: the father in a dark suit, to which is pinned an unidentified order or medal. He holds a small Bible clasped to his breast. The woman is handsome, in a white lacy blouse buttoned to the top of her graceful neck, with masses of hair piled high on her head. The young daughter is quite simply beautiful, an angel.

Text: would not have recognized, but for the signal distinctive wedding ring on her finger. "Mrs. Fortesque," I blurted out, as we stood amongst the milling crowd in the shade of the souk. "I had no idea—" but stopped when I saw the blush originating from beneath the missionary wife's veil spread to her ample and attractive sun-browned bosom (a pendant black enamelled cross its sole decoration), with the attendant rush of blood turning the aureoles—modestly without cinnabar—to the precise same shade of red so favored by the local women. I saw, at the same time, the fleshy peaks slowly stiffen and stand, that motion drawing forth a corresponding response on my part, something I hardly had conceived feasible, after the trauma of the operation of four days ago, with the insertion of the papyrus strips to prevent rejoining of the separated parts while the healing occurred. "I should perhaps explain myself," she said, regaining her composure. "The local rules are very strict; were I not, when attending to my public tasks and duties outside the house, to attire myself with what we consider wanton and promiscuous display, it would be here viewed as flagrant immodesty, and punishable, before the crowd, by the

CARD NO. 19

Description: An ossuary chapel, where the style of the classic Romanesque interior is partly obscured by the encrustation of thousands of skulls and skeletal parts, that form, or cover, the interior architecture. This photograph taken at the crossing, facing the nearby altar, where, instead of a crucifix or a monstrance, an enamelled or painted rectangular metal plaque stands upright, its left side white, its right black.
Text: that the crucifix was now exchanged for a small pendant medallion, half black, half white, the symbol of the local cult. The thought of Mrs. Fortesque having gone, so to speak, over to the other side was shocking, and at the same time extremely piquant and arousing, with my recently acquired knowledge of what that fully entailed for the woman involved. Having just come to the rendezvous from my daily session with the local doctor, who was treating me with that disgusting metallic green and gold powder, the source of which I was loath to ponder on, I scarcely thought myself physically capable of what was to follow, given my general and peculiar state. Nonetheless, when the missionary's widow, after furtively glancing about only to find the chapel empty—no surprise, since it was midday and most families were at home, doors shuttered for the day's largest repast—reached for and embraced me, the last thing I had awaited, I found myself responding in a most unexpected fashion. "But the children—your late husband—" I stammered, as she pushed me back against a column, so the decorative knobs of tibiæ and the like bruised my spine, with her bare breasts crushed against my chest and her hot searching lips

CARD NO. 20

Description: A statue, whose dimensions are given as 26 by 10 by 10 [cm, it is assumed], these last representing the base. A female goddess, in flowing robes, very much gravid, standing in a bronze boat formed like the body of a duck, whose head is the prow. Within its open beak it holds a cube.
Text: certain? It's only been a month . . ." I lingered at these, my own words, astonished at the assertion. "Of course I am," she snapped back, then containing herself with difficulty, lowered her tone, and continued, "I've not been with anyone, before or since," she said, bitterly smiling. She was very much enceinte, astoundingly so, in a way that would have been impossible had I been responsible for her state. I kept on looking at her in bewilderment. My first thought was "propulsive force—perhaps; generative principle—never!!" Still holding my hand lightly, she followed up, saying, "It does seem impossible, doesn't it? Not just the time—I mean, given what had happened to you, in addition. Think, though, was anything odd done to you then, or about that time? I mean . . ." At that, the thought of the daily calls to the doctor snapped into mind. Once I had found out the disgusting source of the gold and green powders, I had ceased from visiting him again. Had our meeting in the ossuary been before or after the "treatment's" short course? I could not remember, for the life of

CARD NO. 21

Description: Another souvenir card assumed to be from the local natural history collection, exhibiting a quite large centipede of unknown type, with several in-

teresting and anomalous features. The alternating black and white divisions of the scale stick beside it marked in tens of millimeters, since centimeters would make the creature ridiculously large.
Text: smooth and horrendously distended vulva with a disgusting plop. The three witches—I cannot think of them as being other than that—hurried to the trestle immediately, clicking the emerald daggers they had for tongues excitedly against their teeth. The multitudinous onlookers and priests held their distance. Mrs. F. seemed to be in a state of shock, but was still breathing with eyes closed. Horrified, I cast a look at Alicia, who stood imperturbed in her youthful nakedness, motionless, still holding the thick black candle cool as you like, as if she were in Westminster Abbey. The bloody caul and afterbirth were snipped at and cut with glassy tongues, and I saw, when the three stepped back, a foul, thick, twitching, segmented thing, snaky, glinting green and gold, thick as a moray eel, writhing between the poor woman's bloody legs. The chief witch nodded to Alicia, who slowly moved forward, setting her candle carefully at her mother's feet. At another signal, she picked up the glistening demonic shape, which unwound itself into a heavy, broad, segmented centipede-like beast of dimensions that left me gasping. Alicia uncoiled the slimy monster, gleaming with ichor, and draped the hellspawn 'round her shoulders, just as if it was a feather boa. Pausing only for a moment, she turned to me with a thin leer, and asked "Want to hold it? It's yours too!" Revulsed, I turned, while she shrugged and set off on the ceremonial way, the crowd bowing to her and her half-brother, sister, or whatever, the belt of hollow birds' eggs—her only adornment—clicking around her slim hips, brown from hours on the temple steps—as she swayed, during

CARD NO. 22

Description: A shining centipede probably of gold, coiled upon a dais of ebony, or some other dark wood, this last encrusted with bejewelled precious metal of arabesque form. The central object's size may be inferred from the various items imbedded in it: Roman cameos, Egyptian scarabs, coins from crushed empires and forgotten kingdoms, some thousands of years old, the votive offerings of worshippers over the millennia we infer the sculpture to have existed. The object is fabulous: an utter masterwork of the goldsmith's art rivalled only by the Cellini salt cellar and one or two other pieces. It almost seems alive.
Text: almost worth it. Calquon and Harrison are dead, what has become of Paul, who thought up all this, I have no idea. I have been subjected to the most hideous torture, and seen the most awful sights, that few can have experienced without losing their sanity. It is deeply ironic after all I have been through, that I by chance only yesterday discovered the object, hidden away in my belongings. What remains to be seen is whether I can bring it back to civilization with myself intact. I cannot trust Alicia, who has clearly let her elevation to high priestess and chief insect-keeper go to her head. During my last interview with her, while she dangled her shapely foot provocatively over the arm of her golden throne, I, in a vain effort to play upon her familial bonds and old self, reminded her of her younger brother, who had not been seen for days. At that she casually let drop that he had been sold on to Zanzibar (where there is, I believe, an active slave market) to ultimately disappear into one of the harems of the Arabian peninsula (Philby may be able to inform more fully). "I never could stand

the little pest," was her remark, so it would be foolish to hope for any sympathy from her quarter. I am being watched quite closely, with great suspicion. Can it be they know? If I ever leave here alive, it will be an absolute sensation. Biding my time, I cannot do anything now, but I can at least try to smuggle these surreptitiously scribbled notes out to the French vice-consul in the city where we bought the mules. He is a good fellow, though he drinks to excess at

An additional 52 cards remain (see photo-copies), which although of great interest, bear no hand-written notes, and therefore are not described here, with the following single exception:

CARD: NOT IN SEQUENCE, I.E. UNNUMBERED BY US

Description: A photographic postal card of a large exterior wall of a stone building of enormous size. The impressive dimensions become apparent once one realizes that the small specks and dots on the stereobate of the vaguely classical structure are in fact people—some alone, others in groups, these last for the most part sheltered under awnings set up on the steps. What most catches the eye, however, is the magnificent low relief work covering most of the wall, depicting, it would seem, some mythological scene whose iconographic meaning is not apparent. It is in character a harmonious mixture of several ancient traditions: one sees hints of the Hellenistic, Indo-Grecian, and traces even of South-East Asian styles. The contrasts of tone make clear that the bare stone has been brightly painted.
The relief itself: It appears a judgment is being carried out. In the background, solemn ringlet-bearded men draped in graceful robes, all in the same pose, all copies of the other. All hold a square object, somewhat in form like a hand-mirror divided into one field black and one field white, and watch with blank eyes the man before them who is strapped to a plank, while a large fabulous beast, part man, part insect, with elements of the order Scolopendra predominating, tears at him in the fashion of the Promethean eagles, and worse. To the right, a young priestess or goddess, nude but for a chain of beads or eggs around her waist, stands contrapposto, with one arm embraced about an obscene creature, a centipedal monstrosity of roughly her own height, leaning tightly upright against her. She is pointing with her free hand towards the tortured man. The expression on her empty face has affinities with several known Khmer royal portrait sculptures. She faintly smiles, as if in ecstasy.

NICHOLAS ROYLE

Hide and Seek

Nicholas Royle lives with his wife and two children in Shepherd's Bush, West London.

He says: " 'Hide and Seek' is about parental anxiety, a preoccupation with which I have become rather familiar. The best story I've read about fears relating to one's children's safety is Alex Hamilton's 'The Baby-sitters,' published in 1966 in Hamilton's collection Beam of Malice, *a book that's well worth seeking out."*

"Hide and Seek" was originally published in Dark Terrors 6, *edited by Stephen Jones and David Sutton.*

—E. D.

It was a way to pass the time and keep the kids happy. Kids. When I was a kid myself I didn't like the word. I didn't like being referred to as one of "the kids." It seemed unrespectful, dismissive. I preferred to be one of "the children." When my own kids were born, I consequently referred to them always as "the children," never "the kids." In fact, to qualify that, it was when the first one was born that I stuck religiously to that rule, which lasted until just after the second one came along. The second and final one, I might add. Nothing I've ever done in my life drains the energy quite like having kids. Don't get me wrong: I wouldn't go back. I wouldn't unhave them. My life has been enriched—immeasurably. Practically anyone who's had kids will tell you the same. Apart from the abusers, the loveless, the miserable. So no, I wouldn't go back, but nor would I have any more. I'm shattered as it is; plus, how could I love another one as much as I adore the two I've got? Mind you, I thought that after the birth of the first one.

Harry, our firstborn, is a handful, as naughty as he is adorable. Good as an angel one minute, absolute horror the next. Would I have him any other way? The standard answer is no. I wouldn't want him any different. The standard answer sucks, however. Doesn't take a genius to work that one out. Sure I'd have him different. I'd have him good all the time. It would make life easier, that's all. However, he's lovable the way he is and if making him any less naughty made him any less lovable, then, no, I wouldn't have him any different.

He's funny. He makes faces and strikes poses I wouldn't have thought a four-year-old capable of. He's a mimic in the making. I love him like—well, there is no like. I love him more than anything or anyone I've ever loved. Before his sister came long. Now I love her the same way I love him. I'm nuts about her. If our relationship is less developed, less complex than the relationship I have with Harry, that's only because he's got two years' head start. Our dialogue is less sophisticated, but we still talk. In fact she's talking more and more all the time. For months, while other two-year-olds were chattering away, Sophie remained silent. She'd point and she'd cry, but she didn't have much vocab. Then it started to come in a rush. Now she knows words I didn't know she knew. Every day she surprises me with another one. The longest sentence she can speak gets longer every day. She's also the most beautiful little girl you've ever seen (takes after her mum—my wife—Sally), but then they all say that.

Sometimes when I'm out with the two of them somewhere I forget that while Harry's walking beside me and holding my hand, Sophie's sitting on my shoulders, and I briefly slip into a dizzying panic. Where is she? Where have I left her? Will I ever see her again? Sure you will, she's on your shoulders, you dummy. It's like forgetting you're wearing your glasses. Don't tell me you've never done that: searched for your glasses for a good quarter of an hour, only to realize eventually they're stuck on the front of your head.

But those moments, those moments when I forget she's there and I don't know where she is, they remind me of when Harry was little. I mean really little, three months or so. When having a baby was still a novelty, when you turned round and saw him lying in his Moses basket and gave a little start because you'd forgotten, you'd forgotten you'd got a kid—or a child.

I had this fear that one day I'd look in the Moses basket and he wouldn't be there. Not that he could climb or roll out of it, he couldn't, but that he just wouldn't be there. That somehow I would have reverted to that pre-parental state. Gone backwards at speed. One minute I had a child, the next minute I didn't. It didn't make any sense, of course, but a lot of stuff goes through your head in those early months that doesn't make any sense.

I was looking after both the kids. Sally was working late, attending a meeting. Harry kept going on about Agnes, one of his little friends. He wanted her to come round. Or to go round to hers. We couldn't do that, I explained, because Agnes's parents had invited us round to theirs the other day. You have to be invited, I explained to him. You can't invite yourself.

Agnes's parents were our closest friends and they lived just two streets away. To stop Harry going on about it, I called them to invite them over. It turned out Agnes's mum, Siobhan, was at the same meeting Sally was at. They worked in the same field. So Agnes's dad, William, was looking after Agnes on his own. Looks like the tables have been turned, he joked. Our wives are out at work and we're left holding the babies.

Then he explained he was trying to finish some work of his own and needed to make the most of Siobhan's being out at the meeting. He was going to try to get Agnes into bed early. Instead, I offered to look after Agnes while he got on with his work. I'll bring her back after an hour or so, I said. Are you sure? He asked. No problem, I said. She's a very easy child.

William dropped Agnes round and she ran into the house, all excited at spending time with Harry and Sophie. William called after her, hoping for a goodbye kiss or hug before he went back home, but she was gone. I saw his crestfallen face, knew how he felt, but knew also that he'd be feeling relieved to have offloaded Agnes for a bit, so he'd be able to get some work done, or just have a break. I locked the door after him: my kids knew about not leaving the house unattended, and no doubt Agnes did too, but it didn't pay to be careless. So there I was now with three of them to keep happy at least until Sally got home. No problem, I'd said to William. No problem, I thought to myself. I loved Agnes almost like my own. Almost. There's always that almost. The love you have for your own kids is different. It's instinctive, fiercely protective. With someone else's kids it's less visceral, more of an affectionate responsibility.

Let's play hide and seek, I suggested. Yes! they all shouted, jumping up and down. Hide and seek. Hide and seek.

Who wants to hide first? I asked. Me! they chorused.

When Harry first started playing hide and seek, when he was two and a half, perhaps, or three, he'd tell you where he was going to hide. I'm going to hide under the bed, he'd say, and you'd try to explain why that wasn't really going to work. Later he would just close his eyes, believing that if he closed his eyes, not only could he not see you, but you couldn't see him either. Eventually he got the hang of it and became quite proficient at the game. He got so that you genuinely couldn't find him for two or three minutes. It was pretty much the only time, apart from when he was asleep, that you could get him to keep still and quiet for more than ten seconds. For this reason we encouraged the playing of hide and seek.

Sophie was still only learning, like Harry had been at her age. And Agnes—well, I was about to find out how good Agnes was at hide and seek.

Who's going to hide first? I asked, as if I didn't know. All three shouted "Me!" and put their hands up, but I knew from experience that if it wasn't Harry, then it wasn't going to work. He'd go into a sulk, wouldn't play properly and everything would start to fall apart. OK, Harry first, I said, raising my arms and my voice to forestall protest. The rest of us count to ten.

Twenty, he shouted as he bounded up the stairs.

I counted loudly enough to drown out his retreat and the girls joined in. Sophie was jumping up and down with excitement. She had just learned how to jump and liked to do it as much as possible whenever there was a situation that seemed to call for it. Twenty, we concluded at the tops of our voices. Coming ready or not. Dead silence from the rest of the house. That's my boy.

Shall we look in the kitchen first, I suggested, in case he managed to sneak past us while we had our eyes shut?

The girls both nodded and I led the way into the kitchen, which smelled of onions and fried minced lamb. Still steaming on the hob was the big pan of chilli I'd made earlier for Sally and me to enjoy in front of the TV when the kids were in bed. The fridge door was a collage of art postcards, Bob the Builder yogurt magnets and photo booth pictures of me and Sally with the kids. Over in the corner, a stereo was playing Porcupine Tree's *Lightbulb Sun* album for about the twenty-third time that day.

No sign of him here, I said. Shall we look in the dining room?

The knocked-through dining room and lounge looked like it usually did when both kids had been home for more than half an hour. Like a cyclone had ripped through the boxes, crates and cupboards filled with toys. A riot of Thomas the Tank Engine, Buzz Lightyear and Woody, Teletubbies and Barbie. Scott Tracey and Lady Penelope masks. Bob the Builder construction vehicles. Britains models and Matchbox Super-fast cars (handed down from father to son). Teddy bears, rag dolls and dozens of assorted soft toys. Full marks to the kids for having out-Chapmanned the Chapman Brothers, who would have been proud of the maelstrom of miscegenation and mutilation.

No sign of him here either, I said, checking under the coffee table and behind the settee. Shall we look upstairs?

Yes!

Upstairs we looked in Sophie's room. We'd recently taken the side off her cot. As a result she could get out of bed and wander in the night, which was marginally preferable to one of us having to go to her if she started crying. Let her come to us instead.

Harry wasn't in Sophie's room.

Sophie and Agnes had already checked out the bathroom. Next was Harry's room. Harry had recently become keen on coloring in and cutting out and sticking down. His masterpieces covered every available inch of wall space. On the floor was a little pile of jagged scraps of paper from his most recent sesssion with the kiddie-proof scissors. I quickly looked under his bed, but could only see his plastic Ikea toy crate-on-castors that I knew was full of dressing-up gear, Batman costumes, old scarves and so on. He wasn't in the walk-in cupboard or the walnut wardrobe.

By now the girls were shouting his name, enjoying the fact that we couldn't find him. We had a quick but thorough look in my and Sally's bedroom, but he wasn't in there either, so he had to be upstairs again. The top floor held my office, another bathroom and the spare bedroom. As soon as we'd looked in all three I began seriously to wonder where he might be. It occurred to me that, although I couldn't imagine how he might have done it, there was the tiniest of possibilities that he could have slipped past us while we were in his room and nipped downstairs. So I ran downstairs and rechecked every possible hiding place. It didn't take long; I knew where they all were by now. I made my way back upstairs like a cop with a search warrant, clearing rooms as I went, mentally chalking a cross on the door, one stroke on the way in, another as I left. Back at the top of the house, I finally admitted to myself that I was anxious.

Harry was good at hide and seek, but not this good. How was it possible, in a house I knew so well, for him to vanish so completely? I forced myself to be calm and to stick to a methodological approach. He couldn't have left the house—the front and back doors were locked, as were the windows. The door to the cellar was kept bolted. The door leading to the crawlspace that was all that was left of the loft after its conversion was not locked, but it was inaccessible behind the ratty old settee in my office and neither of our children had ever shown the slightest interest in it. I looked down at Sophie and Agnes. Their eyes were wide with excitement. Sophie was jumping up and down, shouting Harry's name.

Follow me, I said, something having made me think of triple-checking his favorite hiding place. In Harry's bedroom I got down on all fours and pulled out the plastic toy crate from under his bed. There he was, in the far corner, still as a statue, scarcely breathing. His eyes met mine and he started to smile.

He crawled out and I hugged him so tightly he protested that it hurt.

I'd lost my appetite for hide and seek, but naturally the kids hadn't and Sophie was insisting on hiding next. I knew if I stopped the game there'd be trouble, so we counted to twenty while she toddled off. It took us less than another twenty seconds to find her, a tell-tale giggling lump under the duvet in my and Sally's bed.

In fairness, I now had to let Agnes go off and hide despite overwhelming tiredness on my part and a growing desire to head back downstairs, open a beer and listen to the news on the radio while allowing the kids to veg out in front of Cartoon Network. I couldn't expect either William or Sally for another fifteen minutes.

. . . eighteen, nineteen, *twenty!*

The first place Harry looked was under his own bed. I think we might have heard if she'd hidden in here, I suggested, but in fact we hadn't heard anything at all. She'd managed to slip out and hide without leaving us any clues.

Let's look in Mummy and Daddy's room, Harry urged.

Sophie instantly copied what he'd said in her more condensed delivery, in which all the words ran together and could only be decoded by remembering what had been said before.

Agnes wasn't in Mummy and Daddy's room. The three of us climbed the stairs again to the top floor. Spare bedroom, bathroom, my office—all clear. Back down to the first floor. Bathroom, Sophie's room—both empty. We trooped downstairs, Harry running on ahead, wanting to be the one to find Agnes. There was no sign of her in the lounge, dining room or kitchen. Back in the hall, I noticed her shoes at the bottom of the stairs. She'd taken them off just after coming into the house.

I checked the locks on the doors and windows, then we ran back up to the first floor. I looked under each of the beds, behind all the curtains, in every cupboard. I added my voice to those of Harry and Sophie. I shouted that her Dad was due to collect her and he'd want to get straight back. It was time to come out. She'd won. (*No, I won!* Harry protested.) Come on, come on out, Agnes!

I ran up to the top floor without waiting for Harry and Sophie. I shoved the settee in the office out of the way and yanked open the door to the crawlspace, shining a light inside. Fishing tackle, rolled-up film posters, Christmas decorations, stacks of used padded envelopes, suitcases full of old clothes I couldn't bear to throw away—but no little girl, no Agnes. I looked under my desk, behind the oversize books on the bottom shelves of the bookcases, in the corner between the radio and the radiator. Running back out of my office I collided with Sophie on her way in. She fell over and started crying, but I ran on, into the spare bedroom. I ripped the sheets off the bed, hauled the TV away from the wall. In the adjoining bathroom I tore aside the shower curtain.

As I took the stairs three at a time back down to the next floor I could hear that both children were crying now. In our bedroom I emptied the laundry basket, fought my way through the dresses in Sally's wardrobe. I made myself stop and stare into the room's reflection in the full-length mirror in case that revealed any hidden detail I had somehow otherwise missed. I ran into Sophie's room and climbed up onto a chair to open the door to the linen cupboard.

I had checked everywhere, every possible hiding place, and she wasn't to be found. She'd gone.

The door bell rang. Sophie's room was just at the top of the stairs, so I could see right down to the front door. Through the frosted glass I could see that it wasn't Sally. Anyway, she would have used her keys. It was William.

NAN FRY

The Wolf's Story

Nan Fry was born in Missouri and grew up in Connecticut. She has an M.A. in Medieval Studies and a Ph.D. in English Literature from Yale University. She is an associate professor in the Academic Studies Department of the Corcoran College of Art and Design in Washington, D.C., where she teaches courses on children's literature, the environment, and wolves. She is the author of two collections of poetry: Say What I Am Called, *a chapbook of riddles she translated from the Anglo-Saxon, and* Relearning the Dark. *Her poems have also appeared in magazines such as* The Wallace Stevens Journal, Poet Lore, *and* Plainsong. *One of her poems was installed on posters in the transit system of Washington, D.C., and Baltimore, Maryland, as part of the Poetry Society of America's Poetry in Motion® Program and was included in the anthology* Poetry in Motion from Coast to Coast.

—E. D.

I was hungry.
You killed all the deer,
cut down my forest and plowed
it under. If I took a lamb,
I was the devil's dog, a slavering
fiend, fair game for your stones,
your guns and poisons, your stories.

You caught one of my pups, tied
him to a stake, and when he cried
and his mother ran to him, you
shot her down.

You shot at me too. I outran
the bullets only to stumble
into steel jaws that bit
and held. I bit back and nearly
broke my teeth. I had to chew
my paw off. I left the bloody
stump in that steel mouth.

When I met her, my leg
had healed, but I was alone—
no mate, no pups, no pack.
I could barely catch mice,
couldn't run fast enough
to get a rabbit.

I was hungry all the time.
I'd eat grass even though
I knew it would come up again,
just for the satisfaction of swallowing,
to ease the ache in my gut.

She was plump and tender—a lamb
with no fleece. I wanted
to sink my teeth in right away,
but I wanted the grandmother too.
My jaws closed on them
like a trap snapping shut.

Full at last, I fell asleep.
The hunter cut me open,
took them from me, and filled
me with stones. They say I died then.

But whenever you hear of children
given stones for supper, I am among you.
My name is Hunger.

ELIZABETH HAND

The Least Trumps

Elizabeth Hand's article "Inside Out: On Henry Darger" appears elsewhere in this anthology, but Ms. Hand is known best for her fiction, which has won her many kudos over the last few years. One could not ask for a better example of her extraordinary gifts than the following richly textured work. "The Least Trumps," a splendid contemporary fantasy about the magic inherent in books and art, has my vote as the best story of the year. It comes from Conjunctions: 39, The New Fabulists *issue.*

—*T. W.*

In the Lonely House there is a faded framed *LIFE* magazine article from almost half a century ago, featuring a color photograph of a beautiful woman with close-cropped blonde hair and rather sly gray eyes, wide crimson-lipsticked mouth, a red-and-white striped bateau-neck shirt. The woman is holding a large magnifying lens and examining a very large insect, a plastic scientific model of a common black ant, *Formica componatus*, posed atop a stack of children's picture books. Each book displays the familiar blocky letters and illustrated image that has been encoded into the dreamtime DNA of generations of children: that of a puzzled-looking, goggle-eyed ant, its antenna slightly askew as though trying, vainly, to tune in to the signal from some oh-so-distant station.

Wise Aunt or Wise Ant? reads the caption beneath the photo. *Blake E. Tun Examines a Friend.*

The woman is the beloved children's book author and illustrator, Blake Eleanor Tun, known to her friends as Blakie. The books are the six classic Wise Ant books, in American and English editions and numerous translations. *Wise Ant, Brave Ant, Curious Ant; Formi Sage, Weise Ameise, Una Ormiga Visionaria.* In the room behind Blakie, you can just make out the figure of a toddler, out of focus as she runs past. You can see the child's short blonde hair cut in a page-boy, and a tiny hand that the camera records as a mothlike blur. The little girl with the Prince Valiant haircut, identified in the article as Miss Tun's adopted niece, is actually Blakie's illegitimate daughter, Ivy Tun. That's me.

Here in her remote island hidey-hole, the article begins, *Blake Eleanor Tun brings to life an imaginary world inhabited by millions.*

People used to ask Blakie why she lived on Aranbega. Actually, just living on an island wasn't enough for my mother. The Lonely House stood on an islet in Green Pond, so we lived on an island on an island.

"Why do I live here? Because enchantresses always live on islands," she'd say, and laugh. If she fancied the questioner she might add, "Oh, *you* know. Circe, Calypso, the Lady in the Lake. . . ."

Then she'd give her, or very occasionally him, one of her mocking sideways smiles, lowering her head so that its fringe of yellow hair would fall across her face, hiding her eyes so that only the smile remained.

"The smile on the face of the tiger," Katherine told me once when I was a teenager. "Whenever you saw that smile of hers, you'd know it was only a matter of time."

"Time till what?" I asked.

But by then her attention had already turned back to my mother: the sun to Katherine's gnomon, the impossibly beautiful bright thing that we all circled, endlessly.

Anyway, I knew what Blakie's smile meant. Her affairs were notorious even on the island. For decades, however, they were carefully concealed from her readers, most of whom assumed (as they were meant to) that Blake E. Tun was a man—that *LIFE* magazine article caused quite a stir among those not already in the know. My mother was Blakie to me as to everyone else. When I was nine she announced that she was not my aunt but my mother, and produced a birth certificate from a Boston hospital to prove it.

"No point in lying. It would however be more *convenient* if you continued to call me Blakie." She stubbed out her cigarette on the sole of her tennis shoe and tossed it over the railing into Green Pond. "But it's no one's business who you are. Or who I am in relation to you, for that matter."

And that was that. My father was not a secret kept from me; he just didn't matter that much, not in Blakie's scheme of things. The only thing she ever told me about him was that he was very young.

"Just a boy. Not much older than you are now, Ivy," which at the time was nineteen. "Just a kid."

"Never knew what hit him," agreed my mother's partner, Katherine, as Blakie glared at her from across the room.

It never crossed my mind to doubt my mother, just as it never crossed my mind to hold her accountable for any sort of duplicity she might have practiced, then or later. The simple mad fact was that I adored Blakie. Everyone did. She was lovely and smart and willful and rich, a woman who believed in seduction, not argument; when seduction failed, which was rarely, she was not above abduction, of the genteel sort involving copious amounts of liquor and the assistance of one or two attractive friends.

The Wise Ant books she had written and illustrated when she was in her twenties. By her thirtieth birthday they had made her fortune. Blakie had a wise agent named Letitia Thorne and a very wise financial adviser named William Dunlap, both of whom took care that my mother would never have to work again unless she wanted to.

Blakie did not want to work. She wanted to seduce Dunlap's daughter-in-law, a twenty-two-year-old Dallas socialite named Katherine Mae Moss. The two women eloped to Aranbega, a rocky spine of land some miles off the coast of

Maine. There they built a fairy-tale cottage in the middle of a lake, on a tamarack- and fern-covered bump of rock not much bigger than the Bambi Airstream trailer they'd driven up from Texas. The cottage had two small bedrooms, a living room and dining nook and wraparound porch overlooking the still silvery surface of Green Pond. There was a beetle-black cast-iron Crawford woodstove for heat and cooking, kerosene lanterns and a small red hand pump in the slate kitchen sink. No electricity; no telephone. Drinking water was pumped up from the lake. Septic and gray water disposal was achieved through an ancient holding tank that was emptied once a year.

They named the cottage the Lonely House, after the tiny house where Wise Ant lived with her friends Grasshopper and Bee. Here they were visited by Blakie's friends, artistic sorts from New York and Boston, several other writers from Maine, and by Katherine's relatives, a noisy congeries of cattle heiresses, disaffected oilmen and Ivy league dropouts, first-wave hippies and draft dodgers, all of whom took turns babysitting me when Blakie took off for Crete or London or Taos in pursuit of some new *amour*. Eventually, of course, Katherine would find her and bring her home: as a child I imagined my mother engaged in some world-spanning game of hide-and-seek, where Katherine was always It. When the two of them returned to the Lonely House, there would always be a prize for me as well. A rainbow map of California, tie-dyed on a white bedsheet; lizard-skin drums from Angola; a meerschaum pipe carved in the likeness of Richard Nixon.

"You'll never have to leave here to see the world, Ivy," my mother said once, after presenting me with a Maori drawing on bark of a stylized honeybee. "It will all come to you, like it all came to me."

My mother was thirty-seven when I was born, old to be having a baby, and paired in what was then known as a Boston marriage. She and Katherine are still together, two old ladies now living in a posh assisted-living community near Rockland, no longer scandalizing anyone. They've had their relationship highlighted on an episode of *This American Life*, and my mother is active in local liberal causes, doing benefit readings of *The Vagina Monologues* and signings of *Wise Ant* for the Rockland Domestic Abuse Shelter. Katherine reconciled with her family and inherited a ranch near Goliad, where they still go sometimes in the winter. The Wise Ant books are now discussed within the context of midcentury American lesbian literature, a fact which annoys my mother no end.

"I wrote those books for *children*," she cries whenever the topic arises. "They are *children's books*," as though someone had confused the color of her mailbox, red rather than black. "For God's sake."

Of course Wise Ant will never be anything more than her antly self—wise, brave, curious, kind, noisy, helpful—just as Blakie at eighty-two remains beautiful, maddening, forgetful, curious, brave; though seldom, if ever, quiet. We had words when I converted the Lonely House to solar power—

"You're spoiling it. It was never *intended* to have electricity—"

Blakie and Katherine were by then well established in their elegant cottage at Penobscot Fields. I looked at the room around me—Blakie's study, small but beautifully appointed, with a Gustav Stickley lamp that she'd had rewired by a curator at the Farnsworth, her laptop screen glowing atop a quartersawn oak desk; Bose speakers and miniature CD console.

"You're right," I said. "I'll just move in here with you."

"That's not the—"

"Blakie. I need electricity to work. The generator's too noisy, my customers don't like it. And expensive. I have to work for a living—"

"You don't have to—"

"I *want* to work for a living." I paused, trying to calm myself. "Look, it'll be fun—doing the wiring and stuff. I got all these photo-voltaic cells, when it's all set up, you'll see. It'll be great."

And it was. The cottage is south facing: two rows of cells on the roof, a few extra batteries boxed in under the porch, a few days spent wiring, and I was set. I left the bookshelves in the living room, mostly my books now, and a few valuable first editions that I'd talked Blakie into leaving. Eliot's *Four Quartets* and some Theodore Roethke; *Gormenghast*; a Leonard Baskin volume signed *For Blakie*. One bedroom I kept as my own, with a wide handcrafted oak cupboard bed, cleverly designed to hold clothes beneath and more books all around. At the head of the bed were those I loved best, a set of all six Wise Ant books and the five volumes of Walter Burden Fox's unfinished *Five Windows One Door* sequence.

The other bedroom became my studio. I set up a drafting table and autoclave and lightbox, a shelf with my ultrasonic cleaner and driclave. On the floor was an additional power unit just for my machine and equipment; a tool bench holding soldering guns, needle bars, and jigs; a tall stainless steel medicine cabinet with enough disinfectant and bandages and gloves and hemostats to outfit a small clinic; an overhead cabinet with my inks and pencils and acetates. Empty plastic caps await the colored inks that fill the machine's reservoir. A small sink drains into a special tank that I bring to the Rockland dump once a month, when everyone else brings in their empty paint cans. A bookshelf holds albums filled with pictures of my own work and some art books—Tibetan stuff, pictures from Chauvet Cavern, Japanese woodblock prints.

But no flash sheets; no framed flash art; no fake books. If customers want flash, they can go to Rockland or Bangor. I do only my own designs. I'll work with a customer, if she has a particular image in mind, or come up with something original if she doesn't. But if somebody has her heart set on a prancing unicorn, or Harley flames, or Mister Natural, or a Grateful Dead logo, I send her elsewhere.

This doesn't happen much. I don't advertise. All my business is word of mouth, through friends or established customers, a few people here on Aranbega. But mostly, if someone wants me to do her body work, she *really* has to want me, enough to fork out sixty-five bucks for the round-trip ferry and at least a couple hundred for the tattoo, and three hundred more for the Aranbega Inn if she misses the last ferry, or if her work takes more than a single day. Not to mention the cost of a thick steak dinner afterward, and getting someone else to drive her home. I don't let people stay at the Lonely House, unless it's someone I've known for a long time, which usually means someone I was involved with at some point, which usually means she wouldn't want to stay with me in any case. Sue is an exception, but Sue is seeing someone else now, one of the other occupational therapists from Penobscot Fields, so she doesn't come over as much as she used to.

That suits me fine. My customers are all women. Most of them are getting a tattoo to celebrate some milestone, usually something like finally breaking with an abusive boyfriend, leaving a bad marriage, coming to grips with the aftermath of a rape. Breast cancer survivors—I do a lot of breast work—or tattoos to celebrate coming out, or giving birth. Sometimes anniversaries. I get a lot of emotional baggage dumped in my studio, for hours or days at a time; it always leaves when the customers do, but it pretty much fulfills my need for any kind of emotional connection, which is pretty minimal anyway.

And, truth to tell, it fulfills most of my sexual needs too; at least any baseline desire I have for physical contact. My life is spent with skin: cupping a breast in my hand, pulling the skin taut between my fingers while the needle etches threadlike lines around the aureole, tracing yellow above violet veins, turning zippered scars into coiled serpents, an explosion of butterfly wings, flames or phoenixes rising from a puckered blue-white mound of flesh; or drawing secret maps, a hidden cartography of grottoes and ravines, rivulets and waves lapping at beaches no bigger than the ball of my thumb; the ball of my thumb pressed there, index finger there, tissue film of latex between my flesh and hers, the hushed drone of the machine as it chokes down when the needle first touches skin and the involuntary flinch that comes, no matter how well she's prepared herself for this, no matter how many times she's lain just like this, paper towels blotting the film of blood that wells, nearly invisible, beneath the moving needle bar's tip, music never loud enough to drown out the hum of the machine. Hospital smells of disinfectant, blood, antibacterial ointment, latex.

And sweat. A stink like scorched metal: fear. It wells up the way blood does, her eyes dilate and I can smell it, even if she doesn't move, even if she's done this enough times to be as controlled as I am when I draw the needle across my own flesh: she's afraid, and I know it, needle-flick, soft white skin pulled taut, again, again, between my fingers.

I don't want a lot of company, after a day's work.

I knew something was going to happen the night before I found the Trumps. Sue teases me, but it's true, I can tell when something is going to happen. A feeling starts to swell inside me, as though I'm being blown up like a balloon, my head feels light and somehow cold, there are glittering things at the edges of my eyes. And sure enough, within a day or two someone turns up out of the blue, or I get a letter or e-mail from someone I haven't thought of in ten years, or I see something—a mink, a yearling moose, migrating elvers—and I just know.

I shouldn't even tell Sue when it happens. She says it's just a manifestation of my disorder, like a migraine aura.

"Take your fucking medicine, Ivy. It's an early warning system: take your Xanax!"

Rationally I can understand that, rationally I know she's right. That's all it is, a chain of neurons going off inside my head, like a string of firecrackers with a too-short fuse. But I can never explain to her the way the world looks when it happens, that green glow in the sky not just at twilight but all day long, the way I can see the stars sometimes at noon, sparks in the sky.

I was outside the Lonely House, cutting some flowers to take to Blakie. Pink and white cosmos; early asters, powder blue and mauve; white sweet-smelling phlox, their stems slightly sticky, green aphids like minute beads of dew beneath the flower heads. From the other shore a chipmunk gave its warning *cheeet*. I looked up, and there on the bank a dozen yards away sat a red fox. It was grinning at me; I could see the thin black rind of its gums, its yellow eyes shining as though lit from within by candles. It sat bolt upright and watched me, its white-tipped brush twitching like a cat's.

I stared back, my arms full of asters. After a moment I said, "Hello there. Hello. What are you looking for?"

I thought it would lope off then, the way foxes do, but it just sat and continued to watch me. I went back to gathering flowers, putting them into a wooden trug and straightening to gaze back at the shore. The fox was still there, yellow eyes glinting in the late-summer light. Abruptly it jumped to its feet. It looked right at me, cocking its head like a dog waiting to be walked.

It barked—a shrill, bone-freezing sound, like a child screaming. I felt my back prickle; it was still watching me, but there was something distracted about its gaze, and I saw its ears flatten against its narrow skull. A minute passed. Then, from away across Cameron Mountain there came an answer, another sharp yelp, higher-pitched and ending in a sort of yodeling wail. The fox turned so quickly it seemed to somersault through the low grass, and arrowed up the hillside toward the birch grove. In a moment it was gone. There was only the frantic chatter of red squirrels in the woods and, when I drew the dory up on the far shore a quarter-hour later, a musky sharp smell like crushed grapes.

I got the last ferry over to Port Symes, me and a handful of late-season people from away, sunburned and loud, waving their cell phones over the rail as they tried to pick up a signal from one of the towers on the mainland.

"We'll *never* get a reservation," a woman said accusingly to her husband. "I *told* you to have Marisa do it before she left—"

At Port Symes I hopped off before any of them, heading for where I'd left Katherine's car parked by an overgrown bank of dog roses. The roses were all crimson hips and thorns by now, the dark green leaves already burning to yellow; there were yellow beech leaves across the car's windshield, and as I drove out onto the main road I saw acorns like thousands of green-and-bronze marbles scattered across the gravel road. Summer lingers for weeks on the islands, trapped by pockets of warmer air, soft currents and gray fog holding it fast till mid-October some years. Here on the mainland it was already autumn.

The air had a keen winey scent that reminded me of the fox. As I headed down the peninsula toward Rockland I caught the smell of burning leaves, the dank odor of smoke snaking through a chimney that had been cold since spring. The maples were starting to turn, pale gold and pinkish red. There had been a lot of rain in the last few weeks; one good frost would set the leaves ablaze. On the seat beside me Blakie's flowers sat in their mason jar, wrapped in a heavy towel; one good frost and they might be the last ones I'd pick this year.

I got all the way to the main road before the first temblors of panic hit. I deliberately hadn't taken my medication—it made me too sleepy, I couldn't drive, and Sue would have had to meet me at the ferry, I would be asleep before we got to her place. The secondary road ended; there was a large green sign with arrows pointing east and west.

THOMASTON
OWL'S HEAD
ROCKLAND

I turned right, toward Rockland. In the distance I could see the slate-covered reach of Penobscot Bay, a pine-pointed tip of land protruding into the waters, harsh white lights from Rockland Harbor; miles and miles off, a tiny smudge like a thumbprint upon the darkening sky.

Aranbega. I was off island.

The horror comes down, no matter how I try to prepare myself for it, no matter how many times I've been through it: an incendiary blast of wind, the feeling that an iron helmet was tightening around my head. I began to gasp, my heart starting to pound and my entire upper body going cold. Outside was a cool September twilight, the lights of the strip malls around Rockland starting to prick through the gold-and-violet haze, but inside the car the air had grown black, my skin icy. There was a searing fire in my gut. My T-shirt was soaked through. I forced myself to breathe, to remember to exhale: to think *You're not dying, nobody dies of this, it will go, it will go . . .*

"*Fuck.*" I clutched the steering wheel and crept past the Puffin Shop convenience store, past the Michelin tire place, the Dairy Queen; through one set of traffic lights, a second. *You won't die, nobody dies of this; don't look at the harbor.*

I tried to focus on the trees—two huge red oaks, there, you could hardly see where the land had been cleared behind them to make way for a car wash. *It's just a symptom, you're reacting to the symptoms, nobody dies of this, nobody.* At a stop sign I grabbed my cell phone and called Sue.

"I'm by the Rite-Aid." *Don't look at the Rite-Aid.* "I'll be there, five minutes—"

An SUV pulled up behind me. I dropped the phone, feeling like I was going to vomit; turned sharply onto the side street. My legs shook so I couldn't feel the pedals under my feet. *How can I drive if my legs are numb?*

The SUV turned in behind me. My body trembled, I hit the gas too hard and my car shot forward, bumping over the curb then down again. The SUV veered past, a great gray blur, its lights momentarily blinding me. My eyes teared and I forced my breath out in long hoots, and drove the last few hundred feet to Sue's house.

She was in the driveway, still holding the phone in one hand.

"Don't," I said. I opened the car door and leaned out, head between my knees, waiting for the nausea to pass. When she came over I held my hand up and she stopped, but I heard her sigh. From the corner of my eye I could see the resigned set to her mouth, and that her other hand held a prescription bottle.

Always before when I came over to visit my mother, I'd stay with Sue and we'd sleep together, comfortably, not so much for old time's sake as to sustain some connection at once deeper and less enduring than talk. Words I feel obliged to remember, skin I can afford to forget. A woman's body inevitably evokes my own, small wet mouths, my own breath, my own legs, breasts, arms, shoulders, back. Even after Sue started seeing someone else, we'd ease into her wide bed with its wicker headboard, cats sliding to the floor in a gray heap like discarded laundry, radio playing softly, *Tea and oranges, So much more.*

"I think you'd better stay on the couch," Sue said that night. "Lexie isn't comfortable with this arrangement, and . . ."

She sighed, glancing at my small leather bag, just big enough to hold a change of underwear, hairbrush, toothbrush, wallet, a battered paperback of *Lorca in New York*. "I guess I'm not either. Anymore."

I felt my mouth go tight, stared at the mason jar full of flowers on the coffee table.

"Yup," I said.

I refused to look at her. I wouldn't give her the satisfaction of seeing how I felt.

But of course Sue wouldn't be gleeful, or vindictive. She'd just be sad, maybe mildly annoyed. I was the one who froze and burned; I was the one who scarred people for a living.

"It's fine," I said after a minute, and, looking at her, smiled wryly. "I have to get up early anyway."

She looked at me, not smiling, dark brown eyes creased with regret. *What a waste,* I could hear her thinking. *What a lonely wasted life.*

I think the world is like this: beautiful, hard, cold, unmoving. Oh, it turns, things change—clouds, leaves, the ground beneath the beech trees grows thick with beechmast and slowly becomes black fragrant earth ripe with hellgrammites, millipedes, nematodes, deer mice. Small animals die, we die; a needle moves across honey-colored skin and the skin turns black, or red, or purple. A freckle or a mole becomes an eye; given enough time an eye becomes an earthworm.

But change, the kind of change Sue believes in—Positive Change, Emotional Change, Cultural Change—I don't believe in that. When I was young, I thought the world *was* changing: there was a time, years-long, when the varicolored parade of visitors through the Lonely House made me believe that the world Outside must have changed its wardrobe as well, from sere black suits and floral housedresses to velvet capes and scarlet morning coats, armies of children and teenagers girding themselves for skirmish in embroidered pants, feathered headdresses, bare feet, bare skin. I dressed myself as they did—actually, they dressed *me*, as Blakie smoked and sipped her whiskey sour, and Katherine made sure the bird feeders and woodbox were full. And one day I went out to see the world.

It was only RISD—the Rhode Island School of Design—and it should have been a good place, it should have been a Great Place for me. David Byrne and a few other students were playing at someone's house, other students were taking off for Boston and New York, squatting in Alphabet City in burned-out tenements with a toilet in the kitchen, getting strung out, but they were doing things, they were having adventures, hocking bass guitars for Hasselblad cameras, learning how to hold a tattoo machine in a back room on St. Mark's Place, dressing up like housewives and shooting five hours of someone lying passed out in bed while a candle flickered down to a shiny red puddle and someone else laughed in the next room. It didn't look like it at the time, but you can see it now, when you look at their movies and their photographs and their vinyl forty-fives and their installations: it didn't seem so at the time, but they were having a life.

I couldn't do that. My problem, I know. I lasted a semester, went home for Christmas break and never went back. For a long time it didn't matter—maybe it never mattered—because I still had friends, people came to see me even when Blakie and Katherine were off at the ranch, or bopping around France. Everyone's happy to have a friend on an island in Maine. So in a way it was like Blakie had told me long ago: the world *did* come to me.

Only of course I knew better.

Saturday was Sue's day off. She'd been at Penobscot Fields for eleven years now and had earned this, a normal weekend; I wasn't going to spoil it for her. I got up early, before seven, fed the cats and made myself coffee, then went out.

I walked downtown. Rockland used to be one of the worst-smelling places in the United States. There was a chicken-processing plant, fish factories, the everyday reek and spoils of a working harbor. That's all changed, of course. Now there's a well-known museum, and tourist boutiques have filled up the empty storefronts left when the factories shut down. Only the sardine-processing plant remains, down past the Coast Guard station on Tilson Avenue; when the wind is off the water you can smell it, a stale odor of fishbones and rotting bait that cuts through the scents of fresh-roasted coffee beans and car exhaust.

Downtown was nearly empty. A few people sat in front of Second Read, drinking coffee. I went inside and got coffee and a croissant, walked back onto the sidewalk and wandered down to the waterfront. For some reason seeing the water when I'm on foot usually doesn't bother me. There's something about being in a car, or a bus, something about moving, the idea that there's *more* out there, somewhere; the idea that Aranbega is floating in the blue pearly haze and I'm here, away: disembodied somehow, like an astronaut untethered from a capsule, floating slowly beyond that safe closed place, unable to breathe and everything gone to black, knowing it's just a matter of time.

But that day, standing on the dock with the creosote-soaked wooden pilings beneath my sneakers, looking at orange peels bobbing in the black water and gulls wheeling overhead—that day I didn't feel bad at all. I drank my coffee and ate my croissant, tossed the last bit of crust into the air and watched the gulls veer and squabble over it. I looked at my watch. A little before eight, still too early to head to Blakie's. She liked to sleep in, and Katherine enjoyed the peace and quiet of a morning.

I headed back toward Main Street. There was some early-morning traffic now, people heading off to do their shopping at Shaw's and Wal-Mart. On the corner I waited for the light to change, glanced at a storefront, and saw a sign taped to the window.

ST. BRUNO'S EPISCOPAL CHURCH
ANNUAL RUMMAGE SALE
SATURDAY, SEPTEMBER 7
8 A.M.–3:00 P.M.
LUNCH SERVED FROM 11:30

Penobscot Fields had once been the lupine-strewn meadow behind St. Bruno's; proximity to the church was one of the reasons Blakie and Katherine had first signed on to the retirement community. I wasn't a churchgoer, but during the summer I was an avid hunter of yard sales in the Rockland area. You don't get many of them after Labor Day, but the rummage sale at St. Bruno's almost makes up for it. I made sure I had wallet and checkbook in my bag then hurried to get there before the doors opened.

There was already a line. I recognized a couple of dealers, a few regulars who smiled or nodded at me. St. Bruno's is a late-nineteenth-century neo-Gothic building, designed in the late Arts and Crafts style by Halbert Liston; half-timbered beams, local dove gray fieldstone, slate shingles on the roof. The rummage sale was not in the church, of course, but the adjoining parish house. It had whitewashed walls rather than stone, the same half-timbered upper story, etched with arabesques of dying clematis and sere Virginia creeper. In the door was a diamond-shaped window through which a worried elderly woman peered out every few minutes.

"Eight o'clock!" someone called good-naturedly from the front of the line. Bobby Day, the graying hippie who owned a used bookstore in Camden. "Time to go!"

From inside, the elderly woman gave one last look at the crowd, then nodded. The door opened; there was a surge forward, laughter and excited murmurs, someone crying, "Marge, look out! Here they come!" Then I was inside.

Long tables of linens and clothing were at the front of the hall, surrounded by women with hands already full of flannel sheets and crewelwork. I scanned these quickly, then glanced at the furniture. Nice stuff—a Morris chair and old oak settle, some wicker, a flax wheel. Episcopalians always have good rummage sales, better quality than Our Lady of the Harbor or those off-brand churches straggling down toward Warren.

But the Lonely House was already crammed with my own nice stuff, besides which it would be difficult to get anything back to the island. So I made my way to the rear of the hall, where Bobby Day was going through boxes of books on the floor. We exchanged hellos, Bobby smiling but not taking his eyes from the books; in deference to him I continued on to the back corner. An old man wearing a canvas apron with a faded silhouette of St. Bruno on it stood over a table covered with odds and ends.

"This is whatever didn't belong anywhere else," he said. He waved a hand at a hodgepodge of beer steins, Tupperware, mismatched silver, shoeboxes overflowing with candles, buttons, mason jar lids. "Everything's a dollar."

I doubted there was anything there worth fifty cents, but I just nodded and moved slowly down the length of the table. A chipped Poppy Trails bowl and a bunch of ugly glass ashtrays. Worn Beanie Babies with the tags clipped off. A game of Twister. As I looked, a heavyset woman barreled up behind me. She had a rigidly unsmiling face and an overflowing canvas bag—I caught glints of brass and pewter, the telltale dull green glaze of a nice Teco pottery vase. A dealer. She avoided my gaze, her hand snaking out to grab something I'd missed, a tarnished silver flask hidden behind a stack of plastic Easter baskets.

I tried not to grimace. I hated dealers and their greedy bottom-feeder mentality. By this afternoon she'd have polished the flask and stuck a seventy-five-dollar price tag on it. I moved quickly to the end of the table. I could see her watching me whenever my hand hovered above something; once I moved on she'd grab whatever I'd been examining, give it a cursory glance before elbowing up beside me once more. After a few minutes I turned away, was just starting to leave when my gaze fell upon a swirl of violet and orange tucked within a Pyrex dish.

"Not sure what that is," the old man said as I pried it from the bowl. Beside me the dealer watched avidly. "Lady's scarf, I guess."

It was a lumpy packet a bit larger than my hand, made up of a paisley scarf that had been folded over several times to form a thick square, then wrapped and tightly knotted around a rectangular object. The cloth was frayed, but it felt like fine wool. There was probably enough of it to make a nice pillow cover. Whatever was inside felt compact but also slightly flexible; it had a familiar heft as I weighed it in my palm.

An oversized pack of cards. I glanced up to see the dealer watching me with undisguised impatience.

"I'll take this," I said, and handed the old man a dollar. "Thanks."

A flicker of disappointment across the dealer's face. I smiled at her, enjoying my mean little moment of triumph, and left.

Outside the parish hall a stream of people were headed for the parking lot, carrying lamps and pillows and overflowing plastic bags. The church bell tolled eight-thirty. Blakie would just be getting up. I killed a few more minutes by wandering around the church grounds, past a well-kept herb garden and stands of yellow chrysanthemums. Behind a neatly trimmed hedge of boxwood I discovered a statue of St. Bruno himself, standing watch over a granite bench. Here I sat with my paisley-wrapped treasure, and set about trying to undo the knot.

For a while I thought I'd have to just rip the damn thing apart, or wait till I got to Blakie's to cut it open. The cloth was knotted so tightly I couldn't undo it, and the paisley had gotten wet at some point then shrunk—it was like trying to pick at dried plaster, or Sheetrock.

But gradually I managed to tease one corner of the scarf free, tugging it gently until, after a good ten minutes, I was able to undo the wrappings. A faint odor wafted up, the vanilla-tinged scent of pipe tobacco. There was a greasy feel to the frayed cloth, sweat, or maybe someone had dropped it on the damp grass. I opened it carefully, smoothing its folds till I could finally see what was tucked inside.

It was a large deck of cards, bound with a rubber band. The rubber band fell to bits when I tried to remove it, and something fluttered onto the bench. I picked it up: a scrap of paper with a few words scrawled in pencil.

The least trumps

I frowned. The Greater Trumps, those were the picture cards that made up the Major Arcana in a tarot deck—the Chariot, the Magician, the Empress, the Hierophant. Eight or nine years ago I had a girlfriend with enough New Age tarots to channel the entire Order of the Golden Dawn. Marxist tarots, lesbian tarots, African, Zen, and Mormon tarots; Tarots of the Angels, of Wise Mammals, poisonous snakes and smiling madonni; Aleister Crowley's tarot, and Shirley Maclaine's; the dread Feminist Tarot of the Cats. There were twenty-two Major Arcana cards, and the lesser trumps were analogous to the fifty-two cards in an ordinary deck, with an additional four representing knights.

But the least trumps? The phrase stabbed at my memory, but I couldn't place it. I stared at the scrap of paper with its rushed scribble, put it aside, and examined the deck.

The cards were thick, with the slightly furry feel of old pasteboard. Each was printed with an identical and intricate design of spoked wheels, like old-fashioned gears with interlocking teeth. The inks were primitive, too-bright primary colors, red and yellow and blue faded now to periwinkle and pale rose, a dusty gold like smudged pollen. I guessed they dated to the early or mid-nineteenth century. The images had the look of old children's picture books from that era, at once vivid and muted, slightly sinister, as though the illustrators were making a point of not revealing their true meaning to the casual viewer. I grinned, thinking of how I'd wrested them from the clutches of an antiques dealer, then turned them over.

The cards were all blank. I shook my head, fanning them out on the bench before me. A few of the cards had their corners neatly clipped, but others looked as though they had been bitten off in tiny crescent-shaped wedges. I squinted at one, trying to determine if someone had peeled off a printed image. The surface was rough, flecked with bits of darker gray and black, or white, but it didn't seem to have ever had anything affixed to it. There was no trace of glue or spirit gum that I could see, no jots of ink or colored paper.

A mistake then. The deck had obviously been discarded by the printer. Not even a dealer would have been able to get more than a couple of bucks for it.

Too bad. I gathered the cards into a stack, started wrapping the scarf around them when I noticed that one card was thicker than the rest. I pulled it out; not a single card after all, but two that had become stuck together. I set the rest of the deck aside, safe within the paisley shroud, then gingerly slid my thumbnail between the stuck cards. It was like prizing apart sheets of mica—I could feel where the pasteboard held fast toward the center, but if I pulled at it too hard or too quickly the cards would tear.

But very slowly, I felt the cards separate. Maybe the warmth of my touch helped, or the sudden exposure to air and moisture. For whatever reason, the cards suddenly slid apart so that I held one in each hand.

"Oh."

I cried aloud, they were that wonderful. Two tiny, brilliantly inked tableaux like medieval tapestries, or paintings by Brueghel glimpsed through a rosace window. One card was awhirl with minute figures, men and women but also animals, dogs dancing on their hind legs, long-necked cranes and crabs that lifted clacking claws to a sky filled with pennoned airships, exploding suns, a man being carried on a litter and a lash-fringed eye like a greater sun gazing down upon them all. The other card showed only the figure of a naked man, kneeling so that he faced the viewer, but with head bowed so that you saw only his broad back, a curve of neck like a quarter-moon, a sheaf of dark hair spilling to the ground before him. The man's skin was painted in gold leaf; the ground he knelt upon was the dreamy green of old bottle glass, the sky behind him crocus yellow, with a tinge upon the horizon like the first flush of sun, or the protruding tip of a finger. As I stared at them I felt my heart begin to beat, too fast too hard but not with fear this time, not this time.

The Least Trumps. The term was used, just once, in the first chapter of the unfinished, final volume of *Five Windows One Door*. I remembered it suddenly, the way you recall something from early childhood, the smell of marigolds towering above your head, a blue plush dog with one glass eye, thin sunlight filtering through a crack in a frosted glass cold frame. My mouth filled with liquid and I tasted sour cherries, salt and musk, the first time my tongue probed a girl's cunt. A warm breeze stirred my hair. I heard distant laughter, a booming bass note that resolved into the echo of a church clock tolling nine.

> Only when he was certain that Mabel had fallen fast asleep beside him would Tarquin remove the cards from their brocade pouch, her warm limbs tangled in the stained bedcovers where they emitted a smell of yeast and limewater, the surrounding room suffused with twilight so that when he held the cards before her mouth, one by one, he saw how her breath brought to life the figures painted upon each, as though she breathed upon a winter windowpane where frost-roses bloomed: *Pavell Saved From Drowning, The Bangers, One Leaf Left, Hermalchio and Lachrymatory, Villainous Saltpetre, The Ground-Nut, The Widower:* all the recusant figures of the Least Trumps quickening beneath Mabel's sleeping face.

Even now the words came to me by heart. Sometimes, when I couldn't fall asleep, I would lie in bed and silently recite the books from memory, beginning with Volume One, *The First Window: Love Plucking Rowanberries*, with its description of Mabel's deflowering that I found so tragic when I first read it. Only later in my twenties, when I read the books for the fifth or seventh time, did I realize the scene was a parody of the seduction scene in *Rigoletto*. In this way Walter Burden Fox's books eased my passage into the world, as they did in many others. Falling in love with fey little Clytie Winton then weeping over her death; making my first forays into sex when I masturbated to the memory of Tarquin's mad brother Elwell taking Mabel as she slept; realizing, as I read of Mabel's great love affair with the silent film actress Nola Flynn, that there were words to describe what I did sometimes with my own friends, even if those words had a lavender must of the attic to them: *tribadism, skylarking, sit Venus in the garden with Her Gate unlocked*.

My mother never explained any of this to me: sex, love, suffering, patience. Probably she assumed that her example alone was enough, and for another person it might well have been. But I never saw my mother unhappy, or frightened. My first attack came not long after Julia Sa'adah left me. Julia who inked my life Before and After; and while at the time I was contemptuous of anyone who suggested a link between the two events, breakup and crackup, I can see now that it was so. In Fox's novels, love affairs sometimes ended badly, but for all the lessons his books held, they never readied me for the shock of being left.

That was more than eleven years ago. I still felt the aftershocks, of course. I still dream about her: her black hair, so thick it was like oiled rope streaming through my fingers; her bronzy skin, its soft glaucous bloom like scuppernongs; the way her mouth tasted. Small mouth, smaller than my own, cigarettes and wintergreen, tea oil, coriander seed. The dream is different each time, though it always ends the same way, it ends the way it ended: Julia looking at me as she packs up her Rockland studio, arms bare so I can see my own apprentice work below her elbow, vine leaves, stylized knots. My name there, and hers, if you knew where to look. Her face sad but amused as she shakes her head. "You never happened, Ivy."

"How can you *say* that?" This part never changes either, though in my waking mind I say a thousand other things. "Six years, how can you fucking *say* that?"

She just shakes her head. Her voice begins to break up, swallowed by the harsh buzz of a tattoo machine choking down; her image fragments, hair face eyes breasts tattoos spattering into bits of light, jabs of black and red. The tube is running out of ink. "That's not what I mean. You just don't get it, Ivy. *You* never happened. *You*. Never. Happened."

Then I wake and the panic's full-blown, like walking into a room where a bomb's exploded. Only there's no bomb. What's exploded is all inside my head.

It was years before anyone figured out how it worked, this accretion of synaptic damage, neuronal misfirings, an overstimulated fight-or-flight response; the way one tiny event becomes trapped within a web of dendrites and interneurons and triggers a cascade of cortisol and epinephrine, which in turn wakes the immense black spider that rushes out and seizes me so that I see and feel only horror, only dread, the entire world poisoned by its bite. There is no antidote—the whole disorder is really just an accumulation of symptoms, accelerated pulse rate, racing heartbeat, shallow breathing. There is no cure, only chemicals that lull the spider back to sleep. It may be that my repeated tattooing of my own skin has somehow oversensitized me, like bad acupuncture, caused an involuntary neurochemical reaction that only makes it worse.

No one knows. And it's not something Walter Burden Fox ever covered in his books.

I stared at the illustrated cards in my hands. Fox had lived not far from here, in Tenants Harbor. My mother knew him years before I was born. He was much older than she was, but in those days—this was long before e-mail and cheap long-distance servers—writers and artists would travel a good distance for the company of their own kind, and certainly a lot further than from Tenants Harbor to Aranbega Island. It was the first time I can remember being really impressed by my mother, the way other people always assumed I must be. She had found me curled up in the hammock, reading *Love Plucking Rowanberries*.

"You're reading Burdie's book." She stooped to pick up my empty lemonade glass.

I corrected her primly. "It's by Walter Burden Fox."

"Oh, I know. Burdie, that's what he liked to be called. His son was Walter too. Wally, they called him. I knew him."

Now, behind me, St. Bruno's bell rang the quarter hour. Blakie would be up by now, waiting for my arrival. I carefully placed the two cards with their fellows inside the paisley scarf, put the bundle inside my bag, and headed for Penobscot Fields.

Blakie and Katherine were sitting at their dining nook when I let myself in. Yesterday's *New York Times* was spread across the table, and the remains of breakfast.

"Well," my mother asked, white brows raised above calm gray eyes as she looked at me. "Did you throw up?"

"Oh, hush, you," said Katherine.

"Not this time." I bent to kiss my mother, then turned to hug Katherine. "I went to the rummage sale at St. Bruno's, that's why I'm late."

"Oh, I meant to give them my clothes!" Katherine stood to get me coffee. "I brought over a few boxes of things, but I forgot the clothes. I have a whole bag, some nice Hermès scarves, too."

"You shouldn't give those away." Blakie patted the table, indicating where I should sit beside her. "That consignment shop in Camden gives us good credit for them. I got this sweater there." She touched her collar, dove gray knit, three pearl buttons. "It's lamb's wool. Bonwit Teller. They closed ages ago. Someone must have died."

"Oh hush," said Katherine. She handed me a coffee mug. "Like we need credit for *clothes*."

"Look," I said. "Speaking of scarves . . ."

I pulled the paisley packet from the purse, clearing a space amidst the breakfast dishes. For a fraction of a second Blakie looked surprised, then she blinked, and along with Katherine leaned forward expectantly. As I undid the wrappings the slip of paper fell onto the table beside my mother's hand. Her gnarled fingers scrabbled at the table, finally grabbed the scrap.

"I can't read this," she said, adjusting her glasses as she stared and scowled. I set the stack of cards on the scarf, then slid them all across the table. I had withheld the two cards that retained their color; now I slipped them into my back jeans pocket, carefully, so they wouldn't get damaged. The others lay in a neat pile before my mother.

" 'The Least Trumps.' " I pointed at the slip of paper. "That's what it says."

She looked at me sharply, then at the cards. "What do you mean? It's a deck of cards."

"What's written on the paper. It says, 'The Least Trumps.' I don't know if you remember, but there's a scene in one of Fox's books, the first one? The Least Trumps is what he calls a set of tarot cards that one of the characters uses." I edged over beside her, and pointed at the bit of paper she held between thumb and forefinger. "I was curious if you could read that. Since you knew him? I was wondering if you recognized it. If it was his handwriting."

"Burdie's?" My mother shook her head, drew the paper to her face until it was just a few inches from her nose. It was the same pose she'd assumed when pretending to gaze at Wise Ant through a magnifying glass for *LIFE* magazine, only now it was my mother who looked puzzled, even disoriented. "Well, I don't know. I don't remember."

I felt a flash of dread, that now of all times would be when she started to lose it, to drift away from me and Katherine. But no. She turned to Katherine and said, "Where did we put those files? When I was going through the letters from after the war. Do you remember?"

"Your room, I think. Do you want me to get them?"

"No, no. . . ." Blakie waved me off as she stood and walked, keeping her balance by touching chair, countertop, wall on the way to her study.

Katherine looked after her, then at the innocuous shred of paper, then at me.

"What is it?" She touched one unraveling corner of the scarf. "Where did you get them?"

"At the rummage sale. They were wrapped up in that, I didn't know what they were till I got outside and opened it."

"Pig in a poke." Katherine winked at me. She still had her silvery hair done every Thursday, in the whipped-up spray-stiffened bouffant of her Dallas socialite days—not at the beauty parlor at the retirement center, either, but the most expensive salon in Camden. She had her nails done too, even though her hands were too twisted by arthritis to wear the bijoux rings she'd always favored, square-cut diamonds and aquamarines and the emerald my mother had given her when they first met. "I'm surprised you bought a pig in a poke, Ivy Bee."

"Yeah. I'm surprised too."

"Here we are." My mother listed back into the room, settling with a thump in her chair. "Now we can see."

She jabbed her finger at the table, where the scrap of paper fluttered like an injured moth, then handed me an envelope. "Open that, please, Ivy dear. My hands are so clumsy now."

It was a white letter-sized envelope, unsealed, tipsy typed address.

Miss Blakie Tun,
The Lonely House,
Aranbega Island, Maine

Before zip codes, even, one faded blue four-cent stamp in one corner. The other corner with the typed return address: W. B. Fox, Sand Hill Road, T. Harbor, Maine.

"Look at it!" commanded Blakie.

Obediently I withdrew the letter, unfolded it, and scanned the handwritten lines, front and back, until I reached the end. Blue ink, mouse-tail flourish on the final *e*. *Very Fondly Yours, Burdie*.

"I think it's the same writing." I scrutinized the penmanship, while trying not to actually absorb its content. Which seemed dull in any case, something about a dog, and snow, and someone's car getting stuck, and *Be glad when summer's here, at least we can visit again.*

Least. I picked up the scrap of paper to compare the two words.

"You know, they *are* the same," I said. There was something else, too. I brought the letter to my face and sniffed it. "And you know what else? I can smell it. It smells like pipe tobacco. The scarf smells like it, too."

"Borkum Riff." My mother made a face. "Awful sweet stuff, I couldn't stand it. So."

She looked at me, gray eyes narrowed, not sly but thoughtful. "We were good friends, you know. Burdie. Very lovable man."

Katherine nodded. "Fragile."

"Fragile. He would have made a frail old man, wouldn't he?" She glanced at Katherine—two strong old ladies—then at me. "I remember how much you liked his books. I'm sorry now we didn't write to each other more, I could have given you his letters, Ivy. He always came to visit us, once or twice a year. In the summer."

"But not after the boy died," said Katherine.

My mother shook her head. "No, not after Wally died. Poor Burdie."

"Poor Wally," suggested Katherine.

It was why Fox had never completed the last book of the quintet. His son had been killed in the Korean War. I knew that; it was one of the only really interesting, if tragic, facts about Walter Burden Fox. There had been one full-length biography, written in the 1970s, when his work achieved a minor cult status boosted by the success of Tolkien and Mervyn Peake, a brief vogue in those days for series books in uniform paperback editions. *The Alexandria Quartet, Children of Violence, A Dance to the Music of Time. Five Windows One Door* had never achieved that kind of popularity, of course, despite the affection for it held by figures like Anaïs Nin, Timothy Leary, and Virgil Thomson, themselves eclipsed now by brighter, younger lights.

Fox died in 1956. I hadn't been born yet. I could never have met him.

Yet, in a funny way, he made me who I am—well, maybe not *me* exactly. But he certainly changed the way I thought about the world; made it seem at once unabashedly romantic and charged with a sense of imminence, as ripe with possibility as an autumn orchard is ripe with fruit. Julia and I were talking once about the 1960s—she was seven years older than me, and had lived through them as an adult, communes in Tennessee, drug dealing in Malibu, before she settled down in Rockland and opened her tattoo studio.

She said, "You want to know what the sixties were about, Ivy? The sixties were about *It could happen*."

And that's what Fox's books were like. They gave me the sense that there was someone leaning over my shoulder, someone whispering *It could happen*.

So I suppose you could say that Walter Burden Fox ruined the real world for me, when I didn't find it as welcoming as the one inhabited by Mabel and Nola and the Sienno brothers. Could there ever have been a real city as marvelous as his imagined Newport? Who would ever choose to bear the weight of this world? Who would ever want to?

Still, that was my weakness, not his. The only thing I could really fault him for was his failure to finish that last volume. But, under the circumstances, who could blame him for that?

"So these are his cards? May I?" Katherine glanced at me. I nodded, and she picked up the deck tentatively, turned it over, and gave a little gasp. "Oh! They're blank—"

She looked embarrassed and I laughed. "Katherine! *Now* look what you've done!"

"But were they like this when you got them?" She began turning the cards over, one by one, setting them out on the table as though playing an elaborate game of solitaire. "Look at this! They're every single one of them blank. I've never seen such a thing."

"All used up," said Blakie. She folded the scarf and pushed it to one side. "You should wash that, Ivy. Who knows where it's been."

"Well, where *has* it been? Did he always go to church there? St. Bruno's?"

"I don't remember." Blakie's face became a mask: as she had aged, Circe became the Sphinx. She was staring at the cards lying faceup on the table. Only of course there were no faces, just a grid of gray rectangles, some missing one or two corners or even three corners. My mother's expression was watchful but wary; she glanced at me, then quickly looked away again. I thought of the two cards in my back pocket but said nothing. "His wife died young, he raised the boy alone. He wanted to be a writer too, you know. Probably they just ended up in someone's barn."

"The cards, you mean," Katherine said mildly. Blakie looked annoyed. "There. That's all of them."

"How many are there?" I asked. Katherine began to count, but Blakie said, "Seventy-three."

"Seventy-three?" I shook my head. "What kind of deck uses seventy-three cards?"

"Some are missing, then. There's only seventy." Katherine looked at Blakie. "Seventy-three? How do you know?"

"I just remember, that's all," my mother said irritably. She pointed at me. "*You* should know. You read all his books."

"Well." I shrugged and stared at the bland pattern on the dining table, then reached for a card. The top right corner was missing; but how would you know it was the top? "They were only mentioned once. As far as I recall, anyway. Just in passing. Why do you think the corners are cut off?"

"To keep track of them." Katherine began to collect them back into a pile. "That's how card cheats work. Take off a little teeny bit, just enough so they can tell when they're dealing 'em out. Which one's an ace, which one's a trey."

"But these are all the same," I said. "There's no point to it."

Then I noticed Blakie was staring at me. Suddenly I began to feel paranoid, like when I was a teenager out getting high, walking back into the Lonely House and praying she wouldn't notice how stoned I was. I felt like I'd been lying, although what had I done, besides stick two cards in my back pocket?

But then maybe I was lying, when I said there was no point; maybe I was wrong. Maybe there *was* a point. If two of the cards had a meaning, maybe they all did; even if I had no clue what their meaning was. Even if nobody had a clue: they still might mean something.

But what? It was like one of those horrible logic puzzles—you have one boat, three geese, one fox, an island: how do you get all the geese onto the island without the fox eating them? Seventy-three cards; seventy that Katherine had counted, the pair in my back pocket: where was the other one?

I fought an almost irresistible urge to reveal the two picture cards I'd hidden. Instead I looked away from my mother, and saw that now Katherine was staring at me, too. It was a moment before I realized she was waiting for the last card, the one that was still in my hand. "Oh. Thanks—"

I gave it to her, she put it on top of the stack, turned, and gave the stack to Blakie, who gave it to me. I looked down at the cards and felt that cold pressure starting to build inside my head, helium leaking into my brain, something that was going to make me float away, talk funny.

"Well." I wrapped the cards in the paisley scarf. It still smelled faintly of pipe tobacco, but now there was another scent too, my mother's Chanel No. 5. I stuck the cards in my bag, turned back to the dining table. "What should we do now?"

"I don't have a clue," said my mother, and gave me the smile of an octogenarian tiger. "Ivy? You decide."

Julia's father was Egyptian, a Coptic diplomat from Cairo. Her mother was an artist manqué from a wealthy Boston family that had a building at Harvard named for it. Her father, Narouz, had been married and divorced four times; Julia had a much younger half brother and several half sisters. The brother died in a terrorist attack in Egypt in the early nineties, a year or so before she left me. After her mother's death from cancer the same year, Julia refused to have anything else to do with Narouz or his extended family. A few months later, she refused to have anything to do with me as well.

Julia claimed that *Five Windows One Door* could be read as a secret text of ancient Coptic magic, that there were meanings encoded within the characters' ceaseless and often unrequited love affairs, that the titles of Nola Flynn's silent movies corresponded to oracular texts in the collections of the Hermitage and the Institut Français d'Archeologie Orientale in Cairo, that the scene in which Tarquin sodomizes his twin is in fact a description of a ritual to leave a man impotent and protect a woman from sexual advances. I asked her how such a book could possibly be conceived and written by a middle-aged communicant at St. Bruno's in Maine, in the middle of the twentieth century.

Julia just shrugged. "That's why it works. Nobody knows. Look at Lorca."

"Lorca?" I shook my head, trying not to laugh. "What, was he in Maine, too?"

"No. But he worked in the twentieth century."

That was almost the last thing Julia Sa'adah ever said to me. This is another century. Nothing works anymore.

I caught an earlier ferry back than I'd planned. Katherine was tired; I had taken her and my mother to lunch at the small café they favored, but it was more crowded than usual, with a busload of blue-haired leaf-peepers from Newburyport who all ordered the specials so that the kitchen ran out and we had to eat BLTs.

"I just hate that." Blakie glowered at the table next to us, four women the same age as she was, scrying the bill as though it were tea leaves. "Look at them, trying to figure out the tip! Fifteen percent, darling," she said loudly. "Double the tax and add one."

The women looked up. "Oh, thank you!" one said. "Isn't it pretty here?"

"I wouldn't know," said Blakie. "I'm blind."

The woman looked shocked. "Oh, hush, you," scolded Katherine. "She is not," but the women were already scurrying to leave.

I drove them back to their tidy modern retirement cottage, the made-for-TV version of the Lonely House.

"I'll see you next week," I said, after helping them inside. Katherine kissed me and made a beeline for the bathroom. My mother sat on the couch, waiting to catch her breath. She had congestive heart disease, payback for all those years of smoking Kents and eating heavily marbled steaks.

"You could stay here if you wanted," she said, and for almost the first time I heard a plaintive note in her voice. "The couch folds out."

I smiled and hugged her. "You know, I might do that. I think Sue wants a break from me. For a little while."

For a moment I thought she was going to say something. Her mouth pursed and her gray eyes once again had that watchful look. But she only nodded, patting my hand with her strong cold one, then kissed my cheek, a quick furtive gesture like she might be caught.

"Be careful, Ivy Bee," she said. "Goodbye."

On the ferry I sat on deck. The boat took no cars, and there were only a few other passengers. I had the stern to myself, a bench sheltered by the engine house from spray and chill wind. The afternoon had turned cool and gray. There was a bruised line of clouds upon the horizon, violet and slate blue; it made the islands look stark as a Rockwell Kent woodblock, the pointed firs like arrowheads.

It was a time of day, a time of year, I loved; one of the only times when things still seemed possible to me. Something about the slant of the late year's light, the sharp line between shadows and stones, as though if you slid your hand in there you'd find something unexpected.

It made me want to work.

I had no customers lined up that week. Idly I ran my right hand along the top of my left leg, worn denim and beneath it muscle, skin. I hadn't worked on myself for a while. That was one of the first things I learned when I was apprenticed to Julia: a novice tattoo artist practices on herself. If you're right-handed, you do your left arm, your left leg; just like a good artist makes her own needles, steel flux and solder, jig and needles, the smell of hot tinning fluid on the tip of the solder gun. That way people can see your work. They know they can trust you.

The last thing I'd done was a scroll of oak leaves and eyes, fanning out above my left knee. My upper thigh was still taut white skin. I was thin and rangy like my mother had been, too fair to ever have tanned. I flexed my hand, imagining the weight of the machine, its pulse a throbbing heart. As I stared at the ferry's wake, I could see the lights of Rockland Harbor glimmer then disappear into the growing dusk. When I stuck my head out to peer toward the bow, I saw Aranbega rising from the Atlantic, black firs and granite cliffs buffed to pink by the failing sun.

I stood, keeping my balance as I gently pulled the two cards from my back pocket. I glanced at both, then put one into my wallet, behind my driver's license; sat and examined the other, turning so that the wall of the engine house kept it safe from spray. It was the card that showed only the figure of a kneeling man. A deceptively simple form, a few fluid lines indicating torso, shoulders, offertory stance—that crescent of bare neck, his hands half hidden by his long hair.

Why did I know it was a man? I'm not sure. The breadth of his shoulders, maybe; some underlying sense that any woman in such a position would be inviting disaster. This figure seemed neither resigned nor abdicating responsibility. He seemed to be waiting.

It was amazing, how the interplay of black and white and a few drops of gold leaf could conjure up an entire world. Like Pamela Colman Smith's designs for the Waite tarot—the High Priestess; the King of Wands—or a figure that Julia had shown me once. It was from a facsimile edition of a portfolio of Coptic texts on papyrus, now in the British Library. There were all kinds of spells—

> For I am having a clash with a headless dog, seize him when he comes. Grasp this pebble with both your hands, flee east-ward to your right, while you journey on up.
>
> A stinging ant: In this way, while it is still fresh, burn it, grind it with vinegar, put it with incense. Put it on eyes that have discharge. They will get better.

The figure was part of a spell to obtain a good singing voice. Julia translated the text for me as she had the others:

> Yea, yea, for I adjure you in the name of the seven letters that are tattooed on the chest of the father, namely AAAAAAA, EEEEEEE, EEEEEEE, IIIIII, OOOOOOO, UUUUUUU, OOOOOOO. Obey my mouth, before it passes and another one comes in its place! Offering: wild frankincense, wild mastic, cassia.

The Coptic figure that accompanied the text had a name: DAVITHEA RACHOCHI ADONIEL. It looked nothing like the figure on the card in front of me; it was like something you'd see scratched on the wall of a cave.

Yet it had a name. And I would never know the name of this card.

But I would use it, I decided. *The least trumps*. Beneath me the ferry's engine shifted down, its dull steady groan deepening as we drew near Aranbega's shore. I slid the card into the Lorca book I'd brought, stuffed it into my bag, and waited to dock.

I'd left my old GMC pickup where I always did, parked behind the Island General Store. I went inside and bought a sourdough baguette and a bottle of Tokaji. I'd gotten a taste for the wine from Julia; now the store ordered it especially for me, though some of the well-heeled summer people bought it as well.

"Working tonight?" said Mary, the store's owner.

"Yup."

Outside it was full dusk. I drove across the island on the rugged gravel road that bisected it into north and south, village and wild places. To get to Green Pond you drive off the main road, following a rutted lane that soon devolves into what resembles a washed-out streambed. Soon this rudimentary road ends, at the entrance to a large grove of hundred-and-fifty-year-old pines. I parked here and walked the rest of the way, a quarter mile beneath high branches that stir restlessly, making a sound like the sea even on windless days. The pines give way to birches, ferns growing knee-high in a spinney of trees like bones. Another hundred feet and you reach the edge of Green Pond, before you the Lonely House rising on its gray islet, a dream of safety. Usually this was when the last vestiges of fear would leave me, blown away by the cool wind off the lake and the sight of my childhood home, my wooden dory pulled up onto the shore a few feet from where I stood.

But tonight the unease remained. Or no, not unease exactly; more a sense of apprehension that, very slowly, resolved into a kind of anticipation. But anticipation of what? I stared at the Lonely House with its clumps of asters and yellow coneflowers, the ragged garden I deliberately didn't weed or train. Because I wanted the illusion of wilderness, I wanted to pretend I'd left something to chance. And suddenly I wanted to see something else.

If you walk to the other side of the small lake—I hardly ever do—you find that you're on the downward slope of a long boulder-strewn rise, a glacial moraine that eventually plummets into the Atlantic Ocean. Scattered white pines and birches grow here, and ancient white oaks, some of the very few white oaks left in the entire state, in fact, the rest having been harvested well over a century before, as masts for the great schooners. The lesser trees—red oaks, mostly, a few sugar maples—have been cut, for the Lonely House's firewood and repairs, so that if you stand in the right place you can actually look down the entire southeastern end of the island and see the ocean: scumbled gray cliffs and beyond that nothing, an unbroken darkness that might be fog, or sea, or the end of the world.

The right place to see this is from an outcropping of granite that my mother named the Ledges. On a foggy day, if you stand there and look at the Lonely House, you have an illusion of gazing from one sea island to another. If you turn, you see only darkness. The seas are too rough for recreational sailors, far from the major shipping lanes, too risky for commercial fishermen. The entire Grand Banks fishery has been depleted, so that you can stare out for hours or maybe even days and never see a single light, nothing but stars and maybe the blinking red eye of a distant plane flying the Great Circle Route to Gander or London.

It was a vista that terrified me, though I would dutifully point it out to first-time visitors, showing them where they could sit on the Ledges.

"On a clear day you can see Ireland," Katherine used to say; the joke being that on a Maine island you almost never had a clear day.

This had not been a clear day, of course, and with evening high gray clouds had come from the west. Only the easternmost horizon held a pale shimmer of blue-violet, lustrous as the inner curve of a mussel shell. Behind me the wind moved through the old pines, and I could hear the rustling of the birch leaves. Not so far off a fox barked. The sound made my neck prickle.

But I'd left a single light on inside the Lonely House, and so I focused on that, walking slowly around the perimeter of Green Pond with the little beacon always at the edge of my vision, until I reached the far side, the eastern side. Ferns crackled underfoot; I smelled the sweet odor of dying bracken, and bladder wrack from the cliffs far below. The air had the bite of rain to it, and that smell you get sometimes, when a low pressure system carries the reek of places much farther south—a soupy, thick smell, like rotting vegetation, mangroves or palmettos. I breathed it in and thought of Julia, and realized that for the first time in years, an hour had gone by and I had not thought about her at all. From the trees on the other side of Green Pond the fox barked again, even closer this time.

For one last moment I stood, gazing at the Ledges. Then I turned and walked back to where my dory waited, clambered in and rowed myself home.

The tattoo took me till dawn to finish. Once inside the Lonely House I opened the bottle of Tokaji, poured myself a glassful, and drank it. Then I went to retrieve the card, stuck inside that decrepit New Directions paperback in my bag. The book was the only thing of Julia's I had retained. She'd made a point of going through every single box of clothes and books I'd packed, through every sagging carton of dishware, and removed anything that had been hers. Anything we'd purchased together, anything that it had been her idea to buy. So that by the time she was done, it wasn't just like I'd never happened. It was like she'd never happened, either.

Except for this book. I found it a few months after the breakup. It had gotten stuck under the driver's seat of my old Volvo, wedged between a broken spring and the floor. In all the years I'd been with Julia, I'd never read it, or seen her reading it; but just a few weeks earlier I started flipping through the pages, casually, more to get the poet's smell than to actually understand him. Now I opened the book to the page where the card was stuck, and noticed several lines that had been highlighted with yellow marker.

> The *duende*, then, is a power and not a construct, is a struggle and not a concept. That is to say, it is not a question of aptitude, but of a true and viable style—of blood, in other words; of creation made act.

A struggle, not a concept. I smiled, and dropped the book on the couch; took the card and went into my studio to work.

I spent over an hour just getting a feel for the design, trying to copy it freehand onto paper before giving up. I'm a good draftsman, but one thing I've learned over the years is that the simpler a good drawing appears to be, the more difficult it is to copy. Try copying one of Picasso's late minotaur drawings and you'll see what I mean. Whoever did the design on this particular card probably wasn't Picasso, but the image still defeated me. There was a mystery to it, a sense of waiting that was charged with power, like that D. H. Lawrence poem, *those who have not exploded*. I finally traced it on my light board, the final stencil image exactly the same size as that on the card, outlined in black hectograph ink.

Then I prepped myself. My studio is as sterile as I can make it. There's no carpet on the bare wood floor, which I scrub every day. Beneath a blue plastic cover, the worktable is white formica, so blood or dirt shows, or spilled ink. I don't bother with an apron or gloves when I'm doing myself, and between the lack of protection and a couple of glasses of Tokaji, I always get a slightly illicit-feeling buzz. I feel like I'm putting something over, even though there's never anyone around but myself. I swabbed the top of my thigh with seventy percent alcohol, used a new, disposable razor to shave it; swabbed it again, dried it with sterile gauze soaked in more alcohol. Then I coated the shaved skin with betadine, tossing the used gauze into a small metal biohazard bin.

I'd already set up my inks in their plastic presterilized caps—black, yellow and red to get the effect of gold leaf, white. I got ready to apply the stencil, rubbing a little bit of stick deodorant onto my skin, so that the ink would adhere, then pressing the square of stenciled paper and rubbing it for thirty seconds. Then I pulled the paper off. Sometimes I have to do this more than once, if the customer's skin is rough, or the ink too thick. This time, though, the design transferred perfectly.

I sat for a while, admiring it. From my angle, the figure was upside down—I'd thought about it, whether I should just say the hell with it and do it so I'd be the only one who'd ever see it properly. But I decided to go with convention, so that now I'd be drawing a reverse of what everyone else would see. I'm a bleeder, so I had a good supply of Vaseline and paper towels at hand. I went into the living room and knocked back one last glass of Tokaji, returned to the studio, switched on my machine, and went at it.

I did the outlines first. There's always this *frisson* when the needles first touch my own skin, sterilized metal skimming along the surface so that it burns, as though I'm running a flame-tipped spike along my flesh. Before Julia did my first tattoo I'd always imagined the process would be like pricking myself with a needle, a series of fine precise jabs of pain.

It's not like that at all. It's more like carving your own skin with the slanted nib of a razor-sharp calligraphy pen, or writing on flesh with a soldering iron. The pain is excruciating, but contained: I look down at the vibrating tattoo gun, its tip like a wasp's sting, and see beneath the needles a flowing line of black ink, red weeping from the black: my own blood. My left hand holds the skin taut—this also hurts like hell—while my right fingers manipulate the machine and the wad of paper towel that soaks up blood as the needle moves on, its tip moving in tiny circles, being careful not to press too hard, so it won't scab. I trace a man's shoulders, a crescent that becomes a neck, a skull's crown above a single thick line that signals a cascade of hair. Then down and up to outline his knees, his arms.

When the pain becomes too much I stop for a bit, breathing deeply. Then I smooth Vaseline over the image on my thigh, take a bit of gauze and clean the needle tip of blood and ink. After twenty minutes or so of being scarred with a vibrating needle your endorphins kick in, but they don't block the pain; they merely blur it, so that it diffuses over your entire body, not just a few square inches of stretched skin burning like a fresh brand. It's perversely like the aftermath of a great massage, or great sex; exhausting, unbearable, exhilarating. I finished the outline and took a break, turning on the radio to see if WERU had gone off the air. Two or three nights a week they sign off at midnight, but Saturdays sometimes the DJ stays on.

This was my lucky night. I turned the music up and settled back into my chair. My entire leg felt sore, but the outline looked good. I changed the needle tip and began to do the shading, the process that would give the figure depth and color. The tip of the needle tube is flush against my skin, but only for an instant; then I flick it up and away. This way the ink is dispersed beneath the epidermis, deepest black feathering up to create gray.

It takes days and days of practice before you get this technique down, but I had it. When I was done edging the figure's hair, I cleaned and changed the needle tube again, mixing gamboge yellow and crimson until I got just the hue I wanted, a brilliant tiger-lily orange. I sprayed the tattoo with disinfectant, gave it another swipe of Vaseline, then went to with the orange. I did some shading around the man's figure, until it looked even better than the original, with a numinous glow that made it stand out from the other designs around it.

It was almost two more hours before I was done. At the very last I put in a bit of white, a few lines here and there, ambient color, really, the eye didn't register it as white but it charged the image with a strange, almost eerie brilliance. White ink pigment is paler than human skin; it changes color the way skin does, darkening when exposed to the sun until it's almost indistinguishable from ordinary flesh tone.

But I don't spend a lot of time outside; inks don't fade much on my skin. When I finally put down the machine, my hand and entire right arm ached. Outside, rain spattered the pond. The wind rose, and moments later I heard droplets lashing the side of the house. A barred owl called its four querulous notes. From my radio came a low steady hum of static. I hadn't even noticed when the station went off the air. Soon it would be 5:00 A.M., and the morning DJ would be in. I cleaned my machine and work area quickly, automatically; washed my tattoo, dried it, and covered the raw skin with antibacterial ointment, and finally taped on a Telfa bandage. In a few hours, after I woke, I'd shower and let the warm water soften the bandage until it slid off. Now I went into the kitchen, stumbling with fatigue and the postorgasmic glow I get from working on myself.

I'd remembered to leave out a small porterhouse steak to defrost. I heated a cast-iron skillet, tossed the steak in and seared it, two minutes on one side, one on the other. I ate it standing over the sink, tearing off meat still cool and bloody in the center. There are some good things about living alone. I knocked back a quart of skim milk, took a couple of ibuprofen and a high-iron formula vitamin, went to bed, and passed out.

The central conceit of *Five Windows One Door* is that the same story is told and retold, with constantly shifting points of view, abrupt changes of narrator, of setting, of a character's moral or political beliefs. Even the city itself changed, so that the bistro frequented by Nola's elderly lover, Hans Liep, was sometimes at the end of Tufnell Street; other times it could be glimpsed in a cul-de-sac near the Boulevard El-Baz. There were madcap scenes in which Shakespearean plot reversals were enacted—the violent reconciliation between Mabel and her father; Nola Flynn's decision to enter a Carmelite convent after her discovery of the blind child Kelson; Roberto Metropole's return from the dead; even the reformation of the incomparably wicked Elwell, who, according to the notes discovered after Fox's death, was to have married Mabel and fathered her six children, the eldest of whom grew up to become Amantine, Popess of Tuckahoe and the first saint to be canonized in the Reformed Catholic Church.

Volume Five, *Ardor ex Cathedra*, was unfinished at the time of Fox's death. He had completed the first two chapters, and in his study was a box full of hand-drawn genealogical charts and plot outlines, character notes, a map of the city, even names for new characters—Billy Tyler, Gordon MacKenzie-Hart, Paulette Houdek, Ruben Kirstein. Fox's editor at Griffin/Sage compiled these remnants into an unsatisfactory final volume that was published a year after Fox died. I bought a copy, but it was a sad relic, like the blackened lump of glass that is all that remains of a stained-glass window destroyed by fire. Still, I kept it with its brethren on a bookshelf in my bedroom, the five volumes in their uniform dust jackets, scarlet letters on a brilliant indigo field with the author's name beneath in gold.

I dreamed I heard the fox barking, or maybe it really was the fox barking. I turned, groaning as my leg brushed against the bedsheet. The bandage had fallen off while I slept. I groped under the covers till I found it, a clump of sticky brown gauze; tossed it on the floor, sat up, and rubbed my eyes. It was morning. My bedroom window was blistered with silvery light, the glass flecked with rain. I looked down at my thigh. The tattoo had scabbed over, but not much. The figure of the kneeling man was stark and precise, its orange nimbus glazed with clear fluid. I got up and limped into the bathroom, sat on the edge of the tub and laved my thigh tenderly, warm water washing away dead skin and dried blood. I patted it dry and applied another thin layer of antibiotic ointment, and headed for the kitchen to make coffee.

The noise came again—not barking at all but something tapping against a window. It took me a minute to figure out what it was: the basket the Lonely House used as a message system. Blakie had devised it forty years ago, a pulley and old-fashioned clothesline, strung between the Lonely House and a birch tree on the far shore. A small wicker basket hung from the line, with a plastic ziplock bag inside it, and inside the bag Magic Markers and a notepad. Someone could write a note on shore, then send the basket over; it would bump against the front window, alerting us to a visitor. A bit more elegant than standing on shore and shouting, it also gave the Lonely House's inhabitants the chance to hide, if we weren't expecting anyone.

I couldn't remember the last time someone had used it. I had a cell phone now, and customers made appointments months in advance. I'd almost forgotten the clothesline was there.

I went to the front window and peered out. Fog had settled in during the night; on the northern side of the island the foghorn moaned. No one would be leaving Aranbega today. I could barely discern the other shore, thick gray mist striated with white birch trees. I couldn't see anyone.

But sure enough, there was the basket dangling between the window and the front door. I opened the window and stuck my hand out, brushing aside a mass of cobwebs strung with dead crane flies and mosquitoes to get at the basket. Inside was the ziplock bag and the notebook, the latter pleached with dark green threads. I grimaced as I pulled it out, the pages damp and molded into a block of viridian pulp.

But stuck to the back of the notebook was a folded square of yellow legal paper. I unfolded it and read the message written in strong square letters.

> Ivy—
> Christopher Sa'adah here, I'm staying in Aran. Harbor, stopped by to say hi. You there? Call me @ 462-1117. Hope you're okay.
> C.

I stared at the note for a full minute. Thinking, this is a mistake, this is a sick joke; someone trying to torment me about Julia. Christopher was dead. Nausea washed over me, that icy chill like a shroud, my skin clammy and the breath freezing in my lungs.

"Ivy? You there?"

I rested my hand atop the open window and inhaled deeply. "Christopher." I shook my head, gave a gasping laugh. "Jesus—"

I leaned out the open window. "Christopher?" I shouted. "Is that really you?"

"It's really me," a booming voice yelled back.

"Hold on! I'll get the dory and come right over—"

I ran into the bedroom and pulled on a pair of loose cutoffs and faded T-shirt, then hurried outside. The dory was where I'd left it, pulled up on shore just beyond the fringe of cattails and bayberries. I pushed it into the lake, a skein of dragonflies rising from the dark water to disappear in the mist. There was water in the boat, dead leaves that nudged at my bare feet; I grabbed the oars and rowed; twenty strong strokes that brought me to the other shore.

"Ivy?"

That was when I saw him, a tall figure like a shadow breaking from the fog thick beneath the birches. He was so big that I had to blink to make sure that this, too, wasn't some trick of the mist: a black-haired, bearded man, strong enough to yank one of the birch saplings up by the roots if he'd wanted to. He wore dark brown corduroys, a flannel shirt, and brown Carhartt jacket; heavy brown work boots. His hair was long and pushed back behind his ears; his hands were shoved in his jacket pockets. He was a bit stooped, his shoulders raised in a way that made him look surprised, or unsure of himself. It made him look young, younger than he really was; it made him look like Christopher, Julia's thirteen-year-old brother.

He wasn't thirteen anymore. I did the math quickly, bringing the boat round and grabbing the wet line to toss on shore. Christopher was Narouz Sa'adah's son by his third wife. He was eighteen years younger than Julia; that would make him eleven years younger than me, which would make him—

"Little Christopher!" I looked up at him from the dory, grinning. "How the hell old are you?"

He shrugged, leaned down to grab the end of the line and loop it around the granite post at the shoreline. He took out a cigarette and lit it, inhaled rapidly—nervously, I see now—and let his arm dangle so that the smoke coiled up around his wrist.

"I'm thirty-four." He had an almost comically basso voice that echoed across Green Pond like the foghorn. An instant later I heard a loon give its warning cry. Christopher dropped his cigarette and stubbed it out, cocking his head toward the dory. "Is that the same boat you used to have?"

"Sure is." I hopped into the water, wincing at the cold, then waded to shore. "Jesus. Little Christopher. I can't believe it's you. You—Christ! I—well, I thought you were dead."

"I got better." He stared down at me and for the first time smiled, his teeth still a little crooked and nicotine stained, not Julia's teeth at all; his face completely guileless, close-trimmed black beard, long hair falling across tawny eyes. "After the bombing? I was in hospital for a long time, outside Cairo. It wasn't just you—everyone thought I was dead. My father finally tracked me down and brought me back to Washington. I think you and Julia had broken up by then."

I just stared at him. I felt dizzy: even though it was a small piece of the world, of history, it meant everything was different. Everything was changed. I blinked and looked away from him, saw the birch leaves spinning in the breeze, pale gold and green, goldenrod past its prime, tall stalks of valerian with their flower heads blown to brown vein. I looked back at Christopher: everything was the same.

He said, "I can't believe it's you either, Ivy."

I threw my arms around him. He hugged me awkwardly—he was so much bigger than I was!—and started laughing in delight. "Ivy! I walked all the way over here! From the village, I'm staying at the inn. That lady at the general store?"

"Mary?"

"Right, Mary—she remembered me, she said you still lived here—"

"Why didn't you call?"

He looked startled. "You have a phone?"

"Of course I have a phone! Actually, it's a cell phone, and I only got it a year ago, after they put up a tower over on Blue Hill." I drew away from him, balancing on my heels to make myself taller. "Jeez, you're all growed up, Christopher. I'm trying to think, when was the last time I saw you—"

"Twelve years ago. I was just starting grad school in Cairo. I came to see you and Julia in Rockland before I left. Remember?"

I tried, but couldn't; not really. I'd never known him well. He'd been a big ungainly teenager, extremely quiet and sitting at the edges of the room, where he always seemed to be listening carefully to everything his older sister or her friends said. He'd grown up in D.C. and Cairo, but he spent his summers in the States. I first met him when he was twelve or thirteen, a gangly kid into Dungeons & Dragons and *Star Wars*, who'd recently read Tolkien and had just started on Terry Brooks.

"Jesus, don't read *that*," I'd said, snatching away *The Sword of Shannara* and shoving my own copy of *Love Plucking Rowanberries* into his big hands. For a moment he looked hurt. Then, "Thanks," he said, and gave me that sweet slow smile. He spent the rest of that summer in our apartment overlooking Rockland Harbor, hunched into a wicker chair on the decrepit back deck as he worked his way through *Sybylla and the Summer Sky, Mellors' Plasma Bistro, Love Regained in Idleness*, and finally the tattered remnants of *Ardor ex Cathedra*.

"Of course I remember," I said. I swiped at a mosquito, looked up, and grinned. "Gosh. You were still a kid then. How're you doing? *What* are you doing? Are you married?"

"Divorced." He raised his arms, yawning, and stretched. His silhouette blotted out the gray sky, the blurred shapes of trees and boulders. "No kids, though. I'm at the Center for Remote Sensing at B.U., coordinating a project near the Chephren Quarries, in the Western Desert. Upper Egypt."

He dropped his arms and looked down at me again. "So Ivy—would you—how'd you feel about company? I could use a cup of coffee. We can walk back to town if you want. Have a late lunch. Or early dinner. . . ."

"Christ, no." I glanced at my raw tattoo. "I should clean that again, before I do anything. And I haven't even had breakfast yet."

"Really? What were you doing? I mean, are you with a customer or something?"

I shook my head. "I was up all night, doing this—" I splayed my fingers above the figure on my thigh. "What time is it, anyway?"

"Almost four."

"Almost *four?*" I grabbed his hand and twisted it to see his wrist-watch. "I don't believe it! How could I, I—" I shivered. "I slept through the whole day."

Christopher stared at me curiously. I was still holding his wrist, and he turned his hand, gently, his fingers brushing mine. "You okay, Ivy? Did I get you in the middle of something? I can come back."

"I don't know." I shook my head and withdrew my hand from his, but slowly, so I wouldn't hurt his feelings. "I mean no, I'm fine, just—"

I looked at my thigh. A thread of blood ran down my leg, and as I stared a damselfly landed beneath the tattoo, its thorax a metallic blue needle, wings invisible against my skin. "I was up all night, doing that—"

I pointed at the kneeling man; only from my angle he wasn't kneeling but hanging suspended above my knee, like a bat. "I—I don't think I finished until five o'clock this morning. I had no idea it was so late. . . ."

I could hear the panic in my own voice. I took a deep breath, trying to keep my tone even, but Christopher just put one hand lightly on my shoulder and said, "Hey, it's okay. I really can come back. I just wanted to say hi."

"No. Wait." I counted ten heartbeats, twelve. "I'm okay. I'll be okay. Just, can you row us back?"

"Sure." He stooped to grab a leather knapsack leaning against a tree. "Let's go."

With Christopher in it, the dory sat a good six inches lower in the water, and it took a little longer with him rowing. Halfway across the brief stretch of pond I finally asked him.

"How is Julia?"

My voice was shaky, but he didn't seem to notice. "I don't know. One of my sisters talked to her about five years ago. She was in Toronto, I think. No one's heard from her." He strained at the oars, then glanced at me measuringly. "I never really knew her, you know. She was so much older. I always thought she was kind of a bitch, to tell you the truth. The way she treated you . . . it made me uncomfortable."

I was silent. My leg ached from the tattoo, searing pain like a bad sunburn. I focused on that, and after a few minutes I could bear to talk.

"Sorry," I said. The dory ground against the shore of the islet. The panic was receding; I could breathe again. "I get these sometimes. Panic attacks. Usually it's not at home, though; only when I go off island."

"That's no fun." Christopher gave me an odd look. Then he clambered out and helped me pull the dory into the reeds. He followed me through the overgrown stands of phlox and aster, up the steps and into the Lonely House. The floor shuddered at his footsteps. I closed the door, looked up at him, and laughed.

"Boy, you sure fill this place up—watch your head, no, wait—"

Too late. As he turned he cracked into a beam. He clutched his head, grimacing. "Shit—I forgot how small this place is—"

I led him to the couch. "Here, sit—I'll get some ice."

I hurried into the kitchen and pulled a tray from the freezer. I was still feeling a little wonky. For about twenty-four hours after you get tattooed, it's like you're coming down with the flu. Your body's been pretty badly treated; your entire immune system fires up, trying to heal itself. I should have just crawled back into bed. Instead I called, "You want something to drink?"

I walked back in with a bowl of ice and a linen towel. Christopher was on the sofa, yanking something from his knapsack.

"I brought this." He held up a bottle of tequila. "And these—"

He reached into the knapsack again and pulled out three limes. They looked like oversized marbles in his huge hand. "I remember you liked tequila."

I smiled vaguely. "Did I?" It had been Julia who liked tequila, going through a quart every few days in the summer months. I sat beside him on the couch, wrapped the ice in the towel, and held it out. He lowered his head, childlike, and after a moment I very gently touched it. His hair was thick and coarse, darker than his sister's; when I extended my fingers I felt his scalp, warm as though he'd been sitting in the sun all day. "You're hot," I said softly, and felt myself flush. "I mean your head—your skin feels hot. Like heatstroke."

He kept his head lowered, saying nothing. His long hair grazed the top of my thigh. He reached to take my hand, and his was so much bigger, it was as though my own hand was swallowed in a heated glove, his palm calloused, fingertips smooth and hard; soft hairs on the back of his wrist. I said nothing. I could smell him, an acrid smell, not unpleasant but strange; he smelled of limes and sweat, and raw earth, stones washed by the sea. My mouth was dry, and as I moved to place the ice-filled towel on his brow I felt his hand slip from mine, to rest upon the couch between us.

"There." I could feel my heart racing, the frantic thought. *It's just a symptom, there's nothing to be scared of, it's just a symptom, it's just—*

"Christopher," I said thickly. "Just—sit. For a minute."

We sat. My entire body felt hot, and damp; I was sweating now myself, not cold anymore, my heartbeat slow and even. From outside came the melancholy sound of the foghorn, the ripple of rain across the lake. The room around us was full of that strange, translucent green light you get here sometimes: being on an island on an island suspended in fog, droplets of mist and sea and rain mingling to form a shimmering glaucous veil. Outside the window the world seemed to tremble and break apart into countless motes of silver, steel-gray, emerald, then cohere again into a strangely solid-looking mass. As though someone had tossed a stone into a viscous pool, or probed a limb with a needle; that sense of skin breaking, parting then closing once more around the wound, the world, untold unseen things flickering and diving, ganglia, axons, otters, loons. A bomb goes off, and it takes twelve years to hear its explosion. I lifted my head and saw Christopher watching me. His mouth was parted, his amber eyes sad, almost anguished.

"Ivy," he said. When his mouth touched mine I flinched, not fear but shock at how much bigger it was than my own, than Julia's, any woman's. I had not touched a man since I was in high school, and that was a boy, boys; I had never kissed a man. His face was rough; his mouth tasted bitter, of nicotine and salt. And blood, too—he'd bitten his lip from nervousness, my tongue found the broken seam just beneath the hollow of his upper lip, the hollow hidden beneath soft hair, not rough as I had thought it would be, and smelling of some floral shampoo.

It was like nothing I had imagined—and I *had* imagined it, of course. I'd imagined everything, before I fell in love with Julia Sa'adah. I'd fallen in love with *her*—her soul, her *duende*, she would have called it—but in a way it had almost nothing to do with her being another woman. I'd seen movies, porn films even, lots of them, watching with Julia and some of her friends, the ones who were bisexual, or beyond bisexual, whatever that might be; read magazines, novels, pornography, glanced at sites online; masturbated to dim images of what it was like; what I thought it might be like. Even watched once as a couple we knew went at it in our big untidy bed, slightly revved-up antics for our benefit, I suspect, a lot of whimpering and operatic sound effects.

This was nothing like that. This was slow, almost fumbling; even formal. He seemed afraid, or maybe it was just that he couldn't believe it, that it wasn't real to him, yet.

"I was always in love with you." He was lying beside me on the couch; not a lot of room left for me, but his broad arm kept me from rolling off. Our shirts were stuffed behind our heads for pillows, I still wore my cutoffs, and he still had his corduroy jeans on. We hadn't gotten further than this. On the floor beside us was the half-empty bottle of tequila, Christopher's pocketknife, and the limes, cloven in two so that they looked like enormous green eyes. He was tracing the designs on my body; the full sleeve on my left arm, Chinese water dragons, stylized waves, all in shades of turquoise and indigo and green. Green is the hardest ink to work with—you mix it with white, the white blends into your skin tone, you don't realize the green pigment is there and you overdo, going over and over until you scar. I'd spent a lot of time with green when I started out; yellow too, another difficult pigment.

"You are so beautiful. All this . . ." His finger touched coils of vines, ivy that thrust from the crook of my elbow and extended up to my shoulder. His own body was unblemished, as far as I could see. Skin darker than Julia's, shading more to olive than bronze; an almost hairless chest, dappled line of dark hair beneath his navel. He tapped the inside of my elbow, tender soil overgrown with leaves. "That must have hurt."

I shrugged. "I guess. You forget. All you remember afterward is how intense it was. And then you have these—"

I ran my hand down my arm, turned to sit up. "This is what I did last night." I flexed my leg, pulled up the edge of my shorts to better expose the new tattoo. "See?"

He sat up, ran a hand through his black hair, then leaned forward to examine it. His hair spilled down from his forehead; he had one hand on my upper thigh, the other on his own knee. His broad back was to me, olive skin, a paler crescent just above his shoulders where his neck was bent: a scar. There were others, jagged smooth lines, some deep enough to hide a fingertip. Shrapnel, or glass thrown off by the explosion. His long hair grazed my leg, hanging down like a dark waterfall.

I swallowed, my gaze flicking from his back to what I could glimpse of my tattoo, a small square of flesh framed between his arms, his hair, the ragged blue line of my cutoffs. A tall man, leaning forward so that his hair fell to cover his face. A waterfall. A curtain. Christopher lifted his head to stare at me.

A veil, torn away.

"Shit," I whispered. "Shit, shit . . ."

I pushed away from him and scrambled to my feet. "What? What is it?" He looked around as though expecting to see someone else in the room with us. "Ivy—"

He tried to grasp me but I pulled away, grabbing my T-shirt from the couch and pulling it on. "Ivy! What happened?" His voice rose, desperate; I shook my head, then pointed at the tattoo.

"This—" He looked at the tattoo, then at me, not comprehending. "That image? I just found it yesterday. On a card. This sort of tarot card, this deck. I got it at a rummage sale—"

I turned and ran into my studio. Christopher followed.

"Here!" I darted to my work table and yanked off the protective blue covering. The table was empty. "It was here—"

I whirled, went to my light table. Acetates and sheets of rag paper were still strewn across it, my pencils and inks were where I'd left them. A dozen pages with failed versions of the card were scattered across the desk, and on the floor. I grabbed them, holding up each sheet and shaking it as though it were an envelope, as though something might fall out. I picked up the pages from the floor, emptied the stainless steel wastebasket, and sifted through torn papers and empty ink capsules. Nothing.

The card was gone.

"Ivy?"

I ignored him and ran back into the living room. "Here!" I yanked the paisley-wrapped deck from my purse. "It was like this, it was one of these—"

I tore the scarf open. The deck was still there. I let the scarf fall and fanned the cards out, facedown, a rainbow arc of labyrinthine wheels; then twisted my hand to show the other side.

"They're blank," said Christopher.

"That's right. They're all blank. Only there was one—last night—"

I pointed at the tattoo. "That design. There was one card with that design. I copied it. It was with me in the studio, I had it on my drafting table. I ended up tracing it for the stencil."

"And now you can't find it."

"No. It's gone." I let my breath out in a long, low whoosh, I felt sick at my stomach, but it was more like seasickness than panic, a nausea I could override if I wanted to. "It's—I won't find it. It's just gone."

My eyes teared. Christopher stood beside me, his face dark with concern. After a minute he said, "May I?"

He held out his hand, and I nodded and gave him the cards. He riffled through them, frowning. "Are they all like this?"

"All except two. There's another one—" I gestured at my purse. "I put it aside. I got them at the rummage sale at St. Bruno's yesterday. They were—"

I stopped. Christopher was still examining the cards, holding them up to the light as though that might reveal some hidden pattern. I said, "You read Walter Burden Fox, right?"

He glanced up at me. "Sure. *Five Windows One Door?* You gave it to me, remember? That first summer I stayed with you down at that place you had by the water. I loved those books." His tone softened; he smiled, a sweet, sad half smile, and held the cards up as though to show a winning hand. "That really changed my life, you know. After I read them; when I met you. That's when I decided to become an archaeologist. Because they were—well, I don't know how to explain it. . . ."

He tapped the cards thoughtfully against his chin. "I loved those books so much. I couldn't believe it, when I got to the end? That he never finished them. I used to think, if I had only one wish, it would be that somehow he finished that last book. Like maybe if his son hadn't died, or something. Those books just amazed me!"

He shook his head, still marveling. "They made me think how the world might be different than what it was; what we think it is. That there might be things we still don't know, even though we think we've discovered everything. Like the work I do? We scan all these satellite images of the desert, and we can see where ancient sites were, under the sand, under the hills. Places so changed by wind erosion you would never think anything else was ever there—but there were temples and villages, entire cities! Empires! Like in the third book, when you read it and find out there's this whole other history to everything that happened in the first two. The entire world is changed."

The entire world is changed. I stared at him, then nodded. "Christopher—these cards are from his books. The last one. 'The least trumps.' When I got them, there was a little piece of paper—"

My gaze dropped to the floor. The scrap was there, by Christopher's bare foot. I picked up the scrap and handed it to him. " 'The least trumps.' It's in the very first chapter of the last book, the one he never finished. Mabel's in bed with Tarquin and he takes out this deck of cards. He holds them in front of her, and when she breathes on them it somehow makes them come alive. There's an implication that everything that happened before has to maybe do with the cards. But he died before he ever got to that part."

Christopher stared at the fragment of paper. "I don't remember," he said at last. He looked at me. "You said there's one other card. Can I see it?"

I hesitated, then went to get my bag. "It's in here."

I took out my wallet. Everything around me froze; my hand was so numb I couldn't feel it when I slid my finger behind my license. I couldn't feel it, it wasn't there at all—

But it was. The wallet fell to the floor. I stood and held the card in both hands. The last one: the least trump. The room around me was gray, the air motionless. In my hands a lozenge of spectral color glimmered and seemed to move. There were airships and flaming birds, two old women dancing on a beach, an exploding star above a high-rise building. The tiny figure of a man was not being carried in a litter, I saw now, but lying in a bed borne by red-clad women. Above them all a lash-fringed eye stared down.

I blinked and rubbed my eye, then gave the card to Christopher. When I spoke my voice was thick. "I—I forgot it was so beautiful. That's it. The last one."

He walked over to the window, leaned against the wall, and angled the card to catch the light. "Wow. This is amazing. Was the other one like it? All this detail . . ."

"No. It was much simpler. But it was still beautiful. It makes you realize how hard it is, drawing something that simple."

I looked down at my leg and smiled wryly. "But you know, I think I got it right."

For some minutes he remained by the window, silent. Suddenly he looked up. "Could you do this, Ivy? On me?"

I stared at him. "You mean a tattoo? No. It's far too intricate. It would take days, something like that. Days, just to make a decent stencil. The tattoo would probably take a week, if you were going to do it right."

"This, then." He strode over to me, pointing to the sun that was an eye. "Just that part, there—could you do just that? Like maybe on my arm?"

He flexed his arm, a dark sheen where the bicep rose, like a wave. "Right there—"

I ran my hand across the skin appraisingly. There was a scar, a small one. I could work around it, make it part of the design. "You should think about it. But yeah, I could do it."

"I have thought about it. I want you to do it. Now."

"Now?" I looked at the window. It was getting late. Light was leaking from the sky, everything was fading to lavender-gray, twilight. The fog was coming in again, pennons of mist trailing above Green Pond. I could no longer see the far shore. "It's kind of late. . . ."

"Please." He stood above me; I could feel the heat radiating from him, see the card glinting in his hand like a shard of glass. "Ivy—"

His deep voice dropped, a whisper I felt more than heard. "I'm not my sister. I'm not Julia. Please."

He touched the outer corner of my eye, where it was still damp. "Your eyes are so blue," he said. "I forgot how blue they are."

We went into the studio. I set the card on the light table, with the deck beside it, used a loupe to get a better look at the image he wanted. It would not be so hard to do, really, just that one thing. I sketched it a few times on paper, finally turned to where Christopher sat waiting in the chair beside my worktable.

"I'm going to do it freehand. I usually don't, but this is pretty straightforward, and I think I can do it. You sure about this?"

He nodded. He looked a little pale, there beneath the bright lights I work under, but when I walked over to him he smiled. "I'm sure."

I prepped him, swabbing the skin, then shaving his upper arm twice, to make sure it was smooth enough. I made sure my machine was thoroughly cleaned, and set up my inks. Black, cerulean and cobalt, Spaulding and Rogers Bright Yellow.

"Ready?"

He nodded, and I set to.

It took about four hours, though I pretty much lost track of the time. I did the outline first, a circle. I wanted it to look very slightly uneven, like this drawing by Odile Redon I liked—you can see how the paper absorbed his ink, it made the lines look powerful, like black lightning. After the circle was done I did the eye inside it, a half circle of white, because in the card the eye is looking down, at the world beneath. Then I did the flattened ovoid of the pupil. Then the flickering lashes all around it. Christopher didn't talk. Sweat ran in long lines from beneath his arms; he swallowed a lot, and sometimes closed his eyes. There was so much muscle beneath his skin that it was difficult to keep it taut—no fat, and the skin wasn't loose enough—so I had to keep pulling it tight. I knew it hurt.

"That's it, take a deep breath. I can stop, if you need to take a break. I need to take a break, anyway."

But I didn't. My hand didn't cramp up; there was none of that fuzzy feeling that comes after holding a vibrating machine for hours at a stretch. Now and then Christopher would shift in his chair, never very much. Once I moved to get a better purchase on his arm, sliding my knee between his legs: I could feel his cock, rigid beneath his corduroys, and hear his breath catch.

He didn't bleed much. His olive skin made the inks seem to glow, the blue-and-gold eye within its rayed penumbra, wriggling lines like cilia. At the center of the pupil was the scar. You could hardly see it now, it looked like a shadow, the eye's dark heart.

"There." I drew back, shut the machine off, and nestled it in my lap. "It's finished. What do you think?"

He pulled his arm toward him, craning his head to look. "Wow. It's gorgeous." He looked at me and grinned ecstatically. "It's fucking gorgeous."

"All right then." I stood and put the machine over by the sink, turned to get some bandages. "I'll just clean it up, and then—"

"Not yet. Wait, just a minute. Ivy."

He towered above me, his long hair lank and skin sticky with sweat, pink fluid weeping from beneath the radiant eye. When he kissed me I could feel his cock against me, heat arcing above my groin. His leg moved, it rubbed against my tattoo, and I moaned but it didn't hurt, I couldn't feel it, anything at all, just heat everywhere now, his hands tugging my shirt off then drawing me into the bedroom.

Not like Julia. His mouth was bigger, his hand; when I put my arms around him my fingers scarcely met, his back was so broad. The scars felt smooth and glossy; I thought they would hurt if I touched them but he said no, he liked my fingernails against them, he liked to press my mouth against his chest, hard, as I took his nipple between my lips, tongued it then held it gently between my teeth, the aureole with its small hairs radiating beneath my mouth. He went down on me and that was different too, his beard against the inside of my thighs, his tongue probing deeper; my fingers tangled in his hair and I felt his breath on me, his tongue still inside me when I came. He kissed me and I tasted myself, held his head between my hands, his beard wet. He was laughing. When he came inside me he laughed again, almost shouted; then collapsed alongside me.

"Ivy. Ivy . . ."

"Shhh." I lay my palm against his face and kissed him. The sheet between us bore the image of a blurred red sun. "Christopher."

"Don't go." His warm hand covered my breast. "Don't go anywhere."

I laughed softly. "Me? I never go anywhere."

We slept. He breathed heavily, but I was so exhausted I passed out before I could shift toward my own side of the bed. If I dreamed, I don't remember; only knew when I woke that everything was different, because there was a man in bed beside me.

"Huh." I stared at him, his face pressed heavily into the pillow. Then I got up, as quietly as I could. I tiptoed into the bathroom, peed, washed my face and cleaned my teeth. I thought of making coffee, and peered into the living room. Outside all was still fog, dark gray, shredded with white to mark the wind's passing. The clock read 6:30. I turned and crept back to the bedroom.

Christopher was still asleep. I sat on the edge of the bed, languidly, and let my hand rest upon my tattoo. Already it hurt less; it was healing. I looked up at the head of the bed, where my mother's books were, and Walter Burden Fox's. The five identical dust jackets, deep blue, with their titles and Fox's name in gold letters.

Something was different. The last volume, the one completed posthumously by Fox's editor, with the spine that read **ARDOR EX CATHEDRA * WALTER BURDEN FOX.**

I yanked it from the shelf, holding it so the light fell on the spine.

ARDOR EX CATHEDRA * WALTER BURDEN FOX & W. F. FOX

My heart stopped. Around me the room was black. Christopher moved on the bed behind me, yawning. I swallowed, leaning forward until my hands rested on my knees as I opened the book.

ARDOR EX CATHEDRA
BY WALTER BURDEN FOX
COMPLETED BY WALTER F. FOX

"No," I whispered. Frantically I turned to the end, the final twenty pages that had been nothing but appendices and transcriptions of notes.

Chapter Seventeen: The Least Trumps.

I flipped through the pages in disbelief, and yes, there they were, new chapter headings, every one of them—

Pavell Saved From Drowning. One Leaf Left. Hermalchio and Lachrymatory. Villainous Saltpetre. The Scars. The Radiant Eye. I gasped, so terrified my hands shook and I almost dropped it, turning back to the frontispiece.

Completed by Walter F. Fox

I went to the next page—the dedication.

To the memory of my father

I cried out. Christopher sat up, gasping. "What is it? Ivy, what happened—"

"The book! It's different!" I shook it at him, almost screaming. "He didn't die! The son—he finished it, it's all different! *It's changed.*"

He took the book from me, blinking as he tried to wake up. When he opened it I stabbed the frontispiece with my finger.

"There! See—it's all changed. *Everything has changed.*"

I slapped his arm, the raw image that I'd never cleaned and never bandaged. "Hey! Stop—Ivy, stop—"

I started crying, sat on the edge of the bed with my head in my hands. Behind me I could hear him turning pages. Finally he sighed, put a hand on my shoulder, and said, "Well, you're right. But—well, couldn't it be a different edition? Or something?"

I shook my head. Grief filled me, and horror; something deeper than panic, deeper even than fear. "No," I said at last. My voice was hoarse. "It's the book. It's everything. We changed it, somehow—the card . . ."

I stood and walked into my studio, slowly, as though I were drunk. I put the light on and looked at my worktable.

"There," I said dully. In the middle of the table, separate from the rest of the deck, was the last card. It was blank. "The last one. The last trump. Everything is different."

I turned to stare at Christopher. He looked puzzled, concerned but not frightened. "So?" He shook his head, ventured a small smile. "Is that bad? Maybe it's a good book."

"That's not what I mean." I could barely speak. "I mean, everything will be different. Somehow. Even if it's just in little ways—it won't be what it was. . . ."

Christopher walked into the living room. He looked out the window, then went to the door and opened it. A bar of pale gold light slanted into the room and across the floor, to end at my feet. "Sun's coming up." He stared at the sky. "The fog is lifting. It'll be nice, I think. Hot, though."

He turned and looked at me. I shook my head. "No. No. I'm not going out there."

Christopher laughed, then gave me that sad half-smile. "Ivy—"

He walked over and tried to put his arms around me, but I pushed him away and walked into the bedroom. I began pulling on the clothes I'd worn last night. "No. No. Christopher—I can't, I won't."

"Ivy." He watched me, then shrugged and came into the room and got dressed, too. When he was done, he took my hand.

"Ivy, listen." He pulled me to his side, with his free hand pointed at the book lying on the bed. "Even if it is different—even if *everything* is different—why does that have to be so terrible? Maybe it's not. Maybe it's better."

I began to shake my head, crying again. "No, no, no . . ."

"Look—"

Gently he pulled me into the living room. Full sun was streaming through the windows now; outside, on the other side of Green Pond, a deep blue sky glowed above the green treetops. There was still mist close to the ground but it was lifting. The pines moved in the wind, and the birches; I heard a fox barking, no, not a fox: a dog. "Look," Christopher said, and pointed at the open front door. "Why don't we do this—you come with me, I'll stay right by you—shit, I'll *carry* you if you want—we'll just go look, okay?"

I shook my head no, but when he eased slowly through the door I followed, his hand tight around mine but not too tight: I could slip free if I wanted. He wouldn't keep me. He wouldn't make me go.

"Okay," I whispered. I shut my eyes, then opened them. "Okay, okay."

Everything looked the same. A few more of the asters had opened, deep mauve in the misty air. One tall yellow coneflower was still in bloom. We walked through them, to the shore, to the dory. There were dragonflies and damselflies inside it, and something else. A butterfly, brilliant orange edged with cobalt blue, its wings fringed, like an eye. We stepped into the boat and the butterfly lifted into the air, hanging between us then fluttering across the water, toward the western shore. My gaze followed it, watching as it rose above the Ledges then continued down the hillside.

"I've never been over there," said Christopher. He raised one oar to indicate where the butterfly had gone. "What's there?"

"You can see." It hurt to speak, to breathe, but I did it. I didn't die. You can't die, from this. "Katherine—she always says you can see Ireland from there, on a clear day."

"Really? Let's go that way, then."

He rowed to the farther shore. Everything looked different, coming up to the bank; tall blue flowers like irises, a yellow sedge that had a faint fragrance like lemons. A turtle slid into the water, its smooth black carapace spotted with yellow and blue. As I stepped onto the shore I saw something like a tiny orange crab scuttling into the reeds.

"You all right?" Christopher cocked his head and smiled. "Brave little ant. Brave Ivy."

I nodded. He took my hand, and we walked down the hillside. Past the Ledges, past some boulders I had never even known were there; through a stand of trees like birches only taller, thinner, their leaves round and shimmering, silver-green. There was still a bit of fog here but it was lifting, I felt it on my legs as we walked, a damp, cool kiss upon my left thigh. I looked over at Christopher, saw a golden rayed eye gazing back at me, a few flecks of dried blood beneath. Overhead the trees moved and made a high rustling sound in the wind. The ground beneath us grew steeper, the clefts between rocks overgrown with thick masses of small purple flowers. I had never known anything to bloom so lushly this late in the year. Below us I could hear the sound of waves, not the crash and violent roar of the open Atlantic but a softer sound; and laughter, a distant voice that sounded like my mother's. The fog was almost gone but I still could not glimpse the sea; only through the moving scrim of leaves and mist a sense of vast space, still dark because the sun had not struck it yet in full, pale gray-blue, not empty at all, not anymore. There were lights everywhere, gold and green and red and silver, stationary lights and lights that wove slowly across the lifting veil, as through wide streets and boulevards, haloes of blue and gold hanging from ropes across a wide sandy shore.

"There," said Christopher, and stopped. "There, do you see?"

He turned and smiled at me, reached to touch the corner of my eye, blue and gold; then pointed. "Can you see it now?"

I nodded. "Yeah. Yeah, I do."

The laughter came again, louder this time; someone calling a name. The trees and grass shivered as a sudden brilliance overtook them, the sun breaking at last from the mist behind me.

"Come on!" said Christopher, and, turning, he sprinted down the hill. I took a deep breath, looked back at what was behind us. I could just see the gray bulk of the Ledges, and beyond them the thicket of green and white and gray that was the Lonely House. It looked like a picture from one of my mother's books, a crosshatch hiding a hive, a honeycomb, another world. "Ivy!"

Christopher's voice echoed from not very far below me. "Ivy, you have to see this!"

"Okay," I said, and followed him.

Honorable Mentions: 2002

Abraham, Daniel, "The Apocrypha According to Cleveland," *The Silver Web* 15.
Addison, Linda D., "Dreams of the Night Bird," *Dark Voices*.
———, "The Comic Cannibals," *In a Fearful Way*.
Aguirre, Forrest and Thomas, Scott, "McKendrick's Bayonet," *Redsine* 10.
Aldiss, Brian, "A Man and a Man With His Mule," *www.brianaldiss.com*.
Alexander, Marie, "Some Divine," *Songs from Dead Singers*.
Ali, Zulfiqar, "Vendetta," *Birmingham Noir*.
Allen, Brady, "Slow Mary," *Strangewood Tales*.
Allen, Nina, "The Beachcomber," *Dark Horizons* 41.
———, "Coming Around Again," *Dark Horizons* 42.
———, "Minding the Gap," *Roadworks* 14.
Allen, Spencer, "Purity," *Wicked Hollow*, October.
Allison, James, "Confounding Mr. Newton," *Strange Horizons* (Web site), June 24.
Almond, David, "Where Your Wings Were," *Counting Stars*.
Andersen, Barth, "Bringweather and the Portal of Giving and Taking," *Strange Horizons* (Web site), May 6.
———, "The Psalm of Big Galahad," *Rabid Transit*.
———, "Show Me Where the Mudmen Go," *On Spec*, Summer.
Anderson, M. W., "Eyes Will Be Watching," *Extremes 4: Darkest Africa*.
Ardai, Charles, "Secret Service," *Ellery Queen's Mystery Magazine*, October/November.
Arnold, Joel, "Bait," *Stones*.
———, "Fetal Position," *Wicked Hollow*, January.
———, "Some Things Don't Wash Off," *Weird Tales* 329.
———, "The Apple Tree Man," *gothic.net* (Web site), July.
Arnott, Marion, "Marbles," *Crimewave 6: Breaking Point*.
Arnzen, Michael A., "Halloween Pie" (poem), *Rogue World* 7.
———, "Tugging the Heartstrings," *Flashquake* 2.2.
Arsenault, T. G., "The Eighth Day," *Random Acts of Weirdness*.
Auden, Miriam, "After the Whale," *Dark Testament*.
Avery, Simon, "The Remains," *Crimewave 6: Breaking Point*.

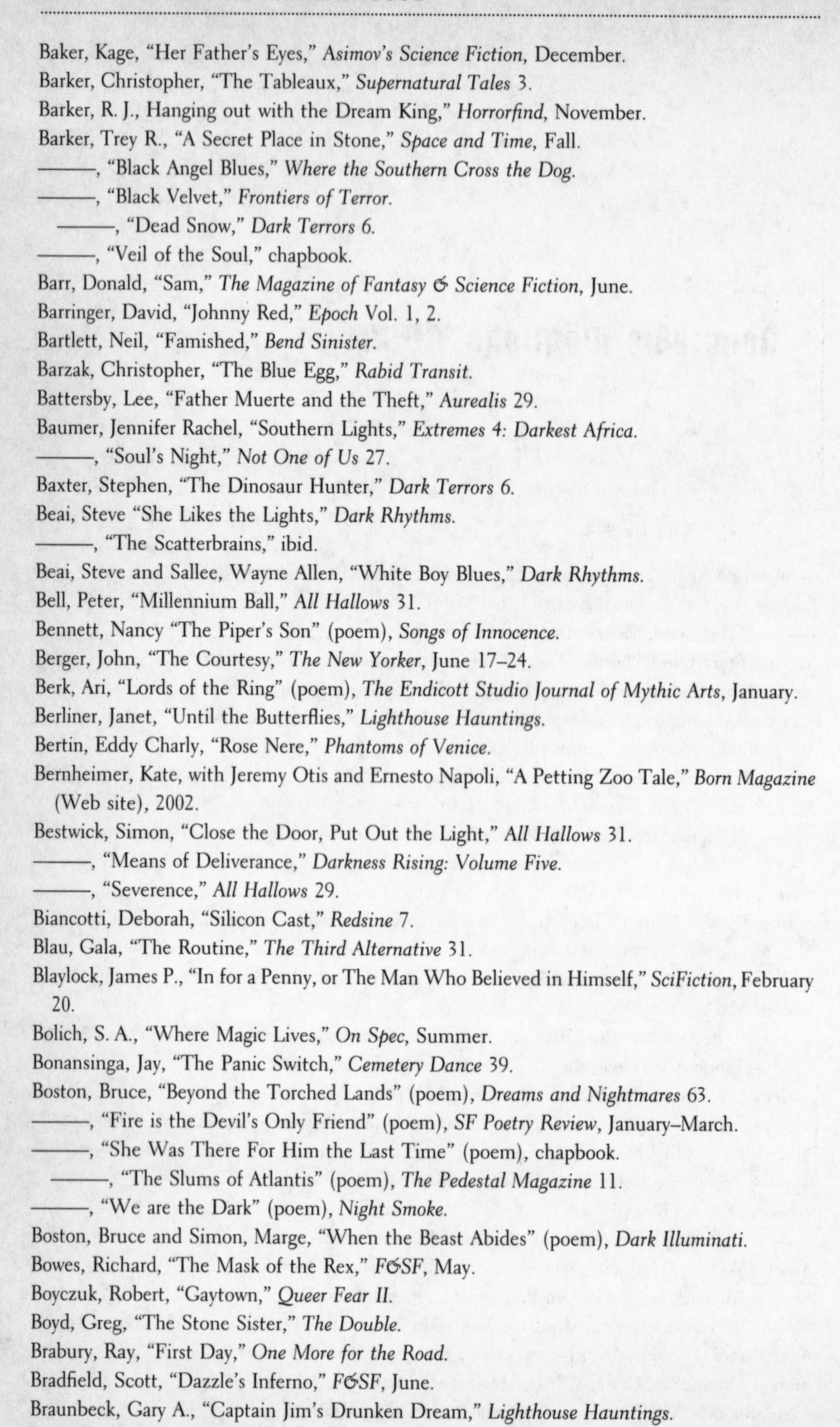

Baker, Kage, "Her Father's Eyes," *Asimov's Science Fiction*, December.
Barker, Christopher, "The Tableaux," *Supernatural Tales* 3.
Barker, R. J., Hanging out with the Dream King," *Horrorfind*, November.
Barker, Trey R., "A Secret Place in Stone," *Space and Time*, Fall.
———, "Black Angel Blues," *Where the Southern Cross the Dog.*
———, "Black Velvet," *Frontiers of Terror.*
———, "Dead Snow," *Dark Terrors 6.*
———, "Veil of the Soul," chapbook.
Barr, Donald, "Sam," *The Magazine of Fantasy & Science Fiction*, June.
Barringer, David, "Johnny Red," *Epoch* Vol. 1, 2.
Bartlett, Neil, "Famished," *Bend Sinister.*
Barzak, Christopher, "The Blue Egg," *Rabid Transit.*
Battersby, Lee, "Father Muerte and the Theft," *Aurealis* 29.
Baumer, Jennifer Rachel, "Southern Lights," *Extremes 4: Darkest Africa.*
———, "Soul's Night," *Not One of Us* 27.
Baxter, Stephen, "The Dinosaur Hunter," *Dark Terrors 6.*
Beai, Steve "She Likes the Lights," *Dark Rhythms.*
———, "The Scatterbrains," ibid.
Beai, Steve and Sallee, Wayne Allen, "White Boy Blues," *Dark Rhythms.*
Bell, Peter, "Millennium Ball," *All Hallows* 31.
Bennett, Nancy "The Piper's Son" (poem), *Songs of Innocence.*
Berger, John, "The Courtesy," *The New Yorker*, June 17–24.
Berk, Ari, "Lords of the Ring" (poem), *The Endicott Studio Journal of Mythic Arts*, January.
Berliner, Janet, "Until the Butterflies," *Lighthouse Hauntings.*
Bertin, Eddy Charly, "Rose Nere," *Phantoms of Venice.*
Bernheimer, Kate, with Jeremy Otis and Ernesto Napoli, "A Petting Zoo Tale," *Born Magazine* (Web site), 2002.
Bestwick, Simon, "Close the Door, Put Out the Light," *All Hallows* 31.
———, "Means of Deliverance," *Darkness Rising: Volume Five.*
———, "Severence," *All Hallows* 29.
Biancotti, Deborah, "Silicon Cast," *Redsine* 7.
Blau, Gala, "The Routine," *The Third Alternative* 31.
Blaylock, James P., "In for a Penny, or The Man Who Believed in Himself," *SciFiction*, February 20.
Bolich, S. A., "Where Magic Lives," *On Spec*, Summer.
Bonansinga, Jay, "The Panic Switch," *Cemetery Dance* 39.
Boston, Bruce, "Beyond the Torched Lands" (poem), *Dreams and Nightmares* 63.
———, "Fire is the Devil's Only Friend" (poem), *SF Poetry Review*, January–March.
———, "She Was There For Him the Last Time" (poem), chapbook.
———, "The Slums of Atlantis" (poem), *The Pedestal Magazine* 11.
———, "We are the Dark" (poem), *Night Smoke.*
Boston, Bruce and Simon, Marge, "When the Beast Abides" (poem), *Dark Illuminati.*
Bowes, Richard, "The Mask of the Rex," *F&SF*, May.
Boyczuk, Robert, "Gaytown," *Queer Fear II.*
Boyd, Greg, "The Stone Sister," *The Double.*
Brabury, Ray, "First Day," *One More for the Road.*
Bradfield, Scott, "Dazzle's Inferno," *F&SF*, June.
Braunbeck, Gary A., "Captain Jim's Drunken Dream," *Lighthouse Hauntings.*

———, "El Poso Del Mundo," *Cemetery Dance* 39.
———, "Have a Drink on Me," *Vengeance Fantastic*.
Brock, Rebecca, "Night Shift," *The Book of More Flesh*.
Brockmeier, Kevin, "A Day in the Life of Half Rumplestiltskin," *Things That Fall From the Sky*.
———, "Passenger," ibid.
Brooke, Keith, "What She Wanted." *Redsine* 7.
Brown, Sherrie, "Haven in Time of Need," *Night Terrors* 12.
Bull, Emma, "Joshua Tree," *The Green Man*.
Bull, Scott Emerson, "Killing is Easy," *Chizine* 14.
Bullington, Jesse, "Charlie's Hole," *The Book of More Flesh*.
Bunn, Cullen, "The Storm Children," *Darkness Rising: Volume Five*.
Burke, John, "A Habit of Hating," *Dark Terrors* 6.
Burke, Kealan-Patrick, "Someone to Carve the Pumpkins," *Horrorfind*, October.
———, "The Quiet," *The Gallows*, January.
Byatt, A. S. "The Thing in the Forest," *The New Yorker*, June 3.
Byers, Richard Lee, "Green Man and Paladin," *Frontiers of Terror*.
Cacek, P. D., "A Book, by its Cover," *Shelf Life*.
———, "In the Spirit," chapbook.
Cady, Jack, "Weird Row," *F&SF*, September.
Caines, Nicola, "The Gun," *Albedo One* 23.
Campbell, Ramsey, "The Retrospective," *The Spook*, February.
———, "The Unbeheld," *The Spook*, July.
Campbell, Ross, "The Price of an Innocent," *Royal Aspirations III*.
Cardin, Matt "An Abhorrence to All Flesh," *Divinations of the Deep*.
———, "Judas of the Infinite," ibid.
———, "The Stars Shine Without Me," *Horrorfind*, July–September.
Carreto, Héctor, "Sometimes at Night My Father Visits Me" (poem), *Prairie Schooner*, Summer.
Carroll, Siobhan "Mrs. Wolf," *On Spec*, Spring.
Castle, Mort, "Disappearances," *Chizine*, January–March.
Catton, John Paul, "Hide and Seek," *Darkness Rising: Volume Five*.
Chadbourn, Mark, "The Fairy Feller's Master Stroke" (novella), chapbook.
———, "Sour Places," *The Children of Cthulhu*.
Chambers, James, "A Wandering Blackness," *Lin Carter's Anton Zarnak Supernatural Sleuth*.
Chapman, Clay McLeod, "The Man Corn Triptych," *Rest Area*.
———, "Rodeo Inferno," ibid.
———, "Second Helping," ibid.
Chapman, Stepan,, "The Comedian," *The Silver Web* 15.
———, "State Secrets of Aphasia," *Leviathan Three*.
Charlton, William, "A Prohibited Area," *Undesirable Guests and Other Stories*.
———, "A Visit to Dublin," ibid.
———, "The Spider," ibid.
———, "The Straw-Man," *All Hallows* 30.
———, "Travelling by Air," *Undesirable Guests and Other Stories*.
Chinn, Mike, "Façades," *Phantoms of Venice*.
Christensen, Paul, "Grackles," *Southwest Review* Vol. 87; 2/3.
Christian, M., "Hush, Hush," *gothic net* (Web site), July.

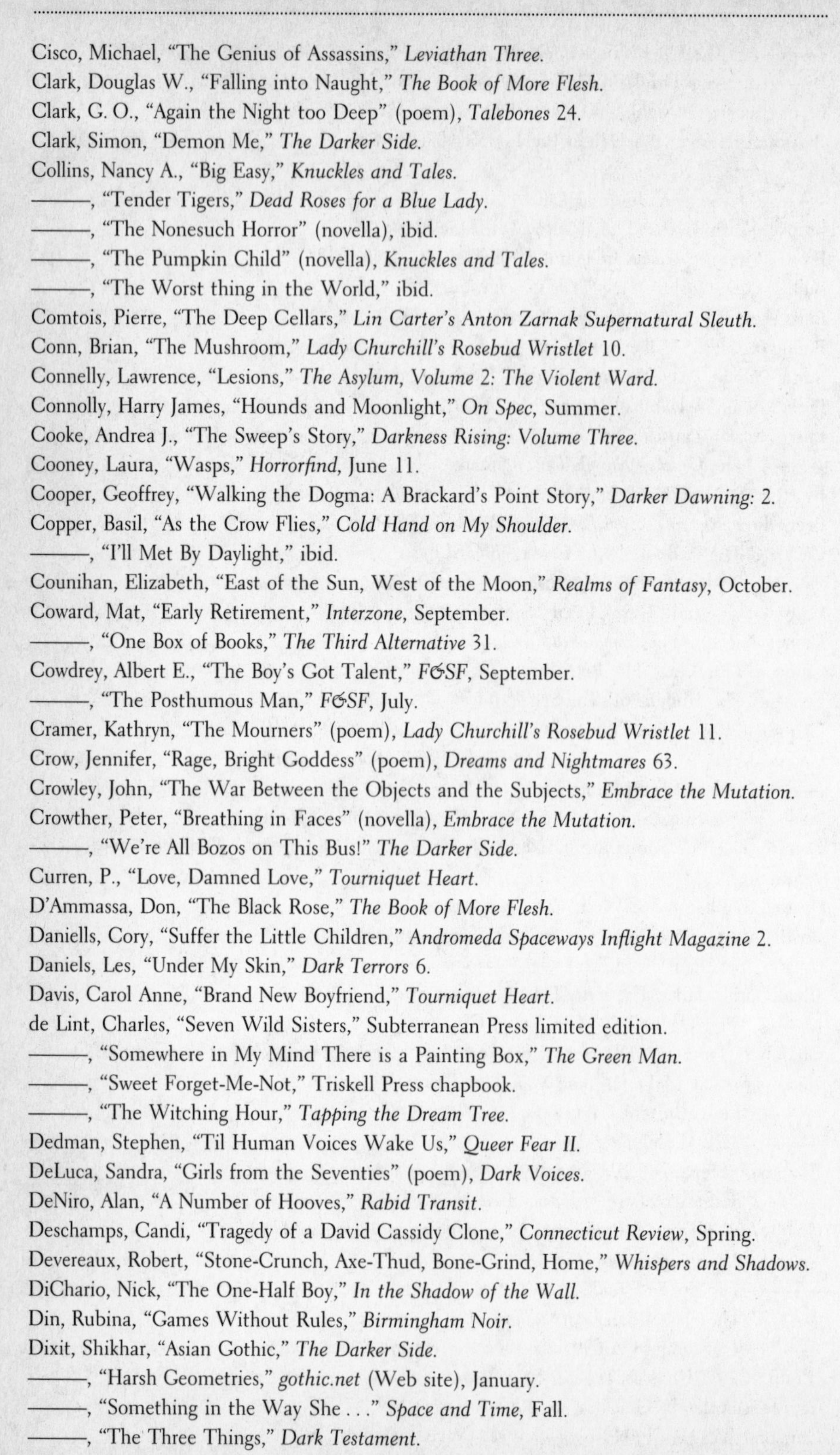

Cisco, Michael, "The Genius of Assassins," *Leviathan Three.*
Clark, Douglas W., "Falling into Naught," *The Book of More Flesh.*
Clark, G. O., "Again the Night too Deep" (poem), *Talebones* 24.
Clark, Simon, "Demon Me," *The Darker Side.*
Collins, Nancy A., "Big Easy," *Knuckles and Tales.*
———, "Tender Tigers," *Dead Roses for a Blue Lady.*
———, "The Nonesuch Horror" (novella), ibid.
———, "The Pumpkin Child" (novella), *Knuckles and Tales.*
———, "The Worst thing in the World," ibid.
Comtois, Pierre, "The Deep Cellars," *Lin Carter's Anton Zarnak Supernatural Sleuth.*
Conn, Brian, "The Mushroom," *Lady Churchill's Rosebud Wristlet* 10.
Connelly, Lawrence, "Lesions," *The Asylum, Volume 2: The Violent Ward.*
Connolly, Harry James, "Hounds and Moonlight," *On Spec,* Summer.
Cooke, Andrea J., "The Sweep's Story," *Darkness Rising: Volume Three.*
Cooney, Laura, "Wasps," *Horrorfind,* June 11.
Cooper, Geoffrey, "Walking the Dogma: A Brackard's Point Story," *Darker Dawning:* 2.
Copper, Basil, "As the Crow Flies," *Cold Hand on My Shoulder.*
———, "I'll Met By Daylight," ibid.
Counihan, Elizabeth, "East of the Sun, West of the Moon," *Realms of Fantasy,* October.
Coward, Mat, "Early Retirement," *Interzone,* September.
———, "One Box of Books," *The Third Alternative* 31.
Cowdrey, Albert E., "The Boy's Got Talent," *F&SF,* September.
———, "The Posthumous Man," *F&SF,* July.
Cramer, Kathryn, "The Mourners" (poem), *Lady Churchill's Rosebud Wristlet* 11.
Crow, Jennifer, "Rage, Bright Goddess" (poem), *Dreams and Nightmares* 63.
Crowley, John, "The War Between the Objects and the Subjects," *Embrace the Mutation.*
Crowther, Peter, "Breathing in Faces" (novella), *Embrace the Mutation.*
———, "We're All Bozos on This Bus!" *The Darker Side.*
Curren, P., "Love, Damned Love," *Tourniquet Heart.*
D'Ammassa, Don, "The Black Rose," *The Book of More Flesh.*
Daniells, Cory, "Suffer the Little Children," *Andromeda Spaceways Inflight Magazine* 2.
Daniels, Les, "Under My Skin," *Dark Terrors* 6.
Davis, Carol Anne, "Brand New Boyfriend," *Tourniquet Heart.*
de Lint, Charles, "Seven Wild Sisters," Subterranean Press limited edition.
———, "Somewhere in My Mind There is a Painting Box," *The Green Man.*
———, "Sweet Forget-Me-Not," Triskell Press chapbook.
———, "The Witching Hour," *Tapping the Dream Tree.*
Dedman, Stephen, "Til Human Voices Wake Us," *Queer Fear II.*
DeLuca, Sandra, "Girls from the Seventies" (poem), *Dark Voices.*
DeNiro, Alan, "A Number of Hooves," *Rabid Transit.*
Deschamps, Candi, "Tragedy of a David Cassidy Clone," *Connecticut Review,* Spring.
Devereaux, Robert, "Stone-Crunch, Axe-Thud, Bone-Grind, Home," *Whispers and Shadows.*
DiChario, Nick, "The One-Half Boy," *In the Shadow of the Wall.*
Din, Rubina, "Games Without Rules," *Birmingham Noir.*
Dixit, Shikhar, "Asian Gothic," *The Darker Side.*
———, "Harsh Geometries," *gothic.net* (Web site), January.
———, "Something in the Way She . . ." *Space and Time,* Fall.
———, "The Three Things," *Dark Testament.*

Donaghue, Emma, "A Short Life," *The Woman Who Gave Birth to Rabbits.*
Donahue, Erin, "Brother and Sister" (poem), *Star*Line,* November/December.
Dorr, James S., "Decking the Hall," *The Asylum, Volume 2: The Violent Ward.*
DuBois, Brendan, "A Lion Let Loose Upon the World," *Pharaoh Fantastic.*
Duchamp, L. Timmel, "The Fool's Story," *Leviathan Three.*
Dudeney, Dicksie, "Death's Head," *Extremes 4: Darkest Africa.*
Duffy, Brendan, "Rent," *Agog! Fantastic Fiction.*
Duffy, Steve, "Glass-Stoppered Bottles" (novella), *New Genre* 3.
———, "Numbers," *Queer Fear II.*
Dunbar, Robert, "Like a Story," *Reckless Abandon.*
Duncan, Andy, "Big Rock Candy Mountain," *Conjunctions:* 39.
———, "The Holy Bright Number," *Polyphony.*
Dunford, Thomas, "Inside Everything is an Engine," *New Genre* 3.
Dunford, Warren, "Slice," *Queer Fear II.*
Dungate, Pauline E., "Angelo's Bar," *Phantoms of Venice.*
———, "Lucy," *Birmingham Noir.*
Dunn. J. R., "Intruders," *SCI FICTION,* November 20.
Eakin, Benjamin Wade, "A Meal for Two," *Dark Offspring.*
Edelman, Scott, "Goobers," *The Book of More Flesh.*
Edwards, Martin, "Bare Bones," *Crimewave 6: Breaking Point.*
Emshwiller, Carol, "The Doctor," *Polyphony Volume 1.*
———, "Grandma," *F&SF,* March.
Engstrom, Elizabeth, "Genetically Predisposed," *Cemetery Dance* 37.
———, "The Goldberg," *Suspicions.*
Estrada, Rafael Pérez, "The Functions of Sleep" (poem), translated by Steven J. Stewart, *Star*Line,* September/October.
Etchison, Dennis, "In a Silent Way," *Embrace the Mutation.*
Evans, R. G., "The Man Who Holds Your Hand Beneath the Pale Moonlight," *WickedHollow,* January.
Evenson, Brian, "Lupe Varga, Deceased," *Angel Body.*
Files, Gemma, "Job 37," *Dark Terrors* 6.
———, "The Narrow World," *Queer Fear II.*
Finch, Paul, "Husks," *The Book of More Flesh.*
———, "The Lamb," *The Darker Side.*
———, "Long Meg and Her Daughters," *The Children of Cthulhu.*
———, "Night of the Pagans," *Roadworks* 14.
———, "Stan the Man," *Tourniquet Heart.*
———, "The Thorn Child," *Songs from Dead Singers.*
———, "The Wages of Sin," *MOTA: Truth.*
Finlay, Charles Coleman, "A Democracy of Trolls," *F&SF,* October/November.
———, "Fading Quayle, Dancing Quayle," *The Book of More Flesh.*
Fletcher, Kay, "Reservoirs," *Supernatural Tales* 3.
Flintheart, Dirk, "Rake at the Gates of Hell," *Redsine* 10.
Ford, Jeffrey, "The Chambered Nautilus," *Say . . . was that a kiss?.*
———, "Out of the Canyon," *The Fantasy Writer's Assistant and Other Stories.*
———, "Something By the Sea," *The Fantasy Writer's Assistant and Other Stories* and *F&SF,* October/November.
———, "Summer Afternoon," *. . . is this a cat?.*

———, "The Weight of Words, *Leviathan Three.*
———, "What's Sure to Come," *Lady Churchill's Rosebud Wristlet* 10.
Ford, John B., "Black Roses and Reputations," *Dark Shadows on the Moon.*
———, "The Infection of Time," ibid.
Ford, Michael Thomas, "Night of the Werepuss," *Queer Fear II.*
Forester, Richard, "Minotaur" (poem), *Prairie Schooner*, Fall.
Forrest, James Stephen, "The Second Most Important Picture," *On Spec*, Winter.
Foster, Alan Dean, "A Fatal Exception Has Occurred At . . ." *The Children of Cthulhu.*
Fowler, Christopher, "Fast Awake," *gothic.net* (Web site), December.
———, "The Torch Goes Out," *The Devil in Me.*
———, "We're Going Where the Sun Shines Brightly," *Dark Terrors* 6.
Fox, Derek, M., "Bones," *gothic.net* (Web site), October.
Friedman, Jeff, "The Golem in the Suburbs" (poem), *Pleiades* Vol. 23, 1.
Friesner, Esther M., "Just Another Cowboy," *F&SF*, April.
Frost, Gregory, "Madonna of the Maquiladora," *Asimov's Science Fiction*, May.
Fry, Susan, "Graveyard Tea," *Writers of the Future* Vol. XVIII.
Futch, James, "Plainfield Dreams," *Plainfield Dreams.*
Gallagher, Stephen, "White Bizango" (novella), *PS Publishing.*
Gallivan, Kevin J. J., "Mrs. Courcy's Folly," *All Hallows* 30.
Garcia, Victoria Elisabeth, "Anthropology," *Polyphony.*
Gash, Donn, "Medicine Man," *Random Acts of Weirdness.*
Gavin, Richard, "Parting the Veils," *Wicked Hollow*, January.
———, "Porcelain and Pretty Lace," *Horrorfind*, September.
———, "Sacred Mutations," *Decadence* 2.
Gay, Anne, "Bride of the Sea," *Phantoms of Venice.*
Gentle, Mary, "The Logistics of Carthage," *Worlds That Weren't.*
Glass, Alexander, "The Ghost in the Valley," *Interzone*, April.
Goldberg, d. g. k., "Final Turn, Last Lap," *Reckless Abandon.*
Goldman, Ken, "The Boardwalk Cats," *Dark Horizons* 42.
Gorman, Ed, "The Cries," *Stones.*
Gorman, Ed and Morrish, Robert, "Lafferty's Comeback," *Frightful Fiction*, March.
Goss, Theodora, "The Rapid Advance of Sorrow," *Lady Churchill's Rosebud Wristlet* 11.
Goto, Hiromi, "From Across a River," *This Magazine*, November/December.
Graham, John, "Oges," *Decadence* 2.
Grant, Gavin J., "Grand Uncle Egbert" (poem), *Full Unit Hookup*, Spring.
Grant, John, "Wooden Horse," *The Third Alternative* 32.
Graves, Rain, "New Orleans" (poem), *The Gossamer Eye.*
———, "The Gossamer Eye" (poem), ibid.
———, "Spider Woman" (poem), ibid.
Green, Dominic, "Blue Water, Grey Death," *Interzone*, January.
Greenwood, Ed, "O Silent Knight of Cards," *Be Very Afraid!.*
Gross, Harold, "Wreckage," *Electric Velocipede* 2.
Gunn, Alistair G., "The Catacombs of Osimus," *Darkness Rising: Volume Four.*
Gwaltney, Jane, "The Meek Shall Inherit" (poem), *Wicked Hollow*, January.
Haines, Paul, "Doorways for the Dispossessed," *Agog! Fantastic Fiction.*
Hall, M. M., "Buttons," *gothic.net* (Web site), May.
Hamilton, Glen Alan, "So Sayeth the Word," *gothic.net* (Web site), July.
Hand, Elizabeth, "Pavane for a Prince of Air," *Embrace the Mutation.*

Hanson, Donna Maree, "The Doctor's Pill," *Redsine* 10.
Harman, Christopher, "Come to Dust," *All Hallows* 30.
Harrod, Lois Marie, "This is a Story You Already Know" (poem), *The Silver Web* 15.
Hartley, James A., "Porcelain," *Frightful Fiction*, June 28.
Hawkhead, John, "The Wrathstone," *Dark Horizons* 41.
Hennessy, John, "The Blood Countess" (poem), *Pleiades* Vol. 23, 1
Hensley, Chad and Pugmire, W. H., "A Clicking in the Shadows," *A Clicking in the Shadows.*
Hernández, Felisberto, "Lands of Memory," translated from the Spanish by Esther Allen, *Lands of Memory.*
Hewish, Dean R., "The Face in the Crowd," *Redsine* 10.
Hill, David W., "Far From Laredo," *Black Gate*, Summer.
Hirshberg, Glen, "The Two Sams," *Dark Terrors* 6.
Hodge, Brian, "De Fortuna," *The Third Alternative* 32.
———, "The Firebrand Symphony," *The Children of Cthulhu.*
———, "Our Lady of Sloth and Scarlet Ivy," *Lies & Ugliness.*
Hodges, Jon, "The Elusive Miss Waldron," *Extremes 4: Darkest Africa.*
Hoffman, Nina Kiriki, "Escapes," *Shelf Life.*
———, "Gone," *Lighthouse Hauntings.*
———, "Grounded," *The Green Man.*
———, "Knotwork," *Vengeance Fantastic.*
———, "Summer Camp Blues," *Talebones*, Spring.
Hopkins, Brian A., "Communion with the Worm," *Cemetery Dance* 41.
———, "El Dia De Los Muertos" (novella), chapbook.
Hopkinson, Nalo, "Delicious Monster," *Queer Fear II.*
———, "Shift," *Conjunctions* 39.
Hoppe, Felicitas, "Knights and Duellists," translated from the German by W. Martin, *Chicago Review*, Summer.
Houarner, Gerard "The Bastard" (novella), *Bastards of Alchemy.*
———, "Children in the Moonless Night," *Visions through a Shattered Lens.*
———, "The Fearnaut," *Horrorfind*, April 2.
———, "The Keeper," *The Asylum, Volume 2: The Violent Ward.*
———, "Like Tears, Cast in the Steps of Her Mother," *Visions through a Shattered Lens.*
———, "The Love in Her Regard," *Decadence* 2.
———, "Those Who Cast Shadows," *Visions Through a Shattered Lens.*
———, "The Unborn," *Dreaming of Angels.*
Houchin, Ron, "Wood Bride" (poem), *Wind* 88.
Howe, Ken, "The Gingerbread House" (poem), TAR 131.
Hudgins, Andrew, "The Afterimage of a Ghost" (poem), *The Georgia Review*, Fall.
Hudson, Ann, "St. Francis Meets Ella Fitzgerald" (poem), *Prairie Schooner*, Winter.
Huff, Tanya, "Playing the Game," *Be Very Afraid!.*
Hughes, Rhys, "Depressurized Ghost Story," *Whispers and Shadows.*
———, "The Evil Side of Reginald Burke," *Stories From a Lost Anthology.*
———, "A Languid Elagabalus of the Tombs," ibid.
———, "Mah Jong Breath," *Journeys Beyond Advice.*
———, "Robin Hood's New Mother," *Redsine* 8.
———, "The Semi-Precious Isle," *Journeys Beyond Advice.*
———, "Story From a Lost Anthology," *Stories From a Lost Anthology.*
———, "The Swine Taster" (novella), *Journeys Beyond Advice.*

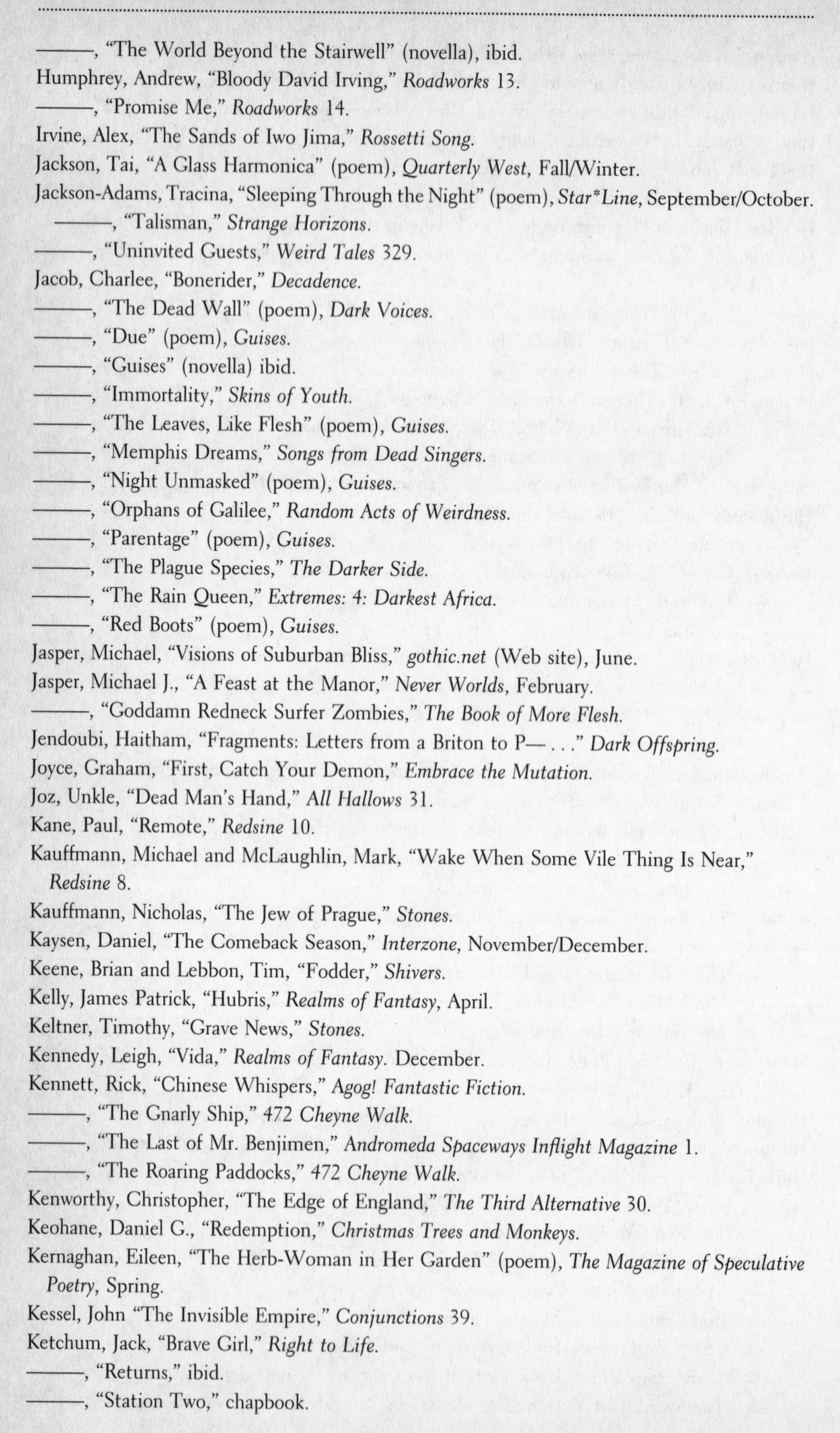

———, "The World Beyond the Stairwell" (novella), ibid.
Humphrey, Andrew, "Bloody David Irving," *Roadworks* 13.
———, "Promise Me," *Roadworks* 14.
Irvine, Alex, "The Sands of Iwo Jima," *Rossetti Song*.
Jackson, Tai, "A Glass Harmonica" (poem), *Quarterly West*, Fall/Winter.
Jackson-Adams, Tracina, "Sleeping Through the Night" (poem), *Star*Line*, September/October.
———, "Talisman," *Strange Horizons*.
———, "Uninvited Guests," *Weird Tales* 329.
Jacob, Charlee, "Bonerider," *Decadence*.
———, "The Dead Wall" (poem), *Dark Voices*.
———, "Due" (poem), *Guises*.
———, "Guises" (novella) ibid.
———, "Immortality," *Skins of Youth*.
———, "The Leaves, Like Flesh" (poem), *Guises*.
———, "Memphis Dreams," *Songs from Dead Singers*.
———, "Night Unmasked" (poem), *Guises*.
———, "Orphans of Galilee," *Random Acts of Weirdness*.
———, "Parentage" (poem), *Guises*.
———, "The Plague Species," *The Darker Side*.
———, "The Rain Queen," *Extremes: 4: Darkest Africa*.
———, "Red Boots" (poem), *Guises*.
Jasper, Michael, "Visions of Suburban Bliss," *gothic.net* (Web site), June.
Jasper, Michael J., "A Feast at the Manor," *Never Worlds*, February.
———, "Goddamn Redneck Surfer Zombies," *The Book of More Flesh*.
Jendoubi, Haitham, "Fragments: Letters from a Briton to P— . . ." *Dark Offspring*.
Joyce, Graham, "First, Catch Your Demon," *Embrace the Mutation*.
Joz, Unkle, "Dead Man's Hand," *All Hallows* 31.
Kane, Paul, "Remote," *Redsine* 10.
Kauffmann, Michael and McLaughlin, Mark, "Wake When Some Vile Thing Is Near," *Redsine* 8.
Kauffmann, Nicholas, "The Jew of Prague," *Stones*.
Kaysen, Daniel, "The Comeback Season," *Interzone*, November/December.
Keene, Brian and Lebbon, Tim, "Fodder," *Shivers*.
Kelly, James Patrick, "Hubris," *Realms of Fantasy*, April.
Keltner, Timothy, "Grave News," *Stones*.
Kennedy, Leigh, "Vida," *Realms of Fantasy*. December.
Kennett, Rick, "Chinese Whispers," *Agog! Fantastic Fiction*.
———, "The Gnarly Ship," *472 Cheyne Walk*.
———, "The Last of Mr. Benjimen," *Andromeda Spaceways Inflight Magazine* 1.
———, "The Roaring Paddocks," *472 Cheyne Walk*.
Kenworthy, Christopher, "The Edge of England," *The Third Alternative* 30.
Keohane, Daniel G., "Redemption," *Christmas Trees and Monkeys*.
Kernaghan, Eileen, "The Herb-Woman in Her Garden" (poem), *The Magazine of Speculative Poetry*, Spring.
Kessel, John "The Invisible Empire," *Conjunctions* 39.
Ketchum, Jack, "Brave Girl," *Right to Life*.
———, "Returns," ibid.
———, "Station Two," chapbook.

Kidd, A. F. "Arkright's Tale," 472 *Cheyne Walk.*
———, "The Psychic Doorway," ibid.
———, "The Sigsand Codex," ibid.
Kidd, Chico, "Ancient of Days," *Darkness Rising Volume Three: Secrets of Shadows.*
———, "Handwriting of the God," *Dark Terrors* 6.
———, "Zé and the Amulet," *Supernatural Tales* 4.
Kiernan, Caitlín R., "Apokatastasis," *The Spook,* March.
———, "Nor the Demons Under the Sea," *The Children of Cthulhu.*
———, "Rat's Star," *From Weird and Distant Shores.*
———, "The Road of Pins," *Dark Terrors* 6.
———, "Standing Water," *The Darker Side.*
Kihn, Greg, "Then Play On," *Horror Garage* 5.
Kilpatrick, Nancy, "Your Shadow Knows You Well," *Dark Terrors* 6.
King, Francis, "Now You See It Now You Don't," *Bend Sinister.*
King, T. Jackson, "A Lesser Michaelangelo," *The Silver Web* 15.
King, Tabitha, "The Women's Room," *Stranger: Dark Tales of Eerie Encounters.*
Klages, Ellen, "A Taste of Summer," *Black Gate,* Winter.
———, "Travel Agency," *Strange Horizons* (Web site), February 11.
Knight, Brian, "Baby Girl," *Dragonfly.*
———, "Dragonfly," ibid.
———, "God's Bug Zapper," ibid.
———, "Wunderland," ibid.
Kopaska-Merkel, David, "Going Down with Jasmine" (poem), *Wicked Hollow,* January.
Kottner, Lee, "The Bear Dancer," *Strange Horizons* (Web site), October 7.
Kritzer, Naomi, "Comrade Grandmother," *Strange Horizons* (Web site), September 2.
———, "In the Witch's Garden," *Realms of Fantasy,* October.
LaBounty, David, "The Mummy of Italy," *The First Line,* Summer.
Laimo, Michael, "The Exploitations of George Frederick Leighton," *The Asylum* Vol. 2.
Lain, Douglas, "The Sea Monkey Conspiracy," *Polyphony Volume* 1.
Lake, Jay, "Eglantine's Time," *Dark Terrors* 6.
———, "Tall Spirits, Blocking the Night," *Talebones,* Fall.
Landis, Geoffrey A., "Old Tingo's Penis," *Interzone,* August.
Lane, Joel, "After the Flood," *The Darker Side.*
———, "The Black Window" (poem), *Talebones* 24.
———, "The Hard Copy," *The Third Alternative* 32.
———, "An Unknown Past," *Songs from Dead Singers.*
Langan, John, "Mr Gaunt" (novella), *F&SF,* September.
Langan, Sarah, "Taut Red Ribbon," *Chizine* 12 (Web site).
Lebbon, Tim, "Black," *Dark Terrors* 6.
———, "Hell Came Down," *The Darker Side.*
———, "Last Exit for the Lost," *Phantoms of Venice.*
Lee, Edward, "Make a Wish," *Horror Garage* 5.
Lee, Tanith, "The City of Dead Night," *F&SF,* October/November.
———, "Flicker of a Winter Star," *Weird Tales* 327.
———, "Midday People," *Dark Terrors* 6.
———, "Persian Eyes, *30th Anniversary DAW Fantasy.*
Libling, Michael, "The Fourth Kiss," *F&SF,* August.
Lifshin, Lyn, "The Ice Maiden Mummy's 24th SOS" (poem), *Connecticut Review,* Spring.

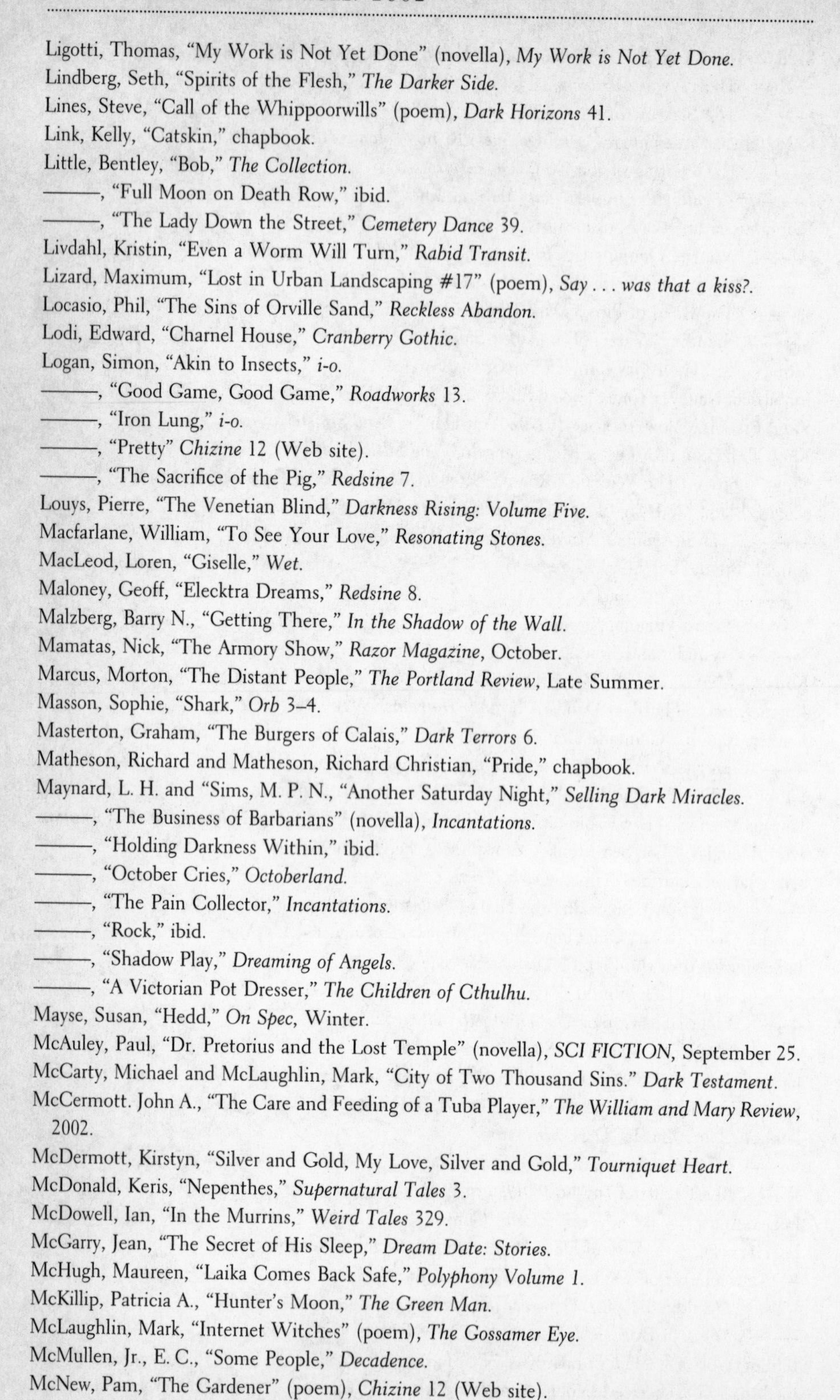

Ligotti, Thomas, "My Work is Not Yet Done" (novella), *My Work is Not Yet Done.*
Lindberg, Seth, "Spirits of the Flesh," *The Darker Side.*
Lines, Steve, "Call of the Whippoorwills" (poem), *Dark Horizons* 41.
Link, Kelly, "Catskin," chapbook.
Little, Bentley, "Bob," *The Collection.*
———, "Full Moon on Death Row," ibid.
———, "The Lady Down the Street," *Cemetery Dance* 39.
Livdahl, Kristin, "Even a Worm Will Turn," *Rabid Transit.*
Lizard, Maximum, "Lost in Urban Landscaping #17" (poem), *Say . . . was that a kiss?.*
Locasio, Phil, "The Sins of Orville Sand," *Reckless Abandon.*
Lodi, Edward, "Charnel House," *Cranberry Gothic.*
Logan, Simon, "Akin to Insects," *i-o.*
———, "Good Game, Good Game," *Roadworks* 13.
———, "Iron Lung," *i-o.*
———, "Pretty" *Chizine* 12 (Web site).
———, "The Sacrifice of the Pig," *Redsine* 7.
Louys, Pierre, "The Venetian Blind," *Darkness Rising: Volume Five.*
Macfarlane, William, "To See Your Love," *Resonating Stones.*
MacLeod, Loren, "Giselle," *Wet.*
Maloney, Geoff, "Elecktra Dreams," *Redsine* 8.
Malzberg, Barry N., "Getting There," *In the Shadow of the Wall.*
Mamatas, Nick, "The Armory Show," *Razor Magazine*, October.
Marcus, Morton, "The Distant People," *The Portland Review*, Late Summer.
Masson, Sophie, "Shark," *Orb* 3–4.
Masterton, Graham, "The Burgers of Calais," *Dark Terrors* 6.
Matheson, Richard and Matheson, Richard Christian, "Pride," chapbook.
Maynard, L. H. and "Sims, M. P. N., "Another Saturday Night," *Selling Dark Miracles.*
———, "The Business of Barbarians" (novella), *Incantations.*
———, "Holding Darkness Within," ibid.
———, "October Cries," *Octoberland.*
———, "The Pain Collector," *Incantations.*
———, "Rock," ibid.
———, "Shadow Play," *Dreaming of Angels.*
———, "A Victorian Pot Dresser," *The Children of Cthulhu.*
Mayse, Susan, "Hedd," *On Spec*, Winter.
McAuley, Paul, "Dr. Pretorius and the Lost Temple" (novella), *SCI FICTION*, September 25.
McCarty, Michael and McLaughlin, Mark, "City of Two Thousand Sins." *Dark Testament.*
McCermott. John A., "The Care and Feeding of a Tuba Player," *The William and Mary Review*, 2002.
McDermott, Kirstyn, "Silver and Gold, My Love, Silver and Gold," *Tourniquet Heart.*
McDonald, Keris, "Nepenthes," *Supernatural Tales* 3.
McDowell, Ian, "In the Murrins," *Weird Tales* 329.
McGarry, Jean, "The Secret of His Sleep," *Dream Date: Stories.*
McHugh, Maureen, "Laika Comes Back Safe," *Polyphony Volume 1.*
McKillip, Patricia A., "Hunter's Moon," *The Green Man.*
McLaughlin, Mark, "Internet Witches" (poem), *The Gossamer Eye.*
McMullen, Jr., E. C., "Some People," *Decadence.*
McNew, Pam, "The Gardener" (poem), *Chizine* 12 (Web site).

Meloy, Paul, "Care in the Continuum," *The Third Alternative* 30.

Miéville, China, "Familiar," *Conjunctions:* 39.

Milder, Scott, "Hat with Flaps," *Strangewood Tales.*

Millar, Sam, "The Barber," *Albedo One* 25.

Minnis, Mike, "Salt Air," *Dead but Dreaming.*

Mohan, Jr. Steven, "Crimes Against Humanity," *Extremes 4: Darkest Africa.*

Mohn, Steve "Kolorado," *On Spec,* Summer.

Monette, Sarah, "Three Letters from the Queen of Elfland," *Lady Churchill's Rosebud Wristlet* 11.

Monk, Devon, "Leeward to the Sky," *Realms of Fantasy,* June.

Moore, James A., "Territorial Markings," *Stones.*

Morden, Simon, "Bon Homme," *Extremes: 4: Darkest Africa.*

Moritz, Blaise, "Penelope" (poem), *The Antigonish Review* 130.

Morlan, A. R., "The Hemingway Kittens," *Shelf Life.*

———, "The Thin Red Line," *Frontiers of Terror.*

———, "Why the Greeks Called 'em Pépōn," *Scavenger's Newsletter,* October.

Morris, Mark, "The Uglimen" (novella), chapbook.

Morrish, Robert, "Memory Lake," *Stones.*

———, "There are Corners in the World Where Lost Things Gather," *Octoberland.*

Mowbray, Chris, "Curtain Call," *Passing Strange.*

Murphy, Hilary Moon, "The Run of the Fiery Horse," *Realms of Fantasy,* June.

Murphy, Joe, "Sweetness and Light," *Dark Terrors 6.*

———, "To Find a One," *Dreaming of Angels.*

Murphy, M. J., "The Dream Queen," *Redsine* 10.

Myrmo, Millen, "Grown Cold," *MOTA 2002 Truth.*

Nassise, Joseph M., "That Cleansing Fire," *Spectres and Darkness.*

———, "The Urge," ibid.

Nathan, Leonard, "Shylock in New York" (poem), *Michigan Quarterly Review: Jewish in America Issue,* Fall.

Navarro, Yvonne, "Do You Dream?" *Freaks, Geeks, & Sideshow Floozies.*

Newman, Kim, "A Drug on the Market" (novella), *Dark Terrors 6.*

Newton, Kurt "The Mothering Hole," *Dark Demons.*

———, "The Projectionist's Nightmare," *Strangewood Tales.*

Newton, Kurt, "Secrets . . . Like Bones in Slippery Dirt," *Dark Demons.*

———, "Something Profound," ibid.

Nicholls, Mark, "I'll Deal With You Later," *All Hallows* 30.

Nicholson, Scott, "Beggar's Velvet," *Whispers and Shadows.*

Nickle, David, "Janie and the Wind," *Cemetery Dance* 38.

———, "Polyphemus' Cave," *Queer Fear II.*

Noel, Scot, "The Hyphenated Spirit," *The Book of More Flesh.*

Norton, Andre, "Sow's Ear—Silk Purse," *30th Anniversary DAW Fantasy.*

Ó Guilin, Peadar, "The Bag," *Reckless Abandon.*

O'Brien, Greig, "Evil Then Became My Good," *Weird Tales* 329.

O'Brien, Tim, "Half Gone," *The New Yorker,* July 8.

O'Leary, Patrick, "The Bearing of the Light," *Conjunctions:* 39.

———, "What Mattered Was Sleep," *SCI FICTION,* August 14.

O'Rourke, Monica J., "Attainable Beauty," *gothic.net* (Web site), May.

———, "Dancing into October Country," *Octoberland.*

Oakwood, Mike, "Baal Out," *Dark Testament.*

Oates, Joyce Carol, "The Deaths," *EQMM*, December.

———, "Madison at Guinol," *The Kenyon Review*, Winter.

———, "The Twins: A Mystery," *Alfred Hitchcock's Mystery Magazine*, December.

Ochse, Weston, "Aliens in the Waste," *Stones.*

Ochsner, Gina, "How the Dead Live," *The Necessary Grace to Fall.*

———, "The Necessary Grace to Fall," ibid.

Okorafor, Nnedi, "Windseekers," *Writers of the Future* XVIII.

Olivas, Daniel A., "Tezcatlipoca's Glory" (poem), *LatinoLA* (Web site).

Oliveri, Michael, "In the Grasp of Fear and Trembling," *Dark Testament.*

Olsen, Lance "Village of the Mermaids," *Leviathan Three.*

Orman, Kate, "And All the Children of Chimaera," *Passing Strange.*

Padgett-Clarke, Kim, "Absolution," *Roadworks* 14.

Park, Paul "Abduction," *Conjunctions:* 39.

———, "Tachycardia," *F&SF*, January.

Parker, Sally, "Generic Story" (poem), *Weird Tales* 328.

———, "Kallisti," *Realms of Fantasy*, April.

Partridge, Norman, "And What Did You See in the World," *Embrace the Mutation.*

Patrice, Helen, "The Nun's Story," *Aurealis* 30.

Patterson, Meredith L., "Principles and Parameters," *The Children of Cthulhu.*

Pearce, Gerald, "Revenant," *EQMM*, December.

Peek, Ben, "Cigarettes and Roses," *Passing Strange.*

Pelan, John, "Armies of the Night," *The Darker Side.*

Pelan, John and Adams, Benjamin, "That's the Story of My Life," *The Children of Cthulhu.*

Peterson, Laurel S., "Bluebeard's Closet" (poem), *Poet Lore*, Fall/Winter.

Piccirilli, Tom "Alchemy" (novella), *Bastards of Alchemy.*

———, "At the Center of a Circle of Vultures," *This Cape is Red. . . .*

———, "Jonah Rose" (novella), *Four Dark Nights.*

———, "Naked Shall I Return," *The Book of More Flesh.*

———, "This Cape is Red Because I've Been Bleeding," *This Cape is Red. . . .*

———, "To the Lonely Sea and the Sky," *Be Very Afraid!.*

Pitt, Darrell, "Trapdoor," *Redsine* 8.

———, "Wind Tunnel," *Orb* 3 and 4.

Platt, John R., "The Day the Laughter Died," *Die Laughing.*

Popkes, Steven, "Fable for Savior and Reptile," *Realms of Fantasy*, February.

Porges, Arthur, "Swamp Demon," *The Mirror And Other Strange Reflections.*

Porter, Karen R., "Reflection" (poem), *Not One of Us* 27.

Powell, James, "The Zoroaster Grin," *EQMM*, January.

Powell, Neil, "Just Curious," *Bend Sinister.*

Pratt, Tim, "Little Gods," *Strange Horizons*, February 4.

———, "The Bicycle Witch," *Realms of Fantasy*, August.

Price, Weston, "Antithesis," *Plainfield Dreams.*

Prill, David, "Dating Secrets of the Dead," *F&SF*, June.

Prince, Martyn, "The Maestro and Monique," *Darkness Rising: Volume Four.*

Proctor, Nancy, "Mr. Neblin's Boy" *Ideomancer*, January.

Prufer, Kevin, "An Angel" (poem), *Boulevard*, Fall.

Ptacek, Kathryn, "Solitaire," *Cemetery Dance* 40.

Pulver, Sr., Joseph S., "Zarnak's Guest," *Lin Carter's Anton Zarnak Supernatural Sleuth.*

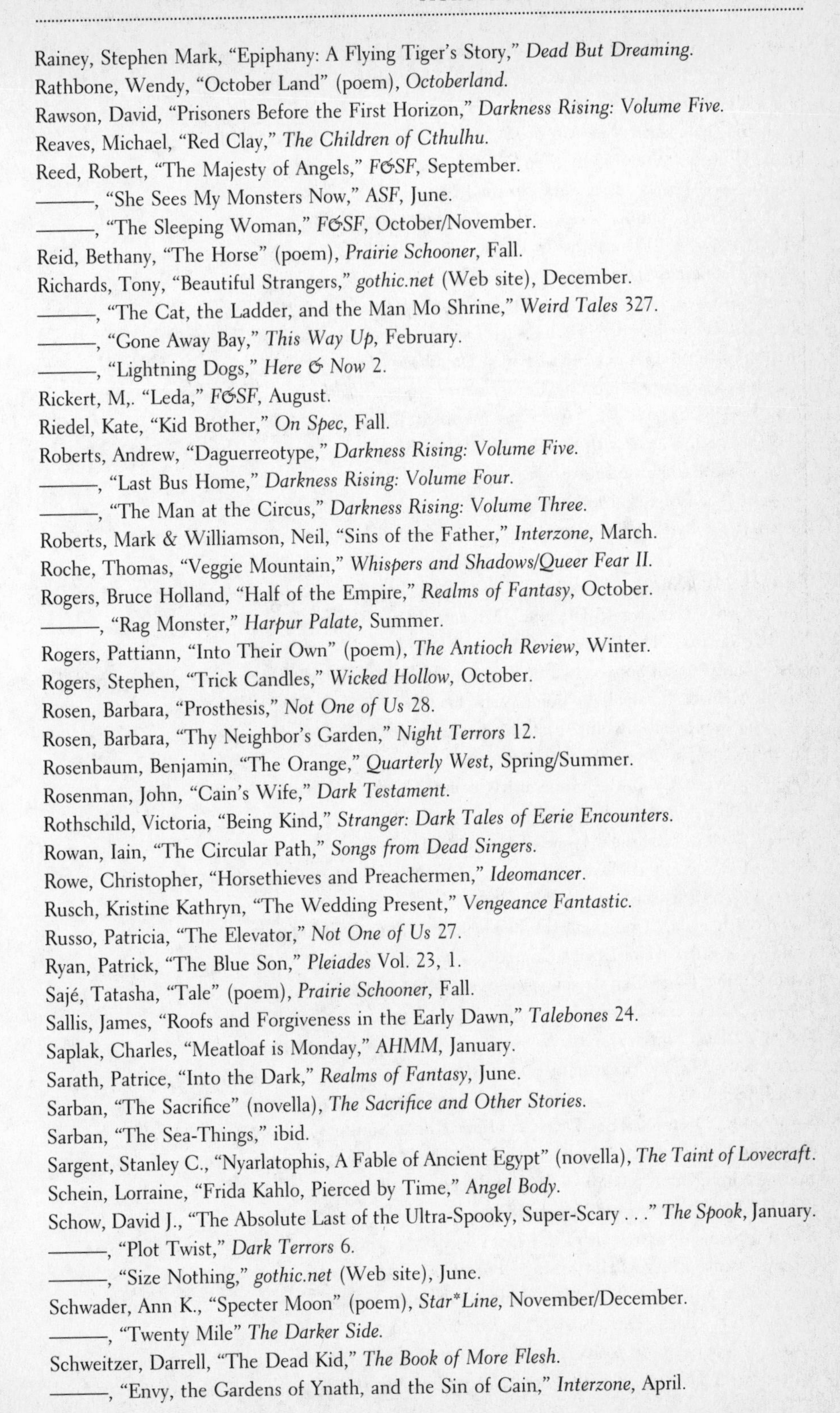

Rainey, Stephen Mark, "Epiphany: A Flying Tiger's Story," *Dead But Dreaming.*

Rathbone, Wendy, "October Land" (poem), *Octoberland.*

Rawson, David, "Prisoners Before the First Horizon," *Darkness Rising: Volume Five.*

Reaves, Michael, "Red Clay," *The Children of Cthulhu.*

Reed, Robert, "The Majesty of Angels," *F&SF*, September.

———, "She Sees My Monsters Now," *ASF*, June.

———, "The Sleeping Woman," *F&SF*, October/November.

Reid, Bethany, "The Horse" (poem), *Prairie Schooner*, Fall.

Richards, Tony, "Beautiful Strangers," *gothic.net* (Web site), December.

———, "The Cat, the Ladder, and the Man Mo Shrine," *Weird Tales* 327.

———, "Gone Away Bay," *This Way Up*, February.

———, "Lightning Dogs," *Here & Now* 2.

Rickert, M,. "Leda," *F&SF*, August.

Riedel, Kate, "Kid Brother," *On Spec*, Fall.

Roberts, Andrew, "Daguerreotype," *Darkness Rising: Volume Five.*

———, "Last Bus Home," *Darkness Rising: Volume Four.*

———, "The Man at the Circus," *Darkness Rising: Volume Three.*

Roberts, Mark & Williamson, Neil, "Sins of the Father," *Interzone*, March.

Roche, Thomas, "Veggie Mountain," *Whispers and Shadows/Queer Fear II.*

Rogers, Bruce Holland, "Half of the Empire," *Realms of Fantasy*, October.

———, "Rag Monster," *Harpur Palate*, Summer.

Rogers, Pattiann, "Into Their Own" (poem), *The Antioch Review*, Winter.

Rogers, Stephen, "Trick Candles," *Wicked Hollow*, October.

Rosen, Barbara, "Prosthesis," *Not One of Us* 28.

Rosen, Barbara, "Thy Neighbor's Garden," *Night Terrors* 12.

Rosenbaum, Benjamin, "The Orange," *Quarterly West*, Spring/Summer.

Rosenman, John, "Cain's Wife," *Dark Testament.*

Rothschild, Victoria, "Being Kind," *Stranger: Dark Tales of Eerie Encounters.*

Rowan, Iain, "The Circular Path," *Songs from Dead Singers.*

Rowe, Christopher, "Horsethieves and Preachermen," *Ideomancer.*

Rusch, Kristine Kathryn, "The Wedding Present," *Vengeance Fantastic.*

Russo, Patricia, "The Elevator," *Not One of Us* 27.

Ryan, Patrick, "The Blue Son," *Pleiades* Vol. 23, 1.

Sajé, Tatasha, "Tale" (poem), *Prairie Schooner*, Fall.

Sallis, James, "Roofs and Forgiveness in the Early Dawn," *Talebones* 24.

Saplak, Charles, "Meatloaf is Monday," *AHMM*, January.

Sarath, Patrice, "Into the Dark," *Realms of Fantasy*, June.

Sarban, "The Sacrifice" (novella), *The Sacrifice and Other Stories.*

Sarban, "The Sea-Things," ibid.

Sargent, Stanley C., "Nyarlatophis, A Fable of Ancient Egypt" (novella), *The Taint of Lovecraft.*

Schein, Lorraine, "Frida Kahlo, Pierced by Time," *Angel Body.*

Schow, David J., "The Absolute Last of the Ultra-Spooky, Super-Scary . . ." *The Spook*, January.

———, "Plot Twist," *Dark Terrors* 6.

———, "Size Nothing," *gothic.net* (Web site), June.

Schwader, Ann K., "Specter Moon" (poem), *Star*Line*, November/December.

———, "Twenty Mile" *The Darker Side.*

Schweitzer, Darrell, "The Dead Kid," *The Book of More Flesh.*

———, "Envy, the Gardens of Ynath, and the Sin of Cain," *Interzone*, April.

———, "How It Ended," *Realms of Fantasy*, August.
Searles, Vera, "The Waiting Room," *The Silver Web* 15.
Sering, Ron, "KOTL," *Cemetery Dance* 41.
Seshadri, Vijai, "The Long Meadow" (poem), *The New Yorker*, June 10.
Shaw, Heather, "Wetting the Bed," *Floodwater*
Shawl, Nisi, "The Beads of Ku," *Rosebud* 23.
Shea, Michael, "The Rebuke," *30th Anniversary DAW Fantasy*.
Shepherd, Lucius, "The Drive-In Puerto Rico," *F&SF*, October/November.
———, "Emerald Street Expansions," *SCI FICTION*, March 27.
———, "White Trains" (poem), *Dark Illuminati*, Issue Zero.
Shepherd, Reginald, "Five Feelings for Orpheus" (poem), *The Iowa Review*, Fall.
Sherman, Delia, "Grand Central Park," *The Green Man*.
Shurtleff, Margaret, ". . . on his dinner plate." (poem), *gothic.net* (Web site), November.
Sidor, Steven, "The Taker," *gothic.net* (Web site), June.
Siegel, Mark, "A Date with Deathe," *Midnight Rose*.
Silva, David B., "Beyond Lake 313," *Frontiers of Terror*.
———, "The Origin," *The Darker Side*.
Silverberg, Robert, "With Caesar in the Underworld," *Asimov's*, October/November.
Silverman, "The Secrets of Lizard Magic," *Mirror, Mirror: Twisted Tales*.
Simmons, William P., "They Never Come Back," *Darkness Rising: Volume Four*.
Simsa, Cyril, "Gazelles in Babylon," *Darkness Rising: Volume Five*.
Singh, Vandana, "The Room on the Roof," *Polyphony*.
Sleigh, Tom, "Spell Spoken by Supplicant to Helios for Knowledge" (poem), *TriQuarterly* 114.
Smith, Michael Marshall, "A Long Walk, for the Last Time," *Dark Terrors* 6.
———, "Night Falls, Again," *Embrace the Mutation*.
Smith, Rob, "The Kiss," *Birmingham Noir*.
Sng, Christine, "Crimes of our Youth" (poem), *Wicked Hollow*, October.
———, "The Marvel of Flight" (poem), *Wicked Hollow*, January.
Snyder, Midori, "Charlie's Away," *The Green Man*.
Soares, L. L., "Second Chances," *gothic.net* (Web site), December.
Sparks, Cat, "Fuchsia Spins by Moonlight," *Redsine* 7.
Squillante, Sheila, "Unmaking the Bed" (poem), *Prairie Schooner*, Summer.
Stableford, Brian, "The Devil's Comedy," *Phantoms of Venice*.
———, "The Face of an Angel," *Leviathan Three*.
———, "Oh Goat-God of Arcady," *The Silver Web* 15.
———, "Tread Softly," *Interzone*, March.
Staley, Shane Ryan, "Apartment 6A," *Luster*.
Stanchfield, Justin, "Little Helper," *Extremes 4: Darkest Africa*.
———, "So Deep Do They Dwell," *Harpur Palate*, Summer.
Stephenson, Robert N., "The Shadow of a Man (Seeking the Child)," *Redsine* 9.
Sterns, Aaron, "At Night My Television Bleeds," *Orb* 3/4.
Stewart, Kristen, "Wishing He was Mine" (poem), *Dark Offspring*.
Stewart, Shane, "Sitting with the Dead," *The Book of More Flesh*.
Storey, Donna George, "Hot Spring," *Prairie Schooner*, Winter.
Suarez-Beard, Beverly, "Bertrand's Bride," *Talebones*, Fall.
Swanwick, Michael, "Dirty Little War," *In the Shadow of the Wall*.
———, "The Sleep of Reason" cycle of stories, *Infinite Matrix*.
Swiercynzski, Duane, "Not All There," *Tourniquet Heart*.

Taaffe, Sonya, "Moving Nameless," *Not One of Us* 27.
———, "Till Human Voices Wake Us," *Not One of Us* 28.
Tan, Cecilia, "Touch Pain," *Asimov's Science Fiction*, February.
Taylor, Seth, "The Love of a Fifty Foot Woman," *Beloit Fiction Journal* Vol. 15.
Tem, Melanie, "The Glutton," *Shelf Life*.
Tem, Steve Rasnic, "The Crusher," *Crimewave 6: Breaking Point*.
———, "Origami Bird," Wormhole Books limited edition.
———, "Outside," *The Children of Cthulhu*.
———, "This Thing Called Love," *Tourniquet Heart*.
———, "What Happens at Night" (poem), *Steve and Melanie Tem's Imagination Box*, CD.
Thees, Lester, "Green Tea with Lizards," *gothic.net* (Web site), March.
Thomas, G. W., "Book of the Black Sun," *Strangewood Tales*.
Thomas, Jeffrey, "300,000 Moments of Pain," *Redsine* 10.
———, "Do You Know This Girl?" *Tooth & Claw*.
———, "The Green Spider," *Strangewood Tales*.
———, "Out of the Belly of Sheol," *Dark Testament*.
———, "Praying That You Feel Better Soon," *Frontiers of Terror*.
Thomas, Michael, "The Beast of Downy Mount," *F&SF*, April.
Thomas, Robert, "The Man Who Could Not Fly" (poem), *The Sewanee Review*, Winter.
Thomas, Scott, "One Window," *The Silver Web* 15.
———, "The Sea Men," *Strangewood Tales*.
———, "The Swan of Prudence Street," *Leviathan Three*.
Thomas, Sharee Renée, "Black River Ritual" (poem), *Harpur Palate*, Summer.
Tiedemann, Mark W., "The Disinterred," *SCI FICTION*, March 19.
Townsend, Alice, "Persephone in America" (poem), *Calyx*, Summer.
Travis, John, "Networking," *All Hallows* 29.
Traynor, Terry, "Mr. Tinky Tink" (poem), *Flesh and Blood* 9.
Tremblay, Paul G., "4'33," *gothic.net* (Web site), May.
———, "The Laughing Man Meets Little Cat," *Chizine* 14 (Web site).
———, "With More Than Eyes," *gothic.net* (Web site), September.
Tullis, S. D., "The Weird Ways," *The Third Alternative* 29.
Tulsa, Chris, "The Birth of Night" (poem), *Prairie Schooner*, Spring.
Tumasonis, Don, "The Houses," *Supernatural Tales* 4.
———, "The Wretched Thicket of Thorn," *All Hallows* 29.
Urbancik, John, "Lâche," *Twilight Showcase*, March.
———, "The Painted Woman," *Decadence*.
Vajra, Lake, "Blue, Frozen" (poem), *Flesh and Blood #9*.
Van Cleave, Ryan, "Overland," *Crimewave 6: Breaking Point*.
Van Dyk, Amber, "Scatter Heart," *Chizine* 12 (Web site).
———, "Sleeping, Waking, Nightfall," *Lady Churchill's Rosebud Wristlet* 10.
———, "The Queen of Hearts," *Wicked Hollow*, April.
Van Pelt, James, "The Boy Behind the Gate," *Dark Terrors* 6.
———, "The Invisible Empire," *The Children of Cthulhu*.
———, "Origin of the Species," *Weird Tales*, Fall.
———, "The Saint from Abidjan," *Extremes 4: Darkest Africa*.
Vance, Steve, "Special Effect," *Cicada*, March/April/*Cemetery Dance* 41.
VanderMeer, Jeff, "The Cage" (novella), *City of Saints and Madmen*.
———, "In the Hours After Death," *Dark Terrors* 6.

———, "The Machine," *Strangewood Tales.*

Vaughn, Carrie, "The Heroic Death of Lieutenant Michkov," *Polyphony.*

———, "The Librarian's Daughter," *Realms of Fantasy*, August.

Vaz, Katherine, "A World Painted by Birds," *The Green Man.*

Vincent, Bev, "Harming Obsession," *Cemetery Dance* 39.

Vine, Mark, "Intro to Children's Lit" (poem), *The Hudson Review*, Autumn.

Volk, Stephen, "A Pair of Pince-Nez," *All Hallows* 29.

Vukcevich, Ray, "Intercontinental Ballistic Missile Boy," *Strange Horizons* (Web site), May 20.

Waggoner, Tim, "Waiting for Courtney' *All Too Surreal.*

Walden, Megan, "Tiger Eyes," *All Hallows* 31.

Wasserman, Jamie, "Prayer (for Natural Causes)" (poem), *gothic.net* (Web site), November.

Watson, Ian "Alicia," *Weird Tales* 328.

———, "The Pleasure Surgeons" (poem), *Dreams and Nightmares* 62.

West, Julian, "Vita Brevis Ars Longa," *Interzone*, November/December.

West, Michelle, "The Memory of Stone," *30th Anniversary DAW: Fantasy.*

What, Leslie, "Blind Date With the Invisible Man," *Polyphony.*

Wilhelm, Kate, "The Man on the Persian Carpet," *F&SF*, February.

Williams, Conrad, "A Door Opens and Closes," *Cemetery Dance* 37.

———, "City in Aspic," *Phantoms of Venice.*

———, "Crappy Rubsniff," *Crimewave 6: Breaking Point.*

———, "Haifisch," *Dark Terrors 6.*

———, "The Intimate," Dusksite.com.

———, "Ubirr," *The Spook*, March.

Williams, Deborah, "Sylvi," *Dark Horizons* 42.

Williams, Drew, "Art and Becoming," *Spectres and Darkness.*

———, "Riding the Dragon," *Horrofind*, January.

———, "Soft, Sweet Music," *Spectres and Darkness.*

Williams, Liz, "Banquet of the Lords of Night," *ASF*, June.

———, "Honeydark," *Realms of Fantasy*, Oct.

Williams, Sean, "The Girl-Thing," *Eidolon: Australian SF Online*, November.

Williamson, Neil, "Amber Rain," *The Third Alternative* 30.

———, "The Happy Gang," *Interzone*, November/December.

Willrich, Chris, "King Rainjoy's Tears," *F&SF*, July.

Wilson, David Niall, "A Poem of Adrian Grey" (poem), *The Gossamer Eye.*

———, "Redemption," *The Subtle Ties that Bind.*

———, "Sushi or Not Sushi," ibid.

———, "Wolf-Child" (poem), *The Gossamer Eye.*

Wilson, Mehitobel, "Fire Breathing," *Dead but Dreaming.*

———, "Growing Out of It," *Skins of Youth.*

———, "Land of Odds, One Mile" *Chizine* 13 (Web site).

———, "The Mannerly Man," *The Darker Side.*

Wolfe, Gene, "Mute," *World Horror Convention Program Book* 4000.

———, "The Waif," *F&SF*, January.

———, "Under Hill," *The Infinite Matrix.*

Wolfe, Ron, "Our Friend Electricity," *F&SF*, June.

Wood, Peter H., "Loschilders Wood," *All Hallows* 30.

Wright, Carolyne, "Clairvoyant's Reading" (poem), *The Iowa Review*, Winter.

Yarbro, Chelsea Quinn, "Inappropriate Laughter," *The Spook*, March.
Yolen, Jane, "Dark Seed, Dark Stone," *Realms of Fantasy*, Feb.
Young, Katherine, "Rusalka" (poem), *Shenandoah*, Spring.
Zumpe, Lee Clark, "Her Horrible Silence" (poem), *Wicked Hollow*, October.

The People Behind the Book

Horror Editor **Ellen Datlow** is the fiction editor of SCIFI.COM. She was the fiction editor of *OMNI* magazine for seventeen years and has edited numerous anthologies, including *Vanishing Acts* and *The Dark.* She has also collaborated with Terri Windling on a number of anthologies besides *The Year's Best Fantasy and Horror* series, including *Sirens*, and for younger readers, *A Wolf at the Door* and *Swan Sister* (for children), and *The Green Man* (for teenagers). She has won six World Fantasy Awards and the 2002 Hugo Award for her editing. She lives in New York City.

Fantasy Editor **Terri Windling** is a writer, artist, editor, and a six-time winner of the World Fantasy Award. As an author, she has published *The Wood Wife* (winner of the Mythopoeic Award for Novel of the Year), *The Winter Child,* and other books, as well as numerous articles and essays on mythology, fairy tales, and art. As an artist, her paintings on folklore and feminist themes have been exhibited at museums and galleries in the United States, Great Britain, and France. As an editor, she has published over thirty anthologies, many of them in partnership with Ellen Datlow, including the *Snow White, Blood Red* adult fairy-tales series. She has been a consulting fantasy editor for the Tor Books fantasy line since 1985. She is the director of the Endicott Studio for Mythic Arts (www.endicott-studio.com) and a founding member of the Interstitial Arts Foundation (www.artistswithoutborders.org). She divides her time between homes in Devon, England, and Tucson, Arizona.

Media Critic **Edward Bryant** is an award-winning author of science fiction, fantasy, and horror, having published short fiction in countless anthologies and magazines. He's won the Hugo Award for his science fiction, and other works of his short fiction have been nominated for many other awards. He's also written for television. He lives in Denver, Colorado. His story collection *Flirting With Death* (Cemetary Dance Publications) will be published soon.

Comics critic **Charles Vess**'s art has graced the pages of numerous comic books for over twenty years. In 1991, Charles shared the World Fantasy Award for Best Short Story with Neil Gaiman for their collaboration on *Sandman* #19, the only time a comic book has won this honor. In 1997, Charles won the Will Eisner Comic Industry Award for best penciler/inker for his work on *The Book of Ballads and Sagas* (which he self-publishes through his own Green Man Press) as well as *Sandman* #75. In 1999, he received the World Fantasy Award for Best Artist? For current information, visit his Web site: www.greenmanpress.com. He lives amidst the Appalachian mountains in southwest Virginia.

Anime and manga critic **Joan D. Vince** is the two-time Hugo Award–winning author of the *Snow Queen* cycle and the Cat books. She has had stories published in all the major SF magazines and has written adaptations of a number of more than a dozen films. Her most recent novel is *Tangled Up in Blue*, a novel in the Snow Queen universe. Her novels *Catspaw* and *The Summer Queen* have recently been reprinted by Tor Books. She's working on *LadySmith*, a "pre-historical" novel set in bronze-age Western Europe. She lives in Madison, Wisconsin.

Jacket artist **Thomas Canty** has won the World Fantasy Award for Best Artist. He has painted and/or designed covers for many books and has art-directed many other covers in a career that spans more than twenty years. He has produced the cover art for *The Year's Best Fantasy and Horror* series since its inception. He lives outside Boston, Massachusetts.

Packager **James Frenkel** has been an editor for Tor Books since 1983 and is currently a senior editor. He has also edited various anthologies, including *True Names and the Opening of the Cyberspace Frontier*, *Technohorror*, and *Bangs and Whimpers*. He lives in Madison, Wisconsin.

BY STEPHEN HUNTER

Hot Springs

Time to Hunt

Black Light

Violent Screen: A Critic's 13 Years on
the Front Lines of Movie Mayhem

Dirty White Boys

Point of Impact

The Day Before Midnight

Target

The Spanish Gambit

The Second Saladin

The Master Sniper

STEPHEN HUNTER

Hot Springs

A NOVEL

SIMON & SCHUSTER
New York London Toronto Sydney Singapore

SIMON & SCHUSTER
Rockefeller Center
1230 Avenue of the Americas
New York, NY 10020

This book is a work of fiction. Names, characters, places, and incidents either are products of the author's imagination or are used fictitiously. Any resemblance to actual events or locales or persons, living or dead, is entirely coincidental.

Manufactured in the United States of America

10 9 8 7 6 5 4 3 2 1

Library of Congress Cataloging-in-Publication Data
Hunter, Stephen, date
Hot Springs : a novel / Stephen Hunter.
p. cm.
1. World War, 1939–1945—Veterans—Arkansas—Hot Springs—Fiction.
2. Gangsters—Arkansas—Hot Springs—Fiction.
3. Hot Springs (Ark.)—Fiction. I. Title.
PS3558.U494 H6 2000 813'.54—dc21 99-088530
ISBN 0-7432-0427-1

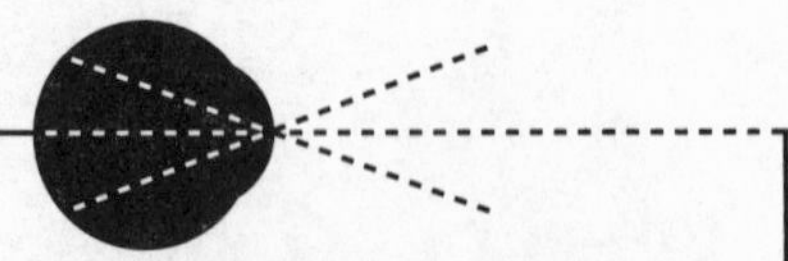

This Large Print Book carries the
Seal of Approval of N.A.V.H.

For my brothers, Andy and Tim,

and my sister, Julie,

who already know the story,

and for my children,

Jake and Amy,

and Julie's children,

Hannah and Sarah,

who will only read it.

My country! America! That is it!

—Audie Murphy, *To Hell and Back*

PART ONE

Wet Heat

CHAPTER 1

Earl's daddy was a sharp-dressed man.

Each morning he shaved carefully with a well-stropped razor, buttoned a clean, crackly starched white shirt, tied a black string tie in a bow knot. Then he pulled up his suspenders and put on his black suit coat—he owned seven Sunday suits, and he wore one each day of his adult life no matter the weather, all of them black, heavy wool from the Sears, Roebuck catalogue—and slipped a lead-shot sap into his back pocket, buckled on his Colt Peacemaker and his badge, slipped his Jesus gun inside the cuff of his left wrist, adjusted his large black Stetson, and went to work sheriffing Polk County, Arkansas.

But at this particular moment Earl remembered the ties. His father took pride in his ties, tying them perfectly, so that the knot was square, the bows symmetrical and the two ends equal in length. "Always look your best," he'd say, more than once, with the sternness that expressed his place in the world. "Do your best, look your best, be your best. Never let up. Never let go. Live by the Book. That's what the Lord wants. That's what you must give."

So one of the useless things Earl knew too much about—how to clear the jam on a Browning A-3 when it choked with volcanic dust and the Japs were hosing the position down would be another—was the proper tying of a bow tie.

And the bow tie he saw before him, at the throat of a dapper little man in a double-breasted cream-colored suit, was perfectly tied. It was clearly tied by a man who loved clothes and knew clothes and took pleasure in clothes. His suit fitted him well and there was no gap between his collar and the pink flesh of his neck nor between his starched white shirt and the lapel and collar of his cream jacket. He was a peppy, friendly little man, with small pink hands and a down-homey way to him that Earl knew well from his boyhood: it was a farmer's way, a barber's way, a druggist's way, maybe the feed store manager's way, friendly yet disciplined, open so far and not any farther.

"You know," Harry Truman said to him, as Earl stared uncertainly not into the man's powerful eyes behind his rimless glasses, but at the perfect knot of his bow tie, and the perfect proportioning of the twin loops at either end of it, and the one unlooped flap of fabric, in a heavy silk brocade, burgundy, with small blue dots across it, "I've said this many a time, and by God I will say it again. I would rather have won this award than hold the high office I now hold. You boys made us so proud with what you did. You were our best and you never, ever let us down, by God. The country will owe you as long as it exists."

Earl could think of nothing to say, and hadn't been briefed on this. Remarks, in any case, were not a strong point of his. On top of that, he was more than slightly drunk, with a good third of a pint of Boone County bourbon spread throughout his system, giving him a slightly blurred perspective on the events at which he was the center. He fought a wobble that was clearly whiskey-based, swallowed, and tried to will himself to remain ramrodded at attention. No one would notice how sloshed he was if he just kept his mouth closed and his whiskey breath sealed off. His head ached. His wounds ached. He had a stupid feeling that he might grin.

"Yes, sir, First Sergeant Swagger," said the president, "you are the best this country ever brought forth." The president seemed to blink back a genuine tear. Then he removed a golden star from a jeweler's box held by a lieutenant colonel, stepped forward and as he did so unfurled the star's garland of ribbon. Since he was smallish and Earl, at six one, was largish, he had to stretch almost to tippy-toes to loop the blue about Earl's bull neck.

The Medal of Honor dangled on the front of Earl's dress blue tunic, suspended on its ribbon next to the ribbons of war displayed across his left breast, five Battle Stars, his Navy Cross, his Unit Citations and his Good Conduct Medal. Three service stripes dandied up his lower sleeves. A flashbulb popped, its effect somewhat confusing Earl, making him think ever so briefly of the Nambu tracers, which were white-blue unlike our red tracers.

A Marine captain solemnized the moment by reading the citation: "For gallantry above and beyond the call of duty, First Sergeant Earl Lee Swagger, Able Company, First Battalion, Twenty-eighth Marines, Fifth Marine Division, is awarded the Medal of Honor for actions on Iwo Jima, D plus three, at Charlie-Dog Ridge, February 22, 1945."

Behind the president Earl could see Howlin' Mad Smith and Harry Schmidt, the two Marine generals who had commanded the boys at Iwo, and next to them James Forrestal, secretary of the navy, and next to him Earl's own pretty if wan wife, Erla June, in a flowered dress, beautiful as ever, but slightly overwhelmed by all this. It wasn't the greatness of the men around her that scared her, it was what she saw still in her husband's heart.

The president seized his hand and pumped it and a polite smattering of applause arose in the Map Room, as it was called, though no maps were to be seen, but only a lot of old furniture, as in his daddy's house. The applause seemed to play off the walls and paintings and museumlike hugeness of the place. It was July 30, 1946. The war was over almost a year. Earl was no longer a Marine. His knee hardly worked at all, and his left wrist ached all the time, both of which had been struck by bullets. He still had close to thirty pieces of metal in his body. He had a pucker like a mortar crater on his ass—the 'Canal. He had another pucker in his chest, just above his left nipple—Tarawa, the long walk in through the surf, the Japs shooting the whole way. He worked in the sawmill outside Fort Smith as a section foreman. Sooner or later he would lose a hand or an arm. Everyone did.

"So what's next for you, First Sergeant?" asked the president. "Staying in the Corps? I hope so."

"No sir. Hit too many times. My left arm don't work so good."

"Damn, hate to lose a good man like you. Anyhow, there's plenty of room for you. This country's going to take off, you just watch. Just like the man said, You ain't seen nothing yet, no sir and by God. Now we enter our greatness and I know you'll be there for it. You fought hard enough."

"Yes sir," said Earl, too polite to disagree with a man he admired so fervently, the man who'd fried the Jap cities of Hiroshima and Nagasaki and saved a hundred thousand American boys in the process.

But disagree he did. He couldn't go back to school

on this thing they called the GI Bill. He just couldn't. He could have no job selling or convincing. He could not teach because the young were so stupid and he had no patience, not anymore. He couldn't work for a man who hadn't been in the war. He couldn't be a policeman because the policemen were like his daddy, bullies with clubs who screamed too much. The world, so wonderful to so many, seemed to have made no place in it for him.

"By the way," said the president, leaning forward, "that bourbon you're drinking smells fine to me. I don't blame you. Too many idiots around to get through the day without a sip or two. This is the idiot capital of the world, let me tell you. If I could, if I didn't have to meet with some committee or other, I'd say, come on up to the office, bring your pint, and let's have a spell of sippin'!"

He gave Earl another handshake, and beamed at him with those blue eyes so intense they could see through doors. But then in a magic way, men gently moved among them and seemed to push the president this way, and Earl that. Earl didn't even see who was sliding him through the people, but soon enough he was ferried to the generals, two men so strong of face and eye they seemed hardly human.

"Swagger, you make us proud," one said.

"First Sergeant, you were a hell of a Marine," said the other. "You were one goddamned hell of a Marine, and if I could, I'd rewrite the regs right now and let you stay in. It's where you belong. It's your home."

That was Smith, whom many called a butcher or a meat-grinder, but who breached the empire on Marine bodies because there was no other way to do it.

"Thank you, sir," said Earl. "This here thing, it's for all the boys who didn't make it back."

"Wear it proudly, First Sergeant," said Old Man Schmidt. "For their sakes."

Then Earl was magically whisked away again and, like a package at the end of a conveyor belt, he was simply dumped into nothingness. He looked around, saw Junie standing by herself.

She was radiantly pretty, even if a little fearful. She had been a junior at Southeast Missouri State Teachers College, in Cape Girardeau, he the heavily decorated Marine master sergeant back on a bond drive before the big push for the Jap home islands. She was a beautiful girl and he was a beautiful man. They met in Fort Smith, at a USO dance, and got married that weekend. They had four days of delirious love, and then he went back to the war, killed another hundred or so Japs, got hit twice more, lost more men, and came home.

"How're you doing?" he said.

"Oh, I'm fine," she said. "I don't want anybody paying me any attention at all. This is the day for the hero, not the hero's wife."

"I told you, Junie, I ain't no hero. I'm just the lucky sonofabitch who walked away from the shell that killed the ten other guys. They're giving me the medal of luck today, that's all."

"Earl, you are a hero. You should be so proud."

"See, most people, let me tell you. They don't know nothing. They don't know how it was. What they think it was, what they're giving me this thing for, see, it had nothing to do with nothing."

"Don't get yourself upset again."

Earl had a problem with what the world thought as opposed to what he knew to be true. It was always getting him into trouble. It seemed few of the combat men had made it back, but because he was a big hero people were always stopping him to tell him what a great man he was and then to lecture him on their ideas about the war.

So he would listen politely but a little bolt of anger would begin to build until he'd be off and some ugliness had happened.

"You can't be so mad all the time," she said.

"I know, I know. Listen to me. You'd think the Japs had won the way I carry on. When is this mess going to be over?"

He slipped around behind Junie and used her as cover, reaching inside his tunic to his belt line and there, where Daddy had carried his sap for putting down the unruly nigger or trashy white boy, he carried a flask of Boone County bourbon, for putting down unruly thoughts.

He got it out smoothly, unscrewed its lid, and in seconds, with the same easy physical grace that let him hit running targets offhand at two hundred yards with a PFC's Garand, had it up to his lips.

The bourbon hit like bricks falling from the roof. That effect he enjoyed, the impact, the blurred vision, the immediate softening of all things that rubbed at him.

"Earl," she said. "You could get in trouble."

Who would care? he thought.

A young Marine captain without a hair on his chin slid next to them.

"First Sergeant," he muttered, "in about five minutes the car will take you back to the hotel. You'll have a couple hours to pack and eat. The Rock Island leaves at 2000 hours from Union Station. Your stateroom is all reserved, but you should be at the train by 1945 hours. The car will pick you and your luggage up at 1900 hours. Squared away?"

"Yes sir," said Earl to the earnest child.

The boy sped away.

"You'd think they could supply you with a combat fellow," said Junie. "I mean, after what you did for them."

"He's all right. He's just a kid. He don't mean no harm."

In fact the young man reminded him of the too many boys who'd served under him, and never came back, or if they came back, came back so different, so mangled, it would have been easier on them if they hadn't come back at all.

"You should be happy, Earl. I can tell, you're not."

"I'm fine," he said, feeling a sudden need for another gigantic blast of bourbon. "I just need to go to the bathroom. Do you suppose they have them in a fine place like this?"

"Oh, Earl, they have to. Everybody goes to the bathroom!"

A Negro servant was standing near the door, and so Earl made his inquiry and was directed through a hall and through a door. He pulled it closed behind him, snapped the lock.

The toilet was of no use to him at all, but he unbuttoned his tunic and slid the bourbon out, and had a long swallow, fire burning down the whole way, rattling on the downward trip. It whacked him hard. He took another and it was done. Damn!

He took a washcloth, soaked it in cold water and wiped down his forehead, almost making the pain there go away for a bit, but not quite. When he hung the washrag up, the pain returned. He dropped the flask into the wastebasket.

Then he reached around and pulled out his .45 automatic.

I carried this here gun on Iwo Jima and before that on Tarawa and Guadalcanal and Saipan and Tinian. He'd done some killing with it too, but more with his tommy gun. Still, the gun was just a solid piece on his belt that somehow kept him sane. The gun, for him, wasn't a part of death, it was a piece of life. Without the gun, you were helpless.

This one, sleek, with brown plastic grips and nubby little sights, was loaded. With a strong thumb, he drew back the hammer till it clicked. He looked at himself in the mirror: the Marine hero, with the medal around his neck, the love of his country, the affection of his wife, with a full life ahead of him in the glamorous modern 1940s!

He put the gun against his temple and his finger caressed the trigger. It would take so little and he could just be with the only men he cared about or could feel love for, who were most of them resting under crosses on shithole islands nobody ever heard of and would soon forget.

"Earl," came Junie's voice. "Earl, the car is here. Come on now, we have to go."

Earl decocked the automatic, slipped it back into his belt, pulled the tunic tight over it, buttoned up and walked out.

CHAPTER 2

They walked out to the car in the West Portico of the White House.

"Your last official duty as a United States Marine," said the young captain, who seemed a good enough kid. "You should be very proud. You accomplished so much. I should salute you, First Sergeant. You shouldn't salute me."

"Son, don't you worry about it," Earl said. "You'll git your chance, if I know the world."

They reached the car, an olive-drab Ford driven by a PFC.

The captain opened the door for Earl and Junie.

Suddenly Earl was seized with a powerful feeling. When he got in the car, the door slammed shut, then it was all over, forever—that part of his life. A new part would start, and where it would lead he had no idea. He was not a man without fear—he'd lived with fear every day for three years in the Pacific—but the fear he felt now was different. It wasn't a fear that threatened to overwhelm you suddenly, to drive you into panic, into letting your people down, that sometimes came under intense fire. It was deeper; it was fear down in the bones or even the soul, it was the fear of the lost. It came from far away, a long time ago.

He shook his head. The air was oppressive, like the air of the islands. The huge wedding cake of the White House office building rose on the left; around, the green grass and trees moldered in the heat. Beyond the gate, black fleets of cars rolled up and down Pennsylvania.

Earl grabbed Junie. He held her hard and kissed her harder.

"I love you," he said. "I really, truly do. You are the best goddamn thing ever happened to me."

She looked at him with surprise, her lipstick smeared.

"I can't drive back," he said. "I just can't. Not now. I don't feel very good. Tell the kid. I'll see you tonight in the room, before we leave for the train."

"Earl. You'll be drinking again."

"Don't you worry about nothing," he said with fake cheerfulness. "I'm going to take care of everything."

If there was pain on her face, he didn't pause to note it. He turned, reached to his neck and removed the beribboned medal, wadded it and stuffed it in his pocket. He reached the street, turned to the left and was soon among the anonymous crowds of a hot Washington late afternoon.

REDS KILL 4 MARINES IN CHINA, a headline on the *Star* screamed.

Nobody cared.

"UNTOLD MILLIONS" LOST IN WAR FRAUD the *Times Herald* roared.

Nobody paid any attention.

NATS DROP TWO yelled the *Daily News.*

OPA OKS 11% PRICE HIKE announced the *Post.*

Earl pushed his way through it all, among anonymous men in straw fedoras and tan suits and women in flower print dresses with their own huge hats. Everybody seemed so colorful. In his years in the Marine Corps he had adjusted to a basically monochromatic universe: OD and khaki and that was it. Yet America was awaking from its long commitment to wartime austerity, the windows were suddenly full of goods, you could buy gas again, makeup on the women was expected, and the men wore gay yellow ties against their white shirts, as if to speak to a springtime of hope.

The medals on Earl's chest and the darkness of his deep blue tunic excited no attention; everybody was familiar with uniforms and the medals meant little. They'd seen heroes. Many of them were heroes. He joined their anonymity, just another nobody meandering up Connecticut toward who knows what. Soon enough he came to a splurge of freedom, which was Farragut Square, with its trees, its benches, its stern admiral staring toward the White House. Pigeons sat and shat upon the naval officer and young men and women sat on the park benches, talking of love and great hopes for tomorrow.

A low growl reached the park, and people looked up, pointing.

"Jets!"

A formation of the miracle planes flew high overhead, southwest to northeast, each of the four trailing a white feathery contrail, the sunlight flashing off the sleek silver fuselages.

Earl had no idea what specific type of plane they were and found the concept of a silver airplane fairly ridiculous. In the Pacific, the Japs would zero a bright gleamy bird like that in a second, and bring it down. Planes were mottled brown or sea-blue, because they didn't want you seeing them until they saw you. They weren't miracles at all, but beaten-up machines for war, and there were never enough of them around. But these three P-whatevers blazed overhead like darts, trailing a wall of sound, pulling America toward something new. Pretty soon, it was said, they'd be actually going faster than sound.

"Bet you wish you had them babies with you in Berlin," a smiling bald guy said to him. "You'd have cooked Hitler's ass but good, right, Sarge?"

"That's right," said Earl.

He walked ahead, the echo of the jets still trembling in his ear. The walls of the city closed in around him, and the next exhibit in the freak show of civilian life was something in a window just ahead, which had drawn a crowd. It appeared to be a movie for free streaming out of a circle atop a big radio. On its blue-gray screen a puppet jigged this way and that.

"Look at that, sir," said a Negro woman in a big old hat with roses on it and a veil, "that's the television. It's radio with pictures."

"Don't that beat all?" said Earl.

"Yes sir," she said. "They say we-all goin' own one, and see picture shows in our own homes. Won't have no reason to go out to the movies no more. You can just stay home for the picture show. They goin' show the games there too, you know, the baseball and that like. Though who'd stay home to see the Senators, I declare I don't know."

"Well, ma'am," he said, "the president himself told me it's just going to git better and better."

"Well, maybe so. Wish my Billy was here to see it."

"I'm sorry, ma'am. The war?"

"Yes sir. Someplace in Italy. He wasn't no hero, like you, he didn't win no medals or nothing. He was only a hospital orderly. But he got kilt just the same. They said it was a land mine."

"I am very sorry, ma'am."

"Hope you kilt a lot of them Germans."

"No, ma'am, I did fight the Japanese, and I had to kill some of them."

"Same thing," she said bitterly, then forced a broken smile upon him, and walked away.

Billy's death on some faraway Neapolitan byway stayed with Earl. Billy was part of the great adventure, one of the hundreds of thousands who'd died. Now, who cared? Not with jet planes and the television. It was all going away.

Get your mind off it, he told himself.

He was feeling too much again. He needed a drink.

He walked along until he found stairs that led downward, which he followed into a dark bar. It was mostly empty and he bellied up to the edge, feeling the coolness of the air.

A jukebox blared.

It was that happy one about going for a ride on the Atchison, Topeka and the Santa Fe. That damn Judy sounded like she was about to bust a gut with pleasure. A train ride. A big old fancy train ride.

Back in Ohio where I come from
I've done a lot of dreamin' and I've traveled some,
But I never thought I'd see the day
When I ever took a ride on the Santa Fe.

The only trains he remembered took him to wars or worse. Now he had a few hours that would take him back to a train ride to—well, to who knew what?

"Poison, Sarge? Name it, and it's yours. One drink, on me for the USMC. Made a man out of my son. Killed him, but made a man out of him."

It was the bartender.

"Sorry about your boy," said Earl, confronting another dead man.

"Nah. Only good thing he ever did was stand up to the Japs at Okinawa. You there?"

"Missed that one."

"Well, he was a bad kid, but he had one good day in his life, when he didn't run from the goddamned Japs. Marines taught him that. I never could. God bless the Marines. What'll it be?"

"You carry Boone County?"

"Never heard of it."

"Must just be an Arkansas liquor. Okay, I'll try that Jim Beam. With a bit of water. Some ice."

"Choo choo ch'boogie," said the barkeep, mixing and serving the drink. "Here's your train, right on time."

Earl took a powerful sip, feeling the muted whack of the booze. It made his fears and his doubts vanish. He felt now he was the equal of the world.

"No, he wasn't no good," said the bartender. "Don't know why he was such a yellow kid. I rode him but good, but he ran from everything. How he ended up in—"

"Mister," said Earl, "I much appreciate this here free drink. But if you say a Marine who stood and fought on Okinawa was no good one more time, I'm going to jump over this bar and make you eat this glass, then the bar, then all the stools."

The bartender, a very big man, looked at him, and read the dark willingness to issue endless violence in Earl's eyes, and swallowed. Earl was a big man too, made almost of leather from his long hard years under a Pacific sun. He was dark and glowery, with leathery pouches under his eyes from too much worry, but he had a bull's neck and those eyes had the NCO's ability to look through you and pin you to the wall behind. His jet-black hair was close-cropped but stood up like barbs of wire on his skull. Under his tunic, his rangy body, though full of holes, was well packed with lean muscle. His veins stood out. His voice didn't speak so much as rumble or roar along, like the Santa Fe. Heated up, he would be a fearsome sight and then some. When he spoke in a certain tone, all men listened, as did the bartender now.

The bartender stepped back a bit.

"Look, here's a twenty," Earl said, peeling off his last big bill. "You put the bottle on the bar, then you go be with some other folks. You can tell them how bad your son was. You can't say it to me."

The bottle came; the bartender disappeared.

Earl worked on the bottle; the bottle worked on Earl. By the time it was a third gone, he was happy: he had forgotten who he was and why he was there. But by the time he reached the halfway point again, he remembered.

Choo choo ch'boogie, came another train song off the juke, driving rhythms, so full of cheer and hope it made him shiver.

> I just love the rhythm
> of the clickety-clack
> Take me right back
> to the track, Jack.

Trains again. What he remembered about trains was they took him to ships and then the ships took him out into the sea.

He remembered the 'Canal, that time it got to hand-to-hand, and he and his young boys on the ridge were fighting the Japs with entrenching tools and knives and rocks and rifle butts. There was no ammo because the planes hadn't come in weeks. The Japs were crazy then; they came in waves, one after the other, knowing the Marines were low on ammo, and just traded lives for ammo until the ammo was gone. Then it was throat-and-skull time, an exertion so total it left you dead or, if you made it through, sick at yourself for the men whose heads you'd split open, or whose bellies you ripped out, or who you'd kicked to death. And you looked around and saw your own people, just as morally destroyed. What you did for something called your country that night! How you killed! How you gave your soul up!

Then, Tarawa. Maybe the worst single moment of the whole thing: oh, that walk in was a bitch. There was no place to go. The bullets splashed through the water like little kids in an Arkansas lake, everywhere. Tracers looped low overhead, like ropes of light, flickery and soft. You were so low in the water you couldn't see the land or your own ships behind you. You were wet and cold and tired and if you slipped you could drown; your legs turned to lead and ice but if you stopped you died and if you went on you died. You tried to keep your people together, keep them moving, keep them believing. But all around you, men just disappeared until it seemed you were alone on the watery surface of the planet and the Japs were a nation hell-bent on one sole thing: killing you.

Earl blinked away a shudder, took another pure gulp of this here Jim Beam, as it was called. Fine stuff. He looked at his watch. He had a trip upcoming on the Atchison, Topeka and the Santa Fe, but where it would take him and why, he couldn't remember.

Iwo, in the bunker. That he would never forget.

He killed his way along Charlie-Dog. His flamethrower people hadn't made it. The captain was hit. There was no cover, because you couldn't dig into the ash; it just caved in on you. He jumped into a nest, hosed it with his tommy. The bullets flew and bit into the Japs. It blew them up, tore them apart. Earl had blood on his face, Jap blood. But he kept going, nest to nest, shooting up the subsidiary positions until he'd finally killed his way to the main blockhouse.

It was secured from within. On top of that he had no weapon, as the tommy had become so fouled with ash and blood it had given up. He could hear the Nambus working from the other side of the blockhouse.

He raced back to the nest he'd just cleared, threw a Jap aside and pulled three grenades off his belt. The Jap things, you banged them to arm them. He grabbed them, ran to the metal blockhouse door, banged them hard and dumped them. He was back dragging the Nambu out from under more dead Japs when the triple concussion came.

The next part was hard to remember, but also hard to forget. He was in the blockhouse. Give this to the Japs, goddamn were they soldiers. They fought to the end, pouring fire out off Charlie-Dog, killing every moving thing they saw. They would die to kill: that was their code. Earl jumped from room to room, or rather chamber to chamber, for the place had a low, dark insect-nest quality to it, and it stunk: shit, blood, food, fear, sweat, old socks, rot, rice. He jumped into a chamber and hosed it down. But he didn't know the Nambu was loaded up with tracers.

When he fired in the smoky darkness, the blue-white tracers tore through all, struck hard surfaces and bounced and bounced again, crazed and jagged. Each squirt on the trigger unleashed a kind of neon structure of pure light, blue-gray, flickery, flung out to embrace the Japs, far more power with the careening bullets than he'd have thought possible. It was like making lightning.

He raced from chamber to chamber, pausing to change magazines on the hot thing in his hands. Odd gun: the mag locked in top, not on the bottom where it would make some sense. It was no BAR; only guys who dreamed up samurai swords and kamikaze planes and human-wave attacks would have cooked up such a silly, junky thing. It even looked slant-eyed. But it worked, always.

In the last room, they waited for him with the predator's eerie calmness. They were out of ammo. He didn't care. They didn't care. What happened they expected, as did he. They faced him; one had a sword out and high, but no room to maneuver in what amounted to a sewer tunnel, illuminated by a gun slit. He sprayed them with light and they danced as their own 6.5s tore through them. When they were down, he changed magazines, sprayed them again, unleashing the lightning. Then he threw the hot little machine gun away.

Earl looked at what he had wrought: a massacre. It was too easy. The Japs were committed elsewhere, their eardrums blown out by the shelling and the gunfire, their sense of duty absolute. He merely executed them in a sleet of fiery light. He heard a moan from the last chamber and thought: one is alive. But then he heard a clank, meaning that a grenade had been primed, so out he spilled, maybe a tenth of a second before the detonation, which shredded the last of the wounded.

He returned to the surface, clambering for breath. Men from his platoon had made it up Charlie-Dog now that the blockhouse guns were silenced but if they spoke to him, he didn't hear, for his ears too were temporarily ruined by the ringing.

"Burn it out," he screamed.

One of the flamethrower teams disinfected the blockhouse with a cleansing two-thousand-degree ray of pure heat; the radiance drove them all back.

The captain was saying, Goddamn he never saw nothing like it, except the captain was from something called Yale and so what he said in that odd little-girl voice of his was "I don't believe I have ever seen a more splendid example of field-expedient aggression." Or something like that.

Earl and his bottle took one more dance. It hit him again, and drove the thoughts out of his head, but then the thoughts came back again.

What was bothersome was the faces. They were vanishing. In one melancholy afternoon in the hospital on Guam after the bad wound on Iwo, he'd done the arithmetic, learned its savage truth.

He had been a sergeant in the Second Marines, then a platoon sergeant also in the Second, and the company gunny sergeant in the Second. When the new Fifth Marine Division was organized in September 1944, he'd been assigned to its 28th Regiment and promoted to first sergeant of Able Company. He had a total of 418 young Marines under him and had been directly responsible to three lieutenants, a captain and finally a major. Of those, 229 had been killed outright. The rest had been wounded, including himself, seven times, three times savagely. None of the officers survived. Of his NCO friends with whom he served at the Marine Detachment in Panama on December 7, 1941, he was the only survivor. Of the company professionals, including officers, from that day, he was the only survivor. Of his first platoon in the Second Marines, on Guadalcanal, he was one of ten survivors; of his company that went into the water off Tarawa, 232 men, he was one of thirty-three survivors; of his company of 216 men that hit the black-ash beach at Iwo, he was one of 111 survivors, but he had no idea how many of them had been wounded seriously. On Tinian and Saipan the numbers were a little better, but only by the standards of the Pacific war.

He knew he should not be alive, not by any law of math, and that the medals he had been awarded were much more for the brute violation of the numbers than for any kind of heroism. Manila John Basilone, the bravest man he ever knew, won the Medal of Honor on a ridge on the 'Canal, stopping a Jap attack with a .30 water-cooled and a fighting spirit and nothing else; he made a bond tour, became a celebrity, married a pretty gal, and was blown to pieces in the black ash of Iwo that first day.

Across from the bar Earl saw himself in a mirror, his eyes black as the black in floodwaters as they rise and there's no high ground left. His cheeks were drawn, and his gray lips muttered madly. He swallowed, blinked, and opened his eyes to see himself again. He saw an empty man, a man so tired and lost he hardly was worth the oxygen he consumed, or the bourbon he drank.

He felt so unworthy.

You ain't no damned good, his father's voice reached him, and he was in agreement with the old man.

I ain't no damned good. Any one of those men was better than me. Why in hell ain't I with them?

Earl took another whack on the bourbon, finished it, looked at his watch. His vision was so blurry he couldn't read it, but given the amount of alcohol he'd drunk, he'd probably missed the train back to Fort Smith, and there'd be all kinds of hell to pay.

He stood up uncertainly, and walked across the bar, and found the men's room. He went in, pulled the door shut, locked the door, took a leak, took out his .45 and thumbed back the hammer.

At no time in the war did he feel as disconsolate as he did now. It wasn't right that he was alive and so many others were dead, and that he had a medal in his pocket that certified him as a HE-RO and they had nothing but white crosses on islands no one would ever visit and would soon forget.

He put the pistol to his temple, felt its pressure, circular. His finger touched the trigger, then pressed it.

The gun didn't fire.

It shivered as it snapped, the small vibration of a hammer falling on a firing pin that leaped forward to strike nothingness. He looked at it, then slipped the slide back a notch, saw that the chamber was empty. He removed the magazine, and found six .45 cartridges, but someone had very carefully taken out the mag and ejected the chambered shell, then replaced the mag. He *knew* he'd loaded it that morning.

Did she do it? She didn't know nothing about guns. Who did it? Maybe he forgot to chamber it? What the hell was going on?

He reloaded, this time threw the slide to fill the chamber and cock it, ease the hammer back to its seating.

He stuffed the gun back in his belt, drew his tunic tight, and unlocked the door.

The lobby of the Carlton Hotel was bright and full of swirling beauty. The light seemed to dance, as if the walls were made of glass. Maybe the VJ Day party was still going on. It was full of pretty young women and their swains, all of them so excited about television and jet planes they could hardly stand it.

Earl slipped through the revelers; everyone was in a tuxedo or a formal gown and gay young things rushed this way and that, hungry for tomorrow to get here.

The boys all were shaven and looked soft; he knew he shouldn't hate them, but he did, and he let that hatred bore through his blur and he felt he needed another drink. Not a fifth of bourbon, but just something to make the pain in his head go away, like a whiskey sour or a gin and tonic or a mint julep. He glanced at his Hamilton and discovered to his relief that he hadn't missed the train; it wasn't yet 7:00. He had time for—

"Sergeant Swagger?"

He turned.

Two men stood beside him. One was a handsome, polished charmer, with a gloss of black hair and movie star teeth, somewhere in his thirties. The other was much older, a gloomy bag of a man, with a sad leathery face and a slow way of moving. He had long arms that his suit only partially disguised and the most gigantic hands Earl had ever seen on a man. His fedora was pushed back carelessly, and his white shirt was gray and spotted. But his eyes were so wary and quick they made Earl think of Howlin' Mad Smith's, or some other old, combat-hard Marine. Earl saw a strap across his chest, under the tie, that indicated the presence of a shoulder holster and from the strain it showed, he knew it carried a big gun.

"Sergeant Swagger," said the first, in tones that Earl then related to his native state, "we've been waiting here for you. Your wife is upstairs packing. She said you'd be along directly."

"What is all this, sir?" said Earl.

"Sergeant Swagger, we've come to discuss a job."

"A job? I got a job. I work in a goddamned sawmill."

"No, a job in law enforcement."

"Who the hell are you?"

"My name is Fred C. Becker and a week ago I won a special election as prosecuting attorney for Garland County, Arkansas."

"Hot Springs?" said Earl. "Now what would you want with me?"

"Hot Springs is the wildest town in America. We have gamblers, we have gunmen, we have whores, we have more crooks than you can shake a stick at and many of them are wearing uniforms and carrying guns. All run by New York mobsters. Well, sir, I'm going to clean up Sodom and Gomorrah and I'm looking for a good man. Everyone I talk to says you're the best."

CHAPTER 3

The city's tallest skyscraper was a spire of art deco, byzantine, glamorous, bespeaking the decadent pleasures of an empire. And from the apartment on the top floor, the empire was ruled.

"It's very New York, eh? I mean, really, one must agree. It's *very* New York," our proud host said to his number-one guest.

"You can say that again," said the guest.

They were quite a pair. One, with the English accent, was in his mid-fifties, five foot ten, solid beef, with a handsome swarthy face. That was our host. He wore an elegantly fitted white dinner jacket, with a rose cummerbund. It fit him like a coating of thick cream poured by a delighted milkmaid. A carnation sparkled in his lapel. His hair was slicked back, and he smoked a cigarette in a holder. He wore a dapper little mustache, just a smudge of one, to suggest not merely masculinity but a certain savoir faire in affairs of business and, as well, the heart. In his other hand, he held a thin-stemmed martini glass. Onyx cuff links gleamed from his cuffs.

"Me," said the other, "now I'm not saying nothing against this, you understand. It's beautiful. It's very beautiful. But I'm a homier guy. I got a place that's what they call Tudor. It looks like a king from your country could have lived there."

"Yes, old man. I know the style. Quite appropriate, I would say. It's actually named for a king's family."

"Yeah," said the guest, "that's me all the way. A real fucking king." He smiled, showing a blast of white teeth.

He was ruddier. He glowed with animal vitality. He wore expertly fitted clothes too, but of a sportier nature, a creamy linen sport coat over a crisp blue oxford shirt, open at the collar. He wore mohair slacks and dazzlingly white bucks. An ascot, a little burst of burgundy silk, completed the ensemble, and in his strong fingers, he clutched a fine Cubano.

"But this is okay," he said again. "It's real swank." He was shorter, more muscular, tanner, more athletic. He had big hands, wide shoulders, a linebacker's pug body. His eyes were especially vivid, as he gobbled the room up. He was not stupid, but he was not really smart either.

"Do you know who did it?" asked his host.

"Did it?"

"The decor. You hire a decorator. You just don't do it yourself. One could never come close."

"Oh," said the sport. "Yeah, a decorator."

"Donald Deskey. The same fellow who did the interiors at Radio City Music Hall. Hence, the wood, the high gloss, the art moderne, the streamline. Why, Cole Porter would be comfortable here."

He gestured with his cigarette holder, and his apartment gleamed before him, cherrywood walls dusky in the glow of muted golden lighting from torchères and sconces, black-lacquered furniture supported by struts of gleaming metal that could have been pried off the *20th Century Limited.* Silk-brocaded drapes billowed in the breeze from the terrace door, and outside the lights of the city sparkled, infinitely tempting.

In the corner of the cherrywood cathedral, a small band played, and a Negro singer with marcelled hair crooned into a microphone. It was up-tempo, smooth as silk, very seductive, about the glories of Route 66 that you'd encounter on the way to Califor-ni-ay. Next to them, another Negro served drinks, martinis mostly, but the odd bourbon or Scotch, to a fast, glamorous crowd. The movie star Dick Powell was there, a craggily handsome head mounted upon a spindly body, a man who beamed beauty and good feeling, and his truly beautiful wife, a woman so unusually comely that in any normal room she would stop traffic. But not this room. Powell's screen girlfriend June Allyson stood off to a side, a small woman, almost perfectly configured but seeming more like a kewpie doll, with her fetching freckles and her spray of blond hair and her crinkly blue eyes.

The other specimens were not so perfect. One was the writer John P. Marquand, surrounded by some admiring fans, all of them exquisitely turned out. Another was the football star Bob Waterford, a gigantically muscular man with a thick mane of hair. He was so big he looked as though he could play without pads. Walter Winchell was expected later. Mickey Rooney was also rumored to be planning an appearance, although with the Mick, one could never be too sure. The Mick burned legendarily hard at both ends of the candle, and he kept to his own schedule. That was the Mick. Then there were the usual assorted politicos, gambling figures and their well-turned-out, even high-bred women.

But the center of attention was another beautiful woman. Her shoulders, pale in the golden light, yielded to the hint of breasts so soft and pillowy that an army could find comfort there, and were cupped as if for display by the precision of her gown, just at the crucial point, where there was but a gossamer of material between her nipples and the rest of the world. She had almost no waist at all, a tiny, insect's thing. Her ample hips were rounded and her buttocks especially firm. The red taffeta evening gown she wore showed all this off, but it was cut to reveal a hint of her shapely legs, made muscular and taut by the extreme rake of her high heels. Her face, however, was the main attraction: it was smart, but not intellectual, say rather cunning. Her features were delicate, except for that vulgar, big, luscious mouth. Her eyes were blue, her skin so pale and creamy it made everyone ache and her hair genuine auburn, like fire from a forbidden dream, a rapture of hair.

"Hi, babe," called the Sporty Guest from across the room, for she was with him.

She ignored him and continued to jiggle ever so seductively to the music, as if in a dreamworld of rhythm. Her dance partner smiled nervously at the boyfriend and Our Host. He was a small, pale boy, weirdly beautiful, not really a good dancer and not really dancing with the woman at all, but merely validating her performance by removing it from the arena of sheer vanity. He had thin blond hair; his name was Alan Ladd, and he was in pictures too.

"I better watch her," said the sport to our host, "she may end up shtupping that pretty boy. You never know with her."

"Don't worry about Alan," said Our Host, who knew such things. "It's not, as one would say, on Alan's dance card, eh, old man? No, worry instead about the blackies. They are highly sexualized. Believe me, I know. I once owned a club in Harlem. They like to give the white women some juju-weed, and when they're all dazed, give them the African man-root, all twelve inches of it. Once the white ones taste that pleasure, they're ruined for white men. I've seen it happen."

"Nah," said the sport. "Virginia's a bitch but she knows if she fucks a *schvartzer* I'll kick her ass all the way back to Alabama."

Our Host aspired to British sophistication in all things, and made a slight face at this vulgarity. But, unfazed and in his own mind rather heroic, he kept on.

"Ben," he said. "Ben, I must show you something."

He took his younger compere through the party, nodding politically at this one and that one, touching a hand, giving a kiss, pausing for an introduction, well aware of the mysterious glamour he possessed, and led his guest to an alcove.

"Uh, I don't get it," said Ben.

"It's a painting."

"I understand that it's a painting. Why is it all square and brown? It looks like Newark with a tree."

"I assure you, Ben, that our friend Monsieur Braque has never seen Newark."

"You couldn't tell that from the painting. Looks like he was *born* there."

"Ben, try to *feel* it. He's saying something. Use your imagination. As I say, one must *feel* it."

Ben's handsome face knitted up as if in concentration, but he appeared to feel nothing. The painting, entitled *Houses at L'Estaque,* depicted a cityscape in muted brown, the dwellings twisted askew to the right, a crude tree stuck in the left foreground but the laws of perspective broken savagely. When Our Host looked at it, he did feel something: the money he'd spent to obtain it.

"It's the finest work of early Cubism in this hemisphere," he said. "Painted in 1908. Note the geometric severity, the lack of a central vanishing point. It predates Picasso, whom it influenced. It cost me $75,000."

"Wow," said Ben. "You must be doing okay."

"I'm telling you, Ben, this *is* the business to be in. You cannot lose. It's all here and the rule of numbers says over the long haul each day is a profitable day, each year a profitable year. It just goes on and on and on, and nobody has to get killed or blown up and sent for a swim with the fishies of the East River."

"Maybe so," said Ben.

"Come, come, look out from the terrace. At night, it is so impressive."

"Sure," said Ben.

Our host snapped his fingers and instantly black men appeared, one with a new martini and the other with a long, thick Cuban cigar, already trimmed, and a gold lighter.

"Light it, sir?"

"No, Ralph, I have told you that you don't hold the lighter right. I have to light it myself if I want it done correctly."

The Negroes disappeared silently, and the two men slipped between the curtains and out into the sultry night.

Pigeons cooed.

"The birds. Still with the birds, eh, Owney?" said Ben.

"I got to like them during Prohibition. A pigeon will never rat you out, let me tell you, old man."

The pigeons, immaculately kept in a rack of cages against one wall, cooed and shifted in the dark.

Owney downed his martini with a single gulp, set the glass on a table, and went over to the cages. He opened one, reached in and took out one bird, which he held close to his face, as he stroked its sleek head with his chin.

"Such a darling," he said. "Such a baby girl. So sweet. Yes, such a baby girl."

Then he put the pigeon back in the cage, plucked the cigar out of his pocket, and expertly lit it, scorching the shaft first, then rolling the end through the flame, then finally drawing the smoke through the thing fully, letting it bloom and swell, sensing each nuance of taste, finally expelling a blast of heavy gray smoke, which the breeze took and distributed over midtown.

"Now come, look," he said, escorting the younger man to the edge of the terrace.

The two stood. Behind came the tinkle of the jazz, the sounds of laughter, the clink of glasses and ice.

Before them curved a great white way.

Lights beamed upward, filling the sky with illumination. Along the broad way, crowds hustled and milled, too far to be made out from this altitude, but in their masses recognizable, a great, slithering sea of humanity. The traffic had slowed to a stop, and cops worked desperately to unsnarl it. Beeps and honks rose with the exhaust and the occasional squeal of tires. Along the great street, it seemed the whole world had come to gawk at the drama of the place, and the crowd seemed an organism its own self, rushing for one or another of the available pleasures.

"Really, it's a good place," Owney said. "It works, it hums, everybody's happy. It's a machine."

"Owney," said Ben, "you've done a great job here. Everybody says so. Owney Maddox, he runs a great town. No other town runs like Owney's town. Everybody's happy in Owney's town, there's plenty of dough in Owney's town. Owney, he's the goddamn king."

"I'm very proud of what I've built," said Owney Maddox, of his town, which was Hot Springs, Arkansas, and of the grand boulevard of casinos, nightclubs, whorehouses and bathhouses that lined it, Central Avenue, which curved beneath his penthouse on the sixteenth and highest floor of the Medical Arts Building.

"Yeah, a fellow could learn a goddamn thing or two," said his guest, Benjamin "Bugsy" Siegel, of Los Angeles, California, and the organized crime confederation that had yet to be named by its investigators but was known by its members, in the year 1946, simply as Our Thing—to those of them that were Sicilian, "Cosa Nostra."

CHAPTER 4

The bar of the Carlton was one of those rooms that made Earl immediately uneasy. It was full of shapes that had no place in nature, mainly circular ones—round, inscribed mirrors, a round cocktail bar, round little tables, rounded chairs with bold striping. It was the kind of a bar you'd expect on a rocket ship to the moon or Mars.

It mi-IGHT as we-ELL be spa-RING

some pretty boy sang over the radio, getting a strange upward twist into words where no such thing could logically be expected. Everyone was young, exuberant, excited, full of life. Atop the prow that lay behind the bar, stocked with enough bottles to besot a division, a young goddess and her pet fawn pranced. She was sculpturally frozen in Bakelite, the struts of her ribs showing, the struts of the fawn's ribs, all of it gleamy, steamy and wet, from the spray of water, somehow rigged to float across her tiny, perky breasts.

"Hey, look at that," said the older man. "Don't that beat a World's Fair in St. Louie?"

Earl hardly glanced at the thing. It seemed wrong.

The sculpture was naked. He was drunk. The world was young. He was old.

The three scooted to the last table in a line, nestled into the corner, under a mirror clouded with inscribed images of grapes, dogs and women. It was very strange. Nothing like this on Iwo.

A girl came; Becker took a martini, the old man a soda water and Earl his regular poison, the Jim Beam he'd grown so fond of.

"You don't drink, sir?" he asked the older man.

"No more," said the fellow. "No more."

"Anyhow," said Becker, returning to business, "I just won a special election that we got mandated because we proved that the poll tax was unjustly administered by the city administration. We being myself and twelve other young men, all of us veterans with overseas duty and a sense of mission. As of next Tuesday, I become the prosecuting attorney of Garland County. But of the twelve, I was the only one to win. So until the next election, in the late fall, let me tell you where that leaves me. Out on a limb. Way, way out."

Earl appraised him. He was so handsome a man, so confident. In fact, he was oddly mated with the sad-sack old teetotaler with the watchful eyes and the big hands. Who were they? What did they want?

"So I'm in a tough situation," Becker continued. "I'm getting death threats, my wife is being shadowed, it's getting ugly down there. Hot Springs. Not a happy place. Totally corrupt. It's run by an old gas-bag mayor and a judge, but you can forget about them. The real power is a New York mobster named Owney Maddox who's got big-money boys behind him. They own everything, they have a piece of all the pies."

"I still don't see where Earl Swagger fits in."

"Well, what I'm getting at, Sergeant, is that Owney Maddox doesn't want anybody messing with his empire. But that's what I'm sworn to do."

"You must think I'd be a bodyguard," Earl said. "But I ain't no bodyguard. Wouldn't know the first thing about that line of work."

"No, Sergeant, that's not it. In order to survive, I have to attack. If I'm on the defensive it all goes away. We have a chance, a window in time, in which we can take Hot Springs back. They're complacent now, they don't fear me because the rest of the slate lost. What can one man do, they think. If we move aggressively, we can do it. We have to blitz them now."

"I ain't no reformer."

"But you know Hot Springs. Your daddy was killed there in 1942 while you were off fighting the Japanese."

"You been lookin' into me?" Earl said narrowly. He wasn't sure he liked this at all. But then this man was the law, after all, by formal election.

"We made some inquiries," said the old man.

"Well, then you learned it wasn't Hot Springs. It was a hill town way outside of Hot Springs, closer to his home territory. Mount Ida, it was called. And I wasn't fighting the Japs yet. I was on a train with two thousand other suckers pulling cross-country to begin the boat ride out to the 'Canal. And I don't know Hot Springs. My daddy would never take us. It was eighty miles to the east, over bad roads. And it was the devil's town. My daddy was a Baptist down to his toes, hellfire and damnation. If I'd gone to Hot Springs, he'd a-whipped me till I was dead."

"Yes, well," said Becker, running hard into Earl's stubbornness, which on some accounts just took him over, for no good reason.

Earl took another hit on the bourbon, just a taste, because he didn't want his brain more scrambled. But he just didn't get a good feeling about Becker. He glanced at his Hamilton. It was getting near to 7:30. Soon he had to go. Where were these fellows taking him?

He looked at the silent old man next to Becker. What was familiar about him?

"Well, Sergeant—"

But Earl stared at the old man, and then blurted, "Excuse me, sir, I don't know if I caught your name."

"Parker," said the old man. "D. A. Parker."

And that too had a ring somehow.

"You wouldn't be related to—nah."

"Who?"

"You wouldn't be related to that FBI agent that shot it out with all them Johnnies in the '30s. Baby

Face Nelson, John Dillinger, Ma Barker, Bonnie and Clyde. Went gun-to-gun with the bad boys of the Depression. Famous, for a while. An American hero."

"I ain't related to that D. A. Parker one damned bit," said the old man. "I *am* him."

"D. A. Parker!"

"Yes, that's me. I'm not with the Bureau no more. And, no, I never shot it out with Johnny Dillinger, though I come close once or twice. I had nothing to do with Bonnie and Clyde. Them was Texas Rangers operating on the fly in Louisiana that caught up with that set of bad apples and did a day's worth of fine work. I tracked Ma and her boy Freddie to Floriday, but I don't think it was my burst that sent Ma to her grave. We believe she killed her own self. I did put eleven rounds into Freddie, and that finished his hash forever. And I did run into the Baby Face twice. We exchanged shots. I still carry not only a .45 bullet that he put into my leg, but the .45 he put it in there with."

He leaned forward, letting his coat slide open. Earl looked and saw a stag-gripped .45, with a bigger set of sights welded into the slide. The gun hung close to D.A.'s body in a complicated leather shoulder holster and harness, well worn. It was even dangerously cocked, sure sign of a real *pistolero.*

"Anyhow, Swagger," said Becker, trying to regain control of the conversation, "what we're going to do is raid."

"Raid?"

"That's it. I'm setting up a special unit. It's young, unmarried or widowed officers from outside of Arkansas, because I can't have them being tainted by the state's corruption, or having their families hunted. This unit will report only to me, and it won't be part of any police force, it won't be set up within a chain of command or anything. We will hit casinos, whorehouses, sports books, anyplace the mob is running, high-class or low. We will be very well armed. We will squeeze them. That's the point: to squeeze them until they feel it and have to shut down."

Becker spoke as if he were quoting a speech, and Earl knew right away that only a part of what the young man planned was for the citizens of Hot Springs. It would be especially for one particular citizen of Hot Springs, namely Fred Becker.

"Sounds like you'll need a lot of firepower," said Earl.

"We do," said D.A. "I have managed to horsetrade for six 1928 Thompsons. Three BARs. Some carbines. And, since I spent the last four years working for Colt, I talked a deal up so we get a deal on eighteen brand-new National Match .45s. Plus we have over fifty thousand rounds of ammunition stored down at the Red River Army Depot, where we'll train for a while. Twelve men, myself, and the only thing we lack is a sergeant."

"I see," said Earl.

"We need a trainer," said Becker.

"I'm too old, Earl," said D.A. "I been thinking

about this for a lot of years. I've been on raids not only in the FBI but in the Oklahoma City Police Department before then. I been in twenty-eight gunfights and been shot four times. I've killed eighteen men. So what I know, I learned the hard way: it's my opinion that when it comes to gun work, the American policeman ain't got a chance, because he ain't well enough trained. So what I mean to do is put together a professional, well-trained raid team. Lots of teamwork, total backup, rehearsal, preparation, train, train, train. I include the FBI, especially now, when all the old gunfighters have been booted out. When the Baby Face went down, he took two fine young FBI agents with him, because they weren't well enough trained to deal with someone as violent and crazy-goddamn-bull-goose-brave as him. Lord, I wish I'd been there that day. They put seventeen bullets into him and he kept coming and killed them both. He was a piece of work. So I want this unit trained, goddamn it, trained to the eyebrows. But I need someone who can ramrod 'em. I get to be the Old Man. I get to be wise and calm. But I need a 100 percent kick-ass piece of gristle and guts to whip their asses into shape, to beat the lessons into them. I need someone who ain't afraid of being hated, because being hated is part of the job. I need someone who's faced armed men and shot 'em dead. I need a goddamned 100 percent hero. Now, do you see what this has to do with Earl Swagger?"

Earl nodded slightly.

"Earl," said D.A., "you was born for this job like no man on earth."

"So it seems," said Earl, looking around at all the bright young gay things sipping champagne, dancing the jitterbug, laughing brightly, squeezing flesh, and thinking, *Goddamn, I am home again.*

CHAPTER 5

West Virginia flowed by; or maybe it was Ohio. It was hard to tell at night, and the train rattled along forcefully. Earl sat in the private compartment watching America pass in the darkness, feeling the throb of the rails on the track. His head ached, but for the first time, after a day of heroic drinking, he felt as if he were more or less sober.

The private compartment was a last kindness from his country for one of its heroes. No lumpy seats for the Medal of Honor winner, no sitting upright, unable to sleep because the metal in the ribs still hurt and his back ached. But he wasn't drinking.

Junie slept in the lower berth. He could hear her breathing steadily. But he just sat in the leather seat before the little round table, feeling the rhythms and flowing onward toward what would be his new destiny. Then she stirred.

"Earl?"

"I thought you were asleep, honey. You should sleep some."

"I can't sleep when you can't sleep, Earl. Are you all right?"

"Yes ma'am. I'm fine."

"Earl, you were drinking, weren't you? I could smell it on you."

"I stopped for drinks while I was walking, yes. I was celebrating. I was happy. I met the president. I was at the White House. I got the big medal. I got my picture taken. Won't have many days like that."

"Earl, the medal. It was in the pocket of your uniform slacks. The ribbon got all wrinkled. I put it back in the jewelry case. You should take care of it. Someday you will give it to a son."

"Well, honey, if I ever have a son, I don't think I'll say to him, 'See what a big man your father was.' So I think if I ever have a son, I'll just let him grow up without me telling him how great I was, since I never felt great one damn day in my life."

"Earl, you are so angry these days."

"I will put it aside, I swear to you, Junie. I know this ain't been easy for you. I know I have become different than the man you married."

"That Earl was handsome and proud and he looked so beautiful in his uniform. He looked like a movie star. All the girls loved him. I fell so hard in love with him, Lord, I didn't think I'd live till sunrise. Then he asked me to dance with him. But this

Earl is more human than that one. This Earl is more man, more real man. He does his work, even though he hates it, and he never yells at anyone. He's a real man, and he's there every night, and some letter won't come telling me he got killed."

"Sweetie, you are some peach. You are the best."

He leaned over in the dark and gave her a kiss.

She touched him, in a way that let him know that tonight would be a very good night for some intimacy. But he sat back.

"I have to tell you something first."

"Earl, I don't like that tone. What is it? Is it those two men who came to see you?"

"Yes, it is."

"That showboaty fellow in the nice clothes? And that sad old man. I didn't like the showboaty fellow."

"I didn't really like him either, but there you have it. Becker is his name, and he'll be important someday. He's actually an elected official, a politician. Them two fellows offered me a job."

"Did you take it?"

"It means some more money. And it means I won't get my fingers chopped off by the band saw. They'll be paying me a hundred a week. That's more than $5,000 a year before taxes. There's a life insurance plan too, plus medical benefits from the state of Arkansas, so there won't be no worrying about having enough money for a doc. They even gave me a clothing allowance. I'm supposed to buy some suits."

"But it's dangerous."

"Why would you say that?"

"I can tell it from your voice."

"Well, it could be dangerous. It probably won't be. Mainly it's training."

"Training?"

"Some boys. I'll be working with young police officers, training them in firearms usage, fire and movement, generalized tactics, maybe some judo, that sort of thing."

"Earl!"

"Yes ma'am?"

"Earl, you'll be training them for war."

"Well, not exactly, honey. It's nothing like a war. It's for raiding gambling places. This fellow is the new prosecuting attorney down in Garland."

"Hot Springs!"

"Hot Springs. Yes. He's going to try and clean up the town."

"We're moving to Hot Springs?"

Well, damn him if he didn't just let it sit there for a while. He let her enjoy it: the idea of moving out of the vets village at Camp Chaffee, maybe getting a place with a real floor instead of wood slats that were always dirty, and that had walls that went straight up to a ceiling, and didn't arch inward or rattle and leak when it rained. The refrigerator would be big, so she wouldn't have to shop every day. The shower would be indoors; there'd even be a tub. The stove would be gas.

"Maybe so," he finally said. "Maybe in a bit. We'd get a nice house, out of town, away from the commotion. It can get plenty hectic in that place."

"I'm not coming, am I, Earl?"

"No ma'am. Not at first. I have it worked out, though. You'll be fine. The paycheck will come straight to you. You can put a certain part of it in a state bank account, and I'll write checks from that for my spending money. You'll get a list of the benefits, and it won't be no time before we can move."

Junie didn't say anything. She stirred, seemed to roll over and face the bunk atop her, and when she finally settled she seemed further away.

"See, it won't work out, having you down there," he said. "Not at first. I'm going to be in Texas for a while, where we're going to train these kids, then we move up to Garland. But I ain't even going on the raids. I'm more the trainer and the sergeant. I have to ride herd on the younger fellows, just like in the Corps, that's all. And there's a security issue, or so they say, but, you know, it's just being careful."

"I can tell in your voice. You'll go on the raids. It's your nature."

"That's not the plan. They don't want a big fancy hero type like me getting shot."

"That may not be the plan, but you have a nature, and you will obey it. It's to lead other men in battle and help them and prevent them from getting hurt. That is your nature."

"They didn't say a thing about that. The reason

we don't want the women down there is just some precautions. It's very corrupt in Hot Springs. Has been for years. All the cops are crooked, the newspapers are crooked, the courts and the judges are crooked."

"I heard they have gangsters there, and whores. That's where Al Capone went and Alvin Karpis and Ma Barker went to relax and take hot baths. They have guns and gangsters. It's where your father got killed."

"My father died in Mount Ida, and he could have died anywhere on earth where there's men who rob other men, which is everywhere on earth. He didn't have nothing to do with Hot Springs. All that other stuff, you can't believe a lick of it. It's old hillbilly boys with shotguns."

"Oh, Earl, you're such a bad liar. You're going off to a war, because the war is what you know best and what you love best. And you're going to leave me up in Fort Smith with no way to get in contact with you and I'll just have to wait and see if somebody doesn't come up with a telegram and say, Oh, Mrs. Swagger, the state of Arkansas is so sorry, but your husband, Earl, is dead. But it's okay, because he was a hero, and this here's another nice piece of plated gold for your trouble."

"Junie, I swear to you nothing will happen to me. And even if it does, well, hell, you got $5,000 and you're still the most beautiful gal in Fort Smith and you don't have to stay in the hut, you could probably find an apartment by that time, when this housing mess is all cleared up. It'll all get better, I swear to you."

"And who raises your son?"

"My— I don't have a son."

"No, maybe it's a daughter. But whatever it is, it sure is getting big in my stomach."

"Jesus," said Earl.

"I wasn't going to tell you until after the ceremony, because I wanted the ceremony to be all for you. But then you went off and you didn't show up all afternoon."

"I'm sorry, sweetie. I never would have guessed."

"What do you think happens? You can't grab me four times a week without getting a baby out of it."

"I thought you liked it when I grabbed you."

"I *love* it. You didn't ever hear me saying no, did you?"

"No ma'am, guess not."

"But it doesn't make a difference, does it?"

"I promised them. I said yes. It's more money. It's a better life."

"Think about your boy, Earl."

But Earl could not. Who'd bring a kid into a world where men fry each other with flamethrowers, machine-gun each other or go at it hand-to-hand, with bayonets and entrenching tools? And now this atom bomb thing: turn the earth into Hiroshimas everydamnwhere. He looked at her, indistinct in the dark, and felt her distance. He thought of the tiny being nestled in her stomach and the thought terrified him. He never asked to be a daddy, he didn't think he was man enough for it.

He was scared. He had a sudden urge, almost overwhelming, to do what he'd never done in the Pacific: to turn, to run, to flee, to leave it all behind him.

He saw his own melancholy childhood, that weary cavalcade of fear and pain. He didn't want that for his boy.

"I— I don't know what to say, Junie. I never thought about no boy or girl before. I just never figured on it."

He had another feeling, one he felt so often: that he was once again failing someone who loved him.

He wished desperately he had a gift for her, something that would make it all right, some little thing.

And then he thought of it.

"I will make you one promise," he said. "It's the only one. I will quit the drinking."

CHAPTER 6

The kid was hot. The kid was smoking. His strawberry-blond hair fell across his pug face, a cigarette dangled insolently from his lips, and he brought the dice, cupped into his left hand, to his mouth.

"Oh, baby," he said. "Jimmy Hicks, Captain Hicks, Captain Jimmy Hicks, Jimmy Hicks, Sister Hicks, Baby Hicks, Sixie from Dixie, sexy pixie, Jimmy Hicks, Baby Hicks, Mamma Hicks, oh, baby, baby, baby, you do what Daddy says, you sweet, sweet baby six!"

A near religious ecstasy came across his face as he began to slowly rotate his tightly clutched fist, and sweat shone brightly on the spray of freckles on his forehead. His eyeballs cranked upward, his lids snapped shut, but maybe it wasn't out of faith, only irritation from the Lucky Strike smoke that rose from his butt.

"Go, sweetie, go, *go!*" said his girlfriend, who hovered over his shoulder. She looked about ten years older than he, had tits of solid, dense flesh, and her low-cut dress squeezed them out at you for all to see. Her lips were red, ruby red, her earrings diamond, her necklace a loop of diamond sparkle, her hair platinum. She touched the boy's shoulder for good luck.

With a spasm he let fly.

The dice bounded crazily across the table and Earl thought of a Jap Betty he had once seen, weirdly cartwheeling before it went in. The Betty had settled with a final splash and disappeared; the dice merely stopped rattling. He looked back at the kid, who was now bent forward, his eyes wide with hope.

"Goddamn!" the boy screamed in horror, for the cubes read three and four, not the two and four or the three and three or the five and one he needed, and that was the unlucky seven and he was out.

"Too bad, sir," said the croupier with blank professional respect, and with a rake, scooped up what the kid had riding, a pile of loose twenties and fifties and hundreds that probably amounted to Earl's new and best yearly salary.

The kid smiled, and pulled a wad of bills from his pocket thick as Dempsey's fist.

"He crapped out," Earl said to D.A., who stood next to him in the crowded upstairs room of the Ohio Club, watching the action. "And he's still smiling. How's a punk kid like that get so much dough to throw around? And how's he get a doll off a calendar?"

"There's plenty more where that came from," said D.A. "You don't go to the pictures much, do you, Earl?"

"No, sir. Been sort of busy."

"Well, that kid is named Mickey Rooney. He's a

big actor. He always plays real homespun, small-town boys. He looks fourteen, but he's twenty-six, been married twice, and he blows about ten thousand a night whenever he comes to town. I hear the hookers call him Mr. Hey-kids-let's-put-on-a-show!"

Earl shook his head in disgust.

"That's America, Earl," said D.A. "That's what y'all was fightin' for."

"Let's get out of here," Earl finally said.

"Sure. But just look around, take it all in. Next time you see this place, you may be carrying a tommy gun."

The club was dark and jammed. Gambling was king here on the upstairs floor, and the odor of the cigarettes and the blue density of the smoke in the air were palpable and impenetrable. It smelled like the sulfur in the air at Iwo and the place had a sort of frenzy to it like a beach zeroed by the Japs, where the casualties and supplies have begun to pile up, but nobody has yet figured out how to move inland. And the noise level was about the same.

At one end of the room a roulette wheel spun, siphoning money out of the pockets of the suckers. A dozen high-stakes poker games were taking place under low lights. In every nook and cranny was a slot and at each slot a pilgrim stood, pouring out worship in the form of nickels and dimes and silver dollars, begging for God's mercy. But craps was the big game at the Ohio, and at even more tables the swells bet their luck against the tumble of the cubes and piles of cash floated around the green felt like icebergs. Meanwhile, some Negro group diddled out hot bebop licks, crazed piano riffs, the sound of a sax or a clarinet or some sad instrument telling a tale of lost fortunes, love and hope.

Earl shook his head again. Jesus Christ, he thought.

"We got to keep moving, Earl," said the old man. "They don't like baggage in a joint like this. You play or you leave."

As they moved downstairs, they passed through the crowded bar. Five girls tended it, hustling this way and that to stay with the demand. Behind them, in the elaborate mahogany structure, ranks of dark bottles promised an exciting form of numbness.

"You want a drink, Earl?"

"Nah," said Earl. "I gave that shit up."

Earl wore a new blue pinstripe three-piece suit and a brown fedora low over his eyes. He had a yellow tie on, and a nice shiny pair of brown brogues. He felt like he was wrapped in bandages but he looked like $50 worth of new goods, which is what he was.

"Probably a good thing," said D.A. "I won sixteen gunfights drunk, but, goddamn, there came a time when I was drinking so much I was afraid I'd wake up in Hong Kong with a busted nose, a beard, a tattoo and a brand-new Chinese family to support."

"Happened to more than a few Marines I knew," Earl said.

They walked out onto the street. Before them, on the other side of Central like seven luxury liners tied up in dockage, the town's seven main attractions—bathhouses—blazed against the night, and even now were crowded with people seeking the miracle power of the waters, which emerged from the unseen mountain behind them at a steady, dependable, mineral-rich 141 degrees.

People had been coming to this little valley for centuries and so the city had acquired an odd clientele: it was for those in need. If you needed health and freedom from the cricks of arthritis or the rampages of the syph you came to Hot Springs and soaked for hours in the steamy liquid, which if nothing else numbed the pain and cleaned out your dark crevices. When you got out, you felt like a prune. Better? Well, possibly. At least you felt different. But as the years passed, the city grew to offer the fulfillment of other needs, all of them elemental, and its clientele by the year 1946 was not merely the old and the infirm but the young and the very firm: there was no human need that could not be satisfied in Hot Springs in a single evening, from sexual to financial to criminal to redemptive.

The city the hot spigots nurtured was spread along the curve of a now-buried creek, the one side buttressed by the bathhouses, the other by the town's commercial strip, which was a hurdy-gurdy boardwalk: oyster houses, restaurants, shooting galleries, nightclubs, casinos, sports books and of course whorehouses. The street was a broad boulevard, and lit so well it appeared to be a kind of limited daylight. Only the mountain, which the U.S. government owned, was invisible, but every other damn thing was there to see.

"It's like Shanghai in '36," said Earl, "except the whores' eyes ain't slanty."

From their vantage point—across Central, standing on the sidewalk before the Fordyce Bath House and looking up and down the street, which ran between the mountains and seemed to be guarded at the north end by a gigantic gateway consisting of the vast Arlington Hotel on one side and the much taller Medical Arts Building on the other—it seemed gigantic. The lights rolled away to either horizon, a mile of sin and hustle. Yet that was only Hot Springs' most visible self. From the main thoroughfare, other roads curved up into the hills, and each block had a whorehouse and a casino and a sports book, sometimes more than one each. Out Malvern, the color turned black, for in Hot Springs sin knew no racial barriers, and the action got even smokier and steamier out there, toward the Pythian Hotel and Baths, the only place in town where the Negroes who actually provided the labor for the place could sample the burning waters.

"Boy, I don't see how Becker is going to close this place down with just twelve of us," Earl said. "It would take a division."

"Well, here's the drill," said the old man. "There's

maybe five hundred sports books in this town, and they're the heart of the operation. Everything feeds off of them. But of them, there's one that's called the Central Book, and all the other books feed off it. It's got all the phone wires and all the race data comes pouring into it; the geniuses in it chalk the odds, and call around town to the other book so that the bets can be laid right up to post time. Then they tab the results, and get them out, and the traffic goes on. It's a great business; the house edge is two percent and the house wins, win or lose. But its problem is it's vulnerable to a wire shutdown. It all depends on how fast they get info from the outside. That's the lifeline. See, here's the deal—if we can shut down that main book, man, we hurt 'em. We *nail* 'em."

"Do we know where it is?"

"Of course not. Lots of folks do, but they ain't gonna be telling us. What we're going to do is hit a variety of places, close 'em down, wreck the machinery, and turn the prisoners over to the cops. The cops won't hold 'em but a day, but the key is wrecking the machinery. You pull those slots off the wall, and you'll see that some of them have been tagged ten or twenty times for destruction by the Hot Springs PD. Somehow, it never gets done. So we smash the slots, wreck the gaming tables, confiscate the money and the slips, and look for financial records or anything that will tell us where the Central Book is. See, it's simple. It's like the war. We take out Jap headquarters and we win."

They were drifting north up Central, and in most of the second- and third-floor windows of the buildings that lined its gaudy west side, girls hung out and called.

"Hey, sugah pie. Hey, you come on up, and we'll teach you a thing or two."

"Come on, baby. Here's where it's so sweet you gonna melt, honey."

"We got the best gals up here, sweetie. We got the prime."

"Care to get laid, Earl?" said the old man.

"Nah. I'll get a dose for sure. Plus my wife has gone and gotten herself pregnant, so I don't need no complications."

"Pregnant? When's it due?"

"Hmm. Truth is, I don't know. She's been that way for a while, only I didn't notice."

"Earl, if I'd a known you had a pregnant wife, maybe I wouldn't have signed you up. This could be scratchy work."

"Don't you worry about it, old man. It's what I do best."

"Shouldn't you be happier? I had a kid, and even though he died young, I never regretted it. Those were happy times. Anyhow, you're going to be a daddy. That's supposed to be a time of joy for every man."

"Ah," said Earl grumpily.

"You'll figure it out, Earl. Believe me, you will."

They moseyed along, past the bathhouses on the

right and the casinos and the whorehouses on the left. In time, the bathhouses gave way to a nice little park, where the city fathers had laid out flower beds and trees and the like. It was so pretty, and behind it rose the mountain which presented Hot Springs with its thermal liquids and turned it into a town like no other.

The sidewalk was crowded, for in Hot Springs nobody stood still. The two undercover men slid through knots of the desperate who'd come to Hot Springs out of the belief its vapors could cure them and knots of the rich, who'd come to Hot Springs out of belief in fun. The former were shabby, scrawny and chalky; they looked half dead already, and they were invisible to the pleasure seekers, who were always sleek and in suits or gowns, with straw hats or veiled hats, usually pink and full, usually hearty and hungry and looking forward to the night's fun. Now and then an HSPD black-and-white would prowl the streets, with a couple of slovenly semicomatose officers looking out, watching the crowd for pickpockets or strong-arm boys.

"We should tell them cops there's gambling going on here," said D.A.

"Why, they'd be shocked," Earl said.

At last they came to a magnificent structure maybe four blocks north of the Ohio Club, literally in the shadow of the Medical Arts Building and the gigantic Arlington Hotel, with its tiers of brightly lit rooms. But as magnificent as the Arlington was, it could not compete with the elegance of the place across the street.

It was the Southern Club. Black marble porticos held up by marble columns announced its palatial ambitions; the whole thing was polished to gleam in the dark like something out of a Hollywood movie set in Baghdad. Inside the foyer, a chandelier glittered, sending slices of illumination into the street; the whole place was emblazoned with lights. Limousines pulled up slowly, letting out their moneyed passengers, and the tuxedo was the order of dress for the men, while the women, usually heavily jeweled, wore diaphanous white gowns that clung to their bodies.

"This is where the high rollers go," said D.A. "This is Owney's masterpiece. Man, the money he makes in there."

"What does he think he is, a king or one of them Egyptian fellows who had a tomb the size of a mountain?"

"Something like that," said D.A. "He's got two casinos in there, three parlors for high-stakes poker, and a lounge where he gets the top stars to come in and perform. I think it's Perry Como this week. He even had Bing Crosby one week. Oh, it's the nicest place between here and St. Louis and here and New Orleans. It's a peach of a place. There ain't no place like it anywhere."

"He's doing well, ain't he?" said Earl, watching the place carefully, as if laying plans for a night attack.

"Let's camp here for a bit and see what we can eyeball."

They found a bench on their side of Central, and watched the show progress, as the slow train of limos each dropped off a matched set of swells. It seemed to be some kind of swell convention. Even Earl in his new blue suit felt underdressed.

"Now let me tell you a little story about where the Southern comes from. In 1940, a bridge washes out above Little Rock, over the Arkansas. So the payroll for the big bauxite operation at the Hattie Fletcher Pit that comes down from Chicago won't be rolling that way, that once. Instead, Alcoa ships the money to Tulsa, and from Tulsa to the nearest railhead, which is Hot Springs. One shipment only, while they're shoring up that bridge over the Arkansas. These payrolls is special, down here in the South—see, in 1940, nobody has checking accounts, so it's got to be all cash money. Over $400,000.

"Anyhow, she rolls into the train yard here at Hot Springs late one Friday night, and fast as you can say Jack Sprat, five very tough cookies hit the train in the yard. They know which car is the mail car and everything. They blow the lock with some kind of specially built bomb device, and climb in. One of the guards pulls a gun, and they shoot 'em all down. Tommy guns, four men shot to death in a second. There's four large vaults in the mail car and they know which one to blow open with nitro; they're out and gone with the payroll in less than three minutes.

Of course the HSPD can't get its cars over here for love nor money; by the time the State Police get a team in it's practically the next morning, and even when the FBI joins up, whoever done it is long gone. Of course they throw up roadblocks, and roust local law enforcement in three states, and put bulletins on the radio and round up all the known armed robbers and shooters in those same three states. But that job was too slick for any local hoods. I don't think Johnny Dillinger himself could have done such a thing, and of course the manhunt don't turn up a damned thing. They just got away as slick as you can imagine. A Marine like you ought to admire it, Earl: it was a commando raid."

"They had to have inside info," said Earl.

"Clearly they did. Now here's the point: two weeks later, Owney Maddox buys the old Congress Hotel, tears it down, and begins to build on this here Southern Club. Where's he get the money? From outside sources? I don't think so; anyhow, Becker can't find no business records and the deed is entirely in Owney's name. Maybe he's tired of sharing with the big boys, maybe he don't want to be tied to them, maybe he sees an opportunity to take the town over lock, stock and barrel. Of course nobody can prove a thing, but there's four widows and a bunch of orphans who got nothing for the deaths of their husbands, except maybe a nice letter from the railroad. And Owney got the Southern Club."

"I hate the kind who pays others to do the killing."

"Well, well, well," said D.A., checking his watch. "Yep, right on time. Back from a nice steak at Coy's. Yes, sir, there's the man himself."

Earl watched as the darkest, fanciest car he'd ever seen pulled down the line of limos. A Negro in livery came out with a whistle, and stopped traffic, so that the car could slide in without having to wait in line.

"It's a bulletproofed '38 Cadillac," said D.A. "It's the biggest in Arkansas. Probably this side of Chicago."

The car was $7,170 worth of black streamline, with its teardrop fenders and its gleaming silvery grille and the white circles of its tires. It was the Fleetwood Town Car Series 75, absolute top of the Caddy line, its V-16 engine displacing 346 cubic inches, its dark sleekness and rakish hood ornament suggesting a hunger to get into the future. The car slid directly to the place of honor, and immediately two more liveried black men rushed out to open the door for Mr. Maddox.

"Just in time for Perry Como," said D.A.

Owney got out, stretched magnificently, sucked in a breath of smoke from his cigarette holder, and ran his other hand over his slicked-back hair. He wore a creamy dinner jacket.

"He don't look so tough," said Earl. "He looks kind of fancy."

"He's British, did you know that? Or sort of British. He came to this country when he was thirteen, and now he puts on airs and calls everybody Old Man and My Dear Chap and Ronald Colman shit like that. But it's all a con. He was running a street gang on the East Side when he was fifteen. He's got a dozen or so kills. He's a tough little monkey, let me tell you."

Hard to match that description with what Earl thought was a toff, a glossy little fellow who paid too much attention to the way he dressed.

Owney leaned over gallantly, put in his hand, and took a long, silvery limb from a lady, and bent to escort her out of the car. She bobbed, then popped up in clear view.

"Now there's a dame," said Earl. "That is a dame."

"That is, that surely is," said D.A. "Now ain't that the goddamndest thing? I know that one and I bet I know our next guest."

The woman stepped sideways, smiling, filling the night with the dazzle of her lips. She was all dessert. She was what all the gals wanted to be, but never could quite make it, and what all the guys wanted to sleep with. Her hair was an auburn cascade, soft as music.

"What's her story?" asked Earl.

"Her name is Virginia Hill. She's a mob gal. They love her in Chicago, where she was special pals with some of the wops that run that town. They call her the Flamingo, she's so long and beautiful. But again, don't let the looks fool you. She's a tough piece of work from the steel towns of 'Bama. She came up the hard way, through the houses. She's a hooker, or used to be one, and she's been around the life a long time. She's twenty-eight going on fifty-eight. And now, the last player. Now, ain't this interesting."

Yes, it was. The third person out of the car was toasty brown, like some sort of football athlete or other kind of ballplayer. He wasn't in a tux at all, but some kind of tan linen, double-breasted, with a yellow handkerchief and a pair of white shoes on. His shirt was storm blue and he wore a white fedora. A cigar was clutched between his teeth, and even from across the street the tautness of his jaws suggested great strength. He radiated something, maybe toughness, maybe self-love, maybe confidence, but some other thing, well off the normal human broadcasting spectrum.

"Who's the punk?" asked Earl.

"That's Benjamin Siegel. Better known as Bugsy, but not to his face. He's a handsome nutcase from the East Side of New York, very connected to the top guys. He was sent out to L.A. a couple of years before the war, where he's been running the rackets and hanging out with movie stars. But it's very damned interesting. What the hell is he doing here, visiting with Owney Maddox? What are them two birds cooking up, I wonder? Bugsy didn't come here to soak his ass in the vapors, I guarantee you."

The three celebrities exchanged an intimate little

laugh and pretended to ignore the gawkers around them, those who felt the power of their charisma. Abreast, they walked up the steps and into the nightclub.

Earl watched them disappear. He squirmed on the bench, feeling a little dispirited. It seemed so wrong, somehow: all those boys dead in the shithole reefs of the Pacific, for "America"; and here was America, a place where gangsters in tuxedos had the best women and the swankiest clubs and lived the life of maharajahs. All that dying, all that bleeding: Owney Maddox. Bugsy Siegel.

"Man," he allowed, "they dress too pretty. Would be a pleasure to git them all dirty, wouldn't it?"

"That's our job," said the old man. "You and me, son. Don't believe they allow no tuxedoes in jail."

CHAPTER 7

Virginia was in a foul mood, not in itself an unusual occurrence, but this morning she was well beyond her usual bounds of anger.

"When are they going to get here?" she demanded.

"I called them. They will get here as fast as they can," said Ben, staring at his favorite thing on earth, his own roughly handsome face in the mirror, as he tried to get his bow tie just right. It was a red number, with little blue symbols of something or other on it. He'd got it at Sulka's, the last time he was in London with the Countess.

"Well, they better shake their asses," Virginia said.

"They" were the squad of bellboys necessary to move the Virginia and Ben show from the Apollo Suite at the Arlington to a limousine to the Missouri-Pacific station for the 4:15, which would take them to St. Louis, where they would transfer to the *Super Chief* on its way back to Los Angeles. So many men were required because wherever Virginia went, she went in style, involving at least ten pieces of alligator luggage. Ben also traveled in alligator and in style, but he disciplined himself to a mere eight cases.

So eighteen suitcases were stacked in the living room of the Apollo Suite, awaiting removal. But Virginia hated to wait. Waiting was not for the Flamingo. It was for the other 99.999999 percent of the world. She decided she needed a cigarette. She walked out onto the terrace and the blinding Arkansas sun hit her. Her sunglasses were already packed. For some reason the sun against her face infuriated her more.

She stepped back into the room, nerves uncalmed by the cigarette. She didn't like to smoke indoors because the smoke clung to her clothes. She was in the mood for a fight.

"This place is a goddamn dump," she said. "Why did we come here? You said I'd meet picture people."

"Sweetie, you did meet picture people. You met Alan Ladd, Dick Powell and June Allyson."

"You idiot," she said. "They ain't *picture people.* They are *Hot Springs people.* Don't you understand the difference?"

"Alan Ladd is big in pictures!" protested Ben.

"Yeah, but his wife manages him and she watches him like a hawk. And she ain't about to help a li'l ol' thang like me! I felt her staring at me! She would have ripped my eyes out, except that if she'd tried, I'd have belted her in the puss so hard she'd see stars for a fucking year. And that Dick Powell, he's like Mr. Bob who ran the company store. Just a big ole politician, slapping the gravy on every goddamn thing! I know his type; big on talk, nothing on getting it done. He'll smile pretty as how-de-do, but he ain't one bit interested in me! I want to meet Cary Grant or John Wayne. I want to meet Mr. Cooper or Mr. Bogart! These are little people. You can't get nowheres in L.A. with little people."

Ben sighed. When Virginia lit up like this, there was no stopping her, short of an uppercut to the jaw, which he had delivered a few times, but she was wearing him down. You can only hit a gal so many times. He wished he had the guts to dump her, but in bed, when the mood was on her, she was such a tigress, so much better than anyone, he knew it was impossible.

"Well, I'm down here on business," he said. "I have a lot to learn from Owney. He has ideas."

"That creep. He's about as British as my Uncle Clytell."

"Sweetie, we'll be back in L.A. in a couple of days. I'll buy you a new mink. We'll throw a big party. Stars will come. But let me tell you! This has been very profitable for me. It's going to get better and better out there. You watch and see where the next ten years take us. We will be so big—"

"You been saying that for six months and you're still the bughouse creep they sent to L.A. to get outta their hair and I still don't have a speaking part! Did you call your lawyer?"

"Well, honey, I—"

"You did not! You are still married to that bag Estelle! You're still Mr. Krakow! Mr. Krakow, would you like some eggs with your bacon and let's take the station wagon to Bloomingdale's, dear, they're having a sale! You ain't moved one step closer to no divorce. You bughouse kike, *I knew you'd lie! You liar! You goddamn liar!*"

She turned, and snatched a $200 lamp off a mahogany end table, lifted it and turned toward him. She advanced, nostrils flaring, eyes lit with pure craziness.

But then his own sweet craziness skyrocketed out of control.

"Don't call me bughouse!" Ben shouted back. Nothing got him ticked faster than that. A white-hot

flash of lightning zagged through his brain, taking all thought and reason from him. He stood, balled his fist and began to stalk his adversary, who approached savagely.

But a knock on the door signaled the arrival of the help, and with a snort, Virginia set the lamp down, opened the door and headed toward the elevator.

Virginia stared stonily at Hot Springs as it drifted by through the Caddy's window. In the broad daylight, it was just another crappy burg, like Toledo or Paducah.

"Virginia," asked Owney, "did you take one of our famous baths? Very soothing."

"I ain't letting no nigger scrub me with a steel-wool mitt while my hairdo melts and my toes wrinkle up like raisins," Virginia said.

"Ah, I see. Well, yes, there is that," Owney replied.

Ben shot him a little look. It said, She's in one of "those" moods.

Owney nodded, cleared his throat, and directed his gaze back to Ben.

"It's a humming joint," said Ben. "You really got something going here."

"So I do. It's called the future."

Ben nodded; it was clear that Owney saw himself not merely as a professional but as some sort of elder wise man, with rare and keen insights. That's why a lot of New York people regarded him as a yakker and didn't miss his pontifications and fake Englishisms a bit. But Ben was curious and had his own ideas.

"The future?"

"Yes. Do you see it yet, Ben? Can you feel it? It's like that Braque hanging in my apartment. You have to *feel* it. If you feel it, its meanings are profound."

Ben's placid face invited Owney onward, and also suggested that Ben was stupid and needed educating, neither of which was true.

"The future. Ben, the wire is dead. The war killed it. It accelerated communications exponentially, old man. We used to control the wire because we controlled the communications. We were *organized.* We could get the race and sports data around the country in a flash, and no other organization, including the U.S. government, was capable of competing. Information is power. Information is wealth. But the war comes along and finally the government understands how important information is to running a global enterprise, and finally they begin to fund research. Once the genie is out of the bottle, there's no putting him back. The next few years will amaze you, Ben. This television? Huge. Person-to-person calling? Instantaneous, without operators or trunk stations. Super adding machines, to make the most arcane calculations the property of the common man. So our great advantage is gone, and with it the source of our wealth and power. We must change!

Change or die! They couldn't see that in New York, but believe me, it is coming. Great change. One must ride it, not fear it, but be able to play it, don't you see?"

Ben nodded sagely. Once in 1940 with the Countess he had stayed at Mussolini's summer retreat and heard that bombastic baldy talk in a similar vein. The future! Tomorrow! Fundamental change!

What did it get him, but an upside-down ride on a meat hook at the end of a piano wire after the gunners got done stitching him, and old lady peasants spitting on his fat carcass?

"Yeah, yeah, I see," said Ben innocently.

"Ben, the future is in casinos. That is where the great wealth will come. A city of casinos, a city we own and operate. That is what I'm trying to build here, slowly and surely, with the long-term goal of making gambling—gaming, we'll call it—legal in Arkansas. It's like a license to mint money. People will come in the millions. They can wander the trails in the afternoons, eat food that's cheap, see the shows—Perry Como and Bing Crosby are just a start—and that night enter a magic world and feel the thrill and the excitement that's formerly been felt only by high rollers and aristocratic scoundrels. They'll pay! They'll pay dearly! Ultimately we will become just another American corporation, like Sinclair Oil or Motorola or RCA. Ultimately, we will *be* America!"

"Talk, talk, talk!" said Virginia. "You chumps, a

Chicago mechanic could clip you and you wouldn't even see it coming. It ain't going to change, Owney. Them old bastards, they got too much riding on the way they do things. They'll kill you before they let you change the fucking rules, without batting an eyelash."

They were talking so furiously none of them noticed the black '38 Ford with two glum detectives following them a few car lengths back.

The train lay like a fat yellow snake, huge and wide and imposing. Its diesel streamline seemed to yearn for a horizon, a plain to cross, a river to vault, a mountain to climb. The engine had a rocket ship's sensible sleekness, and a small cab twenty feet off terra firma. It issued noises and mysterious grumblings and was attended by a fleet of worshipful keepers. Conductors and other factotums prowled the platform, examining documents, controlling the flow into and off the thing. The crowds rushed by.

Amid them, but indifferent, and smoking gigantic cigars, the two lords stood in their magnificent clothes, waiting imperially. It would take time for the boys to get the luggage into the compartment and now Owney and Ben were contemplating history.

"This is where that train was jacked, isn't it?" asked Ben.

"It is indeed, old man."

"Nineteen forty-one?"

"Nineteen forty."

"What was the take?"

"I believe over four hundred thousand in cash. The Alcoa payroll for the Hattie Fletcher bauxite pit. In Bauxite."

"In Bauxite?"

"Yes, old man. They named the town after its only product, which is bauxite. The bauxite of Bauxite rules the world, that is, when applied to aluminum by some alchemical process I couldn't possibly understand, and then built into lightweight ships, planes and guns. We won the war with aluminum. The miracle metal. The metal of the future."

"Damn, sure is a lot of the future here in Hot Springs! It was at this station?"

"Not in the station, per se. It was the mail car, and the train was over in the freight docks. You can't see it from here, but this is really a yard. There are several other tracks, controlled by the tower, and warehouses on the other side. You'll see when you get aboard."

"The crew? They've never been caught?"

"Never. They must have been out-of-towners. No local thief could operate at that level of perfection."

"I heard they were Detroit boys, usually work for the Purples. Some done some time with Johnny D back in the wild times. Good people with guns. I heard Johnny Spanish himself."

"I thought he was dead."

"Nobody will ever kill Johnny Spanish. He's the best gun guy in America."

"Well, if you say so. I thought *I* was the best gun guy in America. I could tell you some *fabulous* adventures I had back in New York before the Great War!"

Both men laughed. Ben took a mighty suck on his cigar, a very fine Havana, and looked around in the late afternoon sunlight. It suddenly occurred to him: where was Virginia?

"Where's Virginia?" he asked, instantly coming alert from his torpor.

"Why, she was here a second ago," said Owney.

"She was pesky this morning. She can get real pesky sometimes," he said, soothing his panic as he eyed the crowd. At last he saw her. She had wandered down the platform to get a cigarette while the boys loaded the bags. But—who was she talking to? He could make out a figure, someone strange, someone he didn't know, but hard to see through the crowds. But then the crowds parted magically, and he saw her companion. A tall, tough-looking gent in a blue suit with a fedora pulled low over his eyes and the look of command and experience to him. Ben smelled cop, and a split second later that little flare of rage fired off in his mind.

"*Goddamn her!*" he exploded, his face white with fury, his temples pulsating, and he began to stride manfully toward his woman.

They spent the morning examining gambling joints from the hundreds in the town, from the smallest, dingiest sports books in the Negro areas out Malvern to some of the more prosaic slot halls on the west side out Ouachita to the elaborate Taj Mahals of Central Avenue. Any one of them could be the Central Book, but how would they know? None of the eight or so they eyeballed, entered, dropped a few bucks' worth of quarters into, seemed remarkable in any way. Then they stopped at a Greek's and had a couple of hamburgers and coffee.

"Is this what cops do?" asked Earl. "They just drive around and look at stuff?"

"Pretty much," said D.A., taking a bite. "But when the shit happens, it happens fast. Just like in the war."

"Okay, Mr. Parker. I believe you."

"Earl, before this is all over, you'll look back on these early days with some nostalgia. This is about as good as it gets."

Earl nodded, and went back to his burger.

Finally, D.A. went off, dropped a nickel and made a call. He came back with a smile on his wrinkled, tanned prune of a face.

"This snitch I got at the Arlington, one of the bellboys, he says Bugsy and the babe are moving out today and the boys are going upstairs to get their luggage and load it up for them. Let's go to the hotel and see if we can't pick 'em up."

Earl threw down his cup of coffee, left some

change at the counter and the two of them went out and got in the Ford.

When they got to the Arlington and parked above it on Central, with the grand entrance in easy view, it didn't take long to pick up the caravan. The limo, which looked like it was thirty feet long, led the way out of the hotel's grand entrance. It was followed by a pickup, full of luggage and black men. And behind that, a third car, a Dodge, where six of Owney's minor gunmen and gofers—they were all from a hillbilly family called Grumley—sat dully, pretending to provide security.

From a few car lengths back, Earl and D.A. followed, taking it nice and easy, and kept contact as the folks in the big limo talked on and on. Earl could see that Bugsy and Owney did most of the chatting. The woman just looked out the window, her features frozen in place. The cavalcade made its way through the heavy traffic up Central, and a traffic cop overrode the light to let it pass, while D.A. and Earl cooled their heels behind the red. By the time they got to the station, the black men had the luggage off the truck and loaded onto a couple of hand carts and were hauling it toward the big yellow train.

"Is that the Atchison, Topeka and the Santa Fe?" asked Earl, as D.A. pulled into a space on Market Street.

"No, Earl, that is not. That is the Missouri-Pacific 4:15 for St. Louis, the first step on the trip back to L.A. Now let's get out and mosey over there and see what there is to see. Probably nothing, but for now I am sick of casing books in Niggertown."

"I roger that," said Earl.

The two split up, and drifted through the gathering crowd as the time of departure approached. Earl lit a cigarette, found a pillar to lean against far down the platform and commenced to smoke and watch. In time, he spotted the two gangsters talking animatedly near the station house, each smoking a gigantic cigar. The two fellows seemed to be having a good enough time. Other than that, nothing much was happening, though more and more people were boarding the train and the conductors seemed a little more frenzied. He glanced at his Hamilton, saw that it was just about 4:00 P.M. The all-aboard would come very soon. His leg hurt a little, as did his left wrist. He flexed his left hand, opening and shutting it, and shifted his weight, trying to keep his mind off of it. He wasn't used to wearing a tie all day, either, and it was getting on his nerves, but he wasn't about to loosen his, even in this heat, until D.A. did the same. He was thinking about a nice hot shower back in his cabin at the Best Tourist Court.

Suddenly someone stood before him, and he cursed himself for his lack of awareness. It was the woman. Her hair was red, and pinned up under a yellow beret. She stood on white, strapped heels in a yellow traveling suit cut right at the knee that showed off more leg than was healthy for anybody. She was staring at him intently, her eyes dark.

"Say, handsome," she said, "did you use your last match to light that butt or would you have one or two others left in the box?"

Nothing shy about this one. And, she smelled great too. Her accent was sugar-dipped, like a fritter hot on a cool Southern morning, and he placed it as either from Georgia or Alabama.

"I might have another one here, ma'am," he said. "Let me just dig through my gear and see."

He stood, pulled the matchbox out from his inside pocket. He deftly opened it, took out a match, and struck it and cupped. He had large hands that protected the fragile flame from any gust of breeze. She came close, cupping his hands in hers, and drew his flame to her Chesterfield.

"There you go," he said.

"Thanks, I needed that." She stood back, inhaled deeply, then exhaled a zephyr of smoke.

"Do I know you?" he asked. "Ain't you in the pictures?"

"Been in a couple, doll," she replied. "But you had to look quick. It's a crappy business unless you know big guys and I just happen to know the wrong big guys. The big guys I know scare the hell out of everybody else. You wouldn't know any big guys, would you, handsome?"

"No ma'am," said Earl, smiling. "I know a couple of generals, that's all."

"Oh, a soldier boy. I thought you might be a cop."

"I used to be a Marine."

"Bet you killed a tubful of Japs."

"Well, ma'am, you just never could tell. It was so fast and smoky."

"My chump boyfriend stayed in L.A. running a sports wire. He's a real hero, the louse. He drags me all the way to this craphole town to meet picture people and they're all small potatoes. It took me ten years to get out of towns like this, and here I am, back again."

"You from Georgia, ma'am?"

"Alabama. Bessemer, the steel town. If you haven't been there, you ain't missed much, sugar. I—"

Earl had the peripheral impression of flailing, of something hot and wild suddenly swarming upon him, animal-like, so fast it was stunning.

"What the fuck is going on?"

It was Bugsy Siegel, his nostrils flaring, his eyes livid with rage. Two flecks of gray gunk congealed in the corners of his mouth. His body radiated pure aggression and his eyes were nasty little pinpricks.

He grabbed the woman, roughly, by the elbow and gave her a powerful yank. The strength of it snapped her neck. He squeezed her arm hard until his knuckles were white.

"What the fuck is this all about, Virginia?" he demanded.

"Christ, Ben, I just got a light from this poor guy," she said as she pulled her arm free.

"Sir," said Earl, "there wasn't nothing going on here."

"Shut up, cowboy. When I talk to you, that's when you talk to me." He turned back to Virginia. "You fucking slut, I ought to smack you in the face. Get to the train. Go on, get your goddamn ass out of here!" He gave her a shove toward the train, and turned after her.

But then he thought better of it, and turned back to Earl. His hot eyes looked Earl up and down.

Earl gazed back.

"What are you looking at, bumpkin?"

"I ain't looking at nothing, sir."

"You fucking dog, I ought to beat the shit out of you right here. I ought to smash you into the pavement, you little nobody. You nothing. You piece of fucking crap." His anger fueled the color of his language.

"Ben, leave the poor guy alone, I started talking to—"

"Shut up, bitch. Get her to the train, goddammit," he barked at two of Owney's Grumleys who'd shown up in support. Earl saw Owney himself with two others back a few steps and around them a cone of onlookers had formed. It was dead quiet.

"Do you know who I am?" Ben said.

"Ben, get ahold of yourself," said Owney.

"He's just a guy on a platform," the woman yelled, pulling away from the two goons.

But now the focus of Ben's rage was entirely

upon Earl, who just stood there with a passive look on his face.

"Do you know who I am?" Siegel screamed again.

"No sir," said Earl.

"Well, if you did, you fucking putz, you would be shitting bricks in your pants. You would be stinking up this joint. You do not want to fuck with me. You don't even want to be in the same state as me, do you understand that, you country fuckhead?"

"Yes sir," said Earl. "I only lit the lady's cigarette."

"Well, you thank your fucking lucky stars I didn't decide to wipe your ass on the railway tracks, you got that, Tex? Do you get that?"

"Yes sir," said Earl.

Bugsy leaned close. "I killed seventeen men," he said. "How many you killed, you pitiful farmer?"

"Ah, I'd say somewhere between 300 and 350," said Earl.

Bugsy looked at him.

"And see," Earl explained further, "here's the funny thing, the boys I killed, they was trying to kill me. They had machine guns and tanks and rifles. The boys you killed was sitting in the park or in the back seat of a car, thinking about the ball game." Then he smiled a little.

At first Bugsy was stunned. No one had ever talked to him this way, particularly not in the face of one of his rampages. And then it struck him that this hick wasn't scared a lick. The guy smiled at Bugsy and—fuck him, fuck him, FUCK HIM!—actually winked.

Bugsy threw his punch with his right. It wasn't a roundhouse, for he was a skilled fighter and knew that roundhouses were easily blocked. It was an upward jab, with the full force of his body behind it, and his reflexes were fast, his strength considerable and his coordination brilliant, all driven by his mottled fury. He meant to punch the cowboy right below the eye and cave in the left side of his face.

He threw the punch and for quite a while—say somewhere between .005 and .006 second—felt the soaring pleasure that triumph in battle always unleashed in him, the imposition of his will on an unruly world, his ego, his beauty, his cunning, all in full expression. He knew important people! He hung out with movie stars! He fucked a countess, he fucked Wendy Barrie, he fucked hundreds of the world's most beautiful starlets! He was Bugsy, the Bugman, Bughouse, friend of Meyer and Lucky, he counted in this world.

Then it all vanished. With a speed that he could never have imagined, the cowboy got a very strong hand inside his wrist to turn the blow, not so much block it, and with his other hand himself strike.

Bugsy was not a coward. He had been in many street fights, and he'd won most of them. He was indefatigable in battle when he had a stake in the outcome, and his rage usually sealed him off from the sensation of pain until hours later. He had been hit many times. But the blow he absorbed took all that away from him. It was a short right-hand punch that traveled perhaps ten inches but it had a considerable education in mayhem behind it, and it struck him squarely below the heart, actually cracking three ribs. It was a hammer, a piston, a jet plane's thrust, an atom bomb. It sucked the spirit from him. The shock was red, then black, and his legs went, and he slipped to the platform, making death-rattle sounds, feeling bile or blood pour from his nostrils to destroy his bow tie. He urped and his lunch came up. He convulsed, drew his legs up to his chest to make the hurt go away, sucked desperately for oxygen and felt something he had not felt in years, if ever: *fear.*

His antagonist was kneeling.

"You know what?" he said. "I only hit you half as hard as I know how. If I see you in this town again, I'll hit you so hard it'll knock your guts out of your skin. Now you get on this train and you go far, far away. Don't come back, no more, no how, not ever."

He stood and looked Owney square in the eye.

"You or any of your boys want to try me, Mr. Maddox, you go right ahead."

Owney and his crew of Grumleys took a step back.

"I didn't think so," said Earl, smiled, winked at the pretty lady and slipped away.

CHAPTER 8

After he regained his voice and his legs, but not his color, Bugsy turned his rage on Owney, demanding to know who the vanished cowboy was. Owney admitted he didn't know at all. As the crew of Owney's Grumley boys led him to the Pullman car and as he nursed the wretched pain in his side, Bugsy passed out what could only be an edict, with the full power of his associates back east behind it: You find out who that guy is. You find out where he lives, who he hangs with, what he does. You mark him well. But do not touch him. I will touch him. Touching him, that's for me, do you understand?

Owney nodded.

Virginia said, "Sugar, you're going to touch him with what now, a howitzer? An atom bomb? A jet?" She threw back her hair, flushed and victorious, and laughed powerfully, a laugh that emerged from a diaphragm as if coated in boiled Alabama sap and grits. "Honey," she said, "you ain't got the guts to face that kind of how-de-do again, let me tell you. Ha! He got you so good! You should have seen the look on your face when he poked you! You poor ol' thing, you done got the white beat off you!"

"Virginia, shut up," said Bugsy. "You were the cause of all this."

"So how was I supposed to know he was Jack Dempsey? Anyhow, you were the idiot that swung on him. Couldn't you see he was a tough guy? He looked tough. He stood tough. He talked tough. And, honey, he sure as hell hit tough!"

"Do you want a doctor, old man?" Owney asked. "We could delay the train."

"And let these hicks laugh at me some more? Let some hick sawbones pick at me? No thank you. Owney, you said you ran a smooth town. You said we'd all be safe here, you owned things, things ran great in Owney's town. And this happens. Some ringer. He had to be a pro boxer. I never saw no guy's hands move that fast, and I never got hit so fucking hard in my life. So maybe this ain't such a safe town and maybe you ain't doing such a good job."

With that he limped bravely up the steps of the Missouri-Pacific and was taken to his Pullman stateroom by a covey of Negro porters.

Virginia followed, but she turned for a last whisper to the befuddled Owney.

"You tell that cowboy to watch out. The goddamn Bugman holds grudges. And tell that sugar boy if he ever comes to L.A. to look me up!"

Shortly, the train pulled out of the station, and Owney hoped that he was forever finished with Benjamin "Bugsy" Siegel, who had come for a "vacation and a bath" at the urging of Meyer Lansky and Frank

Costello, who were big in New York.

"All right," he said when the train pulled out, addressing Grumleys present and elsewhere, "now you know what's going on. Find out who that guy is and find out fast. But don't touch him! Something's going on and I have to know what the fuck it is."

He was troubled: change was coming, he knew, and to ride it out he had to keep things running smoothly down here. Hot Springs had to be a smooth little empire, where nothing went wrong, where boys from all the mobs could come and have their fun, and mix and get together, without problems from the law. That's what he was selling. That was his product. Everything he had was tied up in that. If he lost that, it meant he lost everything.

"Mr. Maddox, he's long gone," said Flem Grumley, one of Pap Grumley's sons and the eldest of these Grumleys. "He just melted so fast into the crowd, we didn't get a fix on him. Who'd have thought a guy would have the balls to paste Bugsy Siegel in the ribs?"

"Find him" was all Owney could think to say.

They drove away from the station in silence. Earl stared glumly into the far distance. His hand hurt a bit. He figured it would be bruised up some in the morning.

"Tell you what," said D.A. finally, "I never saw one man hit another so hard. You must have boxed."

"Some" was all Earl said.

"Pro?"

"No sir."

"Earl, you're not helping me here. Where? When? How?"

"'Thirty-six, '37 and '38. I was the Pacific Fleet Champ, middleweight. Fought a tough Polak for that third championship on a deck of the old battlewagon *Arizona* in Manila Bay."

"You are so fast, Earl. You have the fastest hands I ever saw, faster even than the Baby Face's. You must have worked that speed bag hard over the years."

"Burned a few speed bags out, yes sir, I surely did."

"Earl, you are a piece of work."

"I'm all right," he said. "But I made a mistake, didn't I?"

"Yes, you did, Earl."

"I should have let him hit me?"

"Yes, you should have."

"I think I know that," said Earl, aware somehow that he had failed. He turned it over in his mind to see what the old man was getting at.

"Do you see why, Earl?"

"Yes sir, I do," said Earl. "I let my pride get in the way. I let that little nothing in a railroad station get too big in my head."

"Yes, you did, Earl."

"I see now what I should have done. I should have let him hit me. I should have let him smack me to the ground and feel like a big shot. I should have begged him not to hit me no more. Then he'd think I'se scared of him. Then he'd think he owned me. And if it was ever important, and he came at me again, he'd sail in king of the world, and I'd have nailed him to the barn door so bad he wouldn't never git down."

"That is right, Earl. You are learning. But there's one other thing, Earl. You threw caution to the wind. That was an armed, highly unstable professional criminal, surrounded by his pals, all of them armed. You are unarmed. If you'd have hit him again, you'd probably be a dead man and no jury in Garland County would have convicted your killers, not with Owney's influence on Bugsy's side. So it was a chance not worth taking."

"I'm not too worried about myself," Earl said.

"No true hero really is. But the heroics are over, Earl. It's time for teamwork, operating from strength, careful, professional intelligence, preparation, discipline. Discipline, Earl. You can teach these young policemen we have coming in discipline, I know. But you have to also show it, Earl, embody it. Do you understand?"

"Yes sir."

"It's not a pretty nor a right thing for me to address a hero of the nation in such a way, but I have to tell you the truth."

"You go ahead and tell me the truth, sir."

"That's good, Earl. That's a very good start."

They drove on in silence for a bit.

"Now they know there's a new fellow or two in town," Earl finally said.

"Yes, Earl, they do."

"And that would be why we are not heading back to the cabins?"

"That is it, exactly."

They were driving out Malvern through the Negro section, and now and then the old man eyed the rearview mirror. On the streets, the Negro whorehouses and beer joints were beginning to heat up for a long night's wailing. Mammas hung from the window, smoking, yelling things; on the streets, pimps tried to induce those of either race or any race to come in for a beer or some other kind of action. Now and then a Negro casino, usually smaller and more pitifully turned out than the ones for the white people, could be glimpsed, but mostly it was just black folks, sitting, watching, wondering.

"Tell me, Earl, what was in your room?"

"Some underclothes for a change, some underclothes drying in the tub. Some socks. Two new shirts. A razor, Burma-Shave. A toothbrush, and Colgate's. A pack of cigarettes or two."

"Any books, documents, anything like that? Anything to identify yourself?"

"No sir."

"That's good. Can you live with the loss of that stuff?"

"Yes, I can."

"That's good, because if I don't miss my guess, starting now them boys are going to turn that town upside down looking for the Joe Louis that poleaxed their special visitor. I paid for the cabins through next Monday; if we check out today or make a big folderol about packing and leaving in a hurry, that's a dead giveaway as to who we are. It's best now just to fade quietly. They'll check everywhere for boys who've left suddenly, left in a lurch, left without paying up. So if we don't do anything to draw attention to ourselves, we'll keep them in the dark a little longer."

"Yes sir," said Earl. "I guess I'm a little sorry."

"Earl, in this work, sorry don't matter. Sure is better than sorry. Remember: the mind is the weapon. Think with the mind, not the fast hands."

Owney's Grumleys turned the town pretty much upside down. He had a gang of former bootleg security boys and did all the heavy hitting he found necessary. There were a bunch of Grumleys, all related, including several Lutes, more than a few Bills, and not less than three and possibly as many as seven Slidells, as well as a Vern and a Steve. The Slidell Grumleys were by repute the worst and they had to be kept apart, for they would turn on each other murderously, given half a chance.

A Grumley visited every hotel, tourist court and campground to examine, sometimes sweetly, sometimes not so sweetly, the registration books. Another Grumley or two—usually a Bill and a Lute—traveled the whorehouse circuit. Madams and girls were questioned, and a few sexual adventures were worked in on the sly by this or that Grumley, but such was to be expected. Grumleys were Grumleys, after all. And still another couple of Grumleys checked the bathhouses. Other Grumleys tracked down numbers runners and wire mechanics and instructed them to keep their eyes open double wide. Owney even had some of his Negro boys—these were most definitely not Grumleys—wander the black districts asking questions, because you never could tell: times were changing and where it was once impossible to think of white people hiding among, much less associating with, Negro people, who knew the strangeness of the wonderful modern year 1946? Even the police were brought in on the case, but Owney expected little and got little from them.

In the end, all the efforts turned up nothing. No sign of the cowboy could be unearthed. Owney was troubled.

He sat late at night on his terrace, above the flow of the traffic and the crowds sixteen stories below on Central Avenue, in the soft Arkansas night. He had a martini and a cigarette in its holder in an ashtray on the glass table before him. Beyond the terrace, he could see the tall bank of lighted windows that signified the Arlington Hotel was full of suckers with bulging pockets waiting to make their contributions to Owney's fortune; to the right of that rose Hot Springs Mountain with its twenty-seven spigots of steamy water for soothing souls and curing the clap.

He held a pigeon in his hands—a smooth, loving bird, its purple irises alive with life, its warmth radiating through to his own heart, its breast a source of cooing and purring. The bird was a soft delight.

He tried to sort out his problems and none of them seemed particularly difficult in the isolate, but together, simultaneously, they felt like a sudden strange pressure. He had been hunted by Mad Dog Coll, he had shot it out with Hudson Dusters, he had felt the squeeze of Tom Dewey, he had done time in New York's toughest slammers, so none of this should have really mattered.

But it did. Maybe he was growing old.

Owney petted his bird's sleek head and made an interesting discovery. He had crushed the life out of it when he was considering what afflicted him. It was silently dead.

He threw it in a wastebasket, gulped the martini and headed inside.

PART TWO

Day Heat

AUGUST 1946

CHAPTER 9

On the first morning, Earl took the group of young policemen out to the calisthenics field in the center of a city of deserted barracks miles inside the wire fence of the Red River Army Depot. The Texas sun beat down mercilessly. They were all in shorts and gym shoes. He ran them. And ran them. And ran them. Nobody dropped out. But nobody could keep up with him either. He sang them Marine cadences to keep them in step.

I DON'T KNOW BUT I BEEN TOLD
ESKIMO PUSSY IS MIGHTY COLD
SOUND OFF

ONE-TWO
SOUND OFF
THREE-FOUR

There were twelve of them, young men of good repute and skills. In his long travels in the gardens of the law, D.A. had made the acquaintanceship of many a police chief. He had, upon getting this commission, called a batch of them, asked for outstanding young policemen who looked forward to great careers and might want to volunteer for temporary duty in a unit that would specialize in the most scientifically up-to-date raiding skills as led by an old FBI legend. The state of Arkansas would pay; the departments would simply hold jobs open until the volunteers returned from their duties with a snootful of new experience, which they could in turn teach their colleagues, thus enriching everybody. D.A.'s reputation guaranteed the turnout.

The boys varied in age from twenty to twenty-six, unformed youths with blank faces and hair that tumbled into their eyes. Several looked a lot like that Mickey Rooney fellow Earl had seen in Hot Springs but they lacked Mickey's worldliness. They were earnest kids, like so many young Marines he'd seen live and die.

After six miles, he let them cool in the field, wiping the sweat from their brows, wringing out their shirts, breathing heavily to overcome their oxygen deficit. He himself was barely breathing hard.

"You boys done all right," he said, and paused, "for civilians."

They groaned.

But then came the next ploy. He knew he had to take their fears, their doubts, their sense of individuality away from them and make them some kind of a team fast. It had taken twelve hard weeks at Parris Island in 1930, though during the war they reduced it to six. But there was a trick he'd picked up, and damn near every platoon he'd served in or led had the same thing running, so he thought it would work here.

He named them.

"You," he said, "which one is you?"

He had the gift of looming. His eyes looked hard into you and he seemed to expand, somehow, until he filled the horizon. This young man shrank from him, from his intensity, his masculinity, his sergeantness.

"Ah, Short, sir. Walter F.," said the boy, dark-haired and intense, but otherwise unmarked by the world at twenty.

"Short, I'll bet you one thing. I bet you been called 'Shorty' your whole life. Ain't that the truth?"

"Yes sir."

"And I bet you hated it."

"Yes sir."

"Hmmmm." Earl made a show of scrunching up his eyes as if he were thinking of something.

"You been to France, Short?"

"No sir."

"Well, from now on and just because I say so, your name is 'Frenchy.' Frenchy Short. How's that suit you?"

"Uh, well—"

"Good. Glad you like it. All right, ever damn body, y'all say 'HI FRENCHY' real loud."

"HI FRENCHY" came the roar.

"You're now a Frenchy, Short. Got that?"

"I—"

And he moved to the next one, a tall, gangly kid with a towhead and freckles, whose body looked a little long for him.

"You?"

"Henderson, sir. C. D. Henderson, Tulsa, Oklahoma."

"See, you're already a problem, Henderson. Our boss, his name is D.A. So we can't have too many initials or we'll get 'em all tangled up. What's the C stand for?"

"Carl."

"Carl? Don't like that a bit."

"Don't much like it myself, sir."

"Hmmm. Tell you what. Let's tag an O on the end of it. But not an S. That would make you a Carlo. Not a Carlos, but a Carlo. Carlo Henderson. Do you like it?"

"Well, I—"

"Boys, say Hello to Carlo."

"HELLO CARLO!"

In that way, he named them all, and acquired a Slim who was chunky, a Stretch who was short, a Nick who cut himself shaving, a Terry who read *Terry and the Pirates,* a smallish Bear, a largish Peanut, a phlegmatic Sparky. Running short on inspiration, he concluded the ceremony with a Jimmy to be called James and a Billy Bob to be called Bob Billy and finally a Jefferson to be called not Jeff but Eff.

"So everything you was, it don't exist no more. What exists is who you are now and what you have to do and how Mr. D. A. Parker himself, the heroic federal agent who shot it out with Baby Face Nelson and put the Barker Gang in the ground, will train you. You are very lucky to learn from a great man. There ain't many legends around no more and he is the authentic thing. You meet him tomorrow and you will grow from his wisdom. Any questions?"

There were probably lots of questions, but nobody had the guts to ask them.

For a legend, D.A. cut a strange figure when at last he revealed himself to the men, this time at one of the old post's far-flung shooting ranges. If they expected someone as taut and tough as jut-jawed, bull-necked, rumble-voiced Earl, what they got was a largish old man in a lumpy suit, beaten-to-hell boots and a fedora that looked as if it had been pulled by a tractor through the fields of Oklahoma, who seemed to do a lot of spitting.

It was after the morning run and the boys had changed back into the outfits they'd wear on the street—that is, into suits and ties, and damn the heat.

The old man didn't give any orders at all and didn't mean to command by force but by wisdom. His first move was to invite the boys to sit. Then he noted that it was hot, and since it was hot he suggested they take their coats off. When the coats came off, he walked among them, and looked at their sidearms, mainly modern Smith or Colt revolvers in .38 Special, worn in shoulder holsters, as befits a plainclothesman. One of them even had an old Bisley in .44-40.

"That's a powerful piece of work, young man."

"Yes sir. My grandfather wore it when he was sheriff of Chickasaw County before the Great War."

"I see. Well, it loads a mite slow for our purposes. Don't get me wrong. A Colt single-action's a fine gun. So's a Smith double. But this here's 1946 and it's modern times. So we're going to learn how to get ready for modern times."

"Yes sir," said the boy. "That is why I came here."

"Good boy. Now, I suppose y'all are good shots. Why, I'd bet all of you shot expert on qualification. Let's see how many did. Hands up."

Twelve hands came up, unwavering with the confidence of the young and sure.

"All of them. See that, Earl? They're all experts."

Earl, standing to one side with his arms folded

and his face glowering in the best sergeant's stare, nodded.

"Yes sir. Been known to use a Smith myself," D.A. said. He threw back his coat and revealed what it had not hidden that effectively: his own Smith .38/44 Heavy Duty, with white stag grips, worn on an elaborately carved Mexican holster off a second belt beneath his trousers belt.

"Yes sir, a fine gun. Now tell me, who can do this?"

He reached in his pocket, pulled out a silver dollar. He turned and lofted the coin into the air. It rose, seemed to pause, then fell. His hand a blur, the old man drew and fired in a motion so swift and sudden it seemed to have no place in time. The ping from the coin, and the speed with which it jerked out of its fall and sailed thirty feet further out, signified a hit.

"You," he pointed to the youngest of the boys. "Can you go get that for the old man?"

"Yes sir," said the boy, the one Earl had nicknamed Frenchy yesterday.

Short retrieved the piece.

"Hold her up," said D.A.

The young officer held up the coin, which was distended ever so slightly by the power of the .38 slug punching through its center. The Texas sunlight showed through it.

The boys murmured in appreciation.

"See," said D.A., "y'all think that was pretty neat, huh? Truth is, it's a miss. Because I hit dead center. Usually when I do that trick for the kids, I like to hit closer to the edge, so when they wear it on a thong around the neck, it'll hang straighter. How many of you could do such a thing?"

No hands came up.

"Mr. Earl, you think you could?" asked the old man.

Earl was a very good shot, but he knew that was beyond his skills.

"No sir," he said.

"In fact," said D.A., "there ain't but four or five men in the world who could do that regularly. A Texas Ranger or two. An old buddy of mine named Ed McGivern, a trick shooter. Maybe a *pistolero* in Idaho named Elmer Keith. See, what I got, what them boys I named got, you don't got. That is, a special gift. A trick of the brain, that lets me solve deflection problems and coordinate the answer between my hand and eye in a split second. That's all. It's just a gift."

He turned to them.

"I show it to you because I want you to see it, and forget about it. I'm a lucky man. I'm a very lucky man. You ain't. You're ordinary. You can't do that. Nobody in the FBI could do that. So what I mean to teach you is how an ordinary man can survive a gunfight, not how a man like me can. You've seen fast and fancy shooting; now forget it. Fast and fancy don't get it done: sure and right gets it done. And take them revolvers back to your lockers and lock them up. You won't be using them no more and you won't be shooting with one hand and you won't be trusting your reflexes. This here is the tool of our trade."

He took off his coat, and showed the .45 auto he had hanging under his left armpit in its elaborate leather harness.

"We use the .45 auto. We carry it cocked and locked. We draw with one hand, clasp the other hand to the gun and grip hard, we concentrate on the sights, we lock our elbows until we're nothing but triangles. We got a triangle of arms between ourself and the gun and a triangle of legs between ourself and the ground. The triangle is nature's only stable form. We're crouching a little because that's what our body wants to do when we get scared. We aren't relying on the ability of our mind to do fancy calculations under extreme pressure and we ain't counting on our fingers to do fancy maneuvers when all's they want to do is clutch up. Every goddamn thing we do is sure and simple and plain. Our motions are simple and pure. Most of all: front sight, front sight, front sight. That's the drill. If you see the front sight you'll win and survive, if you don't, you'll die.

"Did I hear a laugh? Do I hear snickers? Sure I do. A man shoots with one hand, you're telling me. All the bull's-eye and police shooting games are set up for one hand. Them old cowboys used one hand and in the movies the stars all use one hand. You don't *want* to use two hands, 'cause that's how a girl shoots. You're a big strong he-man. You don't need two hands.

"Well, that there's the kind of thinking that gets you killed."

He withdrew another silver dollar from his pocket, turned and lofted it high. The automatic was a blur as it locked into a triangle at the end of both his arms and from the blur there sprang the flash-bang of report; the coin was hit and blasted three times as far back as the previous dollar. Again, Short retrieved it. He held it up. It was no souvenir. It was mangled beyond recognition.

"You see, boys. You can do it just as fast two-handed as one."

They worked with standard Army .45s without ammunition for the first day. Draw—from a Lawrence steer hide fast-draw holster on the belt right at the point of the hip—aim, dry-fire. Then cock, relock and reholster. That was D.A.'s system, the .45 carried cocked and locked, so that when you drew it, your thumb flew to the safety as the gun came up on target, and smushed it down even as the other hand locked around the grip and you bent to it, lowering your head and raising the gun until you saw the tiny nub of front sight and the blur of the black silhouette before you.

Snap!

"You gotta do it right slow before you can do it

right fast," he would say. "Ready now, again, ready, DRAW . . . AIM . . . FIRE."

A dozen clicks rose against the North Texas wind.

"Now, again," said the old man. "And think about that trigger pull. Control. Straight back. That trigger stroke has got to be smooth, regular and perfect."

On and on it went, until fingers began to get bloody. Even Earl pulled his share of draws and snaps, aware that he among them all could not complain, could not stop. But there were so many troubling things about it.

Finally a hand went up.

"Sir, are you sure about this? I could draw and shoot much faster with my Official Police. I don't like losing my Official Police."

"Any other questions?"

There was silence, but then one hand came up. Then another. And a third.

"The sights are so much tinier than my Smith. I can't pick them up."

"I heard automatics jammed much more than wheelies. It makes me nervous."

"I think I'd feel better carrying at the half-cock, and thumb-cocking as I drew, like I did with my old single-action."

Mumbles came and went.

And even Earl had his doubts. He didn't like walking about with a pistol on safe. To shoot he had to hit that little bitty safety, and under pressure, that might be tough. He didn't like the idea of pointing a gun at somebody set on killing him and getting nothing out of the effort.

"Earl, how 'bout you?"

"Mr. D.A., you're the boss."

"See, men, that's Earl. That's a good Marine to the last, supporting his old man no matter how crazy. But Earl, if I wasn't the boss, what would you say? Come on, now, Earl, tell these boys the truth."

"Well, sir," said Earl, "under those circumstances I'd say I'se a bit worried about carrying that automatic with the safety on. You got to hit that safety to shoot fast and I know in the islands, we many times had to shoot fast or die. No guns in battle are carried with the safeties on. There may not be time to get them off."

"A very good point, Earl. They're all very good points. Which is why today we make the change. You have to understand what don't work as compared to what do work. Let's head back to the indoors."

The unit trooped back to the explosives disassembly building, which had been appropriated as a classroom. There, against one wall, was a shipping box of cardboard, maybe two feet by two feet, swaddled in tape and labels. Earl looked at the label and saw that it was from something called Griffin & Howe, in New York, and searched his memory for some familiarity with the place, but came up with no answer, though the words had a tone he knew from somewhere.

"Coupla you boys, load this up to the table," commanded D.A. and two of the officers did so, by their effort proving that the box contained a considerable amount of steel.

"Earl, would you please open the box for me."

Earl took out his Case pocketknife and sawed his way through the cardboard and staples and tape. When he got it open, he saw that it contained a nest of smaller boxes from Colt's, of Hartford, Connecticut, each about eight inches by six inches, and beside the Colt's logo, it said National Match Government Model.

"Now, I worked for Colt's for a number of years, so I got a deal on these guns. Then I had 'em shipped to Griffin & Howe, a custom gunsmithy in New York. Earl, take one out, please, and show it around."

Earl pulled one box out, pried the lid off it. Inside, a Colt government model gleamed blackly at him, but he saw immediately that the cardbord of the box was slightly mutilated in one spot, where it meant to hold the pistol snugly, as if something larger than spec had been pushing at the box. He pulled the pistol out.

"See what you got?" D.A. asked. "You tell 'em, Earl."

"The sights are much bigger," Earl noted right away. Indeed, the target pistol's adjustable sights had been replaced with a bigger fixed version, a big flat piece with a cut milled squarely into the center; at the front end, instead of that little nubby thing, there was a big, square, wide blade.

"Oversized rear, Patridge front sights. What else, Earl?"

Earl gripped the pistol and his hand slid up tight to nest it deep and his thumb naturally went to the thumb-safety, which had been enlarged into a neat little shelf with the soldered addition of a plate. His whole thumbprint rested squarely on it. No way he was going to miss that thing.

"Now dry-fire it," the old man said.

Obediently, Earl pointed in a safe direction, thumbed back the hammer, pressed the safety up for on. When he plunged it down with his thumb, the thumb met just two ounces or so of resistance, then snapped downward with a positive break. Earl pulled the trigger, which broke at a clean four pounds, without creep or wobble.

"That is a fighting handgun," said the old man. "The best there is. Completely safe to carry cocked and locked. Its ramp polished and smoothed so that it will feed like a kitten licking milk. A trigger job to make it crisp to shoot. A fast, seven-round reload in two seconds or less. A big-ass .45, the most man-stoppingest cartridge there is, unless you want to carry a .357 Magnum, which would take you two years to master, if that fast. And finally, the shortest, surest trigger stroke in the world. Gents, that's the gun you'll carry, it's the gun you'll shoot, it's the gun you'll live with. It's the gun you'll clean twice a day. It's the gun that'll win your fights for you if you treat it well. I should tell you it was all thought out by a genius. Not me, not by a long shot. But that's what the Baby Face did to his .45s. He was a killer and some say even crazy, but he had more pure smarts about guns of any man since old John Browning himself."

Draw, aim and fire.

Draw, aim and fire.

Two hands, the safety coming off from the thumb's plunge as the second hand came to embrace the first in its grip, the rise of the front sight to the target.

"You don't got to line it up," said the old man. "What you're looking for is a quick index. You have to know that the gun is in line; you don't got to take the time to place the front sight directly between the blades of the rear sights. You got to flash-index on the front sight. You see that front sight come on target and you shoot."

Draw, aim and fire.

Draw, aim and fire.

Earl was surprised how well it worked, once you got the hang of it. It helped that his hands were so fast and strong to begin with, and that he'd fired so many shots in anger and so shots in practice meant nothing. But clearly, he had some degree of exceptional talent: the pistol came out sure, it came up and BANG it went off, almost always leaving a hole in the center of the target.

"Forget the head, forget the heart," counseled the old man. "Aim where he's fattest, and shoot till he goes down. Center hit. Clip him dead center. If he don't go down, if he's still coming, shoot him through the pelvis and break his hipbone. That'll anchor him. Some of these bigger boys take a basketful of shooting before they go down. That's why you have to shoot fast and straight and a lot. Usually, the man who shoots the most walks away."

D.A. watched with eyes so shrewd and narrow they missed nothing. This boy, that boy, this boy again, that one again: little flaws in technique, a tendency to flinch, a lack of concentration, a finger placed inconsistently on the trigger, a need to jerk, or, worst of all, an inability to do the boring work of repetition that alone would beat these ideas into the minds. But D.A. was patient, and kind, and never nasty.

"Short, you are very good, very fast, I must say," he said to the young Pennsylvanian, who, to be sure, was the best of the youngsters, a very quick study.

Short was fast too. Not as fast as Earl or the old man—in time, the old man believed *nobody* would be faster than Earl—but fast. He got it right the first time and kept it right.

Henderson, from Oklahoma, was a bit more awkward. Tall and blond, with arms too long and hands too big, he was all elbows and excess motion. He didn't have the gift for it that Short and some of the others did. But Lord, he worked. He got up early to practice dry-firing and he stayed up late practicing dry-firing.

"You are a worker, son," said D.A.

"Yes sir," said Henderson. "That's what my people taught me." He drew against phantom felons until his fingers were bloody.

"Now this," said Earl, a few days later, "this is the real McCoy."

He held in his hands the .45 caliber Thompson M1928 submachine gun, with its finned barrel, its Cutts compensator, its vertical foregrip, its finely machined Lyman adjustable sight.

Five other such guns lay on the table, sleek and oily.

"Mr. D.A. got a deal with the Maine State Police, which is why these guns all say Maine State Police. This will be our primary entry weapon, not merely for its firepower, but more than anything for its psychological effect. You find yourself on the other side of a gun like this, the thought goes, you don't wanna fight no more. Didn't work with the Japs but it should work with these here Hot Springs hillbillies."

The men looked at the weapon, which he held aloft.

"It's a recoil-powered, open-bolt full automatic weapon. That open-bolt business is important, because it means it can only be fired with the bolt back. You forget to cock it, you are S.O.L. If it don't have a magazine in it, it can't fire, unless you have done stuck a cartridge with your fingers up in the chamber, then cocked it, and I ain't never heard of no man doing that but it's my theory that if there's a way to screw up, some recruit will find it, no matter how well hidden. Don't never put a shell into the chamber because everybody will think it's empty and that's how training accidents happen. You'll have plenty of chance to bleed up in Hot Springs, no need to do it here.

"Now, this evening, I'll teach you how to break it down, how to clean it, how to reassemble it. You will clean it and reassemble it each time you fire it, and the reason for that is the same as the one I gave you earlier: you want to treat it well so it will treat you well. Now, how many men know how to shoot this gun?"

A few hands went up, mainly from the older men who'd joined the unit from State Police agencies.

But so did Frenchy's.

"Frenchy Short, do tell. Well, young man, you come on up here. Where'd you learn to shoot the tommy?"

Frenchy came up.

"My mother knew the police chief of our town. She arranged for me to shoot all the guns for my fifteenth birthday."

"A birthday present. Damn, ain't that something. Come on, Frenchy, show the boys."

So Frenchy went to the firing line, inserted a stick magazine and leaned into the gun.

The Colt Police Silhouette target loomed twenty-five yards downrange, the shape of a man with his wrist planted on his hip.

"Get ready, boys!" Earl said and Frenchy found a good position, and pulled the trigger. Nothing happened. Then he remembered the actuator up top, drew it back with an oily slide of lubricated metal, reacquired the shooting position, and pulled the trigger. Nothing happened.

"Shit!" he said.

"Safety," said Earl.

Frenchy fiddled, eventually turned some lever.

Again he brought the gun to his shoulder.

One shot rang out. The magazine fell to the ground.

"Shit!"

"Now, see, Frenchy here thought he already knew. He didn't wait to learn. He already knew and he wanted to show off. You don't show off at this work, 'cause it'll get you killed. Got that? This is about teamwork, not hey-look-at-me. Also"—he winked at Frenchy—"when you load the mag, you gotta slap the bottom to make sure the mag lock has clicked in. Sometimes it don't lock up all the way but the spring tension holds the mag in place, and you think it's time to bebop. But it don't bebop, it only bops, once. Frenchy didn't know that, the mag kicked loose. So what does he now say to Baby Face Nelson who is walking toward him with a sawed-off? *Slap* that mag hard, *hear* it lock in."

Earl locked the magazine in, gave it a stiff smack with his palm, then drew back the actuator, then spun and shouldered it.

"Plug your ears, boys, but open your eyes. I'm using tracers so's you can watch the flight of the bullets."

He leaned into the gun with a perfect FBI firing position and fired half a magazine and even though his left wrist was stiff with ancient pain, he gripped the foregrip tightly, pulling it in. That was the whole key to the thing. The gun shuddered, the bolt cycled, the empties flew in a spray, the gun muzzle stayed flat though blossoming with blast and flash and spirals of gas, the racket was awesome as the bullets sped off so fastfastfast it seemed like one continuous roar. It was so bright that no flash could be seen but the chemical traces in the tail end of the bullets still igniting, trailing for a split second the incandescence of the round's trajectory. It was there and not-there at once, the illusion of illumination in the form of a line of simple whiteness, almost electrical, straighter than any rule could draw; the line traced from the muzzle to the target without a waver to it. Twenty-five yards downrange Earl's gun gnawed a raggedy hole in the center of the silhouette.

"Great, huh? Well, guess what, that's all wrong.

Never fire more than three-round bursts. In the movies they wail away like that, but that's because right behind the camera they got a bohunk with a case of .45 blanks ready to scoot out and reload when the camera's off and the star's taking his Camel break. You will carry all your ammo, and you don't want to use it up for nothing, and unless you are a genius, every goddamn shot after the third is going into the trees. I happen to be a genius. Maybe Frenchy is too. But no other birds here appear to be. *This* is how we do it."

He turned again, brought the gun into play and tapped out three short three-round bursts. Each burst scored the head of the target, each leaked its flicker of flame. By the end, there was no head, only shredded tatters of cardboard.

They worked with Thompsons in the afternoon and the .45s in the morning for several days. They worked hard, and some got the swing of it faster than others, but by the end, each of them was edging toward some kind of proficiency. The tracers, an old FBI training trick, made it easier for a buddy to read the trajectory of the rounds and advise you when the muzzle roamed, throwing bullets to no particular destination. But Earl warned them only to use the tracers in training, never in battle, because first of all they were a dead giveaway to your position and secondly the trace was incendiary and if fired into dry wood buildings or sage or other undergrowth or dead leaves or whatever, would light up a fire. No problem on an island like Iwo, but not good in a city like Hot Springs, where most of the casinos were old wooden structures.

On the fifth day, Earl introduced them to the BAR.

"Now this here gun is a real Jap-killer. It fires big .30 government cartridges at about twenty-three hundred feet per second and they will tear up anything they hit. If you got a boy behind soft cover, this will punch through and get him. Against cars or light trucks, this here thing is The Answer. Twenty-round clips, effective range out to one thousand yards, gas-operated, man-portable, but no lightweight. About sixteen pounds. They usually come with bipods for support, but the first thing that happens is the bipod is junked. These guns already got their bipods junked. Each squad in the Marines or the infantry had one of these guns; they were the base of fire, set up to cover all squad maneuvers and offer long-range suppressive fire.

"We will use these guns sparingly. They will fire through three walls and kill someone across the street going to the bathroom. But you should know them, anyhow, in case we come up against some real desperadoes, who are hunkered in good and solid and want to shoot it out to the last man. That's when the BAR comes into play. It ain't a John Wayne gun. You don't spray with it like you see in the movies. It's got too much power for that."

But the boys found it much easier to shoot than

the Thompsons, for the reason that it was heavier, and its weight absorbed the recoil better and because the longer .30 governments were much easier to load in the magazines than the stubby .45s for the Thompson. They'd shoot it at the hundred-yard range, and quickly became proficient at clustering five-round bursts center mass on the silhouettes.

Half days were spent on weapons they'd be least likely to use, the Winchester 97 shotguns and the M-1 carbines. And then they took Sunday off, and most went into Texarkana for a movie or some other form of relaxation while Earl and D.A. plotted the schedule. Everybody knew what was coming next.

The fun part.

CHAPTER 10

Owney never held his meetings at the same place twice. It was a habit from the old days. You didn't want to fall into a pattern, because a pattern would get you killed. If you have a Mad Dog Coll hunting you, you learn the elementary lessons of evasion, and you never forget them.

Thus most of the higher-ranking Grumleys, the bigger casino managers, the head bookmakers, the wire manager, his lawyer, F. Garry Hurst, the men who ran the men who ran the numbers runners, and so forth and so on, were used to being banged all over town when Owney convened them.

They never knew when the call would come and what travel it would demand. So today's mandate was usual in the sense that it was no more unusual than any other mandate. He called the meeting for the bathhouse called the Fordyce, on Central, which had been temporarily closed for the occasion.

They sat naked, swaddled in sheets, under an ornate glass roof, multitinted and floral. It was somehow like sitting *in* flowers. It was daytime, as befit business. Sunlight streamed through the window above, incandescent and weirdly lit by the hyacinth-tinted glass. Each had bathed in the 141-degree water until each had felt like a raisin. Then each had been subjected to a needle-pointed shower that ripped open their pores. Now they sat in a steam room, looking like Roman senators in togas, except that the vapors swept this way and that. Outside, Grumleys patrolled to make certain no interlopers or accidental eavesdroppers were in the vicinity. A couple of Grumley gals even moved into the women's bath area, so as to make sure no ladies lurked there.

The meeting was businesslike, though the Owney on display here was not the cosmopolitan Owney the host, anxious to put on a display of savoir faire for an important out-of-towner, complete to a version of a British accent derived more from an actor than from actual memory. In the privacy of his own sanctum, where his power was absolute and his prestige unchallenged, Owney devolved to the tones of the East Side of Manhattan, where he had been nurtured from the age of thirteen through the age of forty-three.

"Nothin'," he said again, chewing on an unlit cigar, another Havana. "You got fuckin' nothin'?"

"Not a dang thing," said Flem Grumley, the senior Grumley since Pap Grumley's clap had kicked in a month ago, declaring that seasoned operative hors de combat. Flem, hardened in the bootlegging wars of the '20s, spoke a brew of Arkansas diction so dense it took years of concentration to master its intricacies. "We's run the town up, we's run it down. These damned old boys done slipped the noose. Damnedest goddamndangdest thang."

Owney chewed this over a bit, shredding his cigar even further.

"Only," said Flem, "only a bit later cousin Slidell, that being Will's boy Slidell, not Jud's nor Bob's, nor—"

"Yeah, yeah," said Owney, to halt the list of Slidell Grumley fathers.

"Uh, yes sir, that Slidell, he done checked back at the Best out Ouachita. Seems a feller rented two cabins fer a week. Older feller, sad-like. A younger feller jined him, tough-like, so it goes."

"There were two of them, then?" Owney remarked.

"Wal, sir, maybe. Manager says them boys

stopped showing up midweek. Never came back. Will's Slidell got the key, checked out each cabin. Wasn't nary much-like. Extry underwear, toothbrushes and powder, a Little Rock newspaper. No guns or nothing. Them boys travel light, even if they's the ones, even if they's wasn't."

"I don't fuckin' like this shit one bit," Owney said aloud. "If they was nobodies, they fucking wouldn't have thought it to be a big deal. They mighta left town, but not before checking out. These guys, they *knew* I'd be looking for them. That fuckin' cowboy who hit Siegel, he *knew* me. He looked at me and said"—and here he lapsed into a passably convincing imitation of the rumbly vessel that was Earl's sulfur-scorched voice—" 'How 'bout it, Mr. Maddox, you or any of your boys want a taste?' He fucking *knew* me. How's he know me? I don't know him. How the fuck he know me?"

Owney gazed off into the vapors as if fascinated by this new problem. That guy had the best hands he'd ever seen.

"That fucking guy, he could hit. I managed a boxer for a few years. Big lug couldn't hit shit. But I know the fight game, and that boy was a hitter!"

"Could they be New York guys? Or Chicago guys?"

"They could be Chicago guys," Owney said. "Bugsy was a New York guy and he sure as shit din't know them. I'd a heard if they was New York. Man, he hit that yid hard!"

"Cops?" someone thought to ask.

"Did you check the cops?" Owney asked Flem Grumley.

"Did, yes sir. Chief says it warn't none of his boys. He ain't hired no new boys. He even called a friend he has in the Little Rock FBI and it ain't no federal thing. No revenooers or nothing like that. Believe me, I know revenooers and these damn boys weren't revenooers. No revenooer ever could hit like that."

"Could they work for the new prosecuting attorney?" somebody asked. "We don't got any sources into what Becker is running."

Flem had an answer: "That boy is so scared since Rufus throwed that dead dog on his lawn he ain't been seen in town! He don't hardly even go to his office!"

There was much laughter.

And that was pretty much it: the rest was old business—a new Chinese laundry near Oaklawn was behind in his payments and would have to be instructed to keep up-to-date; the Jax brewery in New Orleans had delivered too much beer but a Grumley had convinced the driver of the truck not to report it; the wheel at the Horseshoe was running wobbly and cutting into the joint odds, though it could be repaired—but thought had to be put into replacing it; the betting season at Hialeah was just getting started and Owney ought to consider putting a new man or two into the Central Book as the wire would run very hot when Hialeah was up and steaming.

But after the meeting was over, the manager of the Golden Sun, a house near the Oaklawn Racetrack, pulled Owney over.

"I heard something, Owney."

"And what's that, Jock?"

"Ah, maybe it's nothing, but you should know anyhow."

"So, spill."

"My brother-in-law runs a craps game in an after-hour joint for Mickey Cohen in L.A. He used to work on that gambling boat they had beyond the twelve-mile-limit."

"Yeah?"

"Yeah, and times are tough since they closed that ship. But Mickey told my brother-in-law that good things are set up."

Owney listened intently. Mickey Cohen was Bugsy's right-hand man.

"What's he mean?"

"He says there'd be jobs for all the old guys, the real pro table crews."

"So? Is Bugsy going to try and get the ship thing going again?"

"No, Owney. It's bigger than that. Evidently, he's bought a big chunk of desert over the Nevada state line. Gambling's legal in Nevada. Nobody goes there, but it's legal."

"I still don't—"

"He's thinking big. He's going to build a place. A

big place. He's got some New York money bankrolling it. It's supposed to be secret. But he's going to build a gambling city in the desert. He's going to build a Hot Springs in the desert. Me, I think it's shit. Who's going to go to a fucking desert to gamble?"

But Owney immediately understood the nature of Bugsy's visit, and saw the threat to his own future. That was Bugsy's game, then. There could only be one Hot Springs. It would be here in Arkansas, where it belonged; or it would be in Nevada, in the fucking desert, where yid punk Bugsy wanted it.

It wouldn't be in two places.

Someone was going to have to die.

CHAPTER 11

D.A. had worked it out very carefully in his mind. He broke the team down into two-man fire teams, and put three of them into each squad, one designated the front-entry team and the other the rear-entry team.

Now it was time to do it, with unloaded weapons but all other gear as it would be, including the heavy vests that everybody hated.

Of course the young Carlo Henderson found himself united with the even younger Frenchy Short, who was full of opinions too important to be kept to himself, which was one reason nobody else would come near Frenchy.

"See," he said, "I would use the shotguns and the carbines. This isn't the '20s. The Thompsons were developed for trench warfare. For spraying. You spray a room, you got—"

"You wasn't ever instructed to spray nothing," said the stolid Carlo. "Mr. Earl told us: three-shot bursts."

"Yeah, well, some of these hicks from the sticks, they'll go nuts if somebody starts shooting at 'em. They'll spray anything that moves. They'll turn one of these casinos into a Swiss cheese house."

"You'd best just do what you're told."

"Ah," said Frenchy. "You're one of them. You probably love all this shit. You probably love that big Mr. Earl throwing his weight around like he's some kind of God or John Wayne or something."

"He seems okay. I heard he was a big war hero."

"Yeah, what'd it get him? Pretend sergeant in Hot Springs, Arkansas, busting down casino doors. Shit. He couldn't do better off a big medal than *that?"*

"What're you even here for if all this is so much crap?"

"Ah—"

"Well?"

"You won't tell anybody?"

"Of course not. You're my buddy. I have to cover for you."

"I got kicked out of Princeton. Boy, was my old man red-assed! He's a big-deal judge, so he got me a job in the police department. What I really want to do is get to the FBI. But not without a college degree, no sir. But if I do well as a cop—"

"Why'd you get kicked out?"

"It's a long story," said Frenchy, and his eyes grew hard and tough with a zealot's fire. "It was another crap deal, believe me. I got blamed for something I absolutely *did not do!* Anyhow, if I can get into the FBI, I can maybe then get into the OSS. You know what that is?"

"The what?"

"The what! Henderson, you're even dumber than you look. It's the Office of Strategic Services. The spies. Man, I would be so good at that! You work in foreign countries and I have a gift for languages and accents. These guys all believe I'm from some Passel O'Toads, Georgia! Anyhow, in OSS you pull shit all the time. In the war they blew up trains and assassinated Nazi generals and cut wires and eavesdropped on diplomats. My uncle did it."

"Well," said Henderson, "you'd best forget about all that and just focus on what we're going to be doing in a few minutes."

"Okay, but I get the Thompson, okay?"

"I thought you didn't like the Thompson."

"I didn't say I didn't like it. I said it was wrong for this kind of work. But I get to carry the Thompson."

"Fine. I'll go first."

"No, I'll go first. Come on, I'm much faster than you, I shoot better than you, I'm quick, I'm smart, I'm—"

"You can't *both* go first and carry the Thompson. That's agin the rules."

"The rules!" cursed Frenchy, as if he'd run up against this one before. "The goddamned rules! Well, fuck the rules!"

The address was Building 3-3-2, in a sea of deserted barracks that spilled across the hardscrabble Texas plain. It looked no different than any other barrack, just a decaying tan building, its paint peeling, its wood drying out, a few of its shingles flapping in the ever-present wind.

That was the target. The twelve officers took up positions in a barracks three doors down, made a preliminary recon, studied their objective, and drew up plans. Stretch, the oldest at twenty-six, a Highway Patrolman from Oregon, was nominally in charge, and he was steady and wise, and knew the wisdom in keeping it simple. It seemed so easy, if only everybody would listen and cooperate.

But almost immediately Frenchy began to undercut him. Frenchy knew better. Frenchy figured it out. Frenchy, charming, loquacious, willful, kept saying, "I'm the best shot, I ought to go first. Really, why not let the best shot go first?"

"Short, can you give somebody else a turn?"

"I'm just saying, the best way is to utilize your best people up front. I'm a very good shot. Nobody has shot as well as I have. Isn't that right? Correct me if I'm wrong. So I ought to be the first-entry guy."

He had very little shame, and no quit in him at all. Finally, to shut him up and get on with the planning, Stretch gave Frenchy the okay to be first man on the rear-entry team, with his partner.

That said, other assignments handed out, and the men suited up, sliding on the heavy armored plates over their suit coats, then donning their fedoras. They got into three cars—two old Highway Patrol Fords, painted all black, and a DeSoto that had once belonged to the State Liquor Control Board—and drove through the deserted streets of the barrack city until they came at 3-3-2 from different angles.

"All teams," said Stretch, into his walkie-talkie and consulting his watch, "deploy *now!*"

The cars halted. The men rushed out. Immediately one fell down, jamming his Thompson muzzle into the Texas loam, filling its compensator with muck. Another, as he ran to the door, banged his knee severely on the swinging steel of the vest, which was really more a sandwich board of heavy metal; he went down, painfully out of action.

But Frenchy, in the lead from the rear car, made it to the door first and fastest. He carried the tommy gun. Carlo, less graceful and more ungainly in his armor, struggled behind.

Frenchy kicked the door.

It didn't budge.

"Shit!" he said.

"Goddammit, you're supposed to wait for me!" Carlo said, arriving, followed by the last four men on the team.

"The fucking door is jammed."

Frenchy kicked it again. It didn't move.

"We ought to—"

But Frenchy couldn't wait. He threw off his heavy armor, smashed in a window, climbed into the frame and dove through it, rolling in the darkness. He stood up.

"Prosecuting Attorney's Office," he screamed. "This is a raid! Hands up!"

"Wait for me, goddammit," huffed poor Henderson, still on the other side of the door.

Frenchy heard them banging. It never occurred to him to unlock it. He did not wait for anybody. He headed down a hall in what was surprising darkness, feeling liberated in the absence of the twenty pounds of armor. The hall led to a wider room, and he raced in, pointing his empty tommy gun at menacing forms which proved to be old desks and tables and chairs. At once the room filled with smoke. The smoke billowed and unfurled, completely disorienting him. He coughed, ran further into the room, all alone, and stepped into a wider space, where the smoke was thinner. All around him things seemed to crash. Before him, he saw shapes. Without thinking about it, he dropped to one knee, put the tommy gun sights on them, and pulled the trigger. The gun's bolt flew forward with a powerful whack.

He recocked, knowing in reality he'd just mowed a few people down, and suddenly a figure appeared before him.

WHACK! he fired again, and a second later noted the surprised face of Carlo Henderson, whom he had just killed. He lurched to the left to a stairwell, kicked it open and raced up it.

"Short!"

He turned. Earl stood behind him, .45 leveled straight at his face for a perfect head shot, and snapped the trigger.

Then Earl said, "Congratulations, Short. You killed three of your own team members, you killed your partner, and you got yourself killed too. Just think of what you could have done if you'd have gotten to the second floor!"

D.A. gathered the young men in the dirt road out front of 3-3-2, invited the fellows to shed the body armor, stack the guns, take off the hats and coats and loosen the ties and light 'em up if they had 'em. It was blazing hot and most of the men had sweated through their clothes. They were a pretty sad-looking bunch: dampened and dejected.

"Now fellows," he said, "I'd be lying if I told you you did a good job. Frankly a bagful of coons locked in a cellar with ten pounds of raw meat might have behaved better. Basically what I saw was a series of mistakes compounding mistakes. I don't know what happened to your communications. Front-entry team at least hung together; too bad you got wiped out by the rear-entry team. Now, as I told you, the deal is simultaneous entrance. That's the trick. You have to be coming from two directions at once with overwhelming force. They have to understand that there is no possibility of victory and that resistance is futile.

"I will admit that we threw you some ringers. Mr. Earl popped a smoke grenade just to confuse the issue. I would say it confused you plenty. Would anyone disagree with me? The back door was locked. Did anybody think to look above the doorjamb? That's where the key was. Instead, at that point, rear-entry team just fell apart. Did rear-entry team walkie-talkie front-entry team? Nah. I was monitoring the radios upstairs. You were out of contact, and when you're out of contact, all kinds of hob can play. Finally, fellows, you can't let yourself get too excited. We had an unfortunate experience where one team member became separated, and got extremely aggressive with his weapon. He was supposed to be in support, but he rushed ahead, brought fire on the other team, then shot his partner, then rushed up a stairwell without securing the zone behind him and got shot by Mr. Earl. Fellows, you have to stay calm. If you let your emotions get the best of you, you become dangerous to your team members. This is about teamwork, fellows, remember. Teamwork, communications, good shooting skills, controlled aggression, sound tactics. That's the core of the art. You got anything, Earl?"

"Only this. I learned this one the hard way. The fight is going to be what it wants to be. You got to be ready to go with it, follow it where it goes, and deal with it. Remember: Always cheat, always win."

Fire and movement.

It was the most necessary training and the most dangerous.

"I saved this for last," said D.A., "because you have to work on your gun-handling skills and your self-discipline before you can even think about such a thing. This is the one where if you screw up, you kill a buddy or a bystander."

The course, as D.A. designed it, was set up in a tempo office building that administered the ranges back when the depot was turning out men for war. Now it was scheduled for destruction when the government's budget would allow it. It could be shot up to everybody's content and all walls but the front one were declared shootable. That gave the men a 270-degree shooting arc.

"You move through in two-man teams, just like on a real raid. The man on the right takes the targets on the right. The man on the left the targets on the left. Short, controlled bursts. Remember, trust your buddy. And, for God's sake, *stay together!"*

That was Earl. He would walk behind each team as they ran the course, as a safety measure.

The guys waited their turns as each two-man team ran the course. Inside the house, they could hear the quick stutters of the tommy guns and the bark of the .45s as each team popped its targets. One by one the teams emerged intact, joyous, and Earl would call up another team.

Finally, it was Frenchy and Carlo's turn.

"Okay, guys, you just take her easy. Short, you listening today?"

"Yes sir."

"Good. Okay, who's on the big gun?"

The two hadn't discussed this. They looked at each other.

"Henderson, you're bigger. You run the big gun. Short, you're a damned good pistol man. You work your .45. Remember, controlled speed, make sure of your targets, keep relating to your partner. Know where he is at all times, and nobody has to get hurt."

"Gotcha," said Frenchy.

The two young officers locked and loaded their weapons under Earl's supervision, then bent and got into the heavy armored vests.

"All right," he said, "muzzles level, we're shoulder to shoulder, we're not rushing, we're all eyes looking for targets. You shoot the black targets. You don't shoot the targets with white Xs on them. That would be civilians. Henderson, remember, three-shot bursts on that thing, dead center. You, Short, you're responsible for the left-hand sector. Henderson, you take the right. Don't hold the gun too tightly. Okay, fellas, I'm right here for you. All set?"

Both youngsters nodded.

"Let's do her good," said Earl.

Frenchy kicked the door, which yielded quickly. They entered, walked in tandem down a long corridor. At a certain point Earl flicked on a wall switch and two targets stood before them. Frenchy, his pistol out, was fastfastfast, putting two shots into the chest of his. A split second later Henderson's three-shot burst tore the heart out of the target on the right.

"Good, good," said Earl. "Now keep moving, don't bunch up, don't stop to admire yourself, keep your eyes moving."

They came to a corner. Frenchy jumped across the hall, his gun locked in the triangle of his arms and supported by the triangle of his legs as he hunted for targets. Carlo came next, dropping into a good kneeling shooting position. Two targets were before them, and Earl felt the boys tense as they raised their weapons, but then relax; the targets were Xed.

"Clear," sang Frenchy.

"Clear," came the answer.

"Good decision," said Earl. "Keep it up."

They moved on to a stairwell.

"Remember the last time?" Earl asked.

That was a hint. Frenchy jumped into the stairwell, covering the back zone, while Carlo fell to the far wall, orienting his Thompson up the stairs. Both saw their targets immediately. Frenchy's .45 rang twice as he pumped two shots into the silhouette from two feet away and Carlo fired a seven- or eight-shot burst, ripping up two silhouettes at the top of the stairs.

"Clear."

"Clear."

The gun smoke heaved and drifted in the smallish space. A litter of spent shells lay underfoot.

"Good work," said Earl.

Frenchy quickly dropped his magazine, inserted another.

"Great, Short. Nobody else has reloaded and some of 'em have run dry upstairs. Good thinking, son."

Frenchy actually smiled.

The team crept up the stairs.

They did another explosive turn as they emerged from the stairwell to confront yet another empty hallway. Down it lurked a series of doors.

"Got to clear them rooms," said Earl.

One by one, the team moved into the rooms. It was tense, close work: they'd kick in a door, scan the room, and find targets that could be shot or targets that couldn't. The gunfire was rapid and accurate, and neither of them made a mistake. No innocents were shot, no bad guys survived.

Finally, there was one room left, the last one.

The two gave each other a look. Frenchy nodded, took a deep breath and kicked the door open, spilling into the room to find targets on the left. One step behind plunged Carlo, who saw three silhouettes behind a table and raised the tommy, found the front sight and pulled the—

Frenchy had a moment of confusion when he felt he should not be moving, but an immense feeling of freedom and speed hit him. It was his armored vest; the strap had popped and the vest slipped sideways, the sudden shift of its weight taking his control from him. The second strap then broke, and the vest fell in two separate pieces to the floor, but Frenchy was too far gone and felt himself sprawling forward as his feet scrabbled for leverage, but instead slipped further on empty cartridge cases.

It was all so unreal. Time almost stopped. The noise of the Thompson became huge and blocked out all other things. He smelled gun smoke, felt heat, even as he fell. He lurched toward the flash and had an instant of horror as he knew, knew absolutely that he would die, for he would in the next instant fall before the path of the bullets and Carlo would not expect him and that would be that.

Shit! he thought, as he plunged toward his death in the stream of .45s.

Yet somehow he hit the ground untouched, stars shot off in his head, and then someone heavy fell upon him and there were muffled grunts.

"Jesus Christ!" Carlo was saying.

"Y'all okay?" asked Earl.

Earl was among them in the tangle on the floor. He disengaged and got up. "Y'all okay? You fine?"

"Gosh darn it!" said Carlo.

"Short, you hit?"

"Ah, no, I— What happened?"

"I almost killed you is what happened," said Carlo, his voice aquiver with trembling. "You fell into my line of fire, I couldn't stop, I—"

"It's okay, it's okay," said Earl. "Just get ahold of yourselves."

"What the heck happened to you? Why were you way out there?"

"The vest broke and I fell forward and my feet slipped on some shells."

"You are a lucky little son of a gun, Short. Mr. Earl, he grabbed the gun maybe a tenth of a second before it would have cut you up. He went through me and he grabbed the gun!"

"Jesus," said Frenchy. A wave of fear hit him.

"Okay, you fellows all right?" said Earl.

"Jesus," said Frenchy again, and vomited.

"Well, see, that's what a close shave'll do to you. Come on now, you're both okay, let's get up and get out of here."

"You saved my—"

"Yeah, yeah, and I saved myself three weeks of paperwork too. Come on, boys, let's get our asses in gear. No need to get crazy about this. Only, Short: next time, check the straps. Do a maintenance check each time you go on a raid. Got that?"

"I never—"

"It's the 'never' that gets you killed, Short."

But then he winked, and Frenchy felt a little better.

There was no officers' club for Earl and D.A. to go to that night, and since neither man drank anymore, it was perhaps a good thing. But D.A. invited Earl out to dinner, and so they found a bar-b-que joint in Texarkana, near the railway station, and set to have some ribs and fries, and many a cold Coke.

The food was good, the place was dark and coolish, and somebody put some Negro jump blues on the Rockola, and that thing was banging out a bebopping rhythm that took both their minds away from where they were. Afterward, the two men smoked and finished a last Coke, but Earl knew enough to know he was being prepared for something. And he had a surprise of his own he'd been planning to lay on D.A. sooner or later, and this looked to be as good a time as any.

"Well, Earl, you've done a fine job. I'm sure you're the best sergeant the Marine Corps ever turned out. You got them whipped into some kind of shape right fast."

"Well, sir," said Earl, "the boys are coming along all right. Wish we had another two months to train 'em. But they're solid, obedient young men, they work hard, they listen and maybe they'll do okay."

"Who worries you?"

"Oh, that Short kid, of course. Something in that one I just don't trust. He wants to do so well he may make a bad judgment somewhere along the line. I will say, he learns fast and he's a good pistol hand. But you never can tell about boys until the lead starts flying."

"I agree with you about Short. Only Yankee in the bunch and he sounds more Southern than any man born down upon the Swanee River."

"I noticed that too. Don't know where it comes from. Any South in him?"

"Not a lick. He told me he had a gift for soaking up dialects. Maybe he don't even notice that he's doing it."

"Maybe. I never saw nothing like it in fifteen years in the Marines."

"Anyhow, I'm asking you because I got some news."

"Figured you did."

"Mr. Becker is getting very restless. He's under a lot of pressure with anonymous phone threats and such-like and townspeople wondering when the hell he's going to do something other than go to his office and close the door without talking to nobody. And his wife is followed by Grumley boys everywhere she goes. We got to deal with that. We got to move, and soon. Are we ready?"

"Well, you're never ready. But we are ready on one condition."

"I think I know what this is, Earl," said the old man gravely.

"So did my wife. She said it was my nature."

"She knows you, Earl. And I know you too, even though I first laid eyes on you three weeks or so ago. You're the goddamned hero. How you made it through that war I'll never know."

"Anyhow, I have to go. The boys have made a connection to me, and they'll be frightened if I ain't there."

"They'll get over it."

"Mr. Parker, I have to be there. You know it and I know it. They need a steady hand, and you've got too much to do setting the raids up with Becker and then dealing with the police and the press afterward."

"Earl, if you get hit, I'd never forgive myself."

"And if one of those kids got hit while I'se sitting somewhere sucking on a Coca-Cola, I'd never forgive myself."

"Earl, you are a hard man to be the boss of, I will say that."

"I know what's right. Plus, no goddamn hillbilly with a shotgun is going to get the best of me."

"Earl, never underestimate your enemy. You should know that from the war. Owney Maddox was called 'Killer' back in New York. According to the New York District Attorney's Office, he killed over twenty men in his time. Once this shit starts happening, he's going to bring in some mobsters who've pulled triggers before. Don't kid yourself, Earl.

These will be tough boys. Get ready for 'em."

"Then you'll let me go?"

"Shit, Earl, you have to go. That is as clear to me as the nose on my face. But I want you to go home and talk to your wife first. Hear me? You tell her like a man. So she knows. And you tell her you love her and that things will be okay. And you listen to that pup in her belly. Look, here's twenty-five bucks, you take her out to a nice dinner at Fort Smith's finest restaurant."

"Ain't no fine restaurants in Fort Smith."

"Then hire a cook."

"Yes sir."

"And you meet us Tuesday in Hot Springs."

"Tuesday?"

"Here it is, Earl. Our first warrant. We hit the Horseshoe at 10:00 P.M. Tuesday night. We're going to start the ball rolling with a big one."

CHAPTER 12

He got back late Friday night; the vets village was quiet and it took him some time to find his own hut. The low, corrugated shapes had such a sameness to them that most of the women had tried to pretty them up with flower beds and bushes, maybe a trellis or something silly like that. But they were still essentially tubes half buried in the earth, passing as housing. Eventually, he got himself oriented—fellow could wander for hours in the sameness of the place, all the little streets just like all the other little streets—and found 5th Street, where he lived in No. 17. He knocked and there was no answer. She must be sleeping. He opened the door because nobody bothered to lock up.

He heard her in what passed for the bedroom; it was really just a jerry-built wall that didn't reach the arched tin roof. She breathed steadily, deeply, as if for two. He didn't want to startle her, so he stayed out of that room and instead remained in the large one.

He moved one small lamp so that the bulb would not shine into the bedroom, and turned it on, looking about as he undressed. It was a fairly squalid experience. The furniture was all used, the tin walls overcurving as if boring in, to crush the life out of all possibility here. She'd worked hard to cheer the place up inside as well as out, to disguise its essential governmentness, by painting and hanging pictures and curtains and what-not. But the effort was doomed, overwhelmed by the odor of the aluminum that encapsulated them and the feel of the give in the wooden slats that made up the floor.

The plumbing was primitive, the stove and icebox small, the place drafty. It was no place to bring up a kid.

He went to the kitchen—rather to the corner where the kitchen appliances were located—and opened the icebox, hoping to find some milk or something or maybe another Coca-Cola. But she had not known he was coming and there was nothing. But then a rogue impulse fired off and he opened a certain cabinet and there indeed, as he remembered, was a half-full bottle of Boone County bourbon.

It took a lot of Earl not to drink it. He was not in the mood to say no to bourbon, because the long pull up the western edge of Arkansas on 71 essentially took him through home ground. The road, two lanes of wandering macadam, crawled through Polk County, where his daddy had been the sheriff and a big, important man. Near midnight, the drive took Earl through Blue Eye, the county seat, nestled in the trackless Ouachitas. He hadn't seen it in years. The main street ran west of the train tracks, lined with little buildings. He'd had no impulse to detour to see what had been his father's office and was still the county sheriff's office; nor had he had an impulse to detour out Arkansas 8 to Board Camp, where the farm that he had inherited as the last surviving Swagger lay fallow. He had faced it once, when he was immediately out of the Corps, and that had been enough.

Ghosts seemed to scamper through the night. Was it Halloween? No, the ghosts were memories, some happy, some sad, really just bright pictures in his mind of this day and that in his boyhood, of parades and hikes and hunting trips—his father was an ardent, excellent hunter and one wall of the house was alive with his trophies—and all the things that filled a boy's life in the 1920s in rural America. But he always sensed his father's giganticism, his father's weight and bulk and gravity, the fear that other man paid in homage to Charles Swagger, sheriff of Polk County.

He tried not to think of his father, but he could no more forbid his mind from doing that than he could forbid it from ordering his lungs to breathe. A great father-heaviness came over him, and he could see a spell of brooding setting in, where his father would be the only thing in his mind and would still, all these years later, have the capacity to dominate everything.

His father was a sharp-dressed man, always in black suits and white linen shirts from the Sears, Roebuck catalogue. His black string ties were always perfect and he labored over them each morning to get them so. Daddy's face was grave and lined and brooked no disobedience. He knew right from wrong as the Baptist Bible stated it. He carried a Colt Peacemaker on his right side, a leather truncheon in his back pocket and he rattled with keys and other important objects when he walked. He carried a Jesus gun also, a .32 rimfire Smith & Wesson stuffed up his left cuff and held there by a sleeve garter. It had saved his life in 1923 in a shoot-out with desperadoes; he'd killed all three of them and been a great hero.

Charles Swagger also had the capacity to loom. It was in part his size but more his rigidity. He stood for things, stood straight and tall for them, and represented in a certain way America. To defy him was to defy America and he was quick to deal with disobedience. People loved him or feared him, but no matter what, they acknowledged him. He was a powerful man who ruled his small kingdom efficiently. He knew all the doctors and ministers and lawyers; of course he knew the mayor and the county board, and the prominent property owners. He knew all of them and they all knew him and could trust him. He kept the peace everywhere except in his own home, and from his own aggressions.

Charles didn't drink every night, just every third night. He was a bourbon drinker, and he drank for one reason, which was to feel himself the man he knew everybody thought him to be and to banish the fears that must have cut at him. Thus, drunk, he became even mightier and more heroic and more unbending. His righteousness in all things grew to be a force of nature. His doubts vanished and his happy confidence soared. He retold the story of the day and how he had solved all the problems and what he had told the many people who had to be put in their places. But when he looked about and saw how little his family had given a man of his nobility and family lines, it troubled him deeply. He corrected his wife's many mistakes and pointed out that her people were really nothing compared to his. He pointed out the flaws in his sons and sometimes—more often as he got older—he disciplined his eldest with a razor strop or a belt. That boy was such a disappointment. That boy was such a nothing, a nobody. You would think a great man like Charles Swagger would have a great son, but no, he only had poor Earl and his even more pathetic younger brother, Bobby Lee, who still wet the bed. He instructed his eldest in his insignificance, as if the boy were incapable of understanding it himself, though the boy understood it very well.

"He has no talent," Charles would scream at his wife. "He has no talent. He needs to find a trade, but he's too lazy for a trade! He's nothing, and he'll never be anything, and I'll beat the fear of God into him if it's the last thing I ever do."

Thus, alone in his hut, that boy, grown to be a man, felt again the temptation of the bottle. Inside the bottle might be damnation and cowardice, but it was also escape from the looming of the father. It beckoned him mightily. It offered a form of salvation, a music of pleasure, the sense of being blurred and softened, where all things seemed possible. But you always woke up the next morning with the taste of an alley in your mouth and the hazy memory of having said things that shouldn't be said or having heard things that shouldn't be heard.

Earl opened the bottle and poured the bourbon out. He didn't feel any better at all, but at least he had not fallen off the wagon. He went back over to the couch and lay there in the dark, listening to his wife breathe for two, and eventually he fell off to his own shallow and troubled sleep.

The next morning she was happy. He was there, it took so little to please her. He listened to her account of the doctor's reports and she asked him to touch her stomach and feel the thing inside move.

"Doctor says he's coming along just fine," said Junie.

"Well, damn," said Earl. "That's really great."

"Have you picked a name yet?" Junie wanted to know.

No. He hadn't. Hadn't even thought of it. He realized she probably presumed he was as occupied with the baby as she was. But he wasn't. He was pretending he cared. The thing inside her scared him. He had no feeling for it except fear.

"I don't know," he said, "maybe we should name him after your father."

"My father was an idiot. And that's when he was sober," she added, and laughed.

"Well, my father was a bastard. And that's when *he* was sober." And they both laughed.

"You should name him after your brother."

"Hmmm," said Earl. His brother. Why'd she have to bring that up? "Well, maybe," he said. "We have plenty of time to figure it out. Maybe we should start fresh. Pick a movie star's name. Name him Humphrey or John or Cornell or Joseph or something."

"Maybe it'll be a girl," she said. "Then we could name her after your mama."

"Oh," he said, "maybe we just ought to make it a new start. It ain't got nothing to do with the past, sweetie."

Junie was showing now. Her face was plumped up, but still the damndest thing he'd ever seen. She was packing weight on her shoulders and, of course, through the middle.

"Honey, I don't know nothing about names. You name the baby. You're carrying the critter, you get to name it, fair enough?"

"Well, Earl, you should take part too."

"I just don't know," he said, too fiercely. Then he said, "I'm damned sorry. I didn't mean to bark at nothing. You getting the money all right? You okay in that job? You don't have no problems, do you, sweetie? Hell, you know what an ornery old bastard I can be."

She forced a smile, and it seemed to be all forgotten but he knew it wouldn't be.

That night he took her into the dining room at the Ward Hotel on Garrison Street, the nicest place to eat in all of Fort Smith.

He looked very handsome. He wore his suit so well, and he was tanned and polite and seemed happy in some odd way, in no way he had been since the war. It warmed her to see him so happy.

"Well," she said, "it does seem like we've come up in the world. You have a car. We get to go out at a fine place like this."

"That's right," he said. "We're on our way. You know, you could probably rent a place in town. You could get out of that vets village. They're going to be building new housing everywhere."

"Well, it seems so silly. Why move now, then move again when we have to go into Hot Springs? I assume I'm coming to Hot Springs sometime."

"Well, yes, that's the plan, I guess."

But a vagueness came across his face. That was Earl's horror: his distance. Sometimes he was just not there, she thought, as if something came and took his mind from him, and gave it over to memories of the war or something else. Sometimes she felt like she was in the *Iliad,* married to a Greek warrior, a powerful man but one who'd shed too much blood and come too close to dying too many times, a man somehow leeched by death. There was a phrase for it that she'd heard in her girlhood, and now it came back to her: "Black as the earl of death." Hill people talked that way, and her father, a doctor, sometimes took her on his trips into the Missouri hollows and she heard the way the folks talked: black as the earl of death. That was her Earl, somehow, and somehow, she knew, she had to save him from it.

The waiter came and offered to fetch cocktails. Earl took a Coca-Cola instead, though he encouraged Junie to go ahead, and she ordered something called a mimosa, which turned out to be orange juice with champagne in it.

"Now where'd you hear about that?"

"I read about it in the *Redbook* magazine."

"It seems very big-city."

"It's from Los Angeles. It's very popular out there. They say California is turning into the land of opportunity now that the war is over."

"Well, maybe we should move out there when all this is over." But the vagueness came to his face again, as if he had some unpleasant association with California.

"I could never leave my mother," she said hastily. "And with the baby coming—"

"I didn't mean it, really. I wouldn't know what to do in Los Angeles. Hell, I hardly know what to do in Hot Springs."

"Oh, Earl."

They ordered roast chicken and roast beef and had an extremely nice dinner. It was wonderful to see him in a civilized place, and to be in such a nice room which was filled with other well-dressed people. The waiters wore tuxedos, a man played the piano, it was all formal and pleasant.

"Now, honey," he finally said.

A shadow crossed her face, a darkening. She knew that tone: it meant something horrible was coming.

"What is it, Earl? I knew there was something."

"Well, it's just a little something."

"Is it about the job?"

"Yes ma'am."

"Well, so tell me."

"Oh, it's nothing. Mr. Parker though, he thought I should come up here and take you on a nice date and everything. He's a fine man. I hope to introduce you to him sometime, if it works out. He's as fine as any officer I had in the Corps, including Chesty Puller. He cares about the job, but he cares about his people too, and that's very rare."

"Earl? What is it?"

"Well, honey, you remember those raids I said I was never going on? Into the casinos and the book joints? Now these young men we have, they've worked damned hard and they've really become very good in the small amount of time. But two weeks. Hell, it takes two years to become a good Marine. Anyhow, these boys, they . . ."

He trailed off helplessly, because he couldn't quite find the words.

"They what?"

"Oh, they just don't quite know enough."

"Enough for what?"

"Enough to do it by themselves."

"I don't—"

"So I said to Mr. Parker, I said I should go along. At first. Just to make sure. Just to watch. That's all. I wanted to tell you. I had told you I was just going to train them. Now I'm going with them. That's all. I wanted to tell you straight up."

She looked at him.

"There'll be guns and shooting? These raids will be violent?"

"Probably not."

She saw this clearly. "No. That is the nature of the work. You are dealing with criminals who are armed and don't want to accept your will. So it is the nature of the experience that there will be violence."

"We know how to handle the violence. If there is any. That is what this training has been about. Plus, we wear heavy bulletproof vests."

She was silent.

Then she said, "But what does that do for me and the child I carry? Suppose you die? Then—"

"I ain't going to die. These are old men with rusty shotguns who—"

"They are gangsters with machine guns. I read the newspapers. I read *The Saturday Evening Post.* I know what's going on. Suppose you get killed. I'm to raise our child alone? He's never to know his father? And for what? To save a city that's soaked in filth and corruption for a hundred years? Suppose you die. Suppose they win? Suppose it's all for nothing? What am I supposed to say to this boy? Your daddy died to stop fools from throwing their money away on little white cubes? He didn't die to save his country or his family or anything he cared about, but just to stop fools from gambling. And if you close down Hot Springs, the same fools will only go some other place. You can't end sin, Earl. You can only protect yourself and your family from it."

"Yes ma'am. But now I have given my word, and I have boys depending on me. And, the truth is, I am happy. For the first time since the war, I am a happy man. I am doing some good. It ain't much, but it's what I got. I can help them boys."

"Earl, you are such a fool. You are a brave, handsome, noble man, but you are a fool. Thank you, though, for telling me."

"Would you like some dessert?"

"No. I want you to go home and hold me and make love to me, so that if you die I can have a memory of it and when I tell our son about it, I will have a smile on my face."

"Yes ma'am," he said. It was as if he'd just heard the best order he'd ever gotten in his life.

CHAPTER 13

Hard-boiled eggs (two), dry toast, fresh orange juice. Then he went over accounts for three hours and made a number of phone calls. For lunch he went to Coy's and had a fillet. On a whim, he stopped at Larry's Oyster Bar on Central and had a dozen fresh plump ones from Louisiana, with a couple of cold Jaxes. He went back and took a nice nap. At 3:00 a girl from Maxine's came over and he had his usual good time. At 4:00 he met Judge LeGrand at the club and they got in a quick nine holes. He shot a 52, best of the week. He was catching on to this damned game. At 6:00 he went to the Fordyce and took a bath, a steam session and a rub-down. At 7:00 he had dinner at the Roman Table restaurant with Dr. James, the head of surgery at the hospital, and Mr. Clinton, who owned the Buick agency; both were on the board of the country club, the hospital, and Kiwanis and the Good Fellows. At 9:00 he went to the Southern, caught some of Xavier Cugat's act, which he had seen a dozen times before, checked with his floor managers, his pit bosses and his talent manager to make certain that Mr. Cugat and his boys were being well taken care of. At 11:00 he walked back to the Medical Arts Building, took the elevator up, got into a dressing gown, and had a martini on the patio, while reading that morning's *New York Mirror,* just delivered from Little Rock. That Winchell! What a bastard he could be.

Owney took a moment before bed and stood at the balcony. He had come a long way. He was unusual in his profession in that he had just a sliver of an inner life. He wasn't pure appetite. He knew he existed; he knew he thought.

Today had been such a good day, such a perfect day, yet such a typical day that he took a little pleasure in it all: how hard he had fought, how tough it had been, and how beautifully it had worked out. So many of them died, like the Dutchman, spouting gibberish as the life ebbed out of him, or Mad Dog, splattered with tommy gun fire in a phone booth, or Kid Twist, who went for a swim in midair after volunteering to rat the boys out; or went crazy, like Capone, down there in his mansion in Florida, a complete lunatic by reports, so hopelessly insane on the corrosiveness of his dose that nobody would even bother to visit him. He remembered Capone, the plump sensualist with a Roman emperor's stubby fingers and a phalanx of legionnaires to guard him everywhere, taking the Apollo Suite at the Arlington because it had two entrances, or, as Alphonse would think of it, two exits. A tommy gun legendarily leaned in a corner, in case Al or a lieutenant had a sudden problem that only a hundred .45s could solve.

"Al, it's safe here. That's the point: it's smooth, it's safe, you can come down here by train and enjoy yourself. A man in your position, Al, he should relax a little."

Al just regarded him suspiciously, the paranoia beginning to rot his mind, turning his eyes into dark little peepholes. He didn't say much, but he got laid at least three times a day. Al was reputed to have an organ bigger than Dillinger's. Pussy was the only thing he really cared about and pussy, in the end, had destroyed him. He was afraid of the needles so he came to Hot Springs, under the belief the waters could cure him. They couldn't, of course. They could only stay the course of the disease a bit. All his soaking in 141 degrees had earned Scarface but a few extra hours of sanity in the end.

Owney finished his martini, turned to check that his pigeons had been fed, saw that they had, and started in, when he was surprised by Ralph, his Negro manservant.

"Sir. Mr. Grumley is here."

"Flem?"

"No sir. The other Grumley. The one they call Pap. He's out of his sickbed."

This alerted Owney that indeed something was up.

He walked into the foyer of his apartment, to find the ghost-white old Pap Grumley supported by two lesser cousins or sons or something.

"What is it, Pap?" asked Owney.

"A Grumley done been kilt," said the old legger, a flinty bastard who'd fought the law for close to six decades and was said to carry over a dozen bullets in his hide.

"Who? Revenuers?"

"It's worse, Mr. Maddox."

"What do you mean?"

"Your place done been raided."

Owney could make no sense of this. One or two of his places were raided a year, but by appointment only. It usually took a meeting at least a week in advance to set up a raid. The police had to be told which casino or whorehouse to raid and when to do it, the municipal judge had to know not to get that drunk that night so he could parole the arrestees without undue delay, the casino had to be warned so that nobody would be surprised and nothing stupid would happen, the Little Rock newspapers had to be alerted so they could send photographers, and the mayor had to be informed so that he could be properly dressed for those photographs. Usually, it occurred when some politician in Little Rock made a speech in the statehouse about vice.

"I don't—"

"They come in hard and fast, with lots of guns and wearing them bulletproof vests. And one of 'em shot a Grumley. It was Jed's boy, Garnet, the slow-wit. He died on the spot. We got him over at the morgue and we was—"

"Who raided?"

"They said they was working for the prosecuting attorney."

"Becker?"

"Yes sir. That Becker, he was there. There's about ten, twelve of 'em, with lots of guns. They come in hard and fast and one of 'em shot Garnet dead when Garnet pulled his shotgun. Mr. Maddox, you got to let us know when there's going to be a raid. What am I supposed to say to Jed and Amy?"

"Where did this happen?"

"At the Horseshoe. Just a hour ago. Then they chopped up all the tables and the wheels with axes and machine-gunned the slots."

"What?"

"Yes sir. They turned them machine guns loose on over thirty slots. Shot the hell out of 'em too, they did. Coins all over the goddamned place. Nickels by the bucketful."

"They were working for Becker?"

"Yes sir. He was there, like I say. But the boss was some big tough-looking stranger. He was a piece of work. He shot Garnet. They say nobody never saw no man's hands move faster. He drew and shot that poor boy dead in about a half a second. Nailed him plug in the tick-tocker. Garnet was gone to the next world before he even begun to topple."

The cowboy! The cowboy was back!

By the time he got there, reporters and photographers were already on the scene. They flooded over to Owney, who was always known for his colorful ways with the language, those little Britishisms that sold papers. There were even some boys from Little Rock in attendance.

But Owney was in no mood for quips. He waved them away, then called a Grumley over.

"Get the film. We don't want to let this out until we know what's happening. And send 'em home. And tell 'em not to write stories until we get it figured out."

"Well, sir," said the Grumley, "there's already a press release out."

He handed it over to Owney.

HOT SPRINGS, August 3, 1946, it was datelined.

Officers from the Garland County Prosecuting Attorney's Office today raided and closed a gambling casino in West Hot Springs, destroying 35 slot machines and much illegal gaming equipment.

The raid, at the Horseshoe, 2345 Ouachita, also confiscated nearly $32,000 in illegal gambling revenues.

"This marks the first of our initiatives to rid Hot Springs of illegal gambling," said Prosecuting Attorney Fred C. Becker, who led the raid.

"We mean to put the gangsters and the card sharks on notice," said Mr. Becker. "There's no longer a free lunch in Hot Springs. The laws will be enforced and they will be enforced until gambling and its vices have been driven out of our city."

Operating on a tip that illegal activities were under way. . .

Owney scoffed as he discarded the sheet: maybe the thirty-foot-high neon sign on the roof of the Horseshoe that said 30 SLOTS—INSTANT PAYOUT! was the tip-off.

"Who the fuck does he think he is?" Owney asked the Grumley, who had no answer.

"Where's my lawyer?" asked Owney and in short order F. Garry Hurst was produced.

"Is this legal?" Owney demanded. "I mean how can they just fuckin' blow down the doors and start blasting?"

"Well, Owney, it appears that it is. Becker is operating on a very tiny technicality. Because Hot Springs Mountain is a government reserve, any illegal activities within the county that are subject to affecting it can be construed to come under injunction. So any federal judge can issue warrants, and they don't necessarily have to be served by federal officers. He can deputize local authorities. Becker's got a federal judge in Malvern in his pocket. There's your problem right there."

"Damn!" said Owney. He knew right away that clipping a federal judge would not be a good idea, just as clipping a prosecuting attorney wouldn't, either.

"Can you reach him?"

"He's eighty-two years old and nearly blind. I don't think money, whores or dope would do the trick. Maybe if you snuck up behind him and said boo."

"Shit," said Owney.

"It's a pretty smart con," said Hurst. "I don't see how you can bring legal action against the federal government, and through that technicality Becker is essentially operating as a federal law enforcement officer. He's got the protection of the United States government, even if the United States government has no idea who he is."

"Okay, find out all you can. I have to know what the hell is going on. And I have to know soon."

Owney headed inside, where Jack McGaffery,

the Horseshoe's manager, waited for him.

"Mr. Maddox, we never had a chance. They was just on us too fast. Poor Garnet, that boy never hurt a fly, and they blowed him out of his socks like a Jap in a hole."

But Owney was less interested in the fate of Garnet than he was in the fate of the Horseshoe. What he saw was an admirably efficient job of ruination accomplished quickly. The roulette wheels and the craps tables could be replaced quickly enough, although a roulette wheel was a delicate instrument and had to be adjusted precisely. But the slots were the worst part.

Usually, the slots were simply hauled away to a police warehouse, stored a few weeks, then quietly reinstalled. Some of them had dozens of TO BE DESTROYED BY HSPD stickers on their backsides.

But this time, someone had walked along the line of machines and fired three or four tommy gun bullets into each. The heavy .45s had penetrated into the spinning guts of the mechanical bandits and blown them to oblivion. The Watlings looked like dead soldiers in a morgue, their glossy fronts cracked or shattered, their adornments of glass spider-webbed, their stout chests punctured, their freight of coins spewed across the floor. Reels full of lemons and cherries and bananas lay helter-skelter on the floor, along with springs and gears and levers. They were old Watling Rol-a-tops from before the war, though well maintained, gleaming and well bugged and tighter than a spinster's snatch, ever profitable. The Rol-a-tops, though, were the proletarians of the gambling universe. More obscenely, a Pace's Race, the most profitable of the devices, was included in the carnage. It was a brilliantly engineered mock track where tiny silhouettes of horses, encased in mahogany under glass, ran in slots against each other, and by the genius mechanics of the thing, the constantly changing odds whirled around a tote board, the odds themselves playing the horses. Its glass shattered, its elegant wood casing broken, its tin horses bent and mangled, the thing lay on its side, all magic having been beaten out of it.

Owney shook his head sadly.

"We kept people out," said Jack. "All the coins are still there. Them boys didn't get no coins, that's for sure."

"But they got $35,000?"

"Sir, more like $43,800 and odd dollars."

"Shit," said Owney. "And all the records."

"Yes sir. But wasn't airy much in them sheets."

Of course not. Owney wasn't foolish enough to keep sensitive documents in casinos.

"But sir," said Jack. "Here's something I don't understand."

He pointed at the walls. Every ten or twelve feet, someone had whacked a hole with an ax. Owney followed the gouges, which circled the main room of the casino, continued up the stairs to Jack's looted office, and followed a track into both the gals' and the men's rest rooms.

Looking at the destruction in the women's room, he said finally, "Who did this?"

"Well, it was an old guy. There was an old guy who came in after all the ruckus was done. He had a hatchet and he went around chopping holes in the wall while the younger boys chewed up the tables and gunned the slots."

"What'd he look like?"

"Like I say, Mr. Maddox, old man. Face like a bag of prunes. Big old man. Sad-like. He looked like he seen his kids drownded in a flood. Didn't say much. But he was some sort of boss. Meanwhile, the tough guy supervised the cracking of the tables, and outside, Becker and his clerk handed out them news releases, answered some questions, posed for pictures. Then they all up and went. Nobody made no arrests."

"Hmmmm," said Owney. He had been caught flat-footed, and someone smart somewhere was behind it. That old man chopping at the walls. He was clearly someone who knew what he was doing. He had a sense of the one place Owney was vulnerable. You could raid on places in Hot Springs for years, and as soon as you closed one joint down, another would spring up, sustained by the river of money that was track betting. But the old man was looking for the wiring that would indicate the secret presence of the Central Book, where the phones poured their torrents of racing data, and Owney knew if he found it, he could dry Owney out in a fortnight.

Goddamn the wire! He was trying to get out of that business but he was still tied to it, it was still his lifeline, and he was still vulnerable to its predation.

One thing was for sure: next time he'd be ready.

"Jack, get Pap in here."

When the old man came, Owney went to the point.

"I want 'em all armed now. Nothing goes easy anymore. They'll never have it as soft as they had it tonight. If they want a war, we'll give 'em a goddamned war. They got guns? We'll get bigger guns. Tell the Grumleys, they will get back for what was done to them tonight."

"Wooo-oooooooo-doggies!" yelped the haggard old sinner, and danced a mad little jig there in the ruined casino.

CHAPTER 14

By three separate cars, the raid team arrived at the courtyard of the Best Tourist Court at around 9:30 P.M. The neon of the Best was spectacular: it washed the night in the fires of cold gas, in odd colors like magenta and fuchsia and rose around each cabin. It looked like a frozen explosion.

In this strange illumination, the men loaded

magazines quietly, slipped into their bulletproof vests, checked the safeties, locked back actuators, tried to stay loose and cool and not get too excited. But it was hard.

Across the street they could see the looming shape of the old ice house, and next to it, the Horseshoe itself, somewhat rickety and wooden like most of the casinos built in the 1920s, with its blazing neon sign thirty feet high atop the roof: 30 SLOTS—INSTANT PAYOUT! and the double green neon horseshoes at each end of the sign.

"Hard to miss," said D.A.

"It's not like a secret or nothing," said one of the boys, possibly Eff—for Jefferson—up from the Georgia Highway Patrol. A designated tommy gunner, he was loading .45s into a stick magazine.

Earl was alive in ways he hadn't been alive for a year. He felt his eyeballs extra-sharp, he tasted the flavor of the air, his nerve endings were radar stations reading every rogue movement in the night sky. He walked around, checking, examining, giving this boy or that the odd nod or pat of encouragement.

Becker pulled in, with a clerk. He seemed especially nervous. He walked among the men smiling dryly, but he kept running his tongue over his gray lips. All he could think to say was "Very good, very good, very good, very good."

Finally he approached the two leaders.

"I like it. They look sharp," he said.

"It ought to go okay," said the old man.

"You, Earl, you agree?"

"Mr. Parker's got it laid out real nice, sir," said Earl.

"Okay. When it's clear, you send a boy out. At that moment I'll call HSPD and announce a raid in progress and request backup. Then I'll call the newspaper boys. I did alert the Little Rock boys to have a photog in the area. But that's okay, that's secure. Got it?"

"Yes sir," said D.A., but suddenly Earl didn't like it. Okay, Owney owned the local rags, but how safe were these Little Rock people? He pulled D.A. aside.

"I'm going to go in early," he said.

D.A. looked at him.

"You'll be right in the line of fire for twelve nervous kids."

"Yeah, but in case somebody in there gets a little crazed or has been tipped off, I might be able to cock him good and save a life or two. This'll probably be the only raid we can get away with that."

"I don't like it, Earl," D.A. said. "It's not how we planned it. It could confuse them."

"I'll be all right," said Earl. "It could save some lives."

"It could cost some lives too," said D.A.

"Look at it this way," said Earl. "We'll never get a chance to pull this trick off again. They'll be waiting for it in all the other places. We might as well do it while we can."

D.A. looked at him sharply, seemed about to say something, but then reconsidered; it was true he did not want a killing on the first raid, for he believed that would turn the whole enterprise inevitably toward ruination.

"Wear your vest," he cautioned, but even as he said it, he knew it was impossible: the vests were large and bulky and looked like umpire's chestpads, and everybody hated them. If Earl walked in with a vest on, it would be a dead giveaway.

"You know I can't."

"Yeah, well, take this."

He handed over a well-used police sap, a black leather strap with a pouch at the end where a half pound of buckshot had been secreted.

"Bet you busted some head with this old thing," said Earl with a smile.

"More'n I care to remember."

Earl looked at his Hamilton in the pink light and shadow. It was 9:45. Between the tourist court and the casino, Ouachita Avenue buzzed with cars.

"I'm sending in three teams in the front and two in the back," said D.A. "I'll move the rear teams in first. I'll run them teams around the ice house, and they'll rally in its eaves, on that southwest corner. At 9:59, they'll move single file down to the rear entrance. We have sledges. At ten, they hit the door, just as the three front-entry teams go through the foyer and fan out through the building. Luckily it's a simple building, without a lot of blind spots or tiny rooms."

Earl nodded.

"That's good," he said. "But maybe instead of going around the ice house, you ought to move 'em around the other side of the casino, sir."

D.A. looked at him.

"Why?" he said.

"It's nothing. But the manager's office seems to be upstairs on that same corner. Maybe he's up there, the window's open, and he hears scuffling in the alley, or somebody drops a mag or bangs into a garbage can. Maybe it ticks something off in him, he takes out a gun, he heads downstairs. The rear-entry team runs into him with a gun out on the stairway. Bang, bang, somebody's hurt bad. See what I'm saying, sir? I think you'd do best to run 'em around that other side of the building."

"Earl, is there anything you don't know?"

"What to name my kid. How to balance a checkbook. Which way the wind blows."

"You are a smart bastard. All right."

Earl checked his .45, making sure once again that the safety was still on, and, from the heft, that indeed the piece was stoked with seven cartridges. He touched the three mags he had tucked into his belt on the back side. He touched his sap.

Then he went among the boys.

"Listen up, kids," he said.

They stopped fiddling with their tommy guns and drew around him.

"Slight change in plan. I'm going to go on and be

in there. I have a favor to ask. Please do not shoot me. You especially, Short. Got that?"

There was some nervous laughter.

"Okay, I'll be in the main room, at the bar. Mark me. If I move fast, it's because I've seen someone with a gun or a club. I say again and now hear this: Do not shoot old Mr. Earl."

Again, the dry laughter of young men.

"You are broken down into your teams, you have your staging assignments and your route assignments. And remember. The fight's going to be what it wants to be, not what you want it to be. You stay sharp," and he moved away from them and disappeared.

Frenchy was annoyed. The last man on the last team. He was backup on the rear-entry team, the third fire team. That made him sixth man through the door. It did get him a tommy gun, however. He felt it wrapped under his coat as he crossed Ouachita, huge, oily and powerful. He waited for the cars to part, then dashed across, as the others had done, one man at a time, the tommy gun secured up under his suit coat, the heavy armored vest rocking against him as he ran. No car lights shone on him; nobody from the Horseshoe saw him, or could be expected to.

He ran to the Horseshoe's northwest corner, then threaded back alongside the west wall of the casino. Inside he could hear the steady clang of the slots, the calls of the pit bosses and the more generalized hubbub of a reasonably crowded place.

He slid along the edge of the building, ducking the wash of lights that shone from the shuttered windows. His eyes craned the parking lot to his right for movement, but there was none at all. Five men had passed this way before him, and at last he joined them, in a little cluster at the southwest corner of the big, square old building.

"Six in," he said.

"Time check," said Slim, who as the second-most-senior man of the unit was running the rear entry team. Slim was a heavyset, quiet fellow from Oregon, a State Trooper out there. He was one of three actual gunfight veterans on the team.

"2150," said his number two, Bear.

"Okay, let's hold here," Slim said, trying to control his breathing. "We'll move to the door at 2158."

They hunched, tensing, feeling the sultry weight of the air. It was all going so fast. Getting across the street and reassembling at the rallying point seemed much simpler than it was supposed to be. No screwups at all.

"One last time, let's go over assignments. I'm one; when the door goes, I pile through it first, with my .45, covering the right side of the rear hall, turning right, moving into the main room and covering the right again."

Two, three and four ran through their assignments, droning on about turns to left or right and sectors to cover with pistol or tommy gun.

"I'm five," said Henderson finally. "I go down the hall, past the casino, turn right, take the stairs up to the manager's office, which I cover. Securing that, I work the men's and women's rooms."

"I'm six," said Frenchy. "I grab the blonde, I fuck her fast, then I spray the room with lead, killing everybody, including you guys. Then I light up a smoke and wait for the newspaper boys and my Hollywood contract."

"All right, Frenchy," said Slim. "Cut the shit. This ain't no joke."

"All right, all right," said Frenchy. "I'm six. I support five up the rear stairs with the tommy, covering the left-hand side of the stairwell. I cover him in the manager's office, and then we check the two rest rooms. I hope there's a babe on the pot in the lady's."

"Cornhole," someone muttered.

"Now what's the last thing we heard?" asked Slim. "What should be freshest in our minds?"

There was stupefied silence.

"Damn, you guys already forgot! Mr. Earl is going to be in there. He'll be at the bar. So you guys especially, three and four, you make sure you do not cover him. No accidents. Got that?"

Taking the silence as assent, he then said, "Time check?"

"Uh, 2157."

"Shit, we're late. Okay guys, single file, follow me. You ready with that sledge, Eff?"

"Yes I am."

"Let's move out."

They scooted down the rear of the building and came to rest in the lee of the door. The alley was dark. All was silent.

"On the tommies, safeties off."

Silently, the men found the safeties of their weapons and disengaged them, while three edged around with his sledge, getting ready to give the door a stout whack just above the handle.

Slim looked at his watch. The second had ticked around, until it reached straight up.

"Do it," he said.

Earl stepped into a well-lighted space. It wasn't nearly as crowded as the Ohio had been that night. A big guy eyed him as he walked through the doorway, clearly a muscleman or some kind of enforcer, but he was so close to the door he felt the palooka would have no chance to react when the fellows spilled through in a few minutes.

He moved on into the big room, which was simply the majority of the building. It was just a space to house the sucker-swindling machinery, decorated along horse-racing lines, with jerseys and crops and helmets and horsehoes festooning the walls. The lights were bright, the smoke heavy, and the slots were set against the walls, where a number of weary pilgrims fed them coins to what appeared to be very little financial gain on their part. In the center of the room a couple of tables offered blackjack, there was a poker game going on but without much energy and a roulette wheel ticked off its reds and blacks as it spun to the amusement of another sparse crowd. But the main action was craps, where the players were louder and more excitable.

"Eighter, eighter, eighter from Decatur."

"No, no, Benny Blue's coming up, here comes the big Reno, I can feel it in my bones."

Perhaps because it was built around dynamic movement, this game seemed to draw the most passion. Its players crowded round, and gave their all to the drama.

"Yoleven, yoleven, yoleven!"

Earl slid to the bar and ordered a beer, which was delivered by a plug-ugly without much sentimentality.

"First one's on the house, long as it ain't the last one."

"Oh, it's going to be a long night, trust me, brother," said Earl, taking a sip of the brew.

He measured the bartender, who looked like a tough cracker, and thought he might have to cool him out. When the man's attention was on other customers, Earl snuck a peek down and under the bar, where he saw, among the bottles and napkins, a sawed-off pool cue, and a sawed-off 12-gauge pumpgun. The weapons were hung under the bar right next to the cash register. At 2159, Earl thought, he'd mosey down and set up there.

Meanwhile, he scanned the crowd, looking for security types. So far only two: the big guy at the door and the barkeep. Maybe there was another someplace but he sure didn't see him.

Smoke heaved and drifted in the bright room. He picked up his beer and moved on down to the cash register, until he was parked just above the cached weapons. The hand on the clock on the wall said ten o'clock, straight up.

Three's sledge hit the door, rebounded once. He caught it and being a strong young Georgia vice detective, swung again, to the sound of wood shattering and ripping. A blade of light fell into the alley as the door was blasted from its hinges and fell wretchedly to one side.

The men scrambled in.

There was a sense of craziness to it, as they stumbled over each other and no one could quite get his limbs moving fast enough. Their eyes bugged as the hormones of aggression flooded through their bodies. They rushed along, bringing the guns to bear, looking hungrily for targets to kill.

Slim was shouting *"Hands up! Hands up! This is a raid!"* and others took up the call, *"Raid! Raid! Raid!"*

Frenchy had but a glimpse of the first two teams as they fanned out and dispersed into the casino's main room. But he churned along in the wake of

Carlo Henderson, his partner, who was strangely animated to grace by all the excitement and moved ahead purposefully, quickly found the right-hand stairwell, and began to assault the stairs, screaming *"Raid! Raid! Hands up!"*

Frenchy was with him when a man appeared at the top of the stairs. Frenchy knew in a second he'd shoot if Carlo weren't in the way, but he couldn't fire and he sat back waiting for Carlo's shots to ring out. But Carlo didn't shoot.

"Hands up! Get those hands up and you won't get hurt!" he screamed, thrusting his .45 in his two hands before him, aimed straight at the heart of the figure, who threw his hands skyward and went to his knees.

Carlo was next to him like some kind of sudden athlete, spun him, leaned him against the wall, spread him and searched him. A Colt .32 pocket model came out and was tossed down the stairwell.

"You stay put!" Carlo demanded, reached up, gracefully snagged the guy in one half a pair of cuffs, wound him quickly around and clipped the other wrist and sat him down with a thump. He was wearing a white tuxedo and Frenchy bet he'd be the manager.

Perhaps that's why when the two men kicked open the casino manager's office and scanned it quickly for threats, they found nothing.

"Clear!"

"Clear on my side!" replied Frenchy.

Next they did the washrooms. A fairly drunk guy

was propped against the urinal; Frenchy gave him a nudge and he fell backward, spraying pee in a wide arc, but the two young policemen, though encumbered in vests and with weapons, were so horrified of the prospect of being splashed, they leapt back and missed the dousing. Frenchy felt a flare of rage, and stepped forward to club the drunk with his tommy gun butt, but Carlo interceded and brought him under control. The drunk lay in his own piss, screaming, "Don't hurt me, don't hurt me!"

"You stay here till we come get you," Carlo screamed. Then he turned to Frenchy. "Come on, goddammit!"

They ducked next into the ladies'. It was clear, except for a closet, which they tried and found locked.

"Smash it?" asked Frenchy.

Carlo pulled really hard. It wouldn't open.

"Yeah," he said. "You smash it open since you want to hit something. I'm going to take that drunk and the guy in the tux downstairs before they run away."

He disappeared.

Frenchy had a weird need to spray the door with the Thompson. Nah, he knew that would be wrong.

Instead, he beat at it until the jamb gave, and pulled it open. Nothing inside except a wash bucket and a mop.

He heard a thump or something coming from outside. He ducked out, searched, saw nothing. He looked into the casino manager's office and it appeared empty.

He thought nothing of it and downstairs he could hear the loud voice of D. A. Parker, "Now, ladies and gentlemen, you just stand clear, we are from the Prosecuting Attorney's Office and don't mean no harm to any citizens. You just relax and you'll be able to go home in a bit."

There was a quiet moment when the world seemed to hang suspended. Then it exploded.

Earl sat calmly as the doorway burst open and the first man through swung his .45 like a scythe and neatly clipped the security man at the door. Great anticipation, great reaction. Earl watched the hand with the gun invert, then flash outward toward the stunned piece of beefcake, heard the odd, meaty sound as the gun made contact with the face, and watched as the enforcer dropped into a puddle. Other raiders spilled into the room, fanned out, and took over the room.

It was good. He was proud. No one was out of control, no one was gesturing crazily or screaming. They simply asserted command. They were professional, and Stretch, who was doing the shouting, had an authoritative voice untarnished by fear or doubt.

"Hands up! Hands up! Show us hands!"

Hands went up; people froze. Even the croupiers and the pit bosses froze with the sudden, overwhelming display of force.

That is, except for the bartender.

Earl knew his man. The bartender reacted with his guts instead of his brain, and, alone among them, he spun and grabbed reflexively for a weapon under the bar.

Earl probably could have broken his arm with the sap. Instead, he thumped him lightly and perfectly, intercepting the plunging limb and striking it at the nearly fleshless bone along the arm's top.

"Ah!" the bartender groaned, driven to his feet by the agony of the blow that had turned the whole left-hand side of his body numb. He sat back, clasping the bruise to him, and in pure animal terror recoiled and tried to go tiny and harmless.

"You be a good boy!" Earl warned.

Earl turned back and saw that the situation was now in complete control. Nobody else moved.

"You okay, Mr. Earl?" asked Slim.

"B'lieve I'm fine," Earl said, taking his badge out of his pocket and pinning it to his lapel.

"You were one inch from catching a tommy gun burst in the guts," one of the raiders said to the bartender, who still groaned at the pain.

Earl leaned around the bar, plucked out the pool cue and threw it across the floor. Then he pulled out the sawed-off pump, pointed it down, and jacked the pump hard, ejecting six twelve-gauge shells. He dumped the empty thing on the bar, its pump locked back to expose the unfilled chamber.

D.A. was there next.

"Now, ladies and gentlemen, you just stand clear. We are from the Prosecuting Attorney's Office and don't mean you any harm. You just relax and you'll be able to go on home in a minute."

"Can we keep our winnings?"

"Anything on your person you may keep. Sorry, but anything on the tables will be confiscated by the Prosecuting Attorney's Office."

There was some grumbling, but as the guns came down and the hands came down, everybody seemed to be making the best of it.

In another second Carlo Henderson appeared with a squawking guy in a white tux, hands cuffed behind him.

"Who the hell are you? What the hell is going on? I am Jack McGaffery, manager of the Horseshoe, and Owney Maddox is going to be plenty jacked at this."

"Reckon he will be, sir. Are you aware there are illegal gaming devices on the property?"

"Naw, do tell? Never noticed a thing, there, Sheriff. By God, Owney Maddox will have your *ass* for this. You ask these folks. He won't—"

"Well, sir," said D.A., "you tell Owney Maddox if he wants to make an appointment with Mr. Becker, to go right ahead. Meanwhile, soon's we get these folks out of here, we're going to destroy the illegal—"

"*Destroy!* Jesus Christ, man, you must be *crazy!* Owney will hunt you to your last day on earth!"

"Don't think you get it yet, McGaffery. He ain't

hunting us, we're hunting him. We're the new boys in town and by God, he will wish we'd never come. All right, fellows, let's get it done!"

They began to herd the citizens out the front doors, while a few other raiders moved the casino staff to one side. Earl stood watching and noted that Frenchy finally arrived from upstairs with his Thompson gun. He hadn't shot anyone yet; that was good.

"All right," Earl commanded. "Peanut, you bring the cars up close and we'll get the axes out and go to town. Y'all, you just sit down over there, and watch what we do so you can give Owney Maddox a good report. Mr. Becker will be here soon. We'll see if you're gonna be arrested or not. I want—"

Earl had a thought before him which was something like "I want you to pay close attention to what a thorough job we do, because we're going to do a lot more thorough jobs before we're done," which was meant for the casino staff as a note of intimidation for Owney Maddox and the Grumley boys. That way he'd know he had some problems and he'd get serious about them.

But that thought never got out.

Instead, from the corner of his eye, he saw something move that shouldn't move at all. It was a shape, a form, a shadow, and no clear outline was visible, for it seemed to emerge from the back entrance in a flash of a second. Earl only recognized that it was a human form and that a hard, cold thing that rose at an angle above it was the double barrels of a shotgun.

Earl could not command himself to draw and fire. No man could move that fast from the rational part of his brain. He simply swept aside the coat, drawing the gun, his thumb flying to and pushing off the safety, his other hand clasping the grip and cradling the first hand, his elbows flying and then locking, almost as if he'd willed it rather than done it, and in the next billionth of a second the pistol reported loudly, kicked against his tight double-handed grip and ejected a spent brass shell.

In the close room the noise was tremendous. It bounced off walls and its vibrations sprang dust from rafters and countertops. It unleashed energy from everywhere, as citizens dove for cover, raiders dropped and pivoted, aiming their weapons off the cue from Earl, and even D.A. got his gun out fast and into play. Only Frenchy stood rooted in place, for Earl's bullet had passed within a foot or so of him before it plowed into the center chest of what appeared to be a vacant, doughy-faced young man in an ill-fitting Sunday-go-to-meeting suit.

His eyes locked on Earl's as the shotgun fell from his hand, and implored him for mercy. The request was too late, for it wouldn't have mattered if Earl fired again or not. The young man went down like a sack of spring apples falling off a wagon, hitting the floor with the crack of bones and teeth breaking; his blood began to pump from his heart across the floor in a spreading satin puddle.

Everybody was yelling and diving and moving at once, but Earl knew it was over. He'd seen the front sight on the chest at the moment he'd fired.

"Goddamn, Mr. Earl," somebody said.

"That damn boy!" said McGaffery. "He didn't have the sense of a mule. You didn't have to kill him, though."

"Maybe he ain't dead," said a raider.

"He's dead," said D.A., holstering his automatic. "When Earl shoots, he don't miss. Good shot, Earl. You boys see that? That's how it's done."

Earl himself felt nothing. He'd killed so many times before, and not only yellow men. He'd killed white men in Nicaragua in 1933, with the same kind of gun that Frenchy carried.

But he felt it in his heart right away, the difference: that was war. This was—well, what was it?

"You killed a Grumley," said the bartender, still holding his bruised wrist. "Now you got the Grumleys on you. Them boys don't forget a thing. Not never. The Grumleys will mark you and dog you the rest of your days, mister."

"I been dogged before, mister" was all Earl said; then he turned to the raiders and said, "Okay, let's get going. You got some busting up to do. Come on."

But he didn't like the killing either. It wasn't a good sign, Grumleys or no Grumleys.

CHAPTER 15

Owney knew the most important thing about his situation was to pretend he had no situation.

Thus, though Hot Springs' insular, gossipy little business, gambling and criminal communities were aflame with speculation about the raid, and the *Little Rock Courier-Herald* and the *Democrat* had run pieces, it was important for him to suggest that nothing was really amiss. He got up, dressed dapperly—an ascot!—and went for a stroll down Central, saying hello in his best Ronald Colman voice to all those he knew, and he knew many people. He was especially British today, even wearing a Norfolk jacket and flannels, with a dapper tweed hat.

"Cheerio," he said wherever he went. "Be good sports. Keep the old upper lip stiff. Tut tut and ho ho, as we say in Jolly Olde."

He attended a luncheon for the hospital board and dropped in at the Democratic Ladies' Club, where he made a donation of $1,000 toward the clubhouse redecorating project slated for that fall. He met Raymond Clinton, the Buick agency owner, and had a long discussion about the new Buicks. They were beauts! He said he was thinking about retiring his prewar limo. It was time to be modern and

American. It was the '40s. The Nazis and the Japs were whipped! We had the atom bomb!

But even as he was going about his public business, he was relaying orders through runners to various of his employees, directing a search, putting pressure on the police, sending out scouting parties, setting up surveillance at Becker's office in City Hall and convening a meeting.

The meeting was scheduled for 5:30 P.M., in the kitchen at the brand-new Signore Giuseppe's Tomato Pie Paradise, where Pap Grumley and several ranking Grumleys, F. Garry Hurst, Jack McGaffery and others showed up as ordered. Everybody gathered just outside the meat locker, where about a thousand sausages hung in bunches and strings. The smell of mozzarella and tomato paste floated through the air.

"No siree, Mr. Maddox," said Pap. "My boys, they been up, they been down. These coyotes have vanished. Don't know where they done gone to ground, but it ain't in no goddamn hotel nor no tourist camp. Maybe they's camping deep in the hills. Shit, my boys couldn't find a thing. We may have to go to the hounds to git on these crackers. Know where I can git me a troop of prize blue ticks if it comes to that. Them dogs could smell out a pea in a pea patch the size of Kansas. One particular pea, that is."

He spat a gob of a fluid so horrifyingly yellowed that even Owney didn't want to think about it. It landed in the sink with a plop.

"You got boys coming in?" Owney, the high baron of New York's East Side, asked in his native diction.

"Yes sir. Got boys from Yell County. The Yell County Grumleys make the Garland County Grumleys look tame. They're so mean they drink piss for breakfast."

Owney turned to Jack McGaffery.

"And you? You made the fuckin' calls I told you?"

"Yes sir. We can get gun boys from Kansas City and St. Paul inside a week if we need 'em. It ain't a question of guns. We can put guns on the street. Hell, there's only a dozen or so of them."

"Yeah, but we gotta find the fuckers first."

He turned to Hurst.

"What do you make of it?"

"Whoever thought this out, thought it out well," said the lawyer. "These boys were well armed and well trained. But more to the point, whoever is planning this thing has thought long and hard about what he is attacking."

"Garry, what the fuck are you tawkin' about?" said Owney.

"Consider. He—whomsoever *he* may be—has certainly made a careful study of Hot Springs from a sociological point of view. He understands, either empirically or instinctively, that all municipal institutions have been, to some degree or other, penetrated and are controlled by yourself. So he sets up what appears to be a roving unit. It stays nowhere. It has no local ties, no roots, no families. It can't be reported on. It can't be spied on. It can't be betrayed from within. It permits no photographs, its members do not linger or speak to the press, it simply strikes and vanishes. It's brilliant. It's even almost legal."

"Agh!" Owney groaned. "I smell old cop. I smell a cop so old he knows all the tricks. You ain't pulling no flannel over this old putz's eyes."

He looked back at Jack.

"The cowboy was the fast one. The rest were punks. But you said a old man was in command. That's what you said."

"He was. But I only heard the name Earl. 'Earl, that was a great shot,' the old man said to the fast cowboy after he clipped Garnet. But no other names were used. The old one was in charge but the cowboy was like the sarge or something."

"Okay," Owney said. "They will hit us again, the bastards. You can count on it. They are looking for the Central Book, because they know when they get that, they got us. Meanwhile, we will be hunting them. We got people eyeballing Becker. We follow Becker, he'll be in contact with them, and somehow, he'll lead us to them."

"Yes sir," said Flem Grumley, "'ceptin' that Becker never showed at his office this morning, and when we sent some boys by his house, it was empty. He moved his family out. He's gone underground too."

"He'll turn up. He's got speeches to make, he's got interviews to give. He wants to be governor and he wants to ride this thing into that big fuckin' job. He's just another hustler. He don't scare me. That goddamn cowboy, he scares me. But I've been hunted before."

"Pray tell, by whom, Owney?" asked Garry.

"Ever hear of Mad Dog Coll?"

"Yes."

"Yeah, well, Mad Dog, he comes gunning for me. He steals my best man, fuckin' Jimmy Lupton, and holds him for ransom. I got to pay fuckin' fifty long to get Jimmy back. He was a pisser and a half, that fuckin' kid. Balls? Balls like fuckin' steel fists. Crazy but gigantic balls. So you know what the lesson is?"

"No sir."

"Bo Weinberg catches him in a phone booth with the chopper. The chopper chops that mick fuck to shit. Don't matter how big his fuckin' balls are. The chopper don't care. So here's the lesson: everybody dies. Every-fuckin'-body dies."

After the meeting, Owney went to his car. He checked his watch to discover that it was five o'clock, 6:00 New York time. He told his driver where to go.

The driver left Signore Giuseppe's, drove down to Central, turned up it, then up Malvern Avenue and drove through the nigger part of town, past the

Pythian Hotel and Baths, past cribs and joints and houses, then turned toward U.S. 65, the big Little Rock road over by Malvern, but didn't drive much farther. Instead, he stopped at a gas station along the edge of Lake Catherine.

Owney got out, looked about to make certain he was not followed. Then he went into the gas station, a skunky old Texaco that looked little changed since the early 1920s, when it was built. The attendant, an old geezer whose name should have been Zeke or Lum or Jethro nodded, and departed, after hanging out a sign in the window that said CLOSED. Owney checked his watch again, went to the cooler, took out a nickel bottle of Coca-Cola, pried off the cap and drank it down in a gulp. He took out a cigarette, inserted it into his holder, lit it with a Tiffany's lighter that had cost over $200, and took a puff.

The cigarette was half down when the phone rang.

Owney went to it.

"Yeah?"

"I have a person-to-person long-distance call for a Mr. Brown from a Mr. Smith in New York City."

"This is Brown."

"Thank you, sir. I'll make the connection."

"Thanks, honey."

There were some clickings and the rasp of interference, but a voice came on eventually.

"Owney?"

"Yeah. That you, Sid?"

"Yeah."

"So what the fuck, Sid? What the fuck is going on?"

"Owney, I tell ya. Nothing."

"I got a boy busting my balls down here. Some hick ex-soldier prosecutor who thinks he's Tom Fuckin' Dewey."

"Not good."

"No, it ain't. But I can take care of it. What I'm worried about is that fucker Bughouse Siegel. Frank and Albert and Mr. Lansky all like the little fuck. Is he behind my trouble down here? Is he trying to muscle me out of the business? It might do him some good."

"Owney, like you said, I asked some questions. What I hear is he is just pissing money away into a big hole in the ground out in some desert. That hot-number babe he's got with him, you know, she ain't too happy. She's been talking to people about what an asshole he is. She has friends. She has a lot of friends and he leaves her alone in Hollywood to go out to the desert and piss some more money into a hole. Only I hear that broad ain't ever alone. She still has the hotsies for Joey Adonis, among others."

"So the Bughouse has that to worry about before he worries about my little action down here?"

"That's what I hear. But Owney, I have to tell you the big guys do like him. They sent him out there. He has their ear. I'd look out for him. He thinks big."

"Yeah, he thinks big, with my thoughts. I gave him his whole idea. He thinks he can fuckin' build a Hot Springs in the desert. There's nothing there but sand. Here, we got nature, we got mountains, we got lakes, we got—"

"Yeah, but in that state, gambling's legal, so you don't get raided. Remember that. That's a big plus."

"We're not *supposed* to get raided here."

"So you said. Owney, the guys, they always say, That Owney, he runs a smooth town. That's why they like to go there. The baths, some dames, some gambling, no problem, no hassles with the law. That's what they like. As long as you provide that for them, you will have no problems."

"Yeah."

"Owney. Best thing you can do is forget about Bugsy, and keep that town running smooth. That's your insurance policy."

"Yeah," said Owney. "Thanks, Sid."

It was on the way back that he had his big thought.

"Back home, sir?"

"No, no. Take me to the newspaper office. And then call Pap Grumley. Tell him to find Garnet Grumley's mother. Or someone who looks just like her."

CHAPTER 16

"So tell me what happened up there, Henderson," Earl asked Carlo.

"I guess I screwed up. I thought I had it covered. I thought we done a good job."

Earl nodded.

The raiders were headquartered in the pumping station of the Remmel Hydroelectric Dam, which blocked the Ouachita River and had thereby created Lake Catherine, and lay between Magnet and Hot Springs, on Route 65, not far at all from the Texaco station where Owney had gotten his call from New York. The pumping station, which was administered by the TVA and run out of Malvern, not Hot Springs, was a large brick building at the end of three miles of dirt road off U.S. 65; though most of its innards were taken up with turbines turning and producing electricity for Hot Springs, the upper floors had surprising space and provided room for fourteen cots, as well as hot showers and indoor plumbing. It was better than most places Earl had slept during the war. D.A. had thought all this out very carefully.

"Tell me what happened."

"Well sir, we done our best. I am truly ashamed it wasn't good enough. But we got up there fast, we nabbed that bird McGaffery on the steps, there was a goddamned pissing drunk in the men's room, and we run him downstairs too, and we checked all the closets."

"So Garnet Grumley could not have been up there?"

"I don't think so," said Carlo. "But if I missed him, then I missed him."

"He was not up there," said Frenchy. "Mr. Earl, we went all through that place. I even beat the lock off the closet door in the ladies'."

"See," said Earl, "I do not particularly care for having to shoot a boy dead, who was after all only doing his job and as it turned out had forgotten to load his shotgun. Either of you killed anyone?"

Both men shook their head no.

"I *swear* to you, Mr. Earl, that fellow did not come from up there," said Frenchy. "He must have snuck in from the outside. Or maybe he came up from the cellar."

"Wasn't no cellar," said Carlo. "And we'd have seen him in the alley if he'd been lurking up there. Mr. Swagger, I do believe it was my fault and I am very sorry it happened. It wasn't Frenchy's. I was number one on our fire team, so the job was mine, and I muffed it. If you give me a next time, I will sure try hard to do a better job."

"Jesus, Henderson," said Frenchy. "He wasn't up there. It's not your fault, it's not my fault. It just goddamned happened is all and everybody is lucky it was him that got killed, and not one of us."

Earl pushed something across the table at them. It was the *Hot Springs New Era,* the city's afternoon paper.

FARMBOY SLAIN IN COP "RAID"
Locals decry "Nazi" tactics
"He was a good boy," Mom says.

"Christ," said Frenchy.

Carlo read:

Raiders from the Prosecuting Attorney's Office shot and killed a local man while invading a local nightclub.

The incident occurred at the Horseshoe Club, on Ouachita Avenue in West Hot Springs, late last night.

Dead was Gar fnet Grumley, 22, of Hot Springs, shot by a raider as he wandered in from the upstairs bathroom.

"Garnet was a good boy," said his mother, Viola Grumley, of eastern Garland County. "He did all his chores and milked his special cow, Billie. I wonder what he was doing in that downtown club. But I wonder why they had to shoot such a harmless, God-fearing boy."

Fred C. Becker, Garland County Prosecuting Attorney, refused to talk to *New Era* reporters.

In a news release his office provided, he claimed that officers shot in self-defense while on a raid aimed at local gamblers.

See *New Era* Editorial, Page 7.

"Boy, I'll bet that one's rich."
"Oh, it is," said Earl.
The two young men flipped pages.

NEW JAYHAWKERS?

In the era preceding the Civil War it was common for night riders to terrorize Arkansans in the name of a just cause, which was more a license to hate. Town burnings, robberies, lynchings and other malicious acts were the order of the day. History remembers these brigands as Jayhawkers and under that same name it consigns them to evil.

Well, a new plague of Jayhawkers is upon us. Unlike their predecessors they don't ride horses and carry shotguns; no, they ride in modern automobiles and carry machine guns.

And, like their brethren from a century ago, they hide behind a supposedly "just" cause, the elimination of gambling influence and corruption from our beautiful little city. But, as before, this is a clear case of the cure being worse—far worse—than the disease.

"Ouch," said Carlo.
"Newspaper morons," said Frenchy.
"Well, they do leave out the fact that the late Garnet spent fourteen months in the state penitentiary for assault and that he had a juvenile record that goes back to before the war," said Earl. "And D.A. says that Viola is no more his mama than you are, Short.

He's an orphan Grumley, raised at the toe of a boot in the mountains, and pretty much your legger attack dog, and little else. So if a man had to die, better it was him than you or me."

"Yes sir," said Carlo.

"Okay, let me tell you two birds something. You are the youngest, but that don't bother me. You are probably also the smartest I got. I don't hold that smart boys ain't no good in combat, as some old sergeants do. But I do know your smart boy is easily distracted, and naturally doubtful, and has a kind of sense of superiority to all and sundry. So let me tell you, that if you want to stay in this outfit, you put all that aside. You put those smart-boy brains on the shelves and you commit to doing what you're told and doing it well and thoroughly. Elsewise, you're on your way back to where you come from, and you can tell your buddies there you were a bust as a raider."

"Yes sir," said Carlo.

"Now rack up some sleep. We're going again tonight."

CHAPTER 17

The Derby was filled that night. At one of the booths, the young, leonine Burt Lancaster held court like a gangster king, surrounded by cronies and babes, his teeth so white they filled the air with radiance.

In another, the young genius Orson Welles sat with his beautiful wife, eating immense amounts of food, an actual second dinner, and downing three bottles of champagne. Rita Hayworth just watched him sullenly as he uttered the words that were to become his signature: "More mashed potatoes, please."

Mickey was there, of course, though without his wife. He was with a chorine who had even larger breasts than his wife. He was smoking Luckies and drinking White Russians and looking for producers to shmooze, because he could feel himself, in his dreams at least, slipping ever so slightly.

Bogie was there, with a little nobody named Bill something or other, a Mississippi-born screenwriter who was lost in the rewrites of Ray Chandler's *The Big Sleep*. Bogie called him "Kid," got him good and drunk, and kept trying to get him to understand that it really didn't matter if anybody figured out who did it.

And Virginia was there, with her swain Benjamin "Bugsy" Siegel, and Ben's best Hollywood friend, Georgie Raft.

"Will you look at that," said Ben. "Errol Flynn. Man, he don't look good."

"He's all washed up, I hear," said Georgie, drunkenly. "Warner's may drop him. Look at him."

Errol Flynn was even drunker than Georgie Raft and his once beautiful face had begin to show ruination. It was a mask of beauty turning inexorably into a burlap sack hung on a fencepost.

"Yeah, well, they didn't pick your contract up either, Georgie," said Virginia.

"I bought my way out of my contract," said Georgie. "I gave Jack a check for $10,000 and walked out of his office a free man."

"I heard he would have paid *you* the ten long to take a hike," said Virginia.

"Can it, Virginia," said Ben.

Raft stared moodily into his drink. For a tough guy, he had an amazingly delicate little face, a nose as perfectly upturned as any pixie's.

"It ain't been easy on him," consoled his best friend from the old neighborhood, where they'd specialized in heisting apple carts.

"Why don't you beat up a casting director, Ben? That is, if you could find one you could take. Maybe you could make Georgie big again."

"I don't know what's the matter with this bitch," Ben explained to Georgie. "Ever since we got back from the South, she's been acting funny toward me."

He looked at her. But goddamn, she was still the female animal in all her surly glory, tonight with a huge wave of auburn cream for hair, meaty big-gal shoulders and breasts scrunched together to form a black slot in the ample flesh into which a man could tumble and lose his soul forever.

"Yeah," she said, "maybe it has something to do with all the times you fly out to the fucking desert and watch Del Webb pour Mr. Lansky's money into a big hole in the ground."

Another row was starting.

"Kids, kids, kids," consoled Georgie. "Let's enjoy ourselves. We have a great table at the Brown Derby in a room filled with movie stars. People would kill to get what we have. Let's enjoy. Garçon, another Scotch, please."

The three friends each retreated briefly to his or her libation, tried to settle down and collect themselves, then returned to conviviality.

"Virginia, it's a big thing I got going. You'll see. The big guys all believe in it. It'll be bigger than Hot Springs."

"Hot Springs is supposed to be in Hot Springs, not in a desert. Owney Maddox is supposed to run Hot Springs. That's the way it's supposed to be, Ben. You ought to know that."

Ben allowed himself a snicker.

"You think Owney's so high and mighty? You think nobody would stand against Owney? Well, let me tell you something, Owney's got some troubles you wouldn't want."

"Owney's okay," said Georgie. "He knew some people and helped me get started out here."

"Owney's finished," said Ben. "He just don't know it yet."

"Owney's a creep but he can take care of himself," Virginia argued, then took another sip of her third screwdriver. She could outdrink any man in Hollywood except for Flynn. "He pretends to be a British snob but he's an East Side gutter rat, just like you two pretty boys."

"Virginia, Owney's got troubles and the big guys know it. I heard about it all the way out here. He's got some crusader raiding his joints and he doesn't know how to get the guy. His grab on that town is shaky and once it slips, you just watch everybody walk away from him. It happened to him in New York, it'll happen to him in Hot Springs. He lost the Cotton Club, he'll lose the Southern. You just watch. He'll end up dead or with nothing, which is the same thing."

"And would you be the guy to take it from him?"

"I don't want nothing in Hot Springs. But I don't want Hot Springs being Our Town either. We need a new town, and I mean to build one in the desert. You just watch me, goddammit."

"Ben, the only thing you've built so far is a hole in the ground for somebody else's money."

"Virginia, you are so rude."

"Don't you love me for it, sugar?"

"No, I love you for them tits, that ass, and the thing you do with your mouth. You must be the only white girl in the world who does that thing."

"You'd be surprised, honey."

"Hello, darling. Your bosom is magnificent."

This was from Errol Flynn, an old pal of Virginia's from some weekend or other. Flynn leaned into their booth, his famous handsome face radiating a leer so intense it could melt a vault door.

"Hit the road, you limey puke," said Ben.

"Hi, Georgie," said Errol, ignoring Ben. "Tough luck about Warner's. They'll drop me next."

"I got some deals working. I'll be okay. Errol, how're you doing?"

"Well, there's always vodka."

"Errol," said Virginia, "just don't doodle any more fifteen-year-olds. Jerry Geisler might not get you out of it next time."

"In like Flynn, old girl. Oh, Benjamin, didn't see you there, old fellow. Still looking for buried treasure? There's a very good map to it in *Captain Blood*."

"You Aussie bastard."

The reference was to one of Ben's more regrettable adventures. With a former lover who billed herself a countess by way of some forgotten marriage to an actual Italian count, he had rented a yacht and gone to an island off the coast in search of pirate's treasure. It had been quite the joke in Los Angeles in the social season of 1941.

"Don't pick on Ben," said Virginia. "He has big

plans. He does know where the treasure is buried and it is in a desert, only it ain't on an island."

"Virginia, you bitch."

"Tut tut, old man," said Errol, moving on to another table.

"You shoulda smashed him," said Georgie. "He can be an asshole. You understand, I can't take him on because he still has Jack Warner's ear, and he might talk against me. I might get another shot at Warner's, so I don't want to do nothing now."

"You're dreaming," said Virginia. "You couldn't smack him because you're afraid of him. He's pretty tough, they say. And genius here couldn't smack him because he can't smack anybody without puking all over his clothes."

"Virginia, leave it alone."

"Did he tell you that story, Georgie? He tries to strong-arm this cowboy in Hot Springs and the guy hits him so hard he can't sit up straight for a week and a half. And I had to listen to him all that time, whinin' like a baby."

"I'll fix that guy."

"Yeah, you'll fix him. You and some army. Ben, why don't we go back right now? Fix him this week. Get it out of the way?"

Ben's eyes clouded and his face tightened.

"I got business to take care of first."

"He's spooked by this guy. So he'll hire goons to clip him, because he don't have the guts to do it man on man."

"I will fix that guy," Bugsy swore. "I will fix him after I fix Owney and after I fix Hot Springs. Forget Hot Springs. Its time is over. The future is in the desert, goddammit, and I will lead the way."

CHAPTER 18

The Belmont lay close to the Oaklawn Racetrack, just south of Hot Springs. If the Horseshoe was your run-of-the-mill joint, with a hundred duplicates on almost any street in town, the Belmont was a step up the food chain. It offered the fancier gamblers a sense of class without quite demanding of them the tuxedoed glamour—with its Xavier Cugats and its Perry Comos—that a place like the Southern Club might. The entertainment tended to be regional, usually a piano combo that played light jazz. It sold cocktails at the bar, not shots, not champagne. Its machines were the sleeker Pace Chrome Comet, which looked as if it could get up and fly, the hottest thing from the year 1939, as its reels spun bells and apples and bananas and oranges this way and that. These machines weren't as tight as the older models, which meant that once or twice a night a line of bells would pop up and pilgrim would be rewarded with a silver cascade of nickels. The house payoff was a modest 39 percent.

It stood in the same hollow as the now deserted racetrack, under a low piney ridge, and it had been done up in the style of the antebellum South, to resemble a wooden plantation house with fake columns and white trim that a Scarlett O'Hara might have designed. A valet crew parked cars; the overhanging elms gave it hushed and muted elegance.

Rather than enter the gates and move into the parking lot, in plain sight of the valets, D.A. elected to infiltrate from the empty racetrack. The three cars discharged their men on the far side, and there the raiders loaded magazines, checked weapons, put on vests and went over their plans for the last time. Becker was already there, this time with two men on his staff and a clerk-driver.

D.A., Earl and Becker hunched undercover in a racetrack portico, examining a diagram of the Belmont with a flashlight.

"Since this is a bigger, more complicated structure," said D.A., "I'd rather have muscle up front. I'd send ten men through the front door and side door—a six-man team and a four-man team—and I'd bolt that kitchen door and leave two men out back to cover it. That way, you got all your force up front and you get it into play."

"I don't want any shooting," said Becker suddenly. "I don't want anyone else getting hurt."

There was a quiet moment.

Then D.A. said, "Well, sir, then I guess we better gather the boys up and take 'em home. I ain't sending men into a dangerous situation with the idea they can't defend themselves."

"No, no," said Becker. "They *can* defend themselves. I just want 'em to *think* before they shoot."

"If they think before they shoot," said Earl, "they may die before they shoot."

"We train 'em to shoot instinctively. They've been trained hard. There won't be no mistakes."

"Like the Horseshoe?" Becker said.

"That weren't no mistake, sir," said the old man. "That was a completely justified legal shooting during the commission of a bonded officer's official duty, and we ought to thank the man who done it, for it probably saved some lives."

Becker seemed to vacillate, almost biting his lower lip like a child.

"It just played bad in the papers, that's what I mean. I have more photogs from Little Rock here," he finally said. "We need the Little Rock papers behind us. They'll get the state behind us. The Hot Springs papers don't matter. But you can't screw up in front of Little Rock reporters. Okay?"

Both officers nodded, and Earl was thinking: This bird wants everything. He wants us to raid without killing and he doesn't want the action to get out of control. He's worried more about the press than the young men who are going in tonight. You can't control this work like that.

"We'll brief the boys," said D.A.

"Excellent. I'll meet up with the photographers."

Becker looked at his watch: it was 9:35 P.M.

"Ten P.M., as usual?"

"We can't set up that fast," said D.A. "Make it 10:30."

"I told the photographers to meet me across the street at 9:45. Dammit, they'll get bored."

"Ten-fifteen then, if we hurry."

"That's good," said Becker. He walked back to his car and his clerk drove him away.

"He's shaky," said Earl. "I don't like that."

"I don't like it neither."

They beckoned the raiders over, and briefly went over the plan.

Earl finally said, "You, Henderson and Short, you'll be the cover team."

He could feel Frenchy's eagerness seem to melt in the dark.

"Want you to slip up and jimmy the kitchen door with a crowbar or something, so nobody can get out. If somebody does get out, he's wanting to get out bad, so you cuff him and cover him closely. Okay?"

"Yeah," said Henderson.

"Remember, be cool, calm, collected. Y'all been doing good. I'll go in after the entry team, but you be listening to Slim, he's the boss. I'm just along for support."

"Yes sir."

The unit moved around the racetrack single file. They could see the Belmont twinkling through the trees and hear the jazz streaming out of it, almost with a clink of cocktail glasses and the late-night odor of cigarettes to it.

"We'll go through the trees up high, on the ridge; then we'll file down and around the building. The entry team will go around front. There's people out there, so you have to control them right away."

But Earl drew D.A. aside.

"That ridge is a little steep," he whispered. "With these vests and the Thompsons, coming down in the dark could be tricky. Somebody could fall, we could get an accidental discharge. See, I'd keep 'em down here and just slip behind the line of sight from the front here on the right. Rally at the corner. Send the teams around, set up, and move fast, real fast."

D.A. looked at him for just a second, and a peculiar light came into his eyes, invisible in the night.

How does he know? he thought.

But then he saw the wisdom in Earl's counsel.

"Yeah, that's good, Earl."

Earl told the team of the new plan.

"You're on safety now. Team leaders, when you get there at the rallying point, you remember to tell your tommy-gunners to go off safety. If they have to shoot, something better come out when they pull the triggers besides cussing. Got that?"

Whispers came in assent.

"Henderson, you got that crowbar?"

"No sir," said Henderson, "but I do have a length of chain and a padlock."

"Good. You all straight?"

"Yes sir."

"You're also in support. If it gets wild, your job is to come in through the back. Got that?"

"Yes sir."

"Short, you got that?"

No answer.

"Short!"

"Yeah, yeah. I'm all set."

"Okay," said Earl. "Let's do it."

Frenchy and Carlo separated from the congregation of raiders. They slithered around the back of the plantation house, keeping low, under the view from the windows. They scuttled alongside the foundation, at last coming to the kitchen door. It was closed already, but the windows on either side were open, and a steamy light and a sense of urgent bustle poured out of each. They could hear Negro men talking among themselves.

Henderson slipped forward, looped the chain around the door handle, pulled it tight, looped it against the doorjamb, and clamped the lock shut. It would hold tight enough to prevent an exit, unless somebody really leaned into it.

The two men crept out to the perimeter of trees and set up in a defensive position about thirty yards in back of the house.

"You better give me the Thompson," said Carlo.

"Not a chance," said Frenchy. "You're fine."

"I can't hit anything at this range with a .45."

"Yeah, well, I have the Thompson and I'm keeping it. Get that straight right now. We wouldn't be in shit squad if you hadn't screwed up. So you don't deserve the Thompson."

"I screwed up? You screwed up! You didn't do a last check, or you would have found that hillbilly."

"I did do that last check. He wasn't up there. That's what you should have said to Earl, not this 'I'm so sorry' crap. If you act guilty, the facts don't matter. You are guilty."

"You should have checked."

"I did check. So here we are, dumped out back so we don't fuck up again."

"Somebody has to do this job."

"Nobody has to do this job. We all should be going in."

Frenchy was really getting steamed. Something about Earl really had him angry. Earl this, Earl that, God Earl, King Earl, Earl the leader of the pack! It was beginning to wear on him.

"What's so special about Earl?" he blurted.

"Earl's a hero and you're lucky to be here to learn from him," was all Carlo could think to say. "Now shut up and pay attention. We should be doing our jobs, not yakking about this stuff like old ladies."

Of course Becker's change in schedule had thrown the whole thing off. They weren't in position until 10:10, and in the darkness it took about four minutes to get organized into the proper squads and fire team, all trying to do it silently while crouching in the bushes under the windows. Fortunately, there was no perimeter security, no patrolling guards, no dogs, for if there had been, surely the whispering, bickering raiders would have been easily spotted.

Finally, with just thirty seconds to go, Earl got them straightened out, and the side-entry squad peeled off to beeline to the side door, which stood unguarded.

Earl looked at his watch.

"Okay," he said, "I'm going to go out and get the valets out of the way."

"You be careful," Slim said.

"*You* be careful," Earl said. "You're going in. I'm just going to roust some teenagers."

Earl stood, slipped out of his vest, which again would blow his cover, and rounded the corner.

He walked up the walk where three kids about eighteen or so lounged smoking under a neon sign that announced VALET. They wore absurd costumes that he could tell from their posture they despised.

"Hi, fellas," he said.

The boys looked up, caught short. Where the hell did this bird come from? But he was so chipper and bodacious the way he strode manfully up the flagstones to them.

"Uh—" the oldest began.

"See, fellas, I'm from the Prosecuting Attorney's Office." He pulled open his suit coat to show the badge pinned over his left breast. "Now we have something just about to happen here, and I don't want none of you boys getting hurt, so why not just step aside a bit, and turn and face the wall, maybe rest your hands up agin it."

"Are we under arrest?"

"Not unless you robbed a bank. Robbed any banks?"

"No sir."

"Ain't that swell."

"I better call Mr. Swenson," said one of the boys, reaching for a phone mounted on the wall.

Earl's fast hands beat him to the destination. He grabbed the phone, and with a snap popped the cord that ran to the receiver. "I don't think that would be a good idea," he said merrily. "Mr. Swenson's going to find out we're here soon enough, believe me."

Using the authority of his body language, he herded them along the front of the casino until they were a good twenty yards from their positions.

"You wouldn't have no guns, would you?"

"No sir," came a reply.

"'Cause I don't want to have to hurt nobody. You just rest up agin the building for a few minutes while this thing happens and everything will be just fine."

Earl turned a bit, and gave a whistle and watched as the raid began.

"There's the signal. Safeties off. Let's do it," said Slim.

He led his five men around the corner of the building to the front door. The door was open and a security officer, talking to a woman just inside the entrance, looked up in surprise. Terry, Slim's number-two man, clubbed him with the compensator on the end of his Thompson muzzle, opening a vicious wound in the side of his face, and he went down. The woman screamed but the raiders rushed past her like McNamara's band and began to fan out into the casino, their guns much in evidence, their fedoras low over their eyes, their square vests like sandwich boards across their bodies.

"Hands up! Hands up! This is a raid!"

The side-door team hit its entry point with the same velocity and urgency. The doors didn't need sledges but merely stout kicks. The men poured in and fanned out on the other side of the room. A team raced upstairs, clearing rooms, finding only gamblers and staff members, but no resistance.

It was over in seconds.

"Y'all go home now," Earl said to the valets. "This place is closed. You find other jobs tomorrow, hear?"

Earl walked in, his badge pinned to his lapel, and seconds later D.A. pulled up in a car.

It had gone exactly as planned: the overwhelming show of force, the speed of deployment, the cleverness of the raiders as they separated gamblers from workers, the pure professionalism of it.

"Clear upstairs," came the call.

"Clear in the kitchen," came another call.

"Now ladies and gentlemen," said D.A., "this here's a raid on an illegal gambling facility by the Prosecuting Attorney's Office. You will be checked and released if there are no outstanding warrants on you. You may keep any winnings you have on your person. We'll have you out of here in no time, if you cooperate with us. And my advice is: if you like to gamble, try Havana, Cuba, because that's where you're going to have to go."

Mr. Swenson, the manager of the place, was brought between two raiders, cursing and spitting. A rotund man, with slicked-back hair and a summer tuxedo, he wore a red carnation in his lapel. Earl plucked it out and inserted it into his mouth, shutting him up.

"When we want to talk to you," he said, "we will tell you. Otherwise you suck on that flower like a lollipop and watch us tear this joint up so you can tell Owney Maddox he's finished in this town."

Then they heard the machine gun fire.

"There they go," said Carlo.

But from the rear, behind the trees thirty yards out, the two young officers saw nothing. They heard glass breaking, doors being shattered and other signals of men moving aggressively against an objective. It was over very quickly.

"That's it?" said Frenchy.

"I guess," said Carlo.

"Well, let's get in there."

But Carlo wasn't sure. He realized now he had no clear post-raid instructions.

"I think we ought to hang here till we're released."

"Come on, it's over. You can tell it's over. I don't want to miss the party."

"There's going to be plenty of party. Let's just sit here a bit longer."

"Shit, sit here in the dark, while everybody else is having a great time? Come on, this is stupid. Who died and left *you* in charge? That's where we're needed, not sitting out here like a couple of Boy Scouts."

Carlo let it simmer. Rather than argue with his partner, he just hunkered yet more solidly against the weight of the tree, saying nothing, moving not a muscle or a twitch, signifying the conversation was over.

"Look," said Frenchy, "we were put out here to cover this back entrance. Nobody's coming out this back entrance. So we're just wasting our time."

Finally, it seemed he was right. There was no more bustle from the kitchen and no evidence of movement or escape from the door.

"All right," Carlo finally said, "let's go."

They got up.

"Put that safety on," said Carlo. "I don't want you roaming around with a live gun."

"Safety's already *on,*" said Frenchy, though of course it wasn't, nor did he have any intention of putting it on, not till the party was over.

The two young men walked to the kitchen door, feeling the bulk of the would-be plantation house loom over them. Carlo bent, unlocked the padlock, coiled the chain, and opened the door, stepping in.

Frenchy followed him and—

Whoa, there.

He caught a peripheral of movement from his left, spun, and saw a second figure leap silently from the window, collect himself, join his partner and start to head off.

Frenchy dashed at them, intercepting them halfway to the trees.

"Hold it!" he screamed. *"Hands up!"*

He braced them from thirty feet with the Thompson, his finger dangerously caressing its trigger, which strained ever so gently against the pad of his fingertip.

But neither man seemed particularly challenged by the heavy gun aimed at him.

"Hey, hey, watch it, kid, them things is dangerous."

The other laughed.

"He's more gun than man, I'd say." They separated slightly.

"Don't move!" barked Frenchy.

"We're not moving? Are we moving? I don't see us moving. Do you see us moving?"

"I'm not moving," said the other. "If a lawman tells me not to move, I'm not moving, no sir."

"Hands! Show me hands!"

But neither man raised his hands.

They were two tough-looking customers in suits with hats drawn down across their eyes, mid- to late thirties, both handsome in a rough way. They were utterly calm. The one on the right was even smiling a little bit. The signals they were putting out utterly confounded him.

"Look, kid, why don't you put that gun down and go inside before somebody gets hurt," said one. "You don't want to do nothing stupid now, do you? Something that you'd regret your whole life? I mean hell, this is just a penny-ante gambling bust that ain't supposed to happen and it's all going to be straightened out in—"

Frenchy fired. The gun shuddered, heaved, flashed, spit smoke and flung a line of empties off to the right, pounding against his shoulder. Three-round burst? No siree bob. He hosed them, blowing them backward like tenpins split by a bowler's strike, and they tumbled to the earth in a tangle of floating dust and gun smoke.

"I don't do stupid things, asshole," he said.

Then he fired another burst, to make sure they stayed down.

Carlo, halfway through the kitchen, got there first. He found Frenchy standing thirty-odd feet from the bodies, screaming hysterically.

"Asshole! Assholes! You fucking *pricks!*"

A tendril of smoke curled out of the compensator of the tommy and a litter of brass shells lay at his feet. The stench of gun smoke filled the air.

"What happened?"

"Fuckin' guys made a move. I got 'em. Goddamn, did I get 'em. Got 'em *both,* goddammit!"

"You okay?"

Clearly he wasn't. His eyes were as wide as lamps and his face was drawn into a mask of near-hysteria. He sucked at the air mightily. He seemed to stagger, then dropped to one knee.

"What the hell happened?" yelled Earl, arriving in a second.

Frenchy was silent.

"He nabbed these two guys making a getaway. He braced them, they drew and he dropped them. Looks like he clipped them both."

Earl walked over to the bodies as D.A. arrived. Two other raiders showed up, and then Becker, alone.

"What the hell is going on, for God's sake? I have two Little Rock photographers and two reporters out front, and they want to know what the hell happened."

"The officer dropped two runaways," said D.A. "They drew on him? Isn't that right, son?"

But Frenchy was silent.

Earl kneeled, put a hand out to each throat to feel for a pulse, but purely as an obligation. Each pulse was still. The two men lay on their backs. Frenchy had shot very well. Dust and smoke still floated in the air, and the blood continued to ooze from a network of wounds, absorbed by the material of the suits, so that each man was queerly damp, a sponge for excess blood. One's eyes were open blankly. The other's face was in repose. A hat was trapped under one head but the other hat lay a few feet away. The wounds were mostly in the torso and gut; both faces were unmarked.

"They drew on you, right?" asked D.A.

Frenchy was silent.

Earl heard the question and did the next bit of very dirty work. He pulled the sodden suit coats away from the bodies and checked for weapons. No shoulder holsters, no hip holsters, no guns jammed in belts, no guns in pockets, no guns in ankle holsters, no guns in suit pockets.

Earl rolled one over slightly, and gingerly withdrew a wallet. It contained what looked to be about $2,000 in cash and a driver's license in the name of William P. Allgood, from Tulsa, Oklahoma. A business card identified Mr. Allgood as an oil equipment leasing agent.

"Shit," said Earl, turning to the next body. That was a Phillip Hensler, also of Tulsa, a salesman for Phillips Oil.

He walked back.

"They wasn't armed," he said.

"Shit," said D.A.

"Oh, Christ," said Becker. "He killed two unarmed men? Jesus Christ, and I've got reporters here? Oh, Jesus Christ, you said they were trained, this wouldn't happen! Oh, Christ!"

"It's worse. One's a goddamn oil salesman, one leases drilling equipment. Both from Tulsa."

"Oh, shit," said D.A.

By this time, the Hot Springs police had arrived, and out in the lot, the gumballs flashed red in the night. A heavyset detective came around the corner with two uniforms.

"Mr. Becker? What the hell is going on?"

"One of my investigators shot two fleeing men," said Becker. "Naturally, we'll want a full investigation."

"Shit," said the cop.

"Y'all get on out of here until we're done," said Earl.

"Hey, buddy, I'm Captain Gilmartin and I—"

"I don't give a fuck who you are," said Earl, ramming his chest square against the fat man's gut, "I got six tommy guns that say you get the fuck off my operation till I let you on it, and if you don't like that, then there's some woods over there and whyn't you and I go discuss this a little further?" He fixed his mankiller's glare against the cop and watched the man melt and fall back.

"Take it easy, Earl," said D.A. "The police can control the crowd and look at the bodies when we're gone."

Earl nodded.

But someone else came up to the mute Becker, one of his assistants.

"Fred, the press guys are really getting difficult. I can't hardly contain 'em. They want to come back here and see what we bagged."

"Shit," said Becker. Then he turned to D.A.

"So you tell me what to do. You *promised* me this wouldn't happen. Now we got a situation where we've killed two innocent men. Unarmed men."

"Well, we don't know nothing about 'em yet," D.A. said.

Earl was so disgusted with Becker's panic that he turned and walked away, over to where Frenchy knelt in the grass with Henderson more or less holding him. He knelt too.

"You saw them make a move?" he asked.

"He ain't talked yet," said Henderson.

"Short. *Short!* Look at me! Snap out of it, goddammit. You saw them make a move?"

"I swear to Christ they did," Frenchy said, swallowing.

"They ain't armed."

"I know they were going to try something. I saw his hand move."

"Why would his hand move? It had nothing to move toward."

"I— I—"

"Did you panic, Short? Did you just squeeze down on 'em because you was scared?"

"No sir. They made a move."

"Son, I want to help you. Ain't nobody here going to do it. That Becker, he'll throw you to the wolves if it makes him the youngest governor in the state of Arkansas."

"I— I know they moved. They were trying something."

"Is there any evidence? Did they say anything? I mean, give us something to work with. Why did you fire?"

"I don't know."

"Did you see anything, Henderson?"

Carlo swallowed. He decided not to mention Frenchy's cursing the dead bodies, his state of lost anger.

"He was just standing there with the smoking gun. They were dead. That's all."

"Shit," said Earl.

But someone was standing over him.

Peanut, the biggest man in the unit, a former detective from Atlanta, loomed over them.

"Whaddaya want, Peanut?"

"Well sir," said Peanut, "I may be wrong, but I don't think I am."

"What?"

"Them boys. The boys Short bushwhacked."

"Yeah?"

"I looked 'em over real careful."

"They're a couple of salesmen from Tulsa."

"No sir. B'lieve one's Tommy Malloy, out of Kansas City, and the other's Walter Budowsky, called Wally Bud. Bank robbers."

"Bank robbers?"

"Malloy's number one on the FBI's most wanted list. Wally Bud is only number seven. But that's who it is, killed deader'n stumps over there."

"Jesus Christ," said Frenchy. "I'm a hero!"

CHAPTER 19

Cleveland was on the phone. Owney didn't want to take it and you never could be too sure about the security of the phones, even if Mel Parsons, who ran Bell Telephone in Hot Springs, maintained that no one could eavesdrop without his knowledge.

Still, Owney knew he had to take the call.

He had a martini, and a Cubano. He sat in his office in the Southern. One of the chorus girls kneaded the back of his neck with long, soothing fingers. Jack McGaffery and Merle Swenson—neither with a club to manage—sat earnestly on the davenport. F. Garry Hurst smoked a cigar and looked out the window. Pap and Flem Grumley were also in attendance, though as muscle slightly exiled to a further circle.

"Hello, Owney Maddox here."

"Cut the English shit, Owney. I ain't one of your stooges."

"Victor? Victor, is that you?"

"You know it is, Owney. What the hell is going on down there? My people tell me some cops knocked off Tommy Malloy and Wally Bud. I'm supposed to tell Mr. Fabrizzio that? Mr. Fabrizzio liked Tommy very much. He knew his dad back in the '20s when his dad legged rum across Superior for him."

"It's nothing. I got some pricks who—"

"Owney, Jesus Christ, this is serious shit. There are people unhappy all over the goddamn place. Tommy was down there because you said he'd be all right. Send your boys down, you said; I run the town, the town welcomes visitors. What the fuck, now I got two dead guys?"

"I'm having some trouble with a local fuckin' prosecutor. It ain't a big thing."

"Oh, yeah? It was pretty fucking big to Tommy Malloy. He's fucking dead, if I recall."

"I got some kind of rogue cop unit. These guys, they're like another mob: they just open fire and to hell with anything else. It's like the Mad Dog is runnin' them. I will take care of it. Mr. Fabrizzio and his associates have nothing to worry about. It's safe for Cleveland, it's safe for Chicago, it's safe for New York. Ask Ben Siegel, he was just down here. He saw the town. Ask him."

"Owney, it was Bugsy *called* Mr. Fabrizzio.

That's why I'm on the phone right now."

"That kike fuck," said Owney.

Now it was official. Bugsy was talking against him. That was tantamount to a declaration of war, for it meant that Bugsy was lobbying for permission from the commission to move against him. Whatever was going on with goddamned Becker, it was helping Bugsy no end.

"Look, Vic, we go way back. You know me to be a man of my word. I'm fuckin' dealing with this. I will take care of it. A week, maybe two, that's all, then we're back exactly doing what we've been doing since '32."

"Bugsy says, once he gets his joint up and running, that's the kind of shit would never happen. He guarantees it. Gambling's legal out there."

"Yeah, but it's a fucking desert. It's full of scorpions and lizards and snakes. Great fun. I can see what you'd be telling Mr. Fabrizzio after a snake bit him onna ass!"

"Well, you got a point there, Owney. Just get it taken care of. And this is advice from a friend. Imagine what your enemies are saying."

Owney hung up, only to get a new call. It was from the lobby, saying that Mayor Leo O'Donovan and Judge LeGrand were here, they had to see him.

"Send them up."

This was troubling. By time-honored fiat, meetings with Hot Springs officials were conducted on the sly, never in observable public spots, particularly a casino. This meant that the two men, who more or less administered the town under his benevolent guidance, were seriously spooked.

He turned to the girl, whose face was pretty but vacant.

"Honey, you go now. You come visit Owney later tonight."

She smiled a bright, fake smile, so intense that he thought he might already have had her. Maybe he had. He couldn't remember.

In any case, as she ducked out, the two town officials ducked in, and didn't even notice Pap and Flem Grumley, who under normal circumstances they would have avoided like a disease. After all, the Grumleys *were* a disease.

Owney offered them a drink, a cigar, and an earnest demeanor.

"Owney," said Leo O'Donovan, His Honor, a watery-eyed old hack who like to parade around the town in his cabriolet behind horses named Bourbon and Water, "I'll come to the point. People are unsettled with this kind of violence. Suddenly, the town is turning into Chicago in the '20s."

"I'm working like hell to locate these characters! What do you think I been doing, Leo, sitting on my hands? You think it's fuckin' good for me when two boys get clipped on my own fuckin' territory? Next thing, we won't be getting the Xavier Cugats and the Perry Comos and the Dinah Shores down here, and then we're screwed."

"Jeez, Owney," said Leo, dumbfounded. "I thought you were *British*."

Under the intense pressure of his situation, he had slipped and let his New York persona show in front of people not in the inner circle.

"Well," he said, somewhat archly, "when one finds oneself in a gangster movie, one must act the gangster, no? No, Garry?"

F. Garry Hurst said, "Absolutely, old toff. Mr. Maddox sometimes *pretends* to be an East Side gangster for the amusement of his staff."

Pap chimed in with, "He's a proper English gent, the finest in these here parts, Mr. Mayor."

The mayor looked at Pap as if he'd just been addressed by a large hunk of dogshit, sniffed and turned back to Owney.

"You have to do something, Owney. The town is coming to a stop."

"Oh, I hardly think that's quite the case, Leo. The girls are still doing their mattress-backed duties, the alcohol is still flowing, the horse wire still thrums with electric information, the fools still bet the horses, the wheel and the dice, Xavier continues to wow them, and Dinah is scheduled for next week. I've just replaced my old Watlings here at the Southern with brand-new Mills Black Cherries, the very latest thing. Fresh from the factory in Chicago, seventy-five of them, the most beautiful machine you've ever seen. I've got the best room in the country. So you see, we really haven't been affected a bit. We've lost two houses out of eighty-five, and less than $100,000, plus around sixty-five slots. It's nothing. It's a trice, a trifle, a gossamer butterfly wing."

The two officials were hardly consoled.

"Owney," said Judge LeGrand, "the mayor is onto something. Like FDR said, the main thing we have to fear is fear its own black-assed self. If people lose their confidence in the town, Hot Springs goes away. It disappears. It turns into Malvern or Russellville or some other bleak little nowhere burg. Like many cities of fabled corruption, it is sustained merely by the illusion of vice and pleasure, which is to say, the illusion of security that such human weaknesses ain't only tolerated, they are encouraged. If that image is damaged, it all goes away."

The judge spoke a harsh truth.

Publicly Owney could only say, "I swear to you both, we will work on this issue."

Privately a million thoughts poured through his head.

"What I'm saying," the judge continued, "is that this problem had better be dealt with quickly. I think for our business interests, what we need is a show of force, a stand, a victory."

"Judge, old man, your sagacity is unmatched. And I say in a response hardly as eloquent but equally as heartfelt: I will take care of this. As I said, we are working on it. For your part, I expect the following: business as usual. The same payments in the same pickups. You enforce discipline with yours so I do not have to enforce it with mine. That is clear?"

"It is," said Leo. "We'll do our part."

"We are all taking the right steps," said Owney, to signify that the meeting was over.

The two men left.

"Any bright guys got any bright ideas?" he asked. "Or do I have to fire you mutts and bring in some heavy fuckin' hitters from Cleveland or Detroit or KC?"

"Now, sir," said Pap, "ain't no damned call to be talking to a Grumley like that. You know us Grumleys go to the goddamn wall fer you every damn time you need us, Mr. Maddox. That's God's honest truth."

He hitched up his pants, stiff with indignity, and launched a gob of something blackish toward the spittoon, which it rattled perfectly.

"Telephones," said Flem.

"What?" said Owney.

"Goddamn telephones. If'n them boys is hiding in secret, and if we follow Mr. Becker but don't never see him leavin' town, and he's there every goddamned time, he's got to be reaching them boys by telephone. You know the boss of the phone company. So whyn't we tap into his lines, and listen to his calls. That way we get to know where they gonna be striking next. And we'd dadgum be waiting for 'em. Radio intelligence, like. We done it to the Krauts in Italy, toward the end of the war. Intercepted their messages, sure as shit."

"You know, Owney, that's very good," said F. Garry. "That's quite good, actually. I'm sure Mel Parsons could provide technical guidance. After all, he's an investor too, isn't he?"

"Yes, he is. Goddamn, that *is* good. Pap, you raised a fuckin' genius."

"I knowed about what happened in Italy in '45," said Flem proudly. "That's whar they court-martialed me."

"They court-martialed you?"

"Yes sir. The second time. Now, the third time they . . ."

It was D.A.'s idea but it was Earl who figured out how to make it work.

He called Carlo Henderson the next morning.

"Henderson," he said, "how'd you like to go on a little trip?"

"Uh. Well, sir—"

"No big deal. Just a little lookie-see party."

"Sure."

"You got a straw hat?"

"Here?"

"Yeah?"

"No sir."

"How 'bout some overalls, a denim shirt, some clodhopper boots?"

"Mr. Earl, I'm from Tulsa, not the sticks. I went to college. I'm not a farmer."

"Well, son, that's fine, because guess what's in this bag?"

He handed over a paper sack, much crumpled, weighing in at around five pounds.

"Uh . . . overalls, a denim shirt, some clodhopper boots and a straw hat?"

"Exactly. Now I want you all dressed up like Clyde the Farmer. I'm going to have one of these federal dam workers drive you downtown. Here's what I want. You just mosey around the block City Hall is on, where Mr. Becker's office is. And the blocks a couple each way."

"Yes?"

"Here's what you're looking for. A phone company truck and man. Parked somewhere in that vicinity, working probably on a pole, but maybe under the street or at some kind of junction box. Now the thing is, you can't let him see you watching him. But if you see him, you watch him close, see, because I think you'll see he ain't really working. He's actually playing at work. But he's got earphones and a rig set up to the pole knobs or some such, don't know what it'd be. But he's really listening. He'd be all dialed into calls coming out of Mr. Becker's office."

"But we don't get calls from Mr. Becker's office."

They got pouches delivered by a fake postman, with the information for that night's raid encoded, a system put together by D.A. with the express intention to avoid a wiretap.

"That's right. We don't. You know it and I know it. Mr. Becker knows it and we both know D. A. Parker knows it, because he thought it up. But *they* don't know it. We could let him tap his butt off, but Mr. D.A. came up with an idea to turn their little game against them. This one could turn into some real damn fun and I don't know about you, Henderson, but goddammit, I could use me some fun."

CHAPTER 20

GANGSTERS SLAIN IN HOT SPRINGS read the headline in the Little Rock *Arkansas Democrat* two days after the raid.

PROSECUTING ATTORNEY'S RAIDERS SEND TWO "MOST WANTED" TO COUNTY MORGUE

Hot Springs—Officers from the Prosecuting Attorney's Office shot and killed two highly dangerous wanted men in a nighttime raid on an illegal gambling establishment here tonight.

The shootings occurred at the Belmont Club, on Oakland Boulevard in South Hot Springs, at approximately 10:30 P.M.

Dead were Thomas "Tommy" Malloy, 34, of Cleveland, Ohio, a bank robber who was listed as No. 1 on the FBI's most wanted list, and Walter "Wally Bud" Budowsky, 31, also of Cleveland. Budowsky was No. 7 on the list.

Both men were pronounced dead at the site.

Malloy, a career criminal since his teens, was wanted on several charges of armed robbery, including the July 5, 1945, robbery of a Dayton, Ohio, bank and trust that left two officers dead and two more wounded. That crime catapulted him to No. 1 on the FBI's list, but he is wanted in connection with at least 12 other charges, including a kidnapping, two counts of assault with attempt to kill and several more counts of fleeing across interstate lines to avoid prosecution.

Budowsky is also suspected in taking part in the Dayton job, as well as several other crimes. Both men served time in the Ohio State Penitentiary.

The editorial was even better.

BECKER: A MAN OF HIS WORD

It seems that when Garland County Prosecuting Attorney Fred C. Becker gives his word, that word is as good as gold.

Elected in a controversial election just last month, Becker has moved aggressively against organized crime interests in Arkansas' shameful bordello town 35 miles to the south, raiding two casinos in the past week. Long

> a haven for gamblers, gunmen and ladies of the night, Hot Springs is becoming downright dangerous for such folk, owing to Becker's crusade.
>
> At the same time, it's becoming a place of pride for citizens who obey the law, worship God and go to church on Sunday.
>
> Becker is to be commended for his efforts and maybe Arkansas would do well to think about hitching its wagon to his star in the 1948 gubernatorial race. If he can clean up Hot Springs, a Herculean labor if ever there was one, then who knows how far he can go?

This was a good day for Becker. The *Arkansas Democrat* was the only paper with a reputation outside the state; it could get him noticed nationally. Who cared what the Garland County rags screeched about or their demands for indictments against the raiders; they had no circulation outside the county, no influence on party politics, no reach to the state's bosses, no connections to the national press.

Already that seemed to be happening. He was onto something. The winds of change were in the air; the tired old men who'd run the country while the boys were off fighting had to step aside now, and whoever saw that first and seized that opportunity would go the furthest. If he became governor in 1948, he would be the youngest governor in the history of Arkansas, one of the youngest governors in the United States. The sky was the limit; who knew where that could take him, particularly if the radio networks began picking up on it.

Already *Life* was sending a man down, and that meant *Time* would follow and probably *Time*'s imitator, *News-Week*. Those magazines were read in Washington, where it really counted. Maybe . . . Senator Becker. Maybe . . . even bigger.

So after his morning news conference—a love celebration, really, in which the Little Rock boys pulled rank on the snippier Hot Springs bumpkins and asked flattering, softball questions—he went back to his office to luxuriate in his success. As a matter of fact, he wasn't an aggressive prosecutor so much as an ambitious politician. There were a number of routine matters before him—moves to prosecute traffic offenders, county statute violators, petty criminals in the Negro section—but all of them could wait.

Instead, he loaded up the bowl of his English briarwood with a fine mild Moroccan tobacco, lit it up, and enjoyed the sweetness and the density of the smoke and the pure pleasure: he concentrated on enjoying the moment, and more than a few minutes passed in this state of high bliss before a knock came at the door.

It was Willis O'Doyle, his number-one clerk, who had ambitions of accompanying his chief as far as his chief could go. O'Doyle had a communiqué from D.A., an out-of-schedule communication unusual in and of itself.

It said, when decoded, "Please call us at 2:00

P.M. tomorrow and order us to raid Mary Jane's, in the Negro section out Malvern Avenue. This will pay very big dividends."

Hmmm, he thought. What the hell is this about?

Earl came to them that very morning.

"All right, fellas," he said. "You want to gather 'round?"

The raiders, sleeping on cots, spent lazy days when they weren't actually scheduled to hit some place. Earl had plans to keep them in shape with various dry-fire exercises but it seemed so pointless because there was so little room in the pumphouse station and they couldn't work outside, because of fear of discovery. So he let them sleep, stay clean, clean their weapons and otherwise occupy themselves until the word came on the target that night.

This was his first urgent gathering since they'd swung into operation.

"We have an opportunity," he said. "In the service, the CO'd just give the order and I'd draw up a plan and that would be that. But this ain't the service, and it's your butts on the line, so I figure you ought to have some say-so in what we do next. Fair enough?"

The men nodded or murmured assent, even the still-sleepy Frenchy Short, now something of a hero for his victory over the two gangsters.

"Y'all know what radio intelligence is?"

"Fred Allen?" somebody said.

"No. *Gangbusters!*"

There was some laughter.

"Not quite," said Earl. "It's what you can do when you break the other guy's code. Or it's what you can do when you know the other guy's broken your code, only he don't know you know. Well, we now got us a chance to play a little radio game, 'cept that it's a telephone game.

"Mr. D.A. knows all the tricks, and he figured Owney's boys would be trying like hell to find us. He figured they'd even try and tap Mr. Becker's phone lines. That's why we don't use telephone lines. Well, goddamned if Carlo Henderson didn't go downtown yesterday dressed like a farmer, and goddamn if he didn't find a telephone crew set up at a junction box where all the prosecuting attorney's lines are shunted through to the big Bell office. So they are listening. Here's a coupla things we could do.

"First, we could just mark it, and make certain we never gave up nothing on the phone. See, that would keep them guessing, and it would cause them to spread out their resources, because mind my words, what they want to do is ambush us.

"Now here's another thing we could do: we could pass out phony information. We could say, See, we're going to Joe's Club. So they'd set up to get us at Joe's Club, only we'd hit Bill's Club. That way we'd be sure to have a raid without no problems. We could probably do that two, three times.

Then they'd catch on, and that game'd be over.

"But there's one last thing we could do. We could pass out the information that we were going to hit Joe's Club. So you can bet they would load up at Joe's Club. They'd love to hit us and hurt us and kill some of us. They'd love to humiliate Mr. Becker and send us home in shame. But here's the wrinkle. We know that they know. So instead of them hitting us, we lure them in, and then we hit them. They think they got us marked, all the time we're marking them. We counterambush and we smoke 'em good. See? Their best shot is blasted, the power and the prestige of Owney Maddox and his hillbilly gunmen is made to look pathetic. We found a place on Malvern that'd work right fine. Called Mary Jane's."

"Hell," said Bob Billy, one of the most aggressive raiders, a Highway Patrolman from Mississippi, "I say we go and kick some fellers upside the head."

Cheers and laughter and agreement rose.

Earl let it die down.

"Okay," he said. "That's fine and good, but understand where you're going. You're going into the fire. Sometimes you can't control what happens in there. Blood will be shed, blood in this room. Know that going in. If it's more than you bargained for, it's okay. But I want a vote, and I want it secret, so nobody feels pressure. I want it written down. A simple no or yes. Because we can't make this work if we don't believe in it."

It was unanimous.

CHAPTER 21

"He's finished," said the Countess.

"But suppose he isn't?" Ben said.

"He's finished. I know he's finished."

"But suppose he isn't? He's a tricky bastard, slippery and smart. He gets out of it somehow. And he hears I been talking against him. And he gets to thinking about it. And he hears about the desert and the building I'm doing and the plans I got. And he reads the writing on the wall. He knows that even though I'm in a different state two fucking thousand miles away, he and I are at cross purposes."

"Don't get paranoid, darling."

"What's paranoid?"

"The idea that everyone is out to get you."

"Everyone *is* out to get me."

"But not yet. Because you are smarter and quicker and you see these things so much sooner."

They lounged by the pool of the Beverly Hills Country Club, beside a diamond of emerald-blue water patrolled by the legends of the movie business, their wives, their children, their managers, their assistants, their bodyguards. The Countess wore a white latex suit à la Esther Williams; her legs were tan, her bust was full, her toenails were red.

Bugsy wore a tight red suit that showed off his extremely athletic body, his ripply muscles, his big hands, his larger-than-life penis. He too was tan, and his hair gleamed with oil, the sun picking it up and glinting off it fabulously. He looked like a movie star, he wore movie star sunglasses and he sipped a movie star's drink, a piña colada, from a tall glass.

Virginia was on one of her trips back east, to visit certain aging relatives or so it was said. He actually wasn't too clear on where she was, but it helped to have her gone, as she could be a pain in the ass. She'd been really annoying of late.

The Countess, by contrast, was a more comforting person. Her name was Dorothy Dendice Taylor DiFassio, the last moniker making her an authentic countess, though the count had long since been abandoned. She was one of Ben's earliest Southern California lovers and she had connections to Italy through her title, and the two of them had some crazed adventures together.

"That is why I need a backup plan and I need it now."

"You'll come up with something."

"I have to be ready. He's now involved with this goddamn crusader. Everybody's talking about it. He got two Cleveland boys clipped on him and right now his name is mud in every syndicate spot in the country. He is so weak now he can hardly keep it going. But I know him. He'll come up with something, he'll get out of it, you'll see."

"You give him too much credit, darling. Look, there's a cute one!"

She pointed at a pool boy. These creatures came from all over America to become movie stars. Most failed but some actually got as far as pool boy. They modeled their bodies and their blond locks around the club, hoping to catch a producer's eye. The one she noticed, though, was beefier than most and not blond at all, but rather dark-haired.

"You, boy," she called.

"Christ, Dorothy," said Bugsy, "are you going to fuck him right here?"

"Possibly. But it would hurt my chances for a table at El Morocco. Boy, come here."

The lad obliged.

"What's your name?" she asked.

"Roy, ma'am," he responded.

"Roy, eh? How wonderful. Roy, I think I'd like a whiskey sour with a lemon twist. Do you think you can remember that?"

"Yes ma'am."

He lumbered off.

"That one's going to be a big star some day," she said. "He's got a certain *je ne sais quoi.*"

"I'll say," Bugsy said. "The way he was staring at my dick shows what a future he's got in this fruit town!"

"Ben, you are so crude. I don't think he's homo."

"The handsome ones are all homo. Anyhow, back to *my* problems."

"Oh, that's right, darling," said Dorothy, "I forgot. Yours are the *real* problems. The rest of us are simply bedeviled by petty annoyances."

"Well, Dorothy, I do not think Roy the Pool Boy is going to pull out a chopper and clip you right here. I am at risk and I've got to deal with this problem."

"Do you want him killed?"

"Ah—difficult. I'd have to get permission. It'd have to go through channels. And everything's so spread out these days. It used to be a few blocks of Brooklyn, now it's everywhere, from coast to coast. Getting things okayed can be tough and time-consuming."

"So what you really want is him eliminated, but not necessarily killed."

"That would be right, yeah. If I could get him sent up for five years or so, he'd have nothing when he got out."

"Hmmm. What are his weaknesses? His vanities?"

Ben thought hard. He remembered the beautiful art deco apartment overlooking the city, the phony English accent, the liveried staff, the sense of elegance.

"He wants to be a British gentleman. He wants to be cultivated. He wants to be like the real Gary Cooper, not the real Cary Grant. He likes furniture, art, food. He wants to be a king. He's tryin' to be bigger than who he is. He's tryin' to forget where he came from and what made him."

"I see," said the Countess. "Quite common, actually. And exactly why I treasure you so dearly: you are what you are to the maximum. There's no hypocrisy in you. Not a lick of it."

"I guess that's a compliment."

"It is. Oh, hello, what's this?"

It was Roy the tall Pool Boy. He held a whiskey sour on a silver platter and he offered it to madame.

She opened her alligator purse and removed a $50 bill.

"For you, darling," she said.

"Thank you, ma'am," he said, bowing a little so that he could get a better look at Bugsy's dick stuffed in his tight bathing suit.

Then he went away.

"A look like that could get him killed in a lotta places on the East Side," said Ben.

"And he is what he is," she said. "Anyway, art? Art? You said art? He collects art."

"Yes."

"Hmmmm," she said. "You know, collecting is a disease. And even the most rational and intelligent of men can lose their way when they see something they must have. This should be looked into, darling. This has possibilities."

CHAPTER 22

"Guns?" asked Owney.

"Yes sir," said Pap. "Not just the six-shootin' guns we carry during the day. Guns."

"Traceable? I wouldn't—"

"No sir. 'Bout fifteen or sixteen years ago, when it was a time of road bandits and generalized desperado work, it was Grumleys what run houses of safety in the mountains. We had boys from all over. I'se a younger man then, and we Grumleys, we took 'em in, and fed 'em and mended 'em. The laws knew to stay far from where the Grumleys had their places in the mountains. So I seen them all, sir, that I did. Why, sir, was as close to him then as I am to you now. Johnny, such a handsome boy. Reminded me of a feller from the movies. Lord Jesus, he was a handsome boy. Beaming, you might say. Filled the room. A laugher, a fine jester. And just as polite and respectful to our Grumley womenfolk as a fine Mississippi gentleman, he was, he was indeed. Oh, it was a sad day when that boy went down."

"Johnny?"

"Johnny Dillinger. The most famous man in America. And that other smiler, the one from the Cookson Hills acrost the line in the territory? He rusticated some time out with the Grumleys too. The newspapers called him Pretty Boy, but I never heard no one call him but Charlie, and even Charles most ofttimes. Charlie was a good 'un, too. Big-handed boy. Big strong farm hands, Charlie had. Charlie was one of the best natural shots I ever seen. He could shoot the Thompson sub gun one-handed, and I mean really smart and fine-like. Would take the stock off. Shoot it one-handed, like a pistol. And Ma. Ma and her boys comes through a time or two. Knew Clyde Barrow and that Bonnie Parker gal too. They was just li'l ole kids. Scrawny as the day was long. Like kitty cats, them two, rolling on the floor. Never could figger on why the laws had to shoot them so many times. Seen the car they was driving. It was put on display up in Little Rock. Took the Grumleys to show 'em what the laws could do if they'd the chance. Them laws, they must have put a thousand bullets into that car, till it looked like a goddamned piece of cheese."

"And you got guns? Enough for this job?"

"Enough for any job, sir. Your Thompson sub guns, five of 'em. Drums. And, sir, we have something else."

"Ah," said Owney, fascinated as always by the old reprobate's unlikely language, part Elizabethan border reiver's, part hillbilly's. They sat in the office of a warehouse near the tracks, where Owney's empire received its supplies and from which point it made its distributions; Owney had declared it to be his headquarters for this operation. Grumleys in overalls with the hangdog look of mean boys about to go off to do some killing work hung around.

"What might that be, Pap?"

"Why, sir, it be what they call a Maxim gun. The Devil's Paintbrush. It's from the First Great War. The Germans used it. It's got belt after belt of bullets, and we've never used it. My father, Fletcher, got it in a deal with a Mexican feller who come to Hot Springs in 1919 for to buy some women to take back to Tijuana. Wanted white gals. Thought he'd make a fortune for his generalissimo. Well, we got this gentleman's Maxim gun, but he never got any white gals. Wouldn't sell no white gal to a Mexican."

A Maxim gun! Now that was some power.

"We'll set it up on the second floor," Pap explained. "When them boys come to call, we'll let them come in and up the stairs. Then my cousin Lem's boy Nathan will open up with the Maxim. Nathan is the hardest Grumley. He served fifteen years of a life sentence, and prison taught him savage ways. Nathan is the best Grumley killer. Onct, he shot a clown. Never figgered out why. I ast him once. He didn't say nothing. I guess he just don't like clowns. He's a Murfreesboro Grumley, and they grow Grumleys hard down there."

"I thought it was the Yell County Grumleys that were so hard."

"Yell County Grumleys *are* hard, naturally. But you take a naturally hard Grumley and you toughen him up in a bad joint, and what you got is something to make your blood curdle. That Mr. Becker would beshat his drawers if he but knew what awaited."

"It's a shame he won't be along. We hear he arrives afterward, always."

"He won't arrive afterward this time. There won't be no afterward," said Pap. "They'll only be blood on the floor and silence."

"That I believe," said Owney, looking at the dance of black madness in the old man's glittering eyes.

"Mr. Maddox," said Flem Grumley, arriving from some mission. "We just heard. My cousin Newt has it from the phone tap at Hobson and Third. They're going to hit Mary Jane's tonight."

"Mary Jane's?" said Owney, unfamiliar with the place.

"It's in Niggertown."

"It's going to be hot in Niggertown tonight," said Pap. "Oooooooo-eeeee, it's going to be hot. We'll even boil us a cat for luck!"

It was a time of waiting. Earl thought it was like the night before when the big transports wallowed off an island, and you could hear the naval guns pounding all through the night, but in the hold, the boys were in their hammocks, all weapons checked, all blades oiled, all ammo stashed, all gear tight and ready, and they just lay there, smoking most of them, some of them writing letters. There'd always be a few boys shooting craps in the latrines, loudly, to drum away the fears, but for most of the boys it was just a time to wait quietly and pray that God would be watching over them and not assisting Mickey Rooney with his racetrack betting the next day.

In the pumping house, the slow grind of the valves almost sounded like the transport's engines, low and thrumming, and taking you ever onward to whatever lay ahead. It was late in the afternoon. These boys were dressed and ready. The guns were cleaned and loaded, the magazines all full, the surplus walkie-talkies checked out and okayed, the vests lined up and brushed clean. The men were showered and dressed and looked sharp in their suits. They sat on their cots, smoking, talking quietly. One or two read the newspaper or an odd novel.

Earl walked over to Frenchy, who stood by himself in front of a mirror, trying to get a tie tied just right. He could tell from the extravagant energy the kid was investing into the process that it was a way of concentrating on the meaningless, like oversharpening a bayonet or some such. Kids always found something to occupy their minds before, if they had to.

"Short? You okay?"

"Huh?" Short's eyes flew to him, slightly spooked.

"You okay?"

"Fine. I'm fine, Mr. Earl."

"You upset?"

"Upset?"

"About dumping them two bohunks. First time you draw live blood it can spook a fellow. Happened to me in Nicaragua in '32. Took a while to get used to it."

"Oh, that?" said Short. "Those guys? No, see, here's what I was thinking. Wouldn't it be better if I was interviewed by *Life* magazine? I hear they're coming down here. Or maybe it was the *Post*. Or even *Look*. But anyway, me and Mr. Becker. He's the legal hero, I'm the cop hero. We're a team, him and me. I think that would be so much better. See, that way the public would have someone to respect and admire. Me."

Earl gritted his teeth hard.

At 8:20 Earl stopped at a Greek's, got a hamburger and a cup of coffee and read the papers. More about Jayhawkers and who they'd kill next. When would indictments be delivered or did Becker's control over the grand jury give his raiders carte blanche to rob and kill whoever they wanted? Who were these Jayhawkers? How come they never met the press or issued statements? How come the good citizens of Hot Springs didn't know who they were or have any explanation of how they worked?

After eating, he got back in his vehicle and began a long slow turn out Malvern, past the Pythian

Hotel and Mary Jane's, and then went onward for another several blocks, just in case.

At Mary Jane's he saw nothing, no commotion or anything. It was just another beer joint/whorehouse with some slots in the bar, like a hundred other Hot Springs places. There was no sense that tonight would be any different than any other night: a few girls sat listlessly in the upstairs windows, but there wasn't enough street traffic yet for them to start their yelling. The downstairs of the place didn't seem very full of men, though later on, of course, it would be different. White boys wouldn't head on down to Niggertown for a piece of chocolate until they were well drunk and had got their courage up. Black men were probably still working their jobs, cleaning out the toilets in the big hotels or running the dirty towels to the big washing machines in the bathhouses or rounding up the garbage.

But Earl got a good glimpse of the place. It was a brick building standing alone on the street, with shabby buildings nearby but not abutting it. Possibly it had once been a store of some sort, before the black people had moved into this part of town and took it over. It had a big front window, shaded, and above there were a bunch of windows that looked down on Malvern. Earl liked the bricks; he'd worry about a wooden building because heavy bullets like those from a BAR would sail clean through and do who knew what damage further down the block.

Earl made three more circuits on his grand trek,

making sure he wasn't followed, making sure that nothing was out of order, that no cops had set up. So far it looked like a go.

At 9:20 he dropped a nickel into a downtown phone box and called D.A., who had a network of snitches he'd been working.

"Are we all set?" D.A. asked.

"Yes sir. The boys are ready. I haven't made radio contact with them yet, but that'll happen soon. Any news?"

"One of my snitches told me that around noon, a truck pulled up behind Mary Jane's, and a bunch of white men got out and hustled in."

"They're loading up. They've bitten."

"He said there were eight of them, in overalls. Earl, eight's a bit. They could cause some serious wreckage."

"Yes sir. I think we can still get it done. I don't want to postpone at this point. We have the jump on them."

"All right, Earl. I trust your judgment on this one. I haven't told Becker yet. He's going to be pissed."

"Yes sir. But this was a good plan and it's going to work and the boys wanted to push it. I still think it's going to be a great night for our side."

"Well, Earl, God bless us. Remember, wear your vest. I'll go to Becker at exactly 10:00 P.M. when you hit, and have him order up medical backup and the police to set up a perimeter."

"Yes sir."

Earl hung up.

He drove around a bit, wondering when the streets would fill up. But strangely they never did. A few white men seemed to mosey around the area but that density of the black throngs that was such a fervid feature of Malvern Avenue, that sense of whores and workingmen and jive joints and housewives and kids, of them all in it together, riding the same ship toward the same far destiny, that was gone.

Finally, at 9:40 he pulled up a few blocks away, parked and went into a small grocery. A few old black men lounged near the cash register where the proprietor sat.

"Howdy," Earl said. "Looking for a place called Mary Jane's. Y'all know where that is? Heard a fella could have hisself a good old time there."

The men looked at one another, then over to the proprietor, the wisest among them clearly, who at last spoke.

"Suh, I'd take my business out of town tonight. There's a strange feelin' in the air. The wimmens been talkin' 'bout it all afternoon. Git your babies in, they been sayin'. There's gonna be bad-ass troubles over there at Mary Jane's tonight. Gun trouble, the worst kind of trouble there is."

Earl nodded.

"Sir, I think you're speaking the truth."

"You look like a cop, suh," said the old grocer.

"Grandpop, I am," said Earl, "and y'all have

picked up on something. Make sure your children are in because it's going to be a loud one, I guarantee you."

"Y'all going to kill any Negroes?"

"Don't aim to, Grandpop. This one's between the white boys."

There was no Mary Jane and there never had been. No one could remember why the place was called by her name. Its owner was a tall, yellow-skinned black man named Memphis Dogood. Memphis had two long razor cuts on the left side of his face, one of which began on his forehead, opened a hairless gap in his eyebrow, skipped his recessed eye and picked up again, running down his cheek. The other crossed it about an inch above the jawline. One—the long one—was delivered by a gal named Emma Mae in New Orleans in 1933. He couldn't remember how he got the other scar, or which came first.

In Mary Jane's, Memphis made the decisions. He rented the slots, ancient, tarnished machines from before the First War, a couple of old Mills Upright Perfections, a Dewey Floor Wheel or two and even one rattly old Fey Liberty Bell, from the Boss—a Grumley cousin named Willis Burr, far beneath even Pap's notice—and bought his liquor as well from the Boss. He paid 48 percent of everything to the Boss. He skimmed a little, but every time the Boss looked at him with squeezed eyes and jiggled the spit in the pouch of his mouth, mixing it with to-baccy juice for a nice hard splat, as if he were puzzling over the figures, it scared Memphis so he swore he'd never do it no more. But he always did.

Memphis ran a fair joint. The gals might act up but usually Marie-Claire, the octoroon, took care of them. She was his main gal, and she packed a wallop in her left fist. His customers were also usually all right. Some of the younger bloods might act up now and then, on booze or reefer, and he'd once had to thump a boy with a sap so hard the boy never woke up and had to be laid out by the tracks. The polices come by to ask questions, but nothing never came of it. Now and then, a white boy or usually two or four white boys, usually drunk, would show up, on the hunt for some colored pussy, because you wasn't no man till you dipped your pen in ink. They were well treated, for it was always known that if you hurt a white boy there'd be all kinds of hell to pay.

On that day, Memphis Dogood fully expected no surprises. He was vaguely aware that something of a political nature was happening in town but those things usually ran their course on the other side of the line. He had no opinions about vice or gambling or prostitution, except that he hated reformers and knew a few who'd preach all day, work up a sweat, then come on down for some relaxation with his gals, so he knew them to be hypocrites. Even a white minister once came down, and he ended up with two gals, and did each of 'em right fine, or so they claimed.

Memphis, at any rate, was sitting in the small back room behind the bar, with a pimp's .25 lying on the table, counting up money from the night before. He also had a sap and a pearl-handled switchknife out. It was the slow season. Might have to let a gal go. Why didn't the Boss cut down from 48 percent to 38 during the slow season when the ponies weren't running? But the boss never would and only a fool would mention it to him. It was a good way to turn up missing. It was said that the floor of Lake Catherine was full of Negro men who'd asked the Boss a question the Boss didn't like.

The door in the back room opened loudly and he heard the labor of men struggling with weight. He knew somehow from the way they breathed that they were white men.

Was it some batch of Holy Rollers, or maybe Klan boys, drunk and looking for a fight?

He picked up his sap and walked back there, but was met halfway by two men with suitcases. Behind he could see two more struggling with a bunch of canvas-wrapped pieces, and behind that two more. All were wearing overalls and had low mountaineer's hats pulled over their eyes. All wore gunbelts loaded up with cartridges and heavy revolvers, man-killing revolvers. They had nearly fleshless faces and gristly semibeards and had a look he knew and feared: of tough, mean, violent crackers, the sort who thought no Negro was human and made up lynch mobs or whatever, and who fought all them terrible battles against the Union in the great war and were still proud that they had stood for slavery and that the bastard Lincoln hadn't made it out of 1865 alive.

He knew them immediately to be Grumleys, but of a more violent breed than the Grumleys who controlled the Negro section of town.

"Say there," he said, swallowing, "just what is it y'all boys think it is that you're doing?"

"Tell you what, nigger," said the first, "you just go on about your business and don't pay us no nevermind, and you'll do just fine. You hear me, nigger?"

"Yas suh," said Memphis, who, though he acknowledged the might of the white man as a natural condition of the universe beyond the reach of change, did not like being treated so arrogantly in his own place, particularly when he paid the Boss 48 percent every Tuesday, regular as rain.

"See, I don't explain nothing to no nigger. You got that, boy? We are here because we are here and that's all the goddamned hell you got to know. You got that?"

"Yes suh."

"We be upstairs. But I don't want you going nowheres, you know what I am telling you? I and my cousins, we are here until we are done, and I don't want nobody knowing we are here and I don't want no nigger making any business about it, do you understand?"

"I do, suh."

A stronger voice bellowed, "Jape, you stop jawing with that nigger and help us get this goddamned thang upstairs. Have the boy hep too."

"You pitch a hand, now, nigger," said Jape, ordering Memphis to assist with the labor. He went quickly over, as directed, and found himself given a large wooden crate, with rope handles. He lifted it—ugh, sixty, seventy pounds, extremely heavy for its size!—feeling the subtle shift of something dense but also loose in some way, like a liquid, only heavier. He could read a bit, and he saw something stamped on it, first of all a black eagle, its wings outstretched, its head crowned and then words that he didn't understand: *MG/08,* it said, and next to that, in a strange, foreign-looking kind of print, *7.92 X 57 MM MASCHINEKARABINER INFANTERIE PATRONEN.*

At 9:45 Earl made a last drive down Malvern for a look-see at Mary Jane's. Again, it was surprisingly empty. A single white man sat at a table to the right, in overalls, with a low-slung hat down over his eyes and a half-full whiskey bottle on the table before him. His fiery glare seemed to drive most people away.

Above, a few gals hung out the sporting house's windows, but they were listless, almost pallid. Earl recognized fear of the paralyzing variety; he'd seen enough of it.

He pulled around the block for a look down the alley. It was deserted. He turned off his headlamps and drove slowly down the alley, pulling up about a hundred feet short of the rear entrance to Mary Jane's, and with binoculars studied the rear of the building.

It was a brick rear with a door that would have to be blown, but no windows overlooked it, so there was no worry of enfilade fire. There was no sign of life along the cobblestones of the alleyway, which shone not from rain but from the liquidation of the moisture in the air against the still warmish bricks. As the night cooled, the slickness would disappear.

Earl picked up his walkie-talkie, snapped it on, and pressed the send button.

"Cars one, two and three, are you there for commo check?"

There was some crackly gibberish, but then cutting through the squawks came the reply.

"Earl, this is car one, we are set."

"Earl, same for car two."

"Earl, I ditto for car three."

"Car one, there's a white boy sitting at a table to the immediate right of the entranceway in the bar. Do you read?"

"Roger."

"'Less I miss my guess, there's your first Grumley boy. So when the initial entry team goes up the way to the door, I want you to leave one man behind at the car with a Thompson and I want that boy zeroed. If he rises from the table with a weapon, he has to go down. Got that?"

"Roger on that, Earl."

"Be careful. Short burst. You ought to be able to bust him with three. Don't let the gun get away from you."

"It won't happen."

"You other two units, you are set. This whole damned thing turns on how fast you git through that back door."

"Yes sir. We are ready."

"Okay, you fellas, you do yourselves proud now, y'hear?"

"Yes sir."

Earl felt like a cigarette. He glanced at his watch. It was 9:57. He flicked a Lucky out, lit it up, took a deep breath and felt good about the thing. What could be done had been done. It was clear there would be some surprises for the Grumley boys.

He slipped out the door of his car, letting it stay ajar, and headed back to the trunk. He popped it. Inside lay his vest and a 1918 A1 Browning Automatic Rifle.

Fuck the vest. He was way down here where there was no shooting. He didn't need the vest.

He took the Browning, slid a twenty-round mag into the well, snapped it in and threw the bolt to seat a round. Then he pulled out a bandolier with ten more magazines for the gun and withdrew four magazines, which he put in his suit coat pockets, two in each for balance. He threw the bandolier back inside and closed the trunk gently.

But he could not help thinking: What is wrong? What have I forgotten? Am I in the right place? How soon will medical aid arrive? Will this work?

But then it settled down to one thing: What is wrong?

The call came from upstairs. It was Nathan Grumley, behind the big German gun, which was mounted on its sled mount just at the head of the stairs, with its belts of ammo all flowing into it.

"Jape, you see anything?"

"Not a goddamned thing 'cept these here fat niggers," Jape called back. He sat alone at a table in the bar. Around him, the slots were unused. The place was practically empty but three boys had bumbled in and he had directed that they stand nonchalantly at the bar. If they didn't want to, he suggested they have a talk with his uncle, at which point he pulled back his jacket which lay crumpled on the chair next to him and revealed the muzzle of his tommy gun. All complied, though one wet up his pants when he saw the gun.

By a clock on the wall Jape could see that it was virtually 10:00. He took another sip on the bourbon, warmed by its strength, finding courage in it. He was a little nervous. The cut-face nigger was behind the bar, looking spooked as shit. Good thing he'd gone behind the bar and cleaned out the baseball bat, the sawed-off Greener and the old Civil War saber like his grandpap might well have carried.

Then, precisely at ten, a car pulled up, its lights off. Jape reached over and slid the Thompson out from under the coat, shucking the coat to the floor. The gun came over until he held it just under the table, ever so slightly scuttling his chair back. He could see some confusion out by the car, but it was dark and he wasn't sure what to do.

"You niggers stay where you is!" he commanded. "Nathan, I think they're here, goddammit."

The sound of the big bolt on the German gun being cranked was Nathan's response.

"We gonna jambalaya some boys!" Jape crooned to the terrified black men.

"I don't want to die," came a gal's voice from upstairs, high-pitched and warbly. "Please, sirs, don't you be hurtin' me."

"Shut up, 'ho," came the response.

The raid team broke from the car and headed toward Mary Jane's.

Jape's fingers flew toward the safety of the gun, and pushed it off. By Jesus, he was ready.

Everything was lovely. Two State Police were bodyguards and there were a lot of guns in the room, carried by veterans who'd waded ashore at Anzio and Normandy and suchlike, so at last Fred Becker felt safe and among friends. He was able to put aside that gnawing tension that was his closest companion through all this mess.

He was meeting with his group of reformers, all men like himself, at Coy's Steakhouse, on a hill just beneath Hot Springs Mountain on the east side of the city. Three national correspondents and a photographer from *Life* were in the room too.

But the circumstances were only nominally political. The young men were here to celebrate Fred's success and what it would mean for them all, as they foresaw their own co-option of the levers of power in the Democratic party in the next election, and their eventual takeover of the city on a thrust of righteous indignation. For Fred and his raiders had given the town hope and loosened the grip of the old power brokers. One could feel it in the air, the sudden burgeoning spring of optimism, the sense that if people only stood up things didn't have to stay as they always did, locked in the hard old patterns of corruption and vice and violence.

All the wives were there. It was a grand evening. It was as if the war had been won, or at least the light at the end of the tunnel glimpsed. Toasts were made, glasses raised, people almost broke into song. It was one of those rare nights of pure bliss.

Then a shadow fell across the table. He looked up to see the long, sad face of D. A. Parker.

"Mr. Becker?"

"Yes?"

"I think you'd best come with me. The boys are working tonight and you're going to be needed down there."

"What? You said—"

"You remember I asked you to make that call yesterday concerning a place on Malvern Avenue. We used that to set up an opportunity that looked very promising," said D.A., hoping to cut off the tirade that accompanied Becker's instruction in any raid plans that masked the prosecuting attorney's deep ambivalence about the use of force and his own physical fear, which was immense.

Fred rose.

"Folks," he said, "honey," acknowledging his wife, "I've got to run. There's work to be done and—"

At that moment came the sound of gunfire. Machine-gun fire. It rattled through the night, a liquefied rip familiar to each man who'd served in a war zone. It could be no other sound. If you've heard it once you know it forever.

Fred's face went bloodless.

"Sounds like the boys are doing fine," said D.A.

CHAPTER 23

What is wrong?

He didn't know. But some weird vibration of distress hummed in his ear. Something somehow was wrong.

Two cars, lights dimmed, pulled down the alley, passing him, coming to rest at the rear of Mary Jane's. Silently, the doors sprang open, and eight members of the rear-entry team got out, cumbersome in their vests with their awkward weapons. Without noise they assembled into a stick as Slim led them to the door, a shotgun out before him and aimed at the knob. Except for a scuffle of feet and the breathing of the men, muted but still insistent, it was quiet.

What is wrong?

Then he knew.

They would know we'd also come in the rear because that's our signature. We go in multiple entrances simultaneously. We swarm in: that's D.A.'s best trick. Therefore, knowing that, they will have to ambush us from the rear.

But how?

There's no room to fire from the building at men this close and there's no sign of men moving in on them. The alley had been entirely deserted this whole time: only Japanese Marines could hide so silently.

Then Earl knew where they'd be.

They'd be down the block. He recalled a truck parked there, on a cross street, a good two hundred feet ahead, and he instantly diverted his gaze down the alley, trying to see through the dark.

Suddenly from the front, the sound of guns firing angrily, long bursts chewing the night apart, bullets blowing into wood and glass.

Then Earl saw movement in the dark. He couldn't make it out clearly: just a sense of movement as one darker shade of blackness moved twenty-five feet and planted itself directly across the alley exit to a cross street half a block down.

He waited, forcing his concentration against the subtly differing shades of blackness.

He thought he saw something squirm and believed it to be a tarpaulin being pulled back to reveal men hunched over the lip of the truck bed, as if settling in to aim.

Earl fired: the BAR chopped through its first magazine in less than two seconds, and far off he saw over the jarring sights the flashes and puffs as his bullets jacked into something metallic, possibly a truck, lifting dust and sparks from it. He slapped a new magazine in fast, and fired another long burst into it, holding the rounds into it, watching them strike and skip off. A shot, then a second, came from the truck bed, and then somehow a gas tank went, lighting up the night in a roiling orange spume and in its concussive force lifting the truck ever so slightly and setting it down. A man in flames with a Thompson gun ran from it, dropped the gun and fell to the alleyway.

Earl looked back to Mary Jane's to see the last of the rear-entry team race into the place.

The car pulled up out front.

They were so tense their breaths came in dry

spurts, like rasps scraping over a washbucket.

"Okay," said Stretch, just barely in command, "you know the drill. Let's go. Peanut, you're on the big gun."

"Gotcha," said Peanut, sliding down behind the fender of the car, raising his Thompson as he fingered off the safety, and checked with the same finger to make certain the fire selector was ratcheted toward full auto. His front sight bobbed and weaved but then stabilized and came to rest on the man slouching at the table in the barroom.

The three remaining men, their loads in their hands, charged up the walk to the storefront. It wasn't far, maybe twenty-five feet. They kicked open the door and screamed "*Raid! Raid! Get your hands up!*"

Jape saw the door open, goddamn! and was so excited he thought he'd piss up his pants. He kicked the table away to brace the Thompson against his hip, feeling his hand curve over the huge hundred-round drum to grab the foregrip and hold it tight.

"*Raid! Raid!*" came the shouts, and as he raised the weapon he had the consciousness of glass or something breaking and it was as if he were being mauled by a lion who leaped at him from nowhere, and from that sensation there came the sensation of drowning, sinking, falling, all of it toward fatigue and ultimately sleep in darkness.

The three at the door were not aware that behind them Peanut had fired, bringing down the barroom gunman with one perfectly placed burst. They were themselves unarmed, except for handguns still holstered. What they carried, two apiece, were buckets half filled with screws, stones, pieces of broken glass and scrap wood, and quickly, each lobbed his burden, one then the other, into the bar to the stairway, where the buckets hit, and emptied their contents in a rattle of things scraping and clanking and falling and crashing. It was no substitute for the sound of human feet in a normal world, but in the superheated one of house combat—gunshots now came from behind too, for some odd reason—it was enough to confuse the gunner upstairs, who now fired.

Nathan, the prison-hardened Murfreesboro Grumley behind the weapon, simply kept the butterfly trigger depressed. The gun, mounted on a securely heavy sled tripod, fired for about two minutes, and it poured down such a hail of 8-mm fire that the floor which absorbed it shattered, while broken flooring nails flipped through the air, amid the clouds of other debris that flew. The gun was so terrifying that D.A.'s plan simply fell apart.

The front-entry team retreated hastily to its car and took up cowering positions. The rear-entry team, all eight men including Frenchy and Carlo, collected in a choke point just out of the beaten zone, unable to think, talk, signal or otherwise function intelligently in the rawness and the hugeness of the sound.

Courage was beyond the question; it was meaningless in the face of such a volume of fire, and the men looked at each other bug-eyed and confused. They needed a leader and he didn't get there for another thirty seconds, though without his vest and with a BAR.

"Get back!" Earl screamed, for he knew that the gunner would soon see he was firing at nothing and would swing fire.

They scuttled backward, and in the next second, the gunner deratcheted his gun from the sled tripod, swung it radically to the right and sent another eight hundred rounds through the wall into the hallway where until that second the men had been.

The gunfire atomized the thin plaster and wood wall that separated the stairwell from the hallway. Dust and chips flew; the air filled with poisonous brew.

Earl waited now until he heard a clink.

That meant a belt had run out and he heard crankings and clankings as Nathan attempted to speed-change to a new belt. But instead of racing out, Earl merely scrunched along the now blasted hallway, raised his BAR along the same axis the bullets had just traveled, and fired an entire magazine upward through the shattered wall of Mary Jane's.

He rammed another magazine in, fired it in a flash. Then he slithered around the stairwell and looked upward. He could see nothing in the floating smoke and plaster and wood powder.

An odd noise came to his ears. He tried to identify it but his ears rang so from all the firing that it took a second or two. Then he had it: it was a steady drip . . . drip . . . drip.

Earl looked and saw—blood. It coagulated on the top of the stairway, paused, then dripped down, drop by drop by heavy drop, until a tide overtook the individual drops and began to drain off the top of the stairs in a jagged track.

"Hey, up there," he called. "This don't have to go on. Ain't no lawmen hurt yet nor no citizens. Y'all throw your guns down and come on out."

He thought he heard the scurrying of men, a hushed argument.

As he crouched there, the blood rolled down the steps with more force, and to his left and right raiders came to flank him, setting up good shooting positions.

The silence wore on, but then they heard what sounded like shuffling.

"Get ready," whispered Earl.

They could track the shuffling down the hallway until at last a figure emerged. It was a Negro girl, about twenty, in a slip and a pair of high-heeled shoes. Her face was swollen, her eyes red and huge. She clutched herself with her arms. Her lips trembled. She seemed shaky on her heels.

"You be careful, missy," Earl said. "You come on down and you'll be all right. We don't mean to hurt you or your friends none."

"Sir, I—"

The bullets hit her in the back, blowing her sideways against the wall; she jackknifed, her eyes rolling up, then fell forward off the top stair. She rolled down the stairway, arms and legs flung this way and that, her head bobbing loosely. Earl grabbed her, and held her close, getting her blood all over him. He felt her struggle to rise, watched her eyelashes flutter as if to make a last claim on life, and then she died in his arms. He was holding her hand so tightly he thought he'd break her fingers.

"Hey, you lawmen," came a low Grumley voice. "You come on up and git more of that. We got lots of it up here fer you too. And we got four more nigger gals up here and they ain't gittin' out alive, 'less you go and get our truck."

"Your truck is blown all to shit," Earl called back. "I lit it up my own self and whoever was aboard is burnt crispy. You hurt any more of them gals and I will personally see that you leave here in a pine box. You come out or you'll toast in hell tomorrow morning, that I swear."

He turned to the closest man to him, who happened to be Frenchy.

"You know where my car is?"

"Yes sir," said Frenchy.

Earl took Frenchy's Thompson and spare magazines, unscrewing the stock bolt as he spoke.

"You head on back there and open the trunk and git me some more of them BAR magazines. I'm clean out. You bring 'em to me, 'cause I may need 'em."

"Can I have my gun?" said Frenchy nervously.

"Go on, git the goddamn magazines!" said Earl, pushing him rudely back down the hallway.

He had the bolt out and tossed the stock away. He turned to Stretch.

"I'm going to head up for a lookie see. Y'all stay here."

"Earl, you ain't got no goddamn vest."

"I can't move with the goddamn vest. You hold here but you wait on my signal. You got that?"

"Earl, we ought to wait till—"

"You do what I tell you!" Earl said, his dark, mad eyes boring into the boy, who turned away under the assault.

Bitterly, Frenchy ran by other crouching raiders out into the alley. Twice he was stopped by men who wanted to know what was going on, but he ran onward.

He got to the alley and saw that each end was now blocked by police cars, whose red lights flashed into the night. A light came on him and he pulled his vest aside to show the badge on his chest, and ran ahead, getting to Earl's car.

He opened the trunk, and found a boxful of BAR mags, all loaded.

Suddenly two policemen and some kind of plainclothes detective were there by him.

"What the hell is going on, bud?" asked the detective.

"We may need backup. They have four Negro girls held hostage upstairs. We killed a batch but there's more."

"Hell, we ain't going in there. Sounds like a goddamned war."

"You go to Becker!" Frenchy said hotly. "He'll tell you to come up and support us."

"I ain't getting no men shot up over nigger whores, bud. You goddamned Jayhawkers started this one, you finish her up. I don't work for no Fred Becker."

"Where is Becker?"

"He's up front posing for photographers and I got a feeling he's pretty goddamned upset over this goddamned battle thing y'all got going in Mary Jane's."

"Yeah, well, fuck you and the mule you rode in on, Zeke," said Frenchy, and then turned and ran with the mags.

He was halfway there when he heard the sound of tommy guns.

Earl slithered ever so slowly up the staircase, climbing over the debris of screws and what-not. When he reached the halfway point he could see over the edge into the hallway. Spread out and gazing resolutely at the heaven he'd never enter lay a mean-looking old

Grumley boy, his eyes black and blank as diamonds. He lay in his own blood and a litter of hundreds of shells. Another boy lay a few feet away, his hands clenched around his belly, which blossomed blood.

Earl pointed the Thompson at him.

"You best show me your hands or I will finish you right here," he said.

"I am so gutshot I am going nowheres, so you go ahead and finish me, you law town bastard," said the man, who turned out to be but a boy of twenty, though his face was clenched in pure adult hatred.

"Lay there then and bleed," said Earl. "It don't make no matter to me."

He slipped up another step, saw that the feed lid on the big German machine gun was still up, meaning it could no longer be fired. He slipped a bit farther forward, grabbed the snakelike curl of ammo belt that lay beneath the gun, and gave it a yank. He held it, then yelled, "Watch out, coming down," and flicked it downward. He signaled with his fingers: three, then he pointed to his handgun.

Obediently, three raiders—Slim, as senior man, Terry and Carlo, who were next in the stick—yielded their Thompsons to others and slid up the steps until they were just below him.

"They must be down at the other end in one of them rooms, but they got them gals. If you have to shoot you use your pistols and you aim carefully, you got that? You shoot at Grumleys, not at motion. They may push the gals out first. Shoot their legs, their pelvises and wait for the girls to break free. Then you go for chest or head. Got that?"

"Earl, they got machine guns!"

"Y'all do what I tell you or I'll get three more birds and you can go wait in the cars."

"Yes sir."

"I'm going acrost the hall. You cover me, you got that?"

"Yes sir."

"You make sure you got your goddamn vests on."

"Yes sir."

"Okay. On the count of three. Ready. Three!"

Earl jumped across the hall, almost slipped in Grumley fluid and empty shell casings, but made it. Just as he ducked into a room, a man at the end of the hall stuck his head out with a tommy gun and blasted a lengthy burst at him, but immediately the three raiders returned fire, driving him back.

"I think I got him," said one.

"I don't know," said another.

Earl, meanwhile, looked around the room. Squashed into the corner and holding on dearly to each other, two more Negro gals cried softly.

"Y'all be quiet now," said Earl. "We're going to get you out, okay?"

One of them nodded.

Earl peeked around the corner and saw nothing. He nodded over to Slim and held out two fingers, cranked his thumb back to indicate he was sending the women over.

Slim nodded.

"Okay," he said, "y'all get over here and get ready to run. I'm going to fire a little bit. They won't be shooting. You just jump over to the stairs and go on down and somebody will take care of you. Don't you pay no mind to the shooting I'm going to do. You got that?"

Both nodded.

Earl stepped out into the hall, and fired half a magazine into the ceiling at the rear of the corridor, watching the bullets tear into the plaster. The two girls dipped across, where they were grabbed by Carlo, who ushered them downstairs.

Frenchy returned to the hallway adjacent to the stairwell, breathing hard. He could see that the action had moved upstairs. He bent over and retrieved Earl's BAR, took one of the magazines, and implanted it. Then he cranked the bolt back.

The thing was heavy, and as he had his pockets jammed with other loaded magazines, he felt quite a burden as he rose. He walked around to where other raiders crouched at the foot of the stairs. He could see three others up there.

"I got Earl's gun reloaded," he said.

"Well, he seems kind of busy just now," said Eff.

"Well, hell, he sent me to get ammo for that gun and so he must need it."

Eff and the others just looked at him.

"Look out," he commanded. "I'm taking it up to him."

Frenchy pushed his way by them and began to edge his way up the steps.

Earl watched the room at the end of the hallway. He heard a motion, like a squirming or shifting, and the next thing he knew a man laid out with a shotgun and fired. He felt the sting of pellet, but fired too, finishing off the magazine. The bullets whacked chunks of plaster off the wall and the Grumley boy slumped and fell amid a white cascade of shattered masonry.

Frenchy started when the gunfire suddenly erupted. At that moment also his foot found a puddle of Grumley blood that had coagulated on the fourth step. Before he knew what was happening, he slid downward, struggled for purchase and fell hard. He clenched as he fell and was aware that he squeezed off a five- or six-shot burst of automatic rifle fire. Men ducked and fell to avoid the shots, and the gun pivoted in his descent, still pumping, and sent a load of bullets through the window, blowing it out in the process.

But then he was down, hard, his ass suddenly hot with pain from the fall.

"Jesus Christ, Short! What the hell are you doing?"

"I fell, goddammit. Is anybody hurt?"

"You are a lucky son of a bitch," someone said.

"You didn't clip nobody down here but you're going to have to pay for a new window."

"Fuck it," said Frenchy. He pushed the mag release button so that the half-empty mag fell out, and replaced it with one from his coat pocket. Then he picked himself up, climbed the rest of the way, and bullied his way between the raiders at the top.

"Earl," he shouted, "I have the BAR."

Earl looked at him, shook his head. But then he nodded, and gestured for the boy to come across.

He stepped into the hallway, and fired, issuing suppressing fire that again chewed into the masonry far at the end of the hall.

When Frenchy made it safely across, he pulled him back and took the BAR. Frenchy reached for the Thompson, but Earl threw it across the room onto the bed.

"You leave it be. Stick near me, and when I drop a magazine, you hand me a new one. You got that?"

"Yes sir," said Frenchy.

But Earl was already leaning out the hallway.

"Slim," he said, "y'all be ready over there. I'm going to work my way down the hall. You weave behind me, clear the rooms. I think they's empty. When I get into the room next to the one they're in, I'm going to shoot through the walls. This .30 caliber should kick right through. I'll shoot high but I'll scare the shit out of 'em. They'll a-come running out, and you boys be ready, you got that?"

"Yes sir," said Slim.

"You ready, kid?" he asked Frenchy.

Frenchy gulped.

Earl stepped out, the BAR locked in the assault position, its butt clamped under his arm, its long muzzle pointing down the hall. Like his caddie Frenchy cowered behind, two mags in one hand, one in the other, others stuffed into his suit coat. It seemed almost comic—the man with the vest cowering behind the man without one—but nobody laughed.

As second in the stick, Carlo let Slim dash forward into the first room, duck in and shout "Clear!"

It was his turn. As Earl moved forward, hunched and urgent, and passed the next doorway, he jumped toward it. Ooof! He stumbled, caught himself, and looked down to discover a Grumley toppled over in a pool of his own blood, his fingers latticed around a belly wound that still pulsated. But Carlo could tell in a second he was dead, and flew on.

He kicked open the door, scanned quickly over the sights of the .45 which he had locked before him at the end of his two tightened arms. He pivoted, finding the room empty, checked behind the door, then dashed to a closet, finding only frilly women's clothes.

"Clear!" he yelled.

"Clear!" came another call, as a third raider worked a room behind Earl's staunch advance.

Finally, there was only the one room left, the last

room on the right. A dead Grumley lay on this floor too, though Carlo wasn't sure when he'd been hit. He couldn't remember many details of the past three or four minutes.

He crouched in a doorway, on his left knee, his pistol fixed on the last entryway, his wrists braced against the wall. Slim was above him in the same position, only standing, and down the hallway, two or three other raiders had taken up positions in doorways.

Earl yelled to the surviving Grumleys.

"We got y'all covered. You come on out and you won't get hurt."

"Fuck you, lawman," yelled a Grumley from inside. "You come in this room, we're gonna start blasting these here nigger gals and we'll all go to hell for breakfast."

"Don't hurt them gals. They ain't done nothing to you."

"No man tells a Grumley what to do, you bastard. Who the hell you think you are! This is *our* town, it ain't yours. You get out of here or by God there'll be blood in rivers spilt. No Grumley goes down easy, you hear me?"

But Earl wasn't listening. Instead he'd slipped into the room next door, oriented his automatic rifle to the common wall with the room where the last Grumley boys crouched with their hostages. He stitched a burst across the wall, about seven feet high. The old wood and plaster board vaporized under the buzzsaw of .30 caliber bullets. The magazine was done in two seconds. Dust floated heavily in the air.

"Another," he yelled, and Frenchy placed the mag in his hand. He jammed it in and fired it off in another single roaring blast.

Dust blew and floated everywhere, like fog.

Screams came from inside the room.

Suddenly the door blew open and a Negro gal sprawled out, thrown out by two Grumleys to draw fire. But she didn't, for the raiders stayed unexcited and reasonable, and in fact after falling to her knees, she got up and ran down the hallway, screaming "Don't shoot me, oh please, sirs, don't shoot me."

Earl fired another magazine, and it was enough.

They all broke from the room, Grumleys in rage and fleeing prostitutes in panic, figures in the foggy dust only readable by body postures.

In the fog, only gun flashes leapt out. Carlo fired at what had to be a man and brought him down as two or three of the gals ran clear. Above him, Slim found a target and fired, and his man fell backward, his finger jacking the trigger of a Thompson, which whittled a nasty gash in the ceiling. Two more black girls fled by, and a last Grumley came out of the room with a shotgun and three raiders shot him simultaneously and he fell down atop still a third.

Dust heaved. From somewhere women howled. Gunsmoke filled the air.

Earl clicked in a new magazine and slid to the side of the last door, then stepped in.

A last Grumley huddled in the corner, behind the large yellow mass of a woman in a dressing gown who screamed and blubbered but could not escape his iron grip. He had a big revolver jammed into her throat.

"I'll kill this sow!" he screamed. "Throw down your guns or by God I'll kill this—"

But as he spoke, Earl flicked the BAR selector switch to semi-auto, brought the rifle to his shoulder like a marksman and shot him where what little of his head could be seen, just above the left ear, not a killing shot, but the rifle bullet had such velocity it spun him around to the wall. The big woman pulled away and fell to the floor and began to crawl, and before the Grumley could get his gun back into play, Slim and Carlo hammered him several times.

It was finally quiet at Mary Jane's.

"Jesus Christ," said Slim.

"Man," said Carlo. "I never saw nothing like that."

"Everybody okay?" asked Earl.

"Mr. Earl, you're bleeding."

"I picked up some pellet somewhere in there. It ain't a goddamn thing. The boys all right? Frenchy, you okay?"

"Yes sir," Frenchy said heavily.

They quickly checked to discover no casualties.

They moved back into the hallway and looked at what they had wrought. Dead Grumleys lay along the hallway, which itself was a corridor of ruin, as so many shots had torn through wood and plasterboard, and the air remained heavy with gunsmoke and floating dust and grit. Empty cartridges in the hundreds littered the floor. The blood had pooled here and there.

"There, boys," Earl said, "y'all take a good look. That is the world you have entered. Now I want you to form a detail and pick up all the weapons. If them Hot Springs detectives get ahold of the Thompsons, they'll just go back to the bad boys and we'll have to take 'em all over again. If that goddamn machine gun is too heavy to carry, Slim, you find someone who knows about such things and strip the toggle bolt. If nothing else, I want that bolt sunk deep in Lake Catherine, so we don't have to worry about it no more. If you can't find no one, you come to me."

"What if the cops—"

"The cops ain't gonna stand agin you tonight. Nobody's going to stand agin you tonight."

As the men spread out to retrieve the fallen guns, another raider came down the hall to Earl.

"Mr. Parker's downstairs, Earl. He wants to see you."

"Yeah, yeah," said Earl. "I'll get there in a moment. I don't hear no ambulances. It's clear now. Tell 'em to get some ambulances in here in case any of these gals are shot up. I think we saved most of 'em."

They could hear a woman wailing loudly downstairs.

"Mr. Earl, you should know: there's a problem."

"What would that be, son?"

"Some women got shot."

"We lost one, by my count. Them Grumley boys shot her."

"No sir. Not here. Down the block at the Pythian Hotel. Two Negro gals sitting in the parlor. Somehow a burst came through the window and kilt 'em both. The Negro peoples are down there all het up, and the cops may have a riot. Mr. Becker is goddamned upset and there's all these reporters here."

CHAPTER 24

The facts were tragic. Mrs. Alva Thomas, forty-seven, of New Albany, Georgia, and Miss Lavern Sevier Carmichael, twenty-three, of New Iberia, Louisiana, had been sitting in the lobby of the Pythian Hotel and Baths when the gunfire down the street had erupted. While most sensible people got down on their stomachs at the sound, the two ladies, in deep religious concentration, declined to do so. God's attention was elsewhere. Each was hit but once. The .30-caliber-model-of-1906 bullets had flown a long way and not lost but a mite of their power when they struck the two women fatally.

The Reverend Tyrone Blandings, of the leading

Negro church in Hot Springs, requested a meeting with Mr. Becker. There he was formally apologized to, and told the county would pay for the shipping and funeral expenses of the two bodies, but that the enforcement of the law must be absolute and sometimes in these confrontations between the sinners and the sinless, unaccountable accidents happened. It was God's will. He must have a plan.

Meanwhile, Mayor O'Donovan empaneled a group of elder Hot Springs citizens to investigate the out-of-control Jayhawkers who turned the city into a war zone. If it had been within the purview of his powers, he informed the newspapers, he would have called a grand jury and issued indictments, but unfortunately it was only the prosecuting attorney who had the legal power to convene such an assembly.

The outstanding warrants on seven of the nine Murfreesboro Grumleys were never acknowledged in the Hot Springs newspapers, though the bigger Little Rock papers made certain this evidence reached the public up front.

The dead were listed, all of them Grumleys or Grumley cousins: Nathan Grumley, forty-two; Wayne Grumley, Jr., twenty-one; Jasper "Jape" Grumley, twenty-three; Bowman Peck, twenty-seven; Alvin Grumley, twenty-eight; Jeter Dodge, thirty-two; Duane Grumley, thirty-two; Buddy "Junior" Mims, thirty-three; Dewey Grumley, thirty-seven; Felton Parr, thirty-nine; and one unidentified body, burned beyond all recognition, presumably that of R. K. Pindell, age unknown, gone missing. Of the eleven, Nathan was clearly the most violent, as he had spent twelve years in the penitentiary on a case of second-degree murder and was suspected of a variety of other crimes, including rape, child molestation and dozens of counts of armed robbery as well as being widely suspected of killing a clown. He was also a known contract killer for Jefferson Davis Grumley, known as the "Boss of Pike County," and brother to Elmer "Pap" Grumley, once known as the "Boss of Garland County," though now thought to be retired.

But each of the other Grumleys or Grumley cousins had at least one and some as many as five outstanding warrants lodged against their names, for crimes that went anywhere from breaking and entering to suspicion of murder. So those Murfreesboro Grumleys, most people acknowledged, were not innocents.

The next evening, Mr. Becker gave a speech before the Better Business Bureau of Hot Springs in the Banquet Room of the Arlington Hotel. Giving speeches was a gift of his, as he had that rare ability to project concern and empathy and at the same time heroic will. He bit his lip when he discussed his dilemma in sending his men in against so dangerous a foe as gamblers and wanted men armed with machine guns, but then in the end decided it was worth it, for the law had to be served no matter the cost. The law was what separates us from the apes, after all. And unlike some men, he felt the weight of the deaths of Negroes as heavily as he felt the deaths of white folks; he was sorry that such a thing had occurred, but he assured his listeners it was unavoidable, as part of his commitment to reform. The gambling and corruption that had marked Hot Springs for a century had to be stopped and he would stop it, no matter what it cost him. Most of the men in the room believed that he himself had led the raid, as he frequently referred to "his boys" and the risks they had taken for Hot Springs and for America. He knew the way ahead was tough but he knew it was the right way.

They gave him a standing ovation.

As for the raiders, early the next morning they were informed that Mr. Becker had decided the best thing for them to do would be to go on vacation for a bit. All their weapons were to be secured and they were to drive back to their training headquarters at the Red River Army Depot, and from there commence a week off.

But of course there were two private chats to be gotten out of the way. One took place between Earl and Frenchy and, surprisingly enough, was initiated by Frenchy, in the ramshackle room that served as Earl's operations center in the pumping building.

"I wanted to apologize," he said early. "I fucked up."

"How's that?" said Earl.

"With those two Negro women. I fired those shots. I was racingup the steps, I tripped on a shell,

I'd just loaded the BAR. I felt it firing. I—"

"You was in a battle zone, why wouldn't you have had your finger on the trigger? At any time a Grumley might have jumped out at you with a gun."

"I'm still sorry. If only—"

"Don't waste no time on *if onlys*. You can run it through your head a thousand times and if this thing or that thing is different, it all turns out different. But maybe it turns out worse, not better, don't forget that possibility."

"Yes sir," said Frenchy.

"Good," said Earl.

"Thank God," said Frenchy, "that they were only Negroes."

Earl said nothing. But then he thought a second, as Frenchy returned to the bunk area, and said, "Just hold on."

"Yes sir."

"I wish you hadn't said that."

"Mr. Earl? I guess I meant, think of the *problems* we'd have if they'd have been white. That's what I meant."

"No, that ain't what you meant. I know what you meant. You meant, hey, they was only niggers."

Frenchy said nothing, but he seemed to squirm with discomfort. Then he replied, "They were only Negroes. I would never say nigger because my parents told me it was uncouth, but still, they were only Negroes. And the truth is, some of the boys are wondering why we went to so much trouble and risked so much to save some black prostitutes."

"Okay, you listen here, Short, and you listen good. Third day on Tarawa, third day after that long walk in through the cold water, I got plugged by a Jap sniper. I like to bled out but two boys from the Ammunition Company that we used as litter bearers, they crawled out and got me. Lots of fire going on. Japs everygoddamnwhere, you hear me? They drug me in, they dumped me on their litter and they carried my bleeding ass back to the aid station. Didn't say a word. Negro boys. I'm dead but for them two, and a few hours later one of 'em hisself was drug in, and they laid him next to me, and he died. I watched him die. Damned if his blood weren't the same goddamned color as mine. Bright red, when it come out, then turning sort of blackish. So don't you tell me they're any goddamned different."

He didn't realize by the end he was screaming, but as Frenchy shrank back further and further it became clearer and clearer and he looked up to see everybody else around him staring, all the guys.

"So any other bird got a complaint?"

There was silence.

"You are good, brave boys. You are as good as any Marines. But underneath, your blood is the same color as any Negro's, so when a Negro dies it's a real hard death. Anybody have any goddamned problem with that?"

"No sir," came a comment.

"Then get your asses back to packing up. We

have to move back to Texas before we can take some time off."

If Earl seemed to have a particularly brutal edge to his voice, they were all unaware of a reason. But perhaps it had to do with a previous discussion Earl had just concluded with D.A., which developed along different lines.

"Earl," D.A. said, "this smells of so many kinds of bad I don't know where to start."

"Start at the top, finish at the bottom," said Earl.

"The kid who killed them two gals? Becker wants him dumped. He wants his ass gone. He says it's the smart move. It'll quieten the Negroes, it'll show we're responsive to community pressures and that we've got hearts and consciences."

"If that boy goes, I go," said Earl intractably.

"Earl, I—"

"If that boy goes, I go. No other way."

"Earl, Becker and some of his people are beginning to think we are out of control."

"I can't fight no other way, Mr. Parker. Fighting's too goddamned tough as it is to do it while being second-guessed by folks who've never done a lick of it and don't have no stomach for it nohow."

"Earl, in truth, you made some faulty decisions."

"I know I did. But it ain't on the boys, it's on me. If mistakes were made, I made 'em. You'd best fire me, Mr. Parker, and leave them boys alone."

The old man just shook his head.

"Damn," he said, "you are a stubborn man. You

don't have some kind of craziness in your head that makes you want to die, to be with your pals in the Pacific? They say that's common. Is that what's going on with you? Is that why you didn't wear the vest?"

"I didn't wear the vest because I had to move fast. The vests ain't no good when you move fast. They're heavy, they're cumbersome, they eat up your energy real fast, and they only stop shotgun and pistol. They wouldn't have stopped that big German machine gun a lick."

"But you keep jumping into the guns."

"It's the only way I know."

"You are a hard piece of work, Earl. But I keep having to say the same goddamned things. You have to wear the damned vest. That's how I want it done. You were to command from outside, not inside. This isn't the Marine Corps. You are a law officer, sworn true, and your job is to follow the instructions of your superior, which is me. Earl, I will not steer you wrong. Don't you trust me?"

"I do trust you. You are a fair and decent man. I have not a doubt about that one."

"But you don't trust Becker."

"Not a goddamned bit."

"He wanted me to fire you too, Earl. I told him if you went, I went. Now you tell me if that Short goes, you go. This don't sound like it's working."

"It's the only way I know, Mr. Parker."

"Call me D.A., goddammit, Earl. Okay, Short

gets one more chance, you get one more chance."

And what he didn't say was that he had only one more chance.

"Now I want you to go home. The boys go home for a week, you go home for a week. And get those goddamned pellets plucked out of your hide, so you won't be so disagreeable, do you understand? And see your wife. The poor woman is probably very upset with you."

CHAPTER 25

They got back to the Red River Army Depot, were paid in cash the money owed them, and left early the next morning for Texarkana and from there to all points for a week of pleasure. Some went home, some, whose homes were too far, headed down to the Texas beaches, but a day away by train, some headed for that lush and Frenchy town, New Orleans.

All, that is, but two of them.

Carlo Henderson was tapped by D.A. late that morning, as most of the others had left. He was in no hurry because he was going to catch a late bus out of Texarkana for Tulsa, where he planned to visit his widowed mother. But that was not to be.

"Yes sir?"

"Henderson, Mr. Earl tells me you're doing very well. You've got a lot to be proud of."

Carlo lit up with a smile. Earl, of course, was a God to him, brave and fair but not a man given to much eloquence in his praise.

"I am just trying to do my duty," he allowed.

"That's important, isn't it?"

"Important?"

"Duty, son."

"Yes sir," said the boy. "Yes sir, it is."

"Good, I thought you'd say that," said the old FBI agent. "Now let me ask you this: what do you think of Mr. Earl?"

Carlo was taken aback. He felt his jaw flop open, big enough for flies to fill, and then he swallowed, gulped and blurted out, "He's a hero."

"That he is," agreed the old man. "That he is. You've heard these rumors that Earl won a medal, a big medal, in the Pacific? Well, they're true. Earl was a great Marine out there. Earl killed a lot of the Yamoto race. So any young man who gits to study and learn and benefit from Earl's bravery and leadership ability, he's a lucky young man indeed, wouldn't you say?"

"Yes sir," said Carlo, for he felt that way exactly.

"But you should know something, Henderson," D.A. continued. "Earl's was the very toughest of wars. Five invasions. Wounds. Lots of men lost on hell's far and barren beaches. You get my drift?"

Carlo did not.

"It takes something from a man, all that. You

can't go through it and come out the same. It wears a man down and exhausts him. It blunts him. Now, son," continued the old man, "I am a mite worried about something. See if you follow me. You ever hear of this thing called combat fatigue?"

"Yes sir," said Carlo. "Section 8. Cuckoo. You can't do your job no more, even though you ain't been hit. So off you go to the nuthouse."

"Them jitters, they don't always make it so you want to go to hospital. Sometimes they make it so you just want to die and git it over with. It's part of combat fatigue. It's called a death wish. You hear me? Death wish."

The concept sounded somehow familiar to Carlo, but he wasn't sure from where. And he wondered where in hell this was going.

"See, here's what can happen," D.A. explained. "A fellow can be so tired he don't want to go on. But he's got too much guts—they call it internal structure, the doctors do, I have looked it up—to quit. So he decides to kill himself doing his duty. He takes wild chances. He behaves with incredible bravado. But he's really just trying to git hisself killed. Strange it is, but they say it happens."

"Is that what's going on with Mr. Earl?" Carlo asked.

"I don't know, son. What do you think?"

"I don't know neither, sir. He seems all right, I guess."

"Yes, he does. But dammit, I have told him three

times on raids to wear the damned vest and he will not do it. I have told him his job is to stay outside and coordinate, over the walkie-talkies. But again, he's got to be right up front where the guns are. And that last stunt. Why, he walked down that hallway in plain sight, daring them boys to shoot him. What a fool thing to do. He could have laid back and with that BAR just opened fire and finished their hash off."

"He was afraid of hurting them colored girls."

"Never heard of such a thing in all my days."

"Yes sir."

Now that he thought about it, Carlo had to admit it did seem peculiar.

"So anyway," said D.A., "I am mighty worried about Earl. I do not want to be a party to his self-destruction. I picked him, I offered him this job in good faith and I expected him to do it in good faith, and not try and get himself killed. Do you understand?"

"I think so, sir."

"Now, there's one other thing as well."

The boy just stared his way.

"You know I respect and appreciate Earl as much as any man on the team?"

"Yes sir."

"And you know I think he's a true American hero, of the type there ain't many like anymore. Mr. Purvis, he was one. Audie Murphy, now there's another. William O. Darby, he was another. But Earl's quite a man, that's what I think."

"I do too, sir," said the boy.

"So I ask myself a question so hard I can hardly put it in words. Which is: Why did he lie?"

"Sir?"

"Why did he lie? Earl told a lie. A flat, cold, indisputable lie and it's got me all bothered, bothered as much as his crazy need to get hisself kilt. I tried to dismiss it but I couldn't. There seemed no point to it, none at all, not even a little one."

"He lied?"

"He did."

"It don't sound like him."

"Not a bit. But he did."

"On what topic?"

"The topic was Hot Springs."

"Hot Springs?"

"I asked him dead-on. Earl, have you ever been in Hot Springs? No sir, he said. 'My Baptist daddy said Hot Springs was fire and damnation. He'd beat our hides off if ever we went to Hot Springs.' That's what he said."

"But you think he has?"

"Shoot, son, it's a pitcherful more than that! At least three times I have planned a certain way, based on my reconnoitering and my experience. And in each damn case, he has at the last second said, Now wait a minute, wouldn't it be better if . . . And each goddamn time his way was better. Better by far."

"Well, I—"

"Better because he knew the terrain or the site of the buildings. The last time was the best. He's in the alley watching the rear entry team, holding it all together on the radio. But suddenly he gets this feeling the team will be ambushed from behind. So he's looking down the alley when they move a truck with gunmen in it down toward Malvern, with an enfilade on the rear to Mary Jane's. How's he know to look there? It's dark as sin, but he knows where to look? How?"

"Ah. Well, I guess—"

"Guess nothing! I asked him straight up and he told me he was just lucky he was looking in the right direction. Bullshit! I swear to you, he goddamned *knew* there was just the slightest incline down that little street, called Guilford, toward Malvern. He *knew* a truck could roll down, no engine involved, just by releasing the emergency brake, and git into shooting position. So that's exactly where he looked and by God when he saw them boys sliding into position he was ready. He emptied two BAR mags into that truck and up she went like the Fourth of July and three more of Pap Grumley's cousins went to hell. He *knew*."

The old man seemed astounded, turning this bit of information over and over in his mind. It fascinated him.

"All right," he said, "here's what I want. You take this week and you turn all your detective skill loose on Earl. Earl's background. Earl's past. Who is Earl?

Why's he working the way he is? What's going on in his head? What do his ex-Marine pals say? What's his folks say? What's his family doctor say? How was he in Hot Springs? When was he in Hot Springs? Why was he in Hot Springs? What's going on? And you report to me. So I can decide."

"Decide?"

"Decide whether or not to fire Earl. I will not be party to his suicide. It's more than I care to carry around on my shoulders. I will not have him using me to git hisself kilt. Do you understand?"

"I am not a psychologist, sir. I can't make that call."

"Well, dammit, I can't make it neither, not without some help. If I fire Earl, the whole goddamned shebang falls apart, that I know. And I got that bastard Becker to answer to. But if I send him ahead and he gets killed, I got my own self to answer to. Both of them are stern taskmasters."

"Yes sir."

"This is a hard job. Maybe the hardest of all. Harder than walking down that hallway in all that dust and smoke with Grumleys with tommy guns at the other end."

The boy's face knitted in confusion, but then he saw that the old man had all but made up his mind that he would fire Earl. That is, unless he could be talked out of it, on the strength of something that he, Carl Donald Henderson, could dig out. And that was what he was good at, digging, ferreting, going through files, making calls, taking notes, comparing fingerprints, alibis, accounts and stories. So in that sense he could help Earl, he and he alone, and the heaviness of the task that had just been offered him filled him with solemnity.

"I will look into it, sir."

"Good. Here's a file on what I have. It'll git you started. There's people to talk to."

"Yes sir. Where am I going, sir?"

"You'd start in his hometown. It's called Blue Eye, out in Polk County."

At the bus station, Carlo used up all his change calling his mother long distance and telling her he would not be coming in after all, he had another assignment.

Then he went to the Greyhound window, and bought a ticket for Blue Eye, on the 4:30 bus that drove up Route 71 through Fort Smith to Fayetteville, and then he bought some popcorn and a root beer and sat for the longest time, watching the slow crawl of the clock hands, reading a John P. Marquand novel that he couldn't keep track of, and trying not to think about the mysteries of Earl Swagger. The file sat unopened on his lap. He could not bring himself to look at it somehow, any more than he could bring himself to take off his Colt .45, secreted in the fast-draw holster behind his right hip. He was just too used to it.

They called the bus at 4:15 and, ever obedient

and respectful of the rules, he was one of the first to board. He sat halfway back, on the right, for it was said that the ride was smoothest there.

And then he saw Frenchy Short.

Yes, it was Frenchy all right, though not in his usual blue serge suit, but dressed far more casually, in denim jeans, a khaki shirt and a straw cowboy's hat, with a carpetbag full of clothes under tow. Was it Frenchy? Yes, it was Frenchy! He almost left his seat to yell a greeting, but then he looked at Frenchy and saw that he too was in line to board a bus.

Then his bus pulled out and Frenchy was gone.

But later, that night, when he got to Blue Eye, he had to ask the driver, "You know that bus that was in the dock next to us at Texarkana?"

The driver just looked at him.

"You know that one? I didn't get a look at it, but where was it headed?"

"That'd be the Little Rock bus," the driver said.

"Oh, the Little Rock bus."

"Yes sir," said the driver. "It heads straight on up 30 through Hope, on up to Little Rock."

"It just goes to Little Rock?" asked Carlo.

"Yep. Well, that's where she finishes. She stops at Hope and Malvern and all them towns. Then she veers over 270 and toward Hot Springs. That's the Hot Springs bus. Most folks take it to Hot Springs, for the track and the gambling. Hot Springs, that's a damned old hot town, you'd best believe it, son."

CHAPTER 26

The aspirin worked well enough on through De Queen but the throbbing began just beyond. He took some more but it didn't seem to help. Particularly, there was a pellet lodged between the layers of muscle on the inside of his left biceps and when it rubbed a certain way it sent a jack of pain through the whole left side of his body, once so bad he had to pull off Route 71 and let it pass. It made him thirsty for a powerful drink of bourbon.

He couldn't stop in Blue Eye because he knew too many folks and too many folks knew him. The next towns up the road offered no promise, small, dying places like Boles and Y City, mere widenings in the road, too small to have a doctor.

Finally, he came to Waldron, in Scott County, a town large enough to support such a thing. Waldron lay in a flatlands between the mountains, essentially a farm town, and it had grown prosperous on the rich loam of Scott. It was large enough to support a Negro district, a servant population to provide comfort to the wealthy white families in the area. Earl drove through it looking for a certain thing and at last found it: Dr. Julius James Peterson, OB-GYN, as the sign said. He parked around back and slunk up the back steps like a man on the run. It was near nine o'clock, but a light shone from within the frame house.

He knocked and after a bit the door opened, though a chain kept it from flying fully wide.

"Yes?" the man said, and there was fear in his voice, as there would be in the voice of any Negro man answering a nighttime knock and finding a large white male on the other side.

"Sir, I need some medical help."

"I'm a baby doctor. I deliver babies. I can't help you. You could go onto Camp Chaffee. There's a dispensary there that's always open if it's an emergency. They wouldn't turn you down. There's a small hospital for white folks in Peverville too, if you want to go that way. I can't let you in here."

"I can't go to them places. I'm by myself. This ain't no raid or night rider thing. I'm a police officer."

Earl got out his wallet and showed both the badge and the identification card, officially stamped with the seal of the great state of Arkansas.

"I can't help you, sir. You are a white person and I am a Negro. That's a chasm that can't be bridged. There are people around here who would do my family great harm if I practiced medicine on a white person. That's just the way it is."

"I guess I ain't like them others. Doc, I need help. I got some pellet riding under my skin, hurts like hell, makes me want a drink bad, and if I start drinking again, I lose everything. I have cash money, no need to make no records. Nobody seen me. I will be quietly gone when you are done. I'm asking a mighty favor, and wouldn't if I didn't have to."

"You say you are not an outlaw?"

"No sir, I am not."

"Are you armed?"

"I am. I'll lock the guns in the trunk of the car."

"Go do that. After I remove the pellet you can't stay here."

"Don't mean to."

"Then disarm and come in."

Earl did as he said he would, then slipped in the door. The doctor took him to a shabbily appointed but very clean examining room. Earl took his shirt off and sat on an examination table that had stirrups of some sort at the end. He didn't like the look of them stirrups.

"I count six in all," he said. "The one in my arm, for some reason it hurts the most."

The doctor, a mild-enough-looking black man of lighter, yellowish complexion and hair that was almost red, looked at the mesh of scars on his body.

"The war?"

"Yes sir. The Pacific."

"Then you know pain and won't go into shock. This will hurt. I don't have anesthetics here."

"Okay. It don't matter. I can get through anything if there's a promise of better on t'other side."

The doctor washed, sterilized a long, sharply pointed probe and began to dig. The first three pellets came out easily enough, though not without pain. The doctor disinfected each wound with alcohol, a flaming sensation if ever there was one, then bandaged each with a gauze patch and a strip of adhesive. The fourth and fifth were deeper and even more painful. But the last one, in the arm, was a bastard. It wouldn't come and it seemed the more the man dug, the further into the muscle it slipped. But Earl didn't move or scream; he closed his eyes, tried to disassociate himself from his hurting, and thought of other places, better times, and his teeth ground together as if they meant to crush each other to dental powder, and then he heard a clink as the last pellet was deposited in a dish.

"You're not from around here?" said the doctor. "No white man would let a black one inflict so much pain on him without the word 'nigger' being spoken at least ten times."

"Funny, never crossed my mind. I grew up in Polk County."

"No, I'd say you grew up in the South Pacific and became more than a man, you became a human being."

"Don't know about that, sir."

"I won't ask you how you got these wounds. I doubt it was a hunting accident. It's not bird season. And I heard tell of a great battle in Hot Springs, but I know you not to be a Grumley sort. So if you carry the badge of the law, I assume you're a good man. I know you're a lucky one: No. 7 birdshot doesn't play so gentle in most cases."

"Been lucky my whole life. What do I owe you?"

"Nothing. It's not a problem. You continue with the aspirin, have another doctor look at it the day after tomorrow. Possibly, he will prescribe penicillin, to fight an infection. But you must go now."

"Sir, I have a hundred dollars. I'm guessing you don't charge poor women who come to you much if anything at all. You ain't no rich doctor, I can tell. So you take this hundred, and it's for them."

"That's a lot of money."

"Hard earned too, by God, but I want you to have it."

He pressed the money on Dr. Peterson, shook his hand, dressed and slipped out the back, in the dark, as he had come.

"Well, ain't we a sight?" he said with a laugh. "You're all swoll up and I am full of holes."

"Earl," she said, "that is not funny a bit."

"No ma'am. I don't suppose it is."

Chastened, he took another sip on his Coca-Cola and then a bite of his hot dog. Under his shirt, his wounds still occasionally stung, particularly the arm, where the doc had dug so deep. They sat at a picnic table in a park in Fort Smith that overlooked the Arkansas River, a meadowy place that rolled down to the water, where the pines sprouted up. There, the black waters rushed thunderously along; there must have been a big rainstorm up north.

But there were no storms here. It was a hot, bright Sunday in August, a year after they dropped the big ones on the Japs, and people frolicked in the shadow of an old courthouse, famous in an earlier century for its public hangings. Adults pushed their babies along the walkways in elaborate strollers; young servicemen from Camp Chaffee spooned with their townie belles. Even Negroes were welcome; it was an afternoon on the Grand Jette, Fort Smith style, complete to points of light in the bright air, and in the green of the pines, and if there weren't monkeys on leashes there were spaniels on them. Everybody was eating Eskimo Pies or hot dogs and thinking about the future and no one looked to the southwest, for in that quadrant of the scene lay the vets' cemetery, newly expanded, hills of rolling white markers that gleamed in the sun so freshly planted were they. One of the state's other war heroes rested there, William O. Darby, the young Ranger major who'd fought the Germans in Italy so hard and then gotten killed by a piece of metal the size of a dime from an artillery shell late in the spring of 1945 while he stood on a hill as an observer. Earl didn't want to go anywhere near that.

"You were in that ruckus all the papers wrote up," she said.

"I was there, yes."

"And that's why you have bandages all over your body."

"I caught some pellet, that's all. It ain't no big thing. Hurt myself shaving worse most mornings."

"Earl, they say that was the most violent gunfight in the history of the state. Fourteen people died."

"Eleven of 'em was bad-boy Grumleys, as low a form as has existed, whose passing is of no note whatsoever. They didn't have to die. They could have surrendered to the law, easy as pie."

"It wasn't their nature."

"No ma'am, guess it wasn't."

He looked at her. Her face had broadened considerably, and her shoulders, legs and arms thickened up a bit. But still and all: a beautiful woman, an angel, full and fair and blond and decent, the very best of America. She licked at her Eskimo Pie, with that special grace that seemed hers alone. She was the only human being on the planet who could eat an Eskimo Pie in the full blaze of afternoon and not spill a drop of it.

Under her breasts, the child seemed eager to come into this world, so forcefully did it thrust itself out and away from its mother. She had worn a red maternity blouse to hide it, but the subterfuge was pointless: that was a lot of baby in there.

"I am so frightened, Earl, that you are going to die for nothing and I will be alone with this child," she said, the last of the ice cream pie gone.

"If it happens, you will get a nice big chunk of insurance money from the state. It'll get the two of you a fine start in a new life. Maybe you'll meet up with a fellow who's around more than I am. And that money is more than my mama got when my old man got hisself bushwhacked back in '42. She got a gold watch, a hundred dollar burial fee, and commenced to drink herself to death in a year. I know you'll do better."

He took another sip on the Coca-Cola. The river wound blackly through the trees, but between here and there, boys threw a ball or sailed planes, girls cradled dolls, moms and dads held hands.

"I am so sorry," he finally said. "I know you didn't sign on for this thing. But I am in it now, and I don't know how to get out of it."

"You could just quit and go back to the sawmill."

"You know I couldn't do that."

"No. You have no quit in you, that's for sure."

"I think I could go to Mr. Parker and see about getting a loan against the money they'll be paying me before this thing is finished. Maybe there's a credit union or something. Also, there's some veterans' rights I got coming I ain't looked into yet. That way I could move you out of that damned Quonset hut in the village and into a nice little place much closer. Say in the towns outside of Little Rock. I'd see you much more often."

"Earl, it seems so ridiculous with the farm."

He sat a long moment, looking again down and across the meadowy grass to the river. Then he said, "I wasn't trying to hide that place from you. It wasn't no secret. I just never got around to telling you about it."

"I wasn't prying. A letter came from the Polk County tax assessors bureau, which had been forwarded by the Marine Corps. It was stamped Open Immediately. I opened it. You owed back taxes on two hundred acres out in Polk, out Route 8. It was past due: $127.50, plus a three dollar penalty. I sent them a check. Then I got to thinking about it and so last week, before all this gun-battle business, I had Mary Blanton drive me out there. We spent the day on the farm."

"It's a nice place, I recollect," he said. "The old man had it up and running pretty tight at one point."

"It's a wonderful place, Earl. The house needs work, mainly paint, but there's a big garden. I counted four bedrooms. The kitchen hasn't been touched in years. It could use some work too. But Earl, there's land. There's farmland which could be leased out, there's a creek, there's a stand of timber where you could hunt and raise your children. There's meadowland and a corral and a fine barn. Earl, honey, we could be so happy out there. And we own it. We already own it. We could move in tomorrow. I don't have to stay in a sewer pipe and take the bus to work. I could teach in Polk County. When the baby comes, he or she'd have a wonderful place to grow up."

"The week I left the Marine Corps," he said, "when I was driving up to Fort Smith for you, last December? I stopped there and spent some time."

"You don't want to go there, do you, Earl? I can tell from your voice."

"I almost burned it to the ground. That would have felt good. I'd love to see that place go up in flames. It's . . ."

He trailed off.

"It's what, Earl?"

"There's a lot of hurting in that place. It's haunted. You see a pretty little farm and I see the place where my brother died. He hung himself in 1940. I hardly knew the boy. I sure didn't do him no good. His big old brother didn't do a pie's worth of good for him. Like everybody else, I let him down. Nobody did him no good. Nobody stood up for him. In the basement of that house my old man used to beat me and so I suppose he beat Bobby Lee too."

"It wouldn't have to be like that. We'd paint it white, I'd get the garden up and running, you could lease out the fields like your daddy did, it could be a good house, a happy house. It could be a house full of children."

Earl finished his hot dog.

"I don't know. I just ain't sure I could face that place. Let me think her over."

"Earl, I know you have a melancholy in you over your childhood. But you have to think of your child's childhood. Do you want him born into a Quonset hut on a military base? Or on a big, beautiful farm on the most beautiful land in the state?"

"That is not an easy question," he said.

"No, it is not."

"I'd sell the goddamned place if I could. But land

is so cheap now, and it's so far out, I'd never find a buyer. When's that goddamned postwar boom going to hit Polk County? Anyhow, I'll think some."

"You'll think *hard* on it?"

"Yes ma'am."

"All right, Earl. I know you'll work it out. I know you'll do the right thing. You always do."

For the next few days, Earl was perfect. There was never a harder-working, more cheerful man, a better husband. He repainted the inside of the Quonset hut apartment a bright yellow, a day's worth of back-breaking labor, but worth it, for the lighter color cheered the place up. He loaded the old sofa up on the roof of his government Dodge and took it to a dump, then went over to the Sears, Roebuck in Fort Smith and bought a new sofa for her, a pretty thing in green stripes. That made the rooms even brighter.

He redug the garden, weeded it, trimmed the hedges. He took her out to dinner, twice. They went for walks. He listened to the baby move and the two of them tried to think up names for it. She wrote long lists and he laughed at Adrian and Phillip, he thought Thomas and Andrew were okay, he liked Timothy and Jeffrey. The problem was, except for Adrian, each of the names had a boy somewhere attached to it, a Marine who'd died or been maimed and was carried out by stretcher bearers screaming for his mama.

But Earl tried not to let any of that show on his face. He tried so hard to be the kind of man he thought she deserved, the kind of man he thought he wasn't. He never told her about the way his father would sneak up on him and whisper something fierce and hurtful in his ear, then steal away, to leave nothing but sunlight and trees blowing in the breeze.

Finally, he drove her to the doctor's office and sat out front during the exam and then the doctor brought him in and spoke to him while she dressed. Earl had seen lots of docs, and this one was no different from any in an aid station, a field hospital or a hospital ship: a grave official type man, with a blur of mustache and eyes that were somehow lightless.

"Mr. Swagger, first of all, the baby and your wife are both doing fine. The health of both seems well within the parameters of what we'd qualify as a normal, healthy term. The baby should be right on time. I'd say first week in October."

"Yes sir, great. That's great news."

"Now I did want to say something to you. There's no cause to be alarmed just yet, but I have noted that the baby is situated a certain way in your wife's uterus. Not abnormal by any means, but at the same time not exactly where we'd expect it to be."

"Yes sir," said Earl gravely. "Does Junie know this?"

"No, she doesn't. I'd prefer her not to know. It would cause anxiety, quite possibly undue. It may not be anything to get alarmed at."

"But it means something. What does it mean, sir?"

"There can be complications. Usually of no consequence. But what happens sometimes in this case is that the child arrives in the wrong presentation. That is, instead of breeching face up, it breeches face down. Then it gets tricky. I want you prepared."

Earl nodded.

"It says in the paperwork you're a state employee. An engineer, a crew foreman?"

"No sir. I work as an investigator for a prosecuting attorney in another county."

"I see. Law enforcement. Is it demanding?"

"Sometimes."

"You were in the war, weren't you?"

"Yes sir. The Pacific."

"Well, then, you've seen some emergency medical situations I'd guess."

"A few, yes sir. I was wounded a few times."

"Good. Then you know what can happen."

"Are you telling me there's a chance my wife could die?"

"A very small one."

"Jesus," he said. "For a damned baby."

"The baby is very important to her, as it would be to any woman. That's part of being a woman, and that's part of what's so wonderful about women. And that's part of the reason I'd prefer her not to know. Sometimes we men have to make the serious decisions."

"Yes sir."

"So what I am saying is that if the complications are grave, I may have to make a choice. I may only be able to save one, the child or the mother. I am assuming the mother would be your choice."

"Ain't no two ways about it. We didn't plan this kid, I ain't settled in this job yet, the timing was all off. And I don't feel much for it. Don't know why, I just don't."

"Many men who came back from a hard war feel the same way. I've heard those words a hundred times. I think it'll change when you hold your child, but to many men who've been in combat, the idea of bringing a new child into a somewhat profane world seems pointless."

Earl thought: You just said a mouthful, Doc.

"Anyhow, here's what's most important. You must be around when the child is born. I don't know what sort of arrangement you and your wife have, with your work so far away, but you absolutely have to be here in case a decision is needed. Do you understand?"

"Sir, I've made my decision."

"Yes, but if the baby comes late at night or when I'm not on call, I might not be here. Any of a dozen things could happen. It's quite common for the delivery to be assisted by the staff resident. That would be a younger doctor, possibly not willing to make the decision that you just made. He might not have the sand to intervene and you could lose them both. So you need to be here. You may have to fight for your wife's life. You may even have to fight your wife for it."

Earl nodded.

"But I can see something on your face," the doctor said.

"Yes sir. The job I'm in, sometimes it gets very complicated and I can't get back. I just don't want to let nobody down."

"Well, Mr. Swagger, you'll just have to decide what's more important to you. You don't want someone else making that decision, do you? No, Mr. Swagger, please, please, try and be here."

"Yes sir," said Earl, feebly, knowing it might not happen that way. "I'll do my best."

CHAPTER 27

Pap Grumley danced a dance of grief and shame. It was a strange mountain dance that somehow connected with people who worshipped the Lord with poisonous snakes or through the speaking of tongues, practices which were part of Grumley life in one way or other.

He was dressed for mourning, all in black, black frock coat, black pants, his black boots, a black hat that could hold twenty gallons, pulled low over his eyes. Eleven coffins filled with Grumleys had been lowered into the ground and words were said over them. All the Grumleys and assorted clans were there, including Pecks, Dodges, Grundys and Pindells. The women and the men were grim in their mourning clothes, their taut mountain faces bleak and severe, their blue eyes gray with pain, their demeanor dignified and stoic, yet hurting massively.

A Grumley preacher said the Lord's words, about how He must have wanted Grumleys in heaven for a peculiar hard job, so He sent for a whole lot of them, to stand by His right hand and help Him spread the Word. But the words he said were not nearly as eloquent as the dance Pap danced.

The spirit moved in him. He tramped in the dust, back and forth, he shivered, he shook, he stamped. The music was unheard by men's ears but came from a part of all the Grumley soul, old mountain music, the whining of a fiddle played by a drunk who'd watched his children die one by one of the pox, and had felt the cold creeping in late at night when blankets were thin and a fiftieth or a sixtieth day of feeding on taters and nothing but had just been finished, with a fifty-first or a sixty-first in view for tomorrow. It was a dance of ancient Scotch-Irish pain and within it lay a racial memory of life on a bleak border and the piping of grief and the wailing of banshees late in the cold night, where a man had to survive on his own for the government belonged to one king or another; it was reiver's music, or plunderer's music, the scream of rural grief, of a way of thinking no city person who didn't fear the harsh Presbyterian God but who had not also run 'shine against the mandates of the Devil City in far-off eastern America, the demon city lodged between Maryland and Virginia, where godless men passed laws meant to take the people's and the Grumleys' freedom and convert it to secret wealth for the castle people, could feel.

"That man bound to 'splode, look to me," said Memphis Dogood. "He is a hurting old boy."

"He may indeed, old fellow. These Grumley chaps take things like this quite seriously," said Owney.

Owney and Memphis sat in the back of Owney's bulletproof Cadillac, which had wound down the miles between the Medical Arts Building and this far Grumley compound in a trackless forest just north of Mountain Pine.

Had the Grumleys known a Negro man was one witness to the privacy of their ceremony it is altogether possible they would have hanged him or tarred him, for the Book is explicit in its denunciation of the sons of Ham, and they took the Book at its literal truth. That was what was so Grumley about them. But Owney wanted Memphis to behold the festival of grief that attended the burial of the eleven Grumley dead on the theory that it might get Memphis more talkative than he had heretofore been.

So the two of them watched from leather seats in

the back of the V-16—Memphis had never seen such a fine car—as the Grumleys, en masse, and Pap, in particular, mourned.

Pap stamped and the dust rose. Pap twitched and the dust rose. Pap did three this way then three that and the dust rose. He danced amid a fog of dust, the dust coating his boots and trousers into a dusky gray. His face too was gray, set hard, his eyes blank or distant. He folded his arms and gripped his elbows and danced and danced the afternoon away. His back was straight, his neck was stiff, his hips never moved. God commanded his legs alone, and had no use for the rest of him, and so deadened what was left until it reached a form of statuary.

"That boy could dance all night," said Memphis.

"And into the morrow," said Owney. "Now Memphis, you are possibly wondering why I brought you out here."

"Am I in trouble, Mr. Maddox? Weren't nothin' I could do, 'splained it to the bossman. Didn't say nothin' to nobody. Them revenooer boys, they knowed you had yo' Grumleys spread all over my place. And they was loaded up for bear. Next thing old Memphis know, the Big War done broke out. Ripped up my place right good."

"I need more. I need the kind of detail a clever man can provide, a shrewd man, who's fooled by nothing in this world. That would certainly be you. A man doesn't last in the brothel profession unless he's a keen judge of character. So you would notice things others might not. Tell me, Memphis, about them. About him."

"You mean they bossman?"

"Yes."

"Suh, I don't mean you no disrespect, but if Grumleys all you got to go agin that boy, then, suh, you be in a peck o' hurt. You be in a tub o' hurt."

"Describe him, please."

"Uh, he mean serious bidness." He scanned his memory for helpful images. "Nigguhs talk about Bumpy in Harlem."

Bumpy Johnson. Owney knew Bumpy well. Bumpy used to sit with his own gunman at a back table in the Cotton Club and even the toughest white mobsters avoided him directly. Yes, he saw the comparison, for Bumpy's every motion and dark, hooded eyes said: If you mess with me, I will kill you.

"Bumpy in Harlem. Yes, I knew him."

"He had that. Whatever Bump had, this boy had it too. Nigguhs can pick that up. A nigguh hafta figger out right quick if a man mean what he say. And this here fella, he surely did. His own dyin' don't mean shit. Don't mean shit."

"We call him the cowboy," said Owney.

"My gal Trina? She say he worked it upstairs so no nigguh gals git shot. All them bullets flyin', he worried about 'hos gittin' shot. Ain't that nuthin'? Ain't no white man like that down here. Hear tell they got some like that up North, but ain't no white man like that down here."

"What do you mean, Memphis?"

"He wouldn't shoot no gals. He shot over they heads. So they don't kill no nigguh gals."

Now this was a new detail that hadn't emerged in Owney's investigations.

The cowboy had something for Negroes? What on earth does that mean?

"And my main gal, Marie-Claire? She say, that ol' Grumley holdin' a gun agin her throat, sayin' he shoot her. Now, suh, you know any white po-lices in America just laugh and say, 'Go'n and shoot that nigguh gal!' Be laughin' all about it! But this here fella, he lif' his rifle, aim careful, and hit that las' Grumley right upside the haid. So Marie-Claire twist away, and them other fellas, they hammer that las' Grumley. Ain't no white cop do that, and nobody know that better than Memphis Dogood, I'm tellin' you right, suh. I gots the scars to prove it."

"You are probably right," said Owney: he knew that in that situation in every city in America the policemen would have simply fired away, killing both the felon and his hostage and therefore accomplishing two objectives: saving themselves any danger, and providing a highly amusing few seconds.

The cowboy loves the Negro people for some reason.

Interesting.

"Well, you've been very helpful, Memphis."

"Thank you, suh," said Memphis Dogood.

"Unfortunately, I can't drive you home."

"Suh?"

"Yes. Can't be seen with you. You know, appearances, all that. Those fellows over there, they'll take care of you."

"Mr. Maddox, them's Grumley boys and—"

"Nothing to worry about, old man. You have my guarantee."

He smiled. The door was opened, and Owney's driver leaned in, put his large hand on Memphis's shoulder, and directed him outward.

Some Grumley boys, young ones, watched, then began to mosey over to Memphis.

CHAPTER 28

Among the many things his colleagues did not know about Walter F. (formerly "Shorty" and now "Frenchy") Short was the following: he was wealthy.

Not rich, not a millionaire, not a playboy, a polo player or a "movie producer," but still he had a private income that would keep him perpetually comfortable to indulge his pathologies, as derived from old family investments in Canadian timber, American pharmaceuticals and railroads and a large interest in a Philadelphia manufacturing company that made, of all things, the little brass ringlets that served as belt notches in the web gear GIs had used in defeating the Axis in the recent war.

So when Frenchy arrived in Hot Springs in overalls, a threadbare khaki shirt, a beat-up coat and a low-slung fedora, a .45 on his belt behind his right hip, his first move would have surprised everyone. It was to go to his apartment.

He kept it in the New Waverly Hotel, and slunk through the lobby, largely unnoticed. He showered, beating off the road dust of the bumpy bus ride. Then he toweled off, and took a nap until later in the evening. Arising, he went to his closet and picked out a nice Brooks Brothers whipcord suit, light for summer, a pair of Weejun loafers, a blue shirt and a red-and-black-striped regimental tie. Under a crisp panama hat, he went out and about the town, a perfectly dressed sporting man whom no one could possibly associate with the grim young posse of Jayhawkers who had so alarmingly shot the town up over the past several weeks.

At first he did what any young man would do in such circumstances. He gambled a little, he had a nice meal, a few drinks, and then he went to one of the finer establishments at the far end of Central, traveling past the Ohio, the Southern, the Arlington and so many other monuments to Hot Springs' principal obsessions, and got himself laid up one side and down another.

That accomplished, he taxied back to the New Waverly and slept for two straight days.

On the third day he made a trip to a surplus store, and made a number of surprising purchases. That afternoon and night, he pleasured and partied again. He made no phone calls, because he had no friends and his family was not particularly interested in where he was or what he was doing, not after the trouble he had caused it; they just wanted him far out of Pennsylvania, for the rest of his life.

On the fourth day, he slept late again, took a light meal in the New Waverly dining room, then repaired to his room. There he opened the paper sack he'd brought from the surplus store the day before, removed his new ensemble and put it on: a new pair of black gym shoes, a black Norwegian sweater and a pair of rugged blue denim work pants. He also had a light tool kit in a brown valise. He slipped out the back of the hotel, and negotiated his way through alleys and lanes and byways, as if he had secretly studied the town's layout on maps (he had) until at last only a fence separated him from his destination.

Someone once said, in discussing the OSS, that aristocrats make the best second-story men and Frenchy was about to prove the wisdom of this judgment. He climbed the fence and moved swiftly to the building, a four-story brick affair. A skeleton crew managed the switchboards, but that bullpen was on the first floor, just off the main entrance. The upper floors were all dark.

Frenchy found a foothold that was a brass hose outlet, and from there made a good athletic move up to a window ledge, used the strength in his wrists and forearms to haul himself up to the roofline of the first-floor rear portico, gave a mighty *oof!* and pulled himself finally to the roof of the portico. He lay there, breathing heavily, imagining himself pulling such a stunt against the German embassy in Lisbon in search of codes or secret agent identities, just like his uncle had done.

But there were no SS men with machine pistols guarding the Hot Springs Bell Telephone office in late August of 1946. They had, as a species, largely vanished from the earth. The only potential opposition for Frenchy was a night watchman who never left his post on the first floor. Why should he? Who on earth would even conceive of breaking into a phone company? What would a thief be after—nickels from the pay phones?

Frenchy was fully prepared with shims and picks to crack the building; after all, at Choate he had famously liberated a biology exam for the first-formers, and made himself a legend among the populace while going blithely unpunished. At Princeton, he had tried the same trick with a physics exam, and gotten caught and expelled (the first time), but getting caught was a function of being ratted out by a bluenose prick who didn't believe in such things.

But—hello, what's this?—instead of having to use his treasury of deviant devices, he found the second-story man's best friend, the unlocked window. In a trice, he was in.

He discovered himself in a darkened office and snapped on his flashlight. He learned instantly that this was the foyer of the personnel office, of no use to him whatsoever. He stepped carefully into the hallway, then taped the door lock so that it wouldn't lock behind him, then left another tiny mark of tape high on the door so he could remember which one it was for his escape plan, and then began to patrol.

He walked down darkened corridors, checking out door titles. BOOKKEEPING. BILL PAYMENT. DIRECTORY PREPARATION. REPAIR ASSIGNMENTS. SALES. And so on and so forth, all the little fiefdoms so necessary for the care and maintenance of a modern monopoly. At last, on the silent third floor, he discovered what he thought he needed: ENGINEERING.

He used a shim to pop the lock, slid adroitly in, and again taped the lock behind him. He sent his flashlight beam bouncing around the room. Only banality was revealed: a number of drafting boards, a number of messy desks, some cheesy, cheery Bell Telephone morale posters on the institutional green walls, the glass cubicle of a supervisor, and finally and most important a horizontal filing cabinet, that is, a wall-length chest of thin, wide drawers, each marked by geographic grid references.

Shit, he said.

Time to get to work, he thought.

Many of his former friends and his family thought that Frenchy was lazy. Exactly the opposite was true; he was capable of very hard work, relentless and focused. His oddity of mind, however, was that it never occurred to him to simply *do* what was required of him; rather he would invest three times more energy and six times more discipline in figuring out how *not* to do it. He was addicted to shortcuts, quick fixes, alternative routes, cutting corners, doing things his own way, no matter what, no matter how much the cost. "Does not follow directions," his kindergarten teacher had written and no keener insight into his personality was ever revealed. It had made for quite a colorful first twenty years on the planet—his was one of those rare, bright but naturally deviated minds. He was cunning, practical, nerveless, self-promoting, rather brave and completely self-possessed at all times, or nearly all times.

So now he applied himself with a concentration that would have astonished his many detractors, who had never been allowed a glimpse of the real Frenchy and who had nicknamed him Shorty. He began at the beginning, and studiously invested close to four hours in running over the diagrams in the drawers which he correctly assumed to be wiring diagrams.

His thinking on this problem was original and far in advance of D.A.'s or Earl's and a prime example of how well, when focused, he could work things out. He reasoned that Owney Maddox's empire was only secondarily an empire of force, violence, debt collection and municipal subversion; primarily, it was an empire of the telephone. Everybody knew this: the racing data had to pour in from the tracks of America, there to be distributed instantaneously to all the minor duchies of the empire, the dozens of nondescript books around town in the back of Greek coffee joints, drugstores, haberdasheries or what have you. The legendary but mysterious Central Book was therefore, as all agreed, the linchpin to the operation. They could only really bring Owney down by taking it out, drying up the info and therefore starving him out in a short while. Earl and D.A. especially knew this.

But Frenchy determined the next step, which is that the Central Book could only be accomplished with phone company collusion. Somewhere, somehow, someone in this building had made secret arrangements for wires to be laid into an otherwise bland building in Hot Springs, and those wires had to be routed somehow so they wouldn't pass through the switchboard that unified the town. A stranger couldn't call an operator and say, "Honey, get me Central Book!" Therefore, somewhere in this building had to be an answer.

He now industriously examined wiring diagrams. He quickly learned that a symbol, a little black diamond, indicated the presence of a phone junction, and suspected that the Central Book would have an unusual concentration of black diamonds. So his eyes searched the schematics for clusters of black diamonds. But the problem wasn't that there weren't any, but that there were too many. It seemed every page had a cluster and sometimes more than one, and often enough he recognized them from the addresses—one, for example, was the Army and Navy Hospital, which made sense, because wounded boys still lingering from the war's effects would be in constant telephone contact with family and loved ones. So what he had to do was hunt for a cluster of black diamonds that had no justification.

This sounds like boring work, and for most it would be. For Frenchy it was pure bliss. It enabled him to forget who he was, what his demons commanded him to do, his paranoia, his fears, his considerable accumulation of resentments, the perpetual nervousness his bravado only partially concealed. He worked swiftly and with great intensity and thoroughness, pausing now and then to write down the address of a diamond cluster he couldn't identify.

On and on he worked, until it was growing light in the eastern sky. He looked at his watch. It was 6:00 A.M., and soon the day shift would come along. He still had five drawers to search, and not enough time to do so.

He determined to come back the next night, and the next too, if need be. Quickly he closed the drawer he was working on, looked to see if he'd left traces of his presence, and noted nothing and stood to rise.

But then he said: what the hell.

He plucked open one of the drawers yet unexamined, and pulled at a pile of diagrams, as if in a blur or a dream. He didn't even look hard at them, but simply let them flutter through his peripheral vision. He saw that somebody had spilled some ink. They'd made a mistake. He passed onward.

But then he thought: there haven't been any other mistakes.

He rifled back, found the page, and Jesus H. Christ Mother Mary of God, there was a concentration of phone lines so intense it looked like a Rorschach ink blot. In it, he saw his future.

He noted the address, and said to himself: Of course!

CHAPTER 29

"No," said Ben, "no, that one has splatters. It didn't have splatters. No splatters."

"What did it have, darling? You have to help me, you cute little booboo," said the Countess.

"You two birds," said Virginia, "you actually think this shit is fun! My feet hurt. We been walking for ten years."

"Virginia, I told you not to wear them really high heels."

"But she looks gorgeous, darling," said the Countess. "She's more edible than any of these paintings, and I love the shade of her pretty pink toenails."

"Dorothy, you're the one they should call Bugsy. You're as screwy as they come."

The threesome stood in the modern wing of the Los Angeles County Museum before a bewildering display of the very latest in decadent art. The painting immediately before them looked like Hiroshima in a paint factory, an explosion of pigment flung demonically across a canvas until every square inch of it absorbed some of the fury of the blast.

"That guy has problems," observed Bugsy.

"He's a bastard. A Spanish prick who collaborated with the Nazis and beats all his women. But he's the most famous artist in the world. He gets a lot of pussy."

Ben leaned forward to read the name.

"Never heard of him," he said. "He ought to take drawing lessons."

"You never heard of him! You never heard of nothing didn't have a dame or a ten-spot attached," said Virginia, bored. Dammit! The spaghetti strap of her right shoe kept slipping off her foot and coming to nestle in the groove of her little toe. There, it rubbed that poor painted soldier raw. She kept having to bend over to readjust it. She did so one more time, and heard boyfriend Ben say to his best friend Dorothy the Countess from directly behind her, "Now *that's* art!"

"You dirty-minded Jew-boy," she said. "Ben,

you are so low. You come to look at pictures and you end up doing close-ups on my ass!"

"He's just a boy," said the Countess. "Virginia, what can you expect? That's why we love him so."

"Yeah, Dorothy, but you don't have to uck-fay him no more. I still do."

The Countess laughed. Her raffish friends filled her with glee. They were certainly more amusing than the dullards she'd grown up with in Dutchess County.

"Anyhow, dear: no splatters?"

"None. Not a one. I'm telling you, it looked like Newark with a tree."

"Newark?"

"I been to that town," said Virginia. "It's New York without Broadway. It's just the Bronx forever. Wops and guns. I wouldn't go back on a bet."

"Newark meaning? What was its quality of Newarkness?"

"Square, dark, dirty, crowded, brown. I don't know why I thought of Newark."

"Oh, it's so obvious. In that little rat brain of yours, darling, New York is still glamorous and adventurous. But if you subtract the neon and the glamour, you're left with nothing but masses of grimy buildings. Voilà: Newark."

"I wish I could remember the fucking name. He told me the name. It just went right out of my head. Virginia, you remember the name? Oh, no, that's right, you were rubbing your tits against Alan Ladd."

"I don't think he noticed. He'd never get me a part in a picture. His wifey wouldn't let him."

"Our attentions are wandering again, are they not?" said Dorothy. "Let us recommit them to the object at hand."

"It may not matter, anyhow," said Bugsy. "He's smack in the middle of a fucking war down there. Eleven of his boys got blown out of their boots in some nigger cathouse thing. Everybody's talking he's going down."

"That cowboy may get him," said Virginia. "Dorothy, did our hero ever tell you how he straightened this cowboy out at the train station in Hot Springs? Guy lights my cigarette, so Benny pulls his tough-guy act on him. But the cowboy ain't buying it. So Ben gives him a poke. Only it don't land, and the cowboy hits Ben so hard it almost makes him bald. Ben cry-babied for a month and a half and I notice he ain't been back to Hot Springs. He ain't going back until somebody takes care of the cowboy."

"Virginia, he hits me harder every time you tell that story," said Ben. "It's her favorite story. She's been telling it all over town. I got New York guys calling me and asking me if I settled up with the cowboy, for Christ's sakes."

"But you haven't. See, Dorothy, he really does fear the cowboy."

"He knew how to throw a punch, I'll tell you that," said Bugsy, remembering the hammerblow to his midsection. "But I'll tell you what else. When I finally get a line on his ass, he will be—hey, hey! There it is! It was like that," he said excitedly. "Virginia, wasn't that it?"

He pointed to a dense, enigmatic work, darkish and lacquered.

Dorothy didn't have to examine the label. She knew a Braque anywhere.

CHAPTER 30

Earl's daddy? they said. Earl's daddy was a great man.

It wasn't like it was now, they said. Back then the law meant something and the law meant Earl's daddy, Charles.

Things are wild now, but they wasn't when Earl's daddy was around. Earl's daddy kept the law. Nobody done busted the law when Earl's daddy was around.

Earl's daddy was a *great* man.

Even if Earl won a big medal killing Japs, he wasn't the man his daddy was. Now that man was a great man.

I don't know nobody who'd stand against Earl's daddy.

You know, Earl's daddy was a big hero in the

Great War. He killed a mess of Germans.

It was nearly unanimous. In Blue Eye, Arkansas, the one-horse town that was the seat of Polk County, the station stop for western Arkansas on the Kansas City, Texas & Gulf run to New Orleans, and a place where the weary traveler could get a cold Coca-Cola off of Route 71, Earl's daddy still cast a big and a bold shadow. You could ask about Earl in a grocery store and in a barbershop or at the police station and what you heard about wasn't Earl at all, but Earl's daddy. He was such a great man, it was said, that his own sons were overwhelmed by him. One ran away and t'other kilt hisself at fifteen. That was a sad, sad day, but Earl's daddy kept going, because he was a man who did his duty and knowed what his duty was. Hell, in the '20s, he killed three bank robbers. And many's the big-city boy or the uppity nigger who thought he could put one over on Earl's daddy and ended up with a knot on his head the size of a pie plate, for Earl's daddy brooked no nonsense, had fast hands, the lawman's will and a leather birdshot sap that seemed never far from his right hand.

Carlo went to the cemetery. There was the big monument that read CHARLES F. SWAGGER, CAPT. AEF 1918 SHERIFF 1920, 1891–1942 and "Duty Above All" in marble bas relief on a pedestal atop which stood the sculpture of a patriotic American eagle, its wings unfurled to the sky, its talons taut and gripping. The wife was nowhere to be found, nor was the younger son.

"Now that one," said a Negro caretaker who noticed the young man, "that one, he was a stern fellow. He didn't take no guff, no sir. He put the fear of God in everydamnbody."

"He was a great man, I hear," said Carlo.

The old man laughed, showing few teeth and pink gums. "Oh, he surely was," he said, "a very *damn* great man!" He toddled off, chortling.

Carl went to the newspaper office, and looked up in the bound volumes the story of the tragic day of Charles's death. Wasn't much. Evidently old Charles had been coming back from his monthly Baptist prayer weekend at Caddo Gap, driving through Mount Ida late, and he saw the door open behind Ferrell Turner's Liquors. He parked his car and got out his flashlight and went to investigate, even if he was in Montgomery County and not Polk. He was close to Polk, just a few miles, he saw what could have been a crime and he went to investigate.

One shot was fired by a burglar and down the old hero went. Probably some damned kids with a stolen gun and some hooch, looking for more hooch before they went off to war. Simple, stupid, tragic; they found him the next day and buried him two days later. It was a shame Earl's daddy had to die so pitifully. Both his boys was gone then, his wife was a drunkard and nobody from the family showed up when that great man was put to rest, but most of the rest of the county was there, great men and small, rich men and poor, man, woman and child, for in some way Earl's daddy had affected them all.

Carlo spoke to the new sheriff, a veteran named Beaumont Piney who'd been training for North Africa when Earl's daddy had gotten killed, and to the mayor and to other politicians, deputies and municipal employees and never got much beyond the recognition of Charles's greatness. But finally, on the third day, and a pointless interview with the county attorney, he heard a voice on his way out coming from down the hall.

"Goddammit, Betty, right here, I said 'Fifteenth,' but you just typed 15-h without no damn *t!* You have to type the goddamn thing over. Can't you be more careful, goddammit!"

The woman sniveled and wept and then the screamer stopped screaming and Carlo heard, "I'm sorry, it ain't nothing, I got to watch my damn temper, please, Betty, I didn't mean nothing, it don't matter."

And the secretary said, "But Mr. Vincent, my name is Ruth, not Betty. And I've worked here three whole weeks."

"Oh," said the man. "My last secretary was named Betty."

"No sir," Ruth said, "she was named Phyllis. Don't make a difference, though. Both Betty *and* Phyllis quit."

"Now don't you quit, Ruth. I don't mean no harm. I just yell too damn much. Here, now, I have an idea. Why don't you take this afternoon off?"

"Well, sir—"

"No, no, I insist. I yelled, you got upset, you got to take a nice afternoon off."

There was some shuffling, but in a second a woman came out, her hat on, her eyes reddened and swollen, and a formidably large, sheltering bear of a man led her out as if he were taking his infirm mother to see the doctor.

The couple walked by Carlo without noticing, and as they went, Carlo finally saw the name on the door of the now empty office: SAMUEL C. VINCENT, ASSISTANT PROSECUTING ATTORNEY.

He walked in and waited in the outer office and waiting room.

In a minute or so, the large man returned, his eyes black with intensity. His hair was a thatch that had never seen a comb and grew in every direction and he wore frameless specs that blew his dark eyes up like camera lenses. He was fleshy, not soft but large and strong. His suit fit like it'd been bought off the rack by someone who knew nothing about suits and it was covered with flecks of burnt ash.

"Who the hell are you, sonny?" he demanded, fixing the young man with a glare.

"Sir, my name is C. D. Henderson. I'm an investigator with the Garland County Prosecuting Attorney's Office," he said. He got out his badge and offered it to the man, whose eyes flashed that way, then back to his face, where they lit square and angrily.

"What the hell problems they got in Garland County bring 'em over here to Polk? Your Fred Becker has enough fun gittin' his picture in the paper all the damn time, what's he need over here? He going to start raiding in Polk now? B'lieve the colored folk run some illegal bingo in their church on Saturday night. That'd be a good raid. Hell, he'd get lots of ink out of that one!"

Carlo let the squall blow past, tried to look as bland as possible.

"Sir," he said, "this isn't anything about that. Mr. Becker don't even know I'm here. I'm here at the request of my supervisor, Mr. D. A. Parker."

"Parker! The old gunfighter! Yeah, he's the kind of boy you'd want if you'd be going to bang down doors and shoot places up! You don't look like no gunfighter to me, son. Do you shave yet?"

"Onct a week, sir."

"You was probably in the war, though. You was probably a general in the war?"

"No sir. Spent two months in Florida in the Air Corps, till they realized I didn't see colors too well. That's why I'm a policeman."

"Well, come on in, but let me warn you, I hope you ain't no fool, because I am not the sort who can stay civil in the presence of fools. You're not a fool, are you?"

"Hope not, sir."

"Good."

The assistant prosecuting attorney led him into

the office, which was not merely a mess but already half afog with pipe smoke. A deer head hung off the wall, but possibly it had died of asphyxiation, not a rifle bullet. In one corner well-thumbed legal volumes lay behind a glass case. The rest was documents, case folders, police reports, everywhere. Literally: everywhere.

"Let me tell you it ain't easy running a county when your prosecutor is a political hack like ours," said Mr. Vincent. "May have to run for the goddamn job myself one of these damned days. Now, sit down, tell me what you're investigating and why you came all the way out to the West." He began to fiddle with a pipe, clearly feeling the room wasn't smoky enough.

"Well, sir, I'm looking into the background of a man born and raised here in Polk County. You may know him."

"Earl. You'd be the johnny asking about Earl. Thought so." He got the pipe fired up, and belched a smokestack's worth of gassy unpleasantness into the air, which hung and seethed. The young man's eyes immediately began to water.

"Let me tell you something, sonny. If Earl's involved in that ruckus over in Hot Springs, it'd be a damned shame. Not after what Earl gone through. I'd hate to see Earl die to make Fred C. Becker the youngest governor in the nation. That would be as pure a crime as any Owney Maddox ever perpetrated. Is he on that raid team?"

"Sir, that is confidential information. No one knows who is on that raid team."

The older man fulminated a little. "No finer man was ever born in these here parts than Earl. He went off to war and won the Medal of Honor. Did you know that?"

"I knew he won a big medal."

"He did. He fought all over the Pacific. He's as foursquare as they come. If you're investigating him, you'd better have a goddamned good reason, or I'll throw you out of my office on your bony young ass myself."

"Sir, he ain't be investigated for no crime. No sir."

"What, then?"

"Well sir, as Mr. Parker explained it to me there's something called a 'death wish.' "

"A what?"

"A death wish. Some men for some reason, they *want* to die."

"Craziest goddamn thing I ever heard of."

Carlo nodded. Then he said, "But I see from them diplomas you went to Princeton University, out east. Hear that's a pretty good school. Did me some reading on what Dr. Freud said about death wishes. I'd bet you'd have run across it too, in your time educating."

Sam Vincent stared hard at the young man.

"Say, I'll bet you think you don't miss a trick, do you?"

"Miss 'em all the time, sir. But I'd bet a dollar against a cup of coffee that someone who went to Princeton and Yale Law School and wants to be elected a prosecuting attorney himself real soon-like, I'd bet he knows more about a death wish than most."

"Well, all right then. I have heard of such a thing. I will say Earl has a melancholy streak to him. Would that be a death wish? Don't know. I do know his daddy encouraged discipline and obedience with both his boys, and wouldn't brook no messy feelings or nothing. They were raised to do the job and see it through, and Earl certainly proved out. But they were both boys for holding things in and maybe that's what D. A. Parker sees as sadness unto death in Earl."

"Yes sir."

"Do you know Earl?"

"Yes sir."

"What do you think of Earl?"

"I—I think he's the bravest man ever lived," said Carlo. "I seen him do some things no man should have the grit to pull." He thought of Earl advancing through the dust with the BAR, daring the Grumleys to come out and shoot at him, letting his people get behind cover in the doorways. He thought of Earl taking that shot on a Grumley to save the Negro gal's life.

"Nobody wants nothing bad to happen to Earl," said Sam.

"Yes sir."

"Is that all?"

"Well. One of the things Mr. Parker wanted me to look into is this: Was Earl ever in Hot Springs? It seems he knows it damned well."

"Never. Never, never, never. Old Baptist Charles thought Hot Springs was hell and blasphemy. He'd have beat the hide off his boy if he'd have caught him in that sewer."

"I see."

"Earl has a gift for terrain. All the Swaggers do. They have natural feelings for land, they're fine hunters and trackers and they have an uncommon gift for shooting. They are born men of the gun. Charles Swagger was a wonderful hunter, got a buck every damned year. Tracked the county up and down, and always came home with game. A wonderful shot. The finest natural shot I ever saw, and I've hunted with some fine shots. Don't know where it comes from, but all them boys could shoot. Earl's daddy was a hero in a war too, and he shot it out with three desperadoes in a Main Street bank in the '20s, and sent them to hell in pine boxes. So if Earl seems to know things, it's just his gift, that's all."

"I see. Let me ask about one last thing. Earl's brother. He had a brother, named Bobby Lee. He hung himself, I believe, back in 1940. You probably hadn't gone off to fight in 1940. Maybe you were here for that."

Sam Vincent's eyes scrunched up and even behind the glasses, Carlo could make out something there.

"What you want to dig all that up for? Poor Bobby Lee. It ain't got nothing to do with anything. That's long over and done."

"I see."

"Hell, Earl was somewhere in the Marines then. It don't mean much."

"You knew Earl?"

"I knowed 'em both. Earl was two years ahead of me at high school and Bobby Lee was ten younger. I was the prosecutor that handled Bobby Lee's death. I was there when they cut him down. I wrote the report. You want to see it?"

"I suppose."

"Betty!" Sam called.

"Her name is Ruth and you gave her the day off."

"Goddamn her. Don't think she'll work out neither. You wait here."

The older man left and Carl sat there, suffocating, as the fog in the air wore him down. He felt a headache beginning and he heard Sam banging drawers and cursing mightily.

Finally, Sam came back.

"There, there it is."

He handed over the file, and Carlo read what was inside. It turned out to be straightforward enough: on October 5, 1940, the fire department was called by Mrs. Swagger and a truck got out to the place fast. The firemen found her crying in the barn at the feet of her son, who had hanged himself with a rope from a crossbeam. Sam arrived and directed that the body be taken down. The sheriff was located and he arrived from a far patrol and took over. Sam made the necessary interviews as brief as possible and supervised as the boy's body was taken to the morgue. The boy was buried without ceremony a day later and the sheriff never talked about it again. The county judge ruled death by suicide.

"No autopsy?" Carlo asked.

"What?" said Sam.

"Didn't y'all do an autopsy?"

"Son, it was open and shut."

"Well sir, I learned my policing in Tulsa under a chief detective inspector named O'Neill and if I'd have closed on a suicide without an autopsy, he'd have—"

"Henderson, you're like all the kids today. You think every damn thing is a crime. It's my job to represent the state in these tragic instances and believe me there wasn't nothing in that circumstance worth an autopsy. I wasn't no greenhorn neither. I'd been assistant prosecuting attorney since 1935. I'd seen a lifetime's worth of squalor and misery and pain and lost life. So I made a judgment."

"But it was irregular?"

"You are a persistent son of a bitch, ain't you?"

"I take great pride in my investigative work, sir. I believe I have a calling at it."

"Okay. You believe in law and order?"

"Of course I do. More than anything."

"Now you listen to me. Law and order. Law *and* order, you understand? That's a easy one. But let me ask you. Do you believe in law *or* order? That one ain't so easy."

Carlo drew a blank. He wished he were smarter and could play ball with this sly dog.

"Seems to me they are the same," he finally allowed.

"Maybe mostly. But maybe not. And if you've got to choose, what do you choose?"

"I don't see how there can be one 'thout the other."

"Sometimes you got to give up on law to save order. Sometimes order is more important than law. By that I mean, sometimes you learn something that might hurt order. It might hurt the way people think on things. They have to trust the man with the badge. He's got to be a paragon, a moral certainty to them. If he has weaknesses, and those weaknesses become public knowledge, well, my God, who knows where it might lead. To doubt, then chaos, then anarchy. The edifice is only as strong as its weakest buttress. So sometimes you make a call: you don't deal with something. You let it pass, you shave a corner, you do this, you do that. Because the idea of the lawman as a man of honor and virtue and courage and decency is much more important than that lawman himself. You understand?"

Carlo did, of course. He now knew what the old

bastard was getting at. He himself knew cops who were drunks or cheats or liars or cowards. But if you made a moral cause of it, and by that cause held the larger issue of the police up to ridicule, you only weakened the structure that supported the community or, even larger, the nation. So a police officer or a prosecutor had to use a certain discretion: there was a time to act, and a time to look away, and that was the heart of it.

"You've been a great help, Mr. Vincent," Carlo said, rising. "I can see the people in this county are well represented."

"Don't be in no hurry, Henderson. You ain't done learning for today. You and me, we got a place to go. You want to learn a thing or two? Then by God so you will. Get your hat and let's go."

The police station was in the same City Hall building but without direct hallway access, for arcane architectural reasons. It was actually outside, so they walked around the corner through small-town America to its entrance. At least half a dozen people said, "Howdy, Mr. Sam," and tipped a hat, and Sam tipped his in return. The trees were in full leaf, so the sun wasn't so hot and a cool wind blew across them.

"Stop and look," Sam said as they stood atop the stairs that led to the station. "What do you see?"

"A small town. Pretty little place."

"Where and how most people live, right?"

"Yes sir."

"It's all stable and clean and everything's right in the world, isn't it?"

"Yes sir."

"It's order. And that's what you and I, we work to defend, right?"

"Right."

"We defend the good folks from the bad. From the monsters, right?"

"Yes sir."

"We defend order. But what happens, Henderson, when you got yourself a situation where the good folk *is* the monster?"

Carlo said nothing.

"Then you got yourself a fine kettle of fish, that's what you got," said Sam. "And you and I, son, we got to clean it up. It's really the most important thing we do. You see what I'm driving at?"

"Yes sir."

They walked in, past the duty sergeant's desk with a wave, back into the day room and the detective squad room—more waves—then past the lockup and the little alcove where there was a vending machine for Coca-Cola and another one for candy bars, down a dim corridor, until finally they reached a room marked EVIDENCE.

Sam had the key. Inside, he found a light, and Carlo saw what was merely a storeroom, boxes and boxes on shelves, the detritus of old crimes and forgotten betrayals. A few guns, shotguns mostly, rusting away to nothingness on the dark shelves. The shelves were labeled by year and Sam knew exactly where he was going.

They went further into the room, to the year marked 1940 on the shelving. Sam pointed to a box on a high board marked SWAGGER, BOBBY LEE. Carlo had to strain to his tiptoes to get it down, though it was light, being composed of little beyond documents and manila envelopes.

Immediately Carlo saw that the documents were mere photo duplicates of the one he'd already read. But the older man grabbed an envelope, opened it, looked at it, and then handed it over.

"Take a gander," he said, "and learn a thing or two."

And Carlo beheld the horror.

CHAPTER 31

"Them two," said Vince Morella, who managed the Southern.

"Yes, I see."

"Shall I send some boys over?"

"No. Not at all. Send over a bottle of champagne. Very good stuff. The best, in fact."

It was between sets in the grillroom at the Southern, beneath the cavernous horse book and casino upstairs. This week's act: Abbott and Costello.

"You sure, Owney?"

"Very."

"Yes sir."

Vince called his bartender over and whispered instructions. Shortly thereafter, at the bar where two men stood drinking club sodas, the barkeep approached with a bucket full of ice and a green bottle.

"Fellows," he said, "this is your lucky day."

"We already ordered drinks," said the older man.

"You didn't order no *alcoholic* drinks. So the owner wants everybody happy and he sent this over, his compliments. Enjoy."

He worked some magic and with a pop the bottle was pried open, its cork caught in a white linen towel. He poured some frothy bubbly into two iced glasses.

"Bottoms up," he said.

The younger of the men, with tight, ferocious eyes, picked up the glass and poured it back into the bucket.

"I drink what I like," he said.

It was the cowboy and his older partner. Owney recognized them now clearly from the train station, where the cowboy had smashed Ben Siegel. They reeked of aggression as they sat at the bar, especially the cowboy. Strong of frame, erect, his bull neck tense, his dark, short hair bristly. Darkness visible: he had a look of darkness, dark eyes, dark features, a gunman's look.

A space had cleared away around him. Though elsewhere in the room, elegant men in dinner jackets ate dinner with their begowned wives and mistresses, here at the bar it was quiet and tense. The bartender swallowed, smiled pathetically and said, "I don't think Mr. Maddox is going to like that."

"I don't give a shit," said the cowboy, "what Mr. Maddox likes or what he don't like."

The bartender slipped away, reported to Vince, who in turn reported to Owney.

"They's asking for it," said Flem Grumley. "We should give it to 'em."

"Yes, yes, let's shoot up the most beautiful and expensive spot between St. Louis and New Orleans. And while we're at it, let's shoot up my roomful of brand-new Black Cherries, clanking away upstairs and paying the house back 34 percent and buying you and yours clothes, food, cars and your children's medicine. How clever."

He fixed Flem with a glare; Flem melted in confusion.

"They want something, else they wouldn't be here, eh, old man? Let's see what it is."

He inserted a Nat Sherman into his onyx cigarette holder, lit it off a silver Dunhill and stood.

"You boys stay here. I don't need any beef around."

"Yes sir," said Flem, speaking for the phalanx of Grumleys who surrounded Owney ever since the Mary Jane's shoot-out.

He walked over.

"Well, fellows," he said, sitting down at the bar, but facing elegantly outward, "isn't this a little brazen, even for you? I mean, my chaps could polish your apples in about seven seconds flat, eh what?"

Neither of his antagonists said a thing for a bit. But then the cowboy spoke.

"You try something fresh and tomorrow they'll bury ten more Grumleys. And you too, friend. And you won't care whether we made it out or not."

As he spoke, he pivoted slightly to face Owney, and his coat fell open, revealing a .45 in a shoulder holster. The thickness of his belt suggested it supported another .45.

Owney looked him over. He had a little Mad Dog to him, with the glaring eyes and the total absence of fear, regret, doubt or hesitation. But he also had a command to him. He was used to people doing what he said.

"Who are you? Still playing mysterious? We'll find out soon enough. You won't remain anonymous much longer. Somebody'll talk. Somebody always does.'

"You'll be finished by that time. You can read our names in the fishwrap at the penitentiary in Tucker."

"I won't serve time at Tucker. Or Sing Sing. Or anywhere. That's what lawyers are for, old man. They can get a chap out of anything. Now, really, what do you want? Are you measuring this place for a raid? Yes, do come, guns blazing, and kill a doctor or a judge or a politician. That'll do Becker no end of good."

"Listen here, Maddox," said the old man. "We come to talk straight out. You can't scare us, you can't bluff us, you can't stop us. We mean to keep coming at you. The more you squawk, the more killing there's going to be. Why don't you just cash in and get out now. You've got your millions. Move off to Mexico or Switzerland or out to Nevada or someplace."

"Well spoken, old fellow. He's got a bit of the philosopher to him, doesn't he? But you see the analysis is faulty: this isn't about money. We all know that. It's about some other thing. It's about who's the boss."

"We don't care much about that," said the cowboy. "We just mean to run you out of town or bring you down. Them's the only two possibilities."

"A third: you could die."

"It ain't likely," said Earl. "'Less you get some real bad boys."

"A fourth," said Owney. "For the old fellow, a nice retirement contribution. A nice nest egg. Well invested, he could live grandly. As for the cowboy here, he comes to work for me. I've heard the reports. You're a good gunman. They say as good as Johnny Spanish, maybe better. You come work for me."

"I bet you even think that's possible," said the cowboy. "See, here's the thing. You're a bully. You like to push people around. I don't like that, not even a little. In fact, it gets my blood all steamed."

It was amazing, and truly rare. Here was a man who seemed literally fearless. His own death had no meaning to him. Owney could read his essential nihilism in the blackness radiating from his eyes. He had Vincent the Mad Dog's contempt for life and willingness to risk his own anytime for any stake in any fight in any street or alley. Memphis Dogood was right: he didn't fear death. And that made him very dangerous indeed.

"Do you really think you can scare me?" said Owney. "I've fought on the street with guns and knives. I've shot it out with other gangs in the most brutal city on earth. When you've had a crazy black Irish boyo named Mad Dog out for your blood, and you're alive and he's dead, let me tell you, you've done something. And Mad Dog's only one."

"Yakkity-yak's cheap. We talk lead."

"You listen to me, cowboy. Oh, hello Judge LeGrand"—he waved his champagne glass in salute to the politician and issued a wondrous smile at the judge and Mayor O'Donovan, who accompanied him—"and you listen intently. The day after the next raid, a bomb will go off. In the Negro town. It'll kill twenty or thirty Negroes. Everybody will think some night riders did it, or some fellows in hoods. The investigation will be, I think one can safely predict, feckless. But you and I, friend, we'll know: you killed those Negroes. And you'll kill more and more.

So I'm afraid you'll have to be the one who leaves town. Or turn the streets red with Negro blood and think about that for the rest of your life, old man. Enjoy your champagne. Cheers."

He rose and walked away.

CHAPTER 32

"Why are you showing me these?" said the doctor, his face pained.

"Well, sir," said Carlo, "I went to the library and I looked up medical journals. I spent three days. Shoot, a lot of it I couldn't even understand. But you wrote a paper published in 1937 called 'Certain Patterns in Excessive Discipline *in Situ Domestico*.' I read it. You seemed to be talking about a similar thing."

"It's the same," said the doctor, who was head of the Department of Pediatrics at the University of Oklahoma, in Norman, in whose office Carlo now sat.

The doctor—his name was David Sanders and he was in his forties, balding, with wire-frame glasses—looked squarely at Carlo.

"That paper didn't do me a bit of good, except that it got me laughed at. A man has a right to beat his children, everybody says so. Spare the rod, spoil the child. To suggest that a child has a right not to be beaten, well, that's radical. I even got some letters accusing me of being a communist."

"Sorry to hear that."

"So I gave it up. It was infinitely depressing and nobody wanted to hear about it. So I gave it up."

Carlo said, "I see you won a Silver Star. It's up there on your wall. So you can't be a coward."

It was, next to degrees and other professional awards, books and photos of fat, smiley babies.

"That was a war. It was different."

"Still, if anybody can help me, maybe you can."

"You want a lot, Officer Henderson." Sanders sighed and looked at the photographs.

There were eight of them. The boy, naked on a morgue slab, from various angles. The rope burn was livid, and his neck was elongated, strangely wrong, clear testament to asphyxiation by hanging. But that was only part of it.

"The welts," said Carlo.

"Yes. This boy has been beaten, many times, with a heavy strap or belt. There's second-degree scar tissue all over his back, buttocks and upper thighs. He's been beaten beyond all sense or reason. Almost daily, certainly weekly, and nobody cared or intervened."

"Was he tortured? Them spots on his chest. Look like cigarette burns to me."

"Oh, I think to his oppressor, the beatings were satisfying enough. The cigarette burns were almost certainly self-inflicted. When I was looking into these matters, I saw a lot of it."

"I don't get it. Why would he do that to himself? Why would he want *more* pain?"

"The victim comes to believe that somehow it's *his* fault. He's the problem. He's no good. He's too weak, stupid, pitiful. If only *he* were gone, it would be all right. So he finds himself guilty and sentences himself to more torture. He finds small, cruel, barely bearable rituals for inflicting the punishment upon himself. He is blaming himself for the crime, not the person who is beating him. It's a fairly predictable pathology. I gather from the elongation of the neck he finally ended it?"

"Yes sir," said Carlo. "This was all back in 1940."

The doctor turned one of the photos over, where the date had been stamped: OCTOBER 4, 1940, POLK COUNTY PROSECUTING ATTORNEY'S OFFICE.

"Well, at least the pain stopped."

"Do most of them commit suicide?"

"It's not uncommon, from my preliminary survey. But the rest? Well, go to any prison and ask the right questions and you'll find out. You raise a child in great pain, he comes to believe pain is a normal condition of the universe. He feels it is his right to inflict it. From what little research I did, I saw what looked to be a frightening pattern: that our most violent criminals were beaten savagely as children. They simply were passing the lessons of their childhood on to the rest of the world."

"Who would do that to a boy?"

"Oh, it's usually the father. I see a father who secretly hates himself, who almost certainly has a drinking problem, who quite possibly works in a violent world, who was almost certainly savagely beaten himself. He considers it his right to express his rage at the world for disappointing him in the flesh of his son. But he's really expressing his rage at himself for knowing that he's not the man the world thinks he is, and he's feeling the strain of maintaining the facade. I don't know. I only know he'd be pitiful if he weren't so dangerous."

"Suppose he was a policeman?"

"Again, I'm just speculating. But he'd be a man used to force. He'd believe in force. His job was to use force."

"This one used it a lot. Not just on his sons. The people in his town consider him a damned paragon, a hero."

"Again, not surprising. Almost banal. Who knows why, really. That's the difference between public and private personalities. We consider that what goes on at home, in the privacy of that castle, to be nobody's business."

"Suppose this boy had an older brother. Would he have been beaten too?"

"I don't know. But I don't think this kind of behavior pattern just starts up suddenly, out of nothing. It's ancient, almost omnipresent. My guess is, he'd have been beaten too."

"That boy—the older brother. He left home at sixteen, went and joined the Marines, and never went home again. What would he feel?"

"Mr. Henderson, I'm not a psychologist or a psychiatrist. I have no X-ray vision. This is all speculation."

"No sir. But ain't nobody know this business like you."

"Well, I'd say, this older brother would feel grief and rage and deep survivor's guilt. You'd expect him to be emotionally crippled in some respect. You'd expect him to have an unhealthy view of the universe—he'd believe that at any moment the world was about to shatter and some huge malevolent force would break in and whip him savagely. That would be difficult to live with. He could easily become a monster."

"Could he become a hero? An insane hero who took amazing risks?"

"Well, I hadn't thought of that. But I can see how the war would be the perfect vessel for his rage; it would give him complete freedom. And when he was in battle, he wouldn't be haunted by his past. So other men would be frightened, but he'd be so preoccupied, he'd actually feel very good because his memories were effectively blocked for once. Was he in the war?"

"He won the Medal of Honor on Iwo Jima."

"Very impressive. What happened to the father?"

"He was a law officer who got himself killed. I

guess he was a little too used to whacking people in the head, and he whacked one boy who had a gun."

"Sometimes there is justice."

"I never thought I'd say it about a dead police officer, but, yes, sometimes there is justice."

CHAPTER 33

"It's there."

"How do you know?"

"I went, I saw."

"How do you know?"

"If you look at it from the outside, you'll see that there's four windows across the back. But if you go where they have the slots and the gambling stuff, you can only see three windows. There's a kind of dead space to the rear. It *has* to be there."

"You're sure?"

Frenchy, back a day early, sat alone with Earl and D.A., just returned from Hot Springs. It was early on a sunny afternoon; outside it was Texas, and nothing but. The temperature was hotter than hell, the atmosphere drier than a desert, and all the wood seemed about to crack from sheer cussedness. The wailing wind picked up a screen of yellow dust and threw it along in front of it. But the three men, sweaty but still in suits and ties, sat in the Assembly Room and talked it all out.

"Yeah, that's it. Plus, if you go out and follow the phone wires, you'll see that there's an unusual number of poles outside in the alley. Where there should be just one pole, there's two, for all the lines. I know. I checked. It's there. It's at the Ohio Club. It makes sense. It's downtown, he can walk to work, he can keep an eye on it, it's close to everything, it's so heavily used that no one would think you could hide a phone room in it. We never would have found it."

"You found it," Earl said.

"Well, *I* found it, yeah. But I'm a genius. I have a very sly mind. Everybody says so."

The boy smiled unsurely as if he wasn't quite sure that this was going as expected. D. A. Parker and Earl looked at him with hard, level eyes.

"Maybe he's right," said D.A. "We should check it out."

"It's the Ohio Club. The Central Book, I'm telling you. Not in the casino but on the same second floor, in the back. It's obvious. I found it."

He smiled in the way a man who thinks he's really winning some points smiles.

"We'll go up there tomorrow and check it out," D.A. said.

"Yeah," said Earl.

"We can close this thing down early next week," said Frenchy. "We take that place out, Owney's licked. You said so yourself. That's the key. What can he do? He has no other place set up and all the horse books die. They die in a matter of days. So what's he do, spend *his* money to keep the town operating. Or bail out? We all know he'll bail. He's *got* to."

He summed it up admirably.

"There's a problem," said Earl.

"What's that, Earl?" asked D.A. "If he's got it, he's right. And Owney won't be detonating no bombs in Niggertown because once it gets out the phone room's closed down, all his boughten judges and cops are going away from him 'cause they know he won't git enough money to pay them off."

"No, that's not the problem." He looked hard at Frenchy. "Now, you got anything to add?"

"What do you mean?"

"You sniffed this out on your own? All by your lonesome?"

"Yes sir."

Earl looked hard again at the boy.

"You lying to me? Short, are you lying? You could get us all messed up if you're lying."

"Hey," said Frenchy fearlessly, "I know that. No, I'm not lying."

"Earl, what?"

"Goddamn you, Short!" Earl bellowed.

Frenchy recoiled, stung.

"Earl, what—"

"There ain't no windows at all atop the Ohio Club. And there ain't no extra phone poles out back."

"Ah, well—"

"Earl, how do you know?"

"I know. I know, goddammit! I notice stuff like that, and by God, I know that!"

"Ahh, well, maybe, uh—" Frenchy bumbled.

"Short, I'm going to ask you one more goddamn time. Where'd you find this shit out? Where? Are you just making it up?"

"Ah. Well, actually, uh—"

For the first time in his life, Frenchy Short wasn't sure what to say. He had a gift for improvisation under stress, that he knew; it had saved him getting cooked a number of times, though alas, a few times it hadn't. But he was also utterly confused, because this great treasure was the home run that would make him a hero, he was sure, and erase completely the ambiguity of the killing of the two mobsters and the awkwardness of the accidental slaying of the two Negro women. It meant he was the star, the best boy, the success.

"Short, you better tell us," said D.A.

"It just makes sense."

"Actually, it don't make no sense at all."

"*Short!* Goddammit, you tell me!" Earl shouted.

"Okay, okay. What difference does it make?"

"It makes a difference, Short," said D.A.

"I broke in."

"You broke in? To the Ohio Club?"

"No. The phone company."

Frenchy explained his thinking, his night mission, his burglary, his discovery.

"Jesus Christ," said D.A. "Do you know what could have happened to us if you got nabbed by the cops?"

"I wasn't going to get nabbed. It's Hot Springs, Arkansas, for God's sakes, not the U.S. Mint."

"Shit," said D.A.

"What difference does it make? I got it, didn't I? Without a problem. No sweat. And it's right, dammit. It's the breakthrough we needed. Who has to know? Nobody has to know. It doesn't matter. I didn't burglarize anything. I didn't *steal* anything. I just looked through some drawers, that's all. Hell, those drawings might even be in the public domain, for all I know."

"I don't know what difference it makes, but we got to tell Mr. Becker. He will have to know."

"But it's good information. It *is* good, isn't it, Mr. Earl? I mean, it's good combat intelligence."

"It is, Short."

"What will happen to me?"

"I don't know."

"Can't you just say you got an anonymous tip?"

"No. Not anymore. Becker wants more control from now on. I can't order up the raids myself. He has to check off. I have to run this by him. We have to see what he says, all right?"

"Look," argued Frenchy, "now that we *know* what it is, it's just a matter of time until we can find something to support it. Once we find that out, we go to Becker and say that that's the primary evidence.

Then we have our cause, we take the joint out, and we're all heroes and we go home happy. It's easy."

"You are a clever little bastard," said Earl.

"I ain't getting into no big lying situation. I will have to run this by Becker. It's his call. If it were my call, who knows, but it's his call, he's the one who has to answer for it, he's the one signing the checks. It may be different now after all that shooting last time out. We just got back from a trip to Hot Springs, looking exactly for this information. But goddammit, Earl, you and I'll git back up there tonight and talk to him. Short, you stay here. Don't you tell nobody. You hear? *Nobody!* Got that?"

"Yes sir," said Frenchy. "But I'm telling you, this can be the big one."

Frenchy spent the day in Texarkana. A movie called *O.S.S.* with Alan Ladd had just come out, and he sat through it twice, though he knew it was phony. It couldn't have been like that in the war. The girl was some new actress he'd never seen, and who wasn't that beautiful, and everyone smoked. But they didn't have the class the OSS people had, Frenchy was sure; his uncle had class, a savoir faire, a mysterious intimation that life was more fun if you cultivated an ironic disposition and could hold your liquor.

When he got back, it was around 6:00. Three of the men had returned already, Bear, Eff and Billy Bob, called Bob Billy for silly reasons, and the four had a kind of hearty how-ya-doin' escapade there, exchanging stories. The three had gone to New Orleans and had a really fine time. When the conversation got around to Frenchy, he got very vague. He just said he'd had a damned good time too.

Then a car pulled in, and it was Earl and Mr. D.A. They welcomed the men back, chatted pointlessly for a while, and finally left. Earl nodded at Frenchy and he joined the two in the office.

They sat. It was darkening, and the old man turned on a lamp that filled the dreary little room with yellow light. Outside a bit of Texas wind moaned.

Finally the old man looked up.

"Here, I got this for you," he said. It was a letter, on the official stationery of the Garland County Prosecuting Attorney's Office. "Mr. Earl had to work like hell to get this. He swore Fred Becker up one side and down the other, and said he'd walk if Sid didn't cough up a letter."

"A letter?" said Frenchy.

"A letter of recommendation. You deserve it," said the old man.

Frenchy looked over at Earl, who just sat there, darkness shading his eyes.

To Whom It May Concern:

Walter F. Short was in the employ of this office as an investigator and warrant-serving officer between July 28 and September 12, 1946. During this time, he performed his duties with exemplary courage and professional commitment. He exhibited a great deal of enterprise in the accomplishment of all tasks given him. He has a great future in law enforcement.

Fred C. Becker
Prosecuting Attorney
Garland County, Arkansas

"It ain't bad," said D.A., "considering at one point this afternoon he wanted to indict you and send you to jail for breaking and entering."

"I don't understand it."

"You been fired, son," said Earl at last.

"I've been fired?"

"Mr. Becker says he's got to allay community fears about us being out-of-control gunmen. He has to tell people that he's taken command of the team, and that the 'bad apples' have been let go. You got the nod as the bad apple. As I say, he wanted to make a public example of you. Earl here got him to see what a bad idea that was."

Frenchy just stared off into space.

"I found the Central Book," he finally said. "Doesn't that count for anything?"

"It counts for not going to prison and walking out of here with a nice letter that'll git you a job anywhere you want. Meanwhile Earl and I have to find some way to justify the raid. We got to do it all legal-like. That's Mr. Becker's order."

"It's not fair," said Frenchy.

"No, it's not."

"It's just politics," said Frenchy.

"Yes, it is."

"You can't let him do this."

"I can't stop him from doing this," said the old man. "I can't stop him from doing anything. He says the governor is leaning on him from above and he's got people in the community leaning on him from below."

Frenchy turned to Earl. "You supported this?"

Earl looked him in the eye.

"Sometimes you get a bad officer above you. It ain't supposed to happen, but it's in the cards. So you got to go along until you get an opportunity to make things right. You got to hold the unit together, you got to put up with the shit, you got to keep running the patrols. You got to take some losses. You're the loss, Short."

"Jesus," said Frenchy. "All these guys, from Podunk City and Hick Town U.S.A., and Toad Pond, Oklahoma, and *I'm* the one that gets canned. Jesus Christ, I *fought* for you guys. I *killed* for you guys. It's just not right. Can I at least *see* Becker?"

"Bad decision," said Earl. "He don't like face-to-face things. Figures, I'd say. Anyhow, he don't like that kind of pressure and he could still indict you for B and E, or maybe even if he wanted to for shooting them two boys out back of that casino. Do yourself a favor. Learn from this, get the hell out of town, and go on with the rest of your life. You're young and smart. You won't have no trouble."

"But I—"

"Yeah, I know. But the key thing here is, don't let it get to you. Take it from me, son. Just start over fresh, and don't let this thing haunt you. Me and Mr. D.A., we're sorry. But it's an outfit thing, a politics thing. Learn from this: it's the way the world works."

CHAPTER 34

Pap Grumley's death, of the commingled impact of grief and clap, pretty much finished the Grumleys as a possibility, as far as Owney was concerned. He would keep the Grumleys around to service his empire, to receive and make his payoffs, to lubricate the machine, to bust the odd debtor and the like, but he knew that without Pap's stalwart leadership and heart, the Grumleys were done as a fighting force. Flem would stay as his factotum, but Flem would never be the man Pap was. Flem wasn't a wartime leader, not by a long shot.

So Owney finally made the decision that he'd been toying with all these weeks. He went to his gas station near Lake Catherine and placed his long-distance call to Sid in New York. He spoke to Sid, told him what was required. Sid did the legwork, made the connections, set up the proper channels and finally Owney reached the party he needed to reach. This was a Mr. A, who himself was speaking from a pay phone to avoid the possibility of federal wiretaps.

"Thank you so much for talking with me, Mr. A. I hate to bother you."

"It's nothing. Talk to me, Owney. Tell me what I can do to help you," said Mr. A.

"I got a problem. I got cops like you never saw. These fuckers, they come inta one a my joints with machine guns and shot the shit out of the place. They killed eleven boys of mine. Chicago, the fat Sicilian, that Valentine's Day thing, it wasn't nothing like this. Down here, it's the South, there are no laws."

"Owney, the boys are talking. You know how it is when the boys talk."

"And that shmata Ben Siegel is talking too. Right? I know he is. It's how a yentzer like that operates."

"Owney, no need to run down the other fellow. Ben is out in L.A., doing his job. You leave Ben out of this."

"Yes, Mr. A," said Owney, slightly stung.

"Owney, you have to take care of this. You ran a tidy little place down there and everybody was happy. People went down there for vacation and they were happy. They played the horses, the wheel, the slots, they met some girls, they laughed at Abbott and Costello, they heard Dinah Shore, it was very nice. Now you got bullets flying and people dying everywhere. You can't do business in a climate like that, you can't have no fun. Things don't grow like we all think they should."

"I agree with you totally, Mr. A. Growth. Stability is the fertilizer of growth, which is the destiny of prosperity. What I have here is a franchise on the future. This is what will be, you'll see. Except for these crazy cops."

"Very good, Owney. You still understand, I see. Now, you want we should send some fellas? I could dispatch some very good Jersey people."

"Nah. Not hitters. Hitters ain't got no stomach for this. Hitters take guys out to the marshes and clip 'em with a .32 in the back of the head. It ain't like that down here. It's a fuckin' war. Plus, hitters'd stand out like fuckin' sore thumbs."

"So what do you need?"

"I need soldiers. I mean real hard-ass fucking soldiers, been in some scrapes, shot it out with the fucking cops, ain't afraid of nothing. Like the scary shit, when the lead flies. There are some boys like that."

"Sounds like you want Marines."

"Nah. What I want is armed robbers. I want the best armed robbery crew. They'd be the boys who could run a thing for me. They could plan and wait and spring a trap and shoot the shit out of it. They'd have the discipline, the long-term, wait-through-the-night guts. Okay. You know who I want, Mr. A. I want Johnny Spanish and his crew. They worked for me before. They worked for me in '40."

"Johnny's retired, Owney."

"Johnny owes me. He hit a big fucking score in '40. Biggest caper of his career. I set that job up for him."

"Whyn't you just call him? I could find the number."

"Mr. A, coming from you, it would be better. He's black Irish. You know, I come from England. The Irish, they got a thing about the English."

"Just 'cause you tried to starve them to death."

"Hey, I didn't starve *nobody.* All the time I have these problems with the Irish. That goddamned Vincent the Mad Dog, another black Irish, want to bust my balls. God, was I glad when he got his ass blown to shit."

"All right, Owney. I can make a call. I can ask a favor. But you know, Johnny and his people don't work cheap. Johnny goes first-class. He deserves first-class."

This, of course, was Owney's problem with Johnny. Johnny and his crew—that would be Jack "Ding-Dong" Bell, Red Brown, Vince "the Hat" de Palmo and Herman Kreutzer—took 60 percent of the take, leaving 40 for the local setup guy. This was unprecedented: in all other similar transactions, the armed contract robbers only got 50 percent. But they were the best, if a little aged by now. So if Johnny came down here for a bit of business and there was no up-front promise of a take, Johnny would need a cash down payment and a big backside splash.

"It has to be Johnny," said Owney.

"It's done. He'll be there before the week is over."

"You got to hurry, Mr. A. These guys are one strike from taking over down here."

"Owney, Owney, Owney. Johnny will take care of it all. You can trust Johnny. We'll look out for you, Owney. You can trust your friends."

CHAPTER 35

Junior Turner, the sheriff of Montgomery County, looked at Carlo Henderson with a grimace of the purest dripping scorn. Junior was a big man in his thirties, with a face that looked like old possum hides hung on a nail in a barn somewhere. His fat belly exploded beyond the perimeters of his belt and there were stains of a disagreeable nature on his khaki shirt. He wore a big Smith & Wesson Heavy Duty .38/.44 in a fancy belt, the only fancy thing about him. Then he turned and launched a majestic gob of Brown Mule from his lips. It took off with a disgusting slurping sound, seemed to elongate as it followed the parabola of its arc, a yellowish tracer bullet glistening with mucus, tobacco curds and spit, until it struck dead center into the spittoon with a coppery clang, rocking the vessel on its axis.

"This here's a small town, my friend. We don't much cotton to outsiders stirring up our business."

Mount Ida, a smear on the roadside consisting of a bar, a general store, a Texaco station and a sheriff's office, stood in the trackless Ouachitas, encapsulated almost totally in a wall of green pine forest, about halfway between Blue Eye and the more cosmopolitan pleasures of Hot Springs. It united the two by a sliver of road called 270, mostly dirt, occasionally macadam, all of it lost and lonely through the high dense trees.

"Sir, I am on official business," said Carlo.

"You say. The official bidness of Garland is bidness. So why'n hell's a little old boy like you rutting around in a crime done happened in our county four years back? It was open and shut. If you read the papers, you know ever goddamned thing."

"I am just following up a loose end."

"Now what loose end would that be, son?" asked Junior, casting a yellow-eyed glance around to his two deputies, who guffawed at the sheriff's rude humor.

"I am not at liberty to say, sir," said Carlo, feeling the hostility in the room.

"Well, son, I ain't at liberty to just open my files to any joe what comes passing this way," the sheriff said. "So mebbe you'd best think 'bout moving on down the road."

"Sir, I—"

But he saw that it was useless. Whatever grudge this man had against Garland County and its representatives, it was formidable and unbridgeable. He knew he was out of luck here. He rose and—

"So you tell the Grumleys if they want to check out Montgomery, they can just go on straight to hell," the sheriff said.

"I'm sorry?"

"You tell the Grumley clan Junior Turner of Montgomery says they should go suck the devil's own black goat's milk. I said—"

"You think I'm working for the Grumleys? You think I'm a Grumley?"

"He got that Grumley look," said the one of the deputies, evidently called L.T. "Sort of narrow-eyed, towheaded with a yellow thatch all cut down. Them eyes blue, long of jaw, a rangy, stretchy boy."

"I think I smell a damned Grumley stink on him," said the other deputy. "Though I 'low, Grumleys most usually travel in packs."

"It ain't common to see a Grumley on his lonesome," said Sheriff Turner.

"I killed a Grumley," Carlo said.

"You what?"

"A couple, actually. It was hard to tell. Lots of dust flying around, lots of smoke. Mary Jane's, it was. I see they're now calling it the greatest gunfight in Arkansas history. I fired a lot, I know I hit at least two, and they went down."

"You kilt a Grumley?"

"I know you heard about that raid. That was us. That was me. That's what this is all about. The Grumleys. Putting them out of business for good. Driving 'em back into the hills where they can have sex with their cousins and sisters and be no bother to good folk anymore."

"L.T., you hear that? He kilt a Grumley," said the sheriff.

"He must be one of them boys working for that new young Becker feller," said the deputy.

"I figgered he worked for Owney and Mayor O'Donovan and that Judge LeGrand and the gambling boys, like all the Grumleys these days. That ain't so?"

"I almost got my butt shot off fighting gamblers with machine guns," said Carlo. "Grumleys all. A Peck and a Dodge too, I believe."

"Grumley cousins," said L.T. "Just as hell-black low-down mean too. Maybe meaner."

"Damnation! Damnation in the high grass! Damnation in July! He's okay! He's goddamned okay," said the sheriff, launching another naval shell of yellowish gunk toward the spittoon, where it banged dead bull's-eye, a rattle that reached the rafters.

"Sheriff's brother was a state liquor agent," said L.T. "That'd be my Uncle Rollo. In '37, some ole boys set his car aflame. He was in it at the time. Burned up like a fritter that fell into the stove hole."

"No man should die the way my brother did," said the sheriff. "Since then, it's been a war 'tween the Turner and the Grumley clan. Which is why ain't no Grumley in Montgomery County."

"I think he's okay, Junior."

"By God, I say, he *is* okay. He's *more'n* okay. He's goddamned fine, is what he be. Son, what's it you want?"

Did Carlo want recollections? The boys provided them. The files, the photos, the physical evidence. It was his for the asking. Did he want to examine the crime scene? Off they went.

In a few hours of cooperation, Carlo learned what was to be learned, which, as Junior said up front, wasn't much. In the crime scene photos, Charles Swagger lay face forward in his automobile, his head cupped against the wheel, his one arm dangling, fingers languid, pointed downward. A black puddle of blood lay on the floor of the Model T, coagulated at his feet. His old six-gun, a Colt's Army from 1904, was in the dust, one of its rounds discharged. Marks in the dust indicated no kind of scuffle. The back door to the warehouse behind Ferrell Turner's liquor store had been pried open, though nothing taken. There really wasn't much to go on, but the final conclusion reached by the Mount Ida detective, one James Fields, seemed to sum it up as well as anything.

"It appears the decedent saw or heard something as he drove through town late. He pulled around back, put his spotlight on the door, and saw some movement. He got out, drew his gun, called, then started forward. He was shot, returned fire once (probably into the air or ground, as no bullet hole was found), then returned to his car as if to drive to the hospital or a doctor's, but passed out. The recovered bullet was a .32 caliber, lodged in his heart. A manhunt and exhaustive search for clues unearthed nothing; the case remains open, though until this officer returns from wartime service it will go on the inactive list."

It was dated January 20, 1943, the day before Jimmy Fields went off to the war he never returned from.

"Ferrell found him the next morning, early," recalled L.T. "Just lying there, like in the photo."

"Nobody heard the shots?"

"No sir. But that don't mean nothing. Sound is tricky this deep in the woods. Ferrell slept about three hundred feet away in his general store but he was a drinking man. He could have slept through anything. Jimmy done a good job. He worked that case hard. If there'd a been anything to find, he'd have found it."

They went to the crime scene, only a couple of hundred feet from the office. There, Carlo stood in the dust behind the liquor store and saw that the warehouse was really more of a shed, secured with a single padlock, which itself could easily be pried loose.

"What's he keep in there?"

"The beer, mostly. It's cool and once a day a truck delivers the ice. It's the only place 'round here that sells cold beer."

"I suppose I could talk to Ferrell."

"Sure, but Ferrell didn't see nothing. But I know you want to be thorough. So, yeah, let's go talk to Ferrell."

That talk was short; Ferrell did know nothing. He'd gone out back early in the morning to open up for the ice delivery and the milk truck and been surprised to find Charles Swagger's old Ford there, old Charles Swagger dead in it. He'd heard no shots.

Carlo asked modern, scientific questions that couldn't be answered by any living man, about bloodstains and trails and fingerprints and footprints and whether there was dust of the kind that was from the ground here found on Charles's boots. Ferrell had no idee; he just called the polices and the boys all come over and Jimmy Fields done took over. The only answers to those questions died with Jimmy in the hedgerow country.

He asked as he had asked everybody: Did you all know Charles?

Charles was a great man, they said. We seen him every damn month on his way to prayer meeting at Caddo Gap.

As the afternoon wore on, poor Carlo began to see his time was wasted and whatever he learned really was of no importance in regard to his original mission, which had nothing whatsoever to do with Charles Swagger, his angers, his violence, his fury, his death, but with Earl Swagger, his melancholy, his courage, his baffling behavior, his possible lie about being in Hot Springs before. It almost made him dizzy. He felt he'd wandered into a madhouse and didn't belong, was learning things best forgotten, that meant nothing except obscure pain in years back, not worth recalling.

At nightfall, he went to say his farewells to Sheriff Junior Turner and thank him for his cooperation. After all, in the end, Junior had done all right by him, once the original misunderstanding was cleared up. But Junior had other ideas. Did he want to come up to the house and eat dinner with all the Turners? Er, no, not really, but Carlo now saw no polite way out of it, and Junior and his boys seemed really to want his company, a rare enough occurrence in his life. So in the end, he meekly said yes, and was hustled off.

And what a dinner. Whatever the Turners did, they ate well. Squirrel stew in a black pool of bubbly gravy, like a tar pit, collard greens, turnips, scrapple, great slabs of bacon all moist with fat, taters by the long ton, in every configuration known to man, chicken-fried steak, big and gnarly and soaked in yet a different variation on the theme of gravy, corn on the cob or shelled and mushed, a mountain of grits slathered in a snowcap of butter, hot apple dumpling, more coffee, hot, black and strong, the attention of flirty little Turner girls, somebody's female brood of cousins or nieces or something (never too clear on exactly who these girls were) and, after dark, corn likker and good storytelling.

It was night. Mosquitoes buzzed around but the Turner boys, all loquacious, were sitting about on the porch, smoking pipes or vile cigars imported from far-off, glamorous Saint Louie, in various postures of lassitude and inebriation. In the piney Ouachitas, crickets yammered and small furry things screeched when they died. Up above, the stars pinwheeled this way and that.

The subject was set by the day's events and it turned out to be the man who was both god and devil to them, who but Charles Swagger, former sheriff of Polk County, a man who walked high and mighty and treated such as them as the scum of the earth.

"He was a proud man," an unidentified Turner said, from the gray darkness of the porch, in a melancholy of recollection, "that you could read on him. But you know what the Book sayeth."

The dark chorus supported this point.

"Yes sir."

"You do, you do."

"That'd be the truth, that would."

"That's what she says. You listen, young feller. Luke's a preacher, he know the Book."

"The Book sayeth, pride goeth before the fall."

"And you know what?" said Junior Turner. "After the fall, it hangeth around too!"

Everybody laughed, including slightly overwhelmed and slightly overstuffed Carlo.

"You saw him often?" he asked, amazed that Charles was so big to them, for after all, this wasn't his county, and his office was forty miles of bad road to the west.

"Ever damn weekend in four," said a Turner. "He'd go on over to that Baptist prayer camp. He been a good Baptist. He been Baptist to the gills. He'd come on through in that old Model T of his, with the big star on it, and he'd stop at Ferrell's store, and have hisself a cold Coca-Cola. You'd see him watching and keeping track."

"He was great at keeping track."

"He stand there in that black suit and he's all glowery-like, you know. Big feller. Big hands, big face, big old arms. Strong as a goddamned blacksmith. Wore the badge of the law. Brooked no nonsense from no man. You'd as soon poke a stick at a bear as you'd rile up Charles Swagger."

"He must have been a worshipful man."

"Well sir," said a Turner, "you could say that. He'd be headed on toward Caddo Gap. He'd be going to worship a cribful. That Baptist prayer retreat camp, that'd be at that Caddo Gap."

"Yes, that would, and the old man, that's where he'd head, to do his own kind of worshipfulness."

And they busted out laughing.

The Turners howled into the night! It was like the drunken deities of a fallen Olympus snarfing out a bushel basket of giggles and guffaws at the latest vanity of their pitiful progeny, that tribe of hairy-assed scufflers and hustlers known as mankind.

"Oh, he was a prayerful man," somebody said.

"He worshipped all right."

"Pass that jug, Cleveland."

"She's a coming, Baxter."

"I still don't—" started Carlo.

Junior Turner delivered the news: "He did worship. He worshipped at the altar of titty and cooze! He drank the sacred elixir of hooch. He tested God's will and mercy by betting it all on the throw of them little old cubes with the dots! What a great man he was."

"That old boy, he was a inspiration to us all."

Carlo was suddenly confused.

"I don't—"

"He didn't go to no prayer meeting at Caddo Gap. No siree, not a goddamn bit of it. He'd come through here and make a big play of how holy he was, and tell ever damn body about the prayer retreat, then he'd roll on out of town, up Route 27 toward Caddo Gap. But goddamn, then he'd cut through the woods on some old logging road and git back on 27 out near to Hurricane Grove and head on his way to where he's really going. Hot Springs, the Devil's Playpen. One day a month, Charles gathered up a hundred or so dollars from the niggers and white trash he'd beat over the head, told his old wife he's going to talk to Jesus, came through here, then cut over to Hot Springs, where he whored and drank and gambled, same as any man. So high and mighty!"

"Jesus," said Carlo.

"He was a man of sin. Vast sin. He had the clap, he had ten girlfriends in ten different cribs. He never went to the quality places, where he'd might like to chance recognition. Nah, he went to low places, in the Niggertown or up Central beyond the Arlington. He's a reg'lar, all right."

"How do you know?"

"Ask Baxter. Baxter knows."

"I ain't a sinner no more," said Baxter, in the darkness. "The Lord done showed me a path. But in them earlier years, I done some helling. I knowed him 'cause I pumped gas for him so much as a youngster when he stopped for his Coca-Cola. I seen him onct, twicet and then ever damn place, ever damn time. He didn't have no badge on then. He wore a gal on each arm, and the smile of a happy goddamned man. Sometimes the cards smiled, sometimes they didn't, but he kept coming back. He had the best life, I reckon. He was a God-fearing man of civil authority twenty-nine days a month and on the thirtieth day he's a goddamned hellion who got his old pecker in ever kind of hole there was to be had in Hot Springs. Great man! Great man, my black asshole!"

"This is the truth?"

"This is God's honest truth," said Junior Turner.

"We all knew it. Not nobody back in his hometown did, but we sure did. So when he got hisself kilt, we figgered it was gambling debts or woman trouble. Whoever done it did a good job of covering it up. But goddamn, he paid the devil his due, that I'll say."

"You didn't investigate?"

"Well, son, I was in combat engineer school at Fort Belvoir, in Virginia that day. My deputies was in—where was you, L.T.?"

"Getting ready for the Aleutians."

"Hell, everybody was some damn place or other. Only Jimmy really was here and by God he'd tried like hell to get in, till finally the standards dropped in '43 and they took him. Jimmy didn't see no percentage in turning the light on Charles Swagger's hunger for flesh and gitting himself involved in what goes on in Hot Springs. Hot Springs, that's a evil town. If Charles went to Hot Springs for pleasure, he knew there'd be a price to pay, and by God, he ended up paying it."

"I see."

"If you want to know who killed him, I'll tell you how to do it."

"Okay," said Carlo.

Junior leaned forward.

"You look for a silver-plated Smith & Wesson .32 bicycle gun. Little thang, .32 rimfire, couldn't weigh more'n ten, twelve ounces. Charles called it his Jesus gun, and he kept it secured up his left sleeve by a sleeve garter. He carried the Colt, a Winchester '95 carbine in .30 government in the car, just like the Texas Rangers love so deeply, but that little gun was his ace in the hole. That was the gun he kilt Travis Warren's little brother Billy with in 19 and 23, during the Blue Eye bank robbery. He shot Travis dead with the Colt, and his cousin Chandler too, but old Billy hit him with a 12-gauge from behind, and knocked him down and bloody with buck. Billy walked up, kicked the Colt across the floor and leaned over to put the shotgun under Charles's chin for a killing shot, and Charles pulled that li'l silver thang and shot that boy slick as a whistle 'tween the eyes. Anyhows, whoever kilt that old man in 1942, he stole that gun. Everyone who knew a thing about Charles knew it was missing. The Colt was there on the ground, you seen it. But the Jesus gun was missing."

Carlo knew it was a bad idea, but he couldn't help from asking.

"Why do they call it a Jesus gun?"

"'Cause when he pulls it on you, you are going to meet Jesus. Billy sure did, at the age of only sixteen."

"Wonder if Billy likes heaven?"

"Bet he do. Plenty of cooze in heaven! All them angel gals in them little gowns. They don't wear no underpants at all."

"Now don't you go talking that way 'bout heaven," warned Baxter. "It could have consequences. There are always consequences. That's the lesson in tonight's sermon."

Eventually, most of the Turners gave up the ghost and retreated to farmhouses or cabins. It suddenly occurred to Carlo that he had no place to stay, he was too drunk to drive and could see no way clear to a happy solution to his problem. But once again Junior Turner came through, and dragged him upstairs to an unused bedroom, where he was told to get his load off and stay the night, Mama Turner would have grits and bacon and hot black coffee in the kitchen beginning at 6:00 and running through 9:00.

Carlo stripped, blew out the candle, pulled a gigantic comforter over his scrawny bones, and his head hit the pillow. He had a brief fantasy about the farmer's daughters, since there'd been so many pretty Turner girls fluttering this way and that, but no knock came to his door, and as a graduate of a Baptist college he wouldn't have known what to do if one did. And then the room whirled about his head one more dizzying time and he was out.

His dreams tossed in his mind, though. Strange stuff, the product of too much white lightning and too much gravy mingled into a combustible fluid. He could make head or tails of none of it, though it disturbed him plenty and once or twice pulled him from sleep. He'd awaken, wonder where the hell he was, then remember, lie back and sail off again to a turbulent snoozeland.

But the third time he awoke, he knew it was for good. He was sweaty and shaking. Was he sick? Was he going to get the heaves or the runs? But his body was fine; it was his heart that was rocketing along at a hundred miles per hour.

He felt a presence in the room. Not a Turner cousin, comely and sweet, but something far worse: a haunt, a ghost, a horror. He reached out as if to touch something, but his fingers clawed at nothingness. The thing was in his head, whatever it could be. What was it rattling about in his subconscious, trying to find a way to poke a hole into his conscious, trying to get itself felt, noticed, paid attention to? Whatever, it was unsettling. He rose, went to the window, saw the Turner yard, bone-gray in the radiant gibbous moonlight, a swing hanging from a tree, a bench close by, where loving daddies could watch their baby sons play, and guard them and look after them, as his had done for him, as most had done for theirs. It was a scene of such domestic bliss and becalmed gentility it soothed him, but the luminous grayness of it suggested a photo negative, something somehow in reverse, and he saw another daddy, Charles the Tyrant, with his immense reservoir of hidden violence, his hatred, his disappointment, his vanity, his egoism, his self-doubt, and he saw him beating a boy child in that ghostly light.

"You ain't no damned good!" he heard the old man scream. "What is wrong with you, boy! You fail at everything! You are such a goddamned disappointment!" *Whack!* the strap across the legs, *whack!* the strap across the back, *whack!* the strap across the buttocks, the thumbs grinding bone bruises into the boy's arms as the larger man pinioned him in endless, suffocating rage.

What happens to such boys? What becomes of them? They become so full of hatred themselves they lash out at the world. They become monsters hell-bent on punishing a world that did nothing to protect them. Or they become so full of pain they don't care if they live or die and off they rush into the machine guns. Or they hang themselves at fifteen, for there is no hope on earth left.

Then at last he saw it.

He tried to push it away but it made such perfect sense now, it unified all the elements, it explained everything now.

How did Earl know so much about Hot Springs?

Because he'd been there.

Why couldn't he tell anyone?

Because he'd been there secretly, tracking someone, setting a trap for someone.

That man was his father.

Earl couldn't be frightened by his father, for by '42 he was a strong Marine sergeant with a couple of boxing titles to his name, and combat in Nicaragua and all over China, not the scrawny, frightened sixteen-year-old who'd fled home in 1930 to escape the father's rages.

But Earl had some last business with his father. He saw how Earl's mind would work. Earl was going to the Pacific and he would probably die. His division had orders to Guadalcanal by that time. He had no expectation of surviving the great crusade in the Pacific, for after Guadalcanal there were another hundred islands, with twisted names, letters in combinations never seen before, an archipelago of violence beckoning, promising nothing but extinction. But he had a powerful debt to pay back to the man who'd beaten him, and worse, the man who'd beaten his younger brother, without Earl there to stop it.

And Earl would know about the Jesus gun, and his father's trick of wearing it in his sleeve, secured by a garter.

In his mind's eye, Carlo saw what he hoped had not happened but whose logic was absolute and powerful: Earl, AWOL from the Corps, tracking his own daddy through the bawdy houses and flesh parlors of Hot Springs in January of 1942, and then at last facing him, facing the monster.

Had Earl been the man who killed his daddy?

It terrified Carlo, more than anything in his life ever had, but he knew he had to find the truth.

CHAPTER 36

It was always about money with Johnny. Johnny expected to be paid very well, very well indeed, and he also insisted on charging Owney a tax for being English. He called it his Potato Famine bonus: $20,000, over and above the agreed-to sum, just because . . . just because all them laddies and lasses had starved in the bogs of County Mayo a hundred years ago.

"Old man," protested Owney, "my people were selling fish and sweeping streets in the slums of the West End at the time. Doubt if they had a ha'penny between them. It was the lord highs what ruined the potato crop and set your people to dying in the river glens."

"Ah," said Johnny, all a-twinkle with blarney, "if you English shopkeeps had the nerve to overthrow them wig-wearing nancy boys and gone and made a proper revolution, mine'd not had to flee to the slums of New York and peck out a new life. We'd all be living in the castle now."

We are living in the castle now, boyo, Owney thought, but didn't express it. You couldn't argue with Johnny, and so the deal was done and Ralph brought Johnny another mint julep. He and Owney sat on Owney's terrace above the rumble of Central late in the afternoon. The cars churned down the broad avenue, the pigeons cooed lovingly.

"I see the mountain's still a fair eyeful," said Johnny, looking out beyond the Arlington to North Mountain, which rose in pine-crusted glory across the way, all twenty-one of its springs still blasting out the steamy mineral water, as they had since time immemorial.

"The town has changed in six war years, eh, Johnny?" said Owney.

"In 1940, she was still a Depression town. Now she's modern. Now she's a beaut. She still lights up the night sky, I'll be betting."

"That she does."

"Now, tell me about these boyos who are plaguing you. They sound like the Black and Tans you Brits sent up to raid on us in the '20s."

"You would know, Johnny," said Owney.

"I would indeed. I was in County Mayo and the pubs of west Dublin running with me brothers with the Lewis guns and the Thompsons, hunting and being hunted in them alleyways. I do hate the Black and Tans. Sure but they made the people suffer. They burned, they pillaged, they tortured. Night riders, anonymous, hard to get at, highly secretive, well armed. Sounds about the same, does it not?"

"Well, almost," said Owney. "These boys don't torture. They don't burn. They sure pillage, though. They've cost me close to a hundred grand in lost revenues in two months."

Actually, it was closer to three hundred grand, but Owney knew if he gave the correct number, Johnny would make a lightning calculation and up the agreed-on cost appreciably. That was Johnny; he held all the cards and he loved it.

Johnny's raven hair was brilliantined back and his olive complexion radiated ruddy good health. He was fit, vigorous, handsome as the bloody devil himself, at forty-seven years old. He wore a double-breasted bespoke suit in gray flannel, and bespoke shoes as well. When he smiled, the sky lit up in the pure glowing radiance of it. Everybody loved Johnny. It was hard not to love Johnny. He'd fought in the Great War, the Troubles in Ireland, where he'd learned his dark skills, and since 1925 had worked his violent magic on these shores. Men wanted to drink with him, women to sleep with him. What an odd glitch it was that a man so gifted by God had this one little thing: he liked money that others had earned, in large piles, and if someone or something got in his way, he had not the slightest qualm about touching the trigger of his Thompson and eliminating them with a squirt of death. It never occurred to him to feel remorse. His mind wasn't built that way. He had killed thirty-nine men, most of them officers of the law or bank or plant security, or German soldiers or British troopies, but occasionally the bullets flew beyond targets and struck the innocent. It didn't matter to him, not one little bit.

"So tell me, Owney, tell me about these dark lads, and we'll get to getting you your money's worth."

Owney explained details of the shoot-out at Mary Jane's, confessing puzzlement at the victory of the men with the lesser guns over the men with the greater guns.

"See, your problem was your ambush site," said Johnny. "The Maxim's a fine gun, as all hearties found out in the Great War, but she's got to have a wide field of fire and has to be laid just right. Shooting down some stairs don't do a fella no good at all; it minimizes what you've got going for you. I can see you've never planned an ambush against trained men, eh, Owney? Nor had that border reiver scum from the mountains."

"I guess not."

"Your hero fellow kept his cool and understood that the ballistics of his weapon allowed him to shoot through wood. He waited till the belt clinked dry, then he enfiladed the stairwell. From that point you were doomed. As Herman will tell you when he gets here, properly deployed, pound for pound there's not a better gun about than a Browning Automatic Rifle."

"So what are we going to do? I'm running out of time. I've threatened to bomb Niggertown to keep them from raiding, but only the cowboy cares about the niggers. Sooner or later, that threat will lose its meaning and even he will have to go ahead. And if they get the Central Book, the money dries up fast, and I am in a world of trouble."

"That would be the checkmate move, then?"

"Yeah, and we could do everything right and on the last day, they could hit that joint and we'd be fucked. So we have to act fast."

Johnny's face fell into a density of concentration. He thought out loud.

"The chances of bumbling into them in another raid are remote. The chances of jumping them in their home ground are also remote. Plus, difficult to handle. No, we've got to find a prize so sweet they'll not be able to resist. We've got to lay a trap so deep they won't ever suspect. We've got to find something that makes them unbearably agitated."

"And what would that be?"

Johnny said, "This Becker. You say he likes to get his picture in the paper?"

"He does."

"Then it's got to be something with splash. Something with style. Something that would get the *New York Herald Tribune* out here and *Life* magazine."

"Yes."

"So much glory that Becker will not be able to turn it down."

Owney thought hard. He didn't have a clue.

Johnny looked at him with impatience.

"Come on, goddammit. Use that thinker you got up there. You're like the Brit generals during the war, you can only think about moving straight ahead."

"I just don't—"

But Ralph was suddenly there, hovering.

"Ralph?"

"Mr. Maddox, Vince Morella is here."

"Christ!" said Owney. "What the hell. It can't wait?"

"He's very insistent."

"Jesus Christ!" He turned to Johnny. "Wait a second. These Arkansas boys, they can't get *nothing* straight."

He rose, went into the living room where Vince Morella stood, holding hat in hand nervously.

"What the fuck, Vince. I'm inna middle of an important meeting."

"Sorry, sorry, sorry, Mr. Maddox, but I think you'd want to hear this right away."

"So?"

"I get to the club this morning, go into my office, and there's a guy sitting there. He's already *in.* He says he wants to meet with you."

"Jesus Fucking Christ, I told you—"

"You don't get it. He's one of them."

Owney's eyes narrowed suspiciously.

"He's—"

"He went on all the raids, knows who they are, where they're quartered, how they operate, what they'll do next, how they communicate. He'll give it all to you!"

Owney's eyes narrowed. Now this he finally understood.

"For money, eh. Somebody always sings for the moolah."

"Not for money. That's why he had to see *you.* For something only you can give him. He's a college kid. His name is Frenchy Short."

PART THREE

Night Heat

CHAPTER 37

Both men were grouchy, dirty and cranky. Road dust clung to them in a gritty film. A shower would be so nice, a sleep. This was their third trip to Hot Springs from Texas in as many days, with the bitterness of a bad scene with Becker and the sad scene with Frenchy Short yesterday. And today was a high killer. Above, the sun beat down, a big hole in the sky, turning the sky leaden and the leaves heavy and listless. No wind puffed, no mercy, as if they'd brought some godforsaken Texas weather with them.

Dressed in farmer's overalls with beaten-up fedoras pulled low over their eyes and .45s tucked well out of sight, they sat on the front porch of the Public

Bathhouse, that is, the pauper's bathhouse, at least in the shade. Other poor people—genuine poor people—lounged about them, too sick to look anything other than sick, come to Hot Springs for the waters of life, finding only the waters of—well, of water. The Public was the least imposing of the structures on Bathhouse Row, but it looked across the wide boulevard of Central Avenue at the Ohio Club.

It was a thin, two-story building, wedged between two others, the Plaza Building and the Thompson Building; its big feature was a kind of mock-Moorish gilded dome, completely fraudulent, which crowned the upper story, and a dormer of windows bulging out over the first-floor windows. It was in the Ohio that he and the old man had observed Mickey Rooney and his big-busted wife number two throwing away thousands of bucks in the upstairs craps game.

"That's going to be a hard place to bust," said D.A.

"I'd hate to do it at night when it's all jammed up," said Earl. "You got all the traffic and pedestrians, you got all the gamblers upstairs, you got Grumley riffraff with machine guns, you got Hot Springs coppers real close by. It could make Mary Jane's look like just the warm-up."

"Night's out. I don't think that bastard Becker would go for another night raid, especially downtown. Too many folks about."

"I'm thinking about five, before the avenue and

the joint fill up. We run some kind of cover operation. Maybe we could get our hands on a fire truck or something. Go steaming in with lights flashing and sirens wailing, be in on them before they figure it out and once we get it, we have the place nailed. Nobody dies. We close down that place, we put the word out among the Negroes to watch real careful for strange white people in their neighborhoods."

The two men sat in silence for a while. Then the old man said, "Let's go get us a Coca-Cola. My whistle could use a bit of wetting."

"Mine too," said Earl.

They walked south along Central, came finally, after oyster bars and whorehouses baking emptily in the noonday sun, the girls still snoozing off a night's worth of mattress-backing, to a Greek place. They went in, sat at the fountain, and got two glasses of Coca-Cola filled with slivers of ice.

"It ain't the how of the raid," said D.A. "It's figuring out the why of it. We have to *justify* it. Short was right on that one."

"Maybe we lay up outside, pick up a runner, and sweat him. When we break him, we hit the place."

"But we got it all set up first? Don't like that. Also, Owney'd track down the runner and kill him and maybe his family as a lesson. I don't like that."

"No, I don't neither. Maybe we find someone who works in the joint who'd testify."

"Who'd that be? He'd become the number one bull's-eye in the town. Sooner or later, we move along. Sooner or later, he'd get it. Some Grumley'd clip him for old timey sake."

"Yeah, that's right. Maybe a Grumley. Find a Grumley to talk. Turn on his kin for a new start."

"But we ain't got no budget to finance a new start. We can't protect 'em. There's nothing we can offer that'll make a Grumley turn. Finally, them Grumleys hate us. We put eleven of 'em in the ground, remember? They might still come looking. It don't matter that Pap up and died hisself off. Flem don't have Pap's grit, but he's just as much a snake."

"We got to find out where they're weakest and attack 'em there."

"Give it to Owney, he knows his business. Ain't no 'weakest.' "

"He is a smart bastard. He's been running things a long time. Goddamn, I hate being this goddamn close and not getting it done."

"We'll get it done, Earl. One way, the other, sooner, later. We'll get it done. That I swear."

They drove back, the long, grueling three-hour pull through southern Arkansas down U.S. 70, through Arkadelphia and Prescott and Hope, making Texarkana by 4:00 and the Red River Army Depot by 5:00.

The boys were sitting outside the barracks, looking disconsolate. There was an Arkansas Highway Patrol truck and three Texas Highway Patrol cars. A group of Highway Patrolmen seemed to be running some kind of operation.

Earl and D.A. walked up.

"What the hell is going on?" Earl said.

"They come to git our guns," said Slim. "Got a piece of paper signed by the Arkansas governor, the Texas governor and a federal judge. Becker signed off on it too."

"Shit," said D.A., pushing past them. "What's all this about? Who's in charge here?"

"You'd be Parker?" said a tall Arkansas Highway Patrol officer. "Parker, I'm Colonel Jenks, commandant of the Arkansas Highway Patrol. Sorry about this, but at ten this morning, I got a call from the governor's office. I went on over there and he'd evidently just chewed the hell out of poor Fred Becker and got him to issue an order. By eleven the governor's staff had taken it before a judge, and by noon they's on the phone, working out a deal with these here Texas boys. They want us to take charge of your heavy weapons and your vests. Y'all can still carry .45s, but—"

"Sir," Earl said to the commandant, "we try and do this work without a base of fire and we will end up in a pickle for sure. That's something I learned in the war, the hard way."

"I ain't saying what you done is bad. Nobody's had the sand to go face-on with them Hot Springs Grumleys and their out-of-town mobsters till you came along. But the governor's gitting heat from all sorts of folks, and that's how governors work. We serve at his pleasure, so we do what he says. That's the way it be."

"Earl," one of the boys called, "it don't seem right. How can we do this work if we don't go in well heeled?"

"Yeah," another said, "if we run into more Grumley bad boys with big ol' machine guns, what're we supposed to do?"

"You got the best pistol skills in the state," said Earl. "You will prevail. That I know."

But it disturbed him nonetheless.

"Can't we make some disposition so that if we get a big raid and it looks scary we can get our firepower back?" asked D.A.

"Sir," said Jenks, "you'll have to work that out with the governor. I can't settle it at this level. Your Mr. Becker will be the one to make that case."

"Only case he makes is to git his picture in the paper."

"I have to get these guns up to Little Rock tonight, and locked in the armory at State Police headquarters. As I say, it ain't my decision. I just do what I'm ordered to do. That's the way it be."

Now the guns came out: the Thompsons, looking oddly incomplete without magazines, three apiece under the arms of State Troopers. Then the Brownings, so heavy that a man could carry but one. Earl recognized, by a raw cut in the foregrip wood where he'd banged it against the doorjamb, the gun he'd carried as he walked down the hall, keeping up a hail of fire, Frenchy behind him, feeding him the magazines.

"Hate to lose that goddamn BAR," said D.A. "That's what keeps 'em honest."

"It ain't fair," screamed a boy, who turned out surprisingly to be Slim, the oldest and the most salty. "They can't be asking us to continue on these raids without no fire support. That ain't right."

"It ain't right," said D.A. "I'll be talking hard with Becker. We'll get this worked out."

"But we—"

"It's not—"

"We depend on—" came a tumble of voices.

"Shut it off!" Earl bellowed, silencing his own men and shocking the Highway Patrol officers. "Mr. D.A. said he'd work on it. Now just back off and show these boys you're trained professionals who obey your officer." That was his command voice, perfected over hard years on parade grounds and harder years on islands, and it silenced everyone.

"Thanks, son," said Colonel Jenks. "Can see you're a man who knows his stuff. Bet I know which one you'd be."

"Maybe you do, Colonel," said Earl.

"Heard nothing but good things about the ramrod down here. They say he's a heller."

"I do a job if it comes to that."

"Good man," the colonel said, as if marking him for future reference.

A sergeant came to D.A.

"Sir, you'll have to sign the manifest. And what about the carbine?"

D.A. scratched his chicken-track signature on the paper and said, "What carbine?"

"Well sir, in the original manifest you had six Thompsons, three BARs, six Winchester pumps and six M-1 carbines. But you only got five carbines."

"Hmmm?" said D.A. He looked over at Earl. This was a mystery, as the carbines had never been deployed, they'd simply stayed locked up down here in Texas. Earl didn't like the carbine, because its cartridge was so light.

"We never used the carbine," said Earl.

"Well sir, it says you had six, but we only rounded up five."

"I don't have no idea. Any of you men recall losing a carbine?"

"Sir, we ain't touched the carbine since training."

"The carbines was never up in Hot Springs."

"Colonel Jenks, what do you want to do here, sir?" asked the sergeant.

Jenks contemplated the issue for at least a tenth of a second. Then he declared, "Call it a combat loss, write it off, and forget all about it. We don't have to make no big case out of it. It ain't even a machine gun. Now let's get out of here and let these men git going on their training."

CHAPTER 38

It took a day to set up through the auspices of a friend of his who was an FBI agent in Tulsa and knew who to call. Carlo ended up paying for it himself, because he knew there was no budget and that D.A. would never approve. But he had to know.

He had never flown before. The plane was a C-47, though now, as a civilian craft, it had reverted to its prewar identity as a DC-3. It left Tulsa's airfield at 7:30 A.M. and flew for seven hours to Pittsburgh. The seats were cramped, the windows small, the stewardess overworked. He almost threw up twice. The coffee was cold, the little sandwich stale. His knees hurt, his legs cramped. In Pittsburgh, the plane refueled, exchanged some passengers for others, and finally left an hour later. It arrived, ultimately, at National Airport just outside Washington, D.C., at around 4:00 in the afternoon.

He took a cab to the Headquarters of the United States Marine Corps, at Arlington Annex, in Arlington, Virginia. It was a set of wooden buildings, shabby for so grand an institutional identity, behind barbed wire on a hill overlooking the capital. In the distance, a white rim of buildings and monuments could be seen, grandly suggesting the greatness of the country it symbolized, but out here, across the river, the warriors of that country made do with less. The only concession to ceremony was the presence of ramrod-stiff Marines in dress blues outside, keepers of a temple, but inside, he found no temple at all. It was merely a busy workplace of men in khaki humming with purpose. It took a bit, but finally someone directed him to the Personnel Records Branch of G1 Division, HQ USMC. A sergeant greeted him in the foyer, and he identified himself and was led in, past offices and work bays, to an inner sanctum; that is, what appeared to be miles and miles of shelves stacked with the manila envelopes that represented each of the men who'd worn the Globe and Anchor in this century. The sergeant took Carlo to a reading room, windowless and bright, where what he had requested had been put out for him.

"What time do you close?" he asked.

"Officer Henderson, we don't close. We're the Marine Corps. Take your time. We run a twenty-four-hour department here."

So Carlo, exhausted and bewildered, at last sat down alone with the ultimate clue in his quest.

Finally, shaking slightly—the effect of the hard day's travel, or his own apprehension?—he opened the battered file that contained the service record book of SWAGGER, EARL L., FIRST SGT., USMC (RET.)

With the service record book, he was able to watch the man progress from lowest grade to highest, across three continents, an ocean and the mightiest war ever fought. The book was a compendium of places lost or destroyed or forgotten about, of judgments tempered and faded but always accurate, and finally of obscure institutional relics and random facts, including fingerprints taken on enlistment, civilian occupation and education, prior service, promotions and reductions—including examinations and recommendations for advancement, pay matters including travel allowances; military justice including time lost through misconduct; inventories of residual clothing and equipment; enlistment and reenlistment data with supporting medical records; foreign and sea service; commanders' ratings on conduct and efficiency; marksmanship scores; specialist qualifications; and awards and decorations. It was in bad penmanship, in a language whose intricacies and nuances he didn't understand. But he did start noticing things: he noticed right away, for example, a discrepancy in birth dates. Earl joined the Corps in Fort Smith, in 1930, claiming to be seventeen, but Carlo now knew he was born in 1915; he was two years underage. That spoke of a boy in a hurry to get away from what Carlo knew was the hell of his life.

The book followed the boy from his first days as a recruit at the brutal Parris Island of 1930. Many of the scores were meaningless to Carlo, for they referred to tests he didn't understand in a numerical progression he also didn't understand. But he understood simple marksmanship, and noted that the boy shot expert in all weapons. PVT. SWAGGER, E. L., was then sent to Sea School, at the Norfolk Navy Yard in Virginia, and then deployed as a rifleman to the Fifth Marines in Nicaragua, working with the Nicaraguan Guardia Nacional in something called M Company, with an enthusiastic unofficial endorsement from the officer in charge, one Captain Lewis B. Puller. "PFC Swagger shows natural talent for combat operations and is particularly proficient in running a fire team of four men in jungle patrol." Then it was two years on the old *Arizona* as a rifleman, later squad leader of the Marine Detachment aboard that craft, whose wreckage now still oozed oil in Pearl Harbor. But rank was slow to come by in the tiny prewar Corps, even if his recommendations were uniformly excellent and each commanding officer would write, in what appeared to be an unusual number of unofficial letters of recommendation, something like, "This Marine shows leadership material and should be encouraged to apply for Officer Candidate School or even an appointment to Annapolis and a regular commission." But Earl never went; he just sea-bagged on, finally promoted to corporal and assigned as a squad leader, then an acting platoon sergeant, with the Fourth Marines in China, from June of 1935 until June of 1939. He was in the Marine Detachment at Balboa in the Panama Canal Zone as a straight-up three-striper when the war broke out.

Carlo read it quickly, almost afraid of what he might find. But the record was uncontaminated with sin. Earl was assigned as a platoon sergeant in Company B, Third Battalion, Second Marines, where he served from February of 1942 until August of 1944. In September of 1942, he landed on Guadalcanal. That was a long and hard campaign. It won him his first Silver Star, and a recommendation for a commission (turned down). After a period of reorganization and retraining in Wellington, New Zealand, he went into it again—Tarawa. There, he was a platoon sergeant, and after the horrible fuckup at Red Beach One, where the Higgins Boats foundered on the offshore reef and he had to wade ashore with his men, taking heavy fire every step of the way, he got his most severe wound, a chest shot from a Japanese sniper on D plus two. That was followed by a four-month recuperation. Nineteen forty-four was the year of Saipan and Tinian, and two more attempts to commission him. His refusal to become an officer was beginning to irritate some, as the battalion executive officer wrote tartly: "Platoon Sergeant Swagger again shows exemplary leadership skills, but his continual refusal to accept the higher responsibility of a field commission is troublesome; he's clearly capable of such responsibility, being not merely aggressive in battle but shrewd in organizational details; but he seems to reject the commission on some vague psychological ground, because his father was a (decorated) officer in the AEF in World War I, and he doesn't want to be of the same 'ilk' as his father. He does not explain this very coherently, but the feeling is clearly deep-seated and passionately held. When the war is over, it is highly recommended that this valuable Marine be offered some kind of counseling to overcome his resentment of the officer class. Meanwhile, he performs his duties with outstanding diligence." In November of 1943, he was promoted to gunnery sergeant and reassigned to Company A, Third Battalion, Second Marines, Second Marine Division, during retraining and reorganization at Camp Tarawa, Hawaii. He served with A/3/2 in the Saipan and the Tinian campaigns.

In September of 1944, he was reassigned to 28th Marines in the new Fifth Marine Division, whose cadre comprised veteran NCOs from earlier Pacific battles. He was also promoted to first sergeant of Company A, First Battalion, 28th Marines. February of 1945 was Iwo Jima. The medal citation was there and Carlo imagined Earl charging up that hill in a fog of sulfur and volcanic grit and gunsmoke, destroying those machine-gun positions, finally entering that concrete bunker for a final up-close battle with the Japs. He killed forty-odd men in a minute and a half, and saved the lives of 130 Marines caught in the bunker crossfire. Amazing. The big one. But he was wounded seven times in that engagement. A severe bout of malaria, accelerated by combat fatigue, didn't help. He was sent to a training command in San Diego in June of 1945, after release from the hospital.

In October of 1945, he was declared unfit for further duty because of his wounds and a disability in his left wrist, which still bore several pieces of shrapnel. He was retired medically with a small pension, in addition to receiving his 52-20 severance package (twenty bucks a week for a year) from the government. In February of 1946 the paperwork on his Medal of Honor citation finally was approved, and in late July of 1946 he was given the award in a small ceremony at the White House.

"Excuse me," he yelled out to the sergeant, "could you explain something to me."

"Yes sir." The young man ducked in.

"When I was in the Air Corps, we called it 'AWOL,' absent without leave. Is there a Marine equivalent?"

"Yes sir. We call it UA, meaning unauthorized absence."

"Now, this particular man, would a record of his UAs be kept here? I don't think I saw any."

"Yes it would. Theoretically. The company first sergeant maintains the service record book. So how diligent the first sarge was, that would determine how diligently the records are kept. Do you have a date or anything?"

"Yes. Third week in January, 1942."

The young man leaned over the service book and began to riffle through the pages.

"Looking here, I can say definitely he was with the Second Marines at New River, North Carolina, before the Second left for the West Coast, departed for the Pacific in July from San Diego and landed on Guadalcanal in September. He was assigned to a platoon all that time. There's no Captain's Masts, no UAs, no disciplinary action of any sort. He was there every day."

"What about, you know, temporary duty? TDY we called it."

"In the Naval Services, it's TAD. No, it would be unusual for a junior sergeant to go TAD at that point in his career, and this one certainly didn't. He was too busy getting ready to kill Japs."

"Leave, none of that?"

"No, sir. Not during the third week of 1942. Wasn't much leave at all given in the Marine Corps in 1942. He was on duty, on station, doing his job."

Carlo felt as if an immense burden had been lifted from him. Involuntarily, his mouth curled upward into a smile, bright and wholesome. He felt himself blushing.

"Well, listen, you've been a big help. I'm very appreciative."

"Yes sir."

He couldn't stop smiling. Suddenly the world seemed beautiful. His future was mapped out: he'd return tomorrow, the team would finish up its raiding, they'd all go back to their departments, the experience would mark him as someone special, and his career would just go on and on. Not out of ambition was he pleased, but out of something else: reverence. He saw what he was doing as divinely inspired. He was doing God's Will. It would be the Just Man who enforced both the Law and the Word, living to standards set by the Book and in the flesh by heroes like Earl Swagger; in their honor, he would live a life of exemplary conduct and—

"Of course," said the sergeant, "you might still want to check with the Historical Section and see what was going on in the Second Marines that week."

After a night in a motel comprising three hours of desperately dead sleep and three hours of fitful turning, Carlo took the cab back to the Arlington Annex to find the G3 (Operations) Division of HQ USMC. Operations was in another of the shambling wooden buildings that were the center of the Marine empire. The building showed hard use: it needed paint and air-conditioning and a general sprucing up; or it needed tearing down.

He walked in, introduced himself and showed his badge, and was accorded a professional respect he somehow felt he had yet to earn. The FBI connection worked here too, and he went without trouble to the second floor, to the Historical Section. In here, a narrative of the Second World War was being officially compiled by a number of civilians and Marine retirees. He was eventually turned over to a man in civilian clothes who was missing an arm, referred to by everyone as Captain Stanton.

"What I need," he explained, "is the regimental record—I guess it would be a logbook or something—of the Second Marines, during the third week of January in 1942. Specifically, Company B, Third Battalion."

"They were mostly still stateside then," said Captain Stanton. "Probably still at New River. Sometime in there they would have moved to the West Coast. They didn't deploy until July for the 'Canal.

"I understand that, sir. I just have to see what was going on in the regiment that particular week. That company, that battalion if possible."

"Okay," said the captain. He retreated to the stacks, while Carlo waited, his suit rumpled, feeling sweaty and somehow uncomfortable. The office smelled of cigarette smoke and dead heroes. In stalls men consulted volumes, maps, made phone calls and took notes. Light streamed through the sunny windows, illuminating clouds of smoke and dust; the atmosphere seemed alive with particles and gases. Was this all that was left of all those young men who'd gone ashore on the beachheads of the Pacific, so many of them dying virgins, shot down in warm water or in cloying sand, never having felt the caress of a woman or the joy of watching a son take a first step? Now, they were here: in a large government-green office, full of old journals and files in cabinets and maps, where their sacrifice and heroism was reduced to words to be published in dusty volumes that nobody would ever read. WakeIslandManilaGuadalcanal BetioSaipanGilbertsMarianasTarawaIwoOkinawa. It all came to this, the lighting of cigarettes, the rumpling of paper, the tapping of the typewriters, the scratching, so dry, of pen on paper. There should be a Marine in dress blues, playing taps endlessly to salute the boys of the broken palms and blazing sunsets and long gray ships and jungles and coral reefs and volcanic ash. This room housed it all, and somehow there should be more, but this is all there was. It was another reliquary of the bones of martyrs, some of them so young they didn't know what the word martyr meant.

"Henderson? You okay?"

He looked up to see Captain Stanton, holding a thick volume under his one good hand.

"Yeah, sorry."

"You were sort of talking to yourself."

"I'm sorry. They deserve so much more than this room."

"Yes, they do. That's why we have to get it all written down, so that it'll be recorded forever. Anyhow, here's the logbook of the Second Marines, January through April, 1942."

Together, they paged through it, finding old orders, directives from command and staff meetings, training schedules, disciplinary records, and a narrative of day-by-day operations. It was the collective diary of thousands of men preparing for a desperate, endless war at the end of the world.

"15 Jan 41: 2nd Marines receives deployment orders from HQ-USMC for Camp Pendleton, California, prior to shipment overseas in Pacific Battle Zone. Operations ordered to commence planning of the redeployment."

Then, for the week of January 17 through January 24, "Elements of 2nd Marines in transit to West Coast"; it continued until early February.

"They were on the move for three weeks?" asked Carlo.

"Son, a Marine regiment is part of a division, which is a formidable amount of men. We're talking about a headquarters element, three infantry regiments of about 3,100 men each, an artillery regiment, an engineer regiment, a tank battalion, a special weapons battalion, a service battalion, a medical battalion and an amphibious tractor battalion. They were understrength, of course, but a division carried a paper strength of 19,514 men. So we're talking about a unit that's folded into a larger unit of at least twelve to thirteen thousand men. Plus all the vehicles and equipment, including the guns. It all has to work together. It's no small thing."

Carlo sat there. A worm began to gnaw at his brain. He rubbed his hand against his eye but it would not go away.

"I'm trying to envision this."

"Envision chaos. Barely organized, confusing, messed up, full of mistakes. You're moving a large body of men and equipment. It's 1942, the war has just begun. Everybody's in a panic, nobody knows what's going to happen next. You're working on a railroad system that's just been converted to troop-carrying duties. It demands coordinating with the railways, assembling trains, picking routes, routing the trains in and around other military traffic and civilian traffic, the coming of blackouts, the beginning of wartime regulation and austerity. The logistics are a nightmare. It's a mess, and none of the officers or NCOs have any real experience in it. Up till then the Marine Corps has pretty much moved only at the battalion level. Now you're moving in units of 12,000 men."

Carlo nodded, let it sink in.

"I take it you were there."

"In 1942 at that time I was a staff sergeant in the First Marines. We were also at New River but we didn't move west until July. Our baptism of fire came later, at Bougainville. It would help if I knew what this was about."

"It's a security clearance and a problem has come up. I'm trying to account for a sergeant's location in the third week of January. I already know he wasn't UA or on temporary duty or leave. He was officially with the regiment at that time."

"That should settle it, then."

"What were the routes taken west, do you recall?"

"Ah, there were many trains, many routes, depending. Since we were staging for the Pacific at

Pendleton, outside of Diego, we usually went a southern route. Let's see. In my case, the train went from New River through Nashville, down to Little Rock, on to Tulsa, down through New Mexico and Albuquerque. We were hung up at Albuquerque a week due to a coal shortage, and then on into Diego."

Little Rock!

"Goddamn!"

Goddamn!

It was the first time in his life of virtue and service that he could remember swearing.

"You look like I just hit you between the eyes with a poleax, son."

"Let me ask you this. Is this theoretically possible? A guy has been in ten years. He's a sergeant. He's been around, in China, Nicaragua and the Zone. He's well-liked, even beloved. He knows all the other sergeants and all the junior officers and they know he really can do his job well. Now his unit is moving west by train, in that huge mess you described earlier. At some place—say, Little Rock—he jumps the train. He's from Arkansas, he has some family business to attend to before he goes to war. It takes him about a week, maybe less. He gets it done, heads back to Little Rock. Sooner or later another train bearing Marines comes through. He puts his uniform back on so he can mingle with them easily enough, and maybe he knows some of them and they know who he is. So he gets out to San Diego a week late. It's not that no one has noticed, it's just that they know this guy will be back, and when he quietly shows up one day, that's that. Nothing is said about it. I know it's against regulations, but this is a combat guy, the best, no one wants to give him any trouble, it's a sergeant kind of thing, something sergeants would let other sergeants get away with. Is that possible? Could that happen?"

"Theoretically, no. We do take attendance in the Marine Corps every morning at muster. But . . ."

"Everyone knows that when they go up against the Japs, this is the guy they want around in a big way. He's got leader and hero written all over him in letters a foot tall. And he's probably going to die in the Pacific. Guys like him don't come back from wars, unless it's by some wild statistical improbability."

"The truth is, what you describe, is it possible? Son, it's more than possible. It probably happened a lot. When we shipped out, we knew we weren't coming back. I did it myself."

CHAPTER 39

He looked like a kid in a movie, one of those things with Dick Powell where everybody sang in a real trilly voice, and the women's hair was all marcelled and they wore diaphanous gowns. They didn't make movies like that anymore, but that's what the kid looked like.

"You're kind of young for this shit, aren't you, kid?" asked Owney.

Frenchy sat in an office inside the corrugated tin of the Maddox warehouse way out on the west side of town. He'd been cooling his heels with a mob of surly Grumleys who looked as if they'd just as soon eat him raw as oblige him by letting him live. They yakked at each other in Arkansas hill accents so dense and fourteenth-century, even accent-master Frenchy couldn't quite figure them out. They also spit a lot, the one thing about this godforsaken part of the country he could never get used to.

He wore gray flannels, a blue blazer with the Princeton crest, blue Brooks shirt, a yellow ascot and saddle shoes. And why not? What else would a man wear for such a ceremonial event? Overalls? He'd secretly sworn never to wear overalls again. That store-bought suit he had worn every day as one of Earl Swagger's boy commandos? That thing should be burned.

"I'm twenty," he said. "I have very smooth skin, which makes me look younger. My mother says it makes me look like a girl. Do you think it makes me look like a girl?"

"Is this some kind of fucking joke? Are they tryin' to pull my leg?"

"My, nasty, aren't we? They said you liked to

pretend to upper-class manners but were really pretty crude underneath. I guess they were right."

"He's got you there, boyo," said Owney's companion, an Irish movie star who looked too much like Dennis Morgan for anybody's good.

"Sir, I don't believe I've had the pleasure," said Frenchy.

"You know who I am, kid."

"I'm Walter Short, of Williamsport, Pennsylvania. You can call me Frenchy, all my friends did, that is, back when I had friends, and even that wasn't for very long. And you would be—?"

"Ain't he but a charmer, Owney," said the Irishman. "Aye, he's a lad, I can tell. It ain't no joke to this one. He's got the look of a gentleman schemer to him, I can see it on him. It's a Brit thing. They love to look you in the eye and go all twinkly on you before they pull the bloody trigger."

"Never you fucking mind who he is," said Owney to Frenchy. "You sing, buster, or you won't be a happy kid much longer. You convince me you got the goods."

"Sure. Let's see: the leader of the outfit is a famous ex-FBI agent named D. A. Parker, one of the old-time gunfighters of the '30s. Killed a lot of bandits, they say."

"Parker!" said Owney. "D. A. Parker! Who's the goddamned cowboy?"

"His name is Earl Swagger. He's more a Marine sergeant than a police officer. Lots of combat experience in the Pacific. Won some big medals. Unbelievably brave guy. Scary as hell. You don't want him mad at you. Oh, yes, you already know that. He *is* mad at you."

He smiled.

"Earl and D.A. really are splendid men. You'd never stop them with those hillbillies you've got changing tires in the garage. If that's the best you've got, I'd suggest a career change."

"Cut the crap, wise guy. Keep talking."

"I'll tell you so much for free," said Frenchy. "You go check it out while I go out and get some dinner. Then, tonight, I'll tell you what I want from you. When I'm convinced you can give it to me, then I'll give you what you want."

"Son, Mr. Owney here could have his boys squeeze it out of your high fanciness in a few minutes of dark, sweaty work, you know."

"The funny thing is, he couldn't. He could beat me for a year and I'd never tell. I know what I'm doing and I know how the game is played. You don't scare me."

"Look at the balls on that one, Owney," said the Irishman, amused. "Lord, if I don't think he's telling some kind of truth. He don't always tell the truth, but this time he is. And he'd take what you give him, Owney. He's a smart one, and he's willing to risk it all to win what he wants. Give the little pecker that."

"Kid," said Owney, who had a nose for such deceits, "why? Why you doing this?"

This was the only time in the long night that Frenchy showed even a bit of emotion under his bravado. He swallowed, and if you looked carefully, you might see a brief, ashamed, furious well of tears in his bright eyes.

But then he blinked and it was gone.

"He should have done more for me. They all should have done more for me. I got a letter. A fucking letter."

And then Frenchy told them everything he could about the raid team except where it could be found and where it would strike next.

Once the original breakthrough had been made, it didn't take long. Owney called F. Garry Hurst with the names Earl Swagger and D. A. Parker. Garry Hurst called associates in Little Rock and within three hours Owney had in his hands files, complete with photographs, that verified against Owney's own memory and the testimony of the two managers who'd seen them the identity of his two antagonists. The picture of D.A. came from a 1936 issue of *Life* magazine, called "The Fastest Man Alive," in which then FBI agent D. A. Parker drew against a time-lapse camera with a timer and was clocked at a move from leather to first shot in two tenths of a second. Among the pictures, one showed the then much younger man holding a tommy gun and looking proud at the final disposition of the Ma Barker gang in Florida. Another revealed that he'd been a member of the team that had brought down Charlie "Pretty Boy" Floyd in Ohio. In a last picture, the man stood tall and lean and heroic as the great J. Edgar Hoover pinned the Bureau's highest award for valor on his chest. In a few years, fearing that he was growing too famous, Hoover would fire him, as he fired the great Melvin Purvis.

The Swagger picture appeared in the *Arkansas Democrat Times:* the Marine, ramrod-straight, in his dress uniform, as the president of the United States put a garland of ribbon and amulet around his neck, the Medal of Honor. Once it would have been the biggest news; by the time of the photo, July of 1946, that is, three months ago, just before all this began, it had only played on an inside page.

"Fuckin' Bugsy didn't know what he was up against," said Owney. "That guy's a war machine. Bugsy's lucky he didn't get himself killed. And I am unlucky he didn't kill Bugsy for me."

"And Earl Swagger is unlucky," said Johnny Spanish. "If we don't kill the poor boyo, then sure as Jesus Bugsy will."

Frenchy was back from dinner, looking extremely pleased with himself. The two men awaited him in the upstairs office, but all the Grumleys had been sent home. Only one lurked outside, with a pump shotgun, and he stepped aside for Frenchy.

Frenchy's mood was peculiar: he had no doubts, no qualms, and he felt, at least superficially, good, even well. But he was aware that he'd crossed some kind of divide and that it really was tricky on this side. He needed to maneuver very carefully here, and keep his goal in mind, and not get hung up. He had to get out of here with something other than just his skin: he had to get something positive, something that would take him where he wanted to go.

At the same time, though he didn't feel it, a pain lurked somewhere. It left traces, like tracks in the snow, as now and then odd images floated up out of nowhere to assail him: how Earl had saved his life when he fell forward into Carlo's line of fire during the training, the rage he felt when he wasn't named first man on the entry team, the oddest sense of happiness and belonging he'd begun to enjoy on the raid team. It was so strange.

This time, Owney was more respectful and less suspicious. He seemed like a colleague. He sat at the desk smoking a cigar and the Irishman sat at his side. Frenchy could see a *Life* magazine article with D.A.'s picture in it and a newspaper clipping of Earl. Drinks were offered, twelve-year-old Scotch whiskey. Frenchy took a cigar and lit it up.

"It checks out, old man," said Owney, who had suddenly transformed himself into a stage Englishman. "But the problem, my new friend, is that it's not enough. Most important: where are they? Second most important: how can we get at them?"

"Oh, I've got that all figured out," said Frenchy, taking a big draft on the cigar, then chasing it with just a touch of the old, mellow Scotch. "I've designed something that's really sharp. I mean, *really* sharp." He raised his eyebrows to emphasize the point.

"Hadn't you best ask the lad his price, Owney?" asked the wise Irishman. "If it's cream he's givin' you, it's cream he'll want in return."

"What do you want, old man? Money? Filthy lucre? Judas got his thirty pieces, how many pieces do you want?"

"Money?" said Frenchy. "You're making me laugh, Mr. Maddox. You have me confused with a greedy little schemer who wants to buy a new Ford coupe. I am *beyond* money."

"That makes him truly dangerous," said the Irishman. "He's bloody Michael Collins."

Frenchy leaned forward.

"I've done my homework. I know how big you were in New York."

"True enough, Owney was the tops," said the Irishman.

"You still know people back there. I mean, big people. Judges, attorneys, bankers. You know them or you know people who know them. People with influence."

Frenchy's blazing ambition filled the room. Or was it his despair or his courage? Whatever, it was almost a little frightening. He leaned forward even further, fixing the two of them with eyes so hot they unsettled. The two gangsters felt the power of his will and his inability to accept that he couldn't get what he wanted.

"I want you to get me a job with the government."

"Jesus," said the Irishman. "I'm thinking the boy wants to be an FBI agent! We should shoot him now."

"No," said Frenchy. "Not at all, not the FBI. It's called the Office of Strategic Services. It's the spies. It's very tony, very Harvard, very old law firm, very ancient brokerage. Most of the people who work for it went to the same schools and they sit and drink in the same clubs. They're special, gifted, important men, who secretly run the country. They're above the law. You think you're important? You think you're big? Ha! You only exist because you fulfill some purpose of theirs. You supply a need and so they let you survive. They answer to no one except their own cold conscience. They are the country, in a way. I want to be one of them. I *have* to be one of them."

"Jesus, Johnny," said Owney. "The boy wants to be a spy."

"You can do it. Earl and D.A. couldn't do it, because they're nothing in the East and no matter how great they are, nobody out East would notice or care. It's a club thing. You have to get into the club. I know you know people. I know you could make three phone calls and I've suddenly got someone going to bat for me. That's what I want."

"I could make a phone call."

"To an important man."

"I could make a phone call to an important man."

"He could go to bat for me. He could *make* them hire me. He could tell them—"

"Yeah, yeah," said Owney. "Wouldn't be easy, but it could be done. Your record, it's okay?"

"If you look close, it's spotty. But from a distance it looks good. Right schools, that sort of thing."

"So, what are you going to give me?"

"Okay," said Frenchy, taking a draft on a cigar. "I'll tell you how to get them."

"We're all ears, boyo," said the Irishman.

"You have to have good men, though."

"We have five of the best," said the Irishman.

"And you'd be one of them, Mr. Spanish," said Frenchy. "Or should I say Mr. John St. Jerome Aloysius O'Malley, armed robber extraordinaire, called Spanish for the olive cast to his skin. As I say, I do my homework."

He sat back, beaming.

"Ain't he the smart one," said Johnny. "A sly boyo, misses not a thing, that one."

"Kid, you're impressing me. You are making me happy. Now make me happier."

"I'm going to make you unhappier. They *know* where the Central Book is. Right now, they're trying to figure out how to hit it. So you don't have a lot of time."

This was Frenchy's specialty, as it turned out. He had a gift for conspiracy, but under that, and far more important, he had a gift for conviction. It was an almost autistic talent, to read people in a flash and understand how to beguile them along certain lines. He knew he had them now, and he even had a moment's pleasure when he realized he could play it either way: he could set these guys up for Earl or he could set up Earl for these guys. Any way he came out on top! It was so cool! He held his own life in his hands; he could do anything.

"How did they find it?"

"They didn't," said Frenchy. "They're not smart enough. *I* found it for them."

He quickly narrated his adventures at the phone company on Prospect Avenue.

"Fuck!" said Owney, devolving to East Side hoodlum. "That fucking Mel Parsons! I knew he was no good! I'll get that changed right away!"

"Barn door and all the animals fled, sport," said Johnny Spanish. "Listen to the boy here. He's smart, he's got some talent. See what he's got to offer."

"Okay," said Frenchy. "D.A. had us quartered at the Lake Catherine dam, in the pump house."

"Fuck!" said Owney, this elemental truth right under his nose at last revealed.

"But he won't go back there. He's smart. When

he goes operational again, he'll find some other place. You'll never find it. And even if you do, what are you going to do? Go in with a thousand Grumleys, kill everybody? There'd be a huge stink, the governor would have to call out the National Guard. What does that get you?"

"Go ahead, sonny," said Johnny.

"So you have to ambush them. But you've got to do it in such a way that when they're finished, it's not going to be a scandal. It's going to be a joke."

"You have the floor, kid. Keep talking."

"What would be a temptation they couldn't resist? That Becker couldn't resist?"

"Now, see, Johnny was talking about that today too. You guys sure you ain't related?"

"Possibly his lordship's triple-great-grandfather fucked me triple-great-grandmother the scullery maid in her bog cottage in County Mayo in 1653," said Johnny.

"I don't think we ever had any Irish servants," said Frenchy, completely seriously. "Anyway, here it is: the Great Train Robbery."

There was a quiet moment. The two men looked at each other.

"Yeah, I thought so," said Frenchy. "That was the biggest thing that ever happened here. October 2, 1940. Five men take out the Alcoa payroll, kill four railway guards and get away clean with several million dollars. In the Hot Springs yard! Big news! Great job! It's even said that a certain Owney Maddox built the biggest casino in the world in 1941 on the proceeds of that job. It's also said that the great Johnny Spanish, the world's smartest armed robber, masterminded the job."

"Have another cigar, kid."

"Don't mind if I do."

Frenchy turned the lighting of the cigar into high drama. He sucked, he puffed, he drew the fire into the long, harsh tube of finest Cuban leaf, he watched the glow, he got it lit fiercely, and finally he expelled a huge cloud which rotated, Hiroshima-like, above his clever young head.

"If Fred Becker *stops* another train robbery and if he *nabs* the team that did it and that's the team that did the *first* robbery and he gets convictions on *them,* by God, then he's a national hero. He's the next governor. He's won what *he* wants to win. See, he only sees the gambling crusade as a vehicle. He doesn't believe in it a bit. It's just leverage to get him to the next level."

Owney appraised the young man. He had the gangster thing. Mad Dog had it. Bugsy had it. The Dutchman had it. It would change over the years to something mellower and deeper, into a strategic vision. But now, raw and unalloyed, this handsome upper-class boy had it in absolute purity: the ability to see into a situation and know exactly how to twist it, where to apply force, where to kill, how to make the maximum profit and get away with the minimum risk.

"So," continued Frenchy, "what you have to do is find some way to plant the possibility that another train robbery's being set up. That Johnny Spanish has been seen in town. Becker will go for it like crazy. He'll go for it fast and recklessly. That's his character, his defining characteristic, that ambition. He'll *order* Parker and Earl to intercede. He has to. They're the only men he's got he more or less trusts. You've got him. Only, when he lunges for the big prize, it's just bait concealing a hook, and you get him right through the gills. You lure the team into that railyard, and hammer it good."

He sat back, took another huge puff on the cigar. The smoke curled around his face, and he took a sip of the Scotch whiskey, but not too much, for he didn't want to blur his sharpness.

"I think he will make a fine agent," said Johnny Spanish. "He's pure Black and Tan, a night rider with a cunning for the devil's work."

"Why, that's the nicest thing anyone's ever said about me," said Frenchy, only partially ironic. He felt suddenly something he had never felt before: that he was home. He belonged.

But Johnny went on. "See, he's got so much upstairs, but in the end, he's a brick shy in the realm of experience."

"What's wrong?" asked Frenchy.

"A night ambush's a devilish hard thing to pull. I've been in dozens so I know. You get your own boys all mixed up with the other fella's. Everybody's shooting at everybody else. Then, you've got a big space like that railyard, with lots of room for maneuver, and it gets even more mixed up. And to put a final ribbon on it, see, they're wearing those damned vests, so they're not going down. By Jesus, boy, you've thrown the babe out with the bathwater. You've got to lure them into a contained area so there's telling what's them and what's us. That, or figure a way to let us see in the dark."

The smile began slowly on Frenchy's face. It flamed brightly, gathering force and power, becoming a ghastly apparition on its own. His smugness was so radiant it became a force of illumination almost on its own. He gloated like a man mightily self-pleased to discover that he'd arrived exactly where he intended all along.

"Old man," he said. "Consider *this*." He reached into his pocket and removed a page clipped from the June 1945 *Mechanix Illustrated.* He unfolded it and gently put it on the desk before them.

UNCLE SAM CAN SEE IN THE DARK read the headline, above a picture of a GI clutching a carbine with what looked to be a spotlight beneath the barrel and one of the new televisions mounted atop the receiver, where a telescopic sight might otherwise go.

"It's called infrared. You beam them with a light they can't see. Only you can see it, through that big scope. They're in broad daylight, only they don't know it. You can hit head shots, and to hell with the vests. You pop a few of them, and the rest turn and run. You litter the place with carbine shells and you vacate. I can get you hundreds of carbine shells. Your police are there in seconds, report no sign of another outfit and that the raid team panicked in the dark and shot the shit out of each other. They're clowns, who's not to believe it? Since you control the cops, nobody will ever work the forensics. Hey, is it swell or is it swell?"

The phone rang.

"Goddamn!" said Owney, reaching for it.

"With Mr. Maddox's connections, it can't be too difficult to get ahold of a couple of these gadgets. You set up on a boxcar. The raid team comes into the yard. Bing-bang-boom! It's over."

"Yeah?" said Owney, into the receiver. "Goddammit, this better be impor—"

His rage turned to amazement.

"Be right there," he said. He turned back to his confederates.

"You work it out with him," he said. "You guys are a team, I knew that from the start. Tell me where to go to get those units and you'll have them next week. I've got to run."

"What's going on, boyo?" asked Johnny Spanish.

"A babe has just shown up and she'll talk only to me."

"Ah, Owney, many's the fine fella who's been undone by a lass. You wouldn't be that kind, would you now?"

"Not a chance. But this one's different," he said, closing the door. "It's Virginia Hill."

CHAPTER 40

"I hate to fly," said Virginia. "It hurts my butt. I hate those little johns. I hate it when you're stuck next to some joe who wants to tell you his life story."

"Virginia," said Ben, "you have to do it."

They were in the lounge at Los Angeles International Airport, sipping martinis. It was a very deco place, all chrome and brushed aluminum, filled with soaring models of sleek planes. Outside, through an orifice now being called a "picture window," planes queued up to take off on the long tarmac. They were silvery babies, their props buzzing brightly in the sun, most with two motors, some few with four. They looked, to Ben at least, like B-17s taking off for a mission over Germany, not that he had ever seen a B-17 or been anywhere near Germany while the shooting was going on.

Virginia took another sip of her icy martooni. The gin bit her lips and dulled her senses. She had to pee but she couldn't find the energy. Her breasts were knocking against her playsuit top, as if they wanted to come out and play. The drink made her nipples hard as frozen cherries. Her brassiere cut into her gorgeous mountains of shoulders. One shoe had slipped half off her foot. Every man in the joint was staring at her, or rather, at parts of her, but that was a necessary condition of her life. Ben's pal, a tough little mutt named Mickey Cohen, lounged nearby, as a kind of sentry. He sent out such vibrations of protective aggression that none would approach, or even admire too openly. Mickey looked like a fire hydrant on legs.

Airplane! Virginia Hill went by train, in her own stateroom, on the *Super Chief* or the *Broadway* or the *Century* or the *Orange Blossom Special!* Elegant Negroes called her "Miz Hill" when they served her Cream of Wheat in the morning, tomato aspic in the afternoon and steak in the evening, all with champagne. It was so nice. It was the way a lady traveled.

"Now tell me again what you're supposed to do."

"Oh, Christ," said Virginia. "Ben, I am not stupid. I know exactly what to do."

"I know, I know, but humor me."

"Ah. You bastard. Why do I put up with this shit?"

"Because of my huge Jewish pretzel."

"Overrated. You might try kissing me a little first, you know. It's not always so good when we try and do it in under ten seconds."

"I look at you and I just can't wait. When you get back, kisses, presents, dinner, champagne, petting. I'll pet! I swear to you on my yarmulke: petting!"

"You bastard."

"Please, Virginia. I am so nervous about this."

"Twenty hours or so, I get to Hot Springs. I check into the Arlington where I already have a reservation. I go to Owney. He of course has to have me up. I tell him I'm on a sort of a peace mission. Ben is worried that Owney will think he's shoehorning in on the Hot Springs business with this desert deal. I'm to assure him that that's not the case and that if Vegas even begins to look as if it might work, you, Ben, will invite him, Owney, out as a consultant and fellow investor. Owney is to consider Vegas his town as much as Hot Springs and as far as Ben is concerned, Owney will always be the father and Ben the son."

"Yeah, that's good. You can do that?"

"In my sleep, sugar."

"Okay, what's next?"

"Then I pressure him about the cowboy. Does he yet know who that cowboy is? Ben has been very embarrassed about what happened to him with the cowboy. It's gotten all around and Ben is being teased about it and being laughed at behind his back. Can Owney please hurry up and find out who the cowboy is?"

"Yeah."

"Ben, I'm telling you, even if he tells me I am not going to tell you. I will not be part of anything against that guy. He was just a guy who lit a cigarette. You swung first. He didn't know who you were."

"Virginia, how many times do I have to tell you? Forget the cowboy. It's got nothing to do with the cowboy. You don't have to protect the cowboy. But you have to put that move on Owney, because he will see through the father-son bullshit in a second, and will know you have a secret agenda. He will believe *that's* the secret agenda. We *want* him to believe that I'm obsessed with the cowboy, that I've sent you there to find out who the cowboy is. That way, he will discount what moves I'm making and consider me a noncompetitor, caught up in some grudge match that don't have nothing to do with business."

"Okay," she said, and took another toot on the martooni. "Too much vermouth. Bartender, gimme another, easy on the vermouth. And two olives."

"She likes fruit," Ben said to Mickey. Mickey didn't say anything. He hardly talked. He just sat there, working on his fire hydrant impersonation.

"Now," said Ben. "What's next? It's very important. It's the point!"

"The painting."

"Yeah, the painting. You might have seen it the first time, Virginia, if you'd been paying attention instead of rubbing your tits up against Alan Ladd."

"He hardly noticed, believe me. His old lady was watching him like a hawk."

"He noticed, I guarantee. Anyhow: look at it very carefully. Get its name. But remember *exactly* what it looks like. In fact, buy a little sketch pad and as soon as possible, sort of draw what it was like. Label the colors."

"This is stupid. I ain't no fancy artist like Brake."

"*Braque,* Virginia. It's French or something."

"This is secret-agent stuff. What do you think, sugar, I'm in the *OSS* or something?"

"Virginia, this is important. It's part of the plan. Okay?"

"Okay."

"We have to know all about that painting. Go back a second time, and check your first impressions, all right?"

"I can't stand that creep *twice.*"

"Force yourself. Be heroic, all right?"

"Ty!" she suddenly shouted, rising.

A small, fine-boned dark-skinned man had entered the bar for his own bout of martoonis; Virginia waved, her voluptuous breasts undulating like whales having sex in a sea of the brand-new miracle product Jell-O.

Ben felt a wave of erotic heat flash through his brain as the two mighty wobblers swung past him, and turned to see the man toward whom she now launched herself.

It was that movie star, Ty Power.

"Virginia," he said, "why, what a nice surprise."

"Martooni, honey lamb? Join us. You know Ben."

"Don't mind if I do, Virginia."

"How's the new picture? I hear it's swell."

Business. Ben sighed, knowing he had lost her for the time being. Then he retreated to his own private recreational world as Virginia pretended to be a movie star and Ty concentrated on her giant breasts and Mickey worked the fireplug routine. He thought about how he was going to kill the cowboy and enjoy every second of it.

CHAPTER 41

Carlo finally reached D.A. late that night from a phone booth in Washington National Airport. It took a pocketful of nickels before the connection was finally established and even then D.A. was only at this mysterious number rarely. But this time he was, though he'd clearly roused himself from a deep sleep.

"Where the hell have you been?" the old man demanded.

"I'm in Washington, D.C. I was checking on Earl's Marine records."

"D.C.! Who the hell told you to go to D.C.?"

"Well sir, it's where the investigation took me."

"Lord. Well, what did you find out?"

"Sir, I have to ask you. Suppose—" He could hardly get it out. "Suppose there were evidence that suggested Earl killed his own father?"

"What?"

He ran his theory by D.A.

"Jesus Christ."

"Sir, if ever a man needed killing, it was Charles Swagger. Heck, it may even have been self-defense and the reason Earl didn't turn himself in was 'cause he knew he'd get hung up in Arkansas and miss the trip to Guadalcanal."

"You tell nobody about this. You understand? Nobody."

"Yes sir."

"If I find a chance, I may poke Earl a little bit on the subject. But that's all. Under no circumstances are we going to indict a man like Earl for something that can't be proven but by the circumstantial evidence in some forgotten Marine Corps file."

"Yes sir."

"Now you get on back here. We may be moving back into Hot Springs very shortly, and we need you."

"Yes sir."

Frenchy was gone. Carlo was still tending to a sick mother and would be back. Two others elected not to return, and after the heavy weapons were confiscated, Bear and Eff left the unit, saying the work was now too dangerous.

That left six men, plus Earl and D.A., no weapons, no vests.

"Y'all have to decide," Earl told them, "if you want to go ahead with this. We're operating on about two cylinders. You're young, you got your whole lives ahead of you. I don't like it any more'n the rest of you, but those are the facts and I ain't sending any man into action who don't believe in the job and his leaders. Anybody got any comments?"

"Hell, Earl," said Slim, "we started this here job, I sure as hell want to finish it."

"I will tell any man here," said Earl, "that all he has to do is come to me in private and say, thanks but no thanks, and I'll have you out of here in a second, no recriminations, no problems, with a nice letter from Fred C. Becker. We ain't fighting Japs. We're fighting gamblers and maybe it ain't worth it for men with so much yet ahead."

"Earl," said Terry, "if you could go through the war and come home and have a baby on the way, and still go on the raids, that's good enough for me."

"Well, ain't that peachy. You may feel different if you get clipped in the spine or get an arm shot off."

"Earl, we are with you. You lead us, dammit, we'll follow."

"Good," said Earl. "You goddamn boys are the best. Carlo will be back soon, that's another gun. Plus, we think we got a real fine idea on where to hit 'em where it hurts the most."

He issued orders: he and Mr. D.A. were going back to the Hot Springs area that night to find another place to hide the unit, and they'd send word for the others to join up in two days or so. For the rest, they were just to train under Slim's guidance, working with the remaining .45s and practicing their pistol skills.

Earl and the old man poked about in the far environs of Hot Springs, looking for a good hide. A trailer camp out by Jones Mills promised something, but was too close to the main road in the long run, and not far from a small casino and bar where surely the presence of a passel of hard-looking young men in the vicinity would be noted.

"A fine sity-ation where the law's scared of getting spotted or jumped by the criminals," fumed D.A. "Ain't never been in nothing like this before. Like *we're* the ones on the goddamned run."

They tried a hunting lodge near Lonsdale, to the north, cut over and tried a fishing camp at Fountain Lake, and still couldn't quite settle on a place. Off toward Mountain Pine was Grumley territory, so no further progress to the west was made; instead, they cut back, drove up the Ouachita toward Buckville; at last they located Pettyview, an agricultural community with almost no street life at all. A quick inquiry by Earl at the real estate office located a chicken farm, abandoned since before the war and up for rent. They drove out and found the site about the best: an old house, an empty barn, six long-deserted chicken houses, piles of bones and shit turned to stone out back, and no neighbor within four miles or so. The barn could easily enough conceal all the cars, lamps didn't have to be lit at night, and the place was available for $35 a month with an option to buy, month to month. D.A. forked over the $70 in cash, and they were in business again.

"Let's head back into town," said Earl. "I want to see how things are going in that colored whorehouse."

"Sure," said D.A. "Who knows what might come of it."

"Want to get there just after dark, so's nobody sees us."

Again D.A. said sure, and they drove on in silence, and D.A. fiddled with the radio, trying to line up on the Hot Springs KTHS beam, which played a lot of the jump blues and new bebop he seemed to have a strange affection for. He liked music with a little juice to it, he'd say.

"Say, Earl," said D.A., "been meaning to ask. Your daddy? He's killed in, where was it?"

"Mount Ida," said Earl. "Nineteen forty-two."

"They never caught who done it?"

"Nope."

"I'd think a man like you'd be gunning for whoever done it. Want to go back and track that dog down and make him pay."

"My daddy was looking to die, and had been for years. That mean boy done him and me and everybody else a damn favor. I'd give the bastard my big old star medal if I found him."

"Earl! Damnation! You shouldn't talk like that! He was your daddy, and a fine upstanding man. A law officer. Shot it out with some bad fellas. A hero in the Great War. I'm surprised to hear you talk as such."

"My daddy was a bully. He'd just as soon thump you as look at you, while he's sucking up to the quality. He always thought he was too good for what he got, and he was ashamed of who he was and who we were. He was a Swagger, from a long line of Swaggers descended from folks who settled this part of the country right after the Revolutionary War. I hope my ancestors weren't the bastard he was."

Bitterness seemed to swirl over Earl, as if he didn't like being reminded of his father. Now he was grumpy and gloomy.

"Could he have been somehow mixed up in any Hot Springs business?" asked D.A. "I mean, Owney and the Grumleys got a lot to answer for. Could that somehow be a part of it?"

Earl actually laughed, though there was a bitter, broken note to it.

"That's a goddamn hoot if I ever heard one! My old man was a drunk and a hypocrite and a whoremonger and crooked to boot and a bully. But see, here's the thing: nothing he knew was worth getting himself killed over. Absolutely nothing. He was a little man. Only thing he knew were all the back roads and paths in Polk County. He got that from all the hunting he done, and all the heads he put up on his wall. He cared more about them heads than he did his own children. What the hell could he have known to interest an Owney Maddox? Mr. D.A., you sure you're still on the wagon?"

"Okay, Earl, just asking. Thought I'd check it out."

Earl stopped.

He looked directly at D.A.

"Let me tell you something. Nobody knows a goddamned thing about my father, and it's best that way. Long gone, buried and forgotten. That's the way it should be. Now, Mr. Parker, I don't like to talk sharp to you, but I can't be talking about my father no more. It makes me want to drink too powerfully, you understand?"

"I understand, Earl, and I apologize."

"Fine. Now let's go check on them Negro people."

They drove on in silence, cruising down Central through South Hot Springs, turning right at the hard angle that was Malvern Avenue and following that up to the Negro section. Night had fallen and it was a jumping street, as usual, with the gals calling down from their windows and the crowds bustling into the beer joints, to run against the wheel or bet the slots. And when they got to it, it seemed even Mary Jane's had found some kind of new life. It was really thrumming, almost like some sort of tourist attraction like the alligator farm or the shooting gallery in Happy

Hollow. It looked like old Memphis Dogood was having himself a time keeping up with his customers, and the lack of girls in windows suggested they were all making their night's nut and more on their backs.

D.A. drove around back, where it wasn't crowded, and parked the car. The two men got out, found the door open and a man out back smoking.

"You, boy," said D.A., "you go on in and find Memphis. You tell him some friends want to see him."

The boy looked at them sullenly, but then rose and obeyed. Soon enough three heavyset fellows escorted the large yellow whore called Marie-Claire out. She looked them over and then said, "It's okay."

"Where's your man?" asked D.A.

"Gone. They come git him. He ain't never comin' back. He in the swamp somewheres."

"Who got him?" asked Earl.

"White mens. Grumleys, mos' likely. Don't rightly know. They come by, tell him they need to see him. Thas all. A few days back. He ain't comin' home, I tell you."

Earl shook his head.

"Sister, maybe he just wandered off with another gal," said D.A.

"And leave his place? Memphis love this place, he ain't never gonna leave it 'cept to be underground, thas God's truth."

She glared at the old man, showing a surprising ferocity for a black woman.

"I think Maddox got to him. Grilled him, then

dumped him. Or had somebody dump him, more his style," said Earl.

Then he turned.

"Sorry, sister. All this bad stuff come down on your place from white folks, sorry about all that. These are bad people and we're trying to clean it up and people get hurt sometimes. Very sorry."

"You was the one shot that Grumley hoozer had the gun to my throat, wudn't you?"

"Yes ma'am. That was me."

"Well, suh, tell you somethin' then. You want to know about Mr. Owney fancy-man Maddox? I know a man might could help you."

"Tell me, sister."

"Yes suh. Ol' man name Jubilee Lincoln. Live by hisself over on Crescent, little ol' house. Spirit call him late in life. He speak fo' God now, run the New Light Baptis' out his front parlor. You might wanna see him."

"Why's that?"

"He know about this. You go see him."

They got to the New Light Baptist Tabernacle half an hour later, finding it a wooden house that had seen better times in a run-down neighborhood that backed into the hills of East Hot Springs.

"Now, Earl, you s'pose that gal went to call Owney Maddox and the boys? And they're waiting for us in there?"

"Don't reckon," said Earl. "I don't see how she could help Owney after what he done to Memphis."

"Earl, you think of them as regular people, whose minds work just like ours. It ain't like that."

"Sir, one thing I do believe is that they are the same."

"Earl, you are a hard, strange fellow, I do declare."

They parked in an alley, and the dogs barked and scuffled. They slipped in a back gate and went up to the door and knocked.

In time, stirrings from inside suggested human habitation. Finally, the door opened a crack, and an old man's face peered out at them, eyes full of the fear that any black man would feel when two large white men in hats showed up knocking after dark.

"No need to worry, pop," said Earl. "Don't mean you no harm. Memphis Dogood's gal Marie-Claire gave us your name. We are what they call them Jayhawkers, trying to push the Grumley boys out of town."

The old man's face lit in delight suddenly. A smile beamed through the eight decades' worth of woeful wrinkles that had meshed his face into a black spider web and for just a second, he was young again, and believed in the righteous way of progress.

"Suhs, I just wanna shake your hand if I may," said the gentleman, putting out a cottony old hand that felt a hundred years old. Earl shook it, and it was light as a butterfly.

"Do come in, do come in. Lord, Lord, you are the righteous, that I know."

"We're just polices, sir," said Earl. "We do our job, and white or colored don't matter to us."

"Lord, that be a miracle on earth," said the old man.

He took them into his living room, which boasted a batch of old chairs and an altar. Up front was a cross. Two candles flickered in perpetual devotion.

"Lord, Lord," he said. "Lord, Lord, Lord."

Then he turned. "I am the Reverend Jubilee Lincoln, of the New Light Tabernacle. That was the niece of one of my flock them Grumleys done kilt. You remember?"

Earl did. The black girl. At the top of the stairs. Crying, her eyes pumping moisture. The shiver in her whole body, the shakiness in her knees.

"I'm sorry," said Earl. "We saved the ones we could. Wasn't nothing we could have done about that gal. It's messy work."

"Alvina was a wild gal, like her mama, suh," said the Reverend Jubilee Lincoln. "Her mama died in a 'hohouse too, sorry to say. The word of Jesus don't mean nothin' to either of them gals, and they paid the price. Her daddy is mighty upset too. That man ain't stopped cryin' all day, ever day, ever since."

"It does happen that way sometimes," said D.A. "Sin begets doom, often as not. But I'm sure she went to heaven. She was walking righteous toward the law when them Grumleys finished her."

"Amen," said the Reverend Jubilee Lincoln. "I want to thank you, suhs. You sent some Grumleys to hell, and specially you sent old Pap Grumley there too, even if you didn't shoot him yo'self. Ain't no white men take so much risk to save cullud gals, as I hear it."

"We tried, Dr. Lincoln," said Earl. "We saved most. It pains us we weren't able to save all."

He couldn't remember the girl's name even. But he remembered the bullets hitting her and how heavily she fell down the stairs and how she died in his arms.

"Them gambler fellas don't give no two nothin's 'bout no culluds," said the old man. "I cleaned toilets and spittoons in the Ohio for fifty years, till I couldn't bend over no more, and nobody never called me nothin' but Jubilee, and nobody never gave nothin' about any of mine or what happened to them, no suh. You two is the only righteous white peoples I ever met."

Earl took a deep breath. Then he looked at D.A. Then he said, "You say you were the janitor at the Ohio?"

"Yes suh. Yes suh, and a hard job it be, specially since they put all them damn phones inside and all them boys sit there takin' inf'mation and smokin' and spittin' and drinkin'. It was a mess most nights."

"Sir? Would you—?"

"Would I what, suh?"

"Would you sign a statement saying you saw a telephone room in the Ohio?"

"That Mr. Maddox and them Grumleys, they like to kill me dead if they find out."

"It would be dangerous, that's true," said Earl. "But we'd keep you protected until it's over."

"Suh, if them Grumley crackers decide to kill a Negro man in this town, nothin' but the Lord Almighty could stop 'em."

"Well sir, we're trying to end that kind of thing. End it for good and all."

The old man considered.

"I reckon, the good Lord's gonna call me to Glory anyhows, soon enough. Been around eighty-seven years. Hell, if it rile them Grumleys up, I be *glad* to do it!"

CHAPTER 42

You could not deny how beautiful she was. How a woman could have hair that red, maracas that melony, a waist that narrow, hips that round and legs that long was something on the level of the truly miraculous. Her lips were like strawberries, her eyes green and forever. Everywhere she went, it might as well be spa-ring.

"Virginia, you look so wonderful, darling," said Owney. "Cocktail?"

"Fabulous," said Virginia.

"Martini?"

"Absolutely dah-vine, sugar. Dip the olives in the vermouth, that'll be quite enough."

"Yes, my dear," said Owney. "Ralph, you heard Miss Virginia. Care to come out on the terrace? It's lovely and the view is quite spectacular."

"Of course. But I want you to show me around. What a fabulous place. It's so New York here. It's a little bit of New York in the heart of little old Arkansas, I do declare!"

"We try, darling. We try so hard."

"Oh, birds! I never would have guessed."

They walked to his pigeons, cooing and lowing in their little cages.

"They're adorable. So soft, so cuddly."

The word *soft,* pronounced by Virginia Hill above the two most perfect breasts in all of the white world, more beautiful than a Lana's, a Rita's, an Ava's, almost knocked Owney out. He needed a drink, and to focus hard.

Ralph arrived.

"Martini, m'dear?" said Owney. "Low on the vermouth, as you requested."

"Sweet as shoefly pie and apple-pan dowdy, I declare." She was really laying on her Scarlett O'Hara imitation with a trowel. She took the drink, winked at Owney through it, and . . .

Gulp!

"That was fabulous. Could Gin-gin have another winky?"

"Ralph, run get Miss Hill another winky."

"Yes sir," said Ralph.

Owney took Virginia to look at Central Avenue, hazy in the falling dusk sixteen floors below.

"Ain't it a sight? Sugar, that is some sight. Can't b'lieve it's in the same South where Miz Virginia done growed up. Winky makes Gin-gin feel good. Where Gin-gin growed up was pure Southern-fried dogshit, complete with them uncles couldn't keep them fingers to themselves."

She threw him a smile, and sort of scrunched her shoulders in a practiced way that seemed to crush the immense breasts together more poetically, as if to mount them on a silver platter and present them for his pleasure.

"Virginia, come sit over here, in the arbor."

They sat. Gin-gin's second winky arrived. Gulp!

"Another, Ralph."

"Yes, boss."

"Now Virginia, I suspect you have a message for me."

"Oh, Owney, you don't miss trick one, do you, honey?" She touched his leg and flashed a mouthful of teeth at him. He vowed that he'd have two of the best gals sent over from the best house tonight, and drown in flesh.

"Well," she said primly, "Ben is worried that . . ."

and off she went, explaining how Ben worried that Owney would take offense at his, Ben's, plans in the desert, exactly as Ben had laid it out for her, with a few breathless giggles, and a few fleshy quivers of the mighty boobs thrown in here and there for emphasis.

"The thought"—Owney laughed when she was done—"that I would take *offense* at anything Ben did in Nevada, why, darling, it's almost *adorable.* Ben is my favorite son. Of all my boys, he's the best, the smartest, the quickest. I'm honored that he's chosen me as his hero and that he seeks to emulate me. Why, what he accomplishes in that desert will be a monument to me, and I'm touched. Virginia, sweetness, do you hear? *Touched.*"

"I sure am happy that you're so happy."

"I'm so happy too. I genuinely *appreciate* the way Ben keeps me informed. In our business, communication skills are *so* important. Why, good heavens, it's almost dinnertime. We'll dine at the Southern. There's a most amusing fellow you'll meet, a business associate of mine."

"Sugar, I can't wait. But can I run to the ladies' first?"

"Why of course, my darling. Wouldn't have it any other way."

She tottered off on her heels, that body that seemed to have stepped off a Liberator fuselage only barely shielded by the artful languor of her gown, her flesh undulating underneath its strictures.

Owney tried to think. He had no buzz on because his own martini was pure spring water. What does this mean? What is going on? What is the hidden message?

"Why, Owney. Why Owney, what on earth is *this?*"

Owney rose, walked in to see Virginia standing awestruck in front of his Braque.

"You didn't see that the last time, Virginia?"

"No, I was trying to make time with Alan Ladd to get a picture."

"Well, then, my dear, that is *art.*"

"There's something about it," she said.

"Ben said it reminded him of Newark."

Virginia burst out with a laugh so spontaneous it shook him.

"That silly!" she said. "That boy don't know a thing."

"No, I suppose not."

"Why's it all square?"

"It's called Cubism, darling. An early modernist movement, which broke down the convention of the narrative and the objective. It communicates the power of ideas over precise information. One can feel its power. Actually when Ben says 'Newark,' in his way he's not far wrong. Braque called it *Houses at L'Estaque.* But it's not about houses. It's really about the power of the universe and how its deepest secrets are hidden from us."

She looked at him all goo-goo-eyed.

"Why, honey, I never knew you were so smart! You sound like a regular Albert Einstein."

"It's not quite e=mc squared, but in its way it's an equally radical supposition, eh?"

He stood there, feeling the pride he drew from the picture. Knowing its secrets made him feel ineffably superior. None of the square Johns from the Hot Springs business community who frequented his soirees had an iota's worth of knowledge about this thing. At $75,000 it had been cheap for that thrill alone.

"*Houses at L'Estaque,*" she repeated. "Ain't that a toot!"

CHAPTER 43

It was too hot for gardening—it was darned near too hot for *anything!*—but Junie wasn't the sort to be stopped by a little heat. So out she went, the baby huge inside her and kicking, her feelings a little woozy, but nevertheless determined.

Arkansas was not rose country. You couldn't get a good rose, at least not here, on this flat plain with its half-buried tubes of homes and no clouds in the sky and the sun hammering down, somehow bleeding the day of color. She hadn't even tried roses. She knew roses would fail in so much direct sunlight.

So she'd planted less aristocratic flowers in the little bed outside her hut on 5th Street in the Camp Chaffee vets village, a mix of hydrangeas, daisies, lilacs and lilies. Now some weeds had come into the garden and it was time to expunge them.

Of course she had no tools, and the dried earth was too hard to attack with a spoon, and so she rooted around and found a ghoulish Jap bayonet that Earl had brought home from the war. It had a long, black blade, a truly horrifying thing, but she put it out of her mind that it had once been used to kill men, and insisted to herself that it was only a tool. With its smooth sharpness, she could penetrate into the soil deeply, twist vigorously and uproot the ugly scruff weeds that had seemed to come up almost overnight.

It wasn't a big job and wouldn't have been beyond her in any circumstances except these, where the heat just pummeled her. But she worked onward, through her discomfort, through her sweat, and in an hour had culled most of them. But her back ached. And her feelings of wooziness suddenly increased.

So she sat back for just a second, wiped her brow, and gathered strength for the last few weeds.

Possibly a mistake. As soon as she did, she looked up. Life was livable as long as you simply concentrated on what was just ahead of you, and let your faith and your love steer you, and did your duty. That she knew.

But, looking up, she confronted a bigger picture:

the rows and rows of Quonsets gleaming dully in the sun, lit up now and then with a wife's attempt to brighten them (as she had) with flowers. The attempts were heroic and doomed. The huts were still government housing, with laundry on lines that ran between them, hardscrabble, almost grassless dirt that lay in the lots, dusty gravel streets.

Would they ever get out?

What about the boom? Would it ever reach them and take them somewhere? But not if Earl was dead in some horrid battle for nothing against gangsters.

Don't think that, she warned herself. She had a deep belief in God, country and her husband, and would never allow herself any willing subversion. But lately, more and more, evil thoughts had been creeping into her brain.

Is this it? Is this what I get? What about all the jobs that were supposed to open up after the war, the explosion in industry and finance, construction and communication? Shouldn't it somehow be for the men who'd fought the hardest, like her Earl? Instead, is he going to throw his life away for nothing?

The man who was her husband was still a considerable mystery to her. He didn't like to talk about the war or his past, but they deviled him savagely. He was a good man, an honest man, but he had a reservoir of melancholy deep inside him that would not come out. When he gets on his feet, she thought, it will be all better. But he was on his feet now, and what he loved best had nothing to do with her, but only with other men, some kind of mission, something that took him so far away not just in emotion but in distance. It would involve guns and killing. He loved her, she knew. She didn't doubt it, not a bit of it. But the question remained: what good was that kind of love, because it wasn't the love of somebody there, somebody to be depended on. It was love as an idea, not a messy reality, love from afar. He was still at war, in certain ways.

The baby kicked.

You stop it, you little thing, she ordered.

He kicked harder, and there came a sudden cramp so intense her limbs buckled and down she went, curling up.

Oh, Lord? Was it time?

But her water hadn't broken, so no, it wasn't time, it was just one of those rogue pains that sometimes happen.

She wasn't sure what happened next. It all went dark. She fell into pain, then numbness. Then she heard a voice and thought it might be Earl's.

"Earl, honey?"

"No, Junie, it's me, Mary, from next door. Honey lamb, you fainted."

Mary Blanton was kneeling beside her, fanning her with a copy of *Redbook.*

"Oh, my goodness," said Junie.

"I don't know anything about being pregnant, Junie, but I can't think weeding in ninety-five-degree weather is recommended."

Junie shook the confusion out of her eyes. Now she felt really icky.

"I don't know what happened," she said.

"Come on, honey, let me get you inside and into some shade. You can't lie out here and roast."

With Mary's help, Junie hobbled inside, where she lay down on her bed.

In the little kitchenette, Mary turned on all the fans, then threw ice into a glass and appeared with a large iced tea.

"Here you go, you sip on that till you get your strength back."

Junie sipped the tea and its coolness hit her solidly.

"Are you okay?" Mary asked.

"Yes, I'm fine now. Thank you so much, Mary."

Mary was the bluntest woman Junie had ever met, and she'd worked in war factories for years while her husband, Phil, was in the Navy. Now he was working in a radio shop by day and going to electronics school at night on the GI Bill.

"Well, I don't know about any husband like yours who'd leave a girl all alone as much as you are. A girl as pretty as you and as pregnant as you ought to be getting special attention, not all by herself in a tin hut, pining away."

"Earl's got a job he has to do. He always does his job. That's the kind of a man he is."

"If you say so, Junie. I never heard of such a thing. It's not how we'd do it up North."

Mary just didn't understand, not being from around here.

"I know he was a hero, but that only goes so far. A man ought to be home when his young wife is going to have a baby."

Junie nodded. Then she started to cry.

Mary held her, muttering, "There, there, sweetie, you just cry it all out, don't you worry."

Finally Junie looked up.

"I am *so* scared," she said.

"About your Earl?"

"Yes. But also about the baby. I can feel it. There's something wrong. I could lose them both."

CHAPTER 44

Earl and D.A. were not demonstrative men. But the confidence they now felt, armed with the Reverend Jubilee Lincoln's signed affidavit and his considerable courage, came through anyway, in the way they walked, in the way they talked, in the way they were. The men realized that something had happened, some breakthrough had been made, and the game was very nearly over, victory in sight. That filled everyone with hope and joy, and even the loss of the heavy automatic weapons and the bulletproof vests and six men seemed not to faze anyone; a general air of lightness and frivolity ensued as they broke down the camp at the Red River Army Depot, loaded up and headed out for the new quarters on the Pettyview chicken ranch.

It helped that the phrase "chicken ranch" was a well-known synonym for whorehouse.

"Hey, we're going to a chicken ranch. Whoo-eee!"

"Bear, would your mama 'low such a thing?"

"Hell, bubba, I was a champeen chicken rassler afore you'se even a glint in your daddy's eye!"

"Boy, the best part of you ran down your mama's leg. Tell you what, you need any help, y'all come to me and I'll show you the ropes."

"Yeah, you guys all talk big, lemme tell you when you get a dose your old dicks gonna swell up like a tire on a hot day. Shoot, saw a feller in Memphis so purple and swoll-up he couldn't get his zipper zipped. Had to walk around with it hanging out. But it was so purple, nobody thought it was a dick; they thought it was some kind of tube or something."

The joshing continued, and someone said to Earl, who was supervising benevolently, "Say, Mr. Earl, we are running low on .45 hardball."

Earl examined the ammunition cache. There was but one case of the .45 hardball left, that is, 1,000 rounds.

"Shit," said Earl. "Well, I doubt we'll need it anyhow."

"Yes sir."

"Lookie here," said Earl, figuring out a scrounger's angle. "I see we got plenty ball tracer we used in the training."

It was true. Four cases of the Cartridge Caliber .45 Tracer M26 remained.

"Look, load up two cases of the tracer in my trunk. Maybe I can work a trade with another agency or something, and lay off the tracer in exchange for some more hardball. Who knows? If we have to, we can always go to tracer, but I don't want to do it inside."

"Yes sir."

"On the 'Canal, I saw ball tracer from an idiot's tommy gun light up a goddamn cane field. It was full of Japs, but if the wind blowed wrong, I know a Marine squad would have been fried up real good."

"Bet you chewed him out, eh, Earl?"

"Hell, boys, couldn't chew him out. That idiot was me!"

They all laughed. It was the first time in anyone's memory that Earl had referred to the war or made fun of himself, a double whammy in the cult of Earl that he had spontaneously created.

D.A. came out of his little makeshift office with a briefcase full of papers, and said, "Y'all ready?"

It seemed they were.

There was a last-minute discussion of routes and timing, for it would be better if everyone arrived later, and after dark, and D.A. told them to keep their lights off as they traveled down the last half mile of dirt road before they reached the farm and not to make the turnoff if there were other cars on the highway.

Each car had an assignment: one would stop for ice, another for groceries and snacks, another for Coca-Colas.

But finally, there was nothing left to do.

"Okay, boys. We'll see you tomorrow," sang D.A., and the little convoy was off.

"Look, that's fine, but something else has come up."

The meeting was at an out-of-the-way ice cream parlor in West Hot Springs, well off the byways of the gambling town. Becker wore his usual suit and had his usual pipe; but this time, besides assorted clerks and functionaries, he had two blunt-faced State Policemen in not so plain clothes as bodyguards.

"Sir," said D.A. patiently, as if explaining to a child, "I'm telling you we can end this thing. We can end it just like we planned. We all agreed very early on that the Central Book was the key. Now we've got a plan that—"

"I heard the plan the first time, Parker. I'm sure it's a fine plan."

"We can do it fast. Our boys are very well trained," said Earl. "They're probably the finest-trained police unit in the country today. We can do it and nobody gets hurt, and it's over. You win. You're the hero. You're the next—"

"Earl," said D.A. sharply.

"Yes sir," said Earl, shutting up.

"The raids still make me uneasy," said Becker. "Too many things can go wrong, too many people can get killed. The community doesn't like the raids. All the killing—it makes people nervous."

"Sir, if you're fighting rats, some rats are bound to die," said D.A.

"Something else has come up."

Earl and D.A. said nothing but exchanged a brief glance.

"A source I trust, not in the police department or the municipal government, says that he was dining with his wife in the Southern Club and he saw Owney with a beautiful woman and a man he recognized from the papers as an Irish mobster called Johnny Spanish."

Earl and D.A. ate their ice cream.

"Sir, there's lots of gangsters come to Hot Springs."

"Not like this one. I made some inquiries. It seems Johnny Spanish—real name John St. Jerome Aloysius O'Malley—is a noted heist expert. An armed robber. He learned his trade in the IRA in the '20s. He specializes in banks and factory payrolls. Very violent, very smart, very tough. He has a crew of four other men, and they do the heavy work but the mob scouts their jobs and puts up the seed money."

The two men were listening numbly. Each by now had an idea where this one was going.

"They say Johnny Spanish was in Hot Springs in 1940. Early October, 1940. Mean anything?"

"The Alcoa payroll job."

"Exactly. So I'm thinking: Owney used Johnny before to raise money for a project—the building of the Southern. Now, you've put a big crimp on Owney financially with your raids. He needs cash to keep operating, to keep up his payments. His empire runs on cash. This would be the *perfect* time for another big job."

"That seems like the sort of thing you'd need a big police operation for," said D.A. "We haven't trained for that kind of operation, Mr. Becker."

"But you have the element of surprise! Now let me finish. I made some discreet inquiries. Alcoa sure isn't coming through Hot Springs anymore, I'll tell you that. But tomorrow night, the Federal Reserve Board is moving over a million dollars in gold up to Fort Knox, in Kentucky, where they're consolidating the gold reserves. They dispersed them during the war, because they thought it was too big a target. A million bucks' worth was moved to the Federal Reserve Bank in New Orleans. Now it's headed back to Fort Knox, under guard of the U.S. Army, and that train is slated to run up the St. Louis & Iron Mountain tomorrow night to Little Rock, where it'll divert to the Memphis & Little Rock and on to Kentucky tomorrow night."

"They're going to stop a train guarded by troops?"

"No. But suppose a bridge would catch fire? You watch. Sometime tomorrow a bridge along the St. Louis & Iron Mountain will catch fire somewhere north of Hot Springs but south of Little Rock. Or some track will be torn up. Or a tunnel will collapse. Something will happen tomorrow. The feds will divert to Hot Springs because it's the biggest yard between New Orleans and Little Rock, and the closest. If that happens, I guarantee you, Johnny Spanish will hit that train, Owney will make a million bucks and he'll go on and on and on."

"You should call the FBI," said D.A. "It's a federal thing. They have the firepower to handle that sort of thing. I still know a few fellas in the Bureau. I'm sure they'd share the credit, Mr. Becker. That could make you look real good."

"Oh, I'd get muscled out. I know how the FBI works. You worked for Hoover. You know what an egomaniac he is."

The dull, pained look on D.A.'s face told the story.

"He's right," he finally said. "They'd push us out and it wouldn't have nothing to do with us. J. Edgar himself would come on down to get in all the pictures."

"Now," said Becker, "look at it this way. If our team does this, brings these fellows down, makes the nab, it has exactly the same effect as closing down the Central Book. Then we can hit the Central Book too, if we have to. But if we get Johnny Spanish and his boys, we link him to Owney, we save the gold, we pin the 1940 Alcoa job on him, just *think* of it!"

Earl said, "I don't like night operations. They're plenty tricky, especially on unknown ground. Everything looks different at night. You got bad communication problems, you have target-marking problems, you have terrain recognition problems. You need perimeter containment, you need experience. Lots of men died at night because their own boys got jittery."

But D.A. responded quickly. "Yes, but Earl, think of the reward. This might be it exactly. This would put us on the map for all time. I can see the look on J. Edgar's face if I showed up on the cover of *Time* magazine. Whoooeee, that chilly bastard would twitch his lips like the strange fish he is and wish to hell he'd gotten there first. Whoooooeee."

Earl saw at that moment his argument was lost. D.A. had connected with the concept in some deep way that called upon his own bitterness and seemed to validate his derailed life. It was the poison of dreams.

"Yes sir," Earl said. "We are short on men."

"I'll call Carlo at his mama's and get him back fast. And hell, I'll go myself. I'm still the best gun in town. Ain't as spry as I once was, but I'm still damned fast."

"That's the spirit," said Fred Becker. "By God, that's the Marine spirit!"

CHAPTER 45

Somewhere along the way, Herman Kreutzer had picked up some expertise in electronics, so he understood Sniperscope M1 right away, and he was the one who talked Johnny Spanish through it, with guidance from War Department technical manual TM 5-9340, classified SECRET! Owney must really have had some juice to come up with something this special this fast.

The system consisted of two units linked by electrical cord: the Carbine, Caliber 30, T3 Modified, which wore the Telescope T-120 jury-rigged by special bridge mount to its receiver, and clamped beneath its forestock the infrared light source, which resembled a headlight, and behind that a plastic foregrip with the lamp trigger switch; and, three feet of cord away, the electrical power supply unit, a large metal box that supported the battery and various vacuum tubes. The whole thing weighed about eighteen pounds, loaded. The scope looked like a thermos jug, the headlamp like, well, a headlamp, and the electrical power supply like a large but utilitarian radio. You couldn't move fast with it, you couldn't maneuver, pivot, twist or switch angles or positions quickly.

"Ah, whoever came up with this gizmo never trekked the alleys of Dublin, that I'll tell you," said Johnny, feeling the heavy weight of the rifle but more peculiarly its awkwardness, for the scope was too large and the lamp completely threw off the balance of the little piece; and the fragility of the connection to the battery housing via the cord made the whole thing even more problematical.

"You'll get the hang of it, Johnny," said Herman, fussing with various switches and consulting the manual. "It's just for sitting in a hole and clipping Japs as they come over the ridgeline thinking everything is hinky-dinky banzai. Okay, I think we're set. Red, get the lights."

Red Brown hit the lights. Jack Bell and Vince the Hat put their cards down. The Maddox warehouse went dark.

"Throw the bolt," said Herman.

Johnny, in the kneeling position, snapped the bolt, lifting a round into the carbine's chamber.

Herman read by flashlight. "Okay, now with your front hand, hit the trigger switch up on the front grip."

Johnny did as he was told.

"By Jesus, it's broken," he said.

"Nah, it's invisible. Invisible to you, to the naked eye. Look through the scope."

Johnny obeyed.

"Nothing."

"Okay, I'm going to try a few of these switches and you keep looking and—"

"My God and sweet Lord," said Johnny. "The blasted thing's glowing like a horror movie. Where's Boris Karloff when you need him?"

"What's it look like?"

"All green."

"What do you see?"

"Hmmm," said Johnny, concentrating. "Why, I see them paint cans you set up."

"Is there a crosshair?"

"Indeed."

"See if you can hit anything."

"Hold your ears, boys."

Johnny loved to shoot and he shot well, as did his whole crew. He babied the carbine, locked it into his shoulder, his other arm braced on his knee, he steadied and waited and then popped off a shot. To his surprise, the carbine fired full automatic; a spray of five bullets launched themselves toward the target in the brief time that Johnny had his finger on the trigger. The burst was sewing-machine fast, a taptaptaptaptap that stunned everybody.

"Yikes," Vince said. "The fuckin' thing's a machine gun."

"It's the M2 carbine," said Herman. "It goes full auto. It's supposed to fire that way. Did you hit anything?"

Johnny looked through the scope again.

"One of them cans is gone. By Jesus, I must have hit the bloody thing."

He fired four more bursts from the curved thirty-round magazine, and in the dark, even with the echo of the shots, they could hear the paint cans tossing and splashing and banging as the bullets tore through them.

"Lights," said Herman.

The lights came on. Johnny had hit all four cans, and the paint, red, exploded out of them, spattering across the corrugated tin walls of the warehouse.

Smoke floated in the air and faraway holes winked as they admitted outside light from the bullet punctures in the tin wall. The stench of burned gunpowder lingered. A red mist floated.

"Looks like bloody Chicago on a St. Valentine's morn," said Johnny.

Much fiddling and experimentation remained. Eventually, Johnny and Herman got the scope zeroed to the point of impact: the infrared lamp had a range of about one hundred yards, but at that range Johnny could put four shots in a target in a second, because his trigger control was so superb and the heaviness of the weapons system dampened the already light recoil of the carbine.

"They got a lot to work on with this thing," said Herman, his brilliance ever practical. "Needs to be lighter, tougher, stronger, with a longer range. They've got to mount it on something more powerful than a puny little carbine. They get it all jiggered up right, goddamn, they are going to have a piece of work!"

"Yeah, well, we can't wait till they get around to that. We go with what we got."

"Johnny, I'm just saying that—"

"Yah, ya big Kraut, you're thinking of them good old days mowing down people with your BAR in the trenches."

"Actually, it was a piece of shit called a Chauchat. Finally we got the BARs but not until—"

"Herman, *concentrate,* you bloody genius, on the night's work. Tomorrow we'll have a nice good visit with them wonderful old days in the AEF, all righty?"

The five men gathered around a plan of the railyard that Owney Maddox had supplied. It helped that they'd worked the same yard exactly six years earlier, although Jack and Vince weren't on the crew then. Quickly enough they came up with a sound plan, based on Johnny's cunning and Herman's sense of infantry tactics.

"We want them in a bunch," said Herman. "We want this over as fast as possible. It can't be a hunt, you know, a goddamn man-on-man running gunfight through the railyard. Get 'em into the zone, let Johnny hose 'em down, move in, mop up, dump a bunch of carbine brass and a few guns, and get the hell out of there. Get our money, go back to Miami."

"Owney'll be there too," said Johnny. "He wants to celebrate the finish."

"Damn, Johnny, that'll slow us down," said Herman.

"But you see, Herman, you smart fella, in this town, Owney owns the coppers. That means they ain't going to be responding to calls from people who hear the gunshots until we're out of harm's way. All right?"

Yes. It was all right.

Johnny Spanish's crew rallied at the deserted railyard canteen at about 10:00 P.M., under cover of dark. They looked like a commando unit, with faces blackened, in blue jeans and dark shirts and watch caps pulled low. They checked the weapons a last time, made sure all magazines were loaded and locked and that they had plenty of quick reloads. Vince had secured one of the larger old one-hundred-round drums for his Thompson 1928 from the Grumleys, who had plenty of drums but no more guns, and was busily cranking the spring—not easy—and inserting rounds to get the thing topped off. Herman and Johnny double-checked the infrared apparatus.

At 10:15, a scuffling announced the arrival of another player, and it was Owney himself, accompanied by his new Best Friend, Frenchy Short. Owney had no long gun, but carried a Luger in a shoulder rig.

"How do you know they'll come from west to east," said Owney. "Maybe they'll set up on the east side of town and come through from that way."

"Uh-uh," said Johnny. "Know why?"

"No."

"The dogs."

"The dogs?"

"All them black families live close up to the track over in the east side nigger section. They all got dogs, and them dogs set up such a racket when they're annoyed. Parker and Swagger are smart boys. They'll know that. They'll come like red Indians, from the west, I tell you. He'll read the land, Swagger will, and he'll see where our government train will have to be and he'll move from west to east, across the gap in the tracks, and that's where we'll hit him. Oh, it'll be a pretty thing. Caught a Brit squad in the open just like this, I did, yes sir, 1924, with me Lewis gun, and you should have seen them feathers fly that night!"

"Yeah, right," said Owney.

"Owney, lad, I'll want you on the flatcar with us. But you stay put once the fun starts, as I don't want to lose track of you and put a hot one between your beauty eyes. What a terrible pity that would be."

"That's encouraging," said Owney, "coming from an Irishman."

"You got any last comments, Judas Junior," Johnny Spanish asked Frenchy.

"The truth is, you should hit Earl first. If Earl goes down, the rest will lose their will to fight. He is the spirit of that unit. Without him, they're just Boy Scouts."

"Odd, but I think I understood that already," said Johnny.

A last watch check: It was now 11:00. The Grumleys had obediently set a bridge afire in Traskwood and the train—it was actually leased, at Owney's insistence, by his great customer, Jax Brewing, of New Orleans, Louisiana—would pull into the railyard around 1:00. Presumably at that time, Earl and his boys would move from their secret quarters and into the railyard, wait for the suggestion of mayhem, and then spring, only to realize in their last horror that they had been sprung.

"Think we'd better be goin', fellas. Good hunting to the lot of you; meet you back here at three and it's champagne for everybody, on his lordship Maddox."

But as Johnny prepared to lead his team out and Owney was consumed in some drama of his own, Frenchy took a moment to speak to the Irish chieftain.

"Yes, lad?"

"Earl? He's—he's actually a—"

"I know, boy. He's a hero. He's the father you never had. Could I cut him some slack? Could I take him in the legs, say? Could I just put him out of action? I've seen the lovesickness in your eyes, boy. But the answer is no, can't do it. As you say, he's the best. Kill the head, the body dies. He has to go first. I'll make it clean. A shame, in another life Earl and Johnny could be the best o' friends, and repair to a pub every night to talk over the gunfights of yore. But no, sonny: he goes first."

"Yeah," he said. "You're right."

"Look at it this way," said Johnny. "Bugsy Siegel has sworn to kill this fine fella. He even sent his girlfriend out just to get the name. Bugsy's still mad. If we don't do it cleanly, Bugs might do it messily. That would be too sad an ending for a hero, eh? At least tonight he goes out like the man he is, a braveheart till the end, no?"

CHAPTER 46

The word came around 5:00; exactly as had been predicted, a bridge had caught fire up near Traskwood, and the St. Louis & Iron Mountain line was shut down until the fire could be put out and the bridge reinforced. All freights were to be diverted over to the Chicago, Rock Island and Pacific lines, which went east and west; a few would be shifted to the Hot Springs railyard.

"That's it," said D.A., getting the news from a messenger sent out by Fred Becker. "We go, then. It's all set. I'd get myself ready now. Becker says that northbound train won't be in until well after midnight, but I want us on site and ready to move well before then."

The men nodded and mumbled; most were glad to be moving out and into the last phase, since the chicken farm, such a joke in the abstract, proved to be a hot, dirty, dusty old place that smelled of hardened chickenshit anyhow, and they were anxious to move onward. Even Carlo Henderson, who'd just showed up that afternoon and hadn't had time to settle in yet, appeared ready to go and didn't need any rest from his journey back.

The teams drove in by different routes, and assembled just west of the railyard and station, on Prospect, behind a grocery store. There was less a need for secrecy this time, because, absent the Thompson submachine guns and the BARs, they were just men in suits with hats, completely nondescript in a town filled with men dressed exactly alike.

Earl checked his Hamilton, saw that it was nearly midnight. They were about a half mile south of fabulous Central, where the clubs and casinos were blazing up the night, so over here it wasn't nearly so busy.

"All right," Earl said. "I want you going out in skirmish teams, two men apiece. Don't go in a mob. Couple teams move on down the block. Don't get caught in the light of the station. Spend a few minutes in the dark and get your night eyes. Go into the yard and about halfway across it there's a little hollow and some open space, under the electric power wires. There's a switching house there, just a little shed, and set there somewhere. That's where we'll rally. We'll hunker up there and wait till the train arrives."

"Earl, suppose they gun the guards?"

"I know if we attack 'em while they've got the guns on the guards they will kill those boys. If we attack 'em before, we got no case and we stop the robbery, but we want a case. So we have to trust they go in and get out fast, and that's when we go. All set?"

They all mumbled assent.

"Anything to say, Mr. Parker?"

D.A., who usually wasn't with them at this point, said only, "You boys listen to Mr. Earl. He's right on this one. I'll be with you the whole way."

"Sure wish I had my tommy gun," Slim said.

"Hell, you couldn't hit nothing with it nohow," someone else said, to some laughter.

"Okay, fellas. Good hunting and be careful. Don't get yourself hurt. Everybody goes home."

They broke down by teams and one by one the teams departed, until only Earl and D.A. were left.

"Well, Earl, you all set?"

"Yes sir."

"Earl, this will work fine. I swear to you."

"I trust you, Mr. Parker."

"Now, Earl, trust me on one last thing."

"Yes sir?"

"When we get to that switching house, and when we get an indicator that there's a robbery going on, I will move out with the boys. I want you and Carlo to stay in the switching house."

"What?"

"You heard what I said."

"What the hell is—"

"Now you listen, Earl. This is going to happen one of two ways. It's going to happen easy or hard. If it happens easy, it's just going to be a matter of 'Stick 'em up, you bastards.' Now if it goes hard, it could be a sticky mess. Then I want you coming in where you can help out the most. You're the only one here with that kind of savvy. And that Henderson kid, he's a rock-solid hand too. So that's what I want you two boys doing."

"Mr. Parker, the boys are used to seeing me up front."

"The boys will be fine, Earl. You have trained the boys well."

"You're just trying to—"

"Earl, this is the way I have figured it out. This is the way I want to do it."

But Earl was worried. He knew the fight would be what it wanted to be, not what D.A. wanted it to be.

Now Frenchy had no place to go. It's the waiting that got to him. Best thing would be to find a whorehouse, get drunk and laid, and wake up tomorrow morning to see how it had gone.

But that wouldn't work. Tomorrow, early, he'd take the bus to Little Rock and from there a plane on to Washington, D.C. The day after, he would go to a well-appointed law firm on K Street where a senior partner named David Wilson Llewelyn would interview him, strictly as a formality. David Llewelyn had served in the OSS during the war and was a close personal friend of a man named Allen Dulles, who had run OSS. He was also a close personal friend of a man called Charles Luciano, recently deported, but a gangster who had made certain the docks ran well in New York during the war. Llewelyn owed Charlie Lucky a favor, particularly when Llewelyn couldn't get the deportation canceled. And Charlie Lucky owed Owney Maddox a favor, for some obscure service years back. Frenchy would be the favor, a prize in a transaction that would satisfy the honor of three important and powerful men, none of whom really gave a shit about Walter H. formerly "Shorty" and now "Frenchy" Short of Williamsport, Pennsylvania.

He felt utterly desolate. He sat in the bar of a place just down from the bus station, a honky-tonk full of smoke and mending GIs on outpatient status from the Army and Navy Hospital, amid girls of somewhat dubious morality and hygiene. He nursed a bourbon, and tried not to see himself in the mirror across the bar. But there he was: a handsome young man in a spattered mirror, very prep-looking, as if he'd just stepped off the Choate campus. Looked younger than his age. Who'd look at such a mild, innocent kid and guess what grew in there? Who knew he had such dark talents, such a twisty, deviant mind, such raw guts, and such a total commitment to himself above all things? You could look at a thousand such boys and never pick him as the one like that.

Frenchy was busy doing something his training would teach him was utterly pointless. He was justifying.

It's not my fault, he was saying to himself. They betrayed me. They did it to me first. They should have fought harder for me. Goddamn that Earl, goddamn him to hell: he knew how good I was and he knew it wasn't my fault I stumbled in the middle of a gunfight and after all I was the one who made everybody look good when I got those two bank robbers who I know were trying to move on me and would have killed me and maybe the whole raid team if I hadn't've stopped them.

His was the gift of self-conviction. In a little while he had reconstructed the past. This new version was much better. In it, he was the secret hero of the team. All the fellas looked up to him. He led all the raids. He got the two bank robbers. But Earl and D.A. were jealous of his success, of his natural heroic style and his cunning and nerve. After all *he* had found the Central Book. So they had to defeat him, destroy him, ruin his chances. The old and the corrupt always tried to destroy the fresh, the energetic, the talented. It happened all the time. It wasn't his fault.

The more he thought about it, the better he felt.

"Anything?" whispered Owney.

He crouched next to Johnny on the flatcar, and crouched behind them, guarding the delicate umbilical between the carbine and the light source, was Ding-Dong.

"I think they're there. I heard something. But I can't see anything yet," Johnny responded.

The only sound was the odd tinkle of running water, as if someone somewhere had left a faucet running. The smell of kerosene, oil and coal filled the air, making it unpleasant to breathe. Odd noises came: the scuttling of rats or possibly hoboes, the movement of yard bulls on their rounds, the clanks as brakemen greased up the journal boxes over the axles. But here, in the center of the yard, it was surprisingly clear: the coaling and watering docks were farther out, on the outskirts.

Johnny Spanish watched through the green glow of the infrared scope. It was strange. The world had been turned inside out, almost like a photographic negative. Light was dark and dark was light, with a crosshair superimposed.

He could see the switching shed, but there was no indication that anything was happening. Because he was looking into a lamp beam, the problem of shadow—though it was green, not black—was disconcerting. He wondered if he should have done more work on the scope, getting a better sense of what was going on in the glowing puzzle that was his night vision through the eyepiece. Could men move into his firing range and he not identify them as men?

No, not really. He could, after all, make out the shape and size of the switching house, could see the little dip behind it, could see the hard steel struts of the power wire pylons. There was no background, because the power of the lamp didn't penetrate that far. He couldn't see what wasn't illuminated, which gave the universe a completely foreshortened perspective, as if the world were but 150 yards deep or so.

"Do you see—"

"Shut up, goddammit! Shut up and be still!" he commanded Owney, who was shaky.

Owney said nothing.

Then, far off, they heard the sound of a train approaching.

"It's time," Johnny whispered softly.

"Ding-dong," said Ding-Dong Bell. "The party's about to start."

CHAPTER 47

Crouched in the dark behind the switching shed, they watched as the train pulled into the yard. It looked like any other train, leaking steam, hissing, groaning, like some kind of large, complex animal. When it finally came to rest, it clanked, snapped, shivered and issued steam from a variety of orifices. A lot of the boxcars said JAX BEER but that meant nothing; trains were thrown together out of all kinds of cars, everybody knew.

In the center of the train there was one long, black car, with lights beaming through from little slots. It looked like some kind of armored car, the exact center of the contrivance, a dark, sealed, menacing blockhouse on wheels.

"That's it," whispered D.A. to Earl.

"Yeah," he said.

It was nearly 2:00 in the morning. Before them for hours had been black nothingness, only the incongruous sound of water running from someplace close at hand, the stench of kerosene. A yard bull had come their way, carrying a lantern, but he was so unconcerned he simply looked into the shed, saw no hoboes hunkered there and moseyed on. But now at last, the train.

"Should we move in?" asked D.A.

"Nah. Wait for them to make a play. It don't mean nothing if you move too early."

"Yeah."

"I'll check the boys."

Earl separated from the old man, and slid almost on his hands and knees along the shallow embankment where each member of the team crouched, low and ready, each man locked in his own private drama.

"Okay?"

"All set, Mr. Earl. You give the signal."

"It'll be a bit yet, you just wait calmly."

"I'm ready."

He gave each man a tap on the shoulder, feeling their aliveness, their vitality. This was it. It would be over after tonight. They all knew it.

The last guy was Carlo.

"You okay?"

"Swell, Mr. Earl."

"Your mama okay?"

"She's fine."

"You get the word from D.A.?"

"Yes sir. But I don't like it much."

"I don't like it much neither but that's what the man says. When the men move out, you head on over to that shed and join up with me. We'll wait and see what happens."

"I got it."

"Good boy."

Earl squirmed back to D.A.

"It's not too late. I can lead 'em. You can come in where *you're* needed."

"No, Earl. This is my party. I've earned this one."

"Yes sir, but—"

Suddenly, a hundred-odd yards away, a door flew open, throwing a slash of light across the yard. There were two quick shots. Figures seemed to scurry back and forth in front of the dark car in the middle of the train, and men climbed in. Another shot sounded.

"Jesus," said D.A.

"That's it," said Earl. "They've done made their move."

"We should go now?"

"I'd give it a few more minutes. Let 'em feel comfortable."

"Yeah."

The door slid closed, and the light went out. Time ticked by, nearly two minutes' worth. Finally, D.A. said, "Okay. Let's do it."

"That's good," said Earl. "You want to be set up when they come out."

Earl scampered down the line.

"Time to move out," he whispered to each man, until he got to the end.

"Come on, Henderson."

"Yes sir," said Henderson.

The men scooched forward, then rose. D.A. was in the lead. Visibility was limited to maybe twenty-five yards at most, but they formed up in good order, a skirmish line with ten feet separating them.

D.A. moved to the center of the line, gave a wave that passed as a sort of signal, and they moved out, crouched, each with his .45 clasped in two hands in front of him, as they had been instructed.

Johnny saw them rise in the green murk.

"Okay," he said.

He felt Owney tense with anticipation.

Now they came. Seven men, like soldiers in the Great War, bent double, moving cautiously across no-man's-land. It reminded him of 1918 and the last big German attack, and the endless killer's ecstasy he'd felt experiencing the delights of the Browning .30 water-cooled, watching the bullets flick out and unleash a storm wherever they struck and in that turbulence knocking the advancing men askew like tenpins, so many of them, and the hot pounding of the gun, the furious intensity of it all, the star shells detonating overhead. This infrared thing: it was his own private star shell.

He tried to pick out Earl. Earl will be in the lead. Earl would be heroic. But the instrument couldn't resolve such details; he could only make out blurs moving with the sure, steady pace of human animation.

"Shoot 'em," hissed Owney as he watched the

carbine barrel tracking ever so gently off Johnny's hold, as the Irishman measured his shots.

But Johnny had nerves of tungsten. That's why he did so well at this business. He let them come onward because he knew that after the first burst, the formation would scatter, and he'd have to track them and take the survivors down running. That meant the further they were from cover, the more time he'd have and the fewer who'd make it back to the switching shed.

He let them come on another minute. Then another. It had a curious, almost blasphemous intimacy to it. The men felt unobserved, he could tell, secure in their darkness. Now and then they'd halt and gently regroup and at odd moments in this process they'd strike poses so bored and languid and unselfconscious, it was as if he were observing them in the shower.

"Shoot, fer Chrissakes!" barked Owney, as the pressure of the stalk proved too heavy for his more brutal and direct style of gangstering.

"Now, now, boyo," crooned Johnny, "just another bloody second. I think I've got the leader all picked out."

It was the bigger fellow in the middle, a drooping, long-armed hulk of a man, who led the boys onward, a little ahead of them. That would be Earl, of course. He was so large. Odd that he'd be so large; the kid had never said he was a large man, but just a fast, tough one, sinewy and quick and raw.

He found his position, and the leader stepped into the crosshairs.

Now, he thought.

They walked slowly through the dark, seeing the train ahead of them in the dark, its flanks illuminated so slightly by the vagrant incandescence of Central Avenue far away, but filling the horizon with light.

There was no movement from the train. Whatever was transpiring was transpiring in silence. These guys were good: very professional, D.A. was thinking.

He glanced to either side, and could see the boys nearest to him and beyond that make out the shape of the boys further away. He was aiming to rally in the hitch of the armored car to the car behind it, then send two men down to the other end, and in that way set up a crossfire. He'd have one or two boys actually under the car too, in case Johnny's men tried to duck out that way. Those boys could nail them easily. He was quite willing to kill all of Johnny's boys. He knew in this business that you had to commit to killing early and stay committed. If you poisoned your mind with notions of mercy, it would cost you a moment's hesitation and that could destroy you in a flash. When the guns came into play, shoot fast, shoot well, shoot a lot: those were the rules.

They were so close now.

The line disappeared or at least got so indistinct Earl could not pick it out against the slight illumination of the train a hundred yards off. There was a sense of blur, of disturbance to the atmosphere, but that only.

"They're going to be okay, I think," said the boy. "They're almost there. It's looking—"

Five short bursts fired so fast it sounded unreal. In the clear part of his brain, Earl made the numb note that somebody had extremely good trigger control and that the weapon's signature had an aching familiarity to it, something he knew so very well, and a fraction of a second later he identified it as an American carbine. But that part of his mind was very far away from the other part of his mind, which was hot and shocked and full of anger and fear and terror at once.

Ambush.

Perfectly sprung, perfectly set up, brilliantly planned.

Again the carbine: short, precise bursts, obviously an M2.

"Jesus, Earl," the boy said, and made a move to run to the aid of his friends. But Earl's first move was to grab the boy and haul him to earth.

"Stay," he hissed, for even though he had yet to articulate it in any meaningful fashion, a number of anomalies struck him at once. Why was the fire so precise? At night it was almost always a question of area fire, sweeping and intense; or it involved a star shell, throwing its illumination across the terrain, so that targets could be marked. Neither of these night-action features presented themselves and though, like the boy, he had a longing to run to the wounded he knew too that to do so was simply to enter the killing zone as defenseless as they.

And now he cursed the lack of a long gun. What he needed, he saw in a flash, was the BAR now locked in the State Police arsenal in Little Rock. With that powerful instrument he could suppress the battlefield, drive the shooters to cover, get his people a chance to get back.

"We need to—"

"No," Earl exploded, "you follow on me."

And with that Earl ran not to the killing zone, but rather to the switching shed, and set up a good supported kneeling position behind it, with just his head and shoulders and the pistol in a good two-handed position.

His ears found the zone and in a second a flash located the position. He could barely see his front sight, but he cranked up a good ten feet from the source of the fire, for he had to throw rounds in long arcs to get them there.

But it was a guessing game. He didn't know where you held to bring a .45 slug onto target from an unknown distance of about a hundred or so yards.

He fired, seven times quickly, put the gun down, and took Carlo's, who, smart as usual, had immediately understood the gist of it, and had prepared his own weapon for Earl, who then, with it, proceeded to lay out another magazine, exactly as Carlo inserted another magazine into the empty gun.

It wasn't much, but from far off came the splatter of shots hitting and kicking up dust and metal fragments, and maybe in that noise a kind of a sound of scurry or discomfort.

Earl had it now, and knew what would come next. He withdrew, knowing that he had but seconds. The boy was baffled.

"What are you—"

Again the carbine snapped out a short burst, and the astonishment came in where the bullets struck. Not near them, but exactly where they had fired from. Three bullets bit into the wood of the switching shed in exactly the location of Earl's foray, and three more spat across the dirt, kicking up clouds and filling the air with gun spray.

"Jesus!" said the boy.

"He can *see!*" croaked Earl. He thought for a second, realized he was zeroed in some sense. But he also figured the gunman would guess he'd move to the other side of the switching house. He didn't. He moved back to exactly where he'd been, took a sight picture, fired to the same point, and withdrew. A burst answered him, and he thought that was the last time that would work.

But next they heard a terrible groaning sound, and two figures spilled into the hollow just behind them. It was D.A., blood on his face, supported pitifully by the husky Slim.

"They done kilt us!" said Slim, and at that moment he made the mistake of rising too high out of the hollow as he addressed Earl, for three bullets popped dust, blood and hair off his head and he pitched forward.

Johnny watched them come, wondered briefly if he should try and hit the leader first but then decided they would scatter at the first shot and that he'd get more of them by going from right to left. He watched the man furthest from him come, settled into his rhythm, tracked him.

It was dead quiet.

He squeezed the trigger and a three-round burst pierced the night. The muzzle spewed burning gas brilliantly but on the scope the flashes registered only as interference across the bottom; he pivoted slightly and in less than half a second fired another squirt, then another, and then another.

It was not like killing.

It seemed to have nothing to do with killing. It was like some kind of ghastly fun, a game, to put the reticle of the sight on forms that had been reduced only to the green light of their heat, squirt them, feel the gentle shudder of the weapon and watch as they seemed to collapse into themselves.

By the time he got to the leader, that fellow had figured out what was going on. It couldn't have been but a second or two. He fired, and the bullets were off mark, one out of three hitting, he knew, by the way the man fell. He was about to squirt him again when another man came into the scope; he diverted and fired again. A hero. Running to his fallen boss! Johnny liked that loyalty in a man, any man, even this man, as he killed him.

Now it was mopping up.

The living had fallen to the ground, presumably confused over the weird accuracy of their antagonist, but still believing themselves to be safe in the dark. They didn't know they were flanked on two sides, or that two more gunners from the train would be moving on them, with instructions to circle around behind, trapping them completely in the hollow behind the switching shed, toward which their own instincts would dictate that they retreat.

He hunted and found a crawler in the dark.

The three-bullet burst centered the boy perfectly, kicking a spray of dust from his coat as the bullets skewered him. Another was intelligently moving not to the rear but to the extreme right, having figured that gunmen would cover the rear. Another good man; with pity in his heart, but not mercy, Johnny took this lad too.

"Are you getting them?" asked Owney, an idiot who wanted a report in the middle of a battle.

"In spades, bloody spades, boyo," he said, and veered back to the center, where the fallen, wounded leader must be. Another boy was now attending to the leader, one he'd probably missed.

Ah, now you two and the night's work is done, thought Johnny.

But detonations suddenly erupted too near them, with the sprang of bullets on metal, and worse, the spray of spattered lead, which lashed out and made them wince.

"By Jesus!" said Johnny.

"Where the fuck did *that* come from?" Owney said. "I think he hit me."

"Nah, he's shootin' from far off, you just felt a whisper of tiny fragments. Stay cool, buster."

The rounds had hit on the flatcar bed a good twenty feet from them, but enough to distract.

Johnny looked into the gloom and through the darkness could only see the flashes far off, in the lee of the switching shed. These seven rounds, however, hit a bit closer, kicking up their nasty commotion but ten feet away.

"He sees us!" said Owney.

"Not a bit of it! He's shootin' blind, the bastard," said Johnny, returning to the scope. He put the reticle on the last flash and tripped a six-round burst. The bullets struck dead on, lifting dust from the ground, pulling puffs of debris from the wood of the house.

"I may have got him," he crowed. "Right in the gizzard."

But he reasoned that the boy, if not hit, would move to the other side of the switching house, so he pivoted slightly, found that locality in his sight. The image was not so distinct as it was at the very limits of the infrared lamp, but he knew it was good enough to shoot. But the next seven shots came from the same side as the first fourteen, and he knew the fella had outguessed him. He pivoted back, saw nothing, but then a flash of motion. Something had slithered into the hollow behind the switching house and in a second, as if on cue, a boy rose, and Johnny potted him, three-round burst, head shots all.

"By Jesus, got another!"

"Is that all of 'em?"

"No, there's one, maybe two more at the shed. They don't even suspect that where they are now there's men all about them, ready to open up on command."

"Let's finish it."

"Give 'em a moment to think. They'll realize they're fooked, then they'll make a break and me boys will do them good and it'll be over. There's no place for them to go, except into the ground."

"You can't hit them from here?"

"From this range I doubt these little carbine bullets can carry into that shed. Herman's Browning rifle will make Swiss cheese of it, though, and de Palmo's Thompson should write an exclamation point to the night's fun."

The three men lay on the bottom of the switching shed, curled around the big levers that controlled the track linkages, breathing heavily.

"Oh, Christ," said D.A. "Oh, Jesus H. Christ, they had us nailed. They ambushed us perfectly, the bastards. Oh, Christ, all those boys, Earl, Earl, I lost all those boys, oh, Jesus forgive me, all those poor boys, such *good* boys, oh—"

"Shut up, Mr. Parker," said Earl. "Think about here and now!"

"He's hit bad," said Carlo. "He's losing blood fast. We've got to get him to a hospital or he'll bleed out."

"There's always a lot of blood. Stanch the wound. Apply pressure. It'll coagulate. If he's still kicking and he ain't in shock, he's got some time yet."

"Yes sir."

"Earl, they had us."

"Yes sir, I *know* they had you."

"What're we going to do?" asked the boy.

"Hell if I know."

"We could fall back on the low crawl."

"Nah. This old man can't crawl none. And they got boys on each side of us, and probably behind us by now. He ain't no dummy, whoever done put this thing together. The bastard."

"Earl, I am so sorry for getting all them boys killed."

"It's a war. War ain't no fun at all, sir," said Earl.

Carlo said, "We low on firepower too."

"Yes I know," said Earl, and reached to see if the old man still had his .45 but he didn't. He did have two full magazines in his coat pocket, however.

Earl calculated quickly. He'd fired three magazines, meaning twenty-one rounds were gone. He had one left, the boy had two left, and the old man two. That's thirty-five rounds in five magazines, with two pistols.

Shit, he thought. We are cooked.

"What're we going to do, Earl?"

"*I don't know!* Goddammit, I am thinking on it."

"We could split up, go in two ways. One of us ought to make it. We get cops and—"

"They ain't no cops coming," said Earl. "Don't you get that? They'd be here by now. This is it. This is all there is. And don't you get it yet? He can see in the dark."

"Earl I am so sorry about them boys I—"

"Shut up, the two of you, and let me think."

Above them, the wall on the left-hand side of the shed exploded, spewing fragments, high-velocity dust, and twenty .30 caliber bullets in a kick-ass blast, which went clean through and blew twenty neater holes in the right-hand side of the wall. The noise banged on their eardrums till they rang like firebells. The smell of pulverized wood filled the air, mingling with the kerosene and the oil.

"Browning," said Earl. "He's about twenty-five yards away over on the left. He can cut us to ribbons if he's got enough ammo."

"Oh, Christ," said Carlo. "I think we bought it."

"Not yet," said Earl. "Not—"

Another BAR magazine riddled the wall, this time six inches lower. A few of its shots spanged off the potbellied stove.

Then a voice called out.

"Say chums, we can finish you anytime." It was Owney, not far away, with that little twist of fake English gent in his words. "You throw your guns out, come on out hands high, and you can leave. Just get out of town and don't ever come back, eh? That's all I'm asking."

"You step out," said Earl to his companions, "and a second later you're dead."

"I'll give you a minute," said Owney. "Then I'll finish you. Make the choice, you bold fellows, or die where you stand."

But Earl was rummaging around in the shed. To Carlo he seemed a man obsessed. He cursed and ranted, pushing aside lanterns and crowbars and gloves, standing even, because he knew the BAR man wouldn't fire as the minute ticked onward until at last—

"Ah!" he said, sinking back down to the ground with a handful of something indeterminate in the dark.

"Now you listen up and you listen up good. Henderson, load up them .45s and get 'em cocked and locked."

Johnny dumped a magazine, even though it had a few rounds left, and snapped in a fresh one so he'd have plenty of ammo.

He went back to the scope.

In the green murk, he saw nothing except the outline of the switching shed sitting atop the little hollow. Some dust seemed to float in the air on the side where Herman had hammered two BAR magazines into it, but otherwise it was motionless.

"Maybe they're all dead," Owney said.

"They ain't dead," said Johnny. "That I guarantee you. No, they're in there like rats in a trap, snarling and trying to figure how to flee."

Owney checked his watch.

"You said a minute. You gave 'em two."

"I did," said Owney. "But I want 'em out. I want 'em found outside, not inside."

Once again he rose and yelled.

"I'm telling you for the last time. Come out and surrender or get shot to pieces in that shed."

The gunfire had provoked the dogs all through the Negro district and their barking filled the air. But no sirens screamed and it seemed as if the universe had stalled out, turned to stone. It seemed darker too, as if the townspeople, hearing the firing, had done the wise thing, turned out their lights, and gone into cellars. No yard bulls or brakemen showed; they too conceded the yard to the shooters, and presumably had fallen back on the control tower or the roundhouse for shelter from the bullets.

"I'm going to give the order to fire," Owney screamed.

"We're coming out!" came a voice.

"Now there's a helpful fella," said Johnny.

He bent into the scope and saw two men emerge, one supporting the other, their hands up. Then a third. The third would be the dangerous one. He put the scope on him, and his finger went against the trigger and—

Exploding green stars!

Brightness, intense and burning!

The hugeness of fire!

He blinked as the scope seemed to blossom in green, green everywhere, destroying his vision, and he looked up from it blinking, to see nothing but bright balls popping in his eyes as his optic nerves fired off, and heard the sound of gunfire.

"He's got night vision, see?" Earl said.

"Earl, ain't nobody got night vision," said D.A. "Talk some sense."

"No, he's got a thing called *infrared.* Some new government thing. They used it on Okinawa. I heard all about it. You can *see* in the *dark.* That's how he makes them good shots. That's how come he head-shoots Slim from a hundred yards in pitch dark. He can see us."

"Shit," said Carlo.

"Now, way that stuff works, it sees heat. Your heat. It shines a light that only he can see. A heat light. But it sees all heat, or all light."

"Yeah?"

"So here's the deal. I give the signal, I'm going to light this batch of flares. In his scope, it's all going to white. He ain't going to see nothing for a few seconds. Then I'm going to lean around the back and keep that BAR boy down with a gun in each hand, fast as I can shoot."

"Earl—"

"You shut up and listen. You take the old man and you run to the sound of the water. You hear that water?"

Yes: the faint tinkle of water, not too far off.

"That water. That's where Hot Springs Creek goes underground. It runs the whole length of Central Avenue underground, about two miles' worth. You and the old man, you get in there and you keep going till you find a door. It's the secret get-out for a lot of places, and the bathhouses drain into it too. You get in there, you get in public and you get the hell out of here."

"What about you, Earl?"

"Don't you no nevermind about me. You do what I say. Here, I want you to take this crowbar too."

He held up a crowbar he'd scrounged.

"There'll be a boy out there, waiting for you. You should see him, his eyes should be blinded by the flares. You have about a second, you throw this bar and you smash him down, then you run on by to the culvert and you are out of here."

"Earl, how do you know about that culvert?"

"*Goddammit!* You don't worry about that, you do what I say."

Owney cried again.

"I'm telling you for the last time. Come out and surrender or get shot to pieces in that shed."

The two of them got the old man to his feet, keeping well away from the window. They came to lodge against the doorway, just a second from spilling out.

"Now are you ready? You ready, old man? I'm going to light these flares and —"

"I'm going to give the order to fire," Owney said.

"We're coming out!" screamed Carlo.

"Good," said Earl. "Look away, don't look into the flares. I'm going to light these things, then you hand me the guns and—"

"He hands the guns to me, Earl," said D.A. "I can't run nowhere. I got nowhere to run. Give me them pistols, boy."

"No!" said Earl.

"I'm *ordering* you, Henderson. Earl, light them damn things. Son, give me the pistols 'afore I pass out. You go, goddamn you, and don't you look back."

Carlo didn't think twice. He handed the two pistols to D.A., who lunged a little away from him and halfway out the door and seemed to find his feet, however wobbly.

"You old bastard," said Earl. "You go down and we'll be back for you."

"You do it, goddammit!" said the old man.

"Shit," said Earl, and yanked five pieces of tape

in rapid succession, which lit the flares. He felt them hiss and burn and their explosive heat. But his eyes were closed, he didn't look into them, he edged to the door and then dumped them on the ground.

"Run!" he commanded, but Carlo was already gone. He followed, and he had a sensation of the old man spinning in the other direction, and he heard the .45s blazing, one in each hand, fastfastfastfast, the old man fired and as Earl ran he saw in the glow a man rising with a tommy gun but slowly, as if blinded himself and Carlo threw the crowbar from ten feet with surprising grace and accuracy and the heavy thing hit the gunman in the chest and hurt him badly so that he stepped back and fell.

The boy ran on and Earl ran too, out of the glow, and they heard the heavy blast of the BAR and answering shots from D.A.'s .45s.

Suddenly it was a dirt blizzard. Around them erupted fragments, dust and debris as the carbine gunner got onto them, and the boy stumbled but Earl was by him, had him, and pulled him down into the stream.

They heard the BAR. They heard the .45s. They heard the BAR. They heard no more .45s.

"Come on," said Earl. "Come on, Bobby Lee. You got to go *now!* It don't matter that it hurts, you got to go *now,* with me."

And Earl had the boy and was pulling him along, in the dark, through the low tunnel.

"Did you get them?" asked Owney.

"I think two got down in some kind of ditch. The one out back, Herman finished him."

"Shit," said Owney. "They'd better not get away. Goddammit, they better not get away. If one got away, you know which one it was."

Johnny yelled. "Herman, lad, circle around and see where them boys gone. You other fellas, you converge on the shed. We're coming ourselves."

Getting the cumbersome apparatus off the flatcar was not an easy thing but with Jack Ding-Dong doing the labor, they managed. Then Jack carried the heavy battery unit, and Johnny walked ahead with the rifle, scanning through the scope. Owney was just behind.

"On the right," said Johnny, and Owney looked and saw a Jayhawker, just a young kid, lying spread out on the ground, his dark suit sodden with blood.

"They're all over the goddamned place. We done a good night's work, we did," said Johnny.

"Over here," yelled Herman.

They walked on, past poor Vince the Hat de Palmo, who was conscious again, in the ministrations of Red Brown, though he gripped his chest as if he'd been hit by a truck there.

"Them flares blinded me," he said to Johnny.

"There, there, lad," said Johnny. "They blinded me too."

At last they reached a culvert, saw the water glittering through it.

"That's where the bastards went. Trust a rat to find a hole. Where does this go?"

"Under the streets," said Owney. "Goddamn. Goddamn, the cowboy got away."

"But he's running scared, probably hurt. He's no problem, Owney. Not for a time. He'll mend, he'll come for you. We'll find him first and put him down. Damn, he's as sly a dog as they come, isn't he? How in Jesus' name did he know of this culvert?"

"I know what I'll do," Owney said. "I'll call the police."

"Johnny, Johnny?"

"What is it?"

"He's still alive."

"Who's still alive?"

"The old man."

"Jesus Christ," said Owney, turning.

He walked with Johnny quickly back to the shed. In the hollow behind it, the old man had fallen. He lay soaked in his own blood, jacking and twitching with the pain. Herman must have hit him five times, and Johnny two or three times before that. But the gristly old bastard wouldn't die.

"He's a tough boyo," said Johnny.

The old man looked up at them, coughed up a red gob, then looked them over.

"So you're the fellows done this work? Well, let me tell you, Earl will track you down and give you hell on earth before you go to God's own hell."

"You old turkey buzzard, why don't you hurry and die," said Owney. "We don't have all night for your yapping."

"Owney, I marked you for scum the first time I laid eyes on you and I ain't never wrong about such things."

"Yes, but how come then I'm the man with the gun, eh, old man? How come you're lying there shot to pieces, bleeding out by the quart?"

"Takes a lot to kill me," the old man said. Then he actually smiled. "And maybe you don't have enough pecker-heft to get it done."

Owney leaned over him and shot him in the forehead with his Luger like a big hero.

CHAPTER 48

They ran crouching through the darkness and in a bit of time the slight illumination of the opening disappeared as the underground course of the stream turned this way or that.

"Jesus, I can't go on," moaned Carlo.

Earl set him down, peeled back his coat and his shirt. The carbine bullet had blown through him high in the back and come clean out the front. He bled profusely from each wound.

Earl tore the boy's shirt, and wadded a roll of material into each hole, the entrance and the exit, as the boy bucked in pain and tossed his head. With the boy's tie, he tied a loop tightly that bound the two crude bandages together. With his own tie, he quickly hung a loop around the boy's neck, to make a crude sling.

"Let's go."

"God, Earl, I'm so damned tired. Can't you go and get help while I rest?"

"Sonny, they will see you when you can't see them and they will kill you. If you stay, you die. It's that simple."

"I don't think I can."

"I know you can. You ain't hit that bad. Someone has to survive to talk for them boys that didn't. Someone's got to remember them boys and what they did and how they was betrayed."

"Will you pay them back, Earl? Will you get them?"

"Damned straight I will."

"Earl, don't. D.A. didn't want you in trouble. D.A. loved you, Earl. You were his son. Don't you get that? If you go down, then what he did don't mean a thing."

"Now you're talking crazy."

"No, no," said the boy. "He sent me to investigate you 'cause he was worried you had a death wish. And then when I found out about your daddy, he told me to get back and not say nothing about it."

"I don't know what you're talking about, but you're wasting your breath. My daddy's been dead a long time."

"Your daddy just died a minute ago and his last wish was that you live and have a happy life, which you have earned."

"You just shut that yap now, and come on."

"Earl, I'm so tired."

"Bobby Lee, you—"

"I'm not Bobby Lee, Earl. I'm Carlo Henderson. I ain't your little brother, I'm just a deputy."

"Well, whoever you are, mister, you ain't staying here."

With that Earl pulled him to his feet, and pushed him along through the hot, sloppy water in the darkest darkness either of them had ever seen.

Hot Springs Creek was a sewer and a drain. It smelled of shit and dirty bathwater and booze and blood. As they sloshed along, they heard the skitter of rats. There were snakes down here, and other ugly things that lived under whorehouses and fed on the dead. Maggots and spiders, broken glass, rotting timbers, all lightless and dank, with the stench of bricks a century old and the banks a kind of muddy slop that could have been shit.

"How much further, Mr. Earl?"

"Not much. I don't hear 'em trailing."

"I don't neither."

"That goddamned infrared gizmo was probably too heavy to carry along down here, now that I think about it."

"Earl, how'd you know of this place?"

"Shut up. Don't be talking too much. Another couple of hundred feet and we'll begin to think about getting out."

"Getting out?"

"Yeah. You'll never make it if we go all the way to the other end. You'll bleed out. It's another mile and a half ahead. But all the speakeasies, the baths, all them places got secret exits, just in case. We'll get through one of them."

"Earl, I am so tired. So goddamned tired."

"Henderson, I don't b'lieve I ever heard you swear before."

"If I get out of here I am going to swear, smoke a cigarette and have sexual intercourse with a lady."

"Sounds like a pretty good program to me. I might join you, but I'd add a bottle of bourbon to the mix. And I don't drink no more."

"Well, I ain't ever had no sexual intercourse."

"You will, kid. You will. That I guarantee you."

He pulled the boy out of the water and up the muddy bank, where he found a heavy wooden door. It seemed to be bolted shut. The boy sat sloppily in the mud, while Earl got out his jackknife and pried at a lock, and in a bit old tumblers groaned and he pulled the thing open two feet, before it stuck again.

He got the boy up, and the two of them staggered

onward through a chamber, up into a cellar, around boxes and crates, and upstairs, and then came out into corridors. The temperature suddenly got very hot, and they bumbled toward a light ahead, and pushed through a door, and found themselves in a moist hot fog with apparitions.

"Get a doctor, get a doctor!" Earl hollered, but what he heard was screams as shapes ran by him, scattering in abject panic, which he didn't quite understand, until a naked old lady with undulating breasts ran by him.

He fell to clean tiles which he soiled with the slop on his shoes and pants as other women ran by, screaming.

And then a policeman arrived, gun drawn.

"Get this boy to a hospit—" he started, but the cop hit him, hard, in the face with the pistol barrel, filling his head with stars and pain, and he was aware that others were on him, pinning him. He heard the click as the handcuffs were locked about his pinioned wrists. Then someone hit him again.

CHAPTER 49

Earl lay in the city jail. No one interviewed him, no one asked him any questions, no one paid him any attention. They let him shower, and gave him a prison uniform to wear, and took his suit out for cleaning. He seemed to just brood and smoke and had trouble sleeping. Late one night, a decent bull who'd been a Marine led him from a cell into an anteroom and let him call his wife, to tell her, once again, he had survived.

"I knew," she said. "They didn't have your name in the papers with those other poor boys."

"That's the one thing they got right, then."

"All those boys, Earl," she said.

"It was just so wrong," he said.

"Earl, come home. That is the devil's own town. You've given it every last thing and what's it got you?"

"Nothing."

"Earl, it's not worth it."

"No, it's not. It never was. All them boys gone."

"Earl, you can't think about that. It'll kill you."

"I know. I should think of other things: how's that baby?"

"Kicking a bit. A little kicker, if you ask me."

"I'm coming home as soon as I can, sweetheart. I will be there when it comes."

"I know you will or die trying," she said.

He watched it play out in the newspapers over the next few days. He thought he was beyond surprise, but even he had trouble believing what came next. The *New Era* had it thus:

JAYHAWKERS AMBUSH SELVES
Seven Die in Railyard Mixup

Members of the Prosecuting Attorney's special raid team evidently got in a gunfight amongst themselves in darkness last night in the Missouri and Pacific Railyard.

Seven men were killed, including D. A. Parker, 65, a legendary FBI agent who shot it out at one time with the gangster chieftains of the '30s.

Sources indicate that Parker was the leader of the unit, known in local parlance as "Jayhawkers," after the Kansas brigands that bedeviled Hot Springs before the Civil War.

"I am exceedingly disappointed in Mr. Parker," said Fred C. Becker, Garland County Prosecuting Attorney. "He was a man of experience but evidently in his advanced age, his mind began to deteriorate and he made a number of bad judgments. Night operations are tricky, as I learned firsthand in Italy in the United States Army. I will forever hold myself responsible for my lack of foresight in not replacing him with more rational personnel. I feel the pain of this loss immensely. And I take full responsibility."

Sources gave this account of the night's events.

Acting on a tip, Parker took his unit to the railyard, where he suspected a train robbery, similar to the Alcoa Payroll Job of 1942, was being engineered.

In the darkness, his men got separated. For some reason, one of them fired and all the others began to fire at indistinct targets.

When it was over, seven men, including Parker, lay dead.

The state papers in Little Rock were kinder, but only a little bit. In all, that seemed the verdict: an idiotic D. A. Parker leading his little ragtag band into the railyard on a fool's errand, where out of sheer stupidity it self-combusted. The Jayhawkers had killed themselves.

Earl knotted the rag up into a ball and tossed it across the cell. He lay all day and night. It was not unlike the war. He just stared at a numb patch of ceiling, trying to work out what had happened and why. He tried not to think of the boys and the brief spurts of fire that took them down so neatly, and how well planned, how ingenious the whole thing was. He tried to exile the grief he felt for the good young men and the rage he felt for Becker and Owney Maddox and this Johnny Spanish, the professional bank robber, who must have set the whole thing up.

He tried so very hard, and he tried hard not to think of the mute coffins, lined up and shipped without ceremony back to their points of origin.

On the third day, he was taken from the cell into a little room, and there discovered not Fred C. Becker but Becker's head clerk, a ferrety little man with eyeglasses named Willis O'Doyle.

"Mr. Swagger?"

"Yeah. Where's Becker?"

"Mr. Becker is working on important cases. He could not attend."

"That bastard."

"Mr. Swagger, attacking Mr. Becker verbally will not do you any good in this room."

"Am I being charged with anything?"

"No. Not if you cooperate."

"Jesus Christ, he gets seven men who fought and bled for him killed and I'm supposed to cooperate?"

"Mr. Becker is as upset as you at the outcome of the action. But he feels with more effective leadership from Mr. Parker and yourself this could have been avoided."

O'Doyle looked at him with placid ideologue's eyes, unaware, uninterested.

"Mister, you don't know much about things, do you?"

"Be that as it may, Mr. Swagger, I am here to inform you that the governor of the state of Arkansas has today officially required that the prosecuting attorney's special raid team officially cease to exist. Mr. Becker has decided to comply with that order. A news release to that effect will be put out this afternoon."

"He can still win, you know. He can still hit the Ohio, even with just a few state cops, close it down, and put it to Owney Maddox."

"I don't think Mr. Becker is interested in further dangerous activities, especially in the downtown area."

"He's given up."

"Sir, it does you no good to assail Mr. Becker."

"If he doesn't do something, he's a loser. He's gone. Nobody'll ever elect a quitter to anything in this state. It's the South, for God's sakes."

"Mr. Swagger, the city attorney was going to indict you on charges of malicious mischief, discharging a firearm within city limits, leaving the scene of an accident, and breaking and entering for that little trick of crashing into the Fordyce. You're lucky he didn't include pandering and sexual deviancy for entering the women's bathing area!"

O'Doyle was a prude; his little face knitted up in distaste.

"But Mr. Becker interceded in your behalf. All charges will be dropped against you and Mr. Henderson. The condition is that you sign a statement acknowledging the events in the railyard three nights ago, and leave town immediately, and never come back. This offer is on the table for the next ten minutes. Mr. Becker wants you gone. Gone forever, so that he can begin the healing. He has many more steps to make on his journey."

Earl just looked at him with contempt. Becker had made some kind of peace with the city, with, presumably, Owney. It was all to be covered up.

"What kind of investigation did they make at the crime scene?"

"It was never considered a crime scene, but an accident scene. The Hot Springs city police cordoned it off, and set about to provide medical help. Unfortunately, so well trained was your team that all the bullets were fatally placed. Seven men were declared DOA. It's been a very bloody summer."

"You could pull that one to pieces with ten minutes' worth of investigation. Did they take up shell casings? Did they do forensics on the bodies? Did they talk to witnesses who heard different kinds of gunfire? Did they even find carbines in the area? Our carbines were taken away, along with every other long gun and our vests. How could we have shot each other with carbines if we didn't have no carbines—"

"I am assured that several carbines were recovered on site, Mr. Swagger. You had better get used to the idea that this is over, and that the best thing for you to do is leave the county and begin again elsewhere. I've spoken to Mr. Henderson. He's seen the wisdom in our suggestion."

"I don't know why you bastards always turn on the men you pay to do your killing for you," Earl said. "But that's the way it happens."

"You understand, you are also forbidden from making contact with Mr. Becker, from speaking to journalists or publishing an account of these events, of publicly identifying yourself as a member of what the newspapers called the Jayhawkers?"

Earl looked at him.

"You are also officially warned that any attempt at misguided vengeance against those you perceive as culpable in this case will be considered a willful violation of this agreement and the law as well, and you will be prosecuted aggressively and to the full extent of our resources. You are to leave town quickly, quietly and completely. You are never to set foot in Garland County again. Your ten minutes are almost over, sir."

Earl just shook his head.

"Mr. Swagger, this isn't merely the best deal you'll get, it's the only deal you'll get. I'd sign off on it, get out of town and get about my life's work, whatever that may be."

"He's just going to write all them boys off?"

"Mr. Swagger, I have other appointments. If this document is not signed in the next three minutes, I will direct the city attorneys to begin legal proceedings against you. With a wife on the verge of a baby, I don't think you want to spend the next few weeks in jail while this thing is painfully sorted out. By the way, your badge, which was in your effects, has been confiscated and destroyed. Furthermore, as you are no longer a bonded officer of law enforcement, you have lost the right to carry a concealed weapon. Sir, I would sign and vanish as fast as possible."

Earl's bull rage suggested to him that he ram the little man's skull against the wall, but he saw what paltry good that would do, and after he smoked a cigarette, he signed the goddamn thing, feeling as if he'd just sold out his oldest and best friends.

"Oh, and one last thing, Mr. Swagger. You will be billed seventy-five cents for the dry cleaning of your suit and tie and the laundering of your shirt and socks."

CHAPTER 50

Becker would see nobody. He canceled all appointments. He sat alone in his office, contemplating his ruin. Of course he lacked the nerve for suicide, and he enjoyed the self-pity too much sober to blur it with alcohol, so he simply stared out the window, sucked on his pipe, and blew huge clouds of aromatic smoke into the air.

Why did I ever try this idiocy? he thought.

What possessed me?

Am I merely stupid or am I colossally ignorant?

The newspapers were really piling on. Even his nominal allies in Hot Springs were distancing themselves from him. He'd been made to look like a bloody buffoon and now Owney would be bigger than ever.

It had all vanished: governor in '48, the youngest ever in the state's history. Maybe the Senate then. Maybe the national ticket. There is nothing more intensely bitter than a fantasy that has sustained one for a decade suddenly being snatched away and crushed by reality. How could he daydream now? How could he settle back in the minutes before sleep and see himself exalted, vindicated, loved, propelled ever onward on good looks, charm and sheer affability? Postwar America was going to take off like a rocket; television was going to rule and that would give the advantage to handsome men; there would be change everywhere, as the young replaced the old, as a new order took over for an old one.

And he had lost.

He would not be part of it.

It seemed so unfair.

He loaded another ton of tobacco into his pipe and forgot himself in the intricacy of the ritual for a while, then finally got everything tamped and squashed in just right, and lit a match and drew in the firecrackly explosion of dense heat. In that alone there was pleasure.

The door opened.

"Mr. Becker?"

"I told you I didn't want to be disturbed."

"It's your wife."

"I can't talk to her."

"It's the tenth time she's called."

"I don't care. Leave me alone."

"What about the two o'clock staff meeting?"

"Cancel it."

"What about your meetings with the mayor and the chamber of commerce?"

"Cancel them."

"What about the newspaper people? The waiting room is full of them. The columnists have tried to bribe me. They're annoying everybody and some of them don't flush the toilet when they're done with it."

"I issued a statement. I have nothing further to add."

"Yes sir. Would you like a glass of water or some coffee or something?"

"No."

"Mr. O'Doyle is back."

"I don't want to see him."

"There are several matters that need—"

"Let the staff decide."

"Yes sir."

"Please go away."

"Yes sir. Oh, this came. I'll leave it here for you, sir."

Becker sucked in the pipe smoke, blew out still more ample clouds of smoke. He almost slipped off into his favorite fantasy, where he stands before a national convention, feeling the power of history as it approves him, and various people who denied him his specialness are seen below the podium, their faces crushed in bitterness. But then caught himself and returned to normalcy, and he was the one who was bitter and would be for a long, long—

This came. I'll leave it here for you, sir.

Now what the hell did that mean?

He looked and saw a large manila envelope on the floor, face down.

What was *this?* Why would she leave it? What was . . . ?

His curiosity momentarily overcoming his lethargy and self-hatred, he went to the doorway and picked the envelope up.

It was first-class, special delivery, from Los Angeles, California, addressed to him personally, and marked HIGHLY CONFIDENTIAL.

What the hell?

He opened it and looked at the contents and—

"Miss Wilson! Miss Wilson! Get the Little Rock FBI on the horn! And fast!"

CHAPTER 51

Earl was escorted to his car by two Hot Springs plainclothesmen whose demeanor indicated they'd be just as happy to beat him to a pulp as to spit. He drove the seven blocks to the hospital with a black-and-white ahead of him and one behind him, and the plainclothesmen behind them.

He parked and went in, and found the boy sitting wanly in the waiting room. His left side was heavily bandaged and his arm immobilized by a sling, and his face appeared pale and forlorn.

"Well, ain't you a sight," Earl said, glad to see the kid was basically all right. That meant he hadn't lost them all. He'd saved one. He'd gotten one through it. That at least he'd done, when he'd failed at all else.

"Howdy, Mr. Earl," said Carlo. "Good to see you."

"Well, sir," said Earl, "guess my last official act is to take you to the station and see that you head back to Tulsa. Then I'm to get out of town and don't come back no nevermore, or these fine gents'll throw me in jail."

"Yes sir."

"Got the car right out here. Can you make it? Do you need a wheelchair?"

"No sir. I'm fine. I lost some blood, that's all, but the bullet passed through without breaking any bones. I been ready to leave for two days."

"Guess all them important boys had to decide what to do with us."

"Yes sir. Heard they was going to throw us into jail."

"But heroic Fred Becker stopped that. Yes sir, that's what I like about Fred, he always stands by his men."

"He's a real hero, that one," said the boy.

They walked out into bright sun, and all the cops were lounging on their bumpers. Earl waved.

"Howdy, y'all. We're going to the train station. Let me know if I get too far ahead of y'all now."

The cops stared at him grimly; now that he was disarmed and beat up badly, he didn't scare them a lick, no sir.

He opened the door for Carlo, then went around and got in.

The hospital was in the north end of town; they drove south down Central one last time to the train station. The eight bathhouses FordyceSuperiorHale MauriceQuapawOzarkBuckstaffLamar gleamed on the left and on the other side of the boulevard, ancient, corrupt Hot Springs marched onward, the Medical Arts Building, the Southern, all the smaller casinos and brothels, on down to the Ohio.

"We could still shut that place down," joked Earl.

"Two men without guns, with a cop escort. That would at least surprise 'em."

"Give 'em a good laugh, wouldn't it, Mr. Earl?"

"It sure would, Henderson."

Two blocks beyond they reached the train station. All evidence of the shootings of four nights earlier had vanished by now; the place hummed with pilgrims come to take the waters. The Missouri and Pacific 4:30 lay next to the station, cutting off the view of the railyard beyond, so at least they didn't have to look at the killing ground, the switching shed or the culvert.

Earl bought the ticket, one-way to Tulsa, $8.50, with just about the last of his cash. Supposedly the state would forward a last paycheck, or so he had been promised, but he'd believe it when he saw it.

The train wouldn't leave for half an hour, so the two men sat down on the bench. Discreetly, the policemen and the detectives set up a watch around them.

"You want an Eskimo Pie, Henderson?"

"Yes sir."

Earl went back inside, got the boy the ice cream and returned. While the boy ate his ice cream, he lit up a cigarette and stared at the train just ahead of him.

"Mr. Earl," said the boy. "How come you knew where that culvert was?"

"What?" said Earl.

"How come you knew where that culvert was?"

"Hmmm. I don't much know. Must have seen a map. What difference does it make?"

"How come you knew how steep the hill behind the Belmont was? How come you knew that street ran downhill not far from Mary Jane's? How come you knew where the manager's office at the Horseshoe was? Mr. Earl, was you in this town before you got here with D.A.?"

Earl didn't say anything. Then he said, "What difference does it make?"

"I have to have this out with you, Mr. Earl. Mr. Parker wouldn't want me to. But I have to know, Mr. Earl. If you murdered your father, I have to know, and then I have to work out what to do next. I can't let a murder pass, no matter that the man who committed it saved my life. I'm a police detective and that's what I'll be till the day I die."

"You are a good cop, Henderson. Wish I could say the same."

Earl lit another cigarette. The boy stared at him intently.

"It makes sense, Mr. Earl. You were going to the Pacific. You thought you were going to die over there. You had to have it out with your daddy, to punish him for beating your brother till he died, then hanging him up in the barn, and beating you till you ran away. But you couldn't disappear during normal duty, because the Marine Corps would keep a record. But when the division moved out for the West Coast from New River, that would be your time, Mr. Earl. You could disappear and come back and your sergeant pals would cover for you. You could get here and wait for him and recon the place and learn it up one side and down t'other. So you meant to beat him up and you shot him instead. You drive him out to Mount Ida, you dump him, you hop a freight, then another troop train, and you're on your way to Guadalcanal and who would know? Is that how it was, Mr. Earl?"

"Say, you are good, ain't you?" said Earl.

"You tell me, Mr. Earl. Mr. D.A. would let it pass as bad old business, but I have to know. I investigated it. I can't get it out of my mind. It kills me to think you done such a thing, but I can't look myself in the mirror if I don't know."

"Wouldn't that be some end? Survive the Pacific, survive all this and get the chair because some young cop has the genius to see into everything?"

"Some people need killing. No doubt about it. Your daddy, he's one of them, from what I can tell. I saw the pictures of that boy. I ain't even sure it's wrong, what you did. But I have to know. I just have to."

The mention of his brother hit Earl like a slap in the face.

"You are right," he said. "Some people deserve killing. And you got everything pretty right too."

He took a breath. "I will tell you this once and I will never speak of it again. I will never answer no questions on this and if you want to believe me or not, that is your decision, but you should know by this time I am not in the habit of telling lies. I only told one that I know of, when I told D.A. I had never been here."

"I believe you, Mr. Earl."

Earl took a puff, blew a blue cloud of smoke out before him. Passengers hurried this way and that, kids squawked, mamas bawled, dads lit pipes, traveling men read the paper, cops kept watch. It was America as it was supposed to be.

Earl sighed.

"I did decide to have it out with that old bastard. Didn't seem right for him to go on and on and both his sons dead before him for one damned reason or another. My topkick covered for me. I jumped train in Little Rock, and was here in Hot Springs for four days. I made it back to Pendleton just fine. Top understood. He was a good man. He didn't make it off the 'Canal, but he was a good man."

"I have it right?"

"Most of it. You only got one thing wrong."

The boy just looked at him.

"It's like everything you say. I learned the town, I learned all the casinos and finally I picked him up, b'lieve it or not, at the Horseshoe. The Belmont was too fancy for him. I knew about the hill behind the Belmont because I can read a goddamned map, that's all. But I followed my father from dive to dive, from joint to joint. It was a Saturday night and I was going to wait till the crowds died down, then jump him and beat the shit out of him. I wanted him to feel what it tasted like, to get a hard, mean beating. He'd never been beaten in his life, but that night, I would have cracked him a new head, that I swear."

The train whistled. It was time to go.

"You better get aboard," said Earl.

"I can't go till I hear it all."

"Then I better finish fast. You sure you're up to this?"

"Yes sir."

"Well, we'll see. The old man finally laid up at a place down at the end of Central. Just another no-name whorehouse at the cheap end of the row. I moved on down and waited. And waited. And goddamn waited. I seen him park his car, I seen him go in, and then nothing. Finally, 'bout four, I went in myself. There's something strange goin' on, but I'm not quite figuring it out. It's all dark, and the whores are just shocked-like. It's a run-down whorehouse, all dark, all crappy, all lousy. No johns nowhere, but some whores sitting in a little room, and I got to say, they's scared. They's almost in shock. 'You see a old man come in here?' I ask. I ask 'em, and they just run away, like they can't figure out what the hell is going on. Damnedest thing. I go upstairs. One by one I open doors. It ain't much different than Mary Jane's, and in a couple of rooms, I find other whores, some of 'em drunked up, some of 'em high on juju-weed, and I'm wondering what the hell is going on.

"Finally I get to a last door. Daddy's got to be in there. I kick the door in, and get ready for the fight of my life, because he was a big, mean sumbitch and he ain't going to stand still while his oldest boy goes to whip-ass on him. But he's just lying there and in the corner, this little gal is crying so hard, the makeup on her face is all run to hell and everything.

"I check Daddy. He ain't dead, but he's almost into the barn. 'Daddy,' I say. He reaches up and grabs my arm and recognizes my voice. 'Earl,' he says. 'Oh, God bless you, son, you come for your daddy in his hour of need. Son, I am kilt dead, get me out of this house of sin, please, son, I am so sorry for what I done to you and your brother, I was a wicked, wicked man. I done such evil in the valley and after and now the Lord has punished me, but for your sake and your mama's sake, git me out of this here house of sin.' "

"What was the valley?"

"Henderson, I ain't got no idea. Maybe he meant 'Valley of the Shadow,' that's all I could figure, and I puzzled on it for many a year."

"Go on."

"Well, I look, and he's shot. Shot above the heart. Had to be a little bullet, 'cause there's a little track of blood, not much. 'What happened?' I ask the girl, and she says, 'Mr. Charles, they busted in on him. They grabbed him and when he drew his little gun, they got it from him and shot him with it, right in the heart. They came to kill him and kill him they did.' This whore was crying up a storm. Mr. Charles, he was so good and kind, he took care of us, all that stuff. 'Who done this?' I asked. 'They done it,' said the whore. 'Gangsters done it. Shot him with his own gun and told me if I squealed they'd kill me and all the gals in the house.' 'Git me out of here,' he screamed. 'I am dying, Lord, I am dying, but son, Jesus, please, get me out of the house of sin.' So that is what I done. I come to beat the man and put the fear of God in him, and I ended up carrying him down two flights of stairs, him crying and telling me what a good son I was and all that, how wonderful I was, how proud he was. Things don't never work out like you expect, know what I mean? I was strong enough to carry him out. But I didn't want to go on the street, so the madam, she takes me down into the cellar, and through a big door and that's how come I got into the underground stream the first time. I carried him to the culvert. 'Thank you, son,' he said. 'Thank you so much.' I went back, got his car, drove it to the station and carried him to it. Time I got him to it, he's dead and gone. His last words was, 'I have been a wicked man and I done evil in the valley and so much evil come from that and I hope Jesus forgives me.' I didn't want him found there. I drove him to Mount Ida, dumped him, tore open the liquor locker behind Turner's. He had his Peacemaker in the car. I jacked off a round so they'd think it was a gunfight, I messed up all the tracks in the dust, and then I lit out cross-country. The next day, I hoboed a train. A week later, I reached Pendleton and four months after that, I hit the 'Canal. That's the true story. I was hunting him, but so was someone else."

"Jesus," said the boy.

The train had begun to pull out.

"Why'd they kill your daddy?" Carlo asked.

"I ain't never figured it. Who knows what that man had got himself into? He was a bad man. He beat and hurt people, he did terrible things. Someone finally caught up to him, I reckon. Before I did."

They rose, and went to the train, where a conductor was calling a last *"All aboard."*

"One thing maybe figures into this," said Carlo. "I only noticed this 'cause I was looking in newspaper files and I happened to make a connection. But you know that robbery? The Alcoa payroll job?"

"Yeah?"

"It was October 2, 1940. Your brother died October 4, 1940. There's something you might think on."

"Damn," said Earl.

Carlo got to the train, and hobbled aboard and for just a bit Earl kept with him as if he didn't want to let his one survivor from the wars escape his protection.

"Earl? Whyn't you let your father just be found in that whorehouse? Why take the risk? Would have served him right."

"You don't get it, do you, Carlo. Them whores. They wasn't like other whores. None of them."

The young man's face, still so innocent, knit in confusion.

"They was all boys," said Earl, stopping at last, spilling his last and most painful truth.

CHAPTER 52

She was an octoroon from the French Quarter, well schooled in the arts, with oval, wise eyes that bespoke the knowledge of ancient skills. So she had the thunderous savagery of the Negro race, but no vulgar Negro features. She looked like a white girl of special, almost delicate beauty, as if from a convent, but her soul was pure African. And she was extraordinary. She took him places he never knew existed. She took him to a high mesa that overlooked everything, and he could see the world from far away but in precise detail, and then she plunged him into a vortex so intense it made that world and its complications vanish.

"My God," he said.

"You like?"

"I like. I see why Miss Hattie charges so much."

"I am very good."

"You are *the best.*"

"I am so pleased."

"No. I am the one that's pleased."

Owney wasn't obsessed with the pleasures of the flesh like some, but now and then, in a celebratory mood, he liked to let go. And this one had really gotten him to let go.

"Ralph will take care of you."

"Thank you, Mr. Maddox."

"Thank *you*. Uh, you were—?"

"Opaline."

"Opaline. Thank *you*, Opaline."

Opaline, wrapped in a chartreuse silk peignoir, her white heels and beautiful shoulders flashing, walked out to dress. Owney rolled over, checked the clock. It was nearly 1:00 P.M.

He went into his bathroom and showered, then took his time dressing. He had no appointments today, the fourth day in the first week of the complete consolidation of his realm. Johnny Spanish and the lads were presumably still celebrating in some dive or other, on his tab, and he didn't begrudge them. All things considered, they had performed exactly as advertised.

Owney decided it would be a tweed day. He chose a Turnbull & Asser shirt in white linen cream and a red tie in the pattern of the 15th Welsh Fusiliers and, finally, a glorious heather suit from Tautz, the leading sporting tailor of the day. He finished with bespoke boots in rich mahogany. It took him some time to get everything just right, and finally, he enjoyed the construction. He looked like an English gentleman off for an afternoon's sporting. Possibly a partridge hunt, or a spot of trout fishing. He didn't shoot partridge and he'd never fished in his life, but in all, it was quite nice.

He walked into the living room.

"Ralph, I'll take my lunch on the patio, I think."

"Yes sir, Mr. Maddox, sir."

He went out, checked on his cooing birds, stroked one or two, attended to their feeding, then sat down. Ralph served him iced tea while the meal was being prepared.

"Telephone, Ralph."

"Yes sir, Mr. Maddox, sir."

He had one final *i* to dot. And the wonderful thing was: his worst enemy would dot it for him.

He reached into his wallet, and took out a note he'd received from the chief of detectives of the Hot Springs Police Department. It had a name and an address on it.

Earl Swagger
17 Fifth Street
Camp Chaffee, Arkansas

The cowboy. The cowboy had somehow escaped, but the police had done what no one else had been able to do: they'd captured the cowboy. He was released today, and ordered out of Hot Springs. But that wasn't enough for Owney. He mistrusted men like the cowboy, for he knew that the cowboy's anger would grow, and that he would never be safe until the cowboy was eliminated. But now there was peace in Hot Springs, and everybody knew it was time for the killing to stop and stability and prosperity to resume. A deal had been reached.

But he knew someone who hated the cowboy even more than he did.

He picked up the phone.

He dialed long distance, and the operator placed the call for him, and he waited and waited as it rang and finally someone answered.

"Owney Maddox here. Ben? Is that you, Ben?"

"Mr. Maddox, Mr. Siegel isn't here. He's in Nevada."

"Damn. I have some information for him. Information he wants very much."

"Do you want to leave it with me?"

"Yes. It's a name and an address for an Arkansas party he's most interested in. It's—"

But suddenly Ralph was hovering.

"Yes, Ralph?"

"Sir, there's some men here."

"Well, tell them to wait. I'm—"

"Sir, they's FBI. And Mr. Becker."

"What?"

At that point, Fred Becker strode onto the patio, with four FBI agents and four uniformed state policemen.

Owney said, "I'll call you back," and hung up.

He rose.

"What the hell is this all about? Ralph, call my lawyer. Becker, you have no right to—"

"Mr. Maddox, my name is William Springs, special agent of the Little Rock office, Federal Bureau of Investigation. Sir, I have a warrant for your arrest."

"What?"

"Sir, you own a painting by the French artist Georges Braque entitled *Houses at L'Estaque.*"

"I do. Yes, I bought it from a legitimate—"

"Sir, that painting was stolen in 1928 from the Musée D'Orange in Brussels. You are in receipt of stolen property which has been transported across state lines, which is a felony under federal statute 12.23-11. You are hereby remanded into custody and I am serving you with a search warrant for this property, for your office at the Southern Club, and for your warehouse complex in West Hot Springs, which agents and state policemen are currently raiding. Anything you say may be held against you. Sir, I am required to handcuff you. Boys"—he turned to his men—"rip this place up."

The cuffs were snapped on Owney.

He shot a look at Becker, who looked back with a smirk.

"You've been ratted out, Owney," said Becker. "You have some nasty enemies in Los Angeles."

"This is a two-bit fuckin' rap," said Owney, devolving to Brooklynese, "and you fuckin' know it,

Becker! My lawyer'll have me outta stir in about two fuckin' minutes."

"Yes, perhaps, but we intend to search very carefully and if we find one thing linking you to the Alcoa payroll robbery or any of twelve to fifteen murders in Hot Springs since 1931, when you arrived, I'll put you away for the rest of your life and you'll never see daylight again. Say goodbye to the good life, Owney."

"Take him away, boys," said the FBI agent.

As they led him away, Owney saw his beautiful apartment being ransacked.

PART FOUR
Pure Heat

CHAPTER 53

Earl drove west, leaving Hot Springs in the rearview mirror. The road ran through forest, though ahead he could see the sun setting. The police convoy followed him to the Garland County line, and stopped there as he passed into Montgomery toward places beyond.

He told himself he was all right. Really, he told himself, he was swell. He was alive. His child would be born shortly. He had survived another war, an unwinnable one, as it turned out, but there was no changing things and there was nothing back there for him but probable death and guaranteed shame and humiliation.

I am not a goddamned avenging angel.

It is not up to me to avenge the dead.

I am not here to punish the evil.

I cannot go back to that town, one man alone, and take on a mob of professional gunmen, gangsters and crooked politicians.

My life is before me. I commemorate my dead by going on and having a good life.

He instructed himself in all these lessons hard as he was able, searching for a kind of numbness that would permit him to go on.

He tried to tell himself his wife and child needed him, this was over and finished.

But the road, darkening quickly, kept taking him back.

And maybe it was the hard truth he'd told the boy about his father.

He couldn't keep his mind in the present. His mind kept changing gears and he remembered that other night in 1942, his father dead in the seat next to him, much later, much darker at night, driving this same road toward Mount Ida, his mind racing, trying to figure out what to do, how to do it, feeling both cheated and relieved, wanting nothing now except to get over this thing, dump the old bastard and get back to the United States Marine Corps.

Then, as now, Mount Ida finally slid into sight, after such a long time, but then it was quiet; now it was much earlier and Turner's general store and liquor store were still open for business and some old boys stood or sat out on the porch before the old buildings.

Earl realized he had a thirst, and pulled off the road.

He walked up to the porch and heard the boys talking.

"Howdy," he said.

"Howdy, there, mister," came a reply.

"Got a Coca-Cola inside? A nice cold one? Got a long drive ahead."

"Yes sir. You go on in, and Ike'll git you a Coke."

"Thanks," he said.

"My pleasure, sir," said the man.

Earl walked in, found an old store with sagging shelves but well stocked, probably the only store this deep in the Ouachita forest, and folks from all around must have come here. He went to a red Coke machine, opened it up, and reached for a nickel. He didn't have one. He had only quarters.

He went up to the counter, asked a boy there for change, got it, went on back to the machine, and got his Coke. He was walking out and to his car when he heard one of the boys on the porch saying, "They say this'll make Fred Becker the governor."

"I thought that boy's all finished," said another. "But he beat 'em. He beat them Grumleys fair and square."

It took a second for this to register. At first Earl had the impression it was another Fred Becker they were talking about and that it was another batch of

Grumleys, but then he realized that couldn't be the truth.

"'Scuse me," he said, "don't mean to butt in. But what's all that about Fred Becker and the Grumleys?"

"You from Hot Springs, sir?"

"Well, I done some work there. That's all finished and I'm heading on to Fort Smith."

"Hell, there's been a war there," said the man. "Fred Becker led a bunch of fellers against the gangsters in Hot Springs."

"B'lieve I heard something about that, yes sir," said Earl.

"Well," said the fellow, "today, he wrapped it up. Done arrested the gangster king himself, Owney Maddox, the big boss of Hot Springs."

"Arrested him?"

"That Fred done it by himself. Say, there's a fellow with some sand to him. They say he shot it out with the Grumleys at Mary Jane's and today he walked up big as life and arrested Owney Maddox."

"On what?"

"You must not have been listening to your radio. No sir, it's all over the radio. They're saying Fred's going to be the next damn governor. He got Owney Maddox on the charge of an art theft, for some kind of painting, and they searched Owney's apartment and they found some payroll slips from Alcoa, so they think Owney done masterminded that job. It's all falling apart on Owney Maddox. He's in jail and he's going to stay there and all them damn Grumleys he got working for him are squirreled good."

"Art theft?" said Earl.

"Some old picture he had. It was stolen, and Fred digged it out, and called the feds and made the arrest. Don't that beat all? It's just like with Al Capone. He's a bad man, but everybody's scared to go agin him, so they finally get him on tax evasion. So they get that Owney on art theft!"

"Ah," said Earl, as if he'd just learned something new.

"You okay, mister?"

"I'm fine," he said.

"'Cause you just look like a haunt walked through you."

"Nah, I'm fine," said Earl. He turned and went to his car.

He climbed in, but couldn't find the strength to turn the key. The Coke suddenly didn't interest him at all.

Fred Becker, hero? Fred Becker, the next governor? Hey, isn't it great about Fred Becker, how he got Owney Maddox?

He sat there, breathing hard.

What about them boys? What about that old man? They believed in their job and they risked their lives for it, and they got cut down in the night and nobody said Jack about it and a few days later it was as if it hadn't happened and nobody remembered a goddamn thing now that Fred Becker was a big hero.

In his head, one bitterness slid into and was absorbed by another. It was just like the war. All the boys go out onto the islands and they fight in battles so horrible it scars a man just to think about it. And they die, and by the time you get back everydamnbody's forgotten all about it and some joker's up front acting like a hero and he had nothing to do with it, not a goddamned thing.

He shook his head. The anger came over him so bad he could hardly stand it. He wanted to fight, to smash something, to howl at the moon, to kill something, to see it bleed and twitch out. It was a killing anger, a hurting anger.

He wanted to go back to Hot Springs and start shooting. But shoot who? They were all gone. Owney was locked up and whoever it was had hit the boys in the train yard, presumably that Johnny Spanish fellow, was off in some gangster hideout.

There was no one to kill. It was the same rage he felt when he went to beat his father and his father was already dying.

Earl got out of the car.

"You didn't drink that Coke up, mister."

"No, I didn't. Feel a need for something else tonight."

"You all right?"

"I am fine, sir."

He walked past them, but this time not into the general store but into the little liquor store next to it. There, in an old frame, was the front page of the

Blue Eye newspaper with its story of the death of the great Charles Swagger, sheriff of Polk County, who'd died stopping a burglary over in Montgomery County, at Turner's liquor store, this very place.

"They never caught 'em," said the liquor store clerk, who was actually the same Ike who'd just stepped through a door.

"So I heard," said Earl.

"Hard to figure, that old guy fighting to save my uncle a few dollars' worth of beer."

"He wore the badge," said Earl. "He knew what he'd signed up for. Don't waste no time worrying about him."

"So what's your poison, sir?"

"You got that Boone County bourbon? Ain't had a lick of that in a time."

"You want the pint or the fifth."

Earl got out his wallet. He had seven dollars left and nothing else coming in soon.

"How much the fifth?"

"That'd be three dollar."

"Give me two fifths then. And keep the change, sonny."

CHAPTER 54

Nobody could believe how well Frenchy shot. Some of them were serious people. Some were ex-paratroopers, many ex-cops or FBI agents, some ex-Marines, all of whom had been in it, one way or the other. But Frenchy outshot them all, two-handed to boot.

"Son, who taught you to shoot like that?"

"An old guy, been in a lot of stuff. Worked it out, this system."

"It's not doctrine, but damn, it's so fast and accurate I don't see a point in changing it. Never would have believed it could be so fast, two hands and everything."

"You get used to it. It's rock steady."

"Wish I'd had you along on my team in Market Garden."

"Yeah, well, I was a little young for that."

"You ever in the for-real?"

"I was a cop in the South. I was in some for-real stuff. In it deep."

"Where?"

"Oh, the South."

"Oh, it's that way, is it? Sure, kid. You are a good hand."

"I was taught by the best," Frenchy said.

He was D.A.'s best pupil, really. The gun came from his holster so fast nobody could see it, was clapped by the other hand and outthrust even as his eyes clamped to the front sight and bangbang, he'd slap two holes in the kill zone, rotate to another, bangbang, and on to another, with the seventh round saved for just in case. These .45s had not been worked on like the ones D.A. had tricked up by Griffin & Howe, they were just old sloppy twenty-seventh-hand service Ithacas and Singers and IBMs, with an old Colt thrown in here and there for good measure, but they went pop every time the trigger was jacked and they felt familiar to Frenchy.

It was the shooting week of CIG training class 004, Clandestine Techniques, up on Catoctin Mountain in Maryland, where the old OSS had trained, a place called Camp Ritchie, maybe fifty miles outside of D.C. It still had a lot of World War II feeling to it, with the old LOOSE LIPS SINK SHIPS and INVEST IN INVASION BUY WAR BONDS posters turning yellow and tatty, the wooden barracks thick with the odor of men having lived in close quarters, all of it nestled safely behind barbed wire and guarded by Marines.

And of course Frenchy was just as good with anything; he could shoot the Thompson, the BAR and the carbine with extraordinary skill. It just seemed to come naturally to him, and it filled him with confidence, so that when the field problems arose, he seemed always to be the one who solved them fastest, even among men who'd been in combat. Soon he was an acting team leader, and he led after Earl's techniques, giving his boys nicknames (that is, nicknaming men who were ten years older than he was, Harvard and Yale graduates, and combat veterans), teasing them, cajoling them, always putting himself out front and when it came time to work, outworking them. He had a funny tic when he explained things to them: he'd listen, then say, "See, here's the thing," then gently point out the way it *should* be done.

Finally, toward the end of the course, an instructor drew him aside.

"You've done damned well, Short. You've impressed some people."

"Thanks."

"Now many of these guys will go under embassy cover to various spots around the world where they'll run agents, or recruit locals, or make reports. Some others will stay here, this'll be their only taste of the actual, and they'll be sent to headquarters, where they'll mainly be analysts."

"Both those sound pretty boring to me."

"Yeah, I thought so. You have a cowboy look to you. Are you a cowboy, Tex?"

"No sir."

"But you have a field operator's brain, I can tell. And real good shooting skills. Real good."

"Yes sir."

"You've been mentioned for Plans."

"Plans?" said Frenchy. "That doesn't sound like much fun."

"One thing you have to learn, Short, is that in this business nothing is what it sounds like. Okay?"

"Yes sir."

"Mr. Dulles sees Plans as a kind of action unit."

"Like a raid team?"

"Yeah, exactly. It'll be working in military or guerrilla-warfare situations, sometimes behind the lines, running operations. Probably high-contact work. Lots of bangbang. Lots of sentry-knifing, dog-killing, bomb-planting, border-crossing. That sound like your cup of tea?"

"Does it ever!"

"You have a problem with Army Jump School?"

"No sir."

"You have a problem with a commando tour with the Brits? Good training."

"Sounds good."

"You have a problem with language studies?"

"Ah—I speak French and passable German."

"Think about Chinese, Short. Or Indochinese. Or Greek. Or Korean. Or Russian, if the big one ever comes."

"Yes sir," said Frenchy.

"Good man," said the instructor.

And so Frenchy's course was set. He was to become a specialist in doing the necessary, not out of sentiment but out of hard, rational thought, carefully measured risk, a burglar's guts and a killer's decisiveness. But at this point he envisioned one more moment in his career with the Garland County raid team, a kind of a last thing that he owed himself. It came some months ahead in the week after he graduated from Clandestine Techniques OO4 at the head of his class and before he reported to Fort Benning for Jump School. He spent it in Washington, D.C., and for several days he roamed the city, looking for out-of-town newsstands, for copies of the Little Rock *Arkansas Gazette* or *Democrat*. He had no luck. But then he went to the Library of Congress and ordered up a batch of backdated *New York Times* and in that way, buried on a back page, learned of the fates of D.A. and the boys. EX-FBI AGENT SLAIN IN ACCIDENTAL GUNFIGHT. He did note that Earl's name was not listed among the dead, nor was Carlo Henderson's, so he assumed that somehow they had survived. It figured. You couldn't kill the cowboy. Maybe Bugsy Siegel would, as Johnny Spanish had predicted, but Owney hadn't been able to, not even with Frenchy's treacherous help.

If you saw him sitting there, in that vast, domed room on Capitol Hill behind the Congress, you would have seen a grave, calm young man, brimming with health and vitality, but already picking up a warrior's kind of melancholy aloofness from the workaday world around him. And at least at that moment—for he had not yet entirely mastered the art of completely stifling his emotions—you might have seen some regret too. Maybe even some sorrow.

CHAPTER 55

Earl started drinking almost immediately. The bourbon lit like a flare out beyond the wire and fell down his gullet, popping sparks of illumination, floating, drifting, pulling him ever so gently toward where he hoped the numbness was. No such goddamned luck. He drank only to forget, but of course the only thing the bourbon did was make him remember more, so he drank more, which made him remember yet more again.

He wasn't headed west on 270 toward Y City, which would take him over to 71 for the pull up toward Fort Smith and Camp Chaffee, where his wife and unborn child, his new life or whatever, awaited. He couldn't do that, somehow. He was in no state to face them and the emotions that he had controlled so masterfully for four days now seemed dangerously near explosion. He knew he was rocky. He turned south, down 27 out of Mount Ida, to 8, and then west on 8. He knew exactly where he was headed even if he couldn't say it or acknowledge it.

By the time he pulled into Board Camp it was nearly midnight. Wasn't much to be seen at all. It was never even as much as Mount Ida. He drove through the little town and there, a few miles beyond toward the county seat of Blue Eye, off on the right, he saw the old mailbox. SWAGGER it said, same as it always had.

He turned right, sank as the dirt road plunged off the highway, watched his light beams lance out in the darkness until at last they illuminated the house where he grew up, where his family lived, where his father lived, where his brother died. The light beams hit the house.

They illuminated broken windows, knocked-out boards, ragged weeds, a garden gone to ruin, peeling paint, the nothingness of abandonment. After his father died, his mother had simply given up and moved to town. He never saw her again; he was in the hospital after Tarawa when the news came that she had died.

Earl pulled into the barnyard and when his lights crossed that structure, he saw that it too had fallen into total disrepair. It needed paint and was lost in a sea of ragweed and unkempt grass. Daddy would shit if he saw it now. Daddy always kept it so nice. Or rather, Daddy directed that it be kept nice. It had to be perfect, and it was one of Earl's chores to mow the lawn and lord help him if he forgot it, or he didn't do it well enough. The lawn had to be perfect, the garden well cultivated, the whole thing upstanding and pretty, as befits an important man.

Earl turned off the lights. He opened the door. Crickets tweedled in the dark and the soft rush of the wind filled the Arkansas night, with maybe just a hint of fall in the air. The house was big, with four bedrooms up on the second floor. Once it had been the leading house in the eastern half of Polk County, maintained by a lot of good land, but somehow, some Swagger granddad or other back in the last century had gotten out of the farming business before really getting into it and committed to the law enforcement business, because the Swagger men were always hunters, always had a kind of natural instinct for the rifle, and a gift for reading the terrain. No one knew where it came from, but they'd been soldiers and hunters for as long as anyone could remember, just as long as they'd lived in these parts. They were never farmers.

Earl tipped the bottle up and felt the bourbon clog his throat and with a mighty gulp he took down two more harsh swallows. The illumination rounds went off in his guts, lighting the target. It made his eyes water. He stood, wobbling just a little, and faced the big house.

It scared him still. It was a house of fear. You walked softly in that house because you didn't want to upset Daddy. Daddy ruled that house as he ruled so much of the known world. Daddy's hugeness was something he could feel even now, his presence, looming and feary and cold and mad, that man who even to this day stalked the corridors of Earl's mind, always whispering to him.

"Goddamn you, Daddy, goddamn your black soul! Come out and fight!" Earl screamed.

But Daddy didn't.

Earl saw that he had finished the bottle. He returned to the car, now glad he'd bought a second one. He found it. He had some trouble with the cap because he was so damned drunk his fingers barely worked, but in a little bit, it came free. By now the bourbon had lost its taste. He swallowed, swallowed some more, and pitched forward. He passed out in the front yard.

Sometime later in the night, Earl awoke, still drunk but shivery in the cold. He was wet; he'd pissed his pants. No, no, it was dew, dampening him through his suit coat. He pulled himself up, shuddered mightily in the cold, seized the bottle and took another couple of pulls. But he didn't pass out. Instead he rose, and in the blurry darkness of his vision made out the car. He wobbled back toward it, unsteadily as hell, and made it all the way, falling only once.

"Goddamn," he cursed to no man, as around him the black world pitched and bobbed, as if he were on some merry-go-round that went up and down just as fast as it went around. He felt like he was going to puke. He flew off in all directions and all six of his hands reached for all six of the handles to the door of the vehicle, and somehow he got it open and plunged into the back seat, and collapsed with a thump as the blackness closed around him again.

He awoke again to a strange sound. His frayed

mind stirred from unconsciousness. He seemed covered in grit somehow. Again the sound: loud, close, familiar. Again the grit, spraying downward on him like droplets of water, except it wasn't water it was—

BANG!

Another bullet tore through the window, puncturing neatly through, leaving a spackle of fractures, a mercury smear across the glass, erupting with a spray of grit that was pulverized glass which floated out in a cloud, then floated down upon him.

"Don't shoot!" he screamed and in a split second realized what had happened. Somehow Owney's Grumley boys had tracked him down. They had him nailed. They knew where he'd go and that's where he went and they found him passed out in the car and they worried it was a trick so they laid up until the light and when he still didn't stir after a bit they fired rounds through the windows and the windshield.

"Don't shoot!" he screamed again, knowing he was finished. He had no gun. He was aflame with pain, head to toe, from the ravages of alcohol. His mind was all jittery with fear. Goddamn them! They had found him!

Earl hated fear and worked hard at controlling it, at testing himself against it because it scared him so much, but now he had no preparation for it, and it just came and took him and made him its toy. He began to cry. He couldn't be brave. He couldn't fight. He was going to end up like his daddy, shot by killers and left dying and begging for mercy.

"You show us hands!" came the cry, *"or god-damn we will finish you good!"*

He looked around. Nothing to fight with. Another shot rocked through the window, blowing out a puff of sheared, shredded glass.

"I'll put one in your gut, mister, you come out or by God I will finish you."

Earl kicked the door open and as he rose felt the shredded glass raining off his body like a collection of sand. He blinked in the sunlight, showed his hands, and edged out. There were at least four Grumleys, all with big lever-action rifles, all laid up behind cover, all zeroed on him.

One of the men emerged from cover.

"You armed?"

"No sir."

"Don't trust him, Luke. Them boys is tricky. I can pop him right now."

"You hold it, Jim. Now, mister, I want you to shuck that coat and show me you got nothing or Jim will pop you like a squirrel. Don't you do nothing tricky."

Why didn't they just shoot him and be done with it? Did they want to hang him, beat him, set him afire?

Slowly with one hand, then the other, he peeled off the coat, and showed by his blue shirt and suspenders that he was unarmed. He kept his hands high. Two of the men approached while two others hung back, keeping him well covered. By the way they handled their rifles, Earl could tell they had handled rifles a lot.

"Turn round and up agin that car," commanded the leader.

Earl assumed the position. A hand fished his wallet out while another patted him down.

"What the hell are you doing here?" he was asked.

"I own this place. Been paying taxes on it for years."

"Hell, nobody owns this place, since old lady Swagger done up n' died in town. This is Sheriff Charles Swagger's old place, mister."

"And I am Charles Swagger's son, Earl."

"Earl?"

"By God, yes," came another voice, "according to his driver's license, this here's Earl Swagger hisself."

"Jesus Christ, Earl, why'n't you say so? Git them hands down, by God, heard what you done to them Japs in the islands. Earl, it's Luke Petty, I'se two years behind you in high school."

Earl turned. The men had lowered their rifles and gazed at him with reverence, their blue eyes eating him alive. Luke Petty looked slightly familiar, but maybe it was the type: the rawboned Scotch-Irish border reiver whose likeness filled the hills a hundred miles in either direction.

"Luke, I—"

"Goddamn, yes, it's Earl, Earl Swagger, who

won the Medal of Honor. Where, Earl, Saipan?"

"Iwo."

"Iwo goddamned Jima. You made the whole damned county proud of you. Pity your daddy and mommy weren't around to know it."

That was another story. Earl left it alone.

"Sorry about the car, Earl. Folks is jumpy and we seen a car in an abandoned place and a man sleeping. Well, you know."

Earl didn't, not really, but before he could say a thing, another man said, "Earl, you look plenty wore out. You okay?"

"Yes, I'm fine. I now and then go on a toot, like the old man—"

"He was a drinking man, yes, I do remember. Oncet boxed my ears so hard made 'em ring for a month," one of the other men said fondly.

"Well, I have the same curse. I'm now living up in Fort Smith and I fell off the wagon. Got so drunk I didn't want the wife to see me. So I somehow turned up here. Sorry to rile you."

"Hell, Earl, it ain't nothing. You ought to move on back here. This is your home, this is where you belong."

"Don't know about that, but maybe. I have a child on the way and we will see."

Then he noticed the stars. Each of these boys was a deputy, each wore a gunbelt loaded with cartridges and a powerful revolver, each had the look of a rangy manhunter to him.

"What're you boys out huntin'? You look loaded for grizzly."

"You ain't heard?"

"How could I? Was drunked up like a crazy bastard last night."

"Earl, you best watch that. Can tear a fellow down. Saw my own daddy go sour with the drink. He died too young, and he looked a hundred when he's only forty-two."

"I hear you on that one," said Earl, who hoped he'd never drink again.

"Anyhow, we're hunting gangsters."

"Gangsters?"

"He ain't heard!"

"Damn, he did do some drinking last night."

"You know that Owney Maddox, the big New York gun what run Hot Springs these past twenty years? The one old Fred Becker caught?"

"Heard of him," Earl said.

"Five bastards busted him out of Garland County jail last night late. Shot their way out. Say it was just as bad as that Alcoa train job or that big shoot-out in the train yard. Killed two men. But Owney's fled, he's free, the whole goddamned state's out looking for him."

"Earl, you okay?"

"Yeah," said Earl.

"You look like a ghost touched you on the nose with a cold finger."

Owney. Owney was out.

CHAPTER 56

It was exactly the kind of operation Johnny Spanish loved. It demanded his higher skills and imagination. It wasn't merely force. On its own, force was tedious. Labor enforcers, racketeers, small-potatoes strong-arm boys, the common soldiers of crime, they all used force and it never expressed anything except force.

Johnny always looked for something else. He loved the game aspects of it, the cleverness of the planning, the deviousness of the timing, the feint, the confusion, the misinformation, and the final, crushing, implacable boldness. It was all a part of that ineffable *je ne sais quoi* that made Johnny Johnny.

Thus at 10:30 P.M. at the Garland County jail in the Town Hall and Police Department out Ouachita Avenue toward the western edge of the city, the first indication of mischief was not masked men with machine guns but something entirely unexpected: tomato pies.

The tomato pie was new to the South, though it had gained some foothold in New Jersey and Philadelphia. It was a large, flat disk of unleavened dough with a certain elastic crispiness to it, coated with a heavy tomato sauce and a gruel of mozzarella cheese, all allowed to coagulate in a particularly intense oven experience. It was quite a taste sensation, both bold and chewy, both exotic and accessible, both sweet and tart, both the best of old Italy and new America at once. Four tomato pies, cut into wedges, were delivered gratis to the jail by two robust fellows from Angelino's Italian Bakery and Deli, newly opened and yet to catch on, to the late-night jail guard shift. The boys hadn't ordered any tomato pies—they'd never even heard of tomato pies!—but free food was one of the reasons they'd gotten into law enforcement in the first place. Even those who had no intention of eating that night found themselves powerless in the grip of obsession, when the odors of the sizzling pies began to suffuse the woeful old lockup. Who could deny the power of the tomato pie, and that devilish, all-powerful, mesmerizing smell that beckoned even the strongest of them onward.

This was the key to the plan. Like many jails built in the last century, Garland County's was constructed on the concentric ring-of-steel design, with perimeters of security inside perimeters of security. One could not be breached until the one behind it was secure. Yet all yielded to the power of the tomato pie.

The guards—seven local deputies and warders and a lone FBI representative since the prisoner, No. 453, was on a federal warrant—clustered in the admin office, enjoying slice after slice.

"This stuff is *good*."

"It's Italian? Jed, you see anything like this in Itly?"

"All's I seen was bombed-out towns and starvin' kids and dead Krautheads. Didn't see nothing like this."

"Man, this stuff is good."

"Best thing is, they deliver to your doorway and it's piping hot."

"It's 'Mambo Italiano' in cheese and tomato. I love the toastiness. That's what's so good. I like that a lot."

At that point, two more men from Angelino's showed up, with four more pies.

"You guys-a, you love-a this-a one, it's got the pepperoni sausage, very spicy."

"Sausage?" said the guard sergeant.

"Spicy," said the deliveryman, who opened the flat cardboard box, removed a 1911 Colt automatic with a Maxim silencer, and shot the man once. The silencer wasn't all that silent, and everyone in the room knew immediately that a gun had been fired, but it reduced the sound of the percussion enough to dampen it from alerting others in the building. More guns came out, and a large fellow appeared in the doorway with a BAR.

"Get against the wall, morons," screamed the commander of the commandos—that is, Johnny Spanish at his best.

"Jesus, you shot—"

Johnny knew the tricky moment was in the early going where you asserted control or you lost it and it turned to nightmare and massacre. Therefore, according to his lights, he was doing the humane thing when he shot that man too, knocking him down. If he'd been closer he would have clubbed the man with the long cylindrical heft of the silencer, but that was the way the breaks went, and they didn't go well for that particular guard that particular day.

Herman grabbed the biggest of the men and said simply and forcefully, "Keys," and was obediently led to the steel cabinet on the wall, it was opened, and the keys were displayed for his satisfaction.

"Which one, asshole?" he demanded.

The man's trembly fingers flew to a single key, which Herman seized. With Ding-Dong as his escort, he headed into the interior of the jail.

Iron-barred doors flew open quickly enough and, deep in the warren, they came to the cage that contained Owney Maddox. That door too was sprung, and Owney was plucked from ignominy. He threw on his coat and rushed out, passing the parade as Johnny and his boys led the surrendered guards back into the jail to lock them up away from telephones so that he didn't have to shoot the lot of them.

"Good work," Owney cried. And it was. For his legal situation had collapsed and it appeared a murder indictment for the four guards slain in 1940 was in the offing. A gun had been found in his warehouse that had been used in that crime and the FBI test results had just come in. Meanwhile, all his well-placed friends had deserted him, and even lawyer F. Garry Hurst wasn't sanguine about his chances of survival. A life on the lam, even well financed as his would be, would be no picnic but it was infinitely preferable to life in the gray-bar hotel.

Johnny's team quickly completed the herding operation, locking the bulls back with the cons. Then they methodically ripped out all phone lines. Owney was bundled into the back of an actual Hot Springs police car, driven by Vince the Hat de Palmo in an actual Hot Springs police uniform, and he disappeared into the night.

Johnny and his boys left in the next several seconds, but not, of course, before they'd finished the pizza.

Vince drove Owney through the night and at a certain point on the outskirts of town, they pulled into a garage. There, the stolen police car was abandoned, and Owney got into the hollowed-out core of a pile of hay bales already loaded on the back of a hay truck, which was to be driven by two trustworthy Negroes in the Grumley employ. The hay pressed in close around him, like a coffin, and the truck backed out and began an unsteady progress through town. It would only be a matter of minutes before sirens announced the discovery of the breakout, but the plan was to get Owney out of the immediate downtown area before roadblocks were set up. They almost made it.

The sirens began to howl just a few minutes into the trip. Yet nobody panicked. The old truck rumbled along and twice was overtaken by roaring police cars. Once it was stopped, cursorily examined, its hay bales probed and pulled slightly apart. Owney lay still and heard the Negro driver answering in his shufflingest voice to the police officers. But the cops hurried onward when they grew impatient with the molasses-slow drift of the driver's words as he explained to them that the hay was for Mr. Randy in Pine Mountain, from the farm of Mr. Davidson in Arkadelphia, and so they passed on.

They drove through the night, though at about thirty-five miles an hour. Owney knew the city would be in an uproar. A certain code had been broken when the two police officers had been shot, which meant that now the cops would pursue him with all serious purpose, earlier arrangements having been shattered. But it could be no other way. Very shortly he'd be transferred to a sounder federal incarceration and there'd be no escape from that. Whatever, he understood, his Hot Springs days were over; his fortune had already been transferred, and the ownership of his various enterprises passed on, through the good offices of F. Garry Hurst, to other men, though the benefits to him would accrue steadily over the years.

But he did not believe that retirement was at hand. He would leave the country, live somewhere quietly in wealth and health over the next few years, and things would be worked out. He had too much on too many people for it to be elsewise. Somehow, he knew he wasn't done; possibilities still existed. It would be explained that he was abducted, not escaped; the deaths of the policemen would have nothing to do with him; a deal would be worked out somehow, a year or two in a soft prison, then he'd be back in some fashion or other.

He had to survive. He had but one ambition now, and that was to arrange for the elimination of Ben Siegel, who clearly was the agent of his downfall. It couldn't be done quickly, though, or harshly. Ben had friends on the commission and was said to be doing important work for them in the West. He was, for the time being, protected. But that wouldn't last. Owney knew Ben's impetuousness would make him somehow overreach, his greed would cloud his judgment, his hurry would offend, his hunger would irritate. There would be a time now, very shortly, when Ben was vulnerable, and he would be the one to take advantage of it.

In what seemed long hours later, the quality of the ride changed. It signified the change from macadam to dirt road, and the speed grew even slower. The vehicle bumped and swayed through the night and there was no sound of other traffic as it wound its way deeper and deeper toward its destination.

Finally, they arrived.

The hay bales were pulled aside, and Owney rose and stretched.

"Good work, fellows," he said, blinking and stretching, to discover himself on a dirt road in a dense forest, almost silent except for the heavy breathing of the drivers.

"Yas suh," said one of the drivers.

"You take good care of these boys," he said, addressing Flem Grumley, who stood there with a flashlight in a party of several of his boys, all heavily armed.

"I will, Mr. Maddox," promised Flem.

"The others arrive yet?"

"Johnny and Herman. The other two haven't made it in yet. But they will."

"Yes," agreed Owney.

The two drivers restored the hay and left with the truck. Meanwhile, Flem led Owney and Vince through the trees and down a little incline. A body of water lay ahead, glinting in the moonlight and from the lights of buildings across the way. It was Lake Catherine.

They stepped through rushes, and eased their way down a rocky incline toward the water, under the illumination of the flashlights guided by the Grumleys.

In time, they came to a cave into which the water ran and slid into it.

"Hallo, Owney lad," sang Johnny, rising to greet the man whose life he had just saved. "It's just like the last time, except we didn't steal any payroll, we stole you!"

CHAPTER 57

The deputies had gone, leaving Earl alone with his headache, his shot-out car windows and his bad news.

He shook his head.

Owney makes it out; he'll get away, he's got some smart boys in town with him, he'll get his millions of dollars out, and he'll go live in luxury somewhere. He won't pay. The dead boys of the Garland County raid team and their old leader pass into history as fools and the man they died to stop ends up living with a swimming pool in France or Mexico somewhere.

Earl felt the need to drink again. This one really hurt. This one was like a raw piece of glass caught in his throat, cutting every time he breathed.

The sun was bright, his head ached, he felt the shakiness of the hangover, the hunger from not having eaten in twenty-four hours, and the emptiness of no life ahead of him and memories of what was done stuck in his head forever.

He wiped the sweat from his brow, and decided it was time to go on home and try and pick up the pieces. Yet something wouldn't let him leave.

He knew, finally: he had to see the place one more time.

See the goddamned barn.

He'd seen it in November when he was discharged and stopped off here before going on up to Fort Smith and getting married and joining up with the rest of America for the great postwar boom. Hadn't felt much then. Tried to feel something but didn't, but he knew he had to try again.

He walked through the weeds, the wind whipping dust in his face, the sun beating down hot and ugly, a sense of desolation like a fog over the abandoned Swagger homestead, where all the Swagger men had lived and one of them had died.

The barn door was half open. He slipped in. Dust, cobwebs, the smell of rotted hay and rotting wood. An unpainted barn will rot, Daddy had always said. Yes, and if Daddy wasn't here to see that the barn was painted every two years, it would rot away to nothing, which is what it was doing. The stench of mildew and decomposition also filled the close dense air. The wood looked moist in places, as if you could put a foot through it and it would crumble. Odd pieces of agricultural equipment lay about rusting, like slingblades and the lawn mower that Earl had once used, and spades and hoes and forks. A tractor, dusty and rusting, stood mutely by. The stalls were empty, though of course a vague odor of animal shit also lingered in the air.

But Earl went to where he had to go, which was to the rear of the barn, under a crossbeam. That is where Bobby Lee had hanged himself. There was no mark of the rope on the wood, and no sign of the barrel he had stood upon to work his last task, the tying of the knot, good and tight, the looping of the noose, and the final kick to liberate himself from the barrel's support and from the earth's woe.

He had hung there, as the life was crushed out of his throat, believing that he was going to a better place.

Hope you made it, Bobby Lee. I wasn't no good to you at all. You were the first of the all-too-many young men I let down and who paid for it with their lives. There were legions of these beyond Bobby Lee, platoons full of them, from the 'Canal to the railyard in Hot Springs, all of whom had trusted him, and there wasn't a damn thing he could do for them except watch them die.

A thought came to Earl. He could find a rope and do the same trick and that would solve a lot of problems for a lot of people, mostly himself. The faces of boys wouldn't always be there, except when he was in a gunfight, to haunt him and sour his sleep, his food, his life.

But Earl was somehow beyond that now. He had a vague memory of shooting himself in the head in a bathroom in Washington, dead drunk, and finding that he'd forgotten to load the chamber, the only time ever in his whole life when he had pulled a trigger and been surprised at what happened.

Bobby Lee hadn't been so lucky. He wanted to leave the world and no secret part of him intervened. He kicked the barrel and he left the world and went to a better world, where no drunken father would take his anger out on him, and beat him and beat him just to express his own rage at what lurked deep in his own mind. October 2, 1940. Earl had been in the Panama Canal Zone at Balboa, on jungle maneuvers, happy in his far-off mock war, his brain consumed with the tactical problems, the discomforts, the need to lead his men, his worry over a captain who seemed a little too fond of the bottle, the—

No, no. *Not* October 2, 1940. That was something else. That was something else. Bobby Lee killed himself two days later, October 4, 1940. Why had he remembered October 2?

Oh, yes. Now he had it: Carlo Henderson had pointed out that the Alcoa payroll job had been October 2. Five men shot and killed four railway guards in the same damned railyard, and got away scot-free with $400,000 that very quickly came back to Owney Maddox, who probably was going to live off it for the rest of his life.

Something nagged at Earl.

Suddenly he wasn't in the dust-choked barn anymore, where his brother died and where the general agenda was rot and ruin, but only in his head.

Daddy must have beaten Bobby Lee really bad on October 3 or October 4. He must have gotten completely drunk and angry and forgotten himself and beat the boy so hard the boy concluded there was a better place to be and it wasn't in this world.

Why October 4?

Well, why not? If it was going to happen, it was going to happen and any one date was as good as another.

Still Earl couldn't put it quite away. It *was* two days after the most notorious crime of the era. His daddy would have been busy on roadblock duty all that—

Well, what about that?

Why wasn't Daddy parked out on some roadblock? A robbery that big, leaving that many men dead, the roadblocks would have stayed out for a week at least. Yet somehow in all that mess, Daddy has a chance to get liquored up and comes home and finds his second son and cannot help but release his deepest rage and beats on the boy so bad that the boy decides this life ain't worth living no more and that he will stop the hurting.

Could Charles have had something to do with the robbery?

It almost seemed possible. For with Charles's secret life in Hot Springs, he'd certainly have come to the notice of Owney and the Grumleys. His weakness made him vulnerable to blackmail, as did his gambling debts. If they needed him, he'd have been powerless to stop them. He was made to order for the taking, with his rigidity, his pride, his secret shame, his alcoholism.

And maybe it wasn't till afterward he learned that four men had died and he hadn't just helped robbers but killers as well. And he'd been so overcome with disgust and self-loathing for what he'd done, he'd laid on a big drunk. The biggest. And God help his child when he got in that way.

But then Earl had a sudden laugh. Standing there in that rotting barn, breathing the choking dust and smelling the odor of rot and shit and rust, he laughed hard.

What on earth could my daddy have known to help those birds? Charles Swagger knew nothing! What the hell value was he? He knew how to sap a drunk and get the cuffs on. He knew how to fix an uppity Negro with a stare so hard it would melt a safe. He knew how to shoot, as he'd proved in the Great War, and in the bank in Blue Eye in 1923, but them boys didn't need shooters, that was clear; they knew how to shoot.

Earl turned, and slipped out of the barn. A cloud had come over the sun, so it was cooler now, and the freshness of the air revived him somewhat as he escaped the dense atmosphere. He allowed himself a smile. His father! A conspirator in a train robbery! That stubborn, mule-proud old bastard with his stern Baptist ways and his secret weakness and rancid hypocrisy! What could he offer such men! They'd laugh at him because they didn't fear him and without the power of fear he had no power at all.

Earl walked over to the porch and sat down. He knew he should leave soon. It was time to go. He had to make peace with his failures, to face the future, to go on and—

But: Who was my father?

Who was he? I don't know. He scared me too much to ever ask the question when the man was alive, and his memory hurt too much to ask it when he was dead. But: Who was he?

He turned and looked into the old house. If there was an answer maybe it was in the house that Charles Swagger inherited from Swaggers before and made his own little invincible kingdom.

Earl rose and went to the door. It had been nailed shut. He hesitated, then remembered that he now owned the place and the door only sealed him off from his own legacy. With a stout kick, he blasted the door open, and stepped inside.

Some houses always smell the same. He'd have recognized it anywhere, though now the furniture was gone, as were the pictures off the wall. The smell was somehow more than the accumulated odors of his mother's cooking and the generations of cooking that had come before; it was more than the grief or the melancholy that had haunted this place; it was more than the bodies that had lived here. It was unique and its totality took him backward.

He remembered himself as a boy of about

twelve. The house was so big and dark, the furniture all antiques from the century before. If his father was home, the house would tell him: there'd be a tension somehow in the very structure of the universe. Daddy might not be angry that day, might merely be aloof and distant, but the danger of his explosiveness would float through these rooms and corridors like some sort of vapor, volatile and nerve-breaking, awaiting the spark that set it off.

Or maybe Daddy was drinking. He drank mostly on the weekends but sometimes, for unknown reasons, he'd drink at night and the drink loosened his tongue and let his demons spill out. Maybe he'd hit you, maybe he wouldn't, but it wasn't just the hitting; he'd be on you, like some kind of stallion or bull or bull rooster. He had to dominate you. He couldn't let you breathe.

What're you staring at, goddammit, he'd demand.

What's wrong with you, boy. You some kind of girl? You just stare. I'll knock that goddamned stare off your face.

Charles, the boy didn't mean nothing.

In my house, nobody stares at me. This is *my* house. Y'all live here because *I* let you. I set the rules. I provide the food, I pay the hands, I keep the law in this county, I set the rules.

Earl walked from room to room. Each was empty in fact but full in his own mind. He remembered everything, exactly: the placement of the sofa, the size and shape of the dining room table, the old brown pictures of Swaggers from an earlier time and place, he remembered them all.

Whoa, partner, he counseled himself. Don't let your hate just fog your mind.

He tried another approach. If you must understand your father, don't think about what made him angry, since *everything* made him angry. Think about what made him happy.

He tried to remember his father happy. Was his father ever happy? Had his father ever smiled?

He had no memory of such an event, but in time he realized that being occupied, his demons quelled momentarily by mental activity, was as close to happiness as Charles Swagger, sheriff of Polk County, ever got.

So Earl knew where he had to go.

Not into the kitchen or the bedroom or the cellar, and not upstairs where the boys slept, but back through the house to his father's trophy room.

That was his father's sanctum. That's where his father retreated. It was a sacred temple to . . . well, whatever. Who knew? Who could say?

Earl opened the door. The old woman had left the room pretty much intact when she left after his death. The guns were gone of course, presumably sold off, and the cabinet removed. Earl remembered standing before it as a child; in fact his one or two pleasant memories with his father seemed to revolve around the guns, which stood locked behind glass. The old man had some nice ones: Winchesters mostly, dark and oily, sheathed in gleamy soft wood, a Hi-Wall in .45-120, a whole brace of lever actions, from an 1873 he'd picked up somewhere to a '92 to an 1895 carbine, all in calibers nobody loaded anymore, like .40-72 and .219 Zipper and a beautiful old 1886 in .40-65; Daddy also had a couple of the little self-loaders, in .401. He had three shotguns for geese in the fall, and he had one bolt gun, the '03 Springfield, which he'd turned into a sleek and beautiful sporter. The guns were treated with respect. If Daddy approved—rare, but it happened—you were allowed to touch the guns. But they were gone. So was the desk, the volumes of works on hunting, reloading and ballistics, the liquor cabinet where the ever-filled bottle of magic amber fluid was kept. So was the map of Polk County, where he had painstakingly tracked his kills with coded color pins each year, yellow for deer, red for boar, black for bear, so that in the end, the map was a tapestry of brightly lit little dots, each signifying a good shot. A blank rectangular space stood on the wall, where the map had been taped for all those years and the paint hadn't faded. Now it was just emptiness.

And she had no stomach for removing the trophies themselves. It was as if Charles's powerful medicine still inhabited them, and looking at them on another wall, he saw they were dusty and ratty, beginning to fall apart like old furniture, their ferocity largely theatrical. Earl nevertheless felt the power of his father's presence.

Charles was a hunter. He stalked the mountains and the meadows of Polk and other nearby counties with his Winchesters, and he shot what he saw. He was a very good shot, an excellent game shot, and he learned the habits of the creatures. He was a man who could always support himself in the woods, and he had that Swagger gift, mysterious and unsourced, for understanding the terrain and making the good read, then finishing up with a brilliant shot on the deflection.

Earl remembered; his father took him hunting and taught him to shoot, and taught him to track, taught him patience and stoicism and a bit of crazed courage, the willingness to ignore the body and do what had to be done. And the odd thing was, they were skills that let Earl survive the dark journey that would become his fate. So he did in fact get something from his daddy, a great gift, even if he never realized it at the time.

He looked at the heads on the wall. Bear, boar, three deer, an elk, a cougar, a bobcat, a ram, all bearing either a graceful furl of horn or a mouthful of snaggly teeth. Like any trophy hunter, his father took only the best, the oldest animals, who had long since passed their genes along to progeny. The taxidermist was a fellow in Hatfield, and he too had the gift.

The animals seemed to live on that wall. They were frozen in expressions of anger or assault, their lips curled back, their fangs bared, the full animal majesty of their power exploding off their faces. It was all make-believe, of course; Earl had been to the shop and the taxidermist was a bald, fat little cracker who smelled of chemicals and had a shop full of marble eyes sent from 34th Street in New York, intricate replicas of the real thing that gleamed and seemed to stare, but were merely glass.

What does this room tell me?

Who was my father?

Who was this man?

He stared at the trophy animals on the wall, and they stared back at him, relentless, if locked in place, still spoiling for a great fight.

What did my father know?

On the evidence of this room, only the pleasures of the hunt. And the pleasures of the land the hunt was conducted upon.

That's what a hunter knows. A hunter knows the land. A hunter roams the land, and even if he's not hunting that particular day, he's paying attention, storing up information, recording details that someday may come in handy.

That's what my father would know: the Arkansas mountain wilderness, as well as any man before or since.

That was the only place he was ever really happy.

CHAPTER 58

Owney was nervous. Across the way, there seemed a lot of activity. Searchlights and the pulsing flash of red gumballs cut the night as the cops stopped cars, threw up roadblocks, sent out search teams and dogs on the hunt for him. But the lake was serenely calm. It lay in the dark like a sheet of glass, glinting with illumination from the various points of light on the shore.

"Don't worry," said Johnny. "It'll be like the last time. It'll go without a hitch."

"I ain't worried about the lake," said Owney. "I'm worried about the forest. How can you remember? It was so complicated. It was at night."

"I have a photographic memory," said Johnny. "Certain things I don't forget and you can take that to the bank." He smiled, radiating charm. He held all the cards, and he knew it.

"And then we talk money."

"There's plenty, believe me," Owney assured him.

"That's the problem. I don't believe you. No matter what I ask for you'll cry-baby and try to jew me down. But I know you've got millions."

"I don't have millions," said Owney. "That's a fuckin' myth."

"Oh, I've done some checking," said Johnny. "I have a figure in mind. A very nice figure. After all, we *are* saving your life. It seems like I should take you for everything, because I'm saving everything."

"Is this a getaway or a kidnapping?"

"Well, actually, it's a wee bit of both," said Johnny. "We won't leave you with nothing."

"No, you wouldn't want to do that," said Owney. "You want me to be your friend after all this is over. I'll get back, somehow, you know I will. I'm Owney Maddox. I ran the Cotton Club. I ran Hot Springs. This is just a little setback. I ain't going into no retirement. I'll be big in the rackets again, you'll fuckin' see."

"Yeah, sure," said Johnny.

"I think I'll move out to California. The opportunities are golden and I got a feeling there's about to be a change in management real soon. A certain party's luck just ran out."

It was almost time.

Johnny checked his watch and went to the mouth of the cave and looked across the lake. Owney followed and sure enough, out of the darkness they saw the white flashing sails of a large craft. That was the core of Johnny's plan. He knew that the law enforcement imagination was somehow drawn to the drama of the high-speed getaway. Thus cops thought of roads mainly, and of airplanes and railways. Crime was modern, fast-paced, built on speed. Who would ever suspect—a sailboat?

It was a beauty, owned by Judge LeGrand, a fifty-footer under two masts and a complexity of sails that pulled it gracefully and silently across the water. The judge entertained on it many times, taking visiting congressmen and titans of industry out for elegant sails across the diamond-blue water, under the diamond-blue sky, swaddled in the green rolling pine hills of the Ouachitas, where they sipped champagne and ate oysters and laughed the evening away like the important men they were, so that when they lost their hundreds of thousands at Owney's gaming tables, they still went home with wondrous tales of Southern hospitality and sleek nights under starry skies.

The boat drew four feet; she was a trim craft, pure teak and brass, with a crew of four to run her and an auxiliary engine—nobody knew about this, it was her secret—that could propel her through the water in the absence of wind and had the special gift of taking her along narrow passages under mechanical power if necessary, and it would be very necessary.

The boat was too cumbersome to dock, so it simply put up at anchor seventy-five feet out and a dinghy, propelled by two oarsmen, slid toward them.

"All right, you boys, let's get aboard," Johnny commanded as the small craft nudged ashore.

They left the cave, scuttled down the bit of hillside and ducked among the reeds until they reached the prow, which was being held steady at a taut rope's end by a crewman. Owney clambered aboard, shivering ever so slightly as the breeze picked up. The boat's insubstantiality annoyed him—he liked things solid—as he found a seat. He felt it continue to slipside and tremble as the others came aboard. But then, quickly enough, they were off and the progress to the bigger boat was easy.

Hands drew Owney aboard.

"Good evening, Mr. Maddox," said Brick Stevens, the boat's skipper, a hot local available bachelor who secretly (Owney knew) was screwing both the judge's daughter and his wife, "how are you, sir?"

"I'll be much better when I'm sipping a piña colada in Acapulco," he said.

"It'll just be a couple of days. The judge sends his best wishes."

"The judge better keep sending his money. I own this town, after all."

"I'm sure the judge realizes that, sir."

After Owney, the five gunmen, encumbered with their weapons, clambered aboard.

"All right, boys," said Brick, "let's go down below. Meanwhile, we'll be off."

They stepped uneasily down the teak steps into what was a stateroom, though not much of one, more a state crawlspace. But inside, yes, it was nice, more teak, with a small bar, lots of liquor.

Owney settled down on the sofa. The others took up chairs and whatever.

"I'm going to turn the lanterns down, fellows," said Brick. "It'll be safer that way."

"How long, skipper?"

"Can't be more than four hours. There's enough breeze and I'll go three sheets. I know these waters like the back of my hand. I'll have you where you want to be by twenty-two bells. That's ten o'clock for you landlubbers."

"We're all landlubbers here," said Herman Kreutzer, holding his BAR loosely.

"You will be careful with that?" requested Brick.

"Sure. But if a State Police cruiser tries to board us, you'll be glad I've got it."

"This is an antique, old man. We can't have it shot up."

"Then sail good, skip."

The skipper ducked back upstairs and in just a few minutes the boat began to edge forward in the darkness as its sails caught and harnessed the wind. It was like a train, in that it seemed to take forever to get going, but then, suddenly, had amassed enormous smooth speed, and flashed across the water.

Owney looked out the porthole. He could see a few lights, but wherever they were, the shore was mostly dark. There was no sound except for the snapping of the sail in the wind and the rush of the water being pushed aside by the boat's knifelike prow.

"We're okay on time?" asked Owney.

Johnny made a show of squinting at his watch, and then a bigger show of making abstract calculations in his head, and finally came up with an answer.

"Absolutely okay."

"Because the longer we hang around, the greater the chance of someone spotting me."

"I know it."

"And you've made the calls, it's all set up, these are reliable people."

"Very reliable. This is the soft way out. It worked before, it'll work again. Think of the last time as a rehearsal. This is the performance. Everything's set. The critics will love it. You'll be a hit on Broadway."

"I don't care about hits on Broadway. I care about hits in Las Vegas."

"It will happen."

"The fuck. Who the fuck he think he is! Braque! I bought that goddamn painting from a legit dealer. How's *I* supposed to know it was hot?"

"Owney, Owney, Owney," crooned Johnny. "You're home free. You'll have your freedom, your vengeance and your wealth. No man in America is better off than you."

The boat skimmed across the smooth water, and Owney settled down and watched as the lights of Hot Springs passed on the right and then got smaller and dimmer until they died away altogether.

Finally, a far shore grew near, nearer still until it seemed they were out of lake. They were, in fact. They had reached the northernmost point of Lake Hamilton. They were at the mouth of the Ouachita River.

Owney heard the captain giving commands. He cut sail and dropped anchor. It took his well-trained crew only a few minutes to rig for running by motor. Quickly they set up the Johnson outboard on the fantail, and ginned it up. It sounded like a sewing machine. Brick took the helm and guided them into the narrow mouth of the river.

But Brick knew what he was doing. It was said he'd run rum for Joe Kennedy in the old days, making a fortune before moving south and joining the horsey set. He was an adventurer too, and had skippered a PT boat in the war. He got a Jap destroyer, it was said, but maybe it was only a landing craft or a cargo scow. But he knew his art: he took the boat up the narrow strait of the Ouachita River, between darkened shores so close they could almost be touched, past the little river town of Buckville. Hot Springs was far behind, and then, up near Mountain Pine, the river shifted direction, widened, and headed west into the vast Ouachita wilderness. The boat gulled along against the current, and the men finally came on deck. Around them was only darkness and the sense of the forest so close and engulfing it almost had them. But they pressed on to the west, passing into Montgomery County. They were headed west toward escape.

In the vast quiet darkness, Owney began to relax at last. He was going to make it, he finally believed.

CHAPTER 59

Where was he? She couldn't put it out of her mind. He was in trouble. They had gotten him. He had survived so much, but he had not survived this last thing with the gangsters.

She called long distance to a newspaper in Hot Springs. Were there any incidents, any killings, anything involving a man named Earl Swagger.

The man said, "Lady, ain't you heard? We had a big prison break down here. The whole town's going crazy looking for Owney Maddox. You ought to call the cops, maybe they'd know."

Eventually she got to a lieutenant of detectives who chewed her out for interrupting them in their important work of capturing this escaped criminal, but he finally told her the last anybody had ever seen of that disagreeable individual, Earl Swagger, he was on his way out of the county and if she loved her husband, she'd make it clear to him he was never to return.

That was a night before.

Where had Earl gone?

She tried to settle herself down, but she just sat there, feeling nauseated and frightened in the darkness. There was nobody to help her. That was Earl's duty. Was he involved in the manhunt for this Owney, a gangster? He had told her he was off, he was out of that business, he'd been fired and he was coming home and that's all there was to it. He was coming home to work in the sawmill.

But she thought he was involved in the matter of Owney. The gangsters had finally caught up with him in some way. She thought of him off in the woods, the gangsters having executed him and dumped him in a grave that would go forever unmarked. Such a cruel end for a hero! It would be so unfair.

In her abdomen, her child moved. She felt it kick ever so gently, and that too was strange. Something about the child frightened her, although the doctor kept saying that everything was fine. But it wasn't fine; small signals of danger—her fainting spells, for example—kept arriving as if the child, somehow, were sending her messages, warning her that he needed help already, that there would be difficulties.

She went to the desk, and got out the map of Arkansas. She looked at the highways. Clearly, it was no more than a few hours—maybe four or five at most—from Hot Springs to Camp Chaffee. There was no reason for Earl to be missing.

She couldn't stay put. She rose, nervous, not knowing what to do. It was near dark.

She went next door to Mary Blanton's and knocked.

Mary answered, a cigarette in her hand, and immediately read the distress on Junie's face.

"Junie, what on earth? Honey, you look awful. Is that critter kicking up a storm?"

"It's Earl. He was supposed to be back from Hot Springs last night and I haven't heard a thing."

"He's probably parked in a bar, honey. You give a man a day off and sure as hell, that's where he'll end up. My Phil'd waste his life among the Scotch bottles if I let him."

"No, Mary, it can't be that. He swore to me he was off the stuff forever. He swore."

"Honey, they all say that. Believe me, they do."

"I'm so afraid. I called the police and the newspapers, but they just told me he left late yesterday afternoon."

"Do you want to come in and wait here, honey? You're welcome. I'm just reading the new *Cosmopolitan.*"

"I'd like to look for him."

"Oh, Junie, that's not wise. The baby's due in two weeks. You never know about these things. You shouldn't be off on some wild-goose chase. And what if Earl calls?"

"But I'll go crazy if I just sit around. I just want to drive down to Waldron and then over to Hot Springs. That'd be the way he'd come, I know. We'll run into him and that'll be that. But I just can't sit there anymore."

"You can't drive alone."

"I know."

"Well, let me get my hat, honey. Looks like the gals are going on a little trip. Wouldn't mind stopping for a beer."

"I'm not supposed to drink, they say."

"Well, honey, there's nothing to stop *me* from drinking, now, is there?"

"No ma'am," said Junie, already feeling better.

"You just watch real good. You have a Coke, and you watch me drink a beer." She winked good-naturedly.

Mary got her hat and the two went out to Mary's car, a 1938 DeSoto that could have used some bodywork. Mary started the old vehicle, and they backed out of the driveway and headed through the maze of gravel roads in the vets village.

"Do you think we'll ever get out?" Mary asked.

"They say they're building more houses. If you had a good war record you can get a loan. But it'll still be a wait."

"All that time when Phil was in the Pacific, I kept thinking how wonderful it was going to be. Now he's back and"—she laughed bitterly, her signature reaction to the complexities of the world—"it's not wonderful at all. In fact, it plain stinks."

"It'll work out" was all Junie could think to say.

"Honey, you are such an incorrigible optimist! Oh, well, at least we won the war, we have the atom bomb, our men are back in one piece and we have a roof over our heads, even if it's made of tin and smells like the inside of an airplane!"

They laughed. Mary could always get a laugh out of Junie. Junie was so duty-haunted, so straight-ahead, so committed to the ideal, that Mary was a refreshment to her, because Mary saw through everything, considered every man who ever lived a promise-breaking, drunken, raping lout, and in her day had riveted more Liberator fuselages than any man in the Consolidated plant.

The camp vanished behind them as they hit Route 71 and followed that road's generally southward course as it plunged down the western spine of Arkansas.

There was little enough to see in the daylight and even less in the twilight. Traffic was light.

"You know, we could miss Earl's car. It would be easy to do."

"I know. Maybe this wasn't such a good idea."

"If it makes you feel better, you should do it. You get few enough chances in this lifetime to feel better."

Small towns fled by: Rye Hill, Big Rock, Witcherville, little dots on a map that turned out to be a gas station and a few outbuildings of indistinct size and meaning. It grew darker.

"Why don't we stop and get that beer," said Junie.

"Hmmm, now I'm not so sure. These boys out here, they may think we're fast city gals out larking about. See, all men think that all women secretly desire them and want to be conquered and treated like slaves. I don't know where they get that idea, but I do know the further you get from city lights, the stronger that idea becomes, although it's certainly very strong in the city too. And the fact that you're carrying thirty extra pounds of baby'll just get 'em to thinking you want a last adventure before you're a mama forever."

Junie laughed. Mary had such a bold way of putting things, which is why some of the other wives in the village didn't like her, but exactly why Junie liked her so much.

She looked at the map.

"Up ahead is a city called Peverville. It's a little larger. Maybe we'll find a nice, decent place where nobody'll whistle or make catcalls."

"Oh, if they don't do it out loud, they'll do it in their heads, which is the same thing, only quieter."

The land here was quiet and dark; it was all forest, and the gentle but insistent up and down of the road suggested they were going through mountains. Occasionally a car passed headed in the other direction, but it was never Earl's old Ford.

"I hope he's all right," Junie said.

"Honey, if all the Japanese in the world couldn't kill Earl Swagger, what makes you think some likkered-up cornpone-licking crackers from Hot Springs could?"

"I know. But Earl says it's not always who's the best. When the guns come out, it's so much luck too. Maybe his luck finally ran out."

"Earl is too ornery. Luck wouldn't dare let him

down, he'd grab it by the throat and fix that Marine Corps stare on it, and it would give up the ghost!"

Again, in spite of herself, Junie had to laugh.

"Mary, you are such a character!"

"Yes ma'am," said Mary.

An approaching car looked to be Earl's, and both women bent forward, peering at it for identification. But as it sped by, a much older man turned out to be the driver.

"Thought we had us something for just a while," said Mary.

"You know, Mary," said Junie, "I think maybe we better head on back."

"Are you all right?"

"Suddenly I don't feel so good."

"Is that critter kicking up a storm?"

"No, it's just that I seem to be cramping or something."

"Oh, gosh, does it hurt?"

Junie didn't answer, and Mary saw from the pallor that had stolen over her features that it did.

"Do you want to go to the hospital?"

"No, but if I could just—"

She hesitated.

"Oh, I'm so sorry," she said. "I made a mess. I don't know."

Mary pulled off, reached up and flicked on the compartment light.

"Oh, God," she said, for Junie was soaked.

Suddenly Junie curled in pain.

"My water just broke," she said. "I am *so* sorry about the car."

"Forget the car, honey. The car don't mean a thing. You are going to have that damn baby right now. We have to find you a hospital."

"Earl!" screamed Junie as the first contraction hit, "oh, Earl, where *are* you?"

CHAPTER 60

The boat was behind them. They had left it at the River Bluff Float Camp, where the river grew too rough to be navigated. Now they traveled through the darkness in a 1934 V-8 Ford station wagon, primer dull, which had come from the Grumleys' store of bootlegging vehicles. It had a rebuilt straight-8 Packard 424 engine, super-strong shocks, a rebuilt suspension and could do 150 flat-out if need be. Revenooers had called it the Black Bitch for years.

Forest was everywhere, and the narrow, winding road suggested that civilization was far, far behind.

Owney kept looking at his watch.

"Are we going to make it?"

"We'll make it fine," said Johnny. "I set it up, remember."

Now there was just this last, long pull through the mountains, along a ribbon of moonlit macadam; and then a final rough plunge down old logging roads, the exact sequence to which Johnny swore he had committed to memory.

"Suppose something goes wrong? Suppose we have a flat tire or have to evade a roadblock, and we fall behind schedule."

"If we're not there, he comes back next day, same time, no problem. It's flexible. I accounted for that. But we have clear road and we ought to keep going. The sooner we're out of here, me boy, the sooner you're enjoying the pleasures of them dusky Mex women."

"Okay, okay," said Owney. "I hate being nervous. I want to fucking *do* something."

"This is the hard part, old man," said Johnny.

"Say, Owney," said Herman Kreutzer from the back seat, "whatever happened to your English accent? It seems to have escaped too."

The gunman erupted in laughter. This annoyed Owney, but until he had reestablished himself, he was subject to such predations. His misery increased.

"Uh oh," said Johnny.

"Oh, shit," said Herman.

Owney felt the sudden infusion of red light as, just behind them, a police or sheriff's car had just turned on its lights and siren.

"Fuck, he's got us," said a gunman.

"We're going to have to pop this boy," said Johnny.

"No," said Owney. "I'll handle it. You guys, you been laughing at me like I'm nobody. I'll show you Mr. Fucking New York rackets."

"Oh, he's a tough one," said Vince the Hat.

"Let the boy operate," said Johnny.

Johnny guided the car to the shoulder and eased to a halt: Owney got out, raised his hands high.

The policeman—no, a sheriff's deputy, or possibly the sheriff himself, for the black-and-white's door read SHERIFF and under that MONTGOMERY COUNTY, ARK.—climbed out of the car, but kept his distance. He was not distinctly visible behind the haze of lights.

"I'm unarmed," called Owney.

He spread his coat open to show that he had no pistol. Then he started to walk forward.

"Y'all just hold it up there," said the sheriff.

"Ah, of course. Meant no harm, sir," said Owney in his best stage British.

"Who are you? Mite late to be pleasure-cruising through the mountains in a big ol' station wagon."

"We were enjoying the sporting possibilities of Hot Springs," said Owney. "Our money having run rather abruptly dry, we decided to head straight toward Fayetteville. We may have taken a wrong turn. Glad you're here, Sheriff. If you'd just—"

He took another step forward.

"You hold it," said the sheriff. "And tell all them

boys to stay in that car. I am armed, and I am a good shot, and I'd hate there to be any trouble, because if there is, one or t'other of you and your boys is going to Fayetteville in a pine box."

"Yes sir. No need for violence. We'll show proper ID and you may verify our identities via your radio. I appreciate that people are jumpy tonight, what with that fellow escaping prison in Hot Springs. We've been stopped twice at roadblocks already."

He kept advancing.

"You hold it there, pardner," said the sheriff, putting his hand to a big gun in his holster, and at the same time looking quickly to the car to make certain nobody had stepped out and all the windows had remained rolled up.

"Sheriff, uh—?"

"Turner, sir."

"Sheriff Turner, I appreciate your nervousness given the drama of the evening. But I wish to assure you I am harmless. Here, go ahead, search me. You'll see."

Owney assumed the position against the fender of the police vehicle; the fellow gave him a quick pat-down and came to the conclusion he was unarmed.

But Owney also saw that he was a professional, and shrewd. He hadn't approached the Ford but stayed back by his own vehicle. No one in the car could get a shot at him, not without opening the doors and leaning out, and he was probably very good with his gun. If they all jumped out of the car, they might get him, but not before he'd gotten two or three of them. And he could then dip back into the woods, pop their tires and make it to a phone to call in reinforcements quick. Sly dog.

"What business are you in, sir?" asked the sheriff, somewhat relaxed that he'd found no gun on Owney.

"Well, I've been known to wager a penny on the ponies, the fall of a card or the roll of a die."

"Gambler, eh? But you didn't do too well in Hot Springs."

"Had a run of bad luck, yes. But I'll be back, you can make book on it."

"Well, y'all be careful. Ain't no speed limit here but you were moving mighty fast. Don't want to scrape you off a tree."

"No, indeed."

"Say, what was the name again?"

"Vincent Owen Maddox."

The sheriff's face knitted with a little confusion, for the name sounded so familiar.

"And you say you're headed to Fayetteville."

"Headed *toward* Fayetteville, old fellow."

"Well, Mr. Maddox—"

Then his face lit with amazement as he realized that the Owen became Owney, and his face set hard, for in an instant he knew who he was up against, and his hand flew fast and without doubt toward the big gun at his hip.

But Owney was faster.

In less than half a second he had a small silver revolver in his hand, as if from nowhere, as if from the very air itself, and he fired one bullet with a dry pop into the sheriff's chest. The big man never reached his Colt and stepped back, for the bullet packed so little impact it felt only like a sting, but in the next second the blood began to gush from his punctured aorta and he sat down with an ashen look, then toppled sideways to the earth.

"All right, you fellows," called Owney. "Get him in his car and get it off the road, chop chop now."

Johnny's gunmen got out of the Ford and dragged the dead police officer to his car. Vince started it, and began to creep along the road until he found enough of a hill to drive it over so that it would tumble off and into the underbrush.

"Say," said Johnny, "ain't you a fast piece of work. Where'd you get that little ladies' gun?"

"When they delivered my suit to the cave, it was tucked in a pocket."

"I don't mean that. I mean, where were you packing it? I didn't realize you were heeled. You sure got it out in a flash."

"I am a man of some dexterity."

"Where was it?"

Owney smiled, and pulled up his coat sleeve. His shirtsleeve underneath was unbuttoned and a black piece of elastic circled his wrist. Quickly he slid the gun under it, then drew the suit sleeve back down over it, where it disappeared to all but the most discerning eye. But Johnny could see it was an old nickel-plated revolver of the sort called a bicycle gun, a .32 rimfire from very early in the century, that lacked a trigger guard and had a one-inch barrel.

"It's a trick another sheriff once taught me," said Owney.

CHAPTER 61

My father knew the land. That's what my father knew. But what good is that? What value is that? What does that get you?

Earl walked out onto the porch, where he could see the sun setting to the west. But it was a quiet twilight in Polk County and no cars had headed on down the road in quite some time.

My father knew the land.

What does that tell me?

But the more Earl hammered against it, the harder it became.

He knew *this* land. What the hell good would that be to train robbers in Hot Springs, fifty odd miles away. He knew Polk County, an out-of-the-way spread of land, mostly mountain wilderness with a few one-horse towns far to the west, hard up against Oklahoma. What was there about Polk County that could be important to these men?

Well, maybe they could hide out in the mountainous trees of the Ouachitas. But there were plenty of trees, mountains and wilderness in Garland County itself or in Montgomery County. What would they need to come an extra county over here for?

He tried to recall what he knew about that robbery, what old D.A. had told him months back. Five armed men, an inside job, four guards killed, a huge payroll in cash taken, and they got away without a trace.

He applied his tactical imagination to it. It was a military problem. You have to leave an area. You are behind enemy lines. You are being hunted in force by all police agencies. How do you do it?

Well, obviously, you drive. But to where? Roadblocks are already out. You can't get far by road. Do you take a train? No, don't be ridiculous. Well, maybe you don't leave. Maybe you go to ground for a month and wait the manhunt out. You have, after all, friends in the area who can hide you. But . . . the longer you stay there, the more likely that somebody will notice something, somebody will talk, somebody will see something.

That leaves a boat. Could you take a boat? Could you ride up the Ouachita River to— well, to where?

That was interesting. You might go by boat, and possibly the cops wouldn't be covering the river or the lake because they'd believe you'd be on the road. But . . . a boat to where? You take the Ouachita to where? It would make most sense to take it south, toward the Mississippi, and he didn't even know if the Ouachita reached the Mississippi. And that took them into the flat part of the state, where—

This was getting him nowhere. It was pointless speculation. Maybe they did take a boat. Where would it get them, which way would they go, who could know now, six years later? And what difference would it make?

He heard a dry light whine from far off. It was so familiar he almost didn't notice it. He'd heard it in the Pacific a million times. He looked into the fading light and finally caught it, a plane, a silver speck up high, where the sunlight still commanded, glowing against the darkening sky, entirely too far to be identified.

An airplane, he thought.

They might go someplace where they could be picked up by an airplane. This suddenly seemed reasonable. You get into an airplane and you're free. It's 1940, after all. There's no radar, because it's still a secret; and the big wartime push hasn't begun, so the system of commercial aviation is haphazard and roundabout, planes come and go every day.

They go to an airplane.

What kind of airplane?

There are four men. They all have automatic weapons and presumably some supply of ammunition. They have clothes because they've been living in the area prior to their raid, and they have the trophy of their efforts, the payroll. Close to half a million, in cash. In small bills, in bags or a strongbox or some such. All that cash, maybe a hundred pounds of it. He had no idea how much a half million in small bills would weigh, but it would be considerable.

So: What kind of airplane?

Not a Piper Cub or any other small puddle-jumper, like the observation jobs he'd seen in the war. Maybe you could land all right, but it would be too dangerous to take off again with all that weight.

Therefore: it would have to be a multiengine plane, a substantial airplane that could carry five men, their equipment, their money. Something like . . . a DC-3? No, too big. But maybe some kind of Beechcraft, twin-engined, like the staff planes the brass had used in the war. You never saw them in combat zones, but behind the lines they were ubiquitous. Heavy, slow, low, but planes that were dependable and could land anywhere it was flat.

So where would you land such a plane?

Obviously, the airports were out, because they'd be watched by cops. You couldn't land that big a plane in a farm meadow, or anywhere near civilization because it would clearly be spotted, and you probably couldn't do it at night, because it would be too dangerous.

So: you had to find a big, flat field somewhere,

but somewhere far from prying eyes, somewhere in the wilderness, in the mountains, somewhere safe and secure, unlikely to be stumbled upon. That would leave out a road, a farm, a park, it would leave out just about anywhere.

Where would you land a plane? And what on earth would his father the hunter have to do with it?

A memory came to Earl. It was indistinct at first, a blurred image from some deep pool where experiences had been recorded. It was from his childhood. He had a vision of a remote field, a valley, yellow and rolling. He was there with his father and a few other men. It was maybe 1927 or '28, he was maybe twelve or fourteen years old. He heard his father's voice, instructing.

"Now you pay attention," the man was saying, in that low rumble that was his voice, "because I don't want to have to say this twice, Earl. You want to look to the treeline. The mule deer is a creature of the treeline. He likes the boundary between the open and the closed. He also likes the wind to be blowing across the open, so that he can smell anything tracking him. He won't go into the full open, particularly during hunting season, because he knows he's being hunted. Don't know how, but he does. He's smart that way. He wants the tender shoots of the margins. This is where you will find him, in the dawn or possibly at twilight. You must be alert, for his moves can sometimes seem magical, and you must be patient, for there is nothing in his mind to distract him, as there will be to distract you, so you must compel yourself to stillness. Do you understand, Earl? Are you listening, boy?"

Of course he was listening. Who could not listen to Daddy? Daddy demanded respect, and Daddy got it. Earl sat with his rifle as his father explained to him, as he was introduced into the rituals of the hunt.

But now he remembered and he saw: a wide field, so remote that to see it was to feel oneself the first white man in the territory in the year 1650-something, and to marvel at it, its length, its yellowness, the low hills that encased it to make it a valley and the far, blue peaks of higher mountains.

A name came out of his memory.

Hard Bargain Valley, a splash of flat yellow in the mountains, called such because some westward pilgrims had thought to winter there and by spring all that remained was food for the crows. Earl remembered the crows wheeling overhead, back and forth, like bad omens. God had made a hard bargain with the pilgrims indeed.

Could you land a plane on Hard Bargain Valley?

Yes, he knew in a second. You could. Easily. A bigger plane too, not a Cub but a substantial twin-engined craft.

Now it came together in a moment, as if all the parts of the puzzle had been sunk in his brain all these years and at some darker deeper level he'd been working on them. Now they fit. They announced themselves with a thunderclap, a vision of purity so intense it almost knocked him back.

Five men, heavily armed, fleeing Hot Springs. They have to get to a remote spot where a plane can pick them up.

There's only one such place within a night's travel. But how will they find it? There're no paved roads in, only a hopeless mesh of old logging trails, some drivable, some not. Who would help them?

It would have to be a man who knew the territory better than anyone. Sheriff Charles Swagger, the great lawman and hunter.

And they'd know about Swagger. He had a secret life in Hot Springs. Once a month, he'd show up for gambling and whoring and sporting with the special, secret vice he loved the best. Owney Maddox, that champion of human weakness, would know this. He'd have the leverage on old Charles and there would be the man, a paragon of public morality for so long, suddenly caught in the grip and crushed into obedience by a gangster.

So Charles would draw up a route. He would then engineer the roadblocks so that the fleeing men could get through them when they reached Polk County. Then he would meet them deep in the forest, and take them the last few miles to Hard Bargain Valley, and it would be a good bargain for them, for the plane would come at dawn and pluck them away and they'd have disappeared forever. The $400,000 would be quickly enough laundered and it would return in a few weeks to Hot Springs, as working capital for Owney Maddox, who would use it to build the Southern, the most elegant and successful casino in America.

Earl could see the last melancholy act too. Charles hadn't known men had been killed in the robbery. He'd gotten in because it was just robbers stealing money from Big Business like Alcoa and the money would go to gamblers, it was just the way the world worked, victimless, corrupt, ancient. But four men had died and suddenly his father is an accessory to murder. It sickens him, and that's why he returns home drunk and bent with anger at himself, and who does he run into but his young son, Bobby Lee, and the boy becomes the focus of his fury, his deep disappointment in himself, all his failures. He beats the boy and beats him and beats him, then passes out. Maybe he beats him to death and strings up the body to hide the crime. Maybe the boy hangs himself. But that is how it had to be. The evil father, the helpless son, the one man who had a chance to stop it fled to another family called the United States Marine Corps.

It was at that point Earl realized that they would do tonight exactly what they did in 1940. Of course. It was the same problem, except the treasure wasn't a payroll, it was Owney Maddox himself. It had worked before. The same route, the same arrangements with a plane, the same destination. Only this time they didn't need a Charles Swagger because they were smart, one of them had paid attention and he could find Hard Bargain Valley on his own.

Earl looked at his watch. It was near 8:00 and the sun was almost gone.

They were going to get away with it, because nobody else knew where Hard Bargain Valley was or could get there in time.

He himself had no idea where it was. It was somewhere in the mountain vastness that even now was fading into darkness and that no one could find who hadn't been there before and didn't know the way and he didn't know the way and there was no map, the map was gone.

Then Earl remembered his daddy's room. The map was gone, yes, but its outline still was described by that bright patch of unfaded paint.

He turned swiftly, walked back through the house and entered the room.

He faced the emptiness.

Nothing. What had he expected? It was just a square of lighter paint, even now losing its distinction as the light failed.

He tried to remember what it showed. It showed Polk, one of Arkansas's most westerly, most poverty-stricken, most mountainous, most remote counties. He tried to think: What is the essential quality of Polk County? He tried to remember as he stared at the square: What did I see here? Remember what you saw. Remember what was here.

He remembered. A big map, with few roads and many creeks, and many blank areas marked UN-

MAPPED. The swirl of color depicting different elevations as the larger forms of the mountains were at least suggested. But what was the pure quality of Polk County by shape?

He remembered: it was very regular. It was, like the sheet of paper that documented it, almost perfectly rectangular, with only a flare to the northwesterly corner and the southwesterly quarter to render the shape irregular. But otherwise it was drawn as if with a ruler, by men who laid out counties from far away without any knowledge of what the land was and therefore in defiance of the land. The borders didn't follow mountain crests or rivers or natural forms in the land; they defied them, they bisected them, they conquered them.

So the rectangle on the wall, it almost represented the pure shape of the county, with those deviations in the corner that were largely irrelevant because neither of them contained unmapped areas.

Earl tried to remember. What else was there? What else marked the county? He couldn't remember anything, any roads, any mountains, any creeks or rivers. It was over sixteen years since he'd really been here. How could he be expected to—

Pins. Pins. The map was festooned with pins where Charles Swagger had taken game and over the years he'd taken a lot of game, and he loved mule deer most of all, mulies they were called, magical creatures of muddy earth color who exploded from stillness to grace to invisibility in the blinking of an eye, and if you even saw one, much less managed to kill one, you felt that nature had been benevolent.

Earl looked away, then looked back again, seeing nothing. Then he edged sideways so that he saw the blank space on the wall at an angle, and could read the texture of it and that's when he saw them.

Of course. The map was gone. The pins were gone. The Swaggers were gone, all of them, dead or cursed, especially this last one, but what remained after it all were the pinholes.

Scanning the empty space from an angle, Earl quickly began to pick them up, here, there, one at a time, little pricks in the plaster, perhaps visible only in this light, with its play of shadows to bring out the irregularities. A prick here, a prick there, two pricks close together and—

That would be it. That had to be it.

A large concentration of pricks lay in the northwest corner of the lightened space, maybe thirty-five or forty. Not in a cluster, but in two parallel lines, suggesting the margins of the treeline defining the valley itself. That's where Hard Bargain Valley would be. That's where Charles Swagger went every year and every year he tagged his mulie buck, in the margins, just off the flat, remote high field of yellow grass, over which crows heeled and cruised, like omens of ill chance.

Earl knew: it's in the northwest corner of the county.

He knew if he could get close enough by car, he

could hump it in if he worked like the devil. He'd need a county map—there was an Arkansas state map in large scale in his car, and with it he could get close enough. It was maybe two hours' driving, maybe four hours of hard hike and climbing. He glanced at his watch. He could make it by dawn with an hour to spare.

He only needed one more thing.

He went into the third dusty stall and bent to the boards against the wall. He remembered hiding here in the long ago, from his father's rages. *Earl!* the old man would cry, *Earl, you get your ass in here, goddammit!* But Daddy never found him though it only forestalled the beatings a few minutes. No one else ever found him there either. He bet Bobby Lee had a secret place too, but this was Earl's.

With a few swift tugs he removed the boards from the wall. He leaned in—as he had when he stopped at the farm months ago, though then to emplace, not remove. He leaned in and dragged it out, a green wooden box wrapped in a tarpaulin, which bore the stamp SWAGGER USMC atop it, denoting that it was a sea chest that had followed its owner from ship to ship and battle to battle. He dragged the case into the barn, flicked on the bare-bulb light and pried it open.

More objects wrapped in canvas lay inside. He removed them, then unwrapped them, seeing each gleam dully in the yellow light. Each still wore that slick of oil that would keep it safe from the elements. He knew the parts so well. The frame and stock group, the barrel and receiver group, the bolt and recoil-spring group, the buffer and buffer pad. They all slid together with the neatness of something well designed. He knew the gun's trickery, all the little nuances of its complexity, where the bolt had to be, how the pins had to be set, when to screw in the bolt handle. Finally he slid the frame and stock group together and locked it in, and the thing assumed its ultimate shape. It took less than three minutes and he held his M1A1 Thompson submachine gun, with its finless barrel and its snout of muzzle, like a pig's ugly nose, its bluntness, its utilitarian grayness, its faded wood and scratched grip. He also had ten 30-round magazines and in the trunk of his car a thousand rounds of .45 ball tracer that he'd meant to trade to some other law enforcement agency.

Now, as in so many other nights of his life these past years, he had to get somewhere by the dawn. In the dawn, the killing would begin.

CHAPTER 62

At last, with a burst of energy from its 324 Packard horses, the Ford wagon got up a little hill and broke free from the trees.

"We're here," said Johnny Spanish, "with more than an hour to spare. Did I not tell you, Owney, you English sot, I'd have it done in time for you?"

Owney felt a vast relief.

He stumbled from the vehicle, taking in a breath of air, feeling it explode in his lungs.

The field seemed to extend for a hundred miles in each way under a starry sky and a bright bone moon. In pale glow it undulated ever so slightly from one end to the other. He could make out a low ridge of hills at the far side but on this side there were only trees as the elevation led up to it.

The last hours had been ghastly. Slow travel down dirt roads, at least twice when the engine seemed to stall, rough little scuts of inclines where all the boys had to get out and Johnny's deft skills alone, his gentleness with the engine, his knowing the balance and power of the automobile, when those alone had gotten them up and to another level.

How had Johnny known so well? It had been six years since, and in that experience that old sheriff had been the guide. He must have some memory. He was definitely a genius.

"You did it, lad," he said to Johnny.

"That I did. You're grateful now, Owney, but come the pay-up time it won't seem like so much. You'll come to believe you yourself could have done it and what I did will seem as nothing. Then you'll try to jew me down hard, I know."

"No," said Owney. "Fair is fair. You boys done two hard jobs in the last two weeks. I'll pay you double what I paid for the yard job."

"Think six times, Owney."

"Six!"

"Six. Not twice times, but six times. It's fair. It leaves you with a lot of what you've got."

"Jesus. It was a one-day job."

"Six, Owney. It was a five-day job, with lots of arranging to be done. Else you'd be looking at the rest of your time in an Arkansas Dannamora."

"Four and it's a deal."

"All right, Owney, because I don't like to mess about. Make it five, we shake on it, and that would be that."

Owney extended his hand. He had just paid $1.5 million for his new life. But he had another $7 million left, and beyond that, $3 million in European banks that neither a Johnny Spanish nor a Bugsy Siegel nor a Meyer Lansky knew a thing about.

They shook.

"Boys, we're rich," said Johnny.

"Richer, you mean," said Owney.

"We're set for life. No more jobs. We can toss the tommies off the Santa Monica fishing pier."

"Believe I'll keep my Browning," said Herman. "You never know when it'll come in handy."

"All right, you lot, just a bit more to do. You know the drill."

They had to secure the field for landing. This involved reading the wind, for the plane landed against it and took off with it. As efficiently as any OSS team setting up a clandestine landing in occupied France, Johnny's boys picked some equipment out of the rear of the big Ford and went deep into the valley. There they quickly assembled a wind pylon and read the prevailing breeze. It was now only a matter of using a flare to signal the aircraft when she came, then turning her, then climbing aboard and it was all over.

While the boys did their work, and then moved the car to the appropriate spot in the valley, Owney took out and lit a cigar. It was a Cohiba, from the island, a long thing with a tasty, spicy tang to it, and it calmed him down.

He had made it. He, Owney, had done it. He was out; he would repair to the tropics and begin to plot, to raise a new crew, to pay back his debts, to engineer a way back into the rackets.

He had an image of Bugsy after the hit. He imagined Bugsy's face, blown open by bullets. Bugsy in one of his famous creamy suits, spattered with black blood, his athlete's grace turned to travesty by the twisted position into which he had fallen. He saw Bugsy as the centerpiece in a tabloid photo, its harshness turning his death into some grotesque carnival. When a gangster died, the public loved it. The gangsters were really the royalty of America, bigger in their way than movie stars, for the movies the gangsters starred in were real life, played out in headlines, whereas an actor's heroics took place only in a fantasy realm. A star in a moving picture could come back and make another one; a star in a tabloid picture could not, and that impressed incredible élan and grace upon the gangster world. It was glamorous like the movies but real like life and death itself.

Then he heard it. Oh, so nice.

From far off the buzz of a multiengine plane. She'd circle a bit, waiting for a little more of the light that was beginning to creep across the western sky to illuminate the valley, then down she'd come. It was a good boy, or so Johnny insisted. A former Army bomber pilot who could make an airplane do anything she could do and had set planes down on dusty strips all over the Pacific. But before that the boy had run booze and narcotics for some Detroit big boys, where he really learned his craft.

High up, the plane caught a glimpse of sun, and it sparkled for just a second, just like Owney Maddox's future.

Owney turned and before him suddenly loomed a shape, huge and terrifying.

It took his breath away.

Don't let me die! he thought, but it was not a man-made thing at all, or even a man. It was some kind of giant reddish deer, with a spray of antlers like a myth. The beast seemed to rise above him. His throat clogged with fear. In the rising light he saw its eyes as they examined him imperially, as if he were the subject. It sniffed, and pawed, then turned its mighty head. In two huge, loping bounds it was gone.

Jesus Christ, he thought.

What the hell was that?

He didn't like it, somehow. The animal's presence, its arrogance, its lack of fear, its contempt seemed like a bad omen. He realized his pulse was rocketing and that he was covered with a sheen of sweat.

"Owney, lad, come out of the field or you'll get cut to pieces by the props of your savior," called Johnny.

CHAPTER 63

The pain came every two minutes now. It built, like a worm growing to a snake growing to a python growing to a sea serpent or some other mystical creature, red hot and glowing, screaming of its own volition, a spasm, an undulation, a sweat-cracking, muscle-killing pure heat. Someone screamed. It was her. She screamed and screamed and screamed.

From her perspective, she could only see eyes. The eyes of the young doctor and they looked scared. She knew something was wrong.

"Let me give you some anesthetic, Mrs. Swagger."

"No," she said. "No gas."

"Mrs. Swagger, you're only a little dilated and you've got some hours to go. There's no need to suffer."

"No gas. *No gas!* I'm fine. I want my husband. Is Earl here? Earl, Earl, where are you? Earl?"

"Ma'am," said the nurse, looking over, "ma'am, we haven't been able to reach your husband."

"I want Earl. I want Earl here. He said he'd be here for me."

"Ma'am, he's got time. It's going to be a bit. We'll get you into the delivery room when you've dilated to ten centimeters. He'll get here fine, I'm sure. I just think you'd be more comfortable if—"

The pain had her again. The snake roped through her body. How could such a little bitsy thing hurt so much? She was so afraid of letting down Earl. But at the same time, where was Earl?

"Ma'am, I'm going to get your friend. She can be with you. That's all right, isn't it?"

"Yes."

Mary swam into view.

"Honey," she said. "I'll call Phil at the shop. He'll go straight home. He'll go to your house and wait on the front steps for your husband."

"Key," she said.

"What, honey?"

"Key. Key in the flowerpot to right of door, third pot. Answer phone."

"Yes. I'll tell him. He'll wait inside and if Earl calls he'll tell him where you are, so Earl can come direct."

"Where is Earl?"

"I don't know, baby. I'm sure he'll be there as soon as he can."

"I'm not strong."

"Oh, yes you are, baby. You are the strongest. You got through this whole thing without Earl, and you'll get through this if you have to. I know you've got the strength in you."

The pain had her again.

"What's wrong, Mary?" she said.

"There's nothing wrong," said Mary, but she flashed an uneasy look at the doctor. "You're having a baby. I have been led to believe it hurts a bit."

"I can tell something is wrong. Don't let them take my baby. They can't have my baby. I don't want the gas. If I have the gas, they'll take my baby."

"No, sweetie, that won't happen."

But again she had a guilty look.

In time the two women were alone as the doctor, the only one on call this late hour in the near-empty

Scott County hospital, went on his rounds, such as they were. They weren't much because "hospital" was entirely too grand a word for this place; it was more a poverty ward with an operating room/delivery room/emergency room attached, because the quality went up to Fort Smith or over to Little Rock with their medical problems.

Mary came over with a conspiratorial look on her face.

"Baby, they don't want you to know, but they want you to take the gas."

"What's wrong? Oh, God, what's wrong?"

"It's called a posterior presentation. The baby is facing down, not up, and he can't come out down."

"Oh, God."

"With another doctor, they might be able to turn him when you dilate some more. Then they'd cut you a little and remove him and sew you up. But they need two doctors. They can't do it with one doctor."

"Don't let them take my baby."

"Honey, you may have to—"

"No, no, no. *No!*" Her hand flew to Mary's and grabbed it tightly. "Don't let them hurt my baby."

"Honey, if they can't get the baby turned, they may have to do something to save your—"

"No. *No!* Don't hurt my baby! Cut me but don't hurt the baby."

Mary started to cry as she held tightly to Junie's wan hand.

"You are so brave. You are braver than any man

who ever lived, sweetie. But you can't give up your life to—"

"No," she said. "Earl will—"

"Earl would make the same decision. He wants you to be with him. You can have other babies. You can't give up your life for one baby. What would Earl do? He'd be by himself with a baby he wouldn't know how to care for."

"No," she said. "I don't want them to hurt my baby. They can't take the baby! Don't let them take the baby. Earl will be here. Earl will save us both."

"Honey, I—"

The pain had her again, and she jacked as it flashed through her.

Earl? Where are you, Earl? Earl, please come.

CHAPTER 64

Earl lay on his back. The dew had soaked through his coat. His hat was a pillow. He could see nothing but sky lightening as the sun came up. A cool wind rushed through the grass that concealed him. He could have been any man on a park bench or a camping ground, stretching, damp, a little twitchy as the dawn came up and a new day began.

But no other man would have a tommy gun cradled in his arms across his chest and no other man would carry nine other stick magazines loaded with ball tracer in the pockets of his coat or stuffed inside his belt—oh, for a Marine knapsack.

But Earl lay calmly, letting his heartbeat subside, letting his body cool. He was at the long end of a desperate journey across the northwest corner of Polk County, guided by an old map and his instincts. The car had taken him along dirt roads through vast forest and a nickel compass kept him oriented toward the section of the county where Hard Bargain Valley just had to be.

When he ran out of road, he took ten minutes to load up his magazines and his weapon, then he headed off on a track trending north by northwest, through strange forest, across swollen streams, and finally up a raw incline. It seemed to take forever; he thought of a night or two in the Pacific, the 'Canal especially, when the jungle had been like this, dense and dark and unyielding. You hated to be in it at night because the night belonged to the Japs, and them little monkeys could make you stew meat if they wanted. But there were no Japs in this jungle, except his own memories, his own fears, his own angers.

The worst part of the ordeal came at around 5:30 when the land, which should have been rising steadily to Hard Bargain Valley, instead seemed to straighten out. He kept his trust going in the cheap compass, but then he wondered if the presence of so much metal in the tommy gun and all the ammo had knocked it askew. But it held to a steady N and he kept orienting himself to the right of that pointing arrow, even though in the dark his doubts mounted fearfully. He had no other choice.

And then, as sweet a sound as he'd ever heard, there came the whine of a cruising plane, holding at about two thousand feet in a steady drone. That had to be it. That was Hard Bargain Valley and the plane that came for its human cargo.

Abruptly he ran into ridge, heavily overgrown, and made his way up it as quickly as he could. Thank God the tommy had a sling, for without one, the going would have been almost impossible. The gun hung on his shoulder, heavy and dense with that special weight that loaded weapons have, as he pulled himself up.

Then he saw it: the broad sweep of valley, flat and only gently undulating, pure natural landing strip, and on the other side other hills, and beyond them, presumably, mountains, for the darkness still closed out longer views.

Earl could see some kind of activity at the far end of the valley. He knew that's where Owney and his boys would be waiting for the plane to land.

Thus he edged down to the valley floor, still shielded for another few minutes by the darkness, and duckwalked out to the center. The plane had to land over him. When it did, he would empty a magazine into the nearest engine, concentrating all his firepower. That would drive it away. It would not land and then he would close with Owney and his boys, and although the odds were one against six it didn't much matter: business had to be taken care of, accounts settled, and there was no one else about to do it.

A shift in the pitch of the engines of the orbiting plane signified that enough light had arrived at last. Earl craned his head up a bit and saw the plane far off to the northwest, one wing tip high, the other low as it fluted in its approach to the landing path. It seemed to waver in the air as it turned, then straightened, then lowered itself. The gear was already down. It was some kind of low-winged twin-engine Beechcraft, a sturdy, prosaic aircraft. The pilot found his angle and seemed to come in on a string, bearing straight for Earl, coming faster and faster and lower and lower.

Earl's fingers flew involuntarily to the weapon's controls, to test them for the millionth time: the one lever was cranked fully forward to FIRE and the other fully forward to FULL. Then his fingers dipped under the weapon and touched the bolt handle on the other side, to check again that it was drawn back and cocked.

The gun seemed to rise to him and he rose from the grass. The butt plate found his shoulder and all ten pounds of the weapon clamped hard against himself as his vision reduced only to that narrow circle of visibility that was the peep sight. He saw: the flat of the receiver top, the diminishing blunt tube of the barrel and the single central blade of sight. The plane seemed to double, then double again in size as it roared at him, dropping ever lower. He knew that the increase in speed was a function of its closing the distance and it seemed to double again, its roar filling the air, and he pulled the gun up through it, sighting on the right-side engine, leading it, and when the computational machine in his brain so instructed, pulling the trigger and holding it down while running the gun on a smooth rotation from nine o'clock up to midnight and then over to two o'clock.

The gun emptied in one spasm, the sound lost in the roar of the plane. He could sense the empties tumbling, feel the liquid, almost hydraulic pressure of the recoil without a sense of the individual shots as it drove into his shoulder, but most of all he could see the tracers flicking out and extending his touch until he was an angry God destroying the world from afar. The arc of tracers flew into the engine and wing root and the plane trembled ever so slightly, then changed engine pitches again as it pulled up, banked right and flew out of the zone of fire. It seemed to dip, for flames poured from the engine, but then the pilot feathered it, and only a gush of smoke remained, a stain he pulled across the sky with him, and he waggled his wings and headed elsewhere.

Owney watched the plane come down. The pilot was good. He was very good. He had his course, his gear had been lowered, his flaps were down, he was coming lower and lower and seemed just a few feet from touching down.

Then a line of illumination cracked out of the darkness and lashed upward; it was so sustained that for just a second Owney thought it was a flashlight beam or some other form of light until he realized he was deluding himself. The streaking bullets caught the plane expertly, speared it, and the plane seemed to wobble. Owney thought it might explode. Smoke abruptly broke from the targeted engine and the plane quivered mightily as fire washed outward. Then the pilot yanked up and away and almost as if it had been a dream, the plane was gone. It reduced in size arithmetically as it sped away, trailing smoke.

"What the fuck was that?" asked Owney.

"It's him."

"Him?"

"The cowboy."

"AGHHHH!" Owney bellowed, a great spurt of anger uncontaminated by comprehensibility. "That fucking fucker, that fucking dog!" His rage was absolute and immense.

But Johnny spoke calmly.

"You just saw some tommy-gunning, old man. Isn't but one man in a thousand can hold the Thompson so perfectly on a moving target, leading perfectly, not letting it bounce off target. I suppose the tracers help some. They verify impact. But the bastard's bloody good, I'll tell you that. I know only one better. Fortunately it's me."

Around him the others had already unlimbered weapons and were quickly readying for action, the usual fitting of magazines and snapping of bolts. Hats and coats were coming off, automatics being checked for full loads.

"That fucking bastard," said Owney. "Oh, that hick bastard! I should have settled his fucking hash at the railway station. Who the fuck does he think he is?"

"Right now, he thinks he's going to kill all six of us, I should imagine. Owney, dear, you stay here. Johnny and his boys will take care of all this. Right, fellows?"

But there was no cheer from the boys. They had read the fine blast of sustained, controlled automatic fire just as surely as Johnny, and knew they were up against a professional.

"We've got the Ford," called Vince the Hat. "We could just get the hell out of here."

"He'd just ambush us. If he knows the way in, he'll know it out. Anyhow, we've got to deal with him now, or look over our shoulders forever. Evidently that railyard business upset the fellow."

"You bastard!" Owney yelled. *"We'll fuck you but good in a few minutes!"*

"Feel better, now, Owney? There's a good lad. You stay here while the men handle it."

"Johnny, what's your plan?" asked Herman Kreutzer, his BAR loaded and ready.

"He's probably slithering toward us right now.

I'd stay wide, separated so he can't take more than one down with a single burst. I'd say let's move now and fast, because if it's only tracer he has, we'll be able to track them back to him better before the light is full up. Herman, you've the heaviest weapon, you'll provide sustaining fire. Take all your magazines. No point in saving them for a rainy day. It *is* the rainy day. Let's form a line abreast and move in spurts. Stay low, keep moving. Look for the source of his fire. When you spot it, Herman, you must pressure him while we move in. Anybody have a better suggestion?"

No one did.

Earl knew they'd come quickly and they did. His every impulse told him to advance. Get among them, shoot fast from the hip, trusting instinct, their panic at his aggression, and luck. It never remotely occurred to him that he might die. His focus was entirely on destroying them.

All his voices were still. He did not think of the father who had failed him or the men he believed he had failed or the wife alone somewhere. He didn't think of D. A. Parker ordering him to get out or the long run through the sewer or the rage that the raid-team tragedy had been turned into farce for the good of a politician. He had no sense of failure at all, but only a sort of battle joy, hard and pure, and the need to get in close, put the bursts into them and punish them for their transgressions and for his own.

He squirmed ahead, low, sliding through the grass. The blood sang in his ears. The air tasted magnificent, like a fine wine, a champagne. The gun was alive in his hands, marvelously supple and obedient. He had never felt this way in the islands or in any of his other fights. There, fear was always around. Now he was shorn of fear.

A burst of fire came. It was duplicated instantly by three others, as Johnny's boys panicked, even though they were so professional. Bullets hurled through the grass, and where they struck, they raised a great destruction. Smoke and debris, liberated by their energy, rose in a fog, obscuring the field, but Earl saw his advantage. He quickly flicked the fire-control lever on his Thompson, setting it to single shot, rose slightly into a kneeling position even as the random bursts filled the air with a sleet of lead, found a good target and fired one round, its noise lost in the general thunder. He shot low, through the grass, so that his tracer might not be seen, and knew he'd made a good shot.

"*Stop it! Stop it, goddammit!*" screamed Johnny.

The firing stopped.

"Jesus Christ, don't panic, boys. You'll make it easy on him."

"Johnny, Johnny—"

"Shut up, Vince, you've got—"

"I been hit!"

It was so. Vince the Hat de Palmo lay on his side, astounded that he was bleeding so profusely. He'd taken it at the ligature of thigh to hip, and the wound spurted wetly, the blood thick and black across his suit. He looked at Johnny as his eyes emptied of meaning and hope.

"Take his magazines, boys," said Johnny. "We may need them yet."

"Johnny, I—"

"Easy, lad," said Johnny to the youngest of his men, shortly to be the deadest. "Don't fight Ding-Dong."

In his last motions, Vince cooperated with Jack Bell as the older man rolled him over and grabbed the two flat drums that were wedged between his belt and his back.

"You'll come back for me?"

"Sure, kid," said Ding-Dong. "You can bet on it." He gave the kid a wink, which Vince may or may not have seen before he slipped irretrievably into blood-loss coma.

In the interlude, Earl squirmed to the left, toward the low hill that rose at that side of the valley. He crawled and crawled and though he hated to crawl, this day it filled him with joy. The sun was now full on them, drying the dew from the stalks of grass.

The grass at the hill was drier, somehow, for the

hillside drained more fluently than the flatland. As he drew near, a plan formed in his mind. This grass was of a different texture, possibly of a different species. He could tell because unlike the soft grass of the valley floor which merely hissed as he crawled through it or the wind pressed rills into it, this grass crackled like dry old bones and sticks in the breeze.

He stood.

He could not see them, for they too had sunk into the grass, or taken up concealed positions behind the odd bushes on the floor of the valley. He chose one such, leaned into his gun and fired a long squirt of tracers into it.

Then he ducked and squirmed away, as someone with a larger weapon than a Thompson brought fire to bear. These bullets whipcracked through the sound barrier as they passed overhead, their snap echoing against the wind. It had to be a Browning rifle. Someone had a Browning at the railyard too.

He'll try and pin me, the others will work around and up the hill and the one other will go around me, yes. That's how it has to be.

"Do you have him?"

"Yes, he's in a gully at the edge of the hills, about two hundred yards off to the right. I saw the tracers come out."

"You keep him pinned, Herman. Red, you and Ding-Dong go high. Try and get to that hillside above him to get the fire down on him. I'm circling around to the back. You'll drive him to me, boys, and if you don't get him, I'll get him square in the belly."

"Let's do it."

Johnny scuttled off, beginning his long arc around to the rear. For Jack and Ding-Dong, it was an easier journey, for theirs was the straight shot to the hillside, and then a climb to bend around and get above him. The grass here was high and it concealed them; they didn't have to crawl but could run, keeping low, particularly as more gullies opened up the closer they got to the hill itself.

As for Herman, he waited a bit, then a bit more, and finally rose and began an exercise called walking fire, which was exactly what John M. Browning had designed his automatic rifle to accomplish. It was originally conceived as the answer to trench warfare and in this role it was the perfect instrument.

Herman was a big man, strong and fearless, and he loved and knew the gun he carried passionately. He could do amazing things with it. Now he rose, wearing two bandoliers with loaded magazines Mexican-style across his body over his suit coat, the gun locked into his side and pinned by his strong right forearm, which pressed it tightly against him. His reflexes were superb. He fired half a magazine and the burst sped exactly to the gully from which he'd seen the original tracers come. The burst lifted a stitch of dust. No man could do it better and the shame of Herman's life was that he'd not been a

BAR man in Europe or the Pacific, for in that classification he'd have been a true genius. It wasn't that he hadn't tried; it was that he had too many felony convictions.

He finished up the magazine, stitching a hem of lead where he wanted it exactly. He dropped the empty mag, neatly and deftly inserted a new one, all the while walking, and was back putting out his bursts in less than a second. If that's where the cowboy was, he wasn't going anywhere.

Owney could hear the gunfire, but the men had disappeared into the grass. There seemed to be a lot of moving around. It was like chess with machine guns where you couldn't quite see the board.

He was nervous, but not terrified. Johnny's crew was the best; they seemed calm and purposeful. They had succeeded at every enterprise they had tackled, often spectacularly. They were the best armed robbers in America, fearless, famous, quality people, stars in their own universe. They would get him. He knew it. They would get him.

But they wouldn't.

He knew that too, at least somewhere deep inside.

Who was this guy? Where was he from? Why was he so good?

It unnerved him. He had been hunted by Vincent Mad Dog Coll. He was the ace of aces, Owney Killer

Maddox, from the East Side. He had shot it out with the Hudson Dusters in 1913, one man against eight, and walked out unhurt, leaving the dying and the wounded behind him. He, Owney, had walked out spry as a dancer, stopped to reset his carnation in his lapel, and gone out for a drink with some other fellows.

Who could scare him? Who had the audacity? Who was this guy?

The BAR bursts ripped up clouds of dust and dirt. The gully filled with grittiness, so that you almost could not breathe. If Earl had been where Herman thought he was, he would indeed have been one cooked fella. The noise, the ricochets, the grit, the supersonic bits of stone and vegetable matter, the sheer danger—all would have shaken even the toughest of individuals.

But Earl had shimmied desperately forward only a matter of a few yards and found a rotted log behind which to hide, even if he knew it was wholly unable to stop the heavy .30s that might have flown his way.

He now did the unthinkable. Instead of seizing the opportunity to put distance between himself and the shooters who were closing in from all sides, he did exactly what they expected him to do, which was nothing. That's what they wanted him to do. He did it. He just didn't do it where they wanted him to do it, not quite. He knew that as the BAR fire kept him nominally pinned, some others would be entering the dry, higher grass of the hillside, in order to get elevation on his position and bring even more killing power. That's exactly what he wanted.

Methodically, he began to tug at the stem of a bush that had grown up just in front of the log.

Jack Bell and Red Brown reached the edge of the hillside, still well hidden. They were rewarded for their efforts.

"Will ya look at that," said Ding-Dong. "Just what the doctor ordered."

"If it was a dame, I'd marry it," said Red, who actually had several wives, so one more wouldn't hurt a bit.

What they saw was a kind of crest running vertically up the hill, one of those strange rills for which only a geologist could give an adequate explanation. What it meant for the two gunmen was a clear easy climb up to the top of the hill, well protected by the geographical impediment from the gunfire of their opponent.

"Okay," said Jack, "you cover me. I'm going to make a dash, then I'll cover you and you make yours."

"Gotcha," said Red.

Both men rose. Jack dashed the twenty or so yards to the beginning of the spine of elevation, even as Red stood and hosepiped twenty-five rounds down the line of the hill, into the area where Herman's bullets had been striking. His too tore clouds of earth upward, and sent grit whistling through the air.

As he fired the last, his partner made it, righted himself, set up close over the ridge, and fired a blast. Red rose under cover of the fire, and sprinted till he was safe.

Both men drew back, breathing hard.

They looked up the hill. Alongside the ridge, it was about two hundred feet up through tall yellow grass, though it was protected the whole way. About halfway was a small strange group of stunted trees, yellowed and sinewy, then another hundred feet to the crest.

"Johnny," Red cried. *"We're going up."*

"Good move," said Ding-Dong. "He'll wait for us, we'll get up there, we'll have real good vision on the guy, we can take him or we can pin him while Johnny and Herman move in on him."

"Johnny's a fuckin' genius."

Herman couldn't be but a hundred or so feet from the edge of the field and the beginning of the hill. His BAR was almost too hot to touch. He'd sprayed steadily for the past five minutes, until he got close enough. He'd seen nothing.

Maybe he's dead. Maybe I hit him. Maybe he's bled out. If he'd gone another way, he'd have run into Johnny.

Nah. He's in there. He got himself into a jam, he's scared, but he's waiting. He's a brave guy. He's a smart guy, but one on five was just too many. He's in there. He can't move. He's real close.

He heard the gunfire from far to the right and judged that it was covering fire from Red and Ding-Dong. Red's yell came a second later.

That was it. If they got above him, the guy was screwed. They could bring fire on him and if they didn't kill him, he'd have to move. Herman would bring him down if he moved.

Herman snapped in a new magazine, waiting for the guy to move. He stood in a semicrouch and was so strong that the fourteen-pound automatic rifle felt light and feathery to the touch. He looked over its sights, through a screen of grass, searching for signs of movement.

He saw nothing, but given the source of the fire, given the speedy response on his part and the volume of fire he had poured in, the man could not have gotten away, unless there were secret tunnels or something, but there were only secret tunnels in movies.

Be patient, he told himself.

Johnny worked his way around in a wide arc to the base of the hill. He was possibly a hundred yards behind the cowboy's position. He squatted in the grass. He hadn't fired yet. He had a full drum, one of the big ones, with a hundred rounds. He could fire single shots, doubles, triples, even quadruples and quintuples if he had to, so exquisite was his trigger control. He could hold one hundred rounds in a four-inch circle in a fifty-yard silhouette if he had to. He could shoot skeet or trap with a Thompson if he had to. He was the best tommy-gunner in the world.

He was a little anxious.

This fellow was very good. He'd obviously used a Thompson well in the war and could make it do tricks. But Johnny knew if it came to shooting man-on-man, he'd take it. Nobody was faster, nobody was surer, nobody could make the gun do what he could make it do.

He squirmed ahead, then heard the gunfire from Red and Ding-Dong. Red yelled something—he could not quite make it out—but knew what it signified. Red and Ding-Dong had reached the hill and were heading up it. When they got elevation, it was all over. It would be all over very shortly. It was just a question of waiting.

Owney heard the firing. There was so much firing from the right-hand side of the field, and then there was nothing. But all the guns that fired had to be Johnny and his boys. He'd only heard one burst that seemed to come from elsewhere.

He could see nothing. Though the floor of Hard Bargain Valley was relatively flat and hard, for some reason the grass grew at different heights upon its surface, and from where he was, it looked like a yellow ocean, aripple with waves. Toward the edges of the valley, small stunted trees appeared in strange places, randomly.

He thought the fighting was going on over there, maybe a half mile down, on the right side. He thought he could see dust rising from all the gunfire.

Suddenly a long burst broke out, and his eye was drawn to what he took to be the position of the shooter. Another came in on top of the first. Each burst chattered for about two seconds, though from this distance the sound was dry, like a series of pops, like balloons exploding, something childlike and innocent.

Then he saw movement. It was hard to make out, but he saw soon enough that two of Johnny's men, visible in their dark suits, were scrambling up the ridge. They seemed well under cover.

Owney grasped the significance instantly. If they got above him, the cowboy was finished. They could hold him down while the others moved in on him.

Johnny, you smart bastard, he thought. You are the goddamned best.

Herman waited and waited. Nothing seemed to be happening. He decided to move on the oblique and come on the cowboy's position from another angle.

Ever so slowly he moved out, angling wide, edging ever so gently through the high grass, keeping his eyes on the area where the man had to be. Once in a while he'd shoot a glance up the ridge that ran up the hill for signs of Red and Ding-Dong. But he saw nothing.

The sun was high now. A bit of wind sang in his ears, and the grass around him weaved as it pressed through, rubbing against itself with a soft hiss.

The grass seemed to be thinning somewhat as he drew near to the beginning of the incline. He slowed, dropped to his knees, and looked intently ahead. He could see nothing.

Where was the bastard?

He wiggled a little farther out, staying low, ready to squeeze off a burst at any moment. The silence that greeted his ears was profound.

He planted the gun's butt under his right arm, locking it in the pit, and stepped boldly out, its muzzle covering the beaten zone where haze still drifted. He expected to see a body or a blood trail or something. But he saw nothing. He saw a log ahead on the left and in the deeper grass some kind of bush and he directed his vision back, looking for—

Something to the left flashed. In the instant that his peripheral vision caught the motion, Herman cranked hard to bring his muzzle to bear on the apparition; it was a living bush and as it rose, fluffs of grass fell off it, the bush itself fell away and then Herman saw it was a man.

Earl fired five tracers into the big man in one second. They flew on a line and he absorbed them almost stoically in the center body, then sank to the earth, toppling forward, then trying to prevent his fall with the muzzle of the Browning Automatic Rifle, which he jammed into the ground. So sustained he paused, as if on the edge of a topple, his face gray and his eyes bulging, the blood running everywhere.

Earl didn't have time for this shit. He put seven more into him, knocking him down. The tracers set his clothes aflame.

Earl turned as fire broke out behind him. Two men with tommy guns lay at the crest of the ridge, and fired at him. But of course they had forgotten to adjust their Lyman peep sights for the proper distance, so while they aimed at him, the extreme trajectory of the .45s over two hundred downhill yards pulled their rounds into the ground fifty feet ahead of him.

Earl slid back to the earth, making a range estimation as he went. Bracing the gun tight against himself, he hosed a short burst high in the air, watched as it arched out, trailing incandescence visible even in the bright air. At apogee the consecutive quality of the burst broke up and each bullet spiraled on a slightly different vector toward the earth. Earl watched them, and saw that they hit just fine for windage but too far back. He needed more elevation. He corrected in a second, fired two shots and watched them rise and fall like mortar shells. They fell where he wanted. He pressed the trigger and finished the magazine, dumped it, quickly slammed another one home, found the same position in his muscle memory and this time squeezed off the entire thirty rounds in about four seconds. The gun shuddered, spewing empties like a brass liquid pouring from its breech, and the tracers curved through the air, riding a bright rainbow. Where they struck, they started fires.

It was Red who saw what was happening first. He felt okay, ducking back behind cover as a rainbow of bright slugs lofted high above him and descended, but without precision. It was absurdly raining light. Still, there was no real chance that any of the rounds could hit a target, as they dispersed widely as they plummeted.

Then he felt a wall of heat crushing over him, and the heat's presence seemed to distend or twist the air itself. To the right a wall of flame seemed to explode from nowhere. He'd never understood how fast a brushfire can burn, particularly on a hillside where the wind blows continually and there is no shelter.

The fire was a crackling enemy, advancing behind them in a human wave attack, throwing out fiery patrols of pure flame and crackling, popping menace. It sucked the air from them and its smoke closed on them quickly. They turned to run, but the fire was all around them and suddenly a lick of it lashed out and set Ding-Dong's sleeve afire.

He screamed, dropped his weapon and went to his knees to beat it out. But more flame was on him and soon he was lit up like a Roman candle, and if the power of the fire would drive him to run, the pain of it took his energy from him, and he fell back, his flesh burning.

Red didn't want that happening to him. He had just a second to decide, and then he scrambled up the ridge and leaped over it, escaping the hungry flames, but before he could congratulate himself, a fleet of tracers rose from nowhere and crucified him to the ground.

Earl spun, changed magazines again, and looked backward for another target. He could see nothing. If there was another man moving in on him from behind he was moving stealthily. Earl didn't have much cover here and in fact there was very little cover anywhere. He emptied another magazine, then another, hosing down the area where another man would be if he existed. That was sixty rounds in about ten seconds, and the tracers sprayed across the area before him like lightning bolts seeking the highest available target. They churned through the grass, setting small fires when they encountered dryness, but generally just ripping up earth and drawing a screen of dirt into the air.

He changed magazines a third time, moved out a little for a slightly different angle and squirted another batch out in another bright fan of searching bullets.

Johnny was too far to shoot when the thing started happening. Then it happened so fast and so unpredictably he was uncertain what to do. He watched the tracers arc out and descend behind the ridge. Smoke rose so fast in the aftermath it was astonishing. The ridgeline caught fire.

But by that time he had gone totally prone and begun to crawl, crawl desperately forward in the highest grass there was, hoping he could get so close he could count on his superior reflexes to carry the battle. He squirmed like a man aflame, whereas it was others who were aflame. Then the cowboy started shooting wildly. He listened as the man pumped out magazine after magazine, but behind him, where he'd been, not where he was now and where he was headed.

He crawled and crawled until the firing stopped.

By his reckoning he was now just twenty yards or so away, and the cowboy had no idea where he was.

He peered through the grass, rising incrementally higher for visibility and suddenly beheld a wondrous sight.

The cowboy had a jam. His empty magazine was

caught in the gun and he tugged it desperately to get it free, his hand up toward the receiver. Then suddenly whatever it was gave, he pulled the magazine out, and dropped it, his hand reaching into his suit pocket for another.

"Hold it!" said Johnny, covering him with the muzzle.

The cowboy whirled but what could he do? He had an empty gun in one hand and a fresh magazine in the other. He was a good two seconds from completing the reload.

"Well, well," said Johnny, walking forward, his muzzle expertly sighted on the big man's heaving chest, "look who we've caught with his pants down. Jam on you, did it? Them damn things is tricky. You've got to baby them or you'll regret it, lad. Come now, let's have a look at you."

The man regarded him sullenly. Johnny knew he'd be thinking desperately of something to do. Caught like this, with no ammo! Him with the big fancy gun, him who'd shot all them other fellers, and now him with nothing.

"Cut me a break, will you, pal?" said the cowboy.

"And live the rest of me life looking over the shoulder? I should think not."

"I just want Maddox. I don't give a fuck about you. Just walk away and forget all this. You can live."

"Oh, now he's dictating terms, is he?" Johnny laughed. He was now about fifteen feet away, close enough.

"I didn't have to kill your boys. They were here, that's all."

"I should thank you for that, pally. Now the take's so much bigger. You've made me an even wealthier man. I'll drink many a champagne toast to you, friend, for your fine work. You are a game lad. You're about the gamest I've ever seen."

Earl just stared at him.

"I know what you're thinking. Maybe you can get the magazine into the gun and get the gun into play and bring old Johnny down. Why do I think not? No, old sod, you've been bested. Admit it now, you've been handled. Ain't many could handle the likes of you, but by God I'm the one man in a million who could do it."

"You talk a lot," said the man.

"That I do. The Irish curse. We are a loquacious race. Maybe I should walk you across the field and let Mr. Owney Maddox himself put the last one into you. He'd probably pay double for that pleasure."

"You won't do that. You won't take the chance."

"Well, boyo, that's the sad truth. But I won't be long. I'll just—"

His eyes lit.

"Say," he said. "I'm a sporting fellow. You're holding an empty gun."

"Let me load it."

"No thank you. But here's what I'll do." He reached under his coat and removed a .45. It was one of the Griffin & Howe rebuild jobs with which D.A. had armed his raid team.

He threw it into the dirt in front of Earl.

"That one's nice and loaded," he said with a smile.

"But it's five feet away."

"It is indeed. Now I'll count to three. On three you can make a dive at the gun. I'll finish you well before, but I might as well give you a one-in-one-thousand chance. Maybe *my* tommy will jam."

"You're a bastard."

"Me mother said the same. Are you ready, fellow?"

He let his gun muzzle drift down until it pointed to the ground. He watched as Earl looked at the gun on the ground five feet in front of him.

"See, here's the thing," said the cowboy. "Fights sometimes ain't what you want 'em to be."

"One," said Johnny.

He meant to shoot on two, of course.

The cowboy's tommy gun came up in a flash and there was a report and for just a millisecond it seemed a tendril of sheer illumination had lashed out to snare him.

The next thing Johnny knew, he was wet.

Why was he wet?

Had he spilled something?

Then he noticed he was lying on his back. He heard something creaking, like a broken accordion, an air-filled sound, high and desperate, a banshee screaming out in the bogs, signifying a death. He blinked and recognized it as a sucking chest wound. His own.

He could only see sky.

The cowboy stood over him.

"I slipped one cartridge into the chamber before I shucked the magazine," he said.

"I— I—" Johnny began, seeing that it was possible. The gun looked empty. It wasn't.

"Think of the railyard, chum," said Earl, as he locked in the new magazine, drew back the bolt and then fired thirty ball tracers into him.

CHAPTER 65

"Twelve," said the doctor.

"Yes sir," said the nurse.

"Mrs. Swagger, you are dilated twelve centimeters. You have another four or five to go. There's no need to endure this pain. Please let us give you the anesthesia."

"No," she said. "I want my husband."

"Ma'am, we've tried but we can't raise him. Ma'am, I'm afraid we've got a problem. You would be so much better off with the anesthesia."

"No, you'll take my baby."

She felt so alone. She could only see the ceiling. Occasionally the doctor loomed into view, occasionally the nurse.

The two put her gown down.

"We do have a problem with the baby," said the doctor. "It may be necessary to make a decision."

"Save the baby. Save my baby! Don't hurt my baby!"

"Mrs. Swagger, you can have *other* babies. This one is upside down in your uterus. I can't get it out, not without cutting you horribly and, frankly, I'm not equipped to do that and I don't know if I could stop the hemorrhaging once it got started, not here, not with two nurses and no other doctors."

"Can't you get another doctor?" someone asked, and Junie recognized the voice of her friend, Mary Blanton.

"Mrs. Blanton, please get back into the waiting room! You are not permitted back here."

"Sir, somebody has to stay with Junie. I cannot let her go through this alone. Honey, I'm here."

Good old Mary! Now there was a woman! Mary couldn't be pushed around, no sir! Mary would fight like hell!

"Thank you, Mary," Junie said, as another contraction pressed a bolt of pain up through her insides.

"Ma'am, there are no other doctors. In Fort Smith, yes, in Hot Springs, yes, at Camp Chaffee, yes, but you chose a small public hospital in Scott

County to have your baby during a late-night shift and I am doing what I can do. Now please, you have to leave."

"Please let her stay," begged Junie.

"When we go back to delivery, she can't come. You may stay here, ma'am, but do not touch anything, and stay out of the way."

"Yes sir."

The doctor seemed to leave, but instead he pulled Mary out into the hall.

"Look," he said, "we have a very complicated situation here. That woman may die. By my calculus, the baby's life is not worth the woman's life. The woman can have other babies. She can adopt a child. If it comes to it, I may have to terminate the baby's life, get it out of her in pieces. That may be the only way to save her life."

"Oh, God," said Mary. "She wants that baby so bad."

"Where is her husband?"

"We're not sure."

"Bastard. These white trash Southern hillbillies are—"

"Sir, Earl Swagger is not trashy. He's a brave man, a law enforcement officer, and if he's not here, it's because he's risking his life to protect you. Let me tell you, sir, if someone broke into your house at night, the one man you'd want to protect you and yours is Earl Swagger. That is why we have to protect his."

"Well, that's very fine. But we are coming up to decision time and I am not authorized to make this decision on my own and I could get in a lot of trouble. If I don't terminate the baby, that woman will die a needless, pointless and tragic death. She needs your help to decide. You help her decide. That's the best you can do for your friend."

CHAPTER 66

The screen of smoke blew across the valley, white and shifting.

Owney had a hope that Johnny Spanish and one or two of his boys would come out of it, laughing, full of merry horseplay, happy to have survived and triumphed. But he was not at all surprised or even disappointed when the other man emerged.

Out of the smoke he came. He was a tall man, in a suit, with his hat low over his eyes. He carried a tommy gun and looked dead-set on something.

Owney saw no point in running. He was a realist. There was no place to run to and if he got into the forest he would be easy to track and he'd be taken down and gutted.

It occurred to him to get into the station wagon and try and run the man down. But this cool customer would simply watch him come and fill him with lead from the tommy gun.

So Owney just sat there on the fender of the old Ford station wagon. He smoked a Cuban cigar and enjoyed the day, which had turned nice, clear, with a cool wind fluttering across the valley. The sun was warm, even hot, and there were no clouds. In the background, the hillside burned, but it seemed to have run out of energy as the flames spread and died, leaving only cinders to smolder.

The man seemed to come out of war. That's what it looked like; behind him, the smoke curled and drifted, and its stench filled the air; the hillside was blackened. There were bodies back there. Five of them. He'd gotten Johnny Spanish and his crew. Nobody ever got Johnny, not the feds, the State Police, all the city detectives, the sheriffs, the deputies, the marshals. But this one got them all in a close-up gunfight. He was something.

The cowboy was finally within earshot.

With a certain melancholy and an idea for his last gambit, Owney rose.

"Lawman!" he screamed. *"I surrender! I'm unarmed! I'll go back with you! You win!"*

He stood away from the car and took off his jacket and held his hands stiff and high. Slowly he pirouetted to show that he had no guns tucked in his belt. He rolled up his sleeves to show that his wrists were bare to the elbow.

He had the bicycle gun stuck in its sleeve garter

against his left biceps, on the inside, just above the elbow. He'd ripped a large hole in the inside seam of the shirt, invisible from afar, so that he could get at it quickly.

Let him get close, he thought. Let him get close. Offer him respect. Show him fear. Relax him. Put him at his ease. When he lowers the tommy gun, go for the bike pistol and shoot him five times fast, in the body.

He smiled as the man drew near.

The cowboy was lean and drawn. His face had a gaunt look, exhaustion under the furious concentration. His suit was dusty, his eyes aglare, the hat low over them. He looked Owney up and down, taking his measure.

"I'm unarmed," said Owney. "You won! You got me!"

It just might work.

Earl was not surprised that Owney Maddox awaited him with his hands high, his arms bare. What else could Owney do? He was out of options, other than killing himself, and Owney wasn't that kind of boy. He was no Japanese marine, who'd cut his own guts out and die with a grenade under his belly so that when you turned the corpse over two days later, the grenade would enable you to join him in heaven. No, that was not Owney's style.

He stopped ten feet shy of Owney.

"You win, partner," said Owney, with a smile. "You are a champ. I'll say that. You are a pro. You handled the best there is, my friend. I'm outclassed."

Earl said nothing.

He raised his tommy gun, and holding it deftly with one hand let it cover Owney.

"You're not going to shoot me," Owney said. "My hands are up. I've surrendered. You don't have it in you for that kind of stuff. That's the difference between us. You can't make yourself squeeze on an unarmed man with his hands in the air. I know you. You're a soldier, not a gangster. You won a war, but you wouldn't last a week on an island with alleys and nightclubs."

Earl just looked him over, then transferred the Thompson to his left hand.

"Take your belt off and throw it over here."

"Yah. See. I knew you weren't the type," said Owney, doing the job with one hand.

"Thought you was English," said Earl.

"Only when I want to be, chum. Come on, tie me, let's get this over. I want to get back in time to hear Frankie on the radio."

But then he stopped. He looked quizzically at Earl.

"I have to know. You're not working for Bugsy Siegel, are you?"

"That guy?" said Earl. "Don't know nothing about him."

"You fool," said Owney. "You have no idea what you've done, do you?"

"Nope."

Owney joined his hands together for Earl to loop them with the belt. Earl knelt to retrieve the belt. As he rose with it, Owney stepped forward and seemed to stumble just a bit and then his hand fled to his arm. He was fast.

But Earl was faster. His right hand flew to the Colt automatic in his belt like a bolt of electricity shearing the summer air. It was a fast that can't be taught, that no camera could capture. He caught the pistol in his other hand and thrust it toward Owney even as a crack split the air. Owney had fired one-handed. Owney had missed.

Hunched and doublehanded, Earl knocked five into the gangster, all before Owney could get the hammer thumbed back on the bike gun for a second shot. The rounds kicked the gangster back and set him down hard as the little weapon fell from his fingers into the grass.

Now Earl knew who had killed his father. Now Earl knew what had happened to his father's little gun. But he didn't care. His old father meant nothing to him now. He thought of his new father, the man who'd died for him in the railyard. Now he'd tracked D.A.'s true killer down and paid out justice in gunfire.

Earl walked over to Owney. Five oozing holes were clustered in a slightly oblong circle on his white shirt under his heart. They were so close you could cover them with one hand, and they were wounds nobody comes back from.

"W-who are you?" Owney asked.

"You'd never believe it," said Earl.

CHAPTER 67

She had borne so much pain she had become numbed by it. Her eyes were vague, her sense of reality elongated, her sense of time vanished. The pain just came and came and came, and had its way, though now and then a moment of lucidity reached her, and she concentrated on the here and now, and then it all went away in pain.

She heard someone say, "She's at fifteen. We've got to do it."

"Yes, doctor."

The young doctor's face flew into view.

"Mrs. Swagger, I have been on the phone all over the state trying to get an OB-GYN, even a resident, even a horse doctor over here. Someone can be here in an hour, I'm sorry to report. So I have to act now, or we will lose both you and the child."

"Don't take my baby!"

"You will bleed to death internally in a very short while. I'm sorry but I have to do what's right. Nurse, get her prepped. I'm going to go scrub."

She had fought so hard. Now, at the end, she had nothing left.

"It's all right," she heard Mary whispering. "You have to get through this. You'll have other babies. Honey, he's right, you've fought so hard, but it's time to move on. You have to survive. I couldn't live without you, I'm so selfish. Please, your mama, your papa, everybody, they are pulling for you."

"Where's Earl, Mary?"

"I am sorry, honey. He didn't make it."

Then she felt herself moving. A nurse was pushing her down the dimly lit hallway. The gurney vibrated and each vibration hurt her bad. A bump nearly killed her. She was in a brightly lit room. The doctor had a mask on. Then he turned away from her. A mask came and she smelled its rubbery density. She turned her face, waiting for the gas, and saw the doctor with his back to her. He was working with a long probe but she saw that it had a pointed end to it, like a knitting needle.

My baby, she thought. They are going to use that on my baby.

"She's ready, doctor."

"All right, give her—"

There was a commotion.

A woman had broken in. Angry words were spoken. Then she heard the doctor say, "I don't care about all that. Get him in here."

The doctor was back.

"Well, Mrs. Swagger, your husband just showed up."

"Earl!"

"Yes ma'am. And he has another doctor with him."

But there was something on his face.

"What's wrong?"

"This is your part of the country down here, not mine. You would understand better than me. I don't understand, but that nurse says if we let this doctor in here, there will be some trouble."

"Please. Please help my baby."

"All right, ma'am. I knew you'd say that."

"The doctor—?"

"The doctor your husband brought. He's colored."

Earl explained it once again.

"Ma'am, I don't care what your rules say. That's my wife in there and my child, and you need another doctor and this doctor has kindly consented to assist and he's delivered over a thousand babies through the years, so just step aside."

"No Negroes are allowed in this hospital. That's the rule." This was the hospital shift supervisor, a large woman in glasses, whose face was knit up tight as a fist as she clung to her part of the empire.

"That was yesterday. There are new rules now."

"And who has made that determination?"

"I believe I have."

"Sir, you have no right."

"My wife and baby ain't going to die because you have some rule that never made no sense and is only waiting for someone to come along and blow it down in a single day. This is that day and I am that man."

"I will have to call the sheriff."

"I don't give a hang who you call, but this doctor is going to help my wife, and that's all there is to it. I'll thank you to move or so help me God I'll move you and you won't like it a bit. Now, for the last time, madam, get the goddamned hell out of our way."

The woman yielded.

The two men walked in the corridor and a neighbor lady was standing there.

"You are not a man to be argued with, Mr. Swagger," said Dr. James.

"No sir. Not today."

A woman rushed to join them. She looked tired too, as if she'd been through it the same as Earl.

"Thank God you got here."

"You're Mary Blanton. Oh, Mary, ain't you the best though. I called and your husband told me what was going on. Dr. James was good enough to say he'd come along."

"Thank God you're here, doctor."

"Yes ma'am."

The young resident came out into the hall.

"Dr.—?"

"Julius James. OB-GYN. NYU School of Medicine, 1932."

"I'm Mark Harris, Northwestern, '44. Thank God you're here, doctor. We've got a posterior presentation and she's dilated all the way to fifteen and she's been in labor for twelve hours. That little bastard won't come out."

"Okay, doctor, I'll scrub. I believe I can flip the baby. I've managed to do it several times before. We'll have to perform an episiotomy. Then you'll have to cut the cord when I get into her so it doesn't strangle the infant in the womb. Then you'll have to stitch her while I resuscitate the infant. Make sure to have . . ."

Earl watched the two men drift away, and they disappeared into the delivery room.

He went back outside, to the waiting room, which was now deserted. The woman who had given him so much trouble was gone.

He couldn't sit down. He tried not to think about what was going on in the delivery room, or the hours since he'd dumped the bodies, called home, talked to Phil Blanton, driven to Greenwood, begged Dr. Julius James to accompany him, and driven here.

"I am worried about the doctor," he said to Mary. "This could be dangerous for him. He doesn't deserve all this bad trouble."

"Mr. Swagger, if they should move against him, they will be moving against you. I don't believe they will do that. They are bullies and cowards anyhow, not men."

"I do hope you are right, Mary."

In time, after Earl paced and Mary sat dumbly, a law officer approached, as if skulking. He wore a deputy's badge and had the look of the kind of old cop who sat in offices all day long.

"Are you the man that brought the Negro doctor?"

"Yes, I am," said Earl.

"You're not from around here, are you?"

"I grew up down in Polk County."

"Then you know this is not how we do things. We keep white and nigger separated. We have laws about it. I have to arrest you and the Negro doctor."

"I think you'd best go on home, old man," said Earl. "I do not have time for all this."

"Mr.—?"

"Swagger. Earl Swagger."

"Mr. Swagger, this is a great principle we are defending. It's bigger than your wife and your baby. We have the future of the nation at stake here."

"Deputy, possibly you know of my father, Charles Swagger? He was a man who done what he said he would do. He was famous for it. Well, sir, I am that kind of man only more so. So when I say to you, go away, go far away, then you'd best obey me or there will be hell for lunch."

The sheriff slunk away.

But he paused at the door.

"Your beefiness may work with an old man like me, Swagger, when all the deputies are out hunting Owney Maddox. But there are some boys at the end of the street getting liquored up who will take a different view."

"I'll deal with them when they come. If they have the guts. And don't you worry none about Owney Maddox. That bill was settled."

Another half hour passed. Mary sat, now hugging herself. Earl walked back and forth, smoking, like a man in a *Saturday Evening Post* cartoon. He kept glancing at his watch, kept looking at the door, kept trying to calm himself down. He was so desperately exhausted he could hardly think straight, but he was in that keyed up state where he couldn't sleep either. He was just a raw mess.

At last the door opened, but it wasn't a doctor. It was a janitor, a black man.

"Sir," he said.

"Yes, what is it, Pop?" Earl asked.

"They's coming. A mob. Seen it before. It happens oncet a while. They done got to set things back the way they was and when they do that, some boy's got to swing or burn."

"Not this time, Pop. You can bet on it."

He turned to Mary.

"I'll take care of this."

"Mr. Swagger, I—"

"Don't you worry none. I faced Japs. These boys ain't Japs. But just in case, I want you down on the floor. If some lead sails through, you don't want to catch a cold from it."

Earl walked out onto a porch.

He watched them come. The old man was right. There were about fifty of them, and from the groggy, angry progress, he could tell there had been much liquor consumed. The mob spilled this way and that, and shouts and curses came from it. He watched as supposedly decent people stepped aside, or stood back in horror, but he noted too that nobody stood up to these boys, nobody at all.

It was now four o'clock in the afternoon. He'd lost most sense of time and wasn't sure how long he'd been here, how long they'd been drinking, how mad they were. The sun was low in the western sky, and flame-colored. The mountains were silhouettes. A wind blew, and the leaves on the trees all shimmered.

On the boys came. He saw shotguns, a few rifles, a few squirrel guns, hoes, shovels, picks. They'd grabbed everything they could fight with. They were killing mad.

The leader was a heavyset man in overalls with a battered fedora and the hardscrabbled face of a fellow life hadn't treated kindly. His compatriots were equally rough, men who'd been purged of pity by bad breaks, brushes with the law, beatings from bigger men, and a sense of lost possibility. They looked like a ragtag Confederate infantry regiment moving out agin the bluebellies at some Pea Ridge or other.

Earl had known them his whole life.

Earl watched them come, standing straight. His hat was low over his dark and baleful eyes. His gray suit was dusty and rumpled but not without some dignity to it. His tie was tight to his throat and trim. He calmly smoked a Chesterfield, cupping it in his big hands.

Finally they were there, and only his imperturbability stood between him and the doctors and his wife.

"You the feller brought that nigger here?"

"I brought a doctor here, boys. Didn't stop to notice his color."

"We don't 'low no niggers in this end of town. Bad business."

"Today, that changes. I'm here to change it."

In the crowd faces turned to faces and low, guttural exchanges passed electrically among them. Like an animal they seemed to coil and gather strength.

Finally, the leader took a step forward.

"Mister, we'll string you up next to that coon in a whisker if that's what you want. Now you stand aside while we take care of business, or by God this'll be the day you die."

"Boys, there's been lots of days when I could die. If this is the one at last, then let's get to it."

He flicked aside the cigarette, and with a quick move peeled off his coat.

He had a .45 cocked and locked in the shoulder

holster that Herman Kreutzer had been wearing, another .45 cocked and locked in the speed holster on his hip that Johnny Spanish had been wearing and a third stuffed into his belt backward to the left of his belt buckle. His shirt pocket was stuffed with three or four magazines.

"I can draw and kill seven of you in the first two seconds. In the next two seconds I'll kill seven more. In the final two seconds, I'll get the third seven. Now if some of you boys in the back get a shot into me, you'd best make it count, 'cause if it only wounds me, I may get a reload or two in, and each time I reload that means seven more of you boys are going down. So I figure a sure twenty-one of you are dead, and probably more like twenty-eight or even thirty-five."

He paused. He smiled. His hand fell close to the gun on his hip, and there wasn't a lick of fear in him.

"Well, boys, what do you say? Are we going to do some man's work today? You will be remembered, I guarantee you that. You will go into history, you can bet on it. Come on, Fat Boy, you're up front. Is this the day you picked to get famous?"

The fat man swallowed.

"Ain't so much fun when somebody else has the gun, is it, Fat Boy?"

The fat man swallowed again, looked back to his mob and saw that it was leaking men from the rear. It seemed to be dissolving.

Suddenly he and four or five others were alone.

"Fat Boy, I am tired of standing here. You make your play or I just may shoot you so I can sit a spell."

The others left and the Fat Boy was alone. A large stain spread across his crotch as his bladder yielded to stress. But he didn't blink or swallow. He peered ahead intently at nothing.

Earl walked down to him.

He reached into his back pocket. The man stood stock-still, quivering.

Earl took out his wallet, opened it.

"I see your name is Willis Beaudine. Well, Willis, here's something for you to remember. If anything ever happens to that good doctor in there, it's you I'll come visit in the night. And Willis Beaudine, don't think you can run and hide. Many a man has thought that and they are now sucking bitter grass from the root end."

He dropped the wallet down Willis's overalls.

"Now scoot, Willis."

Willis turned and in seconds disappeared. Odd a fat man could move so fast.

Earl picked up his coat, threw it over his shoulder and walked back into the hospital waiting room.

Dr. James was waiting, along with Mary.

"How's my wife?" Earl demanded.

"Your wife is just fine, Mr. Swagger," the doctor said. "She's not bleeding anymore, and she's going to recover very nicely."

"And—"

"Yes," he said, "congratulations. You have a son."

EPILOGUE

1947

CHAPTER 68

He didn't have any trouble finding Beverly Hills but Linden Drive proved difficult. Finally, he stopped on a street corner where a kid was selling Maps of the Stars.

"You're almost there, sir. Three blocks up to Whittier Avenue, then left and Linden is the next one on the left."

"Thanks, kid." He handed the boy a quarter.

The house was big. A star's house should be big. It had that Southern California Mexican palace look to it, with a crown of red tiles over white stucco, some kind of towerlike or churchlike assemblage in the front, immaculate gardens and lawns. He'd seen something like it in China, but the ones in China had all been smashed to rubble by Mao's Pioneers or Chiang's shock infantry.

He parked, checked his watch, saw that it was exactly 7:00 and went up the flagstone walk toward the dark wood front door, a massive slab of carved oak. It was still, and the sun was oozing through the trees toward the Pacific on one corner of the sky. It was so quiet here, the plush quiet of a very rich neck of the woods, where voices were never raised, dinner was served at 8:00 and the only noise would be the solidity of the Cadillac limo doors being gently shut by butlers or drivers.

He knocked, and a man answered.

"I'm here to see Mr. Siegel," he said. "I think he's expecting me."

"Yeah, come on in," said the fellow, some sort of flashily dressed Hollywood type. "I have to pat you down. Just to be sure. You know."

"No problem," said Frenchy.

He turned, assumed the position, and felt the quick, frightened run of hands across his body. It wasn't well done. He could have brought in at least three pieces if he'd wanted to.

"I'm a director," said the man. "I never thought I'd end up frisking guys. But if you're Ben's friend, you move in Ben's world."

"What would you do if I had an automatic?" asked Frenchy.

"I don't know. Probably scream, then faint."

Frenchy laughed.

"This way. I'll tell him you're here. He's upstairs with Virginia's brother and his fiancée."

"No problem. I'll wait. I've got plenty of time."

The man led Frenchy to some kind of living room at the rear of the house, or maybe it was a den. Who could tell in a house so big and plush? It was full of rococo touches, like a statue of Cupid, on tiptoes with his little bow and arrow in bronze. Some English dowager looked as if she were Queen Mab in an oil painting over the mantel but the coffee table had a French country look to it. Then a huge picture window displayed a rose trellis across the backyard about twenty-five feet, festooned with bright explosions of blossoming fire, like gunshots frozen, somehow. It was June and the roses were out. He studied the trellis in some detail, looked at the lay of the yard, the height of the wall, the location of the gate and even the lock on the gate. All very interesting.

In time, the man himself came into the room. Frenchy had never seen him before. He was shorter than he'd imagined, with a movie star's tan and white teeth, his blond-brown hair brilliantined back like George Brent's, his muscular, broad-chested body creamily bulging against the beautifully tailored glen-plaid double-breasted suit he wore, with a tie perfectly tied, perfectly centered. His eyes were bright and sharp and everything about him radiated sheer animal heat.

"I'm Ben Siegel," he said. "And Mr. Lansky said

I should see you but not to ask the name."

"My name is a Top Secret," said Frenchy.

"You with the feds?"

"Not the feds that you need to worry about. Another outfit. We work overseas. Handling things. Very hush-hush. I just got back from someplace I can't even tell you about, or I'd have to kill you."

Ben looked him up and down.

"You're pretty young for that kind of thing, ain't you, kid? Shouldn't you still be sipping milk from a carton in the school cafeteria?"

"I'm smarter than I look and older than I seem."

"Okay, so? What's this all about? How're you in with Meyer?"

"I don't know Lansky. I know some people who know some people. Calls were made because favors were owed and I had something you might find useful. It happens also to be useful to me. That's why I'm here."

"Is this a touch?"

"It won't cost a cent."

"Okay. Sit down, Mr. Mystery Man."

"Thanks."

Siegel sat on a flower print sofa; Frenchy sat in a high wing chair, also flowery.

"So?"

"You want the name of a man in Arkansas. I happen to have some experience in Arkansas."

"You don't look like a country boy."

"I'm not. But I spent some time there and I

worked for a law enforcement unit and I met the man you want to know about. I know all about him."

"How did you know I wanted to know about him?"

"You remember a guy named Johnny Spanish?"

"Yeah, whatever happened to Johnny?"

"Big mystery. But whatever happened to Johnny also happened to your old friend Owney Maddox."

"I hear Owney's in Paris," said Siegel.

"Somehow, I don't think so. I don't think he's in Mexico, Rio, Madrid or Manila, either."

"I've heard that too."

"Anyhow, Johnny Spanish told me of your interest in this individual."

"The cowboy. He packed a punch, I'll say."

"So I hear."

"Fuckin' yentzer hit me so hard I can still feel it. I sometimes wake up dreamin' about it. So what's the bargain?"

"I know who he is. I know where he is."

"What do you want in exchange?"

"A good night's sleep."

"I don't get it."

"Put it this way. This man and I were colleagues at one point. Then we had a policy disagreement and I was forced to make certain other arrangements. I don't know if he knows about them. I don't know what he knows. He could know everything, he could know nothing. It didn't matter when I was overseas, but now it looks like I'm going to be in the States for a bit, while I go to a language school. I don't want to worry about him showing up for a discussion."

"I get it."

"So our interests coincide. I give you him. You pay off your debt, and I don't have to worry about him coming to collect his debt."

Bugsy looked him up and down.

"You may be a guy who can handle himself but you really fear him, huh?"

"He is very good. The best. Better than me, and I'm very good and getting even better each time out. But I'll never get to his level. He's a natural. He's also capable of throwing everything in his best interest away on some obscure notion of honor. In other words, the most dangerous man alive."

"Maybe I ought to charge *you*."

"No. You want him. I've heard the story a hundred times. It's a famous story. It'll probably end up in the *Saturday Evening Post* and then the pictures. You can't afford in your line of work to let something like that slide. That's why you've hired private eyes, bribed newspapermen, tried to infiltrate the Hot Springs police department."

"Say, you *are* informed, ain't you?" Bugsy was clearly impressed.

"I know some folks."

"Okay, spill it. Just a second. Hey, Al, get down here!"

The Hollywood gofer appeared a moment later.

"Yes, Ben."

"Write down what this guy says. Okay, go ahead, Mystery Man."

Al got out pad and paper and began to take notes.

"His name is Earl Swagger," Frenchy said. "He lives on Route 8, in Polk County, Arkansas, with his wife, just west of a little town called Board Camp, maybe fifteen miles east of the county seat, Blue Eye. The name is on the mailbox. It's his father's old place. He's got it painted up real nice now, I hear. And he and his wife had a little boy about ten months ago, so they're all very happy. He's just been appointed a corporal in the Arkansas State Police. You failed to find him on your own because part of the deal that was made when they closed down the Garland County raid team after Johnny Spanish blew it away was to destroy all the records, so that nothing exists on paper."

"Okay," said Ben.

"He's a former Marine first sergeant. He won the Medal of Honor on Iwo."

Bugsy's eyes squinted in suspicion.

"No wonder you don't want him on your tail."

"What else can I do? Perform some service for him and believe that it'll protect me from his wrath? Not in this world, pal."

"Yeah, well, this will make you real happy. I will send some guys out there. Very tough guys. They will jump this Earl Swagger with crowbars and smash him in the head. They will drag him someplace in the woods, and, on my instructions, they will break every bone in his body. Every single one. It'll take hours. They will smash his fuckin' teeth out, break his nose, blind him, punch out his eardrums. The last words he hears will be, 'Compliments of Ben Siegel, who remembers you from the train station.' Then they'll leave him there, and either he'll die tied to that tree or he'll be found and he'll spend the rest of his life in a wheelchair, blind, deaf and dumb. He will remember Ben Siegel, that I guarantee."

It was a little of Ben's famous craziness—the Bugsy part of him—that just leaked out.

Frenchy noted it, then stood. The two men didn't shake hands, and Ben walked him to the door.

"And if anybody ever asks you, kid," Ben said, "you tell them about the day you learned what kind of man Ben Siegel was."

"Yes sir," said Frenchy.

He went to his car and drove away.

Sometime later, Ben was reading the paper on the sofa. He sat with it in his lap, waiting for Chick Hill to come downstairs with Jerri. Al Smiley, his pal, sat next to him.

"This has been a very good day," Ben said. "A very good day. I get to scratch an itch that's been bugging me for over a year. The Flamingo is raking in the dough. I can pay off my debt to Meyer. Virginia will be back tomorrow. Hey, Al, life is good."

"Life *is* good," said Al.

"I always win. Nobody outfights me!"

Outside, the shooter steadied the carbine on the trellis. He wasn't trembling at all, but then that was his gift. At moments like these, he held together. Always had. Always would. It was what he was meant to do.

Front sight. That was the key.

Trigger pull. Squeeze, not yank. The carbine was light, a little beauty of a rifle, powerful as a heavy .38 or one of those Magnums.

He saw Ben Siegel's face against the front sight. Then the face faded to blur as the sight blade became hard and perfect.

The gun recoiled; he didn't hear the blast.

Ben had just the impression of being punched hard and also a brief awareness of glass shattering. Then he—

The gunman fired again, watched as blood flew from the neck. He wasn't aware of the man next to Bugsy collapsing in a heap on the floor.

He shot again and again into the face, watching as the whole beautiful head quivered each time it absorbed a bullet, then settled back, more broken, bloodier, the jaw askew, the cheekbone smashed.

A dog was barking.

The gunman left the trellis and walked up to the window itself, standing close to the eight bullet holes clustered in the heavy glass, each with its silvery webbing of fracture.

Ben lay with his head back on the sofa, his hands in his lap, a whole backed-up toilet's worth of blood corrupting the beauty of his suit and the flowers of the material of the furniture. His tie was still tight and perfect.

The dog barked again.

The shooter put the little rifle to his shoulder one more time, aimed carefully and squeezed the trigger. He fired through the punctured glass, and it collapsed like a sheet of ice. He hit Benjamin Siegel in the eye, blowing it out in a puff of misted blood and bone fragments, and it spun wetly through the air and landed with a revolting sound on the tile floor.

Frenchy lowered the carbine.

"That's for the cowboy," he said, "you fucking yentzer." Then he turned and coolly walked around the house, through the neighbor's yard, dropped the carbine into the back seat of his car, and drove away to the rest of his life.

CHAPTER 69

Earl sat with his son in the rocker on the porch. He held the boy close and rocked gently. The sun was bright and shone off the whiteness of the newly painted barn. He had done a lot to the old farm, including painting all the buildings that same brilliant white, mowing the high grass, planting a garden. He had a plan for plowing the field in the next spring, to put out a small crop. He wanted to buy some horses too, because he wanted his son to ride.

He checked his watch. He wasn't due on duty for another hour and Junie was in taking her nap. The State Police black-and-white was parked in the barnyard, next to an old oak.

A Little Rock newspaper with two items of interest lay on the floor of the porch, next to the rocker. BECKER SETS GOV BID one headline had read; and far below it, in the corner, another bit of news from the old days: WEST COAST MOBSTER SLAIN.

Neither had anything to do with him. Both seemed far away, and from another lifetime, not even his own. His life was now entirely different from that one, more settled. The rigors of duty, a necessary job; the effort it took to keep the farm running and to help Junie, who was still recovering from the strain of her labor; and the requirements of this new thing, which pleased him so much more than he could ever have believed, this business of being a father.

The infant squirmed against him, made some unidentifiable sounds, and looked him square in the eye. There was something about the boy that impressed his father. He looked at things straight on, seemed to study them. He didn't say much. He wasn't a crier or a bawler, he seemed never to get into accidents or do stupid things like putting his hand in a fire or grabbing the hot teakettle. He never awoke in the night, but when they went in, early, he was always awake already, and watchful.

"You are something, little partner," he said to his son.

The boy was ten months old, but he still had the warmth of a freshly baked loaf of bread to his father's nose.

The boy wanted to play a game. He reached out and touched his father's nose and his father jerked his head back and made a sound like a horse, and the boy's face knit in laughter. He loved this game. He loved his daddy holding him.

"Ain't you a pistol! Ain't you a little pistol, buster! You are your old daddy's number-one boy, yes, you are."

He had an idea for the boy. No one would ever raise a hand against him, and no one would ever tell him he was no good, he was nothing, he was second-rate. He'd already talked to Sam about it. This boy would go to college. No Marine Corps for him, no life of war, of getting shot at, scurrying through the bush. He would have a good life. He would be a lawyer or some such, and have a life he loved. He'd face none of the things his poor old dad had just survived. No sir. That wasn't for boys. No boy should have to go through that.

"Da—" said the boy.

"There you go, little guy! That's it! You know who I am. I am your old damned daddy, that's me."

The boy's toothless mouth lit up in a smile. He reached out to touch his father's nose again, and the game recommenced.

But then Earl noticed the presence of two small boys standing just off the porch as if they'd just come sneaking out of the treeline to the left and were pleased with their stealth.

"Well, howdy," he called.

One was a slight youth, blond and beautiful; the other was bigger and duller, with the sad, slack face of someone vacant in the mental department.

"Howdy, sir," said the smaller, sharper boy.

"What you-all doing way out here?"

"We come out on our bikes. We's goin' 'splorin!"

"You find anything?"

"We's looking for treasure."

"Ain't no treasure out here."

"We gonna find treasure someday."

"Well, maybe so."

"You a police?"

"Why, yes I am. I am in the State Police. I haven't put my uniform on yet. You boys look thirsty. You want some lemonade?"

"Lemon," said the big boy.

"Lemon*ade,*" corrected the smaller one. "Bub ain't too smart."

"Not smart," said Bub.

"Well sir, this here's my baby boy."

"He's a cute one," said the boy.

"What're your names, fellas?"

"I'm Jimmy Pye. This here's my cousin Bub."

"Bub," said Bub.

"Okay, you all stay there. I'm going to go in and pour you two nice glasses of lemonade, you hear?"

"Yes sir."

Earl walked into the house and set his son into his playpen, where the boy just watched.

He opened the refrigerator and got out a pitcher of lemonade that Junie always kept and poured out two tall glasses.

But when he returned to the porch, the boys were gone, having moved on in their quest for treasure.

Acknowledgments

In Hot Springs in 1946 there was indeed a veterans' revolt, in which returning GIs, led by a heroic prosecuting attorney, fought and ultimately vanquished the old line mob and gambling interests that controlled Arkansas's most colorful town. However intense it was—the old newspapers suggest it was very intense—it was not nearly so violent as I have made it out to be. Moreover the lawyer who led it—who as I write still lives and who had a most distinguished career—was in every way a better man than my Fred C. Becker. And even the English-born New York mob figure, reputed to be Hot Springs' secret Godfather, was far and away a gentler, better fellow than my nasty Owney Maddox, and is still thought well of in Hot Springs.

So I take pains to separate the real historical antecedents from my grossly fictionalized versions of them. *Hot Springs* is meant to reflect not the reality of the GI Revolt but only my fabrications upon its themes, with the exceptions of the real figures of Benjamin Siegel and Virginia Hill.

The rest is what I do, which is write stories, not histories, and whenever stuck between the cool plot twist and the record will choose the former. I am responsible for all of it, though I should mention those who helped me along the way.

Foremost of these is Colonel Gerry Early, USA Retired, of Easton, Maryland. Gerry, a personnel officer, volunteered to research Earl's Marine career and, with the help of Mr. Danny J. Crawford, Head, Reference Section, Marine Corps Historical Center, Washington, D.C., gave me the great pleasure of reproducing what I feel certain is Earl's record exactly as it would have been had he lived in a world outside my head. It's also a nice tribute to the professional NCOs of the United States Marine Corps in the '30s, who were to prove their worth (and earn glory) in the Pacific. This was long, hard work and I am indebted to them both.

My good friends Bob Lopez and Weyman Swagger were again there to help me. Lopez also introduced me to Paul Mahoney, who collects vintage cars, and Paul helped me with the cars of the '40s. And Paul, in turn, introduced me to Larry De Baugh, an eminent collector of vintage slots, who briefed me and showed me such devices as the Rol-a-Top and the Mills Black Cherry. My colleague Lonnae Parker O'Neal was generous in helping me get the nuances of Southern black speech patterns of the '40s. My *Washington Post* cellmate, the gifted Henry Allen, was of assistance in helping me work out the culture of the '40s, even as he was preparing his own millennium project for the *Post,* in which he attempted to and did in fact answer the following most interesting question: What would it have been like to be alive in each decade of the century? Our mutual supervisor, John Pancake, Arts Editor of the *Post,* was his usual helpful self in not paying terribly close attention to my comings and goings. I could just say, "John, you know, the book," and he'd nod, acquire a distressed expression, and then wearily look in another direction as I marched out.

Fred Rasmussen, of my old paper *The Baltimore Sun,* is a railroad buff par excellence, and he plied me with details on the mythic trains of the '40s, as well as with other railway details.

Some of Earl's comments on fighting with guns are drawn from the wisdom of Clint Smith, the director of Thunder Ranch, the firearms training facility in Mountain Home, Texas. They are used with Clint's permission.

I should mention some books, too. I helped myself with great enthusiasm and no permission whatsoever to the recollections of Shirley Abbott, whose wonderful memoir *The Bookmaker's Daughter* is certainly the most colorful record of the Veterans' Revolt and Hot Springs in the '40s we have, though of course that is not its primary focus. Her father was the head oddsmaker at the Ohio Club. There were many other books I consulted, on and off, most of them purchased at Powell's, the legendary bookstore in Portland, Oregon, where I was taken by Scott LePine of Doubleday, one of the best publisher's reps in the business.

Another book that deserves special mention: *Thompson: The American Legend,* a compendium edited by Tracie L. Hill. It's very expensive but every fan of these fabulous old beauties will get a great kick out of the sentimental journey into the gun's times and culture.

Then there's *Albion's Seed: Four British Folkways in America,* by David Hackett Fischer, which was so enthusiastically recommended to me by Paul Richard of the *Post.* It's an examination of the English roots of American culture, with a section on the Scotch-Irish borderers, who became the American Southerner, and ultimately, for my purpose, the Swaggers and the Grumleys.

In Hot Springs, Bobbie McClane, who runs the Garland County Historical Society, was unfailingly kind and helpful to me. So was Bill Lerz, who helped me find photos of those troubled days. On a less official note, Stormin' Norman, who rents motorbikes at the train station, took me on a wholly more salubrious tour of the town, pointing out where